THE KING MUST DIE...

Gratillonius felt no fear. He had a task before him which he would carry out, or die; he did not expect to die.

In the middle of the court grew a giant oak. From the lowest of its newly leafing branches hung a brazen circular shield and a sledgehammer. Dents surrounded the boss, which showed a wildly bearded and maned human face.

Gratillonius sprang to earth, took hold of the hammer, smote the shield with his full strength. It rang, a bass note which sent echoes flying. Eppilus gave him his military shield and took his cloak and crest before marshalling the soldiers in a meadow across the road.

The priestess of Ys laid a hand on Gratillonius's arm. Never had he met so intense a gaze, out of such pallor, as from her. In a voice that shook, she whispered, "Avenge us, man. Set us free. Oh, rich shall be your reward."

It came to him, like a chill from the wind that soughed among the oaks, that his coming had been awaited. Yet how could she have known?

The storehouse door crashed open and Colconor strode forth. He had outfitted himself well for a barbarian—conical nose-guarded helmet, scale coat reaching to his knees, calf-length leather boots reinforced with studs. His left hand gripped a small round shield. The longsword shone dully in his right.

POUL ANDERSON

THE KING OF YS

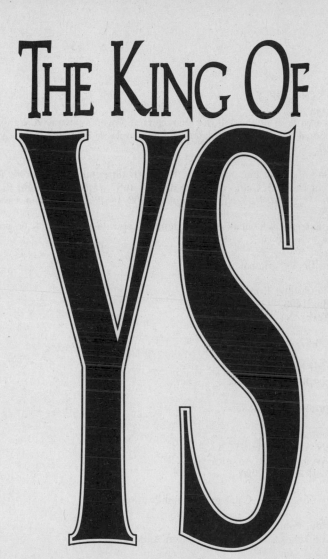

KAREN ANDERSON

THE KING OF YS

The King of Ys has been published in slightly different form as *Roma Mater*, copyright © 1986; *Gallicenae*, copyright © 1987, *Dahut*, copyright © 1988, and *The Dog and the Wolf*, copyright © 1988, by Poul and Karen Anderson.

A Baen Books Original.

Baen Publishing Enterprises
P.O. Box 1403
New York, NY 10471

ISBN: 0-671-87729-1

Cover art by Carol Russo
Maps by Karen Anderson

First printing, July 1996

Distributed by
SIMON AND SCHUSTER
1230 Avenue of the Americas
New York, NY 10020

Library of Congress Cataloging-in-Publication Data

Anderson, Poul, 1926-
    The king of Ys / Poul and Karen Anderson.
        p.   cm.
    ISBN 0-671-87729-1 (trade pbk.)
    1. Ys (Imaginary place)--Fiction. 2. Kings and rulers--Fiction.
I. Anderson, Karen.   II. Title
PS3551.N378K5   1996
813'.54--dc20   96-13680
                                                                CIP

Printed in the United States of America.

I ROMA OCCIDENTALIS

CALEDONIA

HIVERNIA

SCANDIA

BRITANNIA
Eboracum

MARE GERMANICUM

MARE SUEBICUM

Londinium A
Tamesis

Gesoriacum

Mosa · Rhenus · Albis

Victula

Colonia A

GERMANIA

Ys · ARMORICA
Mosella · Confluentes · Moguntiacum
A Treverorum

SARMATIA

Sequana
Liger
C Turonum
GALLIA
Regina · Vindobona

L Parisiorum

SINUS AQUITANICUS
Danuvius

Lugdunum · RAETIA · Augusta V · PANNONIA · Aquincum

Burdigala

E U R O P A

DACIA

Lucus A · Mediolanum
Garumna · Aquileia

Portus C · Rhodanus

LIGURIA · Padus

DALMATIA

Salamantica · Narbo M · Ravenna
Avela · Caesaraugusta · Massilia

ITALIA

Olisipo · HISPANIA · Tagus · Iberus · Tarraco

CORSICA

Roma

THRACIA

Ossonoba · BALEARES

MACEDONIA

Gades · Carthago Nova · SARDINIA

THESSALIA

Tingis · MARE · EPIRUS

MAURETANIA · Stagna · Hippo R · SICILIA · Carthago · Syracusae · ACHAEA · Athenae

LIBYA
Libyca Palus
Pallas Palus

INTERNUM

Tritonis Lacus

AFRICA

OCEANUS ATLANTICUS

KA 96

LEGEND

····· Antonine Wall ʌʌʌʌʌ Boundary of Roman Empire
······· Hadrian's Wall ◆◆◆◆ Boundary between West and East

Roman Name	Modern Site		
(Names on the map are shortened to reflect modern forms. They are here given in full; if the map shows only the second of two words, it is in **bold** type, e. g. C Regina = Castra **Regina**)			
	Confluentes	Coblentz	
	Danuvius	Danube	Narbo Martius	Narbonne
	Eboracum	York	Olisipo	Lisbon
Albis	Elbe	Gades	Cadiz	Ossonoba	Faro
Aquileia	near Trieste	Garumna	Garonne	Padus	Po
Aquitanicus, Sinus	Bay of Biscay	Germanicum, Mare	North Sea	Pallas Palus	former swamp
Armorica	Brittany	Gesoriacum	Boulogne	Portus Cale	Oporto
Augusta **Treverorum**	Tréves, Trier	Hippo Regius	'Annaba	Raetia	Switzerland
Augusta Vindelicum	Augsburg	Iberus	Ebro	Rhenus	Rhine
Avela	Ávila	Libyca Palus	former swamp	Rhodanus	Rhone
Aquincum	Budapest	Liger	Loire	Salamantica	Salamanca
Burdigala	Bordeaux	Limonum **Pictavum**	Poitiers	Sequana	Seine
Caesaraugusta	Zaragoza	Londinium Augusta	London	Stagna	former lagoons
Caesarodunum		Lucus Augusti	Lugo	Suebicum, Mare	Baltic Sea
Turonum	Tours	Lugdunum	Lyon	Tamesis	Thames
Carthago	Tunis	Lutetia **Parisiorum**	Paris	Tarraco	Tarragona
Carthago Nova	Cartagena	Massilia	Marseille	Tingis	Tangier
Castra **Regina**	Regensburg	Mediolanum	Milan	Tritonis Lacus	former lake
Colonia Agrippinensis	Cologne, Köln	Moguntiacum	Mainz	Vindobona	Vienna
	Mosa	Meuse, Maas	Ys	Baie des
	Mosella	Moselle, Mosel		Trépassés

II GALLIA

BRITANNIA

OCEANUS BRITANNICUS

Dubris
Gesoriacum
Turnacum
N Atrebatum
Samara
S Ambianorum
Rotomagus V

BELGICA

Colonia A
Confluentes
A Treverorum

Corvorum Insulae
A Baiocassium
Cosedia
I Abrincatuorum

D Remorum
L Parisiorum

LUGDUNENSIS

Gesocribate
Vorgium Fanum Martis
ARMORICA
Ys
C Redonum
D Venetorum
Corbilo
C Aurelianum
C Turonum

P Namnetum

L Pictavum

A Lemovicium

SINUS

Lemanus Lacus
Genava
Lugdunum
Vienna

Carantonus

AQUITANIA

NARBONENSIS

Burdigala
Duranius

AQUITANICUS

Garumna

Arausio
Nemausus Arelate
LIGURIA

HISPANIA
Oiarso
Roscida Vallis
Tolosa
Carcaso
Narbo M
Massilia

KA 96

Roman Name	Modern Site				
Arar	Saône	Darioritum		Nemetacum	
Arausio	Orange	**Venetorum**	Vannes	**Atrebatum**	Arras
Arelate	Arles	Druentia	Durance	Oiarso	Oyarzun
Augustodurum		Dubris	Dover	Padus	Po
Baiocassium	Bayeux	Duranius	Dordogne	Portus	
Augustoritum		Durocortorum		**Namnetum**	Nantes
Lemovicium	Limoges	**Remorum**	Reims	Roscida Vallis	Roncesvalles
Britannicus,		Fanum Martis	Corseul	Rotomagus	
Oceanus	English Channel	Genava	Geneva	Veliocassium	Rouen
Carantonus	Charente	Gesocribate	Brest	Samara	Somme
Carcaso	Carcassonne	Ingena		Samarobriva	
Cenabum		**Abrincatuorum**	Avranches	**Ambianorum**	Amiens
Aurelianum	Orléans	Lemanus Lacus	Lac Léman	Scaldius	Scheldt
Condate		Limonum		Tolosa	Toulouse
Redonum	Rennes	**Pictavum**	Poitiers	Turnacum	Tournay
Corbilo	St. Nazaire	Matrona	Marne	Vienna	Vienne
Corvorum Ins.	Channel Is.	Nemausus	Nîmes	Vorgium	Carhaix
Cosedia	Coutances				

Identifications on previous maps are not repeated.

IV ÉRIU AND ALBA

CALEDONI

PICTI

DAMNONII

Dál Riata

NOVANTAE

Maia

Dál Riata

QÓIQET NULAT

Mona

Emain Macha

CONDACHT

Mag Slecht

MÍDE   Tallten

ÉRIU

Boand's River

Temir

Clón Tarui

Mona

Ruirthech

Deva

QÓIQET

Dun Alinni

Segontium

VOTADINI

Deva

Sinand

LAGINI

ORDOVICES

Cassel

Siuir

MUMU

SILURES

Isca

Isca
Silurum

Sabrina

Isca

Isca
Dumnoniorum

DUMNONES

KA 96

Ancient Name	Modern Site				
Alba	Scotland; Britain	Dun Alinni	near Armagh	Qóiqet Lagini	Leinster
Boand's River	Boyne	Emain Macha	near Kildare	Qóiqet nUlat	Ulster
Cassel	Cashel	Ériu	Eire	Ruirthech	Liffey
Clón Tarui	Clontarf	Mag Slecht	in Co. Cavan	Sinand	Shannon
Condacht	Connaught	Maia	Bowness-on-Solway	Siuir	Suir
Dal Riata in Alba	Argyll	Míde	Meath	Tallten	Teltown
Dal Riata in Ériu	Antrim	Mumu	Munster	Temir	Tara

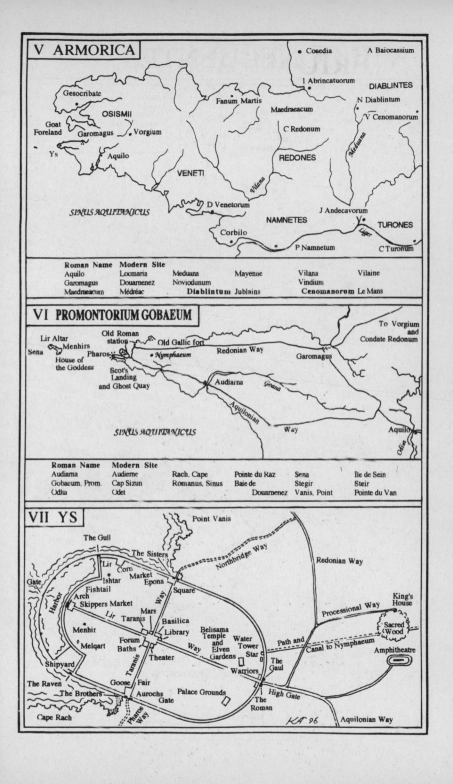

V ARMORICA

- Cosedia
- A Baiocassium
- I Abrincatuorum
- DIABLINTES
- Gesocribate
- N Diablintum
- OSISMII
- Fanum Martis
- Maedraeacum
- V Cenomanorum
- Goat Foreland
- Garomagus
- Vorgium
- C Redonum
- Ys
- Aquilo
- REDONES
- VENETI
- *Vilana*
- *Meduana*
- SINUS AQUITANICUS
- D Venetorum
- J Andecavorum
- TURONES
- NAMNETES
- *Liger*
- Corbilo
- P Namnetum
- C Turonum

Roman Name	Modern Site				
Aquilo	Locmaria	Meduana	Mayenne	Vilana	Vilaine
Garomagus	Douarnenez	Noviodunum		Vindium	
Maedraeacum	Médréac	**Diablintum** Jublains		**Cenomanorum** Le Mans	

VI PROMONTORIUM GOBAEUM

- To Vorgium and Condate Redonum
- Lir Altar
- Old Roman station
- Old Gallic fort
- Redonian Way
- Sena
- Menhirs
- Pharos
- *Nymphaeum*
- Garomagus
- House of the Goddess
- Scot's Landing and Ghost Quay
- Audiarna
- *Geana*
- *Aquilonian Way*
- SINUS AQUITANICUS
- Aquilo
- *Odita*

Roman Name	Modern Site				
Audiarna	Audierne	Rach, Cape	Pointe du Raz	Sena	Île de Sein
Gobaeum, Prom.	Cap Sizun	Romanus, Sinus	Baie de	Stegir	Steir
Odita	Odet		Douarnenez	Vanis, Point	Pointe du Van

VII YS

- Point Vanis
- The Gull
- The Sisters
- Northbridge Way
- Redonian Way
- Lir
- Corn Market
- Gate
- Ishtar
- Epona
- Square
- King's House
- Harbor
- Fishtail Arch
- Skippers Market
- Way
- Mars
- Basilica
- Processional Way
- Menhir
- Lir
- Taranis
- Library
- Belisama Temple and Elven Gardens
- Water Tower Star
- Path and Canal to Nymphaeum
- Sacred Wood
- Melqart
- Forum Baths
- Theater
- Way
- The Gaul
- Amphitheatre
- Shipyard
- Taranis
- Warriors
- The Raven
- Goose Fair
- Aurochs Gate
- Palace Grounds
- High Gate
- The Brothers
- The Roman
- Cape Rach
- Pharos Way
- Aquilonian Way
- KA 96

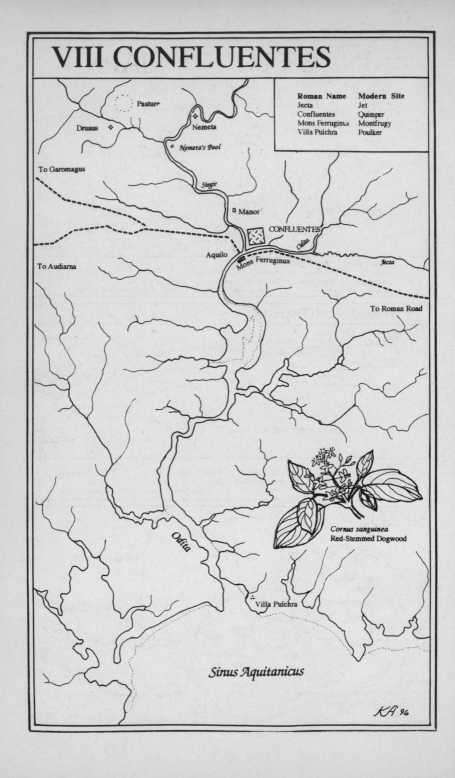

VIII CONFLUENTES

Roman Name	Modern Site
Jecta	Jet
Confluentes	Quimper
Mons Ferruginus	Montfrugy
Villa Pulchra	Poulker

Pasture

Drusus

Nemeta

Nemeta's Pool

To Garomagus

Stegir

Manor

CONFLUENTES

Odita

Aquilo

Mons Ferruginus

Jecta

To Audiarna

To Roman Road

Odita

Cornus sanguinea
Red-Stemmed Dogwood

Villa Pulchra

Sinus Aquitanicus

KA 96

INDEX TO THE MAPS

Numbers refer to the first map on which the name is identified or shown.

Abonae	VIII	Deva (river)	III	Mide	IV
Africa	I	Deva (town)	III	Moguntiacum	I
Alba	IV	Druentia	II	Mona (1 and 2)	III
Albis	I	Dubris	I	Mons Ferruginus	VIII
Anderida	III	Dun Alinni	IV	Mosa	I
Aquae Sulis	III	Duranius	II	Mosella	I
Aquileia	I	Dumovaria	III	Mumu	IV
Aquilo	V	Durocortorum Remorum	II	Narbo Martius	I
Aquincum	I	Eboracum	I	Nemausus	II
Aquitanicus, Sinus	I	Emain Macha	IV	Nemetacum Atrebatum	II
Arar	II	Ériu	IV	Noviodunum Diablintum	V
Arausio	II	Fanum Martis	II	Odita	VI
Arelate	II	Gades	I	Oiarso	II
Armorica	I	Gallia	I	Olisipo	I
Athenae	I	Garomagus	V	Orcades Insulae	III
Audiarna	V	Garumna	I	Ossonoba	I
Augusta Treverorum	I	Genava	II	Padus	I
Augusta Vindelicum	I	Germanicum, Mare	I	Pallas Palus	I
Augustodurum Baiocassium	II	Gesocribate	II	Pannonia	I
Augustoritum Lemovicium	II	Gesoriacum	I	Portus Cale	I
Avela	I	Goana	VI	Portus Namnetum	II
Board's River	IV	Goat Foreland	V	Qóiqet Lagini	IV
Borcovicum	III	Glevum	III	Qóiqet nUlat	IV
Britannia	I	Gobaeum, Prom.	VI	Rach, Cape	VI
Britannicus, Oceanus	II	Hippo Regius	I	Raetia	I
Burdigala	I	Hispania	I	Rhenus	I
Caesaraugusta	I	Hivernia	I	Rhodanus	I
Caesarodunum Turonum	I	Iberus	I	Roscida Vallis	II
Caledonia	I	Ingena Abrincatuorum	II	Rotomagus	II
Calleva Atrebatum	III	Isca (r., Siluria)	III	Ruirthech	IV
Camulodunum	III	Isca (r., Dumnonia)	III	Salamantica	I
Carantonus		Isca Dumnoniorum	III	Samara	II
Carcaso	II	Isca Silurum	III	Samarobriva Ambianorum	II
Carthago	I	Isurium Brigantium	I	Scandia	I
Carthago Nova	I	Jecta	VIII	Scot's Landing	VI
Cassel	IV	Juliomagus Andecavorum	V	Sena	VI
Cassiterides Ins.	III	Lemanus Lacus	II	Sequana	I
Castra Regina	I	Libyca Palus	I	Sinand	IV
Cenabum Aurelianum	II	Liger	I	Siuir	IV
Clón Tarui	IV	Liguria	I	Stagna	I
Colonia Agrippinensis	I	Limonum Pictavum	I	Stegir	VIII
Condacht	IV	Lindum	III	Suebicum, Mare	I
Condate Redonum	II	Londinium Augusta	I	Tallten	IV
Confluentes Rheni	I	Lucus Augusti	I	Tamesis	I
Confluentes Oditae	VIII	Lugdunum	I	Tarraco	I
Corbilo	II	Lugovallium	III	Temir	IV
Corstopitum	III	Lutetia Parisiorum	I	Tingis	I
Corvorum Insulae	II	Maedraeacum	II	Tolosa	V
Cosedia	II	Mag Slecht	IV	Tritonis Lacus	I
Dacia	I	Maia	IV	Tumacum	II
Dalmatia	I	Massilia	I	Vienna	II
Dál Riata in Alba	IV	Mauretania	I	Villa Pulchra	VIII
Dál Riata in Ériu	IV	Matrona	II	Vindobona	I
Danuvius	I	Mediolanum	I	Vorgium	II
Darioritum Venetorum	II	Meduana	V	Ys	I

Although this novel is fantasy, its surroundings are real. The places and peoples of history shaped the setting in which it occurs. To cite only one example: Ys would lack many important cultural traits without the Phoenician mercantile expansion that built Carthage and Cartagena. These maps would be much emptier if they omitted matters not mentioned in the story.

ROMA MATER

This tale is all for
Astrid and Greg
with our love.

I

~ 1 ~

At noon upon that Birthday of Mithras, the sun blazed low in an ice-clear heaven. As Gratillonius looked south, he saw its brilliance splinter into rainbow shards amidst his eyelashes. Hills afar, ditch and earthworks nearby, terraced fields below, lay whitened and still. Smoke rose from Borcovicium fort and the settlement huddled against its ramparts, but so straight that it scarcely marred the purity. When he turned his gaze north, there was nothing of man save the shadow of the Wall, huge and blue, down a cliff whose own shadow filled the hollow underneath. Heights beyond were dark with forest in winter sleep. Light flashed starlike off icicles. A few crows aflight set their blackness against his breath, their distant cawing against his heartbeat, and that was all that stirred.

For a moment he felt wholly alone. The summer's warfare was not only past, it was unreal, a dream he had had or a story told him in his childhood, fading out of memory—but what, then, was real?

A glance right and left brought him back. Foursquare, the murky bulk of a tower blocked off most westward view; but eastward, vision ran along the walkway past the two intermediate observation turrets to the next milecastle, and the next, until the Wall swung under the horizon: fifteen feet from base to battlements, seventy-seven miles from sea to sea across Britannia. Metal made small fierce gleams where men stood watch down that length. Cloaks and drooping standards splashed their colors athwart its gray. Below them, some two hundred Roman paces from him, the legionary base rose in a gridiron of streets and lanes which seemed doubly severe next to the paths twisting between houses in the vicus. Everything he saw belonged here.

And so did he. His body rested easy under helmet, mail, greaves. Beneath them, his tunic hung lower than the skirt of studded leather straps; a scarf protected his neck from chafing by armor; woolen half-breeches, stockings inside the hobnailed sandals, fended off the season; all was familiar. Sword at hip, stick cut from the mainstem of a grapevine, were as much limbs of his as were arms and legs. Because the day was holy, he had not yet taken food, nor would he until the Mystery at eventide, and hunger somehow spurred awareness of his own strength. The chill in the air made it feel liquid, it bathed him

1

within and without. And now trumpets sounded, echoes rang, high noon had come.

To most in the army, that signalled no more than a change of guard. It called Gratillonius to prayer. He faced the sun again, removed his helmet and set it on the parapet. A scarlet horsehair crest, attached for the round of inspection which he was on, scratched his wrist and scritted. He raised his arms and began the office—soft-voiced, because such was seemly and it would be his heart that the God heard—"Hail, Mithras Unconquered, Saviour, Warrior, Lord, born unto us anew and forever—"

"Centurion."

At first he barely noticed, and did not imagine it meant him. "—hear us, You Who did slay the Bull that Its blood might make fruitful the world, You Who stand before the Lion and the Serpent—"

"Centurion!" yelled in his ear.

Rage flared. Had the contumely of the Christians swollen to this?

An instant before snatching his vinestaff and giving the intruder a slash across the mouth, Gratillonius checked himself. It behooved an officer both of the Halidom and of Rome to curb a temper he knew was too quick, and not profane his devotions with violence. He shot a glare which made the fellow step back alarmed, and continued.

The words were soon finished. It was as well, he thought, when anger seethed in him. He turned to confront the stranger, and beheld the insignia of the Sixth Victrix. His mind sprang. Although that legion was based at Eboracum, closer than either of the other two in the island, it had not joined them against Picti and Scoti raging down from the north, but stayed behind. Supposedly that was to stand off any Saxon raiders. However, some few of its men had accompanied Maximus as bodyguards, couriers, confidants.

No matter yet. Gratillonius picked up the stick that marked his rank, tucked it under an elbow, and rapped forth: "Attention! Have you no better manners than to interrupt a man at his worship, soldier? You disgrace your eagle."

The other stiffened, gulped, abruptly recovered and answered, "I beg the centurion's pardon. No bishop ever told me this is a time for services. I had my orders, and only supposed the centurion was deep in thought."

Insolent knave indeed, Gratillonius knew. He sagged a little, inwardly. Of course he was dealing with a Christian. Most legionaries were, these days, or pretended to be. This very year the rescript had arrived that banned the old faiths, along with tales of how the authorities were despoiling Mithraic temples first. Men at war on the uttermost frontier paid scant heed, and Maximus knew better than to enforce such a decree...until today, when the immediate danger was past?

Within Gratillonius, his father drawled anew, "Son, you're too rash, you always court trouble. No sense in that. She'll come on her own,

2

never fear. Better just court girls." A curious tenderness followed. Gratillonius must even quell a smile as he said:

"I should take your name and remand you to your unit for punishment drill, if not a flogging. But since you admit ignorance, I'll be merciful. What do you want?"

An awakened caution replied. "Mine is...the honor of addressing Gaius Valerius Gratillonius, centurion of the Second...is it not? I asked the squad where you were."

"Which is here. Speak on."

The messenger donned importance. "The Duke of the Britains sent me. You are relieved of your regular duty and will report to him at once in the praetorium."

"The Duke? What, not at Vindolanda?" Gratillonius was surprised. The old fort and settlement, close by but somewhat behind the wall, was where the grand commander had generally stayed when in this area.

"He is making a progress of inspection and...other business, it seems. He summoned you by name."

What could that mean? A mission? The blood thrilled in Gratillonius.

~ 2 ~

The close-packed buildings of the strongpoint shaded streets and turned the lanes between into tunnels of cold and gloom. Nonetheless several men were passing time off watch with a dice game on the verandah of their barrack. But they were Tungri, auxiliaries such as formed the permanent garrisons of the Wall; regulars only arrived in emergencies like this year's. Well wrapped in furs, the barbarians doubtless found the dry air a blessed change from their native marshlands. Their speech went croaking and hawking through a quiet otherwise broken by little more than footfalls, although those rang loud enough on frozen earth.

Entering on the west, Gratillonius must pass the headquarters block standing sheer around three sides of its courtyard. He halted to salute the basilica, for it held the legionary shrine and standards: not his legion, true, but equally Rome's. The sentries saluted him in their turn. The smartness of it pleased, now when the Tungri had reminded him of the slovenly ways he found when his vexillation first came here. Maximus had done marvels in restoring discipline. To be sure, Gratillonius thought, the long campaign helped; poor soldiers were apt to become dead ones.

Memory ranged across the months that were past: the march up country through springtime rains to a stone wonder he had never seen before; settling in, getting to know the hills and heaths, exploring what often sleazy pleasures the civilian villages had to offer; shamefaced

3

purification before he sought the Mithraeum, but then, for no good reason that he could see to this day, his elevation in grade—well, they said he had fought valiantly, but that hardly sufficed, and most likely it was that pious Parnesius had recommended him to the Father, and after all, the congregation had grown so pitifully small—

The warring itself was somehow less vivid. It had been an endlessness of expeditions from this base to seek whatever band of painted Picti or gaudy Scoti had been reported, of weather wet or hot, of troubles with supply trains and troubles among the men such as a centurion must handle, of having them shovel trenches and ramparts for encampments they would demolish the next dawn, of finally—most times—coming upon the enemy and going to work, of the dead afterward and the wounded, the wounded.... You did what you and the surgeons could for your own, and tried to keep your men from being needlessly cruel when they cut the throats of tall dark highlanders and fair-skinned warriors from over the water. There was no safe way of bringing prisoners to a slave market, and you could not risk that any would recover from his injuries. You had seen too many homesteads plundered and burnt, slain men, ravished women who wept for children carried off because the Scoti did do a brisk trade in slaves; and this was not only north of the Wall, among tribes friendly to Rome, but south of it, in territories thinly peopled but still subject to Caesar. The foe came around every defense in their leather coracles. So as leaves withered and fell, Gratillonius killed his last opponent (hail rattled on helmets; its pallor across the ground made blood spurt doubly red) and Britannia lay at peace. But thus it had been again and again in the past, and surely would in the future.

He curbed his mind, squared his shoulders, and strode onward. Forebodings were foolishness. The truth was that Maximus had prevailed, had reaped so widely among the wild men that they would not soon come back, and had something to tell an infantryman who was chafing at the sameness of garrison life. What better omen than getting that word on the holiest day of the year?

The praetorium was almost as large as the principia. When Gratillonius identified himself, the guard called a man to guide him. Inside, the warmth of a hypocaust radiated from tiled floors; frescoes on the walls glowed with flowers, fruits, beasts, Homeric Gods and heroes; more servants than soldiers passed by. But such was usual, Gratillonius knew. His own commandant's house in the base at Isca Silurum made this one on the far frontier look impoverished. Maximus had the reputation of living austerely wherever he was.

Another legionary of the Sixth stood at a certain door. Upon learning who had appeared, he opened it and waited at attention until bidden to speak. "Gaius Valerius Gratillonius, centurion of the seventh cohort, Second Legion Augusta," he then announced, and gestured the newcomer in. The door closed. Gratillonius saluted.

Light, straggling bleak through a glazed window, got help from lamps. It showed lavishness neglected. Two men sat at a table whereon were beakers, bescribbled notebooks of thin-scraped wood, a map drawn on parchment, an inkwell and quill, a waxed tablet and stylus. One man, big, young, freckle-faced, was clearly a native. He had donned Roman garb for this occasion, but a mustache flared, his ruddy hair was bound in a knot, a golden torque gleamed around his neck. His companion, whom Gratillonius knew by sight, was the Duke of the Britains.

Magnus Clemens Maximus hailed from the uplands of Hispania Tarraconensis. It showed in his height and leanness, hatchet features, olive skin, hair stiff and black and slightly grizzled. It also softened his Latin as he said, "At ease, centurion. Take off your cloak and helmet." The steel of him was in his voice, though, and his eyes were always probing.

To the tribesman he added: "This is the officer whom I have in mind to lead your escort." To Gratillonius: "You have the honor of meeting Cunedag, a prince among the Votadini and Rome's loyal ally. Your assignment will be to accompany him and his following to the Ordovices, on your way back with your century." Smiling: "Look well, you two. I trust you both like what you see."

Gratillonius sped through memory. Dwelling north of the Wall, the Votadini had formerly been subjects and, after the tide of empire ebbed southward, had stayed on reasonably good terms. Indeed, their leading families claimed Roman descent and often bestowed Roman names. He had not met Cunedag before, but had heard of him as a useful warlord throughout the year's campaigning.

The chieftain's gaze searched over the centurion. It found a man of twenty-five, medium tall for a Briton—which made him overtop most Italians—and robustly built. The visage of Gratillonius was broad and square, clean-shaven, with craggy nose and wide-set gray eyes. His complexion was fair, his close-cropped hair auburn. He moved like a cat. When he spoke, the tone was deep and rather harsh.

"You have won a high name," said Cunedag in his own language. "I think we shall travel well together."

"Thank you, lord. I will do my best," replied Gratillonius. He used the tongue of the Dumnonii, which was not too alien for the Northerner to understand and chuckle at.

"Good," said Maximus, sensing the accord. "Prince, we have talked a long while and you must be weary. The centurion and I have matters to discuss which can scarcely interest you. Why do you not seek your guestroom, or wherever else you like, and rest until we meet at the evening meal?"

Cunedag, an intelligent barbarian, took the hint and uttered a stately goodbye. A gong summoned an attendant to lead him out and a second man to bring Gratillonius a goblet of wine and water. The officer took the vacated stool at his commander's word and peered across the clutter on the table. His pulse drummed anew.

Maximus stroked fingers across his prow of a chin. "Well, soldier," he said, "you must be wondering how I even knew who you are, let alone found a rather special task for you."

"The Duke surely has many ears," Gratillonius ventured.

Maximus shrugged. "Fewer than he could use. In this case, you've become a friend of Parnesius, and it happens that I am acquainted with his father and have kept my eye on the son. Parnesius praised you to me: less your valor, which any dolt could show, but skill and coolness overriding a temperament hot by nature, a talent for improvising, a gift of leadership." He sighed. "That is a gift, you know, a mystery. God's hand touches a man, and that man turns into one whom others will follow though it be past the gates of hell. Would I had more like that to follow *me!*"

A chill tingle passed through Gratillonius. The provinces of the Empire bred men who claimed the purple by right of the sword, and Britannia was among them. Here the legions had first hailed great Constantinus, almost a hundred years ago. More recently there had been Magnentius, rising in Gallia but born in Britannia and supported by Britons; his failure and its terrible aftermath need not discourage later dreams. As warfare ended and winter closed in, legionaries had time to think, wonder, mutter...fifteen years was a long time to keep as able a leader as Maximus off on the frontiers...he declared that he held the Sixth in reserve at Eboracum against Saxon attack, and maybe that was true, but it was likewise true that the Sixth had come to be his adoring own...the real rulers of the West were not the co-Emperors but a barbarian, a woman, and a churchman...the hour might be overpast for putting a man of proven metal on the throne....

Maximus's voice levelled. "I've kept your detachment, together with that from the Twentieth and all the sundry oddments, on the Wall to make sure our pacification was nailed down. The Picti wouldn't worry me by themselves. Their little quarrelsome packs will never do more alone than snap up some loot, take a drubbing, and scatter back to lick their wounds. But lately the Scoti have been leagued with them, and—the Scoti are a different breed of wolf." He scowled. "Somebody in Hivernia has been behind the last onslaught, somebody powerful and shrewd. I would not have put it past him to deliver a surprise blow just when we thought we were safely finished."

Maximus tossed off a laugh and a swallow from his cup. "Well, he didn't. Now he couldn't possibly before spring, and one may doubt he'll care to try again that soon. So the vexillations can return to their legions: a cold trek, but not one that I think they'll mind. On your way, Gratillonius, I want you to guard Cunedag on his. At Deva you and your century will part company not only with the Valeria Victrix troops, but with your fellows of the Augusta. Proceed with Cunedag into Ordovicia, stop where he wants, and do whatever is necessary to establish him."

"Would the Duke explain why?" Gratillonius requested.

"It won't likely be a severe task," Maximus said. "I have had negotiators there, and on the whole, the clans will welcome him. See here. Stationed where you are, you must know how law and order have been breaking down in those parts, leaving people well-nigh helpless before the Scoti, not to mention home-grown brigands. I can't have that sort of thing at my back when—" He broke off. "Cunedag possesses a fairly sound grasp of both military and political principles. He'll take charge. Your century shouldn't have a great deal to do, nor need to linger long, before it can return to Isca Silurum."

"I understand, sir," Gratillonius said. "In part."

"Never fear, you'll know more before you leave. Half a dozen men, both Roman and tribal, are set to instruct you. Meanwhile," and Maximus smiled, "you can get to know Cunedag better this evening at supper."

Gratillonius stiffened. He must summon up as much of himself as he had ever needed in combat in order to say: "I regret that I cannot accept the Duke's invitation."

Maximus raised his brows. "What?"

"Sir, this day is sacred. I may only take part in the feast of the God."

"Oh." Maximus was silent for a space. When he spoke, it was like the winter outside. "I had forgotten. You are pagan."

It prickled in Gratillonius's armpits. "Sir, I do not worship Jupiter, if that's what you mean."

"But Mithras. Which is forbidden. For your soul's good, understand. You'll burn forever after you die, unless you take the Faith."

Gratillonius bridled. "The Duke has not yet seen fit to close our temples."

Maximus sighed. "As you will, as you will. For now, at least. After all, Parnesius is obstinate too. But he serves Rome well, like you and, I dare hope, me. Come, let us drink to the well-being of our Mother."

The wine was excellent, unlike what was issued the troops. Yet its sweetness dimmed on Gratillonius's tongue as Maximus frowned, lowered his beaker, stared into the shadows that filled a corner, and murmured: "Little enough well-being is hers any longer. You've never seen Rome, the City, have you? I have. Our Mother is fallen on evil days. There are more ghosts than living folk in her streets, and the Emperor reigns from Mediolanum, Augusta Treverorum, or...anywhere except poor, plundered Rome. The Emperor of the West, that is. No, today the joint Emperors of the West, the first a plaything of his Frankish general, the second of his mother, and the West divided between them. And even the Augustus of the East feels Constantinople tremble beneath him. It is but four or five years since the Goths rode down the Romans at Adrianople. Have you heard about that, centurion? The Emperor Valens himself died on the field. His successor Theodosius must needs buy the alliance of those barbarians, Arian heretics, those that are not still outright heathen—" He straightened. His voice clanged forth: "By the Great Name of God, Rome shall not suffer this! Mother, your hour of deliverance draws near."

Then immediately he was again the self-contained man whose patience had forged victory. He raised his cup, sipped, regarded Gratillonius over the rim, and smiled afresh before he said, "Be not alarmed, centurion. I've no wish to scare off the few trustworthy men left me. Rather, I've work in mind for you, more challenging and more glorious than the mere delivery of a leader and his warriors to some ragged hillfolk. Indeed, that assignment is essentially a final test of you. If you carry it off as well as I expect—"

Leaning forward: "I've made inquiries about you, of course, since Parnesius's mention of you drew my attention your way. Now I wish to talk freely with you, explore what sort of *person* you are."

"A very ordinary soldier, sir," Gratillonius replied uneasily.

Maximus laughed, straightened on his stool, crossed shank over knee. Such putting aside of dignity, by the Duke himself, caught at Gratillonius's heart. Eagerness rekindled in him. "Oh, no, you don't, lad!" Maximus crowed. "You'll never make that claim stick, not after this summer. And I hear you did well in the South, earlier."

"That was nothing unusual, really, sir. Sometimes Scoti or Saxons came visiting, and we went out to meet them. Otherwise it was plain patrol and camp duty."

"Um-m, I've heard of a fire in town, and a young legionary who risked his life to rescue the children from a burning house. I've also heard how that same fellow gets along well with natives, whether they be his familiar Silures and Belgae or the half-tame dwellers in these parts."

"Well, I'm of Britannic blood myself, sir."

"Unusual— No, you are a regular, of course, not an auxiliary. Almost a namesake of the Emperor Gratianus."

The centurion felt his muscles grow tense. Likening his family to that Scythian-loving sluggard! "Pure chance, sir," he stated. "My folk are Belgae, living near Aquae Sulis since before Claudius. Naturally, we've long been civilized, and a forebear of mine gave the name a Latin form, but we've kept our ties to the land."

Maximus seemed a trifle amused. "Have you no ancestors who were not Belgae? That would be strange."

"Of course there were some, sir. Soldiers stationed in Britannia, Italians, a Dacian, a Nervian. And a couple of Gauls, though they were female, brides brought home."

Maximus nodded, once more grave. "Sound stock throughout. You are of the curial class, I understand."

Gratillonius grimaced. Maximus hastened to bespeak happier matters: "Your grandfather had a distinguished military career, did he not? And your father went into trade out of Abonae, and prospered. That took

8

real seamanship—those tides in the estuary—and fighting skill, too, when pirates infest the waters."

The Duke must have queried Parnesius closely indeed, to dig out things casually related over a span of months. The voice quickened: "His main business was with Armorica, true? And he took you along on his voyages."

"Well, between the ages of twelve and sixteen, when I joined the army, I used to go with him, sir," Gratillonius replied.

"Tell me about it."

"Oh, we'd coast along Britannia, taking on cargo here and there, then cross over to a Gallic port—maybe as far east as Gesoriacum—and work our way west, stopping off to trade. Sometimes we'd leave the ship and travel inland to markets in places like Condate Redonum or Vorgium—" Gratillonius shook himself. Those joyful years were far behind him and his father both.

Maximus's tone sharpened. "Did you ever visit Ys?"

"What?" Gratillonius was startled. "Why...why, no. Does anybody any longer?"

"We shall see. You appear to have an ear for language. Did you acquire fluency in any Gallic tongues? I'm interested especially in whatever they use on the western end of Armorica."

"I got along, sir. That was quite a while ago, and I haven't returned since." Gratillonius began to realize what Maximus was driving at. The hair stirred on his neck and arms. "But I ought to regain it pretty quickly. Those dialects aren't too different from the southern Britannic, and I had a Dumnonic nurse when I was small." Awkwardly: "She stayed on in the house for my younger siblings, and we used to talk in her speech, she and I, till I enlisted—and afterward, when I was home on leave. I do hope old Docca is still alive."

The wistfulness flickered out, for Maximus was saying low, while he stared before him as if his vision could pierce the wall and fly away over Europe. "Excellent. The Lord is gracious to me, a sinner. It may actually be Providence that you are an infidel; for there could be things yonder that are not for a Christian man to deal with."

A fire leaped up in the breast of Gratillonius.

~ 3 ~

Once the temple had not been as far as it now was from a vicus of several hundred veterans, artisans, merchants, innkeepers, harlots, wives, children, hangers-on, a settlement akin to the rest that clustered south of the Wall, from sea to sea, within a mile or a few of each other. But nearly two hundred years had passed since Caledonic invaders laid the Borcovicium region waste while Rome writhed at war with itself. After Severus restored things, rebuilding was done farther uphill, next to the military base. Perhaps in awe, the reavers had spared the Mithraeum. Thus it stood alone on a knoll near the ditch, only brush surrounding its temenos. Northward, darkness rose like a tide toward the battlemented horizon the Wall made; southward, the ground rolled off in ridges which the setting sun reddened. Frost creaked underfoot, voices mumbled through smoke signals of breath, silence everywhere else deepened with cold.

Arriving early for the service, Gratillonius found Parnesius among those who waited outside. His friend was wrapped in a cloak but had not drawn the hood over his black hair. It curled back from his forehead to show the tiny brand of initiation which Gratillonius also bore, both now faint; hot iron had made larger and deeper marks on their bodies when they first entered the army. Beneath the religious sign, Parnesius's eyebrows formed a single bar over his jutting nose. "Hail," he said, more cheerfully than might be suitable at this hour. "How went it with the Old Man today?"

They clasped forearms in the Roman manner. "Lad, you're all aquiver," Parnesius exclaimed.

"How I wish I could tell you," Gratillonius replied. "It's— oh, wonderful—but he made me vow secrecy for the time being. When I can talk, when actual operations are in train, then I'll be far from here."

"Well, I'm glad to see you're glad. Although— Come." Parnesius plucked at the other's mantle. "Step aside for a bit, shall we?"

More men were climbing the trail hither. While they numbered under a score, they were of many sorts, not only soldiers but workmen, serfs, slaves. Rank on earth counted for nothing before Ahura-Mazda.

As it did not before the Lord of the Christians...but they welcomed women to their services, passed fleetingly through Gratillonius. His father, his brother, himself followed Mithras; but his mother had been Christian and so, by amicable agreement, were his sisters raised. Could that alone be the reason why Christ was triumphing?

He thrust the thought away and followed Parnesius off as he had followed this comrade in arms, and the still more experienced Pertinax, on days when they could "take the heather"—fare off with a native guide to hunt, fish, be at ease in clean and lonesome country. "What have you to say?" he asked. " Time's short." Because the service was conducted on sufferance, military members had better be in their quarters by curfew.

Parnesius looked off and beat fist in palm. "I'm not sure," he answered roughly. "Except...I couldn't help getting hints when he quizzed me about you. And...Pertinax and I have had an offer...but we'll stay on the Wall, we two. You're going south, aren't you? Not just back to Isca, but on to Gallia."

Gratillonius swallowed. "I'm not supposed to say."

"Nevertheless—" Parnesius swung about and seized him by the shoulders. His gaze probed and pleaded. "He wouldn't have told you outright, but you must have a fair idea of what he intends. You must be aware you're to guard his back while— Well, what do you think about it? The next war will mean a great deal more than this last one, you know. Don't you?"

"I am...a soldier," Gratillonius answered most carefully. "I follow my orders. But...an Emperor who is a soldier too might be what we all need."

"Good!" cried Parnesius, and pummeled him lightly on the back. "And here in the North, Pertinax and I'll hold fast. Ho, I see him coming. Hail, Pertinax!"

But then the Father appeared, and men ranked themselves for the ceremony.

The Mithraeum was plain and low. It could not hold even as many as the remnant who were gathered. However, it was not meant to. The junior initiates, Ravens, Occults, Soldiers, did not attend the holiest of the rites. They joined their seniors in hymning the sun as it departed.

Flame glimmered across a green southwestern heaven, and went out. More and more stars gleamed forth, and lights along the blackness of Wall and fortress. Elsewhere the world sheened phantom gray. The song ended. The three underling ranks formed their squad and saluted while Lions, Persians, the Runner of the Sun, and the Father whom he attended went inside.

There was no space for a pronaos. There was, though, a vestibule, where Gratillonius and his fellows changed into their sacred garb. For him it was robe, mask, and Phrygian cap, because in the past year the elders had promoted him to Persian. Solemnly, they entered the sanctuary.

Lamplight amidst restless shadows picked out the altars that jutted into the narrow nave. At the end of the chamber, reliefs depicted Mithras slaying the Bull and His cosmic birth with the signs of the zodiac around. The stone was pierced so that illumination behind created the halo about his head. Flanking were the graven Dadophori, the brother figures, one with torch held high, one with torch down and guttering out. It was very quiet. After the chill outside, air felt merely cool. The sweet smoke of pine cones breathed through it.

The celebrants crossed the floor of oak planks and birch logs to their benches along the walls. The Father took his place before the Tauroctony. He was an aged man, as was the Heliodromos who served him. Their deaths would surely spell the end of worship here.

Gratillonius raised up his heart. However men blundered, Mithras remained true to His world; and meanwhile he, Gratillonius, had his own victory ahead of him.

II

Imbolc marked the season of making ready for the year's work, the lambing that would soon begin, spring sowing later, fishing whenever Manandan and the merfolk would allow. People took stock of what supplies remained in household and farmyard. On the coasts they gathered seaweed to cut up and strew on their fields, as well as shellfish when the tide of Brigit stood at its lowest. Yet the day itself and the vigil of the day were hallowed. Along the shores of Condacht and Mumu, live periwinkles or limpets were buried around each house for luck on strand and water. Many tuaths elsewhere did no work that called for the turning of a wheel, such as carting; it might bewilder the sun on his homeward course. Families wove new talismans of straw and twigs and hung them about dwellings for protection against lightning and fire. They celebrated the eve with the best feast their stores could provide, putting some outside for the Goddess, Who would be traveling that night, and grain for Her white cow. They reckoned, however, that Brigit was also pleased if the food went to the needy, or to those parties of youths and maidens that carried Her emblems from home to home across the land—as long as the gift was given in Her name.

Anxiously they watched for weather signs. Rain was welcome, to soften the ground and hasten growth of new grass; but storms were ominous, and if the hedgehog did not appear, that meant he was keeping his burrow in expectation of more winter followed by a hard summer. This year, what happened was so shifty across Ériu that no one knew what to await. Wisewomen said it portended strange doings and great changes; druids generally stayed silent.

On Temir was the most splendid of all festivals, for it was the King's, and Niall maqq Echach bade fair to became the mightiest since Corbmac maqq Arti, or even to outreach that lord. Not only his household and following were on hand, learned men, ollam craftsmen, warriors, their women and children; not only free tenants of both his and theirs, and families of these, from end to end of Mide; not only kings of the tuaths over whom he held sway, and their own attendants and underlings. From Condacht, whence the forbears of Niall had sprung, came many to greet their kinsman. From Mumu, where he had friends, came not a few. From the Lagini came some, more in hopes of mildening him toward themselves than in love. From the Ulati, alone among the fifths, came not a man, unless it be a few outcasts begging. But then, in Emain Macha they held a revel too, which they said was as royal and sacral as this.

Throughout the day of the vigil Niall had been taken up with welcoming his guests as they arrived, in such ways as became their standings and his. Now at eventide he would open the festivities.

Bathed and freshly clad, in stately wise he walked from the King's House to the point where the southward-running of the Five Roads to Temir came up on the hilltop. There his chariot awaited him. Its matched gray horses snorted and pawed; Cathual the driver must keep tight reins. Niall mounted easily. When the wheels groaned into motion, he stood steady amidst the rocking and jouncing. His spear swayed like a ship's mast. Sunlight streamed level to make its head shine as if newly bloodied.

From here Niall saw widely over his domains. Down along the road clustered the booths and tents of lower-ranking folk for whom the buildings had no space. Many were striped in colors, and pennons fluttered above some. On the next summit loomed the hill fort sacred to Medb. Heights round about were still bright, but hollows were filling with shadow. Though leafless, forest hid Boand's River to the north; yet the air, damp and turning chill, bore a sense of Her presence among the spirits that thronged nigh. Westward land dropped steeply to the plain, its pastures winter-dulled, save that mists had arisen to beswirl them with molten gold. The sun cast the same hue on clouds above that horizon, with heaven violet beyond them. Ahead of Niall bulked the Great Rath, its lime-whitened earthwork and the palisade on top likewise aglow.

People crowded the paths to watch him and his guards go by. Men's tunics and cloaks, their breeches or kilts, the gowns of women were vivid in red, yellow, blue, green, orange, black, white; gold, silver, amber, crystal, gems glistened around brows, throats, arms, waists; spears, axes, drawn swords flashed high in reverence; on shields, round or oval, the painted marks of their owners twined or snarled or ramped. Children, dogs, pigs ran about among the grown and joined their clamor to the shout that billowed for the King.

Well did he seem worthy of hailing. His chariot of state bore bronze masks on the sides; the spokes of its two wheels were gilded; at either rail hung the withered head of a Roman, taken by him in the past summer's warfare. Cathual the charioteer was a youngling short but lithe and comely, clad in tunic of scarlet; headband, belt, and wristlets were set with silver. From the shoulders of Niall swung a cloak of the finest wool, striped in the full seven colors permitted a king; his undershirt was of Roman silk, his tunic saffron with red and blue embroideries; rather than breeches he wore a kilt, dark russet to show off the whiteness and shapeliness of his legs, with shoes of kid on his feet. His ornaments outweighed and outshone all others.

Finest to see was himself. At some thirty years of age, after uncounted battles against men and beasts, Niall maqq Echach remained without any flaw that might cost him his lordship. Taller than most he reared, wide in shoulders and slender in hips, skin fair even where weather had touched it and not unduly shaggy, wildcat muscles flowing beneath. Golden were his long hair and mustaches, his close-trimmed beard.

13

His brow was broad, his nose straight, his chin narrow; eyes gleamed fire-blue.

Behind the chariot paced his hounds and his hostages, the men's attire revealing his generosity. They wore light golden chains, that everyone might know them for what they were, but strode proudly enough; their position was honorable, and most times they went unhampered. Behind them, and also in front of the chariot, walked his warriors. Closest to him were the four bodyguards and the gigantic champion, bearing helmets and dress shields of polished bronze; but the rest were hardly less brilliant, in tunics like their master's, axes glimmering and spearheads nodding on high.

Folk cheered themselves hoarse to see the power of King Niall. Few were so close as to make out the grimness upon his lips, the bitterness in his face.

The procession turned where a gate stood open in the Great Rath and a bridge had been laid down across the ditch. It went over the lawn within, past the lesser enclosure of the Royal Guesthouse and the embanked mound whereon rose the King's quarters. A ways farther on, it halted. There the Mound of the Kings lifted itself athwart the outer palisade.

Niall did not dismount and climb its grassy slopes. That was only done when a new King was taken. Then he would stand on the sacred slab at the top, make his three turns dessiul and widdershins, receive the White Wand, invoke the Gods. On this holy eve, Cathual guided the chariot past the Phallus below, five lichenous feet of standing stone. A fighting man stationed at that menhir swung a bullroarer to proclaim that this was truly the King who came by.

The procession went on, out a northern gate, past other stones to which Niall dipped his spear, past the Rath of the Warriors, between the small mounds Dall and Dercha, on to the Feasting Hall. Niall's Queen, his sons, his counselors, their chief servants stood waiting. Cathual drew rein and the overlord sprang down. He gave his weapon to the charioteer and first greeting to the druid and the poets, as was seemly. Thereafter he received the salutation of the others according to their status.

"Now we've a time to wait," he said. "Is it a good sign that we are free of rain the while?"

"It is that," answered the druid, Nemain maqq Aedo, gravely, "but other signs have been such that you will be wise to sacrifice more than is wont tomorrow."

Niall scowled. "I did so last year, at both Imbolc and Beltene, and meager gain did we have of it."

Some people looked aghast at this defiance of the Powers. Nemain simply raised his hand. He was gaunt, snowy-bearded, his eyes dimmed by years and by peering into mysteries. Unlike everyone else, he wore a plain white robe and blue cloak; but his staff was carved with potent

14

ogamm signs. "Speak not rashly, dear heart," he said. "If you failed to overrun the foe—then, sure it nonetheless is that you brought home alive yourself and most of the men, with not so little plunder. Would it not have been easier, now, for the Mórrigu to let you lie raven-food under the Roman Wall? The signs I have read, in stars and staves and secret pools, are signs of mighty deeds, of a world in travail with a new birth. Give freely, and receive back honor."

Flame flickered up through Niall's sullen mood. "Warfare already again this summer?"

"That is as may be. Thus far the red wind only whispers, and I know not from what quarter it is blowing."

Niall's glance flew about, south toward the Lagini, north toward the Ulati, east toward Alba across the water, which the Romans called Britannia. There it lingered.

Breccan, his eldest son, advanced. "Father, dear," he cried, "you'll be taking me along, will you not?"

Niall turned and regarded him. The sun had just set, but light remained in heaven to make the boy shine forth against a world going dun. Breccan was tall for his fourteen years but not filled out; his limbs thrust spidery from the garments that covered his slip of a body. The hair tumbled flax-white past huge blue eyes and a face whose beauty was redeemed from girlishness by the down on its upper lip. Yet he moved with a certain coltish grace; few could match him in a race afoot or on horseback; he was fierce in the games that his kind played and in practice with weapons.

"You are a stripling," Niall said, though he smiled more kindly than he had done since his return. "Be patient. You'll be winning fame aplenty in due course."

Breccan swallowed, stood his ground, and said stoutly, "Seven years it's been since I took valor. You told me then that I should have to wait no longer than that." He appealed to the Queen. "Mother, did he not indeed?"

She, who was in truth his stepmother but had always gotten along with him, smiled in her turn. "Niall, darling," she said, "I remember you promised he should—fare widely, those were your words—after seven years. And did not yourself do the same?"

Niall's countenance darkened. She made a mistake when she reminded him of his own stepmother and how Mongfind schemed his destruction for the sake of her sons by his father.

Laidchenn maqq Barchedo spoke softly: "It is to the glory of the King when someone recalls his exploits. This is also true of deeds done together by brothers among whom there was faith."

For a heartbeat Niall's mouth tightened. But he could not gainsay an ollam poet, who moreover was a guest and the former pupil of his foster-father. Nor did the man from Mumu intend anything but good.

He merely called to mind that the sons of Mongfind had themselves never conspired against Niall but had become his trusty followers; and that he had no right to suspect his wife of urging Breccan into early battle, to get him out of the way of her sons.

The king eased. "We shall see," he told the boy. "Do you begin by learning how to wait. You will do enough of that in war." Suddenly he grinned. "And likewise you will know chills, rains, mud, growling belly, weary feet, grumbling men, and baggage trains gone astray. Not to talk of dripping noses, runny guts, and never a woman for your bed!"

Gladness went through the listeners like a wave. For the first time since coming back to Ériu, himself seemed cheerful. Well, this was the eve of Brigit, and She a healing Goddess.

Meanwhile guests had come crowding about. Men gave their weapons into the care of attendants, for it was gess to go armed into this house. The very eating-knives must be solely in the hands of the servers who would carve the joints. Their shields the men turned over to the steward. Aided by household staff, he bore them inside. There the royal senchaide directed where they should hang, in order of dignity, so that each owner would go straight to his place without scrambles or quarrels. It took a knowledge of lineages and histories through long generations. Dusk had deepened before all was ready and a horn blew invitation.

Magnificent was the Feasting Hall on Temir. The earthwork that sheltered it was not round but seven hundred fifty feet in length, ninety feet in width; and the building left scant room between. Although it had stood for more than two years, and would be torn down this year before a new one was raised for the next Harvest Fair, it did not much show wear. Peeled upright poles making the walls were still bright, ties and chinking still solid; winds had not disturbed the intricately woven patterns of the thatch.

Within, the double rows of pillars upholding that high roof would be reused, as great as they were and as thickly carved with magical figures. Lamps hanging from the rafters and a fire in a pit at the middle gave light to see by, reflecting off gold and burnished bronze. Down the length of the nave, servers stood ready to carve the meat that kitchen help were bringing in from the cookhouse. Guests took benches along the aisles, before which were trestle tables bearing cups of mead. Foremost, at the center of the east side, was Niall's place, flanked by the men of greatest honor. Fifty guards stood in attendance, also disarmed but their shields and helmets asheen in unrestful shadows.

The Queen and other women sat opposite. Unlike most homes, at Temir it was not usual for them to join the men at feast. Instead, they dined in the Royal Guesthouse. This, though, was time sacred to a female God and to the fruitfulness of the coming season. Besides, some of them flaunted scars from battles, and had brought back several of the skulls which stared emptily from the walls. Medb Herself could take pride in celebrants like these.

The surf-roar and clatter of people finding their seats died away. Looks went to the King's companions. Before anyone touched food here, always a poet spoke.

Laidchenn stood up, rang the chimes on the baton that declared what he was, lifted from its carrying case a harp he had already tuned, and cradled it in his left arm. There had been no questions but that he would take the word, among those poets who were present. Not only was he a visitor from afar, he was from the school of Torna Éces. A barrel-chested man with bushy red hair and beard, richly but a little carelessly clad, he did not seem one who could call forth such icy-sweet notes as he did. Power pulsed in his deep voice when he looked straight into the eyes of Niall and chanted:

"Lúg, bright God, of war the Lord,
Long-Arm, hear my harp!
Hark to tales that I will tell,
Talking unto all.

"Heaven sees how Temir's holy
Hilltop now bears Niall,
Never conquered, as its King,
Keeping warlike watch.

"See him seated in his splendor.
So it was not once.
Well that men should know how much
Might wring wealth from woe."

A happy sigh went over the benches. Listeners knew they were about to hear a grand story.

And Laidchenn told it; and those who had heard it often, growing year by year, found newness, while others found wonder.

Niall, sang the poet, Niall, descendant of Corbmac maqq Arti, son of Eochaid maqq Muredach who was called Magimedon—Niall was born of dark curly-haired Carenn, a princess whom his father had carried away from Alba. In those days his grandfather still ruled. Eochaid had a wife named Mongfind, daughter of a Tuathal king in Mumu, who was a witch and a ruthless woman. She bore him four sons, Brión, Fechra, Alill, and Fergus. Because Niall showed early promise, Mongfind plotted to do away with him, lest he succeed to lordship instead of Brion or a brother of Brión. She had him carried off, a small boy, while his father was gone warring. When Eochaid returned, Mongfind persuaded him that the loss was due to Carenn's carelessness, and Eochaid let Mongfind make a menial slave of his erstwhile leman.

But Torna, great poet in Mumu, knew by his arts what had happened, and foresaw what was in Niall. He rescued the child and fostered him. When the early signs of manhood were upon Niall, Torna sent him back to reclaim his own. Eochaid, now King, joyously received this son he had thought lost, and Carenn was released from her bondage.

Once Eochaid wished to test the five youths. A blacksmith's shop caught fire, and he commanded them to save what they could. Brión fetched out the chariots, Alill a shield and sword, Féchra the forge trough, Fergus merely some firewood; but Niall rescued anvil, block, sledges, and bellows, the heart of the smith's trade.

On another time when they were hunting and had grown sorely thirsty, they came upon a well deep in the forest. However, its guardian was a hideous old hag, who would give a drink to none unless he lie with her. No son of Mongfind could make himself do that; at most, Brión achieved a hasty kiss. But Niall led her aside and laid her down. Then rags and shriveled skin fell from her, she came forth radiant in youth and beauty, for this was the Goddess Who bestows sovereignty. Afterward Niall made his half-brothers pledge fealty to him before he would let them drink. They abided honestly by that, and Brión presently fathered a line of chieftains.

But meanwhile Mongfind lived and schemed. Through her magics—and, no doubt, kinsmen in Mumu of whom Eochaid had need—she kept him from putting her from him. Upon his death, she succeeded in having her brother Craumthan maqq Fidaci chosen as his successor.

He, though, proved to be no clay for her molding, but instead a man who laid a firm grip on the land and warred both in Ériu and across the waters. After years, despairing of aught else, Mongfind sought to poison him. He required that she drink first of the cup she proffered; and so they both died. Spells were still cast on certain nights to keep quiet the ghost of Mongfind the witch.

Throughout this time, Niall had been at the forefront of battles. In council his words were shrewd, later wise. It was upon a tenant's daughter, Ethniu, that he begot his eldest child, Breccan; but she was lovely and high-hearted, and everybody mourned when she died in giving birth. Niall soon married well—behold how his sons by the Queen are already shooting up! Thus after the death of Craumthan four years ago, it was no surprise when the Mide men chose him to be their King.

And he has wrought deeds that will live in memory as long as valor is cherished. Besides much else closer to home, he has harried the coasts overseas, bringing back huge booty. When the Cruthini of Alba, whom the Romans call the Picti of Caledonia, threatened the settlement of Dál Riata, Niall made alliance with its mother kingdom for its rescue; then, having cast the Cruthini back, he made alliance with them in turn. In Ériu, too, he called warriors to him from far beyond the bounds of Mide. No vaster hosting has been seen since the Cattle Raid of Cóalnge, than when the men of tribes conjoined roared down to the Wall of Rome.

And this time it was not Cú Culanni who stood alone in defense, it was Cú Culanni reborn at the van of attack. Many a Roman soldier sprawls headless in the heather, many a Britannic estate lies plundered

18

and burnt, many a slave has gone to market and today herds sheep or grinds grain for a worthy master; and if the Wall of Rome still stands, why, the more glory to reap when we return!

"Never shall the hero Niall
Kneel to any other.
Witness, all you Gods, my words,
Aware I tell the truth."

The last notes shivered away. Cheers thundered from benches to ridgepole. The King took from his arm a heavy coil of gold. Standing up, he put it in the hands of Laidchenn. "Have this of me in token of thanks," he said amidst the din, "and let me ask of you that you abide with me a long while—forever, if I may have my wish."

Flushed, breathing hard, eyes asparkle, Niall sat back down. The druid Nemain stroked his beard and murmured, "Your fame grows by leaps, darling."

Niall tossed his head. "What a poet says is true. He may find fresh words for the clothing of truth—but—you would not be denying that I wedded the Goddess of the land, would you?"

"I would not," replied Nemain, "nor speak against anything I have heard tonight; for indeed truth is a lady who has many different garments to wear. I would simply lay caution upon you. Not qualm, only caution, for sadly would we miss our lord should he fall, and worst if it was needlessly."

Niall did not hear. Again his head was aflame with dreams. Long though the nights still were, he did not look for much sleep in this one, if any; for among the gessa laid on a King of Mide was that sunrise must never find him in bed on Temir. It did not matter. He *was* the King.

As host, he should make a speech of welcome. Rising, he lifted his goblet—Roman glass, loot from Alba. Out of full lungs, he shouted: "It's glad I am to see so great and fair a company here, and glad Herself must be, and every God. If I name not the kings and nobles among us and their honors, it is because dawn would break well before I was done. Let us instead make merry, let us no more grieve over our losses or brood on our wrongs, let us look ahead to a year of revenge and victory!"

III

His father's house felt strangely empty to Gratillonius.

Or not so strangely, he thought. When he arrived the evening before, joy was too tumultuous for him to pay close heed to his surroundings. Notified in advance, Marcus had had a feast prepared for his soldier son. The food was local, fish and meat and dried garden truck, but seasoned with such things as pepper and cloves, scarce these days, while the wines were from Burdigala and Narbonensis, not a mediocre Britannic vineyard. If the tableware was of poor quality and the attendant an untrained yokel, talk between the two men made up amply for that. When it turned to Gaius's older brother it grew evasive—Lucius was "studying in Aquae Sulis; you know what a bookish sort he's always been, not like you, you rascal"—but then the news quickly came that his youngest sister Camilla had married an able farmer, Antonia and Faustina continued happy in their own homes, and another grandchild was on the way. And his old nurse Docca had earlier hugged him in arms crippled by rheumatism, and he learned that three or four more of those who had been dear to him in his boyhood were still above ground.

Soon after supper weariness overwhelmed him and he went to bed. It had not been any route march to get here, only a few miles from Isca to the Sabrina, a ferry ride across the broad rivermouth, and a little way inland beyond that. He had, though, been at work since dawn preparing, as he had been for days previously. It won him an early enough start that he could justify spending two nights at home before he began his journey in earnest.

Thus he awoke ahead of sun and household. When he got up, the air nipped and the floor was cold. He recalled that the place had been chilly yesterday too, nothing but a couple of charcoal braziers for heat; he had avoided asking why. Fumbling his way through murk, he drew aside a curtain that, as spring approached, had supplanted shutters. On the leaded window, bits of leather were glued over three empty panes. The glass must have been broken in some accident or juvenile mischief. Why had his father, who always took pride in keeping things shipshape, not had it replaced?

Sufficient moonlight seeped through for Gratillonius to use flint, steel, and tinder. When he had ignited a tallow candle, he dropped the curtain back to conserve warmth and took care of his necessities. Clad in tunic and sandals, candlestick in hand, he padded forth in search of all he remembered.

The house reached shadowy around him. It had grown, piece by piece, for almost two hundred years as the family prospered; but his grandfather had been the last to make any additions. Doors were closed on this upper story, though only he and Marcus occupied bedrooms. (Once the hall was a clamor of footfalls and laughter.) Well, no sense in leaving chambers open when servants were too few to keep them dusted.

Gratillonius went downstairs. The atrium was still elegant, peacock mosaic on the floor and Theseus overcoming the Minotaur on a wall. Colors glimmered where the candlelight picked them out of darkness. However, most of the heirloom furniture was gone. Replacements were conscientiously built, but by carpenters, not artists.

An ebony table was among the few ancestral pieces remaining. Upon it lay several books. They were copied on scrolls, not bound into modern codices, because they too had been in the family for generations. Gratillonius's left hand partly unrolled one. A smile passed faint over his lips. He recognized *The Aeneid*. That he had enjoyed reading, along with other hero stories, as he did hearing the songs and sagas of the Britons from those backwoods folk who knew them yet—and did emphatically not enjoy Fronto and other bores he was supposed to study so he could become a proper Roman. Learning Greek turned out to be impossible for a boy who could be rambling the woods, riding, swimming, boating, fishing, playing ball or war with his friends, alone in the workshop making something—later, hanging around neighbor Ewein's daughter Una— Finally his tutor gave up.

Lucius was different, of course. Their mother had been proud of him.

Sadness tugged at Gratillonius. He left the atrium, went down a corridor to the west wing, and opened a door he knew well. Behind it was a room Julia had used for sewing and such-like lady's work. And for prayer. Her husband let her have a fish and Chi Rho painted on a wall. Before them each day, until a fever took her off, she humbly called on her Christ.

Gratillonius's free hand stroked the air where her head would have been were she sitting there. "I loved you, mother," he whispered. "If only I'd known how to show it."

Maybe she had understood anyway. Or maybe she now did in whatever afterworld had received her.

Gratillonius shook himself, scowled, and went out. He wanted to inspect the kitchen and larder. That wasn't supposed to be any concern of his. But every soldier developed a highly practical interest in grub. Though supper had been fine, what were ordinary meals like, in this house where they couldn't pay to fuel the furnace? Gratillonius meant to make sure that his father was eating adequately, if perhaps frugally.

He should have looked into that on earlier visits. Even before he enlisted he was aware of a pinch that strengthened year by year. But his awareness was only peripheral, as stoic as his father was and as lost as he himself was in dreams of Una, the lightfoot and golden-haired—until she perforce married elsewhere, and he flung himself into the army— She no longer haunted him, much. He should have become more thoughtful of his own kindred.

Yet regardless of Isca's nearness, his appearances here had been infrequent, the last one three years back. And they had been short. He'd spent most of his furlough time ranging the Silurian hills, forests, remote settlements where men were friendly and girls friendlier; or else he'd be off to the baths and frivolities of Aquae Sulis, or as far afield as smoky Londinium. The recollection hurt him, on what might well be his last sight of home and these people, hurt him both with guilt and with a sense of having squandered a treasure.

21

When he had finished his tour, the sky showed wan through glass. The cook and the housekeeper yawned their way forth, too sleepy to greet him. He could forgive that in the former, who had been here longer than he could recall, but the latter was a young slattern. Gratillonius considered giving her a tongue-lashing for insolence. He decided against it. She would merely be the surlier after he was gone. Besides, maybe she was the best Marcus could find. The older man had bespoken a dearth of good help. Not only was the countryside population dwindling as small farms were swallowed up by plantations or abandoned altogether by owners whom taxes and weak markets had ruined. Those folk who stayed were generally bound by law to the soil, and serfs seldom raised their children to much pride of workmanship.

As he re-entered the atrium, Gratillonius met his father coming from upstairs, and was especially filial in his salutation. "Good morning," replied Marcus. "I hope you slept well. Your old bed is one thing I've managed to keep."

Touched, Gaius gave him a close regard. The dawnlight showed a face and form resembling his own; but Marcus's hair was gray, his countenance furrowed, the once powerful body gaunt and stoop-shouldered. "Thank you, sir," Gaius said. "Could we talk today ...privately?"

"Of course. You'll want a walk around the place, anyway. First, though, our duties, and next our breakfast."

They went forth together onto the verandah, sought its eastern end, lifted arms and voices to Mithras as the sun rose. It stirred Gaius more than rites in a temple commonly did. He paid his respects to the God and tried to live by the Law, because that was upright, soldierly, everything this man at his side—and this man's stern father, once—had tried to make him become. But he was not fervent about it. Here, somehow, a feeling of sanctity took him, as if borne on those rays bestorming heaven. Tears stung his eyes. He told himself they must be due the wind.

Everydayness came back. The men spoke little while they had their bread and cheese. Afterward they dressed against the weather and left the house. "Let's begin at the stable," Marcus suggested. "There's a colt you'll appreciate."

Gaius looked about him more closely than yesterday. The house stood firm beneath its red-tiled roofs, and likewise did the farm buildings to either side, around a cobbled courtyard. But he saw where whitewash had flaked from walls, the cowpen and its barn gaped almost empty, a single youngster went to feed pigs and chickens where formerly the grounds had roared with life.

The wind shrilled and plucked at his cloak. He drew the garment tight against those icy fingers. Northward he saw the land roll in long curves to the woods where boys went—sometimes in defiance of orders from parents who feared Scoti might pounce from the river and seize them for slaves—and where Gwynmael the gamekeeper had taught him how to read a spoor and set a snare. Closer in, the acres were cleared, but most had gone back to grass and brush, still winter-sere, although quickened by the faintest breath of new green. Through an apple orchard he discerned a cultivated field, dark save where wind-ruffled rain puddles blinked in the sunshine. Rooks and starlings darted above, blacker yet. A hawk high overhead disdained to stoop on them. Its wings shimmered golden.

A thought struck Gaius. "I haven't seen your steward, Artorius," he said. "Has he died?"

"No—"

"Good. He used to tell me wonderful stories about his days as a legionary. That was what started me thinking I'd want to enlist, myself." Gaius forced a laugh. "After I did, I discovered what a liar he'd been, but no matter, he's a grand old rogue."

"Too old. Nearly blind. I retired him. He's moved in with a son of his."

"Um, who do you have now?"

Marcus shrugged. "Nobody. Can't find a competent man and couldn't afford him if I did. I'm my own steward. The villa's no longer so big or busy that I can't handle it."

They neared the stable. A hound sprang forth, baying, until a word from Marcus brought it to heel. A white-haired man shuffled out behind the creature. He stopped short, blinked, squinted, and quickened his pace. "Why, bless my butt if that's not the young master!" he cried in Belgic dialect. "We'd heard you were coming, but I thank the Gods just the same. Welcome, lad, welcome!"

Gaius took a hand gnarled into a set of claws, regarded a visage withered and well-nigh toothless, and remembered how Gwynmael had drifted like a shadow down forest paths till his bow twanged and the arrow found its mark. He hadn't been nearly this aged three years ago. Well, Gaius thought with pain, you grow old, suddenly you can't run fast enough, and Time the Hunter overtakes you in a pair of leaps. "Are you working here?" he asked in the vernacular.

"So 'tis, so 'tis. I'm no use any more for chasing off poachers or bringing back venison. But your dad's a kindly sort and lets me pretend to earn my keep being his head groom. That's easy, because except for a boy I'm the only groom, heh, heh. Not that I could've carried on in my real job after our woods got sold off." In his shock at hearing that, Gaius hardly noticed when Gwynmael fondled the hound's ears and said, "Splendid dog, eh? Remember Brindle, what coursed the stags so well? Here's a pup from the last litter she bore. Too bad we can't let this 'un do what his blood meant him for." Taking the centurion's elbow: "But come inside, young sir, come in and look at what we got in a stall. Juno foaled him last summer, and if he don't live up to his promise, why, he's the biggest braggart in horsedom."

The stable was dim and warm, smelling sweetly of hay and animal, pungently of manure. Gaius stopped to stroke the two beasts he knew, mare and gelding—their noses were silk-soft, and Juno whickered for pleasure—before he went on to the stallion colt. That was indeed a superb creature, like a cross between flesh and wind. "Epona Herself 'ud be glad to ride him when he's full-grown," Gwynmael said. He had never made any bones about his devotion to the ancient Gods of the Belgae.

"What sire?" Gaius asked.

"Commius's prize stud," Marcus told him.

"Really? Commius the senator? He must have charged you a pretty solidus."

"He did, but I should profit eventually. You see, I think I can fence in most of what land we have left, take out the scrub, sow pasturage, and breed horses. Blooded horses, for riding. Skilled help may not be too hard to come by in that business: veteran cavalrymen from the eastern provinces, especially, or their sons."

"But who could pay the price you'd have to set?"

"The army. I may have swallowed the anchor, but I still get word from overseas, as far as Constantinople. Given the new Asiatic saddles, horsemen are the soldiers of the future. Cataphracts could roll the barbarians back—though we won't get them in Britannia during my lifetime. However, I expect we'll begin to see more and more cavalry in Gallia, and here I'll be, prepared to export." Marcus's smile turned grim. "Also, rich men everywhere will want fast mounts in case of raiders or uprisings."

His moods gentled. He touched Gaius's arm. "I'll need this fellow for breeding," he murmured, "but I'll set aside the best of his get for you."

The son gulped. "Thank you," he said unsteadily. "I'm not sure whether—oh, we have to talk about all this."

They went out and set off toward the Roman road. Little used, the wagon track alongside which they walked was not very muddy. Rounding the orchard, Gaius saw two men, no more, at work in the grainfield. They were plowing with ards drawn by cows. Gaius halted. "Where's the proper gear?" he wondered.

"Sold, like much else," Marcus replied.

Keen as its coulter there rose before Gaius the memory of a wheeled moldboard plow and the mighty oxen that pulled it. Rage rose acid in his throat. "But this is wrong, wrong!"

"Oh, the villa hasn't enough land under cultivation to need better equipment."

"You've sold...still more? Besides the woods?"

"Had to. They slapped an extra assessment on me for waterworks, after Tasciovanus went bankrupt, Laurentinus suicided, and Guennellius disappeared—ran off to Londinium and is hiding in its proletary, some say."

"Who bought your land?"

"Commius. Who else?"

Fury lifted higher. Commius the gross, Commius the crooked, Commius the unmerciful squeezer of tenants, servants, slaves, Commius who bought his way to senatorial rank—everybody knew that was a question of bribing the right people—and thus escaped the burdens of the curials, Commius who thereupon had the gall to boast how public-spirited he was because he maintained a theater, whose pornographic shows must swell business at the whorehouse everybody knew he owned—

"Calm down," Marcus advised. "His sort, they come and go. Rome's had them since first the Republic began to rot, if not earlier; but Rome endures, and that is what matters." When he grinned, his leathery face looked, briefly, wolfish. "In fact, last year, at a series of council meetings, I had the pleasure of frustrating him. He wanted to close our Mithraeum as the Emperor had decreed. I got my friends behind me and we agreed that if that was done, we'd see to it that his precious theater was shut down too. Those plays pretend to show myths of the ancestors, you know, and we'd claim this made them not 'educational displays' but pagan ceremonies. An Imperial inquiry would have turned up more about his affairs than he could well stand—investments in commerce and industry such as are forbidden a senator, for instance. He stopped calling for any religious prohibitions. It was marvelous, seeing him flush red and hearing him gobble. The God does send His faithful a bit of fun once in a while."

But the God's faithful die or fall away, year after year, and ever fewer take their places, Gaius thought.

The somberness dampened his wrath. "At least you've lowered your tax by selling off," he ventured, "and with this horse-breeding scheme you may win back to something better...for Lucius and the grandchildren he'll give you."

Marcus's mouth drew tight. They trudged on in silence, except for the wind. Finally the father said, tonelessly, looking at the far hills: "No. I didn't tell you earlier because it would have spoiled our evening. But Lucius has turned Christian. He's studying under the bishop in Aquae Sulis, with the aim of becoming a churchman too. He talks about celibacy."

Gaius's feet jarred to rest. Emptiness grew from his heart until it engulfed him. "Not that," he whispered.

Marcus stopped likewise and squeezed his shoulder. "Well, well, don't take it overly hard. I've learned to live with it. We've stayed on speaking terms, he and I. It *was* his mother's religion, and is that of his sisters and their husbands and...Maximus, who cast back the wild men.... I can't blame him greatly. If he'd waited till I died, he'd have been trapped in the curial class himself. Taking Christian holy orders now is his way out of it."

Out! thought Gaius. The army was another way, and he had chosen it, although that would not have been allowed if he were the older boy. Since Diocletianus, a son and heir must follow in his father's

25

occupation. The law was frequently evaded, but the curials—the land-owners, merchants, producers, the moderately well-off—were usually too noticeable. Once it had been an honor to belong to their class. They were the councillors and magistrates; they did not endow the grandiose spectacles that Caesars and senators and ambitious newly rich did, but they underwrote the useful public works. That had been long ago. The burdens remained; the means were gone.

"I hoped to be free of it myself, you know," Marcus was saying. "That's why I went into sea traffic. High profits for men who didn't mind the risk. Your grandfather approved—and he was a man of duty if ever there was one—and got me started. But at last...well, you know. It had taken all my father's influence, and a stiff bribe, to get permission for me to become a navicularius when I wasn't the son of one. Then your uncle, my older brother, died, and the guild was only too happy to 'regularize' my status. That laid this estate on me. It's devoured everything I had."

"I do know. But I've never quite understood how."

"I didn't explain because I didn't want to whine at you, who were young and had neither gift nor wish for this kind of thing. I did have my good, quiet Lucius, who was supposed to inherit anyway. It's the taxes and assessments. I barter for my everyday needs, of course; we all do. Not much good silver circulates, and I try to put by a little against real need. But meanwhile the Imperium wants its cash. The taxes in kind, they get higher all the time too, as the number of farmers shrinks. In my seafaring days I was a sharp bargainer, you may recall; but I don't have Commius's talent for grinding wealth out of the poor underneath me."

Abruptly Marcus lifted his head, glanced at Gaius through crow's-footed eyes, and laughed. He might almost have been standing at the prow of his ship as a gale blew up. "At ease, boy, at ease!" he said. "You're safe. The law will scarcely haul a battle-proven officer back to the farm, especially when you're known to none less than Duke Maximus. He'll probably get you senatorial rank. As for this place, why, if my plan pays off, I should have a chance of joining forces with my sons-in-law after they inherit. Between us, we might yet put together a villa that will last."

"But if you fail to?" Gaius breathed.

"I won't consider that till it's upon me, which the God forbid. At worst, I'll never do what too many broken curials have, slunk off under changed names and become underlings, even serfs. No, your old man will die a Gratillonius."

"I would help you if I could. I hope you know that, father. But...I'm bound afar, and what will happen to me I cannot foresee."

"Let's go on," said Marcus. A while of walking passed until he remarked, "You've told me nothing but that you're off to Gallia on a special mission for the Duke. Crossing the Channel before equinox—

Did he give you the funds you'll need to persuade a skipper to take you?"

Gaius smiled. "Better than that. A writ letting me commandeer a naval transport. And I mean to cross by the shortest way, from Dubris to Gesoriacum, where one can scarcely get lost in anything less than an oatmeal fog. Cutting out that hazard makes the added overland travel worthwhile."

"Then your march will take you through Londinium," said Marcus, also trying to lighten the mood. "Give the fleshpots a workout for me."

Gaius shook his head. "We won't stop after today, except for sleep. We've this breadth of Britannia to cross, and then it's more than four hundred miles over Gallia, and...the task is urgent."

Marcus squinted into the wind. Some distance off, Gaius's legionaries had pitched their tents in a vacated field. That was all they had done, being too few for the labor of constructing a standard camp, but they had done it properly. The leather was drawn so taut over poles and guys that the air got no purchase on it but must be content with flapping a banner.

Metal gleamed on statue-like sentries. Men detailed to camp chores were in plain tunic and trousers, but neat. The rest were outside in full battle dress, drilling. When they hurled their javelins, it called to mind a flight of bright birds. Tethered pack horses stood placidly, used to the sight, but the centurion's mount and remount, more spirited, stirred as if impatient for action.

"Four tents," Marcus counted. "Thirty-two men, eh? Not much."

"I chose them carefully, the best I have who aren't bound to wives. Most are Britons; we'll understand each other's thinking. I didn't order them to follow me but offered them the privilege of volunteering. They're eager. Over-eager, maybe, but I think the march will shake them down into a crack unit."

"Still, I can hear in your voice you'd have preferred a larger force."

"Maximus sent direct word to my commandant that I was to have no more than this. He...can't spare many."

"So I've been suspecting.... But he obviously doesn't expect you'll meet serious opposition."

"No. Yonder fellows will be my bodyguards and, um, the presence of Rome. That should suffice."

"Where?"

"Father, I'm not supposed to tell—"

"Four hundred-odd miles of Gallia. Not south, because that's where the main action will be. Also, your experience has been with Armorica, as Maximus must know. Westbound, you'll fetch up at Gesocribate, or else fairly close. But Gesocribate already has an ample Roman presence. And I don't think the Duke of the Armorican Tract would welcome troops dispatched by the Duke of the Britains— certainly not before he knows which way the cat is going to jump. Therefore he's doubtless not been informed, nor is he meant to get the news until too late for him to do anything about it." Marcus nodded. "M-hm. Your task is to secure a critical area and thus help assure that Armorica will stay safe—for Maximus."

Gaius's bark of laughter flushed a hare from a briar patch. It lolloped off as if a fox were at its tail. "Father, you're too shrewd!"

"I told you I get word from outside." Marcus bleakened. "For some time, now, I've caught the smell of war on the wind, stronger and stronger. Civil war. Maximus will get the Britannic legions to hail him Augustus. The Sixth may be doing it in Eboracum at this very hour. He'll cross to Gallia and try for the throne."

"Wait, wait! He didn't say that to me. He said only that affairs of state are approaching a crisis and Rome will need a loyal man in Armorica."

"Loyal to him. You're not stupid. You know what he meant."

"He is...a valiant leader, father. And intelligent and just. Rome perishes for want of right governance."

"Those sound like words you got from him," Marcus said, low in his throat. "Oh, we could do worse. Provided the struggle doesn't wreak the kind of harm the last such did, or give the Northfolk their chance to invade."

Gaius recalled Parnesius. "The Wall will abide, I swear."

"Scoti sail past it. Saxon galleys sweep in from the eastern sea."

"Against them—Rome will have new help."

Once more they halted. Marcus's gaze probed like a sapper's spade. "That's your task," he said finally.

Gaius swallowed hard and nodded.

"I believe I know where. I'd liefest hear it from your lips, son. Mithras be witness that I'll keep the secret."

Gaius thrust the name forth. "Ys."

Marcus drew a sign before him, the Cross of Light that marked the shield of his warrior God. "That's an uncanny place," he said.

Gaius mustered courage. "It's been left alone so long that all sorts of wild stories about it have sprung up. What do we know for certain? What do *you* know, father?"

Wind roared and whistled. Clouds were appearing over the horizon. Their shadows raced across winter-gray hills and the few springtime-wet croplands. A solitary willow nearby lashed its withes around. At their removes, the manor house and the soldiers' camp looked very small. The hawk wheeled scornful overhead.

Lines deepened in Marcus's brow and beside his mouth. "I was never there myself," he said. "I did speak with Britannic and Gallic captains who'd called. But they were just three or four, and none had done it more than once. The Ysans don't seem to want any trade with the outside that they don't carry on for themselves. No more involvement of any kind with Rome that they can avoid. Not that they act hostile.

My talkmates said the city is still more wonderful than they'd heard, Ys of the hundred towers. But even in the joyhouses there was always...an otherness."

"It's a foederate of ours," Gaius reminded.

"After a fashion. And only in name for—what? These past two hundred years? When did the last Roman prefect leave?"

"I'm not sure." Gratillonius straightened. "But I will be the next."

"Keeping Ys neutral, at least, and a counterweight to people elsewhere in Armorica who might otherwise side with Gratianus and Valentinianus against Maximus."

Gaius responded louder.

"And, I hope, taking a more active part than hitherto in measures against pirates. Ysan commerce has shrunk with Rome's. From what little I recall or could find out these past months, Ys trades mainly with its Osismiic neighbors, overland; but once it was the queen of the Northern seas. I should think it'd welcome guidance in rebuilding security and commerce. Father, I don't see how any living city can be the kind of witch-nest those rumors tell of. Give me a few years, and I'll prove as much to the world."

Marcus Valerius Gratillonius smiled, more in pride than in pleasure. "Good for you, son. Sink or sail, you're a Roman!"

And how many such are left? he did not ask. Men who have hardly a drop of blood in them from Mother Rome, and who will never see her whom they serve. Can she hold their faith, today when new Gods beckon?

IV

~ 1 ~

It was good to be on salt water again. Gratillonius braced himself at the taffrail of the transport, near a swan's-head figure that decorated the after section, and looked happily about. Forward of him was the deckhouse, on top of which two men strained to hold their steering oars against seas running heavy. It hid from Gratillonius the main deck, with lifeboat, cargo hatch, crewmen, and his soldiers. The mast rose over it. Square mainsail and triangular topsail bellied against swift gray clouds and malachite waves. Gratillonius could also glimpse the spar that jutted out over the prow and the artemon sail it bore.

No other craft was in sight. Their whiteness dulled by spindrift, the cliffs of Britannia were sinking under the horizon, though he could still make out the pharos that loomed over Dubris. Ahead, hillscape was shouldering out of Gallia, likewise vague and distance-dimmed.

The ship rolled and bounded like a live creature. Waters rushed, boomed, clashed. The wind skirled and flung briny spatters across his lips. Timbers and rigging creaked. Gratillonius's muscles rejoiced in the interplay that kept him erect. Tomorrow he'd be on the road again, and that was good too, because he'd fare through country new to him until he reached magical Ys. But Mithras be thanked that first he got this brief voyage.

He laughed aloud at himself. Had the Gods really carved out a strait at the Creation in order that Gaius Valerius Gratillonius could have a day's worth of feeling like the boy he once was?

The captain strode around the deckhouse. His blue uniform was hidden beneath a cloak he hugged to him in the cold. Approaching, he said through the noise: "Come forward with me, centurion. A fight's brewing between your men and mine."

"What? How?"

"Several of yours are miserably seasick, and when one of them puked on the deck, the sailors didn't want to clean it up. Then they started mocking those landlubbers."

Gratillonius bridled. "What kind of discipline do you have in the fleet?"

The captain sighed. "They resent being forced out this early in the year, in this tricky weather. I do myself, frankly, but I realize you have your orders, whatever they are. Now do come along. It'll work better if we both take charge."

Gratillonius agreed and accompanied the other. On the broad expanse around the mast, men stood at confrontation. They were not all there were in their units. Some deckhands would have been flogged if they left their duty stations—though they too gibed and made obscene gestures. Half the legionaries huddled shivering, turned helpless by nausea. The rest had reflexively formed a double rank; their weapons were stowed but their fists were cocked. The sailors bunched loosely, about an equal number. They were not professional fighters. The garrison commander had ruled that the danger of Saxons was so slight at this season that he wouldn't subject any of his too few soldiers to the real hazard of the crossing. However, each crewman bore a knife, and fingers had strayed to hilts.

Quintus Junius Eppillus stood before his troops, growling at a sailor who appeared to be a leader. Eppillus was a stocky, paunchy man in his forties, big-nosed, bald on top, a Dobunnian with considerable Italian in his bloodlines, Gratillonius's appointed deputy. His Latin came hoarse: "Watch your tongue, duckfoot. The bunch o' you watch your tongues. You're close to insulting not just us, but the Augusta."

The sailor, a tall redhead, leered and answered with a thick Regnensic accent: "I wouldn't do that. I only wonder why your legion allows fat

30

swine like you in it. Well, maybe they've gotten tired of sheep, and pleasure themselves now with swine."

"Take that back before I remove some o' those rotten teeth from your turnip hatch."

"Very well, I'll take it back. You're not swine. It's just your fathers that were. Your mothers were whores."

Cynan, who was young and of the still half-wild Demetae, yelled a battle cry. He broke from the army rank and threw himself on the sailor. They went down together, to struggle for possession of the knife and each other's throats.

"Stop!" Gratillonius roared. "Eppillus, break that up! Nobody else move!"

The legionaries who were standing froze. The captain grabbed a belaying pin and bloodied a head or two among his tars. They retreated in confusion, babbling excuses and pleas for mercy. Eppillus gave the combatants a couple of efficient kicks. They separated and crawled to their feet, gasping, spitting, and shuddering.

"Attention!" Gratillonius barked. He lifted his vinestaff of authority, which seldom left him. "Captain, I want that man of yours whipped."

"Five lashes," the skipper agreed. "The rest of you bless whatever saints you know about. Hop to it!" The redhead was immediately seized. He didn't resist, doubtless realizing he was lucky to escape with nothing worse. The captain turned to Gratillonius. "We'll make the same example of your fellow, eh?"

The centurion shook his head. "No. He must be in shape to march. But we can't have this kind of conduct, true. Keep still, Cynan."

The vinestaff cut a crimson line over the youth's cheek. "Go to the horses and stay there till we land. The rest of you who were involved, except the deputy, hold out your right arms." He gave each wrist a blow that raised a welt but would not be disabling. Eppillus possibly deserved punishment too, but not enough to make it worthwhile compromising his dignity.

Fingers plucked at Gratillonius's ankle. He glanced down and saw that his follower Budic had crawled to him. They youngster's ash-pale hair fluttered around eyes hollowed by misery. He lifted a hand. "Here, sir," he mumbled.

"What?" asked Gratillonius.

"Strike me, sir."

"Why, you didn't do anything." Gratillonius smiled. "You were too upchucking sick."

The blue gaze adored him. "But...I might have...when that...that sailor said what he did...about our legion. And surely I failed my centurion, me, useless when he needed his men. Please, sir. Make it right."

Gratillonius quelled an impulse to rumple those locks, as if this were one of his small nephews. "It is already right, soldier. Just remember and learn." He paused. "Oh, and be sure you shave before we march tomorrow. I want this outfit smart."

31

Adminius snickered at his comrade's discomfiture. "Spruce," he said, "not peach-fuzzy. I'll guide yer 'and if it's been so long you've forgotten 'ow." He was from Londinium, given to teasing country boys like the Coritanian Budic.

Stripped and triced to the stays, the deckhand choked off screams as the lead-weighted cords of the whip reddened his back. Cynan slunk down the hatch. Gratillonius gave the captain a discreet grin and muttered, "Fresh air's the best medicine against seasickness. He'll be where it's warm and stale."

"You're sharper than you look to be," the captain said. "Uh, best we absent ourselves for a while, you and I."

"Right. Let them regain control on their own. It takes hold firmer, that way."

The commanders sought the captain's room within the cabin. There he lifted a flagon from its rack and offered wine, thin sour stuff that didn't call for watering. "Military honor isn't high in the fleet," he admitted, "and it drops year by year. I can't blame the men too much. Time was, you may know, when Rome had a navy in these parts. Now there's just some tubs like this one, that the Saxon galleys can sail or row rings around. They land anywhere they will, the heathen do, and when next we pass by, all we find is ashes and corpses. That wears the spirit away, I can tell you. How do the inland legionaries feel?"

"Not so badly," Gratillonius replied. "We did win our war last year, and afterward my particular detachment had fun getting a new chief installed among the Ordovices. No one objected to him, so we'd nothing more to do than hike around in the hills showing the eagle and proclaiming the news officially. People were delighted to see new faces, and laid themselves out to be hospitable."

"The girls especially, I hope?"

Gratillonius laughed. "Well—Anyhow, we came back to Isca Silurum and settled into winter quarters. It's our home, you know; has been for hundreds of years. The older men generally have wives and children in town, and the younger men are apt to acquire their own after the usual pleasures of courtship. On furlough, you can reach Aquae Sulis in a day, baths, foodshops, joyhouses, theaters, games, social life, even learned men for those who care to listen. It's no Londinium, but still, in season you'd think half the world was jostling through its streets." He drank. "No, a man could do worse than join the army. Not that we don't keep the troops in line. They gripe. But they'd be appalled if we let their...strength fall away from them."

The captain gave him a narrow stare and said low, "From time to time the legions raise up an Emperor. That must be a heady feeling."

Gratillonius veered from the subject. The communities where he had sometimes overnighted, on his march through Britannia, were abuzz with rumors about Maximus, like beehives which were being toppled. He didn't want to give any hint of confirmation, most particularly not to this man who would often be crossing the Channel. If the governors of Gallia got sufficient advance warning to mobilize, the fighting could become disastrous.

"I trust we'll make port before dark," he said. "I wouldn't care to spend the night hove to."

"The wind's not from too bad a quarter, though stiffer than I like. You talk as if you've been a mariner yourself."

"Oh, more of a supercargo, on my father's ship when I was a boy. We called two or three times at Gesoriacum. But that was years ago."

"And a kid would scarcely see much. Can you stay over? The circus is small, but gets a canvas roof in bad weather, so it may be open tomorrow. Pretty good spectacles, not like those wretched bear-baitings which are the best we see in Dubris. In Gesoriacum they know how to stage an animal fight, and once I saw actual gladiators."

Gratillonius grimaced. "No, thanks. Torture and killing, for the amusement of a lot of rabble who'd loose their bowels if they saw teeth or a sword coming at *them*—I don't even permit my men to draw blood when they must touch up the horses."

"I hope you're not so softhearted in combat," said the captain, miffed.

"No insult intended. Anyhow, I can't stay. We've got to be off in the morning."

"Really pressing business, eh? Well," said the captain as his irritation passed, "I know a whorehouse in town that keeps late hours."

Gratillonius smiled. "Again, no, thanks. It's the hostel and an early bed for me." He grew serious. "Also, frankly—and, again, no offense— I'm trying to stay clean. Aside from prayers, it's the only chance this trip gives me to honor the God."

"Why, you could've stopped off at any church or shrine along the way."

Gratillonius sighed. "The Mithraeum in Londinium was closed— closed forever. Does Gesoriacum have one anymore?"

The captain sat straight, or as straight as the heeling ship would allow. His eyes bulged. "What? You're joking!"

"Certainly not. I serve Mithras. Doubtless you serve Christ. What matter, as long as we both serve Rome?"

The captain made a V of two fingers and jabbed them in Gratillonius's direction. "Out!" he shrilled. "Go! It's unlucky enough having a pagan aboard, without sitting here and drinking with him. If you weren't an officer on a mission, I swear I'd have you thrown overboard. Don't think I won't report you when I get back. Now go! Out of my sight!"

The centurion did not argue, but rose and went forth onto the deck, into the wind.

Dusk was falling as the ship glided between jetties and docked at the naval wharf. The soldiers collected their gear and tramped down the gangplank under the stares of the crew. Gratillonius had them wait in formation while the horses were unloaded, a process which called forth words that sizzled. In the meantime he queried the harbormaster, who had come from his office to watch this unseasonal landing, about accommodations for the squadron. To his relief, he learned that most of the garrison were away on joint maneuvers with those of two other towns. Their barracks would thus have plenty of available beds.

Marching his men there, he found the prefect of the cohort that had stayed on guard and presented his written orders. They declared that he was on a mission of state, as directed by the Duke of the Britains, with rights to food, lodging, and whatever else his band required along the way. The prefect refrained from asking questions. These days there were many curious comings and goings. His only inquiry was: "Do you require a room for yourself?"

Gratillonius shook his head. "I think I'll put up at a hostel, and return about sunrise to take your guests off your hands."

The prefect chuckled wryly. "You may as well be comfortable."

Gratillonius made somewhat of a nuisance of himself, seeing to it that his men would have decent quarters and, though it was well past the regular hour, an adequate meal. Not until they were seated in the mess—complaining about food meant for auxiliaries from some forsaken far corner of the Empire—did he leave. It was quite dark then, but the prefect assigned him a guide with a lantern. The wind had chased most clouds away before lying down to rest, letting stars and a partial moon add their light. Air was cold, breath smoked and footfalls rattled, but a breath of spring softened it and leaf buds were pale upon trees.

The inn for official travelers was a two-story building, its tile roof rime-whitened. A stable and a shed flanked the courtyard in front. It stood outside the city, on a highway leading south. Beyond that pavement reached cropland, out of which remnants of two houses poked ghostly. Like many other Gallic cities, Gesoriacum had shrunk during the past several generations, cramping itself within its defenses. Walls, towers, battlements gloomed under Draco and the Milky Way.

Passing by the stable, Gratillonius heard a noise that brought him to a halt. "What on earth?" He listened closer. Someone behind the door was weeping—no, more than a single one. The sounds were thin. His skin crawled. He did not think he had ever before heard such hopelessness.

The door was merely latched. He opened it. Murk yawned at him. The sobbing broke off in wails of terror. "Come along," he ordered his escort. "Be careful about any hay or straw, of course."

34

"Don't hurt us!" cried a child's voice. "Please don't hurt us! We'll be good, honest we will!"

He followed the words without difficulty. This was Belgica, whence the forebears of his own tribe had come to Britannia, and language hadn't changed much on either side. Fair-skinned and flaxen-haired, the children might have been playmates of his boyhood.

They numbered five, three boys and two girls, their ages seeming about nine or ten. They were dirty and unkempt, but not too poorly clad; two of them sported brightly colored wool scarves that their mothers must have given them at the farewell. Some horses in the building kept it warm. But it had been altogether dark here, and the children were penned in a stall. Slats nailed around and over it confined them, and made it impossible for them to stand upright.

Lanternlight glistened off tears on cheeks and, elsewhere, caused shadows to dance monstrous. Gratillonius hunkered down. "Don't be afraid," he said, as gently as the tightness in his throat allowed. "I won't hurt you. I'm your friend. What can I do for you?"

A girl's skinny arms reached out between the bars. He took her hands in his. "Oh, please," she stammered, "will you take us home?"

He couldn't help it, his voice harshened. "I'm sorry. I'm very sorry. I can't—now—but I will see if there is anything I can do, sweetheart. Be brave, all of you."

"You're not Jesus?" came from a boy. "I heard Jesus is the God in the city. I heard He is kind."

"I am not He," Gratillonius said, "but I promise Jesus will always watch over you." He kissed the hands he held, rose, and turned his back. "Goodnight. Try to sleep. Goodnight." The wails broke out anew as he left the stable and shut the door.

"New-taken slaves, sir," the escort observed.

"That's plain to see," Gratillonius snapped. He strode quickly to the hostel and thundered its knocker.

Candleglow spilled around the ruddy man who responded. "What do you want?" he asked. Gratillonius was in civil garb. "It's past suppertime."

"I'll have supper regardless," Gratillonius snapped. "For your information, I'm a legionary officer traveling on Imperial business. Furthermore, I'll have an explanation of those kids caged outside."

"Oh." The manager thought for a moment, then jerked his thumb over his shoulder. "He's in there, he can tell you better than me. Come in, sir." He didn't require credentials, doubtless reckoning that the soldier who had accompanied the stranger was sufficient.

Gratillonius bade that man farewell—be courteous to subordinates who deserve it, more even than to superiors—and followed the hostelkeeper into a long room feebly lit by candles. Their burning tallow filled it with stench, like an announcement of the poverty into which the Empire had fallen. Four guests sat benched around one of several tables. "Hail," called a portly fellow. "Welcome." Judging by his robe and the rings that sparkled on his fingers, he was the leader of his companions, who wore ordinary Gallic tunics and breeches. They were having a nightcap.

Gratillonius ignored the greeting. The manager asked him to register—name, rank, avowal that he was on an errand of the state—before taking a pair of candles and guiding him on upstairs. "We don't get many so soon in the year," he remarked. "You say you're of the Second Augusta? Isn't that off in Brittania? Well, well, these be uneasy times, and me, I know to keep my mouth shut. Here you are, sir. I'll go after my wife. Can't make anything fancy, I'm afraid, but we do keep a kettle of her good lentil soup on the hob. We'll get you something pretty quick, sir."

He left Gratillonius a light and departed. The centurion glanced around the room. Little was in it but a water jug, basin, chamber pot, and a pair of narrow beds. At this slack season, he'd be alone. He unpacked the small bag he had carried, stripped, scrubbed as well as he was able, dressed anew, and said his prayers—well after sunset, but better than not at all.

When he returned downstairs, the portly man called to him again: "Hoy, there, don't be so aloof. Come have a drink with us."

Briefly, Gratillonius hesitated. But...he had sought here not for the sake of comfort, as the prefect supposed, but in hopes of picking up more gossip, a better feeling for how things were, than he could likely get in barracks. Parts of the Continent were devastated or in upheaval, while he had scant exact information. "Thanks," he said, and took a place beside the inviter. A youth, son or underling of the keeper, scuttled forth with a cup, and he helped himself from the pitchers on the table.

"My name's Sextus Titius Lugotorix," the portly man said. "My attendants—" He introduced them. They were a ruffianly-looking lot.

"Gaius Valerius Gratillonius, centurion on special assignment."

Lugotorix raised his brows. Seen close up, his face carried a gash of a mouth and eyes that were like two hailstones. He smelled of cheap perfume. His affability was undiminished. "My, my, you're the silent one, aren't you, friend?"

"Orders. What are you doing here?"

"I'm a publican."

"I thought so."

"We were delayed—some bumpkins got obstreperous and we had to teach them a lesson—and didn't reach Gesoriacum till the gates had closed for the night. I suppose you walked around the city wall, from the military post? It wasn't worthwhile persuading the guard to let us in, when this hostel is so close by." Lugotorix winked and nudged Gratillonius. "And free."

"I didn't know your business entitled you to government accommodations."

36

"The governor has authorized me. Specifically authorized me."
Lugotorix rolled a pious glance ceilingward. "After all, the state must
have its internal revenue."

"Those youngsters in the stable—you're dragging them to the slave
market?"

A man laughed. "Not exactly dragging," he said. "Give the little
buggers a taste of the whip, and they run along so fast their leashes
nearly choke 'em."

Lugotorix peered at Gratillonius. "Did you take a look? Well, don't
get mawkish, my friend." He drained his goblet and refilled it. A certain
slurriness suggested he was a bit drunk. "They weren't abused, were
they? Properly fed, I swear, and you saw for yourself they have a warm
sleeping place and clean straw. Why damage the merchandise? Not
that it'll fetch much. Hardly worth the trouble of collecting and selling.
But I'm a patriot like you, centurion. I feel it's my duty to the state
to crack down on tax delinquents. I'm very patient, too, especially
considering that this is my livelihood and I have mouths of my own
to feed. I give those families plenty of time to find the money. Or if
they can't, I'll take payment in kind, cattle or grain or whatever, marked
down no more than necessary to compensate me for the added incon-
venience. But they snivel that they'd starve. What can I do then but
confiscate a brat? It helps keep the rest honest. If you let somebody
evade his taxes, soon you must let everybody, and the government will
have no more internal revenue."

"What will become of the children?" Gratillonius asked slowly.

Lugotorix shrugged. "Who knows? I pray they'll land in nice Christian
homes and learn the Faith that will save their souls. See what a good
work is mine in the sight of God! But I do have to take the best offer
I get, you realize, or else how could I meet my own obligations to the
state? And whelps like that don't command any large price. They have
to be housed and fed for years, you know, before they're grown to
field hands or maidservants or whatever."

A man leered. "Got a whorehouse in town where some of the
customers like 'em young," he said.

"I don't approve, I don't approve!" Lugotorix maintained. "But I
must take the best price I can get. Besides, those rustic brats are
seldom pretty enough. We may have one this time, but believe me,
she's a rarity."

Her hands had lain in Gratillonius's.

He gulped his wine more fiercely than it deserved. The Empire
still did fairly well by its officers, most places. In return, his immediate
duty was to sound out these people. They must travel rather widely
and hear news from farther yet.

"Well, never mind," he achieved saying. "Look, I'm bound west to
Armorica. I can't tell you more. Now I have, um, been out of touch.

If you can give me some idea of what to watch for along the way, I'll be grateful. So will...Rome."

Flattered, Lugotorix rubbed his chin and pondered before he replied: "We don't hear much from those parts. Courier service across them has gotten precarious, at least for private messages. Official dispatches have nearly absolute priority, and I understand they aren't too sure of getting through anymore. I actually know better what's been happening in Massilia than in Baiocassium, say.... You shouldn't have trouble here in Belgica. It suffered little from the Magnentian War, and the Germanian province eastward has stayed quiet too—good Germans, those, not Hun-like Franks. You should find Belgica easy; and, if I do say so myself, it's concerned citizens like me who keep it that way. But beyond, as you enter Lugdunensis—my information is that the more west you go, the worst conditions get. I trust you're not alone?"

"No, I have soldiers with me."

"Good. Just the same, watch out. I don't *think* the Bacaudae would attack a military unit, but you never know, these days. The word I have is that they're growing ever more brazen."

Gratillonius searched his memory. He had encountered the word before, but only the word, and that was back when troubles were a not quite real thing that happened to somebody else. "Bacaudae?" he asked. "Bandits?"

"Worse than bandits," Lugotorix said indignantly. "Rebels. Men, if you can call them men, who've fled their obligations, gone into the woods, and don't just live by robbery and extortion—no, they have some kind of organization, they call themselves 'Bacaudae'—'the Valiant'—and they war against the very state. Wolves! Vermin! Crucifixion would be too good for them, if we still did it."

"It was not too good for your Saviour, was it?" Gratillonius murmured.

Luckily, perhaps, that was the moment when the boy carried forth his meal. He ordered it put on a different table, and made clear that he wanted to eat by himself and go to bed immediately afterward. Lugotorix quacked a few questions—what was the matter?—but, getting no response other than a glower, soon quit.

There was no more to learn from him, Gratillonius thought, and so there was no need to spend more time at his board. Nothing could be done for the children except to beseech that Mithras—or Christ, or whatever Gods had stood over their cradles—would at last receive their weary spirits. The faith of Gratillonius was pledged to the man who could save Rome. Later that man would set about restoring her true law, making her again the Mother of all.

3

The military highway dropped well south before meeting one that bore west, but pavement offered faster going than most secondary ways in this rainy month. Gratillonius set no fixed daily goals. He took his men as far as they could make it under the given conditions without becoming exhausted. That usually meant about thirty miles, since they were spared the labor of constructing a wall and ditch at the end. It took a gauging eye to know when he should call a halt, for he was on horseback. He would have preferred to share the footwork, but dignity required he ride, as it required a private tent. The men expected it and didn't mind.

They made a brave sight on the march. Gratillonius ranked them four abreast so they wouldn't be slowed by any civil traffic they met. To spare hoofs without the trouble of sandalling them, he rode on the graveled side-strips when those were provided, while three men at the rear led the pack horses. On the highway, Eppillus named a different man each day for the honor of striding in the van, holding the standard on high and with the bearskin over his armor. Everybody wore full battle gear; in sunny weather, light flashed off helmets, mail, javelin heads, the oiled leather of shield facings. Gratillonius displayed silvery coat and greaves, together with crest athwart his helmet and cloak flowing away from his throat, both as vivid a red as the eagle banner. Hobnails crashed down in drumlike unison, but the lines were not rigid, they had that subtle wheatfield ripple that bespeaks men whose trade is war.

At first they travelled through country such as Gratillonius had heard described. It was smooth terrain, grazed by livestock or worked by gangs of cultivators. Aside from woodlots, trees were few. Hamlets generally amounted to a pair of long houses, half-timbered and thatched, divided into apartments for the dwellers and, in winter, their beasts. Carts trundled along the roads, driven by men in smocks and wooden shoes. Other passersby rode mules, or walked carrying baskets or tools. What few women appeared were afoot but seemed unafraid. When they saw the squadron, people gaped, then often waved their hats and cheered. Every fifty or sixty miles the highway passed through a small town. This country lay at peace.

Yet Gratillonius noticed how hastily those towns had been walled of late, with anything that came to hand, even tombstones and broken-up monuments. And they had shrunk. Deserted buildings on the outskirts, stripped of everything valuable, were crumbling into grass-grown hillocks. The inhabitants looked poor and discouraged, save those who sat in taverns getting drunk. On market days the forums remained half empty. As for the hinterlands, the farmers ate better, but most of them were serfs. Or worse; Gratillonius remembered the publican. Whenever he passed a villa—a fundus, they called such an estate in Gallia—or a latifundium, a plantation which had devoured many a farm, he thought a malediction.

He would have liked commandeering fresh rations from those places as the need arose, but that was too chancy. Instead, he levied on military warehouses. Sometimes he had trouble getting what he wanted, because the garrisons were composed of alien auxiliaries with their own ideas about diet. His requirement was for what would keep in this wet climate, while being nutritious and easy to prepare: parched grain, biscuit, butter, cheese, dry sausage, preserved meat, beans, peas, lentils, pickled cabbage, dried apples, raisins, wine. That last was apt to be poor, and the water that would dilute it to be muddy, but beer was too bulky for what you got out of it. Not that he allowed drunkenness. However, it was wise to let the men have a treat at day's end, while supper cooked or in their tents if rain forced a cold meal.

The first night out was mild. They pitched camp in a pasture and grinned and winked at some towheaded youngsters, driving cattle home, who stopped to stare timidly. Gratillonius ordered a kettle of warm water brought him when it was ready, sought his shelter, removed his armor, and sighed in relief. Give him a scrub and a change of linen, and he'd be ready for a drink himself. He insisted the troops keep clean too, but if he bathed out in the open among them, it would be bad for discipline.

Budic carried the water in, set it down by Gratillonius's bedroll, and straightened. He could stand upright in an officer's tent, though his blond hair brushed the leather. He saluted. "Sir," he said in a rush, "may I ask a great favor?"

Gratillonius laughed. "You may. You won't necessarily get it."

"If...the centurion would allow me an extra ration of bread and cheese...and if, when the chance comes, we could lay in some kippered fish—"

"Whatever for?"

It was getting dim in here, despite the flag being folded back. Did the boy blush? He certainly gulped. "Sir, this is Lent."

"Lent. Ah. The long Christian fast. Are you sure? I've gathered the Christians can't agree among themselves how to calculate the date of their Easter."

"I didn't—didn't think, I forgot about it, in all the excitement of departure, and then on the march I lost track of time. But that terrible happening on the ship, it shocked me into recalling—this, and all my sins, like lust when I see a pretty girl or anger when some of the men bait me—Equinox has just passed, with the moon new. Lent is already far along. Please, sir, let me set myself a penance, and also do right in the Faith." Budic swallowed again. "The centurion is not a Christian, but he is a pious man."

Gratillonius considered. He wanted everybody fit, not weakened by a growling belly; and special privilege might well cause discord. Yet this was a deprivation, not a luxury. He doubted others would want it, he having picked men he knew weren't holy-holy sorts—men who, Christian or Mithraist, would not feel uneasy about there being no observance on the Sundays that both religions made their sabbaths. Budic he hadn't known so well, the lad being newly enlisted, an orphaned rustic; but Budic had fought like a wildcat beyond the Wall, been a good if overly earnest trailmate on the way home, and would have been crushed if his leader had passed him over for this expedition. Young, strong in spite of his gangly build, he should get along, no matter his curious practice. Maybe he was so fervent because Christians were scarce where he came from, and other children had jeered at him. Maybe he enlisted partly in hopes of finding friends.

"You may, if it's that important to you," Gratillonius decided. "Just don't act sanctimonious if nobody else follows your example. Go tell the cook."

"Oh, sir!" Adoration blazed forth. "Thank you, sir!"

Presently Gratillonius emerged to find the squadron at ease except for sentries and kitchen detail. The campfire crackled, raising savory fumes out of a pot suspended above. A low sun gilded the earth. Grass was dry enough to sit on, but several men, with goblets in hand, stood clustered before Budic and teased him.

"You mean you didn't think to get a special dispensation?" asked Adminius. "Why, the bishop was 'anding 'em out like 'otcakes at a love feast. Dibs on yer porkchops."

Cynan sneered, which made the mark of his punishment writhe on that cheek. It marred his dark handsomeness, and must still hurt, but should heal soon. Probably he wasn't quite over his resentment. These Demetae were inclined to be broody sorts. "I suppose somebody among us may as well get in good with Jesus," he said, "though I hear this countryside is still blessedly free of Him." He heard Mass when that seemed expedient, but made no bones about reckoning the faith one for women and soft city dwellers. Himself, he sought the temple of Nodens when he could.

"Can't stop and dicker with any cleric we might come across." Adminius's thin features split in a gap-toothed grin. "Tell you wot, though, Budic. If we do meet one, I'll 'elp you grab 'im up and sling 'im over a 'orse, and 'e can oblige you as we travel."

The youth reddened. He doubled his fists. Eppillus's burly form pushed close. He had sensed trouble brewing. "That will do," the deputy rumbled. "Leave off the jibes. Every man's got a right to his religion."

The tormentors drifted away, a little abashed, to mingle with their comrades. "Thank you," Budic said unevenly. "I, uh, may I ask what your belief is? I've never seen you at...our services."

Eppillus shrugged. "I follow Mithras, same as the centurion and two others amongst us. But I admit that for luck I look more to a thunderstone I carry." It was a piece of flint in the form of a spearhead,

41

found near a dolmen many years ago. He chuckled deep in his hairy breast. "Could be that's why I've never made better than second grade in the Mystery. But I'm too old to change my ways, when there's no wife to badger me out of 'em."

"I thought...you would be married."

"I was. She died. Two kids, both grown and flown the nest. I've got a bit of a farm still, back near Isca, and when my hitch is up—couple years to go—I'll find me a nice plump widow." Eppillus grew aware of Gratillonius, who had stood quietly listening. "Oh, hail, sir. Budic, don't stand there like a snow man in a thaw. Go get the centurion his wine."

Gratillonius smiled. On the whole, this episode seemed to bode well.

~ 4 ~

The land began to rise after they crossed into Gallia Lugdunensis. Roads must curve, climb, swing back down again, around and over hills that were often steep. Nevertheless, the legionaries continued day by day to eat the miles.

Or the leagues, which were what waystones now measured. Unlike Britannia, Gallia had reverted from Rome's thousand paces to the larger Celtic measure. Gratillonius didn't know just when or why that had happened. But he did know that the Gallic provinces, together with the Rhenus valley, had been the richest, most populous and productive territories in the Empire. What they wanted, they could likely get—including a new Emperor?

Certainly this land clung unhindered to its own old ways. Cynan had been right; Christianity was a religion for towns. Frequently Gratillonius spied a cella, a Celtic temple. Even smaller than a Mithraeum, it consisted of a single square room surrounded by a porch. Public rites took place in the temenos outside; the chamber could barely hold one or two persons who had some special need of their Gods.

Now and then the legionaries passed a hill fort, earthworks raised on a height before ever Caesar arrived. Most were deserted, their outlines time-blurred, but Gratillonius observed that some had lately been refurbished, refuges against the failure of everything Roman.

Spring rolled northward apace. Trees leafed, hawthorn hedges bloomed white, wildflowers bejeweled meadows gone intensely green, larks jubilated aloft. Where fields lay under cultivation, the first fine shoots thrust out of furrows and orchards were riotous with blossom. Views became splendid from the ridges, down over dappled valleys where rivers gleamed and changed in spate. Rain turned into scattered showers, after which rainbows bridged the clouds. Most days were clear, warm, full of sweetness. They grew swiftly longer too, which made for better time on the road, although Gratillonius liked the gentle nights and would sometimes stroll from camp to be alone with the stars.

Speech changed across the country, shifting from dialect to dialect until you could say that Caletes and Osismii spoke distinct languages. However, he could always make himself understood, whether or not anybody knew Latin—which many farmers, who never went more than a few miles from their birthplaces, did not. Barely enough commerce still trickled along that he could obtain information about conditions ahead. Thus advised, he twice took shortcuts over local roads that were adequate. The gravel on them was washing away and not being replaced, but in dry weather they still served.

The neglect was a sign of much else. The farther west the men came, the more desolation they saw. At first it was not unlike parts of Britannia, vacant huts, acres gone back to weeds, squalid serf shacks well away from the mansions of the honestiores, towns listless and half empty. The larger towns had garrisons, which saw to such things as the maintenance of bridges, but these were auxiliaries from as far away as Egypt, foreign alike to Roman and Celt, generally sloppy. Or, worse, the troops were laeti, Germanic or Alanic barbarians who had forced their way into the province and carved out settlements for themselves: men surly, shaggy, fierce, and filthy, on guard more for the sake of their own kin than for the Empire to which they gave nominal allegiance.

Thirty years had passed since Magnentius failed in his try for the throne. The ruin left by the war was not yet repaired, nor did it seem likely ever to be. Why? wondered Gratillonius. Nature was no less generous here than erstwhile: rich soil, timber, minerals, navigable rivers, fructifying sunshine and rain. The Gauls were an able race, to whom Rome had brought peace, civilization, an opening on the rest of the world. Her armies and navies easily kept prosperity unplundered by outsiders. In return she asked for little other than loyalty, obedience to laws that were more tribal than Roman, a modest tribute so the engineers and soldiers could be paid. Gauls grew wealthy, not only from agriculture and mining but from manufacture. Art and learning waxed brilliant in their cities. Gallia became the heartland of the Empire. Why could she not now recover? What had gone wrong?

Gratillonius didn't ask his questions aloud. The men were already oppressed by what they saw. In camp they didn't sing or crack jokes, they sat wistfully talking about their homes. The centurion heartened them somewhat with a speech on the marvels awaiting them at Ys, but he was hampered by the fact that he didn't know just what those were.

The more they marched, the grimmer it was. The road ran near the coast. Saxon raiders had been coming yearly out of the sea, in ever greater fleets whose crews would go ravaging far inland. The Duke of the Armorican Tract could do little to check them. His forces were depleted, and the shore forts had never been as tightly interlinked as those of Britannia. If a detachment was not simply too small to fight a barbarian swarm, it was seldom fast enough to catch them before they had wrought their havoc and were off elsewhere. They took care to demolish message towers, so that Roman signals of fire by night and smoke by day were no longer visible at any very useful distance; it looked to Gratillonius as if the army had given up attempts at rebuilding.

Otherwise the Saxons were as insensate as wildfire. They slaughtered men, ravished women, made quarry of children. Having clumsily sacked, they burnt. Were a place too poor to rob, they kindled it anyway, for sheer love of destruction. Gratillonius came upon ash heaps that had been houses, buildings of brick and stone rooflessly agape, towns where a few who fled had returned to squat in the ruins and tell their tales of horror, defensive walls broken and never repaired, orchards chopped down, fields charred, harbors empty of their fishing boats. He glimpsed livestock skeletons, strewn human bones which nobody had come back to bury, wandering beggars who had once had homes, three or four women who had gone mad and went about unkempt, ragged, and gibbering. Wild dogs were more dangerous than wolves. One rainy day at the remnant of a manor house, he saw a peacock dying of chill and starvation, its tail dragged down in the mud, and wondered why the sight moved him so.

Scoti out of Hivernia had been arriving too. They were fewer in number than the Saxons, not as wantonly cruel, and their leather coracles could hold less loot than German galleys. They did their share of damage, though, especially by carrying off able-bodied young captives for slaves.

Not every stronghold had fallen, not every farm stood abandoned. A measure of civilized life went on, however wanly. The land itself was beautiful, wide beaches, long hills and dales whose grass rippled and trees soughed in the wind off the sea. Birds filled heaven, gulls, gannets, cormorants, ducks, geese, swans, cranes, herons, a hundred smaller sorts and the eagle high above them. Fish flashed in every stream, bats and swifts darted about at dusk while frogs croaked in chorus, lizards basked on sunny rocks. Squirrels streaked like meteors, hares bounded off, deer browsed in the distance. At least wildlife was coming back.

At Ingena Gratillonius planned to turn south of west, inland, toward Vorgium. There he would collect fresh supplies and have the men put their equipment in top form before the last leg of their journey. The military commander, a grizzled Italian, counselled him against it.

"Yonder's only a husk, scarcely a village, after what the Saxons did to it—Osismiis, that was once the finest city in Armorica, after Ys," he said. Gratillonius felt a shock of hearing how the Roman name had fallen out of use, even for this man. "A few Mauretanians stationed there yet, but they don't keep proper stores, they rely on outside supply mostly. No, I'd say you should head south from here to Condate Redonum.

It's about your last chance to restock, if you're bound west. I suppose you've business among the Veneti?"

"Farther north," Gratillonius evaded.

"Well, then, first proceed to Fanum Martis. Don't bother exchanging courtesies with the garrison, they're a lot of scruffy Egyptians. It's a detour, but you'll make better speed, because you'll have trunk roads to there and then down to Redonum. Thence it's secondaries, but gravelled and well kept up, because the Osismii and sometimes the Ysans use it for their wagons. A good deal is through wildwood, but you should have no trouble; I scarcely think Bacaudae will jump Roman regulars. At the coast you'll come from Garomagus—m-m, the ruins of Garomagus—and from there another good secondary road will take you down to the maritime station near Ys. That's ruined too, been ruined for a long time. However, I hear the Ysans maintain the roads through their hinterland, and they should certainly allow you passage if that's the way you're going."

A thrill passed through Gratillonius. "I've heard tell about Ys," he said carelessly. "Things hard to believe. What's it like in truth?"

The commander frowned. "Who knows, anymore? A city-state on the west coast. I've never been there, but people say its towers are the eighth wonder of the world."

"Surely you know more, sir."

The commander scratched his head. "Well, let me think. I've heard it began as a Carthaginian colony, back before the Celts arrived. The colonists interbred first with the Old Folk, those who're said to have raised the great stones, and afterward with the Osismii. They grew prosperous on trade. Julius Caesar made a foederate of Ys, but relations were never close and the last Imperial resident departed, oh, one or two hundred years ago, I guess. Ys no longer even pays tribute. Lately the Duke asked it to cooperate in the defense of Armorica. I hear the answer he got—in polite words, no doubt—was that by patrolling its own waters Ys was doing the best possible service to Rome. He hasn't the manpower to enforce anything on the city; it's well protected by its wall and there'd be no way to close its sea lanes. Besides, maybe the Ysans are right. I don't know. I told you I've not been there myself."

"Few seem to. Odd. I should think curiosity alone—"

The commander pressed lips together. "I should too, now you say it. But that isn't the case. I never wondered much about Ys either, even when I was young and lively. You see practically no mention of it in any records. I've read Caesar and Tacitus and Plinius and—and many more—and nowhere have I found a word about Ys, not in the *Gallic War* itself, though native tradition insists Caesar paid a visit in person." He sighed. "Christ and all angels help us, there's something damnably strange about Ys. They have a grisly kind of royal sacrifice, and nine witch-queens who go out on a desert island and work black

45

magic, and— Well, I don't want to talk about it. I've troubles aplenty as is."

Gratillonius did not pursue matters.

At sunrise he led his men onward. After two days they came to Fanum Martis, where the tower dedicated to the war God loomed huge and empty above houses, many of which were also deserted.

There they swung south. In that direction they found ample traces of former habitation. Armorica had once been thriving and well populated, except for the heavily forested interior; but little remained. Land rolled gently, taken over by grass, brambles, young trees. Often the travelers spied megalithic monuments. Gauls said Gods, or elves, or wizards, or the Old Folk had raised those gaunt menhirs, solitary or in cromlech circles, those massive dolmens and passage chambers. Once the party made camp by one of the latter. Gratillonius took a torch inside and came upon relics of a family who had sheltered there—a well-off family, whose glassware gleamed while furniture decayed and silver corroded on the earth. He wondered what had happened to them. Thieves had not dared enter this haunted place afterward. Gratillonius left the things where they were, out of respect for the dead, and did not mention them.

None of his followers had volunteered to accompany him, though he knew they would have done so if asked. Gratillonius was not himself afraid. He didn't think Ahriman would deign to employ mere spooks, and in any event they must flee from the light of Ahura-Mazda which Mithras bore. He could not understand why otherwise rational people had all those vague superstitions about Ys.

Next morning the soldiers rose at first light as usual, paid their various devotions, got a meager breakfast, struck camp, and marched. They reached Condate Redonum before noon.

This riparian city too had withdrawn behind fortress walls; but those were unbreached, the houses within unplundered, if dirty and dilapidated. More life flowed over the cobbles, between buildings and across the forum, than Gratillonius had seen for some time. After passing through areas where folk tended to be dark-haired, here he found them again generally fair, as well as robust and rather tall.

Most were local Redones, but quite a few were Osismii come from the west to market. Gratillonius observed the latter with special interest; their country bordered on Ys. The men ran to sweeping mustaches and hair in long braids. Their clothing was of good stuff and frequently fur-trimmed. They carried themselves boldly. Gratillonius recalled that the honestiores had never taken root among them, nor had there ever been many curials to grind between the millstones.

In contrast, the garrison appalled him. It was mainly of Frankish laeti. They were big men, armored in conical helmets and leather reinforced with iron rings. Sword and francisca, the dreaded throwing-ax, were their principal weapons; shields were small and round, garishly

46

painted. They swaggered about pushing others out of the way, daring anybody to defy them.

Gratillonius sought the military prefect at headquarters. That Iberian could only say, "I'm sorry. I'll see to it that you get what you need, of course, but in this confusion it may take a little time, and meanwhile I urge you to camp well away from town. Our people have gotten used to the Franks, if not exactly liking them, but your men could too easily get into a fight. You see, it happens they're holding one of their festivals tonight."

"Hm-m. Drunk and rowdy."

"To say the least. They're heathen, did you know? They'll swill themselves into madness and believe they're inspired by Mercurius— Wotan, they call Him, chief of their Gods." The officer grimaced. "It won't be as bad as the quarter days. Then they go out in the country and make human sacrifices. True, that does take them out of town. Redonum won't be safe tonight. But what can we do?"

Gratillonius thought furiously that he knew very well what *he* could do. Still, he must not lose men in the chastising of Franks...who were allies against barbarians from outside.... His mission lay before him, in glorious Ys.

Next day his troop marched westward.

V

At midnight the Nine left the House of the Goddess and set forth. They bore no lanterns, for the moon was nearly full and the sky clear. Their weather spell had seen to that. But there was a wind, whistling and cold from the east, over the island and away across Ocean. This too was the will of the Nine, for it was such a wind as rode with the souls of many among the dead. The Gallicenae would need every unseen power they could raise to strengthen them in that which they were about to do.

Sena was small, flat, treeless. Moonlight lay hoar on harsh grass, darkling on rocks, ashimmer on tide pools and the kelp strewn around them. It frosted the manes of waves as they rolled and tumbled, it made white fountains where they crashed on outlying reefs and rocks, it glimmered off the coats of seals that swam along as if following the procession. It drowned most stars; those that were left seemed to flicker in the wind.

The women walked slowly, silent save when a cloak flapped or a pebble gritted underfoot. The wind spoke for them. Forsquilis led.

She stared before her, blind and deaf in trance. Vindilis and Bodilis guided her by either arm. They were those who could hold themselves steadiest when next to such a vessel of strangeness. The other six followed in file. Quinipilis was in front, as befitted the oldest, the presiding one. Fennalis came after, and then her daughter Lanarvilis, then Innilis, then Maldunilis. Last was Dahilis, who crowded a little as if the bulk ahead could somehow shield her from the terrors that prowled about. A covered firepot she carried glowed out of airholes like red spider eyes.

It seemed long, but was not, until the Queens reached the Stones. Those two pillars, rough-hewn and raised by the Old Folk, stood close together near the middle of the island. The beak of the Bird, the more pointed head of the Beast—vague resemblances—were some two man-heights aloft. Vindilis and Bodilis helped Forsquilis in between them. They engulfed her in shadow; hardly any of her was now to be seen other than the manyfold linen windings of her headdress, phantom-wan. She laid her palms against the rock and stood motionless except for quickened breath.

The rest ranged themselves in a circle, Quinipilis facing the seeress. The aged woman lifted her arms and countenance on high. "Ishtar-Isis-Belisama, have mercy on us," she called in a voice still strong. "Taranis, embolden us. Lir, harden us. All Gods else, we invoke You in the name of the Three, and cry unto You for the deliverance of Ys."

Her prayer used the ancestral speech because of its sacredness and potency, but thereafter she returned to the vernacular: "Forsquilis, Forsquilis, how go you, what find you?"

The priestess between the Stones answered like a sleepwalker: "I go as an owl. The treetops beneath my wings are a net wherein the moon touches buds and new leaves with argent. It is lonely being a spirit out of the flesh. The stars are more far away than ever we knew; the cold of those vastnesses comes seeping down over the world, through and through me.

"I see a glade. Dew sparkles on grass around a camp where a fire burns low. Metal gleams on its guardians. I glide downward. The forest is haunted tonight. Do I glimpse the antlers of Cernunnos as He walks amidst His trees?

"They are soldiers, yon men, earthlings only, naught in them of fate. Am I misled? Did the gods not hear us or heed us? Oh, surely these men are bound hither and surely that is a sign unto us. Yet— Bewildered, I flutter to and fro in the air."

Suddenly her voice came alive: "A man steps forth from darkness. Was it him that I espied under the boughs? Sleepless, he has walked down a game trail to sit by a spring and love the sky. Sleepless—he knows not why—but I know him! Now when he is drawn this near, his destiny has reached out of the future and touched him.

48

"He feels it. He looks upward and sees my wings beneath the moon, the moon that turns his eyes to quicksilver. The dread of the mystery in him comes upon me. I fly from his terrible gaze. It is he, it is he, it is he!"

Forsquilis shrieked and fell. Quinipilis stood aside while Bodilis and Vindilis pulled her out into the open and stretched her carefully on the ground. The rest clustered about. Between dark cloaks and blanched headwraps, most visages were paler than was due the light.

Bodilis knelt to examine the unmoving woman. "She seems in a swoon," she said.

Quinipilis nodded. "That is to be awaited," she replied. "Our Sister has travelled along weird ways. Cover her well, let her in peace, and she should arouse soon."

"Meanwhile, what shall we do?" asked Lanarvilis.

"Naught," quavered Maldunilis, her wonted placidity torn apart. "Naught save abide...abide that moment."

"Surely *something* else," was Innilis's timid thought. "Prayer?"

Fennalis stroked her hand, responding, "Nay, I think not. We have held rites since sunset. It were not well to risk the Gods growing weary of us."

Bodilis said slowly: "Hold, Sisters. Belike those same Gods have given us this pause. We can think on what our wisest course may be."

Wrath flared in Vindilis. "What mean you?" she cried. "We held council and made decision at equinox. We cast our spells and tonight we know they've wrought well. What else remains but to curse Colconor?"

"That...that is such a dreadful thing," Dahilis dared say. "Mayhap we shouldn't—"

Vindilis turned on the girl as if to attack. "You dare?" she yelled. "Has he won your heart, little traitress?"

"Please, darling, please," Innilis begged. She tugged at the sleeve of the older woman, whose anger thereupon abated somewhat.

Dahilis helped by blurting, "I meant no cowardice, in truth I did not. It was but that Bodilis said—oh—"

"Bodilis said," declared that one, "we should take heed this last time ere we do what cannot be undone. Magic is ever a two-edged sword, ofttimes wounding the wielder. I loathe Colconor as deeply as do any of you, my sisters. But we have called his death to him. May not that be enough? Need we hazard more?"

"We must!" Lanarvilis exclaimed. "If we stand by idle at this pass, well shall we deserve it that our whole enterprise comes to grief." She crooked her fingers aloft like talons. "Also, I want my share in the death."

Vindilis hissed agreement.

"Calm, Sisters, calm, I pray of you," urged Fennalis. "I've no wish myself for black sorcery. Yet if 'tis needful, 'tis needful."

"I believe it is," Quinipilis told them. "Forsquilis is most profound in the lore, aye, but over the years that have been mine I've had to do certain deeds, and watch others done. You, Bodilis, are wise, but it is the wisdom of your books and philosophers. Bethink you. Thus far we have at best brought a man who *may* prevail, and thereafter prove a better King than Colconor."

"He could never prove worse," whispered gentle Innilis.

"This man may choose not to fight," Quinipilis went on. "If he leads soldiers, he is on duty he would be reluctant to set aside. If he does fight, he may lose. I doubt me Colconor's strength has much dwindled since he won the crown."

Bodilis nodded thoughtfully. "True. If then the soldiers slay him who killed their comrade, why, we would be rid of the monster, but how shall we have a new King? The sacred battle may never be of more than one against one. Ys beholds too much desecration already. I believe that is why the powers of the Gallicenae are fading and failing."

"Oh, nay." Innilis shuddered and crept close to Vindilis, who laid an arm about her waist.

"Fear not, my sweet," Vindilis assured her. "We will cast our spell in righteousness, that the hero shall indeed take lordship and redeem us."

Dahilis clasped her hands together. "The hero!" Her eyes shone.

Forsquilis groaned, stirred, looked up with merely human sight. Her colleagues aided her to sit, chafed her wrists, murmured comfort. Finally she could rise.

"Feel you that we should go on as we've planned?" Quinipilis asked. "And if you do, have you the strength?"

The witch straightened. Teeth gleamed between lips drawn thin. "Yea and yea!" she answered. "Wait no more. Our might sinks with the moon."

The Nine had, earlier, brought wood and laid it on a blackened site near the Stones. Dahilis had had the honor of carrying the fire: for the Sisterhood had agreed, upon Quinipilis's proposing, that Dahilis, youngest and fairest of them, should be the bride of the new King's first night. She prayed to Belisama while she emptied glowing charcoal onto kindling. The wind made flames leap quickly.

From under her cloak Forsquilis took a silver vessel whence she dusted salt across every palm. The Queens licked it up in the name of Lir. Quinipilis called on Taranis while she drew forth a knife, nicked her thumb, and flung drops of blood onto the fire. They spat when they struck the coals. Each by each, the Sisters passed before her and made the same sacrifice.

They joined hands around the blaze. It roared, streaming and sparkling on the wind. Red and yellow unease below, icy white above, were all the light there was; everywhere else reached blindness. Sang the Nine:

"Winter wolf and sheering shark,
Whip and tautened traces,
Shame by day and fear by dark,

Hobnails down on faces,
Worms at feast in living hearts,
Dulled and rusted honor—
From his spirit, let these parts
Rise to curse Colconor!

"May he fall as falls a tree
When its roots are rotten
And a wind whirls off the sea,
Angry, Lir-begotten.
Lord Taranis, in Your sky
Hear the tempest clamor.
Long those poisoned boughs reached high.
Smite them with Your hammer!

"Belisama, may our spell
Make You come and take him
Down to doom, and there in hell
Evermore forsake him.
Hitherward his bane we draw
In this vengeful springtime.
Stranger, heed the holy Law
All throughout your King time."

Aboard their boat at the dock, looking beyond the House, the fishermen who had brought the Nine hither saw the fire. They did not know what it portended, they had only obeyed when called upon, but they shivered, muttered charms, clutched lucky pieces, and made forfending signs; and they were Ferriers of the Dead.

VI

~ 1 ~

West of Vorgium the hills became long and steep. Forest thinned out until there were only isolated stands of trees, and none wherever heath prevailed over pastureland. The soldiers were rarely out of sight of one or more megaliths, brooding gray amidst emptiness. Winds blew shrill and cold, drove clouds across heaven and their shadows across earth, often cast rainshowers. Yet here too it was the season of rebirth. Grass rippled like green flame, mustard and gorse flaunted gold, flowers were everywhere—tiny daisies, blue borage, violets, hyacinths, cuckoopint, speedwell, primrose, strewn through filigree of wild carrot and prickle

51

of blackberry. Only willows had thus far come to full leaf, but oak and chestnut were beginning, while plum blossoms whitened their own boughs. Bumblebees droned, amber aflight. Blackbirds, starlings, sparrows, doves, gulls filled the sky with wings and calls.

Farmsteads were apt to be far apart, tucked into sheltering dells: a thatch-roofed wattle-and-daub house for people and animals together, perhaps a shed, a pigpen, a vegetable garden, an apple tree or so. Mainly folk in these parts lived by grazing sheep and, to a lesser degree, cattle. They were all Osismii, and Gratillonius would not have been able to speak with them had he not picked up some of their language as a boy. It used many words unique to itself, words he thought must trace back to the Old Folk. Invading Celts, centuries ago, had made themselves the leading families of the tribe and mingled their blood with that of the natives, but more thinly, this far out on the peninsula, than elsewhere in Gallia.

Some words, he thought with an eerie thrill, must stem from another source, from Ys. They resembled none he had heard before, but stirred vague memories in him of names he had met when studying the history of the Punic Wars.

Although folk were friendly, much excited to see legionaries, he didn't stop for talk except one evening when he chanced to camp near a dwelling. There he learned that the neighborhood had suffered little from raiders, being too poor to draw them, but the western shore was an utter wreck apart from Gesocribate and Ys. The former was tucked well into a narrow bay and Roman-defended. The latter fronted on Ocean, but— The farmer signed himself to his Gods in awe of the power protecting that city. He would be glad to come under its guardianship. Unfortunately, Ys claimed only a few eastward miles of hinterland.

Disturbance crept about within Gratillonius. What forces indeed did such a minikin state command, that it endured while Rome crumbled?

He found himself thinking about that again when his squadron reached the coast and spent a night at Garomagus. He and his father had called there several times, in years as lost as the lives they had found. Small but bustling, the town once embodied those industries, that prosperity, which ringed its great bight: ceramics, metalwork, salt, and garum, the fish sauce Armoricans exported to the farthest ends of the Empire. Now, as sunset smoldered away, Gratillonius stood fingering a shard of a jar, among the burnt-out shells of buildings surrounding a forum where only he and the whimpering wind had motion.

He saw no bones lying about. Survivors who crept back to town after the final sack must have buried their kindred before abandoning their homes. Stains still darkened a fountain gone dry, where the heathen had held a sacrifice, and rubbish littered pavement. A book sprawled mildewing outside a church, its cover stripped of jewels, its vellum capriciously slashed. Gratillonius bent over to peer at the rain-blurred pages and recognized Greek letters and ink drawings. A Gospel. Christian or not, the dead book saddened him. He carried it into the church and laid it on the altar.

Later the moon rose, a day past the full. Unable at first to sleep, he wandered from camp. Following the stream beside which the town had nestled, he came to the mouth and turned onto a beach. Wavelets on the bay glimmered and lulled, sand scritted underfoot. The air was not very cold. He made out stars, old friends, the Bears, the Dragon, the Lion that heralds the northward-swinging sun. Tonight they seemed remote and alien. Did they really rule over the fates of men? Most people believed so. If they were right, then the star of Ys—Venus?—was still ascendant; and the Mars of Rome was sinking?

Without having pondered the matter, which could have led him to question seriously a tenet of his religion, Gratillonius had always doubted astrology. At most, he supposed, whatever planet a man was born under might influence him; but so would the heritage of blood and circumstance that he had from his parents. Manhood required him to make his own fate.

But if the blind circle of the spheres was not what kept Ys alive: what did? He should have learned far more than he knew before embarking on this mission. The knowledge had, though, not been there for him, in any chronicles he could find or any spoken accounts he could elicit. Ys kept itself wrapped in enigma—how?

For no good reason, he remembered another evening a few days back, and a great owl he had glimpsed above a glade. Why should that make him shiver? He turned from shore and sought his tent.

~ 2 ~

Out of what had been Garomagus, a road ran almost due west along the coast, twenty miles or a bit less to the Gobaean Promontory. It was merely graveled, like most secondary Roman routes, but well maintained. The troops started early and marched with redoubled briskness. This night they would be in the fabulous city.

They had covered half the distance when they came to a pair of stones flanking the track. Ten feet tall, those granite pillars were not prehistoric; weather had softened their squared edges, but the characters chiseled into them were still legible. Gratillonius dismounted to read. On the southern column, a gracefully curving alphabet was unknown to him. On the northern he found Latin, surely the same message. His finger traced what his lips murmured: *"In the names of Venus, Jupiter, Neptunus, here I mark the frontier of land that has been of Ys since time immemorial, along this Redonian Way. Hold me and my sister sacred, for we bear the Oath, forever binding. Raised DCLXXXVIII*

AVC obedient to orders of the SPQR, year XIII since the Sign came upon Brennilis, who with C. Julius Caesar did make the Oath."

"Old," Gratillonius whispered. "Four and a third centuries. But the wording—I've seen things like this elsewhere, from nearly that far back—the wording here is—" a chill went up his spine—"unusual."

Eppillus looked around. "Boundary marker, eh?" he grunted. "Where are the sentries?"

Grass waved in a salty breeze, down to a cliff's edge on the north, with water agleam beyond it under a clear sky, and southward up to the spine of the peninsula. Afar in that direction, the men could just spy a flock of sheep near some wind-gnarled trees, but no other sign of habitation. Out where sunlight winked on whitecaps, sails showed boldly colored across the arc of vision. They were too remote for Gratillonius to be certain, but he supposed they belonged to fishing boats. Ys took little from its modicum of thin-soiled hinterland; it communion was with the sea.

"I don't imagine the city feels any need of pickets," he answered slowly. "Relations with the Osismii, and with Rome, have been peaceful. Trade must go unhindered, and across a long stretch, too. 'Redonian Way.' That seems to mean the Ysans think of this as their road to the Redones in eastern Armorica—nowadays to Condate Redonum—though those tribesmen seldom get to these parts."

"But what about pirates?" the deputy argued. "Pirates could land and walk on in."

"They don't. Something keeps them away. I don't know what."

"The old Roman Gods?" Cynan asked from his place as today's standard bearer. "Do They still have power...in this place?"

"Those are not Roman, those Gods the stones bespeak," Gratillonius said. "They're only Latin names. Romans used to suppose any Gods they met were the same as their own, but it was never true. You, my friend, must know better, must know Sulis is not really Minerva or— See, the inscription puts Venus first. A mother Goddess? Maybe. If we could read it, the second stone would tell us something very different from the first, about the Gods of Ys."

"The demons!" Budic exclaimed. He raised his arms. "Christ Jesus," he beseeched, "watch over us, drive off the powers of darkness."

"Fall in," Gratillonius snapped. "Forward march."

Mithras, Lord of Light, ride with us, Your soldiers, he thought as he sprang back onto his horse. He could not make it feel like a prayer. Had he wandered so far, into such foreignness, that the God of his fathers no longer heard him?

Angry at his weakness, he tried to thrust the question away. What was there to fear? Most likely less than anyplace else in the Empire, here where robbers dared not come. However lonesome, the landscape was gauntly beautiful. Ys of the marvels awaited him, and would scarcely deny him obedience. His demands would modest in any case, simply

54

that Ys remain at peace, and help keep the rest of western Armorica at peace, while Maximus campaigned. The leaders of the city could not fail to see how they too would benefit by an Emperor strong and able.

And afterward—why, that grateful Emperor ought at the very least to bestow senatorial rank on a man who had served him well. Perhaps he would lift the man's entire kin out of the curial class. And the officer would go on to mighty deeds, power, wealth, undying fame.

With an abrupt shock, Gratillonius realized that he did not know what his ambitions were. Hitherto he had been content to live day by day. When he thought about the future, he hoped for eventual promotion to senior centurion, followed by retirement in a home he would acquire somewhere among his Belgic tribesfolk. There he would have a woodworking shop for pleasure, horses, dogs, a cat to sleep on a sunny windowsill. Of course, he would already have married and begotten sons.... Never before had he imagined the world open to him. Did he truly want it?

A bulk ahead drew his attention. "Keep on," he ordered, and turned his horse off the road onto a point of land. What he found was the remains of a fortress on the brink of a precipice. Ditched and triple-walled, it was from before the Romans, and long unused. Grass billowed across ridges and mounds that had been earthworks. Yards below, waves foamed and growled; overhead, a gull cruised mewing.

The sight was like an omen of mortality. Gratillonius drew the sign of Mithras, wheeled his mount, and hastened back to the van of his party.

The end of the headland wasn't far now. He knew this road went to a maritime station the Romans had built, back when they maintained a constant presence; later the Ysans manned it for them. From there, he supposed, the way would turn south till it went down to the bay where the city was. Impatience leaped in him. He wanted to gallop straight across. But that wouldn't be dignified. Besides, grass and brush might well conceal footing dangerous to a horse. His heels prodded the animal into a trot while he reined in his spirit.

At the bend in the route he diverged for a look down a side path. Under granite of the promontory, above rage of water among rocks and reefs, he saw the ruins of the station. Holes knocked in walls—whether by enemy rams or by storm-driven surf—gaped full of darkness. Rain had washed away the soot of the fire that consumed roof and dock; he glimpsed only a few charred timbers from either, tumbled and bleached like driftwood.

"This happened years, maybe decades ago," he muttered. "Ys is supposed to be safe. But already then—"

Eppillus trod forward to stand by his leader and see. "Maybe their Gods are dying too," he said. Yet the rusty voice and the barrel-shaped figure somehow called Gratillonius back to hopefulness. Here was reality, prosaically Roman. Whatever ghosts haunted this country were no more solid than those cloud shadows which the sea wind sent scudding over it.

55

"We'll see," the centurion answered. "Onward!"

Southbound he passed a hillock which he suspected covered more wreckage. He scarcely noticed for tower tops were coming into view ahead. When he reached the descent, there was Ys.

From this height the road swept to a deep dale, walled on both sides by the land. Thus protected, the northern slopes were fit for more than rough pasture. Orchards and woodlots stood around the red tile and white walls of wealthy homes, the thatch and clay of clustered cottages. Brown plots amidst the greenness showed where gardens would soon be bearing. The southern side of the hollow was less occupied, because it climbed steeply to form another headland. Between those two nesses was the bight which Ys filled. Eastward the valley ran lengthy, well populated, toward distance-blue hills.

Soldier's training made Gratillonius first survey the terrain. A branch way plunged directly down to a short bridge between this promontory and the wall around Ys. Another road led from the eastern city gate, inland. An arm of it swung north, and then east under the heights, to a grove of oaks, after which it became a mere trail.

On the near side of the shaw, Gratillonius spied three large wooden buildings around a courtyard giving on that road. Beyond the trees, in a low swale, was an amphitheater, modest in size but clearly Roman save for—something subtle, some difference he could not identify from this far off. There the highway went south, and then east again out of sight. Elsewhere ran several dirt roads, and a graveled one out onto the southern cape, which held a pharos at the tip. From the far hills, down the middle of the valley, cutting through the grove, gleamed a narrow canal.

His gaze sought Ys. Strange, he thought as he caught his breath—part and parcel of the strangeness everywhere around—that he and his father had traded as close as Garomagus, yet not until now had he glimpsed Ys of the hundred towers.

Thus they bespoke it around Armorica. If the count was not really that high, if this was in fact a rather small city, what matter? Ys soared out of the sea.

Its wall formed a rectangle about a mile long, to which were added semicircular ends of a diameter slightly less. The shore arc snugged close between the two forelands, and there the rampart loomed fifteen feet. Westward its elevation above water would depend on the tides, which Gratillonius knew to be large. He could only wonder how deep those foundations lay. Red-brown, the material must have been quarried from the cliffs. A band of color below the parapet, a frieze, relieved the murkiness. Twin turrets lifted battlements over each of the three landward entrances. Along the western arc, if he gauged rightly, a fourth pair stood about a hundred and ten degrees apart, to guard the harbor and its marvelous gate.

He could not discern that basin from here, because too many buildings were in the way—towers indeed, high, narrow, reaching for the sky out of the crowd of lesser structures. Mosaics and patternings formed brilliant fantasies up their sides. Glass, gold, even tiled and patinaed copper caught the early afternoon sunlight and flung it back in a dazzle. A slight haziness, borne in from Ocean, made the sight a dream. He could scarcely believe that human beings dwelt yonder, not elves or Gods.

But the first of the Caesars had walked those streets, the first Augustus had ordered those outer defenses erected. Gratillonius had come to reclaim a heritage.

The knowledge thrilled in him. "Silence!" he cried at the amazed swearing of his men. "Dress ranks. We'll enter in Roman style."

The Ysans had paved this section of the way, since gravel would have washed downward. Hoofs rang on stone. Gratillonius tightened knees against the hairy warmth of the horse. Weight pulled hard on him, hauling him on toward the sea.

Faintly through the wind he heard a trumpet call, and another and another. Watchmen had glimpsed his soldiers. The land portals stood open and he supposed townsfolk would soon be swarming forth—past the smithies and carpenter shops and other worksteads that stood just outside along the eastbound road—unless an official delegation forced itself in front of the crowd.

But the first human motion he spied was at the oak grove. Several people came from the house. For an instant they paused in the courtyard to stare. Then a man took the lead, loping out while the rest scurried after. Clearly they meant to intercept the newcomers.

Gratillonius thought fast. Amidst what scanty information he had been able to gather, much of it doubtless false, was a story that the King of Ys spent the three days and nights around full moon in a sacred wood, and that at all times he must hold himself prepared to fight any challenger for his crown. Last night had ended the period in this month; but he might have lingered for some reason. If not, those might be priests of importance...and priestesses? Gratillonius identified women among them. Probably he would do best to meet them as they wished, allay whatever fears they had, ask that they accompany him into town.

A rutted track offered a shortcut between this road and the one that led to the grove. He gestured to his men and turned off, angling downward.

~ 3 ~

The parties met nearer the shaw than the city. They halted a few feet apart. For a space there was stillness, save for the wind.

The man in front was a Gaul, Gratillonius judged. He was huge, would stand a head above the centurion when they were both on the

57

ground, with a breadth of shoulder and thickness of chest that made him look squat. His paunch simply added to the sense of bear strength. His face was broad, ruddy, veins broken in the flattish nose, a scar zigzagging across the brow ridges that shelved small ice-blue eyes. Hair knotted into a queue, beard abristle to the shaggy breast, were brown, and had not been washed for a long while. His loose-fitting shirt and close-fitting breeches were equally soiled. At his hip he kept a knife, and slung across his back was a sword more than a yard in length. A fine golden chain hung around his neck, but what it bore lay hidden beneath the shirt.

"Romans," he rumbled in Osismian. "What the pox brings you mucking around here?"

The centurion replied carefully, as best he was able in the same language: "Greeting. I hight Gaius Valerius Gratillonius, come in peace and goodwill as the new prefect of Rome in Ys. Fain would I meet with your leaders."

Meanwhile he surveyed those behind. Half a dozen were men of varying ages, in neat and clean versions of the same garb, unarmed, their own hair braided but beards closely trimmed. In form they resembled Osismii, except for tending to be more slender and dark, but the visages of four were startlingly alike, long, narrow, curve-nosed, high-cheeked. Brothers? No, the gap between a gray head and a downy chin was too great.

Nearest the Gaul stood one who differed. He was ponderous of body and countenance. Black beard and receding hair were flecked with white, though he did not seem old. He wore a crimson robe patterned with gold thread, a miter of the same stuff, a talisman hanging on his bosom that was in the form of a wheel, cast in precious metal and set with jewels. Rings sparkled on both hands. In his right he bore a staff as high as himself, topped by a silver representation of a boar's head.

The women numbered three. They were in ankle-length gowns with loose sleeves to the wrists, of rich material and subtle hues, ornately belted at the waist. Above hung cloaks whose cowls bedecked their heads. Gratillonius guessed their disheveled appearance was due to haste, after his sudden advent, rather than to carelessness.

The Gaul's voice yanked him from his inspection: "What? You'd strut in out of nowhere and fart your orders at *me*—you who can talk no better than a frog? Go back before I step on the lot of you."

"I think you are drunk," Gratillonius said truthfully.

"Not too full of wine to piss you out, Roman!" the other bawled.

Gratillonius forced coolness upon himself. "Who here is civilized?" he asked in Latin.

The man in the red robe stepped forward. "Sir, we request you to kindly overlook the mood of the King," he responded in the same tongue, accented but fairly fluent. "His vigil ended at dawn today, but these his Queens sent word for us to wait. I formally attended him to and from the Wood, you see. Only in this past hour was I bidden to come."

Gratillonius laughed. "He was sleeping it off, eh?"

The man shrugged and smiled. "After so much time alone with three of his wives—" He grew serious. "Let us indeed go meet with the rest of the Gallicenae and leading Suffetes. This is an extraordinary event. My name is Soren Cartagi, Speaker for Taranis."

The Gaul turned on him, grabbed him by his garment, and shook him. "You'd undercut me, plotting in Roman, would you?" he grated. A fist drew back. "Well, I've not forgotten all of it. I know when a scheme's afoot against me. And I know you think Colconor is stupid, but you've a nasty surprise coming to you, potgut!"

The male attendants showed horror. A woman hurried forth. "Are you possessed, Colconor?" she demanded. "Soren's person when he speaks for the God is sacred. Let him go ere Taranis blasts you to a cinder!"

The language she used was neither Latin nor Osismian. Melodious, it seemed essentially Celtic, but full of words and constructions Gratillonius had never encountered before. It must be the language of Ys. By listening hard and straining his wits, he got the drift if not the full meaning.

The Gaul released the Speaker, who stumbled back, and rounded on the woman. She stood defiant—tall, lean, her hatchet features haggard but her eyes like great, lustrous pools of darkness. The cowl, fallen down in her hasty movement, revealed a mane of black hair, loosely gathered under a fillet, through the middle of which ran a white streak. Gratillonius sensed implacable hatred as she went on: "Five years have we endured you, Colconor, and weary years they were. If now you'd fain bring your doom on yourself, oh, be very welcome."

Rage reddened him the more. "Ah, so that's your game, Vindilis, my pet?" His own Ysan was easier for Gratillonius to follow, being heavily Osismianized. "'Twas sweet enough you were this threenight agone, and today. But inwardly— Ah, I should have known. You were ever more man than woman, Vindilis, and hex more than either."

"My, my lord, you rave," stammered Soren. "Be calm, I pray you, for your own sake and everyone's."

"Calm—after what *you* said to me when yon invaders came in sight?" Colconor's shout was aimed past him, at a younger woman: tall, well formed in a rangy fashion, her face recalling Minerva in its cold regularity and gray eyes. "You adder, you sorceress, you—you Forsquilis, trafficker with devils—" Then she returned him a look that sent a shudder through the centurion.

"Colconor, dear, please, please," begged the third woman. She was big and plump, with brown eyes and pug nose. Her manner was mild, even timid. Was she less formidable than her companions? "Be good."

59

The Gaul gave her a leer that was half a snarl. "As you were good, Maldunilis? 'Twas your tricks more than aught else that kept me belated in the Precinct. But meseems you too were conspiring my betrayal—"

He swung on Gratillonius. "Go, Roman!" he roared. "I am the King! By the iron rod of Taranis, I'll not take Roman orders! Go or stay; but if you stay, 'twill be on the dungheap where I'll toss your carcass!"

Gratillonius fought for self-control. Despite Colconor's behavior, he was dimly surprised at his instant, lightning-sharp hatred for the man. "I have prior orders," he answered, as steadily as he could. To Soren, in Latin: "Sir, can't you stay this madman so we can talk in quiet?"

Colconor understood. "Madman, be I?" he shrieked. "Why, *you* were shit out of your harlot mother's arse, where your donkey father begot you ere they gelded him. Back to your swinesty of a Rome!"

It flared in Gratillonius. His vinestaff was tucked at his saddlebow. He snatched it forth, leaned down, and gave Colconor a cut across the lips. Blood jumped from the wound.

Colconor leaped back and grabbed at his sword. The Ysan men flung themselves around him. Gratillonius heard Soren's resonant voice: "Nay, not here. It must be in the Wood, the Wood." He sounded almost happy. The women stood aside. Maldunilis seemed shocked, though not really astonished. Forsquilis breathed what might be an incantation. Vindilis put hands on hips, threw back her head, and laughed aloud.

Eppillus stepped to his centurion's shin, glanced up, and said anxiously, "Looks like a brawl, sir. We can handle it. Give the word, and we'll make sausage meat of that bastard."

Gratillonius shook his head. A presentiment was eldritch upon him. "No," he replied softly. "I think this is something I must do myself, or else lose the respect we'll need in Ys."

Colconor stopped struggling, left the group of men, and spat on the horse. "Well, will you challenge me?" he said. "I'll enjoy letting out your white blood."

"You'd fight me next!" yelled Adminius. He too had been quick in picking up something of the Gallic languages.

Colconor grinned. "Aye, aye. The lot of you. One at a time, though. Your chieftain first. And afterward I've a right to rest between bouts." He stared at the women. "I'll spend those whiles with you three bitches, and you'll not like it, what I'll make you do." Turning, he swaggered back toward the grove.

Soren approached. "We are deeply sorry about this," he said in Latin. "Far better that you be received as befits the envoy of Rome." A smile of sorts passed through his beard. "Well, later you shall be. I think Taranis wearies at last of this incarnation of His, and—the King of the Wood has powers, if he chooses to exercise them, beyond those of even a Roman prefect."

"I am to fight Colconor, then?" Gratillonius asked slowly.

Soren nodded. "In the Wood. To the death. On foot, though you may choose your weapons. There is an arsenal at the Lodge."

"I'm well supplied already." Gratillonius felt no fear. He had a task before him which he would carry out, or die; he did not expect to die.

He glanced back at the troubled faces of his men, briefly explained what was happening, and finished: "Keep discipline, boys. But don't worry. We'll still sleep in Ys tonight. Forward march!"

By now people were spilling out of the city. Three of Soren's attendants stood in line across the road to keep them from coming farther. This combat would be a rite, not a spectacle. The other three ran ahead, passing by Colconor, to make things ready. Evidently all of them were household staff in yonder place. Since their attitude was not servile, that must be an honored position.

The Speaker walked at Gratillonius's left, the women at his right. Nobody talked.

It was but a few minutes to the site. A slate-flagged courtyard stood open along the road, flanked by three buildings. They were clearly ancient, long and low, of squared timbers and with shingle roofs. The two on the sides were painted black, one a stable, the other a storehouse. The third, at the end, was larger, and blood red. It had a porch with intricately carven pillars.

In the middle of the court grew a giant oak. From the lowest of its newly leafing branches hung a brazen circular shield and a sledgehammer. Though the shield was much too big and heavy for combat, dents surrounded the boss, which showed a wildly bearded and maned human face. Behind the house, more oaks made a grove about seven hundred feet across and equally deep.

"Behold the Sacred Precinct," Soren intoned. "Dismount, stranger, and ring your challenge." After a moment he added quietly, "We need not lose time waiting for the marines and hounds. Neither of you will flee, nor let his opponent escape."

Gratillonius comprehended. He sprang to earth, took hold of the hammer, smote the shield with his full strength. It rang, a bass note which sent echoes flying. Mute now, Eppillus gave him his military shield and took his cloak and crest before marshalling the soldiers in a meadow across the road.

Vindilis laid a hand on Gratillonius's arm. Never had he met so intense a gaze, out of such pallor, as from her. In a voice that shook, she whispered, "Avenge us, man. Set us free. Oh, rich shall be your reward."

It came to him, like a chill from the wind that soughed among the oaks, that his coming had been awaited. Yet how could she have known?

The storehouse door crashed open and Colconor strode forth. He had outfitted himself well for a barbarian—conical nose-guarded helmet, scale coat reaching to his knees, calf-length leather boots reinforced

61

with studs. His left hand gripped a small round shield. The longsword shone dully in his right.

"Well, well, you're here 'spite of being a Roman," he gibed. "Let's have done fast. I've business with yon traitor wives of mine."

"My lord, your demeanor is unseemly," Soren protested. "It cannot please the God."

Colconor spat. "I've given Taranis deaths enough whilst I was King. Think you He'd want a lackey of Rome instead?"

"Kneel." Soren pointed to a spot below the tree. Gratillonius and Colconor obeyed, side by side. An attendant brought water in a bowl, another a sprig of mistletoe. Soren used the herb to sign the contestants as he chanted a prayer in a language Gratillonius did not recognize at all.

Thereafter: "Go forth," said the Speaker for Taranis in Ysan, "and may the will of the God be done."

Colconor led the way between the red house and the stable, in among the trees. Gratillonius followed, never looking back. Light rays struck between branches still largely bare. Shadows welled up in the farther depths of the grove. Last year's leaves rustled underfoot, smelling of damp. Moss and fungi grew on fallen boles. A squirrel darted ruddy, like a comet foretelling war. Gratillonius heard a pig grunt—wild, sacred to whatever mystery dwelt in this place?

Near the middle of the shaw was a grassy space, narrow but clear. Colconor stopped and faced about. "Here I'll kill you," he said in a voice gone flat.

Gratillonius raised his oblong Roman shield. Javelins would be useless under these conditions, and he bore just the shortsword in his fist, the dagger at his hip. Fleetingly, he wished he had had a chance to swap his parade mail for workaday armor. He smiled bleakly at himself. This was good equipment despite the damageable ornamentation. It was with such gear that Rome's legionaries had conquered much of the world. However, they did it in disciplined units, each a single many-legged machine. With two men alone, the barbarian outfit was as useful, maybe better.

Mithras, he thought, I stand as a soldier, obeying my orders. Into Your hands I give my spirit.

Then at once he became entirely seized by the business before him.

The fighters circled, seeking an opening. It was always an odd feeling to Gratillonius when he looked into the eyes of an enemy. A perverse comradeship—

Colconor lunged. His sword whirred down. Gratillonius moved his shield slightly to intercept. The blow thudded loud, radiated back through handle and arm, pulled the strap hard across his shoulder, but the metal rim of the plywood stopped it. He stabbed. Colconor was skilled too. The point smote into the soft pine of the Gallic shield and stuck for an instant. Colconor twisted it while he slashed at that wrist of

Gratillonius. So confined, the long blade was awkward. The centurion had time to block it with his own shield. He freed his weapon and tried for a knee. Colconor recoiled. Blood wet a ripped trouser leg, but from a minor cut.

Colconor bayed. He kept his distance, sword leaping, crashing, seeking. Gratillonius must stay on the defensive, unable to counterattack with his smaller blade. His shield did not catch every blow. Two rang on his helmet, one hit mail, one slid along a greave. They hurt.

Coldly, Gratillonius peered beyond his foeman, found what he sought, began maneuvering. A frenzied Colconor dogged his step-by step retreat. Gratillonius got his back against a great trunk. Colconor yelled and hewed, right, left, up, down, metal a-clang among the rising shadows. He bounced about like a wolf slashing at a bull.

Gratillonius spread his feet right-angled and tensed his knees. Abruptly he released the left. He pivoted, and Colconor nearly ran past him. Gratillonius jabbed.

Colconor drew back...and now it was he who stood pinned against the tree.

Gratillonius gave him no time to work his way out of the trap, but moved in. The longsword dinned on his helmet. A shallow slash opened on his forearm. Then he was close. He feinted at the legs. Colconor lowered his shield to cover. Gratillonius drove the boss of his own straight into his enemy's belly. Scales or no, wind whooped out of Colconor. Gratillonius brought the top edge of the shield aloft, catching Colconor beneath the chin. Bone crunched. Red ran forth. Colconor wailed.

Gratillonius saw a rare opportunity. He drove his sword upward and home. It entered at the cheek and went on. He felt bone give, and next the soft mass of the brain. That was a chancy stroke, but therefore unexpected. Blood gushed from Colconor's mouth and nose. His face became a Gorgon's. He crumpled and flopped. Gratillonius withdrew his sword and reinserted it beside the larynx, to complete the task.

For a while the centurion poised over the corpse. Breath went in and out of him, cool and cooling. He felt sweat chilly on his skin and smelled it, an arrogant odor. His mood was calm, though. He had done what he must—good riddance to bad rubbish—and inspection showed his wounds to be trifling.

He'd not wipe his steel on Colconor's greasy, death-fouled clothes. Squatting, he used earth and old leaves. Meanwhile he considered what might happen. King of the Wood? That doubtless entailed duties, he didn't know what, but seemed to bestow a certain amount of power as well. Thus a prefect who was also the monarch should be able to carry out his mission very handily.

Regarding the slain man, he realized that Ys would expect him, too, to fight future challengers, until at last one of them bested him. He shrugged. Surely he could cope while he finished his work here.

Later he surely could leave. At worse, he and his men might have to cut their way out, or send for reinforcements; but he would regret that if it happened. The Ysans were probably decent people, on the whole. He'd try to do well by them.

Today he'd be busy with whatever ceremonies they held. He said a belated noontide prayer, added a word of thanks, and stooped to close the eyes below him and straighten out the body. Colconor had been brave enough to deserve that much.

As he performed the office, Gratillonius noticed anew the chain around the fallen man's neck. Wondering at something so delicate on someone so uncouth, he gave it a tug and drew forth from under padding and mail the object it held—an iron key, longer in the shank and more intricate in the prongs than he had ordinarily seen.

A talisman? Gratillonius felt the unknown touch him, cold as the wind. With reverence he laid the key back on the breast. Rising, he sought the red house.

VII

~ 1 ~

When he strode into sight, his men drew blade and gave him three honest cheers. Soren led the Ysan males in genuflection. The women remained standing. Maldunilis's soft features offered shyness, uncertainty, but from Vindilis and Forsquilis blazed an exultation terrifying in its savagery.

At once events swept Gratillonius along. Soren conducted him into the house. He saw that the columns of its portico represented a man, bearded and majestic, who bore a hammer like that which hung at the Challenge Oak, and attributes such as eagles, wild boars, and stylized thunderbolts. The name Taranis he recalled from former visits to Gallia, as well as the same image. So the Ysans had made Taranis their chief God? Gratillonius suspected matters were not that simple.

Within, the right half of the house was a feasting hall, high-raftered and gloomy, where fire licked out of trenches in a clay floor and smoke stung eyes before escaping from a hole overhead. Pillars upholding the roof formed two rows of idols, some clearly Celtic, others impossible for him to identify. Wainscot panels behind the built-in benches along the walls seemed to depict heroic tales. Banners hung from the crossbeams, sooted and frayed with age. Magnificence so rude must have stayed in use because ancientness made it holy. "Is this the temple of the God?"

64

Soren shook his head. "No, Taranis has a splendid marble fane in the city, and many lesser shrines. This is the House of the King, also known as the Red Lodge. Once he was required to live here always, with each Queen spending a night in turn. But for centuries, now, it has only been during full moon, and he summons those wives or other persons whom he will." He paused before adding, grimly matter-of-fact: "Of course, wherever he may be, he must come back when a challenger strikes the Shield. The resident staff dispatches a messenger."

Again a prickling went through Gratillonius's skin. Colconor could have left at dawn today for the comforts and pleasures of town. In that event, the Romans would have entered Ys directly, and might well have settled matters with the city magistrates before even meeting the King, who would most likely have decided to accept what he could not easily or safely change. Instead, though, three of his—wives?—had kept him carousing, and at the same time piqued him, as subtly and cruelly as a bullfighter, until he stormed forth when he saw the newcomers and, in besotted fury, forced the quarrel that ended in his death.

And just how had he done so? Gratillonius knew himself for a short-tempered man, and the insults he suffered were unforgivable. Yet he was a legionary officer on duty. For the sake of Rome, he should have armored his pride in dignity and merely returned contempt—not plunged headlong into action of whose consequences he had no idea. What demon had entered him?

A burning log cracked. Flames and sparks leaped high. Shadows moved monstrous in dimly lit corners, and it was as if a rustling went though the blackened banners overhead.

Gratillonius ran tongue over lips. "You must understand, Priest Soren—"

"No, my lord, I am simply the Speaker." The interruption was bluff but not discourteous. "I serve Taranis by leading certain rites and by helping govern the worldly affairs of His temple. Otherwise I am a Councillor of the Suffetes and the director of a Great House—an industry. You, sir, are the ordained one, high priest and, in a sense, Incarnation."

"You must understand," Gratillonius persisted, "that I am a Roman citizen in the service of the state. I am also a votary of the God Mithras. Never ask me to compromise my conscience about either of these things."

He could not be sure, in the dusk, whether Soren showed a flicker of unease. The man did reply steadily: "I do not believe we need fear that. If I am not mistaken, Mithraists may and do honor other Gods. For the most part, a King does as he will. Apart from meeting his challenges—and I would not expect any to you for a long while, my lord—apart from that, a King's reign is very much what he himself makes it. Ys is old. Through the hundreds of years it has seen many different kinds of men on its throne, Romans among them. But come, please."

65

The second half of the Lodge was divided into smaller rooms. These had been modernized, with glass windows, tile floors, frescoed plaster, hypocaust heating. Furniture was comfortable. It included a remarkable number of chairs, with arms and backs. Gratillonius remarked on that and was told that such seats were common in Ys, and not confined to the rich, either.

There was no space for a full-panoply bath, but a large sunken basin had been filled for him. Servants helped him out of his armor and undergarments. He sank gratefully into hot, scented water. His encounter had strained him more than he realized, and Mithras knew what would come next. He needed a rest.

Emerging, he had his injuries poulticed; just the cut on his arm received a precautionary bandage. Thereafter he enjoyed a skilled massage, was anointed, was guided to a new chamber where new raiment lay. Resembling Soren's but more sumptuously worked, the robe fitted him well, as did the soft shoes. He supposed the house kept several wardrobes in different sizes. His pectoral was a gold sunburst, hung from a massive chain and set with pearls and rubies. However, instead of a staff he would bear a full-sized sledgehammer, whose oaken haft and rounded iron head were dark with antiquity. True to his religious vows, he declined the laurel wreath offered him.

More men bustled around than before, making preparations. Soren had gone to oversee matters in the city, and no Ysan present had much if any Latin. His halting Osismian won Gratillonius a little information from the chief steward, about what was happening and what to expect.

Trumpeters and criers went through the streets. "*Allelu, allelu!*" resounded between walls and up into heaven. There followed words in the ancestral language of Ys, which had been Punic. Few other than sacerdotes and scholars knew it today, but it was sanctified. The message then repeated in the vernacular. "*The King is dead, long live the King! In the names of Belisama, Taranis, Lir, come ye, come ye unto the coronation of your lord!*"

The steward's account continued from the immediate past to the present and immediate future.

From the temples of the Three, Their images rolled forth on wagons never used for aught else, drawn by paired white horses for Belisama, black for Lir, red for Taranis. Folk garlanded themselves and heaped the wains with what greenery and blossoms they could find. Led by drums, horns, harps, they went singing and dancing out the gates and to the amphitheater. The clear weather, which gave no cause to unroll the canvas roof, seemed to them a good omen. Some must stay behind, though, making ready for a night's wild revelry.

The royal feast would be more sedate. Huntsmen tracked down a boar, out of the half-wild swine that ranged the Wood. At risk of life, they captured it in nets and hung it above the body of Colconor. There they cut its throat and bled it, down onto the fallen King. Stewed in a sacred cauldron, its flesh would be the center of a meal here at the Red Lodge.

Taken aback, Gratillonius asked what would become of the human remnant. Ys, he heard, was like Rome in forbidding burials within city bounds; and the cemetery out on Cape Rach, under the pharos, had long since grown to cover as much land as could be allowed. Dead Ysans were taken to sea on a funeral barge and, weighted, sent down to Lir. But a former King lay in state in the temple of Taranis until he was burned, which was too costly for anyone else. A warship took his ashes out near the island Sena. There they were strewn, given to Belisama (Ishtar, Isis, Ashtoreth, Aphrodite, Venus, Nerthus...), the Star of the Sea. As for his conqueror, following the victory feast, he spent his first night in this house. Thereafter he was free to move to his city palace. If he chose, he could visit his Queens in their separate homes, or call them to him—

"Queens!" burst from Gratillonius. "Hercules! Who are they? How many?"

"The Nine, my lord, the Gallicenae, high priestesses of Belisama. But, um, the King is not compelled—save when 'tis Her will— Forgive me, great sir, a layman should not talk of these matters. They touch the very life of Ys. The Speaker will soon rejoin you and explain what my lord needs to know."

Dazedly, Gratillonius received a herald, all in green and silver and with a peacock plume on his head, who announced that the processional was beginning. They must want their new King consecrated immediately, he thought. Well, they believed that somehow he embodied a God, or at least the force of that God, upon earth.

Outside, it was late afternoon, and the air boisterous. Soren waited with several fellow dignitaries of his temple. Nearby stood the legionaries. He had made arrangements for them to march along and have seats, later to be quartered in town: unusual, but then, every King was unique. How many had fought, won, reigned, fought, perished, how many ghosts were in this wind off the sea of Ys? Long hills, stark headlands, glimpsed towers and gleam of waters beyond, seemed remote to Gratillonius, not altogether real; he walked through a dream.

Where Processional Way, which led to the Wood, met Aquilonian Way, which ran out of the city's eastern gate, the Gods received their King. The idols of Taranis and Belisama were handsome work in marble, twice life size, done by Greek sculptors whom the Romans brought in as a gesture of alliance in earlier times, He the stern man, She a woman beautiful and chastely clad. The emblem of Lir was immensely older, a rough granite slab engraved with Celtic spirals. Later Gratillonius would learn that that God was never given human shape. Sometimes folk described Him as having three legs and single eye, in the middle of His head, but they knew that was only a way of bespeaking something strange and terrible.

A jubilant crowd followed the wagons. Gratillonius had a feeling their joy was not pretended. Colconor appeared to have made himself hated—mostly among the first families of Ys, whom he daily encountered, but their anger would have trickled down to many commoners. And yet there had been no thought of overthrow, assassination, anything but enduring that which the Gods had chosen to inflict.

Unless— Again bewilderment laid hand on Gratillonius.

As the servant in the house had said they would, the throng moved eastward, down onto low ground, and neared the amphitheater. It was Roman-built, a gracefully elliptical bowl of tiered benches within an outer wall of marble whose sheerness was relieved by columned doorways and sculptured friezes. Nevertheless Gratillonius confirmed the impression he had gotten on the promontory, that it was alien. The proportions were not...quite...classic. The portals were pointed. The fluting and capitals of the pillars hinted at kelp swaying upward from the sea bottom. The friezes mingled seals, whales, Northern fish with fabulous monsters unlike centaurs or gryphons, and with curious Gallic symbols. How much mark had Rome ever really made on Ys?

The people swarmed in right and left while the sacred cortege entered by a centrally southern archway, through a vaulted passage and out onto the arena. This was not sanded, to take up blood, but paved. A spina told Gratillonius that chariot races were held. That low wall ran down the middle of the arena, leaving space clear at either end; there rose posts for the hoisting of scorekeeping markers. In the middle, however, this spina broadened into a cornice, a balustraded stone platform. Stairways led up to it, as they did to the boxes in the stands reserved for magnates. That meant, Gratillonius realized, this place did not see beast combats—nor human, he felt sure.

When benches had filled with brightly clad spectators, the Gods made a circuit of the arena before stopping under the cornice on the south side. Gratillonius noticed that Belisama was in the middle. Soren told him to bow to Them as he, accompanied by the Speaker, went up onto the platform. Acolytes followed, bearing ewers, censers, evergreen boughs. Behind them, a rawboned graybeard carried a bronze casket. It was a position of honor; his robes were blue and silver, and Soren had introduced him as Hannon Baltisi, Lir Captain.

Standing aloft, these celebrants waited until a hush had fallen. The lowering sun still spilled brilliance down into the bowl, though shadows lengthened and chilled. A trumpet rang, high and icy sweet. From the middle northern archway came a band of girls and young women, gorgeously cloaked above white gowns, bearing tall candles in silver holders. "The vestals, virgin daughters and granddaughters of the Queens, those who do not have vigil today," Soren murmured to Gratillonius. They moved wave-like to ring the spina while they sang:

68

"Holy Ishtar Belisama,
Lady of the starry sky,
Come behold Your sacred drama
Taught to men by You on high.
You the Wise One are our teacher.
Spear-renowned of ancient days,
Hear the words of Your beseecher.
Mother, come receive our praise.

"Great Taranis, heaven-shaker,
Lord of sky and inky cloud,
You the rain- and thunder-maker,
Wrap not this Your day in shroud.
Shed Your light on Your procession.
Bless us with Your golden rays.
Giver of all good possession,
Father, come receive our praise.

"Lir of Ocean, dawn-begotten,
Lifter of the salty tide,
Be Your servants not forgotten
When in hollow hulls they ride.
Lord of waves and rocks, bereaving,
Draw us into safer ways,
And, our fears of wreck relieving,
Steersman, come receive our praise.

"Threefold rulers of the city,
Star and Storm and Ocean Deep,
For our praise return us pity
While we wake and while we sleep.
Grant we keep our worship faithful,
Sung aloud in sacred lays.
Turn on us not faces wrathful.
Holy Three, receive our praise."

And now arrived the Nine. Those whom Gratillonius had met this
day were become as strange to him as were the rest, in gowns of blue
silk bordered with figures akin to the friezes, white linen wrapped high
over their heads and pinned by orichalcum crescents, faces stiff in
solemnity. Pace by pace they approached the stairs and ascended one
by one. A tall old woman led them...they seemed to be going in order
of age...Soren spoke the name as each paused before Gratillonius, bent
her head above folded hands, then entered a rank forming on his left
hand and stood like soldiers, war captains of the Goddess, nothing
further of humility about them....Quinipilis, Fennalis, Lanarvilis, Bodilis,
Vindilis, Innilis, Maldunilis, Forsquilis—
   Dahilis.

Dahilis rammed through Gratillonius. He would not confuse that name. O Gods, she was so much like Una the neighbor girl whom he loved when he was fifteen and ever since had sought to find again, for Una must needs marry wealth in Aquae Sulis if she would help her father stave off ruin.... Dahilis reached to the base of Gratillonius's throat. She was slender though full-bosomed, her hue very fair save for the tiniest dusting of freckles over a short, slightly flared nose; her mouth was soft and a little wide, dimples at the corners; her face was heart-shaped, high cheekbones delicately carven, chin small but firm; her dress brought out the changeable blue-green-hazel of big eyes under under blond brows; her movements kept an endearing trace of coltishness, as young as she was.... When she looked at him, her look was not like that of any of the others, proud or rapt or victorious or wary. A blush crept up from her bosom, her lips parted, and he heard her catch her breath before she moved on.

Invocations sounded forth, first in Punic, next in Ysan. Gratillonius could not make himself pay close heed. Reality struck him in the stomach when the Lir Captain opened his casket and held it out to the Speaker, who lifted forth a key on a fine golden chain. Gratillonius knew that key. "Kneel," Soren commanded, "and receive the Power of the Gate that is the King's."

Gratillonius obeyed. When the loop went over his head and the thing hung from his neck it felt heavy, and as if so cold as to freeze his heart through the pectoral and robe. That passed over. He forgot it in the next moment, for out of the casket Soren had brought a crown.

"Receive the sigil of your lordship and the blessing," the Speaker said.

"No, I cannot," Gratillonius whispered.

Soren almost dropped the circlet of golden spikes. "What?"

"I told you I follow Mithras," Gratillonius replied in hasty Latin. "When they raised me to Soldier of the Mystery, I was thrice offered a crown and must thrice refuse it, vowing never to wear any, for the God alone is Lord."

"You shall—" Soren broke off. Glances clashed. He made a wry mouth. "Best not risk a disturbance. The Key is what truly matters. Hannon, keep silence. Gratillonius, may I briefly hold the crown above your head? Answer, quick!"

I must not let them order a Roman about, passed through the centurion. "Do that and nothing else. Or I'll fling it from me. My legionaries sit yonder, still armed."

Soren flushed. "Very well. But remember Colconor."

Gratillonius heard a buzz go around the seats at the change in the ceremony, but it died away and everything further was soon completed. Afterward the maidens led the Queens out; Suffetes came down from their boxes to meet the new King in the arena; the amphitheater emptied; last, the Gods of Ys went home to Their temples, to abide the future.

70

2

After sunset the wind loudened and bleakened, driving rain clouds before it low above the land. The first few spatters were flying when the magnates bade their host goodnight and departed with their lantern bearers for the city, a mile hence. Gratillonius left the door and paced the length of the hall.

It had been a polite gathering, but cautious and formal, when neither side knew what to make of the other. He was no desperate adventurer or runaway slave, he was an agent of the Empire, come to serve its purposes; and though he promised those would enhance the welfare of Ys, he could not blame its leading men if they took that incident of the crown as a bad sign. He had to win their trust. Before he could do so he must understand them in some measure, and what his position among them really was. Well, he thought, tomorrow I'll begin, I'll take my earliest few steps into the labyrinth.

He grew aware that the household staff had assembled before the wall that divided the two portions of the lodge. Flickers of firelight and lamplight showed them expectant. What, more procedures? He stopped and waited.

The chief steward touched his brow, salutation to a superior. "Is my lord ready for bed?" he asked.

"Oh, I...I'm not sleepy, but suppose I may as well—"

"Presently comes the bride of my lord's first night."

"Uh?" No, he would not reveal perplexity. Had he, with his limited knowledge even of Osismian, misunderstood something? Well, let that happen which the Gods willed. Certain it was that he had slept solitary for months. He felt sudden heat in his loins. Of course, if they went by precedence of age—maybe he could blow out the lights and use his imagination. "Aye," he said, as calmly as might be, "let us do what may beseem this occasion."

Servants guided him to a well-outfitted chamber, helped him disrobe, brought in a flagon of wine, cups, cakes and cheeses and sweetmeats, several lamps, incense which they set burning, and left. Abed, unable to lie down, Gratillonius sat with arms folded across nightshirted knees. Warmth from the floor, fragrance from the sandalwood and myrhh, enfolded him. Noise of wind and rain sounded remote beyond the shutters. Much louder was his heartbeat.

Nine wives— He wondered wildly what his duty was toward them. He had married them in a heathen rite and because he had no choice if he was to carry out his mission. When he was done here and could go home, need he legally divorce them? He should ask a Mithraic Father. Yet meanwhile they were human, they could feel pain, and, O Gods, there would likely be children—

Faintly there reached him a hymeneal hymn. It could only be that. His pulse quickened still more. Who had arrived? Wrinkled Quinipilis, bitter Vindilis, handsome Forsquilis, what could happen with any of them? Somehow they had *known* he was on his way hither.

The door opened. "May all Gods bless this holy union," said the steward. Dahilis entered. The steward closed the door behind her.

Dahilis.

She stood as if frightened. One small hand fumbled at the brooch of a rain-wet cloak. She swallowed before she could speak. "My lord King, is...is Dahilis, his Queen...is Dahilis welcome?" Her voice was a little thin, but the timbre caused him to remember meadowlarks.

He surged from the bed and went to take both her hands in his. "Welcome, oh, indeed welcome," he said hoarsely.

The cloak came off. He took it and tossed it aside. She had changed to a simple gown of gray wool whose belt hugged it against her slimness. Her hair was piled high, held up by a comb. He saw that it was thick and wavy, sun-golden with just a tinge of copper. He clasped her shoulders, looked down, and said in his lame Osismian, which he tried to give an Ysan lilt: "How wonderful that you, you, should seek me this night."

She lowered her gaze. "They, the Sisters, they decided it when—when we called you, my lord, called you to deliver us."

He did not want to think about that, not now. "I will strive to show kindness...unto all— Fear me never, Dahilis. If ever I blunder into wrongdoing, tell me, only tell me."

"My lord—" She received his embrace, she responded, the kiss lasted long, she was not skilled but she was quick to learn, and eager.

"Well, uh, well," he laughed breathlessly, "come, let us sit down, refresh ourselves, get acquainted."

Her glance was astounded. "Col—" she began, and checked herself. Colconor, he thought, Colconor would never have troubled to put her at ease. (Supposing that he, Gratillonius, could do it in this first encounter.) "Already you are being kind," she whispered.

They took chairs opposite each other at the table. He felt in a remote fashion what a curious arrangement that was. But naturally, she was used to it. He poured wine. When he was about to add water, she made a shy negative gesture, so he refrained too. Her cup trembled as she lifted it. The drink was dry and full-bodied, warming both flesh and spirit. He thought he would readily learn to like taking his wine like this.

"Do you speak Latin?" he inquired in that language.

"I can try," she gave him back with difficulty. "We study it in vestal school. But I've seldom had any practice since."

He smiled. "Between the two, we'll get along." And thus they did. Sometimes it required much repetition or search for a word, but that became part of a game they played, helping them feel more comfortable with each other; and he found himself actually beginning to acquire Ysan.

72

"I know well-nigh nothing, Dahilis," he said. "You understand, don't you, I did not intend to take the Kingship. I stumbled into it." Her look sharpened, and he hurried on before she could respond. "I do not even know what questions to ask. So let us talk freely, dear. Will you tell me about yourself?"

She dropped long lashes. "Naught is there to say. I am too young."

"Tell me anyhow."

She lifted her eyes. A bit of mischief danced forth. "If you will do likewise, good my husband!"

He laughed. "Agreed. Not that we can say much in an hour or, or two. How old are you, Dahilis?"

"Seventeen winters. My father was King Hoel, my mother Tambilis. Queen Bodilis was her daughter too, my older half-sister, by King Wulfgar. But mother died in my fifteenth year...and the Sign came to me."

And Colconor, then reigning, took her.

"There is, is scarce anything else, my lord," Dahilis said, "but I think I shall be glad you are King. Pray won't you speak of your own life?"

When ever was a man loth to parade his exploits before a lovely girl? thought Gratillonius. Nevertheless he kept the tale laconic. Her eyes widened and widened. To her, Rome must be as glamorous as Ys was to him. And he travelled on affairs of Rome....

When her clothing fell to the floor, he saw that above the cleft of her breasts was a tiny red crescent, its horns to the left, like a birthmark. She noticed his attention drawn to it from other sights, touched it, and said diffidently: "This? 'Tis the Sign. Ever when a Gallicena dies, it appears on one of the vestals. That consecrates her a priestess. I know not why Belisama chose me out of all the rest—but oh, this night I thank Her that She did."

And afterward she snuggled close to him and murmured drowsily, "Yea, I do thank Her, truly I do thank Her, that She made me a Queen of yours. Never erenow have I known what glory She may bestow."

His lips brushed along the summery odor of her hair. "And I thank Her too," he said.

VIII

~ 1 ~

"It were well that we talked together, unheard, you and I," said Quinipilis. "Would it please you to walk the wall? Then I could also show you somewhat of this your newly-won city."

Gratillonius looked more closely than hitherto at the eldest of the Gallicenae. With five-and-sixty winters behind her, she still bore herself tall. A once opulent figure had become stout, her hands were gnarled by the aging that had made her gait rocking and painful, her visage was furrowed and most teeth gone; but underneath abundant white hair, gathered in a Psyche knot, gray eyes gleamed wholly alive, while good bones and arched nose held a ghost of her youthful comeliness. She was simply clad and leaned on a staff whose ferrule was plain iron. Her house was unostentatious, requiring just a pair of domestics, for she used only a part of it. Yet he felt he had never encountered anyone else more truly like a queen.

And her note borne to him at his palace, written by herself in excellent Latin, had less requested his presence than summoned him. He believed he could not well decline. His few days in Ys had overwhelmed him more than they had taught him. He badly needed advice. Still, not knowing what she wanted, he had come in some uneasiness.

"Is that what my lady intended?" he asked.

Quinipilis brayed a laugh. "Oh, ho! Did you fear me dragging you from lovely Dahilis to soothe my lust? Me, barren, crippled, my face like forty leagues of bad road?" She patted his arm. Her palm was warm and dry. "Nay, I gave up that three reigns agone. King Hoel and I were good friends, no more. As I hope you and I shall be, Gratillonius."

"As you were not with Colconor," he ventured.

Her mood darkened. "Never. Oh, he had me, again and again, for well he knew how I abhorred it from him. However, that was less bad than what he made the rest of the Sisterhood suffer. He had the animal cunning to sense it would be dangerous to goad me overmuch. And indeed, at the last—" She shook her head. "No matter. 'Tis behind us, thanks be unto you. We should take counsel for the morrow, foremost concerning that Sisterhood."

"I will be grateful, my lady."

"Then let us begone. A mummy like me does best to use the morning, for she is weary by afternoon."

"Could we not spare you, stay here and talk Latin?" asked Gratillonius in that language. "I'm told all educated Ysans know it, more or less, but don't suppose your slaves do."

"Servants, boy. Temesa and her husband are free, and well rewarded," Quinipilis replied sharply in her mother tongue. He was already able to follow it fairly well, though his speech stumbled. "We have no slavery or serfdom in Ys. Too much have we seen of what they have done to Rome."

"I've heard of Ysans capturing and selling folk."

"Aye, abroad, among the barbarians. Ys lives mainly by her ships. Most are fishing craft and merchantmen. A few are raiders. But do stop spilling my scanty time and come along. I'd fain point out this and that, and see how you respond. 'Twill tell me things about you. And I want to make you practice Ysan." She grinned. "Besides what you've been cooing at Dahilis."

Gratillonius felt himself redden. He helped her on with her cloak and resumed his own. Otherwise he wore the shirt, decorated jacket, breeches, and low shoes that were everyday male garb in the city. They were of fine material but of colors more subdued and cut more simply than was usual among the well-to-do here. As King he could have carried a sword, but was content with the knife at belt which was all that unauthorized persons were allowed to have on the streets. He did not care to be conspicuous this day. Best might be if he went unrecognized—though that was unlikely, when his companion was one whom everybody must know.

They left the house. Like its neighbors, it was of rectangular outline. Dry-laid sandstone blocks and red tile roof glowed mellow beneath rays of a sun that was as yet not far above the eastern towers. It gave directly on the street, and the flower garden behind it was minute, for even this wealthy district was crowded. Most homes nearby were larger, rising two or three stories, smoothly stuccoed, figured with inlays or frescoes. What those showed might be scenes but were often ideals: spirals, Greek keys, geometric arrangements. The effect was brilliant in the clear, cool air, as if jewels had tumbled out of a great coffer.

Not being a commercial thoroughfare, the street was narrow, nonetheless paved and clean. Ys required the hauling away of rubbish. Upon inquiry Gratillonius had learned that the sewers did not drain into the sea, which would have angered Lir, but into tanks of fuller's earth in chambers excavated below the city. From time to time these were emptied and the muck carted inland, where farmers were glad to have it for their fields.

Most people he saw as he walked were menials, in vivid liveries, on errands to and from markets and the like. The rich who dwelt hereabouts were already off to their businesses, while their wives were indoors managing the households. He met an occasional artisan carrying tools for some task, and flocks of children too small to attend any of the various schools, and sometimes an elderly person or a leisured youth. Where leaded windows stood open, he glimpsed a few pets—a songbird, a cat, a ferret. Ys lacked room for larger creatures, except draught animals admitted only onto major routes.

To him, folk generally looked happy. Well, he thought, why should they not? The city-state is at peace, safe, less prosperous than formerly but in no dire want, seemingly well governed. True, for years it lay in the shadow of Colconor, but the harm he could do was limited, and now I have plucked him out of the world.

"Yours seems a nation the Gods have favored," he said.

"They've sent us our share of grief," Quinipilis answered, a bit harshly.

"Whence came Ys? I've heard tell it stems from Carthage of old, but little else. 'Tis a puzzle to me how Ys could flourish this long a while and remain obscure abroad."

75

"Bodilis can best recount the history. She's the scholar among us. Seek her out." Quinipilis paused before she added: "Seek them all out, and soon. Aye, liefest would you lie with Dahilis only; that's graven upon you. And we are seldom jealous of each other, and...the yoke of Colconor united us. However, we brook not scorn. If naught else, that would through us dishonor the Goddess."

"I, I will do my best, my lady. But I've so much to learn, so much to do—"

She smiled at him. "Verily, if you be the man of duty I suppose." A chuckle. "Feel no pity for yourself. They may not be equally well-favored, but nine wives with incomes of their own should fulfill the daydreams of the friskiest young fellow. Well, eight, though I trust you'll reckon me a helpmate. That had better suffice, you know."

He sensed an underlying meaning. "Nay, I do not know."

She turned grave, almost motherly. "You are the King; the Father is in you. We are the Queens; the Mother is in us. Never will your manhood fail with any of these your wives. But never will you have your way with any woman else."

He stopped short. "What?"

"That is the law of Belisama, Who is present at every act of procreation." Her voice went steely. "Colconor tried, and could not, and that is one thing which made a monster of him, though he did find tricks whereby his whores in Old Town might give him pleasures of a low sort." Again the tone softened. "I think you will be too proud for that."

"It...it is not a wish for— Nay. A man is more than...a penis. But, but I have heard that only daughters—"

Compassion spoke. "Aye. We bear no sons. Ever. This too is the law of Belisama; for we are Hers." Quinipilis squeezed Gratillonius's hand. "Surely it is honorable to father Queens."

Stunned, he accompanied her in silence when she walked on. "You shall, my dear, you shall," she said presently. "Those of us who are of childbearing age will open their wombs for their liberator as they would not for Colconor, no matter how that maddened him. The Goddess gave unto Her first priestess in Ys the secret of an herb which bars conception—"

Mithras lives, he thought. Mithras will not leave me bound forever by a heathen spell. When my task here is done, He will free me, and I will go home and beget me sons to bear the name.

He squared his shoulders and rallied his spirit. If nothing else, he had Dahilis, he had Dahilis.

Cheer mounted as he passed through more and more of the city, its variousness and plenitude.

The street climbed gently in this eastern end of town, unlike the steep downwardness of its western half. Near the end he could look over roofs to Elven Gardens; arbors, topiaries, early-blooming flowers.

Adjoining, the temple of Belisama was like a miniature Athenian Parthenon—he had seen a drawing in a book—although its marble was not painted but left pure. That was somewhat northward; southward lifted the dome of his palace.

The street gave on Lir Way, the principal east-west avenue, and suddenly he was in a millrace of traffic, walkers, riders, porters, oxcarts, mulecarts, donkeycarts, a clattering, a chattering, creaking, calling, whistling, singing, laughing, swearing, dickering, hoping—city folk, farmers and herders out of the hinterland, fishermen, merchant sailors, traders, now and then a party of Osismii or Veneti trying not to be yokels, one party of Redones trying to be Romans, bound for the marketplaces or on other business.... Few actual transactions went on in this vicinity. It was full of blocky apartment buildings, with statues at intervals to lend stateliness, heroes, animals, chimeras, each with a hint of something neither Greek nor Roman.

Lir Way debouched on the pomoerium, the space kept clear under the city wall for defensive purposes. Beyond that paved ring, and High Gate standing open, Aquilonian Way ran out broad past the amphitheater, bent southward to climb the heights, turned east again and sought the distant hills. Immediately in front of the pomoerium, two large edifices flanked the avenue, Warriors' House on the left as a barrack for marines, Dragon House on the right as quarters and conference rooms for their officers. Gratillonius gave Quinipilis his arm when they crossed to the wall and went up the staircase on the north side of the gate.

The tower there was generally called the Gaul. Its bulk, battlemented and severe, reminded Gratillonius of the milecastle at Borcovicium and its kind. This, though, was not mortared in their fashion, but of closely fitted, dry-laid granite blocks, their edges rounded off by the weathers of many a lifetime. And so was the entire wall around Ys. He wondered why.

Sentinels recognized Quinipilis, realized who Gratillonius could be, and slanted their pikes, crashing the butts downward, in salute. She waved back cheerily. They wore studded skirts like his men, but helmets were peaked, shoulderpieces and greaves flared, cuirasses loricated and engraved with spirals, shields oval, swordblades of laurel leaf shape, cloth never red but blue or gray, insignia abstract—a foreignness Gratillonius found faintly disturbing, as he did not that of Scoti or Picti or Saxons, because this was more subtle.

Quinipilis led a southward course, over the arch above the gate, past that twin tower called the Roman, on around the half-circle of this end. "I've heard your state has had no army since Caesar made it his protectorate," Gratillonius remarked.

"Nor do we, nor did we ever," Quinipilis snorted. "Why should our men squander their best years in drill, or we pay a pack of flea-bitten mercenaries? Nay, what you see is a cadre of professionals, marines,

77

who double as peacekeepers at home. Besides them, every sailor has training for combat afloat or ashore."

"Suffices that, in times like these?"

"Aye. Not for an empire, but then, we've no wish to rule over outlanders. Have you Romans not had enough woes with your Gauls and Jews of yore, your Goths and Vandals today?" He was surprised that she knew of such rebellions, and a touch disconcerted. His task was to keep the Ysans loyal to Rome—to Maximus—and to that end, much history was preferably ignored. "True, our ships afar may at times meet peril, but no oftener than yours. And as for our defenses, what need we fear when the Gallicenae command the weather?"

Once more he halted in startlement. "My lady, can that be? I mean, well, surely you have the love of your Gods, but the Gods do not always answer human prayers."

Likewise stopping on the walkway, Quinipilis laughed; it made him recall hearing wolves. "You misheard me, boy. I said we *command* the weather. Oh, we abuse our power not, lest the Three take it from us. We call upon it only in the worst need. But no few reaver fleets were wrecked among the skerries, until the barbarians learned to leave us be. Landward, you can see, is merely a narrow arc of wall to hold, should attack come from that side; and our sea lanes will stay open for supply. Not that we've had many threats on land either. Caesar himself, flush from his crushing of the Veneti, knew better than to dare an outright conquest of Ys."

Gratillonius stood for a spell, silent in the breeze that blew tangy off Ocean. A merlon lay sun-warmed under his hand. When he had on a previous circuit leaned over and glanced down through the crenel beside, he had seen the frieze that ran around the wall. A mosaic of colored stones, it showed sacrificial processions, mythical battles, visions out of the deeps that glittered quicksilver to worldedge.

His glance shot to and fro. Bleak and windswept, the headlands enclosed Ys, Point Vanis reaching away on the north, Cape Rach on the south extending more than two miles westward. At the far end of the latter, beyond its clustered necropolis, he saw the pharos tower. Rocks stood rugged out of the waves, reefs lurked just below, surf burst white and green.

The promontories were of the same dark-red granite as the wall. However, he had learned that Ys stood between them on a downward-sloping shelf of sandstone. Its softness was easily quarried— those caves underneath had yielded much building material as they were enlarged— but it was just as easily gnawed by great tides and murderous currents. Indeed Ys had need to stay friends with Lir.

Well, had it not done so? Did wonder not nestle within its rampart? From this elevation, the city was speckled with silver, sunlight off rainwater in multitudinous rooftop catchbasins. He had been told that these drained into bottomless tanks below ground, set in fine sand within clay cisterns. Water passed through the filtering material to central wells, whence people drew it. In this wet climate there was never a lack. Nonetheless, beyond the Gaul and Warriors' House another water storage place rose high, a tower into which the canal discharged through a culvert. There ox-driven Archimedean screws raised the fluid, where-after pipes delivered it to the homes of the rich and to public troughs, fountains, baths. He had heard that the canal ran from a spring in the hills, sacred to Belisama, its shrine tended by virgin daughters and granddaughters of the Gallicenae.

He recalled his wandering mind to its surroundings. Turrets at the wall did not match the height of numerous buildings in the middle and lower town. Those soared from levels of stone to upper stories of wood, flamboyantly ornamented, taller than the Emperors had ever permitted in Rome. If the climb was wearisome to a lodging on a tenth or fifteenth floor— one dwelt in Ys! Gulls winged white between those pinnacles; tops sheened many-hued, tile, patinaed copper, painted gilt.

A faint drumming came up to Gratillonius, the blended noise of wheels, feet, hoofs, machines, pulse-beat of the living city.

"Shall we go on?" Quinipilis suggested.

Where the arc straightened out to run almost due west, Cape Rach thrust a mass inward that had been too large to chisel away. The architects had taken advantage of this; they need not build a causeway as they must on the northern side. Flanked by those towers called the Brothers, Aurochs Gate opened on Taranis Way, which ran northward to intersect Lir Way at the forum and thence onward to Northbridge Gate and its defending Sisters. Down on the left, the plaza of Goose Fair bustled with countryfolk bringing their products to market. Savoriness drifted in smoke from foodstalls, merchants cried their wares from booths.

"You've a livelier commerce than aught I've seen elsewhere, even in Londinium," Gratillonius observed.

Quinipilis shrugged. "'Twas better aforetime, when the Roman peace kept traders safe and Roman money was honest. But still we cope."

"Roman money? You strike not your own?"

"Nay, what sense in that? Formerly Roman currency was taken everywhere. Now, if we made coins for ourselves, they must either be good, and vanish into hoards like sound Roman gold and British silver, or else be as worthless as Roman billon. Gold, silver, and bronze circulate within the city but seldom leave it. For most dealings we're back to barter."

Quinipilis drew breath. "Yet we have wherewithal for bargaining," she said. "Our soil is poor, but its sheep yield a wool long, fine, well-nigh as precious as Asiatic silk. We must import most raw materials, but from them we fashion ships and boats, metalwork and jewelry, cloth, pottery, glassware, of a quality that makes them much desired. Our waters are the source of salt, preserved fish, garum, whale oil, tusks, and such-like exports.

"Though scarcely a foreign ship calls here anymore, ours still fare widely, if quietly. When our merchantmen do not sail off trading for themselves, they carry freight for others, from Britannia to Hispania. Our adventurous young men travel out among the barbarians to get amber and furs or to be slavers, pirates, mercenaries—never against Rome, dear—and those who live return at last carrying wealth. Aye, Ys endures."

Gratillonius's glance flew northward. "On Point Vanis I've seen the wreckage of a station that was Ysan as well as Roman," he said roughly. "It was meant to serve ships when your sea gate must be shut. What happened to it?"

The old woman's staff thudded harder on the stone as she walked. "'Twas night three score years agone, in the reign of my father Redorix, when I was a girl. Suddenly, there a score of Saxon warcraft were. The Gallicenae had not foreknown. The crews landed, harried widely about, destroyed the maritime post as you saw. Redorix died in battle against them. Our men cast them back at the wall, and they made off. The Gallicenae sought Sena and raised a gale they hoped would avenge us, but they never knew if it did or no."

She sighed. "Prefect of Rome, I will not lie to you. Ys was always less than omnipotent; and now, ever more are our ancient powers flickering and fading. Once any high priestess could heal any sickness by laying on of hands; today, seldom. Once her soul could range afar through space and time; today, few of us can have a vision, and for those who do, it may as well be false as true, with Forsquilis alone granted some measure of assurance. Once—ah, but you too have seen your God in retreat, have you not?"

She clutched his wrist. "We wanted you for more than a liberator, Gratillonius. We hoped for a redeemer. May you be he, and not a destroyer we brought upon ourselves."

His throat felt tight. "I will do my best," he said, "but remember I am pledged to Rome."

They walked on in silence to the western arc of wall and along it to the Raven Tower. There a sentry forbade promenading civilians to go farther. Behind him, on the stone curve that ran onward until the sea portal interrupted it, Gratillonius saw bastions upon which stood rain shelters of leather and light timbers. Beneath them, he knew, were ballistae and catapults. He could have demanded access; but he had already been there and Quinipilis was starting down a stairway to the pomoerium. He came after. Let her be the guide throughout.

While the top of the wall was everywhere level, ground dropped sharply beneath the western half of Ys, which was thus overshadowed. Buildings on his right crowded time-worn, mostly bare of decoration; here was Old Town, where industry and poverty intermingled. On his left, the shipyard extended to the harbor. Quinipilis went along its fence until she reached a street which ran beside it in the direction of the water, called the Ropewalk because it doubled as that. This she took. It was not in use today. Looking into the shipyard, Gratillonius spied a single small vessel under construction, albeit there were facilities for several large ones. As the Queen had said, Ys too felt the hard times that afflicted the Empire.

Where a launching ramp went down to the basin, the waterfront began. Its curve paralleled that of the city wall to seaward, a grand sweep two thousand feet in length, set back five hundred feet. Hard against its stone wharf, warehouses belonging to the great traders reared proud. But their inlaid facades were faded, and for the most part they seemed almost empty of men and goods. A number of hulls rested between the floating piers that reached out from the dock like fingers. None at this end were big, mainly fishermen in for unloading or overhaul. Their crews were off on leave, and only a few workers moved among them.

Nevertheless the harbor was a noble sight. Water sparkled as if dusted with crystal, lapped, gurgled. Gulls rode it like white boats or skimmed above in a snowstorm of wings. Some young boys were joyfully swimming, oblivious to the coldness of the water; it was a skill that sailor folk desired. Behind lifted the sheer cliff of the wall, ruddy-dark but its upper battlements brave with flags and the cloaks of watchmen.

Halfway along the waterfront, Quinipilis stopped. Here was a break in the line of buildings, for here began Lir Way. It started off through a triumphal arch, raised by the Roman engineers who built the wall but not to commemorate any victory in war. This was the sign of the saving of Ys, of the Pact between the city and its Gods. Beyond, the square of Skippers' Market was astir as dealers took seat in their booths.

The priestess, though, gazed outward, to where the western entry stood open. "That is the masterwork of all," she said low.

"Aye," Gratillonius agreed in awe.

Fifty feet wide, the gap in the wall faced upon illimitable reaches, Ocean itself. The doors on either side were beginning to close as the tide flowed higher—enormous oaken doors, iron-bound and sheathed in copper weathered green, silent and easy on their hinges despite the mass. Hemp and leather sealed their edges. On the bottom, when they shut, they would press against a sill carved out of the rock shelf that upbore Ys.

As yet, ample space remained between them for an incoming merchantman. Few Romans would willingly put to sea this early in the year, but Ysan mariners were more bold. The craft was leaner and handier than most in the Empire. Gilt trim, horse-headed stempost, red- and blue-striped sails were like a defiance of any dangers. Those sails were being furled, since the wind was not straight from the west and the wall had therefore laid calm on the basin. Towboats darted from their piers on spidery oars. Already their coxswains were shouting bids for the job of bringing the ship in. A customs officer and his amanuensis came out a door and took expectant stance. Oh, there was still life in Ys!

"You have been on the gate?" Quinipilis asked.

"Yestereven," Gratillonius replied. The memory thrilled in him afresh.

~ 2 ~

That was the final rite confirming him as King. Lir Captain and a delegation of sailors, deckhands as well as officers, called on him at the palace when the tide was nearly full. They took him out on the wall to the northern edge of the portal. There he looked downward, at the sea, and they showed and told him how the gate worked.

It was as simple as a heartbeat, and as vital. High on either side, aslant, jutted a great stone block. The feline heads into which these two were sculptured had blurred in the centuries, but their strength abided. Through each, a chain passed over a sheave within. One end of the chain was fast to its adjacent door. From the other end depended a giant bronze ball, cased in padded leather, hollow so that it floated.

"Without this, half the city would lie drowned at high tide," Hannon declared gravely. "Given a spring tide and a hard storm behind it, neither would the eastern side escape. Look. The doors are shaped so that they continue the curve of the wall. This helps them resist the force of the waves. They angle inward from bottom to top. This makes them *want* to close.

"As the water rises, likewise do the floats, giving ever more slack on the chains and thus letting the doors draw ever more near together. When they do shut, water level in the basin is still some three feet below the wharf. The tide outside goes on flowing, of course, until it may crest close under the battlements; but our city rests safe behind its gate.

"You see the floats are sheathed. This is to keep them from damaging themselves and the wall when storms fling them about. From time to time that protection must be renewed, as must the caulking along the edges and bottoms of the doors. This is done at the lowest low tides, on the calmest days. At that, 'tis difficult, dangerous work. The divers who do it are both well paid and honored. For they keep us alive.

"Now when the sea ebbs, the floats drop, pulling out their chains by their weight, hence drawing the doors open again."

"A marvel!" Gratillonius exclaimed. "Indeed the eighth wonder." And even then it perplexed him that this was all but unknown beyond Ys.

"The Romans wrought well," said Hannon, "but only by the leave of Lir; and He set conditions upon that."

"Um-m-m...when the doors do stand wide...could not an enemy fleet enter? Or what if there is violent weather?"

Hannon beckoned. "Come." He led the way down a stone staircase. Meanwhile, with a huge hissing sound, the gate closed. Gratillonius heard surf rumble outside; he saw the basin tranquil beneath him.

The stairs ended at a ledge halfway down the wall. There stood a capstan, from which a cable ran through another cat's head to the inner top of this door. Hannon pointed to corresponding structures on the opposite side. "At need," he said, "we use these to pull the portal shut against the weight of the floats. And we've a further security—which is in your hands, O King. Follow me."

He was rather brusque with his lord, Gratillonius thought. But that was understandable. He spoke for his God and his guild. Besides, like everyone before him in his present office, he was a retired skipper who had dared seas from here to Africa, here to Thule.

The doors, like the wall which they matched, had such a large radius of curvature that the inner surface they presented to the harbor was not far from being flat. A narrow, railed walkway reached across either, each terminating in a platform at the juncture. There Hannon and his party took Gratillonius.

On the southern door, a mighty beam—it must have been hewn from an entire oak tree—stood upright, pivoted above a lead counterweight. A cable ran from its upper end to a block high above, and back down to an equally solid cleat. Hannon stepped to the southern platform, released the cable, lowered the beam. The counterweighting was so well done that he could swing the mass up or down by himself. The beam crossed over both doors and settled into a massive iron U bolted to the northern one.

"This holds the portal tight against aught that may seek to come through," Hannon said. "We've less dread of pirates than of storms. Even in good weather, you've seen, the doors swing slightly to and fro as the floats bob on the waves. In a gale, those floats are mightily stirred. Descending into the troughs, they'd fain drag the doors wide apart. Did that happen, especially at high tide, the sea would pour in and wreak catastrophe on Ys. But the bar keeps the gate fast."

Stapled to the northern door beside the U was a chain on which hung a heavy padlock. Solemnly, Hannon passed it through holes in the beam and the iron, tightened it, and put the hasp of the lock through two links. "Lord," he said, "bring forth the Key."

The Key Colconor bore—and Kings before him and before him, back to the time when Ys and Rome and the sea made their treaty—Wordless, Gratillonius drew it from off his bosom and its chain of gold over his head. Hannon had him close and reopen the lock, release the bar and haul it back upright and secure it.

"That is our final safeguard," said the old man. "In times of threat, from war or weather, we shut the gate, lower the beam, and by the lock make sure that no evil chance can somehow fling it loose from its holder and free the doors to the waves. Always, save if he must needs leave Ys, the King bears the Key upon his person. It is his sacred duty to make fast the gate like this when danger nears, and unlock it when the threat is past. Thus went the word of Lir, Taranis, and Belisama."

Half numbed, Gratillonius donned the emblem again. "But what if I were elsewhere, leading your men off to battle, perhaps?" he mumbled.

"Then the Key awaits your return in the Temple of Lir, and I or another high person uses it. As for its loss, the Gallicenae keep the only duplicate; where, is known but to them." Hannon gave him an austere smile. "You understand this is all ceremonial, a repeated sealing of the Pact, rather than absolutely necessary. If we must, we can change the lock. Fear not. Our Gods do not forsake us."

~ 3 ~

Standing beside Quinipilis, Gratillonius recalled those words. Unthinkingly, he murmured them. She gave him a keen look. "But someday we may forsake the Gods," she said.

"For which others, do you think?" he asked very quietly.

Her laugh was bitter. "I've no fear of Christ. Nay. I feel sorry for the minister the Romans have forced on us. Poor little lonely man."

"I must tell you that I serve Mithras." In haste: "He does not forbid me to honor your Gods, if my acts keep within His law and I hold him in my heart to be supreme."

"Hm. That may bring you trouble, lad." Quinipilis brooded. "But I'll not fret about your Bullslayer either. Nay, what plagues me is a fear that we of Ys may become Gods unto ourselves."

She began walking again, he beside her. The northern half of the dock was given over to large ships, civil or naval—a number lay empty, idle—and to office buildings ornate behind colonnades. At the end of the basin, woman and man turned left, back toward pomoerium and wall. Below an ascending staircase stood the temple of Lir. Older than the Roman work, small but thick-built, it was pillared with rough-hewn gray stones akin to the menhirs found throughout Armorica.

The two climbed up past the Gull Tower and continued the circuit of the city bulwark. Quinipilis breathed hard and leaned heavily on her staff. Gratillonius offered his arm. She smiled and let him help her. "You should not exhaust yourself for my sake," he said.

She smiled. "Be not sorry. At home I can rest as long as I wish. Ere many years have fled, I'll be resting snug forever. Let me now enjoy my good-looking young escort."

"You have seen much, my lady," he said with care. "Methinks you've thought much too, and won wisdom thereby. Will you share it with me?"

"Ha! Scarce would I call myself wise, a hard-drinking hag like me. Anyhow, wisdom lies in nobody's gift. We must each forge it for ourselves, alone, as best we can."

"But you have known the life of Ys for over half a century. Will you not tell me of it? I do want to be good for your people, but I am wretchedly ignorant."

She regarded him for a time. "The omens were unclear when we called you hither," she said slowly. "But I dare think it likely that we did well." Her mood lightened. She cackled a laugh. "Aye, why should the garrulous crone not gossip as we walk?"

While she narrated, the wall grew straight again beneath their feet and brought them to the higher and newer part of the city, where its powerful families dwelt. At Northbridge Gate the landside length began. They went above the portal. Between those turrets called the Sisters, it gave on a short bridge across waters wild among rocks, to the northern cape. There ran Northbridge Way, along which he had come.... The pair continued east and then south.

They passed Star House, a Grecian-like building set in a garden near the wall, next to the Water Tower where astronomical observations took place. Those were essential. Although the secular calendar of Ys had become Julian, the religious calendar remained lunar. The holiest festivals were set by the moon and the planet Venus, which were Belisama's; the clans of the Suffetes each took name from one of the thirteen lunar months.

"The learned foregather here," Quinipilis remarked. "Philosophers, scholars, poets, artists, mystics—'tis a setting better for their discourse than a tavern. You'll often find Bodilis amidst them. Belike you'd enjoy it too. You carry yourself soldierly, lad, but I suspect you use that pate for more than a helmet rack." In Ys the idea was current that consciousness resided in the head.

Mainly, in slow sentences broken by pauses when she must wheeze for air, she spoke of her men. The talk went on past the Water Tower, down the staircase at the Gaul, back through the streets to her house. There Gratillonius bade her farewell. His mind awhirl but his heart warm with the feeling that he had made a friend, he sought home to the royal palace and Dahilis.

~ 4 ~

Now these were the Kings whom Quinipilis knew.

Redorix. He was a landholder near Vorgium until a barbarian raid left him widowed and ruined. Unable to mend his fortunes under the laws of Diocletianus, he went to try his luck at Ys, and overcame him who kept the Wood. The reign of Redorix lasted nine years and was fondly remembered, for he was personable and conscientious. On one

85

of his Queens he begot a girl who received the name Gladwy—the name her mother had borne as a maiden, which was the custom for first borns of a high priestess. A great horseman, Redorix sought to organize a cavalry troop among the Ysans, but this was not very successful and disbanded after his death. That happened when Saxon rovers appeared. There had been no forewarning, either through agents abroad or visions sent the Gallicenae. Folk wondered if this meant the Gods were failing, of if They were angry because too many Ysans had abandoned strict ancestral ways in favor of pleasure and luxury. The Saxons laid waste the maritime station and neighboring homesteads. Redorix led his riders against them and perished in the charge. They assailed the city but could not take it. Archers, slingers, catapults, and boiling kettles wrought havoc on them from the wall. At length they gave up and departed before navy ships out on patrol at sea should return. The Gallicenae raised a storm to hound them, but never knew if it had destroyed the galleys or not. Already Roman commerce was slumping so badly that no effort occurred to rebuild the station.

Calloch. Whenever a King died otherwise than in combat at the Wood, Ys must find a successor as soon as might be. The King was expected to lead his men in war, where his death was not the evil portent that demise from sickness or accident would be. He must always be a foreigner, lest grudges fester and feuds flame in Ys. In Condate Redonum a delegation bought an Osmisian slave, a gladiator. Calloch was happy about this; he would live better, and probably longer, than as a fighter in the arena. For six years he defended himself ably. Else he was not outstanding, and had the sense to stay in the background, letting the Suffetes govern unhindered by him. He begot a number of children, of whom two, by Ochtalis, would become the high priestesses Fennalis and Morvanalis.

Wulfgar. This was a Saxon adventurer, outlawed among his folk for a manslaying that, he claimed, was righteous. Most Ysans believed him, for despite his heritage Wulfgar proved another good King, forcefully taking leadership but considerate of the magnates and mild to the lowly. His greatest service was the enlargement of the navy, which had dwindled under the Roman peace. An enormous strength kept him nineteen years alive. In his reign an aged Queen died, and the Sign appeared above the breasts of young Gladwy. For her religious name she chose Quinipilis. She and Wulfgar much enjoyed each other, and of their three daughters, one would become Karilis. He also begot Quistilis-to-be by Donalis, Lanarvilis-to-be by Fannalis, and Tambilis-to-be by Vallilis, as well as numerous girls to whom the sign never came. These also served as vestals for the required term. Free on their eighteenth birthdays, some married, some renewed their vows and became minor priestesses, some went into curious byways of life: for a strangeness always lay over the Sisterhood. Meanwhile Wulfgar cut down challengers until word got about and none came for a long time.

Then at last a second Queen died, and the Sign marked a daughter of his own. She took the name Tambilis. Horrified, he would have refused, but when they were alone in the bridal chamber, the power of the Goddess descended. Unable to help himself, he made Tambilis his, and she became the mother of Bodilis. It was afterward thought that Wulfgar lost the will to live, as easily as he fell to the man who next arrived.

Gaetulius. This was a Mauretanian auxiliary stationed at Vorgium, who deserted when he saw no future worth having in a military career. While the Gallicenae missed Wulfgar, they did not hold his death against his killer. Such was the will of the Gods; and the slaying of the old King, the crowning of the new enacted the rebirth of the year and of all beloved dead. Gaetulius, though, proved to be a gaunt, ascetic man with a certain streak of cruelty and a temper apt to flare in violence— perhaps because he found himself hemmed in whenever he tried to accomplish something noteworthy and could never make his way through or around the opposition. On Quistilis he fathered Maldunilis-to-be, on Donalis he fathered Innilis-to-be, besides unchosen girls by different Queens. Quinipilis could never bring herself to like him. She discovered she was with child so soon after Wulfgar's death that she was not sure but what it was his. Features and nature revealed it to be of Gaetulius, and the infant grew to womanhood and became Vindilis. The reign of Gaetulius lasted for eleven years.

Lugaid. This was a Scotian from Mumu. He said he was of royal blood, driven out by a feud, but nobody ever learned much about him, for he was a brooding, solitary man. Against the Law of Belisama, Quinipilis regarded him as Wulfgar's avenger. Else he meant little to her. He was not a bad King, and when the mood struck him he sang and played the harp most wonderfully, but otherwise he attracted small love; and it was whispered that, alone, he carried out eldritch rites. By Karilis he fathered Forsquilis-to-be. The mother died in childbed and the girl was fostered by grandmother Quinipilis. The reign of Lugaid was for only four years.

Hoel. When a boy in the tribe of the Namnetes, this person had been sold into slavery for taxes. He ran away and drifted venturesomely about for a long while before coming to Ys and, almost on impulse, taking the Kingship. Handsome and cheerful, he quickly won hearts. He was intelligent, too, but content to stay first among equals, suggesting and persuading rather than invoking the full powers that were his in law. A great sportsman, reveler, and lover, he was likewise strong in battle. (While its wall and its high priestesses protected the city of Ys, its commerce more and more required warlike help.) Hoel took charge of convoys at need. He also led punitive expeditions which taught Scoti and Saxons a lesson they did not forget until after his death. Indeed, under him Ys prospered as it had not done for generations. Trade picked up southward, especially, with his native Namnetes and on down the gulf as far as Hispania. The wealth and the Southern influences that this brought were not an unmixed blessing—said the old and the moody: for they loosened morals and undermined patriotism. Yet Hoel was deeply mourned when he fell, not least by his wives and their plentiful daughters.

Colconor. This was an Osismian farm hand who fled (after having ravished the wife of another, or so the rumor went) and joined the Bacaudae. There he flourished brutally for several years before he decided to become King of Ys; surely, with his strength, he could hold that position until none dared go up against him. Soon he was hated, less for having struck down good King Hoel than for his coarse and overbearing ways. He was just shrewd enough to avoid provocation immediately unbearable. There did come to be an unusual number of challengers, as had happened in the past when Ys fell under a wicked man, but for five years he prevailed over all. None of the Gallicenae bore him a child, though he had them often and savagely—except for Maldunilis, and hers did not come to term, an ill omen. In his reign Tambilis died and the sign came upon youthful Estar, offspring of Tambilis and Hoel. Estar took the name Dahilis. Colconor had special delight in using her. But whatever he did, he found her spirit too sunny to break, as he found that of her fellow Queens too hard or, in the case of Maldunilis, too loose and lazy. This deepened his rage, as it did his loneliness. In Old Town he had his cronies and toadies, among them harlots who could amuse him despite his impotence outside the circle of the high priestesses. On these people he squandered much of the royal treasury. Perhaps it was not perfect justice that blame fell upon him for the decline in trade and the renewed rise of piracy and banditry since Hoel's time. These things were happening everywhere else, and in general the affairs of Ys went on independently of him. But rightly was Colconor blamed for causing the death of Tambilis, through abuse and heartbreak. Whispers of knife or poison went through Ys. This, though, would have been sacrilege, which might well cause the Gods to end the Pact and Lir to send His waves through a shattered gate. Slowly the Nine groped their way to an answer. If Suffetes could in secrecy persuade men to come strike the Shield, then it would be lawful for Queens to cast a spell drawing hither one whose chances were better and causing him to do battle. The omens they took were ambiguous but did not forbid. And so they gathered on Sena, the holy of holies, and there they cursed Colconor.

Gratillonius.

~ 5 ~

About sunset, clouds blew out of the west across heaven. It was already dark when Soren Cartagi raised a bronze knocker and brought it back down on the door of Lanarvilis.

The homes of the Gallicenae were not together, nor were they far apart, in the neighborhood of Elven Gardens and the temple of Belisama. Outwardly plain, they were inwardly Roman, from the time when they were built. Yet that time lay almost four hundred years in the past. Each of the nine dwellings had descended from Queen to successor Queen, each of whom had left her traces that never quite went away. Here the knocker, worn smooth by lifetimes of hands, was in the form of a serpent that bit its own tail....

The door opened. The steward saw who stood at the threshold and brought hand to brow. While Soren was in civil garb, few ever failed to recognize that broad hook-nosed visage and heavy frame. "Our lady awaits you, my lord," the steward reported, and stepped aside. Soren entered. His two lantern-bearers followed. The steward guided the party through the atrium and rooms beyond to a certain inner door, which he swung wide. When Soren had passed through, he closed it and led the escort off. Nobody would venture to question what went on in private between the Speaker for Taranis and a high priestess of Belisama.

Windowpanes in this chamber were full of darkness, but lamps gave ample soft light. It fell on blue carpeting, crimson drapes, fine furniture inlaid with walrus ivory and upholstered in leather. Flagon and cups on a table were cut crystal; a plate for cheeses and spiced mussels was millefiori glass. Lanarvilis took what pleasures she wanted, so they be permissible. What she wanted the most was not.

She rose from a settee and went to meet Soren: a tall blond woman, small-bosomed and thick-haunched, her nose too wide and her blue eyes too small, but not ill-looking when she took trouble about her appearance. Today she had had her tiring maid do her hair up in an intricacy of knots and braids, topped by a jeweled comb. Ointments and powders gave fresh coloring to a face whose bearer neared her fortieth year. Gold shimmered under her throat, above a gown cut low; those folds of rich brown fabric were kind to a woman who had fivefold been a mother. She took both his hands in hers. "Welcome and blessing," she said.

"Elissa!" he blurted, half dazed. "You're beautiful tonight. What witchcraft made you a maiden again?"

Her smile mingled enjoyment and sadness. "I was Elissa once," she murmured; "but that was long ago. I am Lanarvilis now. Elissa is my daughter by Lugaid, finished with her vestalhood, soon to wed and make me a grandmother."

"For an instant I forgot," he said harshly. "Only an instant. It shall not happen more."

"Oh, Soren, dear, forgive me," she begged, contrite. "'Twas myself I felt I should remind. I did wish to receive you well—in celebration—but mayhap 'twas a mistake." She released her hold on him. "Come, be seated, take refreshment."

They placed themselves on the settee, separated a foot or two. She poured. The wine gurgled and glowed. It was a choice Aquitanian, whose fragrance met them before they tasted.

He looked from her, across the room to a mural of Diana the Huntress. "I've been stewing ever since I got your reply to my message," he said. "Why could you not see me earlier?"

"I'm sorry." This regret was calm, with an undertone of resolve. "Three Sisters were needed for a certain emprise, and Vindilis asked that I be among them. What is your desire?"

"I decided 'twould be wise to talk beforehand about this Council the King summons. You and I have worked well together over the years."

"We have that." She regarded him. "But what is in your mind?"

"Let us prepare ourselves against surprises."

"Why, there should be none. For us, at any rate. This Gra—Gra-lo—Gra-til-lonius has met the leaders of Ys severally, well-nigh since he won the crown—since he took the Key. We've all accepted his purpose. The assembly should but ratify our agreement."

Soren scowled. "He's been less than candid. *Why* has Rome sent a prefect, after letting generations go by? Gratillonius speaks vaguely of troubles anticipated and the desirability of keeping Armorica out of them. Methinks he knows more than that, and does in truth plan a surprise later."

Now when Lanarvilis smiled it was not womanly but an aspect remote from humanness, the look of Knowledge. "Aye," she said evenly. "'Tis that which concerned Forsquilis, Vindilis, and myself this day."

He started. "Forsquilis! Did she learn—?"

Lanarvilis nodded. "We believe so. Politically, I deem it very plausible."

He set his glass down most carefully, lest he smash it. "Will you tell me?"

She did.

At the end, he drooped his lids, stroked his beard, sipped his wine, and said in measured tones: "I'd guessed, of course, though I could not be positive. I daresay Gratillonius withholds the news in hopes of first making his grip the firmer. Think you, like me, that 'twill be a shrewd stroke, telling him in Council that we know already? Thus taken aback, he may be the easier to deal with. For sure 'tis, we've no figurehead King here."

"He does not wish us ill."

"Nay, but he has his own aims—or Rome's, whatever Emperor's those may come to be. They may not prove the best for Ys." Soren barked a laugh. "If naught else, let us ride the current to our advantage. We may perchance wring substantial concessions out of the Imperium."

Woman again, Lanarvilis laughed too and touched his hand. "Ever were you the calculating one, Soren."

"I seek the welfare of my city, my house, my sons, and myself," he replied. "What else is there to strive for?"

Her gaze darkened. Unspoken was the truth that they would have wedded, had not the Sign come upon her a single month before the end of her vestalhood.

"Oppose this King when you feel you must," she said. "But lay no plots to confound him. I tell you, he is not evil. Else would the Gods have allowed our summoning of him?"

He stared at her through a silence before he breathed, "Then you did indeed, you Nine."

"Certes." Her tone stayed level. "Did you never suspect?"

"Oh, aye, aye," he stammered. "And yet...was deed like that done any time before in Ys?"

"Nay, and best 'tis that it not be noised abroad. Mere rumor will die away. The new King knows—Quinipilis told him, on purpose—albeit she doubts he can yet believe it. You do."

"I must." Soren passed hand over eyes. "That morning—" he whispered. "What did you do to entrap Colconor? He was strong, and you meant to weaken him as much as might be, but—" He beat fist in palm. "A-a-ah, I've heard of his wallowings in the Fishtail brothels—"

The calm went out of Lanarvilis. Tears trickled, blurring the malachite so carefully painted around her eyes. "Soren, dear, *I* was not there. I knew, I helped plan it, aye, but...but never could I do such a thing to you."

Bitterness lashed: "Why not? What difference? We're not the boy and girl who babbled endearments under a midsummer moon. Your satisfactions have been plain to see on you. I daresay you await more of them from Gratillonius."

She drew herself straight and retorted, "You've taken your own pleasures, Soren Cartagi, and well I know 'tis not been with your wife alone. Should I embalm my spirit? Lugaid was no bad man, and Hoel was grand." Anger collapsed. She struggled not to weep. "But oh, how often with them would I pretend to myself 'twas you. And I tried with Colconor, but as nasty as he was...'twould have been wrong to have even the memory of you present...whenever he took me, I would go away anyplace else."

"Oh, Elissa," he croaked. They reached.

She drew back before they had quite met. "Nay. Nay. We are what we've become. 'Twould be desecration."

He slumped. "True." After a while he stirred. "Best I depart."

She had rallied. "Not yet, Soren. We *are* what we are, Speaker for Taranis and high priestess of Belisama, in Ys. I said we should not conspire against the new King. But let us think how best we may cope with him."

IX

~ 1 ~

Unwontedly solemn, Dahilis asked, "Beloved, have you an hour to spare for me this morning?"

Gratillonius clasped her to him. How wonderfully slender and lithe she was. His free hand cupped a breast, roved down across the curves of hip and belly, rested briefly on golden fleece, returned to chuck her under the chin. "What, immediately again?" he laughed. "I'll need that hour to recover my strength, as spendthrift of it as you've made me."

"I mean talk, the two of us alone." He heard what a need was hers, and read it in the lapis lazuli of her gaze. "Oh, I understand you are engaged, you've been around among people like a whirlwind since first you arrived, but if you have any time free— It concerns us both, and the whole city."

He kissed her. "Of course, of course," he did his best to say in Ysan. "It was never my wish to leave you behind. If you too would discuss affairs of state, why, every magnate and officer should be as delightful."

At his movement, an object stirred between his shoulder blades— the Key that he must always wear but had put at his back, out of the way. Somehow, shifting it onto his chest again felt like closing a door. He pushed the thought off, banned it from Dahilis and himself.

They left the bed to which they had impulsively returned after breaking their fast, and sought the bath. Dahilis became playful once more, giggling as she soaped him and her and rinsed them clean, diving about in the warm water like a seal. They toweled each other as well but did not call anyone to help them dress. He would summon his barber later, he decided. He slipped on a robe, cloak, and sandals. She took an equally simple white gown belted at the waist, slippers on her feet, a fillet on her head. The yellow tresses she had merely combed and let hang free. Many young women of the best families often used plebeian styles these days, rather than the traditional elaborate coiffures. Ready to leave, she seemed to him a maiden, almost a child.

Hand in hand they wandered down a hallway on which opened the doors of luxurious chambers, across the mosaic of charioteers which floored the atrium, past servants who touched the brow, and out into the morning. Uniquely in Ys, the palace had a walled garden around it, not large but so intricate in its hedges, bowers, topiaries, flowerbeds, paths that one could walk long about and never feel cramped. The building and the outbuildings behind it were likewise of modest dimensions, but ample for their uses and pleasing to behold. The northern and southern sides of the palace formed ideal rectangles, their plaster flaunting vigorous images of wild beasts in a forest. Sculptures of a boar and a bear flanked a staircase leading to the portico and the main door, whose bronze bore reliefs of human figures. The upper story was set back above a roof of green copper, and itself carried a dome, on top of which the gilt figure of an eagle spread wings.

It was a glorious day, springtime in bloom, each breath like a draught of cool wine. Dew still glittered on leaves and moss, newly born blossoms, crushed shell that scrunched softly underfoot. Birds were everywhere, redbreast, warbler, finch, linnet, wren, singing in a chaos of joy. High overhead, white as the cloudlets they passed, winged a flight of storks, homeward bound.

Dahilis walked mute, her trouble again upon her, until she and Gratillonius reached the wall. Vines growing over its sandstone did not hinder the warmth of sun that it had begun to give back. He spread his cloak over the dampness on a stone bench and they sat down. He laid a hand across the fist she had made in her lap. "Tell me," he said.

She stared before her, unseeing, and spoke with difficulty: "My lord, my darling, I can no longer abide here. Grant me that...that I may go to my own house."

"What?" he exclaimed, dismayed. "I thought you happy."

"Oh, I was. Gladsome beyond measure. But—it is not right...that I have the King all to myself. Five days it has been. Six nights."

He clenched his teeth before saying, "Well, true, I suppose we should—"

"We must! You are the King. And they, they are my Sisters in the Mystery. They too are of Belisama. Oh, do not anger Her! I would fear for you yet more than I already do."

"I will certainly give them proper respect," he forced out.

She turned her face to him. He saw tears on her lashes. "Do more than that," she begged. "Cherish them. For my sake at first, if naught else will serve. Later for their own. They are my Sisters. They bore with my childhood flightiness, they were gentle and patient when I grew too restless to study what I ought, the older were like my mother unto me and the younger like loving elder sisters in the flesh. When my father Hoel fell, they upbore me in my grief. When my mother died, they did more, for the Sign was upon me that same night, and—And they consoled me, gave me back my heart, after Colconor until they had schooled me in how to endure him. And at last it was they, they, they who had the bravery and the skill to bring you. I was their acolyte. Yet me only have you honored— It is not right!"

She fell into his arms and sobbed on his breast. He stroked her, crooned wordlessly, at length murmured, "Aye. Indeed. It shall be as

93

you wish. And you speak truly, I've been unwise in this. I can but plead that I've been too taxed with my business among men to think, otherwise, of aught than you, Dahilis."

She gulped her way to self-mastery and sat straight. He kissed the salt off her cheeks and lips. His mouth slipped on down to the angle between jaw and ear; he kissed the softness of her skin there, too, and drank odors of her warmth and her hair. "Th-thank you," she whispered. "You are ever kind."

"Nay, now, what else could I be, toward you? And I've agreed you are right. Can you explain to...the rest...that no insult was intended?"

She nodded. "I'll go about today doing that, since tomorrow comes my Vigil."

"What's this?" he inquired.

"You did not know?" she replied, amazed. "Why, I took it for given that my learned lord— Well, then, Sena is the sacred isle. Always must at least one of the Gallicenae be there. Save at a few certain times, Council meetings or the Crowning and Wedding, when all of us are needed here. Oh, and in war, for safety's sake, though I scarcely believe even the fiercest pirate would dare— We go out for a day and a night by turns, on a special ferry. The crew are navy men whose officers decide they've earned this honor for a month."

He forebore to ask what the high priestesses did yonder. That might be a knowledge forbidden him. Instead, he regarded her in some slight bemusement before saying, "You've depths I did not suspect, my sweet."

The bright head shook. "Nay, nay. I'm a shallow little person, really."

"You're unjust to yourself."

"I am truthful. The deaths of four aged Queens did not touch me, I was only sorry and missed them for a time. Not until my father was slain did I understand what sorrow is."

"He surely adored you."

A smile quivered. "He spoiled me, he did. You are much like Hoel as I remember him, Gra—Gratillonius." Her Latin weak, she occasionally had trouble keeping the syllables of his name in place. He found it easiest to chop along in Ysan when with her, telling himself he needed the practice.

"Even afterward," she continued, "when I'd stopped mourning him aloud, I'd not real thoughtfulness in me. I expected to serve out my vestal term, and then after I turned eighteen belike marry a pleasant young man, the sort who was in my daydreams." Her smile writhed away. "But mother died, and the Sign came, and—" She stared beyond him. Her fists doubled anew.

"That must have been horror," he said.

Bit by bit, she eased. "At first. But my Sisters took me in charge, Bodilis foremost. She's my true sister, you know—half-sister—also daughter of Tambilis, though her father was Wulfgar. But the rest comforted me too, and taught me. Colconor was seldom there for long. When he was finished he'd dismiss me, or fall asleep and snore if it was night. Then I could go home next morning. And when he used me—however hurtfully or, or shamefully—I could leave him. I sent my spirit back through time, or forward, to when things had been better or when someday they would be good once more. Forsquilis taught me how. And most days he let me alone, I could live my own life."

"Tell me," he said, trying to help her back to gladness, "how did you pick the name Dahilis? I know your mother called you Estar. How do any of you Gallicenae choose your names when...you have been chosen?"

"They come from places. They bring the blessing of whatever spirit is tutelary. My name means 'of Dahei.' Dahei is a spring in the eastern hills where the nymph Ahes indwells. I picked that because it is cool and bubbly, hidden among trees. When I was a girl and my mother or Bodilis took me along on a trip to those parts—'tis beautiful country-side—while she meditated I would seek the spring and give Ahes a garland and ask her for happy dreams at night."

She sighed, but no longer in misery. "Could we go together sometime, Gratillonius? I'd like to show you."

"Of course, when I can find leisure. There's too much on hand now. Hm. You need not feel overly hurried about passing my message on. Your Vigil on Sena shall be postponed. I should have told you, but you make me forgetful of everything outside. And it was preoccupying, making those arrangements—when I was ignorant of all the ins and outs—for a full Council. It meets tomorrow." He grinned. "That requires your presence."

"As a matter of form," she said humbly. "I can offer nothing."

"Your presence, I repeat. We'll need the loveliness."

"Oh, my own only!" They embraced. "I did not know," she breathed in his ear. "I thought, yea, the new King will carry a better day for us on his shoulders, he cannot help but do that. I did not look for joy such as you've given. Last night after you were asleep, I prayed to Belisama Mother. I prayed you be spared for many, many years—and whatever happens, I might die before you. Was that terribly selfish of me? I'll come back in the sea and wait for you. Always will I wait for you."

"Now, now, I have many a battle in me yet," he boasted. She strained against him. Arousal stirred. "M-m, I've a meeting with some Suffetes at noon, but that's hours hence. Shall we?"

She crowed in glee. "And you thought you'd need more time!"

"With any woman but you I would." Briefly, he wondered. Quinipilis had bespoken the power of the Goddess....

As she skipped along beside his more dignified pace, she said laughing, "Could we wait long enough for you to be shaved? Later you might grow a beard. 'Tis the style in Ys."

He rubbed his chin. "I might. These past days my whiskers have been sprouting at a furious rate."

"Well, but do put the razor to them this time. When I call on my Sisters and explain, best would be that I not flaunt marks on my face. Not but what they won't know from my gait, dear stallion!"

~ 2 ~

The Forum of Ys had never been a marketplace. It merely received that familiar name from the Roman engineers who reconstructed it as they did much else while the wall against the sea was going up. At the middle of the city, where Lir Way and Taranis Way crossed, it was a plaza surrounded by public buildings. These were likewise on the Roman model, marble-sheathed, colonnaded, stately, albeit of no great size. The temple of Taranis, the baths, the theater, and the library were still in use. The basilica was also, less often, despite having seen no Imperial official permanently in residence for the past two hundred years. The temple of Mars had echoed empty almost as long, until Emperor Constantinus I required Ys to take in a Christian minister. Then it became a church.

Budic went looking around the square. Mosaics of dolphins and sea horses ringed a triple-basined fountain at the center. No water splashed; on festival nights, pump-driven oil did, set alight to leap and cascade in fire. At noon today, not many folk were about. They stared curiously at the young soldier. He was out of uniform, but height, pale-blond hair, tunic falling down to bare knees—a garment his Coritanic mother had sewn for him—identified him as a foreigner. Though sunlight descended mild, his calves felt the breeze as a cold caress. His sandals slapped the pavement too loudly.

Because the former temple faced south, the Christians had cut a new entrance in its western side. Mounting the stairs to the portico, he found that door open and passed through. Before him was a stretch of bare floor, the vestibule, ended by a wall—which its peeling plaster revealed to be wooden—that subdivided the great chamber where the pagan rites had taken place. A door in it was also open, giving Budic a glimpse of the sanctuary. It was nearly as devoid of furnishings. The altar block stood in the middle beneath a canopy replacing the cupola of a proper church; the cross upon it was neither gilt nor of especially fine workmanship. At the far end were a table and a couple of seats.

An aged man was languidly sweeping in there, hunched over his besom. Budic halted at the divider. "I b-beg your pardon, sir," he ventured.

The other stopped, blinked, and shuffled forward. "What would ye?" he asked. His Latin had a heavy Redonic accent. "Be ye a believer?"

"I am, sir, though only a catechumen."

"Well, ye're young yet. Can I help ye, brother in Christ? I be Prudentius the deacon."

Budic declared his name and origin. Too bashful to seek higher, he asked, "C-could I see a priest?"

"Priest?" The old man blinked. "Haven't got any priest. What for? How big d'ye think our congregation be? I only get the name of deacon because I'm baptized and have time to help out with the chores. All the rest of the believers are busy making their livings."

"Oh. Then the bishop? If I may?"

"Haven't got a bishop either, not here in this nest of heathens. Eucherius is the chorepiscopus. I'll go ask if he can see ye just now. Wait." The man went off. Budic shifted from foot to foot, gnawed his thumbnail, stared into the sacred room he must not enter before he himself had received baptism. That wouldn't likely be for years and years—

The oldster reappeared. "Come," he said, and led the way through a door in the original transverse, marble wall on the left. Having followed a corridor past an unused space, they reached another door. The deacon signalled the soldier to go in.

Beyond was poverty huddled in what had been opulence. The chamber where the pastor made his home, once the temple treasury, was too big for him. However, decent if modest furniture occupied a part, and a threadbare carpet warded off some of the chill. Windows were glazed. At the north end, where a smokehole had been knocked through the ceiling, was a kitchen, crude but sufficient for cooking. Soot from it had obliterated ancient decorations above and had grayed murals. Several books rested on a table, together with writing materials; pens, inkwell, thin slabs of wood, a piece of vellum off which earlier notations were scraped.

Budic halted and made awkward salute. Two people sat on tall stools at the table. That must be why the deacon had questioned whether the chorepiscopus would receive a new visitor. One person was a short, frail-looking man, gray, Italianate of features, stoop-shouldered in a robe much darned and patched. He blinked nearsightedly and smiled uncertainly. "Welcome," he said in Latin.

"Father—" Budic's voice entangled itself.

"I stand in for the bishop, your proper father in Christ. But let me call you 'son' if you wish. My name is Eucherius. Where are you from?"

"I am...I am a legionary...of those who follow Gratillonius, he who is your King. My name is Budic."

The pastor winced and signed himself, as many Christians had taken to doing. The woman across from him turned and asked in a husky, excited tone: "A man of Gratillonius? Do you have a message from him?" Her Latin was excellent.

"No, honorable lady," faltered Budic, unsure how to address her. "I came on my own account. Father, having leave today, I inquired my way here. We were long on the march. We got no time for anything but hasty private prayers. I've much on my soul, to confess and repent."

"Why, of course I'll hear you." Eucherius smiled. "You come like the flowers of the very Paschal season. But you have no more need to hurry. Join us. I imagine you too, Lady Bodilis, would like to know this young man better. Eh?"

"I would that," said the woman.

"Budic," said Eucherius, "pay respect—not religious, but civil—to Queen Bodilis of Ys."

Queen! A woman of the infamous Nine? Yet...a woman of the centurion's? Dazedly, Budic saluted her.

She was a handsome woman, at least: tall, well formed, singularly graceful in her movements. Dark-brown, wavy hair lay braided around features blunt-nosed, wide in the cheekbones, full in the mouth. Her eyes were large and blue under arching brows. The gown she wore was of rich material, soft green in color, sleeves worked with gold thread, its leather belt chased in undulant patterns. A silver pendant in the form of an owl hung on her bosom.

"You can take a goblet from yonder shelf." Eucherius pointed. "Come share this mead that my lady was so generous as to bring for the warming of these creaky bones. Don't be surprised. She and I have been friends since first I came here, and that was ten years ago, was it not, Bodilis?"

A fit of coughing seized him. She frowned in concern, reached over to clasp his hand. Budic fetched a wooden vessel for himself and diffidently took a third stool, one of the ordinary low sort from which he would have to look up at the others. Bodilis gestured at the flagon. Well, a queen—whether or not she was a heathen priestess—wouldn't pour for a common soldier, would she? Budic mustered courage and filled his cup.

Bodilis smiled at him. This close, he saw fine lines crinkle at the corners of eyes and lips. "We share no faith, the pastor and I," she explained, "but we share love of books, art, the wonders of earth and sea and heaven."

"Queen Bodilis has been more than a companion in my isolation," Eucherius wheezed when he was able. "She saw to it that I got proper furnishings and enough to eat. The pagan Kings had done nothing about that, and—and there are no more than a score of Christians in Ys. Otherwise this church serves what transient Gauls and sailors are believers. My predecessors dwelt in wretchedness. I trust that speeded their salvation, but—but— Hers is a noble soul, my son. Pray that she someday see the light, or that God will reveal it to her after she dies."

Sardonicism tinged Bodilis's smile. "Beware," she said. "Do you not skirt heresy?"

"The Lord forgive me. I must remember—" Eucherius gave Budic his full attention. "When I can, I travel to Audiarna—Roman-held town,

the closest, on the west bank of a river that otherwise marks the frontier—
You'd not know the geography, would you?... There I make my own
confessions, and obtain the consecrated bread and wine. But I cannot
travel often. My health—"

He straightened as best he could, with an apologetic look. "Now
it's you who must forgive, my son," he finished. "I didn't mean to
appear unmanly and chattery, before a soldier at that. It's only, oh, to
see a *Roman* again— Are there Christians among your fellows?"

Budic nodded. Eucherius beamed.

"Drink, lad, and let us talk," Bodilis counselled. "We've each a bundle
of news to exchange, I'm sure."

Budic sipped. The mead was dry, delicately flavored with blackberry.
"I'm just a rustic from eastern Britannia," he demurred. "This journey
has been my first. Well, my vexillation was on the Wall last year, but
that was fighting, and garrison duty in between. Nobody told us
anything."

"The Wall last year! Where Magnus Maximus rolled back a barbarian
midnight." Her tone sank. "Although— What do you know about him?
What sort of man is he?"

"I *am* only a roadpounder—a common legionary, honorable lady,"
Budic faltered. "I know nothing about great matters. It is enough to
follow my centurion."

"But you heard talk," she said fiercely. "You are not deaf."

"Well, camp and barracks are always full of rumors," Budic attempted
evasion. "The lady is very well informed about Rome."

Bodilis laughed. "I try. Like a snail reaching horns out of the shell
into which it has drawn itself. Word does come in. I'm here today to
share with Eucherius a letter lately arrived from Ausonius. He too
hears talk."

"Let us get acquainted," the chorepiscopus urged.

His story soon emerged, as glad as he was of fresh company. He
was a Neapolitan who, after attaining the priesthood, had been sent
to the school of rhetoric which Ausonius then maintained in Burdigala,
for he showed promise. Exposure to ancient philosophers and to the
attitudes of his teacher bred in him a doubt that man since Adam is
innately depraved—especially newborn children. When he expressed
such ideas on his return home, he was quickly charged with heresy,
and had no influential clergyman to argue on his behalf. Though he
recanted, his bishop afterward trusted him with no more than the work
of a lowly copyist.

Then it chanced that the bishop received a letter from his colleague
and correspondent in Gesocribate. Among other things, the writer
lamented that the ministry at Ys had fallen vacant some time ago and
there seemed to be no man both competent and willing to take it over.
Thus the Church had lost even this tenuous contact with the city—the
comings and goings of its traders were altogether unmonitored—and

there was no guessing what the powers of darkness wrought around the Gobaean Promontory.

The Italian bishop wrote back proposing Eucherius, and this was agreed to. The feeling among Eucherius's superiors was that in the midst of such obstinate pagans any errors into which he might again stray would make small difference, while he ought to administer the sacraments sufficiently well to whatever few Christians came by. Also, serving in yonder post would be an additional penance, good for his own soul.

Hence he was elevated to chorepiscopus—"country bishop," as slang put it—with authority to govern a church, teach, lead services, give Communion and last rites, but not to baptize or consecrate the Bread and Wine.

Reaching the city, he learned the language, but remained lonesome, not so much scorned as ignored, until Bodilis's desire for knowledge brought him and her together. She tried to get him membership in the Symposium, the gathering of thinkers at Star House, but the vote failed. For his part, he put her in touch with Ausonius, and those two exchanged letters even though the poet had since joined the Imperial court and attained a consulship.

Eucherius's own correspondence was perfunctory, confined to his ecclesiastical masters. Beguiling his empty hours was the labor of a treatise on the history and customs of Ys. These had come to fascinate him as greatly as they appalled him; and—who knew?—one day the information might help a stronger man guide this poor benighted people back from the abyss.

Tears stung Budic's eyes. "Father," he blurted, "you are a soldier too, a legionary of Christ!"

Eucherius sighed. "No, hardly." He shaped a wan smile. "At best, a camp follower, stumblefooted and starveling, always homesick."

"I hear it is lovely at Neapolis," Bodilis said low to Budic. "Hills behind and a bay before, utterly blue; the old Grecian city nestled between; and that Italian light and air about which we can only dream in our gray North."

"We must forsake this world and seek our true home, which is Heaven," Eucherius reproached. Another spell of coughing racked him, more cruel than the first. He put a cloth to his mouth. When he laid it down, the phlegm on it was streaked red.

~ 3 ~

Eppillus having given them leave, Cynan and Adminius set off to see a little of Ys and sample its pleasures. For guide they had Herun, a young deckhand in the navy. They had made his acquaintance at Warriors' House, where the legionaries were quartered together with men of the professional armed service. Those of the latter who were not on duty or standby generally stayed at home, but for the present the Romans had no place else to sleep than the barrack.

While at liberty one wore civil garb, and no steel save a knife whose blade length could not exceed four inches. Adminius thoughtfully tucked a cosh under the tunic he hung on his wiry frame. Cynan was gaudier in the clothes of his native Demetae, fur-trimmed coat, cross-gartered breeches, saffron cloak flapping in the gusty air; from his left shoulder a small harp hung in its carrying case. Herun was attired in Ysan male wise, linen shirt, embroidered jacket open to display a pendant on his breast, snug trousers. The predominant Celtic strain in him showed on big body and freckled face; the beard trimmed close to his jaws and the hair drawn into a horsetail down his neck were coppery.

"Methought we'd go around by Aurochs Gate and Goose Fair, thence wend north for the Fishtail," he said, slowly and carefully so as to be understood. "Thus will you pass some things worthy of a look ere we settle down to carouse."

"That sounds well." Adminius turned to Cynan and translated into Latin. Meanwhile the three dodged through the traffic on Lir Way and took a street quiet and narrow which wound among the abodes of the wealthy.

"You've seized onto a mickle of our language in the short span you've had," observed Herun.

Adminius grinned his snaggle-toothed grin. "A cockroach scuttlin' about the docksides of Londinium 'ad better be quick, if 'e'd not get stepped on," he replied.

"Mean you that yours was a hard life?"

"Well, my father's a ferryman on the River Tamesis. Early on, the count of 'is brats began to outnumber the count of 'is earnings. From the time I could walk, I scrabbled for whatever I wanted, over and above my mother's boiled cabbage. That was a lawless as well as a poor quarter, but on the same account, chances would come now and then. To snatch them, I 'ad ter be able ter understand men from around 'alf the world, it seemed. So I got a sharp ear and tongue."

Herun frowned, laboring to follow. As yet, Adminius perforce spoke haltingly, with a thick and unique accent, using many words that might be common elsewhere in Armorica but were strangers here. It helped that the mariner had encountered some of them on his travels. Patrolling widely around the peninsula, sailing convoy in periods of special danger, Ysan warcraft often put in to rest or resupply. They usually chose small harbors where there were no Imperial officials to encumber transactions.

"At length you enlisted?" Herun guessed.

Adminius nodded. "I'd made enemies in Londinium. Besides, the legionary's life is no bad one, 'speci'lly when you're good at scrounging and at slipping through cracks in the rules."

"What are you gabbling about?" demanded Cynan.

Adminius returned to his kind of Latin: "Aow, nothing but my biography. Don't fret. You'll soon be slinging the lingo too."

Cynan's dark features stayed fixed in a scowl. "Maybe then those warlocks won't strip my purse—when I've learned how to counter their spells."

"Now, now, don't sulk. It was an honest game. The dice just weren't friendly ter yer. I took my share." Adminius jingled his own pouch. Like Rome's, the Ysan armed services were paid in coin as well as in kind. Most of what he had were sesterces, of depleted worth but preferable to bagsful of nummi. They would serve for such minor dealings as an evening on the town. "And I'm not the chap that won't stand a chum a treat."

Cynan bridled. "I ask no alms."

Adminius ran fingers through his sandy hair. "Mighty near a 'opeless case, ain't you? Why'd you come along if not for a bit o' fun? Consider it a loan. Let the next bout be yours." He slapped the other on the back. "Barracks too dull for yer, eh? Well, you'll feel cheerier after you've 'ad a drink and a wench."

The street passed a walled enclosure, within which rose a domed habitation. Four sentries stood at a grillwork gate: on either side, an Ysan marine and a Roman legionary. Herun saluted in his fashion, Adminius waved at his friends, as they passed by. "Is this the royal palace?" Cynan asked.

"Got ter be. You know we don't assign anybody ter anywhere else, so far. You and I'll be drawing this duty soon."

"I understand how the centurion—the prefect—wants men of his on guard. But why not more? And why have natives at all?"

"Eppillus was explaining that ter me. Gratillonius ain't just the prefect now, 'e's the flinking King. It'd be an insult if 'e didn't let 'em watch over their King. And we wouldn't like it if 'e didn't let us 'elp."

Cynan pondered. "That feels true in me," he agreed after a space. "He's a wise one, no?" Resentment flickered afresh. "At least when my turn comes I won't be cooped up indoors."

"Easy, lad, easy. Are you really that eager ter start in again on drill and digging latrines? Never fear. Give 'im time ter get the lay of the land, and 'e'll find plenty for us ter do, 'e will."

Terrain began dropping fast. Except for the residential towers, buildings grew less lavish and more old. Ever higher did the rampart rear in view and, under a declining sun, fill the ways with shadow. The last sellers, buyers, brokers, and hawkers were leaving Goose Fair. Its stones boomed beneath hoofs and wheels; echoes rolled hollowly. The Brothers at Aurochs Gate were outlined black athwart heaven.

Herun turned right, through streets that became mere lanes, half-roofed by overhanging upper stories between which they twisted. Cobblestones lay lumpy underfoot. More people were about than in New Town—sailors, workmen, housewives, fishwives, children in skimpy tunics, individuals less easily recognizable. Their garments might be flamboyant, rough, or sleazy, but were always cheap. They themselves bore marks of toil and sometimes of past sickness. Yet there was no sign of hunger or alley-cat poverty as in Londinium, nor did the quarter smell sourly of refuse and unwashed bodies. Sea air blew through all Ys, tinged with salt and kelp, chill where walls blocked off sunlight. Gulls cruised white overhead.

The three men halted before a small, rudely cubical structure of rammed earth on a patch of ground defined by four unshaped boundary stones. Between wooden roof and door was inset a solar emblem of polished granite. Despite repairs and replacements which had been made as need arose, the wear of centuries was plain to see. Herun genuflected in reverence.

"What's this?" Cynan asked; his Ysan was sufficient for that.

"The Shrine of Melqart," Herun said. "Thus did the founders of the city name Taranis when first they came hither, long and long ago. Later He got temples more grand, and now this is only open on solstice days, with but a single man to make sacrifice. Elsewhere in Old Town, and not unlike it, is the Shrine of Ishtar—Belisama—which opens at the equinoxes. We honor our Gods in Ys."

He conducted his followers onward. Adminius paraphrased his explanation for Cynan. The Demetan traced a sign in the air. "Well might they honor their Gods," he said low, "they who live on the sufferance of Ocean.... But you're a Christian, you don't understand."

"I ain't that good a Christian," Adminius confessed.

Farther on was another reserved space, this for a megalith man-high, lichen-spotted, darkling. "Menhir Place," Herun said, again bending his knee. "The pillar was here before the city. Out in Armorica have I seen works of the Old Folk that Celts have chiseled their glyphs into, and lately Christians likewise. But our forefathers, and we, ventured not to trouble this that was raised to a God unknown."

Adminius shivered a bit. As if continuing his earlier sentence, he muttered, "I know when somewhere is 'aunted.... Wish I'd brought my cloak. It's gotten futtering cold."

Beyond the harbor end of Lir Way and the respectable buildings there, the Fishtail began. It was quite a small slum, less mean than any counterpart in the Empire. Nevertheless dwellers went ragged, slinking or truculently swaggering. Beggars wailed, decrepit whores gestured weary invitations, children shrieked mockery, narrow stares out of hard faces followed the strangers. "'Tis less grim than you might think," Herun said, "and the inn we're bound for is easy on the purse."

It occupied what had once been a fine home. Plaster was mostly gone from bricks, few good tiles remained among cheap newer ones, mere bits were left of relief sculptures beside the entrance. Within, the former atrium, now the taproom, showed fragments of mosaic in

103

its clay floor. The soot and grease of centuries hid nearly all fresco color, but a stain going halfway up the walls was unmistakable.

"Wotever 'appened 'ere?" Adminius wondered.

"Ancient damage done by the sea, I think, before the rampart was raised," Herun said. He gestured at a table. Four men sat benched there, drinking. They were weather-beaten, knobby-handed, coarsely clad. "Greeting," Herun called to them, and they grunted a response. He and his comrades took the opposite end, ten or twelve feet from them. "Fishers," he whispered. "Decent in their way, but given to over-weeningness. Best we leave them be."

Candles added what they could to light that seeped in through thin-scrapped membranes stretched across windows. The air was acrid with smoke, heavy with odors from tallow and an adjoining kitchen. A man who must be the landlord sent a boy pattering over to ask what the newcomers wanted. "The mead is not bad," Herun recommended. "Beware the wine." He gave their order, and paid when the goblets arrived. "Be this round on my reckoning. Hail and haleness."

A woman emerged from an inner room and made hip-swaying approach. She was comely enough, aside from greasy hair and shabby gown. "Why, Herun, dear," she warbled through a broad smile, "welcome. Where have you been all this time? Who are your friends?"

"Mayhap you've heard the Romans are back amongst us," the mariner replied. "They came with the new King. Here are two of them, Adminius and Cynan."

She widened her eyes. "Romans! Ooh, how *won*derful!" She sat down opposite them, next to Herun. "Be you welcome too, you sightly fellows. If 'tis a romp you'd have, you've sought the right place. I am Keban."

"Where are the others?" Herun asked. "This is seldom a busy hour for you."

"True." She cast a surly glance at the fishermen. "They *say* the catch was poor and they've naught to spend on more than a stoup or two. Well, as for the girls, Rael is under the moon; says she feels too badly to do *any*thing. Silis got pregnant and has not yet recovered from having that taken care of. So I'm by myself." Suggestively: "I long for company."

"You shall have some," Herun laughed. "But first let's give you the drink you expect." He signalled the potboy.

Adminius told Cynan more or less what he had heard. The youth's nostrils flared. He gripped his cup till knuckles stood white above the wood, drew shaky breath, and said deep in his throat: "By the Hooded Three, but I've gotten a need on that march we made! What would they say if I laid her down right on the floor?"

"They'd say you were a fool, wearing out yer knees when a straw tick goes with the rental. 'Old it in a bit, lad. You'll enjoy it the more."

The door opened and banged shut again. A man strode in with a sailor's rolling gait. His garb was rough too, and bore a slight smell of fish. Medium tall, he was broad and powerful; his shoulders, chest, and arms might have fitted a bear, his hands were like capstans which had each raised five anchors. Rugged features and green eyes stood within hair and beard whose blackness declared him still fairly young, however much wind and sun and spindrift had turned his skin to leather.

The fishers rose, reseated themselves, and made gestures of invitation. He smiled and waved but steered for the Roman end of the table. "'Oo's that?" Adminius asked.

"I know him a little," Herun murmured. "His name is Maeloch."

"Why do they defer to 'im? I thought you said their sort make way for no one."

"He is a Ferrier. A Ferrier of the Dead. No bad wight, no bully, but have a care of his pride."

"Mead!" the man roared in a voice to carry through gales. He reached the table, looked down at Herun, and touched his breast. The navy man did likewise. It was the formal Ysan salutation between equals. "Well met," Maeloch rumbled genially. "Who be these strangers?"

"You'd not heard?" Herun replied.

"Nay, I've been at sea this sennight past. Great run of mackerel off Merrow Shoals, if ye can ride out the weather. Now I've a raging thirst and a rampant stand."

"Your wife—"

"Ah, Betha nears her time again. Another mouth to feed; but still, I'd not risk harming the sprat by pounding on her." Maeloch went to rumple Keban's hair. She purred and rubbed her cheek against his thigh. He planked himself down beside her. The mead came for the two of them. "Hail and haleness, all!"

Goblets lifted, except for Cynan's. He glowered, and angrily asked Adminius for translation.

Meanwhile Maeloch's right hand fondled Keban, his left wielded his drink, and he drew from Herun an account of what had happened. It did not quite seem to please him. "A new King aye, that's long overdue," he growled. "Colconor was offal. Were it not that no Ysan may, I'd've challenged him myself—well, nay, I suppose not; that would've meant forsaking my Betha." He nodded stiffly at the legionaries. "But if this King is a swab for Rome— Well, we can hear ye out, ye twain, after I've done my first tupping."

"I want her now," Cynan exclaimed. "Adminius, you said you'd help. Make her price good while I—" He scrambled to his feet, swung past the table end, and tugged at Keban's gown. "Where do we go?"

Surprised, she could only titter. Maeloch tensed. "Hoy, what's this? Let her be!"

"The soldier's want seems more urgent than yours," Herun said hastily. "They were many days on their way hither, these guests. Come, drain your cup and let me buy you another."

"What, me betread wet decks...after a Roman?" Maeloch heaved his bulk up like a spyhopping whale. He stepped over the bench. His right hand closed on Cynan's tunic and cloak, under the throat, and hauled the Briton around. His left fist drew back. "Belay that and begone!"

Cynan whitened. He hissed. His knife came forth. "Let me go, you filthy fishmonger!"

Herun and Adminius exchanged glances. They leaped, Ysan to Ysan, Roman to Roman. From behind, each threw a lock on the arms of his man. Neither could have held it long, but their voices prevailed: "Stop, easy, easy, you are mad, would you bring the watch down on us, let's talk, let's be civilized—" When they felt thews slacken a little, they released their grasps. The antagonists backed a few steps apart and stood with heads thrust out between shoulders, breath harsh in mouths.

Herun: "Maeloch, hold. He's scarcely more than a boy. Believe me, I know these wights, they've not come to oppress or levy on us. Fain would they be our friends. In the names of the Three, peace!"

Adminius: "Get yer 'ead out o' yer arse, Cynan! If the centurion 'eard you'd started a brawl over a 'ore, this early in the game, 'e'd 'ave yer flogged till beetles could dance on yer ribs. Sit down. We'll call for a new round, and maybe toss a coin to see 'oo goes first."

Everybody eased—also the fishers at the far end, who had sprung clear and made ready for general turmoil. A much relieved landlord offered a free serving. This brought men together. In the beginning they laughed too loudly and slapped each other's backs too heartily, but soon they felt fellowship. Maeloch and Cynan could do no less than swap a rueful handclasp in the Ysan manner. Between Herun and Adminius, the full story of the legionaries came forth, from the war at the Wall and onward. It fascinated the fishers, and required more mead for soothing of gullets. If most purses were lean, Herun and Adminius stood ready to buy. The tale reminded Maeloch of a song about a boatman who had lured a shipful of marauding Saxons onto a reef. He sang it for his Roman mates. Not to be outdone, Cynan unlimbered his harp and offered a ballad from his homeland. He did it well. The company shouted for more.

Keban sat by herself, waiting. One hand cradled her cheek, the fingernails of the other drummed the table.

~ 4 ~

Soon after Imbolc, Niall maqq Echach, King over Mide, left Temir accompanied by his body servants, warriors, learned men, and eldest son Breccan. He did not follow the Queen and their children to that one of his halls which she sought. Instead, he made progress around his realm—sunwise, as he must under gess—and was more than a month about it. This was not very commonly done after the first time, when a King was newly consecrated; but Niall said he had been so much away at war that he should get to know his folk better and right any wrongs they were suffering.

Indeed he listened, and not only to the powerful men who gave him lodging. Although he never gainsaid the judge in any district, which was not within his right, he heard disputes brought to those worthies, and sometimes offered advice in private before settlement was decreed. His gifts were generous to the poor as well as lavish to the mighty. He was grave or boisterous as occasion demanded, thus making friends among men; and after a night or three, many a young woman came to feel a warmth for him which glowed from her into her father, brothers, or husband.

Some people murmured that he was being shrewd. Although the weather was fair for this time of year and there was no reason to expect lean months, sooner or later they came. The blame for it was less likely to fall on the King if he was well beloved. Restless Niall might not be at home then to defend himself against charges of evildoing that had angered the Gods. Moreover, his repulse last summer, while not inglorious, called for explaining if he would have warriors follow him willingly on his next adventure.

That he planned one was beyond doubt. Already at Temir he had been in secret talk with men of several different kinds. While his train made its slow way through the countryside, messengers often came speeding with word he did not reveal. Thereafter he was apt to ride off, gazing afar, with none but his guards along and they forbidden to speak to him.

Gossip buzzed. It swelled to a tide when Niall entered Qóiqet nUlat without asking leave of any lord therein, sought Mag Slecht, and made blood sacrifice to Cromb Cróche and the twelve lesser idols. Although he wended back peacefully enough, word of this caused swords to be whetted.

And so in due course he reached the sea, rode down to Clón Tarui, and took lodging at the public hostel there. Day after day he abode, still meeting quietly with men who came and went, but still keeping his own counsel. Since the River Ruirthech that emptied into the bay just south of this place marked the border of the Lagini, the idea arose that Niall had in mind to enforce the Bóru tribute. It had gone unpaid for many years. True, his following here was too small to overcome a whole Fifth of Ériu; but was he making a threat, or was he sending forth scouts and spies to gather knowledge for a campaign in summer? When hints or questions reached him, Niall simply smiled.

The day came at last when he and Breccan had gone hunting, and returned toward eventide. They had started a red deer in the woods northward and chased it down in a breakneck halloo; Breccan's sling had knocked half a dozen squirrels from their trees; everyone was weary and happy. Through cleared lands they now rode, broad and gently rolling acres of pasture and field, bestowed on the hostelkeeper so that that person might give free guesting to travelers. The small round houses of tenants huddled here and there, wattle-and-daub beneath cones of thatch through which smoke seeped into the wind. It had been a day for rainsqualls and continued blustery, although a low sun struck rays like brass through the wrack that scurried overhead. Horses and hounds plodded in the mire of the road. But when the bay gleamed in sight, and the great oblong of the hostel, whinnies and bellings arose, hoofs and feet pounded, the huntsmen forgot how wet and cold they were and lifted a shout of their own.

Suddenly Niall stiffened on the horseblanket. Out of the brume upon the eastern sea, a pair of sails had appeared, above a lean hull—a currach, bearing down on Clón Tarui. "It's reckless early in the year they've been abroad," said a guard.

"It...is...not, I am thinking," Niall answered. "*Hai!*" He struck heels against his mount. The beast plucked up strength and broke into gallop. Breccan's alone could keep pace; the warriors fell behind. Niall did not heed. Nor did he stop until on the shore.

By then the currach was near. It was large, two-masted, the leather of it holding a dozen men. Sails rattled down on their yards, oars bit water, and the craft drove up onto the strand. One man leaped forth first. Niall sprang from horseback. They ran to each other and embraced.

"Ah, welcome, welcome, darling!" the King cried. "It's grand you are looking—and all the lads home alive, too! How went the quest?"

The newcomer stepped back. He was bony, sinewy, auburn hair and beard slightly grizzled around a face that weather had seamed and bedarkened. Despite that and his drenched garb, he bore himself with an easy arrogance. "Bucketing over the sea and trudging over the land," he laughed. "Yet well worth the trouble. What you thought might come to pass has done so indeed, indeed. The Roman soldiers have hailed Maximus their lord, and he has left for Gallia with the most of them."

"Ha-a-ah!" Niall roared.

"Slow, dear master, slow. It does not seem they will be stripping their defenses bare for this—not soon—and I'll be giving you some news about the Saxons, also."

Niall smote fist in palm. "Nonetheless—!"

The skipper arrived to pay his respects. Niall greeted him well and spoke of venison at the feast tonight. Meanwhile the thin man's glance fell on Breccan, who stood aquiver. "And might this be your son, my lord?" he asked. "It's long since I saw him last, and he a babe in arms."

"It is he," Niall replied. "Breccan, my dear, you will not be remembering, but here is Uail maqq Carbri, a trusty man who has gone on many a mission for me—though never, maybe, one that needed as much boldness and wiliness as this."

"Och, it was not that hard, so don't you be daunting the lad about such things," Uail said, cockily rather than modestly. "I know my way about over there, and the speech—a bit of the Latin, too. It was mostly to wander as a harmless pedlar, watching, listening, sometimes getting a soul drunk or furious till his tongue ran free. There was no big secret."

Niall's look blazed across the waters like the last stormy sun-rays. "Maximus withdrawn," he breathed. "We'd likely not be wise to strike Alba this year, at his heels—not yet—but southward, Roman will be at war with Roman—" Again he bellowed. "Ha-a-ah!"

Breccan could hold himself in no longer. And he saw his chance. He seized Niall's hand. "Father," he cried, "I am going along, am I not? You promised! I shall help you get your revenge!"

Niall swept the slender form to his breast. "You shall that!"

He let go, stood for a heartbeat or two, frowned, then shrugged. "It seems Medb will have it so," he muttered. Straightening, he turned to Uail and the sailors. "Come," he said, "make your boat fast and let's be off to the hostel. The keeper is the widow Morigel, and a fine table she sets. Afterward...I will be querying you about everything you have learned."

Breccan danced and whooped.

X

~ 1 ~

The chamber in the basilica where the Council of Suffetes met could have held many more than it did this day. It was ornamented only by its stone paneling, but that was superb, mica-sparked granite, veined marble, mottled serpentine, intricate onyx. Large windows admitted ample greenish light. Under the barrel-vaulted ceiling, sound carried extraordinarily well. On either side of a central passage, padded benches in tiers looked down to the farther end. There stood a dais whereon rested a throne. Behind it, the wall curved to form a bay. Against that wall were statues of the Triad, ten feet tall, Taranis on the right, Belisama in the middle, Lir represented on the left by a mosaic slab out of which stared a kraken.

When everyone else was seated, Gratillonius entered, magnificently robed, bearing the Hammer, the Key in view on his breast, but his head encircled by a fillet rather than the royal crown. His legionaries followed in full armor. The crash of hobnails resounded along the passage. At the dais they deployed right and left and came to attention behind it, in front of the towering Gods. Gratillonius mounted the platform and took stance before the throne. Silence thundered down upon the gathering. He raised the Hammer and intoned as he had been taught: "In the name of Taranis, peace. May His protection be on us."

The Nine sat together in blue gowns and white headdresses at the left end of the foremost benches. Vindilis rose, spread out her arms with palms downward, and responded: "In the name of Belisama, peace. May Her blessing be on us."

By this Gratillonius knew that today she would lead the Gallicenae, speaking for them except when some other had reason to enter the discussion. He wondered why they had elected her instead of, say, wise old Quinipilis. In Vindilis's hatchet features he read an intensity that might prove troublesome. But the Queens moved in their own ways, which it was not for anyone else to question.

Vindilis reseated herself. At the right end of the interrupted arc, Hannon Baltisi stood up. The gray beard flowed from his furrowed countenance over a robe worked to suggest a heavy sea, white manes on green waves. He was not a priest, for the God Whose worldly affairs he guided had none, unless one reckoned every skipper of Ys. But his it was to say, as Captain, "In the name of Lir, peace. May His wrath not be on us," and bring the butt of a trident booming down on the floor before he too sat.

Gratillonius handed the Hammer to Eppillus, whom he had designated his Attendant, and stood for several pulsebeats looking the assemblage over. Beside the high priestesses, it numbered thirty-three, all male and all drawn from the thirteen Suffete clans. (He had learned that those corresponded somewhat to the Roman senatorial rank, save that nobody could buy or wheedle or even earn his way into them. Entry was strictly by birth, marriage in the case of a woman, or adoption in the case of a child.) Soren Cartagi was conspicuous among them in the red robe and miter of his role as Speaker for Taranis. Like Hannon, he represented the corporation of his temple, though he had no ritual part in the proceedings today. He could also, if he chose, argue on behalf of the Great House of Timbermen which was his.

Three men belonged ex officio to the Council—Adruval Tyri, Sea Lord, head of the navy and marines; Cothortin Rosmertai, Lord of Works, who oversaw the day-by-day administration of city business; Iram Eliuni, Lord of Gold, whose treasury function had become almost nominal. The Sea Lord wore ordinary Ysan clothes of good material, his colleagues had decked themselves in togas.

A few more togas were visible among the rest. The majority had selected robes, or else shirt and trousers. Not every garment was sumptuous, for Suffete status did not necessarily mean wealth. The delegates from guilds had themselves been fisher, sailor, wagoner, artisan, laborer, or the like. Even some heads of Great Houses had been poor in their youths. However, most had not, for these firms generally stayed in the same families through many generations.

Thirty-three men. Gratillonius's gaze searched across them. No two were alike; and yet— The aristocrats of Ys had consciously set barriers to inbreeding. None could marry within his or her clan. Brides from outside were usually made welcome. A couple might adopt a promising youngster from among the commons or the Osismii, in hopes of invigorating the bloodline. Nonetheless, again and again he met the "Suffete face," narrow, high-cheeked, aquiline, a memory in flesh and bone of lost Phoenicia.

Well. Best to start. He remained standing but assumed an easy posture. "Greeting," he said in Ysan. "First will I thank you for your forbearance. This honorable Council meets four times annually, I hear, around equinox and solstice. Thus you've but lately completed a session, and have affairs of your own awaiting your attention. Although the King possess the right to order a special assembly when he sees fit, I have striven to make clear that mine today is for the welfare and safety of Ys, and not capriciously in future will I call you back. Rather will I hold frequent private conference about our shared concerns as these arise; and ever will you find me heedful of you."

He smiled. "I trust we can finish within a few hours. You know why we are here. 'Twould expedite matters if we, or at least I, used Latin. Else must I slowly mangle my way through your language, which does it no credit. My hope is that soon I shall be in better command of it. Meanwhile, has anybody aught in disfavor of Latin?"

Hannon lifted a hand. Gratillonius recognized him. "Myself, no," he said in an Armorican seaman's form of that tongue. "There must be some who've not wielded it since school days, but if they may talk Ysan, well enough. My lord King, when you've trouble understanding something, I suggest you ask for translation. Likewise for whoever don't follow you very readily."

"We need a single interpreter," Soren pointed out, "or we will be babbling into each other's mouths."

"I propose Queen Bodilis," came from Vindilis. "She's both learned and quick-witted. Are you willing, Sister?"

"That I am," replied Bodilis in scholar's Latin.

Gratillonius regarded her. An attractive woman, he thought, seems to be in her mid-thirties, best years of a woman's life, my father always told me. The knowledge that he would bed her stirred him—unexpectedly, when Dahilis sat right beside her. Bodilis returned his glance with calm, candor, and a slight smile.

He cleared his throat. "Thank you," he said. "Let me begin by explaining my purposes. I've already done that as best I was able, to several among you. But for the rest, it could be that what you heard at second or third remove has suffered in transmission. Afterward we can discuss everything, and I hope at the end you'll formally ratify my program, and then take a share in it."

Increasingly, he felt sure of himself. This did not seem too different from addressing the soldiers of his century on the day of a mission. He wondered for an instant if, somehow, the fact of cooperation with Bodilis had heartened him. However brave a front he presented, when he first entered this chamber the strangeness of all that was around him had been daunting.

"I realize you've had well-nigh every sort of man for King in Ys," he went on. "As for myself, you know I am a legionary: Gaius Valerius Gratillonius, centurion, hitherto serving in Britannia. There, last year I helped kick the Scoti and Picti back from the Wall. I've heard what pests the Scoti are to you also. I'm a Briton, Belgic, of curial family; and I've visited Armorica in the past.

"Now you should be quite clear about this, that I did not come here with any intention of making myself your King. It happened. Frankly, I'm still not sure just how it happened. But we've got the fact of it before us, solid as your headlands. And...it may be through the favor of the Gods. Not many people seem to have liked Colconor." That drew a few chuckles. "I don't know if I can be another Hoel, but I mean to try."

He took up earnestness as he would have taken up his shield: "My task was, and is, to be the prefect of Rome in Ys. You haven't seen my like since time out of mind. Nevertheless, the treaty—the Oath— remains in force. Ys is a foederate of Rome. It has duties toward Rome, which it may be called upon to fulfill. And Rome has duties toward Ys, which I am also here to see fulfilled. To that end, it may prove valuable that I've won the powers of your King.

"Not that I intend to abuse them, nor throw my weight around as prefect. My assignment is simple. There is reason to fear trouble in the Empire. Gallia in particular may well be in upheaval. I cannot imagine you'd want Ys drawn into that. As far as possible, your city has always kept aloof. My task is to lead you in staying at peace. No more, no less. For that, we cannot sit passive. If Roman Armorica— western Armorica, at least—if it becomes embroiled, Ys can hardly stay out. And Rome, which I serve, will take yet another wound, a wound that could prove hard to stanch.

"What Ys must do is lend its aid to the cause of peace, of order. Legates and governors elsewhere may wish to take sides in the fight. We need to keep them home. A word here, a bribe there, a show of naval strength yonder—that should suffice. What exactly shall we do? I plan to work that out in concert with the leaders of Ys, and then get it done.

"That's all. Later we'll consider together what else we can undertake, in the better day that I believe lies ahead. But first we must weather the storm that's brewing. I want your agreement to this, followed by your best efforts—under me, the prefect of Rome and now your King—to carry out the mission. For the welfare of Rome and of Ys!"

"Thank you."

He folded his arms and waited. After a hush, Soren said, "My lady Bodilis, could you put that in Ysan for the benefit of any who may not have caught every word?"

"I can paraphrase," replied the Queen. "Meanwhile let each of us be thinking of what this portends."

She stood and spoke. Gratillonius admired her handling of the matter; she seemed to express things more clearly and compactly than he had himself.

When she finished, a buzzing went along the benches, until Sea Lord Adruval declared bluntly, "We can't navigate in a fog. And foggy you've been, O King, when we talked before. What is this menace we're supposed to prepare against?"

"I have not said, because I am not party to secrets of state, nor am I a prophet to read the future," Gratillonius answered. "What my commander gave me to understand was that great events will soon happen, and they may get violent. I pray it be less bad than the Magnentian War, and the outcome better. But we must wait for word, and hold ourselves ready to act on it."

Vindilis did not signal request to be recognized. Silence fell immediately upon all others when the spokeswoman of the Gallicenae announced in a steely tone: "I can tell you more than that. Gratillonius's superior, who dispatched him to us, is Magnus Clemens Maximus, Duke of the Britains. The legions in that diocese have hailed him Augustus. They have crossed over to Gallia and are warring for the purple. Gratillonius,"— her eyes burned at him—"you are not stupid. I suppose he never told you outright, but you must have understood; and you are Maximus's man."

The Suffetes gasped. Thundersmitten, the King of Ys cried, "How can you know?"

"By the same means we knew of your coming." Vindilis gestured toward the woman on her left. "Forsquilis went in a Sending."

"What's this? Priestess, we've only your naked word."

Soren's ruddy visage darkened. "Do you call the Gallicenae liars?" he shouted. A growl as of shingle under surf lifted around him.

Quinipilis rose, leaned on her staff, raised her free hand for attention. "Be not hasty," she said in Ysan. "Gratillonius is new among us. He means well. And he *is* King and prefect. Give him a chance to learn."

The centurion wet his lips. "I'm certainly willing to listen," he said. "Do explain."

"That were best done in private," Vindilis answered, "Between Forsquilis and yourself."

"Well—that is, if the lady agrees—" Gratillonius's look went to the Pallas Athene face of the seeress. No expression relieved the coldness of its lines when she nodded. But Dahilis, even in this moment, flashed him an impish grin and jerked a thumb upward.

"Aye, this is no place to reveal a mystery," said Bodilis in Ysan. "The Power reaches beyond speech. Let us go on with the business of our assembly. At eventide Forsquilis can show the King what she chooses."

A mollified Soren agreed: "Very well. Shall we stipulate that the Empire is again at civil war? Since Maximus could not arrange to rally Armorica behind him as he has the Britannic legions, it is to his advantage that Armorica stay neutral while he campaigns east and south of it. Gratillonius's orders are to assure this. He may be right about it being best for Ys too, provided we do not provoke resentment in the Imperium, should Maximus fail. Let us discuss it, and then go on to ways and means."

Gratillonius stood soldierly and helpless while debate began.

~ 2 ~

He could not guess what awaited him at the house of Forsquilis. They walked there in silence, unaccompanied, after the meeting dissolved. Dusk lay blue upon the world; the earliest stars trembled forth. From this high part of the city he could see over the battlemented bowl of night which it had become, to a mercury glimmer in the harbor basin and the vast sheening of Ocean beyond. Right and left gloomed the headlands; out on Cape Rach, fire burned atop the pharos, red, unrestful as a seeking eye. Air was cool, slightly sweetened by a lilac in a stone basin at her doorstep, and wholly quiet.

Lamplight spilled yellow across the paving as a manservant bowed the two inside. "Dinner is ready, my lady and lord," he said. Savory odors confirmed it.

Forsquilis glanced at Gratillonius. He saw that her eyes were gray, like those of the Minerva—the Athene whom she so much resembled. No, he thought confusedly, that Goddess wears a helmet and carries a spear and shield. But what Gorgon's head may this woman bring forth, to turn men into stone?

Her Latin was fluent: "I sent a messenger during the day, directing a repast be prepared. Does this please the King?"

He attempted a jest. "Can't you read the answer in my mind?"

Her solemnity reproved him. "No, unless by strong magic, which might not work; and without dire need, it would be no decent thing to do."

Flushing, he gave his cloak to the servant, as she did hers, and they went directly to the triclinium. Atrium and corridor showed bucolic scenes that he suspected she had never bothered to have altered, nor had those who lived here before her, for they looked old. The dining room likewise was antique; but perhaps she found jarring whatever

114

pattern was on the floor, since reed mats covered it. The furnishings were table and chairs, Ysans never having reclined at their meals. On a richly decorated cloth stood costly ware. He wondered if this was on his account and ordinarily Forsquilis ate austerely. Her slenderness suggested it.

He wondered, as well, just why she reverted to her mother tongue while they settled opposite each other: "Difficult has today been for you. Shall we now take our ease and refresh ourselves?"

"You are...considerate," he responded, deciding to stay with Latin. Why burden himself needlessly in a taut situation? "I'll try. Though it has for certain been difficult. Pardon me if I can't put matters aside at once."

It was not that the Council had, in the end, denied him support. It was that that had been considered, and finally given, almost as if he, the prefect, were a mere courier—at most, an ambassador: as if Ys were not subordinate to Rome but deciding independently that its interest lay in emerging to some degree from the secrecy it had kept around itself.

For the first time, he saw Forsquilis's lips curve upward. "Think you 'twas my fault? Well, in a way. But would you not have done the same if you could, for Rome?"

A servant in livery of black and gold brought bowls and towels for the washing of hands. Another poured unwatered wine, a third set forth appetizers, boiled shrimp, pickled eggplant, raw fish, sauce of garum and minced onion. They ate well in Ys who could afford it, not gluttonously but well.

Gratillonius lifted his beaker. Relief swept through him. "Right! And there's no real conflict between us. I admit being, m-m, surprised. It's hard to believe you'd know what Maximus is doing before I myself have heard. I held back the information about his intentions because, frankly, I wanted the upper hand, if anything untoward happened. But you'd have gotten it as soon as I received whatever word he sends. He will be good for the Empire, and that means he'll be good for Ys."

"We trust so, we of the Sisterhood. We called on the Three to give us the right king, and you are the one They brought."

Gratillonius felt a shiver. He was of Rome, a soldier, a civilized and educated man. Maximus had ordered him here for excellent, logical reasons. He must not believe it had really been the work of alien Gods, and witches, and— He might have dismissed the idea if Forsquilis had raved at him or made mystical passes or done anything but sit there, more and more fair to behold, talking quite evenly— No, not that either. In her tone, in her eyes, there went ghosting something else. He could imagine that she lived on the fringe of the Otherworld.

He snatched after ordinariness. "Well, let's see if we can slack off as you propose. You've heard about me, but I know nothing about you. Tell me."

Her look dwelt long and seriously upon him. "Dahilis spoke true," she murmured at last. "You are a kindly man. You may well prove a second Hoel." And then it was as if a shudder of her own went beneath the controlled exterior. "Although the omens were obscure," she whispered. "But we live in such an age of breakup—"

He *would* not peer into those dim and lawless depths, not yet, not yet. He took a fragrant gulp and a pungent bite. They brought him back to the understandable earth. "You were wife to Hoel?" he asked.

She nodded. "The Sign came upon me when Quistilis died, a year before he did. I was fourteen. He was gentle. But I was bearing his child when he fell. What Colconor did, that caused me to lose it."

A red lump on the floor or in the bed or the privy, that might have stirred for a minute, Gratillonius thought. Freezingly: She tells it in such calm, as if it happened to somebody else long ago. Her soul was withdrawn. Will it ever return?

"May I ask how old you are?" he said.

"Twenty winters."

"Dahilis was not much younger.... You are wise beyond your years, Forsquilis."

"I had nowhere else to go but into the arcane," she told him quietly.

—She showed him a little after the meal, during which they had discussed safe matters. (Not that that was dull; each had endlessnesses to talk about.) A curtained chamber, dark save for a lamp made out of a cat's skull, held within its weaving shadows a shelf of scrolls and codices, a female figurine in clay that she said was from ancestral Tyre, inscribed bones, herbs dried and bundled, flints that perhaps had been shaped by the Old Folk as some said or perhaps were thunderstones as others said.... "These things are not needful in themselves, Gratillonius." Her eyes glistened huge in the murk. "They are but teachers and helps. As I wait entranced, my spirit fares forth. It is a power that once belonged to every Queen. But in this age when the very Gods are troubled and faltering, it has only come to me. Do you remember an owl, of the great sort called eagle owl, at midnight above a glade in Armorica—?"

—In the bedroom she said gravely, "Let us hallow ourselves. Belisama be with us." When she unwound her headdress, he saw that her hair was golden-brown. When she let her gown fall, he saw that she was shapely.

The Bull arose. Fleetingly he remembered Dahilis. But this would be her wish.

All at once Forsquilis laughed aloud and pointed. "Oh, but the goddess has been generous!"

Ugliness stabbed: how could she tell? She had known just Hoel and Colconor, had she not? Maybe, during the reign of the beast King, maybe her Sending had prowled into homes more happy?

116

No. He would not think further. He could not. The Bull was in him, the Bull was he.

Astonishment followed. With Dahilis he had gone slowly at first, soothing her fears, finding his way toward what pleased her. He had looked for this Athene to be likewise, if she did not simply lie there and accept. But she was hastily up against him, her hands seeking and urging. When he laid her down and entered her she yowled. In the morning he recalled the changeableness and unknown depths of the sea. His back was clawed red.

XI

~ 1 ~

A light rain turned the world cool and horizonless on the afternoon when Gratillonius came to call on Bodilis. She admitted him herself. "Welcome, lord King." Her tone and her smile made him believe she meant it.

Entering, he threw back the cowl of his cloak and undid the brooch. Beneath, he wore everyday Ysan garb lately tailored for him. Raindrops sparkled in the auburn curls of the beard he was growing. It still itched sometimes, but he had decided he should show his people every sign he could of his oneness with them. "I am sorry—" he began.

"O-oh, mother! Is *he* the King?" An eight-year-old girl darted from a doorway, tawny locks flying about an elven countenance.

"Now, Semuramat, bow like a proper lady," Bodilis said. Although warmth pulsed in her voice, the child obeyed at once, whereafter she stood staring out of enormous eyes.

"Greeting," the man said in Ysan. "I am...in truth your new stepfather. For this is your mother, is she not? What is your name?"

"S-s-semuramat," the girl whispered. "My lord."

He saw her tremble. The Queens had kept their daughters away from Colconor as much as possible, which became nearly all the time; but there would have been an aura of hatred and terror. "Be not afraid, Semuramat," Gratillonius urged. "I expect we shall be happy together. Hm. Do you like horses?" She nodded twice and thrice. "Well, suppose you come for a ride on my saddlebow as soon as I have a free hour, and we'll get to know each other. Afterward we may perchance look into finding you a pony."

Bodilis laughed. "Don't overwhelm the poor creature!"

117

"I'd fain be the friend of this household," he replied earnestly. "As I was about to say, I'm sorry to have let seven days go by since the Council, ere sending word I would visit you now if you desired. You may have heard how I've been at work, getting to know the city's defenses above all. Three of those days I wasn't even in town, but riding around the hinterland on inspection. At night I'd fall asleep as if into a well." Alone. Not that purely male companionship and concerns were unwelcome, however much he missed Dahilis.

"Go back to your work, dear," Bodilis directed. When Semuramat had pattered off, she explained to Gratillonius, who was hanging his cloak on a peg: "My servants are presently out to fetch what's needful for a worthy supper. I've ever made my daughters help in the house. Princesses should have skills too."

"And discipline, of a loving sort," he approved.

She regarded him for some while before murmuring, "So you understand that also. Few are the men who'd show your regard for a woman's feelings. Oh, mine were never hurt; well did I see why you must stay absent. Yet it gladdens me what you have revealed of yourself."

The compliment made Gratillonius flush. He had been returning her look with pleasure. She was simply clad, in a gray-blue gown with silver stars embroidered on the neckline and sleeves. A belt of crimson mesh snugged the cloth around fullness of bosom, hip, and thigh. He admired the strong bones in her face, and her eyes were like those of Dahilis, her half-sister. There seemed to be no tensing, no qualms in her. She took his hand as naturally as if they had been man and wife for years. "Come," she said, "let us talk."

They passed from the entryroom to the atrium. He saw that, while its floor was antique Roman, the frescoes were not. Their colors bright and fresh, they depicted a vividness of dolphins in waves, sea birds skimming overhead. The style was not quite representational; elongated lines and curves hinted at more than this world knew. Seeming him notice, she said with a touch of diffidence, "Mayhap I should not have covered up the old art. I did first copy it onto vellum, that future generations may have a record. But it was tedious stuff. Whoever inherits this house from me can get rid of mine if she dislikes it."

"What?" he exclaimed. "You painted it yourself?"

"I dabble at things. But come onward. 'Twould be most honorific to receive you in this chamber, but 'twill be more—real—if we seek to my scriptorium." Bodilis laughed. "Besides, Semuramat is not allowed there, not till she grows older and more careful. She's a darling, but she'd pester the life out of us."

"I gather you've other daughters."

Bodilis nodded. "Two. They are both wild to meet you, of course. But Talavair is standing vigil at the Nymphaeum, and Kerna is at her studies in the temple. She'll be home for supper."

"The girls are...Hoel's?"

118

"All three. The Sign came upon me in Lugaid's reign, but he fell almost immediately afterward. Talavair will finish her vestal term this year. She has a young man picked out for herself. A year hence, I may well be a grandmother!"

"What of—Kerna, is that her name?"

"Oh, she's just fifteen, and studious. She intends to renew her vows at age eighteen and become a minor priestess. Not that that debars marriage. However, most men are reluctant to take a wife whose duties will often have her away from home. Former vestals who enter the priesteshood most commonly do so after having been widowed."

They had left the atrium and gone down a hallway beyond. The layout of this house was similar though not identical to that of Dahilis's or Forsquilis's, and unlike the usual Roman. Bodilis opened a door and led Gratillonius through. He found a room nearly as spacious; later she would explain that she had had the wall removed between two former bedchambers. Lamps of a shape as graceful as her gait brightened the dullness that today seeped through windowpanes. One burned on a table, beneath a legged small pot that it kept warm. The oil was olive, nearly odorless. Flagons of wine and water stood beside it, glass goblets and earthenware cups, a plateful of titbits. Shelves around the walls held scrolls, codices, the portrait bust of a woman solemn and beautiful, ivory and bone miniatures of fleet animals. A much larger table filled the far end of the room. Writing materials littered it, open books, brushes and paints, botanical specimens, shells, rocks, a flute, a cat asleep in the middle of everything.

"Pray be seated," Bodilis said. "Would you thin your wine according to your taste?"

"What's in the pot?"

"An herbal infusion. I seldom drink wine save at supper, and then little." Bodilis smiled. "I fear you'll find me drab company."

"Contrariwise, I think." They took chairs. "I'm no heavy drinker myself, most times. May I try a cup of your brew?"

The tisane was fragrant and sweet-acrid, good on a chilly day like this. "I heard aright; you are a scholar," he remarked.

"Well, I enjoy learning things. Also out in the open—I love to ramble about the countryside or go forth in a boat—but nearsightedness does somewhat hinder me there."

"You seem to work on something literary."

"Translating the *Agamemnon* into Ysan. A pity that scarce any of us today read Greek, but better my poor words than no Aeschylus at all."

"How did you learn?"

"I taught myself, from a textbook and lexicon I had sent me. Eucherius, the Christian minister, gave me more instruction, and corrected my pronunciation. They still use Greek where he hails from in Italia." She grew quietly ardent. "Oh, Gratillonius, you have so much to tell too!

What the folk of Britannia are like, their tales and songs and— For me 'tis twice wonderful that you are come."

He dropped his glance downward, into his cup, as if to seek an omen in its murkiness. "I think you will be mainly the teacher," he mumbled. "The Ysan language—"

"Already you handle it rather well. I might be able to help with vocabulary. We make much use of synonyms, for example."

"And the history, the lore, everything below the surface. That is why I—I wanted to visit you first."

"Ask me what you will," she sighed, "but remember I lack the wisdom of Quinipilis, the forcefulness of Vindilis, the witchcraft of Forsquilis, the charm of— Well, I'll try my best."

He heard pain in her voice, raised his eyes, and saw lines at the corners of her mouth, as if she struggled not to show what she felt. It came to him: I'm a blundering ass. She thinks I don't see anything in her but her mind. I never meant that. Jupiter thunder me, no! But if I instantly say she's lovely, she may suppose I'm only snorting after yet another new female body.

He groped his way forward. "Ah, let's talk a while like ordinary human beings. I want to know you, Bodilis. Tell me of your life."

She shrugged. "Naught to tell. 'Tis been well-nigh eventless."

He guessed that, of the Nine, she had had the most resources, the broadest reaches of escape for her spirit, during Colconor. He did not care to think about it. Instead— He tugged his chin. The whiskers were still too short, but he oughtn't scratch his face. Slowly, he said, "You remarked on your middle daughter's wish to remain with the temple after she's free to leave. Was that yours too, when you were a girl?"

The glance she gave him was startled. Then, inch by inch, she leaned back, smiled on him, finally found words. "Aye. The Sign did come upon me when I was the age that is Kerna's now; but ever had I been a child moody and solitary."

"Was that because of...the circumstances of your birth?"

Again she regarded him closely for a spell. "Gratillonius," she breathed at length, "you are a remarkable man. You truly are."

"Nay," he tried to laugh, "'tis but that a military officer must needs gain some skill in guessing about people." He sobered. "Would you liefer not talk of this? I shan't press you."

She reached to stroke his hand. "Why should I hang back? Dahilis must have told you things, and...and if the Gods are willing, we will be together, you and the Sisterhood, for many years." Her look drifted off and came to harbor at the bust. "You know my father Wulfgar begot me on his daughter Tambilis. It was the will of Belisama, no sin among the Gallicenae, but I am told he fell to brooding, and within a year lay dead at the hands of Gaetulius. Certain it is that this left a shadow on my mother, who did not regain gladness until Hoel came. By him she had Dahilis-to-be, you recall. But hers had been a somber house for me to grow up in. I fled into my books and my walks and—all you see around you. My wish was to become a minor priestess, for life."

"Instead you became a Queen," he said low.

She colored. "Hoel made me, too, happy. Not that his was any great intellect. He confessed I could bewilder him. But he was gusty and kind and well knew how to make a girl purr. And his friends, his visitors, how they could talk of marvelous things and mighty deeds! He loved to invite foreigners to the palace; they blew in like winds off the sea. Later I began to frequent Star House—"

She broke off, snapped after air, finished bleakly: "Under Colconor, the Symposium kept my soul alive."

"Oh, my dear!" he said in pity.

She shook herself, confronted him, and retorted, "I ask no balm, Gaius Valerius Gratillonius. My life has been better than most on this earth, despite everything." Her tone softened. "And now you are King."

Silence fell. He drained his cup and filled a goblet with wine, undiluted. Once more she looked away from him. Blood went in and out of the cheek he saw, like drumbeats. He knew what she was thinking of, and surely she knew that he did.

He cleared his throat. "Well. I see. Um-m...whose is yonder bust?"

"Why, Brennilis." Her relief was plain to hear. "Brennilis of the Vision, Brennilis of the Veil. 'Tis uncertain whether the portrait was done in her time or is imaginative, but I like to believe this is indeed how she appeared."

"Who was she?"

"You know not?"

"I am an ignoramus, remember."

"Well, then," she said cheerfully, "what better way to pass the hours ere we dine than for me to relate a little of the history of Ys?"

~ 2 ~

The oldest records were fragmentary, but tradition held that the site was discovered by Himilco when he came exploring up from Carthage some eight and a half centuries agone. Returning, he recommended that a colony be founded there. What Carthage required was a way station and naval base for its trade with the far North. Britannic tin, Gallic furs, German amber, honey, hides, tallow, timber, walrus and narwhal ivory, together with the Southern goods which paid for them, needed protection as well as transport.

No mere outpost could long be maintained at such a remove. Hence it must be a town, capable of feeding and defending itself. Since few of the then prosperous Phoenicians were willing to leave home, they recruited widely about the Mediterranean lands. Prominent among those who immigrated in the early decades were Babylonians fleeing the

Persians who conquered and destroyed their city, and Egyptians resentful of Persian rule.

Legend said that when Himilco was first investigating the region, men of his were slain in their camp every night. At last he tracked down the monster that was doing this thing, and the sailors put an end to it. The creature had laired in a passage grave. The Old Folk whose bones lay there, grateful to be at peace again, promised that settlement here should flourish as long as the dwellers were likewise at peace with the Gods; but if ever there was a falling out, the sea would reclaim its own.

Perhaps because of this, the city was consecrated to Ishtar, for She was powerful over all the elements and was the Star of the Sea. Soon afterward the mixed colonists identified Her with Isis and established an order of priestesses to serve Her.

Otherwise the community was subject to Carthage, though at its distance this was nominal, amounting to little more than a governor from the motherland. As it grew and enlarged its own trade, wealthy men began to chafe under even so light a yoke.

More or less at the same time as the founding of the city, the Celts had arrived, overrunning the aboriginal population and intermingling with it to produce the Gauls. The aristocrats of the new tribes were generally descended from the invaders. It was natural for the city to make alliance with neighbor natives against further newcomers. Wars and raids had harmed those nearby folk enough that they were willing to accept Punic leadership.

By now the name "Beth-Ishtar" or "Beth-Isis" had become shortened to "Ys."

The city was often endangered, more than once besieged. Yet, supplying itself by sea, it outwaited the enemy Celts, who never were very good at sitting still. Water was the worst problem, a fact that may have enhanced the sacredness of its sources in the minds of the people—although the Gauls venerated springs and streams too. The constant need for fighters and workers, in a commonalty still small, bred repugnance for the practice of sacrificing children to Baal Melqart, and eventually its discontinuance. However, prophecy and tradition agreed that from time to time some great blood offering must be made the Gods.

Gradually warfare eased off. While rivalry with the seagoing Veneti remained strong and occasionally flared into battle, Ys developed ties to the Osismii, as that mingled breed of Old Folk and Celts called themselves. Intermarriage became frequent, deities were identified with each other, rites and institutions conjoined, the very language of the city Gallicized.

In Ys the Triad became paramount among Gods. Ishtar-Isis most often bore the name Belisama, which meant "the Brightest One." Melqart assumed the name and attributes of the Celtic sky God Taranis. Lir,

Whose cult was more ancient than colony or tribe, took unto Himself the awe and dread of the sea.

These evolutions were not barbarizations. They went hand in glove with political changes. Increasingly occupied against Rome, Mother Carthage gave Ys even less consideration. Finally the magnates expelled the governor and established a Council of Suffetes on the Phoenician model. For the head of state, they took from various Gauls the idea of the King of the Wood—who was ordinarily no more than a figurehead, and whose death in battle replaced the former sacrifice of children.

The Sisterhood of the Nine grew from both Punic and Celtic roots. It was recruited from among the daughters and granddaughters of Queens, albeit most of the latter were born to ordinary men. Such a girl took holy orders at age seven and served as a vestal until age eighteen. She generally lived at home, but went to temple school and, when old enough, spent days and nights on end in religious duties within the city or at the Nymphaeum. At the close of her term, she was free to do whatever she liked—unless first the Sign had appeared on her and she had been wedded to the King and enrolled in the Gallicenae. After the third generation a given line of female descent was released from all obligation, for then the blood of Incarnate Taranis was thinned down to mere humanness.

If she chose, upon completion of her vestalhood a princess could renew her vows, or at any later time, and become a minor priestess. The temple would also accept other volunteers who qualified, train them, advance them according to what abilities they showed; but of course no such outsider would ever become a Queen.

Ys looked upon vestalhood as a divine privilege. It had its worldly benefits as well. Besides an excellent education, a maiden received a generous stipend. On going into civil life she got additional gold and goods, as dowry for herself or investment capital if she did not elect marriage. The temple could well afford that, for much of the wealth of the state flowed into it from holdings, offerings, and bequests.

Ysan commerce waxed. The city commanded only meager natural resources, other than what it wrested from the waters, but skilled workers turned imported raw materials into wares that, exported, won high prices. Merchantmen on charter and adventurers among the barbarians brought in wealth of their own. When Rome finally sowed salt where Carthage had been, it made no large difference to Ys...although some folk wept.

For a hundred or more years afterward, the city prospered. It had no imperial ambitions; it was content with its modest hinterland and outlying island of Sena. Nor did it need more than a small, efficient navy, chiefly for convoy and rescue duty—when its Gallicenae could raise a storm at will. Its ships went trading and freighting throughout the North; likewise throve its manufactures, brokerages, entrepots; and its poets, artists, dreamers, magicians.

Yet the sea at whose bosom it lay was ever rising....

The Veneti had always been troublesome. When Julius Caesar came conquering, Ys gave him substantial help against them. When he had crushed and decimated those foes, he visited the city in person.

What happened then would be hidden from the future. Brennilis of the Gallicenae had had a vision while in a prophetic trance, and somehow she prevailed upon the tough and skeptical Roman. He actually appointed a soldier to slay the King of the Wood and succeed in that office—a young favorite of his, thus a sacrifice on the part of them both. Other things which were done required eternal silence: for Belisama had revealed that a new age was come to Ys. Archivists of the city believed that this was why Caesar made no mention of it in his writings.

The upshot was that Ys became a foederate of Rome, paid a reasonable tribute, accepted a prefect and his staff, enjoyed the benefits of the Roman peace, and otherwise continued its wonted life.

To be sure, as Armorica was Romanized, there were effects upon this city too. On the whole they were benign. Indeed, Rome saved Ys from destruction. The Vision of Brennilis warned that sea level would mount and mount until waves rolled over everything here, were measures not taken. As defensible as it was between its headlands, this site ought not to be abandoned; but already people were moving to higher ground.

From the time of her revelation, onward through her long life, Brennilis was the effective ruler of Ys. In her old age she won for her people the help of Augustus Caesar. To her he sent his best engineers, that they erect a wall against the waters. They did much else while they were there, but the wall and the gate were their real accomplishment, for which the city gave them a triumph.

That labor did not go easily. Besides the sea to contend with, they had the folk. The Romans thought it ridiculous that the wall be built as high as Brennilis demanded; they did not live to see tides eventually surge where she had foretold. Nor could they understand why they must not use enduring concrete. They insisted on it, and not until storms had repeatedly wrecked their work and snatched lives from among them did they yield. True, they then wrought honestly, in dry-laid blocks of stone so well shaped and fitted that a knife blade could not slip between. But they never understood why.

Brennilis and her Sisters did. In her Vision, Lir had told her that Ys must remain hostage to Him, lest it forsake its Gods in the eldritch days to come. He would only allow a wall that He could, at need, break down, for the drowning of a city gone faithless.

The gate was no defiance of this; Ys required one if it would receive ships as of yore. Sealed in copper, oak endured for many a decade. Sometimes the doors must be replaced—machinery and multitudinous workers doing it in a few hours of the lowest tide and deadest calm, followed by three days and nights of festival—but the necessity came seldom, and Ys abided.

Yet also, as lifetimes passed, it drew ever more behind the Veil of Brennilis. This too had been part of her apocalypse, that the Gods of Ys were haughty and aloof, that They would not demean Themselves to plead for worshippers against a new God Who was to come, but would, rather, hold Their city apart unto Themselves. For all its splendor and prosperity, Ys grew obscure. Chronicles which described it gradually crumbled away without fresh copies having been made, burned in accidentaly fires, were misplaced, were stolen and never recovered, were scraped clean so that the vellum might be reused for a Gospel. Curiously few Roman writers ever referred to it; and of those who did, their works had a similar way of becoming lost.

A part of this may simply have been due regained autonomy, as Roman commerce and government began to fall apart. Longer and longer grew the periods during which the Emperors saw no reason to send a prefect; at last, none came. Payment of the tribute was more and more often delayed by bad communications; at last, Septimius Severus remitted it altogether, in thanks for help the city had given against his rival Albinus. That was the final intervention of any consequence that Ys had made. Thereafter it looked to its own.

But it was not totally isolated. The storms that racked the Empire inevitably troubled Ys as well. Trade shrank, Scotic and Saxon raiders harried the waters and the coasts, inland barbarians pressed westward, evangelists of Christ led men away from the Gods of their fathers. Among the Gallicenae arose a feeling that they had come to the end of still another age. What would the new one bring? None could foreknow. Like a creature of the sea, Ys drew into its shell and waited.

~ 3 ~

By candlelight in the bedroom. Bodilis showed no mark of being past her youth, save for maturity itself. Smiling, she went to Gratillonius. "How can I best make you welcome?" asked her husky voice.

She responded to him, in movement of loins and hands, in soft outcries; but always there was something about her that cared more for him than for herself; and before they slept, she murmured in his ear, "I pray the Goddess that I be not too old for bearing of your child."

XII

~ 1 ~

Suddenly fog blew out of the west. Then wind died while cloud thickened. *Osprey* rolled to the swell, the eyes painted on her bows as blindfolded as eyes in the skulls of the men aboard her. Barely did sight reach from stem to stern, and the masthead swayed hidden. It was as if that formless gray also swallowed sound. There was nothing to hear but slap of waves on strakes, slosh in a well where the live part of the catch swam uneasily about, creak of timbers and lines and of the sweeps where crew toiled—and dim and hollow, at unknown distances and in unsure directions, those boomings which betokened surf over the rocks around Sena.

Maeloch drew his hoooded leather jacket tighter. Leaving the prow of his fishing smack he went aft, past the four starboard oarsmen. Sheeted fast, the lugsail slatted to the rocking. Despite chill, air was too dank for breath to show. As Maeloch neared, the helmsman slowly changed from a phantom to a mortal like himself, beard as wet as the sail, leathery face stiffened by weariness.

"How fare ye?" Maeloch asked. "Need ye a relief?"

Usun, his mate, shrugged. "Not so much as the deckhands. Might be one o' them and me should spell each other."

"Nay. While we keep sea room, their task is but to maintain steerage way. Should we find ourselves drifting onto a skerry or into a snag, aye, they'd better row their guts out. But worse will we need an alert steersman. My thought was ye might want to change with me and go stand lookout for'ard."

Usun sagged a little over the tiller. "If ye, who captain us through this passage on those nights, if ye be lost—"

"Who'd not be, as long as we've wallowed in this swill?" Maeloch snapped. "Would Lir fain destroy us, why couldn't He ha' sent an honest gale?"

"Ha' ye gone mad?" Usun exclaimed, shocked. "Best we join in vowing Him a sacrifice if He spare us."

"He got His usual cock ere we set forth."

"I—I've promised Epona—"

"As ye wish." Maeloch's rough countenance jutted on high. "Myself, I'll deal with the Gods like my fathers before me, straightforwardly or not at all."

Usun drew back. Ever were the Ferriers of Dead an arrogant lot, not only because they enjoyed exemption from tax and civic labor but because—the source of their privileges—they met the unknown, on

126

behalf of Ys. But Usun, who was himself along on such crossings, had not thought the captain's pride would go this far.

Maeloch filled his lungs and shouted: "D'Ye hear me, out there? Ahoy! Here I stand. Drown me if Ye will. But remember, my eldest living son is a stripling. 'Twill be years till he can help bring ye your wayfarers. Think well, O Gods!"

The fog drank down his cry. Louder snarled the surf, and now there was in it a hiss of waves as they rushed across naked rock. Two crewmen missed a beat. The vessel yawed. Usun put the steering oar hard over. His own lips moved, but silently.

Something passed alongside. A splash resounded. Maeloch trod to the rail and peered downward. Foam swirled on darkling water. Amidst it swam a seal. Twice and thrice it smote with its rear flippers. The front pair kept it near the hull. It raised its head. Great eyes, full of night, sought toward Maeloch's.

For heartbeats, the skipper stood moveless. Finally Usun saw a shiver pass through him too. He turned about and said, well-nigh too quietly for hearing: "Stand by to give what helm I call for."

But striding off, Maeloch trumpeted: "Pull oars! Full stroke! We're going home!" The seal glided beneath and beside him.

When he reached the bows, the creature swam on ahead, until he could barely see it through the swirling gray. Once it glanced back at him and made a leap. Thereafter it started off on the larboard quarter.

"Right helm!" Maeloch roared. "Stroke, stroke, stroke! Give it your backs, ye scoundrels, if e'er ye'd carouse ashore again!"

Dread was upon the men, they knew not what this portended, nor knew what to do save obey. To and fro they swayed on their benches. Their breath loudened. Sweeps groaned at the tholes, throbbed in the waves. "Steady as she goes," Maeloch ordered. The seal swam on.

Surf crashed to starboard. On the edge of sight, a reef grinned. Yet *Osprey* had clearance enough. "Might that be the She-Wolf?" Macloch muttered. "If 'tis, we've tricky navigation before us." The seal veered. "Left helm!...Steady as she goes."

Stroke, stroke, stroke. The waters bawled, seethed, sank away and sighed.

—The sun must have been low when the mainland hove in view, shadowy at first, later real, solid, the southside cliffs of Cape Rach. Men dared utter a ragged cheer. With their last strength they brought the battered and tarry boat into her home cove and laid her to at Ghost Quay. Oars clattered inboard. Feet thudded on close-packed stone as sailors climbed onto the dock, caught mooring lines, and made fast to iron rings set in boulders. The hull rolled, rubbing against rope bumpers hung on a log secured to the wharf.

At the stempost Maeloch slowly lifted his hand, waved, let the arm drop again, and watched the seal depart.

127

Usun sought him. A while they stood in silence. Fog seemed thicker still, or was it only that night drew near? They could make out a pair of companion smacks at the quay, rowboats drawn onto a strand which had become cobble-hemmed and tiny at high tide, nets across poles. A track wound up the steeps, to join roads toward the pharos and Ys. A second trail went under the scarp. At its end, a deeper dimness showed where those few rammed-earth cottages were that bore the name Scot's Landing. A hush had fallen. Cold gnawed in through garments and flesh.

"Ye men'll sleep aboard," Maeloch said at length. "We've our catch to prepare for market in the morning, ye know." Only he and Usun among them dwelt here, where some were boatowners like him and all were haughty—however poor—and a little strange, concerned less with affairs of the Fisher Brotherhood and the city than with things that were their own. "But I'll dispatch boys to tell your kin ye came back safe."

"How did we?" one sailor whispered.

"I know not."

"You...a Ferrier of the Dead...know not?"

"What I do those nights is a mystery to me too," Maeloch answered starkly. "Ye've heard what folk tell, that Gallicenae who've died may return in the shape o' seals, abiding till those they loved ha' fared out to Sena. No dream has told me if this be so or not. But when yon swimmer appeared, I had a feeling we should follow her.

"Goodnight."

He left the craft and trudged toward his home. There his wife Betha kept vigil, among their living children and the babe that was great within her. For his sake she was invoking Belisama, Our Lady of the Sea—and, silently or by secret tokens, beings about whom the fisher women never told their men.

~ 2 ~

The day was bright when Innilis came to the house of Vindilis; but within lay dimness and quiet. "Welcome," said the older Queen, with a smile such as was rarely seen on her gaunt countenance. She took both hands of Innilis in her own. To the servant who had admitted the visitor: "We twain have matters of discretion before us. Let none disturb."

The servant bowed. "Never, my lady." This was not the first time he had been so commanded. As half-sisters, both daughters of Gaetulius, unlike though they were in aspect, this pair might be expected to cherish one another. In any event, it was not for him to question what the Nine did, or even wonder.

Vindilis led the way. Innilis must hurry to match her strides. They passed through the atrium. Like Bodilis, Vindilis had had the walls of hers painted over; but these now bore only spirals and Greek keys, black on white.

Beyond was what she called her counsel chamber. Light fell greenish through leaded panes to reveal mostly bareness: a table, a few chairs, a broad and backless couch upholstered in red. A niche held a statuette of Belisama. On a shelf below it were a lamp and an offering of evergreen. Refreshments waited on the table.

Innilis bowed to the shrine and signed herself. After a moment, Vindilis did likewise. The image had nothing of serenity. Rather, it showed the Goddess spear in hand, dress and unbound hair flying, astride a night wind like a stream or a snake —Her persona as the Wild Huntress, leading through the air the spirits of women who died in childbed.

Vindilis turned to Innilis, laid hands on her shoulders, kissed her on the lips. "How went it?" she asked, more softly than was her wont.

"Oh—I—" Innilis looked away. Her fingers, fragile as reeds, twisted together. "He was not unkind. Not knowingly." In haste: "I'm sorry to arrive this late. Three people begged my help at the same time."

"You could not well refuse, if you had no duties more urgent," said Vindilis. "Nor would you ever. Be seated. Here, let me pour you some wine. 'Tis that sweet Narbonensian you like." As she bent to pick up the flagon, light sheened on the silver streak in her hair and the raven coils around it. "What were their needs, those people? Illness?"

"For two." Innilis settled herself. "One is a man I've seen erenow. His dropsy was coming back. I gave him foxglove; that helps. But, poor soul, he has scant strength anymore to earn his living. I think soon the temple must consider him and his family deserving of aid."

"You may be too tender hearted, as often erstwhile." Vindilis sat down opposite her guest. "Go on. You need talk for easing of your mind. Let me be your physician and prescribe it."

Innilis shook her head, drank unsteadily, and replied: "The second was the worst. A girl with a raging fever, none knew why, least of all myself. I could but give her tisane of willow bark, for cooling of her poor little body, and invoke the Mother."

"If any of us can heal any longer by the Power of the Touch, 'tis you, Innilis. You She still heeds. As well She might."

The younger priestess reddened. "I am not worthy. Yet I pray that She will.... The third was an old man on his deathbed. He wanted a blessing."

"*Your* blessing."

"Oh, but 'tis only a rite of comfort."

"That is just why 'tis best coming from the one of us whom everybody loves."

"I...I spent a while more at his bedside. That is what really delayed me. I had my harp along, and gave him some songs he liked. If only my voice were better." Innilis's was high and thin.

129

Vindilis regarded her for a spell that lengthened, her own chin cupped between hands. After fourteen years of consecration, Innilis hardly seemed changed from the thirteen-year-old girl on whom the Sign had appeared in the reign of Hoel—not even by the daughter she had borne him. Short, slight, ivory-skinned, lips always parted beneath a tip-tilted nose, eyes large and blue, she let her hair flow freely, a light-brown cascade down her back, like a commoner maiden, save when occasion demanded she dress it. Her gown today was glowing saffron, but jewelry lay nowhere on her.

Vindilis, clad in silver-accented black with a Gorgon's-head pendant, lifted goblet. "Drink again, darling. I know 'twill not be easy for you to tell me about yesterday."

Innilis's lashes fluttered wildly. Red and white pursued each other above the fine bones. "There is, is naught to tell," she stammered. "I said he...was courteous, told me he re-re-regretted he'd not been able sooner to...pay me his respects, and—" Her words trailed off.

"What further?" Vindilis asked sharply.

Innilis spread her hands, a gesture of helplessness. "What could there be? What know I to talk about with a man? We both tried, but long silences kept falling, until supper came as a release. Then he suggested— What better had we to do? I told you he meant well."

Vindilis sighed, considered, abruptly set her vessel down hard and inquired, "Should I tell you first about my time?"

Innilis nodded, mute, staring down at the tabletop.

Vindilis leaned back, crossed her legs, frowned into space, crooked a finger as if summoning memory to report in full. Her tone was impersonal:

"Well, he arrived at the hour agreed, mid-afternoon. That was earlier than with you, but we knew we had much to discuss. He'd taken the trouble to ask about me beforehand, and actually said he was sorry I'd dismissed Runa for the day; said he looked forward to meeting another daughter of Hoel, who must have been a good father. And he said he'd gotten a feeling that Quinipilis paid me less heed when I was a child than she did her older girl—Since Karilis-to-be was by Wulfgar, whom she liked, and I by Gaetulius whom she did not care for—and Gratillonius wondered if this was why I was reckless and rebellious in my school days. But when he saw his prying was offensive to me, he stopped, and after that our discourse became intelligent.

"He started by asking what we priestesses, both high and minor, *do,* other than conduct our rites and the affairs of our temple corporation. Naught boorish in that question; he begged pardon for his ignorance and said he hoped to remedy it. So I talked of counselling the troubled, healing the sick, teaching the young, taking part in the public business day by day as well as when the Council meets—everything, save that he sheered somewhat away from our spells, the thought of those making

130

him uneasy. Ha, this may be a whip wherewith to chastise stout drayhorse Gratillonius, if he gets over-frisky!

"But now he was merely appealing for my help. Nay, wrong word. In soldierly wise, he put it to me that he and I, all the Nine and their lesser Sisters, should work with him for the safety and well-being of Ys. That talk went on for hours. When at length we took a repast, neither of us noticed what we ate or drank. Yea, methinks I could come to like Gratillonius, as much as lies in me to like any man."

Silence entered and pressed inward. Finally Innilis breathed, "Also after he—he spent the night?"

Vindilis laughed, with neither mirth nor bitterness. "We went to bed, of course. I'd told him the Goddess would be angered were not the sacred marriage consummated, except with a Queen like my mother who's so old the moon no longer rules over her. He was taken aback, but then smiled a bit and said, 'I carry out my orders.' When he began to feel of me, I asked that he mount at once. He did. He took a time about it, as busy as he'd been with others, but wrought no harm, and was satisfied with the single doing. At least, he lay straight down to sleep. In the morning I told him men do not arouse me; Hoel tried often and failed, Colconor was disgusting, Gratillonius might do best to leave me in peace. Could we not be partners, aye, and friends? Dahilis, or anyone, would be welcome to all such honors due me. He laughed and kissed my hand. We parted amicably."

Vindilis's brow darkened. "Although," she said in a harshened voice, "I must needs conceal what I felt, knowing that the same evening he would seek you."

Innilis lifted her gaze. "Oh, but I told you he was kindly." Her speech wavered.

"Once and no more, as with me?" pounced Vindilis.

"Nay—but—"

Vindilis sucked air in between her teeth. "Ah, well might I have foreseen. 'Tis my fault, I should have taken more of his goatishness on myself...for you. Though you are too beautiful—"

"I, I never besought him. He might have stopped, but I never thought to ask. And he was so eager, and between times he looked at me so mildly, stroked me and murmured. I—it seemed not to matter that it had hurt."

Vindilis reared in her seat. "Badly?" she grated.

Innilis made fending motions. "Nay, nay. Be not angry. Please. 'Twas but that he is big and I was, well, dry at first...and later, when I was not, I remembered how Hoel sometimes gave me some pleasure, and I thought mayhap Gratillonius—"

Vindilis rose, came around behind Innilis, stood smoothing the long brown tresses and crooning, "Poor sweetheart, poor little sister-wife." In Hoel they had shared a father for the child that each bore. "You were very brave. Now rest, be at peace, be happy. 'Tis over and done

131

with. Presently we'll find a way to take the burden off you too. He may well have been inflamed because you reminded him somewhat of Dahilis. And surely she will be our ally, whether she know it or not."

Vindilis bent over to pass lips across Innilis's cheek. Her fingers plucked at the silken cord and amber button which closed the neck of Innilis's gown. The younger woman turned her head. Mouths met and lingered. In Colconor they had shared misery which brought them together.

Afterward on the couch, Innilis said through tears, "This *must* be right. The Mother *must* smile on us."

"She has not cursed us, throughout these years, has She?" Vindilis replied drowsily. They had been over this ground before.

"Nay. She has kindled love in us." Innilis clenched a fist. "But oh, if only we need not keep it secret!"

~ 3 ~

Wind whooped above glittery waters, made sails dance, drove white pennons across a vast blue field. It stung tears from the eyes of Gratillonius when he squinted into it. Between that and the glare, he could just make out a low, dark streak in the west: Sena, where again today Dahilis stood her lonely watch.

"Uh, you were saying, sir?"

Eppillus's rusty voice recalled Gratillonius to himself. He grinned, half abashed. "Pardon. My mind wandered."

"Well, the centurion has a peck o' things to think about. And they don't sit still neither, do they? Wriggle around like worms, I'll bet."

"The more reason to use this chance. Come." The two men resumed their walk atop the wall. Passing the Gull Tower, where a sentry saluted, they went above the harbor basin toward the gate. "The seaward defense is holding a practice. I wanted you to watch, and tell me what you think."

On the bastions, rain shelters had been dismantled and removed. The war engines crouched amidst the men who served them, spaced at intervals, three bolt-shooting catapults to each great stone-throwing ballista. Gratillonius and his deputy stopped at the first they encountered, which was of the former sort. Light by comparison, it did not require the recoil-absorbing wall reinforcement of the latter kind, and was much easier and faster handled. "Heed us not," the King told the team officer. "Get on with your business."

"Aye, my lord," said the Ysan. "We're about to start. 'Twill go quicker for the following rounds, but skeins get slack in damp weather—as my lord knows, being a soldier."

He called for winding. The men at the lever arms threw their weight into the work, twisting two vertical strands which, with the frame, flanked the trough. Meanwhile others were bringing ammunition and

132

stacking it. "Hold," the officer ordered. The winders withdrew their levers from the sockets. Pawls clicked into notches. For a moment the wind alone gave tongue.

With a small hammer, the officer tapped the right skein. It sang, a deep bass note. Into the sinew and horsehair of which it was braided had been woven something resonant. Head cocked, the officer listened until the sound died away, before he struck the mate and heard it out. "Hm," he said, "not quite balanced yet. Give this'n a half turn more and we'll try again."

Equal tension was necessary so that the missile, when loosed, would not rub against the groove, and when free would fly straight. Eppillus whistled to behold such a method of gauging. Gratillonius smiled wryly. He would never command Ysan artillery. His ear was too poor; at home, his fellow centurions had requested him to refrain from singing in their presence.

Satisfied, the chief had the casting arms inserted in the skeins. The strong bowstring linking their opposite ends was to propel a slide which in turn pushed a long, iron-headed bolt down the groove. The machine had already been laid for elevation and direction. Now a windlass creaked, drawing the string back against the resistance of the skeins, until the side engaged a locking mechanism at the base of the slotted beam. The chief undid skein pawls. "Would my lord like to send the first shot?" he asked. "Methinks 'twould bring us luck."

Gratillonius nodded, stepped forward, pulled the trigger that released the engagement. The catapult whirred and thumped. The bolt sprang forth, nearly too fast to see.

Other engines had likewise begun to shoot. Their targets were several rafts anchored at varying distances. Boats rested nearby on their oars, bearing scorekeepers, eventually to haul rafts and spent missiles back. But the exercise would go on all day while tide ebbed and flowed. Afar, a naval galley stood by to warn off any merchantmen that might appear.

Eppillus's small eyes bulged with fascination. These designs and procedures had countless differences from the Roman. Gratillonius must nudge him twice to get his attention: "Move that paunch of yours, you. We want to inspect every emplacement on this arc."

They did, walking to the gate and back to the tower, where they descended. Thrum, shouts, horn signals rang in their ears till well after they had passed the temple of Lir. "I don't think we need look the south side over," Gratillonius decided. "They're quite satisfactory, wouldn't you say?"

"I would. Oh, a funny style they've got, but I've seen Romans shoot worse. Naming no units, by your leave, sir. I'd say between their engines and their warships, they're plenty secure to seaward."

Gratillonius frowned. "That's a thing I want to talk over with you. We may have very little on hand in the way of navy, from time to time. Remember, our mission is to make sure not only of Ys, but this whole end of Armorica. That may call for a show of force at certain places. I'll send discreet letters to their officials as soon as I know what the situation is in the east, but those may not be enough. Meanwhile, what's keeping me busy is preparing for contingencies here." His chuckle was rueful. "Ysans can be as stubborn and slippery as any Imperials."

Eppillus rubbed his bald spot. "Hm, well, I'm no seaman, o' course, but I'd still hate to row up at that artillery. And I suppose the city infantry would be on the wall too. Plus every civil mariner in town, eh? Not that a sailor who's never been on a parade ground would be worth too much if a real army hit him."

They walked on by the ancient sanctum of Ishtar and through the mean streets of the Fishtail. Gratillonius had said he wanted to go by an obscure route, where he would less likely be recognized and detained by petitioners, gawkers, or Suffetes. Eppillus was the guide through this quarter. His familiarity with it amused Gratillonius—although doubtless the old roadpounder spent more tavern time gabbing about his past life than in gambling or wenching.

"That's the main business before us today. I've been dismayed at how little I've gotten to see of my own men. But with everything else besieging me— How are they doing?"

"Haven't our honor guards been smart, sir?"

"They have. And when I've asked them the same question, they say, 'Fine, sir.' What would you expect them to tell me under those circumstances? I'm counting on your honesty."

Eppillus stroked the broken bridge of his nose. "Well, we've had our problems, but they're mostly behind us and I needn't pester the centurion with 'em. Sitting around in barracks wasn't good for the boys. The centurion will understand. Now that we're busy again, not just drill but patrols and field exercises, why, they're shaping up fast. Give me another ten, twelve days and I'll have them back in crack condition."

"Splendid!" Gratillonius felt it would do no harm if he slapped the burly shoulder beside him. "We'll proceed to the royal palace and talk at length. I've things to tell you. Between us we can work out the right ways to use our troops. When we're done, I'll see to it that you go back to Dragon House with a bellyful of the best food and wine Ys has to offer. Which is plenty good, believe me." For the sake of Roman prestige, Gratillonius had insisted that his deputy be lodged among the marine and naval officers.

"I know. Thank you, sir." Eppillus gusted a sigh. "Though I got to admit those fine things are kind of wasted on me. I'll settle for a stoup o' Dobunnic red, a roast o' pork, a heap o' cabbage, and a slice o' bread—fresh from the oven, if my wife was baking that day."

"When you return home and retire to your bit of a farm, eh?"

"Mithras willing. I'll stick with the centurion till he leaves here. When will that be, sir?"

"Mithras knows. In two or three years, let us hope. The trick will be to stay alive till then."

—At the palace, a stranger waited.

A Roman. A military courier. He bore the first communication Gratillonius had received, other than rumors out of the hinterland. It was a letter directly from Maximus.

~ 4 ~

When Forsquilis heard what the King wanted to speak of, she raised a palm. "Nay, not here. Come with me to the secretorium."

In her chamber where flamelight flickered through the eye sockets of a cat's skull, shadows made the small female image from Tyre seem to stir, herbs sharpened the air with their memories of wildwood, she sat down facing him. Her hands rested quietly on her lap, her visage bore the calm and pallor of Pallas, but the gray gaze was darkened in this dusk and stars of red fire-glow moved within it. "Now say," she commanded.

In his mind Gratillonius clung tight to the handfast world outside. "Maximus reached Gallia on the day you declared. His legions have swept all resistance before them. Not that there was much. His opposition had little more to set against them than poorly trained auxiliaries. Some legionary units did arrive, hastily called from the eastern frontier or out of Hispania, in time to give battle—but of those, whole cohorts went over to the eagles of Maximus. He writes that he was in danger of outrunning his supply train, and this was among the reasons he had no chance to dictate a message earlier. Flavius Gratianus, co-Emperor, was in Lutetia Parisiorum. Maximus marched on that city. When he got there, the garrison rebelled and foreswore Gratianus. Maximus entered without hindrance. Gratianus had fled. Maximus is—was—making ready to pursue, defeat him decisively, lay grip on the whole of Gallia and Hispania."

"What will he have you do?" she asked low and tonelessly.

"Oh, I'm to send back a report by his courier, continue in my mission, keep him informed. We'll soon have a new and better Augustus, Forsquilis."

"And what would you have me do?"

"I think you know already." Gratillonius must moisten his lips. His armpits were wet enough. "Ys looks well prepared. Aye, not only to defend herself but to carry out the task Rome has given her. Yet...'tis unforeseeable what may happen. The Empire is in turmoil. Its legions guarding Britannia and the East are stripped to the bone. Beyond the frontiers prowl wolves."

"You said we could stand off attack. Not that I think any barbarians would be so mad as to try."

"But Rome, Rome—"

"Ah." Forsquilis sat quite still. Misshapen glooms danced in silence. At last: "You ask that the owl fly forth again."

"Aye."

"And, if need be, the Nine take a hand, seek to order the tides of time." He mustered courage. "You did it with me."

"That was for Ys," she answered sternly.

"If Rome falls, can Ys long endure?" he pleaded. "Bethink you how alone she will stand, while darkness deepens and the sea rises higher."

She was mute another while.

"This is a strange thing you seek," she then said, like one who talks in her sleep. "But these are strange years. I must think. Later I must meet with my Sisters. I will call you here when we have decided." Her eyes came back to him and focused. "Go."

He left. Not until he was outdoors did he let himself tremble.

~ 5 ~

The temple of Taranis was a majestic edifice on the west-northwest edge of the Forum—Roman-built on the colonnaded Roman model, save that it enclosed an open courtyard, its temenos. Only the south wing of the building was given over to worship. The rest held offices, treasury, a hall with sumptuous kitchen nearby for the sacred banquets of the seasons, and a conference room for the Speaker.

There Soren Cartagi privately received Queen Lanarvilis. On the wall behind his chair of state, under an inlaid Sun Wheel, hung weapons of war, surrounding a gold-trimmed Hammer. On the wall to his right a mosaic depicted the God victorious over Tiamat of the Chaos; windows, above a writing table, occupied the left side; bookcases flanked the entrance which he faced. For Lanarvilis, a throne of equal dignity had been brought. However, this day he and she wore plain silk with simple embroidery.

His fist lay knotted on the chair arm, his mouth was stiff, he must wrench the words out: "Thank you for coming, my lady. Believe me, I've no wish to ask about...what concerns you yourself. But for the good of Ys—after you have spent time alone with our King—can you tell me aught new?"

Faintly, she flushed, although she held her own voice level. "Those before me spoke truth. He is a well-intentioned and able man."

"For Rome."

"The cause of Rome is the cause of civilization: which means that 'tis equally Ys's."

Soren shook his head. "Always have you thought more highly of Rome than it deserves, my dear. You dream of a greatness, a grandeur of soul as well as domain, that has long since died, if ever it truly lived. I've dealt with the Empire; I know."

"Soren," she said quietly, "let not your resentment speak for you. Whatever you think—and I myself am not so dewy as to believe in any human perfection—still, the fact is that Gratillonius has our welfare at heart, is moving strongly to assure it, and seeks our advice, inquires about our wishes. He spent hours talking with me, and listening, too, as if I were a man."

"What was the drift of this?"

"Well, he...he'd heard you and I often confer and work together on behalf of our temples. Thus much of his querying concerned you. You've been polite but aloof, he said. And he needs your active help, the more so when the Lord of Works is in opposition to him."

"Indeed?" Despite everything that roiled in his breast, Soren's interest awoke. "How is this?"

"Gratillonius wants fortifications on the headlands. Immediately."

"Hm." Soren tugged his beard. "Little can be done that fast."

"Well, he spoke just of mantraps, with here and there a dry-laid piece of wall to protect archers and slingers. He fears an assault from the sea while our navy is off supporting our envoys to the Roman governors." Lanarvilis laid finger to chin. "Nay, 'fear' is wrong. He wants precautions taken. They will require a work levy."

"Ah. Does he understand what that means?"

"He does. I had him describe it to me."

Soren hesitated. "I intend no offense, dear, but in your desire to think well of him, you may have credited him with a better grasp of matters than he has. Would you tell me what he said?"

"Why—" She paused, shrugged, and recited: "Taxes to Ys may be paid in money, in kind, or in labor. The labor is limited to public works, to a short maximum period in any year, and to times when it will inflict no undue hardship. Since most construction was completed long ago and needs little maintenance, no such levy has been imposed on the poor for generations."

Soren smiled grimly. "I can see why Cothortin Rosmertai digs in his heels. 'Twould upset his administrative routine. Does Gratillonius realize that?"

"Certes. And he's not such a fool as to ride down a Lord of Works whose future friendship will be worth having. He asked me if I could lend my good offices—and prevail upon you—to persuade Cothortin. I agreed. I'll speak to my Sisters also." Warmth: "Glad will they be to have this additional token that the Gods meant well by us when They answered our call."

Soren winced. "You admire him, then. And not only because he is Roman."

Again she flushed, but lifted her head and replied proudly: "Aye. Had the Sign come upon my daughter"—by Lugaid—"while Colconor reigned, I would have made her kneel, and with this hand slashed her throat, lest he get her. Yestereven Gratillonius cleansed me of him. As he is cleansing all Ys."

Soren scowled. "He may yet scrub too hard, he with his foreign God. 'Twould not be the first time the Three withdrew Their favor from a man."

Pain crossed Lanarvilis's face. She rose and reached toward him. "Oh, Soren! Close that wound in you. Speak no ill omen. Bethink your sons and the city that shall be theirs."

He hunched his shoulders. "So be it," he growled. "I'll help. For Ys. And for you who wish it."

~ 6 ~

"Ah-h-h," Maldunilis breathed. "That was good. You wield a mighty sword." She giggled. "How soon will you sheathe it anew?"

Gratillonius lifted himself to an elbow and looked down at her. Afternoon sunlight came through the windows to glow across an expanse of sprawled flesh. They had gone to bed shortly after he arrived, for there seemed nothing else to do. Innilis had at least, shyly, proposed a game of draughts....Maldunilis was tall and plump, with brown eyes and reddish-brown hair now lank from sweat. Although her father had been Gaetulius, the heavy features recalled grandfather Wulfgar. Yet she was by no means ugly, and had shown her new husband a certain lazy sensuality which made the Bull roar loud within him.

"Give me a while," he laughed.

She raised herself too. The copious breasts slithered around as she reached for a bowl of sweetmeats on a stand beside the bed. Their fragrance blended into the closeness of the room. No matter that she kept the largest domestic staff of the Nine, always a measure of slovenliness prevailed in this house.

She offered him a confection. "Thank you, nay," he said. "I've small tooth for such." She fluffed up pillows to lean against and munched it.

"Aye, maybe best you keep your appetite," she answered. "The cooks are preparing a feast." Archly: "'Twill take hours. How shall we spend them?"

Well, he thought, since I've set aside the time till sunrise, why not dawdle about? Gods know I need a rest, a little freedom from responsibility. She's a simpleton, but amiable and a pretty good lay. Unlike some.

The tiny crescent on her bosom seemed abruptly to burn. How did the Sign come to Maldunilis, of all Gallicenae daughters? he wondered. The ways of Mithras could be mysterious, but the ways of Belisama—of

138

the Three Who brooded over Ys—were those of the wind, lightning, the sea deeps, falling stars, death in the night.

He sat straight in the rumpled bedding, crossed arms over knees, and suggested, "Shall we get to know each other better? Tell me of yourself."

She yawned, scratched, fumbled after a second sweetmeat. "Why, naught's to tell. I was never a, a scholar like Bodilis or a seeress like Forsquilis or a politician like Lanarvilis or— I am only me. I do what I am supposed to, and harm nobody." She smirked. "Command me, my lord."

"Oh, surely something," he protested, while observing that she did not even ask for his story.

She put a hand on his thigh and slid it along an insinuating path. "I can tell you that I love to futter. Hoel enjoyed me."

He could not forbear to bark, "Colconor?"

"Aye. He wasn't very heedful, but nor was he as bad as they said. Once he saw I liked having him on me, and I'd willingly do *whatever* he wanted—as I would for you, O King—he did no worse than spank me sometimes, and that only made this big bottom of mine tingle. He'd have treated me better yet had I given him a child. And I did open my womb, I left off the Herb, but the babe dropped out of me early." Maldunilis nuzzled Gratillonius. "I'm sure you can give me one that lives."

He froze.

"What's the matter, my lord?" She sounded plaintive.

His breath came hard and harsh. "That day—in the House of the King, ere I arrived—"

She nodded. "Vindilis and Forsquilis and I were keeping him there. Waiting for you."

"But—but for them it was a necessity—like Brutus striking down Caesar because he hoped to save the Republic. You—"

She smiled. "Why not enjoy? That was why my Sisters picked me for the third. Colconor would know I wasn't feigning. Instead it doubled the pleasure to know I helped prepare the way for you, his conqueror."

The most horrible thing, he thought in a distant part of himself, the ghastliest thing was her innocence.

It thundered in his head. He rolled around and sprang to the floor. Tiles felt cold beneath his feet. Somehow he could chatter, "Pardon me, this is not courteous. Of a sudden I've remembered pressing affairs of state. I must begone."

Her face screwed up. "But my feast!" she wailed.

"Eat it in health. Invite somebody else. Do what you will. I must away." He scrambled into his clothes.

She blubbered a bit. However, she made no effort to keep him, just sat in bed watching while her hand travelled absently between bowl and mouth.

He strode out into the street. A clean wind blew off the sea. He would go to his palace, he decided, take a hot bath, don fresh raiment. Only there in Ys was it permissible to keep horses. He would have one saddled and gallop off across the hinterland, alone.

His Queens—Nobody remained but Fennalis, and she was the mother of Lanarvilis. Flat-out against the Law of Mithras, to lie with both daughter and mother. He would explain that to Fennalis sometime soon as kindly as he was able. They said she was a friendly sort, usually cheerful, bustling about upon charitable works. Besides, with seven living children by Wulfgar, Lugaid, Gaetulius, and Hoel, she might well be past the rule of the moon. Dismiss Fennalis. He had carried out his duty by the lot of them.

It didn't matter which had known beforehand of that whore-hearted conspiracy to entrap a man. Dahilis had not. She had merely appealed to her Gods for deliverance.

Ignoring persons who hailed him, Gratillonius stalked through Ys. He would ride the roads above the sea until his horse could go no more. Then he would return, bathe anew, dress well, and seek the house of Dahilis.

With her he would abide as long as the Gods allowed. Let people say whatever they chose. Was he not the prefect of Rome?

XIII

The word had gone forth around Mide: again this year would the King at Temir carry a spear abroad. Let ships and currachs gather at the mouth of Boand's River. Let those noble landowners who owed him warlike service make ready themselves and their men, to meet well provisioned once seed was in the ground and cattle on their way to upland pastures. Let any other man who was free to do so and wished for adventure, glory, and plunder come too. Niall maqq Echach would await them and lead them—this time not to Alba, where fighting and loot had been splendid but where the Wall of Rome still stood—this time south to golden Gallia!

First there must be the rites of Beltene, welcoming in the summer and striving to make it fruitful. Throughout Ériu, folk would rise before dawn to gather the dew for its powers of cure. Women washed their faces in it to make themselves fair, men their hands to make themselves skillful. Women then drew the magical first water from the well and left flowers behind; men set up a bush before the house, and prepared to defend it against whoever might steal it and the luck it carried; youngsters plucked healing herbs, together with blossoms for shrines, horse bridles, every place that might please the Goddess. Later in the day came exchange of gifts, balls bearing the signs of the sun and moon, followed by hurling-games played with these, which could well lead to brawls and bloodshed. Youths and maidens went in procession around the countryside, singing, acting out Her coming, celebrating her gifts of life and light. Families made no marriage pacts, because that would have been as ill-fated as it was to be born this day. However, many couples plighted troth of their own for the year to come or renewed it, and made love upon the earth.

Food was cold, for all household fires had been put out the evening before. At sunset the dwellers in each neighborhood left their revels and solemnly gathered on the highest ground nearby. While bards or poets sang and druids watched for portents, a chosen man kindled new flame with flint and steel, to make twinned bonfires. Into these folk cast their festival bushes and whatever they had that seemed unlucky, so that fortune might consume misfortune. Farmers drove their cattle between the blazes, for protection against murrains. Those who thereafter went home carried along some of the needfire to relight their hearths. The hardier stayed on till sunrise, for doings that left them weary and a little dazed the next day.

In these observances, every king of a tuath and his queen took a leading part. The King and Queen on Temir must do so on behalf of the whole land. Niall had foreknown he would have no time to himself on the day and night of Beltene; and immediately afterward would come the whirlwind of busking for his expedition. Yet he had felt the need of some calm counsel.

Therefore he had walked out upon the eve preceding the holy dawn. He went in company with his druid Nemain maqq Aedo and with Laidchenn maqq Barchedo, who had become chief among his poets.

As busy as he had been, this was late in the day. Weather had brought rainshowers, though free of the cold east wind or frost that would have boded ill for the coming season. Now clouds drifted low and leaden beneath an overcast that quite hid the sun and laid an early twilight in the valley. Breezes plucked fitfully at grass and leaves. Odors of growth had given way to dankness. Homebound rooks cawed afar, otherwise silence abided the night.

Niall took the northward road, between the Rath of Gráinne and the Sloping Trenches, thence downhill. Well kept, it was not unduly muddy or rutted; but at this hour it stretched empty, nothing bordered it save meadow and coppices, no firelight gleamed from houses in view. The sole brightness, and it wan, came off the spearheads of Niall's four guards, who encompassed the three great ones at a respectful distance, and off a golden torc around the neck of the King. Although he was still magnificently clad, after receiving guests who arrived during the day, dusk was fading all colors.

"Best we not linger outside overly long," counselled Nemain. "The síd will soon be opening and letting their dwellers loose." The eve of

141

Beltene was second only to that of Samain as a time when unhuman beings went abroad through the dark.

Niall tossed his bright head. "We can turn our cloaks inside out and bewilder them," he said.

"So do people suppose," Laidchenn answered; "yet I could tell you many a story, my dear, about those who put overmuch faith in that trick. Even washing in one's own piss is often not shield enough. For Those Beyond may have deeper ends than leading us astray or altogether out of the world."

"Well, what I have to say is quickly said," Niall snapped.

"Then say it," murmured the druid.

The King's mood gentled. He stared before him, down into the gloom toward which he walked. Trouble freighted his tone: "This I could not utter in the hearing of others, lest they think I was afraid and so, themselves, falter. But to you two, my hearts, I can speak without misunderstanding. And what I have to ask of you is whether you can read any warning signs, in this night before us when sorcery reigns, or whether you can cast any guardian spells—for my warfare after I am off upon it."

"Have you cause for dread?"

"I have not. Would I of my free will take men who trust me on a venture I deemed unwise?"

"Nevertheless you are uneasy," said Laidchenn.

"It is about my son, my son Breccan. He burns to prove himself. A while ago, in a gladsome moment, he lured me into a promise that he could come along on this voyage."

"Surely you, of all men, will not begrudge your boy his chance to win fame."

"But he is so young—"

"No younger than yourself, when you returned from Torna's house to claim your birthright."

"I was stronger than he is. Och, he will grow to be a goodly fighter if he lives. But at present he has still his mother's slimness." Niall's voice wavered, seemed to speak of itself, as if he could not stop it. "And, O Ethniu, your face—"

"You loved her."

"As Diarmait loved Gráinne. I do yet, though she be fourteen years in her grave. Breccan is all that remains of her." Niall's hand slashed swordlike though the air. "Enough!" he barked. "This grows unmanly. I, your King, am calling on you two for your counsel and help."

"Is that right for Breccan's own honor?"

"Hold!" said the druid. "Our lord simply asks Laidchenn—asks what may be done to stave off needless woe. Had King Conaire been better advised, he would not have broken the gessa upon him and thereby come to perish in Dá Derga's hostel. Let us take snares from the path of the young stag; wolves he can battle himself."

His staff thumped the ground as they trudged on mute. Ahead of them an oakenshaw enclosed the road. Its outer trees stood limned against heaven, branches reaching like the arms of gnarled giants, while between them gaped darkness. Wings ghosted overhead and vanished among those shadows. Somewhere a belated cuckoo called.

Laidchenn started. "That cry! An evil sign at just this time."

"It is not evil for us," Niall replied, "for it came from the right, which means luck."

"Before we can take thought and cast the yew chips for divining," said Nemain, "we must know more of what you intend. You have not given out much."

"Lest word somehow reach the Romans and warn them," Niall explained.

The druid nodded his white head. "That is clear. However, with us two you can feel safe, darling, else why have you sought us? Now tell us where in Gallia you mean to raid."

"From the supplying you have ordered," observed the poet shrewdly, "I doubt you plan on the north coasts."

"You are right," Niall answered. "They have been well picked over. Besides, I seek no clash with Saxons, like two flocks of carrion crows quarreling over some bones."

"Have a care," warned Laidchenn. "Those are birds of the Mórrigu that you bespeak."

Niall laughed, which shocked his friend afresh, before he asked, "Sure, and may not a man jape a little with his own family?"

The druid nodded, though his demeanor had turned solemn. Niall's claim to lordship rested on more than his having often fed the flocks of the Triple Goddess of war. Many men believed that the hag with whom he had lain as a youth had not only been the Sovereignty of Mide, but Herself.

"Well," said the King, "it's of more than Saxons I am thinking. Foremost, there is Ys."

They went under the oaks. It was not quite so dark there as it looked from outside, but murky enough, the sky a blue-gray glimmer behind barricading leaves, boles and boughs heavy in shadow. "Ys!" exclaimed Nemain. The name cracked through stillness. "Heart of mine, you are not thinking of attacking Ys, are you, now?"

"I am not," Niall declared. "That would be madness. That wall and those guardian witches— Indeed I have no wish to fall on Armorica at all, at all. Ys is a Roman ally. War among the Romans should cause it to reach a protecting hand over its whole end of the peninsula. We will steer wide of Ys. And this is one thing I am hoping you can help me do, keep the favor of Manandan while we are that far out at sea."

"Where do you mean to go?" Laidchenn asked.

"Around and southward, to the mouth of the Liger and up that river. There lie rich farmlands, towns, a city. With strife drawing men away, they should be thinly defended—worse off than Alba, where last year's fighting will have left the Romans wary and prepared." Despite that which gnawed in his breast, exultation made Niall laugh. "Oh, fine shall our harvest be!"

The trees thinned out. Not much more light straggled through, when dusk had been deepening. Sufficient remained for the men to glimpse an eagle owl depart from the shaw: sufficient to flicker across great wings and glisten on great eyes before the bird disappeared from sight, southbound.

Nemain halted and stood staring after it. Uneasily, his companions drew close to him. "What is the matter, wise one?" breathed Niall at last.

The druid bent his thin shoulders. "I do not know. I felt something uncanny there. Come, best we turn about at once and get into shelter before full night has fallen. It will be very dark."

—Obedient to his gess, Niall rose at the dawn. Fireless, the hall was dolmen-black. Straw rustled dryly under his feet. He groped at a bolt and pushed the shutters from a window. The sky had cleared; the first silver flashed through drifting mists and back off dew; though chill, the air already smelled green. He took a long draught of it.

Suddenly he stiffened. From a beech tree nearby he heard the melodious cry of a cuckoo—too early, too early in the morning, and a harbinger of death if heard from within a house on Beltene.

Yesterday the cuckoo had promised better. Well, signs were often unsure. Niall turned from the window. Nemain would be taking omens and Laidchenn making a powerful song, for the sake of Breccan. The King must remain undaunted.

XIV

~ 1 ~

From the harbor and the markets, through the Forum and over the high ground where the wealthy dwelt—from the philosophers at Star House to the marines in Warriors' House—from Scot's Landing under the cliffs to the noisy workshops outside High Gate—from the mansions on the heights above the canal to the hamlets of the valley floor—the whisper flew around Ys and its hinterland. Something tremendous was afoot. This morning the state barge bringing a Queen back from her Vigil on Sena had not, first, taken another out to replace her. All the Nine were gathered together in the temple of Belisama.

In various ways, a few men knew that this was at the behest of the King. None but he knew why.

When Gratillonius left the palace he went alone. A King here could do that if he chose, could walk about or ride abroad, be a man among men. It was the Emperors who sat in a shell of splendor, god-kings with humanity under their feet, those who were not merely gloves on the hands of ruthless real men. Through Maximus, when his victory was complete, Rome would gain back her soldier-Emperors of old.

In a plain, hooded cloak, Gratillonius followed the streets as they wound down to Lir Way and upward on the other side. Traffic had begun to bustle along the thoroughfare. Some persons recognized him and touched fingers to brow; when he noticed, he acknowledged with a nod and passed on. Two or three approached, clearly hoping to ask favors. His dismissing gesture sent them off. The King might be on sacred business.

It was not the practice for him to hear petitioners or give alms, anyhow. Such things were handled by the Suffetes, Great Houses, guilds, temples. Occasional rulers in the past had distributed largesse or heard complaints...occasionally. Thus far, Gratillonius had not, if only for lack of time. Besides, it was not what a centurion did. Lately, at odd moments, he had wondered if he should institute a regular court—twice a month, perhaps—open to whoever had found no better recourse. But he would be unwise to rush into that, without more knowledge of the city and its customs than he yet possessed. Magnates might resent what they felt as an intrusion on their ancient functions. His mission required that he keep them cooperative, and already there was friction aplenty.

Such children as had tagged after him at a distance gave up when he, seeking calmness, entered Elven Gardens. A wall with guarded portals kept the general public out of these exquisitely contoured and cultivated grounds. He found himself alone. If any else were present, the intricacy of paths, hedges, bowers kept them well off, despite this preserve being less than a hundred yards across.

Stillness underlay birdsong. Flowerbeds were hallways, hedges walls, trees roofs; each petal and leaf seemed in perfect place, as though sculptured. Nowhere were trails, staircases, arched bridges wider than for two people to walk abreast, and nowhere could he see more than a few paces before their curves went out of his view. Yet he had no sense of crowding. Sunlight and shadow made secret depths. A statue of a nymph or a faun, or a fountain where stone dolphins played, or the chiming of a streamlet would leap out at him. The forenoon coolness was full of fragrances.

At the farther end he came forth before the staircase to the temple. It climbed steeply, unrailed, from surrounding flagstones. There he had an overlook across much of the city, its towers agleam between shouldering headlands which had turned emerald and gold, the sea beyond whose daughter Ys was, sails like wings beneath the burning Wheel of Taranis. It was not the first time since his arrival here that beauty had taken him by the throat, and he was a hardened roadpounder.

He mounted to the building. It resembled the Parthenon of Athens, in smaller size, though a close glance showed aliennesses—columns more slender, with capitals suggestive of kelp and surf; a frieze of women, seals, cats, doves, blossoms, sheaves, in a style that flowed like water or wind; the marble left bare, weathered to the hue of pale amber.

Bronze doors stood open. Gratillonius entered into a foyer radiant with mosaics of the Mother's gifts to earth. Attendants waited, minor priestesses—who were mostly in their later years—and young vestals. Among the latter he noticed one he had not seen before. Therefore she could be no child of any of his wives. Her mother must be dead; judging by her apparent age, her father had been Hoel. She was of plain appearance and seemed a little dull-witted. He gave her no further thought.

The women greeted him ceremoniously. He replied as he had been taught to and let a maiden take his cloak. Beneath, in deference to this place, he wore a scarlet robe trimmed with ermine, the Wheel embroidered in gold upon the breast. Above it, out in view, hung the Key. That last was as much emblem as he really needed.

A senior led him through a corridor around that great chamber where the threefold image of the Goddess oversaw services. At the rear was a room for meetings. It was amply impressive. In somber stonework, the four walls showed Her leading Taranis back from the dead to His reconciliation with Lir; present at the act of generation, while dandelion seeds blew and bees flew past the bed; triune as girl child, woman, and crone; in the van of the Wild Hunt. Windows above illuminated the high white headdresses of the Gallicenae. Blue-robed, they sat benched in a half-circle before the dais onto which Gratillonius stepped. His guide closed the door and departed.

Gratillonius looked down into the faces of his wives. Briefly, he was daunted. What strangeness was it that had fallen over them? Wry old Quinipilis; lean, intense Vindilis; Forsquilis, half Athene and half she-cat; sensuous, indolent Maldunilis; shy Innilis; stout, kindly, gray Fennalis; her daughter Lanarvilis, earnest and in some hidden way sorrowful; Bodilis, beneath whose warmth and learning he thought he had sensed steel; darling Dahilis—

No, *she* had nothing but love in her gaze. And as for the rest, he must not let his feelings about them, especially about certain of them, unduly influence him. In their own view they had acted righteously, after intolerable provocation. Seemingly they knew things and wielded powers that were beyond him—that was why he was calling on them—but he should not stand in awe of them, either. He had knowledge and abilities of his own.

Muscle by muscle, Gratillonius relaxed. He smiled. "Greeting," he said. By now his Ysan was adequate, and daily improving. "My thanks for heeding my summons. I think you understand 'tis for the good of

146

the people. I, a man and a foreigner, am still ignorant of much. If we ought to begin with a prayer or a sacrifice, tell me."

Fennalis stirred on her seat. "We cannot," she snapped, "with you in this house, you who follow a God Who does not hear women."

Startled, Gratillonius grabbed after a handhold within himself. What possessed this generally cheerful little person? Offense at his never having slept with her? She had seemed to accept his awkward explanation that it was against his religion—ruefully, he suspected, but no more than that, for she was in fact past childbearing age. Usually bustling about on her charitable works, carelessly dressed, she was the last of the Nine whom he would have expected to show intolerance. Her snub-nosed features had stiffened.

"I...I revere Belisama, of course," he tried to respond, "and all the Gods of Ys."

"They sent him to us!" Dahilis cried. Appalled at her own brashness, she covered her mouth; but her eyes still shone defiant.

Quinipilis laughed. "Shall we save the squabbles for long winter evenings when there's naught else to do?" she said. "This council has business more interesting. At the same time, nay, Gratillonius, we need no rite. Such may come later. Today we are but met to reach a decision."

"It is a very grave decision, however," Lanarvilis replied. "Questions of statecraft...We should have other men on hand, the Speaker for Taranis, Lir Captain, the Sea Lord—"

"I will certainly be in conference with them," Gratillonius promised. "I'll have them out to the Wood when, shortly, I stand my full-moon Watch there. But first I must have the willingness of the Gallicenae."

Vindilis scowled. "That turns on the willingness of the Gods. Who dares try to read Their minds?"

"Aye," said Bodilis softly. "And even without hubris, what may stem from a terrible deed? Agamemnon did not truly sacrifice Iphigenia for a fair wind—the Gods wafted her away to safety—but Clytemnestra knew this not, and so murder led to murder until the curse on the house of Atreus was fulfilled."

"Hold on," Quinipilis admonished. "'Tis no delicate balancing of ifs and maybes we have before us, 'tis a practical question not unlike the last such that we Nine faced. Meseems we came rather well out of that one."

Bodilis smiled a little. "I agree. My inclination is to do what the King asks. Without Rome, what is Ys? I only urge that we think first."

Maldunilis looked bewildered. "What is this? Nobody has told me," she complained.

"You didn't trouble to listen," Dahilis said in scorn.

"I—I think—no, wait—" After Innilis had tried several times, her Sisters realized that she hoped to utter a word and indulged her. "That's...not fair to Maldunilis. Did anybody ever seek her out and ask what she thought? I've no real understanding of it myself. I don't. Gratillonius wants us to raise a tempest...against some barbarians who aren't our enemies...Well, why?" She sank back in confusion. Vindilis gave her hand a reassuring clasp.

The man saw that matters were getting away from him. He cleared his throat. "It may be best to lay everything out in plain sight, no matter how much you already know," he said. "Forsquilis, will you explain what you have discovered?"

The seeress nodded. All eyes turned her way. Though she remained seated, it was as if she had stood up, tall and prophetic.

"You remember Gratillonius asked me to make a Sending, widely about," she told them. "The Empire is at war with itself. Our fleet is off to keep western Armorica at peace. But might barbarians, then, take the chance to strike at Ys? Or might a Roman faction? We needed forewarning.

"With your consent, I agreed. My spirit flew forth over land and sea, to look and listen. What it found, I reported to him but not erenow to every one of you. Hark ye."

The centurion was still unsure what truth lay in her. He believed her sincere; but lunatics as well as charlatans infested the world. Nevertheless he had gotten his glimpses of the unexplainable; and his duty was to use every possible weapon for Rome. After sleepless nights, he had decided to try this.

If Forsquilis could really send her ghost abroad and understand what it heard, no matter in what language, then it might well be that the Gallicenae had those other powers they claimed.

She was so calm about it! "There are no plans against Ys. The Armorican Romans mean to stay quiet. Some resent our show of naval strength, regardless of its being made as a polite hint rather than a threat. More of them, though, find in it a godsend, the very excuse they longed for to avoid the risk of taking sides; and they have prevailed on the rest. Barbarians are astir along the denuded eastern frontiers, but that is remote from us.

"It is in Hivernia that I found fresh grief being prepared for the West. A chieftain—a king, a great king, the master behind last year's attack on Britannia—means to take advantage of civil war in the Empire and launch an onslaught up the mouth of the Liger—very soon."

She ceased. Stillness descended while each priestess withdrew into herself.

Then: "Oh, wonderful!" Maldunilis piped. "The River Liger, 'tis well south of us, is't not? Won't the Scoti sail far around Ys?"

Forsquilis nodded. "They've abundant respect for us."

"'Tis a piratical raid, you told me, not an invasion," Lanarvilis said. "Is it then any concern of ours?"

"'Twill be a massive raid."

Gratillonius regained the word: "That's my fear. Portus Namnetum lies not far upstream, a vital harbor for this entire region. Because of the war, 'twill be poorly defended. If the barbarians take and sack it, as well they may, not only will shipping around Gallia Lugdunensis suffer. The whole Liger valley will lie open to later attacks." His forefinger tried to draw a map in the air. "Can you not see Armorica, Ys, cut off, and Rome suddenly bleeding from a huge gash of a wound? I ask you to defend the well-being of your children and grandchildren."

"Or that of Maximus?" Fennalis challenged. "You'd have us wreak harm on folk who wish us none."

"But who intend doing hideous damage elsewhere to those who never harmed *them*," Bodilis retorted.

Quinipilis nodded. "We need to kill them where we can as we need to kill foxes in a chickencoop, though the chickencoop happen to be our neighbors'."

Bodilis laughed. "You might have found a metaphor more dignified, dear. But I agree. I cannot believe the Gods of Ys would forbid a strategy of defending civilization itself."

"Under our King!" Dahilis shouted.

"The Nine alone cannot—" Lanarvilis began, and broke off. "Well, you said you would consult with Soren, Hannon, the leading Suffetes ere anything is decided."

"I am aware I must have their support," Gratillonius answered. "But I cannot speak meaningfully with them unless first I have yours."

Forsquilis shivered. "My Sending has felt cold winds blowing out of the future," she mumbled. Aloud: "The Gods have granted Ys a proven leader. Let him lead."

"We should...give him his chance...this time," Vindilis said slowly. A dark fire burned in her. Innilis clung to her hand.

Fennalis made a slight shrug. "'Twould be foolish of me to cross my whole Sisterhood. Very well. You may be right."

"Pray somebody tell me what 'tis we're to do!" Maldunilis begged.

Gratillonius gave her, and all of them, his reply.

~ 2 ~

An eerie thing happened as Niall maqq Echach was leaving Ériu.

His warriors were gathered where Boand's River met the sea. Tents, which had settled over the hills like a flight of wild geese, were now struck. Grass would soon heal campsites, for the season was well on; it had taken a while after Beltene to finish work and trek here. Wagons and chariots stood ready to rumble home. Banners lifted above bright spearheads where men surrounded their tuathal kings. The currachs that would bear most of them were still beached, but several ships lay

149

anchored in the shallows. Everyone waited for the Temir King to board his.

Racket and brawling were silenced, clangor was hushed. Rain misted. The cool smells of it came from earth, growth, cattle, smoke out of wide-strewn shielings, the waters that beckoned ahead.

Niall strode forth. The grayness around could not subdue the saffron in his tunic, the woad in his kilt, the gold at his throat, the steel on his spear, least of all the locks that streamed from brow to shoulders. His left fist gripped a shield painted the color of fresh blood. Behind him came his son Breccan and his guardsmen, hardly less brilliant. Beside him on the right walked his chief poet Laidchenn maqq Barchedo, on the left his chief druid Nemain maqq Aedo.

His ship lay before him. She was a galley of the Saxon kind, clinker-built, open save for small decks fore and aft, seats and thole-pins for rowers along the bulwarks. Oars lay ready across the benches. Down the middle stretched mast, yardarm, and sail, bundled together on two low racks, not to be raised unless a following wind should arise. The stempost lifted proudly, carven and gilt, a Roman skull nailed on top. Black the hull was, rocking and tugging at its stone anchor, eager to be off to war. Cargo filled the bilge, supplies and battle gear laid down on planks.

Niall had come near enough to hear eddies rustle and chuckle, when the thing came to pass. Out of the gray rain flew a raven. It was the largest any man there had ever seen, its wings like twin midnights. Arrow-straight it glided, to land on the upper rim of Niall's shield and look into his face.

Heavily though that weight struck, the shield never wavered. Not for one step did the King falter. The point of the beak was an inch from the bridge of his nose and could in two pecks take out his eyes; but their blue looked straight into the jet behind that beak, the while he said low, "Hail and honor, if this be She Whom I think."

A gasp and a moan blew through the host. Breccan yelled and stumbled back before he mastered his terror. The guardsmen milled in confusion till their captain spoke a command and got them back at their lord's heels. Laidchenn raised the chiming rod that proclaimed him a poet, inviolable, before he went on along beside Niall. The knuckles were white where Nemain clutched his staff.

Niall stopped at the water's edge. "I promise You many slain," he said, "but this You know I have given and will give. Is there anything else that You are requiring?" The bird did not stir nor blink. "Is it that You have a word for me, darling? I listen. Ever have I listened, and when at last You call me, I will not be slow to come."

The grisly beak moved, touched him lightly on the forehead. Wings spread. The raven went aloft. Thrice it circled low above Breccan maqq Nélli. Then it flapped back up into unseen heaven.

Men were casting themselves to the ground, making signs against evil, vowing sacrifices. Niall and his company stood firm. He did shift the spear to the crook of his right arm, and laid that hand upon the shoulder of his son.

After a time Nemain said softly, "This is a wonder and an omen. I am thinking that that was the Mórrigu Herself."

"As Medb, She has...favored me," Niall answered. "I remember tales of how She has thus appeared to armies before a battle."

Breccan clenched his fists. "What happened to them afterward?" he cried. His voice broke in a squeak. At that, a blush drove the pallor from his face, like rage overwhelming fear.

"Why, some won the day and some fell," Laidchenn told him, "but always it was a battle from which fateful issue welled."

Niall regarded Breccan. "Her message was for you too," he said.

"Choosing him for undying fame," Laidchenn offered.

"Choosing him, at least," Nemain muttered into his beard.

Niall shook himself. "Enough of this. Quickly, now, before the lads give way to terror. Sing some heart back into them, poet!"

Laidchenn rang his chimes, took forth his harp, smote the strings. Men roused from their bewilderment when they saw and heard, for he commanded unseen dominions of his own, whence words came forth to blast, blight, or bless. The trained throat spoke from end to end of the hundreds:

"Well may it be that this means
Mighty ones at work,
Willing we all gain honor.
I invoke victory!"

Niall raised his spear on high. His call rolled out. "The Mórrigu is with us! Rejoice!"

The kings who were gathered saw their King run into the water. It sheeted white about his knees. One-handed, he grabbed the ship's rail and swung himself aboard. There he immediately seized a red cock which lay trussed in the prows. With his sword he cut those bonds, so that the bird fluttered and cawed wildly in his grasp. "Manandan maqq Leri, you will be granting us the passage of Your sea, that we may bring You glory!" He put the victim against the stempost. A sweep of his blade beheaded it. The death struggle laved the Roman skull with blood. "Onward!" he roared to his men.

A cheer lifted, ragged at first, but ever louder and deeper. Weapons flashed free. Standard bearers whipped their poles to and fro until banners were flying as if in a gale. Breccan shuddered in exaltation. Laidchenn and Nemain kissed him on the cheeks, then stood waving farewell as he embarked and the guards followed. Readymaking went swiftly. The anchor came up, the oars bit, the King's galley stood out to sea.

151

That was the signal for the rest to start. They swarmed. The fleet was on its way.

Even in this weather, that was a grand sight. The ships were not many, and aside from Niall's had no more crew than needful. They were meant mainly to carry home loot and captives. But the currachs were everywhere, lean and low, coursing like hounds around horses. Some of those leather hulls could hold only four or so warriors, but in others were better than a dozen. As they got away from land and met real waves, they no longer simply spider-walked; they danced, they skimmed, they soared. Chants of oarsmen went back and forth across unrestfulness, surf-sounds.

Those not at this work were busy getting things shipshape. By the time they were done, the salt was in their nostrils to whip their blood alive. They agreed that the raven had been a marvelous vision, a holy vision, foretelling slaughtered foes, plundered lands, and return to fame. Breccan was so rapt in dreams of it that Uail maqq Carbri, skippering the royal ship, relieved him of duty just to keep him out from underfoot.

Dim on the right, Ériu would be Niall's guide for the first few days. At eventide, whenever possible, his folk would camp ashore. Given their numbers, they need not fear attack by the Lagini, since it would be clear that they were peacefully passing by. However, wind, fog, seas, or rocks might sometimes force them to lie out overnight. After crossing the channel where it was narrowest, they would use Alba the same way—more or less; there was no sense in anything but a straight dash across the Sabrina firth, and safe campgrounds would be hard to find in Roman country.

At the southwestern tip of Dumnonia the men must either hope for a spell of fair weather or settle in and wait for it. Ahead of them would be days and nights on the open sea, as they steered clear of Armorica and its Ysan she-druids, then turned east for the Liger mouth. True it was that they could be rowing that whole while, watch and watch, or sailing if Manandan was kind. But they must see sky well enough to hold a course. Otherwise—"We might blunder our way to Tír innan Oac," Niall had laughed. "Likeliest, though, we'd only gladden the gulls and sharks, and they have not any great name for the returning of hospitality."

The plan was quite sound, he went on to say. Armorican fishermen regularly worked farther out than he proposed to go. Jutish traders and pirates regularly made trips as long, also beyond sight of land, between their homes and Alba. And had not his Milesian ancestors sailed the whole way up from Iberia?

The voyage met no worse trouble than kept men on their mettle— until the first night beyond Dumnonia, in the very Ocean.

Heaven was clear, the moon full, so that vessels need not keep dangerously close together to stay in sight of each other. This was twice good, because they had gotten the wind for which rowers longed and were under sail. It crooned low and not too cold, when you ran before it; waves whooshed and gently rumbled, gleams and silvery traces swirling over the obsidian of them; ships rocked, surged, talked to themselves in creak of timbers and tackle. Niall, who stood a lookout himself, had finished his turn and was about to go join the crew who slept nested together down the length of the hull. Muffled in a cloak, he took a moment of ease on the foredeck. Starboard, larboard, aft, his fleet came along like leaping dolphins. The eye sockets of the trophy skull gaped toward Rome.

Something caught his gaze. He turned his head upward. Broad wings slipped by. An eagle owl...at sea?

It swung away and vanished eastward. Niall said nothing to the other man, who had not seen. That night the King slept ill.

~ 3 ~

In the morning Eppillus took the legionaries out on Redonian Way to the far side of Point Vanis. The whole thirty-two were present. Gratillonius had relieved the honor guard of duty, observing that he would not be at the palace for a while. After his required stay at the Wood, he would be busy in and around Ys, and lodging in Dragon House so he could readily confer with officers of the armed forces.

The Romans tramped smartly off. It was a clear, calm day. Sunlight glared on their metal. A few fleece-ball clouds drifted overhead as lazily as bees droned about wildflower blossoms. On the promontory the grass was thick and intensely green, studded with shrubs and boulders. Under Northbridge, the sea churned and roared among rocks between the headland and the wall of Ys; but everywhere else it reached in sapphire brilliance, its calm broken only where it went white over reefs. Far and far away, a streak of darkness marked Sena. The pharos at the end of Cape Rach, beyond sky-striving Ys, seemed in its loneliness to be calling to the isle of the Nine.

Where Redonian Way bent east, Eppillus barked: "Halt! Fall out." He turned to face the men. "You've been wondering what this is for. Well, I didn't know myself till yesterday when the centurion told me. We're going to do a little drill, boys, a little war game. That's how come I ordered you each to bring a baton. Save your real swords. You might be needing 'em."

"Eh?" said Adminius. "D'you mean we're expecting an attack? Why, just last night, down in a 'ore'ouse, I was talking with a chap back from Condate Redonum, and 'e was telling 'ow it's all serene. Maximus is way off south by now, driving the opposition before 'im."

Eppillus squirted a jet between his front teeth, to spatter on a breast-high wall of dry-laid stone about ten feet long. A couple more were nearby. Already they looked as ancient as a beehive-shaped rock shelter for shepherds in the distance. "This wasn't built against no Roman troops," the deputy said. "What use in that? It's to protect archers and slingers from enemy coming up out o' the water. One thing you'll do today, my fine fellows, you'll learn and learn well where the lilies are."—as Romans called mantraps of the kind that Ysan laborers had dug for them. "Wouldn't want a stake up your arse, would you?"

"Saxons!" Budic exclaimed.

Cynan shook his head. "No such rovers anywhere near," he replied. "The fishers know. I was talking myself—with Maeloch; you remember Maeloch, Adminius—he and I've gotten to be pretty good friends—"

"As broody as you both are, I can see that," the man from Londinium said with a gap-toothed grin. "Wot d'you do, sit around arguing whether Lir or Nodens is 'arder ter please?"

"Silence!" Eppillus rasped. He planted his legs well apart, put hands on broad hips, and glowered at the troops. "Now listen close, you braying jackasses. I don't want to have to say this twice. Ask your stupid questions today. Later on, each one costs an hour's pack drill. Got me?

"Well, then. Maybe once in a while one or two o' you's come up for air out o' his beer and noticed how the centurion's got work started on land defenses. The city could stand off any barbarians that might land, sure; but he don't aim to *let* them land and go around scorching the countryside. That'd make a hungry winter for us, wouldn't it? Did any such thought ever stir in your dim little minds?"

Having captured their full attention, he relaxed his stance and lowered his tone. "Ah, the centurion's a deep one, he is. But I didn't understand how deep, myself, till yesterday, when he called me in. Brace yourselves, boys. This is uncanny.

"Somehow, he didn't say how, he knows there's a big fleet o' Scoti at sea. It's bound for the Liger mouth, to loot and lay waste that whole fine country. The garrisons there are stripped because o' the war. Gratillonius don't figure he can allow this, not at the back o' Maximus Augustus." He drew breath, hunched forward, dropped his voice close to a whisper. "Well, somehow, and believe me, I didn't ask how— somehow he knows a great storm's going to come out o' this clear blue sky, and blow the Scoti onto the rocks around Ys and drown them!"

Rocking back on his heels, thumbs hooked in belt, he let the men mumble their amazement, clutch their lucky charms, speak their hasty prayers. When he judged the moment right, he grinned and said:

"Easy, now. You've got nothing to be scared of, less'n you're a Scotian. After last year on the Wall, I don't suppose any o' us in the Second Augusta bear those headhunting devil-cats much love. Our job is to make sure o' them. You see, all their boats may not be wrecked. Some crews may make it ashore. If we let them go, we'll have a dangerous nuisance on our hands, or worse, for months to come. If we don't—if we cut 'em down as they straggle up from the water—why, not only will we be saving ourselves future trouble, we'll be doing Mother Rome a whopping big favor. Every Scotian we nail is one that won't ever go raiding again."

Cynan cleared his throat. "Question." Eppillus nodded. Cynan turned and pointed over Ys, toward Cape Rach. "I mentioned I've become friendly with a fisher captain. I've visited him and his family in that tiny village down under the southern cliffs. They don't call it Scot's Landing for nothing, deputy. It's the only good place to put in hereabouts, aside from Ys itself, and pirates have used it in the past."

"That was long ago, wasn't it?" Adminius protested.

"What matters," Cynan snapped, "is that Scoti still use it now and then. Not for hostilities, no. But small traders from Hivernia drop in to do business without paying Ysan duties. Or Scotic fishers blown off course come to refill their water casks."

"I know," Budic interposed. "They are from the south of Hivernia. Many are Christian. Father Eucherius was telling me about them."

Cynan sneered. "Is it impossible for a Christian to be a pirate? Besides, surely, if he's not a fool, the chief of this Scotic fleet that Gratillonius...foresees—surely he's provided himself with information about these waters and pilots who know them, even if he doesn't intend anything against Ys."

Adminius rubbed his chin. "M-m, you've a point there, chum."

Cynan's somber stare challenged Eppillus. "This is my question," he said. "Why are we being assigned here? Why not down at Scot's Landing?"

A smile relieved the heaviness of the deputy's features. "Ho, a damn good question, soldier. I'm going to tell the centurion you asked it. He's said he needs leaders from among us. You might make vinestaff someday."

Cynan did not return the smile, simply folded his arms and waited.

"Well," Eppillus explained, "the centurion knows what you do, and more. He's made ready. The fishers are a tough lot, nobody you'd care to meet in a brawl. Ysan marines will be on hand too, to help them hold Cape Rach. The centurion himself will stand by in town, at the head of a striking force which'll go wherever it's needed the most. But that leaves this place."

He pointed. What had once been a path, worn away by neglect and weather to a poor excuse for a trail, dropped down between brambles, over the edge of land and out of sight. "That goes to the ruins o' the Roman maritime station," he said. "Possible place for boats to put in. Maybe not likely, but possible. The centurion wants to cover all bets. He's decided to place a few men here, few but good. That's us, and you'd better measure up. We'll have Ysan sharpshooters with us, and we can send for reinforcements if we need them—like I told you, he'll be standing in reserve—though I hope we won't."

"With luck," said Adminius, "we won't get any custom."

Eppillus laughed. "Oh, I'd like some, not too big for us to handle by ourselves, but enough to look good when the centurion writes his report. Bonuses, promotions, and such, you know. I expect Maximus will be generous to them as deserve it. New-made Emperors always have been, I hear." He rubbed his hands. "Maybe extra acres for my bit of farm when I retire?"

Straightening: "All right! If there are no more questions, let's get cracking."

~ 4 ~

No barge of state took the Gallicenae out to Sena. That would have been too dangerous—after dark, when few sailors dared come near the rocks around the island, and on a mission as dread as was theirs. None would do to navigate but Ferriers of the Dead.

Just past the full, the moon stood low above the cliffs. It threw a shuddery bridge over waters otherwise dark as heaven, closer to hand flecked by foam-gleams that were like fugitive stars. Quiet though air and sea were, whiteness snapped its teeth across the reefs strewn everywhere about. The stillness seemed to deepen the chill that always followed sunset, out away from land.

A pair of boats could carry eight women with sufficient rude dignity. Oars creaked, not loudly, almost the sole human sound. The smack *Osprey* went first. Two of her passengers sat silent in the bows near the lookout, two in the stern, where Captain Maeloch had the helm. He knew this passage so well that in fair weather he would merely need warning of something unexpected, a driftwood log or a piece off a wreck.

Dahilis had settled closest to him, legs curled beneath her on a cushion, at the larboard rail. She could not have been altogether lost in meditations, for from time to time she glanced up to where his beard jutted athwart the Bears. For his part, he stole some looks at her. Very fair she was with her cowl thrown back, hair aglow in the dimness. Above her reached those stars called the Maiden. Finally their glances chanced to meet, and turned aside in confusion and she smiled at herself while he scowled at himself.

Low and flat, the island drew nigh in sight. A small stone building with a squat tower made blackness behind a dock where a lantern glimmered red. The lookout finally did call soft words as he gestured, and Maeloch gave orders and put his helm accordingly. The boat thudded against rope bumpers. The lookout sprang off with a line which he made fast to a bollard. Maeloch tossed him another line for the stern and lifted and secured the steering oar. Flamelight showed that it was old Quinipilis who had had today's Vigil and now stood waiting.

Dahilis rose. Maeloch offered his arm. "Let me help you, my Queen," he said softly.

"Thank you," she answered, which many of the wellborn would not have troubled to do.

He guided her over the deck, jumped to the wharf, and gave her support as she followed. No matter the unknown deed in which she was about to take part, impishness broke forth and she whispered, "That was needless. I'm no cripple. But I enjoyed it. I hope you did."

"My Queen—" For one of the few times in his life, he was taken aback. Hastily: "Um, 'tis not for me to do aught but obey here. However, best will be if ye ha' done ere moonset. The tide will've gotten tricky—nasty rips. But we'll abide your pleasure."

"I think not 'twill take very long, that which we go to," she replied, serious again. "Remember, you and every fisherman, sail not out tomorrow, nor till the King gives you leave."

"We'd no thought of that," he said, "after being told how all ye Nine will come back with us tonight."

Quinipilis beckoned. Dahilis went to join her Sisters. Slowly, in single file, they walked off. Harsh grass, gray under the moon, wet kelp, pools where strange small creatures scuttled, were the other signs of life upon Scna. But three seals followed along the shore till the trail went inland, then lay afloat as if awaiting the high priestesses' return.

At the Stones Quinipilis set her lantern down and lifted her arms. She led the women in their prayer to the Three and in the sacraments of salt and blood. They kindled no wood this time, for their doings were apart from the element of Earth. Rather, they sacrificed Fire to Air by raising the lantern hood and blowing on the flame till it burned furiously, then to Water by quenching the candle in a bowlful of brine. Hands joined, they danced solemnly around the menhirs while they chanted:

"Wind of the West, awaken! The wolf is again a-prowl.
The ravening reaver of sheepfolds has lifted his head to howl,
And the watchmen shudder in summer
    to hear those wintry sounds.
Wind of the West, awaken! Unleash now on him your hounds.

"Calling on Lir, we loose you to harry our enemy
That dared to depart from the heathlands
    and hunt upon His sea,
And His waves shall answer your whistle,
    and come to course the beast
Wildly through brakes of spindrift, relentlessly to the East.

"Calling on Lord Taranis, the Guard of the city wall,
We order up horror and havoc, lest what is worse befall,
And we lend your hand His hammer
    where storm-flung squadrons go
Onto the waiting skerries, that heavy may be the blow.

157

"Calling on Belisama. Our Lady of Life and Death,
Whose kisses put warmth in the newborn
    and stop the old man's breath,
And Whose stars betoken Her peace
    in the dawn and the sunset skies,
Doom will we deal to sea wolves. O Wind of the West, arise!"

XV

~ 1 ~

On his second and third nights at sea, Niall again glimpsed the owl. It came out of the eastern darkness, swung silently above the Roman skull, turned back and vanished in empty distances. Other men saw it too, and muttered of it to comrades who had not. Before fear could spread through his fleet, the King commandeered a currach and had himself rowed to the nearer vessels. "It is nothing to frighten us at all, at all," he declared to them. "No natural bird, surely; but it's done us no harm, has it, now? Maybe a poor wandering ghost, such as we've charms against. Maybe a scout for the witches of Ys, but if so, it's telling them we mean no harm to their country. You'd not be letting a single fowl scare you, would you, my darlings?"

The bold beauty of him, as he stood spear in hand and seven-colored cloak about his wide shoulders, breathed courage into everyone. What further thoughts he had, he kept to himself.

It had been easy to get about thus on the water, for the airs had turned crank, foul when any whatsoever blew, and craft crawled forward on oars. Everywhere stretched Ocean, barely rocking beneath a cloudless sky, and sunblaze blistered fair skins. Niall could only guess where he was. However, he said, one more day must certainly put them well south of the peninsula, after which they could seek land. There they would get their bearings and, hugging the shore, proceed to the Liger mouth.

But on the night before this change of course—the third night, some hours after the owl had passed by—clouds began piling up in the west. Like black mountains they were, and ever more tall they grew, while stronger and stronger became the wind that skirled from them. By dawn it was a full storm.

No man saw that sunrise. There was naught but a faint lightening of what had been utter murk. Heaven was hidden. Wrack flew beneath like the smoke of burning houses. Monstrous were the waves, towering over hulls as they rushed and rumbled by, their backs white with foam, the hollows of them shading from green on top to abyssal black in the troughs. Their crests blew away in blinding froth. Wind filled the world. It struck fangs of cold into the bones of men, it lashed them with bitter scud, it grabbed their garments and sought to drag them leeward to their drowning. Often a burst of rain and great hailstones flew down upon it and streaked across the fury round about.

Niall's folk could do naught save hold their galley head on to the seas. Those who were not at the oars were bailing—buckets, cups, helmets, boots, whatever might keep the water a-slosh no higher than their ankles. The ship pitched, bow down till the stempost flailed amidst spume, bow up and a flood of tears from the eye sockets of the skull. Timbers groaned in anguish. Otherwise the warriors were helpless, driven before the tempest toward wherever it would have them.

Niall went back and forth, balancing himself against the surging as a lynx would. Labor was gess for him, the King; his part was harder, to keep heart in his followers. "Good lads, brave lads, it's fine you are doing. Sure and Manandan is proud of you. And what a tale you'll have to tell by your hearthfires!"

But once when he was aft, he let himself falter. Nobody was in earshot, in this tumult, besides Uail maqq Carbri at the helm, and he a close friend and indomitable. His back to the blast, Niall peered right and left. He made out a few currachs, riding better than the galley but no more able to hold a course. The rest of the fleet was lost to sight in gray chaos, scattered, perhaps much of it already broken and the crews sunk. His shoulders slumped. "I wonder if we should give Manandan a man, that He soften his anger at us," he croaked.

Uail, the old mariner, shook his head. "We should not," he answered through the racket, "for I am thinking this is no work of His, but of Lir, His father. And Lir is the truly terrible— no handsome charioteer but a Force that will not be swerved by anything in human gift."

Niall shuddered. "Who raised Him?"

Uail shrugged, squinted into the storm, devoted himself to his tiller.

Niall started forward again, bench to bench. His son Breccan was among those bailing. Without the brawn to row, bare-legged under a kilt, the prince kept on somehow when grown men had crumpled up, worn out and numbed by the cold. He looked aloft at the King. His golden hair was plastered to his cheeks, as sodden as the shirt that clung to his lanky frame, and his eyes seemed enormous, dark-shadowed by weariness, in the face that was his mother's. The rhythm of his pail checked. He flashed a grin and a thumb-sign of defiance at his father, before he bent back to his task and sent another load of water over the side.

"Medb with us!" Niall shouted. "I did well to bring you!" After that he was cheerful—

—until the first white spurtings and bestial growls told how the fleet had drifted in among reefs.

Uail bawled orders which the roars of Niall passed onward against the wind. Regardless of the danger of getting swamped, the danger of tossing about was worse. Oars churned. Many a wave dropped away from a blade, hissing in mockery, and the stroke smote air. Yet the ship did get turned around. She could not fight her way west, but she could wallow along under some measure of control, claw off the rocks that surrounded her, seek to keep alive.

Save when rainsqualls whooped by, the skies had paled somewhat and Niall could see farther than erstwhile, through a weird brass-yellow light. The gale had slackened just a bit too, so that there was less spindrift to whip his eyes. Yet whistling and bellowing and deep sucking noises filled his ears while the seas ran even heavier. He witnessed currach after currach dashed against a skerry and its ribs smashed to splinters. Men would tumble out of the wreckage, flop for a ghastly moment, and go under, unless the surf rolled their bodies onto a ridge. Flotsam from a second galley, sundered, her crew and cargo spilled, went swinging past. At the edge of vision he spied a low-lying duskiness which he knew from mariners' accounts was the island Sena.

More craft were getting through than lost. Let them understand the King was too, and rally after they had passed these shoals! Niall fetched men from the bailers, Breccan among them, and had them step and secure the mast. That was long and perilous toil. Once the pole fell, caught a man's arm against the rail, made mush and shards of it. He swooned from the pain. Cooly, Breccan cut a strip of clothing and bound the hurt lest he bleed to death. Meanwhile his fellows got the mast in place. Raising sail would have been madness, but the King's banner fluttered aloft, color streamed in the spray, a hoarse cheer lifted through the hull.

Though the sun remained withdrawn, Niall reckoned the time as late afternoon.

Standing lookout in the bows, he was the first to make out the shadow ahead. It grew as the stormclouds had done, rising, solidfying, until ruddy cliffs and the turmoil at their feet were unmistakable. The mainland.

Chill struck Niall in the breast. Then wrath leaped on high. He raised a fist. "I see. It is you yonder who have done this to us," he said between clenched teeth. "Why, why, why?

"Well, you shall mourn for it."

Wind continued to slacken, clouds to thin, the range of eyesight to stretch. The seas were still enormous, impossible to go against, but at least men could work partly across them, could pick the general direction in which a vessel was to be forced landward. Niall saw what he supposed were all the survivors of his fleet, or most of them—less than half the grand host which had sailed from Ériu, battered, awash, the strength wrung out of their crews, but alive, alive.

He saw which way they were setting. If only he could yell across the waters! His flag was a forlorn signal which few would likely fathom.

He could merely do what seemed best, or least bad. Niall moved aft. Amidships, he squatted, tapped Breccan on the shoulder, and said to the dear face: "Lay off that. Tell everybody to stop, take a rest, try to get warm. I think soon we'll be fighting."

"Oh, father!" It was a joy to see the joy that flamed in the youth. Breccan caught Niall's hand between both his. Niall rumpled the wet hair and went on to Uail astern.

"You've a plan, master," said the steersman.

Niall nodded. "I wish I had a better one. It seems the witches of Ys have been working for our destruction. How likely would it else be that we were blown straight onto this deadly ground? Medb, come help us get revenge."

He swept a finger around. "Look," he said. "We cannot beat back west. Seamanship would have us bear as much north as we may, try to round Armorica and win to the Alban Channel. With her weight and draught, this ship is able. But wind and waves are opposed, and overwhelming to the currachs....Have we any more galleys left us? I see just the poor currachs, riding on top of the sea and thereby debarred from making more than a little way across it....One by one, they are bound for yonder headland."

"For Scot's Landing beneath it."

"I know. Remember how much I inquired before we left home."

"Since they are forced onto a lee shore, those with men aboard who know it pick the only safe spot. The rest follow."

"It is not safe," Niall said grimly. "I think Ysan fighters are waiting there to slay them as they debark."

"That could well be." Uail regarded his King. "You've a plan, master," he repeated.

"I do that. *We* can work north. Never would I willingly forsake men who've trusted me. Have you not told me of another landing beyond the city?"

"I have. It is on the far side of Point Vanis, as they call that part. The Romans had a station there, but Saxons destroyed it and nobody has used it since."

"We will. If the Ysans plotted this, as I do believe, then they expect that whoever came through the reefs alive will seek haven at Scot's Landing. There they'll stand prepared. Now our lads, however wearied, should give a good account of themselves. But I doubt they can force a passage to the heights and refuge in the hinterland. The Ysan aim must be to kill most and drive the rest back to the hungry waters. We, though—here we've a shipful of the finest warriors in Ériu. We'll dock at the old station, hurry overland around the city, strike the Ysans from behind, scatter them, and join our comrades. After that, the enemy should sit earthed behind his defenses till the weather clears and we can fare homeward."

"Homeward?... Well, it took Lir Himself to make Niall maqq Echach retreat. We'll bring back our honor if nothing else." Uail hesitated, even while he strained at the oar. "But what if the other approach is guarded also?"

Niall's head lifted haughty as his banner. "Why, we'll cut our way through."

"Row, you scuts!" Uail cried. "Stroke, stroke, stroke!"

Four currachs, which happened to be far enough north, managed to follow. Doubtless the foe was watching and would guess the intent; but given his need to man the southern harborage, could he stem *this* tide? The hope of rescue, vengeance, and glory swelled higher in Niall than ever did lust for a woman.

Passing the headland, where the pharos stood like a sinister phallus, he was almost unaware of the white fury of water churning between it and the city wall. This was his first sight of Ys. He caught his breath.

The rampart shot up sheer, a cliff itself, topped by crags that were turrets. The very smoothness of that height, the marshalling of battlements above, even the frieze of playful, colorful shapes aloft in the granite, made it more awesome than the ruggednesses which abutted on it. The gate was shut—barred and locked, Niall had heard—and the floats that opened it at low tide dashed back and forth, up and down, on waves that ramped and foamed. When one of those padded balls struck stone or metal-sheathed wood, a drum-boom rolled huge and hollow through the wind, with an iron rattle from the chains.

Behind the wall rose towers like frozen cataracts, rainbow-hued; and on the slopes beyond were terraces, gardens, gracious dwellings; and suddenly, briefly, Niall thought he saw why the Romans in Alba had given him such stubborn resistance.

He had his men to save. The galley drove onward.

~ 2 ~

Another cloudburst struck, fiercer and longer than any before. Rain slanted down in sheaves of spears, hail skittered off stones and made hoar the grass it had flattened; wind shrilled till a soldier's head rang in his casque. At last, as quickly as it had come, it went. The gale was dropping too. Through a brief rift in heaven, a sunbeam smote out of the west, from low above the waves, and shattered dazzlingly on them.

Eppillus trudged to the path and a little way through its mud and cascades, for a look below. When he saw, he stopped and whistled softly. Somehow during the squall, a ship of the Saxon kind and four boats had made fast at the ruins of the wharf. They were vomiting warriors.

"Son of a bitch," he muttered to himself. "More than we bargained for." Slipping and swearing, he climbed back up and trotted across to where his legionaries stood ranked. Native archers and slingers stared over their defensive walls, read his visage, and readied their weapons.

"If we wanted a fight, Mithras has been mighty generous," he rasped. "We can't hold the path against as many as are coming. Scoti are like goats anyway. Most o' them 'ud scramble around and take us from the rear. Budic, boy, hit leather." He jerked a thumb at a horse tethered nearby. "Go tell the centurion we got a hundred or worse bandits on our hands here and could use whatever reinforcements he can spare us."

The Coritanian snapped a salute, leaped to the saddle, and was off. To the rest, Eppillus continued: "What we'll do is deploy in a half circle beyond the barriers. I drilled you in the maneuver; now let me stir those pea soup memories o' yours. It breaks the line, but just the same, man for man you're better than any two unarmored barbarians. Besides, the idea is to let the lilies and the sharpshooters take some o' them first. I expect they'll get together after that and go hooting away inland. Whoever they've happened to point themselves at, stand firm. Everybody else watch me. When I swing my sword over my head, like this, you run to me, around any enemy. We'll take tight formation while he's busy with those first few of us and hit him wherever he looks ripest for it. Got me? All right, to your posts. Hang in there for Mother Rome, not to speak o' your flea-bitten necks."

He stumped to his place at the middle, directly opposite the trailhead. Though the wind was falling off, its chill bit through metal, wool, and flesh. Drenched, grass moved sluggishly under its flow. A second sunbeam pierced the tattered, flying gloom and lit wildfire over the wetness. He remembered such weather from his boyhood in Dobunnia—but there the countryside was tamed, neatly kept, graced with trees along the roads, and in the paddocks where cattle grazed red, farmsteads such as the one which waited for him—not bleak and open above a city where sorceries laired; and the storms came in honest wise, of themselves. Eppillus swore, spat, planted his flat feet firmer on the ground, and loosened blade in sheath.

The Scoti appeared. Leading them was a very tall man. His shield was blood-colored. The sea had not dimmed the brightness of his steel, garish clothes, beard, or the locks that streamed yellow from under a helmet. His billowing cloak half concealed a younker who bounded on his right. Behind him spilled his followers. Their weapons whirled, their yells resounded, thinned but sharpened by the wind.

Before drawing his own sword, Eppillus dropped hand to a pouch at his waist and squeezed it. The shape of the thunderstone within was comforting. "Sweat us out some luck, will you?" he said. "Mithras, Lord o' Battles, into Your keeping I give my soul. Come on, stone, I know you can do your job."

As he observed, his heart bounded for joy till he thought it must be making the hair on his chest quiver. The foe had forgotten even such schoolboy discipline as their sort had shown in Britannia. They swarmed forward any old way, howling at the wide-spaced Romans.

Bows twanged. Slings snapped. Barbarians lurched, stared and scrabbled at arrows in them, fell to earth and lay writhing while blood pumped forth. Skulls shattered in a gush of brains where lead smote. Beneath other men turf collpased, pits opened, their screams rose faintly from the stakes at the bottom whereon they were skewered. Why, this alone may panic them, Eppillus thought.

No. Their leader shouted. His sword flared aloft, a beacon. The wild men heard, and saw, and rallied to him. He has the magic, Eppillus thought. I've seen it before. The centurion has some, but this fellow got all there was to get.

The stripling loped ahead, probing for traps with a spear. In a loosely gathered pack, the Scoti came after. They were too fast for missiles to inflict many more casualties. Reaching the wall on their right, they overran it and butchered its Ysans in passing. The tall man stayed in their van. His sword flickered back and forth like lightning. Drops of blood dashed off it into the wind. He turned left and made for the center of the defense.

He's aiming straight at *me,* Eppillus realized. He knows what he's doing. It's like last year over again.

The deputy waved his blade on high. From the corners of his eyes he saw his men leave their posts and converge on him. Good soldiers, good grumbly roadpounders. But here came the Scoti.

Roman javelins flew. They stopped too few of those bastards.

Still ahead of his warriors, the tall man reached Eppillus. His blade whirred. The deputy's shield caught the blow. Its violence tore through hand and arm and shoulder to rattle his teeth. He shoved the boss forward. The Scoti buckler intercepted that. Eppillus brought the top rim of his shield upward, trying for the jaw. The tall man swayed easily aside. His sword swung underneath.

Eppillus felt the impact as something remote, not quite real. Abruptly his left knee gave way. He shifted weight to the right foot and stabbed. His point went into red-painted wood. The barbarian cut him across the forearm. His hand lost its grasp, he let go of his sword. His shield overbalanced him on the crippled left leg. As he fell, another blow took him in the neck.

Battle thundered over him. Armor or no, he felt ribs break. It didn't hurt, nor was the blood that ran out of his wounds anything but warm. He was afar, a boy, lying at ease in a meadow where honeybees buzzed. Dimly he heard shouts, clash of iron, thud and grunt and saw-edged shriek. He tried to think what it meant, and could not, and gave himself up to sleep in the great summer.

3

Those of the Scoti who put their currachs alongside Ghost Quay and sprang onto it made a mistake. Ysan marines stood there, full-armored, shield by shield in the Roman manner. From that fortress the laurel-leaf blades darted out. Archers and slingers on the path above sent a steady hail. Soon the close-packed stones were buried under corpses and entrails, while the water beneath foamed red.

Others among the incomers sought east of the wharf. They could beach their leather boats under the trail that led to Scot's Landing, though time was lacking to secure these and most soon drifted away. Meanwhile the crews must climb a steep and rocky slope to the path— where poised the sailors of Ys. That became a desperate battle.

Holding the high ground, the shellbacks finally prevailed. Such of the barbarians as survived withdrew to the water's edge, panting and snarling. A lull fell over the combat.

The wind was likewise dying down. Waves still ran gigantic, casting whiteness yards aloft where they burst on reefs and cliffs, but their ferocity was spending itself. The storm had done its work; now nature would fain rest.

Maeloch wiped his ax on the shirt of a dead foeman. Rising, he leaned on the weapon, drew long breaths, stared outward.

"What be ye thinking about so hard, skipper?" asked Usun at his side.

"I wondered what'll become of the enemy fallen," Maeloch answered.

Usun was surprised. "Why, I suppose the funeral barge'll take them out and sink them, same as with anybody else but a King."

"Aye. But after that, what? Will they knock on our doors call us to ferry *their* spirits off—and to where?"

Usun shivered, he who had lately filled edged metal with furiousness. "Gods, I hope not! They'd find scant welcome on Sena. Can we cast a spell to keep them down, d'ye suppose?"

"Not ye nor me, mate. Let's ask our wives to try. 'Tis the women that stand closest to death, like they do life."

~ 4 ~

Dahilis had never altered the house she inherited from her mother. To her its softly tinted pastoral frescoes had once been signs of love and peace, afterward of refuge, lately of joy. She did fill vases with flowers in season; and in her bedroom she had replaced an ivory image of maternal Belisama with a wooden one. It was crude, but it had been carved for her when she was a child by an adoring manservant.

In dimness scented by roses, she knelt before the niche, raised her hands, and begged:

"All-holiest, ward him. If he must go to the fight, ride before him, Wild Huntress. Keep him safe, Protectress. And if he is hurt—he is so brave, you know—make him whole again, Healer. For the sake of Your people. Who else is more wise and good? Oh, let him live many, many years. When time comes for the Sacrifice, may it be me who goes instead of him. Please."

Her voice dropped to a whisper. "But not ere—well, you know."

The last few days, while Gratillonius was too busy to visit her, she had been sick in the mornings; and for more than a month, she had had no courses. She could hardly wait to tell him.

~ 5 ~

The King's reserves were standing by at Warriors' House, with horses bridled and saddled just outside High Gate. Thus when Budic delivered his news they were on their way immediately.

Galloping up the road onto Point Vanis, they saw the Scoti swarming down. What was left of the legionaries, about two dozen, followed closely but no longer pressed the attack. Maybe if Eppillus had been in command—but he wasn't. The knowledge rammed into Gratillonius. Indeed an overwhelming force had landed here. It must have been more skillfully led than barbarians usually were, too. Plain to see was that, in spite of their losses, the Scoti had outflanked the Romans before those could dress ranks, killed several, and held the remainder off by rearguard action. Since they were not bound east toward safety but south toward Cape Rach, their intention must be to aid their fellows at Scot's Landing. If they took the Ysans there in the back, they might well clear that whole area and evacuate every raider who was alive.

"By the Bull," said Gratillonius, "it shall not be. Ghost of Eppillus, hear me." He cast reins over his horse's nose, a signal to the well-trained beast that it must not stray, and jumped to the ground. In their strange bright armor, his marines did likewise. They assumed formation and quick-marched to intercept the Scoti.

There was no mistaking the enemy chief, a tall, golden-haired man, like some pagan God of war. I'm going after him first, Gratillonius decided. Once we've taken him out, the rest will be dung to our pitchforks.

Now it was the Scoti who were outnumbered—and unarmored, fatigued, many among them already wounded. As the marines advanced, the legionaries did too, from behind. The chief shouted and beckoned. His followers rallied around, formed a primitive shield-wall, started chanting their death-songs. They would not perish easily.

Gratillonius at its center, the Ysan line made contact. Everything became delirium, as always, except that the marines and the legionaries worked in coordinated units. Gratillonius could see his target man over the heads of the others, but in the chaos that man had gotten elsewhere

166

and was hewing away at Romans. "Ha-a-a! Ha-a-a!" Clang and bang, tramp and stamp, thrust and parry, Gratillonius pushed inward.

A last, violent gust of wind went over the headland. A raven flew upon it.

Gratillonius was never sure afterward what had happened. He remembered a woman, titanic and hideous, lame, swarthy, sooty, a cast in her left eye, who wielded a sickle that mowed men like wheat. But that could not be right, could it? Surely the truth was just that somehow the Scoti battled their way through the onslaught, heaped casualties in windrows, won back to the trailhead and thence to the sea. Gratillonius had taken a blow on the head which, helmet or no, left him slightly stunned for a while. He must have suffered an illusion. That others had had the same was not uncommon in combat.

In the end, after they had done what they could for their own injured and cut the throats of whatever foes lay crippled, he and his troop stood at the brink, looking down. They saw the galley beating along the point on oars. The coracles trailed after. "That remnant is not in simple retreat," Gratillonius deemed. "They still aim to give reinforcement below Cape Rach. Well, we'll see about that."

He almost regretted the killing. If Rome had civilized Hivernia, long ago when that was possible, what soldiers for her its sons would be!

~ 6 ~

Hulls rolled, pitched, yawed, shuddered. Spray sheeted over the bows. Yet close in to land the seas were no longer too heavy to row against, with the currachs in the galley's pathbreaking wake. The reefs farther out took most of their rage. It would have been mortally perilous to venture there. Niall had another reason as well for staying near the cliffs. "The shortest way is the swiftest," he explained to Breccan. "The sooner we reach our people at the harbor, the fewer of them will die."

The boy hugged cloak around shoulders. Legs braced and hands clutching rail, they were standing together on the foredeck. Bailing was not immediately needful—a boon, when the crew were dwindled and so exhausted that turns taken on the benches were brief indeed. "Can we truly help them?" Breccan wondered.

"We can, if the Mórrigu be with us still." Awe tinged Niall's voice. He had seen the Mother of the Slain at work on the battlefield. "This game is not played out, darling. I think that not all the players are human." His gaze brooded over the waves. "What we'll do is engage the enemy yonder while those of our men ashore who've lost their boats—the which they'll have had no chance to make fast—come aboard. Thereafter we'll stand out, escorting what currachs are left. With more men, this ship can get about readily again. The currachs may want towlines from us to escape the maze of rocks we must thread; or if any get wrecked, we can try to rescue the crews."

"Will not the Ysans pursue? I've heard tell of their war fleet, and they know these waters as we do not."

"Those ships are elsewhere, my heart. Otherwise, they would have attacked us before ever we could make any landings. For the masters of Ys knew we were coming. It can have been none but their she-druids that caused us to be blown here." Niall's fist smote the rail. "May each be raped by a demon, and may the whelps he gets on them tear them apart in the birthing."

Breccan looked troubled. "Father, always you told me to honor a worthy foe. And they've been bonny fighters here. They have."

"They set on us with their magical tricks when we meant them no hurt whatsoever." Niall sighed. "Ah, but Ys is fair and wonderful. Let us escape, and I'll forgive the folk if not their rulers." A smile crossed his lips. "Why, someday I'd like to come back, in peace. Behold. Let your eyes revel."

They had rounded the point and were about to pass the city at a distance of several hundred yards. High and high the walls gleamed, and the towers beyond; it was as if the voyagers had truly crossed Ocean and come to Tír innan Óac. The very rowers stared and marveled as they toiled.

Breccan shaded his brow from the spray. "Father, something is different. See, there on top. The little sheds are gone, and—what *are* those things?"

"You've the eyesight of youth," Niall said. "Let me try— Cromb Cróche!" ripped from him. "Those are killing machines! Helm over, Uail! Get us away!"

The air had gone quiet and cold. Waves ran noisily, but not so much as to smother the deep drone and thud which sounded from either side of the sea gate. Boulders the size of half a man came flying, tumbling, arching over with a horrible deliberation. Six-foot shafts, their iron heads murderously barbed, flew straight between them.

A splash erupted alongside. The galley rolled on her beam ends. Aft, Niall saw a direct hit on a currach. And it was no longer there, merely bits of it afloat, and two men who threshed about for a small span until they went under.

"Row!" Niall bellowed. "Pull out of range before they target us!"

Two bolts smote the larboard planks. Their points protruded into the hull. Their shafts dragged, waggled, got in the way of oars. Another pierced a currach, which filled and drifted useless. Men of the third boat drew close and tried to save those who clung to the wreckage. A ballista stone sank it.

"We cannot help," Niall groaned. "We'd only die ourselves." Nor did any chance remain of giving aid at Scot's Landing. The galley must now get so far from Ys that her crew would have all they could do to

168

keep her off the skerries. By the time she could labor around to the south shore that battle would be over.

"Manandan, I offer You a bull, white with red ears and mighty horns, for every lad of mine who comes home," Niall cried. Surely some could win back to such vessels as had not floated away, and thereupon ride it out, maintain sea room, finally steer for Ériu. Oh, let it be so!

Niall drew sword and shook it at the city. A sunset ray broke through clouds to glimmer along the iron, and to make brilliant the armor of the Ysan artillerymen. Tears mingled with salt water beneath the eyes of the King.

"Father, don't weep," Breccan said. "We did well—"

A bolt took him in the stomach, cast him down into the bilge, and pinned him there. His blood spurted forth. For a moment he struggled, flailing arms and legs, like an impaled beetle. He choked off a scream. Then he mastered himself and forced a smile.

Niall reached him, knelt, and tried to pull the bolt free. It was driven in too hard for even his strength. Useless, anyway. Breccan was sped. "Father," he gasped, "was I worthy?"

"You were that, you were, you were." Niall hugged him and, again and again, kissed the face that was like Ethniu's.

Soon Breccan lay quiet, save that the ship made limbs and head flop. His blood and shit sloshed about in the bilgewater.

Niall rose. He clambered back onto the foredeck. Three splashes in the waves, followed by no more, showed that he had drawn beyond reach.

He raised the sword he had dropped when Breccan was hit. He lifted it by the blade, in both hands, letting the edge cut his right palm till red flowed down the steel. None was in his countenance, which was as white as the eyeballs of his dead boy. Looking toward the beautiful city he said, low and evenly:

"Ys, I curse you. May the sea that you call yourself the queen of rob your King of what he loves the most and may what he loves afterward turn on him and rend him. May your sea then take yourself back to it, under the wrath of your Gods. And may I, O strange and terrible Gods, may I be he who brings this doom upon you. For my revenge I will pay whatever the price may be. It is spoken."

Trailed by the last of its currachs, the ship went in among the rocks. Three boats got away from Cape Rach to join them, but one was presently ripped open and the men drowned. Darkness fell. The survivors found anchorage of a sort. In the morning they started home.

XVI

~ 1 ~

Ys jubilated. That evening the Fire Fountain was kindled in the Forum. Its jets and cascades of flame would make luminous the next six nights, for which the Nine had promised fine weather—part of the celebrations, both solemn and sportive, that would give thanks for victory.

In certain houses happiness was absent. Among them were those which had lost a man in battle. Some other people had their different misgivings.

At sunrise Gratillonius left the palace. He did not seek the gate for its ceremonious unlocking; the waves were still running too high. Instead he went alone, in a hooded cloak, unrecognized by such few persons as were abroad this early, to the Forum. Oil to the fountain was turned off just as he came onto the plaza; a little smoke lent acridity to remnant mists.

Mounting the west stairs of the former temple of Mars, he heard the voice of Eucherius the Christian pastor quaver out of a bronze door left ajar. He frowned and halted. Evidently the daily Mass was not over yet. He recognized the blessing that followed Communion, having caught snatches of Christian liturgy throughout his life. A coughing spell interrupted it. Well, then, they'd soon be done in there. It would be bad manners to enter just now. Gratillonius composed himself.

Half a dozen worshippers came out. The catechumens, who did not number very many more, had already heard the part of the service that was permitted them and gone off. These, the baptized, were four women and two men, of humble station and getting along in years. They didn't notice him. When they had passed by, he went into the vestibule. At the inner door he looked beyond, into the sanctuary, where Eucherius and old deacon Prudentius were occupied. Softly, he hailed.

"Oh—the King!" The small gray man was astonished. They had been introduced, but as hastily as Gratillonius felt was halfway polite. He had had too much pressing business. Eucherius left Prudentius to put away the portable tabernacle of the Host which in Ys was little more than a wooden box in the usual turret shape. The chorepiscopus trotted forward to take his visitor by the forearm. "Dare I hope—?" His shy smile faded out. "No, I fear not. Not yet. Were you waiting outside? You would have been warmer in this room. It's open to everybody."

"I don't belong," Gratillonius answered. "But I thought I should give you a sign that I respect your faith."

The pastor sighed. "You wish I would respect yours. Well, I do. From everything I have heard, it is an upright creed. I am sorry—I should not be, but I am—that I may not concede you more than this."

"I've come on a matter touching yours."

"I can guess what. You are indeed a virtuous man. Let us go talk." Eucherius led the way through the corridor around the sanctuary to his quarters. There he offered bread, cheese, and water; he had nothing better. Gratillonius partook sparingly.

"Eight of my soldiers died yesterday," he said. "Seven were Christian. Their legion and funeral society are away off in Britannia. It behooves me as their commander to see that they get the kind of burial they wanted. When I inquired, I learned that no Christains are ever laid in Ysan soil."

Eucherius expressed sympathy before he nodded. "True. Any burials near the city have long been forbidden, since men decided the necropolis should spread over no more valuable land. Not that the faithful could well rest there. And pagan sea funerals—" He grimaced, as if in actual pain. "Ah, poor souls! Father, forgive them, for they know not what they do. They mean well, too, but—but even Queen Bodilis, who has been so benevolent to me— My son, you have at least seen the outer world. How can you partake in these gruesome rites?"

"It's not forbidden me as a Mithraist. The Lord Ahura-Mazda created many beings less than Him but greater than men. Besides, I don't agree the Ysan practices are bad. They sacrifice no humans, like the Germans." Gratillonius drew aside from the combat in the Wood. "Nor do they sanction those obscene things that get done in the name of Cybele." Irritation roughened his tone. "Enough of that. Graves are allowed inland. Some farmers and shepherds, who'd rather keep their dead close by, bury them on their own property. Why doesn't your church maintain a plot?"

"None has been granted us. We have nothing but this building. I doubt anybody would sell us an ell of ground to consecrate, supposing I could raise the money. They would be superstitiously afraid of offending their Gods."

"I see. What do you do, then?"

"There is a churchyard outside Audiarna, the Roman town at the southeast border. It's not too far, about a day's journey by wagon. I have an arrangement with a carter, and with my fellow minister yonder." Another fit of coughing racked the thin frame. Concerned, Gratillonius noticed how bloody was the sputum. Eucherius gave him a sad smile and murmured, "Forgive me. I should not detain you, who must have much else to do. Send one of your soldiers who is a brother in Christ, and between us he and I will take care of everything."

"Thank you." Gratillonius rose, hesitated, and added, "If you have any needs in future, ask. I don't think you'll find me unwilling to help."

"Save where it comes to propagating the Faith?" replied Eucherius gently. "Regardless, yours is a noble spirit. Do you mind if I pray to my God that He watch over you and someday enlighten you? As for— charitable works or the like—oh, Bodilis may have some ideas." His eyes burned fever-brilliant in the gloom. "Give her my love."

~ 2 ~

Soren Cartagi sent an urgent message to the royal palace. The King should promptly meet with the Nine, as well as with Lir Captain and the Speaker for Taranis. "No surprise," Gratillonius snapped. He set the hour of noon and dispatched the courier to inform everybody named. At the time, he escorted Dahilis to the basilica. Twenty-two legionaries followed them. Some limped, some displayed bandages. Eight more lay dead, and two were an honor guard on the last journey of their seven Christian comrades.

The King wore a robe of splendor; the Key hung out in sight on his breast. He had better cut a potent figure. When he had mounted the dais before the eidolons of the Triad and, having formally opened the session and heard the invocations, gave the Hammer over to his Attendant, he was much too aware that that man was not Eppillus. Recovering himself, he nodded gravely at the eleven faces that looked up into his.

"Well met, I trust," he said. "Though belike 'tis matters of import you would bring forth, let us strive to move them expeditiously. We all have many urgent duties, both secular and religious. The Gallicenae should resume their cycle of Vigils, while those in the city attend not only to the Gods, but to the hurt and the bereaved among our folk. My lords, your Great Houses and those who serve them have many calls on your attention in the wake of recent events. As for myself, I must see to public business that has gone neglected, as well as re-establishing communication with our navy and with Roman officials throughout Armorica."

Hannon Baltisi stirred his rawboned length on the bench. "Well may you do that last, O King," he growled, "as heavily as we've paid out for the benefit of Rome. Can you get us any reimbursal of the debt?"

Gratillonius had expected this. Lir Captain was devout to the point of fanaticism. In his days as a shipmaster, he said, he had often encountered the Dread of Lir. He had also seen, spreading through the Empire, a Christianity from which he awaited nothing but evil. "Methought we'd talked this out beforehand," Gratillonius replied mildly. "Ys dare not let barbarians lay waste the civilization which nurtures her also. We had the means to prevent it, and did, at remarkably small cost for the harvest we reaped."

"Nonetheless, cost! And never have I agreed that our action was necessary. While Ys remains true to Him, Lir will guard her. Why should we make enemies among tribes with which we could very profitably trade?"

"We may do that, now that we have chastened them. I know their kind; they respect naught but strength." Gratillonius drew breath. "If we are to discuss policy, we should have summoned the whole Council of Suffetes."

"Nay," rumbled Soren. "That's for later; and in honesty I must say I think you, lord King, are more nearly right. But you are wrong in other ways. You have forgotten the primal charge laid upon the King of Ys."

Gratillonius nodded. "He is the high priest and in a sense the Incarnation of Taranis. Aye. But you know that *this* King is also your prefect."

"And he is no Colconor!" Dahilis cried. Glances turned to her. She reddened, touched her lips, then squared shoulders and gave back a defiant stare.

Gratillonius smiled. "Thank you, my dear," he said. "Let me remind this honorable assembly, 'twas understood when first I mounted your throne that I'd have much on my hands, things too long ignored that must be set aright, new things for which there is an aching need. 'Twas with your consent that I devoted myself to them. What's happened since shows that you were wise to go along with me."

"That's past," Soren declared. "The time has come when you should in earnest assume your sacral duties."

"Gladly will I, insofar as Mithras allows."

Teeth flashed in Soren's beard. His burly form hunched forward. "Then why do you refuse to lead the thanksgiving sacrifice today?"

"I explained that to the priest who asked me yestereven." That had been one of those Suffete men who, otherwise occupied with their own everyday affairs, were initiated into certain mysteries and therefore authorized to conduct the rites of Taranis. The Speaker was among them, but tradition decreed that once he had taken that office he no longer acted as a flamen.

"He should have approached me earlier," Gratillonius reproved. "Then I would not have committed myself to be elsewhere at the time set. 'Tis a holy commitment which I cannot break, just as it appears the hour for your ceremony is now unchangeable. Well, my presence is not absolutely required. Choose a priest to take my place. As for me, surely the God will think Himself best served by a man who has first honored the claims of manhood."

"And what, pray, mean you by that?"

Here comes the crisis, Gratillonius thought. Beneath his robe he tautened himself like a soldier before battle. He kept his voice calm: "You may have noticed that Quintus Junius Eppillus, my deputy, is

173

not here. He fell in defending Ys. As do I, he worshipped Mithras. This day he shall have the burial he deserves."

Soren scowled. "The necropolis was closed lifetimes ago."

"He should not lie there in any case, nor be cast to the eels. Such is not the way of Mithras. I'll leave him on Point Vanis, looking toward the Britannia to which he longed home, but forever guarding this land."

A gasp went among the Gallicenae, save for Dahilis, who had already been told, and Bodilis, who was clearly perturbed. "Nay!" shrilled Vindilis. "Forbidden!"

"It is not," Gratillonius retorted. "That's grazing commons. A headstone will do no harm. Rather, 'twill recall his bravery on behalf of Ys."

Hannon bit off word after word: "It seems my lord King is misinformed. The necropolis was not closed merely because 'twas encroaching on land needed by the living. 'Twas draining down into the sea. Why think you we haul our sewage from pits, 'stead of letting cloacas open in the bay? Coruption of His waters is a mockery of Lir. Men at sea must beg His pardon ere they relieve themselves. Let Ocean have clean ashes of a fallen King; let His fish otherwise have clean, undecayed flesh."

"One grave high on a foreland will not—"

"The precedent!" Lanarvilis interrupted.

Quinipilis raised her staff and suggested, "Could you not lay your friend to rest inland, Gratillonius? I'm sure almost any landowner would allow, aye, believe 'twas lucky and pay honors ever afterward to the dead man."

That was the sticking point, precisely because it was reasonable. Gratillonius had picked the gravesite on impulse, out of sentiment, a wish to give good old Eppillus some small compensation for the farm he would never return to. Only later, when he explained to Dahilis why the priest had left with such a scandalized expression, did she remind him of the prohibition. He had quite forgotten it until then.

Now he could not compromise. His authority had been challenged at its foundation; if he failed to maintain it, he would soon fail as the prefect of Rome.

"I fear that would be to break a vow I made before my God," he stated. "Moreover, with due respect, 'twould be wrong if Eppillus—the memory of Eppillus—became a yokel godling. His soul has earned more. Nay, he shall lie in earth which his blood has hallowed. It will not be a precedent. I will proclaim that this memorial is unique, revering every man who ever gave his life for Ys."

He folded his arms just beneath the Key. "This is my will," he told them most quietly. "Bethink you, my ladies and lords." He made no gesture at the motionless iron rank of his men.

Not much further was said. Hannon himself had no more desire for a confrontation than did Gratillonius. One by one, the gathering mumbled assent.

Still, success was exhilarating, giddying. Gratillonius wanted to make them happy too, make them again his well-wishers. He raised his palms. "Let me give you the glad tidings," he said. "Queen Dahilis is with child."

A murmur, not really surprised, went among the women. Bodilis and Quinipilis, at her sides, embraced her.

Goodwill rushed over Gratillonius. Let bygones be bygones. If Colconor had been wronged, the swine wasn't worth avenging. Certainly that incident should no longer encumber the King in his politics and his daily relationships.

"Hear more, O Sisters of her," Gratillonius continued. "'Tis true I've perforce postponed many of my tasks; but as her time approaches and she is hampered, why, we shall all get to know each other better."

Vindilis flushed as if struck. Fennalis sneered. Quinipilis frowned and shook her head slightly. Bodilis bit her lip. Lanarvilis and Forsquilis stiffened. Maldunilis and Innilis seemed to accept, and Dahilis was radiant—she had felt so guilty about having him to herself when he was with any woman whatsoever—but he realized in some dismay that somehow he had said the wrong thing, and it could not very well be unsaid.

~ 3 ~

Sunset cast scarlet and gold over the half of heaven that reached above Ocean. Water glimmered and glowed beneath the cliffs. Sounds of surf came muted. A breeze ruffled the grass on Point Vanis. It came from the north, cooling the day's warmth, bearing a smell of salt and maybe, maybe, of fields in Britannia.

Six legionaries bore the freshly made coffin of Eppillus to the grave that had been dug and lowered it down. Then they saluted, wheeled, and marched back to the city in formation. As Christians, they could give no more honors to their officer. Four stayed behind: Gratillonius, Maclavius, and Verica, the Mithraists in their vexillation, together with Cynan, who had offered his help. Funerals were not forbidden to non-initiates; after all, wives, daughters, mothers, young sons, companions had farewells to make.

Not before had the believers held a service. That might have been disruptive, on the march and during the settling in and the preparations for war. They had contented themselves with private prayers. This evening they stood together in the presence of eternity.

The three rankers took the spades they had carried and filled the hole. At first clods fell on wood with a sound like footfalls; afterward the noise was muffled, until the low mound had been patted down to await wildflowers. A headstone would come later. Gratillonius had not yet decided what the epitaph should be. Name, position, unit, of course—and perhaps, the old Roman "STTL...*Sit tibi terra levis*.... May the earth lie light upon you."

175

Meanwhile he spoke the sacred words. Holding the grade of Persian within the faith, he could do that, though best would have been if Eppillus could have had his valediction from a Father. "—Since this man our comrade has fared from among us—"

The soul was surely bound for Paradise. How long its trek would be, no mortal could tell. Eppillus had talked of feasting with Mithras; the God must set a grand table! But seven gates stood on the road to the stars, each guarded by an angel who would only let the soul pass when it had undergone a further purification. To the Moon it would leave its vitality, to Mercurius its voracity, to Venus its carnality, to the Sun its intellectuality, to Mars its militancy, to Jupiter its pride, to Saturnus the last of its selfhood; thus would it attain the eighth heaven and the Light, to be forever One with Ahura-Mazda. Gratillonius found the thought of Eppillus trudging on that pilgrimage peculiarly lonely.

But farewell, farewell.

Colors died in the sky. It shaded from silvery in the west to royal blue in the east. The earliest stars trembled forth.

"Let us go back," said Gratillonius.

Cynan plucked at his sleeve. "Sir," he murmured, "may I have a word with you, apart?"

Surprised, the centurion looked into the somber young visage a heartbeat or two before he nodded. They went off to the trailhead above the cliff, up which the enemy had stormed. Peace breathed around them.

"What do you want, Cynan?" Gratillonius asked.

The Demetan stared outward. His hands wrestled each other. "Sir," he forced from himself, "would it be...possible...for me...to join in your rites...hereafter?"

"What? But you're a Christian."

"It means nothing to me," Cynan said hurriedly. "The centurion knows that. Else why would I be here? I offered to my tribal Gods, they seemed more real, but—I always wondered, and then the other day—" His tongue faltered.

"What happened?" Gratillonius prompted.

"You know!" Cynan exclaimed. "That ghastly giantess who entered the battle."

A prickling went through Gratillonius's skin. "What? Did you have that, that delusion?"

"Not me alone. I've talked with others."

"Well," said Gratillonius carefully, "I suppose the Scoti may by some kind of magic have called in some kind of creature to help them at the last. Little good did it do them."

Cynan clenched his fists and twisted about to face his leader. "Sir, that isn't it! I'm not afraid of Halfworld beings. But I saw...I saw an old, animal horror, and it lives inside me, inside everybody, and...and nothing can keep it from us but a God Who is not mad. Will you teach me about yours?"

Gratillonius forgot military discipline and hugged him.

Stepping back, his wits restored, the centurion said, "You'll certainly be welcome to worship with us if you'll accept the discipline. But just as a postulant, a Raven. If you do well, I have the power to raise you to an Occult. No more. Initiation into the true Mystery needs a Father."

"Someday I'll find one," Cynan replied ardently.

It burst upon Gratillonius like sunlight through clouds: Why not?

Votaries of Mithras were scattered through the Empire, their congregations isolated, often persecuted. There must be some in the cities and barracks of Armorica, not to speak of Britannia and the rest of Gallia. In Ys they could find tolerance, the Brotherhood free and open. Not that they could settle here as a general thing, but they could come for prayer, elevation, heartening upon earth, strength for the wayfaring afterward. Moreover, most being soldiers, such ties with them would help him draw together a defensive webwork for the whole province.

He could not found or lead a Mithraeum. That required a Father. But he could cherish the dream and work for its attainment.

~ 4 ~

With the round of the Vigils broken, Bodilis volunteered to be the first who started afresh. The order of rotation was not important. What mattered was to have a Sister on Sena—always, apart from special circumstances—in communion with Our Lady of the Sea and the souls whom She had taken unto Herself.

Bodilis thought she might be the best of the Nine to go forth after the gale, simply because of having both strength of body and an orientation toward natural philosophy: for she did not expect that the cycle could in fact be immediately resumed. She proved right.

Though morning seas rolled as gentle as rocks and riptides allowed, the barge of state that bore her could not make land. The wharf was gone, except for a few splintered bollards. It would have been dangerous for a vessel of any size to approach. Instead, a jollyboat carried the high priestess to shore. Its oarsmen waited while she walked to the building and, afterward, around the entire island.

That took a pair of hours, during which the sailors kept reverent silence. From time to time they glimpsed her, in a cloak of the blue that was Belisama's color, moving over rocks and treeless flats. Before them was the sight of the building and the damage it had suffered. It was a small, squared-off structure of dry-laid granite from which a tower jutted, on the east end of Sena. Billows dashing over the low ground had displaced several blocks at the bottom, visibly though not

177

enough to cause collapse. On the frontal western side, window glass was shattered, shutters torn off, the oaken door a-sag on its hinges.

The calm of this day became a chilling reminder of what had passed. Waves lapped, chuckled, glittered green, azure, white, streaked with dark tangles of kelp. A few seals cruised to and fro, close in to shore; it was as if their gazes too followed Bodilis. Gulls, guillemots, puffins, cormorants winged beneath cloudlessness. Through the air went a current of summer's oncoming warmth.

She returned and had the men bring her back to the barge. There she nimbly climbed the rope ladder to the deck and sought the captain. "We go home at once," she told him. "The place is unfit. It needs restoration."

The officer was bemused, a little shocked. "How, my lady?"

Bodilis smiled. "Be at ease. This is not the first time over the centuries that that has happened. The worst was in the era of Brennilis, when Ocean destroyed everything. It was among the warnings by the Gods against making the wall around Ys otherwise than according to Their will. These repairs ought take no more than some days. Furnishings and holy objects shall be replaced as well, likewise stocks of food and water—aye, in particular the cistern must be emptied, cleansed of salt, supplied with fresh sand and charcoal. The Stones abide as always. However, the hearthsite there would benefit from attention."

The captain tugged his beard. "But what of the House itself, my lady? Restoring yon blocks will be hard labor, impossible for women to do, if the Queen will pardon my saying so." A thought struck him. "Could the King's soldiers lend their skills? The Romans are the greatest engineers in the world."

"Nay. Even Brennilis's Romans were only permitted to draw up plans and give advice. Among men, none but husbands or sons of former vestals may ever betread this island above high-water mark, and then only when the necessity is beyond doubt and after they've been blessed in certain ancient rites. At that, once they are done, all we Nine must come out and reconsecrate everything. Gratillonius is a good man, but he would never be able to understand—" Bodilis broke off. "Come, unship the sweeps, let us begone."

XVII

~ 1 ~

After the victory celebrations, Ys settled back down into the ways of peace. Those did not mean idleness. Besides workaday tasks and repair of storm damage, there were preparations for the great midsummer festival. However, folk no longer tensed themselves against the morrow. The Scoti were broken, the Saxons would surely heed that lesson, the Romans of Armorica stayed quiescent, and—word trickled from the palace, to which couriers brought letters—Maximus was campaigning, successfully, in the South. A person dared again take a certain amount of ease.

Even Gratillonius did. Most of the time he kept busy. He must confer with the individual Suffetes, try to win their confidence, wrangle over ends and means, defense, outside relations, how to refill city coffers that Colconor had emptied, what reforms were desirable in a civil service ossified with age, countless petty details. Without compromising the status of King or prefect, he also tried to make the acquaintance of ordinary people, their needs and wants, strengths and failings.

Still, he could now take some recreation, set up a woodworking shop for himself, go riding, hunting, sailing. He could devote more attention than erstwhile to Dahilis. (As yet, aware that he had blunderingly given umbrage to his other wives, but unsure how to make amends, he met them only publicly, when at all. Dahilis too kept silence about the matter. He knew, and knew that she knew, that to some extent they were selfishly grasping what time remained to them before her fruitfulness was so far along that they had better sleep apart.) He and his soldiers, Mithraist and Christian, could properly observe that Sunday whose holiness they shared.

He could instruct Cynan in the Faith.

He received the Demetan in a room of the palace meant for private talks. On the upper floor, it was small and plain save for frescoes of pastoral scenes, narrow-windowed, sparsely furnished. The first day when Cynan came happened to be rainy, which cast a dimness as if this were indeed a crypt of the Mystery. A servant showed the visitor in, closing the door after him. Cynan snapped a salute. In Roman tunic and sandals, painstakingly barbered and scrubbed, he could not altogether hide surprise at sight of his chief.

"Greeting," said Gratillonius from his chair. "At ease. What's the matter?"

"The centurion is...very kind," replied the newcomer huskily.

Gratillonius studied the darkly handsome face, the muscular body, the hillman beneath the civilized shell, before he murmured, "At ease, I said. Outside this room we are legionary and officer. But here—the first thing for you to learn is that in Mithras are no worldly ranks. No high or low, rich or poor, free or slave." He smiled. "So what's bothering you?"

Trembling, Cynan blurted: "You aren't like before, sir! I didn't really see it till now, but you aren't."

Gratillonius considered. He wore Ysan shirt, jacket, and breeches, as he usually did except when overseeing his troops. Though close-cropped, auburn mustache and beard had reached their full growth. As yet his hair was too short to draw into a horsetail, but it fell beneath his earlobes and was confined by a fillet. Aye, he found himself thinking in Ysan, the lad may well wonder what sorcery beyond the sea gate has flowed its tide over me.

"I have to be King oftener than prefect, remember," he said in his plainest Latin. "Remember also, Mithras doesn't care about your outside. Only your inside, your spirit, counts. Do sit down." When his guest had obeyed, he himself poured wine for them both. "Let's talk."

He couldn't lighten the mood. Cynan wasn't that sort; and, of course, this wasn't that kind of occasion. Gratillonius could, though, seek to penetrate the bashfulness—and the fierce pridefulness—that stood between them. "Before we start," he went on, "we should know each other better. I picked you to come along, back in Isca, because I'd seen you fight like a demon beyond the Wall. But why did you volunteer?"

Cynan stiffened. "It was an adventure, sir."

"Can you look me in the eye and smile when you say that? Listen, son, if you're afraid to be honest, Mithras will not make you welcome. And if I punished you for your honesty, He would disown me."

Blood pulsed up into the young countenance. A fist clenched. "Very well, sir!" the Demetan cried. "I wanted to travel and fight, not do drill at headquarters. But I did not want to travel with Maximus and fight Romans. My home village was near the coast. I came back from hunting in the glens and found the Scoti had been there. What they hadn't plundered, they'd burnt. They killed the men, my father, my older brother. They gang-raped my mother. They bore off my young brother and two sisters for slaves. I swore I'd live for revenge. I lied about my age and my Gods, to join the army. I gloried when we cut down the vermin in the North, and again here—oh, sir, you were Vengeance itself! Then that troll-thing on the battlefield—and afterward, when you gave Eppillus his honor—*That's* why I've come to your God!" He covered his face and wept, long, coughing sobs: no Roman now, a Celt.

Gratillonius let him have it out, and comforted and calmed him, and could finally begin:

"I'm not the best by a long shot to explain the Faith. A lot I don't understand myself. I only rate as Persian, the fourth grade. But maybe it's good for you to hear about it first in simple soldier lingo.

"Persian...The Faith came from Persia, Rome's old enemy, but a worthy foe. Often a man learns more from an enemy than a friend. And, of course, it wasn't always war; and others than Persians were believers; and as the ideas moved into the Empire, Greek thinking, and later on Roman, worked them over.

"Before and above all, forever, the One from which Everything comes—" He checked himself. The concept of Time—Aeon, Chronos, Saturnus, the Source, the Fountainhead—was for the higher ranks, those allowed into the sanctuary. You didn't pray to the Ultimate anyway.

"Above all Gods," Gratillonius said, "is Ahura-Mazda. He's also called Ormazd, Jupiter, Zeus, many names. Those don't mean much; He Is, the High, the Ever-Good." He found himself slipping into the words of the Lion from whom he had received instruction. Well, they were doubtless better than any he could put together. "Below all Gods is Ahriman, Evil, Chaos, maker of hell and devils and misery. The story of the world is the story of the war between Ahura-Mazda and Ahriman. So is the story of your soul, lad. They war for it the same as They do for the whole of Creation. But you don't have to stand by helpless. You can be a soldier yourself.

"Then your Commander is Unconquered Mithras.

"He is the God of light, truth, justice, virtue. Because these come into being, suffer, and die—like mortals, or like the sun that rises and sets and rises again—you'll see Mithras shown with two torchbearers, the Dadophori. One torch is upright and burning, the other is turned down and going out.

"Our Lord Mithras was born from a rock, which some say was a cosmic egg. It was on the banks of a river, underneath a sacred tree. Only shepherds witnessed this, and came to adore Him and bring offerings. But Mithras was naked and hungry in the cold winds. From the fig tree He plucked fruit and from its leaves He made Himself garments. Then His strength came to Him."

Gratillonius paused before saying slowly: "This happened before there was life on earth. I don't understand that myself. But why should a man be able to understand the Eternal?

"The first battle of Mithras was against the Sun. He overcame His noble foe, and received the crown of glory from Him. Thereafter He raised up the Sun again and They swore friendship.

"His second battle was against the Bull, the first of living creatures that Ahura-Mazda made. He seized It by the horns and rode It, no matter how much He was hurt, till It was worn out and He could drag It to His cave. It escaped, and the Sun sent the Raven as a messenger, bidding Mithras kill the Bull. Against His will, He did this. He and His dog tracked It back to the cave where It had returned, and He took It by the nostrils with one hand while with the other hand He plunged His knife into Its throat.

"Then from Its body sprang life upon earth, from Its blood the wine of the Mystery. Ahriman sent his evil creatures to destroy this life, but in vain. A great flood covered the world. One man, out of the humans alive in those days—one man foresaw it in a vision, and built an ark that saved his family and some of every kind of being. Afterward Ahriman set the world afire, but this too it survived, thanks to the labors of the Lord Mithras.

"Now His work on earth was done. With the Sun and His other companions, He celebrated a last supper before He ascended to Heaven.

181

Ocean tried to drown Him on His way, in vain. He is among the immortals.

"But He's still our Commander in the war against evil, that shall end on the Final Day when Ahriman is destroyed, and the righteous are resurrected, and peace reigns eternal."

For a while was silence. Unaccustomed to speaking at such length, Gratillonius had gone hoarse. He didn't think it would be impious to take a long drink of wine, not much watered.

"I have heard a little of this before," Cynan said low. "But you make it...real."

"If so, I'm glad," Gratillonius answered, "though it's no credit to me. Thank the Spirit. You think about this. Ask questions. I'll have more to tell, the next few times we meet. After that, if you still feel you want to join—and mind you, if you don't, I won't hold that against you, because every man has to find his own way—if you still do, I'll initiate you as best I can."

~ 2 ~

Dahilis wished to visit the nymphaeum and seek a special blessing upon her unborn child. To her delight, Gratillonius said he would come along. The distance was less than ten miles, so no servants or provisions were needed, other than a basket of food for a light midday meal. He did take three of his legionaries, explaining that, while there was nothing to fear, they maintained the royal dignity. Dahilis laughed and clapped her hands in glee. She had long hoped to know the Romans better, her husband's trusty men. These were Maclavius, Verica, and Cynan.

On horseback, the five of them went out High Gate. Beyond the smithies, tanneries, and other clangorous or malodorous industries forbidden within town, they turned off paved Aquilonian Way onto a path running due east along the middle of the valley, beside the canal. This cut through the southern edge of the Wood of the King. Though the day was glorious and the leafage all green and gold, Dahilis shivered in the shadows of the oaks and reached to take Gratillonius's hand. She recovered her merriment as soon as they were again in the open.

"Isn't it beautiful?" she exclaimed. "Aren't the Three good and kind, that They made this for us?" She gestured around. Beneath a vault of light where a few clouds wandered and many wings beat, the valley sides lifted intensely verdant. Pastures were starred with wildflowers. Orchards stood rich near farmhouses thatched, earth-walled, but snug and neatly whitewashed. Groves and gardens framed mansions—red-tiled, tawny-plastered, glass agleam—on the heights. Dwellings of lesser size and luxury but in the same pattern, wide-strewn over the slopes, radiated a sense of well-being. A breeze lulled warm, bearing odors of blossom, growth, soil. Canal water glittered and chuckled above its bed of fitted stones, between its narrow banks where moss made softness; frogs leaped, dragonflies hovered lightning-blue. High and high overhead, a lark caroled.

Gratillonius smiled on her. "No doubt," he answered, "but it suffers by comparison with you." Indeed she was lovely. Her head was bare and she had not piled her hair in the elaborate coiffure of a noblewoman but let it flow free, like a maiden's or a commoner bride's, past the pert features and down her back, as yellow as the loosestrife nodding in the grass. A gown of silver-worked samite was belted close around a slenderness which the life within had, thus far, not changed. Skirts hiked up for riding astride, her legs might have been turned on the lathe of a master craftsman who was also a Praxiteles, save that they seemed about to start dancing. How tiny were her sandals!

"Oh, my," she laughed, "you're becoming quite the courtier, darling. Beware lest you lose your proper Roman bluntness."

The path climbed leisurely, leaving homes behind and passing through rail-fenced meadows where cattle grazed. Ysan territory held scant plowland; the city got its grain from the Osismii. An occasional boy or girl dashed to gape at and hail these remarkable passersby, the big man in his fine tunic and breeches, the three in flashing metal, the fair lady. Dogs clamored. Dahilis waved and warbled greetings.

They stopped in a shady place to eat and rest. Dahilis served forth the bread, butter, pickled fish, hard-boiled eggs, wine. Cynan shook his head, walked off, stood gazing into the distance.

"Isn't he well?" the Queen asked, concerned.

"He practices certain austerities before a religious rite," Gratillonius replied.

"Oh." She shied from the subject. Verica and Maclavius were nothing loth to entertain her. Seeing that she winced at mention of war, they talked instead about their Brittanic homelands. Her eyes grew still more huge. "I do hope we can go there someday, Gratillonius, beloved, you and I—to *your* country." The centurion refrained from saying how unlikely that was, or how risky and wretched.

The unguarded frontier was not far when path and canal bent north and wound steeply upward. The waterway became natural, a string of small, chiming falls and whirly pools. Forest grew thick, casting sunflecked duskiness, and the air turned cool. When at last he came forth and saw the Nymphaeum, which he had done just once before and then briefly, Gratillonius was almost startled.

This was no mere pergola. The grounds occupied a couple of acres, the nearly flat bottom of a hollow under the hilltops, open to the south. North, east, and west the terrain rose somewhat higher, slopes and crests covered with wildwood. On the east side the holy spring welled from a heap of boulders whereon stood a statue of the Mother in Her serenity, shaded by a giant linden. All the waters flowed together to make a broad, clear pond, whence issued the stream that fed the canal.

Swans floated upon it. Around it, and in a swathe leading to the building on the west side, a lawn reached silk-smooth, aglow in the afternoon light; peacocks walked there. The grass was bordered by flowerbeds, hedgerows, bowers, laid out with a sweet simplicity. The Nymphaeum itself was of wood, as befitted these surroundings, but on colonnaded classical lines, painted white. Modest in size, it was nonetheless large-windowed, airy, exquisite. A pair of cats, sacred to the Goddess, lay curled in the portico, while Her doves cooed above.

Here, said belief, the female spirits of nature came, to bathe on moonlit nights and flit frolicsome among the trees by day. Here too would stag-horned Cernunnos often come, drawn by their beauty, to this one place in the world where the forest God was not terrible; it was said that breezes at dawn and sunset were His lovesick sighs. No few wedding parties sought the Nymphaeum, and mothers-to-be like Dahilis, and folk weary of spirit, beseeching benison. Gratillonius's band dismounted, secured their horses, and approached in a reverence that was joyous.

Priestesses other than Queens, and descendants of Gallicenae serving their vestalhoods, occupied the house by turns. Seven, robed in plain blue and white, they came out while the newcomers went up the stairs. The girls among them gasped and squeaked as they recognized the King. The aged leader bade him a welcome grave but not awed. When Dahilis spoke her desire, the old one smiled and laid a gnarled hand on her shoulder. "Verily shall you have a blessing, child—at once, or as soon as you have rested from your journey if you need that." The leader looked at Gratillonius. "'Tis a solemnity not for men. Could you absent yourselves an hour or two? You may like to accompany your steeds to the guardhouse; that's a pleasant stroll in this weather, and the warders would be glad of a chat. Afterward you shall sup with us and spend the night. Aye, you may stay as long as you wish."

"I thank my lady," said Gratillonius. This was exactly what he had counted on. "Duty demands return to Ys tomorrow, but until then we gratefully accept the hospitality of the Goddess."

"Guide them, Sasai," directed the leader, took Dahilis's elbow, and led the Queen inside.

A girl of sixteen or seventeen advanced awkwardly and, mute, proceeded down the stairs. Gratillonius recalled her; she had been at the temple of Belisama when he came to ask a storm of the Nine. She was tall, heavy-hipped, thick-ankled. Her head was small, with stringy brown hair, thin lips, underslung chin, and too long a nose. When he drew alongside her, she reddened and cast her glance downward.

His men led the horses behind him on a woodland trail that began at the rear of the Nymphaeum. Quietness brooded. He wanted to be friendly. "Sasai, is that your name?" he asked the maiden.

"Aye, lord," she mumbled, always watching the ground.

184

"Who is your mother?"

"Morvanalis. She is dead."

Gratillonius swore at himself. Of course. He had met all the children of his wives. With an effort, he remembered who Morvanalis had been, the full sister of Fennalis, both born to Calloch and Ochtalis. As for the girl, judging by her age—"Your father was Hoel?"

"Aye, lord."

Silence stretched. He searched for words. Finally: "Are you happy, Sasai?"

"Aye, lord," said the monotone.

"I mean, well, do you think you will continue in service of the Goddess after you turn eighteen?"

"I don't know, lord."

Gratillonius sighed and gave up. The poor creature must be dull-witted as well as homely and ungainly. He doubted she could catch a husband or shift for herself. So let her take the vows of a minor priestess; Belisama would shelter her.

The walk was short to the guardhouse and its stable. A dozen marines were barracked there, in case of danger—not that misfortune had ever stricken these hallowed precincts or the wildest of men dared to violate their peace. The warders were indeed pleased to have company and broke out the mead. Gratillonius had already met some and convinced them that the new King could be a comradely sort. Romans and Ysans sat yarning longer than he had expected, until he must hurry back.

Dahilis sped down the lawn to hurl herself into his arms, never mind stateliness. "Oh, beloved, it was so wonderful, and the omens—the omens— She'll be like none ever before—*your* daughter!" She stood on tiptoe and crammed her lips against his.

—Supper with the women was simple but savory. Once grace had been said, talk became animated. Soon Verica and Maclavius were at their ease too. Cynan, fasting, had gone straight to the guestroom he would share with them.

At sundown the other three soldiers left the triclinium and went forth. The superior had given them permission to pray to Mithras, if they did it off the grounds. They found a glade where the last rays streamed level between boles. On the way back, despite piety, Gratillonius felt cheerful enough to be jocular: "Don't oversleep, boys."

Again Dahilis waited outside for him. "Shall we take a walk ere we retire?" she proposed. He was willing. Hand in hand they sauntered about through the dusk, under the early stars. No nymphs appeared, but she was amply sufficient.

In their own chamber she slipped off sandals and belt, pulled gown and undergarments over her head, let everything fall and reached toward him. A single lampflame cast glow on cheekbones, eyes, the dear vessel that was her belly. Elsewhere shadow caressed her. She smiled. "Why stand you there like that?" she breathed. "See you not how I want you?"

"Is it...seemly...here?"

"You marvelous fool!" she trilled. "Where is it more right to make love?"

When they did, he felt as though Belisama were truly present.

~ 3 ~

Gratillonius had told his dreams to wake him at dawn, and they obeyed. Windowpanes were gray; the room brimmed with murk, chill, and silence. He cold barely see Dahilis beside him. On the pillow, in its flood of tresses, her face looked like a child's. How long were those lashes. Babywise, she was curled up under the blanket. He rose as easily as he was able, but the leather webbing under the mattress creaked aloud.

Her eyes fluttered open. He stooped to kiss her. "Hush," he whispered. "I go to my sunrise prayers, and maybe afterward a jaunt in the woods. Sleep on." He had not told her his real intent, because he knew it hurt her to be reminded that his faith debarred her. If he did now, she would be too excited to rest, and that might not be so good for the unborn. She smiled and closed her eyes again.

He had clean garb in a bag, which he donned, but when he was shod and combed he took something additional and threw it over his arm. Soft-footed, he left the room and groped his way to a rear door. None of the priestesses or vestals was awake; their services were at noontide, full-moon midnight, and the heliacal rising of Venus. His men awaited him outside. They also wore white tunics, together with military cloaks against the cold. Wordless, they gave him the Roman salute and formed single file, Cynan last. Stars glimmered yet in the western heavens, but the east was lightening. Mists drifted over pond and turf. Dew laved sandaled feet. Only the clear ringing and clucking of water had voice.

The day before, scanning the heights, he had decided to go northeast. The trail was barely a trace, gloom loured between the trees, men rustled through underbrush and stumbled on roots, but the rivulet they followed sang and glistened for a guide. It took a while to find the sort of place for which Gratillonius had hoped, but then it was perfect, as if Mithras Himself had chosen it. The hillside broadened to form another hollow, like the one where the Nymphaeum stood save for being tiny. Issuing from a spring a little farther up, the stream ran bright, here a whole three feet wide and better than ankle-deep. Beech, hazel, thorn crowded around, night still in the depths among them but crowns silvery under the dawn. They did not grow too close for free movement. Instead, masses of convolvulus twined stems and lifted white chalices. Dew was brilliant on those leaves.

"We are come," said Gratillonius. "Let us prepare ourselves."

Following an invocation he gave, he was first to strip and wash himself in the purifying water. Maclavius and Verica went in next, then stood on either side of Cynan while the postulant did likewise. These three resumed their tunics, heedless of being wet and cold, but Gratillonius had donned a robe and Phrygian cap.

"Kneel," he said, laid hands on the head of the recruit, and asked for divine favor.

Radiance burst forth. The sun cleared the eastern treetops. Gratillonius, Maclavius, and Verica said the morning orison; Cynan stayed aside.

The Mithraist legionaries had brought flint, steel, tinder, dry wood, and an object which Gratillonius had had a smith make for him. As they, whose rank in the Mystery was Soldier, started and blew on the blaze, Gratillonius the Persian led Cynan through memorized responses. They rang firm into the quiet.

The bed of the fire was soon hot. Maclavius took the branding iron by its wooden handle and held it in the coals. "Kneel," ordered Gratillonius again, "and receive the Sign." Cynan obeyed. Gratillonius accepted the iron from Maclavius. Cynan watched unflinchingly. Verica came from behind to brace him by the shoulders. Gratillonius strode from the fire with the iron red in his right hand. His left brushed back a lock that had fallen over Cynan's brow. For an instant, looking down into those eyes, he recalled how he had slashed this face on shipboard. The weal was long gone. The brand of the Sun would never go, quite, though in time it would fade to as pale a mark as was on him and the other two men. Speaking the Word of Fire, he put the iron to the forehead. Breath hissed between Cynan's teeth, the sole token the Demetan gave. A roasting smell marred the air. Gratillonius withdrew the iron, gave it to Maclavius, and bent to help Cynan rise. "Come," he said. Together they went back to stand in the stream. Gratillonius scooped a handful of water and let it run over the angry red sigil. "Be welcome, Raven, to the Fellowship," he said. He embraced the new brother and kissed him on both cheeks. They returned to earth, wading through the convolvulus. "It is done," Gratillonius said.

A cry ripped across his awareness. Swinging about, the men saw Dahilis under the trees. Her hair was disheveled, her gown mud-stained. Tears coursed down her countenance.

"What are you doing?" Gratillonius roared in his shock, and heard Cynan snarl: "A woman, at this holy hour?"

"I couldn't sleep, I followed your tracks in the dew and went on upstream, I thought we— O-oh," she wailed, "oh, I'm sorry, I'm sorry, but 'tis dreadful what you've done. I dared not speak till now—" She lifted arms and gaze heavenward. "Belisama Mother, forgive them. They knew not what they did."

187

As ever in crisis, Gratillonius's mind leaped to action. He confronted the men. "She has not profaned the ceremony," he said in Latin with all the authority he could muster. "This is no Mithraeum, just a site that was suitable, open to anyone, and she did not interrupt. Mithras is satisfied. You be too." Inwardly, he could only hope he was truthful. He himself had not been instructed in the deepest lore of the Faith.

When he saw them glowering but calm, he went to stand before Dahilis. His arms longed to hold her close and dismiss her despair. Instead he must fold them and say levelly: "We have done no harm, no sacrilege. We held an initiation. That requires flowing water, and there is none in Ys." A sardonic part of him remembered that city Mithraeums commonly drew it from a tank. But of course there was no Mithraeum in Ys.

"Don't you...don't you *see*?" she stammered. "This stream—from Ahes—it flows to join Her most sacred water—and, and you, your male God—"

He decided that it would not be unwise to close his fingers gently on her forearms, look straight into the lapis lazuli eyes, and say, quite sincerely: "My dear, in the end all Gods go back to the One; and as for me, I am the high priest and avatar of Taranis, Her lover. If I have done wrong, on my head be it; but I deny that I have. Ask your Sisters. Meanwhile, fear not."

She gulped, shuddered, straightened. He wished he could console her. Abruptly her smile kindled, however tremulous. "Why, I am, am with you always, Grallon—Gratillonius, beloved," she said. "Cynan, I'm sorry if I...disturbed you...at a wonderful moment...and belike naught was profaned. And, here is the spring of Ahes, *my* nymph, my patroness. Surely she'll listen when I ask her to intercede with Belisama— Shall we be friends again, we five?"

The King thought in a leap of joy: With so high a heart, she may well fulfill the omen she spoke of, she may well bear us a daughter who'll be remembered when Brennilis herself is forgotten.

Dahilis looked about. "Why, see the convolvulus," she exclaimed as vivaciously as might be. "Is't not fair? Could you wait a little, kind sirs, while I gather some?" She became busy doing so. Her chatter went on: "'Tis medicinal, but we grow it not in the city or nearby, for 'tis apt to overrun gardens. My Sister Innilis has told me her supply's run short, for ever does she go about as a healer among the poor in Ys. Belisama's Cup, they call this flower. Know you why? The story is that once, long, long ago, a wagon was hopelessly mired. She came by in the guise of a mortal and told the carter She would help him free it. He laughed and asked what payment She wanted. 'I give My gifts for love,' She answered, 'but now I thirst. Would you give me some of your wine?' Said he, 'Well, I'd not grudge a woman that, but alas, I've no cup with me.' She plucked a convolvulus flower, he filled it, She drank, and thereupon the wheels rolled onto firm ground. Aye, the Goddess can be tender."

And terrible, Gratillonius thought. Dahilis loaded her arms. The dew on leaves and blossoms was cool, almost cold, like moonlight.

~ 4 ~

Innilis needed pretty things around her. The house that she inherited she had had painted rosy pink on the outside; within, the walls became pale blue trimmed with gold, where they did not carry paintings of blooms and birds. Delicate objects filled the rooms, statuettes, crystal, silver, as well as gauzy hangings. Most she had not bought, for she lived quietly and spent much of her stipend on alms and charitable works; she had received it from people who rejoiced to behold her joy. Two servants, man and wife, sufficed her. They were apt to go about their work he smiling, she singing.

Ocean sheened as if polished beneath a late sun when Vindilis arrived. Innilis let her in. They two could merely exchange salutation and looks while the woman attendant stood by. "Welcome, oh, welcome," Innilis whispered. She drew breath and turned to the servitor. "Evar, the Queen and I have m-m-much to discuss. We'll sup—after dark, I suppose. I know not when, I'll tell you at the time, it need only be a light collation. Come." She hastened from the atrium. Vindilis strode at her side.

In the conference room, they closed the door and curtained the windows. Thereafter the kiss went on and on. "'Tis been so long," Innilis half sobbed, her cheek upon Vindilis's small bosom.

"Aye," Vindilis replied into the fragrant brown hair. Nobody else in Ys had heard her croon. "But this time is ours. We've done our duty, now we may have our reward."

Innilis stepped back, keeping hands linked with hands, stared up into the gaunt visage before her, and said sadly, "Not yet may I take much ease, dear darling. Those men worst hurt in the battle—many wounds have become inflamed—men lie tossing on their beds, sometimes raving, while their wives and children know naught to do save pray."

"And call on you," Vindilis added. "'Tis ever thus. You, the Sister of mercy."

Innilis shook her head. "Nay, you know better. Bodilis, Fennalis, Lanarvilis—"

"They do what they can, but the grace of the Goddess is in your touch." Innilis flushed. "You've had your work too."

"In truth." Vindilis's tone hardened. "Our King would fain turn everything topsy-turvy. Along with much else, he wants changes in management of the public treasury, starting with inventory of every coffer, religious and civil alike. I must agree 'tis not necessarily a bad thing. I'd no idea how slipshod record-keeping had become in the Temple. Yet the Nine shall retain control of its finances. Quinipilis and I are overseeing the work. Her strength flags early in the day, so most of it falls on me." She laughed. "That's why my note said we should meet here. At my house, some female prothonotary is like to burst in at any moment with a question."

Innilis's smile lighted the chamber. "Well, you *are* here," she sighed and swayed close again.

They undressed each other with many endearments and little jests. There was a broad couch. They sank onto it. Hands, lips, tongues went seeking, caressing. Time passed unheeded.

The door opened. Dahilis came through. She carried a basket full of Belisama's Cup. "Innilis, dear," she called happily, "Evar told me you—" She dropped the basket and choked off a scream.

Vindilis bounded to her feet. "Shut the door!" she hissed.

Numbly, Dahilis did. Her glance went from the lean, crouched form with fingers crooked like talons, to Innilis huddled back on the couch, an arm across her breasts, a hand over her loins, mouth parted, eyes widened till the blue was ringed in white.

Vindilis stalked forward. "You meddlesome witling." Her fury was like the iceberg that flays a ship. "How dared you? How dared you?"

Dahilis retreated. "I didn't know."

"Vindilis, darling, she couldn't have," Innilis quavered. "I should have told Evar...not to let anybody in, not even a Sister....I forgot. I was so glad y-you were coming...I forgot. 'Tis my fault, mine alone!" She cast herself down on a pillow and wept.

Vindilis halted. "Well, I might have noticed and seen to it, but I didn't," she said. "Whatever the blame, we'll share it, as we've shared our hearts."

Dahilis squared shoulders. "Belike this was... the will of the Goddess," she said. "Certes 'twas never mine."

"I'll yield you that." Vindilis picked up her cloak and covered her nakedness. Grimly: "What we must decide is how to cope with the matter."

Dahilis went to the couch, knelt beside it, threw arms around Innilis. "Cry not, little Sister, cry no longer," she begged. "I love you. I love you best of all my Sisters. Never will I betray you, nay, not to my lord himself."

Vindilis let her continue murmuring, soothing, stroking hair and brow, while she reclad herself fully. When at length Innilis was quiet, save for gulps and hiccoughs and nose-blowing, Vindilis fetched a nightgown from the bedroom. Dahilis helped Innilis draw it on. Its fluffiness made her seem a child. She sat up near the head of the couch, the other two sat on the foot, and they looked back and forth through dimming light.

"I thank you for your loyalty, Dahilis," said Vindilis.

"Well, you were kind to me in the past," responded Dahilis.

"Less kind than I might have been. I see that now. But 'tis not my nature." Vindilis paused. "Nor is it my nature to care for men."

Dahilis cast a troubled regard at Innilis, who faltered, "I, I know not what my nature is. Hoel and Gratillonius—but they never taught me!"

Dahilis bit her lip. "That may be my doing. I've been...greedy... about him. I fear that's offended the Goddess."

Vindilis bridled. "Think you *this* has?" she challenged. "Nay, we twain gave each other the strength to endure Colconor. Thus we could carry out our duties, and not go mad. Love is the gift of Belisama. Should we spurn it, for a man who cares naught?"

"You wrong him," Dahilis protested. She clenched her fists. "Aye, there I think is your sin, that you turn your back on the King the Three sent to deliver us. Innilis—you, at least—oh, do!"

"I can try," came the whisper. "If he will. But never can I forsake Vindilis."

"That may perhaps be— Who am I to say? Who are we?"

Slowly, Dahilis unclenched her hands. She stroked them over her belly, once, and calm flowed after them. Rising, she looked straight at the two and said:

"I promised I'd keep faith with you, and I will. But we must find what is right. Let us think where we may seek. Tell me when you feel ready. Until then, farewell, my Sisters."

She walked out. The hem of her skirt scattered the spilled flowers.

XVIII

~ 1 ~

A short way north of Warriors' House where fighting men on duty had barracks, the Water Tower raised its great bulk higher than the adjacent battlements of Ys. A conduit under city wall and pomoerium led the flow of the canal there, ox-turned machinery pumped it to chambers near the top, whence pipelines redescended beneath pavement and carried it off to certain temples, important homes, fountains, and baths. The pipes were ceramic, because people here had a notion that lead was slow poison. Otherwise, and mainly, they depended on catchbasins and storage tanks with sand filters; rainfall kept those well enough filled.

The roof of the Water Tower held an observatory. Many Ysans did not trust in astrology, but many others did. In any case, stars and planets were vital to timekeeping, navigation, religious rites. Moreover, there was an ancient tradition of gathering knowledge for its own sake. This work requried a building hard by to contain instruments, library, scriptoria, auditorium. The Romans who remodeled Ys gave it a new Star House, in an Athenian style modified for the Northern climate. It came to be the meeting place of philosophers, scholars, poets, artists, visitors who had interesting things to tell, citizens whom the Symposium voted into membership.

A King could not be denied. Few had availed themselves of the privilege—more than once or twice, at any rate. Gratillonius wanted to, but had not hitherto found time. Now he could go.

A supper would be followed by free conversation, which might well outlast the night; but first the afternoon was for formal discussion. Word that the King would attend had brought well-nigh everyone who belonged. Decently clad though never sumptuously, most wearing togas, they reclined like the ancients on couches arranged in a circle, a couple of dozen men and Queen Bodilis. Between each pair, a small table bore dilute wine, raisins, nuts, cheese, which barefoot youths— noiselessly, always listening—kept replenished, not for the gratification of stomachs but to maintain clear heads while the drink lubricated tongues. The room was austere unless one considered the beauty of its marble and onyx or the extraordinarily clear, almost color-free window glass.

Today the president of the symposium was Iram Eliuni, otherwise Lord of Gold. A short, bald-headed, fussy man, he was not without humor as he said, "Fain would I begin by lodging a complaint against our distinguished guest, Gratillonius the King. For generations my office was a sinecure, and I have had leisure to cultivate learning. Of late, he insists the treasury *do* something."

He cleared his throat and proceeded: "However, that is not the topic chosen for this gathering. 'Twas agreed by the committee that faith—that which men believe is the nature of God and Spirit, the meaning and destiny of Creation—that this is the highest and deepest question to which our souls can aspire. Moreover, if men be sane and righteous, belief will determine how they think, how they behave. In sooth, if you know not the faith of a man—or a woman, of course, my lady Bodilis—then you understand that person not at all. Is this stipulated? Aye. Accordingly, we shall in mutual respectfulness investigate each other's religions. Gratillonius?"

Forewarned, the Roman could answer readily: "You wish me to explain mine? Well, to be frank, I doubt I can say much which this group knows not already. Mithraism was widespread when Ys was close-knitted to the Empire. You must have descriptions. I'll be glad to talk about whatever you want to hear, as long as 'tis allowable for me, but I really think 'twill suffice to assure you afresh that I can and do honor the Gods of Ys...barring minor matters of ritual which count for naught... and if I've overstepped my bounds, 'tis been for lack of information, not of goodwill." He looked around the circle, face by face. Bodilis, in a gray gown, wore perhaps the gravest expression. "Let me make a request," said Gratillonius. "Let me ask you first about your religion. I pray you, enlighten me."

"Where'd we begin?" asked a hoarse voice. Several men smiled. The inquirer was among the four regular members who belonged to no Suffete family—an artisan, but in his free time an experimenter who studied the behavior of material objects.

"Perhaps by starting with history, which you recall we've talked about, Gratillonius," suggested Bodilis.

"We have," the centurion replied. "Sirs and my lady, I've knocked about in the world. I know how often the Romans of old were mistaken when they reckoned a foreign God to be the same as Jupiter or Neptunus or Whoever. Thus far I've not been able to make entire sense of your Ysan pantheon. No disrespect; I simply haven't."

"For example?"

"Oh...some of your Gods appear to come from the South or from Asia, but some are Gallic. And yet not Gallic. Taranis Himself—here in Ys He has taken the primacy from Lugh and the hammer from Sucellus, neither of Them having any cult among you as far as I know " Gratillonius ventured a smile of his own. "Help me understand what I have become!"

Esmunin Sironai said, almost inaudibly out of his thin chest: "I trust you realize that we, at least we who are educated, do not take ancestral myths for literal truth, as if we were Christians. They are symbols. As different languages, or different words in one language, may denote the same thing—albeit with subtle variations of aspect—so, too, may different Gods represent the same Being. They change with time as languages do, They develop, according to the evolving needs of Their worshippers. The very heavens change through the eons; nevertheless, the reality of Heaven endures." He was the chief astrologer, once tall, now frail, white-bearded, nearly blind. Under his direction his students, who loved him, continued his researches: for he was not satisfied with Ptolemaeus's depiction of the universe.

"Mayhap 'twould help if the chronicle of the Gods were set briefly forth," propounded Taenus Himilco. "Parts you will have heard, Gratillonius, but not the whole, nor in orderly wise."

A murmur of assent went around the circle. "Do you do this," Iram Eliuni decided. "You are best qualified among us." Of aristocratic appearance and bearing, with a seat on the Council of Suffetes, Taenus was also a landholder near the Wood of the King. He knew not only what city dwellers thought, but what countryfolk did.

At Gratillonius's urging, he commenced:

"In the Beginning, Tiamat, the Serpent of Chaos, threatened to destroy Creation. Taranis slew Her. But She was the mother of Lir, Who therefore waylaid Taranis and killed Him. Heaven and earth were plunged into darkness until Belisama descended into the underworld. At a fearful price, She ransomed Taranis and brought Him back; and

She made peace between Him and Lir. A condition of this peace was that Taranis must die over and over, until the End of All Things, though He would ever be reborn. This mystery we enact in Ys. Formerly 'twas by yearly human sacrifice. Today 'tis in the person of the King. He dies in battle, he is resurrected in the victor, who fathers new life upon the Gallicenae, the chosen of the Goddess.

"In a sense, therefore, every daughter of King and Queens is divinely engendered. Only nine at a time are actual avatars. The rest live common human lives. Likewise do persons born of congress between other divinities and mortals. We have families claiming descent from, say, Teutatis, Esus, Cernunnos—mine—or from female deities by mortal lovers, Epona, Banba.... 'Tis mere ancestry, unattested save by legend. More meaningful, mayhap, though vague as sea-fog, is a tale that in the Ferriers of the Dead flows blood of cold Lir...."

Silence fell. Gratillonius nerved himself to break it: "The Ferriers. I've heard of them. But nobody wants to speak of it. What does happen to the dead?"

"That no one knows. The stories are many, many. Ghosts haunting their homesteads, barrow-wights, the Wild Hunt— dim Hades or utter oblivion— Here in the city and along the coast, we bury our dead at sea, as you know. Their bodies. The Ferriers have the task of bringing the souls out to Sena, for which terrifying reason they are exempt from tax or civic labor. Yonder, 'tis thought, Belisama judges those souls, though some say Lir shares in it. Many say that certain are reborn—that dead Gallicenae, especially, may become seals, which linger until they can accompany their own beloved into the Beyond— But we do not pretend to know."

"As you Mithraists do," Bodilis said coolly.

Gratillonius flushed. "I know not what will become of me," he snapped. "A man can but strive to earn salvation."

"A *man*. Is it denied to any who are not washed in the blood of the Bull? That would admit only the wealthy to Heaven."

"Nay!" exclaimed Gratillonius, doubly stung that she should be the one who gibed. "The Taurobolium—that ugly business where the worshipper stands in a pit and the blood bathes him—that's for Cybele. The Great Mother, they call her."

"You were sanctified by the blood of a King. Why should others not be sanctified by the blood of the bull?"

"As you will. 'Tis not required among them either. The rites are open to women." Gratillonius stopped himself from admitting how closely the Temples of Mithras and Cybele had often cooperated. He had never liked that cult, where men driven hysterical had been known to castrate themselves. Let women follow Christ, Who was good enough for his mother. "When we slay a beast to Mithras, we do it with dignity, as He did."

"I pray you, I pray you!" Iram cried. "This is a comparison of views, an exchange of cognizances. Debates, if debates are desired, must be arranged separately."

Gratillonius suppressed his temper. "Well, about human destiny," he said, "many of my fellowship believe 'tis controlled by the planets, but I confess to doubts about that. Could the learned Esmunin enlighten us?"

"I am not in the least sure of the horoscopes I cast," replied the old man, "although I do my best as duty demands. If there is fate, then methinks 'tis on a grander scale, the forces of it all but incomprehensible to us. The apparition of comets, enigmatic eclipses, procession of the equinoxes—"

It became fascinating.

~ 2 ~

Gratillonius would happily have stayed as late as the last philosopher, but soon after the meal Bodilis plucked his toga and said low, "Come away with me. We've things to talk about."

Despite lingering resentment, he knew she would not request this idly, and made his excuses. No armed guard was necessary hereabouts; a lantern bearer sufficed, a boy who did not know Latin.

"I'm sorry I angered you," Bodilis said in that language. "But given the opportunity, I thought I must."

Astonished, Gratillonius glanced at her. Stars threw more light on her face than did the glow bobbing ahead. He studied its strong molding as if for the first time until, confusedly, his gaze roved off, past the towers to the vast glimmer of Ocean. The night was cool. Footfalls rang.

"You see," she said presently, "you do not understand free women. If you're to reign as we both hope, you need to. I gave you a taste of what you've been giving us."

"What do you mean?" he protested. "My mother, my sisters—no slaves they. Nor most of those I've known."

"But not equals either," she retorted. "We Gallicenae are. Never forget that."

"What have I done wrong?"

She sighed, then smiled and took his arm. "Not your fault, really. Everywhere else, unless perhaps among some of the barbarians, women are underlings. The Romans honored their matrons, but gave them no voice in affairs. The Greeks shut theirs away in houses; no wonder that became a nation of boy-lovers, as dull as they made their poor women! Your cult won't admit them. The Christians will— but subservient, looked at askance as vessels of temptation, denied any possibility of ever administering the sacraments. How could you know?"

The Great Mother—no, She was a screeching Asiatic. Tonight, around him, Gratillonius felt the majesty of Belisama, to Whom belonged moon and stars.

He swallowed. "Did I insult the Nine? I didn't mean to. Dahilis said nothing."

"She wouldn't. She's too loving. Nevertheless I suspect she has urged you pay more heed to her Sisters."

"Well—she has—but—"

"Ah, I speak of pride, of what is due, not of lust, though the flesh does have its just demands. Think back, for example. When you announced Dahilis was pregnant, and this would release you in due course to service the rest of us— Do you like being patronized?"

"No! But—but—"

She laughed softly and held his arm the tighter. "Dear Gratillonius. You've never been a man more than now when you flounder helpless. Do you imagine I'd have bothered trying to teach Colconor? Why, Hoel himself could not understand. He might have—he was not stupid—but he would not make the effort, he would not patiently listen. In you there is hope."

"I will...listen, as long as seems reasonable...and try to do what's right," he said carefully, "but I will not humble my manhood."

"Nobody asks that of you. It's simply that we will not humble our womanhood."

They went on in silence until they reached her home. There Gratillonius tipped the boy and dismissed him. Inside, servants had gone to bed, as short as the nights were growing, but had left a pair of lamps burning in the atrium. Light fell amber upon Bodilis. She whirled about and seized him. "Come," she said huskily, "don't wait, the hours are wearing away."

She had been good before. This time she was magnificent.

~ 3 ~

Rain came misting out of the sea, to hide the towers of Ys and make its streets twilit ravines. Dahilis and Innilis felt it on their faces, like the kisses of a thousand ghosts. They drew their cowled cloaks as tight as they were able while walking. Despite the apprehension in them, they were glad to reach the house of Quinipilis.

The high priestess let them in herself. She had thrown a shawl over a gown often patched; wool stockings and straw slippers were on her rheumatic feet. Carelessly combed, her hair made a white lion's mane. "Welcome!" she hailed. "Stand not there getting wetter, come inside where 'tis halfway warm. I've mulled wine on the brazier, or I can brew up some tisane if you'd liefer." She waved them through and rocked after them. "Pardon my appearance. Your note asked for a private talk, so I gave the staff this day free. Ordinarily I do not meet folk until I've gotten my jowls neatly tied up against my ears."

"We, we meant not to cause you trouble," whispered Innilis.

"Nonsense, child. You've given me unassailable cause to stay away from the temple and slop about here. Toss your cloaks anywhere." Quinipilis led the way to a room off the atrium. Like the rest of her establishment, it was somewhat garishly decorated. The furniture was battered but serviceable. "Be seated. At ease, as our good centurion would say. We've the whole day if we want, not so?—and a kettle of soup cooking. Made it myself. My cook's no slattern, but she *will* put in too few leeks."

They sat down and, for a space, sipped mutely from their beakers. Across the rim of hers, Quinipilis squinted at the guests. When she deemed the moment ripe, she said: "The trouble is yours, plain to see, and a bitter grief in you. Tell me whatever you wish."

Twice Innilis tried to answer, and could not. She shrank back in her chair, clutched her cup, and fought against tears.

Dahilis squeezed her hand before taking the word, low but almost steadily, looking straight into the eyes of Quinipilis: "'Twas my thought that we seek your counsel, you, the oldest and wisest of us. We wanted Vindilis along, but she refused—sought to keep us from going— If you find her more aloof and haughty than ever, that will be the reason."

"Age in itself brings no wisdom, dear. But I have seen a thing or two in the past. Say on."

"This is a thing that could destroy. Yet I d-dare not call it wrong. I found out by sheer chance, unless 'twas the will of the Goddess.... Innilis and Vindilis are lovers."

Quinipilis bared what was left of her teeth in a soundless laugh. "Ho, is that all? I've known for years." Innilis gasped. The wine splashed from her cup and stained her lap. Quinipilis ignored that, smiled at her, and said kindly. "Fear not. I'm sure none else has suspected. Me, I'm curious about people. Their bodies speak more honestly than their tongues. I've learned a bit of the language."

"But what shall we do?" Dahilis pleaded.

Quinipilis shrugged. "Need we do aught? This cannot have been the first time in the centuries. Nine women to one man may be sacred, but 'tis not natural. Yet Ys has done rather well throughout its history. 'Tis only that its folk have inherited, from their Carthaginian forebears, an abhorrence. I believe Belisama understands."

She gazed afar. Her voice dropped. "Poor Innilis. And poor Vindilis. I was never the mother I should have been to her, my Runa, Vindilis-to-be. There was Lyria, you remember, my daughter by Wulfgar whom I'd been so fond of. Aye, 'tis fair to say I loved Wulfgar; and you cannot remember, being too young, what a bright, beautiful child Lyria was. Then Gaetulius slew Wulfgar, and on me begot Runa. Oh, I never hated the little one; she could not help having the father she had. I

197

did my duty by Runa. But to Wulfgar's daughter Lyria I gave my love. And then in the reign of Lugaid the Sign came upon Lyria, and she took the name Karilis, and she died in giving birth, and to the grandchild who is now Forsquilis I passed on the love I had borne for her mother...."

She shook herself. "Enough. 'Twas long ago; and who can command her heart? Do your duty as a Queen. Whoever else may be in your life, provided 'tis not adulterously another man, that person is your own."

"But I hate keeping a secret like this from Gratillonius," Dahilis mourned. "It touches him so deeply, though he know it or not. And, and he is the King we prayed for. We owe him our loyalty."

"What loyalty has he shown us?" demanded Quinipilis.

"Why, why, he has been—kind and sage and strong—" Dahilis's cheeks burned. "Aye, certain things he's neglected, but that's my fault as much as his, and Bodilis told me she's spoken to him and he paid close heed—"

"That is well," said Quinipilis. "Mistake me not. I like him very much. I fear lest he lose the favor of the Three. Mayhap this...between you and Vindilis, dear Innilis—mayhap 'tis Their punishment of him, even though it began ere he arrived. If They do no worse, we should give thanks for mercy."

"That's my terror too," Innilis forced forth. "That the Gods are affronted as They were by...the earlier King. When Dahilis discovered us—could that be Their sign, Their warning?"

Quinipilis came to attention like an old hound that has caught wolf-scent on the wind. "Eh? What's this? Meseems you've more on your minds than you've yet told."

"We do," Dahilis answered. Struggling for every word, she related how Gratillonius had held his Mithraic rite in a stream hallowed to Belisama, and afterward been unrepentant. "He swore 'twas no harm; and he *is* so strong and clever that, that I made myself believe him—but then this next thing happened, and I cannot sleep for fright— Counsel us what to do!"

"Hm. Hm." Quinipilis tugged her chin. "This is bad, I think. He's already defied Lir, d'you see, by burying that soldier of his on Point Vanis. And I scarce imagine Taranis is pleased that Gratillonius has dawdled about getting Him daughters on the rest of the Nine. The Gods are patient, but—"

She rose and paced, hands clasped behind her back, though an occasional wince showed that each step cost her pain. The younger women sat dumb, their stares following her to and fro. Finally she halted, loomed above them—her tall form against the window seemed to darken the room—and said:

"He is worth saving. The best hope, I swear, Ys has had in my long lifetime, or longer than that. Wulfgar and Hoel were good men too, but they lacked the skills of war and governance that seem to be

Gratillonius's, nor, in their day, did such storm-driven tides beat on our gate as are now rising. If he refuses to expiate his sins, we Nine must do it for him. Is that not ever the lot of woman?

"How? I cannot tell. In matters like this, I'm a simpleton: too much earth in me, too little fire, air, or seawater. Let me ask of Forsquilis. Young though she be, that grandchild of mine is deep into strange things. Well do we know."

Dahilis and Innilis shivered.

"'Twill take time, doubtless," Quinipilis went on. "Meanwhile, we'll do what we can to make amends and fend off divine anger. First, I'd say, Gratillonius *must* rightfully honor and make fruitful those of the Gallicenae who are able. If he'll not take the first step toward that, they—we—shall have to."

Dahilis bowed her head. "I've tried," she mumbled. "And, and Bodilis says she did reproach him, and afterward he and she— How glad I was. He keeps telling me, though, he keeps telling me he'll...see to the matter...when I've grown heavier. What else can I do?"

Quinipilis rasped a chuckle. "What, need the Crone instruct the Wench? Your blood knows the answer." She sighed. "You've been too proud, all you lasses. You've concealed your hurt. Have you thought that that might have overawed him? Belike he's unaware of this, he tells himself he only wants Dahilis, with whom he's in love. But underneath—he knows you have powers—and...every man dreads failing with a woman. Which he never will with any of you; but does he truly realize that?"

She laid a knotted hand on the head of Innilis. "Seek him out," she urged. "Set fear aside. Open yourself to joy. Ah, I remember."

"I w-w-will do my best." The words came high and thin.

Quinipilis stood a while looking down at Innilis. It was as if that look went past clothes and the skin beneath, to flesh which had been torn and knitted poorly, to frail ribs and narrow hips. Whatever of the restorative Touch that had once belonged to every Queen lingered in Innilis, it sufficed not for the healing of herself.

Finally the old woman said low: "I was forgetting. The birth of your child by Hoel nearly killed you; and Audris is sickly and not quite right in the wits. Aye, a strong reason for you to seek where you did." Stooping, though the motion wrenched a groan from her, she hugged the other. "Take what time you need, girl. Nerve yourself. Let others go before you. Dahilis will be your ally. And there is the Herb. If the gods did not smite the Nine for bearing Colconor no child, why, surely they'll condone you safeguarding your health, mayhap your very life. But when you feel ready, go to him. Never be afraid of loving him."

XIX

~ 1 ~

Festivals surrounded Midsummer. In part they were religious. On the Eve, bonfires blazed around the countryside after dark, while folk danced, sang, coupled in the fields, cast spells, asked welfare for kith and kine, house and harvest—across Armorica, across Europe. In Ys, day after day processions went chanting to rites at every fane of the Three. Most were parades as well, where the Great Houses, the Brotherhoods, the Guilds turned out in their best, where the marines marched smartly and, this year, the King's legionaries outdid them. There were traditional ceremonies: the weavers presented Belisama with a brocaded robe, the horsebreeders gave Taranis a new team for His wagon, the mariners sailed forth and cut the throat of a captured seal that Lir might have the blood—the single seal that Ysans were allowed to kill throughout the year. There were other offerings to other Gods, deeds ancient, secret, and dark.

Midsummer was likewise a season of secular celebration. It was a lucky time to get married in. It was a time for family reunions, grandiose feasts, youthful flings that elders winked at. The short, light nights were full of song, flutes, drums, dancing feet, laughter. Green boughs hung above every door. People forgave wrongs, paid debts, gave largesse to the needy. Few slept much.

Yet Midsummer was also worldly, political. The day after solstice was among the four in the year when the Council of Suffetes always met.

Often this had been scarcely more than an observance, soon completed. Behind its strong wall and, belief went, the subtle Veil of Brennilis, Ys had been free of many things that aggrieved the earth. But nothing is forever.

On the dais of the basilica chamber, Gratillonius raised the Hammer and said: "In the name of Taranis, peace. May His protection be upon us."

Lanarvilis rose to say: "In the name of Belisama, peace. May Her blessing be upon us." So the Nine had chosen her for their principal speaker at this session, Gratillonius thought. Why? Because she's a good friend of Soren Cartagi, who generally opposes my policies?

Hannon Baltisi stood. "In the name of Lir, peace. May His wrath not be upon us." The trident butt crashed on the floor.

Gratillonius gave Adminius the Hammer to hold. A while he stood watching the faces before him—long, narrow Suffete faces for the most part, but not altogether, certainly not on stout Soren or craggy Hannon or, except for traces, any of the Gallicenae. They returned his reconnaissance. Stillness deepened. Best get started, he thought.

200

"Let me begin by thanking you for your patience and support in these past difficult months," he said. Flashing a grin: "Today we can talk Ysan." A few lips flickered upward, not many. "We've weathered a mighty storm. The seas still run high, but I know we can reach safe harbor if we continue pulling together." Don't remind them how they quibbled and bickered and sometimes came near rebellion. They never quite went over the brink. That's what counts.

"We broke the Scoti. They'll not come again soon, if ever! We kept ourselves from embroilment in the Roman civil war, and kept Armorica out of it too, by our direct influence on our near neighbors and theirs on people farther east. For this, Magnus Maximus is grateful. I have letters from him, which some of you have read and all are welcome to. Having served under him, I can tell you that he rewards service; and he is not far now from winning his Imperium.

"But we have work yet undone, we in Ys. I think the Gods have laid a destiny upon us. We have become the outer guard of civilization itself. We must not fail in our duty."

Hannon barely signalled for recognition before he stood up, gray-bearded patriarch, and snapped: "Aye, we know what you want, you. To keep our whole strength marshalled, however the cost may bleed us. For what? For Rome. King, 'twas I who showed you the mystery of the Key, and loth I am to clash with you—for you are at least an honest man—but why should Ys serve Rome, Christian Rome who'd forbid us to worship our Gods—and yours, Grallon, yours?"

Adruval Tyri, Sea Lord, heaved his burly form erect. As head of the navy, and a former marine, he could say: "Hannon, with due respect, what you speak is walrus puckey. A grandmother of mine was Scotic, my mother was half Frankish, I've travelled about both trading and fighting, I *know* the barbarians. What d'you want? That we haul in our warships, keep none in commission save the usual coast guard, and thereby avoid offending the Saxons? I tell you, if you buy the wolf off with a lamb, next twilight he'll be back wanting the ewe. The Gods have given us a King who understands this." He ran fingers through thinning red hair. "Heed him, for Their sake!"

Hannon glowered and growled, "What do you wish in truth, lord?"

They returned to their benches. Gratillonius cleared his throat. "This," he said. "We've a Heaven-sent opportunity. Armorica has been spared war, thanks largely to Ys. 'Twill accept our leadership, eagerly, at least until such time as the Imperial issue is decided. I'd have us work with the Roman authorities throughout the peninsula. We can help them rebuild signal towers and establish a line of beacon fires ready for ignition. We can keep our fleet on standby for them, who have almost none—for, if the Scoti are no longer a menace, the Saxons remain, and are worse. In exchange, the Romans can defend our land-ward frontiers."

Soren stirred. "What need have we of that?" Rumbled the Speaker for Taranis. "What on land endangers Ys?"

"The threat to Rome, if naught else," Gratillonius replied: "which is the threat to civilization, I tell you. Sirs and ladies, Ys cannot feed herself. Trade is her life. Let Rome fall, and this your city will starve."

Lanarvilis rose. Grace had never imbued her long body or heavy haunches; but the blond hair lifted on high like a helmet as she said quietly: "I would not gainsay the King—not at once, on a single point of issue—but mothers must needs look further ahead than fathers. So I ask this assembly, although we may indeed find some cooperation expedient—ultimately, does Ys the free want to rejoin that Rome which has become a slave state? Had we not better keep our distance and trust in our Gods? Bethink you."

She sat down. Gratillonius swallowed hard. The worst was, he couldn't deny to himself that her question was quite reasonable. If it had not happened that his own Mother was Rome— Clearly, his rampart for her would be years a-building. Well, a mason necessarily went brick by brick. Today he might lay two or three. He cleared his throat for a response.

~ 2 ~

In ancient times the King had stayed always at the Sacred Wood, whither the high priestesses sought by turns, and whatever men he invited. Gradually it came to be that he visited the city to preside over various ceremonies; and these visits lengthened. When Julius Caesar's man won the crown and refused to sit yawning in the primitive House, he merely confirmed and completed what had been the case for several reigns before his. Thereafter the Kings moved freely about and inhabited a proper palace in Ys.

Yet while Taranis thus allowed His law to be lightened, it could not be abolished. The King must return to meet every challenger, slay or be slain. Moreover, save in war or essential travel or when a major ritual coincided, he must spend the three days and nights around each full moon out in the Wood. His presence there being the sole requirement, most sovereigns had taken a wife or two along, and sent for friends, and passed the time in recreations which ranged from decorous to debauched.

Dahilis felt horror of the place. Beneath those shadowing oaks Colconor had killed her father and might have killed Gratillonius, whose blood would also someday nourish their roots. After she confessed this, just before his initial Watch, he had kissed her and gone off to sleep alone.

The duty was otherwise not irksome. Free of distractions, he studied material from the archives, practiced the language, conferred at length with magnates he summoned, pondered the tasks before him, and maintained his regular exercises to keep fit. About the underlying finality he was unconcerned. He awaited no rival soon. Such advents were, in fact, generally years apart. Any fighters who did come, he felt confident he could handle. Eventually his strength and speed must begin failing; but he did not mean to be here that long, although at the present stage of things he saw no sense in planning his departure.

The morning of his third moon dawned already hot. Clouds banked murky in the east and rose higher hour by hour, while a forerunner haze dulled the dwindling western blue; but no breeze relieved the wet air or freshened its musky odors. Soren and the priests who officially escorted Gratillonius sweated beneath their robes so that they stank. They were as grateful as dignity permitted when he offered them beer at the House. He, who had tramped and fought in armor, suffered less, but was glad to strip down to a tunic after they were gone.

Servants had carried along pens, ink, parchment. That last was costly stuff for the letters he meant to write to various Imperial officers of the region, but papyrus was not to be had, as disrupted as trade routes were on both land and sea, while wood was simply too plebeian. Well, he thought, this material should be impressive, emphasizing the capabilities latent in Ys and, by the bye, offsetting his awkward style and vagrant spelling. Only afterward was it to occur to him that Bodilis could have corrected those.

The hall was the most nearly cool place to be. He ordered a table and chair brought in and settled himself down to work. It went slower and harder than he had expected. After a while his jaw and back ached from tension. He wasn't sure why. Maybe a ramble in the grove would help. He set off. That was about noon.

At once he was alone. Utterly alone. Around him the trees brooded, huge boles, twist-thewed branches, claw twigs. Their leaves made a gloom through which a weird brass-yellow light struck here and there, out of a sky gone sooty and steadily darkening further. Silence weighed down the world, fallen leaves too sodden to rustle underfoot, brush stiff as though straining after any sound, never a bird call or squirrel chatter or grunt from a wild boar whose blood was to wash the corpse of a King, nothing astir save himself; but fungi glimmered like eyes. Even the canal, when he reached it, seemed to flow listless, tepid, forbidden to quench his thirst.

Gratillonius scowled. What was the matter with him? He was no superstitious barbarian, he was a Roman....But Romans disliked wilderness. It was beyond their law. In its depths you might meet Pan, and the dread of Him come upon you so that you ran screaming, blind, a mindless animal, while His laughter bayed at your heels....A Presence was here. He felt It as heavily as he felt the slugging of his heart. It might be of Ahriman. Best he return.

As he did, he heard the first muttering of thunder.

He breathed easier after he got back to the Sacred Precinct, its courtyard flagged and swept, open to heaven and onto Processional Way, with a view beyond of the heights, garden-garnished homes, pastureland above the cliffs of Point Vanis where Eppillus kept his long watch. Yet he was still beset by portents he could not read. As he stood there, clouds covered the last western clarity, gray yonder, blue-black where they mounted out of the east. Summer's verdancies were discolored, bruised. Dominant in the courtyard reared and sprawled the Challenge Oak, shield hanging from it dully agleam with brass that the hammer had smitten over and over. Between its outbuildings loomed the House, crimson hue somehow bringing forth the brutal mass of timbers, grotesqueness of images that formed its colonnade. When Gratillonius looked away toward Ys, the city at its distance appeared tiny, fragile, a fantasy blown in glass.

Suddenly as a meteor flash, he became aware of the three on the road. How had he overlooked them? They were almost here. He forced steadiness upon himself. A wind sprang up, soughing in the treetops and tossing them about. The hammer swung on its chain, hit the shield, belled in a mumble. Lightning flickered afar. Thunder rolled more loud.

The three halted before their King. Under their cowls he saw Forsquilis, Vindilis, Maldunilis. He could not quell a shudder.

"Greeting, lord," said Forsquilis. "We have come to attend you during your sentinel stay."

He sought to moisten his lips, but his tongue had gone dry too. "I thank you....However, I did not ask for...your company."

Vindilis's look smoldered in the bony face. "You hardly would," she replied. Did a whiplash of spite go through her tone? "Not of us three out of the Nine."

Forsquilis lifted a hand. "Peace." Calm, resolution were upon her Athene countenance. The gray eyes took hold of Gratillonius's and would not let go. "Aye," she said, "just we three, who held Colconor here until his doom could find him. That was needful evil. The hour has come to set it right."

Maldunilis sidled close to tug Gratillonius's sleeve. "We'll be sweet to you, yea, very sweet," she said, and giggled.

Lightning flared anew, brighter; thunder boomed; the shield rang. Gratillonius felt a surge of anger as heartening as the wind. "Now look you," he snapped, "I accept your intention as good, and mayhap I have been neglectful, but we'll settle all this in rational wise, later."

"We will not," Forsquilis answered. While her tone was level, she had let go of her cloak, and it flapped at her shoulders like great wings. "This is something that must be, lest the time-stream flow still worse awry. I have made a Sending. It did not reach the Gods, that is not in my power, but it did come near enough to hear Them whisper. Follow me." She strode toward the House. Numbly, Gratillonius obeyed. Vindilis and Maldunilis flanked him.

Beyond the doorway, the hall gaped cavernous. The staff had lit fires in the trenches against the approaching storm, but their light only bred shadows which seemed to make move the carven pillars and wainscots, the tattered banners from battles long forgotten. Smoke stung nostrils and blurred vision. The crackling of wood was merely an undertone to the halloo of wind outside.

"Go," Forsquilis ordered the assembled manservants. "Be off to town, fast, ere the downpour catches you. Come not back till the moon has waned."

Gratillonius confirmed with a stiff nod. What else could he do?

"We'll see to you," Maldunilis tittered in his ear. "Oh, we will." His flesh crawled at her touch.

When they were alone with him, the three shed their cloaks. Underneath, they were royally dressed. As one, they confronted him. "Lord King," said Forsquilis gravely, "in us—you and your Queens—the Gods are on earth. We are seed and soil, weather and water, the cycle of the year and the tides, of the stars and the centuries. We engender, we give birth, we nurture, we protect, we dream, we die, we are reborn in our children at the springtime and we die again in the harvest at autumn. If ever in this we fail, Ys perishes; for we are Ys.

"Therefore let that which was done here in hatred be now done in love. Let the wombs that were shut be opened. Let the dead quicken. Taranis, come unto Belisama."

Lightning burst. Its flare through doorway and smokehole made wan the fires. Thunder wheeled after, down and down heaven. Hailstones rattled before the wind, whitened the ground, clamored on the shield In a mighty rushing, the rain arrived.

It was as if Gratillonius stood aside and watched another man go into the arms of Forsquilis. Then there was no Gratillonius, no woman, there was only that which happened, which was everything that there was.

—Lamplight glowed throughout the bedchamber, but its Roman accoutrements seemed unreal, infinitely remote; and the light was not soft in the eyes of Forsquilis, it turned them yellow, like a hawk's. Her visage had become Medusa's, gold-brown locks spread snakish over the pillow, she wrapped long arms and legs about him and cried out as her hips met his plunging.

—"I did wrong to bid you go away," Vindilis breathed in the dark. "Give me another daughter, a new babe to cherish."

"But you told me you liked not—"

"I should have told you what I do like. Hoel could not understand, but Bodilis and Dahilis say that you listen."

"I do. For I want you—you, not just a body lying still—"

"Let us try, let us see. Give me your hand to guide—"

—The sleepy noontide sun cast richness over Maldunilis where she lay. "We're going to drain you dry, you know," she laughed, and somehow that was not impious, for the Gods have humor too and it is not always ironic or cruel; love and death have their ridiculous moments, that the spirit may be refreshed. With Forsquilis and Vindilis playful on either side, Gratillonius saw that Maldunilis honestly desired him and was quite ready to adore him. His ardor torrented.

—The Bull was in him, he was the Bull, rampant among his cows, although in glimpses of self-awareness he knew it was a bull seal he had been thinking of, out on a rookery reef near Sena.

—The last night ended as dawn paled the sinking moon. All four were so weary and sore they could barely drag themselves to their feet. Nonetheless Gratillonius and Vindilis, aye, Vindilis went forth to stand in dew and wildflowers across the road. "Now do you believe?" she asked quietly.

"I seek to," he answered.

Across her dark head, lifted against the sky, the white streak gleamed like a warrior's plume. "We have been Gods. Belike 'twill never happen again. Flesh would burn to ashes. Nay, we shall return to what we were, perhaps a little wiser, a little stronger, but always mortal. Yet we have been Gods."

The sun rose, bearing the glory of Unconquered Mithras. Gratillonius gasped.

He was silent when Speaker and priests led him and his Queens back to Ys. Dahilis met him at the palace, kissed him, said in tender mirth that he had earned a good long rest. She took him to a room curtained and cool, and left him by himself.

A sunbeam struck through. Gratillonius went to that window, opened it, leaned out, holding his palms and his branded brow up to the light. "Nay, I do *not* understand!" he cried. "What came upon me? What was it?" He heard, surprised, that he had called in Ysan. He fled to Latin. *"Tene, Mithra, etiam miles, fidos votis nostris nos!"*

XX

~ 1 ~

Adminius was the new deputy to Gratillonius. Few would have thought the lean, snaggle-toothed scrounger and japester a wise choice, but he quickly vindicated the centurion's judgment, laid his authority firm upon his remaining twenty-three fellows, kept them in sharp form, maintained cooperation with the Ysan regulars and popularity among the Ysan folk.

The municipal theater at the Forum operated, on grants from the Great Houses, during the four months around Midsummer, when daylight could provide illumination after working hours. For the most part it offered classical drama, music, readings; dance, gymnastics, and sports were for the amphitheater outside of town. Not until a month after solstice did the soldiers have leisure to go. Gratillonius kept them too busy strengthening defenses and executing joint maneuvers with the marines.

Finally, though, Adminius announced a party. "We'll march down in formation, 'spite of being civil dressed, impress everybody proper, and take in the show. Don't be afraid. It's the *Twin Menaechmi*, lots of fun—dirty jokes in there too, if you're quick enough on the uptake. I sneaked inter a performance once when I was a brat in Londinium. Afterward we'll 'ave a banquet at the Green Whale. Some of you already know 'ow good a table Zeugit sets. The city's paying, by way of a bonus for our services in the late unpleasantness. And then you're free to go waste yer substance in riotous living—but I want you back in barracks and fit for duty at sunrise, d'you 'ear?"

It was therefore a shock when a spokesman for the patrons announced that the theater was proud to present the *Agamemnon* of Aeschylus in a new Ysan-language translation by the most gracious Queen Bodilis.

"Wot the Sathanas!" Seated on the right of his contingent, Adminius turned to his neighbor opposite, a portly and patrician Suffete. "Excuse me, sir," he said in the vernacular, "aren't they doing Plautus this eventide?"

"Nay, that is tomorrow." The man smiled superciliously. "I daresay our way of counting days straight forward, rather than backwards from ides and nones, is confusing to Romans."

"Oh, bloody Christ." Adminius addressed his men in Latin: "Sorry, boys. I got the date wrong. Wot we'll be seeing is...m-m. I think it's an old Greek tragedy."

Scowls and growls went among them. Cynan, beside the deputy, started to rise. "Well, let's go," he said. "I'm in no mood for—"

Adminius grabbed his arm. "We stay. This is a civilized country, and we owe it ter Rome and the legion ter make a good impression on the natives. You'll take in some culture, s'welp me 'Ercules, if I've got ter 'old yer noses and pour it down yer flinking gullets."

A disapproving buzz went along the close-packed benches. Sullenly, the men resigned themselves. At least they would be able to follow the lines, more or less; none of them knew Greek.

The theater was of the Roman kind, a semicircular bowl before a stage, roofless although with arrangements for spreading a canvas top in wet weather. However, differences were many, most of them more subtle than its comparatively small size. The upper gallery was point-arched, supported on columns slim, unfluted, their capitals in the form of breaking waves. A box aloft there was empty, reserved for the Gods. Female roles would be taken by women, not prostitutes but honored artists. In a well below the stage sat an orchestra with horns, flutes, syrinxes, sistrums, cymbals, drums, harps, lyres. It played for a while, a heavy, moody music; then, as the cloth-of-gold curtain was rolled down, it fell silent, until a long trumpet call resounded.

Scenery portrayed the front of a cyclopean palace, altars before it. A backdrop showed night, slowly brightening to day as layers of gauze were withdrawn. An actor stood peering outward. He bore spear, shield, archaic armor; the great helmet descended to make his mask. After a space motionless at his sentry post, he sighed and began: "O Gods, relieve me of this weary watch, this year-long waiting like a guardian hound with no more rest than elbow 'gainst the roof above the hall of the Atreides! Too well I've learned to know the midnight stars—"

Cynan's eyes widened. "Mithras!" he whispered. "That's the way it *is*."

"Shh," Adminius cautioned. But when the beacon fire blazed afar to proclaim the King's return, he himself let out a cheer.

Thereafter the soldiers spoke never a word; but often they drew breath or smote knees with fists.

When finally Clytemnestra had scorned the chorus and starkly told Aegisthus that they twain would rule; and another trumpet call died away; and the audience applauded and went out into the sunset street— Adminius said, "Wow!"

"Those women, those poor brave women." Budic was not ashamed to shed a few tears.

"What happened next?" Cynan wanted to know. "That Orestes they spoke of, he must have done something. Are there more plays?"

"I've heard Greek plays go in threes," Verica answered. "Maybe Queen Bodilis has translated the rest. Or maybe she will."

"Well, anyhow, she did a damn good job on this one," Maclavius declared. "Especially seeing she's a woman. Only a man who'd been a soldier could've written it."

"He understood more than soldiering, I can tell you," said Budic with the loftiness of youth.

"That was a lucky mistake you made, deputy," remarked Guentius, and general agreement murmured from the rest.

Adminius laughed. "Fine, fine! We might as well appreciate wot's around us. I've a notion we'll be 'ere quite a spell."

~ 2 ~

Summer advanced in triumphal procession. Colts, calves, lambs, kids grew long in the legs and full in the haunches. Apples, plums, cherries burgeoned in orchards. Freshly cut grass filled hayfields with fragrance. Bees droned about heather, clover, gorse, replacing the tribute men had exacted from them earlier. Carts laden with produce trundled out of Osismiic lands, to return full of wares from workshops and the sea. Poppies and cornflowers bejeweled roadsides. Children grew scratched on the hands and purple about the lips, gathering wild blackberries. Young storks, geese, ducks flopped overhead, in training for the trek south. On clear nights the Swan, the Eagle, and the Lyre stood high.

While he still had much to do, most of it of his own making, Gratillonius began discovering time for himself. More and more Ysans, great, humble, and ordinary, were coming to accept him as a man when he was not being the sacral King. He could poke around town, ask people about their work, listen to legends related by granny or gaffer, put a child on his knee and tell it a story while dinner was cooking in some house where he was a guest. He could whistle up his crew and take the royal yacht, a trim and swift little galley, off for a day on the water. With a few bodyguards he could go a-horseback, hunting or simply exploring, well past the frontier. He could sit up late over wine, talking with scholars, philosophers, men of affairs, visiting skippers, everybody who had something worth listening to; and Bodilis was not the sole woman among them. He could participate in sports, watch contests and shows, hear music and readings, wander into books, lie on his back in the open and look at the clouds and find images in them until he drowsed off. He could practice his handicraft.

That last was especially precious to him, because so long denied. As a boy on his father's villa, he had been forever making things. As a soldier, he became the one in the cohort to see when some job of repair was tough or some tricky apparatus needed devising. However, this was limited, since the engineers and other specialists had their pride. Mostly Gratillonius had whittled, cut leather, that sort of thing. Now he had his own workshop, a shed by the stable behind the palace. (None but the King was allowed to keep horses inside the city). He filled it with hand tools, lathe, whatever he ordered. Although no joiner— he hoped eventually to teach himself that fine art—he fashioned furniture, household oddments, items for garden and travel, serviceable and not bad-looking. From the royal hands, they made welcome gifts.

He had been thus busied all day, a while after the inland Celts had celebrated their feast of Lug. Evening closed in. Smiling, pleasantly at ease, he put things in their places and left the shop. Outside, the sun was down and dusk settling in. Swallows darted after mosquitoes, shadows against violet. Most flowers had finished blooming, but trees and hedges made the air sweet, while rose mallow stood pale against walls. Before him, he thought, lay supper with Dahilis, just the two of them, and whatever might follow. He divided half his nights among the other five Gallicenae who expected it, Bodilis, Forsquilis, Vindilis, Maldunilis, Lanarvilis, when they were not having their courses or he was not elsewhere. It was never tense with them anymore, and sometimes it was very good, and they seemed content to let him be with Dahilis otherwise, as least until such time as it would endanger her child. The fullness upon her made her, if anything, more dear to him than ever, if that was possible.

Entering by a back door, he smiled at a servant who saluted and went down a hall lit by wax candles in bronze sconces, to the bedroom and its adjacent bathing basin. There he would cleanse himself and change into fresh clothes, not formal but colorful, cheerful, matching her spirit.

He entered and halted. She was there, dressed for the street. Beside her was Innilis, clad in a gown of sheer silk richly bordered with floral patterns. A star in gemmed silver gathered it low above her breasts, so that the Sign of the Goddess was plain to see. The women stood hand in hand. Lamplight darkened the window but gleamed off the rich brown hair of Innilis, delicate features, teeth white between lips always slightly parted.

"Uh, greeting," Gratillonius said, taken aback.

Dahilis came to him. "Darling, I go home this eventide," she told him. "Today did my Sister here seek me and give me the joyful news that she feels ready to be your true Queen."

Gratillonius stared across her shoulder at Innilis. "What a surprise!" he blurted, and noticed he was embracing Dahilis. "I had no wish, well, no wish to force aught on anyone."

"I know." Innilis clasped fingers together. "You were kind to wait while I...while I sought the Goddess within myself."

"'Twas not easy for her," Dahilis murmured against Gratillonius's collarbone. "Help her. I'll call again tomorrow. But we Nine, we've agreed Innilis should have time, days, in your company. Be good to my little Sister. Oh, but I know you will."

Strange, passed through Gratillonius, strange that Dahilis thinks of Innilis as her little sister, when Innilis is—what?—a decade older, and has borne a child, and— But she does look so vulnerable. No, more than that, she already carries a wound that has never healed. I'm sure of it, though I can't think what it might be.

"Well, my lady, you honor me," he found his way to saying.

Dahilis drew him forward until the three of them stood with arms entwining bodies. She kissed Gratillonius and Innilis. "Goodnight," she said between laughter and tears. "Have a splendid night." She departed.

"Um, uh—" Gratillonius searched desperately for words.

Innilis raised eyes that had been downcast. "Do as if I were Dahilis," she suggested.

"Why, why—" The Bull awoke. By Venus, she was beautiful! "Aye, indeed," Gratillonius exclaimed. "First let's have a bit of wine, and then maybe you'd like to share my bath, and later, we'll dine and talk—"

—And hours afterward—he had been as heedful and patient as he was able, until she began astounding him with passion—she whispered through the dark: "I was afraid. But now I love you too."

"Me *too*?" he asked.

She caught her breath. "Have we not all of us...others...we love?"

"Ah, well." He slid a hand down her flank and laid it to rest. "I'll inquire no further if you'd liefer I didn't."

"Oh, dear Grallon." She kissed him fleetingly, wearily, happily. For a moment, before sleep overtook her, resolution spoke: "No more am I afraid. I will leave the Herb aside, in hope of your child."

XXI

~ 1 ~

Summer welled forth in its final great warmth, light, and greenness. Fields stood ripe, sickles labored, wagons creaked behind oxen. Osismiic villagers brought in the last sheaf, gave it a name and the place of honor at festival, next day burned it and buried the ashes, that no witch might use them to wreak evil and that the God might come back to life at springtime. Soon asters bloomed defiant purple; but it would not be long before the first tinge of yellow was on the birches, and already the storks were leaving, while other migratory birds gathered to make ready in clangorous flocks on hills and at meres.

There was less observance of the season in Ys, but folk were nonetheless aware that another year was passing away. Though business bustled for a term at Goose Fair and the Cornmarket, where the Osismii brought foodstuffs to trade, and at Epona Square, where the horse dealers came, and in flour mills, breweries, bakeries, smoking and pickling establishments: Skippers' Market stood empty, windswept, no further merchant ships awaited. Fishermen drew their boats ashore and settled down to caulk, pitch, mend; most also sought odd jobs in town. Housewives polished lamps and saw to oil supplies. Those who could not afford this increasingly expensive commodity dipped wicks into tallow. Husbands stored away firewood bought from lumbermen. Suffetes who were well-to-do, which not all were by any means, prepared for a round of social events, now that work in the Great Houses would be damping down. Poor people looked to them and to the temples for help during the cold months, not that many in Ys ever knew dire want. The temples themselves made ready for rites immemorially old.

The full moon before autumnal equinox came early that year, in the middle of these happenings. It was the night when Forsquilis went forth alone, as the vision granted to her Sending had enjoined.

She left Ys by Aurochs Gate on the south. None of the sentries there or in the flanking towers called the Brothers challenged her;

portals stood open in times of peace. They recognized her, though, cowl thrown back to bare those sharply pure features to the moon, silver coronet around her brows, hair blowing loose; they dipped their pikes in awed salute, and when she had gone they dared not mutter about her mission, whatever it might be.

Wind prematurely whetted and skirling drove clouds in tatters across the sky. The moon seemed to fly among them. It touched their darkness with ice. Water swirled and snarled as she crossed the shouldering rock between city wall and headland. Beyond, along Pharos Way, rime glimmered on grass; gravel scrunched underfoot, a sound small and lonely and soon lost in the wind. Forsquilis followed the road west. The gap sundering rampart and promontory grew wider as she fared, until the western arc swung north and waves ran unhindered. Cape Rach reached somewhat farther. At its end, the lighthouse fire flickered and streamed like a candle flame. Ocean rolled beyond, around, out past Sena to the edge of the world. The crash and long-drawn rumble of surf on rocks came faintly.

She stopped short of the pharos. Here the road passed through the necropolis. Long had that stood forsaken. Headstones leaned crazily or lay hidden in weeds, names and remembrances blurred off them by centuries of weather. Tombs bulked and gaped. Some were made like miniature Roman temples, some like the dolmens and passage graves of the Old Folk. All were lichenous and eroded, gray beneath the hurtling moon. Forsquilis sought among them, stumbling over the gravestones, until she found the one she needed. It was the largest, a small mausoleum, the entrance Grecian-pillared; but no one could now make out what friezes had been carven above.

Forsquilis stopped. She raised her arms. The cloak fluttered at her shoulders as if trying to flee. "O Brennilis who sleeps within," she called, "forgive that I trouble your rest. It is the whisper of the Gods that sent me hither upon this night. No other sign has been granted me, save omens unclear and portents darkling, which say that your Ys is again at the end of an age. The Old is dying. Time travails with the New, and we fear Its face which we have not seen. For Ys, Brennilis, your Ys that you saved when you walked in sunlight, the sunlight you have forgotten—for Ys, Brennilis, I, Forsquilis your successor, beg a bed for the night with your dust, that in dream I may behold what must be done so Ys may live after I too am gone from the sun. Brennilis, receive your Sister."

She went to the door. If ever it had been locked, the lock was long corroded away. Bronze flaked off beneath her fingers. The door groaned and sagged open. Lightlessness waited. Forsquilis went in to the dead.

Rain blew out of hidden heaven and sea. Its noises and its bright gray engulfed the city. Water blinded windowpanes, drummed on roofs, swirled and gurgled in streets. No fire seemed able to fend off a raw dankness. It seeped through walls into lungs and marrow.

In what had been the temple of Mars, the Christian pastor Eucherius lay dying. His bed was a straw tick on the floor of the chamber which he had made his cell. A lamp guttered nearby; everywhere else the too-large room was full of the dark. Light touched eyeballs, bridge of nose, grizzled beard stubble. It lost itself in the hollows under his cheekbones. The Chi Rho and fish he had drawn in charcoal on the wall, to see above his feet, were swallowed up in thick, swaying shadow; but they were crude anyhow, barely recognizable. He had been no draftsman.

He plucked at the blanket. Slime rattled in his lungs and bubbled red on his lips. Bodilis must bring her ear almost to that mouth before she could hear him. "My lady Queen—" He stopped and struggled for air. "You are wise." Again he must toil to fill what was left of his lungs. "You are pagan, but wise and virtuous." He coughed and gasped. "Aristoteles, Vergilius—

"Maybe you know—

"One hears so many...tales of ghosts—

"Do souls...on their way...to judgment—

"Ever linger a while—

"Only a little while?"

She wiped away the sputum and stroked the thin gray hair. "I know not," she answered in the same Latin. "Who does? But in Ys, many of us believe Gallicenae can be reborn as seals, to lie off Sena waiting for their own dear ones, watching over them. Do you want more water?"

He shook his head. "No, thank you....I feel I am drowning....But I...must not...complain." Coughing shook him. "Gratillonius,...you have seen...enough men die,...worse hurt...than me." This time his fight was lengthy. "If I am being...contemptible,... please tell me,...and I'll try...to do better."

"No, no." The centurion squeezed the minister's hand, very carefully, so frail it was. "You are a man, Eucherius."

He had come in answer to Bodilis's summons, after she had heeded the plea of the deacon, who found the chorepiscopus lying swooned, with blood caking down the front of his coarse robe. It was not certain how long Eucherius had been thus alone. She washed him and gave him a fresh gown and tucked him into bed. Presently he regained awareness and courteously refused the healing Touch that Innilis might possess. Most likely Innilis would have failed regardless, as she did oftener than not in desperate cases. Hot infusions gave some brief strength. A courier was on the way to Audiarna. Gratillonius doubted the chorepiscopus would survive a trip over the mired road for Christian last rites. Meanwhile old deacon Prudentius, exhausted, had perforce tottered off to his rest. Bodilis and Gratillonius kept vigil.

Eucherius twitched a smile. "You are good too," he said. "As for me,...it would be very pleasant...to see Neapolis again,...dreaming before the blue bay,...my mother's house,...the small crooked streets,...a garden where...Claudia and I— But God's will be done."

Of course it shall be done, Gratillonius thought. What else? Ahura-Mazda reigns, and beyond Him, inexorable Time. Well, people babble in their death throes.

"Look after my poor," Eucherius begged. "Get Prudentius...home to Redonia...to die...with his kin...and in Christ."

"We will, we will," Bodilis promised, weeping most quietly, keeping sight of it from him.

He scratched at her hand. "My congregation,...they who thirst for the Word,...who shall comfort them now?"

Gratillonius recalled his own mother at her prayers. The remembrance overwhelmed. "I'll bring in a new shepherd for your faithful as soon as possible," he heard himself declare.

Eucherius lifted his head an inch off the pillow. "Is that a promise?"

"It is. Before Mithras, it is." What else could Gratillonius say, with the deep eyes of Bodilis turned on him?

"Good. Good... Also for you... Not only your chance of salvation,...my son." Eucherius cawed. "Could a...totally pagan Ys...hope for much alliance...with Rome?"

Startled, Gratillonius thought: But he is not maundering!

Eucherius sank back. "May I...pray for you two...by name,...as I do...for all Ys?"

Bodilis knelt on the stone floor and embraced him. Abruptly a measure of resonance was in his voice: "Our Father, Who are in Heaven—"

The cough that seized him shivered every bone. Underneath it was a hideous rattling, gurgling noise. With each convulsion, blood gouted from his mouth. Bodilis ignored it, held him close.

He slumped back. Waxen lids fell half over his eyes. He answered no call or sign; he seemed barely to breathe; to the touch he was clammy and cold. Bodilis cleansed him again as best she could. She and Gratillonius stayed at their post. Eucherius died shortly before his confessor arrived from Audiarna.

~ 3 ~

"The military season draws to a close. A winter campaign would be possible, of course—you have read your histories—but it is not really feasible, for either Theodosius or myself. Why dare the unpredictables of weather, supply, and sickness? Instead, by tacit consent, we withdraw to our headquarters and govern the territories we hold, pending spring. After all, in this game the prize is the Empire. Neither of us wants to dissipate it.

"I could almost wish that Gratianus were not a victim of the war. More than vengeance for his fallen colleague, Theodosius has prestige to consider. Else he might have made agreement already. As matters stand, he has given to his eldest son Arcadius the title of Augustus to which I aspire. We shall have to see what God desires.

"He helps those who help themselves. Christ keep me from sinful pride. Yet I cannot but feel that our successes to date show that the ultimate victory of our cause is in His plan for our Mother Rome. While campaigning may have ended for the nonce, we must not relax our efforts on every possible front. To do so would be sacrilegious.

"You have done remarkably well, C. Valerius Gratillonius. I have commended you for it before, and I will not forget it in future. However, as a soldier you know that duty has not ended until the enemy has passed beneath the yoke.

"I thought I had assigned you a minor station on the periphery. I was wrong. You yourself have shown your importance. Now a great part of my strategy for the coming year turns on you.

"Armorica must remain stable, fending off any barbarians or other invaders but else quiescent. I know better than to call troops from it, but I cannot permit my opponents to try. Moreover, in view of your success against the Scoti, I want you to extend a webwork of defensive cooperation not only north along the Saxon shore, but south as far as the Liger estuary. In these past months, wittingly or unwittingly, you have through your negotiations and shows of force, and the secondary effects of these, drawn an outline of it across the peninsula. Now I order you to begin on the actual structure.

"The Duke of the Armorican Tract has consented to this. Herewith his letter of authorization to you. His agreement was given reluctantly and under pressure. You will understand that no such official enjoys handing a crucial commission to an unknown quantity such as you. I also suspect he is less than enthusiastic about the cause of Magnus Maximus. He is, though, intelligent enough to realize what an opportunity this is for Rome. The attention and strength of his command have been concentrated in the east and the interior, and he feels this must remain so. Terrible though the devastations wrought by pirates have been, an overland invasion of Germans would be worse, as experience has shown. Therefore he has scamped the coast defenses. Now at last, God willing, something can be done about them. Do it well, and you will make your mark—"

Gratillonius laid down the letter. While he had it well-nigh memorized, he had thought he would do best to read it aloud to Soren Cartagi. "I could go on," he said, "but certain details are confidential, and surely you see the general drift."

The speaker of his cult, otherwise head of the Great House of Timbermen, nodded heavily. Outside this conference room of the palace,

215

the day reached bleakly bright. Wind whooped. "I do," he said. "You'd fain leave Ys."

"I must," Gratillonius replied. "To Condate Redonum and elsewhere —a circuit with my soldiers, to carry my warrant and knit the region together as it should always have been."

"Ah. You'd not be content with couriers as hitherto?"

"Nay, I cannot be. The Romans are unorganized and demoralized. They have responded to my calls for a united front against the barbarians with assent but little action and no vigor. Where it comes to choosing sides in a conflict for the Imperium— And yet Rome must have one master, and he an able man. Can you not see?"

Soren stroked the beard that fringed his massive countenance. "Well do I see. Ys shall serve the ambitions of your war lord."

"For the common weal—" Gratillonius left his chair, prowled the room, stood for a while staring out at the wind, turned and thrust his gaze against that of Soren. "Hark," he said, "I called you in to talk about this not only because of your position in *my* Temple. You are a leader among the Suffetes. They listen to you closer than to most. Help me, and together we may do as much for Ys as Caesar did."

"I have wondered how much that truly was," Soren murmured. He straightened where he sat. "No matter; too late. But you, the King of Ys, propose to go faring about, abandoning your sacral duties, for two or three months, on behalf of Rome. This has never been."

Gratillonius gave him a tight grin. "I do not propose to do it, good sir. I am going to do it. What I have hoped for is your support, your explanation to the Suffetes and public that 'tis for their own welfare."

"And if that support is not forthcoming?"

Gratillonius shrugged. "Then I go anyway. How do you plan to stop me? But I should think you'd liefest not rive the state asunder."

Soren glared. "Be careful. Be very careful, my lord. 'Tis happened erenow that Ys has had Kings who overreached themselves. Suddenly challengers appeared at the Wood, one after the next in rapid succession, until those Kings fell." He raised his hand. "Mistake me not. Here is no threat, simply a warning."

Gratillonius's temper, never the strongest part of him, flew into flinders. Somehow he kept their heat from igniting him; but he planted fists on hips, loomed over Soren, and ground out of his teeth: "Enough, sir. 'Tis you who are reckless. Not yet have my Gallicenae called down on me the curse they did on Colconor, whom I slew. Nay, I have spoken with them, and they are willing for me to go. A new age is upon Ys, upon the world.

"Enough of provincial selfishness and dragging of feet. My sword and the swords of my men lie sheathed. We will draw them for Rome, when and as necessity dictates. Bethink you how many blades you can summon on that day."

Soren's breath rasped. I must not drive him into a corner where all he can do is try to fight his way free, Gratillonius comprehended. Again he turned away to the window and the wind. After a moment he said, quite low:

"Sir, we really should not lie in strife as too often we've done. I know not why you've been hostile to me; myself, I've ever wished for friendship. But in your words, no matter. What does matter is the lives of our Mother cities. They are conjoined. Let us set aside any bitterness, yea, any pride, and seek to serve them."

It took an hour or more, but he won grudging acceptance.

XXII

~ 1 ~

At equinox all the Nine must be in Ys, attending the Council and carrying out certain rites. They took advantage of it to meet by themselves in the temple of Belisama.

Quinipilis opened proceedings. Through the greenish light from the windows, between the four walls whereon were depicted aspects of the Goddess, the old woman limped to the dais. Her staff and her breathing rattled loud in the stillness. Painfully she climbed up, turned about, leaned on the stick, and peered down at her Sisters. In blue robes and high white headdresses, they looked back, each in her own way. Bodilis sat calm and expectant, Lanarvilis alert, Dahilis wide-eyed, half afraid and half defiant. The crisis had aroused some excitement in Maldunilis, but in Fennalis largely the indignation that had frequently seized her these past months. Innilis huddled close to Vindilis, who held her hand. Forsquilis kept a distance aside, her countenance unreadable. She had been very quiet since the last full moon.

"Ishtar-Isis-Belisama, Your presence be with us, Your peace dwell within us, Your wisdom speak through us," Quinipilis prayed. Ritual response murmured from the benches. When the invocation was finished, she began:

"This is a grave matter, perhaps more than the cursing of Colconor; for it concerns that new King whom we ourselves, under the Gods, did summon to slay him and join with us in holy wedlock. Yet the first thing I would say is this—do not be daunted, my dears. We will find our way."

"The same way as erstwhile?" asked Fennalis.

"What mean you, mother?" exclaimed Lanarvilis, appalled. "Not to bring early death on Gratillonius!"

"Nay!" shrilled Dahilis. She curbed herself. "You, you cannot mean that, Fennalis, you who are ever so kindly and helpful."

The little plump woman stiffened. "I did not counsel it," she declared. "However, somebody must needs set the thought forth. Else we'll slink around it terrified, as we did when it touched Colconor, far too long."

Quinipilis stood stoutly above. "Well, then, let us clear the air," she directed. "Why should we even consider ridding Ys— and ourselves—of Gratillonius? He's able, forceful, honorable, and better prepared to cope with the outside world than any other King in living memory. *I* think him Heaven-sent. But say on, unabashed. This is the hour for plain speaking."

"Understand me," replied Fennalis, "I hate him not. In truth he is all you maintain. But his soul is harnessed to Rome. Bodilis, you've told the tale of the Atreides, how a curse may hound generation after generation, bringing woe on whole peoples. Is there a fatal flaw in this King? Think only of his leaving Ys."

"Not till after Council and festival," Dahilis said quickly. "And we agreed!"

"What choice had we, as suddenly as he put it before us?"

"There is naught absolutely requiring his presence throughout the autumn," Bodilis reminded them. "A King has always been excused from his Watch in the Wood when a great holy time is on hand, or a great necessity such as war—and who judges the necessity but himself? We can safely assume no challenger will appear. If any does, well, we can house him in the Red Lodge to await Gratillonius's return. He promised us he'd come back before solstice."

"Nonetheless I'm uneasy," Lanarvilis admitted. "What if he perishes on his travels?"

"Ys has met contingencies erenow in her history," said Bodilis. "The Key remains here. Not that he'll likely encounter any mischance he can't cope with."

"Be that as it may, this journey of his is but a single violation of ancient ways," Fennalis pursued. "We have heard, secretly between us, how he insulted a stream consecrated to Belisama. Everyone knows how he buried a corpse where its rottenness would drain down into Lir's sea. And—" She reddened, gulped, plowed ahead: "And he made mockery of the sacred marriage."

"He did not!" Dahilis cried.

"That...breach...has been healed," Innilis whispered. "Has it not?" Her glance strayed downward. No doubt remained that she was with child.

"Indeed he has been filling gaps," said Maldunilis smugly.

Fennalis flushed deeper. "Has he?"

"You and I are too old for more children," Quinipilis stated.

"Just the same—" Fennalis choked on her words.

Bodilis leaned over to stroke her hand and murmur, "We know. We feel the hurt to your pride and, aye, your loneliness every night.

But Sister mine, remember Wulfgar—my father, who died of my birth as surely as my mother could have done—because she was his daughter. And Wulfgar was sheerly heathen, a sacrificer of horses to Thor. How much more does a civilized man with a stern faith, like Gratillonius, look on incest as deadly sin? He knows, too, how of old it brought damnation on Grecian Oedipus and plague on his kingdom, innocent of wrong intent though he and his mother had been. Why, in Ys, too, 'tis abhorred."

Fennalis's features worked. "The royal marriage is different. The Gods Themselves choose the Gallicenae. They know what They do! Oh, aye, since I am no longer under command of the moon, he may claim lawfulness in shunning me." She forced a smile. "And I hope you'll agree I've no large vanity to wound. I was ever homely and dumpy and, once past girlhood, resigned to it." She paused. "But what if, in future, when some of us here have passed on...what if then the Gods confront Gratillonius with the full meaning of Queenship?"

"They wouldn't!" Dahilis wailed.

A shiver went among the rest. "Will They, ever?" Innilis asked desperately. "What would make Them that angry at him?"

"He has already affronted Them," Fennalis said. Now her tone held pity; she might almost have been speaking to one of the poor families to whom she ministered, telling them that their breadwinner's illness could prove mortal. "That is why we are gathered—true, my Sisters? We've bespoken the burial and the misuse of Belisama's waters and his forthcoming journey. Can we be too quick to forgive his treatment of us?" Still more gently: "Dahilis, darling, I'm sorry. I blame not you, as young and loving as you are. But he did, for months, deny his other wives. If he has lately become more dutiful, he has not repented the past, nor done penance for any of his transgressions." Her voice lifted, ragged. "Will the Gods bear with that?"

"Aye," said Quinipilis, "there is the real question. You've done well, Fennalis, to force it thus out into the open. What shall we do? Disown the King?"

Dahilis's denial was merely the loudest of those that arose from seven pairs of lips and, after a moment, the eighth.

Quinipilis nodded. "Good." Strictness descended. "If he will not do expiation—and in the conscience that is his, he cannot—then we must do it for him. But hear me, Gallicenae. We are not ourselves without guilt. *You* are not."

Innilis caught her breath. Vindilis let go her hand, flung that arm around her waist, and lifted the free hand for attention. Her visage turned from side to side along the tier, eagle-proud. "You have heard what is between us twain," she said. "We will not forsake it. We cannot. I even believe we may not."

"I think, I hope we have all come to understand, since hearing yester'en," answered Bodilis. That had been at a rite of purification for the Nine alone, when they made confession of everything they knew that might stand between them and the Goddess. Thus had Forsquilis ordered. "We shall keep your secret because we must. Yet is this not itself a faithlessness toward the King our husband?"

"I wonder, too, how many of you besides Innilis have opened your wombs to him," said Quinipilis. "Oh, the Herb is yours to use as you see fit, Her gift to Her high priestesses. But to refuse Gratillonius children, as though he were horrible Colconor—"

"I haven't," piped Maldunilis. "'Tis but he's not futtered me often enough."

Laughter jerked through the room, less mirthful than startled.

"I have not either," said Bodilis. "But after each of us has decided—for herself—'tis the Goddess Who disposes. Thus far only Dahilis and Innilis—" She sighed. "Let us search our souls. Meanwhile, how can we set right that which has gone wrong?"

Silence lengthened. One by one, gazes sought Forsquilis.

She rose and, through the deepening twilight, approached the dais. There she helped Quinipilis down and guided the dowager to a seat before taking the high place. A while she stood beneath the Resurrection of Taranis, like an eidolon, before she said, low and slow:

"You know what I did in our need, that I sought the tomb of Brennilis and slept next to her bones. You know that hitherto I have kept silence about what dreams came to me; for they were weird and ambiguous, and still am I unsure whether I have seen through to their meaning. But this is what I believe they foretold.

"The Gods are troubled, even as are we mortals. Therefore They will stay Their anger and at Their appointed time make peace with us, that Ys may abide and keep holy Their names.

"This is the sacrifice They require. At the Turning of the Sun, one among the Nine shall not be here as always erenow, but must keep Vigil on Sena. She will receive a hard test. If she endures it well, then shall she be purified, and with her the sacred family, Queens, King, and daughters. Thus did I hear the Word."

Ere anyone else could speak, Vindilis called: "I will go!"

Forsquilis shook her head. "I fear not. For the Word was that she must bear the morrow beneath her heart. I can only think this means she must be heavy with child."

To and fro went their looks. Winter solstice was but three months hence; and for most of that span, Gratillonius would be gone.

Dahilis swallowed twice or thrice, thereafter said almost merrily, "Why, that is myself. Of course I'll go."

"Oh, nay, darling, nay!" protested Fennalis. "You'll be too near your lying-in. You know how apt we are to be weatherbound yonder, in winter perhaps days on end."

"Fear not. As close as I can reckon it, my time will be half a month or more after solstice."

"Hm. I've consulted records. Both Bodilis and you surprised your mother Tambilis, despite your having different fathers. Early births run in that bloodline."

Dahilis had attained calm. "The Goddess will care for me."

Hesitantly, reluctantly, Bodilis said, "Remember the tradition."

"What tradition?" Dahilis asked, bewildered.

"You may never have heard. 'Tis a story ancient and obscure. I sought it once in the archives, but too much is missing after centuries, and I could neither confirm nor disconfirm. The story is that Brennilis was born out on Sena. Thereupon a seal gained human voice, to prophesy that any so born thereafter would bring the end of the age which Brennilis was to make begin. It may be a mere folk tale."

The others hearked back. The law was simply that one and only one from among them must be on the island, save on the high holy days or in periods of peril. She could be any of the Nine; and more than weather worked to keep Vigils out of orderly cycle. There could be strong obligations elsewhere, illness, the frailties of age, advanced pregnancy, evil omens— In spite of every precaution it had happened a few times in the past that a high priestess was dead when her relief arrived; and this called for the same hecatomb against disaster as when a King died in bed.

Sight converged on Innilis. Vindilis held her close, close. She stared out of that shelter and said in a thin tone, "I've been chosen. Have I not?"

"It seems you have," answered Forsquilis. Compassion stirred beneath steeliness. "Take courage. It may be hard, but it shall be glory unto you, and unto your new daughter."

Innilis blinked back tears. "Well, I will go. Gladly."

Vindilis's lips brushed her cheek.

"I have a word further," said Forsquilis as though it hurt to talk. "In my dreams was a sigil, white-hot from the fire, and it sealed a book with wax made not from honeycomb but from the fat and blood of sacrificed humans." To horrified exclamations: "Nay, the grisly rites of old are long behind Ys." She smiled, briefly and bleakly. "Moreover, such a seal would not hold in this real world. 'Twas a sign for me."

She braced herself before continuing: "I have thought, I have sought, I have prayed and offered; and this is how I read the vision. We must pledge our faith beforehand. We must take the Great Oath—by the Ordeal—that we will indeed hold a Vigil at Midwinter, which never was before, and that none shall stand it but she whom the Gods have marked out. Then shall all again be well with Ys."

Anew the Nine fell mute. They had undergone the Ordeal when they plighted fealty to each other and to their purpose ere they went forth on Sena and cursed their King. That had not happened for generations earlier. They fasted and thirsted and scourged....

Dahilis gripped her belly. Light-boned as she was, the unborn swelled and burdened her. "Oh, please," she implored. "Not me. I could lose her."

Quinipilis stood up and made a gesture of blessing. "I daresay 'tis uncalled for in your case, youngster," she said. "And in Innilis's. Your situations are patent." Her wrinkled countenance went from side to side, haughtily. "As for the rest of us, we can very well endure it again. We *are* the Gallicenae."

~ 2 ~

His last night in Ys Gratillonius spent with Lanarvilis. This was not by chance. Dahilis was now forbidden him, save for a kiss and a promise, until after she became a mother. The remaining six out of the Nine he had begun visiting in turn, at their homes so that he might at least have Dahilis freely about in the palace during the day. Everybody concerned realized that, for any of numerous reasons, a turn must occasionally be postponed or exchanged. His forthcoming absence was just the first and most obvious example. Still, he had been surprised and somewhat dashed when the message came that it would not be Forsquilis who received him, but Lanarvilis.

He put on civil garb and his best face, to seek her house about sunset. She met him in the atrium sumptuously clad in a low-bosomed scarlet-and-gold gown that flattered her figure, the blond hair coiled about her head and caught by a garnet-studded silver frontlet. "Welcome, my lord," she said, and held out a hand.

He took it, as was Ysan style. "Thank you, my lady. I regret I could not arrive sooner. Preparations for departure tomorrow sunrise—"

She chuckled. "I foresaw, and ordered a supper that would take no harm from waiting. Shall we to it? We've much to talk about."

They went side by side through this most luxuriously appointed of the Queens' dwellings, past drapes of Oriental opulence, big-eyed Egyptian portraits, exquisite Grecian figurines, and—somehow not incongruous—Roman busts, Marius, Caesar, the first Augustus, Hadrianus, they whose workmanship had shored up, enlarged, repaired their state. Although the food and wines served in the triclinium were no Lucullan feast, they were excellent. A boy stood in the background softly playing a lyre.

"My lady is most generous," said the King after they were settled.

"The Gallicenae desired a worthy sendoff for you," Lanarvilis answered. "We discussed it, and the choice fell on me."

He sipped from his goblet, a taste rich and tart-edged, as cover for his close regard of her. The countenance—green-eyed, slightly wide in the nose and heavy in the mouth, past the freshness of youth, withal by no means bad-looking—was amply mobile but told him nothing. Best might be if he took the initiative. "You do it elegantly," he said. "However, methinks you were elected for more than the table you set."

Unsurprised, she nodded. "Can you guess why?"

222

"Well, you are the closest of the Nine to the mundane affairs of the city. Quinipilis doubtless was once, but her years are upon her. The rest have their special interests. For yours, you occupy yourself with the business of the Temple corporation. You are often in conference with Soren Cartagi, who's not only Speaker for Taranis but a power in the economy and politics of Ys. Hannon Baltisi, too, Lir Captain— you've taken a lead in reconciling them with me, or to me. In that it's helped that you have more knowledge of the Roman world than perhaps anyone else among your people. Were you a man, Lanarvilis, I'd call you a statesman."

"You cannot, simply because I am a woman?" she said in an undertone. Promptly, aloud: "Your words do me honor, my lord. Aye, the sisterhood did feel I might best represent them this eventide—not least because I am, as you know, favorable to Rome. Rome has given civilization so much—the Roman peace—"

As her voice trailed away, he added, "That peace which is falling apart, but which I hope to help restore."

"True. Therefore 'twas felt we should talk freely, you and I. Tell me, for you've been taciturn about it, what your plans are for your journey."

"If I've said little," he replied carefully, "'twas on account of there being little to say. How can I lay plans ere I've learned, in detail, what the actual circumstances are? 'Twould be scant use sending Ysan agents unaccompanied. No matter how honest their intentions, they could never quite see, quite understand."

She smiled. "I do, at any rate to the extent of agreeing 'tis a Roman military man who must go. But can you say somewhat of your aims afterward?"

He had no hesitation about that, and the meal passed in conversation as good as with Bodilis—not the same, largely down-to-earth, but scarcely less intelligent. The wine flowed more readily than either of them noticed.

—Her bedchamber adjoined a room of blue carpeting, crimson drapes, furniture with inlays of walrus ivory and upholstery of leather. There they went for dessert—honeycakes, spiced fruit, a sweet Falernian to drink—and private talk prior to retiring. They sat together, leaning against the cushions on a couch that had a back, the refreshments on a low table before them. He rested an arm across that back, hand on the warmth and smoothness of her shoulder. She leaned close to him. Several beeswax candles burned; their light picked out the fine lines in her brow and radiating from her eyes, the mesh across the skin beneath her throat; and the flesh under her chin had started to sag; yet she was a handsome woman.

"Your scheme looks sound to me," she said softly. "I will so tell my Sisters, and we'll ask the Gods to favor your enterprises."

"You can do better than that," he responded. "You can work on the secular powers, Suffetes, Guilds, aye, common folk. If Ys is to take the lead in Armorica that duty calls for, and reap the rewards that faithful service calls for, Ys must be whole hearted about it."

"What can I...we...do?"

"Persuade them. Make them see 'tis their destiny. You, Lanarvilis, you could begin with Soren Cartagi—" He felt her stiffen. "Why, what's wrong?"

"Oh, naught." She leaned forward, took up her goblet, drank deep. Staring before her: "Soren is an honorable man."

"Did I say otherwise? Look you, I've always regretted it when we've been at odds. I cannot think why. He's learned, able, aye, and a patriot. He should know where the real welfare of Ys lies. For myself, I'm willing to yield on many matters. But if I seek discussion, he soon breaks it off. What is it that makes him clash with me, over and over? Can you, his friend, milden him?"

"I can try." Again she took a long drink, before turning her head and saying, eye to eye: "But you do us, your Queens, an injustice. You never trouble to imagine how we already labor for you."

Caught short, he had no better return than, "What? Well, I know you pray, and...and you tell me 'tis your doing I am here, although—"

"Nay, more than that, and more. But I verge on secrets." Lanarvilis brought her attention back to the cup. Her laugh was uneven. "Desist. We've been political quite long enough, and morning comes far too early, and you must be away and I to my penance. Let us be happy while we may."

"Your penance?" he asked sharply. "What mean you?"

She bit her lip. "I misspoke me."

Concern rose in him. During these past difficult months she had been steadfast, neither toadying nor accusing, just quietly going about her work on behalf of the city and its Gods. Her spirit was a soldier's. "Dear, tell me. Is aught amiss?"

"Yea!" she flung forth. "And we must set it aright, we, the Nine. As soon as you are gone...certain austerities begin."

"But what *is* the matter?" he pleaded. "I should know, that I may help. I am the King."

Metal rang: "You are the King. A man. Do you admit me into your mystery of Mithras? Then ask no more about this."

He took a while to say, unwontedly humble, "So be it. However, here I am, and here I will be again. Always feel free to call upon me."

"Oh, Grallon—Gratillonius!" She put down her cup and cast arms about his neck. Her breath was heady with wine. "Enough, I said. Let's forget all else and be only ourselves. Surely we've earned that much."

—Very late, as lamps were flickering low, he raised himself on an elbow and looked down at her where she lay half asleep. Drowsiness crept over him too. But the thoughts, the images stole by behind his eyes, before his soul. Of the seven who were fully his wives, might this be the strangest?

Dahilis, of course, was purely loving. Maldunilis enjoyed, in her lazy and slipshod fashion, and was in truth not a bad person. Bodilis was...comradely, altogether a woman when they embraced but otherwise a friend who had a great deal to impart; between him and her he felt bonds of loyalty growing like those between him and his father or him and Parnesius or— With Innilis he came to the frontier of enigma. She was sweet, acceptant, sometimes responsive, delighted to be bearing his child...and beyond her defenses he glimpsed a shadow, a thing which he could not bring himself to ask about because he was afraid of hurting her. Vindilis seemed (though what was a seeming worth?) a little more comprehensible, whatever wounds she bore being encased in armor, out of sight and never bespoken. About anything else she talked with him like man to man; that included their joinings, where they had found ways which suited him sufficiently and left her, well, not disgusted. Forsquilis— He had looked forward to spending this night beside Forsquilis. Whether or not it was true that a King was powerless except among the Nine, Gratillonius must needs keep abstinent on his coming travels, since Ysans as well as legionaries would accompany him. Forsquilis might actually have made him welcome such a rest. He knew she was the deepest into the unknown of all the Gallicenae; but whenever they were alone, that soon ceased to make any difference.

Lanarvilis, though— He lowered his head to brush lips across the down that covered her cheek, as soft as moonlight. She had learned how to take her pleasure with him, as she took it with her home, art collection, food and drink, the spectacles and recreations and social occasions which Ys so abundantly offered. As for her work in administration and statecraft, doubtless she had a strong sense of duty, but doubtless it was also something she enjoyed, perhaps in the same way he enjoyed making a piece of craftsmanship grow between his hands. Then what was lacking in her life? From time to time Gratillonius had caught a sense of terrible emptiness. This, too, was a thing about which he did not venture to ask.

She stirred beneath his caress. "You *are* a good man," she mumbled. "I'll do my best, for you and your Rome."

XXIII

~ 1 ~

The Black Months were upon Armorica. As Midwinter drew nigh, day shrank to little more than a glimmer between two huge darknesses, the sun wan and low and oftenest lost in leaden clouds or icy rain. Weather slowed the last stage of journeying, and dusk had fallen when

Gratillonius saw Ys again from the heights of Point Vanis. It sheered sharp athwart the tarnished argency of the sea. Beyond, mists drifted past the pharos flame, the sole star aloft.

He reined in to give the headstone of Eppillus a Roman salute. Metal clinked, leather creaked, horses snorted wearily at his back. "Dress ranks!" he heard Adminius bark. "We'll enter in style, we will." With a rattle of shields and stamp of hobnails, the soldiers obeyed, also the Ysan marines who reinforced them. The deputy had extended his authority over those, not overtly as against their own officer, but by sheer weight of example on the march.

If there had been no trouble, quite likely that was thanks to the sight of disciplined troops. Saxon pirates had ended their raiding till spring, but the woods housed Bacaudae the year around—ever more numerous, it was said, and certainly apt to be desperate in this season.

Gratillonius turned downhill. The horse of Bomatin Kusuri came alongside. He had represented Ys before the Imperials of Armorica. Well qualified he was, Mariner delegate to the Council of Suffetes: more than that, a man reasonably young and entirely vigorous, himself a skipper whose trading and occasional slaving voyages had made him the familiar of folk from Thule to Dál Riata. Gratillonius and he got along well.

"Ha!" he said in his bluff fashion. "Is it a true parade when nobody's out to watch? Well, I'm as glad of that. Best to arrive quietly."

Gratillonius glanced at him. In the murk he saw only the hulking body, the flamboyant sweep of mustaches; barbarian-bestowed tattoos were shadowed. "I daresay you're eager for hearth and bed."

"Well, now, my lord, between the twain of us—mind you, I say naught against my wife, she's a fine woman, though I could wish she'd nag me less to put on her kind of airs—but as long as we are coming in unheralded— Should she ever ask, would you tell her I had work to clear away, and therefore lodged this night in Dragon House?"

"But there's nothing we can't take care of tomorrow."

"Save for a bit of sport, without getting jawed for it afterward. We've been going hard, this trek. For safe return, methinks I should make a thank offering to Banba." That fertility Goddess had, in Ys, become the patroness of harlots. "Pour her a libation or two, haw!"

Gratillonius frowned. Lying went against his grain as well as his faith. However, the chance was slight that Bomatin's wife would ever inquire of him, no matter how much she tried to shine by reflection from the King.

"You, my lord, have a choice ready for you—" The seaman checked himself. "Forgive me. I meant no disrespect. 'Tis but that we've fared and worked shoulder by shoulder all this while, you never throwing your weight around more than necessary. I've sometimes forgotten you're also the Incarnation of Taranis."

"I understand," said Gratillonius, relieved. He would have hated to give a reprimand or, worse, a cut of the vinestaff. Yet if he did not maintain the dignity of the King, could he remain effective as prefect? He had two dozen legionaries to support his governance of a city ancient, proud, and secretive. It was not what he had awaited when he left Isca Silurum, ages agone.

"We did a good job," Bomatin said. After a silence broken just by clopping hoofs and thudding feet, surf on reefs and cliffs as they neared the water: "Did we not?"

"The future will tell," said Gratillonius, which ended talk.

Riding onward, he found his own mind less on what had happened than on what lay ahead. Immediately ahead. Had he entered by daylight he would have gone straight to Dahilis. No, the dear lass would have come forth to meet him, running as fast as the weight within allowed, laughing and weeping for joy. But she was doubtless asleep, or ought soon to be, and rousing her might be a little risky, now when her time approached....

The sentries at High Gate, and up in the Gaul and the Roman, cried hail. "Quiet," Gratillonius ordered. "No sense in a tumult. Everything went well. Tomorrow in the Forum I'll tell the people. Tonight we're wearied and need our rest."

He left his horse to the military grooms, bade his men farewell as became a commander, and walked off, still in wet cloak and muddied centurion's outfit. Windows gleamed here and there, out of surrounding houses or aloft in towers. Even nowadays, when oil had become costly, Ysans liked to keep late hours; they would burn tallow if they must. Despite gloom rapidly congealing to night, broad Lir Way was easy to walk on, and when he turned off in the direction of Elven Gardens, Dolphin Lane was so known to him that he walked its narrow, wall-enclosed twistiness with never a stumble.

Glass was aglow at the house of Bodilis. He banged the knocker, which was in the form of a fouled anchor, blurred by centuries of hands (and what had each of those callers been seeking?). It was no surprise that she opened the door herself. She usually let her servants go home when they had cleaned up after a supper simple and early. Then she was likely to stay awake far into the night, reading, writing, creating.

What caught at Gratillonius's throat was how beautiful she was. A blue robe, wrapped around and held by a sash, hugged the full but still graceful figure. Her hair fell in soft and lustrous waves past the broad, blunt, alive countenance and eyes that were like Dahilis's. Lamplight and beeswax candlelight from behind could only touch a curve, a tress, the hands that reached forth, but somehow he saw. "Oh, you, you," breathed the husky voice, "welcome home, beloved!"

He embraced her, mouth to mouth, till he heard a slight gasp and realized he was straining her breasts too hard against his coat of mail.

He eased his grip, let palms rove across shoulders, back, hips, while the kiss went on.

"Come in," she said finally, let him by, and closed and barred the door behind them. "How are you? What have you...what have you accomplished, King?"

"I am well." He glanced down at himself and snorted a laugh. "Though mired and sweaty and, in general, unfit for polite company....Dahilis! How fares she?"

"Excellently."

"A-a-ah-h-h."

Bodilis hesitated. "I took for granted you'd seek her first."

He felt his face grow warm. "We arrived later than we foresaw. Best leave her undisturbed. I knew you'd tell me the truth."

Bodilis laughed, low in her throat. "And once any fears for her were allayed—why, you've been long on the road."

He gave her a crooked grin. "I have that."

Her eyelids drooped. "'Tis been long for me too."

He strode forward. She fended him off, playfully, seductively. "Nay, wait half a heartbeat! Would you not like refreshment first? You wouldn't? Then let's at least remove your armor and wash you clean. I'll enjoy doing that."

—They lay on their sides, close together, each with a hand on the haunch of the other. As yet they felt no need to draw up the blankets. Recklessly many lamps illuminated her in gold. Outside, rain had begun, a susurrus against the shutters.

"Aye, on the whole, things have continued as erstwhile in Ys," she said. "Well, poor Innilis has been having a bad time, as she did when carrying Hoel's child. Sickness, pains—but no worse than before, if we remember aright, and the first birth is commonly the hardest, and we Sisters have been taking care of her. I think—if you seek her out tomorrow as a friend, simply a friend...that will cheer her much."

"Of course I will."

"Of course. You are you." Bodilis's expression intensified. "She needs every help she can get. This solstice she takes Vigil on Sena."

"What?" asked Gratillonius, bemused. "I thought...on the quarter days...all you Gallicenae were here."

"Hitherto true. But the age born of Brennilis is dying, and—" Bodilis laid fingers across his lips. "Search no further. This is a thing that must be, that Ys may live."

Chill struck through him. She sensed it, smiled, flowed nearer. "'Tis well, not ill. A duty to carry out, like standing on the Wall. Surely you've overcome worse hazards this trip. Tell me."

He hung back. She nibbled his earlobe. "Oh, do, Gratillonius. I'm afire with curiosity."

He became eager to oblige. It was a line of retreat from that which had no name. And this was Bodilis whom he had sought, Bodilis, because she was the one who could both meet his body's needs and then discourse widely and deeply—more so than he could always follow, but that was itself a rousing challenge— He set Innilis aside.

"The tale goes on and on, like the miles," he said. "I've kept a daily record which I want you to read, if you'll overlook my lame language. For now, though—you're not sleepy?—well, let's bring in some wine and lie at ease while we talk. Interrupt me whenever you wish."

She did, in questions and comments that heightened his own understanding of what he had seen and done; but mostly she led him on. The story came forth of his march to sad Vorgium, which had once been prosperous as Ys; to Condate Redonum, where he privily broached ideas for putting the Frankish laeti in their place; south as far as Portus Namnetum and Condevincum, to consider mutual assistance between the hinterland resources of those neighboring cities and the navy of Ys; back north to Ingena and thence along the route he had followed earlier, until he branched off it to visit the tribune in charge at Gesocribate— "On the whole, we reached agreements in principle. 'Twill take years to build the machinery and get it working properly, I know. Still, we've made a fair start."

"*You* have," she murmured, and again her caresses went seeking.

~ 2 ~

Vindilis had moved in with Innilis. None thought the worse of this, or even of their sharing a bed. The younger woman was so often ill and in pain; she should not be left to servants who loved her but were ignorant and clumsy about such matters. In truth, nothing untoward happened, as weak as Innilis had become, beyond kisses, and those grew to be as between mother and child.

A cry in the night or a feverish tossing would wake Vindilis. She then did what she could. All vestals studied the elements of medicine, and priestesses of every grade who showed any gift for it were trained as full physicians. Vindilis practiced little. Her hands were cunning enough, but the Touch of the Goddess was not in them, nor had there been comfort in her manner. This last had changed of late.

The worst attack thus far ended a fitful sleep. Vindilis bounded onto a floor cold beneath her feet and bent over the other. Shutters blocked off any light from outside, but she always left a lamp burning when they retired. The untrimmed wick streamed smoke and a purulent, guttering flame. She could just see that Innilis lay hunched, arms and knees drawn against a now swelling belly. Her hair was lank with the sweat that studded a face blotched, yellowish, sunken in around the bones. The reek drowned any woman-fragrance. Sobs and hissings went between cracked lips. Vindilis put a hand on the brow and felt heat, though Innilis shuddered as with chill.

229

"Darling, darling!" Vindilis hurried to pour water from a jug, lay arm under neck, raise mouth to cup. "Here, drink." Innilis gulped and retched. "Nay, slowly, sip, sip, oh, my poor sweet."

Eventually she could ease the patient back onto the pillow. She went after her cloak. Both slept nude, for whatever warmth and consolation that might give. "Don't go, please don't go," Innilis moaned. "Stay. Hold my hand. It hurts so."

"Abide a little minute or two. I go to fetch powder of mandrake I've had brought. 'Twill give you some ease."

Innilis's eyes widened to ghastly white. "Nay! No drug. It might hurt the babe."

Vindilis bit a back a curse upon the babe. "I think not. In any case, you can't go on like this."

Innilis clutched herself below breasts that were ripening to full loveliness but too sore for fondling. "Nay, Grallon's child, and, and she and I together on Sena. I can endure. I must." Her face turned toward a niche where a small image of Belisama was barely visible in shadow. "Mother of Mercies, help me."

Vindilis threw the cloak over her shoulders and fastened the brooch. "Well, you can at least quaff a pellitory infusion. That's never hurt you, and it should cool you off." She took the lamp. "I'll need this. Be not afraid in the dark."

Innilis shook her weary head. "I am not." Vindilis suspected she lied. "Please come back soon."

"Very soon." Vindilis kissed her cheek and went out.

A door opened and Innilis's daughter Audris came into the corridor. "What is the matter?" she asked. "Is Mama sick again?"

"Aye," said Vindilis. "Go back to bed."

The girl's face screwed up. "I want to see my Mama!"

This child of Hoel was ten years old, two more than Vindilis's Runa by the same King. So unforeseeably did the Sign come upon a maiden. Runa, though, was already as tall, and bright and lively. Audris had something of her mother's looks, except for being towheaded, but still talked like an infant, seemed unable to learn much, and fell into occasional fits. Hers had been a frightful birth. Vindilis had wondered over and over how her half-sister's next would fare.

"Back, I said!" the high priestess yelled. "Back to your room or I'll hit you! And stay there!"

Audris gaped at the snarl above the lampflame, whimpered, and fled.

Dawnlight stole down the smokehole in the kitchen. Vindilis stirred up a fire banked under the hob and fed it with dry sticks and chips to hotten it fast. She keep decoctions readymade, but needed warmth to dissolve honey. That would hide the taste of the willow bark she added to the pellitory. It was supposed to endanger the unborn and Innilis would have refused it on that account; but she required a strong febrifuge—and, yea, a pinch of mandrake. Vindilis paced from flames to wall and back, to and fro, to and fro, while the dull light sharpened and the potion heated.

When she returned, Innilis had slipped partway into unconsciousness. "Here, beloved, here I am, always, always," Vindilis whispered. She raised the head and urged the liquid down. Thereafter she laid herself in the bed, damp and stinking though it was from sweat, and held Innilis in her arms and crooned lullabies until sleep came.

The lamp was nearly burned dry, but no need to refill. The servants would arrive shortly and throw back the shutters. Vindilis knew she would get no more rest until nightfall. She might as well wash and dress. Not enough hot water was left for bathing, but she preferred it cold.

The most direct way took her through the adjacent room, where Innilis had spent much of her leisure in happier days. A large bronze mirror on the wall caught what light there was and sent it off silver bowls, painted vases, bright draperies, bits of artwork. Another image of the Goddess, standing in a niche, was pretty too, benign, perhaps a trifle vapid; but abruptly, as the light struck ivory, it seemed to leap forth in the terrible majesty that was Hers.

Vindilis caught her breath. She turned, went to the niche, threw herself bruisingly hard prostrate on the floor. "Ishtar-Isis-Belisama," she begged, "spare her. Take whom else You will, how You will, but spare Innilis, and afterward I will seek only to serve You."

~ 3 ~

On the road, Gratillonius had promised the legionaries and marines leave for a homecoming feast. Preparations took several days. They included reserving a favorite tavern down in the Fishtail, where prices were low and rowdiness expected; providing it with a couple of pigs to roast and a barrel of better wine than the landlord dispensed; engaging musicians, entertainers, a few strumpets to help out the regulars; inviting friends from the city and environs. This depleted the company fund, but that didn't matter much. Ys furnished the Romans, as well as her own fighters, necessities and services for which they had been wont to pay in Britannia. Furthermore, it gave them a wage, modest but in honest coin. The King had insisted on that, pointing to their proven value as guardians against foes and patrollers against crime. The move was popular with merchants, since it got money out of the city coffers and back into circulation.

On the appointed day, Adminius led the troops forth. Otherwise he set his rank aside, and the passage was no march but a roaring romp. This was in the afternoon, in order to have daylight for the jugglers, acrobats, dancers, prestidigitators, and dancing animals. The weather was overcast but cold and dry: a blessing, as performances would have proper space in Skippers' Market rather than being crammed into the tavern. "Did the Nine arrange it for us?" joked Guentius.

"Quiet!" said Budic. "Don't mock sacred things. You know they never cast spells like that except at the most awful times."

"What? You, the superpious Christian, defending pagan faith?" Cynan gibed.

Budic's young countenance flushed like a girl's. "No, of course not. Although it is a decent sort of paganism. Queen Bodilis— But you don't want to insult our comrades, I hope."

"I was talking Latin," Guentius retorted. "Didn't you notice?"

"Some of them know it," Cynan decided. "Budic's right. Lay off."

Cheerfulness prevailed. When the show ended, as the early dusk was falling, men flocked to the inn and settled down to await the meal whose smoke and savor enriched the air. Goblets thumped, dice clattered, women squealed and giggled, voices lifted hoarse in talk and, presently, song.

—"Ah, 'tis fine to be 'ome again," sighed Adminius in Ysan. His left hand hoisted a beaker, his right gave the girl Keban a preliminary feeling over.

Herun of the navy raised brows across the table. "'Home,' said you? We're happy to have you amongst us. However, yearn you not for your Britannia?"

Adminius shrugged. "God knows when we'll get back there, if ever. And frankly, 'tis no great loss. I could end my days 'ere quite contented. Might do so regardless, when I'm discharged."

"Hm." The sailor stroked his gingery beard. "If you truly mean that, you'll be looking about for a wife. I've a sister you might like to meet."

"Not so fast!" laughed Adminius, while Keban looked miffed.

"Nay, nay. She's young, hardly more than a child. Our parents will want to know any suitor well ere they give consent. For that matter, no girl in Ys may be married against her will, unless a vestal— Um, but a worthy man with Roman connections would be a welcome visitor."

—Said Maeloch the fisher to his friend Cynan: "Aye, do come stay with me when ye can get furlough. Ye know the house is small but snug, and though we're not rich, my Betha is a spanking good cook. The boys as well as myself—not to bespeak our neighbors—we'd love to hear ye yarn about your trip. We can promise to keep your whistle well wetted the while."

"Thank you," said the soldier. "It cannot be till after the Midwinter Council. The centurion wants the whole two dozen of us for a guard."

Maeloch's rough countenance tightened. "What, looks the King for trouble?"

"Oh, no threat, surely."

"Better not be. They'd have us, the whole folk, the seamen 'fore all, to reckon with, did they lay finger on our King or little Queen Dahilis."

232

Cynan's usual dourness broke in a smile. "You've grown fond of him, then?"

"With reason, with reason. He's brought honor back to the Key, order to the holy family; he's rid us of the Scotic pirates and strives to get something real done abut the Saxons; he's dealt fair and square with commoners like me, and now, I hear, he means to hold a court every month where anybody can bring a plea; and...he's made Dahilis glad, Dahilis who ever talks kindly."

"Well, 'tis good to hear you say so. As for the Council, I think he just wants his legionaries for an honor guard, same as before, to help overawe opposition there."

"Aye, even down under the cliffs we hear as how some magnates, Soren Cartagi of the Timbermen foremost, mislike the way he'd link us back to Rome. *I* say, when a storm is rising, break out your sheet anchor and make fast the rode." Maeloch's fist thudded down on the table. Its thick planks trembled. "Enough. Let's drink!"

XXIV

~ 1 ~

There was no wind on the night before Solstice Eve, nor was the air unduly cold. A swelling moon frosted thin, feathery clouds, among which a few stars blinked. Ashimmer like polished obsidian, Ocean heaved slowly, as if breathing in sleep. Sounds of surf rolled faint through deserted streets. The pharos light might have been a candle flame.

Then hour by hour a haze began drawing over heaven out of the west. As the moon sank toward it, a ring came aglow up there and stars withdrew from sight. Shadows blurred, lost themselves in the general darkness.

The moon was low beyond hidden Sena when abruptly a clatter and banging arose. It seemed thrice loud and harsh in this quietude. A cat on the prowl squalled and fled. Had the dead swarmed in from the necropolis to rattle their bones through Ys?

"Open, help, open, ow-w-w!"

A maidservant unbarred the door on which the knocker had beaten. Ghostly in nightgown, she peered at the small figure which jittered on the cobbles. After a moment: "Oh, but 'tis Audris. What are you doing her at this hour, child?"

"Fennalis come quick!" the girl keened. "Mama sick, Aunt Vin'ilis tol' me get Aunt Fennalis, quick!" She herself wore merely a shift pulled over her head. The paving must have numbed her bare feet.

The high priestess was swiftly awake. Unlike most of her Sisters, she kept an attendant always in her house, because she had become hard of hearing and might not be roused by a belated appeal. Aside from lacking the Touch that Innilis seemed, erratically, to have, Fennalis was the best physician in the city, responsive to the great and the lowly alike.

She paused for no more than sandals, gown, cloak, and medical kit. "Audris, stay," she ordered the yammering visitor. "Blodvin, tuck her into my bed, warm her some milk, sit beside her. If she throws a fit—drools, rolls her eyes, strains backward—put a towel in her mouth lest she bite her tongue, but panic not." Fennalis took a lantern that the maid had kindled from the nightfire and trotted forth. Wan light wavered across the snub-nosed features, gray bristle of hair.

The way was short but steep to the home of Innilis. Its door stood open. Fennalis passed through. Candles burned everywhere. She set her lantern down and stood panting and wheezing.

Vindilis came into the atrium. She was naked. Blood bespattered her, dripped from her hands. "At last," she rasped. Heedless of stains, she gave Fennalis support while she well-nigh dragged the older woman along.

"A thump, a scream. She may have started out of bed to go to the pot. Or mayhap— Her mind has sometimes wandered. I suppose she fell off the edge onto the floor. There she lay, writhing and screaming. I saw the waves going down her belly. Somehow I got her back into bed, and lights lit to see by. The waters gushed forth. They were tinged red. Blood followed. I've tried to stanch it. Small success."

They reached the bedroom. Splotches and footprints went crimson across the floor. Sheets, blankets, mattress were soaked. Innilis half sat against a heap of pillows. Her jaws were wide, straining for air, making a Gorgon mask. Eyes stared, blank with pain and terror.

Fennalis regained her breath. She bustled to the bedside, kissed the brow beneath her, and murmured, "How goes it, Sister?" while she removed the cloths Vindilis had tucked between the thighs.

"Oh, it hurts, it hurts," moaned Innilis. Vindilis clenched fists together but kept aside, out of the way.

"Hm. Naturally it would," said Fennalis. "I think you did succeed. No issue now to speak of. Blood always looks like more than it is."

"But too much nonetheless," Vindilis replied in the same grating monotone as before.

Fennalis nodded. "To be awaited. The suddenness and all. I daresay injuries from the first birth never healed aright."

Innilis reached to scrabble after her. "Help me!" she cried. "Save me. I don't want to ride in the Wild Hunt!"

"You shan't."

"Certainly not you." Vindilis came around to lean over the head of the bed, stroke the face that was bent away from her, drop kisses and tears down into the hair. "You are a Queen. Whatever happens to us, Belisama takes us home to Her sea, She, the Star of it."

"Stop that nonsense," Fennalis snapped. "We can get this over fast if we go about it rightly. Vindilis, curb yourself. Stand yonder. Help her kneel....Now, child, bear down."

Innilis shrieked. *"Nay!"*

"Yea," said Fennalis. "Harken. You're not going to lose it. You've done that already. Your task is to get rid of it."

"Oh, my babe, the King's babe!"

Fennalis slapped Innilis on the cheek. "Stop that. Get to work. Vindilis, support her while I unpack my kit."

—When at last Innilis lay simply weeping, Fennalis made her drink from a vial. To Vindilis the physician said: "Opium. Scarce as cocks' eggs nowadays, but I've saved out some for special cases. 'Twill ease her, and can do no harm now."

"Nay." Vindilis stared at that which lay on the floor, quiet after a brief stirring. "It can do no harm now."

"When Innilis is soundly asleep, we'll sponge her off and shift her to the couch in her receiving room. Ease your mind. I don't believe our Sister is in further peril, though belike she'll be slow to regain strength. The servants will be here before dawn."

Fennalis yawned mightily. "Then at last we twain can go tumble into bed and sleep till noon."

"Nay," said Vindilis again. Weariness barely dulled the iron in her voice. "Not till well afterward. Have you forgotten?"

~ 2 ~

The state barge daily set forth at sunrise, or as soon thereafter as ebb tide had started opening the sea gate. This time, fetching Maldunilis back, it carried no replacement. For the next three days, all the Nine would be in Ys, attending to rites and Council. Or thus it had been hitherto.

The last feather-clouds departed. By afternoon the sun shone in a sky gone milky; shadows stretched pale from the south. A breeze sprang up, cold, gradually strengthening until it whittered in streets and raised whitecaps on a darkly greenish-gray sea.

Seven of the Nine met at the temple of Belisama. They dismissed the vestals and minor priestesses, save for one who was to stand outside and admit Dahilis when she arrived, and went on into the main chamber of worship. Chill and dimness lay within, barely lighted by windows whose glass was the hue of underwater; for lamps and candles had been extinguished. They would be rekindled at midnight—would shine from every observant house in the city—to welcome home the returning sun. Grain of stone and mosaic scenes of myth were vague in vision. At the far end, behind the high altar, the images of the triune Goddess towered pallid and stern. Silently, each in her own way, the Gallicenae prayed for mercy.

After a while Dahilis slipped in, clad like the rest in sacral blue and white. Tears gleamed below the tall headdress. Her voice came thin: "I'm sorry, I beg pardon I'm late, but—but—"

Quinipilis approached her, looked close, and said, "Come, best we seek our meeting room at once."

"Nay, I m-m-must make my devotion—"

"You shall, for the whole Sisterhood and people."

"You don't understand! Listen!"

"Hush. This is no place for news. Come."

Numbly, Dahilis followed the old woman, while the others trailed after. They went down the corridor to the chamber behind the sanctuary and entered. It was scarcely warmer, but better served by its windows; the Four Aspects on the walls stood forth in vividness.

Several cried out. On the dais, red-robed, Key in view on his breast, Hammer against hip, Gratillonius waited. He had used the rear entrance—not that anyone would have dared refuse him admission after a single look at his countenance.

Vindilis first got her wits back. Her words attacked like a stooping hawk. "My lord, what is this? Arriving without right is sacrilege. Begone!"

The square, massive visage hardened still further, the powerful body seemed to take stance as if readying for an enemy charge. Rougher than had been his wont, his answer rolled forth. "I have every right. I am the King of Ys. He Whose avatar I am is Belisama's lover."

Dahilis stumbled forward to stand under the dais, confronting her Sisters. They could see how her breath labored, almost how her heart galloped, beneath the child-bulged gown. She raised her palms. "Hear me," she beseeched. "I never intended— But 'tis my fault. Mine alone. When the m-message came to the palace...about poor Innilis—I was so shocked I blurted unthinkingly—"

"And I sensed something more behind that, and thundered it out of her," Gratillonius said. "She strove to hold back, but she'd already let slip she must go hither at this time, about a matter more grave than the loss of an infant. I said I would come too, my legionaries at my back if need be, and have the truth. That—" He faltered. For a moment he stood gnawing his lip, then whispered, "That broke her will."

"Nay, wait, wait," exclaimed Quinipilis. She rocked up to hug Dahilis to her ample bosom. "There, dear, there, 'twas indeed no sin of yours. You were helpless."

"She was sensible," declared Fennalis. "Better give the man his way, and a while to calm down, better that than an open breach, right in the sacred building."

"True," growled the centurion. "She has a wiser head on her, young though she be, than some I could name. Now can the lot of you sit down and we talk this over like reasoning beings?"

"I fear 'tis too deep for reason," said Bodilis; but she took the lead in urging that they try. To Maldunilis she must utter a stiff "Be quiet or I'll throw you out" before that Queen controlled her dread of what these events might portend. The rest won sooner to a stoic peacefulness.

"Well." Seeking to ease things a little, Gratillonius leaned on the long haft of the Hammer. "I hope you understand my wish is to do my duty as your King. But I have other duties too, as the prefect of Rome...and as a man. It grieves me to hear what Innilis has suffered. If I have not hastened to her bedside, 'tis because of this business. To be frank, I am yet unclear about it. I know only that she was supposed to spend the solstice day and night on Sena, but the task has fallen on Dahilis."

"I will fulfill it, oh, I will," Dahilis vowed.

Gratillonius's anger burst forth anew. "Alone, in your condition? Have you seen the sky? Foul weather's on the way, if ever clouds gave signal. You could be trapped out yonder for days, no boat able to live through the waves and reefs. Madness!"

It was as though fire flickered behind ice in the gaze of Forsquilis. "Nay, Roman," she said to the man with whom she had made love this past night. Intensity caused her to tremble. "'Tis the command of the Gods. To learn it I have guested the dead; to carry it out we have thirsted, fasted, and scourged; no more may we deny or defy it than you may spit on the sacrifice of your Mithras. Or less—for He would send you alone down to hell, whereas the wrath of our Gods would fall upon all Ys. It is required that a Sister take Vigil at this Midwinter while bearing within her a child. That was to have been Innilis. Now it must needs be Dahilis."

"You went behind my back." Gratillonius raised the Hammer. "Why, why, why?"

"To expiate the sins against Them, among which yours, O King, wax rank," said Lanarvilis quietly, almost sorrowfully; and she explained.

"But—but that is— See here!" Gratillonius roared. "If I've erred, I'll make whatever amends you want...if they be seemly....*I* will!"

Silence answered, save that Forsquilis shook her head. Dahilis had gone dry-eyed. She sat straight, hands serene in her lap, resoluteness upon her.

"Mithras will protect you! He is just, and He is above—" Gratillonius stopped. He knew implacability when it stared at him.

He had two dozen soldiers. Most ordinary Ysan men would recoil from assaulting him, he trusted; even some of the marines might hang back. In any event, given speed and determination, his company could fight its way clear and on to safety in Audiarna, bearing Dahilis along—

No. He foresaw what that would do to her. And it would irretrievably wreck the still frail structure of defense he was building. His mission was to save Armorica for Rome, not tear it asunder.

"Forgive me. I meant no insult to the Gods of Ys." A while he stood, head bowed, both hands on the butt of the Hammer to upbear his weight, which seemed to have grown boulder-huge. The Key dangled free from his neck.

Finally he shook himself, squared his shoulders, and said, "Very well. So be it. But Dahilis shall take no needless risk."

"Do you doubt that the Goddess will look after her?" Vindilis challenged. "Or if not, who shall fathom Her ways? That which has happened may indeed have been Her will making itself manifest."

"Then do you doubt its fulfillment, whatever we mortals may do?" Gratillonius retorted. "I ask merely that one or two of you—or somebody—accompany Dahilis, and stand by against...troubles such as we have had already."

"None of us may," answered Quinipilis. "Gratillonius, my dear, you're a kind man in your fashion, and I feel what wound is in you. But 'tis a condition of this sacrament, and we are bound to it by the Great Oath, that none among us may betread Sena tomorrow, other than the chosen high priestess and her unborn. And of course nobody else ever may."

Gratillonius pounced. "Ha! What of the workmen—*men*—who repaired the storm damage?"

"That was a holy necessity," Lanarvilis replied. "First they underwent rites of purification and consecration. Afterward the entire island was rededicated. Think not we can evade Belisama's commandment by falsely praying over anybody at this late hour."

His response came as no surprise to himself. It had been rising like a sea tide. "*I* am sanctified," he said.

Horror hissed around the room.

"I am the King. I am Taranis on earth," he followed. "If the King's presence on Sena is unheard of, why, likewise is a Midwinter vigil."

"The King—in Ys—must preside over the festival," Fennalis protested.

Gratillonius fleered. "Are they backwoodsmen here, to believe their celebrations rekindle the sun? Nay, those are but celebrations. I've asked about them. All I'm supposed to do is take part in a ceremony. Somebody else—a priest or Soren, my Speaker—he can do it as well. Has naught like this ever happened erenow in your history?"

"There have been two or three times," Bodilis confessed. "A King was ill, or at the frontier when invasion threatened, or—"

"You see?" Gratillonius cried. He drew breath. "Fear not," he said in a level tone. "I've no wish to profane anything. I'll keep away from the mysteries. But...come worst to worst, I am a good man of my hands, a farm boy who has helped birth many an animal, a soldier who knows how to treat many a hurt. The sailors who ferry you there set foot on the wharf, at least. Would you refuse your sacral King what you grant them?" Most softly: "I am going. I have spoken."

238

Bodilis stirred, raised her hands, gazed beyond the walls as her mind felt its way forward. "Hold, wait," she said. "Sisters, a God does dwell in our King. Who can be certain that Belisama wants not him also?...I told you, Gratillonius, the matter is too deep for reason. Yet while sunlight never reaches the ocean depths, it illuminates the waves.... Aye, listen. 'Tis true that outsiders may walk on the wharf. Indeed, the ground below high-water mark is allowable. That law is for the sake of mariners who may be driven onto a lee shore, but does not explicitly ban others." She met his glance. "Can we, together, find a compromise?"

Hope blazed in him. "I think we can."

The face of Dahilis was like sunrise.

XXV

~ 1 ~

The barge of state was impressive not in size, for its length was a bare sixty feet, but in appearance. The graceful hull was blue with silver trim. At the prow lifted a carven swan's head, at the stern a fishtail, both gilt. A deckhouse amidships, though wooden, was built and painted to resemble a Grecian temple in miniature. While the vessel was oar-driven, she bore a pole for the flying of a flag—heavy silk, gold-fringed, dolphin argent on azure, the annual gift of the Needle-workers Guild. The crew were navy men, periodically chosen by their captains as an honor.

She departed Ys somewhat late on solstice morning because seas were running heavy, causing a chop in the very basin. When ebb had swung the doors safely wide, a trumpet sounded, men ashore cast off lines, the galley stood out. From quay, wall, towers, folk watched this unprecedented faring in awe.

Beyond the shelter, the craft rocked, pitched, shuddered. Wind drove strong, hollowly hooting, thrumming the stays, making waves roar white-maned along until they burst in a crash and a fountaining on the rocks everywhere about. It harried a wrack low and wolf-gray out of murk rising ever higher in the west. Spindrift flung salt onto lips. Chill slashed.

The galley toiled onward, picking a way through the safe lanes. Lookouts strained their vision overside, the steersman and his standby poised taut, rowers changed frequently so as to keep at peak strength. Slowly the shining spires of Ys sank away aft, until flying brume swallowed sight first of them and then of the mainland. No birds were aloft except a cormorant that followed afar, a hovering and soaring blackness. As the barge approached Sena, a score or more seals appeared and accompanied it.

The interior of the deckhouse was a cabin, snug and well appointed, dim today when windows perforce were shuttered. Gratillonius and Dahilis shared a seat. Most of the time she leaned close and he had an arm about her, bracing her as the vessel rolled and plunged. Whoosh and boom of waves, creak and groan of timbers, occasional shouts of the men filled the room. Yet they could talk. They needed to, for yesterday he had spent the evening on his preparations, whereupon she passed the night at the temple, in purification as well as sleep.

"How much may you tell me of what you shall be doing?" he asked.

"'Tis to be a Vigil like any other—in form, at least," she replied. Earnestly: "You do understand what that means, do you not? On behalf of Ys, communion with the Goddess, prayers for the people; and yea, devotion to Lir, since 'tis Taranis Who is with Her everywhere else. At the House of the Goddess I drink Her wine and eat Her bread; more than that I must not say. I then walk to the two Stones that the Old Folk raised near the middle of the island, and perform certain rites. Then I go to the far western end and give Lir His honors. After that I return to the House for orisons, meditation, another sacred meal, and rest until sunrise. After dawnsong I am free, and soon the barge comes to bring my Sister and take me home." She squeezed his hand. "To you. This time, with you."

"Hm!" He scowled. "I mistrust the weather."

"Oh, but we're not supposed to endanger ourselves. We do whatever looks safe, and are excused from the rest. The House is stoutly built. Its tower is for refuge when a storm dashes the waters clear across land. I am sure, though, I'm sure the Gods want a full sacrament at this of all Vigils. They will provide."

Her faith tugged at his heart. He almost wished he could share it. But in the Gods of Ys was too much of the ancient darkness from which They had risen. "When can I see you?"

She turned her countenance up toward his to give him the gift of her smile, which she thought of as a present to herself. "Well, the door of the House is in view from the wharf. You'll have sight of me as I go in and out. And I of you. I don't think Belisama will mind if we wave at each other."

How dear she was. Hair tumbled in a golden cataract past features whose fine bones might be of the Suffetes but whose flared and tip-tilted nose, wide and soft mouth just parted over flawless teeth, fair skin and underlying liveliness were belike from her father Hoel. The great dark-blue eyes she shared with Bodilis; the light that danced within them was her own. Her voice was likewise low: not husky, however; its music, again, uniquely hers. Never before had he known a woman could be so merry and still so loving. He leaned down toward her. The sweetness of tresses and flesh dizzied him.

She blocked his lips with gentle fingers. "Nay, darling, we mustn't, not till we're back home." Laughter purred. "But I don't think She will blame me, either, for looking forward."

He sighed. "Suppose we're weatherbound."

"Then the priestess must carry on the round of services as best she can until she is relieved. I mustn't come to you. We'll make up for that after our girl is born."

"But what if that happens meanwhile?" he fretted. "That's why I'm here, you know. Unless worse befall. I will not stand idly by if you need help, Dahilis. I will not. Afterward let the Gods fight it out with me."

"Hush!" she said, scandalized. "You...you shouldn't be...hostile like that, darling. The Mother loves us. I know She does. And I am not due quite yet. Oh, aye, if bad trouble strikes, of course I may seek your tent. My Sisters and I talked this out last night. This Vigil is not for, for punishment. 'Tis to set things aright, that the Gods may again be free to bestow blessings on Ys."

He cleared his throat. "Um, I meant no offense. Certainly not... But the House will be better shelter for us."

She shook her head violently. "Nay! A man would desecrate it. 'Twould have to be purified and consecrated anew, as 'twas after the carpenters and masons had finished. Meanwhile the poor dead had to wait in the Twilight." Dahilis drew a sharp breath. "The workers were there by divine consent. If you broke in unasked— Nay, I dare not think what vengeance the Gods might take on you. On *you*. Please, beloved, nay, promise me you'll not!"

"Ah, well, we speak of what we trust is unlikely," he evaded. In haste to change the subject: "But what's this about the dead? I remember the funeral barge went out more than once while the repair work was going on."

He could barely hear her whisper through the din: "That was only their bodies. Later the Ferriers bring their souls to Sena for judgment. On such a night the Queen in the House must stay wakeful till morning to pray for them."

"Have you?" Instantly he regretted his heedlessness.

She nodded. He couldn't tell whether she had gone pale, but her eyes were more big than ever, staring straight forward. "Surely. At sundown I have suddenly *known* there would be the landing, and the whisper of the names, and—and been glad to have light around me after I lit lamps on the altar— This is a mystery."

"I'm sorry," he mumbled. "I'd not cause you distress for the world and Heaven."

She embraced him, carefully chaste but altogether forgiving. Her spirits soon lifted afresh. His did too, somewhat.

The barge came in with difficulty through the wild water. Watching on deck, Gratillonius admired the skill of captain and crew. Rowers strained: the master gauged wind and waves, gave hand signals; a stentor bellowed the orders. They caught a billow and rode. As it crested, the steersman put his helm hard over; larboard oars snapped up out of harm's way while starboard oars brought the hull about; the steersman's partner disengaged the left rudder oar and hauled it free; strokes boomed against rope bumpers suspended from the bollards. Immediately sailors leaped off onto the wharf, lines in hand, and made fast. Two aboard ran out a gangplank which their fellows ashore secured.

The captain gave Dahilis the salute of deference. "Thanks be to Lir that He brought us here in safety, and to Belisama that She gave us you, O Queen, to convey hither," he said formally. The wind tattered his words.

She inclined her head to him. "And I thank you on behalf of the Gallicenae and Ys," she replied likewise, then could not resist laughing: "'Twas a pretty show!"

Gravity returned: "The hour is late, on this shortest day of the year. I must commence at once. Farewell."

Gratillonius escorted her to the wharf. Small and alone she looked against the gray-green tumult that battered the island, the dreariness of rock, scrub, and sere grass beyond. Sacral gown and headdress were woolen for winter, as was the cloak she hugged to her, but cold sought inward. A moment her gaze dwelt on him. "Fare *you* well," she said, "forever well."

Turning, she walked off, over the planks and along a short path to the House of the Goddess. From her left hand dangled a bedroll, from her right a bag of other necessities. Despite the burden and even through the garments, he was aware of how dancingly she moved. Her unborn had never dragged her down much. She had often, delightedly, said what a quick and easy delivery should be hers, and what a fine, healthy babe— "Come, Gratillonius, put your hand here, feel her kick, already she wants out. Oh, she'll make the world remember her!" And only a few days ago, Dahilis had felt the lightening.

She glanced back and waved, as she had promised, before she disappeared in the somber bulk of the House. Rushing rags of cloud brushed past its towertop. The western half of heaven had become a cavern.

Someone diffidently touched Gratillonius's arm, "Your pardon, my lord." The King glanced around and recognized a young man named Herun. "We have to set up your camp without delay."

"Oh...oh, indeed," said Gratillonius. "So you can start back. Trying that after dark would be deadly in this weather, I'm sure."

"In truth, lord. As 'tis, likeliest the gate will be shut, or too narrowly open to attempt. But given such a tide, we can make Ghost Quay if we've light to see by. It happens often enough."

Gratillonius must oversee the work and take a hand of his own, as newly invented as it was. None less than Bomatin Kusuri, Mariner Councilor, had helped him devise his shelter yesterday, and gotten craftsmen to prepare what extra parts were required. In effect, a Roman army tent went up on the wharf, tethered to bollards and piles. Meant for eight men, it would be less warm for one, though roomier. However, its leather would fend off any blast that did not tear everything loose; a rug would lie beneath; he was well clad, in fisherman's tunic, trousers, boots, with jacket and gloves and ample changes in reserve; he had candles, lantern, oil, tinder, punkwood, flint, steel.

Nevertheless it was a swine of a job to erect the tent. Leather flapped into faces, cords flew about like slavedrivers's whips. Men said no profane word, but obscenities were plentiful. Afterward, watching for Dahilis, Gratillonius realized she must have gone out again, inland, while he was thus engaged. He had not seen her greeting to him.

Finally the task was over. He said his appreciative goodbyes. The crew embarked, cast loose, fended off, departed. He stood watching the galley dwindle; a brave sight, but how fragile amidst the surges and surfs, like Dahilis beneath this sky.

Having sadly given up on seeing her again for hours, he busied himself settling in. There were things to stow, food such as didn't need cooking, water, wine, bedroll, towels, washbasin, comb, teeth cleansers—the list went on, ending with what he had brought to pass the time. A book could have been too easily blotted, ruined; and he possessed no musical gift whatsoever. He did, though, have waxed tablets and a stylus, for noting down any thoughts that occurred to him about Ys and Armorica. Mainly he had brought pieces of wood, and tools to carve them into ornaments for furniture and toys for his stepdaughters. And why not for his own daughter as well, his and Dahilis's? She'd not appreciate more than a rag doll at first, but later she would enjoy, say, a tiny wagon....

Gratillonius smiled as he crossed his legs on the rug. He reached for a whetstone. Several of his blades needed sharpening, and no servant of his had quite the right final feather-touch.

Wind gusted, screeched, noisily flapped the door-folds, which had been tied back to admit light. His pleasure drained from him. He should not be doing work as mechanical as this. It freed his mind to wonder how Dahilis was, alone with her gods at Midwinter.

~ 3 ~

Gratillonius did not notice her. He and the sailors were struggling to put up his tent. Dahilis wished she could linger till his glance wandered her way. But already she had had to be hasty in the first communion

243

rite. More than half the short day was gone, while clouds drew downward, ever darker, and wind grew more fierce. She must be back before nightfall was complete, so she could see to kindle fire—on the hearth for herself, in lamps for herself and the Goddess.

"Belisama, Queen and Mother, watch over him," she whispered, and started forth.

For a space the footpath followed the shoreline. Castoffs of the tide lay strewn, kelp, shells, dead fish, pieces from the many wrecks that these waters had claimed over the years. Beyond churned and foamed the sea itself, nearly black save where it burst in gigantic whiteness. Growl and roar were like drums beneath the war horn of the wind. Seals swam in the turmoil. They kept turning their heads inland—toward her? The path bent that way, then west again; she lost sight of them.

It hurt to turn her back on the Kindly Ones. It hurt to leave Gratillonius behind. It hurt!

Dahilis halted with a gasp. The pain started at the small of her back and came around to grip her in the belly. It was like the pangs of lightening, but those had been brief and mild. This laid hold of her inmost depths. She barred a cry behind her teeth. Dear Isis, had the birth begun so early?

The cramp passed. A while she stood shivering. Best return, start the fire, wait. If this went on, seek Gratillonius.

Nay. Dead Brennilis, speaking through the mouth of Forsquilis, had warned that the trial would be severe. This was not worse than she, Dahilis, could endure. The pains might well be false. In any event, likelihood was that she could move about freely, most of the time, for hours and hours yet. Let her do so, and win her man forgiveness.

And the Sisterhood and Ys, of course.

She strode on. The wind was now straight in her face. She tasted the salt spray that flung the length of Sena. It sought to tear the cloak from her shoulders. She could barely hold the garment together; it fluttered and snapped frantically. The cold probed through every opening. Her gown made valiant defense, but the wind flattened it against her and her babe, jeered as it lifted the hem, swirled up from underneath. The low, scudding clouds had given way to a roiling leadenness above, a monstrous gloom ahead. Leafless bushes flicked their twigs above stones and patches of withered grass. Hoot and howl streamed around her.

But there were the two menhirs, where she had helped bring Gratillonius and, later, bring him the aid he needed against the reavers out at sea— A second spasm coiled through her. She waited it out.

Shakily, she approached the Bird and the Beast. She said the words, she danced the sunwise dance, she ate the salt and gave the drop of blood, she asked leave to depart and peace on the Old Folk. It seemed a good omen that the next attack held off until this was all done.

After that, though, she lost count of how many stops she must make on her way west. Belike the wind slowed her, she thought: thrusting, battering, chilling, as if Lir had sent it to keep her away from Him. The flat landscape seemed everywhere the same. As she went on, it grew vague in her sight. The wind was lashing such tears from her eyes. Spray flew ever thicker. Its bitterness caked on her lips. Snow that was half sleet began drifting against her. Horizon and sky were lost.

"Lir," she appealed, "Lir, are You really angered that he buried his friend, in the name of their God, above Your sea? You can't be. You are Captain and Helmsman. You understand what manhood is."

But Lir had nothing of humanity about Him. He was the storm that whelmed ships, the lightless depths that drowned men, the waves that flung them onto rocks for gulls to eat what the eels had not. Well did He nourish great whales, and dolphins to frolic about sailors and seals to watch over them. Well did He raise great shoals of fish and the winds that bore rich cargoes homeward. But He was Ocean, the Son of Chaos, and Ys lived only on sufferance of His, only because it had made itself forever a hostage to His wrath.

Let her appeal and appease— She sank to knees, to all fours, and could not quite hold back a cry. Some births came fast. This, her first, too early at that, this birth ought not to, but, "Belisama, Mother, help me."

Dahilis lurched back to her feet. The drift around her grew more white as everything else grew blacker.

Then ahead, at endless last, she spied the tip of the island. Surf ramped beyond it; she heard the boom and long, withdrawing snarl, she could well-nigh feel them through her bones. That was farther out than she must go. She need only descend a few tiers of rock to one that jutted out above high-water mark. Upon it stood an altar, a block of stone, sea-worn until ledges and carven symbols were nearly gone. There she must give Lir His honor. Afterward she could return to the House of the Goddess.

She picked her way down carefully, half blinded as she was. Wind raved, snow and spindrift flew. Her womb contracted. She bent herself around the anguish. Her heel slipped on wetness. She felt herself toppling, helpless. It seemed to go on and on, while she stood aside and watched. Shock, pain, those too struck somebody remote.

—They waited patiently until she crawled back from wherever she had been. That was a slow battle. Often she slid back downward. A birth pang would drag her up again. The agony in her right leg resisted this, as the wind had resisted her walking. But when she did break free, it became her friend. It was something other than a confusion of wind, snow, water, darkness, and noise. Her mind clung to it. Don't let go, she begged. If you do, I'll slip away from this, and I mustn't.

Scrabbling, her fingers hoisted her gown. The right foot was bent awry. Fractured ankle. She would dance no more, not soon. How long had she lain unaware? Not long; her head was unhurt, mayhap saved by the cloth wrapped around it, though that had come loose. Nonetheless, thought fumbled through drift of snow and scud. Her garments were drenched, weighting her when she tried to raise herself on her hands. Water sheeted. The tide was coming in swiftly. With the wind behind it, surf would reach around the altar of Lir. It might pull her off to Him, or it might simply kill her and the child.

She must find shelter before the chill reached her womb. Already she felt numbness stealing inward. She tried to get up on the sound foot and hop. That knee buckled. She fell on the broken ankle. Bright lightnings cast her back into the dark.

It was closing in on the world when she next regained herself. Another cramp pulsed through her. She felt it more keenly than she now felt the broken bones. "Hold," she muttered. "Abide. We'll go to him." His right name eluded her. It was lengthy, Latin, unmusical. Her tongue remembered how Ysans sometimes rendered it. "Grallon. Oh, Grallon."

Dahilis began to crawl.

When she had hitched her way over the terraces, onto the flatland, she could not find the path. Whiteness lay thin upon rock and soil. It flowed along in the air, on the wind, through the deepening dusk. The crash and rush of the sea behind her filled her skull. She must get away from the sea. Somewhere yonder were Grallon and Belisama. "Be not hasty," she told her daughter. "Wait until he can help us." She knew little else, but she did know that she must creep onward, each time that the pains allowed.

~ 4 ~

As twilight fell, Gratillonius grew more and more uneasy. Ignoring cold, he sat in the entrance of his tent. It opened toward the building. He did not see her, he did not see her. By every hell of every faith, she ought to be back. Ought she not? The island was small. Any healthy person could walk it from end to end in an hour or so. Allow as much for the return. She did have her duties along the way, but they couldn't be too elaborate, could they? A slight snow had begun, dry flakes borne nearly level out of the west. It hindered vision. He might miss sight of her. He didn't want that.

His woodcarving forgotten, he waited. Thoughts tumbled through him, memories, mother, father, the farm, camp, girls who seemed to have gone unreal, the Wall, Parnesius, combats that no longer mattered—where *was* Dahilis?—Maximus's will to power, the march to Ys, Dahilis, Dahilis, things he needed to do, also among her Sisters—what in Ahriman's name was keeping her?—how he might disengage himself from Ys after his work in Armorica was done, but not

246

from Dahilis, no, he must win her over to Rome, and where *was* she, what was keeping her? The snow streaked denser than before.

Finally he realized he'd better start fire while he could still see. That meant closing the tent against the gusts that had been whirling about in it. The consequent gloom, and his own impatience, cost him several failures before he had ignited the tinder, blown it to life, kindled a punkstick, and brought that to a candle. Then it took a while more to get his lantern going. It was a fine big one, bronze with glass panes, but awkward in the ignition. He'd be stupid not to use it, however, for a naked flame might well die when he reopened the tent flaps.

It did. He blinked at night. Not dark already! He should stand outside and let his eyes adapt. The wind savaged his face. Waves bawled unseen; he felt the wharf tremble to their blows. With the slowness of a torturer, some vision came to him. He discerned the House not as a mass but as an abyss, blacker than black. If Dahilis had entered it while he wasn't looking, she must be asleep in there.

The knowledge struck into him like a swordthrust. "Asleep?" he yelled. "Can't be!" Not as early as Midwinter nightfall was. She had spoken of an evensong; surely that required lamps. And she would have lighted a hearthfire. But never a glimmer—

He fought himself till the breath sobbed in his gullet. He'd missed sight of her. Shutters and door blocked light. If he went there, she would be aghast. She was supposed to seek him, should necessity come upon her. Stand fast, Gratillonius, stand your watch, keep your post.

Snow hissed. Blindness deepened. He raised his hands. "Mithras, God of the Law, what shall I do?"

A still small voice replied: Look for the smoke.

Gratillonius's heart stumbled. The smoke of sacrifice, the smoke of the hearth, it rose. However swiftly wind snatched it away from its outlet, firelight from beneath it should glimmer on it...and on the flying snow...but there was no light. None whatsoever.

A faraway part of him recalled moments of commitment to battle. In them had been a certain eerie bliss. You had no more thinking to do, nor hoping nor praying. You only drew sword.

He fetched the lantern and carried it by the lug, as low down as might readily be so that he could pick his way up the path. Wind, snow, night had receded to remoteness; he barely heard the sea. The door of the House bore a knocker formed like a triskele. He thudded it hard as he was able. "Dahilis, Dahilis, are you within?" The noise disappeared.

"The sacrilege is mine," he said, mainly for her sake, and opened the door.

Shadows wavered misshapen around a single room. From the Roman-tiled floor a wooden staircase led up into the tower. But that was for refuge. Here he saw a hearth, an oven, utensils, chair, stool, table, cabinet...rug on the floor, lamps and candlesticks on a shelf, hangings

247

to relieve the bleakness of stone walls...at the far end, what might be an altar...closer by, a single bed, and tossed onto it the rolled sheets and blankets he knew.

"Dahilis!" he roared. Echoes laughed.

So, he thought.

She would need a fire, but he didn't know when he would come back with her. He laid out the nicely stacked kindling and sticks. From a jug he drenched them with lamp oil. Let that soak in, that he might be able to start a blaze immediately when he had brought her here to shelter.

Fire....He could be a long time while searching. Best that he take several tallow candles to recharge the lantern. He snatched them off their shelf and stuffed them into the pouch at the belt of his Ysan garb. Down with them he put flint, steel, tinder, and punk, just in case—though he'd need some kind of windbreak before trying to start anything burning. Across his left arm he slung a wool blanket, while he took a firm grip on the lantern, ready to keep it level should he trip. Then he set forth.

"Dahilis!" he cried. "Dahilis!"

The wind whistled, the waves resounded, his voice was lost. As he left the House behind, he glimpsed a seal that had come ashore to lie on the strand. Its gaze followed him till he was gone into his darkness.

He didn't know this damned island at all. There should be a footpath of some kind, but where? Snow had laid enough of a veil over the ground that he couldn't tell by looking. He only knew that it wasn't under the hummocks and tufts of winter grass or the bare, snickering bushes; but those grew sparsely. Besides, she might be anywhere.

It would do no good to run around yelling like a scared pup. Best he weave his way to and fro across the narrow land, guiding himself as best he was able by whatever clues there might be, such as the noise of the waters north and south. At that, he could easily miss her, if she didn't hear him and call an answer. Well, if so, he would work back again. Come daylight he could see farther than by the feeble glow he carried.

But it would be a long night.

—"Dahilis, Dahilis!"

—He came upon a pair of menhirs. Much taller than he, close together, one bluntly pointed and one with a beaklike projection near the top, they must be the Stones about which he had heard words let slip. They might be something toward which she would seek. At least they were things, here in the middle of nothingness. He cast around and around. She was not there. His voice was giving out.

—The snowfall ended in a last, spiteful sleet.

—He could only croak, like a crow with a bad cold.

—When he replaced the candle, fatigue made his hand shake so that he nearly dropped it.

—The wind slackened, but chill strengthened. Heaven was lightless. Gratillonius began to hear surf at the western end of Sena.

—He came upon her quite suddenly. Another shadow he wasn't sure of; a turn for a closer look; he stubbed his toe on a rock; and there she lay. Ice had formed in crackly little patches on her drenched garments. She was huddled around her unborn. Her face was bloodless and peaceful. The lids were not entirely shut, lantern light flicked off eyeballs. As he stooped above, he saw the wrecked ankle. O Mithras! Belisama, why did You let this happen?

He knelt beside her. His hand sought beneath her gown, his ear to her nostrils. Faint, faint...but she lived, the weather had not yet killed her....Almost as faint was the throb farther down. What, was her daughter trying to be born?

You will have to wait your turn, child.

It was less that strength came back to Gratillonius than that he ceased to feel weariness. He got the blanket around Dahilis, both arms under her, thumb and forefinger crooked again at the hand of his lantern. Rising, he began to walk. Meanwhile he, or someone inside him, laid plans. He must know his every move beforehand, for time would be short. His father, in mariner days, had instructed him about death from cold, what the danger signs were, what to do for a victim. An army surgeon on the Wall had similarly lectured to young officers from the South, as winter approached. Dahilis was far gone.

Belisama, Belisama, help her. Surely you love her too.

Did an owl swoop overhead? The merest glimpse—

The House loomed forth. He supported part of her weight on a thigh while he got the door open. As he entered, his light sent shadows bounding hunchbacked around the room. He kicked her stuff off the bed and laid her on the mattress. Wind whined outside, found the door ajar and skirled through. Water dripped from Dahilis's cloak and hair. He had set the lantern on the floor. To start a fire, oil or no, would take longer than he could afford. She must have warmth at once. His fingers flew, stripping the wet garments from her. Dahilis flopped like a jointed doll.

Now, off with his own clothes. The bed was as narrow as a grave, but that was all right; she needed him, the heat of his body, close against her. He grabbed a couple of dry blankets and threw them over both while he found a place for himself. He must cling, and the frame dug painfully into his hip, but no matter, no matter in the least.

His lips touched her cheek. It was like kissing ice.

A change went through her, a shivering, a dewiness on the skin. The breath he could barely sense turned irregular and faintly, faintly, infinitely remotely, labored. He stamped on the horror that wailed within him and reached under her jaw, seeking the pulse. The jaw fell. He heard sounds and caught smells much too familiar.

249

It was so weak a death struggle that it was almost a surrender. (Belisama, Your will be done.) Gratillonius rolled from the bed, found the floor, bent over her. Again his fingers searched for the pulse in her throat. He couldn't find it. Eyes rolled back and half shut, blank, her face gaped slackly at him. He laid a palm over a breast and caught the slightest of motions. She was still breathing just a little.

The hand went down to her swollen belly. Did he feel a beating, as if against a door? He wasn't sure. He was no physician. Yet he remembered slaughtered beasts and slain barbarians. Caesar himself had made Roman law of what was olden practice. In cases like this, one must try to save the child.

Maybe she wouldn't have wished it, had she known what it was going to cost him. He couldn't ask her.

Time hounded him, closer even than before. The unborn were quick to follow their mothers into death. He had heard of some that were delivered but became defectives, worse than poor Audris. He could stay here and fight for Dahilis's life and almost certainly lose; and then her daughter was best left at peace in the dark. Or he could try for the rescue of her blood, not herself. The odds against that looked long also, but not hopeless. As fast as she was going, he must make his decision *now*.

He took the lantern again and went out, down to his tent, unaware of the wind and the cold.

When he came back, he used the flame to start candles, and thereafter kindled fire. Often he interrupted himself to attend Dahilis. His ministrations had no effect. When he ceased to feel her breathe, he used a bronze mirror he had found in her kit. Of course she had a mirror along, like any woman who wants to please her man.

At first it misted over. Soon that was so little that he crouched holding it in place below her nostrils. When it dried, he flung it clanging across the room.

He would have liked to kiss her farewell, but this was not Dahilis. He dropped a towel over the face. As for that which lay naked, he would not think about what it had been. He hoped he would not think about it. He hoped his farmer and craftsman skills, his rough knowledge of anatomy, would serve. A man could only try.

He had—how long? Three minutes, four, five? No more. Arrayed on the table, which he had dragged to the bedside, lay his small sharp knives.

~ 5 ~

Seas ran high on the morning after solstice, but wind had fallen off and skies were clearing. Dawn was barely a promise when Forsquilis and her companion came down the cliff trail to Ghost Quay and along the path to Scot's Landing. At Maeloch's door she smote the wood with her staff, whose iron finial was in the shape of an owl. The knock, knock, knock sounded loud amidst the clash of waves on rocks.

The door opened. The fisherman stood unclad, battle-ax at the ready. "What the squid-futter—" he growled, and then saw. The lantern that the other woman bore cast across the austere features of the high priestess, hooded in her cloak. Behind them, water gleamed under the first thin light in heaven.

"Oh! My, my lady Queen!" He shifted the ax blade to cover his loins. "I thought—'twasn't the Summons—pirates? My lady Forsquilis!"

"We have not met," she said levelly, "but you know me by sight and I you by repute. They call you both the boldest and the most knowing among the fishers. I command you to a faring as momentous as any of yours with the dead—or more, because on this hinges the morrow of Ys."

"What?" Behind his shaggy beard, he gulped. "My lady, that's plain recklessness. Look." His free hand gestured at the chopping and leaping.

The eyes beneath the cowl would not let him go. He saw how haggard she was, as if she had been awake this whole night. "Go we shall, Maeloch," she said, "and faster than ever you travelled erenow."

He thought before he answered: "I've heard as how Queen Dahilis went out to Vigil yesterday, like none ever did before. And the King at her side. Will you relieve her?"

"One might say that."

"Why...why, I'll go, be sure I will, if little Queen Dahilis needs help. But the others may balk."

"Are they Ferriers or not?"

Maeloch squinted past the lantern at her who bore it. "This is Briga, of my household," Forsquilis explained. "She goes too."

She was a sturdy, blond young woman, clearly an Osismian. Such often came to the city and worked a few years, earning dowries for themselves. Sometimes they got married there, or seduced. Briga's free arm nestled a very new babe against her large bosom. Her countenance declared both fear and a doglike trust in her mistress the witch.

"Make haste!" said Forsquilis's whipcrack voice.

Maeloch mumbled excuses, retreated to get dressed, came forth again to beat on neighboring doors and bawl men off their pallets. When they saw the Queen, their grumbles quickly ceased, though she stood in place like an eidolon. Enough of them heeded the call to make a crew for *Osprey*, as they did at a Summons. Most of the regular deckhands lived elsewhere.

The smack lay beached under a roof for the winter; but the Ferriers of the Dead kept gear and supplies always aboard their boats, and were swift to fetch rollers and launch this one. She was off soon after the sun had cleared the Bay of Aquitania. The passage went better than the sailors had feared, though amply difficult. The tide was with them and the wind cold but easy, swinging around widdershins until after a while they could raise the sail to help them at their oars. Sundogs danced in a crystalline heaven. Given such brightness, the helmsman readily kept off reefs.

Briga huddled under the bows, miserably seasick, caring for her infant between trips to the rail. Forsquilis sat nearby, impassive. None ventured to address her. A sailor even forgot her when he pissed over the leeward side a short distance off. His ritual apology to Lir reminded him. "Hoy, my lady, I'm sorry!"

She gave him the phantom of a smile. "Think you me a vestal?"

He wrung his callused paws. "I should've taken the slop bucket aft. But this crossing, we know not why, 'tis got me all muddled.... We do head straight back home, don't we, my lady?"

Forsquilis nodded. "I shall abide. The rest of you will return."

"Ye—?" He looked down at his feet, braced wide upon the pitching deck. "But 'tis festival time."

Her own look went beyond the horizon. "There are signs to seek, rites to begin. In another day or two the barge can safely come fetch me."

He saw that she wanted to be by herself, saluted awkwardly, and went about his duties.

—The rocks around Sena made approach so tricky that perhaps no skipper but Maeloch could have accomplished it today. When at last he brought *Osprey* to the wharf, his men slumped exhausted on their benches.

Forsquilis rose. "Rest a while," she said. "We drove relentlessly west. You can go easier eastward, homeward. Wait here."

She sprang ashore, no need for a gangplank, and made for the House of the Goddess. Her cloak rippled blue. Gulls dipped, soared, creaked through the salt wind. Out amidst the skerries, where waves crashed and foam burst, were many seals.

—The door stood open, the windows were unshuttered, the room was bright and barren. On the bed lay a form covered by a blanket. The floor had been scrubbed clean. Gratillonius sat in a chair next the bed. In his arms he rocked a newborn girl. Her crying was loud and furious.

Forsquilis entered, darkening some of the light. Gratillonius looked up. Auburn hair and beard seemed doubly vivid against a face drained and congealed, nothing behind it but weariness. "I have brought a nurse for her," said Forsquilis. "Come down to the boat. I will see to all else."

XXVI

~ 1 ~

He came awake believing it was Dahilis who roused him. Happiness filled him like sunshine. His heart felt bird-light. Oh, my dear darling!

He opened his eyes. Bodilis withdrew the hand that had been shaking him. Gratillonius remembered. He cried out and sat up in bed.

Dim day entered the chamber through its panes. Bodilis stepped back. She was clad entirely in white, no jewelry, a coif over her hair. "I'm sorry," she said low. "But you must arise. You've well-nigh slept the sun through a round."

He recalled vaguely that Fennalis had given him a potion after he reached the palace. Earlier than that, sailors had borne a wrapped form on a litter from the quay toward Wayfaring House. Earlier than that he had been at sea, a rough passage....His memory was full of jagged gaps where mists and fragments drifted.

"We cannot delay further," Bodilis urged gently. "You are the King. The Gods require Their due. And then there is the infant."

Dahilis's daughter. "How is she?" grated out of him.

Bodilis smiled a tiny bit. "Lustily yelling and kicking, the last I saw. Amazing, in view of—" the smile died—"the circumstances. But yours is strong blood, and her mother was no weakling. Now do get up, Gratillonius. You have your duties."

His whole body ached, as if he had spent a night in combat. His mind moved heavily. His spirit wanted to go away, home to Britannia or off to war or anywhere else. But he was the King. He was the prefect of Rome and a centurion of the Second.

Bodilis guided him to a hot bath. While he lay in it she brought him bread and wine. He had no appetite, but partook and gained strength. A massage afterward by his burly body servant pummeled some sluggishness out of his muscles. Bodilis stood by as attendants arrayed him in crimson robe and royal finery. "Where are we bound?" he asked.

"To the temple of Belisama," she replied. "It was decided to have both sacraments together, inasmuch as the mother is gone and you soon have your Watch to stand."

"Both?"

"First the naming and hallowing of the child."

He nodded. Dahilis and Innilis had told him about that while they were expecting theirs. "I am to do what the mother would have done?"

"This is custom when a Queen dies in childbed."

He remembered thoughts he had had while he waited in the House of the Goddess and afterward aboard ship. "Very well."

Side by side, he and Bodilis went forth. The day was overcast, a silvery gray deepening toward lead as the unseen sun declined. The air lay quiet and raw. His legionaries stood marshalled to escort him. They saluted. "Oh, God, sir, I'm sorry," Adminius said. His lean features worked. "We all are."

"Thank you," said Gratillonius, and walked on.

"'Bout face!" Adminius shouted. "For'ard march!" Hobnails hit paving like a roll of drums.

Traffic stopped when people saw who was coming. Nobody ventured to draw near or even utter a greeting. Gratillonius and Bodilis moved within a shield-wall of quietness.

"We know almost nothing of what happened," she said softly. Her arm was tucked in his. "From what the fishers and the maid Briga and...others here in the city...had to tell, we can guess at some of it. What do you wish to relate?"

In faint surprise, he noticed that talking didn't hurt. It was merely a task he performed. Most of him was trying to understand what the thing itself meant. He could not yet really realize that he would never see Dahilis again, and that his last sight of her must forever be—what it had been. "When she had not returned by nightfall, I went in search. It took hours to find her. She lay with a broken ankle, in labor, unconscious, nearly frozen to death. I carried her back, but I could not *bring* her back. As soon as she died, I did my best to save the child. Any sin, profanation, blasphemy is mine alone. She was entirely innocent."

Bodilis's grasp tightened. "We shall purify and dedicate the island over again. As for your deeds, I dare hope—we Sisters have decided we dare believe—the justice of the Gods is satisfied. They need but look into your spirit. And as for the sacrifice They demanded, we believe Dahilis must have made that. It was not what the Nine awaited, and mayhap not what the Three intended, but surely it was an offering precious enough."

Bitterness seared his gullet. He wanted no part of any such Gods. He refused the load of guilt They would lay on him. Let Mithras be his witness. But he would keep silence, he would duly go through Their rites, for Rome, and because he did not want to wound Bodilis. She must already be inwardly bleeding.

They reached the temple. The soldiers clanked up to form a double line on the stairs. King and high priestess went on in. "The ceremonies will be brief and simple," she reassured him. "It is not like a Bestowal of the Key. A new Queen is presented to the people, and they make merry, only after the soul of the former Queen has crossed over."

"What?" he asked, startled out of reverie. Before she could dispel his confusion, they were inside.

Vestals were ranked along the aisles. Their clear young voices lifted in a hymn. It chimed through the twilight of the sanctuary. Minor priestesses flanked the altar at the far end. From under her coif Bodilis pulled a gauzy veil across her countenance and went to join her Sisters. They waited behind the altar, beneath the tall strange images of Maiden, Mother, and Hag. Lamps on the marble block threw gleams off a golden basin which rested there. The white vestments everywhere around made the temple ghostly.

Gratillonius paused a moment before he concluded he should advance. He did so at a solemn pace. In front of the altar he halted and stood empty-handed, bareheaded. Neither Hammer nor crown had been laid out for him. Here in the holy place of Belisama, he bore just the Key.

A high priestess came forward to face him across the stone. Veil or no, he recognized Quinipilis. Through she spoke steadily, the youthfulness that had hitherto lingered in her voice was gone. "King and father, we are met to consecrate your child. Because her mother has departed, yours is the benison. Let her be brought unto us, and do you give her name and First Sign."

A senior underpriestess approached carrying the infant, which slept, red and wrinkled and how very small. You would not have thought that anything so small was hard to bring into the world.

Quinipilis whispered: "Do you know, Gratillonius? Dahilis was Estar."

He knew, and knew that generally the first born of a Queen received the name that she herself had borne as a vestal. But he had known her as Dahilis, and this creature he had out from her body was all that remained to him of her. Alone with the dead on Sena, he had pondered the question. It had been something to fill the hours.

Quinipilis took the blanket-wrapped babe and held her out. "Draw a crescent on her forehead," she directed low. "Say: 'Ishtar-Isis-Belisama, receive this Your servant Estar. Sanctify her, keep her pure, and at the last take her home to Yourself.'"

Gratillonius dipped his right forefinger into the water that glimmered in the basin. He traced an arc on the diminutive brow. His voice rang loud: "Ishtar-Isis-Belisama, receive this Your servant Dahut. Sanctify her, keep her pure, and at the last take her home to Yourself."

The hymn faltered. Breath rustled and hissed among the priestesses. It was overridden by an angry scream from the awakened child. She struggled to get free of her swaddling.

Gratillonius met the unseen stares of the Gallicenae and growled in an undertone, "I want her mother uniquely remembered in her. 'Tis lawful, I believe."

"Ah, aye," answered Quinipilis. "Contrary to usage, but...the law is silent....Be you Dahut." She returned the babe to the elder, who took it away to soothe.

Gratillonius's intent was clear. Dahilis had taken her sacral name from the spring of the nymph Ahes, to whom she had had a special

255

devotion. The prefix "D" was an honorific and could be retained. The suffix could not, but "-ut" formed a commemorative ending. Thus did Dahut come to Ys.

The hymn ended. Quinipilis straightened as much as she was able, raised her arms, and cried: "Let the divine wedding commence!" Echoes flew around the hush.

Wedding? Gratillonius stood hammerstruck. Now?

But of course. How could he have forgotten? He must have wanted to forget. When a Queen died, the Sign came immediately upon a vestal. Eight women stood before him; and Forsquilis was on Sena.

He would not! Dahilis was not even buried yet!

The spectral forms came from behind the altar to surround him. Quinipilis stayed where she was. One of the others moved, stumbling a little, next to Gratillonius.

"Kneel," the old priestess commanded.

He could go. They were nothing but women here. Outside waited his Romans. Thus easily could he betray his mission. Gratillonius knelt beside his chosen bride.

As if from far away, he heard a prayer. A new hymn swelled. More orisons followed, but they were mercifully short. He and she were bidden to arise. He obeyed the order to lift her veil. At the same time, his wives threw back theirs. The song soared triumphant.

He had seen the homely, timorous face before, but he could not recollect when or where.

"Gratillonius, King of Ys, in homage to the Goddess Who dwells in her, and in honor to the womanhood that is hers, receive your Queen Guilvilis—"

~ 2 ~

There was a modest banquet at the palace, which the Gallicenae shared. Directly afterward the seven each kissed the new Sister and left. Servants requested her benediction and reverentially escorted the pair to a bedchamber swept, garnished, and lighted by many lamps and wax candles. Celebrations would come later, when the spirit of the former Queen had departed.

Talk had been scant at the table. Gratillonius said nothing whatsoever. She sat by her husband, eyes downcast, eating as little and as mechanically as he did. While goodnights went on, Bodilis had drawn Gratillonius aside and whispered in Latin: "Be kind to her. Poor child, she never wished for this. Nobody imagined it. The ways of the Goddess are a mystery."

"What is her lineage?" he asked hoarsely.

"Her father was Hoel, of course. Her mother was Morvanalis—full sister to Fennalis, but that makes her no closer than a cousin to Lanarvilis.

Morvanalis died a few years after this girl was born. The child was good-natured but dull. I remember how she suffered the teasing of brighter classmates uncomplainingly, and sought her few friends among menials and animals. Everyone took for granted that when she finished her vestalhood—that would have been next year—she would take vows as a minor priestess, unless some man of humble station offered to marry her for the dowry the Temple provides. Instead— Don't blame her, Gratillonius, Treat her gently." Bodilis's gaze went deep into him. "I believe you have the strength to do that."

I believe I shall often be drawing on the strength that is in you, he thought.

Incense sweetened the air in the bridal chamber. The flames gave warmth as well as amber light. Beyond the shutters, a night wind lulled. Guilvilis stood in her white gown at the middle of the floor, hands clasped above her loins, head bowed. It was a small head with rather thin, dull-brown hair and a protruding nosetip. Her figure was tall, bosom low, hips and legs heavy; her movements were awkward.

I have to say something, Gratillonius decided "Well,"

She stayed mute. He began to pace, back and forth in front of her, his own hands clenched together behind him. "Well," he said, "fear not. I shan't hurt you. Indeed, tell me what would please you."

He could barely hear: "I know not, lord."

His cheeks heated. Without meaning to, he had asked that which it took an experienced woman to answer, and every vestal was a virgin. He cleared his tightening throat. "Might you like something in the way of comforts, pleasures, enjoyable tasks, freedom from uncongenial ones? Anything?"

"I know not, lord."

"Um-mf. It seems...nobody told me what your name was before."

"Sasai, lord." She had not moved an inch from her passive stance.

"Ah!" It came back to him. "Aye. You were at the Nymphaeum and guided me to the guardhouse when—"

When Dahilis and I went there to ask a blessing on her babe, and that night we made love.

I will *not* hate this person here.

Gratillonius moved to a nacre-inlaid table where stood cups and carafes. He poured wine for himself without adding water. "Do you care for drink?" he asked. "Make free."

She glanced up, and hastily away. "Thank you, nay, lord."

He tossed off the cup in a few draughts that lit fire in his stomach. He'd need help getting to sleep. At least this was not the same room, the same bed where Dahilis and he had taken their joy. "How came you to pick the name Guilvilis?"

"It...oh...Queen Lanarvilis said I could. 'Tis from a hamlet in the hills, she said. The house of Suffete Soren owns p-p-property there."

"Hm." Gratillonius rubbed his beard, refilled his vessel, drank more slowly. A thawing had begun to spread through him. "I take it...when the Sign appears...you tell somebody, and word goes to the—the rest of the Nine—and they meet with you?"

"Aye, lord." A finger strayed up to touch her gown above the shallow curve of breasts. "I woke from sleep, from a flash like fire, and, and—" She swallowed. He saw tears. "I was so afraid."

A certain pity touched him. He took another swallow, set the cup down, went to stand before her. His left hand he laid on her shoulder, his right he put beneath her receding chin, to raise her face toward his. "Be not afraid," he said. "'Tis the grace of the Goddess."

"They...were good to me—but— Oh, why was it me?" she quavered. "Naught do I know."

"You'll learn," he said. "Belisama must have known what She was doing." Inwardly, he wondered. He patted her back. "Be of brave heart."

She half moved to put her arms about him, but withdrew them, a jerky, frightened motion. "My lord is kind. O-o-oh..." She gulped, snuffled, somehow kept from sobbing.

He let her go and sought the wine. It gave him the courage he had been needing. His back to her, he said, "Well, 'tis been a hard day for you, Guilvilis. Shall we to our rest?"

"Aye, lord."

Still looking away and drinking, he said, after a space: "You must understand something. I have had a great sorrow. All Ys has, but...as for myself...take it not amiss—we'll simply sleep this night, and...for a while to come."

"Aye, lord."

Perhaps the Goddess had shown him a mercy. This mooncalf would make no demands on him, ever.

He finished his wine and turned about. She had undressed and stood naked at the bedside. There was more paunch than he had seen on most young women, but her complexion was clear, but her buttocks were huge and her legs like tree trunks, down through the ankles to the big feet. Ankles— The crescent above her breasts smoldered red.

She ventured the faintest of smiles. "Whatever the King wants," she said tonelessly.

"We'll sleep," he snapped. He went about blowing out the lights as if he were the bride, not the groom. The bed creaked and rustled when she entered it. In the dark he removed his own clothes, left them on the floor, and felt his way.

He lay down and pulled sheet and blanket over him. Wine or no, he feared lying awake through the night. The incense cloyed. He turned on his side. It had been toward her, he suddenly knew—sheer habit. She stirred. He felt her nearby warmth. A scent of clean hair and flesh pierced the sweetness. His hand fell upon hers.

258

His member awoke. No! he cried, but it swelled and throbbed. No, this isn't decent! Heat boiled in him. She sensed his restlessness and, herself, turned. He made a motion to keep her off. His palm encountered a breast and closed over its softness. The nipple hardened and nudged.

O Dahilis! The Bull shook horns; Its hoofs tore the earth. Blind though he was, Gratillonius knew how Guilvilis rolled over onto her back and spread her legs. He was not Gratillonius who mourned, he was he who cast himself between her thighs, thrust straight through her maidenhead, heard her cry aloud and took delight, hammered and hammered and hammered. Gratillonius stood aside, at his post of duty, hoping that afterward the Gods of Ys would allow him to sleep.

~ 3 ~

The funeral barge was fifty feet in length, gold-trimmed black, with a low freeboard and a broad flat deck. Stempost and sternpost terminated simply in spirals. A staff amidships bore an evergreen wreath.

When possible, she went out every third day, bearing the dead of Ys from their homes or from Wayfaring House. Often that was not possible, and sometimes their hostelers must lay them to rest in the brine vats. Always, though, in the end, they went to sea.

This morning was bright and calm, sun frosty in the south. Wavelets glittered sapphire and emerald, marble-swirled. They lapped against cliffs, wall, hull. Oars chirked and splashed as the barge passed the gate on an ebbing tide. Gulls dipped and hovered. Seals glided among the reefs.

The dead were laid out shrouded, each on a litter with a stone lashed to the feet. Deckhands went quietly about their work. The loudest noise, and it was low, was the ringing of a coxswain's gong, timing the slow strokes of the rowers. Passengers stood aside or sat on well-secured benches. For the most part they were kinfolk who wanted to say a final goodbye, clad in more subdued fashion than was ordinary. Three were ever on hand: a trumpeter, a drummer, and some one of the Gallicenae.

Upon this faring the whole Nine were aboard, and likewise the King, to follow their Sister. They stayed in a group near the bows, mute, looking inward or else far outward.

The barge travelled no great distance, because the bottom dropped rapidly. When the captain deemed they were over the deeps, he signaled. The trumpeter blew a long call, the gongbeat died away, the rowers merely held their vessel steady.

The captain made ritual request of the high priestess in charge. This time she was Quinipilis, who because of frail health had not come along in years. Blue-clad, her headdress tall and white, she trod forward, lifted her hands, and spoke with more strength than anyone had awaited.

"Gods of mystery, Gods of life and death, sea that nourishes Ys, take these our beloved—"

Having finished the invocation, she received a tablet from the captain and read the names aloud. They were in order of death, as were the bodies. At each, sailors lifted that litter and brought it to a chute on the larboard side. "Farewell," said the high priestess, and the men tilted their burden. A shape slid down. The water leaped a little and closed again.

—"Without a name." Innilis caught her breath and reached after Gratillonius's hand. He took hers. "Farewell." Still weak, barely able to go through with the parts that had been hers, she sat down again.

—"Dahilis." He felt his other hand taken, glanced aside, and saw Bodilis. The shape dropped from sight. "Farewell." The men carried back its bed.

—A trumpet call flew forth over Ocean. The drum marched underneath. There was a silence, save for the waves and mewing gulls. "About and home!" the captain ordered. Oars toiled, the gong resumed, the galley turned landward.

—The declining sun changed the waters to molten gold whose light sank into the wall and the towers of Ys and radiated back. Shadows had begun to lengthen. Their intricacy made sculpture of the brutal headlands, made a weaving of mystical signs, while the city glimmered between like a dream.

When the boat had passed through a now narrowing gateway, it found the harbor basin full of mist and blue shadings. High and high overhead, an albatross caught sunlight on his wings. A murmur stirred in the coolness. Traffic noises muted to a single sound, the breathing of a woman about to go to sleep.

The barge docked and passengers got off. On the quay, under a proud, time-crumbled facade, stood a few men in robes of office. Among them were Soren Cartagi, Speaker for Taranis, and Hannon Baltisi, Lir Captain. A touch surprised, Gratillonius accompanied his Gallicenae to meet them.

Soren offered salute. "My lord," the Suffete said, "not hitherto have I had opportunity to bespeak my sorrow."

By immemorial law, neither he nor Hannon were permitted on the barge until their own final journeys. "Aye," said the gray skipper, "she was dear to everybody, but most to you."

Soren's gaze travelled to Lanarvilis, then back to Gratillonius, and held steady. His heavy features gave less away than his voice. "You will have memories, King," he said. "They burn you, but may you later warm your hands at them on cold nights." He cleared his throat. "Enough. What I—what we here wish to tell you is this. We think the Gods have worked Their will and are at peace with Ys. In a certain measure you've bought that, lord. And you *are* a good King. We'll fight you no more."

Lanarvilis smiled as though she had foreknown.

Soren lifted a finger. "Mind you, lord," he said, "we may well find you wrongheaded in future and ourselves in opposition to you. We must stand fast for what is right. But 'twill be loyal opposition, for the welfare of Ys."

Gratillonius took a moment to marshal words. "I thank you," he said. "More than you know, I thank you. We'll go on together."

Abruptly he realized that he meant it. Despair was for cowards. He still had work to do, battles to wage, dreams to dream. The life that been in Dahilis flowed on in Dahut. Her tomorrows, which he must make sure of, were his renewal.

His next Watch would begin on the Birthday of Mithras.

XXVII

Maeloch awoke. Night engulfed him, save for fugitive red gleams from the banked hearthfire. The single room of his home was full of chill and odors, woodsmoke, salt, kelp, fish, humanity, sea. Again it knocked on his door, a slow one, two, three.

He sat up. His wife Betha stirred beside him. The straw tick rustled. He heard a child of theirs whimper, terrified.

Knock, knock, knock. "I come," he called.

"The Summons?" she breathed.

"Aye, what else?" he replied, lips close to her ear. "The island's been hallowed anew, I hear. And 'twas a while in the doing; we'll have a load this trip."

He always kept seagoing clothes where he could find them in the dark. Best not to light a torch at these times. You mustn't linger. Nor did you want to see too well.

"Who has the Vigil?" he muttered as he fumbled. "Queen Bodilis? Meseems I've heard 'tis she. Pray hard, Queen Bodilis."

The command had gone on down the row of cabins that was Scot's Landing. Clad, Maeloch gave Betha a quick, rough kiss and went out. The moon was full, the air mild. Light glittered and torrented on small inshore waves, flickered and shimmered across the swells beyond, made flags of the foam on skerries. Only the brightest stars were clear in sight. Orion strode opposite the hulking murk of the cliffs, thence the River of Tiamat flowed across heaven past the North Eye and back into unknownness. Frost glistened on thatch roofs. A breeze wandered from the southeast, winter-cold, not strong, but you could lift sail and get help for your oars on the way to Sena. Well, They made sure before They called the Ferriers of the Dead.

Among the men gathering by moonlight, Maeloch recognized two fellow captains. Three boatloads, then. So many had not crossed over since the battle in summer.

Fishing smacks were soon launched. *Osprey* and the others lay alongside Ghost Quay. Gangplanks thudded forth. The wind and the sea murmured.

Maeloch spied nothing but moonlight on shingle, cliffs, and waves. He heard nothing but the sounds of the night. Yet he felt a streaming across the planks, and saw how hulls settled down into the water. They would bear a full cargo tonight.

The stars wheeled in their silence.

Osprey rode no lower. "We are ready," Maeloch said. His breath smoked white. "All hands aboard."

The three boats stood out. Sails blundered aloft. The trimming was tricky, and oarsmen must keep their benches, but it gave a little more speed for passengers who had waited long. Maeloch walked around issuing low-voiced orders as needed. Otherwise nobody spoke. The companion craft were like swans afloat.

Moonlight sleeked the coats of seals.

—The boats maneuvered in among reefs whose treachery the moon betrayed, and made fast at Sena dock. The House of the Goddess loomed black, apart from glimmers of lamplight where the high priestess was praying. The island stretched ashen.

Men who had been securing lines came back aboard and stood aside. Maeloch drew back the hood of his leather jacket, to uncover his head, and took stance near the gangplank. The moon shone, the stars gleamed.

As the souls debarked, *Osprey* rocked ever higher in the water.

Maeloch heard them blow past, breaths in the night, bound for he knew not where. "I was Dauvinach," came to him barely...."I was Catellan....I was Borsus....I was Janatha...."

The sea and the wind sighed.

—"I was Rael," he heard. "I was Temesa."

—A whisper went by without a name.

—"I was Dahilis."

—When it was done, the Ferriers of the Dead cast loose and made for their homes.

GALLICENAE

I

~ 1 ~

The child knew only that she was upon the sea. It was enough to overwhelm her with wonder. That this was the Blessing of the Fleet lay outside her understanding as yet, like nearly all those sounds her father made: "—And how would you like to come along, little one?" What spoke to her was the strength of his arms and the laughter rumbling in his breast as he took her up and held her close.

Already fading out of her were the marvelous things that happened at the docks, people in bright robes, deep-chanted words followed by music that sang, chimed, whistled, quivered, twanged, boomed, as the procession went from hull to hull. The gray-bearded man in the lead was frightening to see, with his long pole and its three sharp spikes that he held on high, but behind him came the Mamas—nine of them, though she was too small to have the use of numbers. Some carried green branches that they dipped into pots that others bore, and then sprinkled oil on the prows. The first had a bowl that swung from gold chains and gave off smoke. When the wind shifted and brought the smoke to the child, it smelled sweet. She and her father stood aside, watching. He was very splendid in his own robe, a great sledge hammer at his side, on his breast the Key that usually hung inside his clothes; but she had no words for any of these things.

Afterward he picked her up again and carried her on board a ship that led the rest forth. The water in the harbor basin was lively, for the gate stood wide and a fresh breeze blew yonder. As her father's yacht passed through, the deck started to roll beneath her. Keeping her feet became a delightful game. The air was shrill and cold. It flung salt spray that tingled on her lips. The planks she stood on were still sun-warmed, giving off a fragrance of new pitch.

Everybody was jolly, men and women and such children as they had with them, none of those as young as the girl. From aft resounded the coxswain's drum, setting time for the rowers, whose oars cracked against the holes. Between strokes they often tossed words back and forth that made them grin. The ship creaked too, stays thrummed, a ruddy pennon at the masthead went *snap! snap!* Gulls mewed, hundreds of them, a snowstorm of wings, dipping and soaring. Other birds were likewise out in their darker throngs, aloft or afloat, and sometimes their cries also cut through the wind.

265

The craft that followed spread formation into a half-moon. Many were bigger than this, whether low and lean or high and round-bellied. Many more were smaller, duller-painted, and the men in them weren't so finely dressed. Some had raised sails, the rest continued under sweeps. Behind them rose the city wall, sheer, murky red save for the frieze under its battlements, and its towers, and the still taller spires inside, whose copper and glass and gilt flung light blindingly back at the sun. The headlands bulked rugged on either side, surf tumultuous underneath. The valley and hills beyond were turning green.

But it was the sea that captured the girl child, the sea. At first she clapped her hands together and shouted. Later she stood silent, aware of nothing else, for this was everything, this was the forever changing boundlessness that she had not known was within herself.

The sky reached pale and clear, only a few clouds scurrying at the edge of the world. Waves rushed and rumbled, long, maned, foam-swirled, wrinkles dancing in webs across their backs. Colors played over them, through them, gray-blue, grass-green, purple-black. Where they broke on the rocks and reefs that lay everywhere about, they bellowed hollowly and sent milkiness fountaining. Torn-off strands of kelp moved snakishly in their troughs. Creatures swam, tumbled, darted, at one with the waves, not only fowl but the sleekness of seals, a few times the silver leap of a fish or the frolicsome grace that was a porpoise. The child did not recognize a piece of driftwood as being off a wreck.

Time was no more, nothing was except the miracle that had taken her unto itself. She did not come back to anything else until the helmsmen put their steering oars over and the yacht turned again landward. The parade was done.

Most vessels headed the same way, wanting their berths prior to commencing the season's farings. A few bore southeasterly, toward fisher hamlets along the coast. The child realized that her adventure neared an end. She did not weep, such was not her nature, but she made her way to the side, the better to watch while she could.

This was on the foredeck, above and forward over the rowers' benches. The bulwark was too high for her to lean over. When a seal drew alongside, she had just a tantalizing glimpse. Nearby squatted a bollard, the anchor rode coiled around it, the hook leaning massive against it. An active creature since her birth, she got a purchase on the hemp and climbed to the top. There she glanced widely around.

Aft she spied a streak of land low in the water, from which rose a single building, dark, foursquare, surmounted by a turret. But she had already seen that. What she wanted to do was look at the seal.

It swam close, easily matching the speed of the oarsmen. The amber-brown of its coat was warm amidst the brilliance of the waves. It did not move like its fellows, intent on prey or whatever else they sought. Rather, as much as possible, it kept gazing upward. Its eyes were big, beautiful, as soft as sleep. Enchanted, the child stared back into them.

A grown-up noticed her on her precarious perch, exclaimed, and hastened to pluck her off it. He was too late. The yacht rolled heavily. It was nobody's fault—these were notoriously treacherous waters—and had happened several times today. The girl was pitched loose and went overboard.

As she fell, the yells from above reached her faintly, unreal, lost in the welcoming noise of the sea. It received her with a single enormous caress. Her thick garments drew her under. A lucent yellow-green blindness enfolded her. She felt neither chill nor fear, merely surprise, a sense of homecoming. The sea tossed her about much like her father bouncing her in his arms. A humming began to fill her head.

Before she could gasp a breath, solidity struck, gripped, whirred her away. Held between the front flippers of the seal, she drank wind and salt scud. And then her father was there, threshing clumsily but mightily through the billows. Somehow it became he that clutched her, kept her face in the air, roared for a line. Scrambling and confusion overran them; and they were back on deck. She released her shock and bereavement in a wail.

He hugged her close to him. She felt his heart slugging behind the iron Key. His voice shuddered. "Are you well, darling? Are you all right, my little Dahut?"

~ 2 ~

The summons came to Galus Valerius Gratillonius in the third year during which he had been Roman prefect and King of Ys. Having read it, he told his majordomo to arrange accommodations for the courier, because he would need a few days to find out precisely what his reply must be. Thereafter he sent for Bodilis and Lanarvilis.

Bodilis arrived first. It was raining. In the upstairs conference room where he received her, a brazier did somewhat to relieve cold, but a couple of lamps mainly cast unrestful shadows that made the pastoral frescoes on the wall dim and unreal, like memories of the summer that was waning. She had left her cloak with the palace doorkeeper. Though it had a cowl, drops of water sparkled in the dark-brown waves of her hair and misted the strong-boned countenance. Two graceful strides brought her to him. He took both her hands—they were warm beneath the dampness—and smiled down into the deep-blue eyes—not very far down.

"It's good to see you again," he said, and brushed his lips across hers, a kiss quick and cool but aquiver. "How have you been, and the girls?" He spoke Latin, and she replied in the same tongue. They ordinarily did when by themselves; she wanted to maintain proficiency in it.

"Oh, Kerna is all agog, planning a feast to celebrate when she finishes her vestalhood, and Semuramat is wild with envy and insists the eight years still ahead of her might as well be eternity," she laughed. Of the three children she had by Hoel, Talavair had completed Temple service and was married, with one of her own on the way. "Una was sound asleep when your messenger came." That was the daughter Bodilis had given Gratillonius last year.

He sighed. "If only I could spend more time in your household."

"No," she said earnestly, "don't think like that."

He nodded. Had Dahilis been less beloved by her Sisters than she was, his lavishing of attention on her would have created stresses he could ill afford. Since her death, he divided his nights as evenly as feasible among the seven Queens with whom he slept, and his days among all the Nine—or, rather, what remained of his nights and days after royal duties and masculine recreations. "Well, we'll have tomorrow, you and I, if the moon be willing. Keep it clear for me."

She smiled. "I've been preparing. But why have you called me here today?"

"Best we wait for Lanarvilis....No, you may as well read this at once." He pointed to a papyrus sheet on the table. It was curled from having been carried as a sealed-up roll. She spread it between her hands and brought it close to a lamp. As she lowered her head, near-sightedly, to scan the writing, she murmured, "Lanarvilis too, and none other? Are we to compare notes on your youngsters? Then why not Guilvilis?"

The jape fluttered forlorn. She had spied the grimness upon him. "It's not that you two—well, you three—among the Gallicenae have happened to bear me offspring this soon," he explained in his methodical fashion. "Although I well know it's no chance pure and simple. You and Lanarvilis took most thought for the future. You both saw that after what...happened with Dahilis, my fathering of more princesses would strengthen my shaken standing in Ys."

"Also," Bodilis said, "we are neither of us young women. Time is at our heels."

"Well, because you are what you are—yourself learned and wise, she versed and shrewd in the politics of the city—I want your counsel before I tell anybody else about this matter."

"Whereas you think poor Guilvilis is neither," remarked Bodilis sadly. "She has nothing to offer you but her utter love."

He bit back a retort that any dog could do as much. It would have been unkind, and not quite true. He must not blame the newest of the Nine for supplanting Dahilis; that had been no wish of her own. Guilvilis was dull, true, but she was humble and sweet and helpful; the first infant she had brought forth, Sasai, was healthy and seemed bright enough; she was carrying a second. "Read," he said.

While Bodilis did, Lanarvilis came in. Blue gown and tall white headdress showed that she had been taking her turn as high priestess at the Temple of Belisama. Nothing less than the wish of the King would call such a one away, and it had better be business vital to the city or the Gods.

Gratillonius greeted the big blond woman courteously, as was his wont. Between them was little of the warmth he had with Bodilis or the wildfire with Forsquilis. Even when they coupled, she held back her inmost self. But they had become friends, and partners valuable to each other in the governance of Ys. "What betokens this?" she asked briskly in her native language.

"A moment," he requested in the same speech. "How fares Julia?" Her sixth and most likely last living child, the babe was frail, often ill. Sometimes, when it fell out that the King visited Lanarvilis while she was keeping Dahut, the beauty, vitality, and willfulness of Dahilis's daughter seemed almost inhuman by contrast, elflike—no, catlike.

"Her fever grew so fierce yesterday that I sent for Innilis, who laid on hands and gave her medicine," replied the mother. "Today she's much better."

"Ah, good. Will you be seated?" Gratillonius gestured at a chair. After two and a half years in Ys, he had come to take that article of furniture for granted, well-nigh forgetting that it was not commonplace elsewhere.

Lanarvilis settled down. He joined her. Bodilis finished reading, passed the letter to her Sister, and likewise sat. For a while, silence took over the room, apart from the susurrus of rain outside.

Then Lanarvilis, whose lips had been moving and forefinger tracing, lowered the papyrus and said with a rueful smile, "I find my Latin worse rusted than I knew. It seems the Augustus commands you to report. But you've been sending him news of your stewardship whenever he required it."

"He wants me to come in person," Gratillonius said.

She drew a sharp breath. "Where?"

"Augusta Treverorum. You may remember hearing how he entered it in triumph early this year"—after he, Magnus Clemens Maximus, scattered the army of co-Emperor Gratianus, who was presently murdered; and Valentinianus made a peace that gave Maximus lordship over Britannia, Gallia, and Hispania, while Valentinianus retained sovereignty over Italy, Africa, and part of Illyricum. The Eastern half of the Empire stayed under Theodosius in Constantinople.

"'Tis understandable," Gratillonius went on. "The issues are settled, the weapons fallen silent, the task no longer to seize power but to wield it. He can learn more, and better, of Ys in interviews with me than from any amount of my clumsy writing."

"And what will he do with the knowledge?" Bodilis wondered.

Gratillonius shrugged. "We shall see. Yet I have ever maintained that Maximus Augustus is the stern physician whom sick Rome needs. He'll heed my advice, if it be sound. This is among the things I'd fain discuss with you two, what my recommendations ought to be."

"He may forbid you to return here," Lanarvilis fretted.

"I doubt that. True, he need no more fear a hostile Armorica at his back. But you know how much is left to do, putting down piracy and banditry, reviving trade, weaving the whole peninsula back together. I'm in the best position to lead that work, and I've proven my loyalty to him."

"You may be gone for a long while, however."

Gratillonius nodded. "Belike so. Even on Roman roads, 'twill be more than half a month's journey, unless I kill horses. And though the conference should not fill many days, I want afterward...to use the opportunity."

"They'll not like it—Suffetes, votaries, commoners, all folk in Ys—having the King take leave of them."

"I've been away erenow. Granted, this may prove a lengthier absence. But no military leader will be called for, and our interior affairs prosper. As for my ceremonial and sacral tasks, they can either await my return or be delegated. I want your thoughts on all this."

Bodilis's gaze grew intent. "What else have you in mind to do?" she asked.

"Well," he said uncomfortably, "you remember that when the Christian minister Eucherius lay dying, we promised him a successor in his church. That's two years gone, and the pledge still unfulfilled, as busy as we've been. I'll seek a man we can get along with."

"That's a small matter, to Ys and in your own head," she responded. "I've come to know you, my dear. What is your true intent?"

"Very well!" he blurted. "You know how I've wished to found a Mithraeum, for the worship of the God Who is mine. I cannot, unless first I've won the rank of Father in the Mystery. My hope is to find a temple where this can be done."

Lanarvilis looked shocked. Bodilis remained calm: "You may search through a vast territory, if I've heard aright about the persecution of that faith."

"Oh, I wouldn't. Mithras is a soldier. First and foremost, He expects a man to do his duty. But if I went as far south as, say, Lugdunum—I'd need permission, but I suppose I can get it—I should at least learn whether any such congregation is left within my reach."

"Would your elevation take long?"

"I trust not. Once, aye, years; but there are so few of us these days, and our needs are so urgent. I promise I'll not seek consecration if it demands more time than Ys can spare."

"I see." She glanced away, thoughtful.

"This is unwise," said Lanarvilis nervously. "Your breaking of traditions has already caused discord in abundance. If now the King, high priest and Incarnation of Taranis, openly gives allegiance to a foreign God—"

"I've made no secret of my prayers," Gratillonius answered. "Never in aught that matters have I failed to give the Gods of Ys Their due. Nor will I." He felt an emptiness as he said that. In his soul he had forsworn Them. "Have we become Christians here, to deny respect to everything divine other than the Lord of our narrow sect?" He forced a grin. "Or sects, rather. They might as well have a dozen different Christs, the way they quarrel about His nature."

Dubious, she yielded. "Well, we can be tactful."

"Aye." Bodilis leaned across the table and laid her hand over his. "Dear, if you are going to Lugdunum, and not terribly belated, would it be too much farther for you to come home through Burdigala?"

"What?" he asked, startled.

Her smile was wistful. "You remember how for years I've been in correspondence with Magnus Ausonius, the poet and rhetor. He's retired to his estate there. If you could bring him my greetings, and carry back an account of him as a person, it would be—almost like meeting him myself."

Pity touched Gratillonius. Her life was not impoverished. More than the perquisites of a Queen, she had the riches of her spirit. But she had never travelled beyond the island of Sena in the west and the frontier of the Ysan hinterland in the east, a few leagues away. The glories of Greece, Rome, all the great civilizations of the Mediterranean and the Orient, existed for her only in books, letters, and the conversation of an occasional visitor. Bound by Imperial law and military discipline, he nonetheless had freedoms she could but dream of. "Why, indeed," sprang from him, "if I can, indeed I will."

~ 3 ~

Again the King stood on the dais in the council chamber of the basilica, at his back the twenty-four legionaries remaining to him, behind them the eidolons of the Triad, and before him the Gallicenae and magnates of Ys. He wore a robe inwoven with gold-threaded tapestry figures to represent the eagle and thunderbolts of Taranis. In sight upon his breast hung the Key, and to his right, deputy Adminius had received the Hammer.

The garb was a part of his message, for at the quarterly meetings he had not dressed quite this grandly, and in everyday life he picked clothing simple and serviceable. It told the assembly that today he was not the blunt-spoken soldier with whom they handled the affairs of the city; he was embodied Power, secular and sacred. Several of the councillors must have anticipated this, for they too were attired in antique vestures or in Roman togas.

Still, after the invocations, Gratillonius used plain language. Oratory was not among his gifts, and while he had become fluent in Ysan, a number of its subtleties would always elude him. First he summarized

271

the situation in the Western Empire and the reasons why he hoped for a better future, at least in those parts where Maximus had control.

"What are the Augustus's plans for us?" growled Soren Cartagi.

"That we shall learn," Gratillonius told them. "I am bidden to his presence."

The news drew the storm of protest he had expected. He let Lanarvilis and Bodilis do most of his arguing for him. Although unprepared, a few joined in on their side, such as Sea Lord Adruval Tyri and Mariner Councillor Bomatin Kusuri. Their grounds were practical. "In Roman eyes, our King is an officer of the army and the state," Adruval reminded. "If he goes not when ordered, that's insubordination. D'ye want a legion coming to winkle him out of here?"

Vindilis's lean features whitened. "Let them dare!" she cried.

"Nay, now, be wise, my Sister," Quinipilis urged. Her voice was unsteady; in the past year or so she had much weakened. "How could we stand them off?"

"The Gods—"

Forsquilis the seeress interrupted in a tone low and carrying: "I think the Gallicenae may no longer be able to raise the Gods in aid; and They Themselves are troubled. For the heavens have moved from the Sign of the Ram to the Sign of the Fish, and the old Age dies as the new comes to birth." Her gaze dropped and her hands passed across her robe, under which a life swelled toward its own forthcoming.

"Will the Emperor let our King return?" asked Innilis. She sounded terrified.

"Why not?" said Bomatin. "He's been doing a masterly job here."

"Doing it for Rome," Hannon Baltisi, Lir Captain, snarled. He raised his arm. "Oh, I agree he's served us well. I don't believe he'd willingly do us an evil turn. But what will he have to say about things?"

"Aye." Soren nodded his massive head. "When Rome was caught up in its tribulations and forgot Ys, we stayed free. Now there's a strong Emperor, the kind who always wants more power—and more cash—and he's become aware of us. What's next?"

Gratillonius decided he had better assert himself. "Hold!" he boomed. "Hear me!" Having gotten silence, he adopted an easy manner:

"My Queens and worthies, bethink you. What's to fear? I served under Maximus when we cast the wild men back from the Wall. I know him for a man able and well intentioned. He'll listen to me.

"Consider what Ys has done for him. We kept Armorica quiet. We saved Gallia from what would have been a ruinous barbarian attack. We have taken the lead in rebuilding defenses throughout the peninsula. Commerce begins to revive as the risks diminish. Folk should soon start reconstructing what's been destroyed. Maximus must be a madman to wish this changed; and he is not. That's the more so when he still has to reckon with the untamed Germani and Alani and, it may be, his fellow Emperors in the South and East. Far from helpless, Ys is in an excellent bargaining position.

"I'd liefer not brag, but this and more we have done under my guidance. And I have been not only your King, but also the prefect of Rome.

"Then be glad if we can renew our ties to Rome the Mother!"

There was some discreet applause, some reservation, several faces that stayed troubled. Hannon Baltisi scowled, cleared his throat, and rasped:

"Well and good, O King, save for this, that Rome has long since become whore to Christ. Need I recall to you how they mock the Gods there, violate temples, smash images, hound worshippers? Will Christ dwell in peace with the Gods of Ys, those Gods who alone hold Ocean at bay?"

Mumbles and whispers passed among the forty-two. The legionaries who formed Gratillonius's honor guard kept still, but he could virtually feel resentment radiate from most of them at such a denunciation of their faith. He weighed his reply carefully. The old man's travels, in his days as a sea captain, had if anything reinforced his fanatical hatred of the Church; but persons more moderate were uneasy, and for cause.

"This is a question among many that I hope to take up with the Augustus," Gratillonius said. "It touches me too, not only in my royal office but in my heart." He congratulated himself on the subtlety of this reminder that he was a Mithraist. Before ground could be broken for the temple of his dreams, foundations must be laid in the minds of men. "But I'm unafraid. The fact is that the Empire continues full of people who are not Christians, a number of them in high positions. Maximus knew my beliefs when he appointed me your prefect.

"Clergy are few and far between in these parts. The Augustus should be satisfied with a new minister here for the Christians among us, just as we had before. That was a harmless man. Fate willing, I'll have a voice in choosing his successor. Rest assured, 'twill be no Ambrosius!"

Bodilis and three or four others recognized the name of the forceful bishop of Italian Mediolanum, and smiled. Relief spread visibly through the rest.

Gratillonius pursued his advantage. "To that end, I may have to search a while," he warned. "Also, 'twould be well that I make myself familiar with conditions throughout Lugdunensis, aye, and in Aquitania—" he saw Bodilis kindle, and tipped her a wink— "so that we'll be ready to cope. This will keep me away for a period of months. I'll be absent at the equinox and mayhap at the winter solstice, as well as other occasions. Yet I'll leave the city in order, fully able to steer itself that long. Surely the Gods will take no offense, when this is for the well-being of Their people."

He knew himself for a hypocrite. But his ultimate purpose was honest, and as a soldier he had never objected to ruses. He sat down

273

on the throne, resigned to a theological dispute. Bodilis and Lanarvilis were primed to conduct it for him. Afterward would come practical topics. What should he say and seek in Treverorum? He sincerely wanted suggestions. If need be, let discussion go on for a few days.

Only a few, however. He must not keep the Emperor waiting.

~ 4 ~

It chanced that this was his night to spend with Innilis. Knowing how he felt, and remembering the mother, his wives tried to shift custody of Dahut so that he could see her when he visited each of them. The effort failed more often than not, since strict rotation was impossible. He might be preoccupied, perhaps out of the city altogether, in the hinterland or on the water or standing his monthly Watch at the Wood. He might have been working hard or late, and in sheer weariness bedded down alone at the royal palace. For her part, a Queen might likewise be overbusied, or having her courses or sick. Pregnancies and childbirth had been intervening too, and bade fair to increase. Forsquilis was now fruitful, Guilvilis was again, and Maldunilis had finally decided to trouble herself about it. Moreover, the two Gallicenae with whom he did not sleep, aged Quinipilis and aging Fennalis, claimed a share in the upbringing of Dahilis's daughter, which for the sake of harmony could not be denied them.

Fortune did have Dahut at Innilis's house when King and Queen arrived on that evening. "Oh, my lord, my lady, how good you're back!" exclaimed the maidservant Evar as they entered. "The little one's been that fretful. She threw such a tantrum I feared she'd hurt herself, I did, and restrained her."

Dread struck. "Is she ill?" Gratillonius demanded.

"Nay, lord, I think not. Like a crazed ferret she's been, for dashing about and throwing things—oh, my, ferrets don't throw things, but my lord knows what I mean— 'Tis but that kids are troublous in their third year. Well, she's not quite in that yet, is she? But ever so far ahead of her age, already speaking, and so much alive. With my lady gone all day— Does my lord want to see her?"

"I do." He brushed past the woman and strode to the room that had been designated a nursery.

When he opened the door, he saw the debris of small destructions strewn about, a broken toy chariot, stuffing ripped out of a rag doll, general chaos. The chamber pot stayed upright; in certain things, Dahut had a feline neatness. The child was curled on the bed, brooding over her wrongs. She had stripped off her clothes. Sunset light, striking through a windowpane, turned her skin to ivory, hair to gold, eyes to lapis lazuli. O Mithras, how she recalled Dahilis!

She gathered her limbs beneath her, again like a cat. "Father," she hissed.

"Ah," he blustered, "we've been having a mutiny, have we? What for? Why have you been such a bad girl?"

She struggled for words. "I wos...wos...*me*."

Did she mean "all alone"? How could he tell? He hunkered down and spread his arms. "Well, well, little rebel, let's make it right again, hey?"

She uncoiled and sped to him. He hugged her withy-slimness. How sweet she smelled! "You mustn't do this, you know," he said into the warmth between her throat and shoulder. "It's not kind to your Mamas, or their poor servants who have to look after you."

"You di'n' come," she gasped; but she shed no tears, she hardly ever did.

"Oh, you were awaiting me? I'm sorry. Your Papa had work to do. Let's get you nicely dressed, and then before Evar brings you dinner we'll play horse and I'll sing you a song—because you're the single human being who does not flinch when I sing, and too soon will that end."

—Innilis ate lightly and simply. Gratillonius liked the fare her kitchen offered, after the frequently elaborate meals he got in Ys. She had learned to give him portions of adequate size. Ordinarily they made small talk over the table and retired early, for although she often showed him affection, they had few interests in common. This evening she spoke earnestly. The glow of beeswax candles lay over the delicate features and in the big eyes.

"Sometimes I fear for Dahut," she said. He could barely hear. "There is something about her."

He harked back to a night on Sena, and a day when a seal had saved the child from drowning, and incidents more fugitive. It took courage to reply. "Mayhap we see the beginnings of a destiny. Or mayhap not. Who can say? I've scant faith in astrologers or fortune-tellers. Let's take each day as it comes. We must anyhow."

"Oh, I thought not of the occult. I meant only—well, I've fretted about this, and talked with Vindilis—Vindilis and others— Do we do right, shunting her from household to household, with never a den where she can snuggle down? Is this why she's wild?"

He frowned. "I know not. How could I? She's my firstborn." Unless he was the casual begetter of a brat or two in Britannia, of which transgression he hoped Mithras had absolved him. "And the King of Ys can't be a real paterfamilias. Has not the Sisterhood always shared in the raising of a princess whose mother died?"

"Aye, but I think never like this. You are different. And Dahut is. I cannot put it in words, I'm too weak and stupid to understand it, but Vindilis says— You *are* the bringer of a new Age, and you did father Dahut."

Different, he thought, indeed different. The daughter of Dahilis is so spirited, so intelligent and beautiful.

—After Innilis miscarried, he had agreed with Vindilis that henceforward she should use the Herb. The next stillbirth could kill her, or the next live birth give another pitiful Audris. Six fertile Queens were ample.

She had not asked him to refrain from making love to her. He had found his way to what was best; much kissing and caressing, then much gentleness, for a single time. About half such joinings seemed to give her pleasure, and the rest no distress. At least, she cuddled close afterward.

This night she stayed awake a while, which was unusual. He could feel how she tensed and faintly shivered against him. "What vexes you?" he asked. When she grew evasive, he pressed the query. In the end she confessed:

"Oh, you, Grallon, fear about you." She seldom gave him his proper name anymore but, like an increasing number of Ysans and Osismii, softened it. "You're bound away."

"I'll return," he said.

She drew a ragged breath. "Aye, since you've promised it. But how long will you stay? You surely yearn back to your homeland."

He lay for a spell, unspeaking. The question haunted him too, but nobody else had raised it. He was astounded that this meek person should. And what in Ahriman's name was the answer?

Of course there was a great deal yet to do in Ys, and he hated leaving a task unfinished. The challenge here called him beyond himself. The making of a useful thing in statecraft was muddled and never really complete, unlike the making of a thing in woodcraft. Just the same, the satisfactions bore no comparison to each other. He had shaped history and law, he had raised bulwarks for the lives of people.... What would come of it all? A barbarian wave had broken itself against Ys, but the tide of barbarism was still at the flow, over land as well as sea. Could he abandon the defenses he had been building?

And yet, never to have a son, if it was true what chronicles and belief said. To abide among aliens until the last death-fight in the Wood made an end of him—

And meanwhile, would those duties truly have been so important? Once the rule of Maximus was firm, his peace would soon reach this far. Likewise, in due course, would his law. What then would be left for the King of Ys? Ceremonies; routines; judgments that made a difference to the parties concerned but were yawnfully tedious for the judge, and as readily rendered by somebody else.

Even now, calm was descending. Though northern Britannia seemed again troubled, the rest of that diocese lay secure. Communications had redeveloped to the point where Gratillonius had had three letters from his father, and sent back replies. To visit the villa once more! Not that he'd accept the wretched curial existence of his free will; but he shouldn't have to. Given the tiniest hint, Maximus Augustus ought to confer senatorial rank on a man who had served him well. And mighty work remained to do in the outer world, reform of the state, subjugation of the barbarians, binding of wounds upon Mother Rome, winning of fame immortal.

Was that his wish?

If not, why not? Ys would never consentingly let its King depart for good. In the past he had wondered about cutting his way free, he and his legionaries or a rescue expedition from outside. But that thought was obsolete—which gladdened him, because he recoiled from any idea of killing his subjects. Come the time, he need merely make a pretext for another journey, and fail to return. It wouldn't hurt the city's institutions too badly. Precedents existed; not every king had died in the Wood. The Suffetes would get somebody—until, no doubt, the Christians came to power here also, and made an end of those bloody successions.

Three years hence, let us say, what reason would Gratillonius have to dwell in Ys?

Well, status, friends, his wives, or certain among them, and Dahut, whom he could smuggle out but would that be the best thing for her?

Innilis nestled against him, weeping most quietly. "Nay, I will abide," he said, and wondered how much of a liar he was, "as long as the Gods allow."

II

~ 1 ~

"Again the tuba, the tuba calling:
'Come, Legionary, get off your duff!'
The hobnails rising, the hobnails falling,
We're bound for glory, or some such stuff.
Farewell, dear wenches! There's time to kiss you
And gulp a beaker before we go.
The Lord on high knows how we will miss you,
So give us memories that will glow."

It was one of the old, interminable, nonsensical songs that men had sung as they marched from Pontus to Hispania, from Egypt to Caledonia, and beyond, in the service of Rome. Footfalls crashed rhythmically beneath its beat. Words rang into the woodlands bordering the highway, until they lost themselves among trees and shadows. This was mostly second-growth forest, beech, elm, hornbeam, though here and there gloomed a huge oak, hallowed perhaps since before the first Caesar, until cultivation died away a hundred or more years ago. Leaves were still thick, full of greenish-gold light, but some had begun to turn color. The air below was windless, cool, scented by damp earth. Overhead were fewer wings than last month; many birds had, by now, departed south.

Riding at the front of his two dozen infantrymen and their pack animals, Gratillonius saw stone pavement run straight before him until, at a dim distance, it went from sight in one of those curves that had been the engineers' reluctant concession to terrain. Behind him lay turbulent Condate Redonum, where soldiers of his had nearly gotten into a fight with members of the Frankish garrison. Ahead, he had been informed, was the Liger valley, rich and well populated as of yore. At Juliomagus he would swing east and follow the great river for a while. His route was not the shortest possible, but almost entirely, it followed roads like this. Spared slogging through mud in the wet season, and most often spared the toil of preparing a walled and ditched camp—because well-secured official hostels stood along the way, near which they could simply pitch their tents—the men should make their best time to Augusta Treverorum.

They were eager too. While they had all become fond of Ys, and several had formed strong ties, the hankering to be back among things Roman was only natural. That had been a large part of his reason for taking the whole twenty-four as his escort, and nobody else. As for the rest of his reason, he wasn't quite sure, but he had a notion that Magnus Maximus would not take kindly to a spokesman native to witchy Ys.

Otherwise his feelings were happy. He also was bound home to his people.

"I'm getting old and my joints are creaky,
The lentils grumble within my gut,
My tentmates snore and the tent is leaky,
And come a combat, I might get cut.
But never mind, we have got our orders.
So cheer up, fellows, for I do think
When we have crossed over foreign borders
There will be wenches, and lots to drink!"

"'O-old!' Adminius cried. The deputy could bring a surprising volume out of his narrow chest. "Battle ranks!"

Gratillonius heard clatter and scramble. He drew rein. Gravel scrunched to silence on the shoulder where he rode. Glancing back, he saw the vexillation quickly bring the animals together and themselves in position either to protect or attack. He'd kept them in crack training.

Adminius trotted over to him. "Being cautious, sir," he said. "Wot does the centurion want we should do?"

Gratillonius peered ahead. No danger was obvious in the mounted man who had come around the curve and was galloping their way. As he spied them, he waved and shouted frantically, and kicked his horse to go faster. The beast was sweaty but not yet lathered; it hadn't carried him far. The man was portly, with black hair cut short and a close-cropped fringe of beard in the Roman style, but tunic and trousers showed him to be a Gaul. Soon Gratillonius made out a dull-red splotch on his left thigh, from which edges of cloth flapped back. A flesh wound. That went with the condition of the horse.

"No pursuit," Adminius deemed. "'E's escaped. Didn't seem worth chasing, I s'pose." He squirted a gob of spit from a gap between teeth. His thin, sandy-stubbled face crinkled in a grin. "Well, they didn't know anybody like us was anywhere near, eh, sir?"

Beneath Gratillonius's calm went an ugly thrill. "We'll wait and hear what he's got to say."

The Gaul halted in front of them. For a moment the only sounds were the whickering breath of the horse and the man's gasps. His eyes rolled. At length he got out, "Romans! Legionaries! God be praised! Quick, and you may yet save us!"

The Latin was fairly good, with an accent that Gratillonius recognized as that of the Namnetes. He had come as far south as their seaport two years ago, when he was trying to link the cities of the littoral in cooperation against barbarians and neutrality in the civil war. "The sooner you make sense and tell me what the matter is, the sooner we may be able to do something about it," he snapped.

"Bacaudae—" the man groaned.

"That's no news. Let's have facts."

The stranger gulped, shuddered, mastered himself in some degree. "My wagon train...goods out of Armorica and Britannia...left Redonum.... Bishop Arator and his attendants joined us there, bound for a conference in Portus Namnetum. We'd been told the route was safe. I b-b-brought guards anyway, of course. But now, in th-th-this forsaken stretch...suddenly, there they were, scores of the vilest robbers springing out of the woods and—" He plucked at Gratillonius's wrist. "God aided me to flee, because I found you. Don't delay! It's only two or three leagues. The guards will fight. You can get there in time. God calls you!"

The centurion spent a flash considering. His mission took primacy. However, his squadron should be a match for any plausible number of outlaws; banditry required suppression; and if word got about that he had been less than zealous in the cause of a prelate, he might as well turn land pirate himself. Worse could be the consequences to Ys.

"On the move!" he barked. Adminius shouted commands. Metal gleamed as the formation reshaped itself and started off.

The Gaul kept his horse alongside Gratillonius's. "Can't you go faster?" he pleaded.

The centurion shook his head. "Three or four miles at a dead run in full armor wouldn't leave the boys fit for much. We'll do what we can. I promise nothing. We may find everybody in your convoy lying

279

throat-cut, and your merchandise gone with your animals. In that case, I can't pursue. We're on urgent business of the state. I can only ask the garrison commander in Juliomagus to try for vengeance."

He felt no great excitement. If he could save yonder folk and kill marauders, that was fine. It depended on how long the guards could hold out. The steady, relentless tramp at his back had carried Rome's eagles across the world.

"Tell me what to expect," he said. "First, what strength did you have?"

The merchant swung his hands and sometimes keened over the loss he might suffer, but piece by piece, the tale came forth. He was one Florus, a dealer in fabrics. With money what it was these days, he most commonly traded rather than bought and sold, which meant he handled a variety, not just cloths but leathers, furs, raw materials. "This trip my best acquisition was a consignment of those wonderful weavings they do in Ys, that have scarcely been seen for many years, oh, priceless...." The train consisted of four mule-drawn wagons; their drivers; the reverend bishop with two priests and four deacons; Florus himself; and six guards, toughs who hired out for this kind of duty despite the law frowning on it. Two were Gauls, three were Frankish laeti, and one was a brown-skinned person who said nothing about himself but might well be a deserter from the army. "We take what we can get, right, Centurion? We make do." The guards had sword or ax, plus a few spears. Their armor amounted to boiled leather jackets, cheap kettle helmets, shields of barbarian type. Then, to be sure, the muledrivers possessed knives, cudgels, whips. And three of the deacons were young and sturdy, equipped with stout walking staffs. "They should be able to fend off the evildoers a while, don't you think? But hurry, hurry!"

"How did you get away?" Gratillonius inquired.

"Oh, I was mounted, by the mercy of God, and when they swarmed out it was clear what they intended, and by God's grace they didn't close a line across the road to the north before I'd gone past. They almost did. You can see where a spear hurt me. Do you have a surgeon with you? Or at least poultices? This kind of injury inflames so readily. It hurts me abominably."

"We're not stopping for anything just yet, friend. Why did you flee? One more *man* defending might make all the difference."

"But I had to get help. God saw to it that I could get help." Florus's voice sank to a mutter. "That means the goods will be safe, doesn't it, O Lord? You'd not let Your faithful servant be ruined, almighty God Who delivers us from evil."

Gratillonius snorted and sent his horse a little ahead.

Slowly the tumult became visible from afar. Noise drifted thin. Gratillonius signalled for double time. He was tempted to speed in advance for a better look. It was getting hard to see any distance as the sun declined and dusk began to seep out of the earth. He resisted the impulse. He had no right to take unnecessary risks. Solitary heroics were for barbarians and fools.

Yonder they grew aware of his approaching force. He saw the struggle die down, like a wave that smashed itself on a reef outside Ys, recoiled in foam, and dwindled away. The next wave was coming....

He reined in and jumped to the ground. The men saw his intention and needed but a minute to tether the horses. "You, keep out of the way!" he told Florus. He unslung his shield from the harness, slipped the retaining strap over his neck, gripped the handle, drew blade and took his place as leader. The squadron advanced.

Nearing, he saw that the battle was almost done. The travellers had given a good account of themselves. Somehow they'd gotten three wagons on the sides of a square, cutting loose the mules, which might well panic. There hadn't been time to bring the fourth around, it stood off where the robbers must have led it, but a crude little fort existed. While three guards held fast at the open side, their comrades and certain of the other men repelled foes who sought to climb over the vehicles or crawl underneath.

Yet they could not long keep off assailants whom Gratillonius estimated to number thirty. As he guessed at once, they were still alive—some of them—only because the bandits lacked proper training and discipline. After being cast back with losses, the outlaws milled around, none wanting to be the first to meet that steel again. They tried to bargain. Gratillonius learned afterward that the bishop had strengthened the will to resist, calling on divine help, while he cleverly strung the talk out. At length the brigands lost patience and made a fresh charge. It failed likewise, though at heavy cost to the defenders.

After that, the attackers had resorted to slings. Kept up, the bombardment would have done its job. The travellers took wounds and a couple more deaths. However, they had enough protection to be difficult targets, and eventually the supply of missiles was exhausted. Yet the defense was now so weakened that the bandit leader could egg his men on to a third assault. It broke through and was in among the wagons when the legionaries arrived.

Gratillonius took his troop toward chaos. The outlaws were Gauls, in ragged, filthy garb, pieced out with hides or old blankets or whatever else came to hand. Hair and beards were matted, greasy manes, out of which glared faces gaunt, scarred, weatherbeaten. Shoes were agape, rudely mended, or mere bags of skin stuffed with grass. The barbarians who raided Britannia were better off. Weapons were spears, knives, pruning hooks, firewood axes, a few swords acquired somehow. The wielders screamed hatred and defiance at the Romans. At the same time, those on the fringe were pulling back, making for the trees, in disorderly fashion. They knew that if they stood their ground they'd be butcher's meat.

Which was exactly what they ought to be. "Right and left!" Gratillonius called. "Circle them!" He leading a detachment, Adminius its mate, his men hastened to bag as many as they could.

Those inside the laager could not readily disengage from opponents who, heartened, fought furiously. It had never been a proper battle at all, but more like a riot. It pushed combatants apart, flung them against their fellows, sent them tripping over each other. Somebody fallen but alive might grab at an ankle or cling to a spearshaft. Wrestlers on the ground further impeded everyone.

First from the soldiers went the terrible flight of javelins. Meant for use against shields, here they struck unprotected flesh. Men fell, writhed, shrieked. Those who tried to help them to safety were themselves delayed. And then the legionaries were upon them.

A fair-haired youth with downy whiskers attempted to dodge past Gratillonius. The centurion gave him the sword between rib cage and pelvis, forcing the blade right and left to make sure of the liver. Flesh resisted softly, heavily, helplessly. The lad went down. Before Gratillonius could pull his weapon free, a full-grown man was at him, weeping, howling, belly wide open as he swung his arms back for an ax blow. Gratillonius rammed the boss of his shield into the solar plexus. Breath whooped from the Gaul. He dropped his ax and fell to his knees. Gratillonius crashed the bottom rim of his shield against the man's temple. The Gaul crumpled.

Gratillonius had delivered a knockout blow he hoped wasn't fatal. He wanted prisoners to bring to Juliomagus for beheading, or whatever the judgment would be—examples. He withdrew his sword. Blood pumped forth. A stump end of gut protruded past the tattered shirt. "Mother," the youth wailed, over and over. Gratillonius went on. The whole episode had taken just a minute or two, scarcely interrupting the rhythm of onslaught.

He saw a cluster of men pass under the trees, disappearing amidst boles and brush. They bore along a figure robed and struggling. He had no chance to think about it. He only had a fleeting perception of one who seemed in charge, slender, swift of motion, uniquely well clad. After that, Gratillonius was busy finishing the engagement.

—The legionaries had suffered no harm worth mentioning. Of the travellers, besides Florus, there survived, slashed and battered but reasonably hale, two Frankish men-at-arms, three drivers, a priest, and a deacon. The rest lay stretched out on the roadside, blood wiped off as best might be, dead or dying. The clergyman had already prayed over them.

And Bishop Arator was missing.

As for the robbers, a full twelve had fallen in battle or, hopelessly wounded, received the mercy stroke. Their bodies were stacked on the opposite side of the road. Nobody had cleansed them, closed staring eyes or tied up fallen jaws, but the kindly shadows were well on the way to covering them. Six captives sat bound to the wagons.

Nobody said much. Most of the survivors were still too stunned. Now and then pain made somebody moan. Otherwise they huddled, shivered, looked emptily before them, clutched the bread and wine that had been passed out. The soldiers were in full self-possession but occupied with making a safe camp, since they would spend the night here. An occasional sentence, grunt, oath sounded beneath the thud of axes, the sucking noise as spades turned wet humus.

Gratillonius and Florus had drawn aside at the latter's request, away from the dead, wounded, captured, the thickening blood puddles. As yet, the sky and the crowns of trees were bright overhead. A few rays slanted golden through the westside gloom. Only a hint of chill was in the air. Crows cawed.

"But the bishop is gone," Florus wailed. "A holy man, a lord of the Church, borne off by a gang of sacrilegious murderers! I'll never live down the scandal, never. And my mules, my well-trained carters, lost! Why could you not make better speed?"

"I told you," Gratillonius said wearily. "If you mean to complain at the garrison, spare your breath. Any competent officer will understand. Be glad we saved what we did and can help you finish your journey."

His command would have to do that. The chances of some other group coming along, whom he could dump the chore onto, were slight, as feeble as traffic had become. He couldn't leave these people without escort when a dozen outlaws were still at large. The delay in his own progress would be excused him. Though the Christians would be aghast at what had happened to a veritable bishop—

"Hs-s-s," whispered from the brush. "Roman, listen."

Gratillonius spun about. He saw nothing but tangled green, murk behind it. Helmetless in the aftermath of battle, the breeze cool upon his brow, did he hear a rustling?

"Hs-s-s," went the voice again. "Hark'ee."

"What's this?" yelped Florus. "Are the murderers back? Help! To arms!"

Gratillonius caught him by the nape and squeezed till he whimpered. "Be still," the centurion said, never looking away from the forest. "Go back to your wagons and say nothing. I'll handle this."

"But—you can't—"

"Begone and shut up, or I'll have you flogged."

He let go. Florus stumbled off, half sobbing. Gratillonius spoke softly: "Who are you?"

"The Bacauda chief. Make no move, if you want your bishop alive."

Something eased in Gratillonius. He heard himself chuckle. "Very well," he said. "Now how shall we go about bargaining?"

The centurion's tent was large enough for two men to sit in, on its floor which kept out the dampness of the soil. Its walls likewise withstood autumnal cold. Outside, a wind had arisen after nightfall, to rush through branches, whirl dead leaves away, rattle the leather of the tent and make its poles tremble. Within, a lantern threw dull highlights onto faces, against monstrous shadows.

"Your price is high," Gratillonius said.

Rufinus shrugged and grinned. "One bishop for six Bacaudae. Take it or leave it. Myself, I think I'm being swindled."

Gratillonius peered at him. His invited visitor was young, about nineteen or twenty he guessed, though the spirit behind the green eyes seemed as old as the night wind. Rufinus was of medium height, much of it in his legs, and wirily built. Features otherwise sharp and regular were marred by the scar of a cut, poorly treated, puckering his right cheek and giving his mouth the hint of a perpetual sneer. Though his beard was still scanty, he kept it trimmed in an unconventional fork. His black hair was also short, and reasonably clean, as were the rest of his person and his clothes. Faded, many times patched or darned, shirt and breeches were of stout material. A deerskin jerkin gave additional protection, and he had doffed a cowled cloak. His footgear was clearly from no shoemaker's shop, but just as clearly made to his measure with a degree of skill. At his belt were a pouch, a knife, and a Roman sword.

"You put me in a cleft stick," Gratillonius said. "Unless I let dangerous bandits go free, what will become of the bishop?"

"He'll be butchered like a hog," Rufinus answered coolly. "Before then, maybe some of the boys will use him."

"What?"

"Well, we seldom see a woman, you know. Though in this case, it'd be revenge more than lust. *I* wouldn't want that withered prune."

Fury thickened in Gratillonius's throat. He could barely stay where he was, and not assail the other. "You rotten snake!"

Rufinus lifted a palm. "Hold on," he said. "I'm only warning, not threatening. "I'd forbid such a thing if I could. But I'm no army officer. We're free men, we Bacaudae. We choose our leaders ourselves, and follow their orders if and when we want to. My gang is enraged. If they don't get their friends back—if, instead, those fellows go off to death, maybe first to torture—I can't stand in the way of their justice. They'd kick me aside."

He leaned forward. His Latin flowed easily despite rough accent, sloppy grammer, and idioms strange to Gratillonius. "As is," he said, "I'll hear curses aplenty when they learn they won't get a ransom besides the exchange. I wonder how you dare hold back stuff that could make you sure of your holy man."

Gratillonius returned a grim smile. "He's not my holy man. I'll have to answer for whatever happens. Leave me this much to show. If you won't, well, I need just report that no meeting took place." He didn't know if he could bring himself to that. Certainly he could not if put under oath. However, he needn't reveal his vulnerability. "Besides, think. You'll have to go far and fast, before the garrison comes after you. This wood isn't too big for them to beat. Four of our prisoners are too hurt to walk much. They'll encumber you enough, without adding boxes of goods."

Rufinus laughed. "Right! That's how come I gave in on that point. I did hope for some solidi, but you win."

He grew serious, with an underlying liveliness that never seemed to leave him. "How's this sound? We meet at sunrise. You keep your men in camp. We're woodsrunners; we'll know whether you're honest about that. We'll show up half a mile south with the bishop. One of us'll stand by him—me—ready to kill if anything goes sour. You release our four disabled buddies and give time for us to carry them well away. Then two of you bring our two hale down the road. You can have their hands tied and leashes on them, and you can have swords, but no javelins. We stop a few yards apart and let our hostages go, both sides. The bishop's slow on his feet, so I'll release him first, but you've got to release ours while he's still near enough for me to dash up and stab him. Naturally, you can pay us back in kind if I play you false. We scamper off into the woods and you return to camp. Satisfied?"

Gratillonius pondered. This was a quick intelligence he dealt with. "The leashes will be long, so your fellows can't bolt off after we let go," he decided. "When they reach you, you can cut the cords."

Again Rufinus laughed. "Done! You're a workman, Gratillonius. Be damned if I don't like you."

In his relief, the centurion couldn't help smiling back. "Aren't you damned already?"

Mercurially, the Gaul turned somber. "No doubt, if it's true what the Christians say. But then I expect the fire for me won't be so hot as what they keep for the great landowners and senators. Do you really know the masters you serve?"

Memories crowded on Gratillonius. He scowled. "Better them than outright banditry. I've seen enough places looted and burnt, women who'd been raped over and over, children and oldsters killed for fun, that I've no lost no sleep after striking down what reavers I could—be they barbarians or Romans."

Rufinus gave him a long look before murmuring, "You aren't from hereabouts, are you?"

"N-no, I'm a Briton. But these past two years and more I've been in Armorica. Osismiic country, that is."

"I don't believe there're any Bacaudae that far west."

"There aren't. Most of it's been picked too clean. Ys alone has stayed well off, because it's got ways to keep the wolves out."

Rufinus sat straight. His eyes caught the lantern light as they widened. "Ys," he breathed. "You've *been* there?"

"I've operated in the area." Gratillonius's instinct was to reveal no more to an enemy than was unavoidable. "Now I'm on a different mission. I planned no fight with you. Nor did those wayfarers you attacked. For whatever you've suffered, blame yourselves."

"Ys, the city of fable—" Rufinus broke off, shook himself, spoke sharply. "I've never been yon way, of course, but I can guess what kind of 'wolves' you're thinking of. Saxons and Scoti for the most apart, hey? And some Gauls who took the chance to go looting around after everything was wreckage—though I'll bet a lot of those were driven to it by hunger. Where was the Roman state that taxed them and ordered them about, where was it when they needed it? But anyhow, they were not Bacaudae."

"Do you mean you're something else than marauders?"

"I do." With bitterness: "You wouldn't care to listen. I'll go now. See you in the morning."

"No, wait!" Gratillonius thought for a moment. "If you'll stay a while, I'll hear you out."

"How's that?" Rufinus asked, surprised. He had gotten up. His movements were apt to be quick, nervous, but deft.

"Well, you see," Gratillonius explained, "I am a Briton, and my time in Gallia has all been at the far western end, except for a march there from Gesoriacum. But I may be, well, in future I may be having business elsewhere. I can handle it better if I know how things are. All I know of the Bacaudae is that they're vagabond gangs of runaway serfs, slaves, every sort of riffraff. I mean, that's all I've heard. Is there more to it?"

Rufinus stared down at the big, blunt-featured, auburn-haired man. "You're a deeper one than you make out," he said low. "I'd give a bit to learn what your business really is. But— Look here. What I've got to tell won't please you. It'll be the truth, but the truth about Rome. I'm not after another fight."

"I don't want any either. Say what you will, and if I get angry, I'll hold it in. I may or may not believe you, but...I've had worse foes than you."

Rufinus's smile glistened forth, bad though his teeth were. "The same right back at you, Gratillonius! Let's." He lowered himself.

The centurion rose in turn. "How about some wine to help our tongues along?"

—The tale came out in shards. Sometimes Rufinus japed, sometimes he struggled not to weep. Gratillonius plied him with drink and questions, and meanwhile tried to fit events together in his mind. Later he would try to understand.

Rufinus was born to a smallholder near the latifundium of Maedraeacum in the canton of the Redones, about twenty miles northwest of Condate Redonum. Albeit impoverished, the family was close-knit and had its joys. Rufinus, the youngest, especially liked herding swine in the woods, where he taught himself trapping and the use of the sling. Yet even before his birth, the vise was closing. The best of the land had been engulfed by the manors. Imperial regulation made needed goods costly when they were available at all. Such transactions were generally furtive, while farmers had no choice but to sell their produce openly, under strict price control. Meanwhile taxes climbed out of sight. Rufinus's father more and more sought refuge in the cup. Finally, his health destroyed, he coughed himself to death one winter.

Rather than let children of hers be sold into slavery for back taxes, the widow conveyed the farm to Sicorus, owner of Maedraeacum, and the family became his coloni—serfs. They were bound to the soil, compelled to deference and obedience, required to do labor for their lord and, after working for themselves, pay more than half the crop over to him. Their grain they must have ground at his mill and at his price. There were no more forest days for Rufinus. Thirteen years old, he was now a field hand, his knees each evening ashake with weariness.

The following year his pretty older sister Ita became the concubine of Sicorus. She could not be forced, under the law. However, he could offer easements for her kin—such as not assigning her brothers to the most brutal tasks—and for her it was a way out of the kennel. Rufinus, who adored her, stormed to the manor house to protest. The slaves there drove him off with blows. He ran away. Sicorus coursed him down with hounds, brought him back, and had him flogged. The law permitted chastisement of contumacious coloni.

For another year, he bided his time. Whispers went along the hedges and in the woodlots; men slipped from their hovels to meet by twilight; news seeped across this narrow horizon. It came oftenest on the lips of wanderers who had made their lifework the preaching of sedition. The Empire had rotted to worthlessness, they said; Frankish laeti at Redonum sacrificed human beings to heathen Gods; raiders harried the coasts, while war bands afoot struck deep in from the East. Meanwhile the fat grew fatter, the powerful grew ever more overbearing. Had not Christ Himself denounced the rich? Was not the hour overpast to humble them and take back what they had wrung from the working poor? The Last Day drew nigh, Antichrist walked the world; your sacred duty was to resist him. Righteous men had sworn themselves to a brotherhood, the Bacaudae, the Valiant....

Ita's death in childbed was the last thing Rufinus endured. After that, he planned his next escape carefully, and found his way to the nearest Bacauda encampment.

—"We're no saints, oh, no, no," he hiccoughed. By then he was fairly drunk. "I learned that soon enough. Some amongst us are beasts of prey. The rest're rough. I give you that. But the most of us, the most of us, we only wanted to live in peace. We only wanted to till our plots of ground, and keep the fruits of our work, and have our honor under the law."

"How do you live?" Gratillonius asked. He had matched the Gaul stoup for stoup, but he was larger and not half starved.

"Oh, we hunt. What a pleasure that is, when we know we're poaching! We raise a little garden truck in the wilds. We rob when we can, from the rich, like that futtering smug trader today, but we swap the loot in honest wise for what we need. And merchants who pass through sections, regular-like, where we are, they pay toll. They're not s'posed to, but they do, undercover, and save 'emselves trouble. And our own people, serfs who've not fled and what few small freehold farmers are left, they help us out, for love."

"For love. Indeed." Gratillonius made his voice heavy with sarcasm. "I'm a farm boy myself. I know farmers. What you say sounds exactly like them."

"Well, we're fighting their war," Rufinus declared. "It's only right for them to pay their share. Food, clothes, that sort of thing. Besides, we protect 'em against bandits."

Gratillonius shrugged. He could well imagine what their protection consisted of. Cotters who declined it were apt to find their roofs ablaze or their throats slit.

Rufinus read his thought and said defensively, "It *can* be for love. How d'you think I got this outfit of mine?"

By charm, Gratillonius imagined. This young man had an abundance of that. Let him enter the drabness that was the life of some isolated, poverty-stricken wife—in and out of it, like bursts of sunshine when wind drove clouds across heaven, like an elf by moonlight— If every Bacauda were as glib, the band today would look a lot less scruffy.

Still, said Gratillonius's stubborn mind, Rufinus was in fact as neat and clean as possible in his kind of existence: which revealed something about him.

The centurion shifted the subject toward matters of more immediate interest. "Well, then, have you Bacaudae a secret kingdom that considers itself at war with Rome, the way the Persians usually are? That doesn't square with what I've heard. But tell me."

"M-mm, no, not really," Rufinus admitted. "We do have emperors— an emperor for each region—but he doesn't do much except lead his own group and be at the head of the gatherings, when several groups meet. We call the head of any other band its duke." His sardonic tone implied that the title didn't mean "leader" but was a deliberate parody of Roman organization. "I'm the duke of mine."

"A bit young for that, aren't you?"

"There are no old Bacaudae," Rufinus said quietly. Gratillonius remembered Alexander of Macedon. For that matter, he himself was twenty-five when he became King of Ys.

"We do make our deals," the Gaul went on in a rush, as the wine sent another tide through his head. "I've heard of bargains struck with Scotian or Saxon. Our folk'd guide 'em to a manor, they'd sack it but in return let the serfs be. And I got friendly with a Scotian—fled his homeland, he did, on account of a feud, and came to us—he told me 'bout Hivernia, where Rome never ruled, where they've always been free—"

Rufinus started, stiffened, once more shook himself. "I'd better not go on," he said. "I might let too much slip out. You're a good fellow, Gra—Gra—Gradlon. But I can't let you in on any secrets of the brothers, could I, now?" He picked up his cloak and lurched to his feet. "G'night. I wish we could be friends."

"I'll take you past the sentries," the soldier offered, rising too. He would have liked to continue the conversation, but it verged on questions that might suddenly make this two-legged wildcat lash out, and his duty was to get the bishop back unharmed.

They walked together into the windy dark, mute. As they parted, they clasped hand to arm.

III

~ 1 ~

About fifteen miles west of Augusta Treverorum there was an official hostel where Gratillonius decided to spend the night, even though sundown was still a couple of hours off. This was doubtless the last such place till he reached the city. Starting at dawn, with nothing to do except swallow breakfast and strike tents, the soldiers should reach their destination early enough next day that he would have no trouble getting them settled in and word of his arrival borne to the Emperor. Besides, he might find no suitable campground between here and there. The hills roundabout were largely given over to vineyards, with scant room between rows. Hazed and dreamy under the declining sun, this country seemed to lie in a different world from Armorica, as did most of what he had passed through. It was as if wars, brigands, and wild men had never been, save in nightmares.

As was common, the hostel maintained an open space for military parties. Having seen his established and supper cooking, Gratillonius sought the house. The dignity of his mission required that he avail himself of it, whether or not it was the kind of fleabag he had found too often along the way.

A man stood outside. He had come forth when the legionaries arrived and watched them set up. As Gratillonius neared, he lifted a hand and said, "Greeting, my son. Peace be with you." His Latin had an odd accent; he could not be a native Gaul, though it shortly turned out that he used Gallic idioms with ease.

Gratillonius halted. Dignity also required he return courtesy, no matter how poor and unkempt the person was who offered it. This one didn't cringe or whine, either. He stood straight, spoke levelly, and looked you square in the eye. "Greeting, uncle." —what soldiers usually called an elderly man who had a bit of respect due him but not too much.

The stranger smiled. "Ah, that takes me far back. I was in the army once. Let me compliment you on the smartness of your squadron. Sadly rare these days. Not many units of old-fashioned regulars left, are there?"

"Thank you," Gratillonius looked closer.

The other carried his years well. While slenderness had become gauntness, the shoulders were wide and unbowed, and if his gait was no longer lithe it remained firm. A snub nose marked a face pallid, lined, and gap-toothed, which you barely noticed after meeting its brilliant blue gaze.

Puzzlement rose in Gratillonius. Why should somebody like that, clearly well educated, go in a coarse dark robe, hardly fit for a slave, belted with a rope underneath a camel-hair cloak—when his footgear was stout though well worn, bespeaking many leagues of use. Had he fallen into poverty? Then he should at least have had the pride left to keep himself clean. Streams, ponds, and public baths weren't that scarce. He had in fact laved hands and feet, but Gratillonius could smell him. Pungent rather than sour, declaring that he spent much time in the open, the odor nevertheless demeaned him...did it not? He shaved, but probably seldom, for white stubble covered jaws and cheeks. Likewise it bristled over the front half of his pate. Behind, hair rose wildly; it would have waved in the breeze if he had washed it.

"Well, you'll want to inspect your quarters before we eat," he said. "Shall we go in?"

Gratillonius stared. "You're lodging here?"

The old man smiled. "I'd rather sleep under God's stars or the roofs of His poor, but—" he shrugged—"a bishop traveling a main highway isn't allowed that."

Gratillonius stood a moment in his neat Roman outfit, confronting the beggarly figure, and wondered whether he had heard aright. Arator had been bedraggled when the Bacaudae released him, but his clothes were of the best, and it didn't take him long after reaching Juliomagus to reappear bathed, barbered, and resplendent. "A bishop?"

"Unworthy though I be. Martinus of Caesarodunum Turonum, at your service. May I ask your name, my son?"

Gratillonius stammered it forth, together with his rank and his legion, scarcely hearing himself. His head was awhirl.

"You are a long way from your home base, eh? I think we shall have considerable to talk about. Come." Martinus took him by the elbow and led him inside.

While he changed clothes in his room, Gratillonius tried to put his thoughts in order. Only recently had he first heard of yonder person, but what he had heard was extraordinary.

Passing through the Liger valley, he had observed that the small pagan temples that elsewhere dotted the landscape were absent, or made into heaps of stone and charred timber. Occasionally he went by the stump of a tree that had been huge and ancient; occasionally he spied, afar, a hut raised by a spring or on a hilltop which must have been a sacred site, where now a single man dwelt. Curious, the centurion had inquired among people he met when he stopped for a night. He learned that the bishop of Turonum and a troop of monks had been going about for years, not only preaching their Christ to the rural population but destroying the halidoms of the old Gods and rededicating these to the new.

"A great and wonderful work!" cried devout young Budic. At last his faith was marching out of the cities.

"Hm," said Gratillonius. "The wonder is that the people stand for it."

Well, he reflected, this Martinus did have the Imperium at his back. Gratillonius himself was technically violating the law when he worshipped Mithras. Had the heathens killed the churchmen, they would have risked terrible punishment. Still, they might have resisted in other ways. Gratillonius well knew how stubborn and sly rustics could be.

It seemed as if Martinus overwhelmed them, simply by being what he was. Gratillonius was unsure how much belief to give stories of miracles wrought by the holy man. They said he healed the sick, the lame, and the blind by his touch and his prayers, that he had even recalled a dead boy to life. They said that once, demanding a hallowed oak be cut down, he had accepted a challenge to stand, bound, where it would fall; as it toppled, he lifted his hand and it spun about and crashed in the opposite direction, narrowly missing and instantly converting the clustered tribesfolk. Maybe so. Gratillonius had seen strange things wrought by his Gallicenae.

He thought, though, most of the force must lie in Martinus himself. The bishop was humble as well as strong. He dwelt outside the city, in a community of like-minded men whom his reputation had drawn to him. Mainly they devoted themselves to worship and meditation.

When they went forth evangelizing, Martinus never ranted or threatened. People told Gratillonius that he spoke to them in their own kind of words, quiet, friendly, sometimes humorous. They told of an incident: he and his followers had torched a Celtic temple, but when the flames were about to spread to the landowner's adjoining house, the bishop led the firefighting effort.

He had never desired his office. When it fell vacant, a trick brought him from his peaceful monastery elsewhere, and a crowd fell upon him and carried him off, willy-nilly, to be consecrated. That was the second time he had been conscripted. The first was long before, he a lad in Pannonia who only wanted to enter the Church, borne away at the instigation of his pagan father and enrolled in the army. Not until the twenty-five-year hitch was up could he give his oath to his God. Thereafter he had been clergyman, hermit, monk— Had that God chosen this means of training him for his mission?

Or was it only, or also, that the Gods of the land were failing, that in some secret way folk knew they had no more reason to honor Them? Gratillonius remembered what Forsquilis had said in Ys....

He re-entered the main room as the kitchen help were bringing out supper. Martinus's entourage sat at table. They amounted to four men, younger than their leader but tonsured and dressed like him. The bishop sat offside, on a three-legged milking stool he had evidently taken along, and ate from a bowl on his lap. The food he had ordered for them consisted of vegetables, herbs, and a few scraps of dried fish stewed together. Prayers preceded the repast. A reading from the Gospels, by a brother who fasted that evening, accompanied it. Gratillonius ate his robust fare in silence.

Afterward Martinus beckoned him over, proffered a bench, and said cordially, "Now, Centurion, do you care to tell us what you've been doing? You must have many curious adventures under your belt."

Gratillonius dug in his heels against liking the man, found himself dragged toward it anyhow, and settled down. "I am...on business of state, reporting to the Emperor," he said.

"I thought so. And we are bound home after business with him. Maybe we can help each other, you and I."

"Sir?"

"I can give you an idea of what to expect. There's been trouble at court, a most cruel strife. God willing, it nears its end, but you'll do best to avoid certain topics. For my part, I'd be very interested to learn more about how things are in Armorica...and Ys."

Martinus laughed at Gratillonius's startlement. "Obvious!" he continued. "In Treverorum I heard incidental mention that Maximus Augustus's prefect at the mysterious city was coming. Who else would you be, you who identified yourself as belonging to a Britannic legion? Take your ease, have a fresh cup of the excellent local wine, and yarn to us."

He and his companions did not join in, sipping merely water, but Gratillonius got from them a sense of cheer, the sort that men feel when they have completed a hard task. He used his own call for more drink to buy time for thought.

How much dared he relate? He had shaded his dispatches to the Emperor, omitting details of religious and magical practices. He had spent hours on the road rehearsing in his mind how he should reply to various possible questions. He would not give his commandant any falsehood. But if he provoked outrage and cancellation of his commission, what then?

"Well," he said, "you must be aware that we're getting matters under control in our part of the country. We'd like to help with that over a wider range." The tale of his brush with the Bacaudae and the deliverance of Bishop Arator, augmented by the exclamations and thanksgivings of the monks, took a usefully long while. He went on to remarks about the revival of trade that was beginning, and finished quickly:

"But it'll soon be dark, and I want to start off at daybreak. You mentioned things I might need to know. Will you tell me?"

Martinus frowned. "The full story would take longer than till bedtime, my son."

"I'm a simple roadpounder. Can't you explain enough in a few words?"

The ghost of a smile crossed Martinus's lips. "You ask for a miracle. But I'll try." He pondered before he started talking.

Nonetheless Gratillonius was bewildered. He could only gather that one Priscillianus, bishop of Avela in Hispania, was accused of heresy and worse. The centurion knew that "heresy" meant an incorrect Christian doctrine, though it was not clear to him who decided what was correct and how. In a vague fashion he was conscious of the division between Catholics, who held that God and Christ were somehow identical, and Arians, who held that They were somehow different. Mithraism was an easier faith, its paradoxes a part of the very Mystery and in any event nothing that directly concerned mortals.

This Priscillianus preached a canon of perfectionism which Martinus felt went too far; fallen man was incapable of it without divine grace. Yet Martinus also felt that this was no more than an excess of zeal. Certainly it spoke against those charges of fornication and sorcery that the enemies of Priscillianus brought. There might have been no large stir had not people by the hundreds and perhaps thousands, despairing of this world, flocked to the austere new creed. As was, Bishop Ambrosius of Mediolanum got the then co-Emperor Gratianus to issue a rescript banning its adherents. They scattered and concealed themselves.

Priscillianus himself and a few followers went to Rome to appeal to the Pope. Among them were women, including two friends of the consul Ausonius. This gave rise to nasty gossip.

The Church had adopted a rule that when internal disputes arose, the final appeal would be to the bishop of Rome. Pope Damasus refused to see Priscillianus. The accused proceeded to Mediolanum, where through an official who was an enemy of Ambrosius they got a rescript restoring them to their churches.

Then they took the offensive, getting charges of calumny levelled against their principal persecutor, Bishop Ithacius of Ossanuba. He fled to Treverorum and found an ally in the praetorian prefect. Intrigues seethed. Maximus revolted and overthrew Gratianus. Ambrosius travelled north to help negotiate the treaty that divided the West.

Ithacius brought his allegations against Priscillianus before the new Augustus. Maximus ordered a synod convened at Burdigala to settle the matter. Much ugliness ensued, rumors of immorality, a noblewoman stoned by a rabble. In the end, Priscillianus refused to accept the jurisdiction of the synod and appealed to the Emperor in Treverorum.

Prelates flocked to the scene, Martinus among them. While he did not say so, Gratillonius got the impression, which later conversations confirmed, that he alone did not fawn on Maximus. Rather, he argued stiffly for what he held to be justice. When the Augustus had him at table and ordered the communal wine cup brought first to him, Martinus did not pass it on to Maximus, but to the priest who was with him; and the Augustus accepted this as a righteous act.

Ithacius saw his religious accusation of heresy faltering, and against Priscillianus pressed the secular, criminal charges of sorcery and Manicheanism. Martinus took the lead in disputing these.

He won from Emperor Maximus a promise that there would be no death penalties. However much the Priscillianists might be in error, it was honest error and deserved no worse than exile to some place where they could meditate untroubled and find their way back to the truth. Gladdened, Martinus started home. The whole wretched business had caused him to neglect his own flock far too long.

—'Wretched' is the right word," Gratillonius muttered.

"What?" asked Martinus.

"Oh, nothing." Gratillonius's glance went to a window. Deep yellow, the light that came through it told him that it was time for his sunset prayer to the Lord Mithras. Besides, after what he had heard, he needed a few lungfuls of clean air. "Excuse me if I leave," he said, rising. "I've duties to see to before nightfall."

The monks took that at face value, but Martinus gave him a look that held him in place like a fishhook before murmuring, "Duties, my son, or devotions?"

Gratillonius felt his belly muscles tighten. "Is there a difference?"

"Enough," said Martinus. Was the motion of his hand a blessing? "Go in peace."

The squadron entered Augusta Treverorum by one of two paved ways passing through a gate in the city wall. The gate was a colossus of iron-bound sandstone blocks, more than a hundred feet wide and nearly as high, with twin towers flanking two levels of windows. Behind it, structures well-nigh as impressive showed above roofs closer to hand, basilica, Imperial palace, principal church; and approaching, the men had noticed an amphitheater just outside that was like a shoulder of the hill into which it was built.

Facades reared grandly over streets, porticos gleamed around market-places, where people in the multiple thousands walked, rode, drove, jostled, chattered, chaffered, exhorted, quarreled, postured, pleaded, vowed, were together, were alone. Feet clattered, hoofs thudded, wheels groaned, hammers rang. The noises were a veritable presence, an atmosphere, filled with odors of smoke, food, spice, dung, perfume, wool, humanity. Litters bore a senator in purple-bordered toga and a lady—or a courtesan?—in silk past a Treverian farmer in tunic and trousers, a housewife in coarse linen carrying a basket, an artisan with his tools and leather apron, a porter under his yoke, a guardsman on horseback, slaves in livery and slaves in rags, a pair of strolling entertainers whose fantastical garb was an extra defiance of the law that said they must remain in that station to which they were born—

Gratillonius had seen Londinium, but it could not compare with this. Abruptly Ys seemed tiny and very dear. He got directions and led his soldiers in formation, giving way to nobody. Before their armor the crowds surged aside in bow waves and eddies.

Space was available at the metropolitan barracks. Maximus kept a large household troop and a substantial standing army. Their cores were legionary regulars, drawn from border garrisons as well as from Brittania. However, more men, auxiliaries among them, had departed for the South with Valentinianus. Thus total Roman strength in Gallia was much reduced. Echoing rooms and empty parade grounds, in the midst of civilian wealth and bustle, roused forebodings in Gratillonius. The Mosella had only about a hundred miles to flow from here before it met the Rhenus, and east of that great river laired the barbarians. Many were already west of it.

He made arrangements for his men. Several whooped joyously when they recognized acquaintances from Britannia, and everybody was chafing to be off into town. "Keeping them taut won't be easy," Gratillonius warned Adminius. "Temptations right and left, starting with booze and broads, leading on toward brawls."

The deputy grinned. "Don't you worry, sir," he answered. "I'll let 'em 'ave their fun, but they'll know there's a 'and on the tether." He cocked his head. "If I'm not being overbold, maybe the centurion'd like 'is own bit o' fun? I'll soon find out where that's to be 'ad."

"Never mind," Gratillonius snapped. "Remember, I want you reporting to me regularly at my lodging."

He proceeded alone to the government inn where he would stay. Temptation—aye, he thought, it simmered in him too; and he realized he had been thinking in Ysan, while certain of his wives stood before him, unclad and reaching out, more vivid than the walls and traffic around.

The room he took was clean and well furnished, if a little time-faded. He unpacked and got busy. First he must notify the palace of his arrival. He had already prepared a note to that effect—writing never came easily to him—and now tied it together with a commendation that Bishop Arator had given him. The letter was embarrassingly fulsome, but explained his not coming sooner and, well, should do his career no harm. Escape from the curial trap—

After he was finished in Ys, if ever he was—

He didn't want to pursue that vision. Hastily, he sought the manager of the house, who dispatched a messenger boy for him.

As Gratillonius then stood wondering what to do, a uniformed centurion entered from the street, stopped, gaped, and shouted his name. "Drusus!" he roared back at the stocky form—Publius Flavius Drusus of the Sixth, whose unit had side by side with his fought its way out of a Pictic ambush. They fell into each other's arms, pounded each other's backs, and exchanged mighty oaths.

"I'm staying here too," Drusus explained, "waiting to deliver a report. Since we won his throne for the Augustus, my vexillation's been stationed at Bonna. Reinforcement for the Fifth Minervia. The war whittled that legion pretty badly, not so much through casualties as because most of it stuck with Valentinianus. The Germani got so uppity that at last we made a punitive expedition. I've been sent to tell how that went; pretty good. Come, we've daylight left, let's go out on the town."

"I'm supposed to report, like you," Gratillonius demurred. "I'd better be here when they call me."

Laughter rattled from Drusus. "Your heels will freeze if you just sit waiting, old buddy. I thought today I'd finally gotten my summons, but no, they told me there the Emperor was suddenly too busy again. You'll be lucky if you're called inside this month. And if the word happens to come when you're out, no sweat. Everything's scheduled hours and hours in advance, because whenever some backlog of state business can get handled, there's so much of it. Enjoy while you've got the chance. I'll go change clothes and be right with you."

Gratillonius sat worrying till his friend returned, and asked as they went forth: "What's happened? Maximus didn't allow this kind of shilly-shallying in Britannia."

"Not entirely his fault," Drusus replied. "You remember how he always oversaw as much as possible personally. Well, he's the same now that he wears the purple. And it worked for a while. Name of

Christ, how we sliced through Gratianus's ranks! But being Emperor is different, I guess. He keeps getting interrupted by new problems."

"Why does he want a direct account of a border clash?" Gratillonius wondered.

"M-mm, don't quote me. I could get in trouble."

"I wouldn't do that to you, Drusus. D'you imagine I've forgotten that day in the rain? All the puddles were red."

Hand squeezed shoulder. "I remember too. Well, nobody's told me anything officially, understand, but when a smell comes downwind I can usually tell whether it's from a rose or a fart. After Gratianus died—and he was murdered, make no doubt of that, murdered when he'd been promised safety at a feast with an oath on the Gospels—" Drusus glanced about. They were anonymous in a throng of people intent on their own lives. "Maximus put the blame on his cavalry commander, but never punished the man.... Anyway. While negotiations were going on afterward, Maximus got the Juthungi to invade Raetia. He had connections to them. Pressure on Theodosius to make a settlement. Valentinianus is only a kid, under the thumb of his mother. But her Frankish general in his turn got the Huns and Alani to harry the Alemanni so close to the Rhenus that Maximus had to move troops to that frontier.

"Which is why I'm still posted yonder, and the Augustus is anxious about whatever the barbarians may be up to, and why. They've gotten a taste of playing us Romans off against each other."

Gratillonius raised a dam against the words that rose in his throat. What was this fellow saying about their Duke, the man who rolled midnight back from the Wall?

Gratillonius told himself that a commander could not always control what his subordinates did, and statecraft unavoidably had its dirty side, and Drusus was a solid sort who might be misled but who should be heard out before any arguments began. "Well, however that is," he said, "why aren't things better organized here? It doesn't sound a bit like Maximus. Can't he get competent officers any longer?"

"It's the Priscillianus mess," Drusus answered. "Before then, we had a pretty smooth mill running. But since that rift spread this far—"

He paused before he sighed and added, "I don't understand any miserable part of it. This town's full of jabber about the First Cause, the Sons of God and the Sons of Darkness, Spiritual Man, mystical numbers, and I don't know what else, except I was there when a man got knifed in a tavern ruckus that started over whether or not the age of prophecy is over. I think Priscillianus has to be wrong when he says men and women should stay apart, never get together. If that is what he says. I don't know. But why all these fights about it? I wonder if Christ in Heaven isn't weeping at what they're doing in His name. Sometimes I almost envy infidels like you."

They had wandered down toward the river. Through an open portal they saw the bridge across it, and vineyards and villas beyond. A fresh dampness blew off it. Leaves blazed with autumn. Gratillonius remembered Bodilis reading to him a poem Ausonius had written in praise of this stream; the author had sent her a copy. *Like a girl-child playing with her hair before a mirror, fisher lads sport with shadowy shapes underwater.* Suddenly laughter welled up in him and he pitched away the cares of the world. They'd climb back onto him soon enough. "Not our department," he said. "How about we find us a place where we can have a drink and swap brags?"

~ 3 ~

Four days later he was in the presence of Maximus Augustus, but as a prisoner.

News had exploded through the city. The Emperor, who had promised clemency for the Priscillianists, was rehearing the entire case. Bishop Ithacius withdrew as prosecutor. It was said that he feared the wrath of such powerful colleagues as Martinus and Ambrosius.

Earlier, the bishop of Mediolanum had come back this far north, ostensibly to see the bones of Gratianus returned to Italy for burial, actually to attend the first trial. Maximus refused him a private audience but received him in consistory, where he in his turn declined the Emperor's proffered kiss of peace and accused the latter of being a lawless usurper. Maximus responded in the course of proceedings with a denial that Valentinianus was his equal; if nothing else, the boy-Emperor and his mother were known to have strong Arian leanings.

Though Ambrosius had since gone home, the qualms of Ithacius were natural. In his place, Maximus appointed Patricius, an advocate for the treasury. Did the Augustus want the property of the heretics?

Gratillonius found a military tribune who was a reliable conduit of information, rather than rumors. What he learned about the goings-on within the Church perturbed him less than what he learned about Maximus. How long must he hang around this cursed city? Most of his time he spent sightseeing, or talking with chance-met men. They were a varied lot, many of them trading up and down the rivers or overland. There grew before him a vision, clearer than ever, of the Empire, how vast it was and how troubled.

The detachment came for him toward evening, when he had lately returned to the hostel after a day's ride in the hinterland. A vintner had hailed him and invited him home for a cup and a gab; there the pretty daughter of the house smiled upon him. Now he sat in the common room prior to supper, more content than he had been, thinking back over the small experience. The door opened. Four soldiers in combat gear tramped through, and at their head a centurion.

"We seek Gaius Valerius Gratillonius, of the Second Legion Augusta," that man announced.

"Here he is." Gratillonius's heart leaped up as fast as his body.

"In the name of the Augustus, come."

"At once. I'll just outfit myself—"

"No. Immediately."

Gratillonius stared into faces gone hard. A prickling went over his scalp. "Is something wrong?" he asked.

The centurion clapped hand to sword. "Silence! Come!"

Household staff gaped, shrank aside, and saw their guest depart surrounded by armed men. Folk outside likewise fell silent as the group strode down the streets to the basilica.

Guarded gates led to a cloistered courtyard where dusk was rising; for the sun had gone below the outer walls. Light still glowed on the upper courses of brick and red sandstone that made up the great building within, and flared off glass in its windows. Numb, Gratillonius accompanied his escort into this citadel of his hopes, past several checkpoints and thus at last to the audience hall where the Emperor was.

The soldiers clanked to a halt and saluted. Gratillonius did too. That was his old commandant there on the throne, the same Hispanic hatchet features and lean body though purple be wrapped around and a golden wreath set above. He hardly noticed the splendor of the room or the several councillors who sat or stood beneath their master.

The officer waited for the Imperial nod before reporting that he brought the person required. "Ah, Gratillonius," Maximus said low. "Step forward. Let us look at you."

The King of Ys posed for what seemed a long while, until he heard: "Know that we have been told such evil of you that we have ordered your arrest. What have you to say for yourself?"

Despite foreknowing he was somehow in danger, Gratillonius felt as if clubbed. "Sir?" Breath sobbed into him. He braced his knees, gave Maximus eye for eye, and declared, "My lord, I have served you and Rome to the best of my ability. Who's spoken ill of me?"

Maximus straightened and clipped, "Your own men, Centurion, your own men. Do you call them liars? Do you deny having trafficked with Satan?"

"What? Sir—my lord—I don't understand. My men—"

"Silence." Maximus nodded at a pinch-lipped person in a drab tunic. "Calvinus, read the report."

That one took up a set of papers and began what soon became a singsong, like a chant to his God. It developed that he was high in the Imperial secret service. His agents were everywhere, in every walk of life, with instructions to keep alert for anything the least suspicious and follow it up until they had sufficient clues to warrant full investigation. As if across a sea, Gratillonius heard how his legionaries, innocently talking in barracks and around town, had spoken of him. There was

299

no need to interrogate any of them; all were ready to boast about their leader and about the wonders of Ys.

Gratillonius heard how he, in a pagan ceremony where the images of devils were brought forth, had wedded nine women who were avowed witches. He heard how he had accepted and openly borne the emblems of a sea demon and a demon of the air. He had sent forth a spirit in the form of a bird to spy upon his enemies. He had ordered magic to raise a storm. He had betrodden an island that was from time immemorial the site of the blackest sorcery—

Courtiers shivered and made signs against malevolence. Lips moved in whispered prayer. The squad that had taken Gratillonius kept martial stiffness, but sweat came forth; he saw it, he smelled it.

At the end, Maximus leaned forward. "You have heard the charges," he said. "You must realize their gravity, and the necessity we are under of finding the truth. Sorcery is a capital offense. The powers of darkness have reached into the very Church; and you are a defiant unbeliever, who bears upon himself the mark of it."

What mark? He had left the Key of the gate behind in Ys, as being too vital to risk anywhere else. He'd grown a beard there, but it was close-cropped like a Roman's. He did wear his hair in Ysan male style, long, caught at the nape to fall down in a tail....He clawed out of his bewilderment and thought Maximus must refer to the brand of Mithraic initiation on his brow, though it had faded close to invisibility and—and Mithraists were loyal Romans.

"You may speak," the Emperor said.

Gratillonius squared his shoulders. "Sir, I've practiced no wizardry. Why, I wouldn't know how. The Duke—the Augustus always knew what my religion is, and it doesn't deal in magic. They believe differently in Ys, true. Well, given my job, how could I keep from showing respect to their Gods? I did—I did ask help from whatever powers they might have, but that was against barbarians who menaced Rome. As for that time on Sena, the island Sena, I wasn't supposed to set foot on it, but my wife—a wife of mine was dying there—" His throat locked on him. His eyes blurred and stung.

"You may be honest." Maximus's tone was steady; and did it hold a slight note of regret? "We had cause for confidence in you, and therefore entrusted you with your mission. But if nothing else, you may have been seduced by the Evil One. We must find out. God be praised, now that the Priscillianus matter nears an end, we have had a chance to hear this news of you. And we have given it prompt consideration as much for your sake—Gratillonius, who did serve valiantly on the Wall—as for Rome's. We will pray that you be purged of sin, led to the Light, saved from perdition." Abruptly the old military voice rang forth. "If you remain a soldier, obey your orders!"

He issued instructions. The squad led Gratillonius away.

In the early morning he was brought from the cell where he had spent a sleepless night. On the way down the gloom of a corridor, he met a procession under heavy guard. At its front walked a gray-haired man, skeletal, eyes fixed luminous upon another world. Four men came after, and a middle-aged woman and a younger who held hands. All were in coarse and dirty garb. They moved stumblingly, because they had not only been half starved but severely tortured. They stank. Lanterns burned smoky in the dank air around them. Hoarsely, they tried to sing a hymn.

"The heresiarch and those followers of his who've been condemned," said one of Gratillonius's guards to him. "They're off to the chopping block. Have a care, fellow, or you'll be next."

—Light was dim also in the interrogation chamber. Gratillonius could just identify scenes of the Christian hell painted on its plaster. How neatly the instruments and tools sat arranged. This could have been an artisan's workshop. Nothing felt quite real, except the chill. Two men waited, the first skinny and wearing a robe, the second muscular and in a brief tunic, ready for action. They studied the prisoner impersonally. He heard through a buzzing in his head:

"—by command of the Augustus. Cooperate, and this may be the only session we'll need. Otherwise we will be forced to take strict measures. Do you understand? We're coping with none less than Satan—"

Surprised at his meekness (but resistance would have been of no avail, when he was so alone), Gratillonius undressed. His nudity made him feel twice helpless. The torturer secured him in a frame so that he stood spread-eagled and took a lead ball off a shelf. It dangled at the end of a thong. Meanwhile the questioner continued talking, in an amicable voice. "—your duty to help lay bare the work of Satan. We do not wish to harm you. Simply as a warning—"

Snapped by an expert hand, the ball smote Gratillonius's elbow. Agony went jagged up that arm. He strangled a scream. He *would* not scream.

"—now tell me, in your own words—"

Whenever he resisted or equivocated, not that he meant to play games but often he wasn't sure how to respond, the blow landed, on joints, belly, the small of the back, until he was a single slab of pain; and worst was that the next attack might come from between his sprangled thighs. Weirdest was that, from time to time, the proceedings would stop, they would bring him water, the torturer would sponge the sweat off him while the questioner chatted about everyday things.

Mithras, Who hates a liar, give me to cling to the truth! "—I did n-n-no such deed, ever. Others may have, I don't know about that, I'm just a soldier, but it was for Rome, everything I did was for Rome."

"He might want a taste of the hook," said the torturer thoughtfully.

The questioner considered. "Once."

When the barbs went into his thigh and out again, Gratillonius knew what it was like to be raped.

"But I cannot tell you more!"

"You've said a good deal already, boy."

"All I could. All." And never screamed, Gratillonius thought blurrily. Never screamed. That much pride is left me. But I don't know if I can keep it after my arms and legs crack out of their sockets on yonder rack, or when he starts hitting me in my manhood.

"Well," said the questioner with a smile, "that will do for today. Please remember how much the state needs your cooperation, you, a soldier; and think what it means to your salvation." The torturer fetched salves and bandages and set about dressing open wounds. "You haven't suffered any permanent damage, you realize. I pray God you don't, dear soul." The questioner stroked the prisoner's wet hair. "But that depends on you."

He called the guards to bring Gratillonius back to his cell.

~ 5 ~

After two days and nights, wherein nothing happened except diminishing soreness and horrible expectations, suddenly he was brought forth. The person in charge was unctuous though uncommunicative. Gratillonius would see the Emperor! First he must needs be bathed, groomed, properly attired....

This time Maximus sat in a room small and plainly furnished, himself simply clad, behind a table littered with papers and wax writing tablets. Apart from two soldiers at the door and the two that led Gratillonius in, he was unattended. Gratillonius gave him a salute, noticing with faint annoyance how awkward it was in his condition. "Sit down," the Emperor directed. Gratillonius lowered his weariness onto a stool.

Maximus observed him closely before saying, "Well, Centurion, how are you today?"

Something grinned within Gratillonius. Aloud he answered, "All right, thank you, sir."

"Good." Maximus ruffled the beard over his craggy chin, stared into space, and proceeded: "You came through interrogation rather well. We've no reason to doubt you were innocent of any criminal intent. Your rescue of Bishop Arator argues in your favor, too. Not being of the Faith, you failed to see the wiles of Satan before you. Meditate on that! But your intentions were patriotic. I expected they'd prove to be. You understand we had to make certain."

Gratillonius spared himself a reply. It would have been too much effort, for no clear purpose.

"Now." Maximus's gaze swung back to stab at him. "Let us hear what you have to relate about Ys."

Surprised, Gratillonius stammered, "The Augustus...has my dispatches—"

302

"If those sufficed, I needn't have brought you here." Maximus barked a laugh. "Since time is lacking, and you're in no shape to take the initiative, I must. Listen well and answer clearly."

His questions were shrewd. At the end, he nodded and said, slow-toned: "Aside from your mistakes—and we pray you've learned your lesson—aside from those, you've done a creditable job. We're minded to keep you at your post. But." He raised a finger. "But we set restrictions on you. You will not further abet the practice of sorcery in Ys. Do you hear? You will not. Instead, you, as the prefect of Rome, will do everything in your power to suppress what is diabolical."

A smile quirked his lips. "I know that won't be easy. You're set among pagans, and they seem to be especially obstinate. I'm not sure any Christian could handle them at all, and certainly I've no Christian officer available with anything like your capabilities. He sighed. "I must use whatever God sees fit to send me."

He grew stern: "We shall not let witches live. Once the last of this Priscillianist obscenity is behind us—we'll be sending agents to Hispania to root it out, down to bedrock—once that's done and the West is secure, look for us to enter Ys and inquire into your stewardship. Therefore be zealous. To drive the lesson home, you'll be led from here to receive five strong lashes, one for each wound that Our Lord suffered upon the Cross. No more, and with an unweighted whip. We are disposed to be merciful."

Gratillonius mustered strength to say, "I thank the Augustus."

"Good," replied Maximus. "Thereafter you may return to your quarters and recuperate. Use the time well. Think about your errors, seek counsel, pray for the grace of the Holy Spirit. Then, whenever you are fit to travel, you may do so."

Dull though Gratillonius's mind was, a flickering went through it. He dared not wonder if he was being wise before he said, "Augustus,"—how weakly his voice resounded in his skull—"you tell me to get advice...from learned men. Well, may I search for it elsewhere than here?"

"What? Where else?" Maximus scowled. "No, do not linger in Caesarodunum Turonum. They're devout there, but you might become confused about certain things."

"I meant farther south, sir. To Lugdunum, Burdigala, places where ...many sages live."

"Are you quite right in your head? You're no student, to sit at the feet of philosophers."

"The Augustus knows...we need a new Christian minister in Ys. That calls for searching. Not just anyone will do."

Maximus fell into thought. "His appointment is not yours to make," he said at length, "but the Church will take your recommendation into account, I suppose. You may prove mistaken. Still, the idea is to your credit." Again he paused. "And as for your personal request—well, why

303

not? It should do your soul good to see more of the Empire, of Christendom, than this Northern fringe. And clergymen who were not involved in the affair here, they may appeal better to your heart." Decision came. "You may travel freely, provided you stay within Gallia, conduct yourself properly, and take no longer than, oh, six months until you return to duty. My secretary will prepare a written authorization."

Wistfulness brushed him. "After all," he said, "we were soldiers together, you and I, soldiers on the Wall. Go with God."

"Thank you, sir," Gratillonius made himself utter.

Maximus's glance went back to the documents before him. "Dismissed."

Gratillonius's guards led him off to the whipping post.

~ 6 ~

Four-and-twenty legionaries, fully encountered, marched out of the rain into the common room of the hostel. They shooed the help away and came to attention, ranked, before the couch where Gratillonius lay on his side to spare his back. Lamplight made their metal gleam against the shadows that had stolen in with eventide. As one, they saluted. "Hail, Centurion!" rolled forth.

He sat up. The blanket fell off him. "What's this?" he demanded.

"By your leave, sir," Adminius replied, "we're 'ere for yer judgment."

"What do you mean?"

The deputy must wrench the words out: "We 'eard wot 'appened, and 'ow it was our stupid fault. Word's got around, you see. Sir, w-w-we wants ter make it good, if we can. Only tell us wot ter do."

Budic's lip quivered. Uncontrollable tears ran down his cheeks. "That *I* should have betrayed my centurion!" he nearly screamed.

"Quiet, you," Adminius snapped. "Bear yerself like a soldier. Sir, we await yer orders. If you can't tell nobody ter flog us, we'll do it ter each other. Or anything you want."

"We haven't yet found out who hurt you," said Cynan starkly, "but when we do, they're dead men."

Shocked, Gratillonius got to his feet. "Are you a Roman?" he exclaimed. "I'll have none of that. They did their duty, under orders, as Rome expects you will. If anything rates punishment, that notion of yours does. Kill it."

A part of him noticed that he hadn't gone dizzy this time, rising. Anger was a strong tonic. But he was recovering pretty fast, too. That knowledge went through him in a warm wave. He looked upon his men in their misery, and suddenly had to blink back tears of his own.

"Boys," he said with much carefulness, "you're not to blame. I never instructed you to keep silence, because I never expected trouble myself. Who would have? And let me say, this show of loyalty damn near

304

makes me glad of what happened. It hasn't done me any real damage anyway, aside maybe from a few extra scars. Give me three or four days more, and I'll be ready for the road."

"To Ys, sir?" Adminius blurted.

Gratillonius shook his head. "Not at once."

"Well, wherever the centurion goes, all 'e'll need is ter whistle us up. Eh, lads?"

The squadron rumbled agreement.

"I'm not likely to require much of a troop in the South, where I'm bound," Gratillonius said, "and as for Ys— Shut in here, I've had time to think. Some of you are likely homesick, after all your while in foreign parts. I can probably dispense with a Roman cadre, the way things are now set up in Armorica. Before leaving Treverorum, I can try to arrange reassignments for you, to your proper units in Britannia."

"Wot, sir? No!"—"Not me."—"Please, I want to stay."—"We're your men, sir."

"You're Rome's men," Gratillonius reminded them sharply. Behind his mask of an officer, he wondered. Barbarian warriors gave allegiance not to any state but to their chieftains. Was the Empire breeding its own barbarians? He thrust the chilling question aside. He could not penalize love.

Also, he could not be entirely sure that there would be no further use in Ys for these roadpounders of his.

"Well, think it over, and quickly," he said. "I told you, I'm starting off soon, and whoever comes with me will be gone a long time." He drew breath. "Thank you for your faithfulness. Dismissed."

"'Bout face!" Adminius barked. "Off ter barracks. I'll follow shortly. Want a private word with the centurion first."

When the rest had tramped out the door, Gratillonius reseated himself and looked up at the thin face. He saw brashness abashed. "Well, deputy, what do you want?" he asked.

"Um, sir, I don't mean ter get above myself, but—could I speak freely, like? Man ter man."

Warmth rose afresh in Gratillonius. He smiled. "Go right ahead. If you overstep, I'll simply tell you."

"Well, um—" Adminius wrung his hands and stared downward. "Well, sir," he said in a rush, "the centurion *is* a man, very much a man, but 'e's been through a 'ard time, after driving 'imself so 'ard, and now means ter begin again, sooner than wot a medic might call wise. It's not for me ter tell yer 'ow to be'ave. But we in the troop do worry about yer. You're getting your strength back, seems. But where's any pleasure? A man can't go on forever with no fun, no little rewards ter 'imself. Not unless 'e's a flinking saint, 'e can't. Could I, or anybody, 'elp the centurion to a bit of re-cre-ation? I'd be that glad, I would."

305

"You're kind," Gratillonius said, "but the food and drink are tolerable in this place, and—I am a marked man, who'd better watch his step. Enough."

"No, not enough! Listen, sir. I know it wouldn't do ter bring a woman in 'ere, or anything like that. But if you go out, would a spy follow? I don't think so."

Gratillonius chuckled. "I haven't made your acquaintance with the sort of house you have in mind."

"No, sir, you're a very serious-minded man. But listen, if you would like a bit of sport, let me recommend the Lion's Den inn at the end of Janus Way. Can't miss it. It's safe, draws a nice class of customer, and the drinks and the games are honest, the girls are clean, and right now they've got the damnedest band of musicians you ever 'eard. That's if you want, of course. I've said my piece. If the centurion 'as nothing else for me, goodnight, sir, and do be good to yerself." Adminius saluted and bolted.

Gratillonius laughed. He hadn't done that since his arrest. It was a grand feeling. What a dear bunch of mother hens he led!

At that, he thought, the deputy had a point. Before setting off on what was, after all, business of the most serious, he'd be well advised to refresh his spirit, get out of this dull dwelling, to where winds could blow the lingering horrors from his head. A vintner who'd been hospitable, and his pretty daughter—

The girl was doubtless chaste—

Gratillonius felt the stirring in his loins. And that had not happened either, following his imprisonment, until now. Fear about it had begun to nag him....

By Hercules, but he'd been long deprived! And he'd spend additional months before coming back to his wives. Into his wives. The visions flamed up. Oh, he'd been told that some or other spell made it impossible for a King of Ys to possess any but the Gallicenae. That was in Ys, though, hundreds of leagues away at the far, lonely end of Armorica, Ys Whose gods he had in his heart forsworn and Who were fading away into myth. What power had They left Them? As he recalled the comfort that lay in a woman's arms and breasts, the forgetfulness of self that lay between her legs, his rod lifted fully. When he regained his feet, it stayed firm.

He cast hesitation aside, fetched his cloak, and went forth into a fine rain that he thought really should steam off his flesh.

—She was a big young blond whose guttural accent somehow excited him the more. He didn't quite make out her name, but she told him she was from east of the border. Hard pressed these days, many half-civilized Germani drifted across the Rhenus in search of employment, and often women trailed along. Roman authorities usually looked the other way, what with a labor shortage acute and worsening. While she talked and her right hand raised the cup of mead he had bought her, her left began to explore his person.

He paid the fee for two turns and they went upstairs. None of his Queens would ever know if he could help it, but if perchance they found out, surely most would understand that a man has needs.

A couple of tallow candles burned in the cubicle where her bed was. Their rankness was exciting too, like animals in rut. His member throbbed. She pulled off her gown and stood smiling at him. Her bosom was heavy above a rounded white belly and a patch that the wan light shaded but that gave off brass glints. He scrambled out of his clothes.

Then he felt the coldness and the shriveling. His knees shook, his pulse rattled.

They lay down and she tried this and that. Nothing availed. Finally she said, "Vell, too bad, but I got to go vork, you know?" He sighed and nodded. There was no mention of a refund.

—He groped his way through night, back toward the hostel. It had been foolish not to carry a lantern. The rain fell heavier than before, with a wind to dash it into his eyes and hoot between walls. Chill sneaked under his cloak.

So, he thought. I am once for all the King of Ys. Anywhere I may be, as long as we both shall live.

Despite himself, he smiled a bit. Then maybe they're not mistaken about other things in Ys, he thought. Maybe the soul of Dahilis is still somewhere thereabouts, waiting for me.

He could almost believe that something of hers had watched over him. He was in search of the highest consecration to Mithras. His hypocrisy before Maximus still tasted nasty in his mouth, necessary though it had seemed. At least now he was, like it or not, free of any further impurity.

IV

~ 1 ~

Even without the need to make fortifications each afternoon and demolish them the next morning, the march to Lugdunum took half a month. It might have gone faster, but Gratillonius wanted to assure himself of complete recovery. He had seen what could happen when men overtaxed their healing bodies. Also, he had been unable to obtain sufficient rations for his squadron in Treverorum, but must needs get them piecemeal at way stations. Several were out of commission, which meant delay while soldiers searched and dickered. Maximus's war had caused some of the damage. More was due to incursions of Franks and Alemanni. The Romans had succeeded in driving those barbarians out ten years ago, then lacked funds and labor for complete restoration.

The countryside was beautiful, but autumn travelled south with the troop, bearing downpours and shivery winds. Journey's end and roofs overhead felt good indeed. Gratillonius gave his soldiers and himself a few days to rest, see the great city, and take what pleasures were available. He knew they would be close-mouthed, and in any event he had not confided his real purpose to them, except for Adminius. The deputy's Christianity was nominal, and his boyhood in the Londinium slums had taught him how to learn much while revealing nothing.

Gratillonius felt it best to keep his own inquiries abut Mithras worship incidental to those about possible clergy for Ys. The latter questions were the merest token. He knew full well that such an appointment could only be made in the North. However, if secret agents demanded a report on him, this should satisfy them.

Whatever guilt he felt had left him as he sat hour by hour in the saddle or lay alone in his tent at night. It was Maximus who was the betrayer. He had not strengthened the Empire, he had split it asunder as Roman slew Roman. He had not given it peace and prosperity, he had raised persecution and fear. He had broken pledge after pledge, to Gratianus, to Martinus, to poor old Priscillianus, to the Senate and the People of Rome; how long would he keep his to Valentinianus? He proposed to violate the ancient compact with Ys. Gratillonius disliked practicing deception, but such knowledge about his commandant had eaten away his resistance to it.

Seeking a better mood, he wandered around Lugdunum and found marvels, stately public buildings, baths, theater, and, outside its walls, sculptured tombs, magnificent aqueducts, an artificial lake for mimic sea battles. While many warehouses stood hollow, commerce still flowed along rivers and roads. Though poverty lurked in tenements and alleys, joviality flourished in taverns, foodstalls, bawdyhouses, odeions, the homes of the well-to-do. Few folk seemed to worry about much besides their private lives, unless they be devout Christians intent on the afterworld.

No Mithraeum survived here, but presently Adminius heard that one was left in Vienna, some twenty miles south. Gratillonius's spirits lifted. He ordered departure the following day. None of the twenty-four asked why, or what else he had in mind.

A considerably lesser city on the left bank of the Rhodanus, Vienna nevertheless possessed its splendors, including a large circus and a temple that Claudius Caesar had erected four hundred years ago. More to the point, military accommodations and civilian amenities were adequate. The troop might be staying for some time.

308

Adminius had ferreted out the name and location of Lucas Orgetuorig Syrus, a wine merchant. Walking thither the day after his arrival, Gratillonius found a house with a moderately prosperous shop. Syrus proved to be an old man whose features, despite generations of intermingling, bore traces of his family's Asiatic origin. When Gratillonius gave him the initiate's grip, his dim eyes widened, then filled with tears, and he came near collapse. Rallying, he took the newcomer to a private room, where Gratillonius made the signs of reverence before speaking those secret words that identified his rank in the Mysteries as Persian.

"Be welcome, oh, very welcome, my son," Syrus quavered. "It's been so long since any of the faithful appeared who were young and strong. Are there more like you?"

Gratillonius nodded. "Three, Father, men of my company. Two have the rank of Occult. The third joined us a couple of years ago. He's only a Raven, of course."

"He has not been advanced? Why not? Advancement should be swift, when we are so few, so few—" The voice trailed off.

"How can it be, Father, with none superior to me where we've been? That's why I've sought you, that, and the hope of your blessing."

"The blessing you have, my son, but...but let us be seated. I'll call for refreshment and we'll talk. Or am I being selfish? Should I first send for Cotta? He's our Runner of the Sun, he deserves to hear. Oh, I must share these glad tidings with him."

"Later, Father, I beg." Gratillonius assisted the frail form to a bench. "Did you wish drink? Permit me to call a servant."

Conversation went haltingly. Syrus had not lost his wits, but they were apt to wander, and twice he dozed off for a few minutes as he sat. Gratillonius learned this congregation existed on sufferance, provided it stay discreet and refrain from any hint of proselytization. It might have been banned altogether, as the Imperial decree required; but Syrus's family had money and his son carried weight in civic affairs. Although himself a Christian, the younger man did not care to see his father's heart broken. Death would close down the Mysteries soon enough.

Gratillonius explained his desire as best he could. "I know it's a great deal to ask, such a promotion, especially when I can't stay here long. It may be impossible. If so, I ask forgiveness for presuming. But if it can be done—if I can be raised to your rank, Father—why, Ys will have a temple of the God, and full celebration of His rites, proper instruction for the young, elevation of worshippers. The faith will live!"

"A wonderful vision, my son," Syrus whispered. "Foredoomed, I fear, but wonderful. Mithras, sentry at the frontier of the dark—" His head drooped, snapped back up; he gulped air. "I must think, study, pray. It is irregular. But, but I wish—how I wish— Can you come to services tomorrow sundown? Bring your fellow believers. It will be a common rite, they too may take part, and welcome, welcome—"

Gratillonius gave him an arm and upbore half his weight when he shuffled off to bed.

—Mithraeums had never been large. The one in Vienna consisted of a single room in Syrus's house. Its windows had been boarded up and plastered over to simulate a cave. Benches along the walls left just a strip of aisle between. A cord at the entrance end marked off the vestibule. Neither font nor image of lion-headed Time stood there, only a basin for holy water. At the sacrificial end, the Bullslaying and the Torchbearers were merely painted above a table that did duty for an altar. Nothing was squalid; wax candles gave light, incense sweetened the air. But of the handful of regular attenders, every head was gray or white.

Yet after the feverish chatter beforehand had stopped and men entered this sanctuary, solemnity brooded over it. The lesser members took stance behind the cord and made reverence as the higher—two Lions, two Persians (Gratillonius the second), the Runner of the Sun, and the Father, all in minimal vestments—passed by. The offering was simply wine raised before the Tauroctony. The re-enactment by the two seniors—of Mithras overcoming the Sun, then crowning Him to be forever after the Unconquered—was bare-bones simple. The liturgy was brief. Subsequently those forward reclined on the benches while Ravens, Occults, and Soldiers brought the sacred meal and served them. That food, at least, was of the best, within the limits of prescribed austerity. Gratillonius savored it, as being like a sign unto him of the soul's ascent Heavenward...when he had tasted nothing holy but prayers for nigh on three years.

Thoughts tumbled through him. Why was he doing this, why was he feeling this? He knew he was not a deeply religious person—no spiritual kin to, say, Martinus of Turonum. Well, but what else had he to cleave to? The Gods of Achilles, Aeneas, Vercingetorix were dead: phantoms at most, haunting glens and graveyards and the dusty pages of books. The Gods of Ys were inhuman. Christ was a pallid stranger. Rome the Mother was a widow, her husband the Republic and their tall sons long since dead in battle, herself the booty of every bandit who came by. Mithras alone stood fast, Mithras all alone.

~ 2 ~

When they consecrated Gratillonius a Father, he felt weariness drop off him like a cloak of lead unclasped, and himself momentarily victorious.

There had been too much he must learn, in too brief a span. He had no gift for acquiring doctrine, words, gestures, arcana; he must hammer them into his head, toiling till dawn grizzled his window and he fell into a few hours of sleep wherein his dreams gibbered. Meanwhile he must ever strive to keep chaste and pious. That was not hard for the body, requiring little more than exercise, cleanliness, and temperance. But his mind was a maniple of barbarian recruits, raw, rebellious, slouching off every which way the instant that the drillmaster's glance strayed off them. He should have had years for his undertaking and done it openly, while the rest of his life went on in everyday wise. Instead, he rammed his way through the teachings, hoped for godliness, and took precautions against the authorities.

Probably no one would ever denounce him. He had entered Vienna quietly, stayed inconspicuous, responded to questions with evasive phrases about a confidential assignment. His men knew nothing and were content to enjoy themselves—aside from Maclavius, Verica, and Cynan, his fellow Mithraists, and Adminius. Those would not give him away. Syrus's congregation had learned silence. However, somebody else might notice how often Gratillonius visited that particular house.

No matter! he told himself. By the time such gossip reached Treverorum, if it did, he'd be back in Ys. Maximus would look upon his establishment of a Mithraeum there as an act of rebellion, which it was, but could scarcely do anything about it for another two or three years, during which anything might happen. Live each day as it comes, like a soldier in the field.

They raised him to Runner of the Sun and he concelebrated the Mystery with Syrus. In his exhaustion, he felt only that he had passed a mark on an endless uphill road.

But when Syrus and Cotta together had finished the rite that made him Father, and for the first time he—with his own hands, farmer's, soldier's, woodworker's hands—lifted the chalice before the Tauroctony, and drank the blessed wine—then abruptly, blindingly, the sacredness of it came upon him. Did the Sun lift out of the night in his spirit, to blaze in terrible majesty from his heart? He knew not. As he spoke the words, he wept.

Everyone embraced him. "The grace of Mithras be with you always, beloved brother," Syrus wished.

That was impossible, of course. After he left the sanctum, he was merely Gratillonius. What had happened within, he could barely remember.

Maybe You will reveal Yourself to me again, God of my fathers, he thought. Or maybe not. I am unworthy of this much. But I will serve You as steadfastly as lies in the power of mortal flesh and grimy soul.

—The Birthday was not far off. Syrus asked Gratillonius to join him in honoring it. The old man cried a little when he heard that that would be unwise. The legionaries had lingered suspiciously long as it was and must be off straightaway. Gratillonius gave him the kiss of peace, and received it.

In the morning the squadron started west toward Burdigala. Gratillonius had another promise to redeem.

Decimus Magnus Ausonius smiled. "You show me the lady Bodilis as still more fascinating in person than in correspondence," he said. "You see, she's had so many questions for me that I failed to question my own assumptions. Thus I came to regard her as a brilliant human being, but one condemned to existence in a stagnant backwater. My mistake. What you have had to tell makes me wonder if Ys may not hold the world's highest civilization. Were I capable of the journey, I would accompany you there, Gratillonius, and explore it. 'Oh, that Jupiter might restore to me the years that are fled!'" His quotation and the sigh that followed were rueful, though quite without self-pity.

"But I talk too much," he went on. "Better to listen. In a sense, Ys is more distant than the farthest land we know of. That mysterious force which has worked for centuries to erase its name from our chronicles— You can remain a while, can't you? Please."

"I should be returning soon, sir," Gratillonius answered.

"You are restless. You hunger for achievement. Well, let us work some energy off you before we dine." Ausonius guided his guest to the door.

Gratillonius went along gladly. Inclement weather had kept people indoors these past two days, during which he—after getting his men barracked in the city—had stayed with the poet. Not that he hadn't enjoyed himself. Ausonius was delightful company. Still erect and lively in his mid-seventies, he had been more than a famous teacher of rhetoric; he had been tutor to ill-fated Emperor-to-be Gratianus in Treverorum, afterward prefect of Gallia, Libya, and Italy, eventually consul. In retirement since Maximus took the throne, he remained active among colleagues, students, civic leaders, a large household and its neighborhood, while from his pen streamed verses and epistles to friends throughout the Empire.

Nevertheless it was a special pleasure to step forth on the portico of the rural mansion, flush lungs with fresh air, and look widely around. Rain and sleet had yielded to sunshine which, although slanted from the south, gave January a pledge of springtime. Grounds swept darkling with moisture down to the bank of the Garumna; mist smoked off the river, roiled by a breeze, half obscuring the vineyards beyond. On a paved path that the men took, doves moved aside from the sapphire arrogance of a peacock.

"A slave told me you have several scrolls in your baggage," Ausonius said. "May I ask what the texts are?"

Gratillonius hesitated. They were from Syrus, aids to his memory of doctrine and rites that a Father must know, and none of lesser rank. When he had no more need of them in Ys, he was to destroy them by fire, with certain prayers. "I'm sorry. It's forbidden me to tell."

Ausonius gave him a close regard before murmuring, "You're not a Christian, are you?"

"I follow the Lord Mithras."

"I suspected as much. Well, I'm Christian myself, but hold that to be no grounds for scorning the ancients or any upright contemporaries who believe otherwise. Surely God is too great to be comprehended in a single creed, and we mortals do best simply to pay our due respects and cultivate our gardens."

Gratillonius recalled poems of Ausonius that Bodilis had shown him. They were concerned with everyday matters, sometimes humorous, sometimes grave, sometimes—as when he mourned the death of his wife or a child—moving, in a stoic fashion. *"Gather you roses, girl, whilst they and you are in flower, remembering how meanwhile time flies from you...."*

Hoofbeats drummed. The men turned to look. Up from the riverside galloped a mud-splashed horse, upon it a boy of eight or nine years. "Why, yonder comes Paulinus," the rhetor exclaimed happily.

Gratillonius had met the lad, Ausonius's grandson, born in Macedonia but now here to get the finest possible education. Being shut in by the rain had made him miserable, despite the elder's unfailing kindliness. The ride had evidently refreshed him, for he drew rein at his grandfather's hail and greeted the men in seemly wise. "Are you ready to go back to your books?" Ausonius asked, smiling.

"Please, can't I ride some more first?" Paulinus begged. His Latin was heavily Greek-accented. "Bucephalus, he's just getting his second wind."

"Discipline, discipline, you must break yourself to harness before you dare call yourself a man.....But in indulging you I indulge myself. Go as you will. 'Good speed to your young valor, boy! So shall you mount to the stars!'" Ausonius quoted with a chuckle. "Meditate upon that line. It should make Vergilius more interesting to you."

"Thanks!" Paulinus cried, and was off in a spatter of wet earth.

Ausonius clicked his tongue and shook his head. "I really must become stricter with him," he said. "Else a rhetorician of considerable potential could go to waste. But it isn't easy when I remember his father at that age."

Gratillonius thought of Dahilis and Dahut. "No, it isn't easy," he said through sudden, unexpected pain. Hastily: "Still, he ought to keep in shape. He may well find need for a set of muscles."

"Oh? Why? We moderns don't revere athletes like the Greeks in their glory. His career should resemble mine, writing, teaching, public office."

Gratillonius's gaze went eastward, toward the Duranius valley through which he had come on his way to Burdigala. Those thickly wooded steeps and hollows lay no great distance hence. Yet little traffic moved there anymore, for fear of the robbers who haunted them. "How long do you suppose that sort of life will stay possible?" he asked harshly. "Why, already—when was it?—about twenty-five years ago, the barbarians cut the aqueducts of Lugdunum itself."

Ausonius nodded. "I remember. It caused the taxes to fail that year."

"Didn't it mean any more to you than that?"

"Oh, these are troublous times, admittedly." The furrows of the old countenance turned downward in sorrow. "My friend Delphinus was fortunate in passing away before his wife and daughter met their fate at the hands of the tyrant Maximus." Ausonius gripped the arm of Gratillonius. "You've intimated that you were a witness to the evil done in Augusta. If you've spoken no more about it, I can understand. But the martyrs are safe in heaven—we must believe—and a measure of justice has since prevailed."

"Really?" asked the centurion, surprised. "How?"

"You have not heard?...Well, I suppose you scarcely could have, on the road as you were." (Or immured in Vienna, Gratillonius did not add.) "I have received letters, including one from a colleague who is in correspondence with Martinus, the bishop of Caesarodunum."

Gratillonius's pulse quickened. "I've met that man. Tell me what happened."

"Why, Martinus was on his way home when he learned of the executions of the Priscillianists, a breach of Maximus's promise to show them mercy. He burned up the road back to Augusta and demanded to see the Emperor. That was denied him. But Maximus's wife, a pious lady, grew terrified, begged Martinus to dine alone with her and discuss it. They say he had never done that with a woman, but consented, and she laved his feet with her tears and dried them with her hair. The upshot was that Maximus did hear Martinus out, a thunderous denunciation, and agreed not to send inquisitors to Hispania, heretic-hunting, as he had planned. In exchange, Martinus celebrated Communion with the bishops who had been active in the prosecution. So you see, civilization, tolerance, common decency won in the end."

A glow awoke in Gratillonius. "By Hercules," he exclaimed, "that Martinus is a soldier yet!"

At the back of his mind went the thought that this boded better for Ys, and for the hopes he cherished, than hitherto.

"Be less pessimistic," Ausonius urged. He gestured. "Look about you. The foundations hold firm. Broad, fertile, well-cultivated acres; flourishing cities; law and order, which reach into the very palace of the usurper. True, the Empire has its difficulties. But the life of the mind goes on, and that is what matters. That is what is eternal."

The mood of the younger man changed as he listened. He wanted to be away, immediately, back into action. He curbed himself. Best he abide a few days more, for his own sake as well as Bodilis's, maybe also for the sake of Ys and Dahut. Let him gather what roses he could and bring them home. If ever he returned here, the flowerbeds might well lie trampled by the hoofs of warriors' horses.

V

~ 1 ~

Ever was there something strange about Mumu, something apart from the rest of Ériu. To this southernmost of the Fifths, it was said, the Children of Danu withdrew after their defeat by the Children of Ír and Éber; now their King dwelt within the Mountain of Fair Women, the síd beyond the plain of Femen. Folk gave more sacrifices to God-desses than to Gods, and believed that by mortal men certain of These had become ancestresses of their royal houses. Female druids, poets, and witches practiced their arts as often as did males, or oftener. Here above all it was terrible to be out after dark on the eves of Beltene and Samain, when the doors between the worlds stood open—so swarmed the dead and every other kind of uncanny being.

Highlands walled Mumu off. Traffic did go back and forth, but less than elsewhere, and war with men of Condacht, Qóiqet Lagini, or Mide seldom became more than a season of skirmishes. The Ulati were far in the north; one scarcely even heard of them. The men of Mumu bore ample spears against each other. At the same time, safe harbors brought about overseas trade in a measure unknown to the neighbor realms. Roman goods arrived from as far away as Egypt: wine, oil, glass, earthenware, in exchange for gold, honey, beeswax, furs, hides. Likewise did the sumptuous fabrics of Ys. Scot's Landing, below that city, took it name not from pirates out of Ériu but from the frequent, peaceful visits of Mumach fishers. The Christian faith got its first foothold on the island among their kinfolk, who claimed that some of the Lord's own apostles had been there.

Missionaries had not yet reached the rugged country about the Mountain of Fair Women when Lugthach maqq Aillelo was king over its allied tuaths. Afterward poets told how Fedelmm, daughter of Moethaire of the Corco Óchae, fought him. Not only did she have warriors at her beck, she was a mighty witch. The story went that she had a friend in the female warrior Bolce Ben-bretnach from Alba. Perhaps as a way to making peace, Bolce sought out Lugthach and laid upon him the demand that he bed her. He could not refuse one with her powers, and thus Conual maqq Lugthaci was begotten. At the birth, the father was away but Fedelmm was present, and to her the mother gave Conual for fostering.

Fedelmm took the infant home. The next night a coven was to meet in her house. Lest harm befall him, she hid Conual in a hole beneath the hearthstone. One of the witches sniffed him and said, "I do not destroy anything save what is under the cauldron." At that, the fire flashed downward and burned the ear of the boy.

From this, some say, came his nickname Corcc, the Red; but others say that was the color of his hair. He also became known as Conual maqq Lárech, because his mother bore the nickname Láir Derg, the Red Mare.

To her came a seer, who read the child's hand and told him: "Always set free any captives you meet, if you are able. Do this and your race will grow great and your fame endure." Conual could scarcely have understood, then, but throughout his life he strove to obey the commandment.

So went the stories. They did not say why Fedelmm soon gave the fostering over to Torna Éces. She may have wished the lad to be free of the dark forces around herself.

Torna was the foremost poet of his day, a man who saw deeply into things and knew promise when he found it. Already he was raising Niall maqq Echach, son of the King of Mide. He had rescued the child from the murderous spite of the King's new wife, Mongfind, the witch-queen out of Mumu.

Conual was only three or four years old when Torna deemed Niall of an age to return to Temir, show that he was not dead as everybody there believed, and claim his rights. Mongfind could wreak no further harm upon him. However, after his father died, she succeeded in having her brother Craumthan maqq Fidaci hailed King.

A better person than his sister, on the whole he reigned well. His grief was that he was childless. When he heard about Conual, who was his cousin, he sent for the boy, meaning to make him an adoptive son. Torna let Conual go, counselling him to remember the kindly duty given him.

The newcomer was soon a worshipful friend of the older Niall and, when big enough, accompanied him to war. Fighting in Qóiqet Lagini, they took a prisoner who proved to be a learned man. On that ground, Conual persuaded Niall he should be released without ransom.

The closeness between the princes aroused all of Mongfind's malignancy. Niall was by then too strong, with too many handfast men, for her to seek his overthrow. It would take very little to break the uneasy peace and let him avenge the wrongs she had done him and his mother Carenn. But she could poison Craumthan's mind against Conual, word by sly word. At last, sick of soul, the king decided he must be rid of the youth.

He could not well have his fosterling slain at home. Instead, Mongfind whispered, he should entrust Conual with a message for a Pictish chieftain in Alba who was tributary to him. As a leavetaking gift,

Craumthan gave Conual a shield whereon stood words engraved in ogamm. Conual took them for a good luck charm.

Having crossed the North Channel and being wearied, he made camp on the beach. Who should chance by but the scholar he had set free? Conual welcomed him, and presently fell asleep. The guest read what was on the shield, as the Pictish lord would also be able to do. The bearer was to be killed. The scholar changed the inscription. Hence, when Conual reached his destination, he was lavishly received, and soon got a daughter of the chieftain in marriage.

Thus the story, and few men would be so rash as to gainsay a poet. Yet naked truth may be garbed in many different words. This tale might be a profound way of relating that Conual Corcc got in trouble at Temir and perforce departed with what small following he could muster, but won high standing in his exile.

Of Niall, the poets told that he became King in Mide after Craumthan and Mongfind destroyed each other with an envenomed drink. Erelong he was warring abroad as well as in Ériu and gaining a mighty name.

Conual Corcc dwelt four years with his wife among her people. He gathered men sworn to him and led them in battle through the great onslaught Niall masterminded and Magnus Maximus repelled. Afterward he brought them and their women down to the country of the Ordovices and Silures. A good many Scoti had settled there as Roman power ebbed out of the hills.

Slowly the tide turned. Before leaving the Wall, Maximus had sent an ally, Cunedag of the Votadini, to take charge in that part of Britannia. Between him and the Second Legion, stationed at Isca Silurum, the Scoti found that they could no longer seize land as their numbers increased, but must fight to keep what they had. Conual Corcc became a leading war chieftain of theirs, who often raided deep into regions the Romans had supposed were safe. Loot made him wealthy.

Yet he was, in his way, a thoughtful man. Torna may have put that into him. Wherever he went, he looked keenly at things, and he turned the memories of them over and over in his head. He considered the farms, manors, towns, fortresses—the tools, machines, books, laws, the sense of a dominion and a history vaster than they could imagine in Ériu. Captives whom he let go spoke well of him upon returning home. In the course of time, truce and trade with Conual became just as possible as war. When he visited a Roman center, he asked endless questions; and to Romans who ventured into his purlieu on peaceful business, he gave hospitality and protection.

It was not that he had any wish to become a subject of their Empire. He understood too well what it was doing to itself. Besides, more and more he yearned for his homeland. But the riches and the knowledge he was gaining here would let him return in strength.

2

It was noon when the legionaries again saw Ys. Sun and sky stood winter-wan, but light gleamed off the few clouds and many wings aloft. Grass on the headlands was, as yet, sere above their stern cliffs. Glimpsed from these heights, the water below ran in amethyst, beryl, flint, sliver. Its noise growled through a shrillness of wind, air alive with salt, kelp, and frost. And there between the steeps rose turreted ruddy walls, soaring and flashing towers. At high tide the sea gate was closed, surf battering under the battlements, and that too was utterly right, a part of coming home.

The soldiers raised a cheer. Riding in front of them, Gratillonius signalled for double-time. Hobnails crashed on paving. Westbound along Aquilonian Way, the men saw ahead to the end of Cape Rach, where the pharos loomed beyond clustered tombs. But soon their road swung north and downward, into the valley. Folk began to spy them and flock forth shouting from homes, farms, orchards nestled in the hills. Sentinels observed afar and sounded their trumpets. Aquilonian Way turned west again at the amphitheater, whose walls barred sight of the sacred grove. Thence the track ran straight between smithies, tanneries, carpenter shops, all the industries required to be where people did not live, until it entered High Gate.

"The King, the King!" Crowds jubilated. Gratillonius's eyes stung. He swallowed hard. Did they truly love him like this? He recognized an occasional face among those that swirled around, Herun the navy man, Maeloch the fisher, several marines who'd been escorts of his or fighters against the Scoti, a wineseller for whom he had once gotten restitution from a swindling wholesaler in Condate Redonum, a woman whom he had once given a judgment against an abusive husband, lesser Suffetes—the magnates would seek the palace for a more formal reception—"Company dismissed!" he rapped. His men broke formation and flung themselves into the throng, searching for comrades and sweethearts.

Gratillonius rode on. An impromptu guard formed, burly commoners who cleared his way for him, genially if not always gently. The press eased off as he turned from Lir Way into the crookedly rising streets along which the wealthy had their houses. Nobody was forbidden to go there, but most Ysans had a feel for what was becoming, an ancient dignity he had never encountered elsewhere.

At the main entrance to the palace he dismounted, gave his horse over to the excited servants, and strode in his armor through the garden —winter-bare, but trees and shrubs awhisper in the wind—to the modest-sized building. Up its staircase he went, between the sculptured boar and bear, under the gilt eagle on the dome, the creatures of Taranis. Bronze doors, intricately figured, were flung wide for him, and he passed the entryroom and came into the atrium.

There they stood, his Queens and their daughters—and Dahut, next to Quinipilis, O Mithras, how the child had grown, and how solemnly she stared from under a golden mane! Also present were the men of the Council, attendants hovering in the background. He halted with a military stamp and clang, raised his palm, intoned, "Greetings, my ladies and worthies," while his heart thuttered and he forced his eyes to swing around, away from the girl who looked so much like Dahilis.

The male grandees didn't matter. Not yet. But what of the Gallicenae? Bodilis smiled at him in unchanged serenity. Tears shimmered on the thin cheeks of Innilis, who huddled close to expressionlessly saluting Vindilis. Lanarvilis's ceremonial gesture showed more warmth. Maldunilis squealed in delight; she was very pregnant. The gaze of Forsquilis smoldered out of her Athene countenance above the infant she bore, whose age must be about two months. How Quinipilis had grown old, the hands trembling that clutched the staff on which she leaned, flesh dried away from the knotted, painful bones, though her grin crinkled wicked as ever. Fennalis too seemed less plump than erstwhile, like an apple that has begun to wither. Guilvilis stood timidly to the rear, her own newest babe clutched to her bosom, her older daughter by Gratillonius clinging to her skirt.

Three stepped forward and confronted him: Soren Cartagi, Speaker for Taranis; Hannon Baltisi, Lir Captain; Forsquilis, whom the Nine serving Belisama must have chosen to be their voice today. "Welcome, King, thrice welcome to Ys, your city," they said together. "May you henceforth long abide in our midst."

"I thank you," said Gratillonius out of an unreasonably dry throat. Seeking to lighten the atmosphere: "And so I intend. You seem well prepared for my arrival."

Forsquilis nodded. Her glance caught his. He nodded back. On the previous three nights, when his band made camp for lack of other accommodation, a great owl had ghosted by.

"How have you and the city fared?" he asked.

Soren shrugged. "There's little to tell, save that— No matter now, no large matter at all."

"What mean you?" Gratillonius demanded.

"Ah, we'd not spoil this hour," Hannon said. He was seldom that cordial. "It can wait. You're the one with the real news, whatever it be."

"News indeed," Gratillonius drew breath. "Too much for telling at once. When I do, I think you'll agree my journey's borne fruit we had need of, knowledge, though some of it bitter on the tongue. Bodilis, I did visit Ausonius." She grew radiant. "As for the rest of what I have to convey, it will require much time and thought of us. Best we wait until tomorrow or the day after."

Soren opened his mouth as if to protest, but Forsquilis cut him off. "We understand," she said. "With no immediate danger, 'twould be foolish to rush into complexities. Come, let's proceed to the banquet we've prepared for our King."

3

When the others departed after the festivities, she stayed.

In his secret self, Gratillonius had hoped for that. After celibate months, the Bull ramped through his blood. A phantom went there as well, memory of failure in Treverorum, fear of new punishment for his sin. Forsquilis was both the most passionate and the most artful of the Nine.

In a candlelit bedchamber, he invested a few moments of extravagant admiration, bent over the cradle of little Nemeta. (After all, he had been unable to keep from hugging Dahut.) The mother ended that herself, pouncing and clutching, purring and mewing.

They well-nigh ripped the clothes off each other. Her beauty flamed at him. He never knew whether he cast her down or she pulled him down. He entered her with a roar, and her hips surged beneath him like the sea.

After the second time they were satisfied to lie talking while strength regathered itself. He half sat, propped on pillows against the headboard that was usual on Ysan beds. She lay curled in the curve of his left arm, her hair spilling amber-brown across his chest. The odor of her was warm and wild.

"Ah," she crooned, "I've missed you, Grallon."

"And I you." His free hand strayed over her breasts. Milkful, they jutted proudly from her slenderness. How golden the light was upon that white skin.

"I'm sure you did," she answered, "especially after—" The words turned into a laugh. Appalled, he felt her fingers on his lips. "Nay, we need speak naught of that. Stallions will be stallions, for which I thank our Lady of the Lovetime."

"Is there aught you don't know, you witch?" he gusted in his relief.

She sobered. "Much. The politics of men and their Gods—" Her look sought a shuttered window...and the night wind beyond? "You have returned a sadder man than you went, my darling. Why?"

Strangely, it was not strange to blurt to this cat-female, as if she were a man or wise Bodilis: "Maximus, Emperor Maximus, I misjudged him. He lives not for Rome but for power, and for power not only over bodies but souls."

From him stumbled the story of what he had seen and endured. Forsquilis held him close.

"So you see Ys is in danger," he ended. "*You* are, your whole Sisterhood. He means to destroy what he calls witchcraft, rip it out by the roots and cast it on the fire."

"And you're to do his weeding for him, eh?" she said low, again looking elsewhere.

"I won't. I am the King of Ys, as...I finally, truly discovered on this faring....But I cannot rise against Rome!" he yelled.

That roused Nemeta, who began to cry. Forsquilis flowed from the bed, took up the babe, soothed and nursed her, the eidolon of young motherhood, while she asked coolly, "What then do you propose to do?"

"I know not." Gratillonius smote fist into palm. "I've thought and thought. I suppose we have two or three years' grace. Maximus must secure his frontier along the Rhenus and make a lasting settlement with Valentinianus—aye, still more with Theodosius in Constantinople."

"And meanwhile," she said, smiling down at her child, "much can happen."

He nodded violently. "'Tis my hope. Already Ys is central to the defense of Armorica. If we can weave such a net of alliances that we are vital, with so many powerful friends in the Empire that he must keep his hands off us—"

"I was thinking of what might happen to Magnus Maximus," she said.

A shiver went through him.

Forsquilis straightened and gave him a level regard. Her tone turned brisk. "Well, these things can await the morrow. We've a third celebration to carry out, I trust, you and I. It should be soon, for you'll need a good night's sleep."

Her words roused fresh lust and gladness. "Oh, we can lie abed late."

She shook her head. "Nay, that would not be meet. You must be up betimes, O King. Too long has your duty been undone."

"What's this?"

"Ah, no large task. 'Tis only that postponing it further would dishonor Taranis." The Queen frowned. "Hm, I'd forgotten, we never told you. Well, soon after you departed, a challenger arrived at the Wood. We've perforce housed him there, fed him, supplied him with harlots and amusements and whatever else befits one who might become King, these past months. High time to end the farce."

Gratillonius sat upright. His muscles tautened. "A fight to the death?"

Forsquilis laughed anew. "Nay, merely a chore, albeit a sacral one. This is a pitiful shrimp of an Osismiian. Clear 'tis, he heard the King would be long away, and knew what a challenger is entitled to, and came to take advantage, with the intent of sneaking off ere you returned. But I divined as much and warned Soren, who ordered a surreptitious watch kept on him. When news of your advent blossomed today, he tried to flee, but was promptly seized. Tomorrow morning you'll kill him and there's an end of the business, aside from the rites that follow."

She tenderly laid her babe, now drowsy, back in the cradle; turned about; glided toward the bed, arms wide. "I believe you are ready now," she whispered. "Come, let's make love. A long, long love."

~ 4 ~

Rain blew up during the night. By dawn its chill drizzle engulfed sky, sea, hills. At the Wood of the King, it dripped off bare oak branches and runneled down trunks and made soggy last year's leaves on the earth. The blood-colored house at the border of the grove was dulled, as if the blood were starting to clot.

There waited Soren in his sacerdotal robes, together with six marines, their horses and hounds. They were the guards over Hornach, who had dared strike the Hammer to the brazen Shield that hung in the yard outside.

His centurion's battle gear moved easily on Gratillonius's frame as he mounted the steps to the portico. Grotesque idol-shaped columns grinned at him. Underneath the roof lay shadowiness through which he peered at his opponent. Hornach was not quite the weakling of Forsquilis's contempt, but he was scrawny; the mail into which they had stuffed him draped limp over knocking knees, the helmet threatened to slide down his nose. Even in this cold, his fear stank.

"Hail!" boomed the seven men and the household staff to the King.

Hornach reached out. "Oh, please," he croaked, "please, I've made a horrible mistake, I'll surrender, abase myself, do anything—"

"Shall we accompany you, sir?" asked a marine. "Wouldn't do to make you chase him. Heh!" he snickered.

"Nay, that were unseemly. 'Tis never been done thus," Soren declared. "We'll put a leash around his waist for you to hold, my lord." A snarl: "Unless you, you wretch, can find the manhood to die as Taranis wills."

"I have an old mother, sir, I've been sending her coins from here, she'll starve without me," blubbered the Osismian. A trouser leg darkened and clung to the shin; he was dribbling piss.

Gratillonius had expected a straightforward fight against somebody like a Bacauda—had deceived himself into expecting it, he suddenly understood. His gullet thickened. "This is no combat, 'tis butchery," he got out. "Unworthy of the God. I accept his surrender."

Hornach went to his knees, weeping, and scrabbled to hug the King's. His guards yanked him back. "That may not be, lord," said Soren, shock clear to see beneath his implacability. "This creature issued the challenge. Worse, he did so in falsehood. Strike him down, in the name of the God."

Gratillonius remembered Priscillianus.

But he was the King of Ys, and here was a rogue who had taken an impudent gamble. "Well," he said, "let it at least be quick."

After praying to Taranis, they hitched a cord around the waist of Hornach. Gratillonius led him on his wabbling way through the brush, until they stood alone in a glade. Rain mumbled in the trees around, washed away tears, sought past armor. Dead leaves squashed underfoot. Gratillonius undid the leash, stepped back, drew sword and brought up shield. "Make ready," he said.

Hornach shuddered, once. His blade jerked forth. It was of the long Germanic sort, and either he had refused a shield—unlikely—or

322

no one had thought to offer him it or he in his terror to voice the request.

"Have at me," Gratillonius invited. Do! screamed within him. "You might win, you know. You might become the next King of Ys." He gagged on his lie.

"Let me go," Hornach pleaded. "I meant no harm. I never did. Let me go, and the Gods will love you."

Not the Gods of Ys, Gratillonius thought. In a moment's confusion: But I in my heart give Them no honor any longer. Why should I do this thing?

Iron answered: Because I will destroy myself, my Kingship, everything that is left me to care about, if I openly flout Their will.

Hornach wailed and half turned to run. Get it over with! thought Gratillonius, and advanced. His opponent twisted around, raised sword, chopped wildly. Gratillonius caught the feeble blow on his shield. The other throat was open to him. He smote.

The trouble then was that Hornach did not die. He flopped on the ground, spouting blood and screams. When Gratillonius bent down to give a mercy stroke, hands tried to wave it off.

Abruptly Gratillonius must vomit.

When he had finished, Hornach lay still.

Gratillonius stood in the rain, plunging his blade into the earth, over and over, to cleanse it. The image of Ausonius said: *"What you have had to tell makes me wonder if Ys may not hold the world's highest civilization."*

I *am* no knacker! he cried into the nothingness and the cold. I am a soldier. Threefold Gods Who robbed the world of Dahilis, will You not send me honest enemies? If You make sport of me, why should I pour out blood for You? Taranis, Lir, Belisama, be warned. I am calling on Mithras to come end Your day, Mithras, Lord of Light.

VI

~ 1 ~

Up from the South wandered spring, and as she breathed upon naked boughs and wet earth there leaped forth blossoms, leaves, new grass, tender herbs, across the length of Armorica. Sunbeams and cloud shadows pursued each other, with rainsqualls and rainbows, till the wind lay down to rest and whiteness brooded huge in the blue. Lambs, calves, foals explored meadows, amazed by brilliance. Wives reopened their homes to air while they scrubbed away winter's grime; farmers hitched ox to plow, mariners bent sail to yard.

Little of the day had entered the house of Queen Vindilis, unless it be a certain bleak freshness. When Fennalis arrived, she gave her brief greeting and led her straight through the austerely ornamented atrium to the private room. Refreshments did wait on its table, nothing more than wine, bread, cheese, and, to be sure, oysters in their opened shells.

Having closed the door, the women made reverence before the image that occupied a niche, Belisama in Her aspect of the Wild Huntress. "Be seated," said Vindilis then. "Avail yourself. How fare you?"

"Oh, you know my rheumatism plagues me in changeable weather, and we get so many bad colds among people at this season that I've scarce had time to think." Fennalis was much in demand as a healer, second only to Innilis. She lacked the Touch that sometimes came to the latter, but she had the sympathy, together with more practical skill. She lowered her dumpy form to the couch, reached for a bite and a sip, chuckled. "*I* know you've not asked me here to put polite questions."

Humor died away as she looked up at the one who stood over her. As usual, Vindilis was plainly clad for a person of rank in Ys: today a gown of pearl-hued wool bordered with a procession in blue of the Goddess's cats and doves, a massive garnet brooch at her throat. Hair drawn back in tight, coiled braids made doubly vivid the white streak through its blackness and emphasized the aquilinity of her features. In the greenish light from the window, her eyes seemed enormous, full of night.

"I thank you for coming," she said, with no softening of her tone. "I believe you'll agree 'tis on a matter of moment."

Fennalis's pugnosed countenance registered puzzlement. She ran fingers through the snowy mane that bristled out of the pins and comb wherewith she sought to control it. "Why me? I'm not wise or strong or, or anything. Oh, if I can help you, dear, of course I'll try."

"I am with child," Vindilis told her.

Fennalis half rose, slopping wine from cup. "What? Why, wonderful!"

"That remains to be seen. Yesterday Innilis examined me and confirmed what the signs had said. The birth should come about winter solstice."

Fennalis sank back and was quiet a while before replying low, "Why are you troubled? 'Twas your choice to leave off using the Herb. Aye, you're not youthful, but you've kept yourself as fit as a lynx. Fear not."

Vindilis snapped forth a laugh. "Does the smith who is forging a sword fear it will cut him down? Nay, what frets him is that it may prove weak in the wielder's hand."

"What mean you?" Fennalis asked, not quite steadily.

Vindilis began pacing, to and fro before the couch. Her skirts whispered. She stared before her as she said:

"I confide in you because you are the only one I can. And you are neither weak nor foolish, Fennalis, underneath those flustery ways of yours. Six children have you borne to three different Kings, and all are still alive. Under Colconor, you could have drawn yourself into the background—he had little yen for you—but instead you stood up to him, again and again, took his abuse, fended the worst of his cruelties off Dahilis as well as your own daughters. And in the end, if you were not the first, neither were you the last who dared call on us to curse him. Since then—"

Fennalis waved her hands. "I am not hostile to King Grallon."

Vindilis laughed anew. "Nor intimate of his, either. You made no secret of your displeasure when he would not truly take you for his wife, and in Council you've opposed more than one proposal of his."

Fennalis sighed. "That's past. He's true to his faith, and so meant me no insult. Whatever dreams had stirred in me have quietly gone away. I am content."

"Are you?" Vindilis swung about and stood confronting her. "The rest are, more or less, aye. Think them over. Bodilis is his favorite, his...his friend. Lanarvilis has her disagreements with him, but not very often anymore. To her, he is Rome, the Roman virtue and the Roman peace she imagines once existed. Quinipilis surely has her doubts, but she enjoys his company and is, anyhow, too old and weary for dispute. To Maldunilis, he has a big cock and is kindly. Guilvilis is his adoring brood mare. Forsquilis—who can ever tell what Forsquilis thinks? I dare not yet be frank with her. That leaves you."

"And Innilis."

"Innilis...will follow my lead." Suddenly the voice of Vindilis had a lullaby sound. "But what shall it be? She also looks on him as a good man, and...sometimes his attentions give her pleasure. The Lady forbid that I ever put Innilis in danger or distress." She signed herself.

"If you are embittered, why are you bearing his child?" Fennalis asked as softly.

Vindilis smiled slightly. "I am not aggrieved. He slew horrible Colconor. He does his best for Ys and for his Queens, and his best is generally excellent." She drew breath. "'Tis not his fault that Innilis and I can snatch only stolen, secret moments. 'Tis not his fault, even, that that aborted get of his almost killed her. Nay, we could be far worse off. I doubt we could be better off."

"But still you oppose him."

"Because he is what he is!" Vindilis cried. "I've not come lightly to this. I've watched, questioned, listened, pondered. I've prayed to the Mother of Stars for guidance. No clear answer came to me, but—what dreams I had, what signs I read in the sea-foam and heard in the sea-wind, all seemed to call me forward."

Fennalis occupied herself as prosaically as might be with slicing the cheese. "At last you decided to have his child," she said.

Vindilis nodded. "What other hold on him can be mine?"

She went to the window and stood staring into it, as if able to see clearly through the small, leaded panes, out beyond the city and across Ocean. "'Twas no easy decision," she said to the woman at her back. "A wish for this was never vouchsafed me. In my vestalhood I meant to renew my vows and become a minor, virgin priestess. What hopes I cherished ran toward things like founding a gymnasium for girls. Understand, Fennalis, I do not hate the minds or the deeds of men. 'Tis their sweaty, hairy bodies that repel me—that, and their supposition that because of what's between my legs, I should forever stay within walls."

Fennalis forbore to mention the freedom that most Ysan women enjoyed. "I remember," she said. "The Sign came upon you and— You were lucky that Hoel was King then. He too was decent."

"Just the same—did you know?—'twas Quinipilis, my mother, who forced me to open my womb to him. Forced me, I say, by endless arguments and browbeatings and—" Vindilis shrugged, grinned. "She was a formidable character in her day, she was. At last I gave in and produced the grandchild she wanted. One. You know well I never paid Runa more heed than I absolutely must. Poor little brat. I hope I'm shrewder these days, more in control of myself."

There was a silence, apart from a *whoo-oo* of springtime wind under the eaves.

"Why do you tell me this?" Fennalis asked at length.

Vindilis turned about. "Is it not clear? I want your counsel, your help. For Ys and its Gods."

The older woman put aside the food with which she had toyed and took up her wine instead. It was more fitting. "You want influence on Grallon beyond your mere persuasions."

"Aye. I need it. We all do."

Vindilis resumed her caged pacing. "Think," she said. "Because he has done so well, authority flows more and more to him. Now he's put the final seal on his Kingship, his halidom, by slaying a challenger in the Wood. That wipes out, from the minds of the people, any last fear that he may not yet have settled his account with the Gods. And he's young, strong, skilled. Surely he'll make short work of any future contestants.

"But he is a Roman!

"What about this new Emperor Maximus, who sent him to us?"

"Grallon explained he won't let Maximus in," Fennalis ventured.

"So he says. Belike he means it. But can he, can Ys hold off the Romans without the help of our Gods? And in spite of the outcome of that fight, I do not believe he is friends with Them. Why, he intends building a temple to his Bullslayer. What will Taranis feel when His priest and avatar bows down to Mithras?"

"That may—I know not—"

326

Vindilis pressed on, like a hunter toward wounded quarry: "Also, what may happen, what will he do, when next the Sign descends? Have you never lain awake wondering, you whom he refused because Lanarvilis is your daughter? Quinipilis has few years left her—mayhap only hours. Which of the vestals will the Gods then choose?"

"It could be any."

"Are you so hopeful?" Vindilis compressed her lips. "Myself, I doubt They will make the matter easy for him. I think They will give him a daughter of one of us. And not your Amair. Not when They have Lanar-vilis's Miraine and Boia. Or...soon Innilis's sad, weak-witted Audris will be of marriageable age; and not long after that, Bodilis's Semuramat or my Runa. The Gods have Their sport with us, don't They, Fennalis? You're old too, after all. Or any of us could die unexpectedly. What *then?*

"I say to you, whatever peace is between Grallon and the Gods is as uneasy as peace between Rome and Ys; and it will erelong be put to the test. We Gallicenae must make ready for that, as best we are able. Therefore I am bearing the King a child. A lure, a hostage, a talisman? I know not. Help me, my Sister."

The energy seemed to go from Vindilis. She lowered herself to a chair opposite the couch, lifted a wine cup, drank, and stared into emptiness.

"I see," Fennalis breathed. "Yours is a noble soul."

"Nay," Vindilis mumbled. "Only one that would fain stay free."

"Belike that's the same thing.... Well, you're right. We must seek to steer the King away from what he might otherwise do. I mean all the Nine, once you and I have found the ways to explain this to them. And, yea, motherhood does confer power, if used wisely."

Vindilis nodded. "As small a touch as proposing a name."

"What?" Fennalis asked. She considered, and nodded in her turn. "Aye. Though 'twas he who wanted the three Roman tags we have."

"Our Sisters were clever enough not to speak against it."

What they thought of were not Maldunilis's Zisa, Guilvilis's Sasai, or Forsquilis's Nemeta. The custom was that the firstborn of a Queen should carry her mother's vestal name onward. But Guilvilis now had Antonia, called after a sister of Gratillonius afar in Britannia; and Lanarvilis had borne Julia, honoring his mother; and Bodilis had Una, though whom that commemorated had not been declared.

"I expect he'll like my suggestion," Vindilis said.

"What is it?"

"Augustina. From that legion that was his."

~ 2 ~

In the two years following his disaster at Ys, Niall maqq Echach waged war over and over in his own land of Mide. Tuaths that thought him weakened, or in disfavor with the Gods, would refuse him his due, and take arms when he fared to demand it. The first several such battles were desperate, for he had indeed suffered heavy loss, the finest of his warriors. Yet he blazed his way through, won victory, made stern terms of peace, brought heads and hostages back to Temir. As word got around, rebelliousness slacked off, while a new crop of young men began dreaming of glory and booty to be gained in the host of this lord.

It was Éndae Qennsalach, King over the Lagini, who had egged on much of this revolt. Bad blood was ancient between his folk and Niall's. Some three hundred years before, Tóthual the Desired had founded Mide, carving the largest part of it out of Laginach territory. Nevertheless, the King of the latter wedded a daughter of Tóthual—but, wearying of her, confined her in a secret place, gave out that she was dead, and got her sister's hand. When the second wife chanced to discover the first, both died of the shame this incest had put on them. Tóthual thereupon raged through Qóiqet Lagini, slaying, plundering, burning, till he got abject surrender. His price was the paying, every second year, of that tribute which came to be called the Bóruma.

So vast was this sum of cows, pigs, cloaks, bronzeware, and silver that it would have beggared the Lagini. Hence the time was not long until they refused. Since then, those Condachtach and Mide Kings who had the claim seldom got it satisfied, and only by collecting it at sword's point after a bitter war. Thus did hatred build up over many lifetimes.

Éndae, always a maker of trouble for Temir, took what he thought was a chance to bring ruin on his enemy. In the third summer, Niall came looking for revenge.

The armies met south of the River Ruirthech. That was a day when clouds blew like smoke, low above the valley, underneath a sky the hue of lead. Rainshowers rushed out of them, drenched men, washed their wounds and their dead, passed away on the keening wind. All colors were dulled except those of blood and gold. Shouts, horn calls, hoofbeats, footfalls, clamorous wheels, clash and rattle of weapons, were somehow muffled. But blows fell as heavy and sharp as always.

Niall's chariot boomed ahead. Grass was thick but slippery beneath its iron-shod fellies; it took all the skill Cathual the driver owned to keep onward full tilt. Behind him the King stood cat-balanced against the rocking and jouncing. Niall roared, stabbed with his spear, smote with his blade, lifted their reddened points on high for a sign to his followers. He himself was a banner, a guiding comet. Above the height of him, hair and beard fell primrose-yellow from the helmet, seven-colored cloak fluttered back from the wide shoulders, gold and amber shone upon the saffron tunic. The handsomeness of his face was twisted into battle fury, wherein eyes glinted lightning-blue, teeth bone-white. Hounds ran alongside, to leap, bay, slash, tear, howl. He seemed as much beast as they, as much war-god as Lúg come to earth. Many a brave man saw what approached and fled, casting his arms from him, wailing the same blind panic into his comrades.

Withal, Niall remained a leader, a part of him watchful and aware. He kept track of the other chariots in his van, right and left. Nearest was that of Domnuald, son by the second of his Queens. This was the lad's first combat, he no more than fifteen summers of age. Hard practice rewarded itself; Domnuald poised easily and struck keenly. Hair like his father's hung wet down cheeks still girlish. O Brigit, Mother of Love, how he recalled Breccan, who died in Niall's arms outside the wall of Ys!

Older sons drove in the wings, themselves already blooded men, restless as stallions, toplofty as eagles. Several nobles had chariots too. More chose to come behind afoot, leading their tenants, with swords, spears, axes, bills, slings, while bows twanged and arrows hissed. The din cut through wind and rain, on up to the hasty clouds. There cruised scaldcrows and ravens, birds of the Mórrigu, gathering at Her feast.

Before Niall, and soon around him, the Lagini fought back. They were equipped and marshalled like his men, and maybe numbered the same. Most of them battled wolfishly well. But they could not make headway. They could not even hold fast. Day had not much dwindled when they were all fled, or captive, or sprawled and emptily staring corpses.

~ 3 ~

Éndae sent a herald to ask for truce. Niall received him as was fitting for one whose person was sacred, and sent him back with word of agreement.

The meeting place they set was near the battleground, a house of the king of the tuath that lived thereabouts. While they waited, Niall and his chieftains took it over and made merry. Dark as the afternoon was, they burned lamps and links without stint. Breaths smoked white athwart shadows crouching, dancing, changing shape, filling every corner and the smoky spaces under the roof. Highlights gleamed, an eye, a smile, a lifted beaker. This was no mead hall, with benches along the walls and a flock of servants. The highest ranking men sat on stools, the rest on the clay floor, and drink passed from hand to hand. Nonetheless, merriment rang.

"Have you a song for us, Laidchenn, dear?" Niall called.

"I have that," answered the poet. As was the custom, he had accompanied the army to watch what happened and afterward put it in words. That was as honorable as to fight, or more so; for what was the use of mighty deeds, did they not live in memory and the fame of them travel afar? "But I ask leave to wait a while."

329

"How is this?" wondered Niall. The buzz of talk died away until rain sounded loud on the thatch overhead.

Laidchenn gestured. He was a burly man with fiery, bushy hair and beard, carelessly dressed, but a man to command awe—chief singer to the King, former pupil of Torna Éces in Mumu. "You know that I, like you, have brought a young son of mine along for the experiencing of his first war, though Domnuald is to become a valiant fighter whereas Tigernach is studying my art under myself. Would you be so kind as to hear the lad's piece? A maiden effort, but burning within him it is, and I think not unworthy of you."

"He is very welcome," said Niall graciously.

Tigernach stood up. He was about the same age as Domnuald, and growing toward his father's body form. Brown-haired, his countenance was plain, somewhat marred by skin eruptions beneath a fuzz of whiskers. He did not shake a chiming rod, for he was, after all, a novice in the craft. Yet melody rippled clear and true from his harp, and boldness—brashness, almost—rose in his tones.

"Lord who harried Lagini,
Star-brilliant in the battle—"

His verse lacked subtlety, the tropes were sparse, and older men winced a bit at its fulsomeness. However, it was properly composed and showed high promise, as spirited as it was. Niall thanked him and gave him a silver brooch. Tigernach blushed so it could be seen in the dimness, mumbled his own thanks, and sat down. Laidchenn glowed with pride.

Of course, there was no comparison to the father's words. They soared, they cried, they sent ghosts shivering up and down backbones. Tears rolled over leathery visages, fists clenched, eyes stared outward beyond the world, as Laidchenn wove his magic.

Meanwhile King Éndae drove up with a dozen well-born attendants. Guards made them wait until the chant was finished and the reward given. A youth at Éndae's side protested. "Hush," said the King. "This is meet and right. Never show disrespect to a druid or an ollam poet. That is a gess upon all men."

He stared glumly into the gloomy day. Rain and mist made vague the encampment of the invaders, though he heard their boisterousness loudly enough. Closer by, servants of the dispossessed labored at the cookhouse to prepare a magnificent meal, or at the pens to feed cattle that would doubtless be herded away.

At last the guards let the newcomers in. When Éndae's champion announced him, and the Laginach King himself entered, Niall did not rise, nor even lift a knee. However, he did in seemly words offer a few seats he had reserved, and call for full cups that the guests be refreshed. Attendants bore off their overgarments and brought dry cloaks for them to wrap themselves in against the chill.

"Well," said Niall presently, "shall there be peace between us or shall there not?"

"That we must see," answered Éndae. He was a lean man, gray of hair and beard.

"Let us begin by knowing each the other," Niall said, and beckoned Laidchenn to name the Mide men on hand, with their honors.

"No such show have I this mournful day," Éndae said, "but myself I will tell you who accompanies me." He gestured. "Here are my sons—"

He came to one about the same age as Dumnuald and Tigernach, also clearly a war-virgin until now: slim, comely, intensely black of hair, white of skin, blue of eye. "Eochaid, youngest who has followed me; but younger still are brothers he has at home, and they growing."

"Why, that is the name my father bore," Niall said with a smile. "Well met, Eochaid, I hope."

He got back a glower. Cruel it was that defeat make rank a lad's first taste of battle.

Éndae hastened on with the introductions. "Now, then," he concluded, "the Gods this day have seen fit to grant you the victory, Niall maqq Echach; but you will be acknowledging that it was dearly bought, and the valor of the Lagini abides. What offer do you make us, that we swear peace with you?"

Niall tossed back his bright locks. "No offer, Éndae Qennsalach. Why should I pay for that which I have won? Henceforward you shall keep your spoon out of my stewpot; and, obedient at last to oaths given long ago, you shall deliver the Bóruma."

Breath hissed between teeth, but men sat still, not altogether surprised—save young Eochaid, who leaped to his feet and howled, "What, would you gnaw us bare, you maggots? Never!" His voice cracked across, which enraged him the more. "We'll pull you from our flesh and stamp you flat!"

"Quiet," Éndae commanded. He reached to pluck at his son's sleeve. "You disobey."

Eochaid was unaware. "Maggots, blowflies, beetles you are!" he raved. "Wait, only wait, and we'll seek your nests and smoke you out!"

Laidchenn surged erect. The bulk of him loomed huge in the flickering gloom, a touch of flame in his beard. He rang his poet's chimes. Men shrank into silence. "Have a care, boy," he warned. "Overwrought or no, you slander honorable foes, like some mad crone in a ditch. Behave yourself."

Eochaid wept. His arms flailed. "Crone, am I? Go back to your sheepfold, old ewe, and let the rams tup you again!"

Horror ran around the room. Before anyone else could rally the wit to speak, Laidchenn's son Tigernach was up also. In him, fury was a winter storm.

"You fling filth like that at my father, at a poet?" he hissed. "Go down in the dung yourself." He made a twin spike of the first two

331

fingers on his left hand and thrust it toward Eochaid. As if something
inside him had foreseen, brooded, prepared, the verses snarled from
him:

"Listen, you light-witted youth!
For that you thus dared speaking
Words unwise and without truth,
We shall soon hear you shrieking.

"Bellowing your bluster out
As if you'd gnawed a nettle,
You'd be shrewder not to shout
But kick an empty kettle.

"Shame there shall be on your face.
It is of your own earning.
Curs will cringe when in disgrace.
May likewise you be learning!"

Eochaid screamed, stumbled backward, fell to his knees, clutched
at his head. On cheeks and brow three great blisters were springing
forth, bloodred, sleet-white, mould-black. He groaned in his pain.

~ 4 ~

Toward sundown the rains blew over and the wind lay down to
rest. Laidchenn and his son walked from the house, away from others
who likewise came forth, off toward the river.

Clouds still towered in deepening blue. Light, pouring level through
the valley, reached to a rainbow. Grass drank those rays and gave them
back in glitter and green glow. They made treetops smolder, water
glimmer. The air was cold and quiet, save as shoes scuffed and slithered
over wetness or voices came faint across distance. Most of those cries
were sounded by carrion birds, scared into darkling clouds by men
who searched the battlefield for kin and comrade.

"You should not have done it," said Laidchenn softly. "I did not
reproach you then, for that would further have undermined King Niall;
but now I tell you, a satire is a weapon more fearsome than knife or
poison."

Stubbornness made Tigernach thrust out his lower lip, though it
quivered. "How did it harm our King, if one who behaved thus in his
presence suffered punishment?"

Laidchenn sighed. "It was too harsh for a grieving, bewildered boy.
His insults diminished none but himself. Surely his father was about
to send him outdoors with a heavy penance to do. Now— The blisters
will heal. They may or may not leave disfiguring scars. But the wound
in the soul will fester for aye. Niall saw this—I could tell—and softened
his demands. Else the damaged, unappeased honor of the Lagini would

332

have forced them into war to the death. After Ys he can, as yet, ill afford that. You have cost him dearly, my son."

Tigernach's will broke. He shuddered, covered his eyes, wavered on his feet. "If the King wants my head for that," he choked, "here it is."

"Not so." Laidchenn squeezed the shoulder beside him, and kept his hand on it as the two walked along. "We understand each other, himself and I. His feelings were clear to me from his glances my way and the words he used. Folk should certainly avenge injuries done their darlings. He is not angry because of your anger on my behalf. He is only...rueful. After all, he did win the day; he did exact good terms; the Bóruma was really too much to hope for, unless in some later year."

Still Tigernach sorrowed. "Indeed, my heart," Laidchenn went on after a moment, "none was more surprised than me at what happened. Who would have thought that you, as far as you are from being an ollam poet, that you could already cast a destructive satire? Did a God seize you, or do you have it in you to become at last as powerful as Torna? Whichever, clear is to see that you have been marked for a fate that will touch many lives."

Tigernach drew an uneven breath and straightened.

Laidchenn gazed toward the river. Mysterious flittings and rustlings went through the reeds along the bank. "Beware," he said. "Henceforward be always careful, and never use your art but on those occasions when you feel sure you must. This day you have made us an unforgiving enemy. Do not do it again without sore need. Your fate will be famous, but perhaps it will not be happy."

VII

~ 1 ~

At high summer, the rain sometimes fell nearly warm through unmoving air. It was heavy upon the day when Queen Lanarvilis received Lir Captain and the Speaker for Taranis. Sight quickly lost itself in that iron-colored cataract; it found no more sky, no more sea, only dim walls along streets where water rushed and gurgled. What filled the world was the noise of the downpour on roofs and paving, and below this, remote and eternal, waves a-crash against the rampart of Ys.

The men gave their hooded cloaks over to the servant who admitted them and proceeded directly to the room where the priestess waited. For them, its numerous candles did not truly fend off gloom, nor its red-blue-ivory-crystal sumptuousness offer comfort. She had attired herself in a loosely cut dress of white silk whose folds and drapes joined with a silver headband to make a timeless dignity. The visitors were in plain civil tunic, trousers, half-boots. Besides the weather being unsuited for robes, they had not wanted to draw notice on their way here.

"Welcome," she said, touching her breast in the salutation between equals. The gaze of Soren Cartagi followed that hand. "Be seated, pray. I've naught set out but wine and water, for your message asked I receive you on grave business. Gladly, though, will I call for better fare, and afterward have you be my guests at supper."

Taking the couch that faced her chair, Hannon Baltisi shook his craggy head. "I thank you, my lady, but best we not linger, the Speaker and me," he said. "Folk might wonder why, and this needs to be secret."

Soren joined his companion. For a moment, play of light tricked the eye, and Soren's hair and beard seemed as gray as Hannon's. As he settled down, they regained their darkness around his broad, beak-nosed visage. It was just the scattered white in them, more of it all the time. He and Lanarvilis regarded each other, forgetting that a third party was present, until she said slowly: "This concerns the King, does it not?"

"Who else?" Soren growled.

Her voice wavered a little. "What's wrong? I read trouble, anger on you, but—but he's done naught that he shouldn't." Flushing, compelling herself to look steadily into the faces, both the faces: "It happens he spent last night with me. After three years wedded to him, I'd have known if aught was awry. Did it touch the city, he'd have told me."

"What had he to say, then?" Soren asked impulsively.

The color mounted in her cheeks. "No affair of anyone else!" She regained self-possession; she had had much practice at that. "Oh, mainly small talk. We played a while with Julia, and he babbled about the latest wonderful thing Dahut has accomplished, and we went on to discuss his journey in autumn. Naught new. His plans remain the same that he set forth at the Solstice Council."

Hannon nodded. Tension gathered in his lank frame. At that meeting he had led the opposition to the King's proposal to make yet another circuit about western Armorica and down to Portus Namnetum, weaving tighter his web of alliances. Gratillonius had been far too much away, neglecting his sacral duties to the point of contumely before the Gods. In the end, a compromise had been reached. Gratillonius would go, but not until after the equinox, and he pledged himself to have returned by winter solstice.

Before Hannon could speak, Soren did: "I beg my lady's pardon. No intrusion—no discourtesy intended. The more so when we are here to seek your counsel and help."

Lanarvilis leaned back in her chair and let her hands lie quietly crossed on her lap. "Say on."

"'Tis this, this temple of his foreign God Mithras he means to build."
Soren choked and coughed.

"Why, I thought that was agreed on. Reluctantly by a number of
Suffetes, aye. But when we, the Gallicenae, having searched our hearts,
our books, and our dreams, could find naught forbidding it, as long
as he stays dutiful toward the Gods of Ys—"

"How long will that be? At the combat in the Wood—" Soren curbed
himself. "No matter that. 'Tis Lir Captain who bears the word today.
I simply came along to give my support, my own plea for yours. You
and I have worked together often over the years, Lanarvilis." He hunched
where he sat.

The older man's voice rolled forth as if once again he trod the deck
of a ship. His look commanded, too.

"Forgive me if I'm curt, my lady. You know 'tis my way.
"Ill did Grallon's wish strike me. Bad enough having a Christian
priest mewling amongst us again. The King can't help that, I give you,
and no true man or woman 'ull pay any heed. But this Mithras, now—well,
in my seafaring days I learned somewhat about Mithras. Mind you,
he's no bad God like yon Christ. He stands for uprightness, manliness,
and He'll let other Gods abide. But He is the Bullslayer, the Comrade
of the Sun. He sets Himself above the rest and lays a law of His own
on His worshippers. Remember how Grallon must needs refuse the
crown after he won Kingship. Not a great thing in itself, maybe, but
a sign of...what else?

"In storm, in fog, in dead calm and sea-blink through endless silences:
I have known the Dread of Lir, my lady. Ys lives on His sufferance.
No disrespect to Belisama or Taranis, nay, nay. We live by Them too.
But the Pact of Brennilis made Ys forever hostage to Lir, did it nay?"

Quietness deepened until the rainfall sounded torrential. Lanarvilis
nodded and signed herself. Soren knotted his fists.

"And Lir wears no human face," Hannon said.

After a heartbeat, he went on: "Well, Grallon aims to take a warehouse
down by the harbor, unused since trade went to hell ere we were
born, he'll take that and make it into a temple of Mithras. You remember
this was after the Council wouldn't let him buy land and dig a cave
out in the hinterland."

They could barely hear Lanarvilis: "The earth is Belisama's. And
Mithras will have no women devotees."

"Taranis makes fruitful the earth," rumbled from Soren.

"Therefore Grallon needs a house in town," Hannon said. "Now
that arrangement seemed to me just as wrong. What gave it Lir for
His honor, Lir Who's so quick to wrath?" He paused, filled his lungs,
stared past the Queen. "Well," he said, "people don't pray to Lir, you
know. We sacrifice, we obey, but He'll have none of our cries, none
of our tears. His sea is already salt enough.

"And yet—well, sometimes He does make His will known, 'stead of whelming those who go against it. He did for Brennilis, long ago. If now we're at the end of the Age she birthed, might He again? I went forth by myself, in a boat, beyond sight of land. I fasted, I thirsted, I held myself sleepless, till—"

He surged to his feet. "Nay, no vision, no voice, only a remembrance. But when I uttered it aloud, soon there came a breeze blowing me back home, and seals and dolphins gamboled all about under the moon."

He placed the big, scarred sailor's hands on his hips, stood astraddle next to the second servant of Taranis, looking down at the high priestess of Belisama, and said: "This is my simple thought. That Lir be honored, let the temple of Mithras also be hostage to Him. When the Romans built our wall, the waters didn't come so high as they do today. In the seaward towers are rooms which're below the waves, abandoned on that account. I've been to see, and one at the bottom of the Raven Tower would do fine. 'Twas never meant for more than a storage cellar; no windows. Dripping wet, but that can be fixed. 'Tis lower than anything he could dig ashore, so 'tis a cave, better than trickery with a warehouse. And—I met Mithras folk when I was young, abroad—the raven is a holy bird to them. What happier sign could Grallon ask for? Or we?"

Again silence, but for the rain. Air slithered, candle flames guttered.

"I see," Lanarvilis finally murmured. Her head was bowed; Soren could no longer read her face.

"You understand, don't you?" the Speaker asked eagerly. "If Gratillonius will accept this, every faction should be satisfied. We'll have interior peace, and peace with the Gods."

She lifted her glance to confront his. "You want my help," she said, flat-voiced, "because you know he is no fool. He'll know that means placing Mithras under Lir."

"Nay, not really. A gesture of respect, and should there not be respect between Gods? Lir gives Mithras this fine site. Mithras, in turn, acknowledges that Lir, that the Three are the patrons of Ys."

Soren leaned forward. Impetuously, he reached across the table between couch and chair. Blindly, Lanarvilis did likewise. Their hands met and clung. Hannon sat back down, folded his arms, rested like a reef outside Sena.

"You want me to...persuade the King," Lanarvilis said.

"First, we suppose, persuade your Sisters," replied Soren. "Make the Gallicenae work together on Gratillonius till he agrees."

"I expect we can," Lanarvilis said.

"You can do so much with him, you Nine," rushed from Soren. "The power that lies in women!"

She withdrew her hands, sat straight, and told him, "Most of that power comes from patience, Soren, from endurance."

He snatched a cup and half emptied it in a gulp, though the wine had not been watered.

Some thirty miles east of Ys lay the head of navigation on the River Odita. Thence the stream flowed south for about ten miles to the sea. These were birdflight distances; it was longer for a man, whether he went by land or water through the winding valleys of Armorica. There a Roman veteran had taken the lead in founding a colony, three hundred years ago. It was actually a little below the farthest north a ship could reach when tide was high; that point was just above the confluence of the Odita with the lesser Stegir. He chose the site because of its handiness to a Gallic settlement and hill fort on the heights behind. Those had long since been abandoned, leveled by man and nature until only traces remained. Houses and small farms replaced them, though for the most part Mons Ferruginus was unpeopled, a woodland through which a few trails wound.

The Roman named the colony Aquilo, from the Aquilonian district of Apuleia in Italy whence he hailed. Sufficiently inland not to fear surprise attack by pirates, it became a minor seaport. Here entered wares of metal and glass, olives, oil, textiles. Out went mainly products of the heavily forested hinterland, hides, furs, nuts, pigskin, preserved meat, tallow, honey, beeswax, timber—but also salt, beneficiated iron ore, preserved fish, garum sauce, and the marvelous things they wrought in gold, silver, ivory, shell, and fabric in Ys.

The fortunes of Aquilo waxed and waned with those of the Empire. However, its leadership stayed in the hands of the founder's descendants. These Apuleii intermarried with their Osismiic neighbors and folk of other cantons until by blood they were almost purely Armorican. In their lives they stayed Roman, even claiming that their ancestor had been kin to the famous writer. They sent their elder sons to be educated at such centers of learning as Durocotorum, Treverorum, and Lugdunum. Eventually they won elevation to senatorial rank. As such, they were no longer supposed to engage in trade; but they had ample relatives to serve as their agents while they devoted themselves to civic and—increasingly of recent decades—military affairs.

Gratillonius had passed through three years before, on his mission of keeping the western end of the peninsula quiescent while Maximus warred. Now, when he returned, Apuleius Vero made him heartily welcome. They had struck it off at once, in spite of the host being a devoted Christian.

After all, the centurion served Rome too; he had fascinating things to tell of the city in his charge; he was making possible a revival of commerce. For his part, Apuleius was well travelled, well read, experienced in the ways of the world. After his student days in the South he had dreamed of a public career, and begun by becoming a confidential amanuensis to the governor of Aquitania. But the death of his father laid on him the duty of coming back and taking over a post in which Gratillonius considered him wasted. Likely Apuleius would have agreed, save that Roman virtue and Christian piety both forbade him to complain against fate.

"You wish to strengthen further the ties between Ys and the Gauls?" he asked when they were alone. "Why? Not that the resumption of dealings hasn't profited everybody. It has, and nowhere more than in my poor Aquilo. However, the Empire is again tranquil, and the barbarians have drawn in their horns since that disaster the Scoti suffered. Can trade not grow of itself?"

He was a slender man in his mid-thirties, of medium height, dark-haired, straight-nosed, clean-shaven, with large hazel eyes whose near-sightedness caused him to wear an appearance of intense concentration. Somehow he seemed to Gratillonius more Hellenic than Roman, perhaps because in his quiet fashion he took pride in a bloodline going back to Magna Graecia. As the man sat, his wife Rovinda came softly in and replenished the wine and nuts they had been enjoying. She was young, comely, the daughter of an Osismiic headman. Since their marriage two years ago, Apuleius had been teaching her the manners of a senatorial matron; but she had never lacked inborn gentility. They had a single child thus far, a girl, and another swelled within her.

Gratillonius weighed his reply. He had rehearsed it in his mind, for he would need it repeatedly, but this was the first time.

"I'm afraid that tranquility is only on the surface, and can't last much longer," he said. "You've heard of the Priscillianist business last year?"

Apuleius grimaced. "Ugly, from what little I know. Unworthy of the Faith. But it's behind us now, praise God. Isn't it?"

"I'm not sure." Gratillonius frowned into a lampflame. The floor of the house was warm from a hypocaust, but the air kept a chill, and outside the shuttered windows an autumn wind wuthered. "The church stays divided, and it and the Empire are woven together. Maximus accuses Valentinianus of heresy. It may be just a pretext. But what a dangerous pretext! No, I don't think we've seen the end of civil war."

"God help us," Apuleius said sorrowfully. "But what can we do, you and I? We're nothing but minor officers of the state. How can you bypass the Duke of the Armorican Tract?"

Gratillonius smiled. "You think I might take too much on myself? Well, I am the prefect of Rome, not of Maximus Augustus but of Rome, in Ys, which is not a province but a sovereign ally and has made me its King. I read that as meaning I've got discretion to act in the public interest as I see it, and answer for my actions afterward...to the proper authority."

"That would be the Duke, wouldn't it? How will he feel about you making his policies for him?"

"I may be cocky, Apuleius, but I'm not crazy. I wrote and got his leave to, m-m, 'do what seems best to develop further those good relations between Ys and the Roman communities on which a start has lately been made.' The Duke's no dunderhead either. He recognizes the facts, no matter how he has to gloss them over. First, he's necessarily most concerned with the eastern and inland parts of the peninsula. I can do in the west what he cannot, and he knows it. Second, he never was happy about Maximus's rebellion. He hinted pretty strongly, in writing to me, that my aims please him."

"I see....But what are they?"

"This: that western Armorica, and as much else of it as I can reach, not get embroiled in any new fighting. That we refuse demands on us to come help kill our fellow Romans, in anybody's cause."

"Which means the cause of Maximus, you know."

Gratillonius nodded. "I think, if we do stand together in this resolution, I think he'll know better than to order us to break it. Later, if he prevails—well, at least we Armoricans will be strong enough to have some say in what happens to us. And he might not prevail."

"Valentinianus is weak," Apuleius mused, "but if Theodosius should take a hand—"

A tingle went through Gratillonius. "It could be. Who knows? In which case Armorica might expect quite favorable treatment. A daydream, maybe. I don't tell myself any nursery tales about us making the difference in what happens. I just think our chances will be better, and Rome will be better served, if Armorica looks after its own, unitedly."

"Under Ysan leadership."

Gratillonius shrugged. "Who else is taking the initiative? Besides, Ys is the natural leader of this whole region." He grew earnest. "Believe me, though—I give you my word of honor—I've no ambitions for myself."

Inwardly, fugitively, he wondered. The world groaned in its need for a man who could set things right. Why could nobody else see what must be done? It was so simple. Government firm, just, obedient to its own laws; military reforms and the taming of the barbarians; honest currency; reduction of taxes, of every burden that was destroying the productive classes; liberation of the individual man from bondage to the estate to which he was born; religious toleration—nothing else, really, than what he had hoped Maximus would enact.

But Gratillonius had no legions to hail him Emperor. He would do well if he could save Ys for Mithras and Dahut. If he was very fortunate, he might save Armorica. Give him that and he would lie down contentedly on his deathbed, knowing he had been a good son of Rome.

Apuleius considered him a while before saying, "I think I'll believe you. To be frank, I also think you talk too vauntingly. What do you and I really know—"a hint of bitterness—"in these backwaters where we sit?"

"I've been out," Gratillonius replied. "Last year, for months, over much of Gallia. I spoke with men as various as Maximus himself in Treverorum and Ausonius—well, an old, learned man in Burdigala."

339

Apuleius sat straight. "What?" he exclaimed. "Ausonius? Why, I studied under him. How is he?"

Gratillonius gladly let conversation go in that direction. Apuleius's admiration for Ausonius was not unalloyed. Arriving in Burdigala while Julianus the Apostate still reigned, himself at the vulnerable, combative age of twelve, he had—as he wryly admitted—changed from an indifferent to a prayerful Christian largely in reaction against the coolness or outright paganism he encountered everywhere around him. Ausonius, he felt, was a man of antiquity, born out of his time, who accepted Christ with the same impersonal politeness he would earlier have accorded Jupiter. And yet, and yet, Ausonius had such riches to give....

The evening ended a trifle drunkenly and altogether cheerily.

~ 3 ~

Morning was lucent. Gratillonius made it an excuse for staying another day. He would take advantage of the weather to do what he had not had time to do on his previous visit, ride around the countryside and get a little familiarity with it—for purposes of military planning if that need should arise, he told Apuleius.

His host smiled, and declined to accompany him. Apuleius was no outdoorsman. He kept fit with methodical exercises, as a duty, but gave his leisure to his books, correspondence, religious observances, family, and whatever intelligent conversation came his way. He offered to assign Gratillonius a guide, but the latter refused in his turn and rode off alone.

The fact was that he wanted solitude, as a man does now and then. It was hard to find when he must always be either the King of Ys, the prefect of Rome, or a centurion of the Second. Therefore he likewise left behind the legionaries who were escorting him, to take their ease with the Aquilo garrison. This consisted of some infantry recruited mostly among the local Osismii and a few horsemen. Younger men of the civil population formed a reserve that would augment it in times of emergency. The Duke had never felt that more strength was needed here. True, pirates often ravaged the estuary—a few years ago they wrecked the lovely villa of the Pulcher family—and occasionally rowed upstream; but to date they had always been driven off short of the city. Ruinous though Vorgium was, the main force in these parts continued to be stationed there.

Gratillonius was soon out of Aquilo. On the left bank of the Odita, it amounted to a few hundred homes—cob, timber, brick, the elegant but small town house of the Apuleii—together with such establishments as a church, a smithy, a marketplace, and a couple of warehouses down by the harbor. Smoke seeped from thatch roofs or curled out of holes in tile coverings; wives went about their tasks with pauses to gossip; wheels creaked; an anvil rang. This late in the year, no merchant vessels

340

lay docked, and Gratillonius did not go out that gate and over the bridge to the west. Instead, he took the eastern portal. The walls around the city were of the old Gallic sort, earth over interlocked logs reinforced with rubble, wooden blockhouses at the corners.

On his right, as he followed a dirt road upstream, was a narrow strip of lowland, behind which rose that long, high hill called Mons Ferruginus. Dwellings dotted it, well-nigh lost to view among the reds, bronzes, golds of autumnal woods. Most migratory birds had departed but heaven was bewinged by crows, sparrows, robins, a falcon afar.

After a short distance, he saw the lesser Stegir flow from the north and join the Odita on the opposite side. Past that was a bridge to cross, whose planks boomed underhoof. On the farther shore the land rolled gently. He left behind him the Odita, which here ran from the east before it bent south, and took a rutted road paralleling the Stegir. It led him through cultivated land, the estate of the Apulcii. He saw the cottages of three tenant families. Beyond them he passed the manor house. Its owner used it mostly as a retreat. Sere weeds and brambles filled much former plowland, with saplings as outrunners of the wildwood in the offing. Lack of markets, lack of labor—how much of this had he come upon!

His spirits revived after the road, becoming scarcely more than a path, took him into the forest. That began about where the channel of the Stegir shifted west. It walled in the farmland on two sides. Mainly it was oak, though beech, maple, ash, and other trees made it at this season a storm of color. There was scant underbrush; deer kept that down, as well as the swine that boys herded. The ground was a softness of soil and old leaves, with fallen boles on which moss grew smaragdine. Squirrels frisked about, small red meteors. Vision faded off into sun-spattered shadows. The air was cool, moist, smelling like mushrooms.

He rode on for a timeless time, letting his thoughts drift. And then, abruptly, a stag stepped into view ahead of him, a glorious beast with a mighty rack of antlers. He reined in. It stopped and stared down the path at him. He had brought a bow along in case of such luck. His hand stole down to unsling it, take an arrow, nock, aim. The stag bounded off. The shaft missed. "Harroo!" Gratillonius shouted, and urged his mount into gallop.

A while the chase thundered over the ruts. Gratillonius's big gelding narrowed the gap. The stag veered and went off among the trees. Gratillonius followed.

Of course it was in vain. He dared not keep on at full unheeding speed where a root or a burrow might cause his horse to snap a leg. The quarry soared now right, now left, until presently the splendid sight glimmered away. Gratillonius halted and swore. His mount whickered, breathed hard, stood sweating.

341

The man's oath was good-natured. He hadn't really expected to take the prey. The challenge had merely been irresistible, and he'd gotten a grand run. Best he return to his route. He wanted to reach cleared country on the far side of the woods and survey it before he must start back.

He had ridden for a spell when it came to him that he should already have been on the road. How could he have missed it? Every direction looked the same, and a haze had drawn over the sky to obscure the sun. What he sought was no spear-straight Roman highway but a track that twisted to and fro like the ancient game trail that doubtless underlay it. He could cast about for hours, randomly seeking a random goal.

He swore with more feeling. The anger was at himself. He had imagined that in the past few years he had learned to control a quick temper, an impulsiveness, that used to get him into unnecessary embroilments. Well, apparently that thing was not dead in him; it had been lying low, biding its chance to spring forth.

"Gone astray, lured off by a deer, like a chieftain in a folk tale," he muttered. "I'll never hear the end of this."

To be sure, if he could get back before dark, he needn't confess.... When he studied the sky carefully, bearing in mind the time of day and year, he established which way was south. The Stegir was certain to be somewhere yonder. Having reached it, he could follow it till it met the Odita.

The quest proved long. The forest floor was only partly clear. Often he must work through or around brush, logs, or pools. When at last he found the stream, the going along it was no better.

The sun went out of sight. Murk and chill welled from the earth. He realized that night would overtake him. To struggle on would be foolhardy. Best he halt soon and make himself as little uncomfortable as possible while he waited for dawn. He had taken with him just a piece of bread and cheese, long since eaten. His belly growled.

The Stegir gurgled around a thicket. Having passed this, he suddenly came upon a hut. A trail, narrow but clear, went thence, doubtless toward the road. Gladness jumped within him. He would still have to spend the night, but here was shelter, and a quick journey come morning. He drew rein and dismounted. His horse's head drooped, as exhausted as the poor beast was.

The hut was tiny, a cylinder of wicker and clay, moss-chinked, under a conical thatch roof. A hide hung from a stick in place of a proper door. He had seen better housing among the Picti. However, the oak whose boughs arched above was magnificent. "Hail," he called. "Is anybody home?" The gloomy depths around blotted up his voice.

The hide crackled aside and a man stepped out. He was tall, powerfully built in spite of gauntness. A crag of nose and headland of chin jutted from a long, hollow-cheeked face; the black eyes were set deep

342

under shaggy brows; the stiff black hair and beard, roughly haggled, were shot with white. He wore a coarse linsey-woolsey robe, belted with a rope. The bare feet were callused and begrimed. Clearly he had not bathed at any recent time, if ever, although an outdoor life made his odor pungent, a bit smoky, rather than sour.

"Peace be with you," he said in Latin. His voice was rather harsh. "Are you lost?" He smiled, showing large teeth. "You seem to be a stranger to these parts, and at this hour I doubt you've come for counsel."

"I am Gratillonius, a soldier, and I have certainly missed my way. Is Aquilo very far?"

"No, but too much for you to reach before nightfall, my son. May I offer you my humble hospitality? I am Corentinus, a hermit." The man looked up between boughs to gray-purple heaven, sniffed the air, and nodded. "We'll have rain in a while. At least my roof is tight."

"Thank you." Gratillonius hesitated. He didn't want to impose on poverty. "Could I, in return, help or—or make a donation?"

"You may make an offering to the Church if you wish. I myself have no needs that God and these two hands cannot fill." Corentinus regarded him. "You must be famished. It's not my habit to eat more than once a day, but I'll prepare you something and—" the laugh rang— "he would be a rude host who didn't share with his guest."

Gratillonius led his horse to drink, unsaddled and rubbed it down, tethered it nearby to graze on some herbage that kept a few withered leaves. Meanwhile he cast mind back over what he knew about hermits. That was hearsay. A practice, said to have originated in Egypt, was spreading northward through Europe, devout Christians going off to be alone with their God, away from the temptations of the world and even the distractions of the Church. Believers, including otherwise pagan countryfolk, often sought out such holy men, who must surely have wisdom and powers beyond the ordinary.

This Corentinus didn't seem quite to fit the picture. If nothing else, he looked too robust; and he must once have been fairly well educated.

Turning from his chores, Gratillonius saw him, robe hiked over knobbly knees, squatting in the burn. Its iciness made no visible difference to him. He murmured—a prayer?—and reached underwater. After a moment he rose. A large trout lay in his hands. Lay! Eeriness touched Gratillonius. The fish was alive; its sheen in the fading light showed it to be healthy; but it did not flop, and it had come straight into that grasp.

"God provides, you see," said Corentinus calmly. He waded ashore and went into his hut. Half stunned, Gratillonius followed. The interior was dark, save for a small, banked fire on the dirt floor, which gave just enough light to work by if you knew where everything was. Corentinus took a knife that rested on a slab with a few other objects. "Be you blessed, little brother," he said, "and be God thanked for His manifold mercies."

With a deft motion he sliced the flesh from one side of the trout and tossed the piece down. Gratillonius sucked in a breath of astounded outrage. He had never condoned cruelty to animals, and this was wanton. Yet the fish only waved its tail. Before Gratillonius could speak, Corentinus had gone back out. Gratillonius came after, automatically. The hermit cast the half filleted creature into the stream and signed the air with the Cross. Gratillonius gasped again. The trout was swimming off as if unharmed—and was it in fact whole, healed?

He grew aware that Corentinus had laid a hand on his shoulder and was speaking in a low tone: "Fear not, my son. What you beheld is no sorcery. It happens daily, unless I am fasting. Thus God keeps me fed. Why He should vouchsafe such grace to me, a wretched sinner, I know not, but He surely has His purpose. Now let's go settle ourselves and talk. You look like a man with good stories in him, and I must admit that in my weakness I can grow weary of seeing nobody except an occasional rustic."

Gratillonius mustered will. He had witnessed things stranger than this, in and around Ys, and some of them had been malignant, whereas Corentinus seemed wholly benign. "Remarkable," he heard himself say.

"A miracle." Corentinus waved. "And yet is not all Creation a miracle? Look around you, my son, and think." He led the way inside and urged his guest to take the stool that was his single item of furniture.

In quite everyday fashion he laid the piece of fish across a mesh of green twigs and hunkered down to roast it above the coals. "It's better baked," he said, "but as hungry as you must be, I won't make you wait for that. You'll find hardtack in yonder box. Dried peas and things too, but, again, I don't want you to endure the time it would take to cook them. No wine or ale available, I fear." He grinned. "Who dines with a hermit must take short commons."

"You are...very kind." The fire, poked up into sputtering flames, picked sights out of shadow. He saw a towel, a spare robe, a blanket hung from pegs in the sooty wall. No bed. Well, he had his horse blanket and cloak, with the saddle for a pillow. The implements he glimpsed were of the crudest, except for that excellent sharp knife. (Corentinus must not want his wondrous fish to feel pain at being carved.) A stone pot, an earthen jug, a grass basket, a couple of wooden bowls and spoons— No, wait. As far as possible from the hearth was a second slab. Upon it, wrapped in fine linen, rested what Gratillonius recognized as book, doubtless a Christian Gospel.

Through the smoke-tang he began to smell cooking meat. His mouth watered. Corentinus looked across at him and grinned anew. Highlights traced the big bones of his face, ruddy amidst murk, and the whiteness of his teeth. "Brace up, lad," he said. "We'll soon have some cargo down your hatch." The Latin had turned accented and ungrammatical, commoner speech.

"How long have you lived here?" the centurion asked.

Corentinus shrugged. "Time ceases to have meaning after a few seasons of seeking eternity." Again he talked like a schooled man. "Umm ...five years?"

"I hadn't heard of you, though I visited Aquilo three years ago."

"Why should you? I'm nobody. You must be far more interesting, Gratillonius."

"What, when you can do magic like this?"

Corentinus scowled. "Please! I said it is no sorcery, no pagan trick. *I* don't do the thing. When I had first fled my sinfulness, an angel of the Lord appeared to me in a dream and told me of the divine favor I was given. I didn't know what it meant, I was bewildered and frightened. After all, the Devil had come in the same guise, no, in the guise of the very Christ, to my holy father Martinus, and tried to deceive him." His tone softened. "Oh, I had to rally my nerve, I can tell you. But what could I do except obey? And behold, my little brother swam quietly into my hands, just as you saw; and I understood that God's mercy is infinite."

Gratillonius wrestled with his honor and lost. He cleared his throat. "I'd better be frank with you," he said. "I'm no Christian myself."

"Oh?" Corentinus seemed no more than mildly surprised. "You, an officer who goes around on what must be important missions?"

"Well, I— All right, sir. I follow the Lord Mithras."

Corentinus looked long at him. "It's well for you that you didn't dissemble, my son. I don't matter, but God doesn't like false pretenses."

"No. My God doesn't...either."

"You may wish to reconsider, after what you've seen this evening."

Gratillonius shook his head. "I don't deny your God has powers. But I will not deny mine."

Corentinus nodded. "I'd begun to suspect you were not of the Faith. Your behavior, your stance, everything. I knocked around in the world before coming here."

"If you don't want me under your roof, I'll go."

"Oh, no, no!" Corentinus raised his free hand. "God forbid! You're a guest. A most welcome one, I might add." He smiled a bit wistfully. "I've no hopes of converting you in a single night, and know better than to try. Let's just swap yarns. But...you spoke of making me some return for hospitality. If you really mean it, then what you shall do is think. Look around you at God's world and ask yourself how it could have come to be and what this life of ours is all about. Think." He paused. "No, I'll not ask that you pray for guidance. You couldn't, if you're as true a worshipper of Mithras as you seem to be. I do ask that you open your mind. Listen. Think."

After a brief silence: "Well, I believe supper is ready; and you haven't yet gotten out the flatbread!"

He insisted Gratillonius take nearly the whole of the food. His share was only a token of friendliness. There was nothing but water to drink.

Regardless, the two men soon fell into talk that lasted through the rain till the sunrise.

Corentinus took fire at what Gratillonius told about Ys. He had been there once, as a crewman on one of the few outside ships that called; he had toured its wonders and, he admitted without breast-beating, its resorts of sin. That Ys was coming back into the Roman sphere struck him as a happy portent.

Indeed, despite his isolation, he was astonishingly well informed. Mention of Priscillianus grieved but did not surprise him; he had known. It turned out that he still got occasional letters from his mentor Martinus.

As for his past, he was the son of a Britannic immigrant to Osismia, born on the fundus of a well-to-do, thoroughly Romanized family. There he received a good basic schooling, though he was more interested in ranging the woodlands or galloping the horses. (He and Gratillonius found kindred memories to chuckle at.) But meanwhile his father's fortune was declining: between the general ill health of commerce, the depredations of the barbarians, and the grinding down of the curials. (Now the two could be grim together.) At the age of fifteen, Corentinus got out from under the ruin and went off on his own. Through what connections remained to him he obtained a berth on a ship, the law being winked at, and spent the next several years as a sailor, a rough man in a rough life.

Finally a storm blew his vessel so far out to sea that the crew despaired of winning back. Most perished miserably in the attempt, in spite of forgetting whatever Christianity was theirs and making horrid sacrifices to other Gods. Corentinus saw visions in his delirium. When at last he reached the Liger mouth, once he had regained strength he made his way to Pictavum, where Martinus then was, Martinus of whom Corentinus had never heard from any human mouth.

This man gave him instruction while he settled into the monastic community. Its books added to his learning. In time he grew restless, and was delighted to accompany Martinus when the latter went to Turonum; to take baptism at the hands of Martinus after Martinus became the bishop; to aid in the effort to evangelize the countryside—until he fell from grace with a heathen woman. Aghast at himself, he asked leave to seek forgiveness through penance, and returned to Osismia to become an anchorite. There it was revealed that, despite everything, God had not cast him off.

—Gratillonius re-entered Aquilo full of thought.

~ 4 ~

As closely as it followed winter solstice, the Birthday of Mithras at Ys gave a glimmer of daylight, barely more than six hours, in a cavern of night. Before sunrise, walls on either side made the pomoerium brim with darkness. Air was bitterly cold. Beyond the rampart growled

346

the sea, and above it skirled the wind. Yet Gratillonius dared hope he saw a good omen in the stars flickering overhead.

Lanterns bobbed, brought faces half out of shadow, made grotesqueries flutter across stone. Buskins clicked, raiment rustled, men kept mute as he led his procession up the stairway. The Raven Tower bulked foursquare out into the surf, its battlements like shields raised against heaven. Sentries, who had been told what to expect, saluted and stepped aside. Lantern-glimmer showed awe on one countenance, misgiving on another, stiffness on the third and fourth. The door stood open. Gratillonius and his followers entered the turret. A stairwell gaped before them. They mounted, came forth on top, looked across the parapet to the dawn.

It whitened above inland hills, turned their ridges hoar, crept down the valley, while stars went out. The towers of Ys caught it in a flash of copper, gold, and glass. The roofs of Ys rose from murk like whales from the sea. Beyond them Point Vanis reared and brightened. Closer by, Cape Rach thrust ruggedly forth. Shifting illumination made it seem as if the old dead were stealing back to their sleep in the necropolis. The pharos smoked briefly—its keeper had snuffed the flame—then gleamed of itself. Ocean sheened, wrinkled, spouted off reefs, out to Sena and on across the curve of the world. Drifts of kelp darkened it here and there; seals tumbled about in the waves.

There were a few minutes to wait. Men stood contemplative or talked in low voices. Gratillonius and his father drew aside, until they looked down on the finger of sea that reached between headland and city wall, cast toward Aurochs Gate. Thus confined, the water dashed noisily against stone and a strip of beach. Gloom still dwelt in that gap, but glints went like fire.

"The moment draws near," said Marcus Valerius Gratillonius.

"At last," answered Gaius his son.

Marcus smiled one-sidedly. "I never believed those historians who put ringing periods in the mouths of leaders when a great event is about to happen. Real people mumbled words worn smooth of meaning."

"Well, we can keep silence." Gaius's gaze strayed west toward the seals and Sena. Did the shade of Dahilis really linger somewhere yonder? Did she watch him now?

Marcus summoned resolution. "Except for this. It's not too late to turn back. Not quite."

Gaius sighed. "It always was. I'm sorry, father."

Since a delegation of Ysan marines, and the legionary Cynan for spokesman, sought him out at the villa in Britannia this past summer and brought him here in the royal yacht, Marcus had questioned the wisdom of establishing a Mithraeum—so lavish, too—in this of all cities. True, the King had overcome opposition, but he had not quelled it in many hearts, and those were only the hearts of men.

Nonetheless Marcus had accepted the instruction and ultimately the consecration that raised him to Runner of the Sun. How strange it felt to Gaius, to be the guiding Father over this man who had brought him into being.

"I understand," Marcus said, almost meekly. He had aged much in the past few years. "Forget my croakings. We'll build Him His fortress."

On the frontier of the night—Day was advancing.

"Good for you, sir!" Gaius blurted.

Marcus plucked at the sleeve of the hierophantic robe. "Afterward we'll have time for ourselves, won't we?" he whispered.

Gaius squeezed the bowed shoulder. "Of course. I promise."

Between royal and Roman duties, the King had had small opportunity thus far to be with his palace guest, and then it had mostly gone to preparing the latter for his role this morning. Fortunately, Marcus had been glad to explore the city and enjoy his grandchildren, Dahut the foremost.

Come spring, he must return home, lest that home crumble from the hands of the family. He and his son did not suppose they would ever meet again. But first they could lighten the Black Months for each other. That was why Gaius had sent for Marcus.

He could more readily have elevated somebody else. Soon he must do so. By issuing invitations during the year, he had gained a congregation for the hallowing of his temple: three Ravens, two Occults, a Lion, two Persians. Additionally, he had seen Cynan through to the rank of Soldier, Verica and Maclavius to Lion. That was all he had.

Light flared. The sun rose over the hills. Gaius Valerius Gratillonius led his men in hymn and prayer.

Before they went below, he raised a hand in salute to Point Vanis, where rested the bones of Eppillus.

Candles in holders of gilt bronze waited inside the tower. With these the party descended. The uppermost room was a watchpost and rain shelter, the next pair were given over to storage. Farther on they echoed empty; those times were past when treasures of Ys had overflowed into them. Walls sweated, air grew dank, flames streamed smoky, as the stairs went down below the surf.

Finally came a space refurbished. Hidden ducts ventilated the fires of a hypocaust that kept it warm and dry. Statues of the Torchbearers flanked a doorway. A mosaic floor in black and white showed emblems of the first three degrees in the Mysteries. On plastered walls glowed frescoes of the tree that nourished infant Mithras and of His reconciliation with the Sun. Benches stood beneath, and a table bearing food, drink, and utensils for the sacred meal. A new wall with its own door shut off the sanctum. With holy water sprinkled off pine boughs, with the incense of pinecones, with wine and honey upon each tongue, the Gratillonii led the dedication.

348

Thereafter it was time to go back above and hymn the noonday sun. It glimmered wan, low in the south. Clouds were gathering, wind shrilled, seas ran white-crested.

The men returned to the Cave of Mithras. Only Father, Runner, Persians, and Lions passed through to the sanctuary; the rest had their lesser devotions to perform in the pronaos.

The King of Ys could well honor the God from the East. Here the Dadophori were sculptured again, in their faces, eyes, postures something not quite Greek or Roman, fluid and sleek, like a wave or a seal. Lion-headed Time stood stern in His own marble, serpent-enwrapped. The font was the carven calyx of a flower. The four emblems in the floor led the gaze onward, past benches above which glistened symbols of the planets, to the twin altars at the far end, where Mithras arose from the Rock, and to the high relief of the Bullslaying that filled yonder wall. The ceiling was deep blue, with golden stars. Candles stood ready in sconces, lamps in niches, to give brightness once they were lit. Soon here, too, resin sweetened the air, along with incense.

Pater and Heliodromos trod forward. Together they led the rites.

Afterward came the Sacrifice, for all initiates. On this unique occasion it began with blood. Cynan, having been duly purified, brought in a caged dove which he had gone to fetch in the course of exercises outside. Marcus Gratillonius took it forth and held it tight while Gaius cut its head off with a clean slash and let it bleed into a golden bowl. Cynan bore this and the remains into the pronaos. Tomorrow he, the Occults, and the Ravens would immolate them. Meanwhile the Gratillonii enacted the subjugation and coronation of the Sun by Mithras.

Finally they officiated over the divine meal which the lower ranks served the higher, a foretaste of the soul's ascent after death. Upon this great occasion it was fare less frugal than customary: beef, subtle seasonings on the vegetables, honeycakes, the best of wines drunk from silver cups. When it was finished, Gaius Valerius Gratillonius gave benediction, and the men departed for the upper earth.

Weather hid the sunset. Nevertheless they said their prayers atop the Raven Tower before they bade one another farewell.

Gratillonius made his voice hearty as he did. Inwardly there remained a wistfulness. He had seen the Spirit enter certain of the worshippers; from Cynan it had fairly flamed. Nothing had touched him akin to the divine fire that lighted his consecration.

Or had it? The God revealed Himself in forms as infinitely various as the forms and signs of love. Was the feeling of completion, of rightness, that Gratillonius did have—was it Mithra's "Well done" to His soldier, while also reminding him that the establishment of a lonely outpost was not in itself any victory?

Night fell upon son and father as they made their way back to the palace. Wind yelled, drove rain and scud before it, filled streets with chill. Under the sea wall, tide ramped and snarled.

VIII

~ 1 ~

The equinoctial gales blew out of Ocean like longings, to wake the soul from winter drowse. When a milder air had borne Marcus off, Gaius Gratillonius felt a redoubled need to be away himself, in action. Luckily—perhaps—there was a call upon him that neither Gallicenae nor Suffetes could deny was urgent. A letter from Maximus had scathingly denounced him for founding a new temple of Antichrist; it had been inevitable that word of that would eventually reach Treverorum. Were it not for pressing demands on his attention, the Augustus wrote, he would recall his prefect, occupy Ys, and extirpate demon worship. As it was, he must content himself with requiring the prompt installation of a new Christian pastor.

The centurion had an idea of what those demands were. Indeed he had better mend fences, both temporal and ghostly. Writing to the Duke of the Armorican Tract, he requested a conference. The reply was that that high official would be in Caesarodunum Turonum for the next several months, and receive him there. It was the civil if not military capital of Lugdunensis Tertia; the Duke doubtless had fence mending of his own to do.

With a few soldiers at his back, all mounted, Gratillonius set forth. He allowed himself and them two days' rest at Aquilo. Otherwise they pushed hard, down to Portus Namnetum and up the Liger valley.

That was lovely country, freshly green and blossomful. Riding through, he felt cheer reborn in him. Why yearn for the barracks in Britannia or hope for a precarious prominence in the Empire? Ys was his home. Its people had become his people. He could see his work on their behalf grow beneath his hands. If he could have no woman besides his Queens, weren't they sufficient and then some? If none of them could bear him a son, did he not have Dahut? The little darling was so bright, so headstrong. She might very well grow up to be another Semiramis, Dido, Cartimandua, Zenobia, but happier fated; her father would lay the foundation for that! And, of course, his other daughters were sweet.

Danger prowled around Ys, but so it did everywhere in the world. As Quinipilis was fond of saying, to borrow trouble was stupid, considering the interest rate on it.

Crossing a bridge from the military highway to the left bank, his party passed through the gate of Turonum and found quarters. He was both relieved and perturbed to discover that the civil governor was absent, summoned to the Emperor along with his counterparts throughout Gallia. At least now he could confer straightforwardly with the Duke.

They got along well at their first meeting. It was privately agreed that neither would send forces to any internecine conflict. They would explain that defense against the barbarians must take precedence. It was true.

As for Gratillonius's need of a clergyman, the Duke recommended him to Bishop Martinus. "He comes into town once a week, usually, from that monastery of his, to lead services at the main church. M-m-m, I know what you are, but it'd be wise of you to attend them then."

Always scout ahead if you can. Gratillonius went for a preliminary look, and was shocked. The church was larger than most, and rather handsome for a building erected in recent decades. However, it was filled with madmen—the sick of mind and feeble of mind, ragged, filthy, some roaring, some shivering, some posturing, some taking attitudes absurd or obscene, while mutters went through the dimness. "San, san, san...I am Jupiter, but they have me locked in hell.... Fintharingly and no, no..."

A deacon explained upon being asked that this was at the order of the bishop. Elsewhere energumens, as such persons were called, wandered starveling, shunned for fear of the demons supposed to possess them, when they were not whipped off with curses, beaten, tormented, sometimes raped or killed. Martinus decreed that they be fed and sheltered in the house of God. Each Sunday he came in among them, clad in sackcloth and smeared with ashes; he lay full length on the floor in their midst, and hour after hour implored mercy for them or wrestled with the Fiend who afflicted them. His touch and his prayers had seemingly freed a number to return to the human world. The rest adored him in their various weird fashions.

Gratillonius thought of his Gallicenae. They too, Innilis especially, had had a measure of luck in coping with insanity. But when they failed, the law of Ys was that the sufferers must be expelled. "It's well done of the bishop," he said.

"Oh, his is a loving soul, sir, underneath the strictness," replied the deacon. "He served in the army, did you know? Conscripted, and spent twenty-five years before he could have the baptism he longed for, but never did his charity falter. When he was stationed at Samarobriva, I've heard—not from him—how one freezing day he saw a near-naked beggar. He'd already given away most of what clothes he had, but he drew sword, cut his cloak across, and let this man have half. No wonder he has power to heal. Of course, he had been a military physician."

Gratillonius decided it would be politic to absent himself until Sunday. Besides, the idea of a man groveling among the crazy repelled him. He hired a boat and went fishing.

On the Lord's day, after sunrise prayers to his own Lord, he was early at the church. This would be far from the first Christian ceremony he had watched, but he wanted to observe everything he could. The energumens were gently but firmly guided out onto the porch, where a couple of priests with the rank of exorcist took them in charge. Trained by now, they gave no trouble. Meanwhile the interior was cleaned and made ready. The congregation arrived piecemeal. A comparative few went inside, most of them middle-aged or elderly, the baptized. Catechumens occupied the porch; of these, a majority were women. There was no objection to those excommunicated for sin or to unbelievers like Gratillonius, if they behaved themselves. Who knew but what the scales might fall from their eyes?

Solemnly, the bishop led his priests and deacons in. Martinus had changed little in a year and a half, save that he was freshly barbered, his sallow face smooth aside from the many furrows, his hair standing white—unkempt still—behind the ear-to-ear frontal tonsure which made his brow seem cliff-high. He wore the same slavelike garb, and went barefoot. His attendants were as humbly clad, and for the most part equally gaunt.

Folk knelt while the ordained led a prayer. There followed a reading from the Prophets. "—*Shall not the land tremble for this, and those who dwell in it mourn, while it rises up like a flood of Egypt and is cast back and drowned?*—" The people joined in singing a short response: "—*Glory unto God omnipotent*—" Standing, they heard the bishop read from an Epistle: "—*The natural man does not receive what the Spirit of God teaches; to him this is foolishness; he cannot know it, because it is only knowable by the spirit*—" A choir sang a psalm. Martinus preached the Gospel. He was no orator. In terse soldierly words, he discoursed on the centurion whose servant Jesus had healed. "—*Lord, I am not worthy for You to come under my roof*—" Gratillonius wondered about that text. For all his devotions and meditations, yonder fellow kept uncommonly aware of what went on around him.

"Silence," enjoined a deacon. While bishop and priests prayed, the offerings of the faithful were brought forth in processional, goods and money. Some were earmarked—for the poor, the ill, a family member in need—and the deacon read aloud the names of those beneficiaries, and Martinus included them in his prayer.

It was the dismissal. Those in the porch left at its end. The doors behind them drew shut. What came next was the Communion service, for the baptized only. Well, Gratillonius thought, we bar our lower ranks from the highest Mysteries of Mithras.

He sought an exorcist, who was helping shepherd the energumens. "I have to see the bishop," he said, and gave his name. "Will you tell him? I'll be at the Imperial hostel."

352

"He receives supplicants—"

"No, this has to be a private talk. Tell him it's with the King of Ys."

The priest gaped and gulped. However, the man before him, big, healthy, well clad, was not obviously a lunatic. To be sure, standing aside as a spectator, he had revealed himself a pagan. But Martinus dealt with many a heathen chieftain in the hinterland. "I can't approach him for some hours yet, sir, not till he's finished his church business, and afterward his charities and austerities. Expect word about sunset."

Briefly, Gratillonius bristled; then he eased off and laughed. Maybe Martinus washed the feet of the poor, but be damned if he toadied to the mighty!

The message that evening, carried by an awestruck boy who had memorized it, was: "The bishop will return to the monastery immediately after worship tomorrow sunrise. He will be glad to meet you at the western city gate and have you accompany him. It will be afoot."

—On this side of the river, the road was unpaved. Rain had fallen during the night, and morning was cold and damp, though warming as the sun climbed. Mist smoked above the water. Dew glittered on grass and young leaves. The hills reached silvery with it. Birds twittered; high and high, a lark chanted its *"hi-hi-hi."* Few people were abroad. While Martinus needed a staff, he strode along without asking Gratillonius to slow down. A few monks who had come with him followed at a respectful distance.

For a time conversation went lively between the leaders. Martinus was ardent to learn everything Gratillonius had done, seen, heard, planned, since their last encounter. But when talk turned to the future, his mood darkened.

"—And so I've got to have a minister of your faith for Ys, soon," Gratillonius finished. "Please don't look on it as a political move. I am what I am. From your viewpoint, too, wouldn't it be best we get a reasonable man like old Eucherius?"

Martinus peered afar. Somehow his thin, snubnosed countenance came to resemble a Caesar's. "God rest Eucherius." His tone was steely. "From what I've heard, he did his pious best. He was weak, though. We require an evangelist there, who will take up arms against Satan."

"But not one who'll, well, antagonize the city. How would that help your cause? Give me somebody I can work with."

"Despite your own paganism." Martinus gentled. "Oh I understand. Yours is a sore dilemma."

"Never mind me. I'm thinking of Ys. And Rome. What good will it do Rome if your man provokes the people into throwing him out? Maximus would— Well, remember what the Priscillianus business cost."

Martinus's knuckles whitened above his staff. "I can never forget," he said low.

Presently: "Let me confess to you." He wrenched the words out. "For we must indeed try to understand each other, you and I, for the sake of the souls in your worldly care, and—and Rome.

"Maximus did agree to call off his inquisitors, and to give the surviving Priscillianists in his dungeons light sentences. However, on this he put a price. As a sign of blessing, I must help celebrate the consecration of Felix as bishop of Treverorum.

"Now Felix was, is, a fine man." Martinus caught his breath. "But to share the Eucharist with Ithacius, the persecutor— Well, in the end, perforce, I did.

"On the way home, I walked through midnight of the soul. It seemed to me that whatever powers of well-doing had been granted me by God must be gone, because of this covenant with evil. Then an angel of the Lord appeared to me and said that I had done what I must and was forgiven." He said that almost matter-of-factly, before he grew stark again: "Nevertheless, I have seen Satan at work within the Church itself. I will never attend another synod of bishops."

They trudged on in silence until Gratillonius had marshalled words: "So you realize how careful we need to be, choosing...a trustworthy servant of God for Ys."

Martinus had recovered calm. "I do. A man devout, learned, civilized, but also virile, familiar with the common folk yet wise enough to cooperate with you for the general welfare and...resistance to tyranny." He gusted a sigh. "Do you know any such paragon? I wish I did!"

Gratillonius's heart leaped. He had spent a great many hours thinking about this. "Maybe I do."

By then they had nearly reached their goal, about three miles downstream from Turonum. Sheer hillsides, honeycombed with caves and burrows, curved backward to wall in a broad, grassy flatland. Primitive huts covered the low area, wattle-fenced gardens among them. Although the community was said to number well over a thousand, most dwelling in caves, few were in sight, nor did smoke rise from any but two or three shacks.

This was the Greater Monastery that Martinus had founded, to which men flocked who had despaired of the world and would seek salvation beyond it. Women came too, but were housed in the city; the bishop clove husband from wife as ruthlessly as he split away fleshliness from himself. Mostly the monks subsisted on donations, or on the proceeds of possessions they had turned entirely over to the Church when they enrolled. What food they grew, what fish they caught, were mere concessions to the body's need of some recreation. They shared a single meal a day, of the simplest kind. Nearly all their waking hours they passed in prayer, contemplation, mortification, reading of Scripture, attendance on the preaching of their master.

Gratillonius could not comprehend how any human being would seek such an existence. Yet as he beheld it, the power of it sent a chill through him.

"Whom have you in mind?" Martinus asked.

The centurion hauled his mind back to realities. "You know him. One Corentinus. We met last year, he and I, when I blundered onto his hermitage, and hit it off. On this trip, I stopped at Aquilo mainly so I could go back there and talk with him again. It went even better. I think he's right for Ys—since we must have somebody—and I hope you'll agree."

"Corentinus...Hm-m." The bishop pondered, while his feet and staff ate the distance to sanctuary. "It may be. It may be. An old seaman, posted to a seafaring folk...I must think. It's clear God has marked Corentinus for some high mission. You know about the miracle of the fish, don't you? Well, then—" More silence, apart from the scrunch of sandals, the song of birds. "I must think, and pray for guidance. But it does seem as though— He'll have to return here, get instructed, be consecrated chorepiscopus. That may take months. However, I could write to Maximus that it's in train."

"I'm afraid he won't be willing, Corentinus," Gratillonius warned. "What he wants to do is sit in the woods and beg forgiveness."

Also, those woods had been full of flowers, fragrances, peace.

Martinus laughed. "He'll take his marching orders if they're issued him. Stay a while, you. Let's talk this over at length. You're a soldier; you can survive our hospitality. If my decision is positive—and I suspect it will be—I'll give you a letter you'll convey to Corentinus on your way back."

Gratillonius bridled. "Sir, I *am* the prefect of Rome and the King of Ys."

Martinus laughed louder. "Why should you not also be God's messenger boy?"

~ 2 ~

Early summer brought a spell of calm, light, warmth. It had prevailed for days when Quinipilis's turn to have Dahut came, and she took the girl out on the water.

"I promised her this, the first chance we'd get," she snapped when her manservant expressed qualms. "Would you have a high priestess break her word? A promise to a little kid is the most sacred kind there is. And nay, we'll not want the royal yacht or any such cluttered-up thing. What you can do is carry my word to Scot's Landing. So get off your arse!"

As he left, the man grinned to himself. The old lady had a rasp for a tongue and a lump of butter for a heart.

Maeloch was quick to arrive from the fisher hamlet under Cape Rach. His *Osprey* was under repair after storm damage. Meanwhile

355

he welcomed extra earnings, and this would be a pleasant job. When he entered the Queen's house he found woman and child on the floor playing with little animals that King Grallon had carved in wood. "Here he is, sweetling," Quinipilis said to her charge. "We can go now."

"Oh, go, go, go!" sang Dahut, and soared to her feet. She was taller than most three-year-olds, wand-slim, wind-swift. Beneath flaxen billows of hair, her eyes were huge, deep blue, in an exquisitely sculptured face. "We go sail!"

"The airs willing, Princess," Maeloch said. "Else must I row." His coarsely clad, burly form, black mane and beard, rumbling voice, caused her no alarm. It did not seem that anything had ever frightened Dahut.

"Well, help me up, oaf," Quinipilis ordered with a nearly toothless smile. As he did, she caught a sharp breath.

"Does something hurt, my lady?" he asked.

"Of course something does. What d'you think 'twould do, in this wreck of a body? Like always having feet in a boiling kettle, if you must know. Let's begone."

"Uh, better if my lady stays home. I'll take good care of the princess, believe me. How I do remember her mother."

"Nonsense! Should I deny me a pleasure because of some verminous twinges? Fetch me my staff. 'Tis in yon corner; are you blind or only drunk? Give me your arm." Quinipilis leered. "I want all Ys to see I can yet snare a lusty young man for escort."

Dahut skipped with them down the winding street. Folk they met, mostly servants in livery, gave deferential salutation. Many recognized Maeloch as well as the Queen. He was not only a fisher captain, frequenter of taverns and sometimes joyhouses like most sailors; he was a Ferrier of the Dead.

"Why d'ye go in this wise?" he wondered.

"On Dahut's account," Quinipilis explained. "She's ever been wild about the sea. Can't get close to it, or out on it, enough."

A grimness crossed Maeloch's weathered countenance. He knew where and how the child had been born. Should that not have left a dread of the realm of Lir within her? Instead, it was as if He had touched her then, and was forever after calling her.

"Her dad takes her when he can," Quinipilis went on, "but he has scant free time, poor fellow. And then 'tis in his yacht. The notion came to me 'twould pleasure her to fare in a small boat."

Maeloch could not keep his forebodings while the bright small presence who already looked so much like Dahilis skipped beside him. "We could land on a skerry I know and spend a while," he suggested. "Might get hungry, though."

"I'm not quite in my dotage! We'll have provisions aboard."

Thereafter Quinipilis must save her breath for walking. "Wan' a' hear a song?" Dahut asked the man. Her hand lay tiny in his. She

356

pointed at the woman, who smiled as if receiving an honor. "Ol' Mama taught me." She lifted a voice clear and true:

"Starfish, starfish, what have you seen
Deep in the water, deep in the green?
I saw the darkness, far from the day,
Where the seals go to hunt and play."

From the Forum, broad and busy Lir Way brought them through Lowtown to Skippers' Market and the triumphal arch. Beyond was the harbor. At early ebb, tide had drawn the sea gate open; but on this mild day, the basin curved almost waveless beneath the city wall. Shallops cruised back and forth, a merchant ship was standing out, more vessels lay docked, bustle went over the stone arc of the quay. Trade was reviving under the reign of Grallon.

A well-stocked boat waited at a slip as Quinipilis had ordered. They went aboard. Maeloch cast off, put oars in tholes, rowed powerfully. They passed between the awesome doors of the gate. He found sufficient breeze that he could step and stay the mast, set sail, pole it out for a broad reach, and merely steer.

It whispered, the breeze, cooling the brilliance that flooded from above and dusted diamond-sparkle across the sea. It stirred, the sea, in low waves that somehow moved as one, like a single huge being gently breathing in its sleep. Today whiteness did not shatter on the cliffs or on the strewn reefs, only swirled and murmured. Otherwise Ocean was a million shifting shades of blue, save where a kelp bed rocked, or a swimming gull or cormorant. Such birds wheeled aloft in the multitudes, seldom crying. Dahut's gaze winged out among them, on past the dim streak that was Sena, to the line where vision met worldedge and lost itself in sky.

Her heed returned when a seal drew near. There were always many of the beasts around Ys, they being protected. Most were plunging through the water or basking on rocks. This one met the boat and swam alongside, a few feet away. Often it looked at Dahut, and she looked back, losing her earlier excitement, becoming mute and motionless though appearing very happy.

"That's strange," Maeloch said after a while. His voice, which could outshout storms, was hushed. "Dolphins'll play thus with a craft, but scarce ever a seal."

Quinipilis nodded. "I think I ken it," she answered as low. Clear sight remained to her. "Yon particularly beautiful coat, a kind of gold under the brown, and those big eyes. Could be the same as was there when the babe went overside. You've heard? I glimpsed it. And a few time since on the beach—"

"A seal saved me and my crew once. Guided us home through a fog, when else we'd sure have run aground."

357

Quinipilis nodded. "We're both wont to signs of the Otherworld, nay? As close as we are to it, in our different ways." She glanced at Dahut. "Sea child."

The girl returned to playfulness when Maeloch dropped sail and rowed to that skerry he had mentioned. It was large of its kind, an islet, bare rock but strewn with weed, shells, bleached and contorted sticks of driftwood. Tidepools gleamed on its lower ledges. She clapped her hands and caroled. Maeloch lay to, hung out rope bumpers, jumped ashore with the painter and made fast to an upright thumb of stone. "Come ye, sweetling," he called. "Nay, first put sandals back on. 'Twouldn't do having the barnacles cut those wee feet."

He assisted Quinipilis, then brought a chair and parasol carried along for her, then set out luncheon, while Dahut scampered round and round, shouting at each new marvel she discovered. After they had all refreshed themselves he led her by the hand, explaining things as best he could. Quinipilis watched, smiled, sometimes talked in an undertone to nobody he saw. At last he said, "Well, Princess, best we be starting home."

Dahut's face clouded. "Nay," she answered.

"We must. The tide's turning. That'll help your poor old Uncle Maeloch, for the wind's down and he'll have to row a lot. But if we wait too long, the tide'll close the gate, and we'll have to make for Scot's Landing, and your poor old Aunt Quinipilis can't get up the cliffs there."

The child stuck out her lower lip, clenched fists, stamped foot. "Nay. I *b'long* here."

"Not the way the sun's putting a flush in that white skin of yours, ye don't. No mutiny, now. Ye can play till I've stowed our gear."

Dahut whirled and sped from him.

When Maeloch returned to Quinipilis he found she had dozed off in her chair, as the aged do. He left her alone while he loaded the boat. Always he kept half an eye in Dahut's direction. She had gone down to the water and become quiet. The rock sloped in such wise that he could see merely the fair top of her head.

Having finished his task, he gave Quinipilis a slight shake. She drew a rattling breath and blinked confusedly. "Dahilis—" she mumbled. Her senses steadied. "Oh, my, such eldritch dreams I was having." Painfully, she hobbled to the boat and got in with Maeloch's assistance.

The sailor went after Dahut. "Time to go," he said, and stopped and stared.

On the ledge beneath him, the girl was side by side with the seal. Maeloch saw that the animal was female. Her narrow, earless head (how much the head of a seal called to mind a human corpse) had brought muzzle against cheek, through a tumble of tresses. The fishy breath seemed to give no offense. Did a murmur, a hum or a tone, resound from the long throat?

"Dahut!" Maeloch bellowed. "What the thunder?"

The two started, rolled apart, exchanged a look. The seal slithered into the water and dived below. Dahut leaped up. The wet body had soaked her gown so that it clung to the curves of her, which were not yet a woman's curves but slender as if to cleave waves. Calming, she walked toward him without protest.

Maeloch squatted to inspect her. "Ye're not hurt?" he grated. "Damnation, whatever happened? Don't do that sort o' thing! A big beast like yon could tear ye in shreds. Saw ye nay its teeth?"

"She came and sang to me," Dahut answered like a sleepwalker.

"Sang? Huh? Seals don't sing. They bark."

"She did so." Sheer willfulness brought the girl back to herself. "She sang 'bout the sea 'cos I wan'ed she should." Turning she called across the luminous, moving miles: "I'll come again! I'll al'ays come again!"

The mood flitted from her. She gave Maeloch an impudent grin, a wink, and her hand to hold. What could he do but lead the daughter of Dahilis to the boat and take her home to her father?

He knew he would never understand what he had seen; but he, who dealt with the dead as his forebears had done before him, need not be daunted by a mystery as tender as this. "She sang, did she?" he asked.

"She did, she did." Dahut nodded violently. "She tol' me 'bout my sea."

"What did she tell you?"

"I 'member. You wan' a' hear?" The treble that lifted toward the gulls was childish, but the words no longer were, and the melody ebbed and flowed. It was not a song that had ever been heard in Ys.

"Deep, deep, where the waters sleep
And the great fish come and go,
What do they dream in the twilight gleam?
The seals will always know.

"Far, far, from the evening star
Comes the storm when the wind runs free
And the cloud that lours with the rain that pours.
The seals will always see.

"High, high is the evening sky,
Deep is the Ocean swell.
Where foam is white in the changing light,
The seals will always dwell."

~ 3 ~

For the past three years, except when it was impossible, Gratillonius had given a day every month to open court. Anybody was free to enter the basilica during those hours, to watch the proceedings or to lay before him a trouble—dispute, complaint, need—that lower authorities had failed to resolve. Turn by turn, he heard them out, and rendered judgment with military briskness. He had neither time nor patience for subtleties, though he strove to be fair. In doubtful cases he generally found for the humble. They had less to fall back on than the well-off.

The setting was impressive. Tiered benches looked down toward a dais on which the King sat enthroned, the Wheel embroidered in gold on his crimson robe, the Key hanging out in view upon his breast, the Hammer across his knees. At a table to his left sat a recorder whose pen ran as fast as words were uttered, on his right a jurist with scrolls containing the laws of Ys before him. Behind the seats four legionaries in full battle gear stood at attention; and behind them loomed the eidolons of the Three, Taranis the Father, Belisama the Mother, kraken that represented inhuman Lir.

On that day, a rainstorm made dim the light from the glazed windows and laved the chamber with its susurrus. Candles in walls sconces and lamps on the desks cast their small glows, uneasy in the drafts. More people than usual had come to observe, for a notorious case was to be heard. The smell of wet wool garments gave sharpness to the air.

Gratillonius heard pleaders in order of arrival. Nagon Demari registered outrage, but Donnerch the wagoner guffawed, when they must wait for several of the lower classes. An elderly woman stated that she did not want the charity of the Gallicenae, for her son's widow could perfectly well pay her support as the son himself had done; having obtained the figures, Gratillonius so ordered. A man found guilty of theft brought friends, whom the magistrate had ruled unreliable, to declare he had been with them on the night of the crime; Gratillonius released him on grounds of reasonable doubt, but warned that this would be taken into account if there was another accusation. A sailor declared that his captain did wrong to make him suffer six lashes for a minor infraction, and ought to pay compensation for the injustice; after several of the crew had testified, Gratillonius said, "You were lucky. I'd have given you nine."

Thereupon it was time for Nagon Demari, Labor Councillor among the Suffetes, and Donnerch, son of Arel, carter. Nagon spoke at length about his beneficence in organizing the longshoremen of Ys into a guild, now that trade was improving, thanks to wise King Grallon. He made a mouth as he said that: a stocky, cold-eyed man who despite aristocratic blood had been born poor and scrabbled his way up in the world till he sat in the Council. "Spare me this and get to the point," Gratillonius snapped.

Nagon looked indignant but explained that handling cargo obviously involved carrying it inland, wherefore carters should belong to the guild, pay its dues, require its fixed charges for their work, and perform such services for the guild as it leadership needed. Donnerch had not only refused these requests, made for his own good, and done so in unseemly language, he had brutally assailed two of the brotherhood who sought to persuade him.

Three newcomers entered the hall. Gratillonius drew a quick breath and raised his hand. "A moment," he interrupted. Louder: "Thrice welcome, honored sir!" with the same repeated in Latin.

Corentinus made salutation. A letter had declared he was coming, but Gratillonius had not looked for him quite this soon. He must have ridden hard, he and the two strong young men who must be deacons assigned him. The new chorepiscopus of Ys had shed much of the forest hermit. Nose, chin, cheekbones still jutted, deep-set eyes still smoldered under tangled brows, but hair and beard were neatly clipped and he had evidently bathed at hostels where he overnighted. His head was bare, the tonsured locks drenched and matted; but the paenula hanging from his shoulders to his knees, off which water dripped, was of good quality, and beneath it the long shanks displayed Gallic breeches tucked into boots.

"We shall hear you out tomorrow—" Gratillonius started to tell those who stood before him.

"Nay," said Corentinus. He used Osismian, but already he could throw in enough Ysan words that he was intelligible to every listener. How had he learned them? "We have arrived early, and God forbid it be in pride. Let us abide your leisure." He folded his height down on a rear bench. Stiffly, the deacons joined him.

Donnerch answered the question in Gratillonius's mind. "Why I know that fellow," he exclaimed. "Hoy-ah, Corentinus!" he waved. The clergyman smiled and made a responding gesture. "I got as far as Turonum, trek before last," the wagoner said, "and he heard about me being from Ys and paid me for a few days of language teaching. I earned it, lord. How he worked me!" He was a big young man, yellow-haired, freckle-faced, ordinarily cheerful.

"*May* we get on with our business, O King?" Nagon demanded.

"If you'll be quick about it," Gratillonius replied.

Presently Donnerch said: "By Epona, but he lies, him! Hark'ee, lord. I'd no reason for paying into his mucky guild and doing his mucky will, did I? And so I told my fellow independent carters. Then this pair of toughs came to call on me. When they started talking about two broken arms, I snatched my mule whip off the wall. I have the cudgels they dropped on their way out, if the King wants to see 'em. Aye, they had me hauled up on charges of assault, but the Magistrate didn't believe 'em, though he dared not call 'em perjurers either. So here we are."

"Perjurers?" shouted Nagon. "Lord, I've come on their behalf because their injuries are too cruel, too grievous, after that barbaric attack—"

"Silence!" Gratillonius commanded. "Think you the King is blind and deaf? I've stayed my hand erenow, Nagon Demari, for there's been much else for me to do, and it did seem you'd bettered the lot

361

of your workers somewhat. But darker stories have grown too many of late. This is only the newest of them."

"Two honest men swear, against this known drunkard and brawler, that he fell on them with a dangerous weapon, unprovoked. Poor Jonan lost an eye. Cudgels? Donnerch could find two cudgels anywhere."

"Getting hurt is a hazard of building empires," Gratillonius said, "and I warn you to stop trying to build yours any bigger. Free carters are not longshoremen. Henceforth, leave them alone. And...Donnerch, mayhap you were needlessly rough. Tell your friends that next time something like this happens, there will be a full inquiry; and whoever has taken arms against a man without real need, he'll know the scourge or the ax. Dismissed."

Donnerch barely suppressed a whoop, Nagon did not conceal a glower. Gratillonius wondered whether he, the King, had won or lost today. He needed all the support he could call on, when he must protect not a mild Eucherius but a forceful Corentinus.

Luckily, just two more cases were left, and those minor. He adjourned before any further petitioners could arrive. In a rear chamber he exchanged his robe for everyday tunic, trousers, hooded cloak. The Key felt momentarily chill against his skin.

Returning, he ignored everybody else that lingered, to greet the chorepiscopus properly and have the deacons introduced to him. Those seemed like vigorous and dedicated men, but well under control of their leader. "It's good to see you again," Gratillonius said in Latin, quite sincerely in spite of awaiting difficulties. "I hope you'll like Ys."

"I do," the minister answered. "Too much. As I rode in, what memories came back." He squared his shoulders. "My friend, I don't know whether you've done me the greatest service or the scurviest trick; but Bishop Martinus said this is God's will, and that must suffice me. Will you show us to the church?"

"Why, you're here too soon. Nothing's properly ready. I'll quarter you in the palace till then."

Corentinus shook his head. "No thanks. The fewer fleshly comforts and temptations, the better. To tell the truth, a reason I pushed hard on the road was fear that you, in mistaken kindness, would outfit our dwelling luxuriously."

"Well, come look, but I warn you, the place has lain neglected since Eucherius died."

"The more merit to us," Corentinus said almost merrily, "as we make it into a fortress of God."

Gratillonius thought of his Mithraeum, also an outpost lonely and beleaguered. Let Corentinus settle in, get some rest, begin to find out for himself what Ys was—not only a seaport with the usual gaiety, unruliness, swindlings, sorrows, vices, ghosts, dreams...though in Ys they were stronger and stranger than elsewhere—not only a city of wealth, power, beauty, industry, corruption, vanity, arrogance, like others...though in Ys these flourished as they had not done elsewhere since the high days of Rome—but a whole society with its own ways and Gods which were not akin to those of any other, ancient, pervasive, and enduring. He, Gratillonius, had not yet fully come to terms with Ys, and he was no Christian. He hoped Corentinus would not break his heart, battering against what the evangelist must needs perceive as wickedness.

They went out into the Forum and the rain. Wind sent the water at a slant, silver that glinted cold across the mosaics of dolphins and sea horses, and downward from basin to basin of the Fire Fountain at the center. The wind hooted and plucked at clothes. It bore a sound and smell of Ocean. Hardly a soul was in sight. Gratillonius led the way across to the former temple of Mars.

"Sir—lord King—" He stopped and looked toward the voice. The speaker was young Budic, who as a legionary of his had today taken a turn in the honor guard at the palace. "Sir, an Imperial courier brought this. I thought I'd better get it to you right away, and you'd be hereabouts."

"Well done," said the centurion of the Second, and took a scroll wrapped in oiled cloth. He kept impassive, though his heart slugged and his throat tightened. Budic stood staring as he walked on.

In the portico of the church he said to Corentinus: "Let me read this at once. I suspect it's something you should know about too."

The chorepiscopus traced a cross in the wet air. "You're probably right," he replied.

The letter was clearly one sent in many copies through Gallia, Hispania, and perhaps beyond.

—*Magnus Clemens Maximus, Augustus, to the Senate and the People of Rome, and to all others whom it may concern, charging them most solemnly and under the severest penalties to carry out those duties laid upon them by Almighty God and the state...*

—*After four years of patient negotiation, it has become clear that accommodation with Flavius Valentinianus, styled Emperor, is unattainable...Intransigence and repeated violations...The abominable heresy of Arius...The cleansing of the state, even as Our Savior drove out money changers and demons...*

—*Therefore we most strictly enjoin the people and those in whose care the people are, that they remain loyal and orderly, obedient to those whom God has set above them, while we lead our armies into Italy and wherever else may prove needful, to the end that the Western Empire, harmoniously with our brother Theodosius of the East, again have tranquillity under a single and righteous ruler.*

~ 4 ~

An autumn storm roared, whistled, flung rain and hail, throughout one night. It made doubly comforting the warmth of Bodilis's bed and body. By morning the weather was dry but the gale still ramped. Man

363

and woman woke about the same time, smiled drowsily at each other through the dimness, shared a kiss. Desire came back. He laughed, low in his throat. "There's no call on me today," he said, drawing her closer.

That was not true. There was always something to clamor for the attention of the centurion, the prefect, the King. Only the day before, news had arrived from beyond the Alps, via the Duke of the Armorican Tract: Maximus was firmly in possession of Mediolanum and Valentinianus had fled eastward out of Italy. Gratillonius then made an excuse to visit the wisest of his Queens, out of turn, for her counsel and afterward her solace.

Nevertheless—"Just you and me," he said in the Latin she wanted to maintain for herself. "Later, let's breakfast with Una, hm?"

"M-m-m," she responded, and in other ways as well.

He often thought that if he could have his wish, she would be his sole wife. She had not the raw ardor of Forsquilis, good-natured sensuality of Maldunilis, dumb eagerness to please of Guilvilis; somehow, in her enough of each was alloyed. She was handsome rather than beautiful, and the years were putting gray into the wavy brown hair, crow's-feet around the blue nearsighted eyes, wrinkliness under the throat, sag in the breasts. But she was no crone, and good bones would endure. Though her monthly courses had not ended, it did not seem she would bear him more children, ever. Well, he had plenty now, and Una was a darling second only to Dahut. Before all else was the *wholeness* of her. She knew things, thought about them, gave him her judgments, submitted to nothing save the truth as she saw it. She was his friend, such as he had not had since Parnesius on the Wall; and she was his lover.

They met; together they went beyond themselves; presently they lay at peace with the universe. Outside, the wind hooted, rattled shutters, carried a noise of waves breaking mightily on the sea wall. Yesterday the King had barred the gate and locked it with the Key that he alone bore, lest the waters fling it open and rage into Ys. He did not expect to free those doors for a while; and few vessels would come thereafter. As winter neared, Ys drew into itself, even as he and his Queen did this day.

She chuckled. "What's funny?" he asked.

"Oh, you," she said. "Dutiful you, hiding away from work like a boy from the schoolmaster. It's good to see you taking your ease, dear, merely enjoying yourself. You should do it oftener."

Reminded, he sat up. "I forgot my morning prayer!"

She arched her brows. "For the very first time?"

"Uh, no."

"I'm sure your Mithras will understand, and overlook it. Belisama does." Bodilis's glance went to the figurine that occupied a niche in her otherwise plainly furnished bedroom. Carved of oak whose grain followed the folds of Her hooded cloak, it showed the Goddess as a woman of middle age, serene, an enigmatic smile on Her lips.

I could adore a deity like that, he thought, if this were Her only aspect.

Putting solemnity aside, "We spoke of breakfast—" he began.

A knock on the door interrupted. "My lord, my lord!" called the voice of Bodilis's chief manservant. "Forgive me, but a soldier of yours is here. He says he must see you this instant."

"What?" Gratillonius swung feet to floor. His immediate feeling was of resentment. Could they never leave him alone? He took a robe off a peg and pulled it over himself. Bodilis rose too, with a rueful look for him.

His deputy Adminius waited in the atrium, wearing civil Ysan garb that he had donned with unmilitary hastiness. He saluted. "Begging your pardon, sir." The lean, snaggle-toothed countenance was full of distress. "I'm afraid I got bad news. 'Ard news, anyway, though I'm sure the centurion can 'andle the matter."

Gratillonius dismissed whatever happiness had still been aglow in him. "Speak."

"You got a challenger, sir. At the Wood. One o' the lodgekeepers came asking where you was, and I thought you should 'ear it from me."

It was as if the wind came in off the street and wrapped around Gratillonius. "Do you know more?"

"No, sir. Should I go look? I can tell 'em I couldn't find yer right away."

Gratillonius shook his head. "Never mind," he said dully. "Let me get shod."

He turned back toward the bedroom. Having covered her own nakedness, Bodilis had followed him and heard. She stood at the inner doorway, the color drained from her face. "Oh, no," she whispered. The hands that groped across his were cold. "Not already."

"The way of Ys," Gratillonius rasped. He brushed past her.

Returning with sandals and cloak, he found she had not stirred. Those widened eyes struck remorse into him. He stopped, clasped her by the shoulders, and said, "I'm sorry. I forgot how terrible this must be to you. A total stranger, who may be another Colconor or, or anything. Don't be afraid." It might be kindly of him to change from Latin to Ysan: "Nay, fear not, heart of mine. I'll smite the wretch ere he can slice a hair off my knuckle. For your sake."

"I dare not pray," she whispered. "This thing lies at the will of the Gods. But I'll hope, and—and weep for you, Grallon, who so loathes this need laid upon him."

He kissed her, quickly and roughly, and went forth with Adminius. The wind shrilled, sent dead leaves scrittling along the street, roused little breakers on rain puddles. It drove clouds before it, making light and shadow sickle over roofs, half veiling the towertops. Rooks winged dark on the blast. The garments of such folk as were out flapped as if they too were about to fly away.

"You'll take 'im, sir, same as you did the last 'un," Adminius avowed. "'E'll've 'ad a scant night's rest in the wet. "E can't be very smart, or 'e'd've waited till later ter arrive."

Gratillonius nodded absently. The rule that the King must respond at once to a challenge, unless absent from the city, was doubtless meant for more than the immediate gratification of Taranis; it gave him an advantage. Frequent changes were undesirable, even when the monarch was a political nullity.

"And if perchance you don't win, God forbid, w'y, 'e won't last out the day 'imself," Adminius went on. "Yer lads'll see ter that."

Shocked before he felt also touched, Gratillonius growled, "No. No legionary will raise a finger against him. That's an order."

"But, but yer the prefect o' Rome!"

"The more reason to maintain law. Including this damnable law of Ys. We *can't* have the city fall into disorder. Don't you see, it's the keystone of everything I've worked to build in Armorica." Gratillonius considered. His mind had become as bleakly bright as the sunbeams. "If I fall, report to Soren Cartagi. He'll be the effective governor for at least a while. Remind him of the need to continue my policies, for the good of Ys. Give him whatever help he requires. When he can spare you, bring the legionaries to the Duke and put them under his orders."

Anguish asked: "Wot about yerself, sir?"

"Let them burn me and scatter the bones and ashes at sea. That's what Ys does with her fallen Kings." And I shall go home to Dahilis. "My brothers in Mithras will hold their own rites for me."

Gratillonius stiffened his neck. "Enough," he said. "I do not plan on getting killed. Forward march! On the double, soldier."

At Dragon House he donned his centurion's armor. All twenty-four of his men formed ranks and followed him out High Gate, battle-arrayed. By then word had spread and the streets were aswarm, ababble. Where Processional Way started north out of Aquilonian Way, a squad of marines formed a line to hold back the crowd. Through the wind, Gratillonius heard shouted wishes for his victory.

That warmed him a trifle. He had much to live for, and live he proposed to do. This challenger would scarcely be another pitiable Hornach, but rather some sturdy rogue prepared to take his chances. Quite possibly he was a barbarian. It would be almost a pleasure to kill a Frank, say. In any case, a fair fight which Gratillonius had not provoked was not butchery. As always, he did not dwell on the possibility that he might lose. To do so would merely weaken him.

The road bent east, under sere hills, and the Wood of the King loomed ahead. The gale had torn off nearly all the leaves that earlier turned it bronze. Now trunks and boughs were winter-gray, though shadows still made a cave of the depths beneath them. Twigs clawed at the sky. Timber creaked. Wind eddied about, wailed and mumbled.

Half a dozen more marines had reached the courtyard of the Shield and Hammer. They saluted the King. Tethered nearby stood their horses, and leashed hounds whined impatient. If either contestant fled, he would be hunted down and brought back for the death stroke.

Red-robed, Soren emerged from the blood-colored house when an attendant called. He had been delayed by no need to equip himself; his was only to lead the ceremonies, before and after. "In the holy name of Taranis, greeting, King of Ys," he said.

For the sake of Dahut, Bodilis, Rome, Gratillonius bent his helmeted head to the God he abhorred. Mithras would understand.

"The challenger has chosen his weapons and is prepared," Soren said. Nothing in his heavy visage bespoke how he wished the combat would go. He was the instrument of Taranis. Turning, he cried: "Come forth, O you who would be King of Ys!"

A wiry, long-legged young man stepped from the gloom within, onto the porch and down the stairs. His movements were quick, suggestive of tension, but there was no hesitancy in them. A forked black beard, well trimmed, decorated clear features marred by poor teeth and a scar puckering the right cheek to pull that corner of his mouth into the hint of a sneer. From the outfits available he had chosen a nose-guarded helmet, knee-length chainmail coat, thick cross-garters over the breeches to protect calves, small round shield, long Gallic sword in a sheath, a javelin in his free hand. Plainly, he meant to make the best of agility against a larger opponent.

Plainly, too, he was not fatigued as Adminius had predicted. Springiness was in his gait and clarity in the green eyes. Browned skin gave a clue. This was an outdoorsman, skillful to contrive shelter and sleep soundly on the wildest of nights. He would be dangerous as a panther; and well he knew it.

He approached across the flagstones, peered, and halted. In Redonic-accented Latin he cried, "Are you the King? But you're the centurion!"

And Gratillonius knew him. "Rufinus!" Rufinus, leader of those Bacaudae whom the legionaries had driven from their prey on the road to Juliomagus—

The young man lifted spear and shield. Laughter whooped from him. "Why, you rascal, you never told me! I'd not've bucked you elsewise. Better to've asked for a place in your command, hey?" He sobered, apart from a savage grin. "Too late now, I suppose. Right? Pity."

"What's this?" Soren demanded. "Know you each other?"

"We've met," said Gratillonius. A knot formed in his guts. "He'll withdraw his challenge if I ask."

"Impossible, as well you remember," said the Speaker for Taranis. "Let us pray."

Rufinus glided close to Gratillonius. The smile kept flickering as he murmured. "I'm sorry, Centurion, truly I am. You're a decent sort, I think. But you should've told me, that night in your tent."

They knelt at the royal oak. Soren signed them both with holy water and invoked the Father God. Wind boomed. A raven flew low overhead.

"We go off by ourselves," Gratillonius said bluntly.

Rufinus nodded. "They've explained."

Side by side, the two men pushed through snickering underbrush to the opening, out of sight from the house, where Gratillonius had killed Hornach and Colconor. Strange that underfoot were rain-sodden leaves and humus; this earth should be gory red.

His mood had not caused him to lose wariness. However, Rufinus attempted no sneak attack, simply leaned on his spear and sighed, "This is too bad. It really is."

"What made you come?" Gratillonius wondered.

Rufinus barked laughter. "I wish I could say a mischievous God, but it was just chance—and myself—though it did seem, one midnight, moonlight hour, that stag-horned Cernunnos danced His madman's dance before me, to egg me on.... Well," he proceeded in a level tone, "you roadpounders gave us brethren a nasty setback, you know. Not just our dead and wounded. You hit our spirits in the balls, and we skulked about for a long spell, living more off roots and voles than plunder and, hm, donations. My standing as duke was in danger, not that it meant much anymore. Bit by bit, I rallied the boys, we got new recruits, till at last I had the makings of a fresh band. What it needed next—you'll know what I mean—what it needed was a blooding, to prove itself to itself.

"Then the news ran this summer, civil war begun again and the Emperor marched off south with his army. I remembered Sicorus. Do you? My landmaster, who debased my sister till she died whelping his get." Fury went like lightning over the face and through the voice, and vanished as swiftly. "We all had things to avenge on Sicorus. The upshot was, one night we came and ringed Maedraeacum manor house in. We let women, children, harmless slaves go out, free; I told the boys that whoever touched them in anything but helpfulness would answer to my knife. Then we pushed Sicorus's overseers in to join him, and set fire to the building. That damaged the loot, of course, but next day we still picked a grand amount of gold and silver from the ashes."

Rufinus sighed once more, shrugged, and finished. "My mistake. I reckoned the Empire would be too busy with its own woes for doing much about this. That's how it was in past civil wars. But it turns out Emperor Maximus had driven his enemies before him right handily. The Roman—the Armorican Duke, is that what they call him? My fellow duke—I reckon he decided he could spare the troops to make an example of us. They scoured the woods for a month or more. Most of my Valiant are dead, the rest are fled. Me, I remembered a centurion who reminded me about wonderful Ys, and decided I'd scant to lose. So here we are, Gratillonius."

Wind brawled, swirled under armor, made the Wood groan. Gratillonius said slowly: "Too late, you thought of asking me for a berth in my service. How could I give you any, after what you did?"

"At Maedraeacum?" answered pride and reason. "Had I no right to bring Ita's ghost peace? Every ghost that Sicorus squeezed out of life? Hasn't Rome made friends of her foes, like you Britons or us Gauls? I could serve you well, King. I'm a good man of my hands. And...My own Bacaudae may be gone, but I know many more, up and down the valleys and off in the hills. Outlaws, but they could be useful scouts, messengers, irregular fighters, for a King who showed them a little kindness."

Gratillonius realized he must not listen. "Try that if you overcome me," he said. "But remember that Rome is the Mother of us all. And be gentle to the Nine Queens and—and their children."

For the first time, he saw complete calm on Rufinus. It was eerily like the peace he himself had felt this dawn after he and Bodilis made love. The wanderer traced a sign with his spear, in the wind. "I promise," he said low.

Thereupon he dropped into a feline crouch and asked, "Shall we have at it, friend?"

"We must," said Gratillonius.

They circled about the glade. Wind keened; the raven, settled on an unrestful bough, croaked hoarsely; fallen leaves squelped. Rufinus moved his buckler to and fro while his arm stayed cocked, ready to cast the javelin. Gratillonius kept his big Roman shield in place and squinted across its upper edge, the sword poised in his right hand.

Glances met and held fast. It was always a peculiar feeling to look into the eyes of a foeman, not unlike looking into those of a woman in bed, an ultimate intimacy.

They stalked, he and Rufinus, each in search of an opening. Now and then the Gaul made tentative movements of his spear. Gratillonius remained stolid. The wind blew.

Abruptly Rufinus cast. Immediately he snatched for the sword scabbard across his back, and charged.

The Roman missile should have sunk its iron head into the Roman shield and hung there, its shaft dragging in the earth. Gratillonius was ready for it. His blade flipped it aside. It spent its malice in a rotten log. Rufinus was upon him. The Gallic sword crashed down. Gratillonius shifted his shield enough to catch the blow. His own weapon snaked forward. Rufinus sprang back. Blood from his left thigh darkened that trouser leg.

He's mine, Gratillonius knew. But let it be quick. Let it be merciful.

Rufinus gave him a wry grin and, again, circled, alert for a chance to pounce. Man for man, outlaw and centurion should be equal. It was not individual Romans but the Roman army that had broken the Gauls. Rufinus, though, had taken a wound not mortal but deep; and whatever carnivore skills he had picked up, he was untrained in the science of killing.

Gratillonius let him attack, over and over, wear himself down, retreat with more blood running out of him. Two or three times he got through the defense, but the injuries that the hare inflicted on the tortoise were minor slashes.

The end came all at once. Gratillonius maneuvered Rufinus up against a thicket, which blocked retreat. Rufinus hewed. By that time the long sword was weakly held. Through the wind, Gratillonius heard how Rufinus panted, while blood soaked his breeches and footsteps. Gratillonius's shield stopped another blow. His short, thick blade knocked the weapon from his opponent's grasp.

A moment Rufinus stared, until his laughter cried out. "Good work, soldier!" He spread his arms, while he swayed on his feet. "Come, what're you waiting for? Here I am."

Gratillonius found he could not move.

"Come, come," Rufinus raved. "I'm ready. I'd've done for you if I could."

"Pick up your sword," Gratillonius heard himself say.

Rufinus shook his head. "Oh, no, you don't," he crowed. "I bear you no ill will, buddy. You won, fair and square. But be damned if I'll let you pretend—*Roman*—you're still in a fight. Make your offering."

To Taranis, Who deigned to be Colconor. And Lir had slain Dahilis.

"Are you playing games with me?" Gratillonius brought forth.

"No," said Rufinus, feebly now as the loss of blood swept him further along. He staggered. "I only...want you...to stop playing games with yourself...and whatever Gods are yours, Roman."

He lurched, sank to hands and knees, crouched gasping.

Mithras forbade human sacrifice.

It was as if Bodilis were suddenly there in the wind and the wet, Bodilis whom Gratillonius would seek back to as soon as he was able. Not losing time in cleaning it, he sheathed his sword. "I cannot kill you, helpless," he said, dimly amazed at his own steadiness. "Nor can I let you lie there. Not if you surrender to me, altogether. Do you understand? I think I can save you if you'll declare yourself my slave, Rufinus."

"I could have worse masters," muttered back around the reborn grin.

Gratillonius knelt and set about stanching the wounds of his man.

~ 5 ~

Throughout the years, Soren Cartagi and Lanarvilis the Queen had held many a private meeting. None was as grim as this.

The gale had died away, but seas still crashed against the wall and gate of Ys, spume flying higher than the battlements. Their sound went undergroundishly through the whole city, as if earth responded to that anger. Starless dark engulfed heaven, save for what towertop windows glimmered alone. Lights and luxury in the room where Lanarvilis received her visitor could not really stave off night.

Motionless in a high-backed chair, she watched him pace to and fro before her. Flamelight sheened on her russet gown and silver fillet. It flickered within her eyes, making them demonlike, though on her face was only compassion for him. He wore his red robe of office, the talisman of the Sun Wheel hung on his breast—so fateful did he think this occasion—but had removed his miter on entering the house. In the uneasy illumination, his hair and beard seemed largely gray.

"Aye, thus it was," he told her in his pain. "He came back upholding the bandit. Said he'd bed him down in the lodge. Ere I could shake off stupefaction and protest, Gratillonius declared himself winner in the combat and that that sufficed; no good would come of slaying a captive. Instead, he would give Taranis a hecatomb of beasts, bought out of his own purse."

Lanarvilis nodded. "The Gallicenae have heard that much, of course," she said softly. "He sent a written account among us—written by Bodilis, with whom he stays closeted in the palace, his Roman soldiers standing by. They've brought the Gaul there too. That is all I know thus far. His words to us were few and hard, no matter that Bodilis tried to milden them."

"I'll give you the rest." Soren's feet thudded on the carpet, a drumbeat above the sea-noise. "I shouted my outrage. Ys lives by Her Gods, Who require Their ancient sacrifices. He replied that—he would fight future challengers, and those who did not yield must take their hazard of death; but he would not believe the honor of any God was served by—he called it murder!" Soren struggled for breath. "'Stand aside,' he said, and began to help the scoundrel to the house.

"I called on the marines to kill the challenger, since this traitor King would not. 'Be still,' Gratillonius said—oh, how quietly. 'It is not meet that anybody die here.' His Romans trod closer, hands on hilts. Yet I—Elissa, Lanarvilis—I saw it was not they that stayed the marines. Our guards too were shaken, but 'twas the King they would obey, this king who scorns the Gods That raised him up."

Soren ground fist into palm. "I swallowed vomit, though it burned my throat," he related. "After the injured man was at rest and a Roman —not our standby physician for a wounded victor, but a soldier with rough surgical skill—was tending him...Gratillonius returned and I sought to reason with him. Whatever his beliefs, I said, surely he could see that this—blasphemy, violation of the Pact—this would make him hated and undermine all he has done for his Rome. He answered that he thought not."

"I fear he was right," Lanarvilis said.

371

"Aye," Soren groaned. "Have you heard? Late in the day, when that Rufinus was somewhat recovered, Gratillonius brought him to the city. Beforehand, he had sent for heralds and told them to proclaim his intent. Folk were packed along Lir Way. He entered High Gate at the head of his marching men and, and a squadron of our marines, he riding, with Rufinus tethered at his saddlebow— Do you understand? He gave himself a Roman triumph; and the people cheered!"

"I heard," Lanarvilis said. "I was not surprised."

"He has won them over. In spite of his alien God, in spite of his protecting that Christian priest, in spite of everything, he's their dear King Grallon, for whom they'll take arms against anybody. How long before the Gods take arms against them?"

"Have you thought, Soren," she asked low, "that we may in truth be at the end of the Age that Brennilis began? That mayhap Ys is once more offered the cup of youth, and if she will not taste of it must soon grow old and die?"

He halted. He stared. "You too?" he breathed at last.

She shook her head. "Nay, my darling. Never would I betray you. But my Sisters and I—other than Bodilis, though she laid certain words of wisdom in that letter—we had Maldunilis brought back from Sena and spoke together. I knew you would seek me out."

His bulk trembled. "What did you decide?"

"It may be that Gratillonius will satisfy Taranis with his hecatomb."

"I think not; for no sacrificial blood will flow in his heart."

Lanarvilis shivered likewise. "Wait and see. Taranis did not cast a thunderbolt this day. But if the Gods are indeed wrathful— Their revenge is often slow, but always cruel."

Soren traced a sign, braced himself, and said, "I'm concerned that all Ys not suffer because of a single man's wickedness. Might you Gallicenae curse him, as you did Colconor?"

Lanarvilis made a fending motion. "Nay! How could we? He may be mistaken, but evil he is not. A curse without passion behind it can no more fly to its target than an arrow from a stringless bow."

"And anyhow, several of you would refuse."

"The whole Nine would, Soren."

"So be it," the man said. "Well, Ys has been saddled in the past with Kings about whom something must be done. I mean not those who were...simply bestial, like Colconor, for to conspire against the Chosen of Taranis is an act of desperation—but some who posed a threat to the whole city. We'll send our agents out through Armorica, bearing gold and promises. Gratillonius will have challenger after challenger, month after month, till one of them cuts him down."

Calm had descended on Lanarvilis. "We guessed that idea would be broached, we Gallicenae," she said, "and we forbid it."

"What?"

"Some of us love him. But put that aside. We too can lay our hearts on the altar when it must be done. Think, though. You and I are the politic persons, the worldliest among those who serve the Gods. Is it not really Ys we serve, Mother Ys?

"Think what Gratillonius has done and is doing. He has strengthened us, within and without our wall. He has quickened our stagnant trade. He has reconciled the high and the low. He has kept us free. Who else has the least hope of holding Emperor Maximus at arm's length? Who else have the Scoti and the Saxons learned to fear? Why, his very Mithras is a counterbalance to that Christ Who would take from us our Gods.

"Dare you imagine that some filthy barbarian or runaway slave can replace him? I say to you, Soren Cartagi, and if you are honest you will concede it—ill shall Ys fare if she loses King Grallon."

Silence followed, apart from the subterranean thunder of Ocean.

Finally Soren dragged forth: "I am...aware of this. I awaited that response of yours. I have even begun talks with my colleagues. Hannon is bewildered with horror, but I should be able to talk him over, along with the rest. We will not rebel, not conspire, but bide our time. Let the Gods work as They will."

He stood quiet for a space before adding. "Yet we, Their worshippers, cannot sit passive. They make us what we are, our unique selves, Ys. How shall we make our amends for this harm that has been done Them?"

"The Nine have thought upon that," Lanarvilis replied gravely. "We, his wives, know what stubbornness is in Gratillonius. But patience, endurance, that is woman's weapon.

"Therefore we will lay the foundations of the future, that ineluctable morrow when he has fallen and we are done with mourning him. We will take triple care that our daughters grow up in the awe of the Gods. First and foremost will we instill devoutness in Dahut, child of Dahilis, whose nurturing we share. Forsquilis senses fate within that girl. Its form is unknown, but its power waxes year after year. We Nine will set upon her brow the sigil of the Three."

Again Soren signed himself.

"It is well," he said, took up the wine cups that stood on the table, handed Lanarvilis one, and took a long draught from its mate.

Thereafter, soothed a little, he sat down opposite her, ventured a smile, and said, "You've lightened a huge burden for me. Thank you."

She smiled back. "Nay, you let it off yourself."

"Well, mayhap, but first you loosened the bonds holding it fast. Ever have you been kind to me."

"How could I be aught else...to you?" she whispered.

They withdrew from the edge of that. "Well," he suggested, "can we spend a while talking of small things? How have you fared since last I saw you? What will you share with me?"

"All I am permitted to," she said.

IX

~ 1 ~

Winter's early night had fallen when three Romans entered an ale-house in the Fishtail district. The first was well known there: Adminius, deputy commander of the legionaries. The second had come occasionally, young Budic; he, who carried a lantern, now blew it out and put it down on a remnant of mosaic. The third was a tall, craggy-boned, middle-aged man, clad in ordinary tunic and breeches, but with his hair shaven off the front half of his scalp.

This taproom had been the atrium of a fine house—long ago, before sea level began to rise, driving the wealthy to higher ground and eventually forcing construction of the great wall. Bits of relief sculpture and hints of frescoes peered out of soot and grease. Tables and benches on what was mostly a clay floor were rough wood, though themselves time-worn, haggled by generations of idle knives. Tallow candles guttered and dripped on the boards, enough light to see by after a fashion. Shadows curtained every corner, flickered across peeled plaster and thin-scraped membrane stretched over windows, parodied each movement. The stench of burning fat mingled with odors of cooking from the kitchen, of sour wine and worse beer.

Withal, it was a rather cheery place. About a dozen fishers, merchant sailors, wherry oarsmen occupied two of the tables. They drank heartily, jested roughly, laughed loudly. A woman sat with one group, teasing them while she sipped what they bought her. As the newcomers entered, another man came in from the hallway beyond. He grinned in lazy wise and secured his belt. The rest gave him a ribald cheer. "Did your ram sink that hull for good this eventide?" shouted someone.

"Nay," he replied, "you know Keban better than that. She'll soon bob back to surface. Me, I'm thirsty. Mead, potboy, none of your horse piss but good, honest mead!" He was young, strong, ruddy of close-trimmed beard and queue-braided hair.

Adminius and Budic recognized him. "That's Herun, of the navy," said the younger soldier in his diffident way, and the deputy whooped, "'Oy, there, 'Erun, come drink it with us!"

Their companion shook his head. "Poor, forlorn soul," he murmured in Latin. "Has he no wife, that he couples with a whore?"

Budic flushed. "W-w-we warned you, sir, what kind of place this is. Should we g-go away?"

374

"No." A smile. "It's not as if I didn't recognize the surroundings."

Herun trotted over. "We got a guest 'ere," Adminius said. "Corentinus."

The mariner halted, squinted through the murk, responded slowly: "Aye, now I know him. Every sennight he preaches at the Forum, from the steps of the old Mars temple. What would a Christian priest among us?"

Corentinus smiled again. "Naught to frighten anybody," he said in Ysan that had become fluent though heavily accented. "I hope to grow better acquainted with folk. These men kindly offered to show me where sailors hang out. After all, I'm a sailor myself."

"Indeed?"

"Or was. 'Tis another kind of sea I ply nowadays. If I pledge not to evangelize, will you let me drink with you?"

A staring, listening stillness had fallen. "'E's a right sort," Adminius declared. "'Oly man, but not sanctimonious, if you take my meaning. Nobody minds Budic or me or most of us soldiers being Christian, so why mind Corentinus?"

Herun recovered himself. "Welcome," he said, a bit grudgingly. "Shall we sit?" He joined the three at a separate table. "Only the mead here is fit for aught but swine and Saxons," he warned, becoming more genial, "but 'tis pretty fair stuff at the price."

The potboy brought a round. Corentinus watered his. "How like you our city?" Herun asked him.

"Oh, dazzling, a whirlpool of wonders," the chorepiscopus replied. "I've never seen aught to rival it, and I've been widely about in my time."

Adminius laughed. He waved a hand around. "This 'ere's 'ardly any palace," he said.

"Nay," Corentinus agreed. "But see you, I've had my fill of elegance. Thanks to the King, I've seen the inside of most wealthy homes in Ys and its hinterland. Beautiful, as I said; but my flock numbers few, and they poor and lowly."

"Get ye no Christians in summer?" growled a man at an adjacent table. "I've met 'em aplenty whilst faring to Roman harbors."

"Aye, aye. They attend services. But my true ministry is to Ys." Corentinus chuckled and shrugged. "Not that my sermons on the steps— my rantings, some call them—draw large audiences. So I thought I would go forth among ordinary folk and get to know them well enough that, God willing, I can find what words will appeal to them."

Herun frowned. "You'll find us a tough lot," he said. "For see you, 'tis by the favor and power of her Gods that Ys lives. Else would the sea overwhelm us."

"God, the true God, He has power to save Ys," blurted Budic.

Corentinus raised a hand. "Belay that, lad. You mean well, but I did promise no preaching this night. Can we not just spin yarns? Or continue whatever else your pleasure is."

"What is yours?" purred a female voice.

They glanced up. The harlot Keban had tidied herself after Herun and come back downstairs. She was pleasant to look upon, in her close-fitting gown over a buxom figure and her deliberately tousled hair. She drooped her eyelids and smiled. "Care for a bit of fun, you?" she went on in Corentinus's direction.

He shook his head. "Not for me, thank you."

She looked about. "Anybody?...Not yet, anyhow?...Well, who'll buy a girl a drink?"

"Allow me," said Corentinus, and gestured her to sit beside him on the bench.

"Huh?" muttered from another table. "Keban, don't you know that's the new Christian priest?"

"Mayhap I can seduce him," she said impudently, and settled down.

Corentinus laughed. "Or I you? We'll see. What'll you have?"

"Wine." She stuck out her tongue at Herun. "Despite what you say 'bout it." To the pastor: "I'm surprised. I truly am. I thought somebody like you would hate me."

Again he shook his head. "Nay," he told her solemnly. "I must hate what you do, but never you, poor child. Tell me, do you never weary of being a thing? Do you ever think what becomes of old whores?"

She defied him; forlornness lay underneath: "What else have I got, unless to be a scullion in some household where the master and, and, all of them'll hump me anyway?"

Budic was appalled. "Why, Keban—" he began, and stopped.

"You've been sweet," she said to him. "Few are."

He withered under Corentinus's sardonic look. The pastor, though, merely declared to the woman: "'Tis never too late for God's grace, while life remains. Did you choose to accept His mercy, I would for my part undertake to find you a decent situation. In due course, my church may found a home for those who were lost aforetime."

The outer door creaked. Boots thudded under the weight of a bear-solid man, roughly clad, who snuffed the link he had been carrying by scrubbing it against the clay and tossed it down. As he approached through the gloom, first Herun, then the soldiers and most of the mariners recognized his rocky visage. "Maeloch!" cried one. "What brings ye hither?"

The fisher captain spouted a laugh. "What d'ye think? A bumper of mead, and— Ah, two girls on hand, I see. Hoy, Keban, Silis, which of ye'd fain be first?"

The former caught at the table edge before her and sat unwontedly silent, but the second, merry, asked, "What, are you that well heeled tonight, Maeloch?"

"Aye, and horny as a narwhal," he said, striding close to rumple her locks. "Been outside o' town this past month, helping Kadrach the cooper." No boats like his, and few ships, put far out to sea at this time of year. Maeloch sobered. "And now I'm done, well, looks to me

376

like a spell o' calm weather ahead, after the blows and high seas we've been getting. Belike there'll soon be a summons for the Ferriers. I'll enjoy myself here, for I'd better be home tomorrow night."

Mirth had retreated as he spoke. Several men drew signs. "Lackwits!" Maeloch said amiably. "Why shrink ye when I bespeak yon duty? Would ye liefer the ghosts spooked about ashore, for aye?"

Since other benches were crowded, he sat down with Adminius and Herun. Opposite were Budic, Keban, and Corentinus. He peered past sputtering candles. "But ye're the Christian priest!" he exclaimed.

"Not precisely my title," the chorepiscopus replied. "No matter. I've heard talk of you, if I mistake me not." He offered his hand across the board, for a clasp in the manner of Ysans who were equals.

Maeloch ignored it, scowled, said harshly, "Why d'ye pester honest men at their hard-won ease?"

"My son, I came not to pester, only to make acquaintance. And ever since I heard of your strange task, I've wished to talk with one among those who do it. Somehow the chance has not come."

"Nor likely will." Maeloch grabbed his mead from the servant and swilled deep. "We're no puking preachers, we're plain working men, but this duty we have from our fathers, 'tis holy, and we'll not speak of it with any who share it not, let alone ye who'd mock it."

"Oh, but I would never mock," said Corentinus quietly. "You have right, 'tis far too sacred a matter. I wish to understand what happens on those nights."

"That ye may scuttle it?" fleered Maeloch. He drank more, snorted, grinned. "Enough, I seek no fight. Keban, honey, are ye ready to frig?"

The woman looked downward. "I don't—sudden-like, I don't feel so well," she mumbled. "I'm sorry, but could I just sit a while?"

Maeloch stiffened. "Next to the priest? What's he been feeding ye?"

"Let her be," Corentinus snapped. "Yonder's a wanton for you." His tone sharpened. "Or is it unthinkable you seek the wife I suppose you have?"

Rage flared. "What business of yours, shavehead? I've heard ye deny the Gods of Ys, the Pact of Brennilis, in the Forum; and I've heard the sea growl in answer at the gate. No more! Get out!"

"Now, wait a bit," Adminius urged.

Maeloch scrambled to his feet and around the table, to stand behind Corentinus and ask, "D'ye leave on your own shanks, or do I frog march ye forth? Quick!"

Corentinus rose, stepped over the bench, looked down an inch or two into the malachite eyes. "Are you that afraid of me?" he murmured.

Maeloch snarled and seized the right wrist of Corentinus. Instantly, the pastor jerked between thumb and forefinger and freed himself; and something happened with an ankle and a shove; and Maeloch sprawled on the floor.

Men swarmed up and around. "No brawl, hoy, let's ha' no brawl!"

"God forbid," said Corentinus mildly. As the fisher climbed back up: "Maeloch, friend, I know you're aweawried, overwrought, and belike I provoked you. 'Twas not my intent. I humbly beg your forgiveness. May I stand you a drink?"

What could a sailor do but accept?

A fresh beaker, drained, had him asking where a priest had learned such a trick for a tussle. "Well, that's a bit of a story," Corentinus said. "Care to hear? Later I'll be happy to teach you the art, if you like."

Men crowded around. Corentinus leaned back, laid ankle over knee, and began: "'Twas from a Sarmatian, on the south coast of the Suebian Sea, back when I was a deckhand. He was a wanderer himself, an outrunner of those Sclavonic and other tribes that're pushing in, now when the Goths and their kindred have pulled out. My ship was adventuring in hopes of getting amber at the source, 'stead of overland. First, you may know, we had to round the Cimbrian Chersonese and pass through the straits to the east. Those're wild and haughty folk there, Angli, Jutii, Dani, not really German although they claim the royal houses of the German tribes stem from them; and they have some mightily curious customs—"

Keban, too listened. Silis sat apart; she had no interest in geography. One hand cradled her cheek, the fingernails of the other drummed the table.

~ 2 ~

Merowech the Frank and his grown sons had been in Condate Redonum buying slaves. They did this four times a year—a healthy young male shortly before equinox and solstice. Everybody in the city knew why; nobody dared speak about it. A few times the Roman authorities had, in private talks, offered to supply condemned criminals free. The Frankish headmen spurned it. They would give their Gods nothing but the best.

Merowech always obtained the victim, using the money collected from the laeti, because the sacred grove stood on his land. It was he who speared the naked body that sprattled strangling from a rope flung over a bough. (The corpse was left for the carrion fowl. Eventually the bones were taken away and stacked on that hill where the midsummer bonfire burned.) To other leading men of the neighborhood fell the honor of poleaxing and bleeding the animals that were also sacrificed, drinking some of the blood and sprinkling the worshippers with the rest. Afterward the carcasses went to Merowech's cookhouse, and everybody feasted in his hall. Thus nourished, Wotan and His sky-riding war band ought to grant victory in battle.

For the vernal equinox an additional purchase was required, a young woman. While the slain kine roasted, the men took her to a newly plowed field nearby. There Merowech swived her, followed by as many more as wished to call Fricca's blessing on their crops and their wives. She then went to work for the household whose turn it was, if she survived. Often she did not.

This day was glorious. Throughout the forest, buds had swelled and burst into leaf, blossom, a tumble of tender colors leading off toward reaches where sunlight speckled shadowiness, a whispering in breezes that were mild and laden with fragrances. The lesser birds jubilated. Overhead passed the great migrators, homeward bound.

Regardless, Merowech, Fredegond, Childeric, and Theuderich rode in helmets and ringmail, weapons at hand. Their dignity demanded it. They were not only the holders of acres broad and rich, they were garrison officers. It was on condition of the Franks providing the principal defense of the Redonian canton that the Romans had allowed them to settle there. Or so the official agreement read. Judging from what his father had told him, Merowech didn't think the Romans had had much choice, as weakened as the Empire was by its internal wars. Nowadays it seemed somewhat recovered, but the precedent had been set; and who could say how long till the next collapse?

A prudent man always went armed. If nothing else, the Franks had their own quarrels. Merowech, for instance, had a dispute over grazing rights under way with his neighbor Clothair, in which bickering half a dozen carls had gotten cut down. Clothair might take it into his head to waylay Merowech; success at that could be worth whatever weregild was negotiated afterward.

Wariness did not forbid mirth, as the warriors rode along the track that twisted toward their farm. They swapped tales of what they had done in town, brags of what they would do elsewhere. When their japes turned to the woman and her expectations, they used their German-laced Latin so she would understand. She gave small response. It was as if she had shed all the tears that were in her. Numbly, hands bound, she trudged along at the end of a cord around her neck, secured to a horse. The man still grimaced to hear, but kept his mouth shut. At first he had cursed the Franks, and when they bade him be still, gibed that he had nothing to lose. A couple of judicious kicks taught him that that was mistaken.

Talk veered to politics. Merowech kept his ears open and his mind well stocked. "Yes," he said, "as nigh's I can guess, the latest news from Italy means Theodosius will indeed bring a host against Maximus. Which one'll outlive that day, the Gods will decide; but we'd best strengthen ourselves. At this coming feast, I mean to broach a thought—"

Abruptly men were on the road, ahead, behind. They numbered about ten, Gauls from the look of them, gaunt, ragged, unshorn, armed mostly with peasant's weapons, knife, wood ax, hook, sickle, sling, just a couple of spears and swords in grimy hands. The exception was a fork-bearded, scar-cheeked young fellow who must be their chief. He bore no marks of starvation or disease, but moved like a cat; though

379

travel-worn, his garb of green had been cut from excellent stuff, a helmet covered his head, a metal-reinforced leather corselet his body; in his grasp were buckler and javelin, across his shoulders a scabbarded blade.

"Halt!" he cried cheerily. "Get down off those horses. Pay your toll and you can go unharmed."

"What's this?" Merowech bawled. "Who in Frost Hell are you?"

"The Bacaudae, the Valiant."

"No, none of them infest these parts."

"We do now. Dismount."

"Donar's whang, he blunders in that!" Merowech growled to his sons in their native language. He had heard about modern cataphracts, but those were afar in the South and East; his kind were fighters afoot. "Snatch your weapons while you jump down, and let fly. I get to cast at him. Then form a shield-burg with me, and we'll go reap them."

In the same motion that brought him to the ground, he released the francisca hung at his saddlebow and hurled it. The dreaded throwing-ax, which flew ahead of every Frankish charge, should have cloven the young Gaul at the throat. But he was alert for it, dodged, launched his spear—and Merowech's round shield had a dragging shaft in it that he could not dislodge.

From boughs and from behind boles on either side, arrows whistled. Childeric howled and sank to his knees, a shaft through his left calf. "Hold, hold!" shouted the Bacauda headman. "No more shooting yet!" He glided nearer to Merowech, his own sword free to meet the Frank's iron. "You're neatly ambushed, dad," he laughed. "Admit it, throw down your arms, and you needn't get hurt worse."

Merowech bristled. "Honor—"

"Oh, stop quacking. What use will you be anybody but the crows if you make us wipe you out? We can do it quite handily, you know. But we want you to carry a message for us."

"I fear he's right, father," Fredegond muttered. "I'm learning his face. We'll get revenge later."

Merowech nodded. "You do have us trapped," he forced from a throat that felt as if noosed. "What do you want?"

"To start with, drop your weapons," said the Gaul. "Then listen to me, and pass on what I tell you."

The Franks made themselves surrender. Horrible humiliations followed. The Bacaudae did them no injury. Rather, they removed the arrow from Childeric and bound up his wound. However, they took from them their arms, armor, horses, money, slaves, everything but undergarments—even shoes, because several of the brigands had only crude footgear.

The man and the woman who had been destined for sacrifice wept, she too, in the embraces of their rescuers. "There, now, there, now," said the leader, who called himself Rufinus, "you're safe, you're free, you'll come along with us to a wonderful city and I'm sure its King will make good places for you."

"What King is he?" asked Merowech.

"You've no need to hear that," Rufinus answered. "But listen to me. I went on a mission to such of my old comrades as I could find in our old haunts. They followed me back. I chose you to catch because of knowing what errand you'd be on. Your Gods gave you no help, though we were spoiling Their sacrifice. Think about that, Frank. Become a little more respectful of civilization."

"You say that, you, a highwayman?"

"We're none like that," Rufinus said sternly. "We're honest folk who want nothing more than to come back under law, a law that is just.

"Listen well. There are going to be more like us in the woods and on the heaths roundabout. In time they'll find wives and beget children. By then they won't be hungry ragamuffins, but well outfitted and dangerous to run afoul of.

"Their first equipment they'll get from...my master. Food? The woods have plenty of game, as shrunk as the population is. Whatever else they need, they'll trade for, or pay for out of some very reasonable tolls they'll levy. They'll harm nobody unless they're attacked, but if they are, they'll punish it hard. Do you hear me?"

"You mean outlaws intend to settle our lands?" Merowech choked on his indignation.

Rufinus laughed. "Not quite outlaws. They'll earn their keep. They'll keep down the real robbers. In case of invasion, they'll be scouts, and they'll harass the barbarians while the cities raise troops, which they'll guide. In a while, I think, they'll be ready to make you Franks settle for just giving animals to your Gods. That'll cost you a great deal less!

"Tell your people at their gatherings. I don't suppose they'll be overjoyed. However, my word may start some of them thinking. We don't really want to teach you the lesson with fire and steel. We've got better things to do."

Merowech stared a long while before he said, "This is no Roman thing. Who's behind it?"

"I can't name him yet," Rufinus replied. "But I will say he's the grandest lord any man could dream of having."

~ 3 ~

On the south side of Ys, between the city wall and the bluffs rising to Cape Rach, was a small crescent of beach. To the east the land mass butted against Aurochs Gate. Thus enclosed on three sides, the strand was often sunless and chilly. An incoming tide could make it dangerous, and the steeps were also a menace to the children whom they tempted to climb. Hence the place was not much used.

Occasionally, on sunny afternoons with ebbing water, Vindilis and Innilis took Dahut there. The girl loved it and was forever begging to go, no matter how raw the weather. She had discovered her chances were best when one of these two Mamas had her in charge. That woman would send for the other one, and the three would walk between those towers called the Brothers, and turn off Pharos Way onto the trail that went precariously down. Thereafter Dahut could do whatever she liked, within reason. Sometimes she wheedled her guardians into allowing what might seem unwise, but they had learned how surefooted she was, and how strong a swimmer. Frequently, though, she would keep motionless for an hour or more, listening to a shell or the surf or the wind, staring out over the deeps where seals and dolphins played, gulls and cormorants winged, ships and great whales passed by.

On this day there was a slight haze, and enough breeze eddied past the headland to make the air nip. It smelled of salt, kelp, clean decay, things less readily knowable. Vindilis and Innilis settled themselves on a driftwood log. In front of them the sand reached coarse, tawny-dark, to a wet edge that was almost black. Beyond glimmered and surged the water, and the wall of Ys curved away, ruddy-hued, dizzyingly high up to the frieze of mythic figures and the battlements. On the other side the promontory bulked westward. Stones and boulders lay jumbled on its flanks, below scaurs where grass clustered silvery. Farther on, sight of land ended and the sea heaved gray-green, bursting white over the reefs. Birds skimmed about, creaking, or walked on the grit, to flap off when Dahut scampered their way.

The Queens had brought a large blanket as well as a basket of refreshments. No servant had carried these; they would not miss an opportunity to be by themselves. Vindilis's aquiline features softened as she brought the cover around them both. Once they sat wrapped in it, arms went about waists. Innilis sighed, almost happily, and laid her head against the taller woman's shoulder.

"How dear a moment this is," she murmured after a while.

Vindilis nodded. "All too uncommon."

"When...we go back up...and you take the child to your house... shall I come along? Spend the night?"

Pain replied: "Nay, that would be too risky."

"Why? Grallon won't be there, in spite of her. 'Tis Guilvilis's night, if he beds with any of us."

"I know. Yet—Dahut sleeps lightly at this stage of her life. Two days ago, with Forsquilis, she was wandering around thrice in the night. Maldunilis told me earlier, giggling, how when father and daughter were both with her, Dahut came in as they were making love."

Innilis flushed. "Really? What did G-Grallon do?"

"Oh, he scolded her mildly, shooed her out, and continued. She can do no wrong in his sight." Vindilis scowled. "You and I— She'd surely babble to him. Whether or not she saw, she has sharp ears and an uncannily quick little mind."

Innilis drooped. "I see. We must go back to stealing our times like chicken thieves."

"The Gallicenae require their secrets kept from the King, now more than ever." Vindilis glanced at the girl. She was piling sand together near the waves. Vindilis brushed lips across Innilis's cheek. Under the blanket, her free hand cupped a breast. "We will have our times," she promised, "and do not think of them as stolen. They are our right. Blame not yonder child. Through her, we may win a happier morrow for ourselves."

"What? How?"

"I know not. But clear it always was, Dahut has been born fateful; and the Gods have yet to claim Their due from Grallon."

"Nay, no harm to him, please," Innilis begged of the wind.

"I too hope 'twill be mere chastisement. We must wait and see. But dearest, if They remain well pleased with us twain, and if Dahut is she who shall make a new Pact with the Gods—" Vindilis held Innilis close.

A seal splashed and slithered onto a rock not far off the beach. Dahut saw, sprang to her feet, strained peering into sunlight and sea-blink. The gown fluttered about her taut slenderness. She called, a wordless quaver. The seal rested quiet. Dahut's head drooped. She turned about and walked toward the women.

Vindilis released Innilis, who reached out from under the blanket and inquired, "Darling, what's wrong?"

"I thought 'twas *my* seal." Dahut stopped, stared downward, dug a toe in the sand, clenched fists. "Twasn't. Just an or'nary ol' bull."

Innilis smiled and, seeking to humor her, asked, "How can you be sure of that?"

Dahut looked up. Under the wild blond locks, her eyes were the hue of lapis lazuli, and as steady. "I know. She taught me."

"Indeed?" said Vindilis. "I've heard you make mention, and heard from others— But what is this seal you call yours?"

"She loves me," Dahut said. "Better'n anybody, 'cep' maybe father."

"Seals are sacred to both Lir and Belisama," Vindilis said mutedly. "I can well believe certain among them have...powers."

Dahut's mood brightened. "Can I get to be a seal? Like her?"

Innilis traced a sign against misfortune. Vindilis said, "Nobody knows. There are stories that—that sometimes good people come back as seals after they die, because the Goddess hears their plea at the Ferrying to Sena. That's so they can wait for those they loved and left behind. But nobody knows."

"I wouldn' be 'fraid to," Dahut declared.

"Peace," counselled Innilis. "Beware of overpridefulness. There are stories that bad people come back too, when the Gods are very angry with them—but as sharks, or things still worse."

Dahut suppressed a retort, flung her head high, and stood straight.

"I think," said Vindilis, "when we go home this evening, I should teach you a new prayer. *Mother of Death, come softly, I beseech.*' You may, after all, not be too young for learning such things." She unbent. "Afterward I'll tell you about a vestal long ago, who by the favor of Belisama had wonderful adventures."

Likewise seeking to please the girl, Innilis said, "That's a splendid fort you're making there."

Dahut nodded. She was not shy about accepting praise. "'Tis Ys," she answered. "I'm making Ys."

And she did, remarkably well, before she watched the tide come in and wash it away.

~ 4 ~

That year huge rainstorms arrived in succession, with lightning and hail. Harvests throughout western Armorica were meager, or failed altogether. There were those who muttered that Taranis was avenging the wrong He had suffered in the Wood. They were not many, though. King Grallon had long since established royal granaries and filled them with the surplus of good seasons, bought from the Osismii. Now the folk for whom his agents provided generally blessed his name. Rejoicing followed his proclamation that as soon as possible, he would commission ships to go fetch more from Brittania and Aquitania. As trade revived—in considerable part because of his measures against bandits and pirates— wealth had flowed into Ys until now the city could readily afford whatever it needed to see it through the next twelvemonth. Thus did disaster not undermine Grallon's authority, but rather strengthened it.

Corentinus therefore expressed surprise when Budic came to his church with word that the King had urgent want of his presence. He said nothing further, threw a hooded cloak over his coarse dark robe, and followed the soldier out. The midday was murky, rain driven thick and chill before a shrieking wind. It scourged faces, forced itself through garments, coursed down ribs and legs, swirled in the streets higher than shoesoles. Often heaven flared, and thunder followed like the wheels of a monstrous war chariot. The sea raged at the gate which the King had locked.

At the palace, the majordomo took the newcomer's cloak and offered him a towel and change of clothes. "I thank you, but nay," Corentinus replied. "Let my wet tracks be a sign to you that here also is no hiding from God. Lead me to your master."

Gratillonius sat in the upstairs room he favored for private conferences. Cups, jugs of wine and water, a lamp stood on the table before him. Next to them lay a papyrus roll. Neither the flame nor the greenish-glassed windows much relieved a dampness in which pastoral frescoes became an irony, nor did a brazier give much warmth. Beneath his everyday outfit of tunic and trousers, Gratillonius huddled in a cape; and that was strange; for cold did not usually trouble him. He had left off any ornamentation. When he looked up at Corentinus's entry, the chorespiscopus saw the strong-boned countenance drawn into haggardness.

"Shut the door," Gratillonius rasped in Latin. "Be seated."

Corentinus obeyed. Gratillonius leaned over the table between them, stabbed a forefinger onto the document, and said in the same tone, "Magnus Maximus is dead."

"What?" Briefly, Corentinus registered shock. He crossed himself, bowed his head, whispered a prayer. When he again met the other man's gaze, his own was firm. "You've just had word?"

Gratillonius jerked a nod. "From the Duke. It happened well over a month ago, but couriers to bear the news were few."

"Theodosius overthrew Maximus, then? He died in battle?"

"No. Theodosius defeated him decisively near Aquileia. I think the Gothic cavalry made the difference. Maximus surrendered and renounced his claim to the throne. That should have been the end, hey? Exile somewhere, to an island, likeliest. Let the man who saved Britannia close his days in peace and honor. But no, soon afterward Maximus and his young son Victor were killed. This letter to me isn't clear as to whether it was beheading at the express order of Theodosius, or murder by stealth." A fist smote the table. The lampflame quivered. "Whichever, we know by whose will they died!"

"God rest their souls," Corentinus said. "And yet He is just, is He not? Maximus's rival Gratianus perished miserably too—and Priscillianus, and how many more?—because of that man's ambition."

"I'd grudges of my own against him. But he was my old commandant!" Gratillonius shouted. "He held the Wall for Rome! He should not have died like that!"

He seized the wine jug and sloshed full a cup. Without adding water, he swallowed. "Pour for yourself, Corentinus," he said. "Drink with me to the memory of Magnus Maximus."

"Is this why you sent for me?"

"N-no. Not really. Though I do want, need, to talk with you, and I expect I'll get drunk, and that's nothing a man should do alone."

Corentinus took a small measure of wine, diluted it well, and sipped. "May I offer a Mass for the repose of those souls?"

"Do. I meant to ask it of you. I thought of a funerary rite before Mithras, but—but Maximus wouldn't have liked that, would he? I'll pay what it costs to have you give my commandant a Christian farewell."

Wind keened, rain runneled down the glass.

"Am I the first you have told about this?" asked Corentinus.

Again Gratillonius nodded stiffly. "I've got to convene the Suffetes and break the news. But first I'd better have a plan to lay before them. Else they'll debate and squabble and bargain, while matters drift. That kind of delay could prove fatal."

"I am no politician or soldier, my son. I couldn't advise you."

"Oh, you can. You've been around in the Empire more than I have. You've got the ear of Bishop Martinus, who's more powerful than he pretends, even to himself. Theodosius has reinstalled Valentinianus, his brother-in-law, as Augustus of the West; but Theodosius is staying on for a while in Italy, and you know very well who's really going to rule. From what I hear, he's a zealous Catholic. You can better guess than I how he'll use the church, and it him."

Corentinus frowned. "Watch your tongue." He paused. "What do you fear, exactly? Won't everyone benefit from peace and a strong Imperium?"

"Once I'd have supposed so," Gratillonius answered starkly, "but I've learned otherwise. And...I belong here now, I belong to Ys. Rome is still my Mother, but Ys is my Wife."

Within the short beard, Corentinus's lips quirked the least bit. Sobering, he lingered over a fresh taste of his wine before he said: "I see. Maximus appointed you prefect. There will doubtless be a pretty deep-going purge of his officials."

Gratillonius drained his cup and refilled it. "I'm not frightened for myself. I honestly think I'm not. But if I'm ordered back and—and obey, what then? Who'll succeed me? What'll he do?"

"Do you fear Roman occupation, the pagan temples destroyed and rites forbidden, Ys rising in revolt and Rome laying it waste as Rome long ago did to Jerusalem?"

Gratillonius shivered. "You've said it."

Corentinus regarded him closely. "Then I'll also say that this strikes me as being a terrible evil. They're not simple rustics in Ys, the kind whose sanctuaries I helped Martinus overthrow. There it was enough to show how the old Gods were powerless to stop us. They'd never been very large in the lives of the people. A spring, a hill, any sacred site meant more; and it can as well be under the tutelage of a Christian saint. The Gods of Ys will not fade away like that. Before yielding up Their worshippers, They would bring Ys itself down in ruin."

"You understand," Gratillonius breathed.

"My holy duty is to win your people to the true Faith. My single hope of doing so without bringing on catastrophe is by persuasion, patience, year after slow year. Not to attack the Gods, but to sap Them. If only you would unlock your heart— But at least, under you, Ys flourishes, open to newness as it has not been in centuries; and your protection is impartial. We need you as our King."

"If you'd write to Martinus—"

"I'll do that, and more. He, in his turn, can convince the bishops throughout Lugdunensis that Ys should be spared. The Imperium ought to heed them. Besides, in worldly terms, better a loyal foederate, a keystone of defense and a cauldron of trade, than wreckage."

Gratillonius eased somewhat, achieved a smile, said: "Thank you. The Duke is on my side already. I don't think they'll dismiss him; he goes back to before Maximus. If you can make the Church our ally as well—" Impulsively: "Listen, Corentinus. You know the Ysan charities are mostly run by the Gallicenae. I know your mission hasn't much to spend. Help me, and I'll endow your good works, generously."

"The thought does you credit," replied the pastor with care, "but the deed could endanger you. Your magnates would see it as yet another defiance of the Gods."

"What I lay out of my privy purse is no concern of theirs, or of Theirs."

"M-m, you realize that such of the poor and unfortunate as you enable us to aid—they will be grateful more to us than you, and this will incline them toward Christ."

Gratillonius laughed and drank. "Manly of you to warn me, but of course I knew it. No harm done. Why should I bar anybody from forsaking the Gods of Ys?"

Corentinus studied him. "Wouldn't you want them to come to your Mithras?"

Gratillonius shrugged. On the heels of his merriment trod pain: "Few ever would. His is no longer a conquering army. We hold the wall for Him while we can, but the foe has marched around it."

He upended his cup and filled it anew. "The Wall!" he shouted. "We stood on the Wall under Maximus. My buddies— How many went south with him? What's going to become of them? Those are men of *mine*. I barracked with them, and pounded the roads and dug the trenches and fought the raiders and diced and caroused with them, and after I'd made centurion I led them, punished them when they needed it, heard out their troubles when they needed that—my Second Augusta and—and there were others with us on the Wall that year, Corentinus. Like Drusus of the Sixth; we saved each other's lives, d'you hear? So they fought for our old Duke, and lost, and what's that Emperor who killed Maximus and Victor out of hand, what's he going to do about them?"

"You are getting drunk in a hurry," Corentinus observed in the sailor's lingo he used when he wanted to.

"I don't expect Theodosius can massacre them," Gratillonius went on. "Too many. But what, then? Think he'll send them back to their bases in Britannia, Gallia, wherever? I think not. He'll be afraid of them, and want to make an example, too. He'll discharge them, maybe. And what are they supposed to do then? They'll lose their veteran's benefits. Are they supposed to starve? Become serfs? Join the Bacaudae? What?"

"A knotty question, in truth," Corentinus agreed. "Christ bade us forgive our enemies, and I should hope Theodosius will, if only for his own soul's sake. But those men *were* mutineers, in a sense, and they'd too likely be an unsettling element in the army. You feel Maximus should simply have been exiled. But how can thousands be?"

Gratillonius straightened. Wine splashed from his cup as he crashed it to the table. "Here!" he exclaimed. "By the Bull, you've hit on it!

Armorica's half empty. What we need most is more people, to make their homes and stand guard over them. And there we've got those fighting men, and here we've got a peninsula at the far end of the Empire where they couldn't possibly be any threat to our overlords."

Excitement seized Corentinus likewise. "Write to the Duke and the governor at once," he said. "Urge them to propose it to the Emperors. Offer the influence, experience, help of Ys in getting settlement started. God willing, you'll have a glad acceptance."

"I'll write tomorrow," Gratillonius roared, "and afterward tell the Council. Now let's drink and sing songs and remember Maximus and all old comrades."

Corentinus smiled—wistfully? "I may not do that myself. But I'll keep you company if you like."

They had been at it for a while, as the day darkened further, when a knock on the door brought Gratillonius there. He opened it and stood aside, still steady on his feet though the flush of wine was on his cheeks and the odor of it on his breath.

Bodilis entered. Her hair hung as wet as her garments. The hands with which she took his were cold.

"I thought you should hear this from me, beloved," she said, oblivious to anybody else. "Word reached me, I went to see, and, and, I think Quinipilis is dying."

X

~ 1 ~

The agony that speared through breast and left arm, the stranglehold that closed on a heart flying wild, gave way to quietness. She slept a great deal, though lightly, often rousing from dreams. Her pulse fluttered weak, like a wounded bird, and she had no strength. Nonetheless she whispered her commands that she be helped out of bed for bathing and necessities. Such times left her exhausted for hours, but her head remained always clear. Besides the wedded couple who were her only servants, the other Gallicenae insisted on abiding in her house, each a day and night in turn. They allowed no more than very brief visits by the many who came, nor did they themselves tax her with much talk. Often, though, they read aloud to her from books she loved.

Rainstorms gave way to fog. As summer waned, Ys lay in a chill dankness and a white blindness that seemed to go on without end. Quinipilis could not get warm, even when the hypocaust had made the floor too hot for bare feet. The Sisters kept her tucked in fleece blankets and rubbed her hands and feet—carefully, as deformed and tender as those had become. They brought soup and upheld her maned skull while spooning it into her.

Innilis had musicians on call, for such times as harp, flute, song might briefly cheer. Bodilis translated some lyrics of Sappho into Ysan, because Quinipilis had admired those she already knew. Whenever she rallied a little, however, the dowager was apt to ask for something more vigorous, renditions from the Greek, original in Latin or Ysan: the clangor of Homer and Vergilius, sternness of Aeschylus and Euripides, comedy of Philemon and Plautus, or (wickedly grinning) the bawdiest bits from Aristophanes and Catullus, as well as Utican the Wanderer and Witch-Hanai of this city. A couple of times she herself recited snatches of Gallic or Saxon.

That was near the beginning of her invalidity. Soon she slipped deeper down, and mostly lay with her thoughts and memories.

Then on the ninth morning she told Fennalis, who had the watch: "Bring my Sisters hither."

"Nay, you'd wear yourself out. I can scarce hear your voice, though you've had a night's rest. Take care so you can get well."

Wrinkles formed a hideous frown. Somehow the words loudened enough. "Stop that. I am not in my dotage, thank you. I am outworn, for which there is no healing." The scowl turned into laughter lines. "I've somewhat to convey to the lot of you—at once, ere the wheels altogether fall off the old oxcart. Prepare me your strongest strengthening draught."

"That could easily kill you."

"Another day or two would do that anyhow, with naught to show for it." Quinipilis must halt a while to breathe. Her fingers plucked at the covers. "Fennalis, I conjure...I conjure all of you...by Our Lady of Passage."

The short gray woman wrestled with herself a moment before she nodded, bit her lip to hold it still, and scuttled out.

Presently there were seven crowded at the bedside. Guilvilis was absent, having the Vigil on Sena. Forsquilis, who was this day's presiding high priestess, had come directly from the Temple of Belisama in her blue gown and white headdress. Innilis clutched the hand of Vindilis, like a child her mother's. Maldunilis wept, striving to hold it quiet and not blubber. Lanarvilis kept stoic. Bodilis kissed the withered lips and stood aside. Fennalis plumped pillows, got Quinipilis half sitting up amidst them, fetched the decoction of foxglove, willow bark, and herbs more curious, held the cup while it went its way, took a post hard by.

Quinipilis's breath quickened and grew noisy. That was almost the single sound. Fog made windowpanes featureless. Within, candles kept shadows at bay, though they filled every corner. A few things were clear to see—a vase of aster and fern from the woods, shelved toys that had been her daughters' when they were small, the hanging sword of King Wulfgar who was her first man, in a niche with a taper at its feet a statuette of Belisama as a young matron holding Her infant. Air lay overheated and sullen.

A hint of blood mounted through the waxiness on Quinipilis. Her glance brightened and steadied. When she spoke, it was clearly: "Welcome. Thank you for coming."

"How could we not come, mother, mother to us all?" replied Vindilis.

"This is our goodbye, of course." Quinipilis's voice was matter-of-fact. She raised a palm against the protest she saw in some of their faces. "Nay, we've scant time left. Let's spill none of it in foolishness. For myself, I'm more than ready to go to my rest. But first I've a thing to deal with—or, rather, leave to you."

"Hush," Forsquilis bade the Sisters. "The Spirit is upon her."

Quinipilis shook her head and coughed out a chuckle. "I misbelieve that, my dear. 'Tis no more than the same vixen that ever made her den in me." She grew serious. "Yet lying here quietly, so quietly, feeling time slip away—that gives one to think, in between the visits of the living and the dead."

The high-crowned head nodded. "You've wondered whom the Gods will choose to reign after you, and why."

Quinipilis sighed. "Aye. I told you I am content to go. But I would have been earlier. Or I could have stayed longer, equally content to watch the seasons pass and the children grow. Is it chance that I must depart just now? I fear very much the Gods are not done with our King."

"Nay!" broke from Bodilis. She slammed control down on herself. "If They are still angry because of—that unfulfilled sacrifice and—other matters—why have They not struck him already?"

Quinipilis closed her eyes. The power of the medicine was flagging. "You can guess?"

"Mayhap I can," Lanarvilis said slowly. "This year agone has been the most dangerous for Ys since the year he came. The Empire has been in upheaval while the barbarians snuffed blood and grew hungry. Then the Imperial peace returned, but the victors would fain destroy everything Ys has ever been. Who could cope save Gratillonius? Even his man Rufinus who should have died in the Wood, Rufinus has proven an instrument for him to begin shoring up our bulwarks. Therefore the Gods have stayed Their hands."

"Until now," whispered Forsquilis.

Quinipilis reopened her eyes. "So I have thought," she told them. "Also this have I thought, that They cannot yet spare him, but They will seek to humble him; and in that They will fail, but They can wound him terribly. He is a good man, under his iron—"

"He came to me yesterday, straight from having been with you," said Bodilis, "and that whole eventide he was swallowing tears."

"Stand by him, Sisters," Quinipilis pleaded. "Whatever happens, never forsake him."

"We can ill do that, like it or not," said Vindilis.

"W-w-we did bring him!" blurted Maldunilis. "We made him King. Could we have a better one? Nay!"

Fennalis began to reply but thought better of it.

"Help him," Quinipilis bade them. "Promise me. Give me your oaths."

"By the Three I swear," said Bodilis immediately.

Vindilis pinched lips together before she lifted her arms and exclaimed, "Hold! Hard is this to say, but bethink you, we cannot foreknow—"

Quinipilis gasped. She slumped into the pillows. Her eyes rolled back. Her breath raced in and out like riptides between reefs, then died away to nearly nothing, then raced, then died. Froth bubbled around her lips.

"Goddess, nay!" screamed Fennalis. She flung herself down on the bed. Her fingers sought to clear the foam away, let air get through. "Quinipilis, darling Quinipilis, are you there, can you hear me?" Only the rattling and whistling answered.

Soon they ended. Fennalis rose. Having signed herself, she beckoned to Vindilis, the blood daughter, who trod forward to fold the hands, bind up the jaw, close the eyes.

~ 2 ~

Lir's fog did not reach far inland. At the Nymphaeum, the end of the rains had brought a last upwelling of warmth and lightfulness. The forest that decked the heights glowed a molten green, a thousand hues which a breeze made ripple and weave. Likewise did the lawn in the hollow drink the sunshine that spilled on it from among a few swan's-wing clouds, and give it back to heaven. Blooms had mostly died, but leaves in flowerbeds and hedgerows lived yet. Brooklets glittered and chimed on their way to the glimmery pond. In the shadow of the linden above the sacred spring, the image of the Mother smiled mysterious.

Forth at noontide from the colonnade of the building came certain vestals, as was appointed for this phase of the moon nearest autumnal equinox. Their garments were as white as the walls and pillars. Their hair flowed loose and their feet danced nimble, for they were young girls, less than three years into their service—descendants of Queens in Ys unto the third generation, whereafter the Goddess released a lineage. More fully clad, a virgin near the end of her term led them, as did an aging woman who had returned to the Temple and become a minor priestess when she was widowed.

Blue sheened on peacocks; three spread their tails, like a salute of banners. The grown maiden put syrinx to lips and sounded the tune, while the girls joined hands and skipped the measure, on their way to do reverence before the eidolon. Their voices rose clear as the pipe-notes.

"Belisama, all-sustaining,
Lady of the golden year,
Now that summertime is waning,
Guard this world You hold so dear.

Soon the leaves must fall to cover
Earth grown weary of the sun.
Bring our lord, our King, our lover
Home to us when sleep is done!"

Suddenly one of them screamed.

The music stopped, the dance jarred to a halt. "What is it?" cried the maiden. "Come here, sweetling." She held out her arms.

The girl touched her bosom, "It, it burned," she half sobbed. "For a heartbeat, it burned." Her eyes widened. Her face went chalky. "I'm well again. I am."

The old woman approached her through the silent stares. "We must look at this." She took the small hand. "Fear naught. We love you."

The maiden mustered courage. "We have our rite to finish," she told the rest. "Follow me onward. Sing your song. Remember, we are children of the Goddess."

The procession resumed, raggedly. Meanwhile the priestess hastened toward the Nymphaeum. Semuramat, daughter of Queen Bodilis by King Hoel, stumbled at her side.

~ 3 ~

The fog lifted. After sunset, a nearly full moon dazzled away from itself the stars that otherwise crowded heaven. So wild was Gratillonius that at length Bodilis suggested they leave her house. "Space, air, a wholesome tiredness of the body, and then you may perhaps win to sleep for a while, my poor beloved." They dressed warmly and went forth.

Silence enwrapped them, save for their footfalls on frosty paving and for the sounds of the sea, rising as they drew nearer. He had ended the ravings and curses and desperate schemes he brought her after the word reached him. Their breaths smoked wan, like the utterances of ghosts. Walls shadowed streets from the moon but not from starshine. Man and woman found their way readily down the lanes that twisted from Elven Gardens, and thence along broad Lir Way, over the deserted Forum, south on Taranis Way to Goose Fair plaza, across it and the pomoerium to a staircase and thus up onto the city wall. Guards at the Raven Tower challenged them; armor shimmered icy in the moonbeams from beyond eastern hills. Recognizing who came, the marines saluted and let them by. Under the high helmets, awe was on faces.

Gratillonius and his Queen walked onward along the battlements, past the war engines that slumbered in their housings, almost to the sea gate. There they stood looking outward.

The moon had cleared the towertops. Above the clustered roofs of Ys, they seemed spires of glass, ready to shatter at the least shaking from the sea, upraised out of a stonefield already sunken. Tonight there was not turbulence. The waters swelled and broke and swelled anew, fluid obsidian over which ran mercury. *Hush*, they murmured, *hush-hush-hush*. So clear was the air that Gratillonius saw a spark out yonder that must be light in the building on Sena, where Forsquilis of the Gallicenae held communion with the Gods.

Bodilis took his arm. "Let us take comfort from such great beauty," she said low.

"Beneath it lies terror," he answered.

"Great beauty is always terrible. Life is."

"Why? What have we done—no, not we, you and little Semuramat—that this has happened?" Gratillonius shook his head. "Oh, I know. You, as close as you were to me, must be hit when They struck. What worse loss than you could I suffer?"

"Dahut," she said.

He snapped after air.

"And you have not lost me," she went on. "Stop treading the same ground. You've pounded it barren. Let me tell you for the twentieth—or fiftieth or hundredth, but the last time—I remain your Queen Bodilis."

"Whom I may never again touch in love."

"That is your choice."

"My choice?" His gaze sought the Raven Tower, black against the sky. Beyond hulked Cape Rach, and at its end guttered the pharos candle. "My faith. Mother and daughter—Mithras forbids. If I denied Fennalis on that account, how can I do otherwise with you?"

"It would be...bad politics."

"No politics tonight, no damned politics! This is of the spirit, as well you should know."

She winced in the colorless light: she, both daughter and grand-daughter of Wulfgar. It was not that her mother had sinned with her father. There could be no incest when the Gods decreed the wedding. It was that he, who could not help himself once Their will was upon him, had afterward lost courage to live, and presently lay dead at the feet of Gaetulius.

Gratillonius saw the hurt he had given, caught Bodilis to his breast, and stammered, "I'm sorry, I didn't mean that, shouldn't have spoken so to you—you half-sister of Dahilis—" through King Hoel: Dahilis, who perished in giving birth to Dahut.

Bodilis stroked his hair, stepped back, and smiled at him. "I understand. These are roads that double back and back on themselves, aren't

393

they? Well, of course I'll long for you, but we'll always stay friends, allies; no God commands our hearts."

"Unless I refuse this marriage. The girl *is* too young. Oh, she's passed her Rite of Welcome; but so short a time ago, she so small yet and—and frightened."

"You will be kind to her. You've been like the father she never really knew."

Now he flinched. Casting weakness aside, he said, more calmly than he had said it before, "Best for her, too, if I balk."

"You would rip Ys apart. This is the holiest rite we were ever given, the renewal of the world."

"I meant, well, carry out the service, but not c-c-consummate the marriage."

Bodilis shook her head. "No, you can't escape that either."

"I did with Quinipilis and Fennalis."

"They were past childbearing age."

"Is Semuramat at it?"

"She will be. And...the bloodied sheet is given the Goddess next morning. No, Gratillonius, dear bewildered man. Unless you'd flee at once, abandon us forever, you must marry Tambilis tomorrow."

He battered a fist against a merlon. That was the name Semuramat had chosen, to honor her grandmother who died in the horrible reign of Colconor. Such was traditional. Yet the older Tambilis had been the mother of both Bodilis and Dahilis.

"At least this time you've said rationally the things you shouted in fragments at the house," added the Queen. She hesitated, glanced out across Ocean, added low, "We do have tonight left us, you and I."

A while he stood, hunched over. Moonlight caught a few tears. Finally he shook his head. "No. Your advice is right, hard but right. Then I dare not—"

"You are doubtless wise," she sighed.

He started back. "Go home, Bodilis," he said. "Rest yourself as well as you can. Your daughter will need you very much tomorrow."

She followed. "What of you?" she asked at his back.

He looked straight ahead. "I'll commandeer a lamp at the tower, and go down into the Mithraeum, and be with my own God."

~ 4 ~

There was the ceremony in the Temple of Belisama, where vestals sang and the Eight stood veiled together with her who would be the Ninth, flanking the altar behind which lifted images of Maiden, Mother, and Hag. The bride came to the groom, they knelt under the prayers and hymns, rose again when bidden; he lifted her veil while the Sisters raised theirs. "Gratillonius, King of Ys, in homage to the Goddess Who

394

dwells in her, and in honor to the womanhood that is hers, receive your Queen Tambilis—" Fennalis, the senior, brought the consecrated wine for them to share.

Public coronation and festivity waited until Quinipilis should have had her sea burial. This day the Gallicenae merely accompanied the King to his palace, where a simple meal was set forth. They talked sparingly, Tambilis not at all. What conversation did take place was mostly reminiscence of the departed.

Afterward, one by one, each of the women kissed the girl and, in their differing ways and words, made her welcome, wished her well, promised her their help and love. By tacit agreement, Bodilis came last. The two clung together a short spell. Gratillonius stood aside, alone.

The guests and their attendants bade him goodnight and left. Dusk was blue beyond the doorway. The household staff were now free to come forth and, through the majordomo, request the benediction of the new Queen. "Blessing on you, blessing on you." Her voice was as thin as the hand with which she touched their heads where they knelt.

Thereafter they escorted the bridal pair to the royal bedchamber. They had cleaned everything that was in it, arrayed green boughs and, in lieu of flowers at this season, clusters of berries. Candles burned in abundance. The broad bedstead carried a richness of furs and embroideries. A table inlaid with nacre held wine, water, fruits, confections. Incense sweetened the air. Frescoes on walls, paintings on shutters, mosaic on floor, gave images of woodland, meadow, lake, sea, cloudscape; beasts real and mythical pranced, swam, flew; youths and maidens were joyful together. Outside, in silence, the stars were coming forth.

The door closed.

Gratillonius turned from it, toward his wife. She stood with arms straight down, fists clenched, staring before her. It came to him that in the chaos of his heart he had not really looked at her. And earlier she had been only Semuramat, daughter of Bodilis, stepdaughter to him, a bright and blithe child with whom he enjoyed passing time whenever he was able. She had, indeed, been like a true older sister to Dahut, more and more so as she blossomed toward womanhood.

At thirteen years of age, she reached not quite to his throat, and much of that height was leg. The rest of her seemed to be mainly eyes, underneath formally dressed hair which had changed from the gold of childhood to a light brown. They were the deep blue of her mother's, those eyes, or of Dahilis's or Dahut's. Her features were delicate, lips always slightly parted over teeth. Because she was often outdoors, summer had tinged her skin and dusted freckles across the tip-tilted nose. Bridal gown and jeweled pectoral hung heavy from her shoulders.

Remembering his first night with Guilvilis, he willed resolution upon himself. There was that which must be done, and shilly-shallying about it would be no kindness. He went to her, smiled, and took her hands. They lay cold in his. "Well, dear," he said, "here we are."

She remained mute. Releasing her left hand, he brought his right under her chin and raised it until their gazes must meet. She blinked and breathed hard. "Be at ease," he said. "You know your old friend. He hasn't changed. I wanted this not myself." Louder than intended: "O Mithras, nay!" Softly again: "We've had a duty laid on us. We'll carry it out like good soldiers, you and I, eh?"

She nodded. It caused his hand, yielding, to slide down her neck. How frail it was, how silken the skin. A blue pulse throbbed.

"Come," he said, "let's be seated, let's drink to a happier morrow." Let her become warmed, at rest, wine-dazed.

She ran tongue over lips. "My lord is, is gracious," she whispered.

He guided her to a settee before the table and, with a faint pressure, caused her to sit down, before he himself did. "What nonsense," he chided, attempting laughter. "We'll have no 'my lord' any longer. You're a Queen of Ys, Tambilis. You'll be a guiding star to the people, a healer, a strong voice in council; you'll command wind and wave; you'll be—with the Goddess. Better I call you 'my lady.'"

He filled two silver goblets, diluting in neither, and urged one into her clasp. "Drink," he said. She obeyed. He saw her grimace and realized that the wine by itself, dry as most Ysans preferred, was harsh on a palate that had usually known water. "I'm sorry. Here, I'll pour some back and weaken the rest. I do think if you take a draught or so you'll feel calmer. And, uh, behold, wouldn't you like these raisins, these sweetmeats?"

Partaking did seem to help. After a few minutes Semuramat—Tambilis gave him a steady regard and said with childish seriousness: "Mother told me you would be kind."

"I promised her. I promise you. As far as lies in my power, I will." And may you never know how I miss her.

"Then do what you shall, Grallon."

His face heated. "Wait, wait, no haste, let's talk a bit, let me tell you something about what to await—"

He avoided grave matters but bespoke feasts, games, foreign visitors with wonderful stories. She drank faster, without noticing. A sparkle awoke. She leaned into the crook of his arm, snuggled against him, as she had done when she was a small girl and he yarning to her in the presence of her mother.

Desire flamed up.

No! he snarled to the Power. You'll have Your way with us, that's fated, but not yet.

"What's the matter?" she asked when his words stopped.

"Naught, naught." He went on with the tale. His loins raged.

—"That had better be all, darling," he said around the dryness in his mouth. Thunders went through his breast. "You need your sleep."

Her nod wobbled, her voice was slurred: "Aye. Thank you, kind Grallon. Now make me a woman."

She caught her wits back to her. "First I should pray to the Goddess, oughtn't I?"

He ordered his arm, that had been about to close tight, to let her go. He stood aside while she went to pray. He had long since had images of the Three removed from this room, but she found a nymph among the revelers who looked older and more modest than the rest. Her slight form took stance before the picture, she raised her hands, and Gratillonius stood fighting off the Bull. He heard:

"Belisama, to Your keeping
I entrust my soul this night.
Guard Your child while she is sleeping;
Wake me to the morning light."

Tambilis turned toward her husband, held out her arms. He went to her through the roaring. She did not know anything else than to let him undress her. Tortoiseshell comb and ivory pins clinked to the floor. He had no skill in loosening hair, and she giggled a bit, while crying a bit, when he tugged a bit too hard. The pectoral and golden bracelets dropped with a clang. The girdle slithered aside like a snake. He shook as he undid the dress and pulled the undergarment off over her head.

Thereupon she stood with an uncertain smile on her lips. Hands flitted for a moment, seeking to conceal, but drew aside. As yet, he saw, her figure was almost a boy's. The crescent of the Sign burned red between tiny breasts. Hips and buttocks had, though, begun to fill out, and above her thighs was a shadowiness that caught glints of light.

Cast her down and have her!

Gratillonius stepped back. "I'll first blow out the candles," he said somehow.

Did the flush upon her cheeks pale? "Nay, please, can we keep them?" she asked. Thus could she see what happened, and maintain bravery.

"If, if you wish." As quickly as he could, he disrobed. When she saw him in his maleness, she gasped, quailed, rallied, stood fast. "Be not afraid. I'll be gentle."

He led her to the bed, drew blankets aside, guided her down, joined her, pulled the covers over them both. She shivered in his clasp. He stood on the wall against the Bull, while he murmured and stroked and kissed. Finally, of course, he must take her.

He *was* gentle. That much victory did he win over the Gods.

It hurt her nonetheless. She shed more blood than was common, and could not help sobbing afterward. He held her close. "There, there," he crooned in her ear, "'tis done, you'll soon be well again, and we need do this no more until you are ready for it, years hence. I will not press you. Sleep, child."

That also was territory he could defend.

XI

~ 1 ~

"Maybe here at last we'll find peace," Drusus said low.

"I can't promise that," Gratillonius told him. "At best, you'll have to work for it, and most likely fight, too."

Drusus sighed. "It'd be worth it. If I could know my kids, anyhow, will have a chance to live their own lives."

Gratillonius regarded his comrade of the Wall with compassion. The centurion of the Sixth Victrix seemed grotesquely out of place in this frescoed, mosaic-floored room. The tunic upon his stocky form was patched and faded. A deep inward weariness bowed the shoulders and looked out of the weatherbeaten, ill-barbered face. There was even a listlessness in his grip around the wine cup that rested on his knee where he sat.

Through doors open to the summer's warmth drifted the sounds of Aquilo, voices, footfalls, hoofbeats, wheel-creak, hammer-clash, together with odors of smoke and of green growth beyond the town. Those too seemed remote from the visitor.

It was Apuleius Vero who found words: "Your life has been one endless march from battle to battle, homeless as the wind, over hill and heath and fields laid desolate, has it not?"

Publius Flavius Drusus cast a glance of startlement at the senator, the antiquated but immaculate toga that wrapped his slenderness and the handsome, still fairly youthful countenance above. "Feels that way, sir," he agreed.

Gratillonius harked back across the years. He had not been much together with this man, but those times were burned into him: combat against the barbarians, fellowship of miles and campfires and barracks, later a chance meeting in Augusta Treverorum and a drunken evening when hearts were unlocked. But Drusus had earlier fought the Saxons as they came reaving out of the eastern sea; he had crossed to Gallia to fight under his Duke Maximus and win for him the Imperium; he had stood guard on the German frontier and campaigned beyond it; he had tramped south over the mountains into Italy and done battle again with legionaries like himself; he had followed his Emperor eastward, and seen their cause go down before Theodosius's Gothic lancers; half a prisoner, he had done hard labor on lean rations through month upon month of autumn, winter, spring; then he had made the trek across Europe to Armorica and a fate still unknown. Gratillonius did not wonder at seeing him slumped.

I hope I can straighten that back of his, the King of Ys thought.

"You may indeed have come to haven," said Apuleius.

"Sirs, excuse me, but I don't understand," the centurion faltered. "I mean, well, all right, we veterans of Maximus have been sent north. We'll get our discharges, and places to stay, and—it's better than we hoped for, back there with the cataphracts on their tall horses herding us along—but what do you want of me? Why am I here?"

Gratillonius smiled. "That's a long story, old buddy," he replied. "Let me just give the gist of it now, because I think dinner time's close and we'd like to relax then.

"This resettlement was my idea, when I heard about the fall of Maximus last year. A priest—chorepiscopus, I mean, name of Corentinus, gave me a lot of help, and we got Bishop Martinus in Turonum and other big men interested, and— Never mind. The upshot is that here we have Armorica, half depopulated, screwed over by pirates and bandits and barbarians who've actually taken up residence. And yonder we had you soldiers, good men, but men that the Emperors could neither trust nor massacre. Let's bring them together.

"I thought of establishing a colony. If it was near Condate Redonum, it'd keep the Franks there in line. But that was refused. Not unreasonable, from Theodosius's viewpoint. He wants you dispersed as well as discharged, so you can't ever get up another revolt. So be it."

As he paused, Apuleius interposed gently: "None of you shall be left destitute. Each man shall receive his plot of land and the basic tools he requires. The tribesmen will surely help him, for they ought to welcome such a strong new neighbor. From among their daughters he can soon find a wife. Praise God for His mercies."

"We'd not every one of us make a farmer," Drusus objected. "Many of us wouldn't know one end of a cow from the other."

Gratillonius laughed. "True. Well, any legionary has skills that're in demand, what with trade reviving hereabouts. There'll be work for all. I can use a few engineers in Ys, as a matter of fact. And if nothing else, the granaries of Ys will keep you from starving before you can support yourselves."

Drusus shook his head dazedly. "My partner in the mud, a king," he marveled.

"Let's get to the point about why we've sent for you," Gratillonius went on. "You owe a heap—I think you'll agree—to my friend Apuleius. He kept up the correspondence and the political pressure and everything else I didn't have the time or the connections for. You see, I knew you'd be with your outfit if you were still alive, Drusus, and knew you could be depended on. So we managed to get a fair-sized number of men in your century assigned to this area."

"No gratitude is due me," said Apuleius. "I only wish to see the district well served, and therefore accepted Gratillonius's recommendation. Aquilo and its environs are poorly defended. We have nothing but a handful of native troops, ill trained, and reservists with no training to speak of. Despite my repeated pleas, the Duke has never stationed any legionary regulars here.

"Well, of course you and your, ah, vexillation are going to be civilians. As such, you cannot, under Imperial law, form yourselves back into a military unit. You will be farmers, artisans, and so on. However, you will not have forgotten your martial trade, and equipment can be gradually obtained. I expect you to hold periodic drills and exercises which will include Osismiic men. Thus you will eventually provide us with a reserve force that is effective."

"Almighty God!" Drusus exclaimed. "You *mean* that?"

"I was never more serious," assured Gratillonius. "I'm hoping you'll take the lead, under Apuleius the tribune, in getting all this organized. Think you can handle it?"

Drusus put down his cup, sprang to his feet, squared his shoulders, and gave the Roman salute. "Sir, I do."

Gratillonius stood up too, refrained from hugging him, but said, "Splendid. We'll discuss details in the next couple of days. First let's enjoy ourselves. Isn't food about ready, Apuleius? My stomach believes it's been sent to hell for the sin of gluttony."

A trifle shocked by the irreverence, the senator nonetheless answered graciously, "Soon, I pray your patience. Would you two like to go to another room and talk? You see, we've developed a custom in my family. Before the main meal, I spend half an hour with my daughter."

"Verania?" asked Gratillonius.

Apuleius nodded. "I'm surprised you remember."

"Why shouldn't I? Charming child." Abruptly it came to Gratillonius: Rovinda, the wife in this house, was again pregnant; but there had been no sign or mention of another infant. Whichever she had borne since Verania must have died, as infants so often did, unless their mothers were Gallicenae who had medical arts and magics and the blessing of Belisama.

Impulsively, Gratillonius proposed, "We'll stay, if you don't mind. She might like meeting newcomers."

"Oh, that would be wonderful," Apuleius said. "You are too kind."

Gratillonius shrugged and laughed. "I'm a father myself, several times over." He regretted it when he saw the flicker of pain across Apuleius's lips, but dismissed remorse; he knew himself for a man not especially tactful nor the least bit subtle.

Drusus sat back down and reached for his cup, looking resigned.

Apuleius went to the inner door and called. A female slave led Verania in. She moved shyly toward him, her gaze big and hazel in the direction of the strangers. Gratillonius's heart lost a beat. O Mithras! Just about four years old, she was a trifle younger than Una, and her coloring was different, lighter; but how those delicate features and that graceful gait recalled the daughter that Bodilis had given him.

Daughter of Bodilis—A year had passed without much blunting his longing for Bodilis as more than a soft-spoken counsellor, a carefully correct friend.

Gratillonius mastered himself. From Dahut he had learned how to court little girls. You didn't stare or beam or gush or grab. You were cheerful, casual, always respectful of the child's dignity; and before long she would listen to you, then come to you, with the dawn of adoration in her eyes.

~ 2 ~

"The centurion will be away," Adminius lamented. "Not the King, 'e don't matter now, but my officer Gratillonius, centurion o' the Second. Slice and gut me, wot a shame! The single thing wrong, that 'e can't be there ter stand me by and lead the celebration afterward. 'E would, you know. I've 'alf a mind ter put it all off till 'e gets back."

He knew that was impossible. The family into which he was marrying would have taken grievous offense. The Powers might too, since the astrological signs were propitious for the date set and none other in the near future. Besides, nobody could say when Gratillonius would return from this latest journey of his.

Adminius found consolation in knowing that his whole Roman squadron would be on hand. This time the prefect had left them behind and travelled with an escort of Ysan marines. In part, he explained, that was to allay a certain jealousy he had seen growing. To take them beyond the frontier not only gave them a pleasurable outing but acknowledged that he was *their* King. And in part, when he was to deal with former rebels, he had better avoid anything that might look suspicious to the Imperial authorities.

The wedding would be an event of some importance, joining the deputy commander of the legionary cadre to Avonis, sister of the naval officer Herun, who with her belonged to the Taniti clan of Suffetes. It would take place at the Nymphaeum, and a Queen would preside. Adminius proposed that his soldiers form an honor guard. They cheered, except for Budic. "What's the matter with you?" demanded Cynan.

The young Coritanean reddened like a maiden. He must gulp before he could mumble, "A pagan rite. The chorepiscopus was warning again, in his last sermon, about d-d-danger to the soul."

"Ha!" Cynan sneered. "Some faith, that won't let a fellow show friendship. When are you due to be gelded?"

"Lay off that," Adminius ordered. "Honesty's too flinking rare as it is....Budic, lad, I won't force yer. But well you know, I'm not the first among us ter settle down with an Ysan wife, and me a Christian too. It's an honorable estate, better than 'oremongering, 'specially when we'll likeliest leave our bones 'ere. You needn't bow down to 'eathen idols—I won't meself—just because you join our party."

Budic caught lip between teeth, shivered, and said, "I'm sorry. I'll come, and, hope Corentinus will understand."

"Good." Mollified, Cynan slapped him on the back. "The centurion would be disappointed to learn you hadn't."

"I thought of that," Budic whispered.

—On the day, the legionaries departed in full and polished armor, up the valley to the hills. The groom rode ahead of them, finely clad, on a white horse, next to his intended father-in-law. Behind followed other kin and well-wishers, together with pack beasts carrying supplies for a feast. The weather was superb. Merriment caroled along the whole way. The bride had fared a day in advance, accompanied by attendants and Queen Forsquilis, that she might be purified and then well rested.

At noon the group reached the sacred site. A vestal guided them by a short woodland path to the barrack. They would sleep there—floor space and pallets were sufficient—before returning home in the morning. While they refreshed themselves and took their ease, the small garrison hospitably carried back the food and wine they had brought, for the women of the sanctuary to set forth on tables which had been placed on the lawn.

At mid-afternoon a procession of girls arrived, led by a full-grown virgin who was near the end of her term of service. Hair garlanded and flowing loose over white gowns, they sang and fluted hymeneals while they conducted the groom and his friends to the Nymphaeum. Beautiful among them danced Princess Dahut. Already she was often here, as well as in other places hallowed to Belisama. It was unusual for one so young, but she was being raised in piety.

Around the greenswarded hollow brooded forest, above it cloud mountains and blue depths, heavy with summer. The air was as sweet as the music. Peacocks walked on closely trimmed grass, swans floated on the pond. That water came from several brooklets out of the hills and the spring at its edge; thence ran a stream which fed the slender canal that joined with rains to quench the thirst of Ys. The spring bubbled from a pile of boulders, atop which smiled a statue of the Mother, shaded by a huge old linden. Flowerbeds blazed with color, hedgerows and bowers drew the eye onward to the building. It was wooden and of no great size, but its white, colonnaded, large-windowed form was as of a jewel.

Adminius uttered a command. The soldiers formed a double rank below the stairs. Forth onto the portico came the aged chief priestess and her coadjutresses, in blue gowns and high headdresses. Gravely, they summoned the groom. He mounted the steps and followed them inside. After him went the rest of the wedding party, and then the choir. The legionaries stayed behind.

Through open doors came sounds of hymn, chant, prayer. Budic strove not to listen. He failed. Those words, those melodies were at once too joyous and too solemn.

They ended in a benediction uttered by a woman's purring voice. The bridal couple appeared, plump blond maiden on the arm of lean sandy man. They descended. As they passed between the soldiers, swords flew from sheaths and *"Ave!"* roared aloud.

The guests followed, the girls, the votaresses. Last was the Queen. Tall and stately walked Forsquilis, her face almost inhuman in its classic lineaments and pallor, save for the faint smile.

Dahut had been named to cry, "Rejoice! The blessing of the Goddess is ours! Rejoice!" Thereupon everything broke up in shouts and laughter. Folk mingled, embraced, made for the laden boards. Forsquilis went back inside. When she returned, her golden-brown hair was coiled around a silver coronet and cloth of gold clung to her litheness. She herself called for drinking to the health and happiness of the newly wed, and in the hour afterward chatted freely with any and all.

The gaiety, and perhaps the wine, soon overwhelmed Budic. Every nuptial feast in Ys, other than the King's, was mirthful, and apt to become erotically charged. Here there could be no stealing off with a newly met woman. However, nothing forbade the vestals to smile, joke, dance, exchange glances, murmur hints. When they attained their majority, most would want husbands, some would want lovers, and surely Belisama breathed higher the fire that She kindled in young hearts. Budic blundered bewildered through a whirl of loveliness.

The sun went under western hills. Clouds burned golden. Forsquilis signalled to the virgins. They formed a line, their feet skipped, their epithalamium lifted, as they brought Adminius and Avonis back to the Nymphaeum. Dahut bore a candle before the two, lighting their way to the flowerful chamber that was theirs for the night.

Festivity outside continued a while. Twilight deepened, stars blinked into view, moon-glow silvered heaven above high eastern darknesses. First the oldest and the youngest yawned goodnight, then presently all revelers departed to their rest.

—Budic awoke. He could not have been long asleep. The barrack was pitchy black and steamy hot. He felt bodies pressed close to his, and for a moment a surging took him; but they were merely two road-pounders like himself, and snored. He rolled over, hoping to regain oblivion. The straw of his pallet rustled. He remembered youths in Britannia, when he was a boy, boasting of what they had done with girls in the hay. He remembered that he had not really been down in peaceful nothingness. Slim forms with voices like the chiming of brooks had undulated through his dreams.

Sweat prickled and reeked in his armpits. His member swelled and strained. Almost, he groaned. *Christ guard me from the demons in this haunt of heathendom!* Useless to lie here. He would only toss about till he roused his mates, who'd swear at him. Maybe some fresh air would soothe. He groped his way to the door, and out.

How solid, how soft the earth was beneath his feet. The night laved his nakedness; he felt every smallest cool ripple in it. The forest smelled of damp and musk. He heard rustlings, chirrings, a hoot, a wing-beat. They seemed to call him. Moonlight dappled leaves and ground. As his night vision strengthened, he saw the path winding off to the holy grounds. Yonder was water. Thirst smoldered in the thuttery thickness that held him by the gullet. He thought confusedly that he would not drink from the pond, for it was given over to the lustful she-devil; but the stream that ran from it, off to the canal and thus the city, ah, he could fling himself belly down, grip the moss in both hands, and bury his mouth in that chilly kiss.

He moved ahead. Twigs fingered him. A moonbeam touched a great fungus growing on a log. It stood forth like a phallus or the flame of the lamp in a bridal chamber. Was it a nightingale that trilled, or a girl's laugh?

The woods opened on the lawn. Budic slammed to a halt.

The full moon hid most stars behind a veil of brilliance. Trees, hedges, grass reached asheen. Above the spring, below the linden, the idol stood livid against shadow. Darkness limned the rich curves of breasts and hips. Argency glimmered and sparkled over the pond. Around it, upon it, out from within it, the nymphs were dancing.

They were not vestals, innocently asleep, they were mist and moonlight made female, shapes that flitted, wove, flickered, soared, twined, caressed, parted to tremble on the edge of flight, came back together to embrace, one with one another and the night and the burgeoning summer. Not with his ears but with his soul, he heard them sing and cry and yowl desire. He knew not whether they were aware of him or cared; but he was about to plunge forth and lose himself in them.

Out of the gloom that bulked against the northern sky trod a man. He was huge, naked, stallion-erected. Each fist held a writhing snake. It was as if stars glittered trapped in his unbound hair. From his temples sprang a mighty rack of antlers. Slowly he paced from the wood toward the nymphs, and their movements turned in his direction.

Budic huddled behind a tree. He could not help himself, he must peer around its trunk.

Moonlight flooded her who came down off the portico and across the lawn. White, white, blue-white was her skin, also nude except for the tresses streaming loose. She held out her arms to the man-shape.

Distant though she was in this dimness, Budic knew that Athene countenance.

The male wheeled and strode to meet her. She ran. When she reached them, they halted and he took both her hands in his. The serpents wrapped around their wrists, moonlight icy along scales. For an endless while, male and woman stood unmoving. Then at last they went side by side into the forest. The nymphs took up their frolic anew.

Lightning through the thunder that filled Budic's skull: Everybody knew Forsquilis was deepest versed in sorcery of the Nine witches, and gossip muttered how she bore the air of a passionate woman and how hard it must be for her to share a single man. None, even Christians, ever dared hint that any among the Gallicenae might betray the King. But what about a God—a demon?

A nymph-shape left the dance and swayed across the dew toward Budic.

He shrieked and fled. Yet he did not re-enter the guards's house when he got there, but spent the rest of the night outside, shuddering, groveling, weeping, and praying.

~ 3 ~

"Have you told anyone else?" asked Corentinus.

Astounded, Budic gaped at him. Dusk gathered around the minister of Christ where he sat on his stool, in the room of his church that he had designated private, like a black-feathered bird of prey on its perch.

"N-no, Father," the Coritanean stammered after a moment. "I p-pretended I'd had nightmares, that was why I was so numb and weak this morning."

"Good." The knaggy head nodded. "No sense in letting rumors get started. They'll force people to take firm stances, which is the last thing we want the pagans to do. Of course, you realize what you saw may well have been just a dream."

"What? No, Father, that can't be. I mean, I beg your pardon, but I do know the difference—"

Corentinus raised a palm to cut off the words. "Peace. Don't fret yourself. It matters little. The forces of Satan prowl always around us. Whether they work as mirage or material, their purpose is the same, to lure us from our salvation. If what you saw really happened, I'll feel sad for that poor benighted woman. But you, my son, you may thank God that He strengthened you to resist."

Budic wailed and covered his face. "No, Father. Th-th-that's why I came—not even to warn you, but, but the vision won't leave me, the lust is fiercer than fire, what shall I do, Father?"

"Ah. Hm." Corentinus rose, bent over the hunched figure, briefly hugged the bright head to his bosom. "Don't be afraid. You have wisdom beyond your years, that you seek help here instead of in a brothel."

"I have sinned that way before. But this, this *called* me."

"I know. I too have heard." Corentinus began pacing back and forth. He made his voice dry:

"Listen, Budic. You've been a pretty good catechumen, and this isn't the first time I've given you some thought. Now, I can't compel your spirit. Only God can do that. But I can, in my left-handed mortal fashion, advise you. So listen, and think.

"Your trouble is that you're devout, but you haven't got the makings of a monk. No disgrace in that. The Lord bade Adam and Eve be fruitful and multiply. What're you waiting for?"

Budic gave him a dazed look. "Where'll I find a Christian wife? I knew I did wrong, going to that pagan wedding. Isn't this my punishment?"

Corentinus smiled. "I'm not sure you did do wrong. I've never reproached any of my flock who married unbelievers. It can't be helped, and grace may come on the spouses. I only require that they allow their children to hear the truth. You, though—you're not the sort who could live with an infidel woman. But you need a woman, in the worst way."

He took stance before he went on, almost sternly: "I have one, if you're Christian enough, man enough, to take her for your wife."

Budic stared up at him. The chorepiscopus seemed to tower as if he spoke from the peak of Sinai. "Who?" Budic whispered.

"You know her well. Keban, the harlot from the Fishtail."

Budic sat dumb-stricken.

"She has repented," Corentinus went on relentlessly, "and she has washed herself clean with her tears, she acknowledges Christ her Lord and Savior. But who among the haughty goodfolk of Ys will have her, even as a scullion? I give her shelter and employment here, but it's made work, as well we both know, and her days are empty, and Satan understands very well how to fill that emptiness with old carnal cravings. I've dreaded that she may fall by the wayside. But if not—what an example to shine before every wretch forsaken in this city of sin!

"Budic, she's still fairly young, healthy, a fit mother of sturdy sons, and reborn in Christ. What she was before is nothing in the sight of God. But is everything in the sight of man.

"Who will have courage to take her under his protection, for the salvation of both, and shield her, and turn his back on the sly, unspoken mockery, till at last it is outlived, forgotten, and an honorable old pair go hand in hand toward Heaven? Might you be, Budic?"

Silence lengthened, underneath harsh breath.

Corentinus eased. "Ah, well, I know better than to force things," he said. "Come, lad, let's share a stoup and talk a bit. I can always use barrack-room gossip. As for any sins of yours, consider them forgiven."

—But later that evening, summoned, Keban entered. In wimple and full, coarse gown, timidly smiling, by lamplight she seemed twice comely. All she did was prepare and set forth a frugal meal, and answer a few inconsequential questions. Yet the glance of Budic followed her everywhere she went.

406

4

Often around the autumnal equinox, storms caused Ys to lock its sea gate, lest waves force an opening and rush through the harbor into the city. When calm was restored, the King freed the portal. It was his sacral duty. Only if he was absent or disabled did Lir Captain take it in his stead.

As usual, he performed the task at high tide, which this day happened to come in the afternoon. "You see," he explained to Dahut, "the doors are hung in such a way that they always want to be shut. As the water falls, the floats that hang from them do too, and draw the doors open. At low water, they would pull so hard that I couldn't get the bar out of its holder."

"But what if you *had* to close the gate then?" she asked.

Gratillonius smiled. "Sharp question!" There was quite a mind below those golden curls, behind those big eyes. "Well, we have machinery, so gangs of men can haul the doors shut against the weight of the balls. Just the same, it's hard work."

Lanarvilis had told him he should let Dahut witness the rite. All the Queens were touchingly concerned about the upbringing of Dahilis's daughter. Delighted, he had sent a messenger to temple school. She came from there in company of Guilvilis, whose turn it was to foster her. He was twice happy that that turn coincided with his night at Guilvilis's house.

Woman and child followed him from the palace. Guilvilis had donned finery, a silken gown that showed to disadvantage her tall, awkward, heavy-haunched figure. The thin dull-brown hair would not stay properly in its elaborate coiffure, but did call attention to small eyes, long nose, undershot chin. In a schoolgirl's brief white dress, Dahut went like wind and waterfall. Gratillonius wore a ceremonial robe of blue-gray wool embroidered in gold and silver thread with sea beasts. In full view on his breast hung the iron Key.

A squad of marines waited in their conical helmets and shoulder-flared loricae. Pike butts crashed a salute on the stones. They took formation behind the King. Traffic on Lir Way was thick and bustle was loud, but a path opened immediately before the procession. Many folk cheered, some signed themselves, a number of youngsters trailed after to watch from the wharf.

The Temple of Lir stood under the Gull Tower, just before the pomoerium. Ancient, it lacked the Grecian exquisiteness of Belisama's, the Roman stateliness of Taranis's. Despite small size, here was brutal strength, menhirlike pillars and rough stone walls upholding a roof of slate slabs. The interior was dark, revealing little more than an altar block within an arch formed of the jawbones of a whale.

Gratillonius entered. The man on watch today greeted him. Every ship's captain in Ys was ordained a priest of Lir; Hannon Baltisi simply presided over meetings of the guild and spoke for it and its cult in

Council. Gratillonius knelt to receive on his tongue the ritual pinch of salt and voice the ritual plea that the God withhold His wrath. Emergence was like release from captivity.

It was a bright, bracing day. When he had climbed the stairs to the rampart heights, he looked out across utter openness. Waters shone blue, green, purple, white-capped, save where they burst on rocks and reefs, brawled against wall and cliffs; there fountains leaped. In this clarity he could see the house on Sena, miles away. Only wings beclouded the sky, hundreds of them soaring and circling on the breeze whose tang washed his face.

He looked inland, across the broad arc of the basin. How still it lay, nine or ten feet beneath the tide, lower yet whenever the combers climbed and broke. Ships and boats crowded the piers. Men were busy with cargo. Mariners of Ys would venture another voyage or two before winter closed in. The knowledge that he had put life back into that trade made a glow in Gratillonius.

And the city behind shone in roofs, towers, on its higher eastern half gardens, temples, mansions. Hinterland stretched beyond, valley and hills where homes nestled, the gaudiness of leaves muted by distance to a tapestry laid over the earth, a sign of ingathered bounty. God Mithras, said Gratillonius, watch over all this, stand guard upon its peace.

Dahut tugged at his hand. "Won't you start?" she piped.

Hauled from his reverie, he laughed and tousled her hair. "Ever are you the impatient one, eh, sweetling? Aye, let's....Have a care! Lean not so far over the parapet. I know you love the sea, but remember, 'tis forever hungry."

He led her past the Gull Tower and the sheltered war engines to that fifty-foot gap in the wall which was the portal. Dahut, who had been here before, cried greeting to the block that jutted from the wall below the battlements. It had the time-blurred form of a cat's head. A chain ran from the inner top corner of the adjacent door, into the block, over the sheave within, and down out of its mouth. Most of the chain hung submerged, for the leather-clad bronze ball at its end floated not far beneath, idly swinging in the waves. Gratillonius heard the thuds when that great weight rolled against the wall. Those dry-laid blocks were well fitted indeed, to have withstood centuries of such battering. And even the doors, oaken though copper-sheathed and iron-bound, had only required replacement twice.

He let go of Dahut's hand. "Now 'tis single file," he said.

A flight of stone steps angled down the inside of the wall to a ledge beside the gate, halfway up. There stood a capstan, from which a chain ran through another cat's head to the inner top corner of the door. Opposite, fifty feet away, was a similar arrangement. "This is the machinery for closing at low tide," Gratillonius explained. "The doors are made so they never swing too widely for that. Follow me onward."

From the ledges, narrow, railed walkways ran across both doors, meeting in two platforms at the juncture. Dahut touched the riveted green plates and black iron reinforcing strips that she passed. "Why must you ever lock the gate?" she asked. "Less'n you want it shut up at low tide."

What a quick person she is! marvelled Gratillonius. "Well, think of a big storm with huge waves. They don't only have high crests, they have deep troughs. The floats drop down as well as bob up. Were it not for the bar, they'd jerk the doors wide. The sea would pour through and do terrible things to poor Ys."

"Thank the Gods that They don't let that happen," admonished Guilvilis. Gratillonius thought, irritated, that man had somewhat more to do with it.

He reached the platform. There a titanic beam, pivoted on the southern door, fitted into an iron U on this northern one. A cable ran from its free end to a block and tackle above. The bar was secured by a chain through it and through a staple, closed by a ponderous lock whose hasp went between two links.

Looking down into the girl's eyes, Gratillonius wondered how he appeared in them. "This is my work," he said.

The marines had deployed along the walkway. Gratillonius unslung the Key from his neck and raised it aloft. "In the name of Ys," he called, "under the Pact of Brennilis that the Gods did grant unto us, I open the city to the sea."

He fitted Key into lock. It turned stiffly, with a clicking as of footsteps. He withdrew the Key and laid it back in his bosom. With both hands he removed the lock and hung it on a single link. Drawing the chain out, he fastened it in a loop by locking the loose end to the staple.

Crossing over to the opposite platform, he uncleated the cable and hauled on it. Cunningly counterweighted, the bar rose easily for all its massiveness. When it was almost vertical, he refastened the cable. Returning, he clasped his hands and bowed before the lock.

It was done. The party went back to the top of the wall. Soon, as tide ebbed, the doors would begin to draw apart. The sea would come hissing through, but gently, by that time not raising the level of the basin too much. Ys would again have the freedom of Ocean.

"I've other matters to attend to," Gratillonius said regretfully. "Guilvilis, there's scant sense in taking the child back to class today. Why not show her about this quarter? The Cornmarket, Epona Square, the Ishtar Shrine, whatever she'd like to see. She's grown enough for it. I'll seek your house this evening."

Dahut skipped for joy.

5

That ended an hour later.

Passing through the narrow, twisted streets near the waterfront, on the edge of the Fishtail slum, the girl halted. "What's in there?" she asked.

Guilvilis looked around. The cobblestones of Crescent Way lay nearly deserted, for dwellers in the tenements that hemmed it in were still off at work. On the right a building lifted four stories high, balconies cantilevered from the upper floor, the lower wall stuccoed and inset with shells which centuries had chipped and discolored. A couple of children had stopped their play to stare at the finely clad lady. A porter with a laden frame on his back had just come around a corner; Ys restricted draft and burden-bearing animals to a few principal thoroughfares. "Where?" the Queen replied vaguely.

"*There,*" said Dahut with exasperation, and pointed.

Opposite stood a building unique to Lowtown. It was of black marble, broad and deep though not high. Pilasters flanked bronze doors on which were life-sized reliefs of a veiled woman and a man with bowed head. The entablature was granite, sculptured into a frieze: a row of skulls and at the center, floating above, an unborn babe.

"Oh," said Guilvilis. "Why, that, that's Wayfaring House."

"What's it?"

"You haven't heard? Well, 'tis, um, 'tis thus. You know dead people get taken out on the funeral barge and put in the sea."

Dahut nodded solemnly. "Father's told me. He says that's where my mother went."

"Well, the barge is supposed to go out each third day, but often the weather makes that too dangerous. Sometimes they have to wait a long while. They did this month, with those awful storms we got. Here, Wayfaring House, here is where they wait."

"Oh." Dahut's eyes widened.

"'Tis all good and quiet for them," Guilvilis said hastily.

"Can we go see?"

"What? Nay, I think better not. Later, when you're older."

Dahut's face drew into an expression the Gallicenae well knew. "Why? You say 'tis good and quiet."

"Well, it is—"

Dahut stamped her foot. "Father said show me everything I wanted!"

Guilvilis searched her memory while the child fumed. "Aye, he...he did that, I think. But—"

Dahut darted from her, up the few broad stairs. The doors were unse-cured. She pulled them apart and was inside before Guilvilis got there.

"What's this?" called the old man on duty. His voice made echoes in the twilight of a huge chamber. He shuffled forward. "My lady, you shouldn't bring a wee one here. Leave her with me. Which beloved would you bid goodbye to?—O-ah." He recognized the woman. "My *lady!*" Touching his brow in reverence: "How may I serve you?"

"I, well, 'tis thus—" faltered Guilvilis.

Dahut dashed past them.

Stone tubs, a few feet apart, covered the floor. She came to the first and looked over its edge.

Brine filled it. Within, full length, lay a dead woman. While a sheet wrapped her body, its soddenness revealed the bony contours. Cords bound wrists and ankles and held her to eyebolts. Hair floated loose. It had been an old woman, withered and toothless. The jaw had been tied up and the eyes closed, but lips and lids were shriveled back, while the waterlogged face bloated around the beak of a nose.

"You shouldn't'a done that, little girl," wailed the attendant.

Dahut made a mewing sound. Like a sleepwalker, she stumbled to the next vat. There was a man more newly dead. He had been young and healthy, though now his skin was ashen. Some mishap had shattered the right side of his head.

"Get her way from that, my lady," the attendant implored. "She's too young for the sight, she is."

"Aye, come, let us go, Dahut, dear, let's go see the Cornmarket and I'll buy you a honeycake." Guilvilis lurched toward the princess. "Cry not, be not afraid."

"Nay," said the man, "these are but the harmless dead. We'll take them to their rest on the morrow, and the Ferriers will bring their souls to Sena and the Gods will make happy those who were good."

Stiff-legged, Dahut walked to the door. She stared before her, never a tear, never a blink. As daylight touched her, it showed a visage with no more color or movement than any in the brine.

Nor did she speak the whole way back to the house, and scarcely at all when Gratillonius arrived there. But when she had gone to bed, and man and wife were about to, they heard her scream.

—He stood holding her in his arms. She had hidden her face against his breast but did not give him back his embrace, only shivered and mewed. By the light of a single candle, he glared at Guilvilis.

"You dolt," he snarled. "You unspeakable clod, lackwit, bungler. What have you done to her? How could you do it, even you?"

She opened and shut her mouth several times, and he thought how very like a fish she looked, before she could stammer. "Y-y-you said take her where she wanted, and, and she got away from me. Oh, I'm sorry!" Tears coursed from her eyes. Her nose dribbled.

"A squid would have had better judgment, more command. And 'tis you who dwell in the home of Dahilis! Take you hence. Leave us ere you do worse harm."

She stared, and now he thought of a poleaxed cow.

"Get you to the nursery." To Sasai, Antonia, Camilla she had borne him in such quick and glad succession. "Dahut and I will be together

411

this night....Not so, darling?" he murmured into the child-fragrance under her hair.

Guilvilis lifted her hands. "I love you, Grallon. I wanted to do what you said. I wanted to please you."

He brushed her aside as he carried his daughter out of the room.

They must cross the atrium to reach the main bedchamber. Every trace of Dahilis was gone. That had been at his insistence. Guilvilis would passively have left the dear things in place. He had ordered them brought to the palace. Guilvilis had acquired a few objects of her own. They were mostly garish. He didn't care.

He heard her weep on her way to the nursery. His anger sank a trifle. Thanks to her, Dahut had seen an unpleasant thing before she was ready for it, and it had given her a nightmare, but surely she could overcome any fears, as lively and self-willed as she was. Sometime soon he'd toss Guilvilis a friendly word or two.

He laid the ivory shape down on the bed. Though there was hardly any light here, she burrowed into a pillow. It was as well, since he must now undress and—better find himself a nightgown, which he generally did only in the coldest weather. Dahut was naked, but, Mithras, she was five years old. Yet, holding her, he had felt the first slight filling out of her slenderness.

"Be not afraid, sweetling," he said. "You saw no people yonder. You saw the husks they've no more use for. 'Tis like a—a dandelion, when the seeds blow away on the wind to become new dandelions."

Still she was mute. He got into bed and held her close. How moveless she lay, except for the faint trembling and catches of breath. Couldn't she cry, talk to him, have it out? Well, she'd always borne a strangeness about her. "I love you, Dahut," he whispered. His lips brushed her cheek. "I love you so much."

She did not answer. He got scant sleep that night.

~ 6 ~

Morning was bright and bleak. The funeral barge departed on the tide.

Dahut saw it from the heights. She had said at breakfast that she wanted simply a crust of bread and a cup of milk—which was true; she must force them down—and that she would make her own way to school—which of late she had been proudly doing. Father had left, and Mama Guilvilis was too crushed to respond. Freshly clad, Dahut set forth. Then she followed side streets to Northbridge Gate and went out on Point Vanis.

Few whom she passed paid her any heed. To them she was merely another lass bound somewhere, uncommonly pretty and curiously intent, but nobody to question. Women and girls walked about Ys as freely, safely as men. However, once on the headland, she left Redonian Way

412

and went along the cliffs. A shepherd, carter, merchant, courier would have been too surprised by the sight of a child alone beyond the city wall. When she glimpsed anybody, she hid behind a bush or a boulder. Sometimes she stayed a while, staring out to sea or downward at earth and insects, before she wandered onward.

The promontory reared stark out of the water and stretched inland nearly bare save for grass turned sallow, gorse, thistle, scattered trees that the wind had dwarfed and gnarled, lichenous rocks. In a few places stood beehive-shaped stone shelters or menhirs raised by the Old Folk to Gods unknown. Wind boomed from the west, a torrent of chill. Clouds scudded before it, gulls, cormorants, a hawk on high. Shadows harried each other across the miles. In between them, sunlight made the waters flame.

Finally Dahut reached a low mound and a headstone, out near the northern end of the point. She sat down to rest. At school she was learning the Latin alphabet. She had not been here since that began. Now, slowly, with a tracing finger, she followed the letters chiseled into the stone:

Q IVN EPPILLO
OPT LEG II AVG
COMMIL FEC

Father had told her that a brave man lay beneath, who died fighting for Ys and Rome before she was born. He put off saying more, and when she asked two or three of the Mamas they put her off too. They seemed uneasy about it.

Abruptly Dahut sprang up. Her glance flung itself around. Against the dazzle on the sea she spied and knew the funeral barge, crawling out upon its oars. She choked down a scream and fled.

Nearby, where the cliffs turned east, a footpath led to them from the bend in the highway. Dahut sought it. Downward bound, it became a mere trail, steep and slippery. Father had held her in the past when they visited. Dahut picked her way alone, breathing raggedly but never losing balance.

A few blocks, canted and overgrown, showed that once a stair had led up. At the bottom were crumbling walls and the remnants of a jetty. Father had said this was a Roman marine station, smashed to pieces and fired long, long ago by the nasty Saxons. Dahut scrambled past the wreckage. Charred baulks and newer driftwood had jammed around the stump of the jetty to form a rough little ness. On this face of the headland the surf did not, today, assault it, though whitecaps smote and whooshed and sent spindrift flying.

Dahut stooped and took off her sandals. Barefoot, she could go out on the logs. Wind ripped at her. She cupped hands about mouth. "O-ho, o-hoo," she called. "Come to me, come to me!"

The wind flung her cry down into the waves.

413

"O-ho, o-hoo! Please come. I need you."

A shape appeared and swam rapidly toward her. It was golden-brown and huge eyed. "Welcome, thank you, welcome," Dahut shouted; and tears started to run. She hunkered down into what shelter an uptilted slab offered. It was of planks, bleached and warped, still held by corroded nails to a pair of snapped-off crossbeams: a piece from the deck of a lost ship.

The seal came aground and slithered over the jumble. Dahut flung arms around her neck. The fish-breath was not foul, it was strong, like a soldier's trumpet. The wetness didn't matter, when such warmth and sleekness were there to lie against. A flipper enfolded Dahut. The seal nuzzled her. Whiskers prickled, then a tongue kissed, a voice hummed deep in the throat behind.

"O-o-oh, I saw the dead floating. They were all ugly an-an-and eels will eat them, *me too*, like my mother that father says was so beautiful, o-o-oh, they come after me in my dreams. I thought one of them was mother."

The seal held her close.

"Nay?" Dahut whispered after a while. "Not really? Never?"

Somehow the seal got her looking outward and opened her to what she saw.

"Papa told me 'bout dandelions—"

Radiance lit the wings of a hovering gull. Its voice was like laughter.

"Aye, shells on the beach, kelp, starfish, but they go back, they all go back."

The waters no longer roared, they sang.

Dahut snuggled. Here, shielded from the weather, held in this comfort, she could let her weariness overwhelm her, she could sleep and be healed. "They all return. Ever'thing returns...." The voice of the seal went lulling. "'Tis mine."

Oh, darling, lie peaceful. The sea is before us,
The mothering, cleansing, all-powerful sea,
And borne on the wind and the foam is a chorus
Of surges and surf to your nest in the lee.
From depths that are darkling the billows lift sparkling,
As eager and salt as the beat of your blood.
No horror shall snare you, but life shall upbear you.
Dear sea-child, the tide of your hope is in flood.

XII

~ 1 ~

There was a man called Flavius Stilicho. His father had been a Vandal who entered the Imperial army and became an officer. Stilicho did likewise, rising high and fast until he was the mightiest general Rome had known for generations. This made him a power in the state. After military and diplomatic exploits in Persia and Thracia, he moved against the barbarians of the North. In Britannia his campaigns piled the bodies of Saxons, Picti, and Scoti in windrows and sent the survivors reeling back.

That spring, Uail maqq Carbri had led a seaborne raid up the channel to the mouth of the Sabrina and along the Silurian shore. Newly reinforced, the Romans fast marched from Isca Silurum, surprised the Scoti, and harvested a goodly number of them before the rest could escape. Uail's outsize currach did keep its load of booty from a town his reavers had sacked, including some captives. Among those was a lad of sixteen, a son of the curial, named Sucat.

Gallia had become an even worse hunting ground. Armorica guarded the approach, strengthened by the newly enlarged navy of Ys. No man of Ériu in his right mind would go there, unless it be as a peaceful trader.

Uail sought Niall maqq Echach, King at Temir, and gave his ill tidings. Unlike most of the chieftains who were on hand, Niall did not rage. Time had taught him patience. If the sun-brightness of his locks had begun, ever so faintly, to dim, the wits beneath were whetted as keen as his sword had always been. He accepted Uail's gifts out of the plunder, and made generous return. "It's kindly your mood is, lord," said the skipper.

Niall laughed. "It is not," he replied. "The Romans must simply wait their turn. I have built up my strength over the years. Now we will build it further still, beginning with an undertaking that men shall remember forever.

Toward that end, he had been seeking the goodwill of his Condach-tach kinfolk. One of these, a tuathal king from the western shores, happened to be guesting him just then, a man named Mílchu. When this man went home, among the gifts he took along was the slave Sucat, whom Uail had presented to Niall.

Alliance was natural. Warfare between the Ulati of the north and the Firi Condachtae south and west of them was as ancient as when

Cú Culanni stood off the cattle raiders of Queen Medb, if indeed the strife had not begun between the sons of Ír and Éber just after they conquered the Children of Danu. Being of Condachtach origin, the royal house that lorded it over the tuaths of Mide had inherited those feuds.

Equally haughty were the Ulatach kings who foregathered at Emain Macha. The chief among them claimed descent from Conchobar maqq Nessa, the lesser ones from the warriors of the Red Branch, as did the landowning nobles.

Tributary to them, between Qóiqet nUlat and Mide, were humbler folk. Ulati had established themselves in these parts as chieftains, but scorned the dwellers, calling them mere Cruthini or outright Firi Bolg, exacting heavy rents, being careless about rights. Often a poor man could only get justice by starving at the door of the rich. Sometimes this, too, failed to shame the defendant, whose well-nourished flesh could endure hunger far beyond the day when scrawniness must either give up or die.

Thus, when the chariots of Niall and his sons rumbled north at the head of a host, victory winged above them. They found few earthworks and strongpoints to overrun. The enemy leaders fought valiantly, but many of their followers, especially bond tenants, were half-hearted and quick to flee. Reinforcements from the King at Emain Macha arrived too late, too little. At the end of the second summer's warfare, Niall had prevailed as far as the headwaters of the River Sinand, almost to the Ulatach lands proper. The petty kings whom he had beaten plighted faith to him. He took hostages from them and went home.

There he would bide a while, waiting to see what happened in Ériu and overseas, before moving onward. Anything else would have been foolhardy. What he had won promised wealth, power, glory, but also unforeseeable trouble. It was more than plowlands, herds, salmon streams, forests for game and timber, gold, weapons, men. His now was mastery over Mag Slecht, the holiest place in all Ériu. He must be careful not to rouse the anger of its Gods or too many of Their worshippers.

~ 2 ~

The months wheeled onward, through winter and spring and again to summer.

Esmunin Sironai, chief astrologer in Ys, predicted a lunar eclipse some three sennights after solstice. His table and formulae went back to the Chaldeans, with much added by the Greeks and no little by his own people over the centuries, hampered though they were by their climate. The Queen who would be in charge of the Temple of Belisama at the time prepared for a special service, and she who would have the Vigil on Sena rehearsed special prayers, for the moon was the

Lady's. Forsquilis arranged to have neither duty; she would be casting spells and taking omens by herself. Bodilis planned to be at Star House.

The weather proved clear. The Symposium met early for dinner and discourse. King Gratillonius had attended such meetings when he was able, but excused himself from this. The word went, very softly, that he intended a rite in his Mithraeum.

At sunset the company entered the Water Tower and climbed a helical staircase to the observatory on top. Esmunin's students busied themselves with armillary spheres, goniometers, and other instruments. The old man sat in a corner wrapped in his cloak. He was nearly blind. "But we will tell you all as it happens, master," they said lovingly. "We will write it down with exactness, that you may draw forth meanings we would never find."

Bodilis went to the parapet. Ys made a basin of darkness, save where fire glowed from windows, but towers still caught light on their uppermost metal and glass. In the opposite direction, the canal drew a thread of silver through the dusk in the valley. Air was as yet warm, moist, full of scents and whispers. And yonder above the hills rose the full moon. Already a gap was out of its limb.

"A-a-ah," murmured voices, and "Goddess, be gentle us-ward," and "Quick, now, set the clock." Nearsighted Bodilis squeezed forefinger against thumb to make a peephole through which she could more clearly see the marvel.

Blackness advanced until it became red. That veil gave way in turn to blackness again as it withdrew from ashen white. It had been an eclipse longer than some, shorter than some. It would go into Esmunin's book, another grain of truth laid down for a harvest he would never see. Bodilis wondered how many learned men in the Empire had troubled themselves to observe this, or watch at all.

A little talk followed, comparison, speculation; but most of the philosophers were ready for bed. Bodilis remained wide awake. As folk descended and said goodnight, she started home, thinking that she would read for a while, or perhaps attempt a little further translation of the *Oedipus*, or perhaps do a sketch for a painting she had in mind. Her place had grown lonesome since Gratillonius ceased sleeping there. Semuramat—Tambilis—was lonely too, but it behooved a Queen to maintain a household; and, to be sure, Tambilis was still studying those things a cultivated woman should know. Kerna and Talavair were good daughters who tried to see their mother often, but they had their families to attend first.

Bodilis had no need of a lantern, so brightly did the moon shine. The streets she took were empty, which made the glimpses she got through the windows of lighted homes seem doubly snug. Her rangy stride sent echoes rattling along the up-and-down twistiness.

It happened that her way led her by a house lately fire-gutted. That was rare in Ys, where only the upper stories of the tallest buildings were wooden. When conflagration did occur, the marines at Warriors' House were as quick to come put it out as they were to come stamp down violent crime. In this case, a high wind and a broken amphora of oil defeated them. The family moved elsewhere, pending repairs.

A man had climbed up to sit on the blackened front wall, whose roof had collapsed. Swinging long legs, he was dressed in forester's wise, coarse shirt, leather doublet, cross-gartered trews. The moonlight showed a silver headband, gold earrings, forked black beard. A scar puckered the face that he kept turned aloft.

The sound she made caught his attention. He came down in a rush via a windowsill and made a sweeping salute of deference. "My lady, Queen Bodilis!" His rather high voice spoke easy Ysan, though with a Redonic accent. "What a grand surprise. How may I serve you?"

She recognized Rufinus. They had met seldom and fleetingly, as much as he was off on errands of the King's about which neither man said much. "What were you doing?" she inquired.

"Watching the eclipse, of course," he laughed. "Such marvels are all too few, and then this wretched weather of ours most likely hides them." Immediately he grew serious. "Afterward I sat trying to think what makes such a thing happen. Surely the Queen knows, but I'm only a runaway serf."

"You've no ideas?" she found herself asking.

"Naught but folk tales. Not erenow have I had leisure to wonder about the world, thanks to King Grallon, best of lords."

Bodilis winced and replied in haste: "Well, 'tis simple enough. The sun and the moon move opposite each other when the angles are just right, and so the shadow of the earth falls on the moon. Have you not noticed that the shadow is curved?"

Rufinus stared. "Why—yea, my lady—but, do understand you to say the world, this earth, is *round*?"

"Indeed. That's well known. Think how a ship goes below the horizon on a clear day. First the hull disappears, then the mast. How could that be, save on a globe?"

Rufinus drew a long breath. His voice pulsed: "True, true! I said I'd never had a chance to think beyond the needs of staying alive, till lately, but— Yea, clear 'tis to see. But more riddles boil forth—" He fell to one knee in his extravagant fashion. "My lady Bodilis, wisest of the Gallicenae, may I beg a favor? May I accompany you to your doorstep, listening to whatever you care to share of your knowledge? If ever you'd make for yourself an adoring servant, here is how!"

Bodilis smiled. "Why, certainly, if you like." As devoted as he was to Gratillonius, this young man would be no menace to her; and he was charming and his appeal was touching. Besides, she recalled vaguely, gossip was that when in Ys Rufinus did not take advantage of the novelty that could attract many a well-born woman to him.

He capered for joy.

The questions he put as they went along showed ignorance, but also a mind amazingly quick to comprehend the truth. At her house she was tempted to invite him in. Few pleasures matched teaching a bright pupil. She thought better of it; but they agreed to meet again when opportunity allowed.

~ 3 ~

That had been a quiet year in Ys. Yet folk came to believe that mighty things were astir in the womb of time. One month the moon had darkened; then in the very month that followed, a comet appeared. For seven-and-twenty nights it followed the sun, drawing ever nearer as a wolf overtakes a stag. Even when clouds hid it, all knew that it prowled above, a maned star trailing tails of ghostly flame.

The Gallicenae met shortly after the apparition. "This fear is nonsense," Bodilis declared. "Whatever comets are—Aristoteles thought them mere vapors in the upper air—the chronicles tell us they've come and gone with less serious consequences than so many thunderstorms."

"The fear may be groundless," replied Lanarvilis, "but 'tis real just the same. 'Twould help were the King on hand, but—" She shrugged. Gratillonius was off to the Romans again, helping Maximus's veterans organize the training of reservists. "Unrest grows. Some mariners are afraid to put to sea. Nagon Demari stirs up the workers."

"And Christian Corentinus makes converts," Vindilis sneered.

"The trouble will die out, won't it?" ventured Innilis.

"One hopes so," Fennalis answered. "Still, 'twould be wise as well as kindly to quell these dreads now if we can."

"That's why I called you hither," Lanarvilis told them, and went on to explain her idea. After some discussion, the Queens reached consensus. Let heralds go forth, promising that at the new moon, some nights hence, the whole Nine would be on Sena, there to divine the will of the Gods and set right any wrongs.

Toward the end of talk, Forsquilis proposed: "We should take Dahut with us."

"What?" exclaimed Maldunilis. "But we can't. She's no Queen. She may well never be."

"True, she may not go ashore with us," Forsquilis said. "But she can abide on the barge, which will wait overnight to take eight of us back." Her seeress's eyes searched them. "It should strengthen that awe of the Gods we want her to feel."

—Dahut was enraptured. The barge of state had always been so splendid, and here she got to ride on it, and to holy Sena! Tambilis, who was familiar with it because of the Vigils she took, led her about and showed her everything, from the swan's head at the prow, through the flagstaff and templelike deckhouse at the waist, to the gilt fishtail at the stern. The sailors made much of the little princess; even those

419

at oars had a grin and a jest for her. It was a brisk day, wind whittering, the sea all gray-green and whitecapped.

The mainland cliffs sank into horizon haze. Low and flat, the island grew in view. Tambilis's pleasure dwindled. She had not told Dahut that she was often terrified yonder, alone after dark with the wind and the sea and Lir.

The barge docked. Guilvilis, who had been on duty, came down from the House of the Goddess to meet her Sisters. Its stonework bulked murky, foursquare, crowned by a turret of equally grim aspect. Beyond reached scrub, harsh grass, naked rock. Dahut tried and tried to see the two menhirs she had heard about, but they were at the heart of the island and she couldn't.

Tambilis bent down to hug her. "You shall stay with the men, dear," said the youngest of the Nine. "They'll want to amuse you, and that's fine, but remember we brought you along so you could think hard about the sacred mysteries."

Bodilis smiled a bit sadly on the two. "You were ever a good girl, Semuramat who was," she murmured.

—While the high priestesses did not believe eclipse and comet were evil portents, neither had they come here as a political gesture. That would have been mockery of the Three. Their sundown rites were solemn. Thereafter they filed inland to the Stones. Wind hooted and bit, waves crashed. Low in the west, the invader star seemed to fly through ragged clouds.

Eight of the women formed a ring around the pillars. Fennalis, the senior, stood in front and called in the ancestral language, "Ishtar-Isis-Belisama, have mercy on us. Taranis, embolden us. Lir, harden us. All Gods else, we invoke You in the name of the Three, and cry unto You for the deliverance of Ys."

Tambilis had carried a firepot. She set alight the wood which a keeper of the Vigil always made sure was ready. The tasting of salt followed, and then the knife, to nick forth a drop of blood that each flung into the flames. Together the Gallicenae sang the prayer for guidance.

Meanwhile the clouds came in hordes out of Ocean, until blackness overwhelmed Sena. The wind loudened, the waves raged.

—By morning a full gale was under way. Noise, chill, and spindrift filled the air. Fury ran free on the waters. There could be no question of return.

The Queens were safe enough. Ascetical though it was, the House gave shelter and held supplies. In the unlikely event that combers washed over the island, the tower offered refuge. Yet this looked like keeping them weatherbound for days. Tasks ashore would go neglected while anxiety tightened it grip on the people, who would see this as another bad omen. Said Forsquilis bleakly: "Once the weather was at the command of the Gallicenae. We ourselves have summoned it. But more and more does the power slip from us. The world blunders blind into a new Age which holds terrors unknowable."

Tambilis and Bodilis went to the barge to reassure the crew and, especially, Dahut. They found the child wholly fearless, out on deck as much as the men dared allow, peering into the wind and chanting some wordless song of her own.

—Next morning the gale had dropped to a stiff breeze, while sunlight straggled down between rain-squalls. The seas remained heavy, and the captain of the barge told the Nine that he could not yet start forth. The reefs were too many, too treacherous. He guessed departure would be possible in another two or three days.

Dahut trilled laughter.

Toward noon, those on the island were astounded to see a vessel bearing in. On eight oars, it was a fishing smack, tarry, battered, but stout. "*Osprey!*" Dahut shouted, dancing in glee. "*Osprey!* Maeloch's come!"

Standing on the dock, Fennalis clutched her cloak to her. "What's this?" she asked. "Whom do you speak of?"

Dahut grew grave. "Maeloch's my friend," she said. "I called to the seal and got her to bring him for us."

"I don't understand," Maldunilis whimpered.

Innilis explained: "Maeloch, a fisher captain, also a Ferrier who knows this passage well. Sometimes he's been the boatman when Dahut's gone out on the water. I've taken her myself down to his home at Scot's Landing, where he fills her with goat's milk and stories."

"She's had me do the same," said Bodilis. "Child, what's this about a seal?"

Dahut paid no heed, and then the boat was close in, its crew looking lively under profane orders. They made fast. Maeloch sprang onto the dock. He drew the cowl of his leather jacket back from his shaggy-maned head, made a reverence like a bear's, and boomed: "Ladies, we'll take ye back. Fear nay. She's a cramped and smelly craft, but the crossing will be quick and safe."

The captain of the barge huffed. "Are you mad?"

Maeloch spread his huge hands. "'Twasn't my thought, mate," he admitted. "A dream came to me last night, and when I stepped out at dawn I saw a seal that swam in a beckoning way. She led us. We might have been skerry-prey without her for a guide; but 'tisn't the first time we did well to follow a seal. She'll bring us to harbor again."

"She *will*!" Dahut cried.

Forsquilis came forward. "This is true," she said into the wind. "I too had dreams. I cannot read them, not quite, but— Come, Sisters, let us embark."

Tambilis sighed almost happily. She must stay behind, today's Vigil being hers, but she would not be entirely by herself. The barge would convey her when the sea had calmed enough for that awkward vessel.

Maeloch beamed. "Aye, welcome aboard, ladies. We'll do our poor best to make the trip easy for ye. I did need to whack a couple of the crew ere they'd go, but they've come to see this is a right thing to do. We ask no reward but your blessing." His hand dropped over the head of Dahut. "For how could we leave the princess waiting here, the daughter of Queen Dahilis what everybody loved?"

~ 4 ~

The tower named Polaris was the westernmost of its kind, in Lowtown although on the mildly prosperous south side of Lir Way. Equidistant from the Forum and Skippers' Market, it contained something of both. Respectable folk occupied the lower stories, the poor and raffish dwelt higher up. When he was in Ys, Rufinus had an apartment on the topmost thirteenth floor.

Thither came Vindilis one winter afternoon. Fog had taken over the city, making its traffic a migration of phantoms, but a breeze from the south had now begun to rend and scatter the blindness. Clumps of it still grayed vision, and air remained raw. In plain black cloak and cowl, Vindilis strode unrecognized.

Approaching Polaris, she got a full view of it save where shreds of mist blurred vision. Less lavishly built and ornamented than some, it nonetheless lifted arrogantly. Marble lions with fish tails for hindquarters flanked the main entrance, whose entablature depicted a ship at sea and its lodestar. The first five stories were of the dry-laid stone the Gods had required, beneath tawny stucco inset with images of Ocean's creatures and plants. Construction above was timber, its paint shading from the same yellow to pearly white. Grotesques were carved into the vertical beams. The tower narrowed as it mounted to its roof. From that bronze cupola, green as the sea gate, curved four serpent heads. Each wall was agleam with window glass.

Vindilis mounted the low staircase, whose granite lay in concavities worn by centuries of feet. Entering, she found herself in a corridor onto which opened a number of shops and workplaces—a wineseller's, a spicer's, a draper's, a jeweler's, and more, including a small establishment selling food. Lamps lightened their dimness. Trade and craftsmanship happened softly. At the middle the corridor was an alcove where a strong man sat by a wheel and crank. A rope went upward. By raising water and other needs, and bringing wastes and rubbish down for disposal, this hoist took some of the curse off living on the higher stories. Adjacent stairs went steeply aloft. Vindilis began the climb.

Doors on the first several residential floors stood mostly shut. Many bore the insignia of families that had lived for generations in the suites behind. Higher on, occupants were more transient. There was a measure of shabbiness, odors of cooking cabbage, loud voices,

422

raucous laughter, children milling in and out of doors left ajar. Everybody goggled at the stranger lady.

Yet no one menaced her, nor did she see outright filth or poverty. Tower folk on the various levels formed their own self-policing communities, often with their own argots and customs. They were apt to scoff at groundlings. It added much to the intricate, many-colored tapestry that was life in Ys.

The thirteenth floor had space for just one apartment. The landing was a narrow strip lighted by a small window. Vindilis scowled at the door. Rufinus had replaced its former knocker with the penile bone of a walrus. Distastefully, she struck it against the wood.

He opened for her at once. Her messenger having told him she wanted to visit, he was neatly attired in a Roman-style tunic. "My lady!" he greeted. "Thrice welcome! Pray enter, let me take your cloak, rest yourself while I bring refreshment."

"Did you think I'd be winded?" she answered. "Nay, I keep myself fit, and forty years leave me somewhat short of senectitude."

Her coldness failed to dismay him. Smiling, he bowed her through, closed the door, relieved her of her outer garment. For a moment they regarded each other, his green eyes even with her black. She had drawn her hair straight back. The white streak through the middle of it seemed to recall the comet of the summer. Whiteness had begun to fleck the raven locks throughout.

"Do be seated, my lady," Rufinus urged. "Would you care for wine or mead? I've laid in cheeses, nuts, dried fruits as well."

Vindilis shook her head. "Not now. I've business on hand that cannot wait."

"Aye, daylight wanes. Yonder door gives onto a balcony. Or would you liefer look through a window in this dank weather? The glass is fairly clear."

"Why do you live in an aerie?" she asked. "I know you could have quarters in the royal palace if you wished."

Startled, he said, "Why, well, I like my privacy. And the view is magnificent. The very fogs—I stand on that balcony under the moon and look down on a city become a lake of flowing alabaster. By day I am kin to the rooks and hawks around me."

"You certainly have changed your ways. Like your language."

"My lady?"

"You neither live like a Bacauda any longer nor talk like one. I'll step outside. What I see should tell me more about you."

Crossing the main chamber, she glanced everywhere around. The bedroom door stood shut. The kitchen was open, and ordinary: a cubicle minimally equipped, plastered and tiled against fire hazard. He kept the place clean. Rather, a hireling doubtless came in and did, for Rufinus had money these days. The atrium doubled as triclinium, with a table and chairs next to a sideboard. The ware on its shelves ran to the fanciful, sometimes the obscene, such as a ewer in the form of Priapus. Another table was of finely carved walnut inset with nacre. Likewise good were a pair of couches. A corner was taken up by his traveling gear, the weapons and tools and forester's outfit with which he fared on the King's missions. Two portrait busts on pedestals flanked it, one the beautiful ancient head of a boy, the second a modern likeness of Gratillonius. Elsewhere sprawled a jackdaw collection of objects, everything from a golden arm ring of Frankish workmanship to an earthen jug which must hold certain memories, whatever they might be.

Passing the central table, Vindilis spied a flute, a couple of books, writing materials, a shingle on which words had awkwardly been penned. "I see you practice your literacy," she remarked.

"I do, my lady, with more patience than is usually mine," he said. "You doubtless know Queen Bodilis was gracious enough to arrange instruction for me. She's promised me fascinating things to read when I'm able."

He hurried to fling wide the balcony door. Vindilis trod forth into a chill that braziers kept from the apartment. She breathed deep. "Fresh air cleanses," she said.

Rufinus smiled. "I pray pardon if my lodgings are stuffy. I get more fresh air than I care for, outside Ys."

The view embraced a semicircle, from the sea portal to High Gate and beyond. Rampart, turrets, triumphal arch, streets, plazas were hers, an interweaving made mysterious by the vapors that drifted through it. Towers like this lanced above, to catch long sunbeams and bedazzle heaven. Afar she saw Elven Gardens and the purity of Belisama's Temple like an island rising out of the mist-lake. The sounds were of wind, wings, bird calls, and, faintly, the pulsebeat of the city.

"Aye," Vindilis mused at length, "you've deeper reasons than you perchance know for roosting here. All this calls to you."

Rufinus blinked. "What?" He cleared his throat. "Hm, can I supply aught that my lady needs for her aeromancy? Shall I absent myself?"

Vindilis re-entered the room, closed the door, confronted him. "Not for that have I come," she said.

"But your message was—"

She smiled sardonically. "My message was to head off rumors. I have no gift for reading the future in patterns of cloud and breeze. If I did, I'd mount the pharos for it. Nay, my aim is to talk with you in private."

Unease passed through him. "Indeed? A surprise. I'm nobody."

"You are he whom the King defied the Gods to spare. That alone makes you fateful. Now you have also become his confidential agent, going to and fro on the earth. Surely you offer counsel as well. Sit down, Rufinus."

"As my lady commands. But first let me pour wine and—"

Vindilis pointed to a chair. "Sit down, I told you."

He folded his long legs and stared up at her. "Does my lady speak for the Nine?"

"Not altogether. Words concerning you have passed among us, but 'twas my decision to seek you out. What I tell anyone else will depend very much on what happens here."

He wet his lips. "I'll not betray my master's secrets."

Vindilis folded her arms and looked above him into the shadows that were gathering as daylight ended. "I need it not. I can guess, broadly, what goes on. The organizing of former Bacaudae into the King's forest rangers. Tasks they carry out at his behest. Linkage with the smallholders, the serfs, belike certain townspeople, the resettled veterans. He's gathering together a native Armorican strength, to protect the country better than Rome does. Yet the Imperial authorities would dislike learning that they are under surveillance and that so much they've mismanaged is quietly being done. *I* will bear no tales to them."

Rufinus had regained balance. "The Queen is shrewd. I beg leave to say no more."

Her gaze smoldered at him. "You may be required to. I think that from time to time you shall be recommending certain courses of action to Gratillonius, proposals that would not have occurred to him of their own accord."

Forgetting her orders, he jumped to his feet. Pallor made the scar on his cheek stand lurid. "Nay!" he cried. "Grallon's my lord!"

"Calm down," she snapped. "Think you his wives would wish him steered toward harm? I've his best interests at heart. And yours, Rufinus."

"Mine? My lady, I'll take no bribe—forgive me—no recompense."

Her smile was hard. "Not even silence?"

He stared. "What mean you?"

"Unwise you were, Rufinus, to take your pleasures freely in Ys."

He stiffened his back. "Why should I not carouse?"

"Wine, song, shows, gambling, aye. But you're never seen in Tomcat Alley, nor do you avail yourself of the girls so readily available in taverns near the waterfront. For that matter, given your status and, yea, your personal charm, I'm sure a number of elegant women would be glad of a little sport with you."

His hands lifted as if to fend her off. "I'm not impotent—"

"I never believed that."

"I've been with women—"

"Doubtless. After all, you came here intending to make yourself King."

"If I choose now to be chaste—"

"Curse me if you must," said Vindilis crisply, "but insult not my intelligence. I suspected early on what you are. The Nine have their means of finding things out when they care to. Shall I name the foreign sailors? Some you brought hither, the young and handsome. That was most foolish. 'Tis sheer luck that your fellow tenants have not paid much heed...thus far. They soon will, unless you grow careful."

The breath rasped in Rufinus's throat. "What concern is this of theirs? Of yours?"

The sharp features softened, and the voice. "It should be none. In olden Greece, I've heard, 'twould not have been, nor for a long time in Rome itself. But Ys is neither. Underneath all the sensuality, its heritage remains, of austere mariners from the South, ruthless charioteers from the East, and—who knows what of the Old Folk?" She laid a hand on his. "Would it were otherwise. But this must needs concern me, because the revelation would destroy your usefulness to the King. It would cast suspicions on him that would wound him in his soul and undermine him in his power. You'd not do that to Grallon, would you, Rufinus?"

He shuddered. Anguish answered: "O Gods, netherworld Gods, nay."

"Then, first, be more discreet," she said. "You can do as you like beyond our borders, though best would be if you use a false name. While in Ys, amuse yourself as you wish, save this." Her tone thinned. "Engage whores, if your fingers will not suffice you."

He reddened. "I can. I have. 'Tis only—I think my nature is, is because I was a boy when I joined the Bacaudae, who seldom see women, and— Nay, I pledge caution in Ys, for Grallon's sake."

Warmth responded: "Then I will accept your wine. Come, light wicks ere dusk overtakes us. Set forth food also, though I eat sparingly. Let us sit down and become acquainted. For I do not abhor you. I understand you better than you imagine."

Heartened, he warned, "Gladly will I plan with you how we may both serve Grallon, my lady. But remember always, he is my lord, to whom my faith is plighted."

"Whom you love," she said softly.

Rufinus flinched. "He does not know."

"Nor shall he ever," Vindilis promised, "if you bear yourself toward me as I hope you will."

~ 5 ~

The Queens were all kind to Dahut, in their different ways, but she came to like Tambilis best and looked forward to her turns at staying in the house of the youngest. This was in spite of the fact that Papa never came there, with his romps and stories and tuneless but bouncing songs, as he did to the other Mamas whenever he was able (though he never spent the night with Fennalis or Bodilis). Dahut tried to find out why that was, but couldn't get any real answer from either one. They certainly smiled and spoke gently enough when they met.

No matter that eight years lay between their births, Tambilis and Dahut shared secrets, played little games together, went on trips, moaned about lessons, giggled at funny things. Tambilis had more learning, of course, which she could not readily explain to Dahut, only saying, "Wait till you get that far." However, she knew there was something mysterious and special about Dahut, which could still less be put into words. "I'm not afraid of you," she said. "You're my own dear cousin."

The Council of Suffetes met around the quarter days. Tambilis confessed to Dahut that she merely listened, sometimes interested, sometimes frightened, sometimes well-nigh falling asleep. On the days themselves, the meetings adjourned for various ceremonies. Tambilis looked on the vernal equinox that year as a liberation.

After services at the Temple of Belisama, she sought Dahut out from among the departing choir girls. She herself had been one of the high priestesses. "Would you like to come with me?" she asked, flushed and proud. "I have the Shrine of Ishtar this time. 'Tis just open two days a year, you know, at spring and autumn."

Dahut joyously agreed and got permission. She had heard that Ishtar was an ancient name of the Goddess and that the Founders had built Her a house when Ys was a new Phoenician colony. Nowadays Her first, simple dwelling stood unused, except when the wheel of the year bore back remembrance.

Hand in hand, the two made their way through crowds that respectfully parted, down into Lowtown. The blue gown and high white headdress of Tambilis only made her look as young as Dahut, who wore a flowing dress of silk, gilt sandals, and above her unbound blond hair a garland of primroses. The day was mild and sunny. Birds winged around flashing towers.

The shrine was small, rammed earth and slate roof on a plot scarcely larger, which was marked off by four boundary stones. When Tambilis had unlocked the door, the interior proved equally plain, clay floor and rough altar block, though the Mirror was polished and the murals of Stars and Moon had lately been retouched.

After prayer, Tambilis seated herself on a bench together with Dahut and waited. In the hours that followed, a number of people came one by one or two by two through the open entrance. Mostly they were humble folk. Some simply wanted to make their devotions. Some approached the Queen and asked for blessing or help—a woman with child, a man who had lost his only son, a woman in search of her husband's forgiveness for adultery, a man soon to sail forth to distant lands, a girl who was deformed and lonely, a boy with soaring dreams.... Tambilis could give the benison. Aid and counsel she was seldom prepared to render, but she knew where they might be found. In this wise Dahut saw what power was the Goddess's.

At sunset, after a final orison, Tambilis closed the shrine. The weight of solemnity fell off her. "Now we are free," she caroled. "Come, let's go to the Forum. They'll be celebrating, you know, and the performers and musicians and, and everybody. There'll be stalls with food and drink and sweetmeats and, oh, all sorts of fine things. Innilis said I can bring you home as late as we want."

"Till dawn!" Dahut cried.

They danced off, Tambilis forgetting that in public a Queen should be stately.

Between the Roman-like buildings that surrounded the central plaza, a throng milled. Their feet hid the mosaics of dolphins and sea horses. Dusk had gone flickery-bright, for the Fire Fountain was playing, oil ablaze, pumped high to cascade in red, yellow, green, blue flames down its three basins. Voices surfed, laughter rang, melodies whistled, throbbed, twanged, drummed. Raiment made a rainbow, and few were the brows without a wreath.

Wandering about, little noticed in spite of Tambilis's garb, the girl passed near what had been the Roman temple of Mars and was now the Christian church. Words slashed through the merriment: "O people of Ys, hear the warning. Terrible is your danger."

Tambilis paid no heed, but Dahut stopped and stared. A tall, raw-boned man stood on the top step of the temple portico. His beard was black but grizzling, his hair abristle behind a shaven slice of scalp that went from ear to ear. His robe was of cloth cheap and rough. At his back, drably clad, clustered a few men and slightly more women. "Amen," they chanted whenever he paused. His speech was quiet, but it carried.

"—yon cheerful ingle is in truth a will-o'-the-wisp leading you on to the burning that waits down in hell—"

The Ysans ignored him, talked, quaffed, japed, kissed.

"I beg you, listen. Ah, well do I understand, my plea tonight will win nobody over. But if you will hear it and think about it—"

Dahut's face paled so that the restless colors took possession of it. "Come," Tambilis said. "No matter that old moldy. Let's go on." Dahut seemed to hear only the preacher.

"I do not scoff at your faith. Your Gods have brought you to much that is wonderful. But Their time is past. Like those unfortunates whom senility has turned mad, They do naught but mislead; and the road They have you upon goes into the Abyss. I love you too much, God loves you too much, to wish that for you. Forswear those demons you call Gods. Christ waits and longs to save you."

"Nay!" Dahut yelled. She broke from Tambilis's clasp, dashed off and up the stairs.

An uneven sigh went over the revelry and damped it down. Many recognized the slim form with the beautiful face that ran to stand before Corentinus. They breathed her name to the rest. Eyes and eyes and eyes turned thither.

"Child," called the chorepiscopus shakenly, "beloved Princess Dahut, do *you* see the truth?"

She stamped her foot, clenched her fists, and shouted up his height: "You lie, old man, you're a liar! The Goddess is good, the Gods're strong!"

"Oh, poor darling," Corentinus said.

"You're horrible!" she screamed. Turning to the Forum, she raised her arms. The light from the Fountain picked out her bright garment and hair, while casting Corentinus into murk. "Don't you listen to him! The Goddess is good, the Gods're strong!"

"Child," Corentinus groaned, "you have but seven years in this world. How can you know?"

"I do know!" she flung at him. "The sea tells me, the seal comes to me, an', an' today—everywhere—" Again she faced the people. "Listen to me. We *belong* to the Gods. If we forsake Them, They will forsake us, and Ys will die. Please be true to the Gods!"

Weeping, she stumbled back down the stairs. Tambilis hurried to embrace her. The crowd swarmed around them. It roared. Corentinus and his Christians stood alone beneath the pagan frieze on their church.

XIII

~ 1 ~

At Lúgnassat, King Niall must by law preside over the great fair at Tallten, its rites and sacrifices as well as its games and worldly dealings. His older sons had fallen into the way of representing him at such other gatherings of the kind as were important. They would be unwise to break that practice, when no warfare had call upon them this year. Besides keeping the glory of their house in view, it gave them a chance to gather news and strike useful bargains. With their north-faring dreams, the lords of Mide wanted no enemies at their backs. About the hostility of the Lagini they could do little; however it seemed that Niall's punitive expedition, and the wealth he took back with him, had sapped the eastern Fifth for a while.

Yet he was now master of Mag Slecht, where stood Cromb Cróche, Who had power over earth and blood. If he wanted the help, the goodwill, of that God, he for his part must not fail to pay honor and make offering. Having given the matter thought, he sent his son Domnuald on his behalf, with a goodly train of warriors and servants, a druid for counsel and magic, a poet for solemnity and power, several bards for entertainment when the company had made camp at eventide. Though still rather young, Domnuald had proven himself in battle against the Lagini and afterward the Ulati. Among his own folk, his cheerfulness and common sense boded well for the future.

As he approached his destination, he departed form the main road and travelled about, collecting the tribute and rents due his father. These he took in the form of kine. To landowners in whose houses he overnighted when that was convenient, he explained his intention of giving the animals, in a huge slaughter, to the Bent One of the Mound. Thus should there come no evil creatures upon Niall or the sons of Niall.

Certain men cast dark looks. After their guest was gone, they rode off with word. Having become a cattle drive, Domnuald's progress grew slow. Nevertheless he ended his journey ahead of time.

The past few days had been hot. Air stewed in the nostrils, clothes clung to skin, breath was heavy and sleep unrestful. Clouds brooded enormous, blue-black, with mutterings in their depths and sometimes a wan flicker of lightning; but the blessed rain did not fall and did not fall. The herd became skittish, hard to control. Men's patience wore thin, until tempers often flared into quarrels.

Mag Slecht was a plain out of which rose small hills. Here the menhirs, dolmens, and cromlechs were many. Such folk as lived thereabouts tended the cult sites and, in return, shared in the sacrificial feasts that outsiders held. Otherwise poor and lowly, they were still regarded as having something eldritch about them.

Domnuald went by their homes without stopping, more hasty than haughty, until his band spied the halidom of Cromb Cróche from afar. Then he galloped his horse ahead of everybody else, up the track through the woods that decked the hillsides, reached the clearing, and reined in.

Awe smote him. He saw a huge circle of grass surrounded by forest. In this windlessness, leaves were utterly silent, as if cut out of green stone, and shadows made caves beneath the boughs. At the center blazed brightness almost too fierce to look at. It was the gold and silver that sheathed a giant standing stone which had somewhat the look of a hunchbacked man. Not much smaller were the menhirs that formed a ring around it, twelve altogether, themselves covered with brass kept bright by the rubbing of worshipful hands.

Domnuald's troop had remained below to set up camp, save for a couple of warriors who followed him more slowly. The trees hid them. Shouts, lowing and neighing of beasts, creak of cartwheels reached him faintly, as if the simmering stillness crushed every noise under its weight. He was alone beneath the thunderheads.

Of a sudden that ended. Three more roads led to this crest. Out from the eastern one trod armed men. Their spearheads flamed in the ruthless sunlight. Domnuald dropped hand to sword hilt where he sat.

The leader strode toward him, a man as heavy as Domnuald was slender, dark as Domnuald was fair. "And who might you be?" called the Mide prince.

"I am Fland Dub maqq Ninnedo," growled the stranger, "king of the Tuath Ben Síde, who hold this land from old. And you would be the upstart from Temir, would you not?"

"I am son to the Mide King, your high lord," Domnuald answered as steadily as might be. "What do you want? The rites are not till day after tomorrow."

"Hear me," Fland said. "You would take over our sacrifices, ours by right since the Children of Danu reigned here. You would glut yourselves on offerings we should have made—"

"The holy meat we will share with all who come," Domnuald cried indignantly. "Do you think the sons of Niall are niggards?"

"Do you seek to buy the favor of our tenants away from us?" Fland retorted. "It shall not be. We, the landholders of three tuaths, say that." He tried to fight down his fury. The breath grated in his throat. "See here, boy. Let us be reasonable. We, my friends and I, we came early so we could catch you, talk with you, beforehand. Surely you and we between us can make a fair division of honor."

Domnuald reddened. "How can I parcel away my father's honor? If you bring livestock of your own to offer, I'll not be standing in your way."

"You have taken as much as the land can spare."

Youth and summer heat broke free like a lightning flash. "And so shall it always be, Fer Bolg!"

As if of itself, Fland's spear stabbed upward. Domnuald's escort, arriving just then, saw their leader topple off his horse, to thresh about with blood spouting and flowing.

Fland stared. "I did not mean—" he mumbled. Wit came back. As soon as the Mide men knew, they would attack. And they outnumbered his. Did he surrender, Niall would not likely take éricc payment for this young life, not though the honor price that a man of Fland's standing must add was high. Best flee north. The King at Emain Macha would have need of warriors before long.

Fland waved and whistled. His companions loped after him into the woods that they knew and the Mide men did not. Behind them, Domnuald maqq Neill's blood ebbed out, slower and slower, like the blood of an animal slain before Cromb Cróche.

~ 2 ~

Landing at Clón Tarui, Conual Corcc left a guard with his ships, his wife, and certain others. The rest of his followers, a large and well-armed band, hurried through Mide to Tallten. They had hoped to attend the fair, but a storm held them past Lúgnassat. Thus they arrived only on its last day, as it was breaking up.

Even so, what they saw was a mighty thing. Here Lúg of the Long Arm had buried his fostermother Talltiu and founded sacred games in Her honor, ages past. Here the Kings at Temir were buried, their grave mounds surrounding Hers like warriors asleep outside the house of a queen. Here the contests still took place, races of every kind, wrestling, hurling, games of skill. Here were music, poetry, dance, both solemn and light hearted. Here was a market to which traders came from all over Ériu and no few countries overseas. Here too was another kind of dickering, for the fair was reckoned a lucky place to make marriages, so that families sought it to discuss arrangements and couples were united in the Glen of the Weddings. Laughter and song resounded through the river valley. Its grass disappeared under tents and booths, and must afterward grow back out of trampled mud. As they arrived and as they left, the lines of chariots and horsemen stretched for miles, not to speak of people afoot.

Above all, the fair was holy. The King himself conducted the great sacrifices; many lesser ones occurred as well. The laws were spoken aloud before the assembled chieftains and ollams. Serious matters were dealt with; an oath sworn or an agreement made here was doubly binding. For a crime committed at the fair, there could be no compounding by payment. Earth-walled fortresses frowned around Tallten, for it was among the royal seats of the realm, but at Lúgnassat season they stood empty; none dared break the peace, enmities were set aside, anyone could come from anywhere and his person be inviolate.

Conual Corcc made his way among the crowds, toward the hall of the King. It loomed on a rise of ground amidst its outbuildings, long and high, peeled studpoles gleaming from whitewashed cob walls, thatch woven in cunning patterns. Life brawled around it, warriors, attendants, artisans, visitors, men, women, children, horses, hounds, fowl—no swine, which it was gess for a King to possess though he could eat them; but prize cattle were there, sleek of red-white-black-brown coats, prideful of horns. Bright was the garb that swirled from shoulders and waists. Steel shone on weapons, bronze over shields, silver off brooches, gold about necks and arms. Talk surged like surf, along with clamor of children, beasts, smithwork, carting, footfalls, hoofbeats. Smoke from the cookhouse told noses that an ox was roasting.

This morning was brilliant. Conual stood taller than most. His hair burned above the hubbub. Folk stared, made way for him and his troop, but did not venture to address a lord unknown to them—until abruptly a voice cried his name. He stopped, looked, and knew Nemain maqq Aedo.

The druid had aged in the years since Conual went abroad. Stooped and skeletal, he leaned heavily on his staff and walked with the care of those who do not see well. Yet he made haste—a path opened immediately in the throng, and a hush fell—until he and Conual embraced.

432

"Welcome, welcome, a thousand welcomes, dear heart!" he cried. "How I have waited for this glad day!"

Conual stepped back. An eeriness cooled his spirit. "Did you, then, foreknow my coming?" he asked.

"Ah, there have been signs, not all of them good, but you strode into my dreams and...waking, I looked into the Well of the Dagdae." Nemain plucked at Conual's sleeve. "Come, let us go aside where we can talk."

"Forgive me, but I should not hang back from greeting the King. That would be an insult."

"It will not, if I enter with you, for I whispered in his ear that I must be off on mystic business. Himself is bidding farewell to his highborn guests who stayed here during the fair. It will take a while."

The sense of trouble grew colder within Conual Corcc. He gave the druid his arm and beckoned his men to keep their distance. A way downslope was a grove of rowan, with a bench for those who might wish to linger among the sacred trees and breathe of their magic. Overlooking the turmoil of leavetaking along the river, it was a haven of peace.

The two sat down. "Know that you have come at a time when grief is upon Niall maqq Echach," Nemain began. "The news has reached him that a son of his was slain at Mag Slecht by tuaths restive after he wrung their allegiance from them. Niall could barely keep showing the world a good face and carry on his duties. Now that the fair is ending, he is free to kill. Already he has sent for his hostages from those three tuaths. Tomorrow he will hang them. His vengeance will not stop at that."

"It's sorry I am to hear this," Conual said. "Who is he that fell?"

"Domnuald—Domnuald the fair, we called him, child of Queen Aethbe."

Conual sighed. "Domnuald, indeed? Ochón! I remember him well. He was only a little lad then, but always bright and merry. May he reach Mag Mell and abide in joy."

"That is too strong a wish to utter at once," Nemain cautioned. "Well, Niall mourns the sorer because Domnuald, of all his sons, reminded him most of Breccan, his firstborn, who died at Ys. You have heard about that?"

"Somewhat. I have been busy, you know, faring, warring, and... dealing...in Britannia."

"You return to claim a dream you have cherished, do you not?"

"I do. It is nothing that threatens Niall. Else why would I seek him first? Rather, he should help me, speed me on my way, for the sake of our common fosterage and the shield I can raise at his back." Conual frowned. "This redoubles the misfortune that has befallen him. As for myself—" He drew breath. "Nemain, dear, could I meet with those hostages?"

"I knew you would ask that," said the druid. "Come."

The prisoners were confined in a shed, tightly bound. Their guards durst not refuse admittance to Nemain, who led Conual in. The three men met his gaze proudly and spoke curtly. "You are ready to die, then?" Conual inquired.

"We are that," replied one, "thinking on what our deaths must cost Niall later."

"Hm, now," said Conual, "your three tuaths can scarcely stand against his might, nor can they look for much aid out of Ulati country. Would it not be better that he seek revenge on the killers instead of laying waste your homeland?"

He spoke with them a bit more. Thereupon he and Nemain went back out and talked at length.

The sun stood past noon when Niall's last guest had left. He slumped on his high seat, drinking horn after horn of ale. Uneasy stillness filled the hall. The rustle of movement and low voices seemed only to deepen it. Abruptly a shout broke through. The chief of the guard announced Conual maqq Lugthaci, who came in, resplendently clad, at the head of his warriors, at his right hand the druid Nemain maqq Aedo.

Niall roared. He bounded from his seat and plunged down the length of the hall to seize his fosterbrother to him. His folk howled, stamped the floor, beat fists against benches and shields, in their joy at seeing darkness lifted from the King.

Conual's followers carried gifts worthy of him, weapons, fine garments, Roman glassware of lovely shape and swirled colors, Roman silver which included a tray whereon were reliefs of heroes, maidens, and curious creatures. Niall made lavish return. Chief among the treasures he ordered fetched from his hoard and gave to Conual were a golden torc and a bronze trumpet whose workmanship drew cries of admiration from everybody who beheld.

Though the feast that day was hastily prepared, it was grand. After Laidchenn had hailed the newcomer in a poem and received a fibula in the form of a charging boar, he said, "Fine this is, but before I know what the deeds of our guest have been, I cannot properly praise them."

The building became still as heed turned toward Conual. He smiled. "That story will take long," he answered. Scowling: "Much of it is sorrowful." Loftily: "But I shall go to wrest out a new fate for myself."

As he related or stopped to answer questions, he never conceded defeat. Yet clear it was that woe had betided the Scoti in Britannia. Under Stilicho's leadership, Romans and Cunedag's Britons had pressed in ever harder. This year, the last Scotic settlers in Ordovician and Silurian lands had perforce abandoned their homes and gone back across the water.

"But mine was not a sad leavetaking," Conual avowed. "I had gathered picked fighting men from among them. Others have I brought with me too. They wait in my ships, for they would be strangers and awkward in this company; but they shall soon be working wonders."

"What is your intent?" Niall demanded bluntly.

Conual laughed. "Why, what else but to claim my heritage in Mumu? I am of the Eóganachta; I will be as great a King as any of them, and afterward greater!"

Niall stroked his beard. "That would please me well, darling," he said. "I fear I cannot offer you help. There is too much on my hands. However, abide here until Nath Í returns from the fair he was attending. Do you remember him? He is my nephew, and now my tanist. He has travelled widely in those parts and should be able to give you sage counsel."

"You are very kind, darling," Conual replied. "So sweet are you that I make bold to ask a further boon."

"You need but ask."

Conual sat straight, looked the King in the eyes, and spoke weightily: "You will recall the command laid upon me, that I am to redeem any captives I meet whenever I can. This day I have met with those hostages whom you have condemned to die tomorrow. What I ask is that you let me ransom them."

A gasp went around the hall. Fists clenched, glances flickered between the two men and the hanging shields and the doorway.

Niall stiffened. The blood came and went in his face. At last he said, word by slow word: "Do I hear aright? My guest and fosterbrother would not mock me, I am sure. Perhaps you have misunderstood. Know, the tuaths for which they stand surety have murdered my son Domnuald. Shall his blood cry in vain for revenge?"

Nemain lifted a thin hand. "Not so," he agreed. "But they who slew Domnuald, Fland Dub and his fellows, have fled beyond the Walls of the Ulati. What honor lies in burning poor little shielings, driving off poor little herds, butchering innocent tenants? The Gods will raise the just man up, and They will cast the unjust down."

"I will pay, in gold, the éricc, and add thereto my own honor price," Conual declared. "Deny me not, if you love me. I may no more refuse to seek the freedom of men in bonds than you may traverse Mag Callani after sunset or let sunrise find you abed at Temir."

Niall hunched his shoulders. "Shall those men go home free, to boast that I dared not avenge my son?" he growled like a wolf at bay.

"They shall not," Conual answered quickly. "I will take them south to Mumu. I think they will serve me well. And we are allies, you and I."

"As for vengeance," Laidchenn reminded, "it awaits you at Emain Macha."

Said the druid: "The ransom that Conual pays will provide Domnuald a burial such as few kings have gotten, and endow honors for him as long as Temir abides."

Niall gusted a sigh. "I yield you this, Conual. But it was not well done of you to trick me into making the promise."

With his pride thus bulwarked, he was presently at his ease, still somber but readier to talk than he had been of late. In the course of the time that followed, Conual remarked, "I was surprised to hear your nephew Nath Í is your tanist. Would you not liefer have a son of yours succeed you?"

"Nath Í is worthy of his father, my brother Féchra, whose ghost ought to be pleased," Niall explained. "Of course, I would have preferred a son of mine. But they all hope to win sword-land, kingdoms of their own." His gaze pierced the darkness gathering around firelight as the sun went down outside. It came to rest on one of the skulls fastened to the wall, a head he had taken in war upon the Ulati. "They shall have that," he said low.

~ 3 ~

Again the year swung toward equinox. Summer died in a last passionate outpouring of warmth, light, green, quick thunderstorms, high stars at night. Life pulsed strong in Ys, trade, shipping, foreigners from inland and overseas, readymaking for festival.

On such a day Dahut went from temple school to the home of Bodilis, whose turn it was to care for her. The time had been long, because first the Queen had had an illness that did not readily yield to medicine or even the Touch, then the princess had been a while at the Nymphaeum. That was customary with royal children, to get them used to the sacred site and its environs before they reached the age of full vestalhood. None had started these visits as young as Dahut, but the Nine had their reasons. Today the King had come back from business in Darioritum. He would not spend the night with Bodilis, he never did anymore, but he would call on her.

Thus Dahut burst into the atrium crying jubilantly, "Mother Bodilis, Mother Bodilis, is father here yet? He is coming, isn't he? He always wants to see me very soon."

She stopped, looked, and breathed, "Why are you sad?"

The woman smiled. It made crinkles around her lips and eyes, radiating into the cheeks as they had never done in Dahut's first memories of her. "Oh, I am not, dear," she answered softly. "I am happy, in a solemn way. Something wonderful is to bless us."

Dahut's eyes, the same blue as hers, widened. "What? I know father will bring me a present. What is it going to be?"

"I fear you must wait. You should have been told erenow, but—"

Footfalls sounded at Dahut's back. Turning, she saw Tambilis enter from the street. The daughter of Bodilis was finely dressed in a gown of white silk embroidered with doves, on her feet gold-inlaid shoes, on her head a garland of roses from which her light-brown hair flowed free past the delicate features. She looked quite different all at once. It was as if overnight she had grown taller, her body filled out and her bosom swelled. Another strangeness was in her as well: she seemed frightened and resolute and lost in a dream.

Bodilis hastened to her. They embraced. "Darling, darling," the mother said. "Are you truly ready and willing?"

Tambilis nodded. "Aye."

"Be not afraid. You are now big enough, and this is Belisama's will, and, and be sure he will deal kindly with you. Be sure of that."

"I know."

Bodilis sobbed forth a laugh. "Come, then. Let me show you what I've had prepared, and tell you what I think will be best, and—" Hand in hand, they left the room and Dahut.

The girl stood where she was. Her face clouded, less with hurt than anger. A servant woman appeared from the inner part of the house. Bodilis must have told her to absent herself. She was an Osismian, blond, plump, one of many who sought to Ys and worked a few years to earn a dowry, unless they could catch a husband here. "Breifa," Dahut snapped, "what is happening?"

The maid was taken aback. "You know not, Princess? Why, tonight the King makes Tambilis really his Queen." She blushed, giggled, squirmed. "Well, he knows not either, I hear. 'Tis to be an unawaited welcome-home gift for him. She is beautiful, the lady Tambilis, nay?"

"Oh," said Dahut tonelessly.

"I could not but overhear," chattered Breifa. "'Twas Queen Bodilis who thought it should be done thus. Messages and such, arrangements, those would be too slow and stiff, they'd take the joy out of this. And Tambilis would be—passive, only a thing, is that what Queen Bodilis said? I remember not. Anyway, better Tambilis sweep him off his feet when he arrives, thinking he has just been invited for a cup of wine and a chat. Then he'll sweep her off hers soon enough, ha, ha!"

Dahut said nothing.

Breifa covered her mouth. "I talk too much, I do. What a bustle 'tis been, making everything right. Rejoice, lady Dahut. Someday you may be a Queen too."

"The Queen...of the man...who kills my father?"

"Oh, dear, I'm sorry. Well, such is the law of the Gods."

Dahut stalked off. She went into the street and stood arms folded, staring from this height out across the city to the sea.

Bodilis emerged, leading Una, her child by Gratillonius, a few months younger than Dahut but smaller and much more quiet. "There you are," the woman said. "I looked and looked for you." She paused. "What is wrong?"

"Naught," said Dahut, gaze held afar.

Bodilis laid a hand on her shoulder. "'Tis disappointment for you, I know, not to see your father this eventide. Be brave. You will soon

437

meet him, I pledge to you. You and Una and I shall stay in Tambilis's house tonight. Won't you like that? And I will tell you why, and you will be happy for him and your friend, I'm sure."

Dahut shrugged and trudged along.

~ 4 ~

At sixteen years of age, Tambilis had completed the education required of her. Each Queen served the Gods and Ys not only in set duties, but according to whatever special abilities she possessed. Tambilis had begun teaching elementary Latin in the temple school of Belisama, where Bodilis instructed advanced students of that language.

The young Queen was strolling about the flowerful intricacy of Elven Gardens during the noontide rest period. She smiled drowsily and crooned to herself. Rounding a hedge, she came upon Dahut. The child sat tracing pictures in the graveled path. What they were was hard to guess, because the stones rattled back together behind her finger.

"Why, why, good day," Tambilis said, astonished.

Dahut looked up like a blind person.

"But you're miserable!" Tambilis exclaimed. She hunkered down to hug her playmate. "What's wrong?"

"Naught," said the dry little voice.

"That's untrue," Tambilis chided. "Hark, you can tell me."

Dahut shook her head.

Tambilis considered. "'Tis the King, nay?" she asked after a moment. "You feel your father slighted you. Well, he did not. 'Twas but that he—he and I—well, the will of the Goddess was upon us. Is. Have no fear. Soon he'll greet you, and he does have the prettiest cloak for you, that he found among the Veneti, and, oh, all sorts of adventures to tell about."

Still there was no response. "Indeed," Tambilis persisted, "you must visit us. We're staying at the palace now while we...get to know each other better. We shall for several days yet." Resignation laid a sudden burden on her voice. "After that, all will be much as it was before."

"I will see him somewhere else," Dahut said.

"But why? My dear, I've not turned my back on you. I love you always." Tambilis searched for words. "'Tis only that time goes, things change. Later you'll understand." Impulsively: "This was not my wish at first. 'Twas Guilvilis who caused it, stupid, clumsy, loving Guilvilis. She mustered courage at last to tell me I did wrong withholding myself when I could gladden him, lighten his cares, and— And, Dahut," glowed from her, "the Goddess gives me joy too, as She will you someday."

Dahut screamed. She scrambled to her feet and fled.

When she was not at her next class, the teacher sent an acolyte to inquire at the dwellings of the Gallicenae. Had she perchance been

438

taken sick? It took hours to establish that she had disappeared, and then to organize search parties. They did not find her until sundown, after she had re-entered the city at Aurochs Gate and was stubbornly walking up Amber Street toward the home of Fennalis. Her clothes were wet, with smells of kelp and fish.

XIV

~ 1 ~

As autumn yellowed leaves, Conual Corcc bade Niall maqq Echach farewell. Since this must at first be a reconnoitering expedition, he left behind most of his men. Just thirty followed him south, among them the three hostages he had saved. His Cruthinach wife came too, for there is magic as well as comfort in women.

Shut off as Mumu was from the rest of Ériu, Niall heard nothing more until spring. When finally a messenger arrived to bid the remaining warriors now seek their lord, it was a strange story that he brought.

A day's travel northwest from the Mountain of Fair Women was the Plain of Femen, where Fedelmm the witch had troubled King Lugthach. It was fertile and well settled, save at one place where forest stood ancient. Few ventured in, for at the middle of the woods reared the Síd Drommen. This limestone outcrop, whose three hundred feet overtopped the trees around, was believed to be the haunt of elves, ghosts, every creature of the Other World. However, swineherds took their animals there in season for the rich mast. Though their trade be humble, it gave them ties to Those Beyond.

Once two of them were in that wood together. Each kept pigs for the king of a neighboring tuath: Dardriu for the king of Éle, Coriran for the king of Múscraige. To his master King Aed came Coriran and said; "We fell into a deep sleep, Dardriu and I. Adream, we beheld the Ridge of the Beings. Before it were a yew tree and a flagstone. Somehow we knew that that was the tree of the Eóganachta, and that he who stands upon the stone shall wax great."

The druid of Aed thought deeply, sought visions, and declared: "The Síd Drommen shall become the seat of the kings over all Mumu. From him who first lights a fire under that yew shall they descend."

"Let us go light it!" cried Aed.

"Let us await the morning," counselled the druid: for it was late, and the sun hidden behind lowering clouds. Soon a snowstorm began, this early in the year.

439

It caused Conual, his wife, and their men to lose their way as they fared down from the north. They blundered into the wood and took shelter below the rock. A yew tree growing there, it leaves withered but as yet unfallen, gave a roof of sorts, letting them kindle a fire. A flat stone at his foot made a place to stand while shoes dried out.

So did Aed find them. Although downcast, the king did not venture to quarrel with the Gods. Conual had, indeed, a birthright claim. Moreover, he was a friend of the mighty Niall, of whom they had report. The upshot was that Aed acknowledged Conual king of the surrounding territory and gave him his own son as hostage.

Thus the story that Niall heard in spring. He smiled and let the men go whom Conual had brought from Brittannia. Among them were several ollam craftsmen—engineers, stonemasons—who understood the Roman arts of fortification. With them Niall sent rich gifts.

A year passed.

For Niall it, like the twelvemonth before, was less warlike than many had been. Both years were nonetheless busy. His sons champed to be off conquering, but their father held them back. "Lay the keel, fasten the ribs, bind the strakes," he said. "When the ship is ready, we will sail." They did not fully understand, not being seamen like him.

Niall did complete the taking over of those nine tuaths which had been tributary to the Ulati. He raised new kings among them to replace those he had felled in battle, and a high King above these: all obedient to him. They were well content, because he returned to them that governance over the sacrifices at Mag Slecht which had been theirs from of old. Despite yielding this, which cost him little and won him much in the way of goodwill, he never let wane his resolve to have vengeance for Domnuald—and someday, somehow, for Breccan.

The hostages that the tuaths gave him he treated so generously that they vowed to fight at his side when he became ready for his onslaught against the Ulati. Likewise would their kinfolk. The kingdom he had founded for these became known as the Aregésla, They Who Give Hostages, a name borne proudly. People began calling him Niall of the Nine Hostages.

—King Fergus Fogae in Emain Macha was fully aware of the storm that brewed in the south. He thought of launching an attack himself, decided that that would be ruinous, and set about strengthening defenses throughout his realm. His poets reminded him of how Cú Culanni had brought Medb and her Condachtae low. Those songs echoed spookily in the hall.

—Next Imbolc came messengers from Conual to Temir. They bore gifts no less than those Niall had sent south, and fateful tidings.

Conual's power had grown like the antlers on a stag. While small, his force of exiles was schooled in ways of war unknown to Mumu. Each battle they won brought new allegiances, thus a larger host to call upon. Without fighting, even more chieftains swore faith to this newcomer whom the Gods had clearly blessed. Lately he had gotten for a second wife Ámend, daughter of Oengus Bolg, king of the powerful Corco Loígde. They holding land on the south coast, Conual thereby gained an opening to the outer world.

The magic that flamed around his name came not least from the seat he had chosen. It was the very Síd Drommen: an audacity that brought not disaster on him, but victory after victory. There he was building a stone stronghold of the Roman kind, impregnable to anything that Gaelic men could bring against it: Liss inna Lochraide, the Fort of the Heroes. Already, in the mouths of the folk, the name of the rock itself was changing to Latin Castellum, which soon got softened to Cassel.

The poet who related these thing to Niall knew better than to say so, but unmistakably underlying his staves was glee, that his lord's rise was so swift that the deeds of the Temir King could not compare.

Niall sat silent a long time, staring into firelight darkness. Finally those who sat close saw his lips move. "The Síd Drommen," whispered forth. "He dared. He *dared*."

~ 2 ~

Forty days after solstice, the diminishing gloom of winter was made bright in Ys. Queen Tambilis bore her first child. Mother and daughter were in the best of health. As he was wont on such occasions, the King decreed festival immediately after the hallowing of the new little Semuramat. Legionaries formed an honor guard when he led Tambilis from the Temple of Belisama to the palace. With them came the rest of the Nine—on as high a holiday as this, the Gods required none to stay alone on Sena—and the magnates of the city with their wives. Wine, mead, and rich food from the royal stores were distributed among the poor, that they too might celebrate. Entertainers of every kind, having anticipated the event, swarmed merrily about. After dark the Fire Fountain blossomed, though weather kept the Forum almost deserted.

In a house near Menhir Place there was no mirth. It was a small but decent house, such as a married soldier could afford to rent. The matron was having her own first childbirth. Her labor started about when the Queen's did. Still it went on. She was Keban, wedded to Budic.

Adminius had excused him from duty, never expecting he would be gone this long. He sat on a bench in the main room, elbows on knees, head bowed between shoulders. A lamp picked furnishings out of the shadows that filled every corner. His breath smoked in the chill. Outside, the night wind hooted, shook the door, flung handfuls of hail against shutters.

The midwife came in from the bedroom holding a candle. She shambled in her exhaustion. Budic raised his face. The youthfulness it had kept through the years was hollowed out. He had not shaved all this while; the whiskers made a thin fuzz over jaws and cheeks. "How goes it?" he croaked.

"Best you look in," the woman said, flat-voiced. "You might not see her alive again. I'll keep doing what I can, sir, but my arts are spent."

Budic rose and stumbled into the other chamber. A brazier gave warmth that sharpened the reek of sweat, urine, vomit, burnt tallow. Enough light seeped through the doorway to show him the swollen form and sunken wet countenance. Her eyes were shut, except for a glimmer of white. Her mouth was half open, her breath shallow. Now and then a feeble convulsion shook her. Helplessly, he laid his palm on her forehead. "Can you hear me, beloved?" he asked. He got no answer.

A sound drew his attention—crash of wood against wall, suddenly loudened storm noises, the midwife's cry of amazement. He went back into the main room. A tall, grizzle-bearded man in a coarse robe and paenula had entered. One knotty hand gripped a staff. Beneath a half-shaven scalp his features jutted like the headlands.

"Corentinus!" Budic exclaimed in Latin. "What brings you, Father?"

"A sense within me that you have need, my son," replied the chorepiscopus.

The midwife traced a warding crescent. Tales had long gone about that this man of Christ sometimes had foreknowledge.

"Need of your prayers," Budic said. "Oh, Father, she's dying."

"I feared that. Let me see." Corentinus brushed past him. Budic sank down on the bench and wept.

Corentinus returned. "She is far gone, poor soul," he said. "This was just a little late in life, maybe, for her to start bearing. I thought she was barren, and beseeched God to gladden the two of you with a child, but—"

Budic lifted his gaze. "Can you pray her back to me?"

"I can only ask God's mercy. His will be done." Corentinus pondered. "Although—" Decision: "He helps us mortals, even unto an angelic summons, but we must do our share. My rough medical skills are of no use here. The Gallicenae command healing powers beyond any I've ever heard of elsewhere. I'll go fetch one."

Budic gasped. "What? But they're feasting at the palace. I know because Cynan looked in on us on his way to parade."

Corentinus rapped out a laugh. "The more merit in the charity, then. Who can tell but what this may start the pagan on a path to salvation? Hold fast, son. I'll be back as soon as may be." He went out into the night.

The midwife shuddered. "What did he want, sir?" she asked. Her Latin was rudimentary.

Budic shook his head, numbed beyond his numbness at the thought of such a raven breaking into the King's banquet and demanding the aid of the Nine.

Whoo-oo called the wind, and more hail rattled over the cobbles. Budic returned to the bedside. Time crept.

The door thumped open. Corentinus loomed above a slight form in a cowled cloak hastily thrown over splendor. Emerging, Budic recognized Innilis. He pulled himself erect and saluted. Behind the two came a servant woman with a box in her arms, and then Adminius in armor that sheened wet.

"Stand aside," ordered the Queen. Budic had never before heard her anything but soft-spoken. She stepped into the bedroom. "Light." The midwife got the candle. "We'll want more than this. I've brought tapers." The servant, who had followed, began unpacking the physician's things from the box. Innilis closed the door.

Adminius looked around. "Filthy weather," he said. "You got something ter warm a fellow's belly? The centurion 'ad us inside, of course. We'd get our share when the fancy part of the evening was done and 'e relieved us guards."

Mechanically, Budic set out wine and water jugs, cups, a loaf of bread and sections of sausage. "He let you go just like that?" he asked.

"'E's our centurion, ain't 'e? Told me ter convey 'is sympathy and best wishes. 'E can't leave the feast, that'd insult some of their 'igh and mightinesses there, but 'e'll stop by in the morning. I came along on be'alf of the boys."

"The priestess Innilis—"

"She honors her calling," said Corentinus.

Toward dawn she trod forth. Her face was pallid, eyes dark-rimmed, hands atremble. "Keban should live," she told the men. "The child—it was a boy—I had to sacrifice the child for the mother, but I think he was doomed in any case. Nay, do not go in yet, not ere Mella has...wrapped him. Besides, Keban has swooned. But I think, by Belisama's grace, she will live. She may be in frail health hereafter, and I doubt she will conceive again. But your wife should live, Budic."

He went to his knees. "Christ b-b-be thanked," he stammered in Latin. And in Ysan, lifting eyes burnt-out but adoring: "How can I thank *you*, my lady? How can I repay you?"

Innilis smiled the least bit, laid a hand on his blond head, and murmured, "The Nine take no pay, unless it be in the coin of love."

"Ever shall I love the Gallicenae and, and stand ready to serve them, whatever their wish may be. By the body of Christ I swear it."

She declined his offer of refreshment and departed with her attendant, promising to visit later in the day. Adminius escorted them. Corentinus stayed behind. "Let us thank the Lord, my son," he said. His tone was harsh.

443

At Imbolc Niall Náegéslach gave out that after Beltene he would fare overseas. Unspoken was: "Let Conual Corcc down in Mumu have his fortress. The Romans threw him out of Britannia. I will carry my sword there."

Remembering what had happened under the wall of Ys, some men were daunted. Most, though, felt no forebodings. In the ten years since, the King at Temir had won back everything he lost, and far more. This foray could well begin laying the groundwork of his vengeance on the city of the hundred towers. Well-informed chieftains knew that the terrible Stilicho had not only himself quitted Britannia, he had taken with him many troops to use against the Germani who threatened Gallia. Complacent and thinly defended, the island east of Ériu offered wealth for the taking.

So it proved. Those who met with the King and followed him in galleys and currachs found easy pickings. From Alba to Dummonia they ravaged. Men they killed, women they raped, slaves and booty they took. What legionaries there remained never got to a place the raiders struck before they were gone, leaving smoldering ruins, beheaded corpses, weeping survivors who had fled and then crept back home. The Britons themselves were ill prepared and fought poorly—save for Cunedag's tough hillmen, whose territories Niall steered clear of. Elsewhere he opened a way for Scoti to return, resettling along the western shores.

In blood he washed away his bitterness. As hay harvest and Lúgnassat neared he went home full of hope, he went home in glory.

He came back to wrath. In his absence, the Lagini had entered Mide and made havoc.

Eochaid, son of King Éndae Qennsalach, led that great inroad: Eochaid, whose first taste of battle seven years ago had become rank with defeat at the hands of Niall; Eochaid, whose handsomeness was forever marred by the scars of the blistering satire which Tigernach, son of Laidchenn, laid on him that same day. Since then he had known victory. He joined the Loígis clans when trouble broke loose with men of Condacht or Mumu, to repel the invaders and harry them past their own borders. He helped bring the allied kingdom of Ossraige to obedience, and collected tribute that subordinate tuaths in the mountains would have denied. Yet always the memory of the humbling festered.

They were, after all, as honor-proud in Qóiqet Lagini as men were anywhere. In Gallia their distant ancestors had been the Gáileóin, the Men of the Spears, which the Lagini claimed was also the meaning of their present name. Having entered Ériu, they formed their own confederation at the same time as the Goddess Macha of the Red Locks built Emain Macha to the north. Their seat of high Kings, Dún Alinni, was the work of Mess Delmon, who cast out the dark Fomóri, and pursued them into the very realms of the dead. The Lagini held

Temir itself until the Condachtae who founded Mide drove them from it.

Long had Eochaid brooded upon this. When the news came that Niall was bound abroad with as large a following as could put to sea, he shouted that this was a chance given by the Gods Themselves. Éndae, his father, urged caution; but Éndae was weakened by age, while the country throbbed with fierce young men eager to hear the son.

Thus Eochaid gathered a host on the west bank of the Ruirthech, which near Dún Alinni flowed north before bending eastward to the sea. His charioteers led the warriors on into Mide, straight toward Temir.

They failed to take it. The sons of Niall who had stayed behind held it too strongly. Yet bloody was the fighting ere the Lagini recoiled. Thereupon they went widely about, killing, plundering, burning. Countless were the treasures, cattle, slaves, and heads they took home.

Niall came back. When he saw the ruin that had been wrought, he did not rage aloud as once he would have done. Men shivered to behold an anger as bleak as the winter during which he made his preparations.

It may be that at first King Fergus of the Ulati breathed easier, knowing that for another year he need not await attack out of Mide. If so, his happiness soon blew away, on the wind that bore the smoke out of Qóiqet Lagini. From end to end of that Fifth Niall and his sons went. They pierced and scattered the levies that sought to stay them, as a prow cleaves waves, flinging foam to starboard and larboard. His ship, though, plowed red waters, and the spray was flames and the whine in the rigging was from women who keened over their dead.

Éndae yielded before his land should be utterly waste. Now Niall exacted the Bóruma; and when he brought it back, chief among the hostages who stumbled bound at his chariot wheels was Eochaid.

Never did Niall show honor to this prince, as he did to those he had from the Aregésla and elsewhere. The Laginach hostages lived crowded into a wretched hut, miserably fed and clad. They were only allowed out once a day to exercise, and that only because otherwise they would have taken sick and died—which some did anyhow. When Niall fared in procession, most of the hostages in his train wore golden chains, the merest token of a captivity which was actually a life full and free in the royal household. The Lagini went in shackles of iron.

On his deathbed a few months later, the druid Nemain reproached the King for this. "You are ungenerous, darling, the which is not like you. Was it not enough to reclaim, in the Bóruma, threefold what that young man reaved us of?"

"I have my revenge to finish," Niall answered. "Let Eochaid meanwhile be my sign to the Gods that I do not forget wrongs done my kindred."

The old man struggled for breath. "What...do you mean...by that—you whom I love?"

445

"Eochaid shall go free," Niall promised, "when the head of Fland Dub is in my hand, and Emain Macha mine, and Ys under the sea."

XV

~ 1 ~

It had become clear to the Nine and many others that Dahut would embark upon womanhood in her twelfth year. Suddenly she was gaining height and shapeliness. There was never any misproportion, outbreak in the clear skin, or loss of self-possession. While always slender, she would be more tall and robust than her mother, though equally graceful and lightfooted. The buds of her breasts were swelling toward ripeness, the curves beneath becoming rich. Golden down appeared below her arms, and under her belly formed a triangle, the figure sacred to the Goddess as the wheel was to Taranis and the spiral to Lir. She strode more than she skipped. Her voice took on a huskiness.

Above, she eerily resembled Dahilis. Great lapis lazuli eyes looked from tawny arches of brow, out of a face where the high Suffete cheekbones joined a chin small but firm. Her nose was short, a little flared at the nostrils, her mouth full and a little wide. Her hair billowed halfway down her back when she loosened it, thick, amber-hued with a tinge of copper therein.

What she lacked was the sunny temper that had been Dahilis's. Despite her beauty and quick-wittedness, Dahut was a solitary child. The Gallicenae and their maidservants had tried to find her companions of her own age, but those grew inclined to avoid her. At home the boys complained that she was too imperious, the girls shivered and called her "odd." Dahut did not seem to care. She preferred adult company when she was not off by herself, which came to be more and more in her free time.

She learned fast, read widely, was earnest in her devotions. Athletic, she walked or ran across long stretches, ranged the woods when at the Nymphaeum, rode the horses her father gave her or drove a chariot he had lately added, was a crack target splitter with bow or light javelin, spent as many hours as she could arrange on the sea, sometimes even demanded privacy to strip and swim in its chill turbulence. Female skills she acquired, but without much interest. Occasionally she made use of Gratillonius's workshop behind the palace, and he laughed that an excellent artisan was lost in her as well as in him. She appreciated good food, drink, garb, together with art, music, theater; but it was as

446

if she found her real pleasure in board games and other mental contests, or simply in listening to the King's conversations with visitors from afar.

His Roman soldiers doted on her. They called her their Luck, and practiced special drills when she was there to see. Likewise, the fisher captain Maeloch was her slave.

The Queens held her precious too, though in various ways and for various reasons. They agreed she must not be spoiled—if anything, more was required of her than of the rest of the princesses—nor should weight be laid on the fact that they perceived a destiny in her, without being able to see what it was. Nevertheless, inevitably, Dahut got intimations of this.

And so in her twelfth springtime she embarked upon womanhood.

It happened when she was staying with Tambilis. Gratillonius did not these days, because Tambilis was near term with her second child, whom she meant to name Estar. Dahut came to her room by dawnlight, shook her awake, and said somberly, "I have bled."

"What?" Tambilis sat up, rubbed her eyes, looked around. "Oh, my dear!" She surged from her bed and hugged the girl close to her. "Welcome! Be not afraid. Rejoice. Come, let me see."

In the guest chamber she examined the cloth that had been for some time laid atop Dahut's nether sheet. A spot marked it, brilliantly red against white, however dim the chamber still was. "Aye, this is your first coursing ever," Tambilis said. "May they be many and all easy. How feel you?"

"I am well." Grudgingly, Dahut pulled off her nightgown at Tambilis's behest and let the woman show her how to wash herself and attach a pad.

"Now you remember what you must do," Tambilis chattered. "And me, oh, the glad load of duties on me! What do you wish for breakfast, darling?"

Dahut shrugged. Well, girls were often upset on this day of their lives. Yet Dahut was calm enough, withdrawn into herself.

"We shall have *such* a festival! We begin with our prayers, of course. I'll help you dress."

Tambilis kept her image of Belisama in a room at the rear of the house. It was a miniature of the Goddess as Maiden, carved out of narwhal ivory and set in a niche painted deep blue with stars. Little of Quinipilis remained in this house; Tambilis favored things bright and dainty. She held up the spotted cloth as she and Dahut gave thanks.

Now the girl did not change lodging but stayed where she was, avoiding company, saying her orisons and meditating upon the mysteries. When the flow had stopped, she bathed in water not from a cistern-well but piped from the Tower, to which it had flowed down the canal from the Nymphaeum. Then it was time for celebration.

Sumptuously arrayed, Dahut went forth from the house into a glorious morning full of songbirds. Ocean sparkled beyond spires washed by

447

last night's rain. Flowers and blossoms dappled the valley and its guardian hills. Airs blew gentle. King Gratillonius waited outside in full regalia, love and pride radiating from him, together with all the Gallicenae in their blue-and-white attire of priestesses. The magnates of the city were there too, surrounded by their families. Light blazed off metal as legionaries drew swords and shouted, *"Ave!"* while Ysan marines crashed pike butts down on paving stones.

Musicians played fore and aft of the procession that went to the Temple of Belisama. Ordinary folk flocked to join it and follow it into the halidom. In that twilit chamber they stood quiet. From the aisle, vestals sang praise.

The Nine stationed themselves behind the altar, before the tall images of Maiden, Mother, and Hag. Dahut knelt and asked their blessing. She received wine, a drop of ox blood, and salt. When she had laid her garland on the block, Fennalis, senior priestess, placed on her brows a coronet of silver studded with emeralds and rubies. In lieu of her mother, her father bowed to the Triune and put a toy into her hands. It was one among many he had made, chosen by her because she was particularly fond of it, a gaily painted wooden horse with jointed legs. This too she laid on the altar and dedicated to the Goddess. That took but a single word: "Farewell."

Again outside after the service, she received the embraces and congratulations of her kin, the cheers of the crowd. She responded sparingly, though she did dimple up repeated smiles. Thereafter Gratillonius brought the party to the palace for a feast. At this she had a final tradition to observe, albeit an event regarded as merry rather than solemn. She gave away the rest of her playthings to her younger half-sisters.

Who should receive what had taken forethought. Bodilis's Una, Guilvilis's Sasai, Lanarvilis's Julia, Maldunilis's Zisa, Forsquilis's Nemeta, Vindilis's Augustina were close to Dahut in years. Guilvilis's Antonia and Camilla were not far behind either; but her Valeria was only five, while Tambilis's Semuramat was two—and that last mother claimed a rattle also, because it was lucky for an unborn child to receive a gift.

Thus went the Welcoming of Dahut. Commoners did likewise for their girls, though usually the blessing was by a minor priestess at a small sanctuary and the meal afterward modest. It was all the same in the sight of the Goddess.

For royal children, though, unto the third generation, more waited.

It happened quietly. In the morning Dahut rode to the Nymphaeum with an escort and a Queen. This one's task would be to stay there for a few days, consecrate the maiden a full vestal, and teach her certain secrets. Dahut would remain longer and receive training in her new duties. Thenceforward she would be at the Nymphaeum a sennight each lunar month, otherwise at the Temple in Ys, as housekeeper, gardener, participant in rites, and student. She would have ample leisure and a stipend which would enable her to live where and how she chose in the city, provided she remain pure. Her service was to end on her eighteenth birthday. Then she would be at liberty to marry, enroll as a subordinate priestess, pursue an independent career, do whatever she wished. Any daughters she might bear, and any daughters of these, must in their turn become vestals like her, enjoying the same advantages—unless, before the term of the vow closed, the Sign should come.

Bodilis had volunteered to be her sponsor at the hallowing. She had been half-sister to Dahut's mother.

The day of arrival went to settling in. Each virgin had a tiny room to herself. A newcomer was subject to japery and giggles in dining commons, but not too many questions. After all, she had been here before, Dahut bore it—neither cheerily nor ungraciously; aloofly—and retired early.

Her religious induction came the next morning, a brief ceremony. Later various instructresses interviewed her. They had already met the new votary, but hoped for closer acquaintance and some idea as to what kinds of education promised most for her. In the afternoon was a dinner more elegant than usual here, where everyday fare was simple. Later, until dark, pipe, drum, sistrum, and voice gave melody for dances on the greensward.

The morning after that, Bodilis drew Dahut aside. "Before I go home, I am to explain to you the secrets," she said. "They're not really close-veiled. That would be impossible." She smiled. "But tradition insists that certain knowledge may pass only between Queen and vestal, and otherwise not be spoken aloud. Let's avail ourselves of this beautiful weather while it holds. Go dress yourself for a ramble and meet me."

Dahut obeyed happily. When she and Bodilis had left the building, she could not forbear to prance about and bay the Wolf Chant. "Ah, you are young still, sweetling," the woman murmured. "Come along."

They took a trail uphill into the woods. A rivulet gurgled beside it. Birds trilled. Squirrels raced ruddy. Sunlight filled leaves with green fire and spattered on the shade beneath. Warmth and savor steamed from the earth.

"There is naught arcane about most of what I shall tell you," Bodilis said. "Special prayers. Cantrips to ward off certain misfortunes and certain creatures. Minor medical skills; we *are* healers, we royal women, though lay physicians practice too. At the least, dignity requires we be able to treat our own lesser ailments. It begins with knowing how to brew a tisane of willow against cramps, albeit many a goodwife can do the same. But let us commence with the greatest and holiest of all, the gift that the Goddess bestowed upon Brennilis and those who should come after."

They emerged where the hillside shouldered out to form a hollow. The spring that fed the stream was not much farther up, and here the water spread some three feet wide, ankle-deep, glittery beneath the sun. That light laid gold over the crowns of the beeches, hazels, and thorns walling in the grassy space. Masses of convolvulus clung to their innermost boles. Within their circle, blue stars sprang from plants with hairy stems and leaves, a cubit tall.

Bodilis signed herself. She knelt before a patch of them. "Here," she said, her tone now grave. "Look closely."

Dahut did perfunctory reverence and hunkered impatient. "Why, that's just borage," she said. "They use it for flavor and color in food. It helps against fever. What else?"

"It is the Herb," Bodilis told her.

Dahut reared back. "What? This?"

Bodilis nodded. "Aye. Our name for it is 'ladygift.' If a Queen of Ys eats a spoonful of these flowers, fresh or dried, a small spoonful, she does not conceive that day. When she wishes a child, she need simply leave off the use—" a fleeting, wistful smile—"and open herself to the King, if she be not too old. It is the bestowal of Belisama, so that the Nine may have sovereignty over their wombs and thus freedom to uphold the law of Ys against any of our random Kings who proves to be bad."

Dahut's fingers stole forward to touch the plant. "But this," she said, "only this? I thought belike 'twas magical vervain."

Bodilis chuckled. "Not that, of all plants! It works to cure barrenness."

"But the Herb should grow in a sacred place—the Wood of the King?"

Both now kneeling, Bodilis took the hands of Dahut in hers, caught and held the maiden's gaze, said slowly: "All the world is sacred, and perhaps the commonplace most.

"The knowledge of what ladygift actually is has gone about underground—that could never be stopped—but 'tis a thing folk do not bespeak. For the Herb, not mere borage but the Herb, is for the Nine alone. To every woman else, this plant is what you said, a simple, a seasoning, a decoration, naught else.

"Remember, Dahut, you must remain chaste until the end of your service. Else the wrath of the Gods would be upon you, and as for the law of man, you could be thrown off the sea cliffs or whipped from Ys into the wilderness. It has happened in the past.

"The ladygift will cease to ward you if you pass your vestalhood unchosen. After that, you must care for yourself, or endure, as has ever been the lot of woman.

"But if ere then the Sign appears between your breasts and you become a Queen: then before each time the King comes to you, or you think he may, until you desire to bear his child—take a few of these little flowers, and kiss them, and swallow them. For the kisses of the Gallicenae raise the Power."

Very early in the shipping season, a large and well-laden merchant vessel stood out from Ys for Hivernia. The crew did not expect to have need for their fighting skills. Strengthened and vigorously used by King Grallon, the navy had scoured these waters clean. Beyond the Dumnonian end of Britannia there was a chance of pirates. However, Tommaltach had assured the captain it was most unlikely that they could bring anything more to bear than a few currachs; and such would not attack a ship with high freeboard, war engines, armored men. The peace of King Conual was spreading fast across Mumu, where folk preferred trade to war anyway. Two years ago, Niall, the King in Mide, had wasted Roman territories. Since then, though, his attention was aimed north; the question was not whether he would fall on the Ulati, but when.

No prudent man would have fared just on the word of a young barbarian. It was borne out by other reports that had come to Ys as traffic between his people and the city grew in erratic fashion. Besides, Tommaltach maqq Donngalii was no ordinary adventurer. His father was king of a tuath and a friend of Conual Corcc. Tommaltach, age about sixteen, was a blooded warrior when he joined a venture to Ys, less in hopes of profiting from gold, sheepskins, and salt pork than to see the marvels. He had taken the trouble beforehand to acquire some of the language, as well as basic Latin. Meeting him, Rufinus readily persuaded him to stay through the winter. During those months, the Gael living in Rufinus's aerie, the two of them had grown close; and Rufinus had gotten a working knowledge of Scotic speech.

After the stark headlands at Armorica, his goal seemed gentle, lushly fruitful, incredibly green. The Ysans anchored in a small bay, made camp ashore, gave presents to natives who approached. Tommaltach dickered for horses. The crew loaded three of these and put Roman saddles on the rest. It took a little while to get the animals used to that. Leaving most of their shipmates on guard, Rufinus and Tommaltach rode off at the head of ten. The journey to Castellum took a pair of easy days, broken at one of the free hostels which kings here endowed.

Rufinus observed carefully as he fared, and beswarmed his guide with questions. This was pastureland where it was not forest, sheep and cattle at graze, only a few small and scattered fields sown in rye, barley, oats. Some wattle-and-daub dwellings stood isolated, but most seemed to cluster inside earthen ringwalls with palisades on top. Towns did not exist. Armies were wild rabble, virtually without body protection, led by noblemen in chariots such as were four hundred years obsolete in Britannia and Gallia.

Withal, throughout Hivernia—Ériu, its people called it—arts and crafts excelled, while respect for learning was so high that the person of a druid or poet was inviolate. Women were almost as free as in Ys, infinitely better off than anywhere in the Roman world. Aside from slaves, who were mainly captives taken in raids, the relationship between master and follower, landholder and tenant, was contractual, either party able to abrogate it at will. Folkmoot and *brithem*—judge—gave out a rough justice; wrongdoing was generally compounded by payment, and a rich man must give more redress than a poor man. When this failed, frequently the aggrieved person sat down at the door of the other and fasted until the latter, who was supposed to starve himself also, yielded. "Unless, I imagine, he outlasts the plaintiff," Rufinus drawled. "Still, you Scoti are not quite the two-legged wolves the Romans think you."

"Ah, it's grand to be home, that it is," Tommaltach exulted. "Not but what I don't mean to be often again in Ys, for the exploring of its wonders and to carouse with you, darling."

Rufinus sighed to himself. This race habitually talked in extravagances. The youth had no idea what they implied to his listener. Tommaltach was beautiful: medium tall, wide-shouldered but supple, the snubnosed, blue-eyed countenance as fair-skinned as a girl's except for a breath of beard, under a tumble of black hair.

No doubt it was just as well. Vindilis had counseled wisely. Less for hospitality than for appearances' sake, Rufinus had from time to time brought a pretty harlot to the tower. He performed competently, thinking it could not be denied that women were better constructed for the purpose, then let Tommaltach have the rest of the sport.

The Scotian left the road, which was dirt but not badly laid out, to swing wide of a dolmen. In Ériu as in Armorica, works of the Old Folk brooded. "Christians chiseled a cross on that," he explained. "Ever since, the dwellers inside have been angry and spiteful." The religion had made considerable headway in Mumu.

Stepping from the hostel at sunrise, Rufinus peered aloft and conferred with Tommaltach and the innkeeper. He did not want to reach Castellum drenched. Opinion was that rain would hold off long enough. Rufinus ordered his men into full battle gear; peaked helmets, cuirasses with flaring shoulderpieces and spiral-ornamented loricae, greaves above leather breeks, studded shoes, leaf-shaped swords, long oval shields. He himself donned a silken shirt with flowing sleeves, jerkin of chased leather, woad-dyed linen trousers, calf-length gilt boots, belt and baldric set with carnelians, over his shoulder a red cloak trimmed in ermine and secured by a cameo brooch. A show counted for well-nigh everything when you dealt with Celts. Besides, Rufinus enjoyed it.

The troop rode briskly on, beneath mountainous clouds through which the sun cast lances. The air was cool and damp. Soon the countryside turned into stands of woodland, meadows between them. Stumps showed that not long ago this had all been forest. "The King is having it logged off," Tommaltach said. "Settlers come, making strength and wealth around his seat." He pointed. "Look, my heart. On the horizon, the Rock!"

Nearing, the travellers saw the limestone mass lift ruggedly, an island in a green sea, its clifftops three hundred feet above. Buildings clustered at its base and strewed themselves out across the plain. Many were larger and better made than Rufinus had seen until now on his expedition. On the heights frowned a fortress. It was the Roman kind, foursquare, turreted, built of mortared stone, a thing that had never before been in Ériu.

Therefore it was twice important to impress the King. "Hoy-ah!" Rufinus cried. "Smartly, on the double!" The horses trotted forward.

Warriors hastened from the dwellings and along the trail up the Rock. They were outfitted like other Scoti. Tommaltach galloped ahead to meet them. They cheered and formed a primitive honor guard.

—Inside the castle, barbarian ways remained strong. The feasting hall was long and lofty. Smoke from a pair of firepits did not escape out the high-set small windows as readily as through thatch. Benches lined the walls. Above them hung painted shields, while skulls grinned from the many niches. Yet there were also finely woven hangings, intricately carved panels on the seats, imaginatively wrought tableware of wood, bronze, silver, gold, a general rude magnificence in which Rufinus found more subtleties the more he looked.

Conual Corcc, a tall man with flame-red hair, was gracious rather than boisterous as he received the Ysans. They distributed gifts from off their pack beasts, things as good as Ys could offer, and got thanks from the King's poet in intricate stanzas. Eventually, at their departure, he made them presents of value exceeding theirs. First they were his guests for over a month, and nothing was refused them.

During that time, Conual and his councillors made numerous occasions for private talk; and their queries were shrewd. "I am an envoy of my lord, the King of Ys," Rufinus said early on. "He has heard of your rise to mightiness. He hopes for friendship, oaths exchanged, benefits shared."

"He is afar," answered Conual. "True, I've no wish to make war on him or on the Romans like Niall of Temir. But what is to bind our two lands together?"

"Trade."

"You've come too soon for that, my dear. The great fairs do not open before Lúgnassat."

"I know. Granted your leave, we would like to take our ship's cargo round about and see what bargains folk wish to strike. But that is not why I am here, the voice of King Grallon. He in his wisdom looks beyond the gains that some Ysan merchants have made at your fairs. He hopes to arrange that many more will want to go, and many of your traders seek to us. We have much to give each other. Ys offers the harvest of the sea; amber from the Northeast, Roman wares transshipped from the South; the products of her own weaveries and workshops. Ériu has the yields of her fertile land, pearls, and also gold, which has long been draining out of the Empire. Surely, as traffic quickens, men will think of more than this."

"Hm. What might hinder?"

"War, pirates, the rapacity of overlords, ignorance and distrust. You, who I hear have spent years in Britannia, you will understand. Consider, King. Think of an alliance between yourself and King Grallon. Imagine missions going to and fro, men becoming well acquainted, making agreements and planning joint ventures. Meanwhile, with help from Ys, your people build stout ships like ours, to trade farther than ever erstwhile and to patrol your home seas."

"It's like a Roman that you are speaking. I follow you, but there are not many in Mumu who could. Just the same— Do let me think. Let us talk more in days to come. Already I know that the message I will be sending back with you will be a kindly one. May you come here again, Rufinus."

~ 3 ~

Apuleius Vero and his wife Rovinda stared enraptured at the presents Gratillonius had brought them. For her there was a woolen cloak from the foremost webster in Ys, warm but light and soft as thistledown, in dusk-blue worked with silvery figures of dolphins and terns. For him there were the poems of Ausonius, done onto parchment by a calligrapher who had access to Bodilis's collection, bound into a codex whose cover was tooled leather with gilt trim.

"Oh," the woman breathed. "It's gorgeous. How can I thank you?"

Apuleius gave his friend a long look. "You *thought* about this, did you not?" he said quietly. "You're less blunt than you let on."

Gratillonius smiled. "I've things for the children too, of course," he told them. "How are they?"

"Very well." A cloud passed over Rovinda's face. She and her husband had lost all but two. She dismissed memories in favor of pleasure. "They'll be overjoyed to know their honorary uncle is back. Their tutor is sick abed, so we've allowed them to stay on the farm. They love the countryside so."

"And they deserve a reward," the father added. "You know Verania is quite the little scholar, when she isn't outdoors. Well, now, Salomon has begun taking a real interest in his own studies. That doesn't come easily to a headlong boy like him. Rovinda, dear, dispatch a slave to fetch them before you turn the kitchen inside out preparing the feast I'm sure you want to welcome our guest with."

"Hold on," Gratillonius suggested. "Why don't you and I walk there? We can easily return with them before dinnertime."

"Aren't you tired after your journey?"

"No, it went smoothly. And from my arriving this early in the day, you know darkness caught us quite nearby. We camped on Drusus's

454

property. He took me into the house and poured with a free hand. A walk will clear my head, if you care to come along."

Apuleius grew pensive. "Hm-m....Very well. I'll let that replace my regular exercises for today. It will be much less tedious." His smile was a trifle forced. "Besides, I planned to take you there when we got an opportunity. I have something for you."

Gratillonius took the package he had not unwrapped. Donning outer garments, the men went forth. Aquilo was abustle. The approximately annual visits from Ys were always occasions in such a small city. The escort were already mingling with the people. He recognized a few former legionaries. Drusus had told him that after six years the resettlement was still working well. The veterans were gradually making the civilian reservists militarily effective—more than Imperial law envisioned. Most of them had married Osismiic women and become farmers, artisans, tradesmen. They had a stake in Armorica. No hostile barbarians would get close to Aquilo, unless as prisoners bound for the slave markets.

Apuleius conducted Gratillonius out the east gate and north on the river road. The day was clear, chill, a wan-bright sun above the heights whose steepness hemmed in this bank. Across the stream, the land rolled away, its northern horizon forested. Scattered farmsteads stood among dun plowfields, sallow meadows, orchards gone yellow and brown. Wind boomed from that direction. A buzzard rode watchful upon its torrent.

Apuleius must raise his voice against the noise. Indoors he would have spoken softly: "You've more than a walk in mind."

Gratillonius nodded. "Privacy."

"Nobody eavesdrops at the house."

"I know. But—your letter urging me to come said only that you've news for me. Now, I've learned your style. You have to be thinking of something unwelcome. I'd have trouble sitting still while we discussed it. This wind ought to flush the fret and anger out of me, so we can have a pleasant evening together."

"I see." Apuleius's Hellenic-like features showed the distress he had been holding back. "The truth is, I have little in the way of news. Mainly it's an accumulation of hints, overtones, mentions, incidents, the sort of word that the tribune at Aquilo, who sees higher authorities now and then and who maintains a rather extensive correspondence—the sort of word he gets, while the prefect in Ys, who is also the King of that nest of pagans, does not."

The wind slipped fingers under Gratillonius's cloak. "I have been notified that Ludgunensis Tertia has a new governor."

"You've probably not heard yet that the Duke of the Armorican Tract is also being replaced."

Gratillonius half stumbled. "What? But he's done well. He and I have kept the peninsula at peace."

"Precisely. He and you. Oh, I'm sure it will be an honorable retirement. No sense in provoking the many who feel grateful. But Honorius—Stilicho, rather—intends that his will, and none other, shall prevail everywhere in the West."

Gratillonius's gullet tightened. "If he means to recall me— Can you make them realize what insanity that would be?"

"My direct influence is slight. I do have communication with some men who are powerful. I will try. Just what I should write in my letters is one of the things we must discuss.

"Your policies were too successful, my friend. The Imperium has had unhappy experiences with such officers. Think back over the course of events since Maximus fell." Apuleius chuckled dryly. "If nothing else, those seven years were seldom dull."

Gratillonius grunted response and fell silent, trying to recall and order them for himself.

—Following his victory, Theodosius reinstated Valentinianus as Emperor of the West, but remained two years more in Italy, organizing its shaken government, destroying every relic of the usurper he could find, before he returned to Constantinople. As chief minister to Valentinianus, he left his general Arbogast.

This man had been the real director of the battle. A Frank and an avowed heathen, he favored barbarians over Romans for high office, pagans over Christians. On both counts, he was soon at odds with Valentinianus, and after a while he got the ineffectual Augustus murdered. Thereupon he proclaimed as Emperor a rhetorician named Eugenius. The real power was his. When Bishop Ambrosius appealed to him to desist from encouraging the cults of the old Gods, he threatened to stable his horses in the cathedral of Mediolanum and draft monks into his army.

After two years that army met the host of Theodosius, bound from the East to regain the West. For two days they fought, until Eugenius was killed and his cause lost. Arbogast fled, but committed suicide soon afterward.

Theodosius marched on to Rome. He was smitten with dropsy and knew he had not much time left on earth. The Empire he redivided, the East going to his son Arcadius, the West to his son Honorius. Thereupon he retired to Mediolanum, made his peace with God as best he could, and expired in the winter that was past, some nine months ago.

Arcadius was an indolent youth of seventeen, under the thumb of his praetorian prefect Rufinus. (Recalling that name, Gratillonius smiled wryly.) Honorius was a boy of eleven, said to be a weakling also. His father had made Flavius Stilicho and Stilicho's wife Serena joint guardians of him. They betrothed him to their daughter Maria.

456

Further strife was ineluctable. Stilicho had begun this season's warring on the Rhenus, where German tribes had gotten troublesome. But after quelling them, he marched to Thracia. There he still was.

—"It's given out that he aims to expel the Goths and Huns from that province," Apuleius said when Gratillonius inquired. "And no doubt he is working toward it. However, I've excellent reason to believe that his real objective is the destruction of the praetorian prefect Rufinus. If he can accomplish that, he will be the master of the whole Empire, both East and West."

"And then—?"

"The event is in the hands of God. But men can take measures."

Beyond the inflow of the Stegir they crossed a bridge over the Odita and followed a road that went north along the tributary stream. An oxcart lumbered far ahead, distance-dwindled; a tenant forked hay into a wooden trough for the cattle in a paddock; at the house behind, his wife strewed grain for free-running chickens: a peacefulness at which the wind gibed.

"I wouldn't look for immediate woe," Apuleius said after a time. "Stilicho will be busy. Even here in the Northwest, surely his first concern must be the Scoti. You know how they took advantage of his departure from Britannia to ravage it, two years ago, and have since been re-establishing their enclaves there."

Gratillonius scowled. His father's home had been spared, but barely. "That was the work of Niall. I hear he's now preoccupied inside Hivernia. Some good luck does drift our way sometimes."

"Who?...No matter. You're in touch with the Scoti as I am not, as I suppose no Roman—no other Roman is. That's one thing against you."

Gratillonius bridled. "See here, I broke the fleet that would have raided up the Liger a dozen years back. True, I'm cultivating relationships with Scoti, but friendly Scoti."

Apuleius sighed. "I don't doubt you. But they see it otherwise in Turonum, Treverorum, Lugdunum, Mediolanum—wherever it comes to mind that the man sent to be Rome's prefect in Ys has become its independent sovereign. For that you are, no matter if you continue piously calling yourself a centurion on special duty."

"How have I subverted any interest of Rome? By the Bull, I've strengthened us!"

"And strengthened Ys. The city that once lay veiled is today chiefest in Armorica, its brilliance and prosperity outshining any of the Western Empire. Nonetheless it remains as alien, as un-Christian, as the seat of the Sassanian King."

"Rome's made peace with the Persians."

"How long can that last? How long will Ys choose to be our ally? You will not reign forever, Gratillonius. You will not reach old age, unless you can end that barbarous law of succession. Ys would be a most dangerous enemy. Already the grievances are building up."

Gratillonius shook his head. "You're wrong. I know."

"You know what they think in Ys. I know what they think who govern Rome. When those men clamp down on the trade you have caused to flourish, how then will Ys feel?"

"Ha? But that's ridiculous! Why in the name of moonstruck Cernunnos should they do any such thing? We gave Armorica peace; we're drawing it out of poverty."

"By means that are...unsettling. The merchants and shippers of Ys, being free agents, undermine the authority of Roman officials, guilds, laws. Men disappear from the stations of life to which they were born. They reappear in traffic that goes unregulated, untaxed, yet scarcely troubles itself to be clandestine. This year Ysans began acquiring substantial amounts of Hivernian gold. It flows about, uncoined, driving the Emperor's money into total worthlessness, thereby making people mutter that perhaps they have no need of an Emperor at all. No, I tell you the authorities cannot indefinitely permit the life of the region to go outside their control. They dare not."

Gratillonius decided to make no mention of his own irregularities. Some Roman officials must have some peripheral awareness of them; but to investigate would take those persons out of comfortable routine, into forests, heaths, slums, barbarian camps. Why force them to that? It could only make difficulties for all concerned—most of all for Rome, because the damned stupid government was not itself doing what was plainly necessary for survival.

"They certainly hold religion against us," he growled. "But we have a church and pastor. We persecute nobody."

"I hear that Honorius is devout," Apuleius said. "When he grows up, he may transform weakness into zeal."

"Maximus once threatened to invade Ys."

"He fell. Stilicho is more formidable."

Apuleius took his friend by the arm. "I don't mean to perturb you," he went on. "I only give you an early warning. You have time to prepare and take preventive steps. I've promised you to serve as your advocate with influential men. I believe we can forestall an order for your recall, because that would risk Armorica falling into chaos, a crisis which Stilicho surely regards as unnecessary at this juncture. But you must do your part. You must be more circumspect. You must forbid smuggling, and curb the most blatant of it. You—" Apuleius stopped.

"What?" asked Gratillonius.

"It would help mightily if you accepted the Faith and worked for the conversion of Ys."

"I'm sorry. That's impossible."

"I know. How often I've prayed to God that He lift the scales from your eyes. It's heretical of me, but I suspect that the knowledge you were burning in hell would diminish my joy in Heaven, should I be found worthy of going there."

Gratillonius reined in a reply. As he had told Corentinus in their generally amicable arguments, he didn't think an eternity of torment was the proper punishment for an incorrect opinion, and saw no righteousness in a God Who did. Corentinus retorted that mere mortals had no business passing judgment on the Almighty; what did they understand?

Apuleius brightened. "Enough," he said. "You have the gist of what I wanted to tell you. Think it over, sleep on it, and tomorrow we'll talk further. Let's simply be ourselves until then. Look, there's the villa ahead."

They walked on. Security from attack and revival of trade had drawn workers out of inland refuges. Maximus's veterans had additionally eased the labor shortage. Agriculture was again thriving around Aquilo, not in the form of latifundia but as sharecropping and even some freeholds. No longer neglected, the land surrounding the Apuleian manor house, which stood near the northwest corner of the cleared section with the forest at its back—this land showed neat fields, sleek livestock, buildings refurbished and permanently in use. At the house itself, whitewashed walls, glazed windows, red tile roof called back to Gratillonius his father's. But here the owner was no curial between the millstones, he was a senator, the closest thing to a free man that Roman law recognized.

The children saw who approached and burst from within, to dash down the garden path and be hugged. Only six, Salomon outpaced his sister regardless. Big for his age, he was coming to resemble his father, though Apuleius must have been a quieter boy. The parents had explained to Gratillonius that they named him after a king of the ancient Jews in hopes that this would cause God to let him live. That had happened, but thereafter Rovinda continued to suffer stillbirths and infant deaths.

Verania followed. At ten she was well made if rather small. She had her father's hazel eyes, her mother's light-brown hair, and a countenance blending the comelinesses in both. Near to Gratillonius, she abruptly blushed and became very polite, her greeting barely audible through the wind.

"Well, well!" he said. "How good to see you two again. I'll spare you any remarks about how you've grown since last. We're doing nicely in Ys. I've much to tell you about that. For a start, here're a couple of little things from there for you."

He squatted on the gravel and opened the package. Its contents were modest, because Apuleius frowned on ostentation. However, they drew a shout from Salomon, a soft cry from Verania. He got a Roman sword and sheath, scaled to his size. "A copy of my old military piece. Someday, I think, you'll lead men too." She received a portable harp, exquisitely carved. "From Hivernia. I know you're musical. Among the Scoti, some of their poets and bards are women."

459

Worship looked back at him, until Salomon sprang up. "I know what we've got for you!" he crowed.

"Hush," said Verania. "Wait till father's ready."

Apuleius laughed. "Why wait? Here we are. Before we step indoors and have a cup of something, let's go see." He linked his arm with Gratillonius's. "You've been so generous to us over the years, so helpful, that we'd like to make some slight return."

Salomon capered and hallooed. Verania walked on the other side of the prefect, not quite touching him, her glance bent downward.

The stable was dim, warm, smelling sweetly of hay and pungently of manure. Apuleius halted at one stall. From within, a stallion colt looked alertly out. Gratillonius would learn that he had overestimated the age, about six months, because it was so large—a splendid creature, sorrel with a white star, of the tall kind that bore cataphracts to battle.

"This is yours to take back with you," Apuleius said.

"By Hercules, but you're generous!" Gratillonius marveled.

"Well, as a matter of fact, my interest in breeding this sort began when you told me how your father's been trying the same in Britannia. I think we're having some success. Favonius is our best thus far. I suspect he'll prove the best possible. You're a horseman. We want you to have him."

"Thank you so much." Gratillonius reached over the bars, stroked mane and head, cupped his hand around the muzzle. How soft it was. "I'll raise him right, and—and when I ride him here in future, help yourself to his stud services. Favonius, did you say?"

"Our name for him. You can change it if you like. It's a rather literary word, meaning the west wind that brings the springtime."

"Oh, it's fine. I'll keep it."

Apuleius smiled in the duskiness. "May he bear you to a springtime of your own."

XVI

~ 1 ~

Tiberius Metellus Carsa was of Cadurcic descent, but his family had long dwelt in Burdigala and mingled its blood with others that pulsed in the city. Its men took to the sea, and he himself inherited the rank of captain after he was trained and a position had opened up. For some years he carried freight between the ports of Aquitania and as far as northern Hispania. At last he encountered pirates. Many such had taken advantage of the strife between Theodosius and Arbogast, and not all were immediately suppressed after the Empire was pacified.

With Carsa in this battle was his oldest son Aulus, born to the trade and, at age fourteen, making his first real sea voyage. The boy acquitted himself well. He was expert with the sling. Though he had not grown into his full strength, from the cabin top he wrought havoc, certainly braining one man and disabling several. Meanwhile his father led a spirited defense at the rail. The upshot was that the reavers took heavy losses and fled before their vessel should be boarded.

That incident decided the owners to put Carsa on the Armorican run.

Those waters were tricky, but the human hazard had much diminished in the decade or so since Ys emerged from isolation. True, lately the barbarians had again been grieving Britannia. However, Ys kept them at arm's length; and now that he had disposed of his rival, the praetorian prefect of the East, Stilicho was dispatching an expeditionary force against them.

Therefore, when shipping season began next year, Carsa sailed the seven-hundred-ton *Livia* down the Garumna and north-northwest over the gulf. His cargo was mostly wine and olive oil, his destination Ys. With him went Aulus.

It was a rough passage, winds often foul, taking a full ten days because the captain was cautious. "I'd rather arrive late in Ys than early in hell," he said. "Although I've heard churchmen declare there is a great deal of hell already in that town."

Young Aulus scarcely heard. He was staring ahead. Wonder stood before him.

The day was chill and gusty, casting saltiness off the whitecaps onto his lips. Waves brawled green, here and there darkened by kelp, bursting white over rocks. Afar lay an island, its flatness broken by a single turreted building. Fowl rode the water and wheeled overhead, hundred-fold, crying through wind and surf, gulls, terns, guillemots, puffins, cormorants. Seals frolicked about or basked on skerries. *Livia* rocked forward under shortened sail, the master peering now at the reefs and now at the periplus fluttering in his grasp, men at the sides ready to fend off if need be. This cape had a grim reputation. It did not seem to trouble the vessels, mostly fishermen, that were in sight; but Roman mariners supposed Ys had a pact with the demons its people worshipped.

The city lay ahead. Its wall bowed out into the sea whose queen it was, filling the space between two looming promontories, the hue of dark roses, up and up to a frieze of fabulous creatures and thereafter battlements and turrets. Farther back, higher still, spires pierced heaven, glass agleam, until the roofs flared into fantastical shapes. As tidal flow commenced the gate was slowly closing. The harbor beyond, docks, warehouses, ships, boats, life, seemed to Aulus a paradise about to be denied him.

Out of the basin hastened four longboats. Shouts went back and forth. Lines snaked downward, were caught and made fast. The Romans struck sail. The Ysans bent to their oars and towed the ship in. Aulus gasped as he passed the sheer, copper-green doors.

In a haze of delight, he watched the tugmen warp *Livia* into a slip and collect their pay; a robed official come up the gangplank, accompanied by two guards in armor unlike any elsewhere, and confer with his father; the crew snug things down for the stay in port and, impatiently, shoulder their bags; the captain at last, at last grant shore leave!

Among the longshoremen, hawkers, whores, strolling entertainers, curious spectators who thronged the dock, were runners from various inns, each trying to outsing the others in praise of his place. They all knew some Latin. Tiberius grinned. "Let's hope our poor devils don't get fleeced too badly," he said to his son. "We'll be here for several days. If we're to ply this route regularly, we need to familiarize ourselves with the port."

"Where'll we stay, you and I?" Aulus asked breathlessly.

"A respectable hostel. I have directions. Get our baggage and we'll go."

On their way, the Carsae found much—everything—to stare at. Nothing, not even those things the Romans had built, was quite like home; always the proportions and the artwork were subtly altered into something elongated and sleek, swirling and surging. The city throbbed and clamored with activity. Most Ysans appeared prosperous. It showed more in bright garments and jewelry than on bodies, except that folk were bathed and well groomed. They tended to be lean, energetic, but basically dignified. Many resembled the aborigines and Celts who had been among their ancestors, but often the Phoenician heritage revealed itself in hawk face or dark complexion. Men usually had close-trimmed beards and hair drawn into a queue; some wore tunics, some jacket and trousers, a few robes. Women's tresses were set according to fancy, from high-piled coiffure to free flow beneath a headband. They generally wore long-sleeved, broad-belted gowns that gave ample freedom of movement, and they walked as boldly as men. The Carsae had heard their rights and liberties were essentially equal. Servants, too, were free agents working for pay, slavery being banned in Ys—an almost exact reversal of Roman practice.

Like the city it stood in, the hostel was clean and well furnished. In the room that father and son got, a fresco depicted a ship at sea and, sky-tall and beautiful, a woman in a blue cloak whose hand upheld a star above the mast.

"Pagans," Tiberius muttered. "Damned souls. Licentious too, I hear. But they have a Christian church somewhere."

"We, we must deal with them...mustn't we?" asked Aulus. They can't be *wicked*. Not if—" He waved an awkward hand at the view in the window. "Not if they made this."

"Oh, we'll mind our manners, you and I. The trade's too profitable. Also, we've got much to learn, and there'll be pleasures as well. Only be sure to keep your soul steady as she goes. I'm told the Armoricans have stories like ours, about sirens who lure seamen onto the rocks. Well, even inside wall and gate, the reefs of hell are underneath us."

Some of the food set before them in the common room was curious, all was delicious—marinated mussels, leeks cooked in chicken broth, plaice lightly fried with thyme and watercress, white bread wherein hazelnuts had been baked, sweet butter, blue-veined cheese, honeycake, and a dry, herbal-flavored mead that sang on the tongue. The serving wench, about Aulus's age, gave him glances and smiles that caused his father to frown.

However, Tiberius responded gladly when a messenger appeared, a boy whose red tunic had embroidered upon the breast a golden wheel. "Captain Carsa?" he asked. His Latin had a peculiar construction. "I am from King Gratillonius. Ever is he desirous of making strangers welcome and hearing from them about the larger world. Therefore is word of them always borne to him. He will be glad to receive you this very eventide."

"Why, why, of course!" Tiberius exclaimed. "But I'm just a merchant skipper."

"One new to us, sir. Let me say as well that a ship of ours returned from Hivernia on the morning tide, and its chief passengers will likewise be at the palace."

Tiberius glanced at Aulus, saw strickenness, and cleared his throat. "Um, this is my son—"

"I understand, sir. He is invited too."

Joy kindled a beacon.

The two put on their best clothes and went with the messenger for a guide. Along the way he pointed out sights till Aulus's head whirled.

Four men flanked the entrance gate of the royal grounds, two in Ysan battle array, two in Roman. Beyond, labyrinthine paths among flowerbeds, hedges, topiaries, bowers seemed to create more room than was possible. The palace was of modest size, but the pride was boundless. Its side walls bore scenes of wild beasts in the forest. A bronze boar and bear guarded the main staircase. Above a copper roof swelled a dome, whereon the image of an eagle spread wings whose gilt blazed against sundown.

Passing through an anteroom, the visitors came into a chamber great and marble-pillared, frescoed with pictures of the four seasons, floor mosaic of a chariot race. Clerestory windows were duskening, but oil lamps and wax candles gave lavish light. Servants glided about refilling wine cups and offering titbits of food. Flute and harp trilled in a corner.

Only a few persons were on hand, none elaborately clad. Seated in chairs as if presiding over an occasion of state, they nonetheless

463

appeared quite at ease. A big, auburn-haired man with rugged features lifted his arm as the new guests entered. "Greeting," he said. His Latin was plain-spoken, with a South Britannic overtone. "I'm Gaius Valerius Gratillonius, centurion in the Second, prefect of Rome, and—" he smiled—"King of Ys. I'd like to hear whatever you care to tell and try to answer your questions, but feel free to mingle with people. We'll have a lantern bearer to take you back."

He introduced the others. Two were female, two of his notorious nine wives. They conveyed no sense of being more than handsome middle-aged ladies—until they joined the conversation as outspokenly and intelligently as any man. A couple of male Ysans were present, an old scholar and the head of a mercantile house. A fairly young Redonian—lean, tough-looking with his fork beard and scarred cheek— was one of those in from Hivernia; Aulus caught his name at once, Rufinus, because it had been famous last year as somebody else's. With him was a fellow not much older than Aulus, defiantly attired in a Scotic kilt and a saffron-dyed shirt secured at the throat by a penannular brooch.

"Sit down," Gratillonius urged. "Drink. You aren't on stage. This isn't the Symposium, eh, Bodilis? Tell me, Captain Carsa, how was your voyage?"

He had a gift for putting company at ease: though Aulus suspected that when he administered a tongue-lashing, lightning sizzled blue. Before long, individuals were freely at converse with whomever they chose. Gratillonius drew Tiberius out about happenings in the South. Since Aulus already knew that, he shortly found himself off in a corner with Tommaltach.

That was the Scotian. His Latin was still somewhat broken, but had a musical lilt to it. Despite his having done battle in his home island, despite his being pagan and unlettered, his liveliness ranged so widely that Aulus felt like a child again. Yet Tommaltach did not patronize him.

—"Ah, you could do well among the girls of Ys, Carsa," he laughed. His glance probed. Aulus's frame was filling out into sturdiness; his countenance was broad, blunt-nosed, regular, beneath curly dark-brown hair. "Can you get away? The hunting's better with two. I'm not talking of some copper-a-tumble whore, you understand; not but what such aren't usually well worth it in Ys. I mean lusty servant women, hoping to marry someday but meanwhile ready for fun if they like you. They're apt to saunter the streets in pairs—"

The Roman wished his face would not heat.

"You could be staying over a while," Tommaltach said, "between two calls your ship makes. My friend Rufinus would take care of arrangements. Sure, and he's a good-hearted man. Your dad should be happy, if you ask him right." Seriously: "It's more than pleasure this would be. It's an e-du-cation. The learning, the folk from everywhere, the marvels, the magic—"

He broke off, turned, and stared. Silence fell upon the room. The girl who had entered, already more than half woman, was so beautiful.

In white raiment, garland of apple blossoms on the loose amber-colored hair, she flowed over the floor to Gratillonius. She murmured huskily in Ysan, then, observing the company, changed to excellent Latin: "Why, father, you didn't tell me you expected guests. I could have left my Temple duties earlier."

The King beamed. "I didn't know you meant to spend the night here, darling. Wasn't it to be with Maldunilis?"

"Oh, she only wants to lie about and eat sweetmeats. I *must* find a place of my own." The girl checked herself, lifted a hand, and said gravely: "Welcome, honored sirs. May the Gods look upon you with kindness."

"My daughter Dahut," Gratillonius announced. "Captain Metellus Carsa, newly from Burdigala. His son...Aulus. I don't believe you've met Tommaltach of Mumu, either. You should have, but it never chanced till now."

Dahut kindled a smile.

Gratillonius laughed. "Well, why do you wait, little flirt? Go brighten their lives for the young men."

Dahut lowered her eyes, raised them again, and demurely joined the elders. However, the time was not long before she was in their corner chatting with Tommaltach and the junior Carsa.

~ 2 ~

Summer lay heavy over the land. Westward, cloud masses loomed on the horizon, blue-shadowed white above a sea that shone as if burnished. Ys glittered like a jewel. Grass greened and softened the headlands, save where boulders or ancient stoneworks denied it. The heights leading east bore such wealth of leafage that most of the homes nestled in their folds were hidden. In between, the valley stretched lush and hushed. Warmth baked fragrance out of soil, plants, flowers. Bees droned through clover.

In the courtyard of the Sacred Precinct, two men fought. Wearing full Roman combat armor, they circled warily, probed, defended with shield or sword, sometimes rushed together for a moment's fury. Their hobnails struck sparks from the slate flags. Neither getting past the defense of the other, they broke apart and resumed their stalking. They breathed hard. Sweat runneled down their faces and stung their eyes. The sun turned the metal they wore into furnaces.

Maeloch the fisher arrived on Processional Way. His stride jarred to a halt. He gaped.

Menservants were watching too, from the porch of the great red house that filled the opposite side of the square. Right and left, its ancillary buildings formed two more boundaries of the courtyard. Black, all but featureless, they radiated that heat which the blood-colored lodge uttered to the vision. The fourth side opened onto the paving of the road. High above roofs, the Wood of the King lifted its crowns, an oakenshaw whose rough circle spanned some seven hundred feet, silence and shadow.

The mightiest of the trees grew at the middle of the courtyard. From the lowest bough of the Challenge Oak hung a round brazen shield, too big and heavy for use. Sunlight dazzled away sight of the wild, bearded visage molded on it, or the many dents made by the sledge hammer that hung beside.

Blows thudded. They did not rattle or clash. Maeloch eased. Both blades were cased in horsehide.

The slender, more agile man saw himself about to be forced against the bole. He turned on his heel to slip aside. Suddenly swift, the large man moved at him, not in a leap but in a pivot on widespread, bent legs that kept his footing always firm. His swordpoint slammed at the other's knee and ran up the thigh below the chain mail. The struck man lurched and gasped a Britannic curse.

"Enough, Cynan!" called his opponent. "If this'd been real, you'd be bleeding to death now."

"Well done, sir," panted the other. "I'm glad you stopped short of my crotch."

"Ha, never fear. I need my roadpounders entire. Besides, your wife would have my head."

Cynan limped. "You did catch me a good one, sir. I'm afraid I can't give you any more worthwhile practice today."

"I've had plenty as is. Come, let's go inside, get this tin off us, wash up and have a drink."

Maeloch, whose Latin was scant, had gotten the drift. His rolling sailor's gait bore him forward. "My lord King," he said in Ysan, "I've sore need to talk with ye."

Gratillonius removed his helmet. He knew this man, as he did every Ferrier of the Dead. "I'll hold public court in a few days," he answered.

The shaggy head shook. "Can't wait, my lord. Aye, ye're standing your Watch. Never kept ye from handling any business you felt like. And—I also deal with the Gods."

Gratillonius met the unflinching gaze and smiled. "A stubborn lot, you fishers. Well, come along, then. Have a beaker while I get clean."

"I thank ye," said Maeloch, as he would have replied to an invitation from a fellow seaman.

The three mounted the stairs to the portico. Its columns were carved into images of Taranis and his attributes, wild boar, eagle, thunderbolt, oak tree. Beyond, the massive timbers and shake roof enclosed a feasting hall. Its pillars and wainscots were likewise carved, but hard to make out in the dimness. Age-eaten banners hung from the crossbeams like bats. The fire-trenches in the clay floor lay empty. Nostrils were glad to inhale cool air.

Gratillonius and Cynan stripped and went on into the modernized section for a bath and fresh clothes. Maeloch accepted a goblet of ale and sat down on a bench built into a side. Three men carried the military gear out for cleaning and stowage. A fourth took a feather duster and went about in search of cobwebs.

Maeloch beckoned to him. "What Queen is here today?" he asked.

The servant halted. "None, sir." Unlike his livery, his voice was subdued. A Ferrier of the Dead, in this house of the killers, raised too many ghosts.

"Why? He's no weakling, our King. Besides, 'tis plain justice to them, one man with nine wives."

"The Princess Dahut wanted to dwell here for the three days and nights of this month's Watch. She wanted no grown woman about."

"Dahut, ye say? What makes the child have such a wish?"

"'Tis not for me to guess, sir. But her royal father agreed."

"Aye, he can deny her naught, I hear. And who'd blame him for that? Where is she now?"

"In the Wood, I believe, sir. She's hours on end in the Wood, both by daylight and moonlight."

Maeloch frowned. "That could be dangerous. What if a sacred boar turned ugly? Nay, Grallon yields her too much there."

"Pray pardon, sir, I must keep on with my work."

Maeloch nodded, leaned back against the smoke-darkened relief of a scene in an ancient tale—the hero Belcar combatting the demonic mermaid Quanis—and pondered.

Lightly clad, Gratillonius emerged with Cynan. He clapped his hands. "Cold mead for two," he called. "More ale for our guest if he wishes. Well, Maeloch, what would you of me?"

The seaman had not risen. "Best we speak under four eyes, my lord," he replied.

"Hm, you are in a surly mood, nay? Then wait your turn. Sit down, Cynan. I'd like to talk about a couple of things," Gratillonius said, pointedly, in Latin. "It was plain, stupid luck that you didn't nail me earlier today with the shield-hooking trick. I've got to overcome my slackness about it. Who can tell what the next challenger will know?"

A man brought the mead, which had been cooled by leaving its bottle in a porous jar full of water. Cynan drank and spoke hurriedly. Despite his centurion's protestations, he soon left.

Gratillonius dismissed the attendants and sat down on the bench beside Maeloch. "Well?" he asked.

The fisher drew breath. "This, my lord. We're angry at ye in Scot's Landing, for that ye had poor Usun and Intil flogged. I said I'd bring the grievance. Usun's my shipmate."

Gratillonius nodded. "I thought that was the trouble," he said slowly. "'Flogging' is the wrong word. Three cuts of an unleaded thong, across those turtle backs, couldn't have hurt much. 'Twas meant for an example, a warning."

"A disgrace!"

"Nay, now. How often have you decked a man who was unruly or foolish, or triced him up for a few tastes of a rope's end, with no lasting grudges afterward?"

Maeloch's huge fists knotted on his knees. "What harm had they done? In this year of poor catches, they took a boat; they fared down the peninsula; they brought back Roman-made wares to sell. But your spies were watching."

"No spies were needed. Those two flouted the law with no special effort to hide what they were about."

"What law? We've aye been free traders in Ys, till ye made that bloody decree. Grallon, I'm nay yet your foe. But I warn ye, ye're going astray. Ye whipped two men and took away their goods. Ye had no right."

Gratillonius sighed. "Hark, friend. Before Mithras, I wish I'd not had to do it. But they forced me. I'd made it clear as the pool at the Nymphaeum, henceforward our traders into Roman territory must go through the Roman customs. These men did not. Liefer than pay tax, they smuggled Ysan cloth to the Veneti, and took those wares in exchange. Let them count themselves lucky the Romans didn't catch them at it. I punished them for the sake of every lad in Ys who's tempted to try the same. If anyone gets arrested, I can do naught—naught, do you hear?—to save him."

Some of the bitterness drained out of Maeloch. Pain rose in its stead. "But why, Grallon?" he whispered harshly. "After all these years, why feed yon sharks?"

"I did not spell out the reasons as fully as mayhap I should have. My thought was that 'twould stir up too much wrath, too much pride. Some among us might go off and make trouble merely to ease their feelings. And we dare not have that. So I simply declared 'tis high time Ys honor her ancient treaties with Rome, and observe Roman law in Roman lands. The fact is— Think, Maeloch. Shiploads of soldiers are now in Britannia. When they've cleared it of barbarians, if they can, what shall they do next? The Emperor, or rather his guardian Stilicho, is already being urged to crush contumaciously pagan Ys. Naught but our usefulness to Rome keeps us free. We must not provoke Rome further. The Council of Suffetes agreed at equinox."

Gratillonius laid a hand on the shoulder at his side. "Bide a while, friend," he went on, softly. "I want you to understand, and make your comrades understand, that this is done for their sake."

He paused before adding: "Let me say at once, confidentially, I know those are poor men, those two, and confiscation of their cargo means hardship for their families. Well, I cannot let them profit by their misdeed, but...between us, surely you and I can work out some quiet way to see them through without undue suffering."

Maeloch choked. "What? Grallon, ye *are* a good man."

A slim form briefly darkened the open doorway. Dahut entered the hall. She seemed to light up its cavernous depths.

"Why, Maeloch," she cried, "dear old Maeloch!" and hurried forward to take both his hands. "Had I but known! You will stay and take supper here, will you not? Say you will!"

Helpless, he must answer, "Aye, Princess, since 'tis ye who ask."

Underneath his words rustled a question. What had she been doing in the Wood, why did she want to prowl it, the Wood where someday a stranger was to kill her father?

~ 3 ~

To the Greater Monastery in the Liger valley, near Caesarodunum Turonum, came a pilgrim. Autumn cooled and hazed the air but decked trees in brilliant vestments. The river glided darkling past the huts that clustered on a flat bank. Hemming this in, hills rose nearly sheer, riddled with caves where monks also dwelt. Many were in sight, coarsely clad, roughly tonsured, unwashed. The newcomer had to search before he found one who was not at prayer or meditation but spading a vegetable garden.

"In Christ's holy name, greeting," he ventured.

"His peace be with you," replied the monk. He saw a young man, fair-haired, rangy, in tunic, trousers, shoes of stout material though showing hard use. A bedroll and meager pack of rations were on his back, a wallet for minor objects at his waist, a staff in his hand. Nothing but a curious accent, not quite Britannic, marked him out from countless wanderers.

"Do you seek work?" asked the monk. "I hear they're short-handed on the Jovianus latifundium." And they did not inquire as to the antecedents of an able-bodied man. Imperial laws binding folk to the soil had succeeded in displacing thousands of them, as farm after farm went under.

The stranger smiled. "Not field work, at least not in any earthly fields. Of course, I'll gladly help if my labor is needed. Where may I find your bishop?"

"Holy Martinus? No, son, you've no call to interrupt him at his devotions. We'll put you up for the night, never fear."

"I beg you. This is necessary. He cannot have so entirely forsaken the world that he would refuse to see a kinsman returned from slavery among the heathen."

Astounded, the monk gave information. The founder and leader of the monastery occupied a single-roomed wattle-and-daub hut, as small and crude as the rest. Its door sagged ajar, to show him prostrate at his prayers. The traveller leaned on his staff and waited.

After about an hour, Martinus emerged. He blinked, for his blue eyes were dimming with age. Thin white hair made an aureole around a face shriveled and shrunken in on itself. Yet he still moved briskly and spoke vigorously. "What do you wish, my son?"

"Audience with you, if you will give me that charity," replied the young man. "I am Sucat, son of your niece Conchessa and her husband Calpurnius, curial in the Britannic town Banaventa."

Air soughed in between Martinus's gums. "Sucat? No, can't be. Sucat perished these...seven years ago, was it not, when the Scoti raided along the Sabrina?"

"I did not die, sir. I was borne away captive. Let me prove myself by relating family history. My father was a Silurian who joined the army and rose to centurion's rank. While stationed in Pannonia, he met and married your niece. Upon his discharge, he brought her to his homeland and settled there. He was a pious man, who despite becoming a curial became a deacon as well—"

Martinus cast himself against Sucat and hugged him with surprising force. Tears burst from his eyes. "God forgive me! Why should I have doubted you? Welcome back, beloved, welcome home!"

He took his visitor into the hut. Virtually its only furniture was a wooden chest and a pair of three-legged stools; but atop the box lay several books. The men sat down. "Tell me what happened, I beg you, and how you escaped and, oh, everything," Martinus exclaimed.

Sucat sighed. "It's a long story, sir. I was carried away with unfortunates—ah, how dare I call myself unfortunate when I remember the poor young women?—I came to Ériu, Hivernia. There I fell to the lot of a chieftain in Condacht—well, he took me to his estate in the far west of the island and put me to tending his flocks. For six years I did."

"You bore it bravely."

Sucat smiled. "It was no terrible fate. True, the mountainside was often wet or cold, but God gave me health to endure that. My owner was not cruel by nature, and some other people did me kindnesses from time to time, and often in good weather little children would seek me out in the pasture, to hear me play on a whistle I'd carved or tell stories I remembered from nursery and school—once I'd mastered the language, of course, which has many differences from ours at home. And then, alone under heaven, I found my way back to God. For I confess to having been a light-minded youth, who forgot Him and trod the paths of sin. Now I said a hundred prayers by day and almost as many by night."

"His mercy is unbounded."

"I might be there still, for escape across that wild land and the waters beyond looked impossible. But a dream came to me at last, and I knew it was from God and required my obedience. Pursuit never found me. I nearly starved, but always, somehow, there was something to eat in time to keep me from falling. They are so hospitable in Ériu.... When I could not ask directions, I guessed, and my guesses led me aright. In the end I reached that harbor on the Ulatach shore which my dream had named, and there was a ship loading for Britannia."

Martinus's military practicality struck through. "What? I've heard the army is cleaning the barbarians out of Britannia."

"It is, though I fear, from what I saw, that that's like weeding thistles. Anyhow, peaceful traders aren't forbidden. This cargo was a pack of the great wolfhounds they breed in Ériu. At first the captain spurned me, as ragged and coinless as I was. But I persisted, and God softened his heart."

"You have gifts of persuasion, it seems."

Sucat flushed. "Well, it was another hard journey on the Britannic side, as devastated as the Westlands are, but home I came in the end. My father had gone to his reward—did you know?—but my mother and various kinfolk remain, and made me welcome with hosannahs. They wanted me to stay forever."

"Why did you not?" Martinus asked.

"I am haunted, reverend father. I cannot forget the people of Ériu—the women who smiled and spoke softly and slipped me a bit of something sweet, the rough comradeliness of men, the innocent children who came to me—even the proud warriors, the majestic druids. It's as if they are all weeping, beseeching, in the night that binds them, crying for the Light." Sucat swallowed. "I believe I have a vocation. Because you are my kinsman, and have made this a famous holy place, a school for bishops and missionaries—I beg you, in Christ's name, take me in, teach me, and if I prove worthy, ordain me."

Martinus was silent a long while. Shadows crept across the floor and lifted in the valley as the sun declined. Finally he murmured: "I think you're right. I think you're in the hand of God. But we dare not presume to know His will, not without much prayer and thought and austerity. Abide here, dear son, and we'll see what we can do for you. I've a feeling already that a great work awaits you, but you'll be long in preparing for it." His voice strengthened, rang: "Yet if I am not mistaken, you'll reach the forefront of ministry; you will be Christ's patrician."

~ 4 ~

Midwinter rites and festival, together with the Council meeting, went past solstice. On the first midnight after they ended, Forsquilis took Dahut out onto Point Vanis.

The air lay windless and cold. Stars crowded heaven; the river of Tiamat foamed across it ghost-white, ghost-silent. By that light the sentries at Northbridge Gate knew the Athene face whose pallor a cowled cloak framed. They presented arms. Mute, woman and girl passed by, onto the short bridge to the headland.

Huge rocks jutted from the water beneath. An incoming tide roared and snarled among them, dashing itself between wall and cliff, spurting whiteness upward out of jet. Hoarfrost grayed the earth ahead. To the west, Ocean bore a faint, uneasy shimmer on its raven immensity. A gibbous moon was crawling from the eastern hills.

Where the road from the bridge met Redonian Way, Forsquilis left both and led Dahut northeast across the foreland. The track she followed wound almost too narrow to walk, between tussocks, gorse, dead thistles, boulders. Dahut stumbled. "I can't see where my feet go," she complained.

Forsquilis, cat-sure of her own way, answered softly. "You shall become one with the darkness, I promise you."

"When? How?"

"Hush. There are those abroad who might hear." Each word blew forth as a tiny white phantom, instantly lost.

The two went on. The moon crept higher. Stars coruscated. Frost brought leaves forth against shadow. Footfalls and the dry rustle of twigs being brushed were the solitary sounds, until sea-murmur deepened and loudened as the walkers drew near the northern edge.

The destination hove in sight. Centuries of weather had worn down earthen walls which once bulked threefold on the clifftop of a small ness. Grass and brambles had bestormed the fortress, covered it over, crumbled it away with their roots; timbers had rotted and rubble fill washed down into the surf; surely the very dead beneath had yielded their bones to the soil.

Forsquilis stopped before the ruin. Casting back her cloak, she raised arms and chanted, not in Ysan but in the sacred Punic of the Founders: *"Mighty ones, spirits asleep in the depths of time, be not wroth. Awake ye and remember. I, a high priestess of Ishtar, bring unto you Dahut, a virgin who bears fate in her womb. Bid us come into your dreams."*

It was as if the sea moaned.

The Queen turned to the princess. "Be not afraid," she said. "Where we go tonight, none but the fearless may enter unscathed."

Dahut straightened. Her hood had fallen off the braids into which her hair was coiled, held by a silver clasp in the form of a snake. Moonlight silvered the right half of her face; the left was in bluish darkness. "You know I am not afraid," she replied.

Forsquilis smiled bleakly. "Aye, well do I know. Of your own free will have you ranged along the borders of the Otherworld, all your brief life; or its creatures have sought you out, but then you never quailed. Ere ever your strange birth, the Gods made you Theirs for some purpose hidden from mortals—and, it may be, from Themselves. Every omen avows it, with never a sign we can clearly read. I have told you how the hope of the Nine has become this: that you, gaining skill in the Old Wisdom that men call witchcraft, may find your way forward to an understanding of your destiny, and make it not terrible but splendid."

Dahut nodded, wordless.

"It is a heavy load to lay on a young girl," Forsquilis said. "Once all the Gallicenae had the gift; but generation by generation, the Power has faded. We can still *sometimes* command the weather, cast a curse, lay a blessing, summon a wanderer, ward off illness or other misfortune, make a death gentle. But Innilis alone has the healer's Touch; I alone can make a Sending or call a demon or lure a God or hear the dead when they speak; and these are fugitive dowers, failing us oftener for each year that slips between our fingers. No longer do the Gallicenae teach a little of the ancient arts to each vestal, all to each new-made Queen. For most, that would be knowledge frightening, troublous, and useless. Give wings to a hare and they will but drag her down, and make her easy prey for the wolf."

"The eagle's wings lift her!" cried Dahut. "They give her the sky and her quarry."

"Well spoken. I pray we have judged you aright, and you yourself. 'Twill be years until we can tell. This night is the barest beginning."

Forsquilis pointed to the earthworks. "Like most folk, you know this as Lost Castle," she said. "You have heard it was built by the earliest Gauls. It is shunned for no single reason—mutterings of bad luck, ghosts, mermaids who slither up from the depths—though I make no doubt you, Dahut, have explored it on your solitary rambles. Did you ever feel a presence here?"

"I am...not sure," the girl whispered.

"Hear what stands in the secret annals, and lock it away in your breast. This was Cargalwen, raised for Targorix, the first of the charioteer kings in our land. Because of a woman, the Old Folk whom he had conquered rose against him. Here on Point Vanis he met them, the sword-hubbed wheels made harvest of them, red rivers twisted down the cliffs to the sea. For a year and a day afterward, the slain lay where they had fallen, and their decay poisoned the air but enriched the soil. When flesh was gone, Targorix had the skeletons laid out on this tip of land, and said that would be the foundation of his stronghold. Human hands did not make it. His druid Vindomarix sang the dwarfs up from below the world and compelled them.

"Mighty for many years were Cargalwen and its lord. But the curse of the Old Folk hounded him. One by one, his sons died. The last and most promising did when he heard a song under the cliffs. He looked, saw a beautiful woman on a rock by the surf, climbed down to meet her, lost footing and fell to his death. Above in the fortress, they heard her laughter ere she vanished beneath the waves. They risked their necks to bring the body back. Crazed with grief, Targorix vowed he would bury the lad himself, in the heart of Cargalwen. Digging, he uncovered a skeleton. An adder nested in the rib cage. It bit him, and so he perished after hours of anguish, on a night of storm when folk thought they heard his soul shriek as it was ripped away.

"The Osismii took new leaders, who made their seat inland. When the Carthaginians arrived, the stronghold lay abandoned. But the earth, the stones, the waters remember.

"Come."

Forsquilis took Dahut by the hand and led her across the ditch, through gaps, over remnants, to the inmost circle. "This will be a long night," the woman said. "Dismiss haste from your spirit. We shall be seeking beyond time."

They sat down cross-legged on the withered grass. Forsquilis turned her face aloft. "Look on high," she said. "See, yonder strides Orion. The Dragon attends the Lodestar. The wheel of heaven is turning, turning, turning. Mount to the Wain, Dahut, enter, be borne down the centuries."

Vision and soul topple into endless deeps aloft.

The moon climbed higher. The witch crooned. Waves clashed and boomed, but as if very distant.

"—Oneness. All is one and one is all. Dream the dreams they dream who are dead."

Frost sends slow shudders through earth. Stones toil upward; on nights yet to come, the stars will shine upon them. Seeds asleep wait for springtime. There is a flicker of aurora in the north, a memory of burnings long ago. Surf rumbles like chariot wheels. A breeze rouses, sighs, seeks lips to kiss.

"What does the night say to you? Nay, tell me not, tell yourself. *Eya, eya, baalech ivoni.*"

Tide turned. The moon stood high and small.

Forsquilis rose. "May the Power be in us," she said. Dahut did likewise, stiff and dazed.

"Join me in the refrain," Forsquilis ordered. "I have taught you."

"I remember it," Dahut said. "Oh, I remember more than ever I knew erenow."

"Beware. Dwell not overmuch on that which comes from Beyond. But you shall feel the Power this night. Together we will summon the wind."

The song lifted. Out there on the headland, it was the loneliest sound in the world. But its undertone was the noise of the slowly retreating sea.

The stars turned, the moon mounted. That breeze which had drifted about began to whistle, ever so faintly. It could have been a melody played on a pipe made from a reed. Haziness blurred the western horizon.

Forsquilis danced while she sang beneath the moon. At first the movements of hands and feet and body undulated like low waves. The music loudened, now and then shrill, as if a gull cried. The swiftening breeze fluttered her cloak. Dahut stood aside near a briar bush, her whiteness limned against remnant walls and the sky. At the end of each strophe, she flung forth her lines: *"—Lords of the elements, Lady of evenstar, Your children evoke you by the right of the Blood!—"*

Clouds lifted in the west. The moon dappled their shoulders. The wind could have been a melody played on a pipe made from a dead man's shinbone.

The dance grew violent. Clouds mounted, blotting out constellation after constellation. Moonlight found whitecaps. They burst on rocks with roar, whoosh, and hiss. Stars flickered in the wind.

Forsquilis grew still. "Enough," she said. Weariness flattened her tones. "The Gods are vengeful toward those who overreach themselves. We have learned that you are born to the Power. Let us go home."

Dahut's voice rang wild: "Nay, let me abide, watch, be here!"

Forsquilis regarded her for a long spell by the wan and waning light. Cloaks flapped and snapped. "As you will," Forsquilis said. "As you must, mayhap."

She set forth toward Ys. Dahut crouched down into what shelter was to be had. The storm strengthened.

—When it had overrun heaven, when rain and sleet slashed in on a keening gale while the sea tumbled and bellowed against the cliffs, Dahut stood naked, arms wide, face lifted to the blast, and shouted laughter.

—Dawn stole aloft in the wake of the storm, the late dawn of the Black Months, on the Birthday of Mithras. It was a light the hue of ice, above weather still roiling murky over the eastern hills. Elsewhere, streaks of cloud blew thin; the hunchbacked moon seemed to race among them. The waters raged like metal poured out of a cauldron, molten yet somehow winter-cold. Dahut stood on the highest cliff of Point Vanis and chanted:

"Green the sea and gray the air,
Flood come forth and wind arise:
Green flood, gray flood, windy cloud,
    All the Sea is one.

"Blackling sea and silver air:
Clouds churn silver, silver tide,
Gales across the reefy cloud,
    All the sea is one.

"Wracking sea and rushing air,
Spindrift, skydrift, gale and blast,
Soar by spray and dive by cloud—
    All the sea is one.

"Sea is mine and mine is air,
Dark of star and wet of moon.
Wave I fling, I pile the cloud.
    All that's sea is mine."

XVII

~ 1 ~

Tommaltach maqq Donngalii returned to Ys with the springtime. Again he came as a partner in a trading venture, and again more for the sake of the visit than for any profit. It fulfilled his wildest dreams when he was received once more at the palace and, there, Princess Dahut offered to show him about the city on her first free day. His heart bounded. That night he lay sleepless.

She guided him to places he had never thought he would enter. A vestal of the first generation had admittance everywhere. Midafternoon found them atop the Water Tower, otherwise reserved for astronomers and philosophers.

Having looked with much respect at the fixed instruments, he let his gaze wander. To one side the city wall curved away beneath this parapet, behind it the blossoming valley. Nestled close was that red-tiled, colonnaded gem called Star House. Not far off, Elven Gardens lifted green and flowery, a chalice for the still more beautiful Temple of Belisama. Other fanes, together with mansions, graced this half of the city. Busy and stately, Lir Way swept down toward the Forum. Towers gleamed into a nearly cloudless heaven. Beyond sea gate and headlands, waters heaved blue and white, past holy Sena to the edge of vision. Sails were out there, and uncounted wings.

His glance went helplessly back to Dahut. She stood at his side, also looking afar. Air flowed cool, mingling odors of salt and flowers, to press her thin gown against a slenderness more full at bosom and hips than he had seen last year. It ruffled the hair that tumbled over her shoulders. The amber of those waves seemed to take into itself the light spilling from the sun.

He sighed. "Wonderful, wonderful. If only I could stay."

She blessed him with a smile. "You will come back, though," she said. "Often."

He shook his head. His Ysan blundered more than could be accounted for by lack of practice during his months at home. "The Gods alone know when I can. 'Twas all I could do to get leave for this trip."

How lightly her fingers passed across his hand, where it gripped the edge of the wall. "You bespoke this not erenow."

"I did not, for I wouldn't be spoiling of the joy. But—my father, my tuath have need of me."

The deep-blue eyes widened. "Say on."

"The Romans advance in Britannia. We cannot be sure what they intend. At the very least, pirates who no longer find good pickings there will turn elsewhere. We must guard our shores. Moreover, King Conual, to whom my father is sworn, means to widen his sway. That will likely call for war. I cannot hang back and keep my honor."

"Oh, poor Tommaltach," she breathed.

He forced a laugh. "Why, glory waits for me, and booty, and many a tale to tell afterward. Will you care to hear my brags?"

"Of course. I will wait so eagerly."

"I too, Dahut," he blurted, "my kinfolk are after me to be marrying. But I'll shy from any such ties—I have hopes—"

Her lashes dipped. "What mean you?"

Hot-faced, he said in a rush, "I may find a way to settle in Ys. A fighting man or, or a merchant factor, or—something. Rufinus promised he'd help. Dahut, when you are free—"

She smiled anew and reached up to lay fingers over his lips. "Hush. I've five more years ahead of me."

"But then—why, Ys might even wish a queen of its own race in Ériu, or—"

Again she silenced him. Her mood darkened. "Speak not of morrows, I pray you."

"Why?"

"They're like yonder seas, when a ship comes in whose pilot knows them not. He must pass through, but he cannot tell what reefs wait beneath." Dahut turned and walked rapidly off. "Come, let's go down."

Gloom and echoes filled the circular stairwell inside the tower. Emerging at its base, youth and girl blinked, as if sunlight were an astonishment. Before them lay Star House. A tall man in a plain gown was about to mount its own stairs.

Dahut stiffened, then strode forward. "What do you want, you raven?" she cried.

Corentinus halted. "Why, 'tis you, Princess," he said as mildly as his rough voice allowed. "What a pleasant surprise. And—aye, the skipper from Hivernia that I've heard about. Welcome, friend."

Dahut stopped before him. "Never call us your friends! This place is sacred. How dare you set foot here?"

"Did you not know? There is to be a meeting of the Symposium. Your father has finally won for me an invitation to attend."

"Why would he do that?"

Corentinus shrugged. "Well, after ten years I've become somewhat of an institution. And my little flock has grown. The magnates of Ys

477

must needs take us into their reckonings. The philosophers have wisely decided to exchange ideas with me, seeking mutual understanding, as civilized men ought. I seem to have come early. Wait, and the King will arrive. He's ever glad to see you."

Dahut's eyes misted. Her lip trembled. "I don't—want to see him—now," she gulped. "Come, Tommaltach."

She led the Scotian off. Corentinus stared sadly after them.

~ 2 ~

Wonder burst over Aulus Metellus Carsa.

Not only did his father agree, after much argument, that he could remain in Ys until the last voyage back to Burdigala in autumn: his term began shortly before midsummer, when festivities were fountaining. True, the captain gave his son into the care of the chorepiscopus, who was to see that the lad led a sober and godly life, pursuing proper studies and being introduced to just such aspects of the city as would be helpful to know about when developing commercial relations further. However, Corentinus knew what it was like to be young. Besides, one could not build goodwill for the firm if one refused invitations from Ysans who were interested in meeting this Roman—some of which invitations came from the very palace—could one?

And then Dahut asked him to be her steersman!

That happened in the course of the merrymaking which followed the solstice rites. It went on for days. After the Council adjourned, King Gratillonius was free to offer his distinguished guest, Apuleius Vero, his full attention.

Not that entertainment had been lacking. On this, his first visit to Ys, the tribune of Aquilo confessed himself bewildered by the endless marvels offered him. Some were of the Roman kind, banquets, games and races and athletic exhibitions in the amphitheater, performances of music and dance and drama in the odeion; but he exclaimed that everything was finer than he had encountered anywhere else, free of coarseness and brutality, yet tinged with a strangeness that freshened it like a sea wind. Other things he beheld were altogether alien. Certain of them he could admire artistically if not spiritually, such as the pagan temples and processions; certain he must deplore, such as men and women dancing together, or the general boldness of females, or the frequent hostility to Christ. But into much he could enter wholeheartedly—library, observatory, creativeness newly reawakened and breaking free of ancient canons, the Symposium, long private conversations with scholars or the learned Queen Bodilis, whipcrack wit, a sense of pridefulness and hope even among the lowliest, a feeling that the horizon was no longer a boundary.

When he told Gratillonius, the King replied, "Thanks. You don't see the underside of things. But never mind; you can guess what that's like. I'll tell you my troubles later, because maybe we can help each other. Now, though, let's enjoy ourselves. We've earned it."

"Have you something special in mind?" Apuleius inquired.

Gratillonius nodded. "I've decided to revive an old custom. It lay fallow a long time because of pirates and the like, but once it was a big event of the season and there's no reason it can't be again. I mean the yacht race."

Traditionally it had gone from the marine station to Garomagus and back, using boats of a single class. Today both terminals lay in ruins, and such pleasure craft as existed in Ys were wildly varied. Gratillonius had devised new rules. Participants would meet outside the sea gate, on the morning ebb. They would round Point Vanis and steer into Roman Bay. The murdered town would be too melancholy a rendezvous, but a short way past it, where the land bent abruptly north, was a fine broad beach. Small vessels could hug the shore; larger ones must stand farther out before turning east, a distance set by hull length and number of oars available, but those could only be used if it proved impossible to sail.

The balancing was crude. Gratillonius did not pretend that this would be a real contest in seamanship. To emphasize that it was simply sport, he sent people ahead to make a feast ready on the beach. The winning crew would receive their wreaths there and everyone would join in celebration before starting homeward.

"Will you be my steersman?" Dahut asked Carsa at the palace, in her fluent Latin.

"What?" he exclaimed, staggered. "Won't you go with your father?"

She tossed her head. "He won't compete, just preside. Anyhow, in that ship of his, with the high bulwarks, with crew babbling and bumbling, I never feel truly near the sea. He's given me my own boat; but he still forbids me to singlehand it." Candlelight glowed on her countenance, in her eyes. Harp and flute lilted around her voice. "He knows you for a skillful sailor. If I ask him in the right words, he'll agree."

That night Carsa lay sleepless.

~ 3 ~

The boat was a twenty-foot currach on the Scotic model, nimble and seaworthy, light enough for two men to row or one to scull. A small deck forward covered a stowage space and gave on a miniature figurehead, a gilt swan, wings outspread as if straining to be free. Otherwise the leather-clad hull was open, save for a pair of thwarts. The mast had been stepped but was still bare.

The day was lucent, the swells gentle beneath a northwest breeze. Vessels danced. Shouts and trumpet call mingled with the cries of the kittiwakes. Carsa accepted a tow from the royal yacht, which was rowed at the beginning, until safely out to sea. What he bore was immeasurably precious. Nevertheless, once he had cast loose and hoisted the azure-and-argent striped sail, he had hard navigation. Often he must grip a sheet in either hand while his knees wedged against the tiller to control the steering oar. He gloried in it, for Dahut praised him.

After he turned the promontory, his task became much easier. Poled out, the sail bellied to the wind. The rudder felt like a live, responsive animal as he wielded it to maintain the proper heading. With shallow draft, a currach could scarcely point up, but on a reach such as this it surged along, lee rail low, parallel to a coast which gradually grew less rugged. Water hissed by, swirled in wake, murmured enormously all around. It was blue, blue-green, violet, snowy-foamed. Leather throbbed, frame and lashing creaked, rigging thrummed. A vast curve of land rimmed most of the world, distance-hazed. Boats and small ships filled its embrace. Afar in the west bobbed the dark hulls and drab sails of fishermen at their labor. Seafowl skimmed past. The air blew keen.

Dahut sat on the thwart immediately forward of Carsa. A rough gown and hooded cloak wrapped her. She looked out at him, radiant. "I'm still surprised your father permits this, my lady," he ventured. "It's not without danger."

"Usually I must have two men with me," she answered, "but today we've a whale-pod around us, and I persuaded him to let me...travel light, in hopes of winning." She grinned. "Fear not. We'll get another tow on the return trip."

"If we should capsize—"

Her glance ignored the floats kept against that chance. "I swim like a seal," she said haughtily. "I am of the sea." Concern flitted across her face. "You do swim? I never thought to ask."

He nodded. "These are chilly waters for learning how."

"I was born to them."

He sensed that this was no matter to pursue and fell silent, content to have her in his sight.

She said hardly anything more herself. Instead, she fell to staring outward, sometimes into the distances, sometimes into the deeps. Her vivacity had left her. He could not tell what was rising in its place.

Time streamed past on the wind. The racers laid Ysan land abaft and entered Roman Bay.

Though Carsa used every trick of seamanship that was his, it became clear this craft would not arrive first at the goal. He nerved himself to say it. "I'm sorry, my lady. We should be among the earlier ones." Dahut shrugged. Her gaze stayed remote.

Now he made out the remnant of Garomagus. An islet guarded the mouth of a stream emptying into the bight. Behind it were roofless walls and gaping doorways. The view east, dead ahead, was more comforting, buildings strewn toylike. He could not be sure, though, which were inhabited, and certainly the signs of civilization were few;

woods had overrun much of the land. It came to him that most of the clearing and plowing must be reclamation after King Gratillonius had given peace to these parts.

He pointed. "Look!" he cried. "The beach we want. The smoke of the cookfires."

Dahut threw back her cowl—light flared over braided hair—and cocked her head. Was she listening to the waves?

"The wind's fallen," Carsa went on after a while, in search of talk. "That northern headland blocks it. However, we'll have enough to make our goal." Several craft were already clustered there. The larger had dropped anchor and employed tenders to bring their people ashore, the smaller were aground.

Dahut shook herself. She regarded him where he stood in the stern, as if across miles or through sea depths. "Don't." Her voice was faint, but he heard her clearly.

Startled, he let his hand slip on the tiller. The boat yawed, the sail slatted. "What?"

Dahut turned from his to peer starboard. Her finger lifted. "Go yonder," she said.

"To Garomagus?" He was appalled. "No, that's ruins. I can't take you there."

She rose, felinely balanced. While she lacked her full growth, the cloak flapped about her shoulders as if she would take wing, and command flared forth cold as northern lights, in the language of Ys: "Obey! Lir speaks!"

He looked around. No help was in sight. The racers were veering away from him, ardent for landing. Laggards toiled too far aft. Nobody heeded this low little vessel. The King doubtless would have, but his yacht was at the destination.

"Christ help me," he pleaded, "I must not bring you into d-danger, Princess."

She scorned the Name. "I have heard Lir in the wind," she told him. "There is no danger. There is someone I must meet. Steer, or be forever my enemy."

He surrendered, inwardly cursing his weakness. "If you will have it thus," he said in her speech. "We cannot stay long. They'll wonder what's happened to you and come searching."

Her slight smile laved his spirit. "We'll join them in good time. And I'll remember your service, Carsa." Then he shuddered a bit, for she added, "The Gods will remember."

Lest he grow afraid, he devoted himself to sailing. The change of course astounded him, so easily it went; he could not account for it. And how peculiar also, he thought, that nobody whatsoever noticed the currach go astray.

To slip in past the isle looked too risky. Besides, he couldn't expect to find a useable wharf. He grounded on the beach just east. Its shoreline turned north, an outthrust of land hiding it from the Ysans beyond. Having struck the sail he sprang forward, down onto the sand, and dragged the boat higher. Thereupon he gave Dahut his arm for her disembarkation. She had no real need of that.

Her visage was white, her eyes enormous, she shivered and spoke unevenly: "Wait here. I'll soon be back."

"No," he protested, falling unawares into Latin, "I can't let you go alone. I won't. What is it you're after?"

"I know not," she whispered. "I have been called." Her utterance rose to a yell. She stabbed two fingers at him. "Abide! Let me go by myself! I lay on you the gess that you not follow, by the power of Belisama, Taranis, and almighty Lir!"

Whirling about, she ran off, over the dunes, through the harsh grass that bordered them, past the snags of a defensive wall, in among the houses. She was gone. A cormorant flew black overhead.

Mechanically, Carsa reached for the anchor rode and made the currach secure. What else could he do?

What else? It struck him in a hammerblow. She had forgotten that he was no pagan, to cower before the demons she called Gods or heed a word she had merely, childishly laid on him. He was a Roman. Anybody might skulk hereabouts. He *would* follow, and be ready to defend her. He wished he had brought his sling. However, a knife was at his belt, and he got the boathook.

Of course, chances were that this place was quite deserted, apart from ghosts and devils. Best would be that she never know of his disobedience. He'd stay cautious....A haze had begun to dim the day. Wind had swung west and blew louder, colder. He summoned up courage to move forward.

Her trail was clear. Dust and sand had drifted into the streets to take footprints; plants grew to be bruised; her tread had splintered potsherds and displaced brickbats, as his did. He was vaguely glad that tracking kept his mind off what surrounded him. Weather had long since bleached the stains of fire and blood, but likewise colors, every human trace. Lichen was patiently gnawing walls which enclosed vacancy.

He found her at the mouth of the stream. It was an abrupt sight, as he came around a building. A few yards away, she knelt on a patch of silver-gray grass, limned athwart the islet beyond. He crammed himself back against the gritty wall and peered with a single eye. Sounds reached him above the shrilling of the wind, mutter of brook and bay, half-heard rolling of Ocean.

She knelt before a seal that had crawled out of the water. Its coat shimmered golden-dark. Her arms were around its neck, her face pressed to its head, hidden from him. He heard her weep. He heard the seal

482

hum, a deep plangency he had not known such a creature could make. A flipper reached to stroke Dahut's locks.

Christ have mercy, to this had the dream-voice called her, she who began the day so blithe. Carsa's knuckles whitened on the boathook shaft. Almost, he dashed to attack the soulless thing and save Dahut.

But she began to sing too. Her tone came thin and small; he was not sure how he made it out through wind and tide and the mewing of the kittiwakes. Somehow he knew that she was turning into Ysan words, for her own understanding, as well as she could in the middle of grief, the song that the seal sang.

"Harken, my darling. Hear me through.
Little I have to tell.
Now at the last I come to you,
To bid you for aye farewell.

"Here what I say ere I depart,
That which I think you ween.
You were the child beneath my heart
When I was your father's Queen.

"Torn from my side one winter night
Out in a wrathful sea,
You are the child whose fate takes flight
Beyond what is given me.

"Kiss me, my sea-child, ere we part
As it was long foreseen.
He that shall rip away my heart
Came down from the North yestre'en."

Carsa stole off. At the boat, he prayed to Christ. Presently, Dahut returned. Beneath the cowl, her face was blank, a visor. As empty was the voice wherein she told him to launch her craft and bring them to the feast.

~ 4 ~

Osprey had fared under oars to the nets placed out the day before. Those having been tended, the smack sailed back, trawling. Her course brought her past Goat Foreland and across the mouth of Roman Bay. Heaven had drawn a veil across earlier brightness, the sun had gone wan and the air mordant. Then wind, stiffening, swung around until it blew almost straight out of the west.

Maeloch swore. Water chopped gray-green. Whitecaps began to star it. Land lay shadowy at the eastern horizon but rose and grew closer as it bent west; even across five or so leagues he made out the cliffs of Point Vanis, which he must round. Spraddle-legged against the rolling of his deck, he growled, "We'll nay be free of another haul at the sweeps, seems." A fisher captain took his turn on the benches.

A crewman laughed. "Well, nor will yon fine yachtsmen."

"Ah, they've hirelings to sweat for 'em," said another.

"Belay that," Maeloch ordered. "Be ye rabble for Nagon Demari to rant at? The Queens, the King, the Suffetes, they're as much Ys as ye and me....We'll try how far we can beat upwind ere we run out of sea room."

The men moved toward the sheets to haul the sail around. He lifted a hand. "Nay, hold a moment." He went to the port rail and squinted. A swimmer had come in sight, outbound from the bay.

"Seal," declared a sailor. "I'll fetch my sling and give him a taste." The animals were sacred, but they had to be discouraged from raiding fishnets.

"Not that 'un," Maeloch answered. "I know her. D'ye see the golden sheen in her pelt? She's the pet of Princess Dahut." Recalling certain things he had witnessed, he drew the Hammer sign of protection with his forefinger, furtively, lest others notice and go uneasy. He himself did not feel threatened, but this was an uncanny beast.

The seal came alongside. She lifted her upper body out of the waves. Her gaze met Maeloch's and lingered for heartbeats. How soft those eyes were.

She swam onward, falling aft of the boat, heading into the boundlessness of Ocean.

"Fin ho!" bawled a man.

Maeloch ran to the starboard side and leaned out. Breath whistled in between his teeth. He knew that high black triangle, seldom though its bearers came this far south. "Orca," he muttered.

The killer whale veered. Maeloch realized where it was aimed. Did the seal? She swam on as if blind. Not that she could escape that rush—"To oars!" Maeloch shouted. "Bring us around! Ye, Donan, get my harpoon!"

Water foamed with speed. The black shape broke surface. Flukes drove it forward faster than Maeloch knew his craft could ever move. He glimpsed its belly, white as snow, white as death.

It struck. He seemed to feel the shock in his own guts. The mighty jaws sheered and closed. Hunger and prey plunged under.

"Belay," Maeloch said dully. "We'll nay see either of them again."

Blood colored the waves, so broad a stain that he could hope the seal had died instantly.

"Stand by to come about," Maeloch said. "We're going home."

It tore from him a croak: "How shall I tell the little princess?"

"Follow her," Bodilis urged.

Gratillonius hesitated. "She'd fain be alone. I've seen her thus erenow."

Forsquilis shook her head. "Something terrible happened this day. I know not what, but I heard ghosts wailing in the wind."

"Never mind that," said Fennalis. "I can tell when a girl needs her daddy. *Go*, you lout!"

Gratillonius reached decision, nodded, and hastened down the gangplank. Dahut had already passed between two warehouses and disappeared.

The Roman youth Carsa stood forlorn on the dock, staring in that direction. His throat worked. He had debarked at her heels, obviously offering—begging—to accompany her. She dismissed him with a chopping gesture and some or other word that crushed him. Earlier, she had quite neglected him, first at the beach when they joined the rest, afterward aboard the royal yacht when her currach was towed. But then, she had shunned everybody, giving the shortest answers if directly spoken to, sitting at the trestle table with food untasted before her or wandering off by herself down the strand. The change from her cheeriness of the morning was like a fall into an abyss. It had spoiled the revel for Gratillonius; he must force himself to be jovial.

True, Dahut had always been a being as moody as Armorican weather. The small girl would flare into furies, the maiden would descend into gloom, suddenly, without any cause comprehensible by him. Her mirth and charm returned equally fast. Yet he had never hitherto watched anything like this. He thought that under a rawhide-tight self-control, anguish devoured her. Why?

Such of the Gallicenae as were in the party had withdrawn to the cabin on the way back and conferred. When the ship came to rest in the harbor basin, they had given him their counsel.

He brushed past Carsa—might have to interrogate that boy, but later, later—and those persons ashore who hailed him. Few tried. Ys had learned to let King Grallon be when he strode along iron-faced. Emerging on the street, he looked left and right. Which way? At eventide, folk off to their homes or their pleasures, the quarter was nearly vacant. He couldn't ask if anyone had seen a desolate lass in outdoor garb go by.

Wait. He did not really know his eldest daughter. No one did. She mingled easily when she chose, but always remained private to the point of secretiveness. However...she would not have headed left to Skippers' Market and Lir Way, nor struck off into the maze of old streets ahead. Wounded, she would seek solitude. Gratillonius turned right.

Dusk welled up inside the city wall. Foul wind and heavy seas had slowed the passage home. Hurrying along the Ropewalk, Gratillonius glimpsed vessels under construction in the now silent shipyard. Their unplanked ribs might have been the skeletons of whales. At the end he swung right again, to the stairs leading onto the top of the rampart, and mounted them.

His heart stumbled. He had guessed truly. Yonder she was.

She seemed tiny below the Raven Tower. Fragments of mist blew above, blurring sight of its battlements. The lower stones glowed with sunset light. Wind had dropped to a whisper, still sharply cold. Ocean ran strong, bursting and booming where it struck, purple-dark in its outer reaches. There fog banks roiled and moved landward. Sometimes they hid the sinking sun, sometimes its rays struck level through a rift. They turned the vapors gold, amber, sulfur, and cast long unrestful shadows over the waves.

Dahut leaned forth between two merlons, clutching them, to gaze down at furious surf and minute beach between the wall and the upthrust of Cape Rach. The noise rolled hollowly around her.

She heard Gratillonius approach and looked to see who did. Her eyes appeared to fill the countenance that was, O Mithras, like Dahilis's. He halted before her. Words were difficult to find. "I want to help you. Please let me try."

Her lips moved once or twice before she got out: "You can't. Nobody can." He could barely hear her through the sea-thunder.

"Oh, now, be not so sure of that." He smiled, put arms akimbo, rocked on his heels, anything that might make his talk more reassuring. "I'm your old Papa, remember? Your first friend, who—" his voice cracked—"who loves you."

Her glance drifted from him, back to the violence below.

Anger stirred. He knew it was at his own powerlessness, and allowed it only to put metal into his tone, as when he the centurion wanted to know about some trouble among the soldiers. "Dahut. Hear me. You must answer. What happened? Your companion missed his proper landing and the two of you came belated to the feast. They were teasing him about it, and he took it glumly. Did he do aught untoward while you were alone?"

When she made no response, Gratillonius added: "If I must brace him to get the truth, so be it. I'll do whatever proves necessary. For I am the King of Ys."

Then she whirled to confront him. He saw horror on her. "Nay, oh, nay, father! Carsa's been—courteous, helpful— He knows naught, I swear, naught!"

"I wonder about that. I wonder greatly. He's a sailor boy. He should not have made a stupid mistake in steering. He should not have been shaken to his roots merely because you fell into a bad mood. Aye, best that Carsa and I have a little talk."

"Father—" He saw her fight not to weep. "S-stay your hand. I swear to you—by my mother—nothing unlawful happened. I swear it."

486

He softened his words again: "I'll believe you, sweetling. Yet something has shattered you today. You cannot leave me in the dark. I *am* the King of Ys; and they say you bear our destiny; but 'tis enough that you are my child by Dahilis, Dahilis that I loved beyond all the world, and still love."

He held out his arms. Blindly, she came into them. He hugged her close. Her cheek lay against his breast. His hand stroked her slimness, over and over. He murmured, and slowly her shuddering eased.

"Come," he said at last, "let's go out where we can be by ourselves."

A few others had been astroll on the wall, and there were the marines at the tower. None had ventured nigh, and Gratillonius and Dahut had ignored them, but he knew what probing pierced the misty glow. He took her hand—it nestled in his like a weary bird—and led her by the guards, on past the war engines in their kennels, to the sea gate.

There they must stop, unless they would descend to the warder's walk. Fog smoked in, ever thicker, hooding them from view beyond a few paces. Its yellow grew furnace-hot to westward, where an unseen sun poured forth a final extravagance of light; but the breeze nipped keenly. Below them, at their backs, the harbor glimmered out of murk. At their feet, surf smashed in a smother of white. To the side, surges went to and fro between the doors, sucking and sobbing.

Dahut stared outward. "We can't see Sena," she said raggedly.

"Nay, of course not." He picked his way forward word by word. "Would you fain?"

She nodded. "That...is where I was born—and mother—"

"I've told you before, and I will again, never blame yourself, darling. She died blessing you. I'm sure she did, blessing you as ever I've since done myself."

"I know. I knew. Until today—"

He waited.

She looked up at him. "Where do the dead go after they must leave us?"

"What?" He was surprised. "Oh, folk have many different beliefs. You, a vestal, you must be more learned than I am about what the wisest in Ys think."

She shook her head. "They only say the Gods apportion our dooms. 'Tis not what I meant. Father, sometimes the dead come back. They are born anew so they can—watch over us— But what happens to them when they die again?"

He called to mind eerie rumors that had reached him over the years. Chill shot along his back and out to his fingertips. "That seal who comes to you—"

"She died. A beast killed her."

"How do you know?" he mumbled.

487

"*She* knew. She told me. I think the Gods saw that—if she stayed—she'd keep me from—from—I know not what, from something They may want of me— Oh, father, where is she now?"

Dahut cast herself back into the arms of Gratillonius. The tears broke loose. She clawed against him and screamed.

He gripped her and endured.

At length, still an animal hurt and terrified, gone to earth in his bosom, at length she could plead, "Help me, father. Leave me not. Be with me always."

"I will,...daughter of Dahilis." He dared inquire no further. Belike he never would, nor she say any more. Yet he felt within himself the strength he had reached for.

"Promise!"

"I do." Gratillonius looked above her tousled head. The sun must have gone under, for hues had drained from the fog and twilight was rapidly thickening. Wind cut through, though, and he spied the battlements of the Raven Tower clear against uneasy heaven, afire with the last radiance of the Unconquered. In a crypt beneath lay his holy of holies. The strength rose higher, defiant of the cruel Gods of Ys.

"I promise," he said. "I will never forsake you, Dahut, beloved, never deny you. By Mithras I swear."

They sought home together.

DAHUT

I

Day came to birth above eastern hills and streamed down the valley. It flamed off the towers of Ys, making them stand like candles against what deepness lingered in western blue. Air lay cool, still, little hazed. The world beneath it was full of dew and long shadows.

This was the feast of Lúg. Here they also kept the old holy times, but the great ones of the city called then on its own Gods. A male procession, red-robed, the leader bearing a hammer, mounted the wall at High Gate. They lifted their hands and sang.

"Your sun ascends in splendor
The brilliance of Your sky
To light the harvest landscape
Your rains did fructify.
These riches and this respite
From winter, war, and night,
Taranis of the Thunders,
Were won us through Your might!

"You guard the walls of heaven,
Earth's Lover, Father, King.
You are the sacrificer,
You are the offering.
The years wheel ever onward
Beyond our human ken.
Bestow Your strength upon us
That we may die like men."

Behind them, where the Temple of Belisama shone on its height, female voices soared from Elven Gardens.

"Lady of love and life,
Lady of death and strife,
Maiden and wedded wife,
    And old in sorrow,
Turn unto us Your face,
Grant us a dwelling place
In Your abiding grace,
    Now and tomorrow!

"You are the Unity:
Girl running wild and free,

Hag brooding mystery,
      And the All-Mother.
Evermore born again,
You, Belisama, reign,
Over our joy and pain
      As does no other.

"You by Whom all things live,
Though they be fugitive,
Thank You for that You give
      Years to us mortals.
Goddess of womankind,
Guide us until we find
Shelter and peace behind
      Darkness's portals."

Ebb had barely begun and the sea gate of Ys remained shut. Never-theless a ship was outward bound. Eager to be off while good weather held, her captain had had her towed forth by moonlight and had lain at anchor waiting for dawn. Mainsail and artemon unfurled, her forefoot hissed through the waves. He went into the bows, killed a black cock, sprinkled blood on the stempost, cast the victim overboard, held out his arms, and chanted.

"Tide and wind stand fair for our course,
      but we remember that the set of them is often to a lee shore;
"We remember that gales whelm proud fleets
      and reefs wait always to rip them asunder;
"We remember how men have gone down to the eels
      or have strewn their bones white on the skerries;
"We remember weariness, hunger, thirst,
      the rotting of live flesh and teeth loosened from jaws;
"We remember the shark and the ice,
      and the albatross lonely above desolation;
"We remember the blinding fog
      and the terrible sea-blink in dead calm:
"For these too are of Lir. His will be done."

The King of Ys, Incarnation and high priest of Taranis, was not in the city, for this was not so momentous a day as to release him from the Watch he must keep when the moon was full. With a handful of fellow worshippers he stood in the courtyard of the Sacred Precinct, by the Challenge Oak, looking toward the sun and calling, "Hail, Mithras Unconquered, Savior, Warrior, Lord, born unto us anew and forever—" The silence in the Wood muffled it.

At the Forum, the heart of Ys, in the church that had once been a fane of Mars, Christians almost as few held a service. Nobody outside heard their song, tiny and triumphant.

2

Rain slashed from the west. Wind hooted. Autumn was closing in, with storms and long nights. If men did not soon take ship for Ériu, they would risk being weatherbound in Britannia until—Manandan maqq Leri knew when.

Two men sat in a tavern in Maia. That was a Roman settlement just south and west of the Wall, on the firth. Roughly clad, the pair drew scant heed from others at drink, albeit one was uncommonly large and handsome, his fair hair and beard not much silvered. Plain to see, they were Scotic. However, they kept to themselves and this was not an inn where people asked questions. Besides, the tiny garrison was in quarters; and barbarians went freely about, Scoti, Picti, occasional Saxons. Some were mercenaries recruited by Rome, or scouts or spies or informers. Some were traders, who doubtless did more smuggling than open exchange. It mattered not, provided they got into nothing worse than brawls. The Imperial expeditionary force had enough to do without patrolling every impoverished huddling place.

A tallow candle guttered and stank on the table between the two Scoti. Its light and the light of its kind elsewhere were forlorn, sundered by glooms like stars on a cloudy night. Niall of the Nine Hostages gripped a cup of ale such as he would not have ordered pigs swilled with at home, were a king allowed to own them. Leaning forward, elbows on the greasy, splintery wood, he asked low, "You are quite sure of this, are you, now?"

Uail maqq Carbri nodded. "I am that, my lord," he answered in the same undertone. Most likely none else would have understood their language, but no sense in taking needless chances. "I'll be telling the whole tale later, my wanderings and all, first in this guise, next in that, ever the amusing newcomer who commanded a rustic sort of Latin—"

"You will, when we've time and safety," Niall interrupted. "Tonight be short about it. Here is a damnable spot to be meeting."

It had been the best they could do. Niall, waging war, landing where he saw it would be possible and striking inland as far and savagely as would leave him a line of retreat, Niall could no more foresee where he would camp than could peacefully, inquisitively ranging Uail. Maia was a fixed point, not closely under the Roman eye; men of Condacht and Mide had bespoken this tavern in the past; they could agree to be there at the half moon after equinox. Nonetheless Uail had had to abide two evenings until Niall, delayed by weather, arrived.

Uail shrugged. "As my lord wills. No men I sounded out, officers or common soldiers, none of them had any word from on high. We wouldn't await that, would we, now? But somehow they were all sure. The word has seeped through. Rome will fight one more season, hoping to have Britannia cleared of the likes of us by then. But no longer. Nor is there any thought of striking at Ériu. They will be needing the troops too badly across the Channel."

Niall nodded. "Thank you, my dear," he said. "I looked for the same. It sings together with what I learned myself, raiding them this year. They were never determined in pursuit when we withdrew. They've not moved against Dál Riata, nest of hawks though it is. We took in deserters, who told us they had no wish to fare off to an unknown battle away in Europe. Oh, it's clear, it's clear, we have nothing to fret about in our homeland from Rome."

"That is good to know, well worth the trouble of finding out."

Niall's fist thudded down on the board. His voice roughened. "I should have been aware already. I should never have havered like this, letting years slip by—" Abruptly he rose. His mane brushed the ceiling. "Come, Uail. Toss off that horse piss if you must and let's begone."

The mariner gaped. "What? It's a wild night out."

"And I'm wild to be off. The fleet lies on the north side of the firth, in a cove where no Roman comes any longer, two days' walk for us from here. If we start at once, we can pass Luguvallium in the dark."

"That would be wise," Uail agreed. Yonder city was the western strongpoint of the Wall. Both men took their cloaks and trod forth.

The rain was not too cold nor the night too black for such as they. Kilts wrapped them from shoulder to knee; at their belts hung dirks, and pouches with a bit of dried meat and cheese; once they were beyond the Roman outposts, no one would venture to question them.

They had walked a while when Niall said in a burst: "I have need of haste, Uail maqq Carbri. I hear time baying behind me, a pack of hounds that has winded the wolf. Too long have I waited. There is Emain Macha to bring down, and afterward Ys."

~ 3 ~

Among Celts, the first evening of Hunter's Moon awakened madness. In Ys, folk no longer believed that the doors between worlds stood open then—if only because in Ys, they were never quite shut—but farmers and gardeners made sure their last harvests had been gathered, while herdsmen brought their beasts under roofs and seamen lashed a besom to every craft not in a boathouse. Within the city, it was an occasion for unbridled revel.

Weather permitting, the Fire Fountain played. Masked, grotesquely costumed—stag, horse, goat, goblin, leather phallus wagging gigantic; nymph, witch, mermaid, hair flying loose, breasts bared and painted—the young cavorted drunken through the streets. Workers of every kind were off duty, and none need do reverence to lord or lady. The older and higher-born watched the spectacle for a time, perhaps, before withdrawing to entertainments they had prepared for themselves behind their own walls. Those might or might not be decorous. Drink flowed, music taunted, and no encounter between man and woman, whomever they might be wedded to, was reckoned entirely real.

Certain classes observed restraint. The King kept Watch in the Wood as usual. Such of the Gallicenae ashore as were not with him held a banquet, and gave a prayer for the ninth out on Sena. Down in Scot's Landing, the Ferriers of the Dead bolted their cottage doors and their families practiced rites that were austere; these were too close to the unknown for aught else.

Yet all, all was pagan.

Corentinus left the torchlight and tumult behind him. He had offered a Mass and sent his congregation to bed. Now he was alone.

Out Northbridge Gate he went, and up Redonian Way across Point Vanis. His long legs crunched the distance. Save for him, road and headland reached empty. This night was clear, quiet, and cold. Stars glimmered manifold before him, Hercules, the Dragon, Cassiopeia, at the end of the Lesser Bear the Lodestar. The Milky Way was dimmed by the high-riding moon and its frost halo. His breath gusted white. Grass, brush, stones lay hoar.

Where the road bent east above the former maritime station, Corentinus left it and made his way west. Soon he came to an outlook over the sea, vast and dark and slowly breathing. A grave was at his feet. He knew the headstone. The one who rested here was no Christian, but had been an honest soldier. This did not seem the worst possible place to stop.

Corentinus lifted his arms and his gray head skyward. "O God," he called in anguish, "Maker and Master of the Universe; Christ Jesus, only begotten Son, God and man together, Who died for us and rose again that we might live; Holy Spirit—have mercy on poor Ys. Leave it not in its midnight. Leave it not with its demons that it worships. They mean well, God. They are not evil. They are only blind, and in the power of Satan. My dearest wish is to help them. Help me, God!"

After a silence, he bent his neck and bit his lip. "But if they are not worthy of a miracle," he groaned, "if there can be no redemption, and the abomination must be cleansed as it was in Babylon—let it be quickly, God, let it be final, and the well-meaning people and the little children not be enslaved or burnt alive, but go down at once to whatever awaits them.

"Lord, have mercy. Christ, have mercy. Lord, have mercy."

II

~ 1 ~

The declaration of King Gratillonius hit the vernal Council of Suffetes like a stone from a siege engine. As prefect of Rome, he told them, he had lately received official word of that which he had been awaiting. The augmented legions in Britannia would take the field again this year, but only for a month or two. Thereafter they would return to the Continent and march south. Anticipating renewed barbarian incursions, mounting in scope and ferocity as time went on, Gratillonius wanted the shipyard of Ys to produce more naval vessels. Yet those would not become Ysan. That would be too provocative. Instead, he would offer them to the Duke of the Armorican Tract, to go under the command of the latter. Their crews would train Roman recruits to man them.

Outrage erupted. Hannon Baltisi, Lir Captain, roared that never would men of Ys serve under such masters, Christian dogs who would forbid their worship, who did not even ask the God's pardon before emptying a slop jar into His sea. Cothortin Rosmertai, Lord of Works, protested that such a program would disrupt plans, dishonor commitments to build merchantmen; in this time of prosperity, the facilities were bespoken far in advance. Bomatin Kusuri, Mariner Councillor, questioned where enough sailors could be found, when trading, whaling, slaving, even fishing paid better than armed service in the Empire did.

Adruval Tyri, Sea Lord, maintained that the King was right about the menace of Scoti and Saxons. They would not be content to rape Britannia but would seek back to the coasts of Gallia. Yet Adruval hated the thought of turning Ysan ships over to Rome. What did Rome do for Armorica other than suck it dry? Would it not be better to build strength at home— quietly, of course—until Ys could tell Rome to do its worst?

Soren Cartagi, Speaker for Taranis, was also a voice for the Great Houses when he said, first, that to help the Christians thus was to speed the day when they came to impose their God by force; second, the cost would be more than the city could bear or the people would suffer; third, Gratillonius must remember that he was the King of a sovereign nation, not the proconsul of a servile province.

Queen Lanarvilis, who at this session was the leader of the Gallicenae, pointed out needs at home which the treasure and labor could serve. And was there indeed any threat in the future with which existing forces could not cope, as they had coped in the past? Had not the Romans now quelled their enemies and secured Britannia? Also in the South, she understood, peace prevailed; Stilicho and Alaric the Visigoth had ended their strife and come to terms. Rather than looking ahead with fear, she saw a sun of hopefulness rising.

Opposition to Gratillonius's desire coalesced around those two persons. When the meeting adjourned after stormy hours, he drew them aside and asked that they accompany him to the palace for a confidential talk.

In the atrium there, he grinned wearily and said, "First I wish a quick bath and a change into garb more comfortable than this. Would you care for the same?"

Soren and Lanarvilis exchanged a look. "Nay," the man growled. "We'll seek straight to the secretorium and...marshal our thoughts."

"Debate grew too heated," the woman added in haste. "You've brought us hither that we may reason with one another, not so? Let us therefore make sure of our intents."

Gratillonius regarded them for a silent moment. Tall she stood in her blue gown and white headdress, but her haunches seemed heavier of late, while her shoulders were hunched above a shrunken bosom. That brought her neck forward like a turtle's; the green eyes blinked and peered out of sallowness which sagged. He knew how faded her blond hair was. Withal, she had lost little vigor and none of her grasp of events.

Soren had put on much weight in the last few years; his belly strained the red robe and distorted its gold embroidery. The chest on which the Wheel amulet hung remained massive. His hair and beard were full of gray; having taken off his miter, he displayed a bald spot. Yet he was no less formidable than erstwhile.

Sadness tugged at Gratillonius. "As you will," he said. "I'll have refreshments sent up, and order us a supper. We do have need to stay friends."

—When he opened the door of the upstairs room, he saw them in facing chairs, knee against knee, hands linked. Taken by surprise, they started and drew apart. He pretended he had not noticed. "Well," he said, "I'm ready for a stoup of that wine. Council-wrangling is thirsty work." He strode to the serving table, mixed himself a strong beakerful, and took a draught before turning about to confront them.

Soren's broad countenance was helmeted with defiance. Lanarvilis sat still, hands now crossed in her lap, but Gratillonius had learned over the years to read distress when it lay beneath her face.

He stayed on his feet, merely because in spite of the hot bath he felt too taut for anything else. The light of candles threw multiple shadows to make him stand forth, for dusk filled the window of the chamber and dimmed the pastoral frescoes, as if to deny that such peacefulness was real.

"Let me speak plainly," he began. "Clear 'tis to see, I hope to win you over, so you'll support my proposal tomorrow. That'll be difficult for you after today, because I put you on your honor not to reveal certain things I'm about to tell you."

"Why should we make that pledge?" Soren demanded.

"Pray patience," Lanarvilis requested gently. To Gratillonius: "Ere you give out this information, can you tell us what its nature is?"

"My reasons for believing the barbarian ebb has turned, and in years to come will flood upon us. Already this year, seaborne Saxons occupied Corbilo at the mouth of the Liger. They're bringing kinfolk from their homeland to join them."

"I know," Soren snapped. "They are laeti."

"Like the Franks in Armorica," Gratillonius retorted. "Rome had small choice in the matter. I mentioned it for what it bodes. There is worse to relate. The reason why I ask for your silence about it is that if word gets loose as to what my sources are, it could be fatal to them."

"Indeed?" answered Soren skeptically. "I know you worry yourself about the northern Scoti, and doubtless you've been wise to keep track of them, but naught has happened aside from some piracy along the Britannic shores, nor does it seem that aught else will."

Gratillonius shook his head. "You're mistaken. I've nurtured relations with the tribes in southern Hivernia for more cause than improving trade. 'Tis a listening post. My informants and…outright spies would be in grave trouble, if it become known what regular use I have made of them. Yonder King Conual of the rising star, he has no hostility of his own toward us; but he is a sworn friend of northerly King Niall. The two wouldn't likely make alliance against Rome or Ys, but neither will wittingly betray the other. Now you may remember my telling you what I found out a while back, that Niall led the reaving fleet which we destroyed."

Soren thought. "I seem to recall. What does it matter?"

"He is no petty warlord. I've discovered that he was the mastermind behind the great onslaught on the Roman Wall, sixteen years ago. Since then, and the disaster he suffered here, he's warred widely in his island. The latest news I've received makes me sure that this is the year when he intends to complete and consolidate his conquests there. After that—what? I expect he will look further. And…he has never forgotten what Ys did to him. He has vowed revenge."

Soren scowled and tugged his beard. Lanarvilis ventured: "Can he ever master naval strength to match ours? Besides a few crude galleys, what have the Scoti other than leather boats? Where is their discipline, their coordinated command?"

Gratillonius sighed. "My dear," he told her—and saw how she almost imperceptibly winced—"like too many people, you're prone to suppose that because barbarians are ignorant of some things we know, they must be stupid. Niall will bide his chance. What he may devise, I cannot foresee, but best would be if we kept him always discouraged. I'm sending my man Rufinus back to Hivernia this summer. His mission will be to learn as much about what is going on as he can; and he's a wily one, you know. If he can do Niall a mischief, so much the better. You'll both understand that this is among those matters whereof you must keep silence."

She nodded.

"Aye," Soren agreed reluctantly, "but you've not shown us that Ys will have need of more navy, let alone that she turn it over to Rome."

Gratillonius drew breath. "What I have to tell you will become generally known in the course of time," he said. "However, by then the hour may be late for us. I've had passed on to me things that are still supposed to be state secrets. If we act on them, we must pretend we are acting on our own initiative. Else my sources will likely be cut off, and the heads of some among them, too."

Soren gave him a shrewd glance. "Apuleius Vero?"

"Among others. He wishes Ys well. Have I your silence?"

Soren hesitated an instant. "Aye," he said; and: "You know I am faithful, Grallon," said Lanarvilis.

The King took another long draught before he gripped the beaker tight, as if it were a handhold on the brink of a cliff, and told them:

"Very well. The peace between Stilicho and Alaric is patchwork. It cannot last. Stilicho made it out of necessity. Trouble is brewing in Africa and he must protect his back as best he can while he tries to deal with that. He's terminating the campaign in Britannia not because the diocese has been secured but because he needs the troops in the South. He wants them as much for protection against the Eastern Empire as against any barbarians. Meanwhile Alaric and his kind wait only to see which of the two Romes they can best attack first. Stilicho is fully aware of that. He expects that within the next several years he must begin calling in more soldiers from the frontiers. Britannia, in particular, may be denuded of defenders."

Shocked, Lanarvilis whispered, "Are you certain?"

Gratillonius jerked a nod. "Most of what I've said is plain enough, once you've given a little thought to the situation. Some of it, such as the African matter or the expectation of transferring legions—those are buried in letters to high officials. Lower officials who found ways to read them have sent the word along a network they've woven for the sake of their own survival; and one or two have passed it on to me. However, all in all, is it such a vast surprise? Is it not more or less what we could have foreseen for ourselves?"

She shivered. Soren grimaced.

Gratillonius pursued: "Think ahead, on behalf of our children and grandchildren. If Rome collapses, Scoti and Saxons will swarm into Britannia, Franks and their kin into Gallia. They'll breed like cockroaches. Here is Armorica, thinly peopled, thinly guarded. At this lonely tip of the peninsula, how long can Ys by herself hold out?"

Stillness took over the room. Night deepened in its window. The candle flames guttered.

Lanarvilis mumbled at last, her head bowed, "Yours is a grim word. I should see what documents you have, but—aye, belike we'd better think how I can change my stance tomorrow."

Soren's fist thudded on the arm of his chair. "You'd give the ships to Rome, though!" he exclaimed. "To Rome!"

"How else dare we build them at all?" Gratillonius replied, flat-voiced. "This is another warning I have from underground. Boy-Emperor Honorius starves for some way to assert himself. His guardian Stilicho is willing to indulge him, if the undertaking be such as Rome can afford. Indeed, Stilicho too would be glad of any accomplishment that impresses the West, the East, and the barbarians alike. To suppress a 'rebellion' in Ys would be easier than to dislodge the heathen Saxons in Corbilo. Nay, we must give no grounds for accusations against us, but keep ourselves too useful to Rome for it to make a sacrificial animal of us."

Soren cursed.

—He left directly after supper. "We've talked enough," he said. "Best I go home now." Gratillonius gave him a glance. The King had dispatched a messenger early on to inform Soren's wife that he would be absent this evening. "I want...to sleep on this." Gruffly: "Oh, I'll hew to my word. Tomorrow I'll urge that the Council consider your proposal more carefully, look into ways and means. But I must devise the right phrases, the more so after what position I took today, eh? Also, remember I'm not sure yet of your rightness, only sure that I disbelieve we've need of everything you want. However, goodnight, Grallon."

He took Lanarvilis's hand and bent slightly above the veins that lumped blue in it. "Rest you well, my lady," he said low. Releasing her, he stumped fast across the mosaic floor of the atrium to the exit. A servant scurried to let him out and hail a boy to light his way with a lantern.

"Good dreams to you, Soren," Lanarvilis had breathed after him.

These had been useful hours, Gratillonius thought, and the meal at the end was amicable. He had won about as much agreement as he had hoped. Next came further maneuvers, bargainings, compromises....He might finally get half what he asked for, which was why he asked for as much as he did....With luck, work might commence year after next, which was why he began asking this early....Aye, time has made this bluff soldier into a very politician, he thought; and realized he had thought in Ysan.

He turned his gaze back to Lanarvilis. Time was being less kind to her, he mused. But then, she was a dozen years older than he.

"Wish you likewise to leave?" he dropped into a silence that felt suddenly lengthy. "I'll summon an escort."

"Are you weary?" she replied.

"Nay. Belike my sleep'll be scant. If you care to talk further, I'd—I have always valued your counsel, Lanarvilis."

"Whether or not I agreed with you?"

"Mayhap most when you disagreed. How else shall I learn?"

She smiled the least bit. "There speaks our Gratillonius. Not that argument has ever swayed him far off his forechosen path." She wiped her brow. "'Tis warm in here. Might we go outside for a span?"

He understood. Sweats came upon her without warning, melancholy, cramps; her courses had become irregular; the Goddess led her toward the last of womankind's Three Crossroads. "Surely. We're fortunate that the weather's mild."

They went forth, side by side. Soren had not actually required a lantern, for a full moon was up. When that happened on a quarter day, the King lawfully absented himself from his monthly stay in the Wood. Light fell ashen-bright on the paths that twisted through the walled garden, between hedges, topiaries, flowerbeds, bowers. At this season they were mostly bare; limbs and twigs threw an intricacy of shadows. The air was quiescent, with a hint of frost. Crushed shell scrunched softly underfoot.

How often he had wandered like this, with one or another of his women, since that springtime when first he did with Dahilis.

"Do you feel better?" he asked presently.

"Aye, thank you," said Lanarvilis.

"Ah, how fares Julia?"

"Well. Happy in her novitiate." Abrupt bitterness: "Why do you ask?"

Taken aback, he could merely say, "Why, I wanted to know. My daughter that you bore me—"

"You could have met with her occasionally. 'Twould have made her happy."

"Nay, now, she's a sweet girl. If only I had the time to spare—for her, for all my girls."

"You have it for Dahut."

That stung. He halted. She would have gone on, but he caught her arm. They faced each other in the moonlight.

"Well you know, Dahut suffered a loss she cannot even talk about," he rasped. "She's needed help to heal her sorrow. I've provided what poor distractions I could think of, in what few hours I could steal from the hundreds of folk who clamor after me."

"She's had well-nigh a year to recover, and been amply blithe during most of it." Lanarvilis yielded. She looked off into the dark. "Well, let's not quarrel. She is the child of Dahilis, and we Sisters love her too."

Her tone plucked at him. He took her hands. They felt cold in his. "You are a good person, Lanarvilis," he said clumsily.

"One tries," she sighed. "You do yourself."

Impulse: "Would you like to spend the night here?"

How long since they had last shared a bed? More than a year. As much as two? He realized in a rush what small heed he had paid to the matter. He would simply hear from another of the Nine that Lanarvilis was giving up her turn with him. That happened from time to time with any of them, for any of numerous causes. They decided it among themselves and quietly informed him. When he did call at the house of Lanarvilis, they would dine and talk, but she gave him to understand that she felt indisposed. He agreed without disappointment. Return to the palace and a night alone had its own welcome qualities, unless he elected to go rouse someone else. Guilvilis was always delighted to please him, Maldunilis willing, Forsquilis and Tambilis usually downright eager.

Her gaze and her voice held level. "Do you wish me to?"

"Well, we did intend speaking further of this statecraft business, and, and you are beautiful." He did not altogether lie, seeing her by moonlight.

She blinked at tears, brushed lips over his, and murmured, "Aye, let us once again."

—They had left the window unshuttered, undraped. Moonlight mottled rumpled bedclothes and unclothed bodies.

"I'm sorry," he said. "I hoped 'twould give you pleasure."

"I hoped so too," she answered. "'Twas not your fault."

He had, in fact, tried for some time to rouse her, until the Bull broke free of restraint and worked Its will. Her continued dryness had made the act painful to her.

"We've had a troublous day," he said. "Tomorrow morning?"

"Nay, better we sleep as late as we can. That meeting will be contentious."

"Nonetheless—"

"Confess we it to ourselves and the Gods, I have grown old."

Bodilis is just a year or two younger! speared through him. *She would be glad of me!*

It was as if an outside voice came: "Would you feel otherwise with Soren?"

Lanarvilis gasped and sat bolt upright. "What do you ask?"

"Naught, naught," he said, immediately regretful. "You are right, we should go to sleep."

He recognized the steel: "Do you dare imagine...he and I...would commit sacrilege?"

"Nay, never, certainly never." Gratillonius sat up also, drew breath, laid a hand on her shoulder. "I should have kept silence. I did for many years. But I do see and hear better than you seem to suppose. There is love between you twain."

She stared at him through the moon-tinged dark.

He smiled lopsidedly. "Why should I resent it? The Gods sealed your fate ere ever I reached Ys. You have been loyal. That's as much as a centurion can ask."

"You can still surprise me," she said as if talking in dreams.

"Indeed, I'd not really take it amiss if you and he—"

Horror snatched her. She clapped a palm across his mouth. "Quiet! You're about to utter blasphemy!"

To that he felt wholly indifferent. He grew conscious of how tired he was. "Well, we need never speak of this again."

"Best not." She lay down. "Best we try to sleep. Soren and I—we've left any such danger behind. It is too late for us."

502

"Nay," Keban said. "Don't."

"What?" Budic dropped his arms from her waist and stepped back. "Again?"

"I'm sorry," she said miserably. "I feel unwell."

The soldier stared at his wife. Several days of field exercises had sent him home ardent, the moment Adminius gave furlough. "What's the matter? A fever, a bellyache, what?"

Keban drooped her head. "I feel poorly."

He regarded her for a space. She stood slumped, her paunch protruding; jowls hung sallow down to the double chin; but that was no change from what she had become during the past four or five years. Nor was her hair, unkempt and greasy, or the sour smell of an unwashed body, or the soiled gown in need of mending. Yet the bones beneath, the eyes, the lips, remained comely; and he remembered.

"You are never quite sick," he mumbled, "and never quite in health.... Well, come on to bed, then. 'Twill not take long, and you can rest there afterward."

"Nay, please," she whimpered. "I would if I could, but not today, I beg you."

"Why not?"

She rallied spirit enough to retort: "Shall I puke while you're banging away in me? I am sorry, but I do feel queasy, and the smells—your breath, your cheese— Mayhap tomorrow, dear."

"Always tomorrow!" he shouted. "Can you no longer even spread your legs for me? You did for every lout in Ys when you were a whore!"

She shrank against the wall. He waved around at the room. Dust grayed heaped objects, strewn clothes, unscoured kitchenware. "May I at least have a clean house, that I needn't be ashamed to invite my friends to?" he cried on. "Nay. Well, be it as you will."

She began to weep. "Budic, I love you." He would not let himself listen, but stalked out the door and slammed it behind him.

The street bustled beneath a heartlessly bright sun. He thrust along its serpentine narrowness, through the shabby district it served. When acquaintances hailed him, he gave curt response. There were temptations to stop and chat, for several were female, wives or daughters of neighbors....But that could lead to sin, and trouble, and possibly deadly quarrels. Let him just find a cheap harlot in Tomcat Alley or the Fishtail or walking these lanes.

Keban would understand. She'd better. She oughtn't to inquire where he'd been. Still, her sobs might keep him awake tonight—

Budic halted. "Christ have mercy," he choked in Latin. "What am I doing?"

It throbbed in his loins. Relief would allow him to repent. But the Church taught that God did not bargain. The pagans of Ys bought off their Taranis, Lir, lustful Belisama with sacrifices; but only offerings made with a contrite heart were acceptable to the Lord God of Israel.

Budic turned on his heel and strode, almost running, to the Forum.

How wickedly merry and colorful the throng was that eddied and swirled over its mosaic pavement, around the basins of the Fire Fountain, between the colonnades of the public buildings! A merchant passed by in sumptuous tunic, a marine soldier in metal and pride. A maiden with a well-laden market basket on her head had stopped to trade jokes with a burly young artisan on his way to a job. A Suffete lady, followed by a servant, wore a cloak of the finest blue wool, worked with white gold emblems of moon and stars; her thin face was bent over a pet ferret she carried in her arms. Silken-clad and Venus-beautiful, a meretrix lured a visiting Osismian who looked moneyed as well as wonder-smitten. An old scholar came down the steps of the library bearing scrolls that must be full of arcane lore. A vendor offered smoked oysters, garlicky snails, spiced fruits, honeycakes. A shaggy Saxon and a kilted Scotian, off ships in trade, weaved drunkenly along, arm in arm. Music lilted through babble and clatter. It came from a troupe of performers, their garb as gaudy as their bearing, on the stairs to the fane of Taranis; flute and syrinx piped, harp twanged, drum thuttered, a girl sang sultry verses while another—shamelessly half-clad in what might be a remotely Egyptian style—rattled her sistrum and undulated through a dance. Young men stood beneath, stared, whooped, threw coins, burned.

The Christian forced his way forward. At the church he was alone.

That former temple of Mars had changed its nature more than once. Entering by the western door, Budic found the marble of the vestibule not only clean but polished. The wooden wall that partitioned off the sanctum in Eucherius's day had been replaced by stone, dry-laid as Ysan law required but elegantly shaped and fitted. Inset murals displayed the Chi Rho, Fish, and Good Shepherd. Corentinus had left the sanctum austerely furnished, which he felt was becoming. However, the cross now on the altar had been intricately carved, with skill and love, by a Celtic believer, and was trimmed with beaten gold. An organ had been installed. It was not that the present chorepiscopus had made many converts in Ys, though he had done much better than his predecessor; and those he had drawn to Christ—like Keban—were generally poor. But the resurgence of trade brought a substantial number of believers to the city each year; and there were some who took up residence as representatives of mercantile interests; and Corentinus was not a man whom one could fob off when he suggested making a donation.

The deacon who greeted Budic was a strong young Turonian whose call sent echoes ringing. "Hail, brother!" He used Latin. "May I help you?"

Budic wet his lips. "Can I see...the pastor?"

504

"You're in luck. In weather like this he's apt to go for a twenty-mile ramble, if he isn't ministering to the needy or whatever. But he has Church business to handle today, letters and accounts and such." The deacon laughed. "If he minds being interrupted, I've guessed wrong. Hold, brother, while I go ask."

Left by himself, Budic shifted from foot to foot, wondered how to say what he wanted to and whether he wanted to, tried to pray and found the words sticking in his throat.

The deacon returned. "Go, with God's blessing," he said.

Budic knew the way through corridors to the room where Corentinus worked, studied, cooked his frugal meals, slept on his straw pallet, practiced his private devotions. This likewise had seen improvement since Eucherius; it was equally humble, but shipshape. The door stood open. Budic entered timidly. Corentinus swiveled about on his stool, away from a table littered with papyrus and writing-shingles. "Welcome, my son," he said. "Be seated."

"Father—" Budic coughed. "Father, c-could we talk in private?"

"Close the door if you like. God will hear. What is your wish?"

Instead of taking another stool, Corentinus went on his knees before the big gray man. "Father, help me!" he begged. "Satan has me snared."

Corentinus's mouth twitched slightly upward, though his tone soothed. "Oh, now, it may not be quite that bad. I know you rather well, I think." He laid a hand on the blond head. "If you have strayed, I doubt it's been very far. Let us pray together."

They stood up. His voice lifted. Budic wavered through responses.

It was immensely heartening. Afterward he could speak, though he must pace to and fro, striking fist in palm, looking away from him who sat and listened.

"—we were happy once, she new in the Faith, we both new in our marriage—

"—since she lost our baby five years ago, and would have died herself, if you hadn't fetched Queen Innilis—

"—denies me. She pleads poor health...says that's why she's such a slattern—

"—lust like a beast's. Sometimes I've just forced her—

"—God forgive me if He can. I've thought how much easier it would be if she had died then—

"—today I set off in search of a whore—"

He wept. Corentinus comforted him. "You are sorely tried, my son. Satan does beset your soul. But you have not surrendered to him, not yet, nor shall you. Heaven stands always ready to send reinforcements."

—In the end, Corentinus said: "The harder the battle, the more splendid the victory. Many a man, and woman also, has suffered like you. But in trouble lies opportunity. Marriage was instituted by God not for pleasure but for the propagation of mortal mankind. Sacrifice of the pleasure is pleasing to Him. No few Christian couples, man and wife, have made this offering. They give up carnal relationships and live as brother and sister, that He be glorified. Can you do that, Budic? Certainly a childless marriage—and it's clear that poor Keban has gone barren—such a marriage thwarts—no, I won't say it thwarts the divine purpose, but it is...immaterial to salvation at best, self-indulgence at worst. If you and she, instead, unite in the pure love of God—it won't be easy, Budic. Well do I know it won't be easy. I cannot command you in this, I can only counsel you. But I beg you to think. Think how little you have now, how impoverished and sordid it is; then think how infinitely much you might have, and how wonderful, forever."

—Budic left the church. The sun had moved well down the sky since he entered. Corentinus's benediction tolled in his head.

Blindly, he walked up Lir Way and out High Gate. Twice he almost collided with a wagon. The drivers swore at him.

He had made no vow. He believed he hoped he would grow able to, but first the turmoil in him must somehow come to rest. A dirt road, scarcely more than a track, went from Aquilonian Way on the right, toward heights above the valley. He turned off onto it, wanting a place where he could be alone with God.

Everywhere around him swelled the young summer. Air lay at rest, its warmth full of odors: earth, greenery, flowers. A cuckoo called, over and over, like the sound of a mother laughing with her newborn. Trees enclosed the path, yew, chestnut, elm, their leaves overarching it in gold-green; sunlight spattered the shade they cast. Between them he had an ever wider view across Ys of the towers, Cape Rach with its sternness softened by verdancy, tumultuous salt blue beyond. Birds skimmed, butterflies danced. Distantly, from one of the estates that nestled on the hillside, he heard a cow bellow; she was love-sick.

Hoofs thudded. Around a bend came a party of riders.

Budic stepped aside. They trotted near, half a dozen young men on spirited horses, their faces wind-flushed—Suffete faces, mostly, but Budic recognized Carsa's among them, the Roman youth who was spending another season here, studying under learned men of the city while he worked to get a commercial outpost well established. They were all lightly and brightly clad. Mirthfulness sparkled from them.

In the van was a horse that Budic also recognized: Favonius, the King's most splendid stallion, already the champion of races in the amphitheater and overland. He whickered and curvetted. The star on his head blazed snowy against the sorrel sheen of his coat.

Upon his back sat Princess Dahut. A woman should not ride an entire, Budic thought confusedly; it was especially dangerous at the wrong time of the month. Gratillonius should not have allowed this. But who could refuse Dahut? She might have been a centauress, as fluidly as she and the animal moved together. Her clothes were a boy's, loose tunic and tight breeches, daring if not forbidden for a girl on an exiguous saddle whose knees guided as much as her hands did. Oh, blue-streaked alabaster tapering down to rosy nails...heavy amber braids, lapis lazuli eyes...

She reined in. Her followers did the same. "Why, Budic," she called. At fourteen and a half years of age, she had lost the lark sweetness of voice that had been hers as a child; the tones came husky, but sang true. "'Tis gladsome to see you. Had you not enough tramping about on maneuvers? What beckoned you hither?"

He stood dumb. An Ysan youth said glibly, "What but the chance of encountering you, my lady?"

She laughed and dismissed the flattery with a flick of fingers. "How went the practicing?" she asked. Looking closer: "You've a sadness on you, Budic. That should not be, on so beautiful a day."

"'Tis naught," he said. "Do not trouble yourself, my lady."

"Oh, but I do. Am I not the Luck of the legionaries?" Dahut's smile grew tender. "'Twould be wrong to query you further, here. May Belisama be kind to you, brave man of my father's, friend of mine.... Forward!" And that was a trumpet cry. The party went on, recklessly fast, back toward Ys.

Budic stared their way a long while after they had vanished from his sight. It was as if a new fragrance lingered in the air.

When Innilis saved Keban's life, I swore I would always be at the beck of the Gallicenae, he thought slowly. Pastor Corentinus didn't like that. Could it be that God has punished me for it? But why? What can be wrong about serving you, Dahut, daughter of my centurion, Dahut, Dahut?

~ 3 ~

At last all was ready. On the mound of the Goddess Medb at Temir, Niall of the Nine Hostages held a mighty slaughter. Smoke rose to heaven from the fires where the beasts cooked, and folk gorged themselves on the meat until many had prophetic dreams. In the morning the host assembled and went north.

Glorious was that sight. In the van rolled the chariots of Niall and his three oldest living sons, Conual Gulban, Éndae, and Éogan. Their horses neighed and pranced, lovely to behold, each team perfectly matched in color of white, black, roan, or dapple gray, plumes on their heads above the flowing manes, bronze hangings ajingle and aflash. The cars gleamed with gold, silver, brass, polished iron. The drivers were only less brilliantly garbed than the riders, who stood tall beside their spar-high spears, cloaks blowing back from their finery like rainbow wings. Behind came the chariots of the nobles, and then on foot the giant warriors of the guard, whose helmets, axheads, spearheads shone sun-bright and rippled to their gait as a grainfield ripples under the summer wind. The tenant levies followed, tumultuous, and the lumbering oxcarts and lowing, bleating herds of the supply train. On the flanks, to and fro, galloped wild young outriders. Clamor rang from horizon to horizon, horns, rattle and clank, shouts, footfalls, hoofbeats, wheel-groan, and overhead the hoarse ravens who sensed that war was again on its way.

At Mag Slecht, Niall paused for another sacrifice. It depleted his cattle and sheep, but he would soon be in Qóiqet nUlat and living off the country. The campaign should not take many days, if all went well, though afterward he and his sons would be long occupied in bringing their sword-land to heel. Meanwhile Cromb Cróche got His blood-feast.

Summoned beforehand, the Aregésla joined him there in numbers greater than he had brought himself. Their chieftains were eager for a share in the fighting, glory, and spoils. Niall warned them sternly to keep obedient to him and make no important move without his leave. Maybe they would heed.

First the warriors traveled west, to bypass a huge stockpen at the Doors of Emain Macha, for it was a strongpoint that would have cost them precious time. A courier brought word that allies were on the move, kinsmen of Niall's in Condacht who had pledged him help. He hastened his pace as much as could be. It was well and good for the Firi Chondachtae to subdue the Ulatach hinterlands, taking their reward in booty, but he wanted to be in possession of the royal seat and its halidoms—the power—before they got there.

After he turned north and later east, sharp fights began, as tuaths rallied against the invaders. He went through them, over them, scarcely checked. More difficult were the many earthworks, the Walls of the Ulati. Garrisons sallied from the hill forts or sent arrows and slingstones in murderous flocks from the tops of earthen ramparts. Most lords would have squandered men trying to take each of these, while Fergus Fogae gathered force to himself at Emain Macha from his entire realm. Niall, who had learned from his battles with the Romans, simply bypassed them. Nowhere stood a cliff of stone from sea to sea, such as had balked him in Britannia. At worst, it was easier to struggle through woods and bogs than to overrun well-entrenched defenders. They could be left for later attention.

In the end, after pushing across the gently rolling countryside, leaving havoc behind, Niall reached the outer guardian of Emain Macha itself. A few miles short of his goal, this wall reared high and green to right and left, as far as eye could see. Where the road made a break, forti-fications hulked on either side, aswarm with armed men. They howled and jeered at the oncoming enemy.

Niall called a halt some distance off. As camp was being pitched, he summoned three of the Aregéslach leaders. "Now you shall prove your worthiness," he told them. "After dark, take a number of your followers aside—quietly, now. Go well off to north or south; we will decide which. At first light, storm the wall. Agile men can climb the embankment, and the seeing will be poor for Ulatach archers. With such a surprise, you can get across at not too great a cost. You will have a running fight, but hasten back to this road and attack at the rear."

It seemed a risky venture, but they could not show doubt before the tall, golden man. Their plans being laid, they in their turn egged on their folk until brawls broke out over who should have the right to go.

Before dawn, wind was driving rain in gray spear-flights. Niall had foreseen this by the clouds and made it part of his scheme. When scouts dashed back to tell of combat noises, he had the horns blown, and his host advanced. Unsure how big the troop was that had assailed them from behind, the Ulati gave it more heed than was necessary. While they were thus bewildered, Niall smote them head-on.

Terrible was the struggle in that strait passage, but also brief it was. With axes and swords athunder at the flanks of their horses, the chariots rolled through and, once in the open again, began harvesting. Romans would not have boiled from their stronghold, desperate, but Niall knew his Gaels. His men seized the chance, forced their way into the works, and laid about them. After some unmeasured time of uproar, he held the guardpoint. Rain ceased, clouds parted, sunbeams struck, carrion birds feasted.

Niall stopped for a day, that he might take stock while his people tended their wounded, buried their dead, and celebrated their victory. The way to Emain Macha stood open, but well he knew that word had flown thither and warfare remained to do. He wanted his host fully prepared. This work included heaping praise on the three Aregésla in the hearing of many and bestowing on them gold, weapons, promises of dominion and high rank. He was careful, though, to keep it clear that his sons would always be above them.

Thereafter he moved onward. King Fergus came forth against him. The armies met on a field which ever afterward bore the name Achat Lethderg—the Place of the Red Goddess, Medb of Temir.

There did Niall break the Ulati. Throughout that day the battle crashed and snarled. Edges grew blunt with striking, men grew so weary that they staggered about, horses that had been stabbed or hamstrung screamed while wounded warriors fought to keep their pain to themselves, wheels and hoofs and feet trampled earth into mud and the fallen into shapelessness from which jutted shards of bone. At last terror came upon the Ulati, and such of them as were able fled any way they could while such of the Firi Mide and Aregésla as were able pursued them like hounds a deer, cutting at them and laughing in glee. Behind them they left their King Fergus, dead in the wreckage of his chariot, and comrades beyond counting. So did Niall prevail.

Too weary for more thanksgiving than a muttered dedication to the Gods of those Ulatach captives whose throats they cut, the warriors dragged themselves into fireless circles and slept where they dropped. In the morning Niall left most of them behind to rest and prepare proper honors for their fallen. With Conual Gulban, Éndae, Éogan, and enough guards to be safe from attack, he drove ahead for a look at Emain Macha.

This was a bright day. Wind whooped over meadows and shaws, which glowed intensely green. Small white clouds ran before it, and birds in their jubilant hundreds. Here and there, water gleamed like silver. Though the air was cool, along it flowed smells of loam, leaves, blossoms, growth—summer. Good it was to ride at ease, taking some stiffness out of the hard-used flesh by balancing against jounce and sway, calling merrily to each other, as charioteers tried which team could show the most paces and prances: they, the victors.

Smoke stained heaven. Niall scowled. "That can only be Emain Macha burning," he said. "Hurry now."

They topped a hill and looked across to the drumlin beyond. There on the ridge, behind its earthworks, the ancient seat of the Ulatach Kings was, and flames consumed the buildings within. "Stop," Niall told his driver Cathual. In a voice gone heavy: "The Ulati themselves have done this. They knew they could not hold it, and would not let us have it."

"So they are indeed brought low!" cried Éogan.

His father shook a silvering head and murmured, "I did not mean the war to end thus. Here something great is perishing. But you are too young to understand."

Higher and higher raged the fires. The smoke of them blackened half the sky. It roiled and swirled, that smoke; uneasy red light played on it from below; shapes came and went within it, darkling visions. Were they chariots that ascended on the wind, and in them Conchobar, Cú Culanni, Amargin, Ferbaide, and more and more, the heroes of the Red Branch departing forever? The sounds of flames afar was like all Ériu keening for her beloved, her defenders.

Chill struck into Niall. He fought it off. "Well," he said, "for good or ill, this is the end of an age. The new one belongs to you, my dears."

Nevertheless he kept himself at the head of things. Notwithstanding that Conual, Éndae, and Éogan would be kings over these conquests, much was left to do before they were firmly in power. He must quell the Ulati who still resisted, and make allies agree to a share of spoils neither unfair nor overly large. Niall did not think he could return home before Lúgnassat, if then.

He even thought about pushing on after the enemy. It was against his better judgment. Driven into corners, the Ulati would be as dangerous as trapped wolves; meanwhile the Midach host would melt away, because men must go back for harvest and other work. What Niall and his sons had won should be ample for their lifetimes. To overreach would be to court the anger of the Gods. Yet...Domnuald was unavenged.

Thus it was with a certain relief that Niall received a present from one of his Condachtach kin when they met. This man had been in a clash to the southwest, where his folk overtook a ragtag company living

510

off the land. Prisoners said its leader, who fell in combat, was Fland Dub maqq Ninnedo, who had fled to league himself with Fergus Fogae. Remembering that Niall had set a price on the head of Fland, the Condachtach chieftain brought it as a gift.

Niall made lavish return. Later, alone by lamplight in his tent, he stared long at the withered thing. Was it indeed what remained of his son's killer? Men lied, perhaps most often to themselves. They said what others wanted to hear, or their hearts did, and soon believed it. How could he know? In the meantime he could only bring home this head to show, which he had not taken with his own hands. It was a thin revenge.

III

~ 1 ~

Morning mist followed a night's rain. The Rock of Cassel reared out of it against gray heaven. Seen from below, blurred to vision, the castle on top no longer looked stark. It was as elven as Ys glimpsed across the sea.

Rufinus and Tommaltach paced the ruts of a road near the foot of the upthrust. Pasture lay empty, a drenched green on either side. Sometimes a sheep bleated out in the blindness that closed in after a few yards. The men could be quite sure that nobody overheard them.

Although each took every chance to practice the language of the other, today each spoke his own—if Ysan be reckoned as Rufinus's; for it is easier to be exact when the tongue moves in familiar ways. "You understand, then," the Redonian said. "I am not here, once again, simply to talk about further trade arrangements, now the Roman expeditionary force is departing Britannia. Trade could take care of itself. My mission is to gather intelligence for my lord, King Grallon."

Tommaltach's young visage writhed. He gripped his spear tighter. "I'll not be betraying King Conual."

"Certainly never." Rufinus stroked fingers across the hand that held the shaft. "Have I not explained, have you not seen for yourself, there is not conflict? 'Tis Niall in the North who'd fain destroy Ys—Ys where you keep memories and friends and dreams dear to you."

"But Niall and Conual are—"

"They are not enemies. Nor are they blood brothers. They have a fosterage in common, little else. Besides, Grallon seeks not the destruction of Niall. He merely wants forewarning, so he can be prepared to fend off any assault."

"What you mean to do is, is underhanded!"

Rufinus laughed. "Truly? Think. Having learned that Niall will likely be gone for some while, I propose to fare up to his country and see whatever I can see, hear whatever I can hear. No more. 'Tis only that in his absence I, a man from Ys, can travel freer than would else be the case. Conual has already given me leave. Indeed, he's charged me with carrying gifts and messages to various people."

"But he supposes—"

"He supposes I will be exploring the possibility of peace and commerce." Rufinus shrugged, spreading his palms wide. "Well, is that a falsehood? Grallon would welcome the event. To you and yonder boulder, I confess 'tis unlikely in the extreme. Conual has told me the same. Yet there is no possibility whatsoever ere we know more about the circumstances at Temir. I am just staying discreet."

Tommaltach sighed and gave in. "You'll be needing guides," he said. "Sure, and I wish I could be that, but we have another season of war ahead of us here, until himself has gotten the oaths he wants."

"I know. May the Gods shield you." Rufinus was silent for a dozen paces. "Guides will be easy enough to engage. And I doubt anybody without powerful cause will attack a band of Ysan marines. I've confided in you, good friend, not because I wish your aid today, but because in future we can help one another."

Tommaltach gulped. "How can that be?"

Rufinus tugged the forks of his beard in succession. "You are son to a tuathal king, and a warrior who has won some fame. Men heed you. Our ships that lie waiting to bear us home—can they be protected by a gess as well as a guard? You could lay one. Also, I am no druid, to read the morrow. It could be that we return here under...difficult conditions. I know not what they may be, but a strong voice in our favor might prove invaluable.

"In exchange— Well, I've spoken with King Grallon. He'd like having a man from Mumu reside in Ys, to handle such matters as may arise concerning Scoti. 'Twould encourage commerce, and thus be to our advantage. Now we understand that this is a thought foreign to your folk, and so we would undertake to support such a man ourselves for the first several years, with a generous stipend—"

Tommaltach gasped. He stubbed his toe, nearly fell, came to a halt, and cried, "I could live in Ys?"

"You could that," Rufinus said, "and be welcome everywhere, among both commoners and Suffetes, on into the presence of the King and his wives and daughters."

~ 2 ~

By Hivernian standards, the estate of Laidchenn maqq Barchedo was magnificent. Southward it looked down a sweep of meadow to an argent streak that was the River Ruirthech; beyond, vague in vision as a fairyland, reached the country of the Lagini, which Rufinus had skirted on his way north. Elsewhere he saw more grazing for great herds of cattle and sheep; shielings near their small fields of oats or barley; woodlots, coppices, primeval forest in the distance. Rain-washed, the land gleamed smaragdine, incredibly lush, under a sky that had gone deep blue save for white flocks of cloud.

Rufinus had the idea from what he had heard that Laidchenn did not actually own this acreage in freehold, as a dweller in the hinterland of Ys owned his home ground, nor as a creature of the state like a Roman on his latifundium. Earth in Ériu was inalienable from the tribe that occupied it, unless a conqueror drove that tribe out altogether. However, King Níall had bestowed the trust here on Laidchenn, from which flowed rich proceeds. Likely the people were pleased. These barbarians revered learned men as much as had the olden Greeks. Laidchenn could safely dwell so near the ancient foes of Mide because a poet was inviolable.

Approaching from the west, Condacht now several days behind him, Rufinus saw a house, long, rectangular in form, loom above its surrounding outbuildings. Moss and flowers brightened its thatch, over peeled studs and whitewashed cob. Hazel trees grew round about; Rufinus recalled that they were not only prized for their nuts, they were believed to be magical.

Hounds clamored but did not attack. Shepherd boys and the like had long since spied the Ysans and dashed to bring word of them. The few armed men who came forth did not act threateningly. At their head were two without weapons. One, thickset, bushy red hair and beard beginning to blanch, carried a rod from which hung pieces of metal that could jangle together, and wore a tunic and cloak whereon the number of the colors showed his rank to be just below the royal. The second was young, brown-haired, pockmarked, more plainly clad, but otherwise resembled the first.

Rufinus's followers kept their seats. It was politic for him to dismount. Leaping down, he raised an arm and said, "Greeting. I am Rufinus maqq Moribanni of Gallia across the water, come here from King Conual Corcc in Mumu, who asked me that I bear word from him to his dear friend, the ollam poet Laidchenn maqq Barchedo. Long have we traveled, inquiring our way. Have I the honor of addressing himself?"

"You do that," said the aging man. "From Conual, are you, now? A thousand welcomes!" He stepped forward, embraced the newcomer, and kissed him on both cheeks.

"You give me more respect than is my due," Rufinus said. "Forgive me if I, a foreigner, am ignorant of the courtesies proper for my great host."

Laidchenn took the bait, though quite likely he would in any case have replied: "You are indeed my guests, you and your men, Rufinus maqq Moribanni, and under my protection. Come, be at ease, let my

513

household see to your needs. Whatever wishes you harbor that we can fulfill, you have but to let us know."

There followed the usual bustle. In the course of it, Laidchenn introduced his companion, who proved to be his oldest son and student Tigernach, and put some innocent-sounding questions about how the strangers had fared and what brought them to these parts. Rufinus appreciated the shrewdness with which his social standing was ferreted out. He took care to slip in a mention that besides speaking the Roman language, he could read and write it; the latter, at least, he would be glad to demonstrate if anyone was interested. This learning placed him immediately under a poet, more or less equal to a druid or a brithem judge. As for his purposes, that was a long story. Wisest was he that he confer with his host before relating it at the feast which Laidchenn had ordered. Some of it might not be suitable for all ears. "Thus, blame not my followers if they are close-mouthed at first. They are not being unfriendly; they are under gess until I can give leave. Anyhow, they know little of the Érennach language, and nothing of the Midach dialects. You hear how awkward my tongue is."

"You do very well," said Laidchenn graciously, "while I lack all Latin."

He put no urgency on his guests, except in making them as comfortable as might be. Rufinus had taken hospitality as he found it in the island, from a herdsman's cabin to the hall of a tribal king, but not since leaving Castellum had he encountered any like this. After a bite of food and drink of ale, he was brought to a bathhouse to steam himself clean. On coming out, he found fresh clothes waiting. The attendant explained that women had taken his own down to a brook to wash, and these were his too. He would have private sleeping quarters: a small bedroom among several in the main building, formed by partitions that did not reach the roof but were amply high. The attendant said a girl was available if desired, and added she was pretty, skilled, and more than happy to make the close acquaintance of a man from abroad. Rufinus replied that he was grateful, but at the moment he had too much wish to meet with the poet. He selected a carnelian brooch from the city's finest jeweler to take along, as a preliminary gift in return for the garments. At the feast he would make his real presentations.

Laidchenn received him in a hut outside, well furnished in a rough fashion. "This is for when I would be by myself to think and compose, or speak with someone privately," he said. "But since the day is beautiful, shall we walk about instead?"

No guards followed. He had no need of any. Those men of his who met the new arrivals had taken weapons simply to mark his dignity. Soon he and his visitor were sauntering alone over the grass. Bees buzzed in clover, which nodded white heads in answer to what the wind whispered. A lark caroled high aloft.

"Now what would you be telling me?" Laidchenn asked.

Rufinus had rehearsed his speech in his mind, careful not to wax fulsome. "I have told how I carry greetings from Conual Corcc. In my baggage are gifts he charged me with bringing you. His affairs prosper, and he wishes the same for his foster-kinsman King Niall and yourself. I have much more to make known, but that can be said before everyone.

"I cannot call on Niall. First, the word they have down in Mumu is that he is making war on the Ulati and will not likely return until late in the autumn, or even winter. Second, it would be rash of me. I will not lie to you; that would cast shame on us both. Here I tell that I am a Gaul as I declared. But I live in Ys, whose King I serve, and my companions are warriors of his."

"Ys!" burst out of Laidchenn. He stopped in midstride, swung around, stared and then glowered.

"Hear me, I beg you."

"I must," Laidchenn growled. "You are my guest."

"Dismiss me if you will; but first please hear me out. Remember, I come by way of King Conual. By and large, Mumu has had good dealings with Ys; and you yourself are a man of Mumu, are you not? My mission was to talk about furtherance of trade and other such matters of common interest. Hearing of Niall's absence, I thought perhaps the Gods had brought me to Ériu in the same year. Well does the King of Ys know what a bitter foe he has in King Niall. He does not share that feeling. He would far rather make peace and become friends. My thought was that here I had a chance to fare north and speak with leading men, who might afterward convey my message, and meanwhile give me an idea as to what hope there is for reconciliation. Conual did not believe it possible, but he approved my intention, and suggested I seek you first, you being the wisest." The scar on Rufinus's cheek contorted with his smile. He spread his arms, baring his breast. "Here I am."

Laidchenn eased his stance. He nodded heavily. "I fear Conual Corcc is right. Niall of the Nine Hostages does not forgive."

"Still, enemies also often exchange words."

"True." Laidchenn ruffled his beard and pondered. "May long life be glorious Niall's, he who has been so generous to me. Yet the Mórrigu has Her own dark ways—as all the Gods do Theirs—and each of us must someday die, and new men bring new times....Knowledge is a drink that never quenches need for itself." Abruptly, enthusiasm blazed from him. "And you dwell in Ys! Ys of the hundred towers!" He seized both Rufinus's hands in his. "You shall stay with me as long as you desire, and we will talk, and—and maybe I can do more than that."

"You are—how does one say 'magnanimous?'—yours is a spirit as large as the sky." It was an odd feeling to Rufinus to realize he meant it.

Thereafter he set himself to charm the natives. That was easy. For the most part, he told about the fabulous city. They bore no special hostility to it. Some had lost kinsman in Niall's fleet, but that was fifteen years ago, seeming now a whim of war and weather; few remained whose memories of the perished were sharp. They would follow Niall if bidden, but the undying hatred was his alone.

Simply by virtue of what Rufinus had learned in Ys and the Empire—he, the runaway serf, bandit, scout, who had picked up his information in fragments, like a magpie—he was reckoned an ollam. Laidchenn conversed familiarly with him, Tigernach eagerly and deferentially, the visiting chieftains and judges almost shyly, everybody else humbly. At meat he received the chine of the animal, second to the thigh served kings and poets; and sat at the upper end of the hall, on Laidchenn's right, his seat just slightly lower; and had the privilege of passing to his host every third ale horn, while Laidchenn's wife sent each third of his to him. He could go wherever he chose, even to the holiest groves, springs and rocks. His counsel and blessing were worth much more than any material goods.

His followers, the marines, benefited. Their company much sought despite their meager stock of words, they made merry with drink, women, hunts, rides, rambles, athletic contests. Rufinus's abstention from love-making raised no doubts about his virility, but instead increased the awe of him. Thus it was doubly effective that most of the time he was cheerful, amiable, as ready to greet the lowliest tenant or rumple the hair of the littlest child as to sit with the mighty and the wise.

In a few days he felt ready to drop a hint. Delightful though this was, he said, summer was wearing on. If he wished to return home with his business completed, he had better go about it, or else risk being weatherbound.

"You are right, my dear," Laidchenn replied. "I have been thinking the same. In the absence of Niall and his three oldest sons, their brother Carpre has the royal duties. He was a colt in the year of the evil, and so has scant ill will toward Ys. Mind you, I would not be saying anything against his faithfulness; but it is no secret that he chafes under his father's hand and longs to win glory for himself. That whole brood does. The eagle's blood is in them."

"Do you think, then, he will receive me?" Rufinus asked.

"He shall that," Laidchenn replied, "for I myself will go along with you."

~ 3 ~

In the high King's absence, Carpre could not reside at Temir, only visit it for ceremonies. Progressing among the homes the family owned around Mide, he was at present a day's journey from the sacred hill, beyond a river which the travelers crossed on a rude wooden bridge. That valley was very fair, with much forest for hunters and swineherds. Similar to Laidchenn's, the estate stood by itself in a great clearing to which roads led between the trees. A palisaded earthen wall, a rath, ringed it in, causing people to seek the grassy space outside for their sports.

Carpre, a young man with the blond good looks said to be his father's, took Rufinus in at Laidchenn's request. His reluctance the man from Ys deemed feigned. Though the prince doubted Niall would ever take any éricc and honor price for what had happened, and therefore no maqq Nélli could—while Niall lived—nevertheless he would consider Rufinus a herald, untouchable in anger, and hear him out. Through the days that followed, Carpre asked questions and listened as ardently as the rest of the Gaels. Again the Ysans had no dearth of frolicsome fellowship.

Again Rufinus kept aloof from it. Besides maintaining the dignity he found so useful, he did not care to waste time in romping, especially with women—time all too limited, during which he might accomplish something for Gratillonius and could at the least gather intelligence. Let him bring back such a bird, to lay at the feet of his master; let him see a smile and hear a "Well done"; then he could go rejoice in those ways that were his.

The blend of rigor and geniality continued to serve him well. At first Laidchenn showed him around, when they were free to stroll. On the second afternoon, coming back from a hallowed dolmen in the woods, they saw half a dozen men being led out the portal of the rath under guard. It was a leaden, drizzly day. Rufinus stopped. "Who are those?" he wondered.

Laidchenn frowned. "The hostages from Lagini," he said.

Rufinus looked closer. The men had nothing on but tunics of the roughest material, ragged and scruffy; hair and beards were unkempt, unwashed; faces were gaunt, limbs lank, skin sallow. The equal number of guards urged them offside and leaned contemptuous on spears while the prisoners began dispiritedly exercising.

"Oh?" Rufinus murmured. He had seen the other hostages whom Carpre had charge of, well fed, well clad, honorably treated. "Have they done wrong, that they must live like penned animals?"

"They have not," Laidchenn sighed, "unless it be the chief of them, and he a high King's son. He led a terrible raid. Niall avenged that on his entire country, yet requires this punishment, too. He knows I think it wrong. A headstrong and unforgiving man, he, indeed, indeed."

Rufinus felt a tingle go up his spine. He knew a little about the antagonism between the Lagini and their neighbors of Condacht and Mide—foremost Mide, whose founders had carved with the sword most of its territory out of theirs. "Tell me more, if you please," he said.

Laidchenn explained, laconically because they were standing in the wet and cold. At the end, Rufinus asked, "Would it be possible for to go talk with that—Yo-khith, is that how you pronounce his name?"

"Why would you?" inquired Laidchenn, surprised.

Rufinus shrugged. "Oh," he said carelessly, "you know how it is laid on me to harvest whatever knowledge I can for my lord." He laughed. "Who can tell but that Eochaid will someday be the go-between for a real peace with Niall?"

"On that day, swine will fly," snorted Laidchenn. He considered. "Well, I see no harm in your curiosity. Come."

The hostages paused to stare, like their warders, as the two approached. Rufinus's heartbeat quickened. The one whom Laidchenn had pointed out, Eochaid, was beautiful. Three discolored patches marred his face, as well as the thinness and grime of captivity, but underneath that it could have been an Apollo's, straight nose, sculptured lips, deep-set eyes whose blue seemed the more brilliant against milky skin and midnight hair. He had kept his tall body better than his companions theirs, doubtless by forcing some kind of gymnastics upon it while shut away; muscles moved feline over the bones. Rufinus felt his sullenness was not from despair, but defiance.

Laidchenn accosted the guards. They could not refuse a poet. Rufinus stepped over to Eochaid. "Greeting, King's son," he ventured.

Breath hissed between teeth. "Who are you that hail me?" The voice sounded rusty.

Aware of listeners, Rufinus declared himself. "I fear I have no ransom for you or anything like that," he added. "But as a foreigner, who is also a herald, I may be able to carry a word from you, and a word back, if you like."

The rest of the Lagini stood by like sick oxen. Eochaid snarled. "What is there to say between Niall and myself, or between myself and that man yonder whose son disfigured me with a satire so that I can never become a king?"

"Well, you can perhaps become free again," Rufinus answered. "Is that not desirable?"

Eochaid slumped. "Why should they ever let me go?"

"Perhaps to carry a message yourself. In Gallia and Britannia, we have suffered from the Saxon. Will his long ships never seek the shores of Ériu? Might it not be best that the Celts form alliance while they still can?" Rufinus reached to clap Eochaid's shoulder. A rent in the garment let his hand touch the flesh beneath. Despite the weather, it was warm, not feverish, but hot. Rufinus squeezed. "Think about it," he said. "I would like to speak further with you, if they let me."

He turned and departed, acutely conscious of the gazes that followed. At his side, Laidchenn muttered, "There was too much wisdom in your talk, my dear. Nobody will hearken."

Rufinus scarcely heard. His head was awhirl. It was not that he had any scheme. He had been acting on impulse. But maybe, maybe he could fish a prize for Gratillonius out of these gurly waters. And in any case, by Venus—no, by Belisama—it was sin to mistreat someone that beautiful!

In the course of the next several days, he sought out Eochaid whenever the Lagini were led forth. The hostage's moroseness soon melted. He became heartbreakingly grateful for news, gossip, advice, japes, whatever Rufinus offered. His fellow captives emerged a bit from their apathy, and the keepers enjoyed listening. All were disappointed when Rufinus asked permission to draw Eochaid aside where they could whisper, because he wished to put questions about the doings in Dún Alinni which Eochaid might not answer in the hearing of foemen. The chief of the guards gave his consent anyway. That was not stupidity. Besides his religious respect for a herald and ollam, he did not see how a meaningful conspiracy was possible.

Nor had Rufinus any in mind. He was merely laying groundwork for something he might well never build. And, of course, he got to stand with arms around Eochaid, feeling the thin but muscular body, cheek against cheek. His pulse throbbed.

What he asked caused Eochaid to say, "This is nothing they do not already know here."

"Doubtless," Rufinus answered. "What we have done is gotten the right to step away like this again. Tell nobody." He tightened his embrace, savoring the warmth. "The time may come when we have real business." He let go. "Be of high heart, my friend."

Throughout his stay he had cultivated the Midach lords he met. A number of them openly wished matters were different. Yet they were sworn to their King, and clear was to see that while he lived there could be no peace with Ys.

The enemy of my enemy is my ally, Rufinus thought, over and over. He tried to imagine how Niall could threaten the city, or any place in Armorica, as long as the strength endured which Gratillonius had raised on land and sea. He failed. Nevertheless—contingencies—and Niall was certainly a scourge of Britannia, Gratillonius's homeland. If he could not be done away with, the next best service to civilization would be to keep him occupied in this island. Would it not? Today he was triumphant (insofar as barbarians could be said to have triumphs) in the North of Hivernia; he was at ease with the West and the South; what was left to oppose him but the East, the Lagini's kingdom?

"Nonsense," Rufinus mumbled to himself in his lonely bed. "You know perfectly well the situation's more complicated than that. His younger sons are sure to go out conquering on their own, whether the old man will or nay. They'll attack other parts of the Ulati's country, and maybe parts of Condacht. He'll have enough to fret about....Still, if the Lagini can add to his woes—his main hostage from them is Eochaid. The rest are well-born but don't count too much. Eochaid, though, free again—Eochaid, young stallion loosed to gallop, blessed by Epona—haw!" he gibed. Who did he think he was? Sophocles, or whatever they called the playwright whom Bodilis had spoken of?

The next day Laidchenn said he could not linger, but must get home and attend to things. The Ysans had better make haste themselves, back to their ship on the Mumach coast, if they wanted a safe sea passage. It was a pity that the peace mission had failed, but it was foredoomed from the start, and at least they would have plenty to tell.

That night Rufinus dreamed he made love to Eochaid in the smiling presence of Gratillonius. He woke in the darkness and lay furiously thinking until dawn grayed it. Then he dozed off, and when clatter in the hall wakened him anew, he saw what he was going to attempt. He might well fail, but the challenge, and whatever hazard might await him, sounded trumpets within his skull.

To Laidchenn he said: "This is a miserable rainy day, unfit for anything but sitting at the fire. If the weather is better tomorrow, I would like to take a last ride through these magnificent woods, where the Beings indwell as nowhere else I have been. Will you grant this? The day after that, we can go."

"I would not call today miserable, only a little damp," replied the Fer Érennach. "But indeed we must give our host proper notice, so he can send us off as befits his honor. Be it as you wish, darling."

After noon Rufinus declared that despite the rain, he felt cramped indoors and would take a walk. While he did, around and around the rath, the guards brought the Laginach hostages forth. Rufinus greeted them and presently drew Eochaid aside, as often before.

This time the captive came back shivering, afire beneath a tightly held face. "What is it?" cried his fellows, and "What did he say to you?" demanded the chief of his keepers.

Rufinus smiled. "Why, I told him a ransom I think my lord the King of Ys may agree to offer, as a step toward uniting the Gaels with him against the Saxons," he answered blandly and grandly. "You will understand that I must not say more than this until later."

"No need to, ever," said the chief. "Red Medb Herself cannot swerve Niall from a sworn purpose."

"There are kindlier Gods," Rufinus told him, and went back inside the rath.

That night he slept very lightly, but awoke vibrant.

When he declined offers of company on his excursion, no one pressed him. From time to time, an ollam must go off alone and commune with his art. Nor did anyone think it strange that he belted a Gaelic sword at his hip. He could meet a wild beast or a crazed wanderer or an outlaw who did not know him for what he was. Carpre asked him to return well before dark for the farewell feast. Rufinus agreed, sprang onto his horse, and rode off merrily waving.

He was, in fact, back early in the afternoon, when the Lagini were being let out. He rode over to them. "In the morning I go," he announced, although that was generally known. "Eochaid, friend, come off a short ways with me, that you may freely tell me whatever is in your heart for me to convey."

This day was also chill, full of mist. The guards watched idly, shivering a bit within their warm clothes, as the prisoner in his rags followed the splendidly attired rider a few yards. Already there those forms became dim and dull. But what was to fear? Half starved, Eochaid could not outrun them; unarmed, he could put up no fight when he was overtaken—

He seized the ankle of Rufinus and pulled. Rufinus toppled from the saddleless blanket to grass. He lay as if half stunned. Eochaid drew Rufinus's sword from its sheath, grabbed the horse's mane, vaulted onto the back.

"Get him!" roared the chief. "Bresslan, Tardelbach, watch the rest!" He plunged forward, spear aimed. A cast shaft flew at Eochaid even as the Lagin was mounting. It missed. From horseback, knees gripping tight, Eochaid swung the blade he had taken. It knocked aside the foremost spear and sent the chief to his knees, blood dripping from a cheek slashed open. Eochaid put heels to belly.

Hoofs thudded away out of hearing. He was lost among the trees, the mists. Before pursuit could get itself together, he would be afar. Hounds or no, it was unlikely that they could find a wily woodsman.

Folk helped Rufinus up and led him to the hall. Laidchenn met him at the doorway. The news had gone ahead. Grimness congealed the poet's face. "Well," he rumbled, "and what have you to say for yourself?"

"He t-took me by s-surprise," Rufinus stuttered. "I'm s-sorry."

Laidchenn drew breath. "I have my thoughts about that. But you are Carpre's guest, and under my protection, however unwise I may have been to give it. Now—man of Ys!—my counsel is that you call your followers and pack your baggage and be off at once. Do not wait to bid Carpre farewell, but thank whatever Gods are yours that he is elsewhere. For the sake of my honor, I will soothe him as best I may. But begone, do you hear?"

"Do you think I plotted—"

"I say nothing other than that the sooner you are out of Mide the better, and never show yourself here again."

"As my lord wills." Beneath his meekness and the whirring of what-to-do, how-to-go, Rufinus exulted.

~ 4 ~

Eochaid knew where the home of Laidchenn was. Everything about so famous a man spread widely. What he did not know was why he made for it.

That was not the shortest way to Qóiqet Lagini, though not overly many leagues longer. Of course, he must dodge about if he would throw his hunters off the track. Yet was this a well-chosen mark to set for himself?

His wonderment was faint, like a lamp flame in a cave where winds roared. His haste, later his wretchedness, made him unable really to think. He had lost count of days and nights, but hunger had ceased to torment him. Often thirst still did, for he dared not cast about after a brook or a spring but must wait to chance upon water. Sleeplessness hollowed his head out; he took rest stops merely to keep from killing the horse, and crouched in his hiding places like a hare that has scented a fox. What naps he did snatch were made uneasy by cold. He was nearly naked. In the beginning, he had perforce kept the sword pressed to him by the arm whose hand clutched his ballocks lest the gallop pound them to mush. The edge cut him and cut him. When first he paused, he slashed up most of his tunic to fashion a crude loinstrap and a wrapping for the blade. Wind, rain, dew traveled with him and guested his fireless camps.

Thus was Eochaid emptied, perhaps to become the vessel of a Power.

At last, at last, from a sheltering grove, he beheld at a distance the house of Laidchenn, and well beyond it the Ruirthech, and beyond that his homeland. Daylight prevailed, though the sun was lost in grayness and a wrack of low-flying clouds. He tried, dully, to think whether he should wait till dark before crossing the open ground, or do so at once. After a slow while, he pushed ahead. No one was likely to get in the way of a harmless-looking wanderer. Besides, seeking to cross the stream at night could well be the end of him. He was not sure how, in his feebleness, he was going to do it by day.

The horse shambled and staggered, half dead. Eochaid hunched on its back. He felt so cold that it was as if the wind whistled between his bones.

Off on the left he saw the dwelling. There they sat warm and gorged over their ale horns, but he could not enter, he must pass by. Inchmeal he began to believe he understood what had brought him. Yonder was the one who had blasted his life. "I curse you, Tigernach maqq Laidchinni," he croaked. "A red stone in your throat. May you melt away like the froth of the river." They were curses poor and weak, such as a base tenant would utter. He himself was poor and weak. He rocked onward.

"Hoy! You yonder! Stop, if you please!"

The call resounded like a voice heard in a dream. Eochaid turned his weary head. He heard his neck creak. The wind skirled. A man afoot was hastening toward him. A cloak in several colors blew back from coat and trews of rich stuff, golden torc, belt studded with amber. The man was unarmed, aside from a staff. Others appeared in the offing, out from under trees around the buildings.

Eochaid's mount lurched ahead. "You must stop!" shouted the man. "For my honor's sake! I want to give you hospitality!"

There was something in the call that Eochaid had heard before. He could not remember what. He thought foggily that anyone trotting, not running, just trotting, could overhaul this wreck that he rode. Maybe he should heed. He drew rein. The horse whickered and stood with head and tail adroop.

The man laughed. "That's better," he said as he came nigh. "I was walking about, making a poem, and saw you. It would be a shame if a wayfarer in need got by the house of Laidchenn—"

He jarred to a halt and gaped. "But you are Eochaid!" he exclaimed. "Eochaid the Fer Lagin."

Below him Eochaid saw the face of Tigernach, the satirist who had ruined *his* face. Those men who were bound toward him would take him prisoner and return him to the kennel.

He slid down off the horse. In his left hand was the sword. He shook the wrappings off as he took it in his right. Did he or the Power strike? The blow was light, as wasted as his body was, but the iron sharp. Tigernach fell, blood spouting from his neck.

Horror yammered among the approaching men. Eochaid dropped the sword and ran. The Power had him. Husk though he was, he sped weasel-swift. Unable to grasp at once what had happened, and then frantic to care for the son of their master, the men were too slow in giving chase. Eochaid vanished into the reeds along the river. While every male in the household beat them as hounds bayed about, until nightfall, they did not find him.

~ 5 ~

Tigernach lived long enough to cough out the name of his killer.

Eochaid crossed the Ruirthech in the dark after all. Having skulked evasive or lain moveless under water with little but his nose above, he found a log that had drifted against the bank. With its help he swam the river. On the far side, he somehow walked until he came on a shieling. The family there was impoverished, but they took him in and shared with him what milk and gruel they had: for the Gods love this. He caught a fever and lay drowsy for days.

That may have been as well for him. A war band from the north side came over and ranged in search. They did not happen on the hovel, and must withdraw when the neighborhood mustered force against them. Belike he had drowned, they supposed, the which was too good for him.

In time, Eochaid became able to make his painful way to Dún Alinni. The news had gone faster. "You cannot stay here, you who have violated the home of a poet," his father King Éndae said. "All Mide and Condacht would come after you once they heard, and this Fifth would itself deliver you up to them." The breath sobbed into him. "Yet you are my son. If I must disown you, I will not forsake you."

And he gave Eochaid a galley of the Saxon kind, and let it be known that men were wanted to go adventuring abroad. There were not a few ruined by the war or despairing of the morrow at home or simply restless and aspiring, who overlooked Eochaid's deed and risked any bad luck that might flow from it because they remembered what a peerless leader he had been. The upshot was that he departed with a full crew and several large currachs besides.

They fared south along Britannia, raiding where they could. That was not often, and pickings were lean. Stilicho's expeditionary force had lately withdrawn, but after expelling the Scoti who had settled there. Though it was against Roman law, the Ordovices and Demetae were now well armed to protect themselves, while the Silures and Dumnonii had a legion not so far away to call upon. Eventually Eochaid and his men settled down for the winter on an island off Gallia, as various other sea rovers were wont to do.

During a spell of fairly good weather he sent a currach back to learn what had happened meanwhile. It returned with ill tidings.

Laidchenn had arrived home shortly before the killing. He was indoors when his folk brought him the news and the body of his son. Loud was the keening; but the poet remained silent until he had a lament ready to give at the funeral feast. The next day he went forth by himself. He climbed the raw earth of the barrow, faced south, and drew his harp out of its case. Sharp with early autumn, the wind at his back blew his words toward the river. Certain black birds circled overhead. When he was done, they also flew that way. Some workmen could not help hearing him. They shuddered.

"Lagini, I sing now.
Wing now to cravens,
Ravens; bespeak them!
Seek them will bold men.
Old men can only,
Lonely, send greeting,
Meeting them never:
'Ever to sorrow
Morrow shall wake you,
Take you like cattle—
Battle-won plunder—
Under its keeping.
Reaping is mirthless,
Worthless is sowing;
Growing dry thistles,
Bristles the plowland.
Cowland lies calfless.

Laughless the hall is.
All is turned sickly,
Quickly, O Lagini."

And every day thereafter, for a full year, did the ollam poet mount the grave of his son to satirize yonder country, its King and its people.

And during that year, neither grain nor grass nor any green thing grew there. Herds starved in barren fields, flocks in sere forests, folk in foodless dwellings. When finally Laidchenn maqq Barchedo reckoned his vengeance complete, and the blight and the famine had lifted, that Fifth of Ériu took long to recover its health. Meanwhile pirates made free of the coasts, raiders and rebels of the interior.

Such was the tale that, above the fire of past wrongs, hammered the soul of Eochaid into a knife meant for Niall.

IV

~ 1 ~

In the dead of winter, people must rise hours before the sun if they were to carry out their duties. It was earlier than for most when Malthi, a maidservant to Queen Fennalis, entered the room where Dahut slept and gently shook her. "Princess. The time is come, as well as I can judge. Waken."

The girl sat up. Light from the lamp in the woman's hand glowed across tumbled hair, white silken shift, the cloven swelling of bosom. She scowled. Her tone came near to a snarl. "You dare! You called me from a dream, a holy dream."

"I am sorry, my lady, but you did order me yesterday evening— You must be in attendance at the Temple today—"

Dahut drew a measure of calm across herself. "Woeful it is, though, being wrenched away just when— Well, have you my bath ready?"

"Of course, Princess, and I'll be laying out your vestments. May I wish you a good morning?"

Rueful humor flitted across the clear brow, the soft lips. "Better 'twould be did I not have to arrive fasting!" Solemnity replaced it. Dahut flowed out of bed. "Honor to the Gods." Before an image of Belisama as Maiden, she offered her orison. At the end she whispered, "You will come again to me, will You not?"

Malthi had lighted a candle for her. She took it out into the hallway. That was less black than expected. The adjoining door stood open, and yellow radiance spilled forth.

Dahut looked in. Fennalis was abed but awake, propped up in a nest of pillows, a sewn stack of papyrus sheets open on the blankets. "Why, greeting, Mama," Dahut said with a smile. The old Queen liked to hear that name from the vestal's childhood. "How naughty. You should be asleep for hours yet, regaining your strength."

525

Fennalis sighed. "I couldn't. At last I called poor Malthi to arrange things." Her white head nodded at the cushions, the nine-branched bronze candelabrum on a table beside her, the booklet under her fingers. "I may as well use the time. Also, it takes my mind off— No matter."

Dahut entered. "Pain?" she asked, concern in her voice.

Fennalis shrugged. "Let's not speak of regaining my strength. It no longer exists."

Dahut set her candle down and regarded the high priestess closely. That stumpy body had been losing its stoutness fast of late. Skin draped emptily past the pug nose and over the withered arms. It was taking on a fallow hue. Nonetheless, her belly made a bulge in the covers. "Oh, dear Mama—"

"Nay, no sniveling. 'Tis high time I got out of the way, and ready I am to go. A kind of adventure, drawing close to the Otherworld. I begin to make out its shores."

Dahut's eyes widened. "In dreams?" she breathed.

"Often I cannot be sure if the glimpses come while I sleep or I wake." Fennalis gave her visitor a sharp glance. "Have *you* been dreaming?"

Dahut swallowed, hesitated, nodded.

"Sit down, if you'd fain tell me," Fennalis invited.

Dahut lowered herself to the edge of the bed. Fennalis reached unsteadily up to stroke her cheek. "How lovely you are," the Queen murmured. "And how strange. What was your dream?"

Dahut stared into the darkness that pressed against the window. "'Twas more than one," she said low. "They began...two years ago, I think, after...my seal left me. I can't be certain, for at first they seemed little different from others, save that I always remembered them. I stood on a seashore. The waters were dark and unrestful beneath a gray sky. The air was windless. No birds flew. I was alone, altogether alone. Yet I was not afraid. I knew this strand and sea were mine.

"The dreams came far apart in the beginning, and I gave them little thought, when so much was happening in my life. Somebody slowly appeared, away off on the horizon. They came toward me, over the waves. Each time they got nearer. At last I could see they were three, a man, a woman, and...something else, a presence, a shadow, but I could feel the might within....

"The dreams seek me more and more often. Now I can see that the man bears a hammer and wears the red robe and Wheel emblem of a King. The woman is dressed in blue and white like one of you Gallicenae. The third—I think has three legs and a single huge eye."

Dahut drew breath before she finished: "This morning just ere the servant roused me, they were so close that I thought I could see what faces were theirs. It seemed to me that the man could be my father and the woman my mother—from what I've heard tell of my mother—"

Her words trailed off. She sat looking at the night.

"The woman may be yourself," Fennalis said.

Dahut twisted about to stare at her. "What? You can, can read it for me? I never thought you—"

"Divination, magic, the Touch, all such wonders, aye, they've passed plain little Fennalis by. Nor was I ill content with that. They are not human sorts of things. I felt no envy of Forsquilis, say. And as for you, my darling, I only wish—" The woman sighed once more. "Nay, I'm still too far from the Otherworld to understand this. I do beg you to be very, very careful."

Dahut straightened. "Thank you, but why should I dread my destiny?"

"You know what it is."

"I know it is *mine*." Dahut rose. Her gaze fell on the booklet. "What is that about? 'Tis new to me." Bending over, tracing with a fingertip, she read aloud: "—Blessed are the poor in spirit: for theirs is the kingdom of Heaven—"

She sprang back as if the papyrus had burned her. "Fennalis!" she cried. "That's Christian! I saw the name of Jesus!"

Calm descended on the woman. "It is. Corentinus has rendered some of his Scriptures into Ysan. He lent me this."

Dahut made a fending sign. "You've been with him?"

"Of late." Fennalis smiled. "At ease, child. We've merely talked a few times, at my request. He knows he'll never convert me. I'm too old and set in my ways."

"By why, then, why?"

"To learn a minim about what he believes, what so many people believe. Surely they have some truth, some insight, and I'd be glad to know what ere I depart."

"They deny the Gods!"

"Well, our Gods deny, or at least defy theirs. Who is the more righteous? Even when young, I—Dahut, my first King was Wulfgar, a rough man but well intentioned, able, and—ah, a stallion of a man; and I was young. Stark Gaetulius slew him and possessed me. Moody Lugaid slew Gaetulius. I could not hate either; both gave me more children to love, and besides, this was the will of the Gods. Still, Hoel came like a big golden sun that drives out winter; and I was not yet too old to have a daughter by him. But horrible Colconor finally cut Hoel down. After five years, Gratillonius delivered us."

Exhausted, Fennalis sank back on the pillows. Her eyes closed. The girl could barely hear: "Someday those Gods you adore will send a man who kills your father. You may become his bride."

"I must go!" Dahut nearly screamed. With anger-stiff strides, she left the room. The candle shook and wavered in her grasp. Her free hand clenched and unclenched.

In a chamber of marble and fish mosaics, lights burned manifold and a sunken bath steamed fragrant. Dahut pulled off her nightgown, flung it on the floor, and descended.

Lying there, she slowly loosened. First her glance, then her hands glided over her body. Just past her fifteenth year, she was nonetheless entirely woman. She caressed the roundednesses, arched her back, mewed, with eyes half shut.

Malthi came in, recalling Dahut to the world. "Princess, 'tis getting late. Better we hurry." As the maiden stepped forth: "How beautiful you are. A pity I must towel you. Many a young man would trample dragons on his way to this task."

Dahut accepted the praise as she did all such words, something pleasant but unsurprising. Back in the bedroom—she had not paused to look in on Fennalis—the servant helped her into the vestal's gown: at this season, white with solar symbols embroidered in gold. Having combed out her hair, Malthi crowned it with a wreath of evergreen laurel, whereinto were woven red berries of holly. Red also were her shoes; but the girdle about her slenderness was Belisama's blue, with a silver clasp conjoining Hammer and Trident.

Taking a lantern, she left the house where she had spent the night and hastened along the street. In its district few had occasion to be up so early. She noticed two or three lights bobbing in the echoful lane. From these heights, she spied more of them down in the working parts of the city and along its avenues, glow-worm small. The air was cold and quiet; breath smoked. A half moon rode among uncountable stars. Towers raised black lances against them. At the top of one a window glimmered lonely. That was where Rufinus lived.

The Temple of the Goddess stood wan, its portico like a cave. Dahut gave her lantern into the care of the minor priestess who was keeping the door, and passed on into the sanctum. It was empty except for her. Lamps along the aisles made a twilight. She advanced to the altar at the far end.

There she lifted her arms. Her duties today would not be sacral, she would take her turn at maintenance and scribe work, but a vestal must always begin with prayer. Its form was not fixed; this hour was called the Opening of the Heart. Dahut looked up to the images of the Triune, Mother, Maiden, and Hag. In the dim and uneasy glow, they seemed to stir. "Goddess, All-Holy," she said under her breath, "come to me. Make known Your will. Embody Your power. Belisama, be Dahut."

~ 2 ~

The men whom Niall had sent south found him at the hostel of Bran maqq Anmerech, on his way to Temir for the festival of Imbolc. A brief and murky day was drawing to its close. Firelight barely kept shadows at bay in the long room where the King sat among his chief warriors. Bran would not offend that nose with the stench of grease lamps, and instead heaped the trench full of sweet fir wood. Gold gleamed, eyeballs glared. Having eaten, the company were at drink while a bard gave them a ballad about an adventure of Niall's great ancestor Corbmaqq.

One did not interrupt an ollam poet, but this was a much lesser sort of fellow. Wet and muddy, the travelers tramped in and greeted their lord. "It's welcome you are," he said. His tone lacked heartiness. He had more and more been brooding these past months. "Bran, fetch what they need and prepare them quarters." That could be done somehow, for the party numbered only ten.

"We have brought such a man as you sent us to find," declared the leader. "Come forward, Cernach maqq Durthacht."

A short but square-shouldered, slightly grizzled person responded. He had a cocky manner and a mariner's gait. Niall's gaze probed him. "You are indeed he who can teach me the tongue they speak in Ys?" asked the King.

"I am that, lord," Cernach answered. His dialect of Mumu was heavy but understandable. "And this is my wife Sadb. I will not be leaving her by herself a year or worse." He beckoned her to join him at his side. She was younger than he, full-breasted, broad-hipped, her hair red and her face comely though freckled. When she smiled, Niall thawed a bit.

"Well," he said, "sit down, the pair of you." A girl brought stools for them, placed at his knees where he sat benched. After mead cups were in their hands, Niall commanded, "Tell me about yourself, Cernach."

"I am a trader captain with my own small ship, harbored in the mouth of the River Siuir. For years I have taken cargoes to and from Ys. I have abided in it, and in my house at home I have received merchant seamen from it, on their way to our fairs or to Cassel. I know it as well as any outsider can know a place so full of magic and poetry; I speak the language with an accent, but readily."

"And you are willing, for rich reward, to share your knowledge with me?"

"I am, also for the glory of having served Niall of the Nine Hostages."

The King peered. "Think well," he warned. "I am the bitter foe of Ys. What harm I can wreak there, I will, and reckon it far too little revenge for the wrongs done me. They begin with the shattering of my fleet and the slaying of my son, when he meant Ys no trouble at all. They have gone on through the unloosing of my foremost hostage, which led to the murder of a son of my head poet and his own withdrawal from my household. That made ashen in my mouth the taste of my victory over the Ulati."

"I have heard this."

"Then you must know that I will learn of Ys as a means toward my vengeance. How that is to happen I know not, but happen it shall, unless I die first or the sea overwhelm the world. Now you have friends yonder, as well as business and, surely, good memories. Would you help sharpen my sword against these? Answer honestly, and you shall go home with gifts for your trouble. A man ought to stand by his friends."

"I will indeed say freely, my lord." Cernach grinned, a sailor's impudence. "I have sworn no oaths with anyone. That is not the way of Ys, unless maybe among the fishers down at the place they call Scot's Landing, and those are an uncanny lot. True, there are men of Ys—and women, ah, women—whom I like; and I have profit of my trade. It would grieve me to see Ys ruined the way Alba is being ruined. However—lord, I said I would be frank—I do not believe you can harm it. It is too strong, its masters too wise and wary. Even mighty Niall could break his heart against that rampart. Maybe I can do you the service of making you see this. Whether or no, well, why should I not play druid and instruct you?"

The warriors stiffened, half appalled. Niall himself tensed. His lips pulled back over his teeth. Then he slackened, rattled forth a laugh, lifted his goblet. "Boldly spoken! It seems I can trust you to do what you agreed, in full measure. Come, drink; and I see that the hostelkeeper is carrying out food after your journey."

—But later, as the fire guttered low, his mood darkened again. "Never seek to turn me from my vengeance," he muttered. "It would spill our time. It could cost you your head. Remember that."

Cernach's wife Sadb leaned toward him. "You have an inward sorrow, Niall maqq Echach," she said softly. "Could I be relieving of it a little this night?"

Niall considered her. At last he smiled. "You could that," he answered. "Let us away."

They said their good evenings and left for the enclosed space given him, his arm about her waist. Cernach looked after them with an expression that became pleased. Bran cleared his throat and said, "I think we can still find a girl awake for you, guest who has gotten such an honor."

On the face of Bran's wife were disappointment and envy. Niall was not only powerful and handsome. The word went among the women of Ériu that he was a lover without compare.

~ 3 ~

When the Suffetes met at vernal equinox, a thing occurred that Ys had never known before. The King brought charges against one of their number.

"—Nagon Demari, Labor Councillor. It has been notorious how his bullies terrorize the waterfront and beat insensible men who resist the demands he makes of them through the guild he heads. Direct evidence has been lacking....Now Donnerch, son of Arel, the independent carter who was taking the lead in forming a new and honest guild, he has been murdered, set on as he passed through the Fishtail after dark and stabbed. This is common news and has caused widespread mourning. What did not come out hitherto is that Donnerch was so robust he did not die at once. He regained awareness and named his two assailants to the patrolmen who found him lying in that alley. Fate made these be legionaries, and therefore they reported directly to me. The Captain of Marines is honest and able, but restricted in what he may do. Without impartial witnesses, the killers need only maintain that Donnerch must have been mistaken, and they would go free. I had them quietly seized and privately interrogated. Torture was not necessary. To me, the Incarnation of Taranis, they confessed as soon as I promised to spare their lives—a pledge the Captain of Marines does not have power to give. They have told me, as they will tell you, that they acted on the order of Nagon Demari."

Uproar. Horror. Oratory. The grindstone that was procedure.

"'Tis a foul bargain, letting hired murderers keep their heads," protested Bomatin Kusuri, Mariner Councillor.

"They shall be taken in chains to Gesocribate and put on the Roman slave market," Gratillonius replied. "The proceeds shall go to Donnerch's widow and children."

He cast all his force and all his power of persuasion and, aye, intimidation into the effort to destroy Nagon. That man had been a thorn in the side of Ys, and the wound suppurating, far too long.

"The testimony's not good enough," declared Osrach Taniti, Fisher Councillor, himself a hard-bitten old salt. "We can't condemn him on the word of two lampreys like those. Mind ye, I'm no friend to Nagon. My Brotherhood's often had to work with his Guild, but we've nay had to like it. However, Nagon has gotten betterment of the longshoremen's lot. Else yon fellows could ha' whistled for a share in this prosperity we're supposed to've gained. That speaks for his character."

"It says merely that every tyrant or demagogue must needs do some service for somebody," retorted Queen Vindilis. "The King has confided in the Nine. We are agreed Nagon is evil."

"We would never wish to ruin the Guild itself," said Forsquilis. "Let honest leadership rebuild it."

"Ah, but who shall name that leadership?" demanded Soren Cartagi. "The King? Beware!" He raised a hand. "Nay, hear me out. None will deny that Gratillonius has wrought mightily on behalf of Ys. Yet time and again he has overreached himself, he has broken bounds that were ancient already when Brennilis lived. He has not been content to be high priest, president of this Council, and war chieftain. He would become dictator. I say this to his face, more in respect than in anger. He is a well-intentioned man, ofttimes mistaken but mayhap more often right. However, what of his successor? What could, say, another Colconor do with power such as Gratillonius would put in the hands of the King?"

There were those, the accused among them, who flatly denied the charges. Argument roiled on throughout the day.

Finally, wearily, a majority voted a compromise. The evidence was deemed insufficient to convict Nagon Demari of a capital crime. The killers might have taken his instructions wrong, or become overexcited. Still, they were henchmen of his, and bad men. His association with them was by itself a grave violation of trust, and gave credence to many more allegations. Nagon Demari was therefore stripped of every office and forbidden to hold any for the rest of his life.

"Stand forth," Gratillonius bade him, "if you have aught to say ere I confirm or dismiss this judgment of the Council."

Left untouched had been the question Soren raised, whether the King himself had exceeded his rights and established a dangerous precedent.

The stocky, sandy-haired man stepped up. He kept his back to the assembly, in scorn. It was the one on the dais whom his chill gaze defied, and the soldiers behind, and perhaps the eidolons of the Three looming above them.

"What is there to say?" he rasped. "You've hounded me for years, and at last you have me between your jaws. Ill was the fate that brought you to the Wood. May a challenger soon come and kill you. You shall not crush the workers who will be cursing your name, nor shall you break my spirit. But here I will not linger, where thanks to you my innocent family can no longer hold their heads high. You will be rid of me, Grallon, because I will take myself away from your pestilential presence. You will not be rid of divine justice."

Gasps went around the chamber. Gratillonius said merely, "Go, then, and live among the Romans. You'll take enough loot with you." The struggle had exhausted him. It was worse than combat. On the battlefield you at least usually had a clear-cut victory or defeat.

He adjourned the session and departed amidst his guards, waving off every attempt to speak with him. Bodilis followed the squad. This was to be a visit he paid her.

Dusk brimmed the city with blue when they reached her house. The soldiers left them and they entered. Bodilis took him to her scriptorium, pending supper. That large room—crammed with her books, writing materials, artistic work in progress, specimens, objects of beauty—was their refuge, now that the bedchamber was denied them. Candleglow fell on small refreshments, wine, water, tisane kept warm by a lamp.

"Won't you shed cloak and robe?" she suggested in the Latin they commonly used when alone together. "They must hang heavy this evening."

"They do that," he sighed, pulled them off and laid them over a stool. Her cat promptly sprang up and sat on the raiment. Bodilis's look followed Gratillonius as he went to pour himself a glass of wine, undiluted, and take a lengthy draught. His light undertunic hung across shoulders still broad and back straight, leaving bare the powerful limbs.

532

Bits of silver glinted in the auburn of his hair and close-trimmed beard. Her locks were quite gray.

"I'm glad this is your evening," he said. "I need your strength."

"Others among us have as much," she answered softly, "and comfort to give you besides."

"But not your...calm, your fellow-feeling. And your wisdom. You can see beyond the politics of what we did today and help me discover what it really means." He sat down and stared at the floor.

She took a cup of herbal brew and a chair facing his. "You speak extravagantly."

He shook his head. "No. I'll set my clumsy words aside, though, and ask for your opinions." It was not the first time in the past decade. The pain of the barrier he had perforce raised between them had long since become familiar; they could talk freely as of old, until he bade her goodnight and sought his bed at the palace.

"Do you wonder what we can best do about Nagon's partisans?" she replied. "We know there will be much resentment. Most of his working men believe that, whatever his faults, he was on their side."

"That was considered beforehand," he said impatiently. "Don't fear any riots. Patrols will be doubled at the waterfront for the next several days. I do wish the Gallicenae would help cool things down."

"You know we mustn't take sides. We serve the Goddess on behalf of everybody."

"I meant in reconstructing the guild. If the Nine were counselors and overseers of that, who could doubt the job was done as honestly as human beings are able?...But we've covered this ground already. I'll do what I can with what tools are allowed me."

"Well, I can propose to my sisters that we reconsider, but it'll surely be futile. We went as far as we should in condemning Nagon. You must have something else on your mind."

"I do." His expression was troubled, almost bewildered. "What certain staunch men said— Oh, I'd given the matter thought before, but hastily. Always there's been too much to do, at once, no time for reflection; and afterward it's too late. But am I being wise, wise not for myself but for Ys? You've made me think back to my history lessons when I was a boy. Marius, who saved Rome from the Cimbri, meant to do well by the people but undermined the Republic—which Caesar demolished in all but name, meaning to repair the state— Am I sapping the wall of Ys? What about the King after me?"

"Oh, darling!" she cried, leaned forward and seized his hand. "Don't talk like that!"

"I'd better," he said grimly. "I'll leave so many behind me, Dahut, Tambilis, the children, maybe you—"

"But you have years ahead of you," she insisted, "as strong as you are. Who has even challenged you since Rufinus, more than a decade ago, in spite of your sparing him? And all the omens foretell a new

Age for Ys. It could well bring an end to, to that which happens in the Wood."

His bleakness did not ease. She hurried on: "Meanwhile, true, we do have serious matters to deal with. You understand—understand fully, don't you?—you will be getting a new Queen."

He hesitated. "Poor Fennalis is ill," he admitted. She had not attended the Council, nor any function of the Gallicenae.

Bodilis studied him. "You shy from this," she murmured.

"Oh, now, I call on her whenever I can. She's cheerful."

"She puts on a good face. But how often have her servants asked you to turn back at her door, saying she's asleep or whatever? That's been at her orders. Gratillonius, lately she's begun vomiting thick, gritty black masses. We know what those mean. She will soon die. We can only try to ease her way a little. You must not hide from the truth."

"What can I do, though?" he groaned. "Which of the vestals will be next? There's no foretelling."

"There can be forethought. What if the Sign comes upon one of your own daughters?"

He stiffened. After a silence that grew long he said, flat-voiced, "That would be very unwise of your Gods."

"Well," she said, more hastily than before, "we Sisters have been considering the girls of the second and third generations. They have their family connections, generally to Suffetes. Whichever of those clans gets the high honor—well, some members will stand aloof, but some will try for this or that advantage. Lanarvilis can best advise you about it."

"Hm." He rubbed his chin. The beard felt wiry. "I'll seek her out."

"First," Bodilis urged, "you should give reverence to the Three. What happened today was truly an upheaval. It may win Their favor, and certainly it'll help calm both Suffetes and commoners, if you recess the Council tomorrow and hold a solemn sacrifice."

He shook his head. "I can't."

She was shocked. "Why not?"

"I've made another promise. It should have been kept earlier, but the word reached me in the middle of my preparations for this day's business, and... Tomorrow at sunset I'll be leading a high rite of Mithras. It would make me impure if I offered first to Anyone else."

"By why is this?" she whispered. "No holy day of His—"

"My father in Britannia has died," he told her. "My initiates and I must give his spirit its farewell."

"Oh, my dear." She rose and reached for him. He got up too. They clung to each other.

~ 4 ~

Joreth kept an apartment on the third floor of that tower called the Flying Doe. She had had its walls done over so that motifs of the sea played across them, waves, dolphins, fish, seals, kelp, shells. Sea-green were the draperies along the windows and the coverings of her bed. Small erotic sculptures decorated the main room. The incense that wafted about lacked the heavy sweetness common in places of this kind; it was subtly wild.

When Carsa entered, he stopped and caught his breath. Daylight through glass limned Joreth's lissomeness against heaven. It smoldered in the amber masses of her hair. She wore a silken gown, close about breasts and hips, flowing of sleeves and skirt, gauzy save where embroidered vines curled tantalizing. "Welcome," she purred, and undulated forward to take his hands in hers. "Be very welcome. What a lovely youth you are."

He swallowed dryness. His heart thuttered.

Enormous blue eyes looked up out of the delicate face. "Aulus Metellus Carsa, nay?" she said with a smile like daybreak. "A Roman from far Burdigala, dwelling among us in Ys. Oh, you must have many an adventure to tell of."

He remembered vaguely how her ancilla had received him two days ago in an upstairs room. Before taking his money and setting this hour, she had engaged him in amiable conversation. It was known that Joreth did not receive men whom she would find unpleasing; she had no need to. Now Carsa realized that the information about him had been passed on, doubtless including that fact that he was sturdy, with curly dark-brown hair and features broad, blunt, but regular. Well, he thought, foreknowledge helped her charm her patrons.

The sight of her was enough, though. Glimpsing her in the streets, hearing enraptured stories from friends, he could at last no longer resist. The price was scarcely within his means, but—

But she was so like Dahut.

She led him to a couch, bade him sit down, poured a fine wine for them both, settled herself beside him. "Come," she proposed, "let us get acquainted. Unlock that tongue of yours."

"You're beautiful!" he blurted, threw his arm about her waist and sought to kiss her.

She held him off with a gesture of her whole body that was not a repulsion but a promise. "Pray wait," she laughed. "You shall have your desire, but I would fain give you the greatest pleasure therein. This is no cheap tavern where you must wolf your girl as fast as your food. You have time ahead of you. Let your...appetite...grow at leisure."

"Looking at you," he mumbled, "I can hardly rein myself in. I was hoping—twice, ere my time had drained out of the clepsydra—"

"Well we'll see about that. Young men are quickly ready again. But Carsa, I tell you afresh, this is no whorehouse. I want to know my lovers in spirit as well as flesh. Else they and I are mere beasts in rut. That is wrong."

He fumbled for words. "Aye. The more so when, when you are of royal birth."

She arched her brows. "You have heard?"

"Somewhat. I cannot really untangle it," he admitted. "These many Queens and Kings through the years. But I'm told you are kin to—to Queen Bodilis."

Joreth threw back her head and laughed anew, a peal to which he thought he heard a certain thinness. "To Princess Dahut, you mean. Deny it not. 'Tis my good fortune that I resemble her."

"And mine," he sprang to say.

"La, you're swift to learn our pretty Ysan ways, Roman," she teased. "I'll enjoy teaching you further. Shall I begin by explaining my descent?"

"Whatever you wish," he answered humbly.

"Well, in the days of King Wulfgar there was a Queen who had taken the name Vallilis. The first child she bore him was to become Queen Tambilis—not the present Queen of that name, but her grandmother. Near the end of her life—she died accidentally, unless 'tis true what some believe, that the Gods Themselves decide the doom of all the Gallicenae—Vallilis bore Wulfgar another daughter, Evana."

Carsa winced. He could not forget the story of Wulfgar. At the death of Vallilis, the Sign came upon Tambilis, his daughter by her. Helpless in the grip of a Power, Wulfgar had possessed her, and she bore him Bodilis. It was not reckoned incestuous in Ys, when the Gods had made the choice. But Wulfgar was said to have been haunted by guilt. He fell to the sword of Gaetulius, though he should have prevailed over the Mauritanian.

Tambilis lived on. When Hoel had taken the crown, she bore him that Estar who became Dahilis after she, the mother, passed away. And Dahilis became, by Gratillonius, the mother of Dahut.

Now a daughter of Bodilis, also by Hoel, reigned as a new Tambilis.... A shiver went through Carsa. This history was as dark, as twisted as that of the house of Atreus. What was he, a Christian man, doing in Ys?

Joreth's voice called him back from his fears: "Evana served out her vestal period and was released. She married a merchant of Suffete class, a man of the Tyri, who are themselves kin to that line of descent. I was her last child and only daughter who lived. Since my grandmother had been a Queen, I too must become a vestal, though that requirement ends with me. My term concluded two years ago, from which you can reckon out that my age now is twenty—not too much more than Dahut's."

"And, and when you became free?" He felt his face grow hot.

Her answer was cooling: "I rejoiced. Poor Dahut, if she is like me in her heart. Aye, in her leisure time she shines brilliant, she is the center of a whirlpool of doings; but 'tis cruel to keep a spirited lass virgin that late. I'd already determined I'd be no household drudge, nor even a fine lady whose husband winks at her lovers. I'd be my own woman, and how else than as a courtesan?"

She paused before adding softly, "Why dissemble, Carsa? I know quite well that I am the desire of men, the envy of my sisters in the life, less for my own sake—albeit I flatter myself I am attractive—than for my likeness to Dahut. Golden Dahut, quicksilver Dahut, who enthralls by her beauty and liveliness, but more, I think, by her strangeness, that slight sea-wind whisper of the Unknown, which she always bears about her."

He remembered the seal, and certain other things. "You...understand much, Joreth."

"'Tis my business to." She leaned close. "What I offer you, Carsa, is a dream. You can keep your eyes open while you pretend to yourself I am Dahut; and I have skilled myself in her ways. But first I must know you as well as she does. Tell me, Carsa."

For a moment he recoiled. How could he thus besmirch that snow-pure maiden? Then he recollected her glances and motions, the wickedness of her wit. Oh, she was pagan through and through, and in all likelihood she knew about Joreth and was amused or, maybe, triumphant.

"Speak," Joreth breathed in his ear. Her fingers went lightly seeking over him.

—He had not stayed abstinent. That was well-nigh impossible for a foreigner resident in Ys, unless he be a very holy man; many of the city's women actively pursued variety. Three of Suffete rank had seduced him in turn. Corentinus had sighed to hear his confessions but not upbraided or penalized him much. Carsa had learned how to boast without being oafish: of the antique splendors and modern diversity in Burdigala, of his education and travels, of how he with his sling had once helped drive pirates away from his father's ship. The ladies had drawn him out and listened with every sign of fascination. They were knowing as well as sightly, those ladies.

They had nothing of Dahut about them.

—Dazed, he stumbled down the stairs. When could he return? He had at least a year before him. This spring his father had left him off, commissioned to establish an office of the firm now that he was familiar with Ys and had useful connections there. He was also supposed to help propagate the Faith....He would justify the trust, he would work like a horse to enlarge the business, so that out of his share he could afford to visit Joreth often. And, God forgive him, he would keep it from Corentinus....

As he stepped into the ground-floor hall, astonishment smote him. Another man was entering. He recognized that medium-tall, supple figure, that countenance blue-eyed and snubnosed, that hair and youthful beard startling black against the white skin. Both walkers halted and stared.

Tommaltach broke the silence. "Well, well!" he said. His Ysan carried a lilting accent. "Sure, and this is a surprise." He grinned. "Or is it?"

Carsa flushed. "What do you want here?" he demanded.

"The same as you just had, I am thinking. Since I'm settled down in Ys—" The Scotian shrugged. "Jealousy would be foolish. We both are only biding of our time, along with the rest like us."

"Time?"

"Come, boy, Joreth can't have robbed you of your mind." Since people were moving to and fro, Tommaltach stepped close and lowered his voice. "In two years, less a few months, Princess Dahut will be free."

"But who will she wed? Not you or me!"

"Oh, I doubt she'll content herself with any one man, ever. —Hold your anger! Don't be striking me. You've seen her more than I have, you lucky rascal. Will you not join me in hoping we shall both be among those she blesses?"

V

~ 1 ~

Although it was an offside room in the basilica at Turonum, for confidential conferences, the space where Gratillonius stood seemed chosen to dwarf him. Quite likely that was true. It would ordinarily have held ten or twenty men. Instead, he was alone—how alone—before two. The amanuensis who sat at a table and recorded words spoken did not count. He was a slave, less real than the images on shadowy walls. Those were recent, in fresh plaster covering whatever paganisms had formerly been depicted. The artist had lacked training. Yet the angular, elongated shapes staring out of their big eyes, Christ with His angels and saints, somehow radiated power; they judged and condemned.

Curtly summoned to report, the King of Ys stood before the governor and procurator of Lugdunensis Tertia. They sat in chairs large and ornate enough to be thrones, their togas warm around them, garments whose antiquatedness made him feel the weight of Imperial centuries. He had now been long on his feet. Entering out of mild weather, he had found his tunic and trousers inadequate against the chill here; it was gnawing inward as his knees wearied.

"You remain obdurate?" asked the governor. Titus Scribona Glabrio was a fat man, but underneath jowls and paunch he carried hardness to match that of his gaunt associate. "In light of the Augustus's decree, handed you to read for yourself, that worship of false gods is banned.

Their temples and revenues confiscated for the use of the state—you refuse your duty to promote the Faith or even to embrace it?"

Gratillonius choked back a sigh. "With due respect, sir," he answered, "we have discussed this at length today. I repeat, Ys is a sovereign nation. Its law requires that the King preside over the old rites. Your church has an able minister there; he and his congregation have my protection; more I cannot do, and remain King."

"You can be recalled, prefect, and as of now."

"Sir, I know. You can arrest me. But I ask you again, what then? Ys will be outraged. It will withdraw from the cooperation that I make bold to say has been priceless to Rome. As for the next King, Ys will do what it's done in the past, when it lost one in some irregular way. It'll find a new man to guard the Wood: purchased slave, volunteer tough, outlaw seeking refuge, makes no difference. What does matter is that he'll be the creature of the magnates, because he'll be ignorant and without cause for loyalty to Rome. Whether you let Ys pull back into isolation or you come and lay it waste, you'll have lost the bulwark of Armorica."

Quintus Domitius Bacca, procurator, sent his words gliding serpentine: "How conscientious have you proven, through, Gratillonius? You encourage trade with the barbarians of Hivernia. I have thrice written to you, explaining how the influx of gold is upsetting the Imperial order, inducing people to hold the Emperor's currency in contempt, bypass normal commercial channels, evade taxes, flout regulations, and seek with increasing frequency to flee those stations in life to which God has called them. But you will not cut it off."

"Sir, you have my dispatches," Gratillonius replied. "I've done what I could about smuggling, but I still think the first job of our sea patrols is protection against piracy and aid to mariners in distress. It is not to stop merchant vessels for random searches. Meanwhile, traveling around, I've seen how by and large the people—all the Armorican tribes—how much better off they're coming to be year by year, safer, healthier, decently fed and housed—"

"Silence!" interrupted Glabrio. "We know of your activities throughout the western half of the peninsula, far in excess of any mandate ever given you. What ambitions do you nourish for yourself?"

Gratillonius stiffened. Anger ignited in him, to burn away fatigue. Nonetheless he chose his phrases with care. "Sir, I've explained that, over and over, not just today but through my letters and visits to your predecessor. I can't understand why you insist on seeing me. Well, I did know what you'd ask and came prepared to answer." Apuleius Vero had warned him four years ago, and repeatedly afterward; he had inquired on his own, and pondered what his discoveries meant. "I believe I did that the first hour today. Why have you been dragging me through it again—I've lost count of how many times, how many different ways—with never a chance to rest or a share in the refreshments brought you? Do you hope to wear me down? Sir, you're wasting your time. I was interrogated under torture once, and that was also a waste of time, for the selfsame reason. There simply is nothing more to tell."

Glabrio flushed. "Are you being insolent?"

"No, sir. I am being truthful, as a soldier should. I *am* still a centurion of the Second."

"A-a-ah," murmured Bacca. The least smile played over his lips. "Shrewdly put. You are not altogether the blunt veteran you act. But we knew that already, didn't we?"

Within himself, Gratillonius eased slightly. They were accepting his reminder, these two, that their authority was limited to civil affairs. His position in Ys had always been anomalous, ambiguous, especially after the fall of Maximus who appointed him. It embraced both military and diplomatic functions. Breaking him would require—to a properly cautious official mind—the concurrence of the Duke at least, and quite possibly of higher-ranking men, perhaps Stilicho. Would those personages really think it worth a cost that might prove enormous?

"There is a certain justice in your complaint, too," Bacca went on. "We may have been thoughtless. Governor, shall we dismiss this man for the nonce? I do have other matters to take up with you in private."

Glabrio put on an appearance of considering before he said: "Very well. Gratillonius, you may go. Hold yourself in readiness for further interviewing tomorrow, should I decide that that is necessary. Farewell."

Gratillonius saluted. "Thank you, sir. Farewell." He wheeled and marched out, aware that he had won his case—for the present, at any rate—and could soon start home. He was too tired to rejoice.

When the door had closed behind him, Glabrio turned to Bacca and demanded, "Well, what is this you want to discuss?"

"It requires privacy, I said," replied the procurator, and sent the amanuensis off.

Thereupon he leaned his sharp features close to his superior's and continued: "That fellow did speak truth. I've been investigating virtually from the day you and I took office, and I know. The only reason to call him here was to take his personal measure. It's formidable."

"I agree." Glabrio frowned. "I do not agree that's good."

"Nor do I. What could happen eventually to our careers, or our own selves, if Ys remains independent, with its influence growing for every year that passes? Now that's been largely the work of Gratillonius. I do believe he has no desire to become another Maximus. He has merely made Ys—alien, pagan Ys—indispensable to the security and well-being of this flank of the Empire. If Rome destroys him, she undercuts the whole bastion he has built for her. And yet the activities and the very existence of Ys subvert the Imperium." Bacca laughed. "Forgive mixed metaphors, but his is a Gordian knot indeed."

"Alexander cut the first Gordian knot across."

"Do you think of having Gratillonius done away with? I'd wager many solidi that any such attempt would fail. His escort, the old Roman legionaries and the young Ysan marines, they keep a close eye on their King. Win or lose, an effort to eliminate him would be recognized for what it was. In fact, I'm afraid that even his accidental death hereabouts would be assumed a murder commissioned by us. No, my friend, we'd better take special care to see that Gratillonius returns intact."

Glabrio shifted his broad bottom on the chair. "I know you," he growled. "You have something in mind. Don't shilly-shally the way you like to. I'm hungry."

"Well, then," Bacca said, rather smugly, "in the course of my duties I have agents keeping track of what happens, and I follow up the more interesting clues myself. Lately there has arrived a malcontent from Ys who was quite high in its affairs until Gratillonius got him removed. We've had a couple of talks, he and I. Today I ordered that he come to the basilica and wait for our summons. Shall I call a slave to fetch him?"

—Bitterly and fearlessly, Nagon Demari confronted the Romans and told them: "Of course I want that brotherfucker dead. Of course I've thought about how to do it."

"Remember," said Glabrio, "we mustn't alienate Ys. We must rather bring the city to obedience."

Nagon nodded. "Right." His Latin was atrocious but understandable and improving daily. "Bring it to Christ. Right. I'm taking Christian instruction, sir. But if you don't want to go in and outright conquer Ys—and that would leave a ruin, with my poor benighted longshoremen killed fighting against you—why, you'll have to send your own man to chop Grallon down. Once he's King, he can work with you to change things gradually."

Glabrio stroked his clean-shaven double chin. "We'll have to be crafty about it," he said, "though we can secretly direct his actions. It helps that Gratillonius himself has much strengthened the Kingship."

"The trouble is," Nagon warned, "you get the Kingship by killing Grallon in the Wood, and he's a troll of a fighter. How long's it been since anybody dared challenge him? A dozen years? In spite of the fact he broke the law to spare that man. He wouldn't spare the next; and meanwhile he keeps in practice. Word gets around."

"Furthermore," Bacca said, chiefly to Glabrio, "some adventurer who did succeed in overcoming Gratillonius would not necessarily be the man we want in Ys. What foreknowledge of him would we have, what hold on him? What rewards could we promise for his cooperation, greater than he might find there for himself?"

"Also," the governor fretted, "if we sent the right man, how do we know he'd win?"

"A succession of men," Bacca said. "I've looked into the law of Ys. It's not unlike the ancient rule at Lake Nemi in Italy. Our guest there has been most helpful in explaining. The King is required to meet every challenger, though just one per day. If he's sick or badly hurt, the engagement is postponed till he's well. Now if a contestant appears *every* day, without surcease, hardy and battle-trained men who have no fear of death—day after day after day, while his lesser wounds and his weariness accumulate—he'll be done."

Glabrio grunted. "A pretty notion. Tell me where we'll find this string of undiscourageable warriors."

"I can!" Nagon cried. "I know!"

"Indeed? Well, before you name them, think. People in Ys are not stupid. Present company excepted, they seem on the whole rather attached to King Gratillonius. An influx of trained fighters such as you propose—no, it would much too obviously be at Roman instigation. It would have the same effect as killing him in this city. Or worse, because the victor, our man, would face a constitutional crisis like that which Brutus did after he met Caesar on the ides of March. The consequences are unforeseeable."

"The maneuver need not be at all obvious," Bacca answered calmly. "Nagon has had a brilliant idea."

Standing before them, the Ysan raised a finger. Vengefulness made ice floes of his eyes. "You may lose a few to start with," he admitted. "But before long you will get the kind of victor that we—you—that Rome can use, and safely, too, everything looking perfectly natural. Listen. Only listen a minute."

—At the hostel, Gratillonius went to its stable. There he saddled Favonius, after which he rode the stallion full speed to the Greater Monastery. He wanted to call on Martinus. Doubtless he'd have to wait till the bishop finished whatever devotions were going on, but then, for a while, he could enjoy the company of an honest man.

~ 2 ~

"Ya Am-Ishtar, ya Baalim, ga'a vi khuwa—"

The aurochs bull lifted his head. Sunlight gleamed off his horns and ran hotly down the great shoulders. Secure under his ward, cows and calves went on cropping the grass in the glade.

"Aus-t ur-t-Mut-Resi, am 'm user-t—"

The young summer filled the forest with greeness and fragrance. Bees buzzed, touching noonday silence no more than did the whisper out of shadows. The bull blinked, drooped his neck, settled down to rest.

"Belisama, Mother of Dreams, bring sleep unto him, send Your blind son to darken his mind and Your daughter whose feet are the feet of a cat to lead forth his spirit—"

The bull's head sank. He slept.

Behind the growth of saplings that screened her, Dahut lowered the hand that had pointed at him as she cast the spell. "I did it," she breathed, half unbelieving. "The Power flowed into me, through me, and—and for that space I was not myself, or I was beyond myself."

Forsquilis nodded. "You have the Gift in full measure, as far as we have tried you," she answered, equally low-voiced. "I failed to throw the net of slumber the first time I sought to after learning how, and likewise the second time. But you—"

She stopped, because the maiden had darted off, around the small trees, between a pair of giants, out into the glade and sunlight. There, gleefully, crowing laughter, Dahut sprang on the back of the bull, gripped his horns, rocked to and fro as if riding him. Her hair flowed wild over the woods-runner kirtle that, with breeks and sandals, clothed her. For a short space the cows regarded her drowsily, then one took alarm and lumbered in her direction. She jumped from her seat and scampered back under the forest roof. The cow returned to her calf.

Forsquilis seized Dahut by the shoulders. Anger made the Queen's face more pale than before and deepened the fine lines that had of late appeared around eyes and mouth. "Are you mad?" she gasped. "You knew not how deeply he sleeps, nor how long he will. He could have been roused, and that would have been the end of you, little fool, tossed, gored, stamped flat."

"But he wasn't," Dahut exulted. "I never feared he would be. The Gods wouldn't let him."

Forsquilis's fury calmed down to grimness. "Are you truly that vainglorious? Beware. Erenow They have found cause to disown mortals They once loved, and bring those persons to doom." She paused. "My fault, mayhap, my mistake. I should have made your trial of this art something less, like putting a sparrow or a vole to rest. But I let you persuade me—"

"Because I am born to the Power, and you know it!"

"Come," Forsquilis said. "Best we start back, if we'd reach the city ere sundown." They had traveled a number of leagues east, beyond the boundary stones, well into Osismiic territory. There were woods in the hinterland of Ys, near the Nymphaeum, but those held too much mystery, too many Presences, for an apprentice witch to risk disturbing.

Side by side, Queen and vestal walked toward the halting place of their escort. Brush was sparse beneath the trees, kept down by grazers such as they had found. Last year's leaves rustled underfoot. Sometimes a bird winged across sun-speckled shade, bound to or from its young in their nest.

"You must learn to be more careful, dear," Forsquilis sighed after a while. "Aye, and more humble. Set beside you, a lynx is cautious and meek."

Dahut flushed. "Not when caged, ardent to be free." She tossed her bright head. "Do you know this is the farthest from home I've have ever been, this wretched day-trip? Why would father not take me along to Turonum?"

"Blame him not. He would gladly have done so, but we Nine together told him he must not yield to your wheedling. You'd have been too long agone from your Temple duties. He has shown you Audiarna more than once."

"That dreary pisspot of a town? Nay, not a town; a walled village, naught Roman about it save a few soldiers, and they natives."

"You overstate things. You often do."

"Outside, a whole world waiting! Ah, it shall be otherwise when the new Age begins, I vow."

"Bide your time," Forsquilis counselled. "Master yourself. Today you bestrode an aurochs. When will you ride your own heart on roads wisely chosen? 'Tis apt to run away with you."

"Nay, 'tis I who choose to ride full speed— Hush!" Dahut snatched at Forsquilis's arm and pulled her to a halt. "Look."

Ahead of them was another opening in the forest, where a spring bubbled forth. Here, too, new growth around the edges hid the pair from sight. Horses cropped, spancelled. Half a dozen men sat or sprawled idle. Metal shone upon them. They were legionaries of Gratillonius's, guards of the royal two on this excursion. Reluctantly, they had obeyed the Queen's order to wait while she led the vestal onward afoot.

Mischief sparkled in Dahut's glance. "Listen," she hissed, "what a fine trick 'twould be to spell them to sleep. Then we could dust them with ants from yonder hill."

"Nay!" exclaimed Forsquilis, shocked. She made the girl look straight at her. "Worse than an unpleasant prank on those who deserve well of us. A base use of the Power, a mockery of the Gods Who granted it. Oh, Dahut, remember you are mortal."

The princess shrugged, smiled wryly, and proceeded ahead. As she came into view of the soldiers, the smile turned dazzling, and she answered their greetings with a flurry of blown kisses.

Budic trod near. His fair skin reddened while he asked awkwardly, "Did all go as you wished, whatever you came here to do, my lady?"

"Wondrous well," she caroled. "Now, let's be off. Let's get into a road and put spurs to our beasts."

He went on one knee and folded his hands, to provide her a step up into the saddle. It was as if the weight he raised were holy.

~ 3 ~

Theuderich the Frank held broad acres some miles out of Condate Redonum. He farmed them not as a curial but as he pleased; the Romans had long since decided it was prudent to wink at their own law rather than try to enforce it upon laeti of this race. After a fire consumed his hall, he rebuilt it on a grand scale, for he had waxed wealthy.

Thus he was at first unwilling to give more hospitality to a single traveler than his honor demanded—a place at the lower end of his board and a pallet on the floor for the night. If not a beggar, the man was plainly clad and indifferently mounted. If not a weakling, being short but broad, he was armed with only a Roman infantry sword and looked no more accustomed to its use than he was to riding. When he asked for a private talk with the master, Theuderich guffawed. Thereupon the fellow drew forth a letter of accreditation. Theuderich recognized the seal and did not trouble calling his slave accountant to read him the text. "Come," he said, and ordered ale brought.

He and the stranger, who named himself Nagon Demari, left the smoky dimness of the hall and walked through a drizzle of rain to a lesser building nearby. "The women's bower," Theuderich said. "It will do for us." Large windows covered with oiled cloth made the single room within bright enough for his wife, his lemans, and their serving maids to work at the loom it held or sit on the stools sewing, spinning, chatting. He shooed out such as were present, closed the door behind him, and turned to his guest.

For a short span, the men studied each other. In his mid-thirties, Theuderich was hulkingly powerful. A yellow beard spilled down from a ruddy face wherein the eyes glittered small by the broken nose. His garments were of excellent stuff but his smell was rank. "You're neither German nor Gaul," he grunted. "What, then?"

"A man of Ys, now in the service of Rome like yourself," Nagon answered.

"Ys?" Theuderich's countenance purpled. He lifted his ale horn as if to strike with it.

Nagon barked a laugh. "Easy," he said. "I've no more love for the King of Ys than you do. That's why I've sought you out."

"Um. Well, sit down and tell me. Speak slow. Your Latin's hard to follow."

Nagon forbore to remark on his host's accent. They hunched on opposed stools. Nagon tasted his ale. It was surprisingly good; but so quite often were Frankish fabrics, craftworks, jewelry. "I can understand your grudge against Ys," he began. "Were you not among those who were set on by what turned out to be agents of its King—eleven years ago, I've heard?"

"Yah," Theuderich snarled. "My father Merowech vowed revenge. On his deathbed, he made my brothers and me swear to pursue it. Not that we needed haranguing. We've suffered more than that one hour of dishonor. Those tame Bacaudae are everywhere about these days, in the woods, the hills, the countryside. They turn our serfs against us. Again and again they've disrupted our preparations for sacrifice, till Wotan no longer gets men on His high days, but only horses. When we've gathered war bands to scour them out, they've faded away, to come back and shoot us full of arrows from cover, or cut the throats of our sentries after dark. And Rome will give us no help. None!"

"Rome has her hands full," Nagon said. "She finds the King of Ys...troublesome." He leaned forward. "Hark, my lord." His life had taught him when and how to flatter. "I have a plan to broach. I came first to you because, while you may not be the supreme leader of the Franks—since this colony of your free-souled folk scarcely has any such man—and you are not even the eldest living son of a great father: still, everybody tells me you are among the strongest and most respected in Armorica. They say also that you are wise, discreet, well able to keep silence until the time be ripe for action."

Theuderich puffed himself out. "Go on."

"Let me ask you a question. Considering what valiant men the Franks are, and what wrongs the King of Ys has done them, and what wealth and glory are to be had yonder, why has none of you ever gone to challenge him?"

Theuderich glowered. His hand dropped to his dagger. "Dare you think we're afraid?"

"Oh, no, never. Surely you have a sound reason."

"Um. Well." Theuderich drank deep, belched, and scratched in his beard. "Well, the fact is that Grallon hound is a legionary of the old kind, what you can hardly get anywhere any more. I've looked into this myself, I have. Men have told me how he's minced his opponents like garlic cloves, and always wins over his sparring partners. What gain in letting him chew up others? Whoever did take him would likely be too badly hurt to get much use out of being King of Ys. Besides, challengers would pester him to his own death."

"This could be changed," Nagon said softly.

Theuderich sat upright. "How?"

"What if Grallon had to fight a man every day? The first few might die—gloriously—but soon he would be tired and battered, easy prey."

Theuderich slumped. "That's been thought of. Can't be done. Ys would never let so many armed strangers in at once; and she's got the force to keep them out. Anyhow, we can't make war on Ys. It's a Roman ally, and we're Roman subjects. Stilicho would be quick to punish us. He may not be too fond of Ys either, but he doesn't stand for that sort of disorder, as—we've learned."

"It could be arranged," Nagon purred. "Suppose the Ysan troops were elsewhere. Suppose then the Franks marched in and established themselves. It would not be an act of war, for how could the Ysans put up a fight? It would be without Roman permission, but also without official Roman knowledge. By the time these doings could no longer be ignored, Grallon would be dead. The new King of Ys would find the Imperial authorities quite willing to pardon any offense against their law, in return for a payment that he could easily make out of the city treasury. Thereafter he could go about lifting the burden off

546

you, his people, that Grallon laid on you. He would be a hero. So would those be who died to prepare the way for him. Their fame would be immortal."

As he talked, Theuderich had begun shivering and panting. At the end, the Frank bayed. "How can this *happen*?"

"We will talk about that," Nagon said. "Pray understand, my lord, the new King need not—must not—become a sacrificial animal waiting for slaughter. His aim shall be to change everything there, piece by piece, until at last he can bequeath the city to Rome, the way I've heard the kingdom of Pergamum was. The Romans will quietly guide him. They won't interfere with his pleasures. Think, nine lovely wives, and the fabulous city itself! In the end, Ys will be Christian, but this King we're talking about cannot be, if he's to lead the rites as he must, unless maybe in his old age he chooses baptism. Oh, a Frankish warrior would be perfect. He'd be an omen foreshadowing the future of all Gallia."

Theuderich stared.

~ 4 ~

One evening before midsummer, a sunset of rare beauty kindled above Ocean. For a timeless time clouds shone with rose and gold and every hue between, against a clear blue that slowly deepened toward purple. The waters breathed calm, giving back to heaven those changeable colors. Whenever it seemed the splendor was about to fade into that night which had already led forth the first eastern stars, fieriness broke free again. Entranced, folk throughout Ys swarmed onto the wall; their murmurs of wonder were as low as the sea's.

Rufinus was one of them. He could have watched from the Polaris, but not as well. On his way, he knocked on the door of Tommaltach, who occupied rooms below his. Together they hastened by the shipyard and up the staircase there. Being important men, they won admission past the guards at the Raven Tower, away from the crowd and onto the stretch where the war engines were. Only a few Suffetes and ladies had done likewise. Those couples or individuals kept well apart, desirous of nothing except the miracle before them. The two comrades recognized Queens Bodilis and Tambilis at some distance, but did not venture greetings.

Finally glory smoldered away forever. People grew conscious of chill in the air and began to descend while they still had light. More and more stars trembled above inland hills. The western clouds had gone smoky.

"Ah, that was a sight of the Beyond, and I thank you for calling me to it," Tommaltach said. "The flames of Mag Mell—though it may be what we have glimpsed is from somewhere greater, from One Who is above the Gods."

Rufinus laughed. "You're too serious for a young lad," he answered. "Come along to my apartment and we'll pour a stoup and be our proper, roisterous selves."

Tommaltach's vision strained into the gathering dusk. "Was Princess Dahut here to see? I do hope so."

As they approached the Raven Tower, several men came from its door. They wore vestments above their clothes. It was not yet too dark to discern the features of Cynan, Verica, Maclavius, a few Ysans—and, in the lead, King Gratillonius, Father of the Mithraic congregation.

Feet halted. Rufinus and Tommaltach touched their brows. "Hail, lord," they said. Gratillonius responded.

Rufinus's teeth flashed in the blackness of his fork beard. "A pity this was a holy day of yours," he remarked. Clearly it was, for ordinarily a believer would just say a prayer wherever he happened to be at nightfall. "While you were underground worshipping the sun, he gave the rest of us the most marvelous spectacle."

"'Twas Mithras we communed with," Gratillonius reminded him, "and His light shone upon our souls." A certain exaltation lingered in him. "My friend, if you would only listen—"

Rufinus shook his head. Pain edged his tones. "Nay, I'll not pretend what is false...before you. Never can I be a communicant of your faith."

"You've told me that erenow, but will not say why. Surely—"

"Never."

Tommaltach quivered. "But I, sir!" burst from him. "I would try my best to understand."

Gratillonius regarded him as closely as the dimness allowed. "Think well," he said. "This is naught to trifle with."

"Nor do I mean to." Tommaltach's voice had lost his usual confident cheer. "What I've been watching— Oh, but 'tis more than that. Since coming to Ys and knowing—you—well, the city, the world beyond, enough to see that I really know nothing— The gods of Ériu are far off, sir, and They seem so small."

"Mock Them not. However—" Gratillonius smiled. He reached forth to clasp the Scotian's arm. "Of course we'll talk, you and I, and if you come to believe in all honesty that Mithras is Lord, why, I myself will lead you into His mysteries," said the father of Dahut.

VI

~ 1 ~

Rain had left the air humid. As the sun declined, vapors reddened its disc, but fog would not likely roll in to cool Ys before dawn. Gratillonius was almost glad to come off the street into the house of Maldunilis.

Zisa, her daughter and his, admitted him with a perfunctory "Hail." This year the girl had had her Welcoming, but to her that stage of life had brought sullenness, perhaps because it first brought fat and pimples.

"How went your day?" Gratillonius made himself ask.

She grimaced and shrugged. "A day at the Temple. You're late. The servants are trying to keep dinner from getting ruined."

"I'd duties of my own," he snapped. Before he could go on to rebuke her for insolence, Maldunilis entered the atrium. That was just as well. Gratillonius stalked to meet her and join both pairs of hands as was fitting.

The Queen looked closely at him. "Again you have a thunderstorm in your face," she said. "What's gone awry this time?"

He gazed back. Over the years she had added flesh to flesh, though her frame was large enough that as yet she did not appear quite gross. Her features remained good in their heavy fashion and her hair was still a burnished red-brown. It was untidily piled on her head, like the raiment on her body. He had grown used to that. He had also grown acceptant of the fact that her interest in civic affairs, or in most things, was weak; she passively accepted the decisions her Sisters reached.

"No need to trouble you now," he said, as often before. "You'll soon hear."

If only this were Bodilis, Lanarvilis, Vindilis for counsel; Forsquilis, Tambilis for instilling fire; Innilis, even Guilvilis for the peacefulness that nurtures. But tonight was Maldunilis's turn with the King. Well, she had her rights, and she was by no means a bad person, and a man ought to shoulder his burdens without whining about them.

She nodded. "Come," she said, "food waits."

She, or rather her cook, set an excellent table. This evening Gratillonius scarcely noticed what was before him, except for the wine. Of that he took several helpings. Maldunilis chattered for both of them; that too was common in their marriage. "—Then Davona—do you know Davona? She's that blond underpriestess who renewed her vows after being widowed two years ago, but believe me, she's a husband-hunting hussy—Davona claimed the foxglove had lain stored too long and lost its virtue, and that was why that poor gangrel we took into the hospice died, but I know she wants to be the one who goes with the gatherers to bless the herb, because there'll be handsome young marines along—

"Grallon, why did you scowl so?"

He shook his head. "'Tis naught. Go on."

"What else? Oh. Well, later that same day I saw my dressmaker. I do need a new outfit for Midsummer, and the price she named—"

Zisa was silent, systematically feeding. Always she watched her parents. Her eyes were small; they made Gratillonius think of a sow's eyes.

549

Sometimes he wished he could like, or at least not dislike, this child of his. The rest were pleasant, certain of them more than that. Bodilis's Una, newly fifteen, and Tambilis's Estar, four, almost rivaled Dahut as she was and had been. Of course, they were her close kin. He shied from that remembrance. Vindilis's Augustina was turning a little strange in her vestalhood, doubtless taking after her strong-willed, aloof mother. The same might be said of Forsquilis's Nemeta, but she was a spirited lass and often cheerful. Tambilis's older girl, Semuramat, and Lanarvilis's Julia were rather solemn, yet never withheld affection from him. Guilvilis's six, ranging from fifteen to three, were very ordinary people who accorded him the same awe, and some of the same love, she did...

Maldunilis finished her dish of comfits. "Are you through, dear? Time for sleep," she said archly.

Gratillonius rose. The wine buzzed faintly in his head, bees in a clover meadow where a youth and his sweetheart had found solitude. "Aye," he answered, "I must be up early."

She giggled. "Indeed you must be up."

He turned his face from Zisa, lest the girl see him flush. Maldunilis had always lacked reticence. He knew what his daughter was thinking— *you are going to futter now*—and would not have cared save that she appeared to gloat over it. Glimpses he had had, looks she cast him, tones and gestures, caused him to suspect she was given to listening at the bedroom door.

Ahriman take that! If what he wanted most was a life free of folk peering, guessing, gossiping, sniggering, proclaiming how much better than he they could do his work, why, then he should long since have slipped away from Ys and become a hermit like Corentinus aforetime. But when his God spoke, Corentinus had had the manhood to obey orders.

Gratillonius accompanied Maldunilis from the triclinium. The wine in his veins helped him ignore everything else. Likewise did the heat that began licking at his loins. Once a Queen of Ys had the King to herself, the Gods entered them both; and Belisama held supremacy over Taranis.

Immediately after the door had closed behind them, Maldunilis flung her mass against Gratillonius. She kissed avidly, mouth wide open, tongue searching. "'Tis been a weary while," she groaned.

His hands wandered. His mind did also, under less control. For the thousandth time, he puzzled over the ninefold marriage that was his. Did the powers of the Gallicenae spring from their pent-up needs? Yet this bulk that he held could belong to any fishwife. Nor did the others claim much more—Innilis's occasional healing, Forsquilis's occasional visions or minor spells—than some barbarian witch might. Together they had summoned him, overthrown Colconor, wrecked the Scotic fleet, or so they believed; but that was, O Mithras, sixteen years ago, and they were frank in their doubts that they could do anything of the kind ever again. They did not *feel* they could. The Age of Brennilis was dying away.

Gratillonius disengaged from Maldunilis and fumbled at his clothes. Let him find whatever surcease was in her, quickly. Most evenings they blew out the lights before they bedded. That was not so common among the Ysans of the upper classes, including his other wives, but this one didn't care and in the dark he could pretend, after a fashion. At this season, though, daylight dawdled. She cast her own garb on the floor. Well, his member responded, and he would pillow his face in the softness between those heavy breasts.

"A moment," she laughed. Matter-of-factly, she slipped the lid off the pot and sat down. Somehow, the gurgling excited him further. No, not all the power of the Nine had left them.

—It was as if lust were a dam, and when it had been broken, care flooded back through him. Lying there in the sweat-dampened sheets, he gagged on a breath.

She stirred beside him. "What's wrong?" she asked.

"Naught, naught," he demurred.

Sometimes she could surprise him. Raising herself to an elbow, she looked down into his eyes and said diffidently, "I know I am a lackwit, but if you want to talk, if that will help, I can keep silence about it."

He sighed. She smiled and stroked his brow, ruffled back his hair. Maybe, if he spoke the matter forth, he really would sleep better.

"No need for that," he told her. "No secret. I'll be setting it before the Council. A message came today from Turonum."

She caressed his head and waited.

"The Romans—" He must gulp and search for words. "The Duke and the civil governor together have sent me a command, me, the prefect of Rome. About a month hence, there'll be military exercises lasting for...a while, they say. It's to be jointly with the regular forces of Ys. Our marine corps and such of our naval vessels as are not out are to report at Darioritum Venetorum and place themselves under the Roman general for the duration of the maneuvers."

"What? Has that ever happened erenow?"

"Never. And Armorica faces no threat these days."

Maldunilis frowned into space. "I don't see— What is bad about this?"

"Why, that it is such a new thing, without any clear cause. Oh, the letter speaks of preparing against the future, and cites our offer to train crews for the ships we'll build for Rome. I cannot refuse obedience and appeal to higher authority. As King of sovereign Ys, I must persuade Ys to do as I, the prefect of Rome, am bidden. The timing is skillful, this soon before our Midsummer Council. I'll catch the Suffetes unprepared and ram an agreement through. I must."

"I'll vote however you want, of course. But surely this is naught bad. Won't our men make a grand showing! Will you go too?"

He shook his head beneath her fingers. "Nay. The order is clear on that. I stay home to look after my 'responsibilities'—Imperial interests. What are they planning, those men?"

"Mayhap only what they say they are."

"You wish to believe that. I'd like it myself. Well, I see no choice before me."

"Then stop fretting." Maldunilis lay back down. Her hand roved across his chest and belly, and onward. "Tonight, be simply Grallon the man."

~ 2 ~

Flowing into the sea about ten road miles from Ys, the River Goana marked the southeastern frontier of the city hinterland; beyond lay Osismia. Nonetheless, Rome claimed Audiarna, the town on its right bank. The inhabitants were almost entirely Gauls, including the small garrison. It had been directed to report with the Ysan marines at Venetorum. That seemed peculiar, since the whole western tip of the peninsula would then be stripped of troops. However, Ysan naval patrols ought to keep pirates away, and there was nothing to fear from inland, was there? Rather, the exercises would be another step toward rebuilding an effective defense for all Armorica.

The day was bright when the newcomers entered Audiarna. Sunlight flashed off pikeheads, high helmets, cuirasses whose lines and ornamentation called deep-water waves to mind. A breeze blew, making banners snap and plumes ripple brilliant. Though numbering a mere few hundred, the marines of Ys were the most impressive sight the sleepy little city could remember. They tramped through its gate and down its principal street in a unison that was not mechanical but flowed, like the movement of a single many-legged panther. Their officers led them on blooded horses. The pack animals that followed were nearly as mettlesome, the supply wagons graceful, playfully decorated, akin to chariots. No tuba brayed; drums thuttered, pipes shrilled, in rhymes whose alienness was of the tides and the winds.

At their heads blazed beauty, a young woman on a great sorrel stallion. Her hair streamed free, gold and amber. Flamboyant as well as impudent, silver-worked blue tunic and kidskin breeks hugged the curves of her; a red cloak winged from her shoulders; a circlet set with gems glittered around her brow. When she drew rein in the forum, a kind of susurrus went through the people who had gathered to watch.

The native company and its Roman cadre had been waiting. Abruptly their outfits looked shabby and their formation ragged. The chief centurion, himself mounted, lifted an arm in salute. The Ysan leader did likewise before clattering over the pavement to utter greetings. At his side rode the maiden, and it was she who spoke first. Being commissioned by a suzerain state and in charge of the superior force, the Ysan would have command over both as far as Venetorum; that concession had helped reduce unwillingness to go. When the centurion formally proffered a vinestaff, it was the maiden who took it and in turn gave it to her companion.

Thereupon she wheeled her steed, rode back to the front of the marines, and cried while the stallion snorted and stamped beneath her: "Comrades of the road, farewell! Now I must return and you continue onward. Yet in spirit I will fare with you always. The legionaries who came to Ys with my father the King call me their Luck. Let me be yours too, as you travel among foreigners and hold high the honor of Ys."

"Dahut!" roared from the men. "Dahut! Dahut!"

"The Nine Gallicenae will watch and pray and work their spells on your behalf," she vowed. "So will every vestal, myself the foremost. Come home in joy. In the names of Taranis, Lir, and Belisama Queen of Battles, be you our strength!"

Again they cheered.

The centurion frowned. It was too much for the chorepiscopus at Audiarna. Although Dahut had used her own language, most of the onlookers knew enough of it to follow; it was not enormously different from theirs. A few registered indignation or made signs and muttered prayers. But many seemed excited, certain among them even uplifted. These also raised a shout.

The chorepiscopus left his church, from the porch of which he had been watching, and pushed through the crowd around the market square. A heavy man, his gray hair tonsured in the style of Martinus, he strode until he stood before the towering horse and the beautiful rider. He raised his arms and bawled in Latin: "O people of Audiarna, soldiers of Rome, what is this work of Satan? Beware of your souls! This pagan witch is not content to flaunt herself in man's clothing like a harlot, she invokes the demons she worships, here in our very midst, we, the subjects of the Augustus. Cast her from you before she leads you down into the fires of hell!"

The Ysan marines growled. Most of them had understood. Hands clenched on weapons.

Dahut quelled the trouble. She threw back her head and pealed forth laughter. Looking down at the cleric, she replied, also in Latin: "Have no fear, old man. If I lead anybody, it will be to nowhere hot, but the sea that is Ys's. Besides, I am leaving now. Let me suggest first, out of kindness, that you study your grammar. What you did to your conjugations was utter horror. But then, your Jesus wouldn't know the difference, would He?"

Before the Ysans could whoop, and so make the Romans angrier, Dahut called to them: "Again, farewell! Fare ever well!" She spurred Favonius and sped from the forum. Her four-man escort had difficulty keeping up. In moments she was gone. The sound of hoofbeats on stone dwindled away. Men blinked at each other, mute, uncertain, as if they had just awakened from a dream.

~ 3 ~

"—Then as the fog lifted, taking soundings we found bottom at forty fathoms. Here fish abounded. We saw thick shoals of little fish like sprats, and rushing to eat them before they dispersed were multi-tudinous cod of twenty or thirty pounds. For three days we fished, cleaning and salting the catch until we bore ample food. Meanwhile, though rarely as yet, we sighted such birds as to make us think land must not be overly far. Our water casks were low and foul, since rain had not come for us to gather in our mainsail as had happened earlier. Therefore we bore on westward."

Bodilis paused in her reading aloud. Gratillonius looked across the table where he and she shared a bench. "Does this still ring true?" he asked.

Maeloch, opposite, nodded his shaggy head. "Aye," he rumbled. "'Tis pretty much a learned man's words, but ye can hear through them that 'twas a plain fisher captain who told him the story. No mermaids, no magical isles, only a nigh endless waste of sea till at last yon crew came to a shore."

Gratillonius thrilled. It was not that he doubted the men of Saphon's smack *Kestrel* had had a strange adventure, three generations ago. Throughout the history of Ys, craft had fared helpless beyond the horizon when a freakish storm sprang out of the east. *Kestrel* was among the few that won back. What kept the tale alive was that the return had been after months, as if from the dead. Gratillonius saw no reason either to question the claim that those men had found land. What he wondered about was how much their description had grown with the telling, year by year, lifetime by lifetime.

When he spoke of it to Bodilis, she said that quite possibly someone had taken down the account in writing, soon after Saphon came home. She offered to search the library. That required patience; scrolls and codices were heaped on shelves in uncounted thousands. Finally, trium-phantly, she found the one document. Having perused it himself, Gratillonius wanted an opinion from a master, preferably also a fisher. *Osprey* happened to be in port unloading a haul.

The library was a curious place for such a tale. High windows between pillars admitted sufficient light into the cool dimness to read by. A mosaic floor depicted the owl and aegis of Minerva. If the Goddess Herself was represented on a wall, bookcases that reached to the ceiling had long since hidden Her. A caretaker padded about, dusting. At another table, a man sat reading and a vestal copied something from a tome, probably at the orders of a minor priestess who wanted information in convenient form. No sound penetrated from the Forum outside. Here was a cavern of mute oracles.

"Go on, my lady, I pray ye," said Maeloch eagerly.

"You may not like what follows," Gratillonius warned.

"Ha? Why not, sir?"

"Because it makes false those wonders that are in the mouths which today tell the story. There is no giant eel, no elven queen in her palace of illusion, no herd of unicorns—naught of the Otherworld at all."

Maeloch grinned. "Why, I'd be surprised if there was. What I've seen of weirdness—and that's more than most—beggars men's brags and boys' daydreams. Ye'd nay ha' bid me hither did the yarn lack *real* wonders."

"Wonders indeed," murmured Bodilis: isles clustered in hordes along the ruggedness of a coast which stretched on and on, immensity behind it, forests of spruce and fir and birch, teeming with elk, bear, beaver, otter, and beasts and birds unknown to Europe, tribespeople broad-faced and black-maned who carried tools of stone. She cleared her throat.

"Hark well," Gratillonius directed Maeloch. "Afterward, think hard. It appears *Kestrel* reached a country huge, rich, and virginal. How much so, we can but guess; yet surely, as you said, the truth will dwarf any imaginings of ours."

The sailor gave him a keen stare. "Ye'd fain outfit an expedition."

"Aye. Two or three ships built especially for the voyage. It seems the way west is difficult but east is much easier, as if Ocean were in truth the world-engirdling river the ancients supposed. Knowing that, we can plan wisely. However, first I need experienced men to tell me if this can likely be done or is a mere fever-dream of mine."

"Ye're nay given to wild notions, King Grallon. Carry on, my lady."

The hope flamed in Gratillonius. Yonder a new land, no, a new world—waiting for Ys, whose seafarers alone had the skill and boldness to reach it—colonies free of hoary hatreds, tyrannies, poverties, menaces, where civilization could be reborn and a palace worthy of elves might arise for Queen Dahut!

"More and more birds did we see," Bodilis read, "and presently driftwood."

A man entered the room and hastened to the table. "Begging your pardon, sir," he muttered in Latin. "Urgent."

Annoyed, Gratillonius twisted about on the bench and recognized his legionary Verica. The two dozen Roman soldiers had stayed in the city when the marines left, to be the core of guardians on its wall and peacekeepers in its streets. Of course, he thought wearily, someone always knew where the King was to be found. "Well?" he rapped.

"Sir, the beacon's lit. Beyond Lost Castle. Nothing's at sea except fishers and a couple of merchantmen. A party worth worrying about must be coming along Redonian Way."

Gratillonius tautened. Few of the signal towers wrecked by barbarians had yet been rebuilt, in these years of peace, but he had worked to have bonfires ready for kindling in a chain along the shoreline. They were intended to warn of pirates. If no hostile fleet was in sight, then an Ysan watcher had been alarmed by what he saw bound overland. Yet apparently no sign burned in Osismiic territory. Such would have been visible from Point Vanis. Which meant the Romans had observed nothing to fear. Which most likely meant that this was all harmless. And yet—and yet the fighting men of Ys were afar.

Gratillonius rose. "I must go," he said. "You two can continue."

"I'd have trouble listening," Maeloch answered grimly. Anguish crossed Bodilis's countenance. For a moment, her hand clutched Gratillonius's.

Verica at his heels, he went out into the Forum and up Lir Way to Warriors' House by High Gate. The bustle and color around him had gone curiously distant, not quite real. He told himself he was foolish to conjure phantoms, that everything could well be a mistake, or benign; but he was no philosopher. He was a military man who needed to make contingency plans.

The barrack echoed emptily to his footfalls. Only a couple of youths were there, from among those newly recruited as auxiliaries in the absence of the regulars. It took a while to devise instructions for them to carry out or pass on to the others, with the aim of getting all his legionaries together and providing some kind of replacements on the wall. Thereafter they were gone for a maddeningly long spell. He sent Verica to fetch his horse Favonius from the palace, and then in Dragon House had the man help him into his armor. Still he must wait.

One by one, though, they arrived, his Britannic Romans. It struck him sharply how none of them was a young man any longer. Even Budic had furrows in his face, while Adminius the deputy was grizzled, nearly toothless, and gaunt as a twig in winter. Just the same, they snapped to their duties and followed him out the gate with a smartness he doubted the Imperial units now at Venetorum could show.

By that time the strangers were in sight, headed down Redonian Way from its southward bend at the old station on Point Vanis. As Gratillonius led his handful to meet them, he saw a score or so detach themselves and leave the road, slanting southeast across the trails that crisscrossed the heights.

This day was sunny. Wind chased small white clouds off an olive sea full of whitecaps that burst against skerries. Intensely green with summer, grass billowed over the headland, around its boulders and megaliths and shelters; sheep made flecks in the distance, driven away by frightened herders. The wind skirled. It bore salt odors. Gulls rode it beyond the cliffs, and a hawk immensely above.

Nearing them, Gratillonius estimated the invaders at a hundred and fifty. It would have meant little—so few would not have dared—when Ys had her usual defenders on hand. Nor could he send to Audiarna for help. That fact chilled him with the knowledge that this must be nothing coincidental, nothing peaceful. Those were Franks.

Big men, mostly fair-haired and blue-eyed, they walked in loose formation behind a few mounted leaders. They had not many pack animals either, nor any wagons, which suggested they did not plan on a long campaign. Some wore nose-guarded helmets and chainmail coats, some kettle hats and boiled leather, but all were well-armed—sword, ax, or spear, and at every belt the terrible francisca. Hairy, slouching, stenchful, they were nonetheless a nightmare sight; it was as if the Roman road shuddered beneath their tread.

Gratillonius reined in and lifted an arm. After a moment, a Frank afoot hoisted a peeled white pole. Gratillonius took that for a sign of truce. Commands barked hoarse and the laeti grumbled to a halt. One on horseback clattered forth from their van. Gratillonius went to meet him.

They sat glowering at each other. "I hight Theuderich, son of Merowech," said the Frank in wretched Latin. He was big, coarse, and golden. "I speak for these men of Redonia whom I lead."

"You speak to Gratillonius, King of Ys, prefect of Rome. What are you doing here? Trespass on an ally is a violation of Imperial law."

Theuderich spat laughter. "Complain in Turonum, or Treverorum or Mediolanum or wherever you like," he gibed. He raised his palm. "Don't be scared. We mean no harm. Let us camp for a bit and you won't have any trouble. We're only here to make sure things go right— that justice is done," he added, a wording he had doubtless rehearsed.

The tension in Gratillonius slacked off a little. It often happened thus, when waiting had finally ended and confrontation was upon him. Alertness thrummed. "Explain yourself."

"Well, my lord," said Theuderich smugly, "the Kingship of Ys is for any foreigner who challenges and slays the old King, like you did, hey? We Franks think the time is overpast for one of our nation to take this throne and set matters right. So we've come in a body. That way, can't be any of your sly Ysan treacheries against our challengers—one each day, right my *lord*? The Gods will decide. We've already asked Them: drawn lots to see who goes first and second and so on. Chramn, son of Clothair, Wotan picked him." He glanced toward the darkling circle of the Wood below them. "I think he's arrived by now."

As if in answer, faint against the wind, from the Sacred Precinct there tolled the sound of the Hammer striking the Shield.

VII

~ 1 ~

"Remember," Gratillonius told Adminius and his other legionaries, "if he wins, he's King. Don't rebel or try to kill him in your turn or

557

do anything but your duty. That is to keep Ys safe and orderly. You're the framework of what watch it's got till the marines and navy men come back. After they do, you can go to Turonum and put yourselves under the garrison commander there."

"We don't want to, sir," the deputy answered. "We got families 'ere, and— And you'll take this swine any'ow, sir, we know you will."

Unspoken behind the faces: But what of the next, or the next, or the next?

Gratillonius had not allowed himself to think about that. He dared not do so yet. Events were moving like a runaway horse; it was less than an hour since the challenge sounded. He turned from the soldiers. In the absence of the marines, theirs was the task of keeping folk who had swarmed to the scene at a good distance down the road. Nobody had brought hounds to pursue a man who fled, but that was unnecessary today. Gratillonius marched at the measured Roman pace to the trees of battle.

The Franks who had accompanied Chramn waited by the rail fence of the meadow across Processional Way. That was just as well. To have them near the Ysans could easily have brought on a riot. As it was, the yells that reached their ears caused them to glare and grip tightly the spearshafts on which some of them leaned. Doubtless they could not make out the words, but threat, defiance, revilements were unmistakable. If a Frankish King brought comrades of his to Ys, they must needs dwell there like an army of occupation. They'd be less disciplined, though; killing, maiming, rape, and robbery would become everyday occurrences.

Chramn stood under the courtyard oak. Red-robed and black-browed, Soren held ready the bowl of water and sprig of mistletoe. From the porch of the Lodge the staff watched, appalled. Behind, wind soughed mightily through the grove.

Chramn leered at Gratillonius. He was young, perhaps twenty, taller by two or three inches and heavier by perhaps fifty pounds of bone and hard muscle. Reddish whiskers fuzzed an incongruously round, apple-cheeked countenance within which the small blue eyes seemed doubly cold. For weapons he bore throwing-ax, dagger, and a longsword scabbarded across his back. A little circular shield was protection incidental to helmet and knee-length hauberk. He would be difficult to get at inside that iron.

Gratillonius halted. Soren must cough before he could ask, "Are you both armed as you desire?" The Frank scowled, and Soren repeated the required questions in Latin. Chramn replied with a noise that must be an affirmative. Gratillonius simply nodded.

"Kneel," Soren directed. The contestants obeyed, side by side as if this were their wedding. Soren dipped the mistletoe in the water and sprinkled them. He chanted a prayer in the Punic tongue Gratillonius had never learned.

The Roman wondered if his enemy was inwardly calling on some heathen God. He formed words in his own mind. *Mithras, also a soldier, into Your hands I give my spirit. Whatever befalls me, help me bear it with courage.* The plea clanked dull, meaningless. Abruptly, of itself: *To You I entrust Ys, my children, my wives, all who are dear to me— because Who else is left to care for them?*

"Go forth," said Soren in Ysan, "and may the will of the God be done." His gaze trailed the pair out of sight.

Chramn joined Gratillonius in passing between the Lodge and a shed, into the grove. Soon huge old boles and densely clustered leafage hid the buildings. The ground was almost unencumbered, except by occasional fallen trees moldering away in moss and fungus. Dead leaves crackled underfoot. Sun-speckled shadow filled the spaces among the oaks, below their arching crowns. For some reason, no squirrel or bird was about, but the wind blustered through branches, making them creak as well as rustle. It smelled of dampness.

At a glade near the center, where grass rippled within a narrow compass, Gratillonius stopped. "Shall we begin?" he said. "Here I killed my two earlier men"—and spared the third; but he had no desire to let this one depart alive.

"Good," replied the Frank. "You think you will kill me too, ha? You will not. You are a dead man."

His voice had taken on a curious, remote quality. Likewise had his expression. The spell of combat was upon him, Gratillonius realized. It did not take the Celtic form, that utter abandon which flung Scoti howling onto the points of their foes. Gratillonius had heard that this could seize Germani too, but Chramn was different. He had not become a Roman machine either. He seemed a sleepwalker, lost in dream, as if already he were among those fallen warriors who feasted and fought in the hall of their Gods, awaiting the last battle at the end of time. Yet he watched and moved with total alertness, all the more dangerous because of having put aside his soul.

Gratillonius drew blade and brought up his shield, ready to shift it as need arose. The two men circled warily, several feet apart. The Frankish ringmail moved supple as snake scales. Chramn's free hand hovered.

It pounced. The francisca leaped from his belt and across the wind. Gratillonius just caught it. He felt the impact through shield, arm, shoulder. The ax stuck in the wood, hampering. Chramn's sword had hissed forth in nearly the same motion as the cast. He bounded forward and swung.

Gratillonius blocked the blow. Chramn tried for a cut lower down, on the leg. Gratillonius fended him off with the big Roman shield while his own short blade worked from around it, probing.

The fighters broke apart. Again they stalked, each in search of an opening. Their looks met; once more Gratillonius felt a strange intimacy.

559

He had given Chramn a slash in the left calf, blood darkened that trouser leg, but it was a flesh wound, the Frank had likely not even noticed.

Chramn charged anew. Shield against shield, he hammered above and sickled below. Several times his edge rang on Gratillonius's helmet or scraped across armor. The Roman could only defend himself, parry, push, interpose, retreat step by step.

The flurry lasted for minutes. Gratillonius felt his heart begin to slam and his breath rasp dry. Sweat drenched his undergarments, reeked in his nostrils. He saw the Frank smile sleepily, well-nigh serenely.

He is a generation younger, Gratillonius knew. He has more strength. He means to attack me like this over and over, till I'm winded and my knees shake and the weight of my hands drags on me. Then I am his.

Gratillonius's glance flickered right and left. He saw what he needed and edged toward it, a tree with lower boughs close to the ground at the rim of the glade.

If he drew well into the grove, the longsword would be hindered, the shortsword not. Chramn knew that. He rushed while his foe was still in the open.

Gratillonius slipped below a branch and went to his left knee. His shield he held slantwise. The limb caused the Frankish metal to strike it awkwardly. He himself had a clear thrust upward from the ground.

His point went under the hem of the byrnie. He guided it with care—time had slowed, he had abundant leisure for precision—and felt it go heavily into a thigh and worked it around to make sure of severing the great blood vessel there. After that he sank it into the belly just above the genitalia.

Chramn pulled free. He lurched back. Gratillonius rose. With his dripping sword, he slashed across the right hand of his opponent, cutting finger tendons. The long blade dropped into the grass. Blood spurted from beneath the hauberk.

"Well," panted Gratillonius, "that's one."

He lowered his heavy arms. Chramn stared and staggered. He would crumple in another half minute or so.

He screeched something and threw himself forward. The shield fell from his left hand, which was still useable. With that hand he grabbed the centurion at the back of the neck. He was losing his footing now, sinking to earth. He kept the hold while he crashed his helmeted head upward, against the chin of his killer.

Blackness erupted.

—Gratillonius gaped at the sky. He looked around, bewildered. A corpse sprawled beside him where he lay. "He was dead," he mumbled. "He hit me." Blood matted his beard. "He was dead. He hit me."

He tried to get up and could not, but crawled between the trees, homing like an animal. Often he collapsed, lay huddled, stirred and crept a little further.

He came back out into sunlight, from behind the house that was red. Men gathered around. "He was dead," Gratillonius whimpered. "He hit me."

Soren called for the physician. Gratillonius was borne inside. A moan lifted from the Ysans, a howl from the Franks. Then Fredegond, son of Merowech, laughed aloud and crossed the road into the Sacred Precinct. He took the Hammer and rang the next challenge.

~ 2 ~

A boat had fetched Tambilis from Vigil on Sena, because at an hour like this all the Gallicenae must be on hand. They met in the house of Fennalis, for the old Queen could no longer leave her bed.

Eight standing crowded the small, simply furnished room. It was hot. Sunlight filled the glass of the west-side window as if with molten brass. Everyone spoke softly; the loudest sound was the labored breath of Fennalis.

"A messenger from Rivelin at the palace reached me as I was leaving home to come hither," Bodilis reported. "I had ordered him to send me immediate word of any change."

"I should have thought of that!" blurted Guilvilis. Tears trickled down her cheeks.

"Cease blubbering," said Vindilis. "What news?"

"Gratillonius has fallen into a deep slumber," Bodilis told them. "Rivelin expects he'll have his wits back when he awakens."

Lanarvilis nodded. "I looked for that from the first," she said. "A blow to the chin—aye, one that did not dislocate or break his jaw—should not do harm like a cudgel at the back of the skull." Her glance went affectionately down to Fennalis. "True? You were ever good with the wounded."

The dying woman achieved a nod and a whisper: "But he'll—be weak—subject to giddy spells—in need of rest and care—for days."

"He mustn't fight again till he's hale," decided Maldunilis, pleased with her own wisdom.

Vindilis frowned. "There's the question, Sisters. *May* he wait that long?"

"Of course he shall," cried Tambilis. Red and white chased each other across her young face. "Else 'twould be no fight. The Gods do not want that."

"But the Franks do," said Lanarvilis bleakly, "and we're ill prepared to deny them."

"What have they been doing since—" Tambilis could not finish. She had run straight here from the dock.

"Those at the Wood returned to their fellows on Point Vanis, bearing the slain," Lanarvilis answered. "At Soren's protest that we had a rite for him, they jeered. They're camped near the bend of Redonian Way. A band of them went down with a cart to fill jugs at the canal, and our folk could do naught about the defilement of the sacred water, but curse them from the battlements. Nor can we keep them from ravaging the hinterland and murdering whomever they catch, if they grow impatient with us."

"What of their dead?" wondered Innilis with a shiver. "Will they burn or bury those—on the forbidden headland? Taranis will smite them for that. Won't he?"

Vindilis compressed her lips before stating, "Grallon held a burial out there long ago. Only today was he stricken down."

"I watched from a Northbridge Gate tower," Forsquilis said. "Nay, I cannot make a Sending by daylight, but a charm did briefly sharpen my sight. The Franks have several coffins with them. Yon corpse lies shut away. Those men who had been at the Wood with him—the chosen against our King, I think—stood around the box. They drew blood from their veins and sprinkled it, then they crossed swords above and roared what must have been a vow of revenge."

"Let us send a herald and appeal to their honor," Tambilis urged.

"Where will he find it?" sneered Vindilis.

"Well, their pride, their boastfulness," said Bodilis. "I follow your reasoning, dear. Tell them that he who insists on doing battle with a man not fully recovered is himself no man at all."

"They might well scoff," Lanarvilis warned. "At best, we do but gain a short reprieve for...him."

"Dare we even seek that—we, the whole of Ys, and we, the Nine who uphold the law of the Gods?" replied Vindilis. "Had the King's foeman not been at the point of death when he delivered that blow, he would have finished Grallon off; and that would have been the will of the Gods, the Frank the new Incarnation of Taranis. How can Grallon delay merely on account of being somewhat weakened, and not violate the law?"

Lanarvilis swallowed hard. "I have talked with Soren," she said as if each word were a drop of gall on her tongue. "He believes this. He says the King must answer the challenge as soon as he can walk to the scene, or be no longer King. There are...many who'll agree, though they love Gratillonius and abhor the barbarian."

Innilis covered her eyes. "Another Colconor?" she moaned. Vindilis laid an arm around her slight shoulders and drew her close.

The older woman's features had gone rigid. She stared before her. "We are foredoomed in any case," she said, flat voiced. "Give him back his full health, and still Grallon cannot possibly win every combat before him. He will grow wearied, and bruised, and— Sisters, what we must do is take counsel among ourselves as to how we shall bear what is coming onto us, and how keep Ys alive while we search for deliverance."

Tambilis wept on her mother's breast. Fennalis sighed on her pillow. Compassion overrode the suffering in her countenance.

562

Forsquilis lifted her arms. Her voice rang: "Hear me. Not yet are we widowed and enslaved. Each victory of our King wins *us* another day and night; and who knows what might happen? We can take a hand in shaping our fate."

"Nay," protested Lanarvilis in something like terror, "we may not cast spells against a contender. 'Twould be sacrilege. The Gods—"

"We were not altogether passive about Colconor, toward the end," said Bodilis, rallying.

"But this—"

"Our lord lies injured. Had it been by cause of war or mishap, we would tend him as best we could and heal him by whatever means we command. Shall our care, our duty, be the less because the harm came to him in the Wood?"

"My thought," Forsquilis agreed. "Innilis, you have the Touch, and I—can fetch certain materials that sometimes help. Let us go to the palace. Nature would give him back his strength in a matter of days. We will simply lend nature our aid."

The fear ebbed from Lanarvilis, but trouble remained: "Is that lawful, now?"

"If not, the Gods will decree we fail," Forsquilis said. "Come, Innilis. I know you have the courage."

Mutely, the other left Vindilis and followed the witch out of the room.

~ 3 ~

The long light set ablaze the gilt eagle atop the dome on the royal house. Farther down, garden wall and the mansions opposite filled the street with shadow, like a first blue wave of incoming night. The crowd gathered outside the main gate waited dumb; rare were the mutters within that silence. Some had stood thus for hours. Most were humble folk, though here and there glowed the cloak of a Suffete or sheened the silk of a well-born lady. Rufinus the Gaul was clad with unwonted somberness. A young Scotian in a kilt stood side by side with a young Roman who had put on a robe for this. They lingered in hope of any word about how their King fared.

"Make way!" called a sudden clear voice. "Way for Dahut his daughter!"

Her vestal gown billowed white around her slimness, so hastily she strode. The hair streaming loose from under a chaplet of laurel seemed almost a part of the deep-yellow rays from across the western sea. In her right hand she carried a twig of mistletoe and a stalk of borage.

People saw her and pressed together to give room as she demanded. A few breathed greetings. Nearly all touched hand to brow. Awe sprang forth on their visages. In several it mingled with adoration.

The four guards at the entrance were legionaries. "Open for me," Dahut said.

"I'm sorry," Cynan replied, "but our orders are to let nobody in."
She bridled. "Who told you that?"

"Rivelin, the physician. He says your father should not be disturbed."

"I countermand it, in the name of the Goddess Who whispered to me while I prayed in Her Temple."

"Let her by," Budic exclaimed. The other two men growled assent. Their years in Ys had taught them that what was lunacy elsewhere could be truth here. Cynan hesitated an instant longer, then turned about and undid the portal himself.

Dahut passed through, up the blossom-lined walk of crushed shell, between the stone boar and bear on the staircase, to the bronze door. She struck fist against the relief of an armored man as if he were an enemy. His breastplate, hollow, rang aloud. A servant swung the door aside. Before he could speak dismay, Dahut had swept past, into the atrium.

A graybeard in a dark robe advanced across the charioteer mosaic to greet her. "Bring me to him," she said.

"He sleeps, my lady," Rivelin demurred anxiously. "His prime need now is for rest. No one should touch him, unless perchance a Queen—"

"Ah, be still, old dodderer. I know where he must be. Abide my return."

Dahut went onward. He started to follow. She spun about, glared, hissed like a cat. Fear took him and he rocked to a halt.

She let herself into the main bedchamber. Drapes made it crepuscular, obscuring the wall's representation of Taranis directing His thunderous, fecundating rain over the earth. Gratillonius lay in a spread-eagled posture, naked beneath a sheet. He had been shaven so his hurt could be examined, washed, bandaged. That would have made him seem years younger, despite the lines plowed into his face, had it not been for a waxy pallor under the tan. Only his breast stirred. He snored heavily, which he scarcely ever had done before.

Dahut stood a while gazing down at him. Her left hand stole forth to take hold of the sheet. She peeled it back and stared a while longer, lips parted over the white teeth.

Thereupon she touched fingertips to him and held them, very lightly, above the heart. With her free hand she stroked the sacred plants across him, brow, eyelids, cheeks, mouth, jaw, throat. Murmuring arcane words, she raised his head and laid the cuttings under it. Stooped over him, she ran both hands along his body, circling motions through the crisp hair on his chest, down the belly to pause at the navel, on until they came together and cupped him at the loins.

"Father, awake," she said low.

Stepping back, she pointed at his head and spoke again, "Awake, awake, awake!" in a voice that sang with assurance.

Gratillonius opened his eyes. He blinked, glanced around, saw her at the bedside, and sat up with a gasp. "Hercules! What is that?"

Dahut leaned close. "Are you well, father?" It was scarcely a question.

"Why, I think—I seem—" He felt of his head. "What happened? That Frank, I did for him but then I remembered no more—but—" He noticed that he was exposed and snatched at the sheet. A healthy red suffused his skin.

Dahut laughed. "You killed him, but in his death throes he gave you a blow to the jaw that cast you from your senses. 'Tis the hour of sundown." Her tone grew steely. "You'll have call for your full strength. The Goddess told me, within myself, to come restore you."

"You have the Touch—you, already?" he asked wonderingly.

"I have my destiny."

He stroked his padded, smooth chin, flexed his muscles, abruptly swung feet to floor and stood up, the sheet draped around him. His look encountered hers.

She lifted her head higher. "My destiny is other than a filthy barbarian wallowing on me," she said.

"You are no Queen," he responded slowly.

"Well, I would be—" Dahut caught his arm. All at once she was a young girl pleading. "Oh, father, you can't fall to those horrible men, you mustn't, everything would fall with you! Drive them off! I know you can."

His features set. "Fennalis will soon leave us," he said in an undertone. "If the Sign does come on you, when I also am dead— Nay!" he bellowed.

Military habits revived. "Go out and wait for me to dress myself. We shall most certainly see about this."

Dahut obeyed exultantly. In the atrium she met Forsquilis and Innilis, who had just arrived and forced admittance. "I've made him whole," she said.

Innilis whitened, her eyes grew enormous. "What? Oh, nay, darling, you cannot have, you shouldn't have—"

Sternness came over Forsquilis. "Hush. There is a fate in her, whatever it be."

Gratillonius entered in tunic and sandals. He barked a few inquiries about the situation. "Come with me," he said then, and went onward.

Trailing after him, wringing her hands, Innilis wailed, "What do you mean to do?"

"Gather a force and destroy them," he flung back.

Forsquilis caught a breath.

"But you've been *challenged!*" Innilis expostulated in horror.

"If we tarry, we'll lose any chance at surprise, and Mithras knows we need every advantage we can scrape up," Gratillonius said.

"The Gods are with us," Dahut added at her father's side.

Forsquilis bit off a reply.

At the gate, Gratillonius spoke tersely to his soldiers. They laid down a shield for him to stand on. Each took a corner and raised him high, his auburn locks catching the sunset, like a Gallic chieftain of old. The people shouted. "Hear me," he trumpeted. "Ys, your city, her

Nine holy Queens, and you her children shall not fall prey to brigands through any vile trick of theirs. Carry this word for me. Every man of Ys who can fight and who cherishes honor, freedom, and his own household, every such man should meet with me at moonrise, bringing his weapons!"

~ 4 ~

The rendezvous was the manor of Taenus Himilco, Landholder Councillor, on the fertile northern slope of the heights, somewhat beyond the Wood. Had the Ysans come in a body they would have betrayed themselves to the Franks, whose fires glowed baleful on the headland above the sea cliffs. Instead, they slipped out by ones, twos, threes as the summons found them and they reached decision and made ready. It stretched over hours, for the moon, waning toward the half, did not appear till almost midnight.

Gratillonius could not have made himself sit still in the darkened house. That would have been unwise of him, anyhow. He went to and fro through the gloom outside, welcoming newcomers, talking, getting the men roughly organized and informed, radiating a confidence that was a lie. He knew how forlorn his venture was. It had nothing in its favor save that it was better than waiting to be crushed.

The time finally came. He read it in the stars and heaved his armored mass onto Favonius. The stallion stumbled occasionally, pushing along under trees. Gratillonius heard more horses move likewise at his back, those ridden by such well-to-do men of fighting age as had been inspired or shamed into joining him. The bulk of his army—he had no good idea how large—was ordinary folk, sailors, artisans, laborers, farmers, shepherds, carters, shopkeepers, a few foreigners who chanced to be on hand and willing for a brawl. He heard the soft swearing of his legionaries as they threaded back and forth, trying to keep the crowd in some kind of order.

When he came out on the nearly treeless promontory, vision got clearer. The moon, wan above eastern hills, with stars and Milky Way turned gray the grass, bushes, rocks, and silvered the waters beyond. A breeze whined chill. Glancing behind, he saw his followers straggle from the orchard they had passed through. Pikes and the infrequent ax or mailcoat glimmered amidst shapelessness. He estimated three hundred men. That well outnumbered the Franks, but those were soldiers by trade, properly equipped and strongly encamped. Gratillonius felt sure it was shrewdness rather than fear of ghosts that had made Theuderich ignore Lost Castle. The ruined earthworks and ditch would aid defense, but without a hinterland for support, a band like his could too easily be trapped and starved on the small jut of land.

Still, the Ysans were no lambs either. As they regrouped, Gratillonius spied Maeloch's bulk and heard him rumble, "Usun, take ye your post here; Intil, ye over here—and the twain of ye remember what ye owe your King, ha?—And the rest of ye—so, so, so—crossbowmen and slingers, at the middle—" The mariners of Ys were trained to fight pirates. Many landsmen had also once prepared against bandits, and had maybe not let their skills decay too much during the past peaceful years. Rufinus had taken charge of several woodcutters and charcoal burners; word had gone a ways out into the hinterland. His former Bacaudae would have been infinitely welcome, but—

Adminius approached the centurion. "We're 'bout's ready as we'll ever be, I think, sir," the deputy said.

"Very well," Gratillonius answered. "Let me repeat, the quieter we move, the likelier it is that most of us will be there to revel around the Fire Fountain tomorrow evening."

"We will, sir, we will! Us boys'll go around shushing the civilians. God be with yer, sir."

Gratillonius clucked to his mount and started off. His chosen route was not to Redonian Way and then due west, but slantwise across the promontory. Though slower and more difficult, it offered a hope of not being noticed too early.

As always when battle drew nigh, doubts and qualms fell away from him. He was committed to action now, and rode at peace with himself. If he lost, if he fell in the fray—well, during the hours at Taenus's home, he had spoken with Maeloch, and the Ferrier had promised passage to Britannia for Dahut and the other princesses, from himself or any surviving son of his. The Gallicenae—the Gallicenae would abide and endure, because they must, but this they had done before, until finally they witched forth a stranger to free them.

Behind his right shoulder, summer's dawnlight crept after the moon.

Time and a mile ebbed away. The Frankish camp grew plainer in sight. Horses and mules were secured at intervals around it. Cookfires were banked, each a small red constellation surrounded by men rolled into their cloaks. A watchfire danced yellow and smoky at the center, and the spearheads of sentries threw back the eastern glow.

At any instant, someone would see the Ysans and cry alarm. Gratillonius swung sword on high. "Charge! Kill them!"

With a yell that went on and on, a growl beneath it, like wind and wave on a shingle beach, the Ysans plunged forward. Gratillonius checked his horse, which neighed and reared. He must hold back, try to oversee what happened, lead his Roman cadre wherever it was most needed, as he had done on that day when Eppillus fell, Eppillus who slept just beyond the bivouac of this new enemy.

The young Soctian Tommaltach dashed past, battle-crazy, shouting and brandishing his blade, wild to be first in the onslaught. Gratillonius could only briefly hope the boy would live. The chances of the young Burdigalan Carsa looked better; he was bound for a slight rise of ground,

567

a commanding position, where he could use the sling that whipped to and fro in his hand.

The men of Ys swept by Gratillonius. They were not altogether a rabble. Shipmate ran beside shipmate, neighbor beside neighbor.

The Franks boiled out of slumber, grabbed their weapons, sprang to form a square. The Ysans should have thrust straight in to prevent it. But they lacked officers. They surfed against the array as it was taking shape, and those in front got in the way of those that followed, and men recoiled and milled about.

They did well even so. Few Franks were in armor. Ax, knife, sword, pike, club, missile worked havoc. Defenders fell and for a moment it was as if the attackers would break the square. Then Theuderich winded a horn in signal, and his men charged in what became a wedge. Slaughter churned. The Ysans withdrew in confusion, leaving their dead and badly wounded to be trampled underfoot or lie ululating. The Franks closed up afresh, howled threats and taunts, moved around as one to collect what mail they had left behind.

Tommaltach went among his comrades like wildfire, blade and war cry aloft. Maeloch spat on his hands and beckoned his followers to pull back together. Rufinus got his to take stance nearby. Crossbow bolts and arrows began to sigh into lightening heaven, seeking prey. More wicked were the slingstones of sailors, herdsmen, and Carsa, splintering temples or knocking out eyes, from every quarter around the foe.

Yet Gratillonius saw from his distance that whatever slight military order his men had had was fast going out of them. They clamored and prowled like a pack of dogs. At best, a few groups retained cohesion, and those could merely keep their places and shoot the last missiles remaining to them. The legionaries at Gratillonius's back cursed aloud.

Theuderich understood equally well. His horn sounded anew. The Franks moved forward and began hewing. Ysans fell, stumbled off, scattered. Gratillonius saw the barbarians bound his way. He was the goal. With him and his veterans down, the Franks could kill at their leisure until their opponents fled. And if he retreated, Ysan resolution would break at once.

He jumped to earth, cast the reins of Favonius over the muzzle, unshipped his shield. "We'll meet them halfway and cut them apart," he said, knowing they would not unless a miracle occurred. They knew it too, but closed ranks and marched with their centurion.

Behind them, the sun cleared the inland hills. It flared off Frankish iron.

Mithras, also a soldier—

What can I promise You for Your aid, not to me but to my Ys, now in this hour without mercy? he thought in an odd, detached fashion. He was not bargaining, but explaining. —Mithras, God of the Light that holds off the Dark of Ahriman, Your chosen sacrifice is a pure heart, and this I do not have; but in token and to Your honor I vow a bull, white and perfect, that in the slaying of him I may tell the world how You at the sunrise of time made it come alive, and that You abide still, Mithras, also a soldier.

What radiance burst forth? The sun should dazzle the Franks, not the Romans.

Gigantic under the sudden blue, the figure of a man strode in advance of the legionaries, on the seaward flank so that they could see he was beautiful and smiling. He was armored like them, in his right hand a shortsword whereon it seemed that flames flickered, in his left grip a shield whereon stood the Cross of Light, and it too blazed; but on his head was a Phrygian cap, which fluttered in the morning wind like a flag.

"Taranis, Taranis!" Gratillonius thought he heard dimly from the strewn Ysans. He knew otherwise, and yet he did not know, he was lost in the vision, all he could do was lead his men onward against the enemy. What it said for them that they held firm and got to work!

The vision was gone. The Franks were shattered. Bawling in terror, they broke ranks, ran, stood their ground when cornered and died piecemeal as the Ysans came over them. Someone—not Theuderich, who lay with his brothers gaping fallen-jawed at the sky while the gulls and scaldcrows circled low—someone winded a horn again and again. In some chaotic, valiant fashion he drew his surviving comrades together, into formation, homeward bound on Redonian Way.

After disposing of the hostile wounded, the Ysans gleefully pursued. They did not seek another clash, but were content to harass from the sides, with arrow and slingstone. Few Franks got as far as the Osismiian border. There they could only save themselves by dispersing, in threes or twos or alone, into the woods, and thus straggle back to their kinsmen and the widows outside Redonum.

VIII

~ 1 ~

In the Council chamber of the basilica, before his ranked soldiers beneath the eidolons of the Three, Gratillonius stood on the dais, robed, the Key out on his breast in plain sight above the emblem of the Wheel, Adminius holding the Hammer near his right hand; and he said to the Suffetes:

"I did not call this meeting in order that we chop law, as some of you have been seeking to do. My position is simple. Let me state it.

569

"We attacked the Franks because they were invaders, come in violation of the Oath that Brennilis and Caesar, Ys and Rome, swore these four and a half centuries agone. Barbarians, they befouled the water that flows from the Nymphaeum, blocked traffic on our main highway, and would surely soon have been wreaking worse. True sons of Ys rallied behind their King to cast them out, and succeeded, with fewer casualties than would have been reasonably awaited.

"Aye, it seems the challenger I should have met in the Wood fell in that battle, to a hand unknown. What of that? He fell on his own misdeeds. Had he survived and come back like an honest man, of course I would have fought him myself. If any living Frank wishes vengeance, let him arrive by himself and strike the Shield; he shall have the full protection of our law until the combat.

"The people cheer. Though it has cost them losses and wounds, they know what they freed themselves from. Will you, my lords, tell them they should have submitted? I warn you against that.

"On the face of it, ours was a desperate venture. Nonetheless it was victorious, and overwhelmingly." (Surely many believe this.) "That shows the Gods of Ys fought with us, and are well pleased. You have heard how most who were there saw a shining vision—I did myself—a sight that dismayed the enemy so that his line broke before us. I, a plain soldier, albeit the high priest of Taranis, I venture not to say more about this. Bethink you, though.

"Enough talk. We should put quibbles aside and get on with coping with the very real troubles and dangers ahead of us."

"'Quibbles,' you call them?" cried Hannon Baltisi, Lir Captain. "If you'd led the attack *after* doing your second combat in the Wood, aye—but you flouted the sacred law. Dare you tell us the Gods smile on your plea of military necessity? They are more strict than that, Grallon. Their patience is great, but sorely have you tried it."

Lanarvilis, who spoke today for the eight Queens that could be present, rose to respond. "We Gallicenae have debated this, and prayed for insight," she said quietly. "It appears to us that our King chose what, in his mortal judgment, was the lesser evil. Oh, far the lesser evil. So must men of goodwill often do. Had the Gods been angered, They could have let him suffer defeat and death on Point Vanis. Aye, They could have made it that the man who slew him was his challenger. Instead, he stands here a conqueror.

"There shall be a festival of thanksgiving as soon as possible, as great as Ys has ever seen. There shall be rites of purification and a hecatomb. Then surely will the Gods forgive whatever sins Their Ys was forced to commit for Their sake as well as her own.

"Thus declares the Temple of Belisama."

"Lir is not that easily appeased," Hannon said.

"The Speaker for Taranis supports the King and the Nine," declared Soren Cartagi.

"And I too, for one," added Bomatin Kusuri, Mariner Councillor.

"And I," joined in Osrach Taniti, Fisher Councillor, "and I make bold to say we twain have some knowledge of Lir's ways."

Once Hannon might have argued further, but old age was overtaking him. "So be it," he mumbled, and sank back. A murmur of assent ran around the benches.

"We do have more perils," reminded Adruval Tyri, Sea Lord. "How could yon Franks have come in, exactly when our forces are elsewhere, save by Roman connivance? What will the Romans try next?" His look was not unfriendly, but it was straight, at the prefect.

Gratillonius sighed. "As yet I know little or nothing about that," he told them all. "I'll be searching out whatever I can." He refrained from mentioning how helpful he hoped Corentinus, through Martinus, could be in that. "Belike some officials overreached themselves, and higher authority will hold them to account for it. Meanwhile, naught else should threaten us in the near future, and our marines and ships are due back soon. What I need from this Council is its agreement that—that we are on the right road."

He got it. The result could scarcely have been otherwise, especially given the temper of the common folk. This meeting had been a formality, although a necessary one.

Following the benediction he must give—how leadenly it always sounded in his ears!—the Councillors went off to their various businesses with scant further talk. As Gratillonius passed the seats of his Queens, Forsquilis left their group and took his arm. "What?" he asked, surprised.

"Come to my house," she said low.

"But the day is yet young, I've much to do, and—Tambilis—?"

"Her courses came upon her yesterday, earlier than usual. She will be the one who resumes the vigil tomorrow, also out of turn. For we took this as still another portent, we Sisters, when we met ere coming here today."

His immediate feeling was pleasure. He knew it for unworthy, but events had kept him abstinent for several days and nights now, and this was the most passionate of his wives. Forsquilis recognized as much. A faint flush crossed the severely chiseled countenance. It drained away at once, her cool reserve in public took her over, and he realized that they had chosen her for cause, whatever it might be. "We must talk, you and I," she said.

There had been no opportunity before. He got back from pursuit of the Franks, day before yesterday, in time to make speeches of thanks, sincere to the men, mechanical to the Gods; and kindle the Fire Fountain at dusk before addressing the wildly celebratory crowd; and, finally alone, give Mithras what devotion he was able. Them sleep rammed him. The following day went to a whirl of work, such as the situation demanded. The Gallicenae had been fully engaged too, conducting services, helping the hurt, comforting mourners.

Forsquilis was not the most learned, wise, or devout among the Nine; but her soul dwelt nearest the Otherworld and sometimes, it was whispered, crossed that frontier. A chill crawled down Gratillonius's backbone. "Very well," he said.

When they emerged on the basilica steps, hurrahs surfed over them. Though Ys was picking up its daily life again, people still thronged the Forum, waiting for a sight of the victor, their rescuer. Gratillonius warmed.

A lean, long-legged figure broke from them and bounded toward him. A legionary made to wave the intruder off. "Let him come," the King ordered.

Rufinus made salutation to him and the Queen. The Gaul wore a sleeveless tunic, for swaddling covered a gash in his left forearm that had required stitches. He moved as lightly as ever, and the green eyes danced with all the wonted mischief. "You said yesterday you'd urgent work for me, lord," he reminded, "but the telling would need privacy. I took this chance."

"Aye. Good," replied Gratillonius. "My lady, would you abide here a moment with the guard?" She nodded slowly. He could see how she tightened beneath the blue gown.

He led Rufinus back upstairs and into a corner of the portico. "I want you to find me a bull, white and perfect," he said in Latin. "Do it discreetly. Bring him to a hiding place nearby—you'll know one, my fox—on the eighteenth day before the September calends, and notify me. Pay whatever it costs. I'll reimburse you."

The sharp, scarred visage grew wary. "Well, that should give time enough. But why just then?"

"That's my affair," said Gratillonius roughly.

"Forgive me, sir." Rufinus steadied his gaze. "I meddle, but a man often has to if he's to serve his master faithfully. The following day is sacred each month to Mithras. I know that much. You plan a thank-offering."

Why did I think I could fool him? wondered Gratillonius. "I pledged it when the Franks were about to break us. You saw what next happened, that sunrise."

"I saw something very strange," Rufinus murmured, "but Ys is a den of strangeness." He frowned, tugged his fork beard, said abruptly: "You'd never get an ungelded bull down into that crypt of yours."

"I know. Regardless of the Christian slanders, blood sacrifices to Mithras are rare and solemn. We—we believers will make ours on the battlefield."

"No, please, I beg you. That'd enrage too many worshippers of the Three."

"I've thought about this too. A man of Mithras does not sneak around. But we need not be offensively conspicuous. By the time our act becomes known through the city, it will have happened, it'll be in the past. I

572

rely on you to help see to that. Afterward I'll defend it against any accusation, and I'll win."

"You will that...among men. The Gods—"

"What, are there Gods that you fear?"

Rufinus shrugged. "I'll do what you want, of course."

Affection welled up in Gratillonius. He leaned the Hammer against a column and clasped the Gaul by the shoulders. "I knew you would. You're as true as any legionary of mine. And you've never done a service higher than this. *Why* won't you enroll with the Lord of Light? You deserve to."

Sudden, astonishing tears stood in the feline eyes. "That would be a betrayal of you."

"What? I don't understand."

"I'd better go." Rufinus slipped free and hurried down the stairs to lose himself in the crowd.

Gratillonius rejoined Forsquilis. "You're troubled," she said.

"'Tis not a matter for women," he rasped. At once he fretted about whether he had given away too much. However, she kept silence, and her face was unreadable.

At her house he dismissed the soldiers and changed his robe for a tunic. This was a warm, cloudless noontide. He stored garments in the homes of all the Nine. Tucking the Key underneath as he was wont, he felt it hard and heavy upon his breastbone. Ordinarily, after these many years, he didn't notice.

He found that she too had donned light, plain garb, a linen gown. It lay pleasingly across curves that somehow blent well with her panther ranginess. Her feet were bare on the reed matting she had over her floors. To him that suggested she did not want the bother of unlacing sandals. Desire throbbed. "Well," he said as merrily as he could, "I suppose your cook has something in preparation, but first—?"

"First we talk." She led him to her secretorium. Window drapes dimmed it. That gave an eerie half-life to the objects round about, archaic female figurine from Tyre, symbol-engraved bones, flint thunderstones, cat's-skull lamp, ancient scrolls....They sat opposite each other. Her eyes, gray by full light, seemed huge and filled with darkness.

"What was that apparition during the battle?" she asked softly.

"Why, why, who knows?" he stammered, startled. Recovering balance: "Such visions have come often erenow. Homer tells how the Gods appeared to heroes who fought under the walls of Troy. The old Romans saw Castor and Pollux riding before them at Lake Regillus. Constantinus claimed the Cross that is Christ's stood once in the sky, and in that sign he went on to make himself supreme. We too, when we met the Scoti in the first year of my Kingship, we'd have slain them to the last man, save that a huge and horrible crone seemed to be there. I thought I saw her myself. You remember. Was it a God, a demon, a delirium? Who knows?"

"You evade my question," she said, unrelenting. "Who, or what, was this?"

"I've heard Ysans say it was Taranis. The Christians among my legionaries speak of an angel. Who knows?"

"You, though. You called on your Mithras, did you not?"

He mustered defiance. "Aye. As was my right. And I am free to believe He answered."

"The attributes of that Being—from what I can discover—" Her calm dissolved. She trembled. "Let it b-be Anybody else Who was there, Anybody."

"What?" He leaned forward to take her hands. They were cold. "How can you say that? When Mithras Himself came to save Ys—"

"Like an outlaw to the last farm where dogs are not at his heels," she gasped. "Oh, Grallon, this is what I have to tell you, that the omens are evil, evil. The Gods of Ys have endured so much. Put down your pride!"

Rage swelled in him. "I ask only that They take heed of my honor, as Mithras does." Her distress checked his mood. "But what are those omens, my dear? Your Sisters looked unafraid enough this day."

Forsquilis gulped. "I did not tell them, nor can I tell you, for 'tis naught so clear as a star falling above the necropolis or a calf born with two heads or even a sortilege on a face in the smoke. Nay, dreams, voices half-heard in the wind and the waters, a chill that gripped me when I sought to pray—I could only tell the Queens that the Gods are troubled, and this of course they knew already. I did not say to them how it *feels*."

She cast herself from her seat, onto his lap, and clung, her face burrowed against his shoulder. "Oh, Grallon, Grallon, be careful before Them! We must not lose you!"

He held her close, stroked her and murmured to her, aware the while that what she wanted was below his reach; but he need not say it in so many words, need he? Let him comfort her as best he might, and afterward stand guard again over her and Dahut and Ys, in the quietly spoken name of Mithras. Her embrace turned into wild, lip-slashing kisses, with clawings to get rid of garments, until they were on the floor together.

~ 2 ~

Torches in the avenue and lanterns up the street, night became a sunrise glow about their eager feet, lit the way for golden youth bound forth to celebrate, and Dahut was awaiting them within her father's gate.

Plangency of harp and flute, the heartbeat of a drum, pulsed in Ys to welcome those whom she had bidden come dance away all darknesses, that morning sun might see how brightly Dahut's dower shone—her father's victory. Golden flashed the eagle wings and bronze the open door, chariots careered within the burnished palace floor, tall the sentry columns reared through incense-dreamy air, and lamplight turned to living gold in Dahut's loosened hair.

Silken gowns and purple edges rippled, flowed, and swirled, silver gleamed and amber smoldered where the dancers whirled. Music laughed and laughter sang around their skipping feet, and Dahut went before them all, the fleetest of the fleet. Fair the well-born maidens were and handsome were the men treading out the merry measure, forth and back again. Close embrace or stolen kiss could cast a sweet surprise; but Dahut was the star that shone before the young men's eyes. Kel Cartagi, Soren's grandson, touched her hand and waist. Then the dance bereaved him of her with its lilting haste. On she swayed to Barak Tyri, on to many more. So Dahut left a swathe of joy and woe across the floor.

When the music paused a while and gave the fevered guest time to cool or drink or chat or flirt or simply rest, Carsa strove to keep a Roman impassivity while Dahut in a ring of other men made jubilee. Tommaltach the Scotian boldly shouldered through to her, cowing with a wolfish grin whomever would demur, ready with such words as run when bardic harpstrings thrum; then Dahut gave him half a glance, and he was stricken dumb. Legionaries duty-freed who hastened at her call, honor guard for her their Luck, stood ranked against the wall, armed and brightly armored from the war that they had won, and Budic's gaze trailed Dahut as the new moon trails the sun.

Soon the music woke again, the dance began afresh. Red and gold and purple twined, unrestful rainbow mesh, till the western stars grew pale and silver streaked the east, when Dahut bade the youth of Ys come follow her to feast.

Afterward she led them out to breathe the sunrise air. Light caressed her slenderness and blazed within her hair. Up onto the city wall she took her company, and Dahut by the Raven Tower looked across her sea.

~ 3 ~

The moon was still down when Gratillonius and his followers went out Northbridge Gate, but starlight sufficed. Redonian Way glimmered ashen and resounded hollowly under their tread. After they passed the bend and turned east, though, murk grew before them. Clouds piled huge over the hills, womb-black save where lightning kicked. Ever strengthening, wind skirled cold as it drove them and the sound of thunder westward.

Muton Rosmertai, Suffete of Ys and Lion of Mithras, shivered. "Yon's no natural storm, bound this way this hour," he said. They were going by Lost Castle. He made a warding at the ruins. A wave-burst on the cliffs below brawled answer.

"We fare in the service of the God," Gratillonius rebuked him.

"Other Gods are angry."

"There is always war among Them," Cynan said. "We are soldiers."

"I am not afraid—not daunted," Muton insisted. By the vague quivery light they saw him puff himself up. He had been a zealous convert, advancing rapidly in the Mysteries because of good works and quick mastery of the lore. However, he was otherwise a dealer in spices, who had never crossed the water or fought a battle. "I only wondered if we are altogether wise, if the cause may be better served by heeding the warnings of Those who likewise are entitled to honor."

"A soldier questions not his orders," said Verica, whom Gratillonius had made his Runner of the Sun. "He carries them out."

"And saves his grumbling for the commissariat," Cynan laughed.

Gratillonius felt uneasy at the talk. Cynan's fellow Persian, Maclavius, delivered the Father from having to command silence and let men brood: "What say we sing? A good route song shortens the miles. *Fratres, Milites*, eh?"

That was in Latin, as most Mithraic hymns were throughout the Western Empire. One by one they took it up, the men of the four high ranks and the half dozen Soldiers, Occults, and Ravens behind them.

"Brothers, soldiers of the Army, now the marching has begun.

And aloft before our ranks there go the Eagles of the Sun—"

The deep cadences laid hold on hearts. Soon it mattered less how the sky above was darkening and the wind had started to sting faces with flung raindrops.

It was not overly far to the meeting place Rufinus had described. Where a trail from inland met the pavement stood a shepherd's shelter, usually deserted at night. Another four lower initiates waited there, under captaincy of the Osismiic Lion Ronach. They had the two mule carts ready which Gratillonius wanted. One was full of articles brought inconspicuously out of the city the previous day, the other carried an abundance of firewood. From the shelter, Rufinus led the bull he had purchased in Osismia. With him was the new member of the congregation, Tommaltach the Scotian, as yet only a Raven but picked to come along on this mission because he could best cope with the beast if it got dangerous.

It was indeed a magnificent animal, Gratillonius discerned, heavily muscled, mightily horned, snow-pure of hue. "Well done," he said, taking the chain to the nosering from Rufinus. "See me at the palace about noon and I'll repay your outlay."

Snag teeth flickered in the fork beard. "May that include what I spent on wine? I'd have to guess."

"Whatever you claim, I'll pay. You'd never cheat me, Rufinus."

"I japed, I japed." Sudden pain was in the voice. It turned matter-of-fact: "Niveus here is gentle for a bull, but watch out if a horse gallops by in sight. He'll want to charge. He tries to inspect every cow he sees, too, I suppose in hopes she's hot. Tommaltach knows him by

576

now. Goodnight." He withdrew so swiftly that it was as though he had melted into the wind.

"We'll scarcely meet either of those troubles the rest of this walk," Gratillonius said. Anything to lighten the mood. He tugged carefully. "Let's go, fellow."

Their progress grew slow. The weather outpaced them. Stars vanished. Lightning leaped, first behind, later overhead, blue-white savagery—no help against the dark. Thunder-wheels boomed down unseen heaven. Wind droned and whined. Raindrops came thicker. Somebody got a couple of lanterns lit, which bobbed cheerless and barely showed the way. The bull snorted, tossed his head, occasionally pulled on the chain. Tommaltach went at his side, spear in right hand, left hand stroking the creature, scratching it behind the horns, while he crooned a Gaelic herdsmen's melody.

"You do have a gift for this," said Gratillonius after a long time wherein nobody spoke. "I've heard about your skill, how you've sported on farms. Will you secure the sacrifice?"

"I'm too lowly, I think," Tommaltach replied.

Gratillonius shook his head. "Nay. This will be the Mystery of Creation, when all men are one." Maybe so. It seemed plausible. The books and memories he had ransacked said hardly anything about Tauroctony in the flesh; the rite was too seldom performed. He had actually discovered more about the Tarubolium of Cybele, but it was a disgusting thing, fit for a cult in which men had often gelded themselves.

His band was to redeem a sacred promise in clean and manly wise. Surely Mithras would also want it done sensibly.

"'Tis honored I am, Father," Tommaltach said.

"You may find you've won the riskiest part," Gratillonius warned.

"Sure, and that helps make me the handfast man of my King."

Gratillonius fled from the worshipfulness in that soft accent, into talk about how best the matter could be carried out. From days on the family farm he well remembered the ways of slaughtering large animals. But it would not be right to stun this bull first with a sledge hammer. He should be fully alive when he died for the God and the people.

Worse, the Hammer was Taranis's, whose high priest the King of Ys was....Lightning ignited the whole sky. Thunder struck brutal blows.

The procession came out on Point Vanis and reapproached the bend of Redonian Way. A sickle moon should have gleamed at their backs and the last stars ahead of them as whiteness entered the east. Instead, night raved. Ys was invisible, save in livid blinks which made the sea ramping under its wall shine like enemy weapons. Gratillonius would only be able to guess at the moment of sunrise.

He lifted his glance. Mithras shall have His honor, he told Them.

At the grave of Eppillus he stopped. "Here will we make the offering," he said. A part of the fight against the Franks had spread this far, and in any event, no spot on the headland could be more hallowed. "But the feast—Ronach, you know. Start the fire."

The Osismian saluted and led the woodcart onward, to a dip near the brink that gave some slight lee. Gratillonius stood by with his fellow officers, holding his cloak tightly to preserve what dignity he might, while Ravens, Occults, and Soldiers groped about, unloading the second cart. Doubtless curses got muttered, strewn seaward by the blast. Much of the freight was furniture and ritual objects to be carried after Ronach, but vestments and sacred implements were there as well.

Gratillonius needed scant change of garb. For this ceremony, unlike those in the crypt, he, the Father, already wore tunic of white wool, sandals, and sword, like Mithras at the first Slaying. He simply doffed his cloak and donned a Phrygian cap. Fleetingly, he thought of taking off the Key. But no, in an obscure fashion he felt that that would be a betrayal. He left it against his breastbone.

The Runner of the Sun, the Persians, and the Lions had more elaborate outfits, which required help. The fumbling seemed to go on for hours. Tommaltach found it ever harder to keep the bull soothed.

Fire glimmered and flapped. Ronach returned. Was the world ever so faintly less black? Sometime about now, somewhere beyond the stormclouds, the Companion of Mithras rose in immortal glory. "Gather, gather," Gratillonius called into the wind. "We shall begin." A flurry of rain struck his face, half blinding him.

The three lower ranks drew away and turned their backs on the Mysteries they must not witness until they had been elevated—apart from Tommaltach, and his attention was on the restless bull. Eyes rolled white, horns made motions of goring, hoofs pawed turf, breath gusted with a sound like waves breaking across reefs below.

Lanterns stood dim under the headstone of Eppillus, which Gratillonius made his altar. The prayers and enactments were stripped-down, simple, because men heard the full rainstorm striding closer, and hailstones skittered ahead of it.

Gratillonius went toward the bull. He drew his sword. "Mithras, God of the Morning—" Wind ripped the words away.

Tommaltach did what he had said he could do. Cat-swift, he seized the great horns and twisted. The bull bellowed. He went down. Earth boomed. Tommaltach sprang back and snatched for his spear, ready to thrust.

The bull rolled off his side, onto belly and knees. Gratillonius pounced. His left hand seized the nose-ring and hauled. The huge head followed, with a roar of agony and rage. Gratillonius struck home, just in front of the right shoulder. The impact was thick. Blood spurted over him.

He got clear before a horn could catch him in the beast's death struggle. Panting, he stood and watched. There were more prayers to say, but not till the bull lay quiet; sooner would be indecent, like gloating.

Lightning smote near Lost Castle, a bolt many-fingered, as if it sought. Thunder drowned trumpetings that turned to sobs, gurgles, finally silence. Hail whitened the headland. Rain came in a wind-harried torrent.

Gratillonius consecrated the sacrifice. He caught blood from it in a chalice, drank, shared with Verica, on behalf of all. The liquid was sticky, hot, and salt. He cut slabs of meat, which his underlings carried off to roast. Much more remained than this tiny gathering could eat. The carcass must be dismembered and burned before the worshippers left. The Ravens would come back later and get rid of the calcined bones.

Unless the storm quenched the fire. His concelebrants trudged after Gratillonius. Those who stayed to tend the fire had stoked it high. Flames rumbled and steamed from a white-hot core. Rain struck, steamed, hissed away. The sacred meal could be cooked at least partly. Father, Runner of the Sun, Persians, Lions could lie drenched on the benches and be served by their slogging Soldiers, Occults, and Ravens, bleakly chewing and gulping in laud of Mithras.

And yet, and yet, they did! When they had finished, Gratillonius rose to give benediction. Suddenly, uncontrollably, he threw his head back and laughed into the sky, at the Gods of Ys.

~ 4 ~

"He refuses to call a Council for dealing with the matter," Vindilis related. "He claims 'twould be needlessly divisive when he claims no desecration occurred. If we must bring it up, he says, we can do so at equinox."

"Shall we?" asked Innilis timidly. Held out on Sena these past three days by the storm and heavy seas that were slow to die down afterward, she had only returned to Ys this morning. Vindilis had kept herself informed, and sought the rosy house as soon as possible. She had wanted to be the one to break the news. Even so, it would strike hard at her beloved.

"Ha!" The tall woman prowled the conference room as if its trim of blue and gold, floral murals, fragile objects of beauty were a cage. Her haggard countenance kept turning to the window, full of cloudy noontide. "A month hence? Well does he know how futile that would be, after such a time. Whatever indignation most of the Suffetes now feel will have damped out into indifference. Already, my listeners tell me, already the common folk are with Grallon. Most say, when they trouble—or dare—to talk about his deed in the taverns or shops or streets—most say he must be right. For is he not their wonderful King, on whose reign fortune has always smiled?"

Innilis, seated on the couch, looked down at the fingers that writhed in her lap. "Could it be true?" she whispered. "Why should the Gods, our Gods be jealous that he sacrifices to his?"

579

"A blood sacrifice on Lir's clifftops, beneath Taranis's heaven? Nay, my darling, you're too loath to condemn."

"What do...our Sisters think?"

Vindilis sighed. "Bodilis, Tambilis, Guilvilis in her halfwit fashion, of course they defend him. Maldunilis is passive as ever, weakly frightened, hopeful this thing will go away. We're keeping word of it from poor Fennalis. Lanarvilis was as shocked as myself, but soon decided political necessity requires smoothing the scandal over. She's trying to mollify Soren Cartagi."

"Soren?"

"Oh, he was wild with fury. He feels this was a treachery against him, after he'd sided with Grallon in Council about the attack on the Franks. Lanarvilis undertook to soothe him enough that he'll at least continue working with the King on matters of public concern, as erenow. 'Tis better than Grallon deserves. I could almost wish those two, Lanarvilis and Soren, would finally share the bed they've longed for all these years."

Innilis gasped.

Vindilis smiled starkly. "Fear not. They never will. There's been too much sacrilege done. *He'll* thrust himself into her—Grallon—as he will the rest of us. Unless we deny ourselves to him. I've done that." A yelp of laughter. "He was polite. Accepted instantly. Aye, relieved." Vindilis halted before the other woman and peered downward at her. "You, though," she murmured, "could punish him thus."

"Oh, nay, I, I'm such a little bag of bones—"

"Beautiful bones, beneath exquisite flesh," Vindilis breathed.

Innilis paled, reddened, paled. Her eyes fled to and fro, never lifting. "He likes me. He's gentle, and, and sometimes— Nay, I beg you, make me not hurt him....What of Forsquilis?"

"She was shaken, took omens, would not tell us what they were but said—if Lir and Taranis strove that dawn to stop the deed, then Mithras prevailed over Them. For her part, she'd stand by her King, whatever may befall him. And off she went, defiantly, arrogantly, to the palace where he was; and nobody saw them again till morning."

Innilis shuddered. "Could she...have spoken sooth?" she whispered.

"It may be. It may be. Taranis and Lir—but Belisama bides Her time. I think She will not wait long."

Seeing terror, Vindilis sat down, laid an arm around the waist of Innilis, drew her close. "Be brave, sweetling," she said low. "She Whom we serve will not strike at us, surely, for his wrongdoings. We must stay together, we Sisters, share our solace, strength, love."

Her free hand caressed the small breasts, then traveled upward to loosen the knot of the silken cord that fastened Innilis's gown at the neck. Her lips fluttered over a cheek, toward the mouth.

"Nay, please," Innilis asked, "not at once. I'm too—horrified—I cannot—"

580

"I understand," Vindilis answered quietly. "Nor do I myself want more than your nearness. I only long to have you by me, hold you in my arms, and you hold me. Will you give me that hour of peacefulness?" Abruptly she seemed frail, vulnerable, old.

~ 5 ~

Dahut arrived at the house of Fennalis while the moon was rising over the eastern hills, ruddy and enormous. As yet its rays streamed unseen, for the sky was still blue, Ocean still agleam with sunset; tower heights flared brilliant, through beneath them dusk had begun to steal like a mist through the crooked streets of Lowtown. Bodilis opened the door for her. An instant the two stood silent, regarding each other. The vestal had not paused to change from her white dress of Temple duty. That, and tresses high-piled, caused her to shine amidst shadows, a lighted candle. The woman was plainly clad, in garb that carried a smell of sweat, her own hair disarrayed. She slumped with weariness.

"Welcome at last," she said tonelessly. "I hoped you could come straightaway when I'd sent for you."

Dahut spread her palms. "I'm sorry. I might have asked leave, but I was to take part in evensong and...this is no time to slight the Goddess, is it? Now when She may be wrathful, and Her moon has reached the full."

"Mayhap. Yet I cannot believe She'd want Her Fennalis to suffer lengthened pain."

"I *am* sorry!" Dahut exclaimed, on the least note of impatience. "I thought Innilis—"

"Oh, Innilis had been here, and failed. You were the final hope. I should have told Malthi to tell you that, but I was tired, I forgot." Bodilis stood aside and beckoned. "Come."

Dahut entered the atrium. It was turning crepuscular. "You, you do realize I know not if I can do aught either?" she said. "When a Queen, a healer Queen, cannot. There was just that moment with my father. Of course I pray the Goddess lend me power to help. Fennalis was always kind to me."

"To everybody." Bodilis led the way toward the bedchamber.

Dahut plucked at her sleeve and asked, "Are none of our simples of any avail?"

Bodilis shook her head, "Nay. Formerly, the juice of the poppy; but she can no longer keep anything down. Hemp smoke gives some ease still, but only when the pangs are not too sharp."

"I knew not. I should have come to see her oftener."

"That would have gladdened her. She loves you. But the young are ever wont to shun the dying."

Dahut lowered her voice. "Death is the single remedy left, isn't it?"

"Aye." Bodilis stopped. She gripped Dahut's arm hard. "I've even thought of giving it to her myself. The books tell that hemlock is gentle. But I was afraid. Belisama calls Her Gallicenae to Her when *She* wills. Pray, though, pray for an ending."

"I will." Dahut's eyes were moon-huge in the gloom.

A seven-branched candleholder illuminated the room. The air was close and full of murk; it stank so badly that the maiden almost gagged. Lately changed, the bedding was wet again, sweat, urine, foul matter that dribbled out despite Fennalis not having eaten for days. Hair lay thin and lank over the blotchy face. The skin of the jowls sagged away from a nose that had finally become prominent. She breathed in uneven gusts. Now and then she made a mewing sound. It was impossible to say whether she recognized when Dahut bent above.

The virgin looked off to the image in a niche beyond the foot of the bed. It showed Belisama the Crone, though not hideous as ofttimes; this aged lady smiled serene and lifted a hand in blessing. Dahut gestured and murmured. Bodilis reverently raised her arms.

It was yarrow that Dahut stroked Fennalis with and laid beneath the head of. The princess could not altogether hide repugnance while she bared the swollen body and passed fingers over; her words stumbled.

Nonetheless, as she ministered, Fennalis grew quiet, closed her eyes, and slowly smiled. Dahut straightened. "I believe you have done it," Bodilis whispered in awe. "Yours is the Power of the Touch. What other potencies do you bear within?"

Triumph rang softly: "I'm glad. The Goddess chose me."

A water jug, washbasin, soap, and towel were in the room. Dahut cleansed her hands fastidiously. "Sleep well," she said to Fennalis, but did not kiss her before leaving.

Bodilis accompanied Dahut to the door. "Please come back tomorrow early," the Queen requested.

"Certes. It will be a free day for me."

"Where are you staying?"

"At Maldunilis's. Did you not know?" In the past year, Dahut had taken to occupying the home of whoever had Vigil. Her clothes and other possessions she stored at the palace, for servants to bring upon demand. Just the same, she talked ever oftener about getting a place of her own.

"I'd forgotten, as tired as I am." The Gallicenae had been caring for their Sister by turns. However, for several days now a fever had confined Lanarvilis and Guilvilis. It was not grave; word was that they would be back afoot tomorrow; meanwhile, double duty fell on the rest. Bodilis had assumed the entire nursing, since she could postpone a number of her usual tasks, such as directing the library or advising on the esthetics of public works.

Dahut hugged her. "May you soon be relieved."

"May Fennalis. Goodnight, dear."

When the door had closed on the girl and the moon-brightened twilight, Bodilis leaned against it a while, eyes nestled into the crook of her arm. "Semuramat—Tambilis," she muttered, "I hope *you* are having pleasure this eventide." Straightening: "Nay, that was self-pity." She laughed at herself for thus talking to herself and returned to the bedroom. "Malthi," she called, "we need you again."

Reluctantly, the serving-woman came to assist in washing Fennalis, changing the bedding, carrying off the soiled stuff. The patient had become able to help a bit, rolling over as needed, drowsily, without showing pain. "I think you can go sleep," said Bodilis at the end of the task.

"You, my lady?" inquired the maid.

"I'll keep watch for a span." Bodilis dossed in an adjoining chamber, the door between left ajar. "I've thoughts to think ere I can await the blind God."

She settled herself in a chair and reached for one of the books she kept on a side table. She had spoken truth. There were certain disturbing questions to consider, after what had just happened. But first she would seek easement. Epictetus lay three centuries dust; it did not matter; his implacable calm spoke still.

"All things serve and obey the laws of the universe: the earth, the sea, the sun, the stars, and the plants and animals of the earth. Our body likewise obeys the same, in being sick and well, young and old, and passing through the other changes decreed. It is therefore reasonable that what depends on ourselves, that is, our own understanding, should not be the only rebel. For the universe is powerful and superior, and consults the best for us by governing us in conjunction with the whole. And further, opposition, besides that it is unreasonable, and produces nothing except a vain struggle, throws us into pain and sorrows."

"Bodilis."

Though she barely heard, a part of her had stayed alert. She put the book aside and went to the bed. Fennalis smiled up at her.

"How fare you?" Bodilis asked.

"I feel at peace," Fennalis whispered.

"Oh, wonderful. Dahut wrought that."

"I have a dream-memory of her, but all was so confused then. Now the world is clear. Clear as the sacred pool—" Words faded away.

"Can I bring you aught? Water, milk, soup, bread?"

Fennalis feebly shook her head. "Thank you, nay." She lay mustering strength until she could say: "I would like—do you remember the story about...the girl, the bird, and the menhirs? My mother used to tell me it when I was little...."

Bodilis nodded. "A Venetic tale, no? Do you care to hear it again?"

"That would...be pleasant—"

Bodilis brought her chair to the bedside and settled back down. "Well," she began, "once long ago there was a girl-child who lived near the Place of the Old Ones, where the cromlechs stand tall and the dolmens brood low and the menhirs are marshalled in their hundreds, rows of them reaching on and on and on. This was so long ago that the great bay there was dry land. Forest grew thick upon it. That was a lonely place to live, loneliest of all for her, because she was the sole child of her father, whose wife was dead, and he a charcoal burner whose hut stood quite by itself in the woods. The girl kept house for him as best she was able. For playmates she had only the breezes, the daisies, the sunflecks that flit on the forest floor when wind stirs branches, and the butterflies that dance with them. She often wished for friends, and longed to go to the Place of the Old Ones. Her father had never let her. When she asked, he said it was haunted. But she dreamed of elvenfolk, unearthly beautiful, who came forth by moonlight and danced, still more gracefully than butterflies, among the solemn stones.

"Now one day when her father was off to his work, the girl took a jar to the spring that bubbled some ways from their hut. She had gone but three steps times three when she heard a peeping sound. She looked, and there was a nestling bird on the ground, a tiny sad scrawny thing that had fallen out. Soon it would die miserably, unless a fox or a badger found it first. The girl felt sorry for it. She picked it up. Looking about, she saw the nest high overhead—"

Bodilis stopped, for Fennalis had closed her eyes and was breathing evenly. "Are you awake yet?" Bodilis asked low. No answer came. After a minute or two, Bodilis was sure the woman had fallen to sleep.

Weariness dragged at her. She yawned, blinked, decided she too might find some oblivion. From the holder she took a candle to light her way.

—She woke. Moonlight streamed steeply through a window to make a pool on the floor. The candle guttered low. Hours must have passed, more than she had intended. Sighing, she rose and shuffled in to see how her patient was.

When she got there, Fennalis opened eyes. As Bodilis watched, the pupils dilated. Sweat broke forth. Breath rattled shallow.

An instant, Bodilis stood motionless. "Were you waiting for me?" she murmured. She sat down on the edge of the bed, leaned over to embrace Fennalis. Sometimes she prayed, sometimes she crooned, while the death struggle ebbed out.

Finally she could stand up, close the eyes, bind the jaw, kiss the brow. Thereafter she groped to the window and stood long staring into the white inexorable moonlight.

~ 6 ~

Sleep had altogether evaded Dahut. At last she wandered forth.

She stood in Lost Castle, Cargalwen, at the outer verge. Behind her hulked mounds that were crumbled houses, ridges that were fallen walls. Darkness lay thick in between, but hoarfrost on grass and stones glimmered along the tops. Beneath her the cliff dropped nearly sheer. Surf boomed and snarled, an incoming tide. Light from the westering moon sheened across black surges, exploded white where waves burst over rocks. In that direction it dimmed stars, but above the hills they were many, Auriga, Gemini, ever-virgin Pleiades, bloody-eyed Bull. A wind wandered, bearing the first bite of autumn. Dahut's garments fluttered. She never noticed that, nor the chill. She had bided thus for a time outside of time.

A flame passed through her, above the cleft of her breasts. She cried out. Then: "A-a-ah. Now, now."

With shaky fingers, she unlaced the bosom of her dress and pulled the cloth aside. By straining her neck backward, she could see what had appeared. Under the moon, the crescent showed not red but black.

She swung about, raised her arms, shouted into the moon: "Belisama, I am ready! Gods, all Gods, I thank You! I am Yours, Belisama, You are mine, we are One!"

The wind strewed her call across the sea.

She stripped the clothes from herself. Naked, yelling aloud, she danced beneath the stars, before the Gods of Ys.

IX

~ 1 ~

"O-o-oh," Tambilis moaned. "Oh, beloved, beloved, beloved!" By the first faint dawnlight Gratillonius saw her face contorted beneath him, nostrils flared, mouth stretched wide, yet ablaze with beauty.

He never quite lost awareness of Forsquilis's caresses, they were in the whole of the tempest, but it was Tambilis whose hips plunged to meet his, whose breasts and flanks his free hand explored, until he roared aloud and overleaped the world with her.

Afterward they lay side by side, she dazedly smiling from a cloud of unbound hair. Her body glimmered dim against the darkness that still filled most of the chamber. Her heartbeat slugged down toward its wonted rhythm.

Forsquilis raised herself to an elbow on his left side. Her locks flowed to make a new darkness and fragrance for him as she lowered her head and gave him a kiss. It went on, her tongue flickering and teasing, before she said from deep in her throat: "Me next."

"Have mercy," he chuckled. "Give me a rest."

"You'll need less than you think," Forsquilis promised, "but take your ease a while, do."

She crouched over him. Hands, lips, erected nipples roved. He lay back and savored what she did. Not for a long time had he brought more than a single Queen to the Red Lodge. Indeed, the last few months he had stood his Watches alone, save for men with whom he did business or practiced fighting, as troublous a year as this had been. Now, though, he had his victories. Of course a difficult stretch was ahead; but he felt confident of coping. Let him celebrate. Let him, also, affirm to Ys that King and Gallicenae were not estranged. Vindilis alone—but he suspected she had largely been glad of an excuse to terminate a relationship they both regarded as mere duty. If anything, she ought in due course to feel more amicable toward him than erstwhile. The fears that Lanarvilis and Innilis nursed would dwindle away when nothing terrible happened. As for the rest of the Nine—

Forsquilis straddled his thighs and rubbed his organ against her soft fur. By the slowly strengthening light he saw her look at him through slitted eyes and her tongue play over her teeth. Eagerness quickened in him. He reached to fondle her. Tambilis, having gotten back some control over her own joints, rolled onto her belly and sprawled across the great bed, watching with interest. There was no jealousy among the Sisters.

Astonishingly soon, even for a King of Ys, Gratillonius hardened. Forsquilis growled, raised herself, moved forward and down again, slipped him in. She undulated. Presently she galloped. Tambilis slid over to lie across him, give him herself to hold close while he thrust upward. Forsquilis's hands sought her too.

In the end they rested happily entangled and let the sun come nearer heaven. He wondered if his sweat smelled as sweet to them as theirs to him. The chill of its drying was pleasant, like washing in a woodland spring. Well, he should soon be free again to range the woods, far into Osismia, riding, hunting, or simply enjoying their peace. The peace for which poor Corentinus yearned. How Corentinus would regard the scene here! Wicked, damned Ys. Gratillonius smiled a little sadly. He had grown fond of the old fellow. And grateful to him for counsel and help over the years. A strong man, Corentinus, and wise, and in touch with Powers of his own; but this he would never allow himself to understand....

"When shall we start anew?" asked Tambilis from Gratillonius's right shoulder.

"Hold on!" he laughed. "At least let's break our fast."

Forsquilis took her head off his left shoulder. "Aye," she said, "we may start getting visitors, insistent dignitaries, early from the city. 'Twould disadvantage us did our stomachs rumble at them."

They sought the adjacent, tiled room. Its sunken bath had been filled but not yet heated. They frolicked about in the bracing cold like

586

children. Having toweled each other dry, they dressed and went out into the hall. Servants were already astir, hushed until they saw that the master had awakened. The carvings on the pillars seemed sullenly alive in the gloom, which hid the banners hung overhead.

"We will eat shortly," Gratillonius told the steward. To the Queens: "Abide a span, my dears." That was needless. They had their devotions to pay, he his.

He went outside. Dew shimmered on the flags of the Sacred Precinct, leaves of the Challenge Oak, brazen Shield. A few birds twittered in the Wood. He walked forth onto Processional Way, where he had an unobstructed view of the hills. Streamers of mist smoked across the meadow beyond. The sky was unutterably clear. Between its headlands, Ys gleamed, somehow not quite real—too lovely?

Gratillonius faced east. The sun broke blindingly into sight. He raised his arms. "Hail, Mithras Unconquered, Savior, Warrior, Lord—"

Praying, he began through the silence to hear footfalls draw near, light, a single person's, likely a woman's. Abruptly they broke into a run, pattering, flying. Did she seek the King to ask justice for some outrage? She must wait till he was done here. He ought not think about her while he honored his God.

"Father! Oh, father!"

She seized his right arm and dragged it down. Dumbfounded, he turned. Dahut cast herself against him. Embracing him around the neck, she kissed him full on the mouth.

He lurched. "What, what?"

She stepped back to shiver and skip before him. Her gown was dew-drenched, earth-stained, her tresses swirled tangled, her cheeks were flushed and radiance was in her eyes. "Father, father," she caroled, "I am she! I could wait no longer, you had to know it from me, father, beloved!"

For a moment he could not feel the horror. It was like being sworded through the guts. A man would stare, uncomprehending. He would need a few heartbeats' worth of blood loss before he knew.

"Behold!" Dahut took wide-legged stance and tugged at her dress under the throat. The lacing was not fastened. The cloth parted. For the first time he saw her breasts bared, firm, rosy-tipped, a delicate tracery of blue in the whiteness. They were just as he remembered her mother's breasts. The same red crescent smoldered between them.

Whatever was on his countenance sobered Dahut a trifle. She closed the garment and said, carefully if shakily, "Oh, 'tis sorrow that Fennalis is gone, but not sorrow either, she suffered so and now she is free. The Gods have chosen. Blessed be Their names."

Again joy overwhelmed her. She snatched both his hands. "'Tis *you* will be my King, you, you! How I have dreamed, and hoped, and prayed—I need not lose you. Ys need not. Nay, together we'll make the new Age!"

The ice congealed within him, or the molten metal, it did not matter which. "Dahut," he heard himself say, word by dull word, "daughter of Dahilis, I love you. But as any father loves his child. This thing cannot be."

She gripped his hand harder. "I know your fear," she answered fiercely. "I've been awake all night, and—and earlier I've thought about it, oh, how often. You recall what happened to Wulfgar. But you're no ignorant Saxon. You know better than to cringe before a, a superstition. The Gods chose you too, you, father, King, husband, lover."

Was she Dahilis reborn? Dahilis had been almost this same age. No, he must win time for himself. "Go," he said. "Into the house. Two of your—two Gallicenae are there. Is it not seemliest you declare it first to them? There are rites and— Meet me later this morning, you Sisters, and we'll talk of what's to be done."

He pulled free of her and shoved her toward the Sacred Precinct. She seemed bewildered at his action. Before she could recover he was striding off, as fast as might be without running, to Ys. Abandoning the Wood before the three days and nights of full moon were up was mortal sin, unless urgency arose. He must assemble the legionaries at once, and any other men he could trust.

~ 2 ~

The barge that carried Maldunilis back from Sena had not brought Innilis to replace her. Instead, the Nine forgathered at the Temple of Belisama. "Aye, the Nine," said Vindilis grimly.

Summoned, Gratillonius arrived about noon. He came alone, onto the Goddess's own ground, but in red robe with the Wheel emblazoned on his breast and the Key hanging out of sight. A hush fell wherever his big form passed along the streets. None dared address him. Rumors buzzed through Ys like wasps from a nest kicked open. He hailed no one.

Elven Gardens lay deserted under the sun. The blossoms, hedges, topiaries, intricate winding paths where sculptures sprang forth, were outrageously beautiful. The towers of Ys gleamed athwart the horns of land, the sea reached calm and blue save where it creamed over skerries or among the rocks around the distant island. Hardly a sound arose other than his tread on the shell and gravel.

He climbed the steps to the building that was like the Parthenon though subtly alien to it. Between the bronze doors he passed, into the foyer adorned with mosaics of the Mother's gifts to earth. Under-priestesses and vestals waited to greet the King. Their motions were stiff and those that must speak did so in near-whispers. Fear looked out of their pale faces.

Gratillonius followed the corridors along the side, around the sanctum to the meeting chamber at the rear. Gray-green light from its windows brought forth the reliefs in stone that covered the four walls: Belisama guided Taranis back from the dead to make His peace with Lir; amidst bees and airborne seeds, She presided over the act of generation; She stood triune, Maiden, Matron, and Crone; She rode the night wind on the Wild Hunt, leading the ghosts of women who died in Childbed. Almost as phantomlike seemed the blue robes and high white head-dresses of the Nine who sat benched before the dais.

The door closed behind him. He mounted the platform.

No word was spoken. He let his gaze seek left to right. Maldunilis, fat and frightened. Guilvilis, onto whose homely visage a smile timorously ventured. Tambilis, taut with woe. Bodilis, hollow-eyed, slumped in exhaustion. Lanarvilis, poised aquiver. *Dahut.* Vindilis, stiff, glowering. Innilis, huddled close beside her, striving not to shudder. Forsquilis, who had been aflame this dawn, a million years ago, gone altogether enigmatic.

Dahut could scarcely sit still. It was as if she were about to leap up and speed to him. Her fists clenched and unclenched. He saw her robe swell, wrinkle, swell to her breathing.

Six of those women had lain in his arms, again and again and again, from the first year of his Kingship; one since the end of that year; one, in shared pain, eleven years ago, then for the past eight years in joy. They had walked at his side, talked gravely or merrily, dealt food and wine and worship with him, quarreled and reconciled and worked with him for the guidance of Ys and the raising of the children they had given him. Now, because of the last and loveliest, they had become strangers.

"Greeting," he said finally.

"Oh, greeting!" piped from Guilvilis. Lanarvilis frowned and made a hushing gesture.

She would force Gratillonius to speak first. So be it. He braced himself. His back arched between the shoulderblades. That was no way for a soldier, tightening up, but this was no battle such as he had ever fought before. His mouth felt dry. He had, though, marshalled some words beforehand, as he had marshalled his fighting men—Christians, Mithraists—who stood by at the palace. Let him deploy them.

"We've a heavy matter on hand," he said. His voice sounded harsh in his ears. "I do not weep for Fennalis, nor suppose you will. She was a good soul who lay too long in torment. We can be glad she is released, and hope she is rewarded. Many people will miss her, and remember how she served them."—in her cheerful, bustling, often awkward, always loving way.

Vindilis's countenance showed scorn. He could well-nigh hear the gibe: Are you quite done with your noble sentiments?

"Because I respect you, I'll come straight to the point," he told her and her Sisters. "Your Gods have seen fit to lay the Sign upon my daughter Dahut. They surely know—as you do who've known me this long—that I cannot and will not wed her. My own God forbids. It is not a thing on which I may yield or compromise. If we all understand this at the outset, we can go on to understand what your Gods intend. You yourselves have found portents of a new Age coming to birth in Ys. This must be its first cry. Let us heed, and take counsel together."

Dahut snatched for air. Tears brimmed her lapis lazuli eyes. "Nay, father, you cannot be so cruel!" Her anguish was a saw cutting him across. He held himself firm between the sawhorses.

Lanarvilis caught the girl's hand. "Calm, darling, calm," the Queen murmured. To Gratillonius, coldly: "Aye, we foreknew what you would say, and have already taken counsel. Now hear us.

"What the Gods ordain for Ys, we dare not seek to foresee. Yet the purpose of this that has happened is clear. It is to chasten you, traitor King, and bring you back to the ancient Law.

"In your first year you broke it, you sinned against each of the Three. You refused the crown of Taranis. You buried a corpse on Lir's headland. You held a rite of your woman-hating God in water sacred to Belisama. Patient were They—though little you ken of what the Gallicenae underwent to win Their pardon for you.

"Your behavior could have been due to rashness, or ignorance; you were young and a foreigner. Likewise, one might overlook your contumacies throughout the years that followed. There were necessities upon you, Rome, the barbarians, even the requirements of that God you would not put from you.

"But thrice again have you sinned, Gratillonius. Against Taranis—aye, 'twas years ago, but you denied Him His sacrifice when you spared your Rufinus—Taranis, Whose own blood was shed that earth might live. The chastisements that came upon you, you shrugged off."

"I should think Taranis wants manliness in men," Gratillonius interrupted. "If we had a dispute, 'tis been composed."

Vindilis took the word: "The Gods do not forget. But They kept Their patience. Lately you defiled Lir's grounds with your bullslaying, in the teeth of His storm. Still the Gods withheld Their wrath. Now, at last, They require your obedience. This maiden They chose for the newest queen of Ys—and belike the brightest, most powerful, since Brennilis herself. Dare you defy Belisama too?"

"I seek no trouble with Gods or men," he protested.

"You'll have it abundant with men also," Lanarvilis warned. "The city will tear you asunder."

Gratillonius hunched his shoulders, deepened his voice: "I think not. I *am* the King, civil, martial, and sacral." Quickly, he straightened where he stood and mildened his tone. "My dears—I dare yet call you dear to me—how can you know this is true what you've said? Why should the Gods force a crisis that splits us, just when we need unity as seldom erenow? For the dangers ahead are nothing as simple as a pirate fleet or a brigand army. I say Dahut is indeed the bearer of a new Age; but 'twill be an Age when Ys puts aside the savage old ways and becomes the Athens of the world."

The girl bit her lip; blood trickled. She blinked and blinked her eyes. He longed, as he had rarely longed in his life, to hug her to him and comfort her, the pair of them alone. "Dahut," he said, "hear me. I w-w-want your well-being. This thing would, would not be right. Nay, you'll be the first princess, the first Queen, who was free to, well, to let her own prince find her."

At the edge of attention, he saw Lanarvilis wince. Dahut shook her head and cried raggedly, "My King is the King of the Wood!"

Bodilis spoke, flat-voiced. "The wedding should be this day. Go through with it. That will calm the city. Afterward we—you will have time to decide."

He felt heat in his brows, chill in his belly. "I know better than that. We twain would be led to the bridal chamber, and once there I would be helpless. First will I fall on my sword. Bodilis, I looked not for you to try and trick me."

She shrank back into herself.

Tambilis stirred. "But *is* it so dreadful?" she pleaded. "You and I—we grew happy. 'Twas at my mother's cost, but—why, Grallon? Why should we not welcome Dahut, whom we love, into our Sisterhood?"

"The law of Mithras forbids," he answered with a surge of anger. "A man without law is a beast. Enough. I told you, this stands not to be altered. Shall we go on making noise, or shall we plan what to do for Ys?"

Vindilis bared teeth. "Because of your sacrilege on Point Vanis, I have denied my body to you," she flung. "What if all we Nine do likewise? You can have no other woman."

"And you, you would not be like Colconor, you would not," Innilis quavered.

Gratillonius was mainly conscious of his sadness for Dahut. He made a one-sided smile. "Nay," he said, "but I told you, a man ought to be more than a beast. I'll have my duties to occupy me."

"I'll never forsake you!" Guilvilis half screamed.

Before anyone could reprove her, Forsquilis leaned forward. It was like a cat uncoiling. "Grallon, you have right, as far as you've bespoken it," she said. "We do not know what this portends. I fear 'tis a war between Gods, but we do not know. King and Queens, Sisters, night is upon us, the stars have withdrawn and the moon has not risen. We must tread warily, warily.

"Grallon speaks truth. He cannot wed Dahut, not while he abides with Mithras. We may in time persuade him otherwise; or we may learn that his insight, into the Gods Who are not his, was better than ours. Neither outcome is possible for enemies. We can only find our way, whatever our way is, we can only find it together.

591

"I have no new omens. Mayhap none of us will be vouchsafed any. But this much I *feel*."

"'Tis plain good sense," Bodilis murmured.

"What should we do, then?" Maldunilis ventured, pitiably hopefully of an answer.

Forsquilis gave it: "Since this is a thing that never erstwhile came upon Ys, we have a right to be slow and careful. We must be honest before the people; I think then they will accept, although—" she actually flashed a grin—"The words we use to tell them, the show we put on for them, those must be artistry. Give Dahut her honors and dues as a Queen, of course; but let the wedding be postponed until the will of the Gods is more clear. Meanwhile, let us not weaken the sacred marriage by an open quarrel.

"I feel that thus we may win through to a resolving, to the new Age itself. But—"

Suddenly Forsquilis rose. Her skirts rustled with her haste as she went to Dahut. The girl got up, bewildered, to meet her. Forsquilis clasped Dahut close. "Oh, darling child," she said, "yours will be the most hurtful part. I sense, it whispers in me, all that is to come will spring from you, how you bear your burdens and, and what road you choose to fare."

Gratillonius saw his daughter cling hard to his wife, then step back with strength. His spirit went aloft, more than was really reasonable. "Gallicenae," he said, "soon I must meet with spokesmen of the Suffetes. Can we decide what I shall tell them?"

~ 3 ~

In the event it was Soren whom he first saw, the two men by themselves in the private room of the palace.

"Nay," Gratillonius declared, "I will not call another Council."

"Why not?" Soren fairly snarled. They stood within fist range of each other and glared. Evening made dim the chamber, which brought forth the whiteness of Soren's eyeballs, streaks in his beard, bald pate. "Dare you not go before us?"

"I'll do that regardless later this month, at equinox. By then we'll know better what's to come of this, and we'll have been thinking. I hope you and your kind will have been thinking. If we gathered earlier, 'twould be a shouting match, not only futile but dangerous."

"You speak of danger, you who'd bring the curse of the Gods down on Ys?"

"Ah, do you sit among Them, that you are sure what They will do—what They can do? Have the Turones fallen to famine or plague since Bishop Martinus tore down their old halidoms and made Christians of them? Here I am, a mortal man; and I go daily out beneath the sky. Let the Gods strike at me if They choose. My business is with my fellow men."

"Those may well become the instruments of the Gods, lest the whole nation suffer."

Gratillonius shook his head and smiled without merriment. "Beware, Soren Cartagi. You think of the worst sacrilege, the murder of the blood-anointed King. I do not believe any Ysan would raise hand against me. That would destroy the very thing you'd fain preserve. Nay, I expect instead the people will rally behind me once they've heard my case and thought on it. For I am their leader, and I am their mediator with Taranis."

"I've something else in mind," Soren rasped.

Gratillonius nodded. "Aye. Another sequence of challenges from outside. Sooner or later I must fall. 'Tis been done in the past, when a King grew intolerable. But you will not do it; you will seek out your colleagues and make them refrain too, as the Gallicenae have already decided to refrain."

Soren folded arms across his massive chest and compressed his lips before he said, "Explain why."

"You know why, if you'll stop to think. Ys is in peril from worse than Gods. I cannot provoke Governor Glabrio further by accusing him of connivance at the Frankish invasion, but there is no doubt. When I sent him a complaint against them, the reply was days late in coming, surly in tone, and dictated by Procurator Bacca—a studied insult It berated me for attacking and killing subjects of the Emperor, rather than negotiating any differences between us. It said my 'murderous blunder' is being reported to the vicarius in Lugdunum, together with a list of my other malfeasances."

Soren stood quiet while dusk deepened, until he said low: "Aye, we know somewhat of this."

"You'd have seen the letter for yourselves as soon as my Watch in the Wood was up."

"What do you propose to do?"

"Send a letter of my own to Lugdunum, by the fastest courier Ys can supply. I may well have to go in person later and defend myself. That will be tricky, mayhap impossible. The Franks were unruly, but as laeti they provided Redonia its strongest defense. Now the flowers of them are reaped, the spirit of the rest broken. Ys remains obstinately pagan, its traders cause folk to desire more than the Empire provides, its freedom undermines subservience.

"Nevertheless, I am a Roman officer. Let Rome's prefect here be slain, and that will be the very pretext Glabrio longs for. He could well persuade the Duke to order an invasion. At worst they'd be reprimanded afterward for exceeding their authority, and their part of the booty would doubtless be ample compensation for that.

"If you are wise, you will do whatever you can to keep challengers out of the Wood!"

"Can you win your case before the vicarius?" Soren asked slowly.

"I said 'twill belike prove harder than any combat for the Key. I am no diplomat, no courtier. But I do somewhat know my way through that labyrinth the government. And I do have influential friends, Bishop Martinus the nearest. It all makes me the sole man who has any hope of keeping Rome off."

"Suppose you fail with the vicarius."

"Well, I'll not tamely let him revoke my commission. Above him is the praetorian prefect in Treverorum, to whom I'll appeal," Gratillonius reminded. "And beyond him is Flavius Stilicho, ruler of the West in all but name. He's a soldier himself. I think likely he can be made to agree that Ys is worth more as an ally against the barbarians, however annoying to the state, than as a ruin. But he will want a fellow legionary overseeing it. And I am the only prefect who, as King, would command the support and obedience of the Ysan folk—and, at the same time, try to preserve the rights, the soul, of the city. Ys needs me."

Soren brooded for a long spell. Gratillonius waited.

Finally the Speaker for Taranis said, "I fear you are right. I must get to work on your behalf, and afterward with you."

"Good!" Gratillonius moved to give him the clasp of friendship.

Soren drew back. Sick hatred stared from the heavy visage. "Need drives me, naked need," he said. "Perforce, in public I shall hold back the words about you that are in my heart. But know, beyond your damnable usefulness against your Romans, you have my curse, my wish for every grief in the world upon your head, blasphemer, traitor, wrecker of lives."

He turned and departed.

~ 4 ~

The funeral barge stood out the sea gate on a morning ebb, bearing death's newest harvest in Ys. Weather had turned gray and windy. Whitecaps on olive-hued waves rocked the broad hull and cast spindrift stinging across its deck. The evergreen wreath on the staff amidships dashed about at the end of its tether. Under the spiral-terminated sternpost, two steersmen had the helm and the coxswain tolled his gong, setting rhythm for the oarsmen below. By its copy forward, the captain kept lookout. Somberly clad deckhands went about their tasks. The dead lay shrouded on litters, a stone lashed to each pair of ankles, along the starboard rail. Elsewhere their mourners sat on benches or gathered in small groups, saying little. Among them on this trip were the King and the Gallicenae, who would be the priestesses because a Sister of theirs was going away.

Gratillonius stood apart, looking off to the dim streak that was Sena. Thus had he often traveled over the years, when someone fallen required special honor, since the day they buried Dahilis. Always at least one Queen had been at his side. Today none of them had spoken a word to him.

When out on deep water, the captain signalled halt. The gongbeat ceased, the rowers simply holding the vessel steady. A trumpeter blew a call that the wind flung away. The captain approached the Gallicenae and bowed to Lanarvilis, who was now the senior among them. Ritually, he requested that she officiate. She walked into the bows, raised her hands, and chanted, "Gods of mystery, Gods of life and death, sea that nourishes Ys, take these our beloved—"

When the invocation was done, she unrolled a scroll and from it read the names, in order of death. Each time, sailors brought that litter to a chute, Lanarvilis said, "Farewell," the men tilted their burden and the body slid down over the side, into the receiving waves.

How small was Fennalis's. Gratillonius had never thought of her like that.

At the end, the trumpet sounded again, a drum beneath. There was then a silence, for remembrance or prayer, until the captain cried, "About and home!" Oars threshed to the renewed gongbeat, the barge wallowed around, it crawled back toward the wall and towers of Ys.

Gratillonius felt he must pace. As he commenced, he saw that the Nine had partly dispersed. Dahut was alone at the starboard rail. His heart thuttered. Quickly, before he could lose courage, he went to her. "My dearest—" he began.

She swung avidly about. "Aye?" she exclaimed. "You've seen what's rightful? Oh, Fennalis, may the Gods bear you straightway to my mother!"

Gratillonius retreated, appalled. "Nay," he stammered, "you, you misunderstand, I only wanted to talk between us—when we land, a chance to explain—"

Her face whitened. So did her knuckles where they gripped the rail after she turned her back on him.

He left her and trudged, round and round, round and round.

A hand touched his. He grew aware that Guilvilis had joined him. Slow tears coursed over her cheeks. "You are so unhappy," she said. The tip of her long nose wiggled. "Can I help? Is there aught I can do for you, lord, aught at all?"

He choked back wild laughter. She meant well. And this could be the start of healing the wound. Whether or no, at least with her he would not fail or flag, he could lose himself in the Bull—even closing his eyes and pretending, maybe—until he lost himself in sleep. "Aye," he muttered. "Excuse yourself from any duties that wait and come to me at the palace." It was where his armed men were. He did not require protection anymore, if ever he had, and soon he would dismiss them, but meanwhile their presence enabled him to overawe some of his angry visitors. "Be prepared to stay a goodly time."

She sobbed for joy. That was the most sorrowful thing he had seen this day.

~ 5 ~

The marines and navy men returned, full of stories about their experiences. Their friends met them with tales to overwhelm those.

Herun Taniti came upon Maeloch and Cynan, among others, in a tavern. This was not their disreputable old haunt in the Fishtail, but the Green Whale. The skipper had prospered over the years, like most working men of Ys, while the naval officer and legionary had pay saved, together with proceeds from modest businesses they and their families conducted on the side.

After cheery greetings and a round of drink—

"Do folk truly, by and large, feel the King does right?" Herun asked. "I should think many would be cowering in fear. How shall the world now be renewed?"

"Well, the fish ha' been running as plentiful as ever I saw, and no storms spoiled the crops, nor did rot strike once they were in, nor a murrain fall on the kine," grunted Maeloch. "I'd say nature steers a straight course yet."

"Such as I've talked with, whether Suffete or commoner, and they're not few in my line of work, they're becoming content again," added Zeugit the landlord. This being a slack time of day, he could sit a while and gossip with these customers. "Many were alarmed at first, but when naught untoward happened, well, they're apt to reckon that dealings with the Gods are for the King, and surely this King, before all Ys has had, knows what he does."

"Young men sometimes get downright eager," put in the courtesan Taltha. She was there as much for her learning and conversational abilities as for beauty and lovemaking. "They talk of a new Age, when Ys shall become glorious, aye, mayhap succeed Rome as mistress of the world."

Zeugit glanced around. The room was spacious, clean, sunny, muraled with fanciful nautical images. Only one other of the tables had men benched at it, intent on their wine and a dice game. Nevertheless he dropped his voice.

"Truth is, few will avow it, but I think the faith of most has been shaken by what's happened; and it could not be shaken so much had its roots not grown shallow. Well, this is a seaport. Under Grallon, 'tis become a busy seaport, strangers arriving from everywhere, with ways and Gods that are not those of our fathers, back when Ys lay for hundreds of years drawn into its shell. More and more of us fare abroad, and carry home not just goods but ideas. Aye, change is in the air, you can smell it like the sharpness before a lightning storm."

"Men who've come to think 'twas not Taranis but Mithras Who appeared on Point Vanis, they're starting to seek initiation into that cult," Taltha said. "Myself, I'll stay with Banba, Epona— They are female. They will hear me." She signed herself. "And Belisama, of course. But it may well be that She has a unique destiny in mind for Princess Dahut."

"Well, between us, I might seek out Mithras too," Zeugit confessed, "save that 'twould harm my business. Also, I'm a bit old for learning new mysteries, or for that little branding iron. No disrespect, sir," he said to Mithraist Cynan.

"No offense taken," replied the soldier in his solemn fashion. "We seek no converts like the Christians, who'd conscript them. The legionaries of Mithras are all volunteers." He paused. "Indeed, lately the King sent a man back who'd fain enlist."

"What, was he unworthy?" asked Herun. "I've heard the cult will take none who're guilty of certain crimes and vices."

Cynan smiled a bit. "We're not prigs. You ken me. Nay, this is an old comrade of mine from Britannia, Nodens, we've marched and messed and worked and fought and talked and gotten drunk together for twenty years or more! I'll name no names. But he is a Christian, like most in our unit. After the battle, he having seen the vision, he went and sought acceptance by Mithras. Gratillonius—I was there, as it happened— he told this man nay. He was very kind, the way our centurion can be when 'tis called for. But he said, first, this man has a wife and children to think about, here in Ys. If he should travel into Roman country, or the Romans come hither, and they learned he was apostate, it might go hard with his family as well as himself. Second, said Gratillonius, this man is sworn to Christ, and on the whole has had a good life. A man should stand by his master or his God, as long as that One stands him true."

"Well spoken," murmured Herun. He stared into his cup. "Although I must think, I must think deeper—" Raising his glance: "What say you, Maeloch?"

The fisher shrugged. "Let each do what he deems right, whatever it be, and we need think no less of him," he answered. "Me, I'll abide with the old Gods. To do else would be to break faith with the dead."

~ 6 ~

Dahut inherited the house that had been Fennalis's, and immediately set about having it made over. For any purpose she chose, she could draw upon the Temple treasury without limit—she, a Queen. Those of her Sisters who saw the accounts thought her extravagant, but forbore to protest at once and commanded that minor priestesses keep silence likewise. Let Dahut indulge herself this much; she had enough difficulties.

Tambilis called on her the day after she moved in. Dahut made the guest welcome, without quite the warmth there had formerly been between them. Tambilis looked around the atrium in amazement. Ceiling and pillars were now white with gilt trim; the walls were painted red, black spirals along the tops; furniture of precious woods, inlaid with ivory and nacre, bore cushions of rich fabric, skins of rare animals, vessels of silver and cut crystal, exquisite figurines, with less regard to arrangement than profusion.

"You have... changed this... made it yours, indeed," Tambilis ventured.

Dahut, clad in green silk whereon inwoven serpents twined, a pectoral of amber and carnelian in front, her hair in a tall coiffure caught by a comb of pearl-studded tortoiseshell, Dahut made an indifferent gesture. "The work's scarcely begun," she said. "I'll have this shabby mosaic floor ripped out; I want an undersea scene. I'll have the finest painter in Ys come in, when I've decided whether that is Sosir or Nathach; he'll do me panels for the walls, the Gods in Their aspects; and more."

"Ah, that's why you've not yet had us here for a consecration."

"Work alone will not make this house ready for that." Dahut curbed her bitterness. "Come, follow me." On the way back, she ordered a maidservant to bring refreshments. Sounds of carpentry in progress clattered, but screens blocked sight of the men.

Since some among them were in what was to be her private conference room, Dahut led Tambilis to her bedchamber. It too had a tumbled, unfinished look, in spite of its new sumptuousness. A niche-image showed Belisama helmeted, bearing spear and shield, though not like Minerva; the gown clung to voluptuousness, the countenance stared ahead in unabashed sensuality. It had been stored in the Temple for generations. No Queen since the original owner had wanted it, until Dahut. She bowed low. Tambilis confined herself to the customary salute.

"Be seated," Dahut said brusquely, and tossed herself on the bed, to lie propped on pillows against the headboard. Tambilis took a chair.

"Well, dear, certes you've been busy," she remarked after silence had stretched.

"What else had I to do?" Dahut replied, scowling.

"Why, your duties—"

"What are they? I am no more a vestal. Nor am I a graduate set free, nor a Queen, mauger they give me the name. They know not what to do with me."

"You can help where asked. Besides, you have your schooling to finish. I was a child at first; I remember how it was, and thought you did too, such friends as we were."

"Aye, the Sisters can invent tasks, meaningless things that any under-priestess could do. I can sit through droning hours of lessons. Is that being a Queen?" Dahut's forefinger stabbed toward Tambilis. "And you, you were at least wedded, already then. And after a while, when you were as grown as I am—" She strangled on rage.

"Oh, my dear." As she leaned forward, reaching to touch, Tambilis reddened.

Dahut saw. She held back, fleered, and asked in a tone gone wintry, "When were you last in his bed? When will you next be?"

"We—you know we decided hostility to him would be...self-defeating. I'll plead for you, Sister mine. I'll work on him as cunningly as I can—as a woman can who does love her man and so has learned how to please him. Be patient, Dahut. Abide. Endure. Your hour shall come."

"My hour for what? When?" The maiden stirred, sat straight, gave her guest the look of a hawk. "Be warned, I will not wait quietly very long. I *cannot*. Belisama summons me."

Tambilis shivered. "Be careful," she begged. "You can...you can engage yourself for a while yet, surely. This house and—well, I know how you've gone forth to hunt or sail or, or otherwise spend your strength till you can rest. Come, borrow that splendid stallion of your father's, as often erenow, and outpace the wind."

That was a wrong thing to say, she saw at once. Dahut paled.

Slowly, she replied, "Another horse, a horse of my own, mayhap. But never, unless the King give me my rights, never again will I fare on his Favonius."

~ 7 ~

A sudden gale sprang out of the west. Wind hooted, driving rain through streets that became gurgling streams. Waves bawled, tumbled, dashed themselves and its floats against the sea gate; but the King had locked it.

Budic sat alone with Corentinus, in the room that the chorepiscopus had for himself at the back of the church. A single lamp picked its scant furniture out of shadows. Shutters rattled; rain hissed down them. Chill crept inward. Corentinus did not seem to notice, though his robe was threadbare and his feet without stockings in their worn-out sandals. Highlights glimmered across shaven brow, craggy nose and chin, eyes as deep in hollows of murk as were his cheeks. "And what then?" he asked.

The soldier had come in search of spiritual help. Corentinus promised him it, but would first have a report on the lately concluded Council. Several men had already told him things—incompletely, however, and Budic had been present throughout as a royal guardsman.

"Well, sir, there isn't much more to tell. Those like Lir Captain, who would not withdraw their opposition, they got their words entered in the chronicle. Queen Lanarvilis, speaking for the Gallicenae, said they'd keep public silence about the marriage issue, for the time being. The Council in general, it voted down censure of the King, which was

599

the least of what the zealous pagans wanted. It didn't approve his action, either. Instead, it entered a prayer into the record, a prayer for guidance and compassion from the Gods. It did declare its support for Gratillonius in his politics, especially his dealings with Rome. That was the end of proceedings. They'd ordinarily have considered other matters, you know, public works, taxes, changes in the laws that this or that faction wants—but nothing of it seemed important. It could wait till solstice, when everybody will know better where he's at."

Corentinus nodded. "Thank you. I'd say Gratillonius got as much as he could possibly have hoped for, at this stage. God aid him onward." His tone softened. "Daily I pray he see the Light. But sometimes— sometimes I don't really pray, because it's not for a mortal man to question God's ways, but I wish for a place outside of Heaven and hell, a kindly place for such as Gratillonius, who hear the Word and do not believe, but who remain upright."

Budic's voice cracked across. "God bless him—for his, his forbearance. He *must* not marry Dahut, God must not let him do such a thing to her, but what's to become of her, then? Father, that's what I'm here about, the wilderness in me—"

Corentinus raised a palm. "Hold! Quiet!" The command snapped like a hawser drawn taut when a ship plunges. Budic gulped and trembled on the stool where he sat.

For a space, only the storm spoke. Corentinus unfolded his knobby length and loomed up toward the ceiling, arms and face raised, eyes shut.

Abruptly he opened them, looked down at Budic, said, "Follow me," and went to the door.

The legionary obeyed, bewildered. Corentinus let them out into the deserted Forum. Rain slashed and runneled. Wind keened. Dusk was setting in. Corentinus strode so fast that Budic could barely keep alongside him.

"What, what is this, sir? Where are we bound?"

Corentinus squinted ahead. His reply was barely to be heard through the noise. "A vessel lies wrecked. Women and children are aboard. We've no time to gather a rescue party before it's pounded apart. But the vision would not have come to me in vain."

Budic remembered a certain night in his home, and stories he had heard from elsewhere. Nonetheless he must exclaim, "What can two men do? The gate is barred. The dock at Scot's Landing—"

"Too far. Too slow." And in fact Corentinus was bound not south, but north on Taranis Way. "God will provide. Now spare your breath, my son. You'll need it."

Tenements of the well-to-do yielded to mansions of the wealthy. Statuary stood dim in the failing light, along either side of the avenue, a seal, a dolphin balanced on its tail, a lion and a horse with the hind-quarters of fish—Epona Square, a glimpse of the equestrian idol— Northbridge Gate, the battlements of the Sisters like fangs bared at unseen heaven—water ramping among rocks under the bridge—the short road that climbed onto Point Vanis to meet Redonian Way—the highroad wan, rimmed by windswept, rain-swept grass and bush, empty of man or beast, here and there sight of a menhir or a dolmen—near the end of the headland, where the road bent east, a blur in the blackness, a gravestone—

Corentinus took the lead down the trail to the former maritime station. Budic stumbled after, drenched, jaws clapping, feet slipping and skidding in mud. Surf crashed against the jetty that it was year by year gnawing away. Under the cliffs, gloom lay thick, the ruin shapeless. Budic tripped over a fragment, fell, skinned his knee. "Father, I cannot see," he wailed into the thunders and shrieks.

A globe of light appeared at the fingertips of Corentinus's uplifted right hand. It was like the ghost-glow sometimes seen at the ends of yardarms, but bright and serene. By its radiance Budic spied a jollyboat banging loose against what remained of the dock. It must have broken its painter or been washed off a strand where it rested and drifted here. Three or four oars clattered in the water that sloshed in its bilge.

Corentinus beckoned. Budic could do no else than creep forward, into the hull, onto the middle thwart. Corentinus climbed into the stern and stood erect. "Row," he said softly but heard with the clearness of a voice in a dawn-dream.

Dreamlike too was Budic's placing a pair of oars between their tholes and pulling on them. Even in dead calm, a man should not have been able to make a boat that size do more than crawl along. For him to row in seas like this, into the teeth of the wind, was beyond the strength of a madman. Yet as Budic put his weight to the task, the hull bounded forward. It mounted the billows to their crests and plunged down their backs like a hunting cat. Corentinus balanced easily. His right hand carried the phantom lantern, his left pointed the way to go.

Night blinded the world. The lonely light swayed onward.

Finally, finally it picked out its goal. A slim craft of some thirty feet lay hard on a skerry, held by snags onto which it had been driven. Waves dashed clamorous over the rock. They were breaking the strakes and ribs of the vessel, bearing those off. Groanings and crackings passed through surf-bellow, wind-howl. Already no refuge was left for the people aboard, save the section amidships. They clawed themselves to the stump of the mast, the tangle of its cordage.

This had been a yacht, Budic recognized. A couple of Suffetes must have celebrated the end of Council by taking their families out on a day cruise; all Ysans reckoned themselves familiars of the sea. The gale had caught them by surprise.

While he himself was no sailor, living here he had inevitably been on the water often enough to have gained a measure of skill. The surges ought to have cast him helpless onto the reef. He maneuvered in and kept his boat as steady as if it were a skiff on a mildly ruffled lake.

Something passed by, on the verge of sight. A shape half-human, foam-white, riding a monstrous wave like a lover? A screech of mockery, through tumult and skirl? The thing vanished into the haze of spindrift. Budic shuddered.

Corentinus hitched up his robe and made a long-legged step to the reef. There he stood fast, though waves boiled higher than his knees. With his left hand he helped the victims clamber from the wreck and scramble over to the boat. Budic would pause in his labors to haul one at a time across the rail.

They filled the hull when all were huddled together. Their weight left bare inches of freeboard. Corentinus came back to take stance astern. By the light he bore, Budic discerned half a dozen men—ha, Bomatin Kusuri, Mariner Councillor—with two middle-aged women who must be wives—the other men were surely crew—and four small children—doubtless the youngest belonging to the Suffete couples, taken out as a holiday treat—exhausted, chilled blue, terrified, but alive.

Rowing did not seem very much more difficult, nor did the boat take on very much more water, than on the way out. Well, now he had the wind behind him. Face full of rain, he could barely see Corentinus give directions. The pastor's robe flapped around his gauntness like a sail that has slipped its sheets; but the light glowed ever steady.

It vanished after they had made landing at the station, and helped the people up the trail, and were safe on Point Vanis.

Abruptly another shadow, Corentinus called in Ysan—not quite steadily, for weariness was overtaking him too—"Give thanks to the Lord, Who has delivered us from death."

"'Twas a demon," babbled a crewman, "I swear 'twas a sea demon lured us, I'd never have let us anywhere near those rocks but we couldn't see the pharos, I think the wind blew it out, and then there was a shining—oh, the white thing that laughed while we went aground!"

Corentinus grew stern. "If you have looked into the abyss and still not seen the truth, at least keep your pagan nonsense to yourself." Milder: "Can everyone walk as far as the city? This darkness hoods us, but we'll keep pavement under our feet. Best we carry the children." He groped about. "Ah, here's a little girl for me. Rest you, sweetling, rest you, all is well again and God loves you."

The party staggered forward. Budic felt how drained of strength he was. Barely could he hold the boy who made his burden. The rescued men must often stop and exchange the other two youngsters. Corentinus paced steadily at his side.

"You've wrought a miracle tonight," Budic mumbled. "You're a saint."

"Not so," the chorepiscopus answered with brief vehemence. "This was God's work. We can only thank Him for the honor He gave us, of being His instruments."

"But why—ships are wrecked every year—why this one?"

"Who knows? His ways are mysterious. A Suffete who embraced the Faith would be valuable in winning salvation for Ys. Or God in His mercy may simply have granted these innocent children their chance to receive the Word and enter Heaven. It's not for us to say." A laugh barked. "And yet—I *am* no saint; may He forgive me—maybe He decided that after everything else that's been happening, high time Ys saw a Christian miracle!"

"Salvation...Princess Dahut, sea-child...D-d-do you suppose this—while she's still free of the deadly sin—this will change her heart?"

Starkness answered the appeal. "We may pray so. I know this much, Budic, I have this much foreknowledge. If Dahut does not come to the Light, she will do such ill that it were better she had died in her mother's womb."

X

~ 1 ~

The gale damped down to a high wind and frequent, violent showers. Seas crashed on the wall and gate of Ys. Bodilis would be confined on Sena for another two or three days, it seemed.

That morning Guilvilis was to lead sunrise rites at the Temple. A rainsquall struck while she mounted the steps—on the far right side of the staircase, as it happened. Near the top she lost footing on a tread which centuries of traffic had beveled and the wet made slippery. She slid, staggered, and went over the edge to the flagstones below. Once and horribly she screamed, then lay moaning like an animal.

A vestal who had also been on the way up saw and scurried to her. Having seen how she writhed and how her left foot thrashed but the right did not, the girl sped back after help. Such few as were present at this hour came in haste. An old underpriestess took charge; she had long been married to a physician, and upon taking new vows after she was widowed had become an instructress in the healing arts. They got Guilvilis onto an improvised litter and into a side room where there was a bed.

"Father must know," said her daughter Antonia, who chanced to have duty. Before anyone could naysay it, the fourteen-year-old was off at full speed to find the King. The old priestess grimaced, and set others to inform the rest of the Gallicenae and fetch the royal chirurgeon Rivelin.

Gratillonius arrived first. He dropped his sodden cloak in the portico and strode aggressively through the vestibule. The Key could be seen to swing on his breast under the tunic which, with sandals, was the only other garb he had taken time to don.

Dim light seeped into the little chamber. A younger priestess and a vestal kept watch. They shrank aside as he entered. He lifted the heavy blankets beneath which Guilvilis lay shivering, and her gown. It became clear to him that her right thigh was broken. He lowered the blanket and stopped above her face. Sweat studded it. She breathed rapidly and shallowly. He looked into her half-opened eyes. "Pupils seem all right," he muttered in Latin. In Ysan: "Guilvilis, do you ken me? This is Grallon."

Her gray lips tried to twist into a smile. He kissed them very lightly. "Poor Guilvilis," he said, "you've never had much luck, have you? But you're as brave a lass as ever I knew. Have no fear. You'll be hale again." He stroked the thin hair, stepped back, and took stance where she could see him, folded his arms, and waited.

Vindilis and Innilis came in together. The tall woman stiffened at sight of Gratillonius. She glared. "Get out, you bird of woe," she said, regardless of how she shocked the attendants. "What can you do here save call more misfortune down on her?"

He stood fast. His reply was flat. "Do you, then, accuse your Gods of penalizing loyalty?"

"Please, please, I pray peace," Innilis implored from the bedside. Her fingers were deft, drawing forth jars, cloths, implements from a bag she had brought. "Beloved, you can best help by standing outside. Let nobody in other than the medicus. Tell the Sisters this is grievous but not mortal, Our Lady of Solace willing."

Gratillonius began to move but Vindilis left ahead of him, in a susurrus of skirts. He paused a moment startled, then thoughtful. He winced a bit when Guilvilis made a jagged noise. Innilis was cleaning and anointing the abrasions, into which fibers from the garment had gotten. "I'm sorry, dearest, I'm sorry," she murmured. "This must be done to stave off infection. I'll be quick, I'll be as gentle as I can."

Rivelin appeared, saluted her and the King, made his own examination. "I fear we have no clean break, but a splintering," he said. "She'll be slow to heal, at best, and mayhap crippled. The sooner we put traction on it, the better. I've need of a colleague to help, a man with strong hands."

"Here I am," said Gratillonius.

"What?" The physician mastered his surprise. Whispers had long gone about concerning surgery the King performed once on Sena; and many had seen him competently treat injuries due battle or accident. "Well, my lord, let me describe for you what force must be applied, and put you through the motions, while we send after the necessary materials."

—When Gratillonius emerged, he found six women gathered in the corridor. His shoulders sagged and he had begun to tremble a bit. Sweat made blots on his tunic below the arms and reeked around him. "It went well," he told his wives and daughter, dull-voiced. "Rivelin is finishing now, with Innilis's help."

"Would you give her naught for the pain? Would you not allow that?" Vindilis snapped.

"Nay, Sister," Tambilis protested.

"Innilis dared not drug her when she had gone so cold," Gratillonius said. "Besides, when we began the work she swooned. Later she'll get something so she can rest quietly. I did not...enjoy myself." His glance sought Dahut. "It must needs be done."

The maiden made no response. "Oh, Grallon," Tambilis whispered, and moved toward him, her hands outheld. Lanarvilis pulled at her sleeve and hissed in her ear. Tambilis halted. Tears in her lashes caught what light there was.

Dahut stirred. "Let me go in to her," she said. "I will give her the Touch. She'll suffer less and heal properly."

Forsquilis frowned. "Nay, best not. Not now, not here. The house of the Goddess, and you unconsecrated— Mayhap later, when Rivelin's let her go home."

"I may not help my sister, I may not keep Vigil—I may not be Queen, thanks to you!" Dahut shrilled at her father.

"I'm leaving," he said. "Have someone keep me informed and tell me when I can call on her."

He walked off. Tambilis half moved to follow, but checked herself. "Patience, my dear," Lanarvilis admonished after the man was gone.

"But he is so alone, so unhappy," Tambilis pleaded. "You act as if this were his fault."

"Was it not?"

"Let that be. Unwise it is to talk about such things," warned Forsquilis. She went to embrace Tambilis. "I understand. All that you are cries out to go to him. I miss him too, the big sad sobersided lost soul. But this is the sacrifice we must make."

"Punish him," Vindilis said, "starve his lust, punish him until he gives in. Not that he will ever again have me. But you others, make him pay. You are the instruments of the Gods."

"He may force himself on us, now that he can't have Guilvilis," said Maldunilis, not altogether fearfully.

Lanarvilis shook her head. "Nay. Give him his due. He is no Colconor. He will not squander the respect we still have for him, nor antagonize us worse at a time when he needs every ally he can find."

"But what shall we do?" asked Tambilis miserably.

"What we have been doing since he spurned his bride—naught. Give him no invitations. Decline any he gives us. Be coldly polite in conference. When at last he seeks us out, receive him likewise. When

605

he speaks of bed, tell him calmly that he has broken the sacred marriage, not we, and we think the Gods have made an example of Guilvilis. That should deter him—that, and his injured male pride. If not, if he does press suit, well, 'tis for each of us to decide, but if outright refusal fails, then I think we should lie down and send our minds away. He is not such a blockhead that he will not know it."

"If I can do that," Tambilis whispered.

Forsquilis bit her lip. "'Twill not be easy," she said. "Remember, though, we do it for him too, that he be brought to make his peace with the Gods."

"How long must we?"

Forsquilis spread her hands. "As long as necessary—or as possible. Meanwhile hope, pray, seek what small spells we might cast. Who knows what can happen?...Dahut, what's wrong?"

The princess had started. She recovered herself. "Nothing," she said. Acridly: "Nothing and everything. A thought passed through me."

"What was it?" Vindilis asked.

Dahut looked away. "A fleeting thing. Let me pursue it further."

"Have a care, child. Take counsel with your Sisters. Ever were you prone to recklessness."

Dahut flushed. "The Gods will watch over me," she said, and stalked off.

~ 2 ~

Weather continued windy, cloudy, raw. The sun blinked in and out of sight while shadows swept a darkling sea where white horses went at gallop until they reared up against the reefs. The noise pervaded Ys, a murmur in Hightown, a rumble and boom and monstrous sighing where the wall stood off the waters. The gate was open, but pilots gave its floats a wide berth.

Tommaltach and Carsa paced the top between Northbridge and the Gull Tower. They had been drinking in Carsa's apartment and decided some sharp air was in order before they supped. Save for the posted guards, nobody else was there. Surf roiled among the rocks below, burst, recoiled in swirls and smothers of foam.

"I wonder that the people take not this as a sign their Gods are angry," said the Roman. His gesture encompassed the bleakness and the time through which it had prevailed. He spoke in Ysan, the language the two young men had in common; as yet, Tommaltach's Latin was halting.

"Why, 'tis naught unusual," the Scotian replied. "You've not dwelt here long enough. At home we'd call it an autumn mild and dry."

Carsa brightened. "Then you think 'twill not make things harder for Gratillonius?"

"Ah, is that what gnaws at you? Well, me too, me too."

"No offense meant, my friend, but you are a pagan, albeit not of the Ysan kind. You understand these folk better than a Christian from the South can."

"I am an initiate of Mithras," said Tommaltach stiffly.

"I know." Carsa laid a hand on the other's arm. "Would that you had taken the true Faith! But what I meant was that you, hailing from among heathens, you can see how the evil works within the souls of men. And you've relieved me. Thank you."

Tommaltach regarded him a while as they walked before he said slowly, "You hope Grallon will—be able to—hold out against marrying his daughter."

"Hope?" Carsa exclaimed. "I pray! Daily, more than daily, prostrate, I implore God to keep her pure." He snapped after breath. "Do you not?"

Tommaltach searched for words, which was unlike him. "Well, if Dahut becomes truly a high priestess of Ys, there goes many a dream. I've never heard that any of them ever took a lover. And if her father says Mithras forbids it, I believe him, though I'm still ignorant of most of the Mysteries. Yet what's to become of the poor darling? How can she ever be free to make her own life? Wonderful beyond wonder, could she become the sort of Queen we have at home. How likely, though, is that? First and foremost comes her welfare."

"Mean you," asked Carsa harshly, "that if her father yields and—the defilement—happens—you would let it go unavenged?"

"He is *my* Father in Mithras," Tommaltach said with difficulty.

"I have sworn before God," stated Carsa, "that if he does it to her, I will kill him."

~ 3 ~

The full moon fled through clouds. They were silver where it touched them, elsewhere smoke and swiftness. The light shuddered over earth. Wind blew icy down the valley, a hollow whistling. It ripped dead leaves off trees and scourged them along the road where Dahut ran.

She turned in at the Sacred Precinct and stopped. Breath gusted in and out of her. A cloak flapped about her shoulders. Its cowl had fallen back and stray locks fluttered from hastily woven braids. The paving of the yard flickered wan as light came and went, between three hulks of blackness. The Challenge Oak and the Wood behind groaned. Now and then the Hammer swung against the Shield and a faint ringing thrilled forth.

Dahut raised her arms. The Red Lodge lay darkened, King and attendants were asleep, but somebody might easily awaken. She began to chant. *"Ya Am-Ishtar, ya Baalim, ga'a vi khuwa—"*

The spell cast, she moved forward soft-footed. A moonbeam showed her lips drawn back, teeth bared, the grin of a warrior in battle.

607

Nonetheless she paused whenever the old wooden stairs creaked beneath her weight; and she moved the doorlatch with utmost caution, and opened the door an inch at a time. As soon as the gap was wide enough she slipped through and at once closed it, as quietly as might be.

A while she listened. Through night sounds muffled by walls, she heard a couple of snores from the benches where men lay. At first the hall was tomb-dark, then she gained sufficient vision to make them out, barely. The pillar idols loomed clearer, more real than they. "Taranis, lover of Belisama, be with me, the beloved of Lir," she whispered.

Cat-careful, she made her way over the floor. A banked fire in a trench warned her off with a few blood-colored stars. At the interior door, she must feel about until she found its latch. The passage beyond was less murky, for windows had been let into this rebuilt half and the weather was not so tumultuous as to require that they be shuttered. Their glass shifted between moonlight milkiness and gaping black, but always blind, nothing truly seeable through them, as if she had gone outside the world.

The door to the royal bedroom stood ajar. She shut it after she had passed through and, again, poised wary for several score heartbeats. The single window here was on the west, and the moon had not yet reached the zenith; thus the brightest that entered was an uneasy gray. She could just see Gratillonius. He lay on his side. An arm and shoulder above the blanket were bare. In the middle of the huge bed, he seemed very alone.

Dahut sat down on the floor to take off her sandals, lest she make a noise. Rising, she unfastened the fibula that held her cloak and lowered that garment, likewise her belt. There remained a gown, which she pulled over her head.

For a moment she looked at her body, ran hands across the smooth curves, smiled. Thereafter she spent minutes studying how the chamber was arranged, estimating distances and directions, planning each movement. Finally she padded to the window. When she had drawn the drape that hung beside it, sightlessness engulfed her.

She glided to the bedside, found the top edge of the sheet, pulled it back, slipped onto the mattress, lay until she was sure Gratillonius had not moved, then pulled the covers over her and edged across to him. He breathed slowly, deeply. The slumber spell held, and for hours it would take more than a touch to awaken him.

His back was to her. She brought her belly close against the warm solidity. A shiver passed through her. She writhed. Her hips thrust. He stirred a little. She drew slightly back and waited for him to sink anew.

Thereupon she raised herself to an elbow and brought her mouth down to his ear. A male odor entered her nostrils. His hair and the regrowing beard brushed her lips.

"Gratillonius," she whispered, "I am here. I could no longer keep from you, Grallon, my darling, take me now." Her free hand slid by his waist, across the ridges of muscle, to the loins. She closed fingers on what she found and moved them. The flesh stirred, thickened, lifted. Heat pulsed. "Grallon, King, lord, lover, here is your Queen."

"Wh-what?" His voice rumbled unsteadily, dazed. "Who? Tambilis?" He rolled around groped, cupped a breast. "You?" Joy throbbed.

She flung herself at him, stopped his tongue with hers, cast a thigh over his. Her hand quivered and tugged, urging the bigness whither she wanted it.

He got to his knees and one palm. "Quickly, mount me quickly," she said in an undertone that could be any woman's.

His other hand stroked. Abruptly it halted. "But you, you're not Tam—Fors—who?" he stuttered. It ripped from him: *"Dahilis!"*

He pulled out of her clasp. His trembling shook the mattress. "Aye, this is Dahilis come back to you," Dahut keened and sought after him. He scrambled, thudded to the floor and across it. Dahut yowled.

Gratillonius hauled the drape downward. The heavy fabric ripped free of its rings. Clouds had briefly parted around the moon. Light cast its patina over Dahut where she crouched on the bed.

Whoo-oo, said the wind.

Dahut clambered to her own feet. Tears torrented, agleam in the night. "I would save you," she implored, "I would have you do the will of the Gods. 'Tis not too late."

She stumbled toward him. He lifted crooked-fingered hands. "To this have your Gods brought you, child of mine?" His tone was dead.

"Oh, father, I'm afraid for you, and I love you so."

"You know not what love is, you who...who supposed a man would not know his dear one in the dark. Go. Depart. Now."

"Father, comfort me, hold me—"

She had come nigh enough to see his face turn into a Gorgon mask. "Go!" he roared. "Ere I kill you!"

Like a bear enraged, he advanced on her. She whirled and fled. Behind her she heard him cry out, "Dahilis, Dahilis!" and began to weep, with the racking sobs of a man unpracticed in it.

Naked, Dahut ran down the road to Ys. She wept also.

More and more, the clouds were swallowing the moon. She should be able to pass unseen through High Gate always open in peacetime, as she had left.

The wind whipped her with cold. Dead leaves tumbled and rattled before her feet. Wings passed overhead, an eagle owl. It vanished with the moon.

~ 4 ~

Vindilis called on Lanarvilis at the home of the latter. They sought the private room. Lamps burned to offset the dullness of a rainy noontide. Their glow brought out the blue and vermilion of lush fabrics, ivory and wood grain of fine furniture, sheen of silver and gleam of glass. Vindilis's gaunt figure, black-clad, was like a denial of it. She sat rigid in a chair facing the couch on which Lanarvilis half slumped.

Vindilis went straight to the attack: "Already the time is overpast for decision. Those of us who honor the Gods and fear Their wrath must close ranks."

"That is...all of us...though we may disagree on what course is wisest," Lanarvilis said.

"There can be no question of wisdom. Prudence is madness. Better Ys defy the whole might of Rome than forsake her Gods."

"What would you have us do?"

Vindilis sighed, while her gaze smoldered the fiercer. "Pray for a sign; but meanwhile make ready for it. I've sought you first because you are pious, my Sister, far more than some among us. Yet you support Grallon."

Lanarvilis straightened. "In his capacity as intercessor for us with Rome. That requires upholding his authority in other respects too. I need not like this nor intend to continue it forever."

Vindilis nodded. "I do not say we should denounce him immediately and call for his overthrow. Nor should we suffer his desecrations much longer. Unless he repent and make Dahut, the Chosen one, the mother of the new Age—make her Queen, and do it soon, then somehow he must be broken. Otherwise Rome will have conquered Ys without drawing one sword."

Lanarvilis frowned. "Go on."

"Let us begin by rallying those of the Nine whom we can. It is bitter to say, but he has deluded certain of us. Poor, stupid Guilvilis; well, the Gods have taken her out of the game for a while. Bodilis— Bodilis wants to believe, with him, that the new Age will be altogether different from the past. Those two we dare not confide in."

Lanarvilis bit her lip. "Shall we plot against Sisters of ours? Nay!"

"I did not call for that. To go on, Innilis is devout, obedient, but she is such a tender and loving person, she hopes this will somehow end happily. We can count on her loyalty, but we must spare her as much pain and anxiety as we can."

Lanarvilis smiled wistfully.

"Maldunilis too wants an easy way out," Vindilis went on, "though in her 'tis due sluggishness and a sort of lazy lust for him. Another King would serve her as well."

"You speak ill of your Sister," Lanarvilis reproached.

"I speak truth."

"Are you quite sure you do?"

"Well, we lack time for pussyfooting. Come a crisis, Maldunilis will stand with us, but not firmly. At best, we can reckon she will not take sides against us, now or later.

"Tambilis is shattered. I fear she loves Grallon more than she adores the Gods. She's young, healthy, will recover and ask herself if she should go on denying him. We must try to make her find the right answer. She feels closest to Forsquilis, unless it be to Dahut. I think you and I, Lanarvilis, should seek the aid of Forsquilis in rallying Tambilis to us."

The other Queen looked uneasy. "But what of Forsquilis herself?"

"Aye, there's ever been an enigma there. We can only appeal to her, in whatever way we deem likeliest to succeed."

"And afterward?"

"The Gods will grant a sign in Their time. We who are entirely true to Them should prepare ourselves; then when we know what must be done, *do* it."

~ 5 ~

Toward evening of the second day after full moon, Dahut appeared at the home of Bodilis. Hitherto she had kept within her own house and bidden her servants turn visitors away.

Weather had abated, going colder but calm, clear in the east and overhead. Westward, though, cloud masses piled blue-black and the sky around the sun was a bleak green. Shadow was beginning to fill the bowl of Ys.

Dahut knocked. Bodilis opened the door. "Welcome," said the woman low. "Oh, thrice welcome, child. I'm so glad you heeded my message. Come in."

Dahut entered. Her stance, face, entire body bespoke resentment. "What do you want?" she demanded.

"That we talk, of course. I've dismissed the staff. Here, give me your cloak, let's seek the scriptorium."

Dahut slouched beside Bodilis through the atrium painted with dolphins and sea birds. "I came because 'twas you who asked. But try me not too hard."

Bodilis squeezed the girl's shoulder. "'Tis life and fate are doing that to you, darling. Have you the courage to meet them calmly?"

Dahut's nostrils flared. She tossed her head.

They passed into the long room full of scholarly and artistic materials. Dahut halted. Breath hissed between her teeth.

Gratillonius remained seated. He offered a smile. "Be of good cheer," he said. His voice was hoarse. "I'm sorry if I frightened you...earlier. You are the daughter of my Dahilis, and I love you. Bodilis lent herself to this little ruse because else you might not have agreed to see me for much too long. We want naught save to make peace."

Dahut stared at the Queen. "You knew?" she asked.

Bodilis nodded. "Your father bared his heart to me."

611

"I have to none other," Gratillonius said with the same roughness. "Nor will I. Sit down, dear one. Have some wine if 'twill ease you."

Dahut sank to the edge of a chair. Bodilis took a third. They sat in a triangle. Silence clamped it tight.

Bodilis broke though. "Dahut," she said gently, "what you sought to do was wild. Thank the Mother, thank Her throughout your life, that it failed. But your father is not angry with you. Not anymore. You are young, wounded, distraught. Come back to us and let us heal you."

A flush passed across the pallor that lay like a mask on the face of the maiden. Fury spat: "What did I wrong? I would have claimed my rights, and the rights of the Gods. *He* refuses them!"

"Would you have consummated the marriage ere the wedding?"

"Since I must."

"That was surely why the Power of the Goddess was not in you."

Dahut moistened her lips and looked into her father's eyes. "You can still make it well between us," she said.

Gratillonius clutched the arms of his chair. "Not in the way you call for," he stated. "Bodilis persuaded me 'twas folly in you, rather than wickedness. Well, learn from your mistake. Take thought."

"We know not what form the new Age shall bear," Bodilis added. "Can we shape it ourselves? We can strive, at least. Imagine a Queen who chooses her King freely, has him to herself, will not lose him in a fight against some wanderer who beds her with the blood scarcely off his hands."

"What would you have me do?" Dahut retorted.

"Be patient while we make our way forward."

"Into what?"

"The unknown."

"Nay, I'll tell you whither you're bound." Dahut sprang to her feet. Poised before them, she jeered: "You'd have me renounce the Gods, the whole meaning and soul of Ys. Where then shall I seek? Your Mithras will not receive me. Cybele is dead. Christ waits. You'd make Christians of us!"

"If need be, aye," said Gratillonius starkly. "I've lain awake nights bethinking this. 'Twould ease most of our troubles. There are worse Gods."

"Nay!" Dahut screamed. She pounced across the floor, snatched the wine flagon off a table, cast it against the wall. It cried aloud as it smashed. Shards flew. Redness like blood spattered over books. Bodilis moaned and half rose.

Dahut crouched back. Her countenance had gone inhuman with rage. "Christ be cursed! Lir haul me under ere I give myself to Christ! But I'll be Queen, true Queen, foremost of the Nine, and the name I take shall be Brennilis!"

She flung the door open and sped from them, out into the sunset.

Next day Gratillonius spoke privately with Rufinus, in the palace.
"We must look to our defenses," he said, using the Latin that was
customary between them.

The Gaul regarded him. "You've no idea of making war on Rome,"
he murmured. "However, if Ys should become a very hard oyster
to open—"

"Ys can become an ally more valuable than it has been," Gratillonius
interrupted. "We've sea power, but hardly any on land. The Franks
may have learned what their proper place is, but they'll forget eventually,
and meanwhile there'll be Germani—Alani, Huns, who knows?—pushing
westward. What I have in mind—this will take years, obviously, and
won't be easy—it's to mesh ourselves with the Armorican tribes,
especially our Osismiic neighbors, somewhat as we've done navally with
Rome. They supply most of the manpower, we supply cadre and much
of the weaponry."

"Hm." Rufinus tugged his fork beard. "How will the Romans take
to that?"

"We'll have to show them how much better it'll work than slovenly
mercenaries and raw reservists. Maximus's veterans have made a difference already, and the former Bacaudae will be priceless in case of
invasion. What we can do for a start—a start toward forming a true
regional militia—is simply to tighten and enlarge that fellowship. You'll
be essential to this. But tell me frankly if you think the idea has merit."

"Quite a conundrum, sir!" laughed Rufinus. The discussion that
followed occupied a couple of hours. They decided the plan was a
least worth pursuing further...after present difficulties had been
resolved.

As he was readying to leave, Rufinus gave the King a long look.
"You're grieved," he said slowly. "More than just your conflict over
Dahut should warrant. Would you care to talk about it? You know I'm
a miser where it comes to secrets."

Gratillonius reddened. "How did you get any such ridiculous notion?"
he growled.

"I've come to know you over the years," Rufinus answered, almost
sorrowfully. "Your tone of voice—oh, everything about you of late—"
He formed a wry half-grin. "Well, I'll be off before you boot me out.
If ever I can help, I am your man." He sketched a Roman salute and
departed.

~ 7 ~

Tambilis visited Guilvilis. Bedridden still, the injured Queen was
seldom free of pain, which lifted in her like a spear, but endured it
dumbly. Her children, the younger ones in particular, provided

distraction of a sometimes chaotic sort. Nonetheless she welcomed her Sister.

"You're sweet to come," she said from the pillow. "They don't all, you know."

Tambilis's gaze went uneasily around the room. Dusk was fading the gaudy, foolish trinkets Guilvilis liked. "Well, they, they do have many duties," she mumbled.

Guilvilis sighed. "They are afraid. I know they are. They fear I got hurt because the Gods were angry with me."

"Oh, now—" Tambilis took hold of the hand that plucked at the blanket.

"Well, I am not afraid," Guilvilis said. "Grallon isn't."

"He comes here too?"

"Aye. Didn't you know? He comes when he can find time. 'Tis kind of him. We've naught to say to each other. He can only sit where you're sitting. But he does come see me. I think his Mithras God will protect us."

Tambilis flinched and drew a sign. "Well," she said with forced cheer, "let me give you the newest gossip from the marketplace."

"Nay, please," Guilvilis replied earnestly, "tell me how he fares."

"But you told me he visits you."

"We can't talk." Guilvilis swallowed tears. "He's been...heavy. Something hurts him. What is it, Tambilis?"

"I have not...seen him, spoken with him...save as affairs of the city or the Temples require....He goes about his rounds. Aye, he keeps very busy."

"Is it this thing with Dahut? How is Dahut?"

"She holds aloof. Ranges alone into the countryside, gone for hours at a stretch. Shuns or scamps all tasks. How can we compel her, if we reckon her a Queen? I tried to speak with her, but she told me to go away. And we were good friends once. May that come again."

"If only Grallon— Could you make Grallon wed her, Tambilis? Then everything would be well, would it not? You're beautiful. He might listen to you."

"Not while I— But I know not if I can continue thus, when he's so sad." Tambilis shook her head violently. After a moment she brightened her voice. "Come, this is useless. Let me tell you of a comic thing that happened yesterday at Goose Fair."

~ 8 ~

The moon waned toward the half. Each night was noticeably longer than the last.

Fog stole in from the sea during one darkness. At dawntide it hid heaven and blinded vision beyond a few yards. It also damped sound;

614

the noise of surf under Cape Rach drifted in its gray as a remote *hush-hush-hush*. Sere grass dripped underfoot. Dankness gnawed.

Out through the swirling, between a lichenous tomb and a canted headstone, came Forsquilis from the necropolis. Her gown and cloak were stained, drenched, her hair lank and eyes bloodshot. A tall form waited. Nearing, she recognized whose it was, and halted. For the span of several wavebeats she confronted Corentinus.

"What do you here, Christian?" she asked finally, tonelessly.

The ghost of a smile stirred the stiff gray beard. "I might inquire the same of you, my daughter."

"I am no lamb of your flock." Forsquilis made to pass by.

Corentinus lifted his staff. "Hold, I pray you."

"Why?"

"For the sake of Ys."

Forsquilis considered the rugged features. The sea mumbled, the fog smoked. "You have had a vision," she said.

He nodded. "And you."

"I sought mine."

Compassion softened his words. "At terrible cost. Mine sought me out of love."

"What did it reveal?"

"That you had gone to beg a remedy for the sickness devouring Ys. I know better than to tell you, here and now, that what you did is forbidden. In your mind, it is not. But I know that you asked for bread and were given a stone."

Forsquilis stood moveless a minute before she asked, "Will you give me your oath to keep silence?"

"Will you accept a Christian vow?"

"I will take your word of honor."

"You have it."

Forsquilis nodded. "You've been many years among us," she said. "I believe you.

"Well, what I may relate is scant. It concerns Dahut. She attempted something. It was impossible, you'd call it fearsome, but she was desperate. I, through my arts, had some forewarning, and...followed along. Dahut failed. She has not yielded, rather she is bound on her purpose though hell and Ocean lie before her."

"Possessed," said Corentinus grimly.

Forsquilis spread her hands from under the waterlogged mantle. "In Ys we would say fated. Be that as it may, this night I sought to learn what I might do toward the rescue of us all."

Corentinus waited.

The Athene face twisted in anguish. "I can do nothing! I *may* do nothing. My lips are locked, my skills are fettered, lest I seek to thwart the revenge of the Gods on Grallon. So did it command me."

"What if you disobey?" asked Corentinus.

"Horror upon Ys."

"As the pagan Gods visited plague on Thebes because of the sin of Oedipus. But yours would do Their harm because of the righteousness of Gratillonius. The true God is otherwise, my daughter."

Forsquilis clenched her fists. "Hold back your preaching!"

"I will, I will. You must, then, stand aside while Gratillonius goes to his doom?"

Forsquilis swallowed, blinked, jerked forth a nod.

"Why do you appeal to me?" Corentinus went on, still quietly.

"Can you help him, somehow, anyhow?" she cried.

The fog was parting, dissolving. A sunbeam lanced through.

"That lies with him," the pastor said. "And with God."

Forsquilis snapped a breath and strode from him. Soon she was lost in the mist. He remained behind to pray for mercy on every soul gone astray.

~ 9 ~

Dusk deepened. More and more stars glimmered into sight. Processional Way was a ribbon of pallor between meadow and heights on the right, the Wood of the King on the left, where wind mourned through the oaks. Ys gleamed faintly ahead.

Dahut rode homeward. Formerly her father would have required an escort for her, safe though the hinterland was these days, but now she claimed independence—not that they had met of late, those two.

A man bounded soft-gaited from the edge of the Wood and loped along at her foot. She clucked to the horse before she knew Rufinus and eased. "What will you?" she greeted him.

Eyeballs and teeth caught what light lingered, sulfur-yellow in the west. "I've a warning for you, Princess." He spoke as coldly as the wind blew.

Dahut sat erect in the saddle. "Well, say on."

"Your father, my King, to whom I am sworn—he is in pain on your account. He is not at war with you, but you are with him."

"Be off, mongrel!"

"I will not until you have heard me. Listen, Princess."

"Queen."

"Listen to me. I've my ways of finding out. We needn't go into what I've learned and what I've reasoned—not yet—not ever, if you behave yourself. But hear me, Dahut. There shall be no plotting against my King. I make no accusations. I merely say it is banned. I am ready to defend him however necessary or—" a dagger slid forth—"if necessary, avenge him. Do you understand, my lady?" Rufinus chuckled. "Surely you, his daughter, are glad to hear this. Let me bid you a very good evening."

He slipped into the shadows. Dahut spurred her horse to a gallop.

616

The day was calm and crisp. Waves rolled almost softly against the wall of Ys and scarcely troubled its open harbor basin. Inland, autumn colors dappled the hills.

Gratillonius stood on the top, above the sea gate, with Cothortin Rosmertai, Lord of Works. "Nay," he told the fussy little man, "the sample taken shows the doors continue sound. However, it does hold dampness. Dry rot will start creeping under the metal. Within—oh, ten or fifteen years, the wood will be weakened. We must replace it ere then."

"Of course, of course." Cothortin pulled at his chin. "Although that's a huge task. 'Tis not been done in living memory."

"I know. Yet the records show how, and we've time to train craftsmen and divers, everyone we'll need. What we should set in train soon is the cutting and seasoning of the oak."

Cothortin pondered. In his fashion, he was competent. "Aye, you're right, my lord. The Osismiic forests—and when conditions are as unsettled as they regrettably are, 'tis wise to be beforehand."

"As it happens," Gratillonius told him, "I've need to visit Aquilo and discuss various matters, such as our policy toward Rome, this month. I can also raise the question of timber."

Cothortin gave a small, anxious sniff. "Should you leave Ys, my lord, under...present circumstances?"

"'Tis a short trip. I'll be back in time to stand my regular Watch."

The longing swelled inside Gratillonius—to be off, away, however briefly, to someplace where the Gods of Ys had no dominion.

XI

~ 1 ~

It was two years since he had last seen Apuleius Vero, when the tribune came to Ys, and four since he had last been in Aquilo. They had corresponded, but sporadically. Gratillonius was no writer, and besides, language must be guarded, in case a letter fell into certain hands. Entering the small city, he observed new construction, streets fuller and noisier, a pair of coasters at the wharf despite the late season. The hinterland had also looked still more prosperous, better cared for, than formerly. What a shame if this should be lost, he thought.

Dismissing his escort to quarters and giving Adminius charge of Favonius, he went on afoot to the house of the Apuleii. A crowd eddied around, people knew and hailed him, the air of welcome was almost overpowering after his loneliness. Word had flown ahead, and Apuleius waited in person at the door. They clasped arms tightly.

"How good to see you again, friend," the tribune said with as much warmth as he ever allowed into his tones. He had grown more gray and his hairline had receded further, but the finely chiseled features were free of any slackness. "Come in, do." He beckoned a slave to take the luggage which an Ysan marine had carried after the King.

They entered the atrium. The same chaste floral patterns as before decorated it, except that one wall panel had been done over; now stems and blossoms entwined a Chi Rho. Gratillonius noticed, too, that while Apuleius's tunic remained of fine woolen fabric, carefully tailored and meticulously cleaned, it lacked olden touches of color and elegance. "I trust you can stay for several days and get well rested," the host said. "You look terribly fatigued. Was it a hard journey here?"

"Not at all," Gratillonius answered. "In fact, refreshing. But you must have seen in my message that I've got serious matters to talk over with you, though I didn't spell them out. We—"

A ten-year old boy erupted from the inner doorway and sped across the mosaic. "Oh, sir, you're here!" he cried.

Apuleius lifted a hand, smiling. "Hush, Salomon," he reproved. "Where are your manners?"

Gratillonius grinned. "Warriors will charge forward," he said, "if you're still like what your father was telling me in Ys. Caution, however, caution is always in order. We may get in a bit of shieldwork this trip, you and I." He was fond of the lad. Abruptly, a blow to the throat, he felt how like a son of his own this of Apuleius was, the son that nine times nine Gallicenae could never give him.

Salomon's blue eyes widened. "You've brought me a shield?" he blurted.

"For shame," his father said. "Greed is a sin, and barbarous as well."

"I don't want to undermine your authority," Gratillonius said, "but it did occur to me that this fellow must have outgrown the sword I gave him last time, and he is about ready to make acquaintance with other gear. Later, Salomon. Uh, how's the rest of the family?"

"In excellent health, by God's mercy," Apuleius replied. "Verania is to market with her mother. They should return soon. Meanwhile, shall we get you settled in? Salomon, go back to your lessons. I will expect better answers this evening than yesterday, when I question you about your Livius, or there will be no excursion to the farm for you tomorrow." He took Gratillonius's elbow. "Come. Wine awaits, and first a slave to wash your feet."

Gratillonius regarded that ceremony as pointless, when he had arrived on horseback wearing boots, but he was long since used to the other man's antiquarian practices. At that, warm water and toweling hands, followed by slippers, soothed. He would have liked a chair with a back to it and undiluted wine, in the bookful room to which Apuleius conducted him, but such things were ordinary only in Ys.

The tribune signed his beaker before drinking. That had not been his custom earlier. "Do you care to tell me at once, in brief, what brings you?" he asked. "If not, we have enough everyday memories to exchange. But you may find relief in speaking forth."

"I would," Gratillonius admitted. "Not but what you can have guessed pretty well. I know how you keep abreast of developments, also beyond Armorica. That's why I've come, for your thoughts and, maybe, your help."

"Suppose you describe the situation as you see it."

Gratillonius did, in words he had carefully chosen and condensed on the way here—the situation with respect to the Imperium. Dahut and the rest, no, he could not talk about that. If rumors had drifted this far, Apuleius had the kindness not to mention them. The whole story might shock him, and Gratillonius needed him calm, Euclideanly logical. Besides, what had any of it to do with Rome?

In the end the listener nodded, cupped his chin, gazed out the window at the pale autumn sky, where rooks rode a bucking bluster of wind, and murmured. "Approximately what I expected. I've already given the matter thought—since hearing of that scandalous Frankish affair, in fact—and made various inquiries. We must talk at greater length, of course, but I think I know what I will recommend."

"Well?" Gratillonius exclaimed. He curbed himself. "I'm sorry." He tossed off a draught. It was Rhenian, tartly sweet. He was a little surprised that he noticed; he had not done so before.

"Best I speak bluntly," said Apuleius with some difficulty. "Your prospects of winning a favorable judgement in Lugdunum are poor. Your enemies in Turonum have connections you lack; and, to be sure, they can make a not unpersuasive case for your having allowed Ys to become a subversive influence. You plan to appeal step by step until at last you reach the Augustus—well, between us, as you yourself put it, Stilicho. This would be a mistake. It could cause proceedings to drag on for two or three years, during which you must often go in person to defend yourself, first here, then there. Such absences would weaken your standing in Ys. You could lose what control you have over events, or it could be pried away from you. Or...anything could happen. Stilicho, for example, is not so almighty as he seems. Greater men than he have fallen overnight; or God may call him from this world. Do not delay."

Gratillonius looked into the hazel eyes. A tingle passed through him. "You do have a recommendation for me."

"We must explore this," Apuleius warned. "However, I feel we will reach much the same conclusions. Send a letter directly to Stilicho. I'll help you compose it and give you one of my own to accompany it, for whatever that may be worth. Far more valuable will be a testimonial from Bishop Martinus, which I believe we can get, and perhaps other prominent Armoricans.

"We do *not* do this behind Glabrio's back. You inform him of your action, as soon as it is too late for him to halt it somehow or dispatch a courier who'll arrive ahead of yours. He then has no grounds for complaint about plots against him, nor any reason to get you summoned to Lugdunum. You may quite likely have to attend a hearing in Treverorum, but that won't be for months, when Stilicho's reply has come. God willing, it should dispose of the business."

"Stilicho may not be easy to reach," Gratillonius said, mostly because he wanted everything laid out plain to see. "The way he moves around, holding the Empire together."

Apuleius nodded. "Like the carpenter on a foundering ship, who dashes about as timbers and cordage come apart in the storm," he answered sadly. Brightening: "But this will be Glabrio's problem in equal measure. Meanwhile you have time to strengthen your position, marshal your advocates."

"You think Stilicho will give me a favorable judgment?"

"At least, he ought not to condemn you out of hand. Your reasoning about him appears sound to me. He is a soldier himself, a practical man, experienced in statecraft; and, I hear, being half a barbarian, he nourishes a wistful admiration for everything civilized—as Ys is, in its perverse fashion."

"What do you mean by that?" asked Gratillonius, startled.

Apuleius sighed, leaned forward, laid a hand on the knee of his guest, smiled like a herald offering truce. "No intent to offend you," he said. "Ys is a wonder of the world. I came back from it so enchanted that it was only after much thought, prayer, austerity I fully understood how it trembles—dances, in its heedlessness—on the brink of hell. And I had been there—" He paused. "*You* are not corrupted, dear friend. In you the antique virtues survive. But you should realize how Ys appears when seen not by its own many-colored lights but by the Light. Pray God it be redeemed before too late."

"Meanwhile," said Gratillonius stiffly, "my job is to keep it on guard duty for Rome."

"True, good soldier. Come, let us put this aside for now, let us drink together and talk of happier matters. Surely you'll have time to share a few innocent pleasures with us?"

—As the men returned to the atrium, Rovinda and Verania entered. The woman was still comely, if somewhat faded. At thirteen the girl had lengthened into thinness, with curves of hip and breast shy beneath her plain gown. She could barely whisper greetings to Gratillonius, while staring downward. Afterward, though, from beneath billows of fawn hair, whenever she thought he was not looking, her gaze followed him always.

Wearying of confinement—his work, which had been undemanding in summer, became nil after Mumach traffic shut down—Tommaltach left Ys, as often before, for a ramble in the countryside. Sometimes on these excursions he was days agone, far into Osismia. On his back were sword and bedroll, in his hand was a spear that doubled as a staff, at his belt hung a few necessities including a packet of food and a sling for knocking down small game. Most evenings, though, he could charm a family into giving him supper, a doss, perhaps a companion for the night.

This morning was clear and chill. Outside High Gate there rose a clamor from smithies and carpenter shops, pungency from tanneries, dyeworks, soapworks, all such industries as were banned in the city, bunched along Aquilonian Way. Their buildings were mostly small, many primitive, cob or wattle-and-daub with thatch roofs, but cheerful well-being bustled in and out of them. A number of men recognized Tommaltach and called greetings. He responded affably. Once their long isolation had ended, Ysans soon became apt to make much of any foreigners.

Having traversed the section, Tommaltach had the amphitheater on his left. Just beyond, Aquilonian Way bent south and went up onto the heights. He followed it. That was a stiff climb. At the top he halted, less to catch his breath than for a look around. From here the road would bear him out of sight of Ys and then, turning again east, presently to Audiarna, at the frontier of the Empire.

Gorse grew thickly at his feet, rustly beneath the wind that shrilled off the sea. Below reached the valley, closely hemmed in but nonetheless, in its peace and wealth, radiating a sense of spaciousness. Harvests were gathered, leaves fallen, pastures sallow; the sobriety of the land brought forth its sculpturing and made the homes on the hillsides gleam like jewels. Exquisite, too, at this distance, lay the amphitheater, the canal a silver thread behind it. The wood of the King squatted there, but one could look away from its darkness.

Westward swept Cape Rach, out to a spire that was the pharos. The tombs in front seemed a mere huddle, moldered into meaninglessness. Closer by, grazing sheep and an occasional wind-gnarled evergreen livened the tawny earth.

Point Vanis was scarcely visible. The towers of Ys crowded it from view. They soared in brilliance, as if cut from crystal, over the city wall, which itself became a ruddy chalice for them. Sea fowl were flocking yonder—drawn by the carts that lumbered out with offal at this time of day, but still a storm of wings which the towers pierced on their way to the sky. Beyond surged Ocean, sapphire, emerald, and leaping ivory, onward to worldedge where holy Sena lay. Sails danced; the sons of Ys were not yet ready to withdraw for the winter from her seas.

"Glorious you are," Tommaltach said. "Would I were a poet, to chant the praise of Dahut's home."

A while later, realizing in surprise how much later, he was pulled from his dreams by a sound of hoofs. The rider approached from the east at a gallop. Sunlight flashed off armor. When he drew close, Tommaltach identified him as a Roman legionary—Guentius, he was. As he came in earshot, the Scotian cried, "What's the haste this fine day?"

"Gratillonius returns," called back the newcomer, and went on downhill.

Tommaltach nodded. He should have remembered who had accompanied Dahut's father to Aquilo. They liked to have a proper reception ready for their King in Ys.

He squinted. Following the horsemen, his gaze had encountered a runner just emerged from the industrial cluster. A woman, young, to judge by speed, grace, and shapeliness. A white gown fluttered loose about her ankles, a blue cloak from her shoulders, as hastily as she went through the wind. Her left hand gathered the mantle at her throat so that the cowl should not fall back, but instead, keep screening. She lowered her head while Guentius neared and went by; his curious glance did not find her face.

Tommaltach ran fingers through his hair, puzzled. The woman stayed on Aquilonian Way. He decided to wait till she reached him. Maybe she had need of male help, and was bonny.

She reached him, stopped, drew away the hood. Sunlight blazed off her braids. The spear dropped from his grasp.

Dahut smiled. A trace of moisture gleamed over a fair skin only slightly flushed. She breathed deeply but easily. "Why, Tommaltach," she said, "would you have left with never a farewell to your friends?"

"My, my lady—" It was he whose heart and lungs shuddered. "Sure, and I'd not— But I'd no idea.... How may I serve you?"

"Come, let us stroll onward, ere folk below notice us and gawk," she laughed.

Numbly, he retrieved his spear. She took his free arm. They paced down the middle of the road. Ys sank from sight. It was as if they had the world to themselves, they and the wind and a pair of hawks wheeling high above.

"Did you intend one of your lengthy wanderings?" she asked.

He gulped and nodded.

"I feared that, when I saw you go past outfitted like this," she said. "'Twas sheer chance I did, unless it be the will of some kindly God. I was off to fetch a horse and make a solitary trek of my own for several hours. But then, instead, I covered me and went on afoot like any nameless girl. Let those who spied her breaking into a dash wonder why." She squeezed his arm against her side. "Belike they think what a lucky scoundrel yon Tommaltach is, that his women pursue him."

622

His countenance burned. He stared directly frontward. "'Tis well I decided to wait, my lady," he pushed out of his gullet.

"Oh, I think I could have overhauled you, long though those legs be. You see, I was determined. Of a sudden, a half-formed thought that had been in me sprang from my brow full-grown."

"Wh-what is that?"

"Did you truly mean to be elsewhere at Hunter's Moon?"

"At—? Oh, Samain. Well, I'd not *meant* to, my lady. It only happens that in Ys I'll have no rites to take part in as at home, and this seemed a good time to travel, before the days grow too short and wet. I'd find me somebody's roof to spend the eve under."

"Are you ignorant of our celebration that night? 'Tis the maddest, merriest revel of the year."

Tommaltach frowned. "I have heard tell," he answered slowly.

"And you'd miss it, a lively young man like you?"

He walked in silence for a while.

"Why this? Why?" Dahut insisted.

Tommaltach summoned resolve. He released himself from her, halted, turned and leaned on his spear, holding it fast with both hands. "'Tis the worst of nights for being abroad," he stated. "Then the doors between the worlds swing wide. All kinds of beings wander free, síd dwellers, the Sky Horse, the Fire Hounds, bogles, werebeasts, evil witches, vengeful dead. The Law stands down and black sorcery rules over the earth. 'Tis the next day and night are joyous, when the wickedness is gone again and the year passes from the Goddess to the Horned One."

Dahut raised her brows. "Oh, surely you've put spooks behind you," she said. "You, who've traveled, met educated people, lived these past months in Ys, and wintered here ere then. Why, you worship Mithras."

"That doesn't mean a man cannot or should not pay respect to the Gods of his fathers and, and the old usages," he replied unhappily.

The slightest scorn tinged her voice: "I've heard that some of the Scotic tribes make a human sacrifice that eventide, to appease the demons. Have you such plans?"

"I have not!" He perceived his own indignation and stood bemused.

Dahut trilled laughter, stepped close, laid hands over his, looked up at him. "Well, set the rest of it aside too. In Ys the time is simply occasion for festival, and has been for centuries. Yet Ys flourishes, Ys is free of ghosts."

"'Tis less sure I am of that than when I first came here—But I'm sorry, I beg my lady's pardon, and her pardon for my rash tongue as well."

She dimpled and beamed. "Ah, you can jest. I forgive you on condition you turn back and keep the night with me."

He could only gape.

"You are not afraid to, are you?" she challenged.

"I am not!" He shook his head violently.

Dahut grew yearning. "Hear me, Tommaltach. Take pity on me. You know how torn my life has been of late. Nay, you cannot truly know, but mayhap you can guess. I, who was young, glad, hopeful, am as trapped and alone between the worlds as any homeless phantom. What shall I do? What can I do? What will become of me? Or of Ys, whose King defies its Gods?" She let go of him, stood with fists doubled at her bosom, and went on bravely: "But I'll not bewail myself. Rather, I'd fain be merry once more, though it be for the last time ever. Why should I sit in my empty house and weep while Ys holds revel?"

"Oh, my lady." Pain made raw his voice.

Dahut blinked her eyes free of tears and smiled anew, a smile that turned mischievous as she spoke. "Going forth to sing, dance, carouse the night away, that will hearten me, will be my message to fate that I am yet unbroken. Who knows? It may turn my fortunes around. The Gods favor the bold. I've heard that you Scotic warriors often kiss your spearheads ere a battle, and go into it laughing. Then you must understand me." (He nodded, stricken mute.) "Now I cannot very well join the frolic openly. Even as a vestal, I was supposed to keep discreet. As one who claims to be a Queen, I should attend the solemn banquet of the Gallicenae, but I can beg myself free of that. My wish is to go out masked, unbeknownst, and mingle with the throng. For both pleasure and safety, I need an escort, a strong young man who'll afterward keep my secret. I could not trust any of Ys with it, but you, Tommaltach, you I trust utterly.

"Will you be my companion on the eve?"

"My lady," he croaked, "I would die for you."

"Oh, that should not be needful. Thank you, dear sweet Tommaltach, thank you!"

"'Tis you I must thank—"

"And you're handsome and lovable too!" Dahut skipped into a dance, there on the highway, arms raised to the sun. She caroled. He stood in his daze and stared.

She took his arm again at last, and got them walking onward. "We'd best start back home erelong, separately," she said. "However, this little while is ours, and so will the whole night be, two moonrises hence." He having partially regained balance, they chattered blithely about plans.

A noise from the rear interrupted them, hoofbeats. They stepped to the roadside and Dahut shadowed her face with the cowl. A woman sped by. She barely glanced at them as she passed, perhaps not recognizing the man either. They knew her, light-brown hair streaming back in disarray from delicate features, tall body that years and two childbirths had matured without causing to grow ungainly—clad in haste, careless of appearance, and her mount doubtless taken from the livery stable among the industries in the same hurry—She thudded on down the road.

"Queen Tambilis," Tommaltach said in wonderment. "What might she be wanting? Oh, of course. Today the King comes home. She's off to meet him."

"I should have known," Dahut hissed. "When I met Guentius, I should have known. But I did not stop to think."

Looking sideways, he saw her gone white; the very irises of her eyes seemed to have paled. Abruptly she whirled from him. "I don't want to see them together," he heard. "I *will* not. Not him and her."

She strode back toward Ys, her pace just short of becoming a run. He followed. "My lady—" he gobbled in his helplessness.

She threw her command behind her: "Abide a while. I must return by myself. Say naught. You will hear later—concerning Hunter's Moon." He jerked to a stop and watched her go from him.

~ 3 ~

Samain Eve was bitterly clear. That was good, for there was much to do. Great folk and their attendants opened the seasonal fairs held for three days all over Ériu. Most tenants could not arrive that early. They must first finish bringing in their flocks for the winter and dig up any root crops still in the ground, lest the terrors of that night wither these. They must douse every hearth and meet on hilltops to take new fire from the blazes freshly kindled, after their chieftains had led them in sacrifice. Meanwhile their wives and children must make houses ready, plaiting together withes of hazel, rowan, and yew to fasten across doorways and windows, setting food outside for the dead who would come wandering by, fetching water from sacred springs or pools, preparing a porridge of certain wild grains and seeds for the family, making sure of enough lamp grease or rushlights to last out the dark.

As the sun lowered, well-nigh everyone hastened indoors. Tomorrow and the day after, they would welcome in the new year. On this night they huddled away from Those who then went abroad. A few of the mightiest druids stayed out to take omens; a few covens met to carry out rites and cast spells handed down from the Firi Bolg and Fomóri; outlaws and gangrels cowered in the bracken; but otherwise the hours of the moon were given over to what was unhuman.

Save for Niall of the Nine Hostages and his charioteer.

Folk at Tallten shivered, muttered, made fending signs. They were not many, mostly warriors on watch in the fortress raths round about. The great fair here took place at Lúgnassat. Samain fair was at Temir itself, and the King should have been there.

Instead he had entered with guardsmen and menials the day before, opened and occupied the royal house, sent messengers to and fro, conferred in secret with those who came; and an eldritch lot they were. His fighting men were picked: tough-hearted old bullies who had

625

followed him for long years, some to the wall of Ys. Likewise the servants were such as recked little of Gods and less of ghosts. The feast had been savage; a quarrel over the hero's portion led to a slaying, which had not happened in living memory.

Niall denied that that was an evil portent. He gave out that his tanist Nath Í could well preside over the first day's sacrifices and games at Temir. He, Niall, would return there at dawn of Samain—the distance was only ten leagues or so—to partake in the Sharpening of the Weapons, the Wedding of the Year-Bride, and whatever else required himself. But this eve he must be at Tallten.

For that was where the Kings and Queens of Temir lay buried.

During the day, his men brought wood to a grave he named. Toward sunset, three women lighted it. Nobody dared watch what more they did. Besides, the mounds hampered sight, though except for the barrow of Lúg's foster-mother at the middle they were not long or high. Unlike the children of Danu at their Brug, these descendants of Ír and Éber rested each in his or her own chamber, alone and prideful.

The sun dropped down to a black wall of forest in the west. It had turned the river fiery. Purple beyond the plain, eastern heaven began to lighten as the moon climbed from below. Bats flitted about. The chill made early dew glimmer on grass and stones.

Through silence came a trampling of hoofs and rumble of wheels. Niall drove forth from the hall. He stood splendidly garbed in a chariot that sheened with bronze. A cloak worked in seven colors rippled from his shoulders. The head of his spear caught the last rays of sun, as did the fading gold of his hair. Also richly attired, Cathual had the reins of two matched gray stallions, animals of Southland breed such as were seldom seen in Ériu and beyond any price.

Ahead of Niall loomed the grave of the Goddess, amidst the ridges that covered his own kin. Shadows blurred them, but wavered as he neared the balefire at the foot of one. There flames roared upward from a white-hot bed. Three black-clad women stared into them.

Cathual drew rein. He must stay where he was, because the horses were uneasy, snorted, nickered, stamped, chafed. Niall descended. He dipped his spear to the women. "Have you made ready?" he hailed them.

"We have that," said the maiden.

"Herself will listen," said the wife.

"Ask no more," said the crone.

"But this I intend."

"It is for you," said the maiden.

"Make your bargain yourself," said the wife.

"You shall not see us again," said the crone.

They departed, went behind the barrow, were perhaps lost in the nightfall; for just then the sun slipped away. Bleak greenish glow lingered a while. The moon rose monstrous.

"Lord," said Cathual, and the firelight showed sweat aglitter on his face, "best you be quick. Sure, and I know not how long I can hold these beasts."

Niall advanced to the head of the grave. He held his spear level above it. "Mongfind, stepmother mine," he said, "wake." The fire brawled. "Behold who has dealt with witches such as once you were, he whose death once you sought. I call you back to the world. I give you blood to drink. I make my peace with you, now at last on this night, that you may turn the hatred that was ever in you against my foes."

He leaned over and thrust the spear downward till it stood at the middle of the mound like a lean menhir deeply implanted. "By this I rouse you, I please you, I compel you!" he cried.

Swiftly, then, he went to stand before the horses. They neighed aloud and snapped at their bits. "Steady, Cathual," Niall commanded. From his waist he drew a shortsword that he had taken off a slain Roman in the year of the Wall. He stepped in and smote. Blood spurted from the neck of the right-hand stallion. The left-hand animal screamed, reared, lashed his forehoofs. Barely did Niall avoid a blow that would have shattered his skull. He wielded his weapon, there between the huge thrashing bodies, and scrambled clear.

Cathual fought the reins while the horses bucked, lurched, stumbled, shrieked in their death throes. Blood reddened the grave. The noises rattled off into stillness. They struggled a while yet, down on the earth, before they lay quiet. The moon mounted higher. It turned the land ashen.

"Now," said Niall. He cut the bodies free. Meanwhile Cathual unloaded a wine cask, two beakers of gold, and a battle ax. Racket lifted anew as he hewed the chariot into pieces which he cast on the fire.

Niall butchered the carcasses. He slashed off steaks and chops; the rest he divided roughly, chunks such as a strong man could lift. Blood-besmeared, he stood at the tumulus and said, "Mongfind, wise-woman, take your sacrifice and be slaked. I am Niall whom you hated, and you are she whom the people so fear that at Beltene and Samain a druid has come to do that which will keep you under. But your sons are long since my faithful followers; and at this turning of the year I have sent the druid away, and instead called witches to my aid and yours.

"Mongfind, come! Help me. Tell me how I may destroy Ys, the city that slew my firstborn son, Ethniu's child. Give me this, and I will unbind you for aye. I will make the law that folk shall offer to you at the turnings of the year, quench your thirst, ease your hunger, and beg your blessing. Mongfind, come to this, the first of your feasts!"

He took back the spear and skewered meat. While he roasted it, Cathual kept the fire fed and broached the wine cask.

627

Thereafter the two men squatted to eat until they could hold no more and drink until they could barely walk. They said nothing; this meal was not for pleasure.

When at last they were done, and the moon high and small and icy in a frost-ring, they cast the remnants of the horses on the fire. It sparked, sputtered, sank low. Tomorrow the birds of the Mórrigu would gorge. Niall planted the ruined spear in the coals. Flames ran up its shaft like the wreathings of a Beltene pole. "I am going to bed now," the King said drunkenly. "Mongfind, follow me."

He and his charioteer helped each other through the moonlight to the hall. Reeling and staggering, all but helpless, they still met no creatures of the night. Guardsmen who sat awake greeted them with shouts of relief, then stepped back, dumbstricken, for these two were entranced. They fell into their beds and toppled into sleep.

In the morning Cathual, hammers and chisels at work in his head, groaned that he had dreamed about a river. There had been woods, and an arrow, and the river flowing forever west into the sea. Everything was confused and senseless, mainly he felt sorrow, grief unbounded, but he did not know why, unless it was that the river flowed always west into the sea. Perhaps he had only had a nightmare. Prophecy was not for the likes of him.

Niall said nothing. Calm though pale, he returned to Temir and carried out his duties. Indeed, he seemed unchanged; men could see that he thought about some great undertaking, but this he had often done.

Only afterward did he reveal that his stepmother had sought him out while he slept. She looked newly dead; a wind he could not feel or hear tossed her gray locks and fluttered her gown; the hands that touched him were cold. Yet she grinned as well as a corpse can and told him, "Seek the Queen who has no King."

~ 4 ~

As ever, the first evening of Hunter's Moon filled Ys with bacchanalia. Then the lowest laborer became equal to the highest-born Suffete, owed no reverence, incurred no blame. Even among temperate families, a gathering in someone's home could well lead to stealing off with somebody not one's spouse, or turn into an outright orgy. If weather was at all bearable, the young took to the streets, unless parents were so strict as to forbid a virgin daughter's going out. Wine, ale, hemp smoke, and giddying mushrooms ruled the night. Lowtown was apt to become dangerous, but violence was rare in the prosperous parts of the city; there were better things to do than fight.

The Fire Fountain played in the Forum. Colored gushes and spurts of burning oil threw uneasy radiance and shadows over the throng that milled about, almost hiding the moon that rose above the hills. Nobody felt the cold. All were too closely together in each other's perfume and sweat, all were too active. Most wore either finery overdone to the point of gaudiness or fantastical costumes. They capered, danced, hugged, kissed, frequently at random; they laughed, shouted, howled, sang. Instruments rang, brayed, tinkled, clicked, hooted, squealed, throbbed, altogether wild.

A goblin mask leered at a girl who pranced wearing swirls of gold skin paint beneath a couple of flimsy veils. Feathers covered a man from head to foot. A lass and lad had partnered their attire to form a bare-breasted centauress. Two youths, the first outfitted as a satyr, the second with antlers and deerskin cape, wagged phalluses of matching immensity. A hideous old witch revealed well turned ankles as she danced with a fellow gotten up to resemble, he imagined, a Hun. A girl with the Suffete face giggled as a burly sailor held her by the waist and felt inside her splendid gown. A visiting Osismiic tribesman carried in his arms an Ysan lady who could not walk because her legs were encased in a fish tail; she rewarded him with a cup brought to his lips and ingenious caresses. The tumult seethed on beyond any person's sight.

One could see what was on the steps of the buildings around the square. Three different groups of musicians played regardless of conflict. Here pipes wailed and drums pulsed frantically in the Phrygian mode, there two kitharas resounded in the Ionian with a drinking song, yonder a trumpet blew a stately Dorian measure—but the words being sung to it were far from stately. Two lithe women in scanty Egyptian garb rattled their sistrums and undulated. A juggler practiced his art. Several couples had spread their cloaks and were in various stages of lovemaking. In the portico of the Christian church, a man stood naked except for a crown of thorns and held his arms straight out to the sides while at his feet three women, wearing exiguous suggestions of Roman legionary gear, shook dice.

Tommaltach frowned when he noticed that. It could be unwise, and was certainly ill-bred, to mock anybody's God. For his part he wore tunic and trews of good stuff, and a gilt mask over the upper half of his face. He cheered himself with a fresh squirt of wine from the leather bottle slung at his shoulder.

"Yaa! Give me some of that!" cried Dahut. She opened her mouth and cocked her head back. He laughed and obliged her. She was in clothing similar to his, sufficiently loose that she could pass for a boy. A full mask covered her head except for jaw and lips (like rose petals they were, those lips). It was an owl's-head image, hollowly staring.

She darted from him, up onto the steps where the dancers were. There she skipped, swayed, snapped her fingers, no less fleet or graceful than they. He gaped in his marveling. She had been wildly gleeful from the sundown moment when they met. Each time she had caught his hand, stroked his back, leaped and trilled before his eyes, burned in memory.

"To High Gate!" called a voice through the uproar. More joined in: "To High Gate! To High Gate!" The processional dance along Lir Way was traditional, after the moon had mounted enough to light it.

Dahut bounded back down. "We go, let's begone," she sang, and tugged at her escort's arm, urged it around her waist. For an instant he was alarmed. Folk who saw a man and boy thus together— But nobody would care tonight, and he and she were both nameless, and besides, she had remarked that many women would be in male disguise. And she was Dahut and he held her.

The musicians scampered to take place at the front of the line that was confusedly forming. They composed their differences and began the saucy "She Sat Upon the Dolmen." Forth they went, and the young of Ys rollicked after. Their dances were manifold. Some sprang or whirled by themselves, some in pairs or rings or intricate interweavings. Dahut and Tommaltach, side by side embraced, kicked their way, with much laughter. When the line had straggled a distance, she signalled to him—somehow he understood—that every few minutes they should link their free hands and gyre around cheek to cheek. He drowned in the warm fragrance of her, spiraled down and down a maelstrom forever.

From its frost-ring the moon silvered towertops, dappled pavement, made the stone chimeras appear to stir as if they too would fain join the lunacy. Echoes boomed. As the avenue climbed, revelers who glanced backward saw past the wall and sea gate to a slowly rolling immensity, obsidian dark but bedazzled by the moon.

Dahut guided Tommaltach. They moved away from the line and into a side street.

"We're, we're drifting off," he faltered.

Her hand in the small of his back, her eager feet bore him onward. "We two," she said deep in her throat. "Follow, follow."

Stunned amidst thunder, he danced with her up the winding narrowness. Music and shouts reached him ever fainter, until they were dream-noise beneath moon-hush, where only the tap-tapping of Dahut's shoes over stone could speak. Houses walled him and her in darknesses broken by glimpses of a pillar or a brass knocker, sometimes a yellow gleam escaping a window shuttered against the cold of Samain Eve.

"Stop," she said, and was gone from him like mist in a wind. But no, she was at a particular door, she turned its latch and swung it wide, lamp-glow spilled forth amber across her. She beckoned. He stood stupefied. "Come," she called, "be not afraid, here is my home."

He stumbled into the red atrium. She slipped off her mask and tossed it onto a chair. The low light died and was reborn in her braids. She smiled at him and returned to take his hands in hers, to look into his eyes. "On this night, aught may happen," she murmured. "I wearied of that vulgar spectacle. Let us celebrate the moon by ourselves."

"My lady," he stammered, "this is—I dare not—I'm but a barbarian, a foreigner, and you a Queen of Ys—"

Her nails bit into him. Lips drew back from teeth, blood drained from cheeks and brow. "Queen," he heard. "This day Queen Tambilis went out with the King to the Red Lodge, and this night she sleeps at his side. How long till the rest betray me too?"

Then immediately she laughed again, crowed laughter, hugged him and laid her cheek to his for one surge of his heart. Withdrawing, she said, "Nay, forgive me, I've no wish to plague you with our politics. Let us merely be gladsome together." Reaching up, she pulled his mask off. "Be seated. My household has this time free, of course, so let me serve you, friend and guest. Forget whatever else we have ever been."

There was actually little to do. Wine and goblets waited on a table, with delicate small foods. She ignited a punk stick at a lamp and brought it to an incense burner likewise prepared. Thereafter she held it in a brazen bowl full of leaves parched and crushed, which she must blow into smoldering life. Placing herself on the couch beside him, she said, "This smoke has its virtues, but it does bear a harsh odor which I hope the perfume will soften. Now pour for us, Tommaltach."

He obeyed. They regarded each other over the rims of the vessels and sipped.

She chatted merrily. After a while he became able to respond.

When she had had him inhale the smoke several times, he felt a boundless, tingling ease and joy. How wonderful the world! He could fling off a whipcrack quip or he could sit and watch her dear lips for a hundred years, just as he chose.

"Wait," she whispered. "I will be back."

He gazed at a lamp flame. There was a deep mystery in it, which he almost understood.

Dahut re-entered. Her hair flowed free, down over the lightest and loosest of belted robes. Blue it was, sea color, a hue that lapped beneath the lapis lazuli of her eyes.

Blue also was a pinch of dried blossoms she cupped in her left hand. She raised her goblet in the right. She bent her head and kissed the borage. She licked it up and washed it down with a mouthful of wine. This was another mystery on this night of mysteries.

She coiled herself at his side and laid her head on his shoulder. "Hold me," she breathed.

He never knew which of them began the kiss, or when.

She took him by the hand and led him to the bedchamber. Moonlight poured through unshuttered glass to mingle with candlelight from a table, quicksilver and gold.

Gravely, now, she guided his fingers to her girdle and thence to the robe.

He knelt before her.

She reached, it was as if she lifted him back to his feet, and that kiss went on and on.

She giggled, though, while they both fumbled with the fastenings of his clothes.

But thereafter she caught him to her, and presently drew him onto the bed, and purred to him, "Yea, oh, yea."

—He did not know if he had caused her pain. "You are the first, the very first, beloved," she told him, shivering in his arms; and a dark spot or two said the same; but she drew him onward, and was quick to learn what pleased him most and to do it.

—Dawn grayed the window. Dahut sat straight in the rumpledness and clasped her knees. Above, her breasts were milk and roses, save for a bruise he had made in his ardor and she had simply bidden him kiss for a penance. She looked down on Tommaltach where he sprawled.

Suddenly her gaze and her voice were an oncoming winter. "Done is done," she said, "and splendid it was, and may we have many more times in the same heaven. But you know—do you not?—that ours was a mortal misdeed, and we must both die, unless you do the single thing that can make the world right again."

~ 5 ~

Gratillonius woke slowly. Fragments of dream crisscrossed his awareness, glittery, like spiderwebs in a forest seen bedewed by the earliest sunlight. They faded away after he opened his eyes. He did not know what hour it was, but brightness seeped by the drapes to make a luminous twilight in the room. Well past dayspring, he guessed drowsily.

And the day? Aye—he chuckled within himself that he was thinking in Ysan—Hunter's Moon ongoing. Tonight it would be completely full. He thought that if this calm weather held, he and Tambilis might walk a ways on the road and enjoy its beauty. That should not count as abandonment of his Watch, provided they return here. Last night they had been too busy.

She slept still, curled toward him, her face dim beneath a tangle of hair. How lovely she was. Most women showed at their homeliest now. He stretched his mouth in a smile while he stretched his muscles—carefully, not to rouse her—and breathed the warmth of her. Let her rest. They had today, tonight, and the following day and night before this retreat ended and he must go back to being King, prefect, centurion. After she met him on Aquilonian Way they had delightedly conspired how he could slough off obligations during this while....

Poor lass, she would have her own troubles to cope with. But together, shield beside shield, they would prevail, make enemies into allies, restore what was lost, and, aye, in the minds of men conquer territory for Dahut, for her to reign happy too.

He slipped out from under the blankets. Air nipped him. He would dress and, after prayers, run around the Wood before they broke their fast.

A sound struck through. He froze in place. It had been faint, muffled, he must have mistaken some clatter from the hall....It sought him again, and again: the hammer-tolling of challenge.

~ 6 ~

At first he could not believe who stood there at the oak. Had he fallen back asleep and into nightmare? No, he thought in a remote place, that could not be. He was too clearly conscious of leafless boughs overhead, scratchiness of the woolen tunic he had flung on, the breeze flowing cold around his bare legs and the flagstones cold beneath his bare feet. Next he thought a mistake must have happened. If Tommaltach was drunk, say, one need not take a childish prank seriously. But Tommaltach stood steady before him, arrayed in a Scotic kilt which was neatly wrapped around his otherwise naked lean muscularity, a long sword scabbarded across his back and a small round shield in his left hand; the black hair was combed to his shoulders, the handsome visage newly scrubbed, the gaze fire-blue—

All at once it wavered. Tears glimmered forth. "Will you not say a word to me?" Tommaltach screamed like a man under torture.

"What can I say?" Gratillonius answered woodenly.

"You could ask me why." Tommaltach sobbed breath after breath into himself. "Or curse me or, or anything."

"You mean to fight me?"

"I do that." In tearing haste. "It must be. You will not do what you should. You will not let Dahut be what the Gods have chosen her to be. You must die, Grallon, though my own heart die with you."

"I, your Father in Mithras." Immediately Gratillonius regretted his words. He had not imagined they would be so cruel. Tommaltach cowered back from them.

He recovered his courage fast. Gratillonius admired that. "I have eaten your salt too," Tommaltach blurted. "Mithras witness, this thing is none of my wish. But men have risen against unjust rulers erenow. And you refuse justice to Dahut."

He loves her, Gratillonius thought. He loves her in the headlong way of young men, the way I loved Dahilis. I knew that already. It was graven on him, as it is on others I could name. But I did not think it would send him crazy like this. Well, he is a barbarian.

Aloud, slowly: "Suppose I agree I've been wrong, and wed her. Will you take back your call to battle?"

Tommaltach's mouth fell open. After a moment he slurred, "Would you be doing that, really?"

"Suppose I do."

Tommaltach rallied. "I cannot be withdrawing, can I?"

Gratillonius gave him a rueful smile. "Cannot, or will not? Well, it makes no difference. I cannot yield."

"Then we must fight." Tommaltach fell on his knees. He covered his face and wept. "Father, forgive me!"

Almost, Gratillonius did. But no, he thought, that would be unwise. Here was an opponent young, skilled, vigorous. Let him at least remain shaken.

"I will dispatch a man to Ys at once," said the Roman tactician. "Making ready will take an hour or two. Be here in time." He could not quite bring himself to add, "Traitor." He turned and went back into the house.

Tambilis waited. Heedless of staring servants, she fell against him. "Oh, Grallon, Grallon!" He embraced her, stroked her hair, murmured that she should not cry because everything was under control.

She drew apart and asked desperately, "Shall I bed with your killer? How could I?"

"Your Gods will strengthen you," he said.

She blenched, as Tommaltach had blenched; and like the Scotian she recovered, to tell him: "Nay, I misspoke myself. I'd not matter. 'Tis you that would be no more."

He constructed a laugh and chucked her below the chin. "Why, I've every intention of abiding in the world for many another year, annoying the spit out of countless fools."

Thereafter he issued his orders and commenced his limbering up—no food, no drink except a little water, before combat. His further thoughts he left unvoiced.

The marine guards with their horses and hounds, and those who held off a clamorous populace down the road; Soren in his vestments; the legionaries in their armor and their distress—it had a ghastly familiarity, another turn of a millstone. Tommaltach seemed calm now; he even bore a faint smile on his lips. Gratillonius wondered how Dahut would receive him unto her, should victory be his. Surely she would grieve at losing her Papa....But she was not going to.

Soren finished the ceremony. He added: "May the will of the Gods be done." Startled, Gratillonius glanced at the heavy features. Implacability responded. In his eyes, Gratillonius realized, I have become another Colconor. That was a lonely feeling.

He dismissed it and led the way into the Wood.

At the glade, he halted. "This is where we usually work," he said. Shake the opponent from any Celtic sense of fate, of possession by his people's female God of war. Remind him that this Roman sword had terminated earlier lives among these huge winter-bare trees. Heaven overhead was nearly white, the sun a frost-wheel casting skeletal shadows. Grass underfoot lay drained of color.

"For Dahut," Tommaltach crooned. "We both fight for Dahut." The words were Scotic, but sufficiently akin to Britannic or Gallic that Gratillonius understood.

"Let us begin and be done," he answered in Latin. He drew his blade, slanted his big Roman shield, shrugged once to make sure his mail was properly settled on him.

Tommaltach's iron gleamed forth. He still bore a smile, and in his eyes an otherworldly look. It was not the sleepwalker's look of Chramn the Frank, but a gaiety beyond anything human. Nevertheless he edged about with the sureness and alertness of a wildcat. Clearly, he meant to offset the mobility of his near nakedness and the length of his weapon against this enemy's armor. Also youth, wind; he could wear Gratillonius down, until the King lacked strength to bring shield up fast enough.

The old badger and the young wolf. How very young a wolf!

Tommaltach kept his sword back, warily, while he circled. Gratillonius turned to face him: smaller radius, easier executed. Clearly, Tommaltach hoped for a chance to strike past the Roman's guard from a rearward angle, into neck or thigh. Clearly, he understood that as he did, he must have his own shield ready to catch the Roman probe. It was light, quickly maneuverable.

Gratillonius retreated inchmeal. If he could lure Tommaltach under a tree, as he had lured Chramn—

Tommaltach refused the bait. He let the distance between them grow. Finally he stood his ground and waited. After all, the King must fight.

So be it. Gratillonius walked forward.

The Scotic blade whirred, whined, struck, rebounded, hunted. Wear the badger down.

But the badger knew how to gauge every oncoming impact, how to shift his shield about and meet it, oh, such a slight shift, consuming hardly any force, while the body kept itself at rest, conserving breath, endlessly watchful.

Tommaltach backed off, panting. Gratillonius marched in on him.

Their eyes met, again the strange loverlike intimacy. Tommaltach yelled and cast a torrent of blows. He forgot about his shield. Gratillonius saw, made a roof of his own, suddenly advanced—by slacking off one of the knees he had held tense, so that he swung forward as if on a wave—and struck. The sword went in heavily, above the left hip. Gratillonius wormed it around.

Tommaltach sank away from the iron. There was an extravagance of blood; there always was. Gratillonius stood aside. Tommaltach gasped something or other, which might or might not have made sense. He pissed, shit, and died.

XII

~ 1 ~

A maidservant admitted Bodilis. Dahut heard and came forth into her atrium. "Welcome," she said tonelessly. The Queen had sent word ahead, and the younger woman had decided to receive her.

Bodilis hurried across the floor and embraced the other. "Oh, my dear, my dear," she said low.

Dahut stood unresponding and asked, "What do you want?"

"Can we talk alone?"

"Come." Dahut led the way to her private room. Bodilis had hitherto only heard tell of it. She looked around at the clutter of opulence and suppressed a sigh.

Dahut flung herself into a chair. She was ill-kempt, in a rich but rumpled green dress. Her eyes were reddened and dark-rimmed. "Be seated," she said, her tone as brusque as the hand-wave that accompanied it. She had made no mention of refreshment.

Bodilis gathered her gray skirt and settled onto a couch opposite, sitting especially straight. "I feared I'd find you like this," she began. "Child, can I help? May I? A friend to listen to you, if naught else."

Dahut stared past her. "Why think you I need help?"

"The terrible thing that happened this morning. Tell me not 'tis left you untouched. The marks are branded on you."

Dahut slumped silent. Outside, wind shrilled through fitful evening light. The room was overheated.

"Your father came so near death," Bodilis said after a while, "and at the hands of your young friend, who did die, at your father's. You must be torn between joy and grief. Worse—let me be frank—you surely understand the Scotian challenged for love of you, in hopes of winning you. Naught else can explain his action."

Still Dahut withheld any answer.

"Beloved, put away guilt," Bodilis urged. "How could you be at fault that he went mad? As well blame the reef where a ship strikes, driven by storm and tide. I do hope you can be—nay, not more careful in future—that you can keep this from happening again. Of course, you could not foresee what he would do. But if you make clear 'twas never your desire, nor ever could be—" Her voice faded out.

Yet she refused to admit defeat. Presently she went on: "Meanwhile, and always, know you have our love, the love of your Sisters. I speak first for myself and Tambilis—"

Dahut stirred. Her look speared at the visitor. "You've seen Tambilis?" she demanded.

"Aye. After the news reached me, I went out to the Sacred Precinct. We talked long together, she and Gratillonius and I. Most of what we said concerned you. Our foremost wish is for your happiness. It truly is. Will you speak with him after he returns? You know not how your coldness pains him."

Dahut turned sullen. "He can end that whenever he chooses. Until then, nay, I will not see him."

"Think further. You'll have time ere he comes back."

"Why, 'tis only tomorrow that his Watch ends."

"But immediately afterward, he intends a Mithraic funeral for the fallen man."

Dahut leaped to her feet. "He *dares?*" she shrilled.

Bodilis rose too. "'Tis not the custom, but he forced assent, pointing out that the required rites are separate from the burial. Tommaltach's will be well away from the city, in earth whose owner gives permission."

"Where will the King find such a farmer?" Dahut asked, calming a little.

"In Osismia. His man Rufinus knows several who'd be glad, thinking that they gain a guardian spirit. He'll guide the party. They'll be gone three or four days—Child, what's wrong?" Bodilis reached to clasp Dahut's shoulders. "You seemed about to swoon."

The young woman sat back down and stared at the floor. "'Tis naught," she mumbled. "You reminded me— But no matter. I am indeed weary. This has been a...trying day for me." She forced herself to smile upward. "You're kind to come and offer comfort. 'Tis like you. But I'd liefest be alone."

"Let me brew you a sleeping potion. Then tomorrow when you have rested, remember your father loves you."

Dahut made fending gestures. "Aye, aye, aye. But if now you'd be helpful, Bodilis, go and let me deal with myself."

The Queen bade a sad goodbye and trudged off.

Dahut paced the house, twisted her fingers together or struck fist in palm, snarled at any servant who passed close. Finally she snatched a cloak off its peg, drew it about her, and went out.

The sun had just set. Sea and western sky glimmered yellow. Overhead and eastward the sky was already as dark as a bruise. Tattered clouds smoked before the wind. They filled Ys with dusk. No other people were in sight, but somebody's pet ferret scuttered across Dahut's path.

The way was short to the home of Vindilis. An amazed attendant let Dahut into its austerity. The Queen entered the atrium from within, saw who this was, and said, "Give the maid your wrap. You will stay for supper, no? But we'll talk at once."

She had been busy in her scriptorium. Candlelight fell on Temple accounts and writing materials. The air was cold; she had her hypocaust fired up only in the bitterest weather. She took Dahut's elbow, guided her to a seat, and brought another around for herself. Face-to-face, knees nearly touching, they leaned forward.

"Why have you sought me?" Vindilis inquired. Her tone was impersonal.

Dahut ran tongue over lips. "I need...counsel, help."

"That's plain. But why me?"

"You are—I think in many ways you're the strongest of the Nine. Certes you're the most—the most devoted. To the Gods, I mean."

"Hm, that's a matter of judgment. I'd call Lanarvilis, at least, more pious than myself. Also, she's ever been the readiest to act in the world as it is, best equipped by temper and experience. She's on Sena, you know, but tomorrow—"

Dahut shook her head. "Please, nay. Mayhap I should confide in her too. But she has ties that I think you're free of."

"True, she sometimes puts political considerations above what I might deem to be more important," Vindilis agreed. "Well, say on, dear, and be quite sure I can keep a secret. 'Tis about the combat today, I suppose."

Dahut nodded.

Vindilis studied her before continuing: "You wish the outcome had been different." Dahut caught her breath. Vindilis raised a palm. "You need not reply to that. Grallon is your father, who bore you in his arms when you were little, made you toys and told you stories and showed you the stars."

"But he's wrong now," Dahut cried, "wrong, wrong!"

"I myself wish Tommaltach had won," said Vindilis. "The will of the Gods is working more strangely than I can fathom." Her words softened. "Oh, understand me, I do not hate Grallon. I am angry with him beyond measure, but when he does fall I will mourn him in my heart ere I brace myself to endure whatever evils he spared me and the new King does not. Yet he was never a friend of the Gods, and he has become Their avowed enemy. Dahut, you will be far from the only Queen whose King slew her father. Think of him, if you will, as having gone off to dwell with his Mithras."

Dahut had regained composure. "Some of the Gallicenae believe we need him still, against Rome." Her voice was harsh. "Do you?"

"Lanarvilis maintains that," Vindilis answered obliquely. "She is reluctant about it, though. Certain among us are wholehearted; they'd fain he never die. And certain others—As for myself, I see the reasoning; but the Gods are not bound by reason."

"And you own that you wanted Tommaltach's victory! I knew you would. 'Tis why I came to you."

"Have a care," Vindilis warned. "You were ever reckless. This is perilous ground we walk."

"That's what I most need counsel and help about." Dahut went on in a rush: "I fear Rufinus. Tommaltach did what he did for love of me, desire of me. Rufinus knows that. He'll wonder if more young men may go the same way. He's threatened me already. He drew knife and vowed to kill me if I plotted against his King. Will he believe I have not? Or will he suppose my mere presence is a mortal danger to Grallon? I fear that smiling man of the woods, Vindilis. Oh, I fear him. Help me!"

The Queen brought fingers to chin and narrowed her eyes. "Rufinus is no fool," she murmured. "Nor is he rash. However, he is very observant...and, aye, very much devoted to Grallon."

"What shall I do?" Dahut pleaded.

Vindilis took both her hands. "Be of good heart, beloved child. Your Sisters will keep you safe. I hear Rufinus will be going off with the King to bury Tommaltach. Those few days' absence should dampen any...impulses. Meanwhile, and afterward, you must cease either brooding alone in your house or haring forth alone into the countryside. Resume your duties as a high priestess. 'Twill be healthful for your spirits. 'Twill also keep you surrounded by people, and in the favor of the Gods. Then in Their chosen time, They will see to your destiny."

Dahut shivered. "But what if, if a man does win the crown—might Rufinus blame me—somehow—and, and seek revenge? 'Tis like a shadow forever across the sun—having him about—after what he told me that twilight."

Vindilis sat quiet for a spell. Then she straightened and said, "I believe something can be done, if you wish it so much. Afterward, let's pray, the will of the Gods can be done. I'll see to this."

She rose. "Enough," she finished. "You did right to come here. Now let us go warm ourselves with a stoup of wine ere we sup. When you return home, I'll have my sturdy manservant Radoch escort you. But first of all, come with me to the tiring room and let me make you presentable. I'll rub your hands and feet, and comb those lovely locks, and you'll feel hope rising anew."

~ 2 ~

Rain lashed from the west, as if Ocean were taking wing. Even Rufinus's aerie was caught in the blindness and noise of it. A single lamp guttered in the main chamber. It stirred up misshapen darknesses more than it relieved them. That lent a ghostly life to the portrait busts of a centuries-dead boy and of Gratillonius. The Gaul sat in a chair, almost on the middle of his spine, legs cocked over a table, and regarded the images while he played on a pipe of narwhal ivory. The notes wailed below the wind.

The door, which had been unbarred, swung open. Instantly he uncoiled, sprang to his feet and backward, stood poised near his weapon rack. A figure entered and closed the door. "Be at ease," said a female voice. It was a command. The newcomer trod forward and retracted the cowl of her drenched outer garment. Black hair turning white in streaks, severely drawn back, and whetted features flickered in sight.

"Queen Vindilis!" Rufinus exclaimed. He saluted her. "What brings you, after—ten years, has it been? How knew you I was in this place?"

"The King returned today. 'Twas a safe wager you'd be with him," she answered dryly. "I thought belike after the journey you'd wish an evening alone; and for my part I wanted this visit known to none but us two."

He hastened to take her cloak and hang it up. "What was that you were playing?" she asked. "An alien mode."

"Scotic, my lady, I learned the tune in Hivernia, where I also got this that can whistle it." He showed her the pipe. The intervals between the stops were greater than on those instruments with which she was familiar.

"What does the music signify?"

He hesitated. "'Tis a threnody."

"For Tommaltach?"

"Aye." His tone harshened. "I know not what possessed him. If it be a human, not a demon, who somehow lured him to his death, I will find out and—"

"But you are not vengeful toward Grallon, are you?" she interrupted.

He grew somber. "Nay, of course not. He did what he must, in agony of soul. He too was betrayed...by someone."

"Did you get Tommaltach well snugged down?" Vindilis asked quickly.

Rufinus nodded. "The King did, with such reverence you'd never have known he was the slayer. I dare hope the prayers lifted the sorrow off him a little....But be seated, my lady, I beg you. May I offer wine?"

Vindilis took a chair and signalled him to do the same. "Mine is no amicable errand," she told him curtly. "You have terrorized Queen Dahut, daughter of the King you profess to love."

"I have not!" he protested. "I only—"

"Silence. We could spend half the night on your slippery contortions around the truth. The fact is, I care not what the truth may be. It suffices that Dahut has plenty to bear without going in fear of you. Therefore you will depart Ys forthwith."

"Nay, now, I'll have justice," he said, appalled. "We'll take this before the King. He'll hear me out."

"We will not. You will not. You know why—you, who call yourself his handfast man."

He lashed back: "You and the rest who deny him, you call yourselves his wives."

Her tone held steady. "Aye, gossip is rife. It is as empty in this case as would be any chatter about justice. Rufinus. I want you away from here, far away. Give Grallon any pretext you like, or none, but go. In return I'll spare him certain facts which *include* your menacing of Dahut."

He sagged. "I would not have harmed her," he whispered. "I warned her off something she might do in desperation."

"So you say. I am not so sure. If Grallon had perished in the Wood—well, Tommaltach was your comrade, but one wonders, one wonders. No matter. You may be guiltless, but you must begone."

"Not forever," he implored.

She considered. "M-m-m....I've a feeling this will work itself out, in whatever way it does, within a year. Aye. A twelvemonth hence, you may send me a letter. If I send back permission, you may return, on the understanding that you will never cause Queen Dahut the slightest anxiety." Relenting a bit: "During that span of time, she may well lose her fear of you, especially if the troubles upon us have ended. I may try to soothe her myself."

"I thank your graciousness," he said bleakly.

She rose. "You have a sennight," she told him. "Give me my cloak."

She left. He stared long at the door. Finally he screamed, "Bitch!" He snatched a javelin from the rack and cast it at the wood. It sang when it struck.

Rufinus filled a goblet and began thinking.

~ 3 ~

Weather cleared. The morning sun stood low to southward. Its rays felt nearly heatless. They shivered over the waters and glinted off hoarfrost ashore. Otherwise land rolled dun, leafless apart from the occasional evergreen, beneath pallid heaven.

Hoofs rang on pavement as a band of men set forth on Aquilonian Way. They were eight marines, whose armor and pikeheads flashed, and at their head, clad in plain wool, Gratillonius and Rufinus. A couple of pack mules followed. Four of the group were young, unwed; they would be gone for months. The rest would accompany the King back to Ys from Audiarna.

Riding on his left, Rufinus cast the rugged countenance a glance. White marbled that auburn beard. "Do you still have misgivings, sir?" the Gaul asked low.

Gratillonius gave him a lopsided smile. "Not really," he said in the same Latin. It was as well for the other man to practice the educated, rather than the serf's version, despite Rufinus having read extensively since he learned how. "I did have my doubts when you volunteered for this mission, but you convinced me." He gestured at a sealed pouch which hung from the adjacent saddle. "The letters are in good hands."

They were his own, and Apuleius's, and ones lately received from such persons as Bishop Martinus and the military commandant at Turonum: whatever prominent Romans had responded to his request for commendations. All would go to Stilicho.

Wherever Stilicho was. If new wars had called the general out of Italy, reaching him would well prove arduous and devious. While Rufinus lacked experience of the Empire beyond Armorica, he should make up for that in toughness and quick-wittedness. Not that he would likely have to fight. Rather, given the credentials he bore, the Imperial highways, hotels, supply stations, and remounts ought to speed him forward. The marines going along were more an honor guard, meant to impress, than a bodyguard. They'd return with whatever courier bore Stilicho's reply north. However, in part they were precautionary. These days you never knew beforehand what might come at you.

"I do question the wisdom of your staying on down there," Gratillonius proceeded. "The more I think about that notion of yours, the less it seems to me that it'll do any good—and you so bloody useful hereabouts. Why should they even allow you to hang around?"

Rufinus sighed. "I've tried to explain, sir, and failed, because I don't have any plan. How could I? But I think I can one way or another talk myself into some kind of appointment, if only because I amuse a few high officers. It'll be lowly, but I'll keep my ears open, and from time to time put in a word on your behalf. I believe the news I'll eventually carry back—the overall picture, the feel of things at Stilicho's headquarters—I do believe you'll find that worth waiting for."

"Never mind. We've covered this ground before. You're bound and determined, and I've no way to prevent, so I may as well accept." Gratillonius laughed. "Frankly, I think you want for a proper sampling of the pleasures in the South. Cool wines, warm clime, hot girls."

Rufinus's mouth stretched wide. "Sir, no! When I've known Ys? It's you, sir, you I want to serve."

Gratillonius slapped him on the back. "I know. I was joking."

"Grallon—lord—be careful while I'm gone. You're in terrible danger. Watch out for— Sir, if you'd just go through with what they want—" Rufinus's head drooped. "But of course you won't," he ended.

"Watch out for your tongue," Gratillonius snapped.

The road turned and climbed. A hare bolted from the gorse alongside. A crow cawed from a bough.

"Well, well," said Gratillonius, "no sense in this. Let's be cheerful. We'll toss a cup together in Audiarna before we make our goodbyes; and I envy you the adventures you'll be having."

The scar twitched as Rufinus sketched a grin. "Well you may, sir. I'll see to that."

They reached the heights. Gratillonius drew rein. "Stop a moment," he suggested. "Take your last look at Ys."

Rufinus sat a long while gazing back at the city where it gleamed against heaven and Ocean.

The afternoon grew mild. Such folk as were able left their work and sauntered about on streets, the wall, the headlands, enjoying its briefness. There would be few more like it, now that the Black Months were setting in.

Carsa meant to be among the strollers. He had little to do once shipping season was past, and often felt restless. Warehoused goods required periodic inspection, and sometimes attention, in this Armorican dankness. Infrequently, a letter arrived from Burdigala, or he sent a report on his own initiative. He was supposed to investigate possible new markets and routes, keep track of existing ones in the region, and familiarize himself with Ys. To that end he talked with what men he found—but outsiders were scarce in winter—and had become a student under certain scholars, pagans though they were. Those were inadequate outlets for his energies.

He was donning outdoor garb in his apartment, on the fourth floor of the tower called the Waterfall, when his knocker clattered. Opening the door, he saw a boy whose brass pendant, a skimming gull, proclaimed him a public messenger. Carsa took the folded papyrus handed him and, alone, unsealed it. Curvily inked Latin characters said: "Meet me at Menhir Place. D."

D? His heart bounded. He told himself this was nonsense, but nonetheless had difficulty securing his sandals.

—She kept him waiting by the ancient stone for a time that felt endless. When she arrived, she was drably clad and hooded, head bowed. Passersby took her for a plebeian girl. None accosted her. This was a poor quarter but not lawless, and besides, sunlight still cleared the city battlements.

When she reached him and looked up, he breathed, "My lady?" while the world spun. He started to bring hand to brow. Dahut caught his wrist and guided the gesture to his breast, salutation between equals. "Nay," she said in an undertone, "betray me not."

"I'd n-n-never," he stuttered.

She bestowed a smile on him. "Of course. But let us be an ordinary couple, pacing along as we talk."

"On top of the wall?"

She shook her head. "I might too easily be recognized there. We can follow the winding ways to Skippers' Market. 'Tis nearly deserted."

"What do you want of me, my lady? Name it, and if I have it, 'tis yours."

Dahut's lashes fluttered long above her cheekbones. "Would that I could give you a simple answer. 'Tis much harder to confess I'd like your company today. You think I'm shamelessly forward. But I am so lonely." She clutched his hand. "So lonely, Carsa."

"You should not be, you."

"I am beset, Carsa, by Gods and men. I know not where to turn. The grisly thing that happened with Tommaltach—I too was fond of him, I miss him, but the ready laugh is stilled and— You are a Roman, Carsa. You stand outside all this. But you are also a kindly friend, a strong man....Will you listen to me, speak to me, till sunset? I must go to the Temple then, but if we could walk about first and quietly talk—"

He took her arm, awkwardly. "I am not worthy," he said, "but, but here I am."

She uttered a forlorn laugh. "Beware. I may call on your company again."

"'Tis yours, always, my lady."

They went on down a lane of violet shadows.

XIII

~ 1 ~

Clouds drove low on a wind that howled as it hunted. Their leadenness blew in streamers around the towertops of Ys. Sometimes a few raindrops stung. Hardly anyone was about in the streets who could have walls between him and the cold.

Though the tide was out, waves battered heavy enough that the King had locked the sea gate. It was doubtless unnecessary. However, little or no waterborne traffic moved at this season, and if the harbor basin was free of chop, vessels within would not chafe at their moorings.

The shipyard lay nearly deserted too. Days had grown so short that it was not worth paying wrights to appear. They sought work indoors, where there were lamps. Maeloch was alone with his drydocked *Osprey*.

His crewmen needed employment during the shorebound months, but he no longer did. Over the years he had modestly prospered; the rebirth of trade increased the demand for fish and also enabled him to make some investments that had paid well. Now he wanted to assure himself that the smack would be seaworthy when next required.

He was examining the hull inch by inch, chalking marks where he should caulk or otherwise restore things. A man passed by on the ropewalk. Maeloch recognized him. "Budic!" he roared. "Hoy, old tavern mate, come have a swig!"

The soldier stopped. He was in Ysan civil garb, tunic, trews, cloak, half-boots, but he had ever kept his hair short and his face clean-shaven. The fair locks fluttered. Standing, peering, he swayed a bit. "Oh," he called back. "You. Well, why not?"

Less than steadily, he advanced to the gate and let himself in. Maeloch guided him to a shed which gave shelter but, with its door open, had light to see by. Budic plumped down onto a stack of planks. From a shelf crowded with tools and supplies, Maeloch fetched an ale jug. Budic quaffed deep.

Retrieving the vessel, Maeloch gave him a long look. Budic's chin was stubbly and his eyes bloodshot. "'Tis early to be drunk," Maeloch said.

Budic shrugged. "I began ere dawn. Well ere dawn." He hiccoughed. "Why not? No duty today for me. Naught at all."

Maeloch settled onto a cluttered worktable and took a pull of his own. "Ye should natheless wait till others are free," he advised. "Drinking without fellowship be a drabble-feathered thing."

"Well, I was on my way into the Fishtail. I'd find somebody. I'd used up what was in my house, you see." Budic reached.

Maeloch hesitated an instant before handing the jug over. "More in a house than cups for passing the time," he said.

"Ha! In my house?"

The bitterness took Maeloch aback. He ran fingers through his white-flecked beard. "Hm. I'd heard— Gossip does go about. But I'd nay pry."

"Why not?" retorted Budic belligerently. "You pried in the past, you, aye, pried, poked, prodded, banged her. She was good then, eh?" He glugged.

"Your friends put that from their minds years ago," said Maeloch in pity.

"Born anew in Christ, aye, aye, that's our Keban."

"We'd ha' honored your wife if ever we'd been guests in your home."

"With her housekeeping? Nah. But she has become a good Christian woman, her. Yea verily, she has that. How gladly she 'greed we sh'd live t'gether like brother and sister, for the glory of God."

Maeloch attempted a laugh. "Now yon's a mighty sacrifice!" He sobered. "Mistake me nay. Poor girl, if she's been as ill as I've heard, 'tis well done of ye. I've off and on found it kindest or wisest to leave my Betha be for a while and seek elsewhere. Ye remember."

"No more. Not for me." Budic shook his head. "I vowed I'd stay pure too. That was after the miracle of the boat. Could I do otherwise, I who'd been in God's own hand?"

Maeloch frowned. "Mean ye that rescue two-three months agone, Bomatin Kusuri's yacht? What tales have come my way ha' been unclear but eldritch." His gaze sharpened. "I knew nay 'twas ye there with Corentinus."

"Who'd ken me in the dark and turmoil? Afterward I said naught, nor did the pastor. For humility's sake. He counselled me thus." Budic had ceased to slur his words. He sat straight and looked afar, rapt. "But I knew the wondrousness of God."

"And gave up women?" Maeloch replied softly. "Well, of course I'd nay question whatever passes 'tween a man and his Gods."

"His God, his one and the only true God," Budic exclaimed. His eyes sought the fisher's. "I tell you, I saw it. I was *in* it. We'd all have drowned but for His help. You're a sailor, you must know that. Then why will you not turn from your demons and believe? I like you. I hate to think of you burning forever."

"I'll believe ye speak straight. But I've witnessed my share of strangeness, aye, lived with it, made the night passage to Sena like my fathers afore me, nay to speak of what's happened on open sea." Maeloch shrugged. "So honor what Powers seem best to ye. Me, I'll abide with mine. They've never wanted more from me than I could spare. Your Christ, though—"

Budic's head wobbled. His momentary self-possession had spun away from him. "'Tis hard, hard," he mouthed. "Yestre'en after I was off duty, homebound down Taranis Way, there came a litter, and riding in it the courtesan J-j-joreth."

Maeloch grimaced. "I know. Her what makes big money playing at being Princess Dahut. May eels eat her."

"Oh, but she was so beautiful. I went back to my house and—and lay awake in the dark, hour by hour, till—"

"And ye'd forsworn any relief. I said already, your Christ's an unreasonable God."

"Nay, His reward f-f-for faithful service is infinite."

"Hm? Ah, well, whatever ye mean by that, let's neither of us preach. I'll stand by my Gods, like I will by my King and my friends, as long as They stand by me."

"Have They that?" Budic cried. "What do They bring but horror? Think of Dahut, think of Gratillonius!"

"True, They're offtimes stern, even grim, but so's the world. 'Tis for us to endure without whining. They give us life."

Budic sprang up. "They do not!" he screamed. "They are blood-drinking demons! The one thing They give you is your doom!"

Maeloch rose more slowly. His huge hand clenched on the Briton's tunic. "Now that's aplenty," he growled. "I'd liefer nay deck ye, boy. Best ye just go. But ask yourself this—when Lir sends fair winds and shoals o' fish, Taranis pours down sunlight and summer rain, Belisama brings love and bairns and hope—ask yourself, boy, what's this Christ o' yours ever done for *ye*?"

He let go and shoved. Budic staggered back against a wall. There he leaned for a minute, agape, as if the unspeakable had at last found words.

~ 2 ~

Scarcely past full, the moon slanted whiteness through windowpanes, down onto Carsa's bed. Dahut raised herself to a sitting position, rising from the blankets like a mermaid from the sea. Moonlight silvered her hair, face, breasts; it made mercury pools of her eyes; but the crescent of the Goddess showed as black as the shadows everywhere around. The young man looked up in adoration.

She sighed. "We must speak seriously," she told him. Her breath was a wraith in the chill.

He smiled and stroked her flank. "This soon?"

"We're belated as 'tis. Three nights together—No matter I go to and fro in the dark, cloaked, hooded, veiled. Folk—servants chatter—they'll soon find that none of them knows where I've been, and they'll wonder, and...Rufinus is gone, but others can spy on me."

He grew grave. "I know. I've thought about little else, save you yourself and my love of you. Tomorrow I'll broach the plan I've made."

"*Now*," she insisted. "The danger is too nigh us both. Either we act at once or you must depart Ys at once, never to return. Else we die. If I left with you, they'd track us down."

He tensed. "I meant to lead you carefully toward my thought. 'Twill be hard for you."

"I know it already." Her voice was level. "You shall challenge the King and slay him."

He started, then likewise raised himself. "Your father," he breathed.

She spread her palms. "My husband, unless you prevent." Her lips trembled. "His will is cracking. Tambilis tells me this, the last Queen who shares his couch. She wishes me well, but she wants the marriage. They all do."

"You too?" he asked. His tone came raw.

"I did at first. But now you— And, oh, Carsa, beloved!" She caught his near hand in both hers. "You believe me, you know I was a maiden, though I did not bleed. But he? And Carsa, I love you."

He snarled. "I swore unto God I'd avenge the abomination, did it happen. Better I strike him down first. I will."

"My Carsa!" She strained against him. The kiss was long and savage.

When they had separated and hearts had quieted a little, her manner turned anxious. "He is a fearsome fighter, a killing machine."

The Burdigalan nodded. "He is. But I'll be no lamb to the slaughter. Let me confess it, I've thought about this, imagined it, ever since the curse fell on you. I'll be shrewder than to meet him on terms where he holds every advantage. Also, his earlier foes were pagan—poor Tommaltach—while I'm a Christian. God will be with me."

"I've fretted over that. How can a man of your faith be King of Ys?"

"I've considered this too." He laughed uneasily. "Have no fears. I've not confided in the chorepiscopus. He'll be shocked, he'll upbraid and belike excommunicate me. Still, I am only a catechumen. And I trust that I can make him see reason. Surely saving you from a union that God forbids will be a worthy deed in His eyes. If He spares me thereafter, I as King—I, wholly Roman—will earn full redemption by leading Ys step by step toward righteousness and Christ." He brought his cheek next to hers. "You first, my darling?"

647

"We'll see," she said under her breath. Aloud: "Oh, Carsa, the wonder of it! Now we have the night free before us!"

~ 3 ~

For an instant Gratillonius hesitated. Summoning courage, he laid hold the serpent knocker on Lanarvilis's door and struck it against the plate. While he waited for response—the time was short but felt long—he twitched his cloak tighter around his plain tunic. The morning was bleak though bright. Mainly, however, he needed something to do.

The door opened. Into the startlement of the woman who recognized him, he said mildly, "I'd fain call on my daughter, the Princess Julia."

"Oh—my lord, she—"

"She is home today, free of duties. I know." Gratillonius went into the house.

"I w-w-will tell her, my lord." The servant scuttled away.

Presently Julia came into the lavish atrium. Even on her free days, she wore vestal white: a plump girl of fifteen with light-brown hair and something of his mother in her features, his mother whose name she bore.

She stopped and saluted him, an awkward gesture. "Welcome, sir." The wariness in her stabbed him.

He ventured a smile. "I wished to congratulate you, my dear," he said; he had rehearsed it in his mind, over and over. "I heard how you won first examination honors in Queen Bodilis's Latin class, and I'm very proud of you." From beneath his cloak, which no one had offered to take, he brought a cedarwood box he had made himself. He had given it all the care and skill that were his, hoping for an hour such as this. "Here's a little token for you."

Julia took it without contact of hands and pulled the lid back. The fragrance of the wood drifted forth. "Oh!" she exclaimed, suddenly large-eyed. Within rested a penannular brooch, silver around twin great topazes. "Oh, father, 'tis beautiful."

Gratillonius's smile widened and eased. "Wear it in joy," he said. "And would you care for a celebration at the palace? Naught solemn, no relics like me, simply whatever friends you invite."

"Father, you—"

"What is this?" They both turned toward the new voice. Lanarvilis entered from the direction of her private room.

"You," she said flatly, and halted in the middle of the floor.

Gratillonius looked her up and down, from crimped ashen hair to pearl-studded sandals. She had covered her height with a gown of rich russet on which embroidered dragons twined; an amber necklace encircled the wrinkliness at the base of her throat but not the stringiness above; tortoiseshell bracelets drew attention to the brown spots that were appearing on her hands. Yet she was not ugly, he thought. He might well have been nearly unaware of the hoofmarks of time, as he was whenever he saw Bodilis. It was that she had become a stranger.

"Forgive me," he said. "I'd no intention of slighting you. I knew not you were present."

"Nay, you chose your time," Lanarvilis answered. "It happened that Innilis and I traded vigils on Sena, because she felt her courses soon to come on her and they've lately been making her miserable. You'd never know about that, nor care."

"I would. But who tells me?" He put down his temper. "We should not quarrel, my lady. I came in friendship."

Friendship of the kind you and I once had, his mind went on, unheard by her. We worked well together, for Ys. It felt good, being members of a good team. And then in bed—oh, we were never in love, either of us. Our hearts were elsewhere. But there were times, again and again, when we surrendered altogether to each other; and between us we created this girl here, and loved her and reared her. How can we now be hostile?

How can it be that I myself, in my inmost soul, care so little, except that it's desirable we stop being hostile?

"He, he gave me this," Julia said. "Because of my examination. And a feast—"

"And what else?" Lanarvilis asked Gratillonius. "The sign has not come upon *my* daughter."

He fought against rage.

His wife shrugged. "Well, best we refrain from open breaches," she said. "We remain yoked to the same load. But, nay, Julia, dear, we shall not cross his threshold until he has granted your Sister her due and the Gods Theirs."

The girl swallowed, blinked, clutched the box to her breast, and fled.

Gratillonius and Lanarvilis stood silent a minute. Finally he said, "Ill is this."

"It is indeed," she replied.

"'Tis not only that you and I and most of the others are divided. The Gallicenae are. Often Tambilis weeps because of the coldness she's met from her Sisters."

"She can mend her ways. You can yours."

"You know that is impossible. Why will you not help me find something we can all accept? The new Age, Dahut the first Queen who's truly free—"

"Go," she said.

He obeyed.

—Cynan was in the guard at the palace gate. His military correctness fell from him when he saw his centurion. He stepped forward. "Sir," he declared unevenly, "we've just gotten the word. Another challenger down at the damned Wood."

649

The moment he saw Carsa in the Sacred Precinct, Gratillonius understood that this day he might well die.

The young man was barefoot, his sturdy frame clad merely in a woolen tunic with a belt where a large knife such as seamen used was sheathed. Stuck beneath the leather was a short staff with a leather strap and attached cord depending from it. In his left hand he gripped a wooden buckler. In his right was a simple sling. A band across his left shoulder supported a bulging, wide-mouthed pouch. It seemed scant equipment against a full-armored Roman centurion, but Gratillonius knew what those weapons could do.

Though Carsa's mouth and nostrils were pinched tight, his visage showed no traces of sleeplessness and he stood at catlike ease. How old was he—eighteen, nineteen? Even unencumbered by mail, a man of forty-two could never come near matching him for speed and suppleness; and strength rippled through the nude limbs.

Gratillonius withdrew to that room in the right-hand building where he outfitted himself. As ever, he declined assistance. It could be his last time alone. He had given Adminius the usual orders ("If he wins, he's King and none of you are to stir against him.") and wanted no further scenes. He had actually hastened off and accepted battle immediately, when he could at least have said farewell to Tambilis, Bodilis, whomever liked him. Better to wait in the hall, among the idols, while the marines formed their barrier across Processional Way and Soren led the houndsmen here.

Underpadding, kilt, greaves, mail, helmet—sword, dagger, big oblong shield, and this time a heavy javelin—"Mithras, hearten me; and should I fall, pardon me my sins, release my spirit, at the end of my Pilgrimage receive me."—The words felt empty, as if the God were gone.

When he came out, air bit at what skin was exposed. The sun hung wan, already far down toward Ghost Quay, making shadows long; somewhere a raven croaked. Gratillonius was more aware of that than he was of the ritual Soren conducted. The Speaker went through the words in a monotone and refrained from any remarks after he finished. Gratillonius looked past him.

King and enemy went in beneath the trees. Twigs made splintery patterns across heaven. What brush there grew was also mostly bare. It crackled at a touch. Fallen leaves rustled louder.

Gratillonius did not seek the glade. No such requirement was on him. He followed traces he knew after these many years, to a place where several half-grown trees made the ground thick and tricky in among the giant oldsters. Halting, turning, he said, "Here we are."

"I expected you'd pick a site like this," Carsa replied in the same Latin.

Gratillonius kept his voice equally cool. "Before we begin—I'm curious—why are you doing this? You had your entire life ahead of you."

"I do yet. The wickedness of Ys is an offense to the Lord. Time to end it."

"Will you, then, lead sacrifices to Taranis and marry the nine high priestesses of Belisama? I thought you were a Christian."

Carsa whitened. "Let's go!" he yelled.

Gratillonius nodded and hefted his javelin.

It was no surprise that Carsa bounded agilely backward. He needed room. Gratillonius abided. If he threw his spear at once, Carsa could likely evade it.

The Burdigalan stopped. Already loaded, its pouch between fingers, the sling snaked free. Carsa's upper body swayed, to put his weight behind the double-pointed lead bullet. His wrist snapped. There was a whipcrack noise. Simultaneously, Gratillonius cast.

The impact of the slug, slantwise from his left, dug it into the thick plywood of his shield. He nearly lost the handgrip. The strap jerked violently against his shoulder. Tears sprang forth. Though their blur he saw the javelin strike the buckler. He'd hoped it would pierce flesh, but Carsa had followed the slower missile in flight. With the swiftness of youth, he'd moved his defense to intercept.

Nevertheless, the iron had gone deep, the shaft dragged, the buckler had become a burden. Carsa dropped it. Gratillonius drew sword and charged.

He'd realized that the whole purpose had been to make him spend his distance weapon. Without it, he could only fight at close quarters. A slinger needed time to reload though, whole chunks of a minute for each shot, time wherein a legionary could cover a fair amount of ground.

The sling snapped again. Gratillonius felt a glancing impact down around his right ankle. It hurt. The greave fended off the worst of it. He crouched low and dodged a bit, back and forth, as he attacked. If a bullet took him between helmet and shield rim, in the face, that was that. A broken foot would be as final, if slower; Carsa need just stand away and bombard him. His shield took another blow, but straight on, merely lancing pain through his knuckles.

Then he was there, but of course Carsa wasn't. The youth had slipped off to one side. Gratillonius saw him behind a screen of saplings and withes. Carsa grinned. While he couldn't well shoot past such a barricade, he could wave his sling tauntingly.

Gratillonius refused the bait. He'd wear himself out pushing through that stuff. He started around it, deliberately, taking his time. Carsa poised. When the chance came, he sent a projectile whizzing. Gratillonius blocked it, too, and advanced, step by easy step. Carsa retreated.

A while they stalked each other among the boles. A slug missed. Gratillonius heard it buzz past. He thought in a distant part of his mind: This is interesting. Can he run me out of wind and legs before I run him out of ammunition? Well, go slow, old son. Play him till nightfall if you can; then the game ought to be yours.

651

Sunlight still touched upper branches, but shadows beneath were turning into murk.

Abruptly Carsa saw a tree that suited him. He leaped, caught a branch, swarmed sailor-nimble aloft. Planting himself ten feet high, where a broad limb stretched nearly right-angled from the trunk, he draped his simple sling over it and from his belt drew the companion piece.

Gratillonius halted. Carsa crowed laughter: "You must not leave me, you know," he called. "We must fight within the Wood to the end."

The staff sling bore a six-foot cord. It required both hands. At short range, its missiles had been known to kill men in armor. If they didn't pierce, the shock sufficed.

Carsa's toes gripped bark. He swayed, superbly balanced. Gratillonius edged aside. Carsa turned to keep him a target.

The cord cracked. The bullet flew faster than sight. It struck another tree. Beneath the heavy thud, torn wood groaned. The lead sank too deep to see.

"That was a gauging shot," Carsa gibed. "Next comes the real thing."

Gratillonius retreated. "Go off if you like," Carsa said. "Shall we continue at dawn?"

Surely he could better endure a night of hard frost than could an older man. He'd scramble about in the branches, keep warm, be alert and strong when his exhausted foe lumbered back into view.

Gratillonius shifted position. What to do, what to do?

The blow erupted.

Suddenly he lost hold of his shield. It dangled by the strap. His left forearm was aflame. Broken? He had no use of that hand. A hole showed where the slug had entered, above the metal boss. It had gone straight through the weak spot left by the earlier hit, with enough force remaining to cripple.

Carsa reloaded. Sunset shone along the arc of his weapon.

Gratillonius reeled to shelter behind the nearest trunk. Slatting and banging, his shield was now more hindrance than help. He slipped it free and dropped it. Briefly he wanted to follow, lie down on it and let the blessed darkness blanket him. But no, Carsa waited.

Gratillonius drew breath, willed pain away, came back around the bole and dashed forward, zigzag. The sling pounced. Agony rived him, to the right of his breastbone. He knew the mail had warded off the bullet—though not its impact; else he'd be dead. He shoved that pain aside likewise, while he trotted on.

Carsa reached into his pouch. Gratillonius halted, a yard or so from his enemy's post.

He had one chance. As a boy on the farm, he had often thrown things, brought down small game with rocks; and in the army he had learned the javelin. He hurled his sword.

It took Carsa in the belly, flat-on rather than by the point, but with power to shove the Burdigalan off his perch. He fell to earth. Gratillonius drew knife and approached.

Carsa rose. He was shaken, the wind thumped out of him. Yet he'd known how to land. The sling had dropped elsewhere. His own blade gleamed forth.

They said in the Fishtail, as they did in the low inns of Londinium, that the winner of a knife fight was the fellow who got carried off to the surgeons. Gratillonius was armored, but he was also shaken, hurt, barely on his feet. Carsa could probe—

Gratillonius closed. He brought up his knee. Greave smote groin. Carsa shrieked. He collapsed and lay writhing. But he still held his knife. He was still mortally dangerous and must be killed. Gratillonius stamped a hobnailed sandal down. He stamped and stamped. He felt ribs crunch and saw the face beneath him turn to red pulp. Finally he broke the apple of the throat. Carsa gurgled blood, flopped, and was quiet.

Gratillonius lurched off through the gathering dusk, to the sacred house. Let the Christians look after their own.

~ 5 ~

Word was that the King had taken severe injuries, broken bones, though nothing from which he could not recover. Most of Ys rejoiced.

The palace guard changed every six hours. On the day after the combat, Budic was among those relieved at noon. Weather hung cheerless. He plodded along the winding street between the houses of the mighty, downhill toward his home. Nobody else was close by.

A woman slipped from a portico and hurried lightfoot to meet him. "Wait, please wait," she called low. He checked his stride. The heart banged within him. When she drew nigh, he saw beneath her hood that she was indeed Dahut.

"Wha—what's this, my lady?" he asked in amazement.

"I saw you pass," she answered, "and— Oh, tell me. How does he fare, my father?"

"You haven't heard?"

"Only what the spokesman says." Tears quivered on long lashes. "That could be soothing lies. He could have a fever or anything."

"Nay, I've seen him. He does right well. But why could you not visit?"

Dahut stared downward. "We are estranged." He barely heard. "We should not be. He swore once he'd never forsake me, but—but he is my father. I'm glad to hear your news. Thank you, dear friend."

"Little enough to do...for you, my lady."

She caught his elbow. Her glance flew up again, to him. "Would you do more? Dare I beg it of you?"

"Whatever you ask," he choked.

"'Tis not much. Or is it? I only ask that you walk me to my house, and talk while we go, but not tell anyone afterward. They'd think me immodest. But 'tis just that I am so lonely, Budic, so full of grief I dare not speak of."

"Oh, my princess!"

She took his arm. "Come, let's away ere we're noticed." A hint of liveliness sparkled beneath the desolation. "We'll be a simple couple, you and I, man and maiden together. You cannot dream what comfort that will give me—you will give me."

XIV

~ 1 ~

Weather turned clear and cold. Early on the second day after his return, Gratillonius went out. He had been tempted to lie longer in the aftermath of what had happened, drowsing when he did not sleep, but that was unbefitting. He compelled himself to walk, no matter what lances every motion sent through him. Tambilis went at his side.

Dawn whitened the inland sky. A few stars lingered in the darkness above Ocean, and the pharos flame burned on Cape Rach. Windows glowed and lantern-sparks bobbed, down in the bowl of Ys.

"Good morning," he greeted the sentries.

"Hail, sir." They wheeled and saluted, Ysans as smartly as Romans. "How's the centurion doing?" Maclavius made bold to ask.

"The medicus tells me I need about a month and a half—"

Gratillonius trod on a patch of ice. Ordinarily he would have recovered footing, but his contused ankle proved slow. He fell. Agony overwhelmed him. For an instant he lost awareness.

He pulled himself back and saw the men clustered around, and the woman. He waved off their solicitude, grumbled, "I can get up all right, thank you," and did, regardless of what it cost him. Sweat was clammy over his skin. "Back inside for me, I s'pose. 'Nother bath. Soldiers, to your posts. Y' 'aven't been relieved yet."

As he hobbled up the path, Tambilis said, "Darling, you *must* take more care. 'Tis no disgrace to be wounded."

"Pity me not," he answered. "I'm alive. I'll get well. Pity that young fellow—those young fellows—who made me bring them down. Whatever possessed them?"

Nonetheless he let her help him undress. It was good to lie in hot water. He declined her offer of opium but accepted a willowbark tisane,

654

with honey and licorice to disguise the taste. He also let her towel him dry and assist him into fresh garb. She saw to it he ate. Thereafter she must be off to Temple duties.

Alone, he fumed. How long would he stay useless? His left arm didn't matter much. It still hurt in its splints and swaddlings, but was merely immobilized—fractured radius, Rivelin had said. The right side of his chest was what incapacitated him, a broken rib or two. Despite a closely fitted leather corselet, any deep breath raised pangs, a cough torment, a sneeze a catastrophe. Rivelin had warned him against excessive manliness; nature was telling him to be cautious, to keep what he did to a minimum. He knew that presently the healing would be far enough along that he could use that hand more. But Hercules! What was he supposed to do meanwhile, sit and yawn?

Too many things called for him. It would be different were he content with a sacral Kingship, like most of his predecessors; but he was not. He had taken charge, instigated, been omnipresent. Doubtless he could hold his monthly court and preside over rites. However, now that his relationship with Soren and a number of other magnates had become one of frigid politeness, he must needs confer oftener with those who supported him, and with key commoners. To avoid an appearance of plotting, which would further antagonize the conservative faction, he had been quietly visiting his friends in their homes, or talking with them in the course of outings through the hinterland. He oversaw public works he had started—repairs to roads and buildings, new construction, preliminaries to the eventual replacement of the sea gate doors—because you can never trust a contractor to get everything right on his own. He led frequent military exercises. He rode circuit well into Osismia, inspecting defenses, listening to tribesmen whom he wanted to stay favorable to Ys. Riding—Favonius needed daily riding.... Well, he must simply delegate tasks. The country wouldn't fall apart if he was absent from its affairs a month or two; he'd made journeys longer than that.

But he was not required to like this!

"My lord, you have visitors," said his majordomo.

Surprised, he looked up from his chair. Guilvilis and Innilis entered. "Why, welcome," he said while his pulse began to race.

Innilis approached and bent over him. Her eyes were huge and dark-rimmed, the thin face paler than usual. "How are you?" she whispered. "Can I do aught to help?"

"You coming here is enough," welled out of him.

She wrung her hands. "I should not. Vindilis—my Sisters will be angry with me. But I could not stay away when you are hurt, when you might have died."

"Thank you. How fares it with you? And Audris?"

"Oh, she is...happy, I believe." On ending her vestalhood, the half-wit girl had found sanctuary as a minor priestess; she could handle drudge work at the Temple and various shrines. "For myself, I—you know how I wish, how we all wish you'd obey the Gods. But I come not to plague you." She stroked his brow.

"And you, Guilvilis?" Gratillonius asked.

The second Queen hobbled forward, leaning on a cane. "I'm well, my lord," she replied with a large smile. "Up and about, as you see."

"She lies," said Innilis gently. "Walking tortures her. The physician fears it always will. Some hip injury, belike." She winced. "I've given her the Touch. 'Tis failed."

Gratillonius felt abashed. "I should have called on you erenow, Guilvilis," he admitted. "But in this last month or two—so much happening—"

"I understand, my lord," The smile turned sad. "And I c-c-cannot easily spread my legs anymore."

Innilis flushed.

"Ask Dahut to see you," Gratillonius advised. "She brought my strength back to me in minutes, after my battle with that Frank."

"The Princess Dahut—Queen Dahut holds apart from us, my lord," Guilvilis faltered. "She—she's sometimes not at her duties, and she never seeks us out."

"Well, ask her!" he snapped.

Innilis drew breath before she said in haste: "I can tell this talk pains you worse than your wounds, Grallon. Set it aside. Let me try if I can Touch you into ease."

She could not. The two women took their leave. Innilis was softly weeping, Guilvilis laid a comforting arm over her shoulders.

Soon afterward, Bodilis came in. She hurried to kiss Gratillonius—the brief, chaste kiss they allowed themselves—and hug his head to her bosom, before she drew up a chair and sat down. "I'd have come at once, dearest," she related, "but had Vigil yesterday, and in these fleeting daylights—Well, see, I stopped at home to get some volumes for you. Here's your beloved *Aeneid*; and you've always told me you'd read our *Book of Danbal* when you found time; and perhaps you'd enjoy my reading aloud these verses—"

She broke off and regarded him closer. "You're suffering," she realized. "Not morose, I expected that, but miserable. What is it, Gratillonius?"

He shook his head and stared at his lap. "Nothing," he growled. "Bad mood, no more."

She learned to catch his hands in hers. "You're an unskilled liar," she said tenderly. "I think I can guess. Dahut."

He sighed. "Well, when my first-born, Dahilis's daughter, avoids me, it does go hard."

Bodilis bit her lip and braced herself. "I meant to discuss that with you. As well have it out now."

He lifted his gaze, alarmed. "What?"

"Dahut. Two different men in quick succession, both known to have been enamored of her, challenging you. The first could have acted on barbarian impulse, but the second—Why didn't she tell Carsa he must spare her father? She's no fool, she has to have foreseen he might attempt your life, for her sake or because the Scotian was his good friend or in sheer youthful madness. Nor does Dahut show the least regret. She scamps her obligations, disappears for many hours on end, is feverishly vivacious far too often. *Why?*"

Shock had rendered him speechless. It gave way to white rage. "Silence!" he bellowed. "How dare you slander my daughter, you slut?"

"Not I," she pleaded. "Tongues are wagging—"

He had raised his hand, he might have struck her, but a spasm of pain jerked his arm down. He sank back. "Tell me who," he panted, "and I'll kill them."

Her voice went stern. "Kill half the populace? Face the truth like a soldier. I didn't say Dahut is guilty of anything. I did not. Nor does anybody else, to my knowledge. But they wonder. They can't help wondering. You would yourself, if you weren't her father."

"Well, I—" He gulped for air. Seldom had he fought a stiffer fight than against this indignation. Finally he could shape a grim smile and respond: "Well, people are like that. This will show us who's loyal."

"We, the Gallicenae, I'll urge that we all advise her to be more discreet."

"Good. She's only young, you know, very young. And bewildered, embittered, poor girl; oh, your Gods have played her false! But this should blow over."

Bodilis shivered. "Unless you receive more challenges."

"No, I hardly will. Remember, I'm exempt till these bones of mine are whole again. Otherwise it'd be no combat. This is not like when I'd merely been stunned by the Frank. We'll have peace, time for the ugliness to die away and be forgotten." Wistfulness touched him. "Time, even, for King and Queens and princess to make peace with each other?"

~ 2 ~

Wind woke anew, with a low gray wrack driven off the sea. His squadmates gave Budic questioning looks when they went off patrol and he told them he wanted to take a long walk. They said nothing, though. He had been moody these past months, especially of late, often absent-minded or staring off at something invisible. Quite likely, they thought, he had been worse shocked by Gratillonius's brush with death than his adored centurion was.

Having changed legionary gear for warm civilian clothes, he left by Northbridge and struck off on Redonian Way, north to Eppillus's grave—where he saluted, as was the custom of his outfit—and then east until beyond sight of Ys. The road was his alone. To the left he glimpsed wild white-maned immensity, to the right sallow pastureland strewn with boulders, here and there a wind-gnarled tree or a lichenous menhir. A few seafowl skimmed about on the blast.

One ancient monument identified a nearby shelter, used in grazing season by shepherds and their flocks when weather got too rough. It was not stone but merely three sod walls open to the south, where the hills partially broke the winds, and a low roof of turfs laid over branches. Inside, he was out of the worst cold but not of the hollow roaring and whistling. Repeatedly, he stepped from the gloom and squinted west up the highway.

She came at last, roughly clad, like an Osismiic woman. Besides a cowl, she had drawn a scarf across her face. That was understandable on a day such as this. Passersby and guards in the city would have paid her no heed—she'd be a countryman's wife, or perhaps a servant on an outlying manor, come to town on some errand—unless they noticed slim form and trim ankles under the wool.

Budic loped to meet her. "My lady!" he cried. "You, dressed thus? And you didn't ride, you walked the whole way. 'Tis not right!"

Dahut pulled aside the scarf and smote him with a smile. "Should I have fared on horseback, among banners and trumpets?" she teased. "I told you I wished a private talk." The gaiety left her. The bright head drooped downward, out of its hood. "Aye, here's a wretched meeting place. You were sweet to come as I asked."

"M-m-my lady did ask, so naturally I— But let's within. I carried along food and a, a wineskin. I should have remembered a beaker for you. I'm sorry. But if you will deign?"

She picked her way fastidiously over dried droppings to a bench. It was small as well as rude; when they sat down, they were crowded together. She refreshed herself with a deftness that bespoke experience. "Ah, that helps. You are so kind, Budic, so thoughtful."

"Why do we m-meet today?"

She passed fingers across the fist on his knee—how moth-lightly! "Why, that should be clear. Thrice we've chanced on each other in the streets, and you've had the charity to walk a way at my side, listen to me, be with me."

"We said naught that was of any moment." He kept his eyes straight before him.

"Nay, how could we? But I felt the strength in you, the caring." Dahut sighed. "How can I bring a man to my house, unless he be always in such full sight and hearing of the staff that we'd have more freedom of speech on the streets?"

"I understand. My house? Keban and I would be honored beyond measure. Only let me know beforehand. It must be swept and garnished for you."

"My thanks. I'm sure your wife is a fine person. But can I open my unhappy heart in her presence? Nay, this poor hut is all I have."

He mustered will and wit. "What would you tell me, then, my lady? I swear 'twill never leave my lips without your permission."

"Oh, fear no secrets. I am only alone, frightened, torn." Dahut drew a ragged breath. It caused him to turn his head and look at her. She caught his glance and did not let go. "Pray understand. I am not sniveling. I can bear whatever I must bear. But how it would help to know that one man at least feels for me! Like...like being at sea on the blackest of storm-nights, among the reefs, but seeing the pharos shine afar."

"Speak," he mumbled.

She leaned against him. "Would you hold me meanwhile?"

"My lady! You are a Queen and I—I am a married Christian man."

"Naught unseemly. Just your arm gentle around me, like my father's when I was small, or like a brother's, the brother I shall never have."

He obeyed. He listened. It tumbled forth, sometimes with tears which he saw her struggle to hold back.

"—the dreadful fate...I rejoiced at what I believed was the benison of the Gods, but my father would not. 'Tis made me think, aye, pain and sleeplessness call thoughts from underground....What should I do? What can I?...He is my father, I loved him, but he denies me now....Was it the Gods Themselves Who drove Tommaltach and Carsa mad?...I have this horror in me, this fear that somehow *I*, all unknowing, I was the bait that lured them to their deaths....Whatever happens will be wrong....Is there no hope?...Budic, hold me closer, I am so cold—"

"You are innocent," he kept protesting, "you are pure, feel no guilt, Dahut. I will pray for you, hourly I'll pray for you."

But in the end he wrenched himself loose. One could not stand upright in the shelter. He shuffled to the entrance. Then when he stood upright, he could not see her within. He hunkered down and said frantically: "Forgive me. I'm weak, I felt a blaze of—of—"

She leaned forward, almost luminous in the dimness. "Of lust?" she murmured. "Is that evil, Budic, dear? 'Tis the power of Belisama."

"I am a Christian!" he shouted. Curbing himself, he went on more steadily, "In Christ is your hope, man's single hope. Put by your heathen Gods. Call on Christ, and He will answer."

"I know naught of Him," she replied—humbly?

He nodded. "I've heard how as a child you mocked at His minister. Be not afraid, Dahut. Saul of Tarsus did worse, until divine mercy overtook him. Ask and it shall be given you."

Her manner turned pensive. "How shall I? What should I seek for? Will you enlighten me, Budic? I trust you, not that old scaldcrow Corentinus."

"He is a saint." Memory stirred, a prophecy uttered on this headland in a night of storm and shipwreck. "Your immortal soul is at stake. Oh, heed! But if you feel shy of him, well—"

Dahut slipped out to join the man. He straightened. Scant trace of distress lingered on the countenance she lifted upward; her gaze was clear. "Will you talk further with me?" she asked.

"Ah, uh, scarcely here."

"Nay. Tell me when you'll next be at liberty, and we'll meet in Ys as erstwhile."

They set a time and place. "Best we start back, my lady," Budic said. "Sundown comes apace."

"Wisest would be that we not enter the city together," she answered. "Go first. I—I'd fain be alone here a short while, here in this place where you've been so kind. 'Tis as if you've left flowers." She lowered her lashes. "I'll think on what you've counselled, and...whisper to your Christ, if I dare."

"Dahut!" he cried in a rush of joy.

She watched him bound off down the road. When he was well away, she snarled and spat. Reflecting further on what had occurred, she began to smile a bit, and when at length she too headed west, she strode with determination.

~ 3 ~

Tide was inbound, but the flow was still easy and the gate open when Forsquilis came home from Vigil. The winter sun was barely aloft. As she descended the gangplank from barge to wharf, another female ran out of a warehouse doorway. The Queen peered through the shadows that filled the basin. "Dahut," she said. "What fetches you?"

The young woman stopped before her. Eyes that seemed enormous caught what light there was. "Please, could we have speech? Alone?"

Forsquilis hesitated before replying, "When?"

"Now. You are too seldom in Ys anymore. I must seize what chance I can."

Forsquilis's tone remained as hard as the air. "Very well. Follow me."

She led the way around the shipyard and up the stair to the Raven Tower. Awed guards let them past. Forsquilis stopped several hundred feet beyond, at the housing of a catapult. She rested her hands atop a merlon, regardless of its chill, and stared out to sea. The waters heaved darkling. Birds filled the pallor overhead with wings and thin screams.

"Say on," she directed.

Dahut's voice grieved. "Why are you so cold to me, Forsquilis? What became of our thaumaturgic studies?"

"I will give you no more arts while you act as you do. Harm enough are you wreaking already, and worse lies ahead."

Dahut caught at the other's sleeve. "What mean you?" she wailed. "What am I save the victim of, of this that's happened?"

"You know full well."

"Think you I willed those horrible battles?" A sob barked in the girl's throat. "Nay, I swear by—by— Oh, I was foolish, heedless. You Sisters have warned me. I'm mending my ways. But I n-never dreamed you would believe the falsehoods about me!"

"I have dreams of my own. They make me glad Nemeta is my sole child." Forsquilis turned and looked straight at Dahut. "Always in them, you are the key that unlocks the doom. It is never clear how, everything is murky and wild, but always you are there at the heart of it. We may not yet be foredone. If you will make your peace with the Gods, They may stay Their hands. But the hope of that seems small."

Dahut stepped back. "*I* have offended Them? I, who wish and pray for naught than that Their will prevail? What of the King?"

"Your father. He who brought you forth when your mother had perished, and nurtured you and to this day loves you. You hate him. You want his destruction. Evil feeds upon evil, till at last it breaks loose and overwhelms all."

"You deny him, you, his wife," Dahut counterattacked.

"Not in hatred." Forsquilis's words softened. "In loving chastisement. In penance for his sin, so the entire wrath not fall on him but some of it be shared. In sorrow and longing. For the sake of Ys."

"Ys, which you forsake yourself. Where do you pass most of your days—and your nights?"

Anger flickered beneath the level response. "I have taken leave of absence from my lesser duties, that by what skills I hold I may seek a resolution of our trouble. None have I found. In the hills, the forests, the deeps, the air, few are my companions, and they are not human. Keep silence about betrayals, you." Surf rumbled against the wall. "And make an end of yours, ere you be betrayed to your own ruin."

Forsquilis walked off to the tower and the stairs. She never looked back. Dahut stayed a long while, first gazing after her, then alone.

~ 4 ~

Rain and sleet scourged the streets. Within a certain mean tavern in the Fishtail, it was night-gloomy, little relieved by a few rank-smelling tallow candles. Hunched over a table opposite Budic, Dahut was herself a shadow. Nonetheless she had dressed as if in poverty, retained a stola over her hair, and smeared herself with cosmetics. A couple of harlots threw resentful glances her way—no other customers were about —but did not interfere.

"This is utterly wrong," Budic remonstrated. "You should never come near a den like this, and outfitted like, like that."

"Quiet." Dahut's reply was just to be heard by him under the muffled storm-racket. "True. A foul place. But we had to meet somewhere, and—'Twill be brief. I've a boon to ask of you—beg of you, dear trusty friend."

"'Tis yours, if I am able."

Anguish made her smile grotesque, but he remembered. "Not hard for you, a man; unthinkable for me. I want a place where I can retire, unbeknownst. A single room will serve, if it have simple furnishings, table, stool, basin, pallet; you know what. Best will be if it also have a separate entrance, or at least a side door onto its hallway. It should be clean, and in a safe neighborhood, but one where folk do not look too closely at their neighbors. Can you find me such a refuge?"

He gaped. "What of your house?"

"I've told you, I'm never by myself there, unless the servants have holiday, and that's only a few nights a year. Even my private room or bedchamber, why, they come in to scrub and dust; they'll notice traces, and certainly be aware whom I receive." Dahut's voice trembled. "You know not how 'tis to be in everybody's eyes. And I above all, I the undesired Queen. Old Fennalis could safely read Christian gospel on her deathbed. But I? Imagine."

He sat upright. "My lady," gusted from him, "do you mean—"

Dahut shook her head slightly. "Forgive me. Bear with me. I'm only a maiden, brought up to worship the Gods of Ys. I'd fain learn more about your Christ. Does He truly call me to Him? How can I tell, unless I can study and, and pray? Things I dare never do at home. You could meet me there too, answer my questions and help me." She wiped at tears. That left pathetic streaks in malachite and rouge. "Or I can be solitary, at peace, free to think. Can you do this for me, Budic? I'm sure your God will love you."

"Why, well, I—"

"You're not rich." She reached under the overgown that helped make her shape unrecognizable, freed a purse, and slipped it across the board. "Here's coin. It should be ample for months, but tell me if you need more. Say you want lodging for a friend—I'd best dress as a boy, 'tis no sin among us in Ys—a lad from afar who speaks our language poorly. He's in the service of somebody else, so he won't use this room often. You can help me devise the full story. You're clever, you've traveled widely, you know the world."

"This is unheard of," he mumbled.

"But not in any way unlawful. I promise you that. Find me my nest, Budic, and if later you can borrow Christian works for me—Say you will, my soldier! Do it for your Luck!"

Resolve grew firm. "Of course I will, my lady."

~ 5 ~

In red robe with the Wheel on its breast and Key laid over that, Hammer to hand, Gratillonius stood before the winter Council of Suffetes and said:

"Hear me out ere you cry havoc. The divisions between us are bad enough. I would not widen them, I would heal them, if I had my way.

662

But what they arise from is conflict between Gods, the commandments of Gods, and I think there is where we must first seek reconciliation.

"I follow Mithras, like my fathers before me. As your King, I have given the Gods of Ys Their honors and dues. I have asked no more in return than that I and my fellows be free in our own worship, like everybody else." He lifted his palm against a murmur. "Aye, even so there have been clashes in the past. Some of you have been outraged. Did you ever stop to think that Mithras may have suffered outrages too? Still, we made peace, and naught that was terrible happened. Rather, Ys has flourished.

"Now we are in a new conflict, the gravest of all. Somehow we must end it, ere it tears the city asunder. I know not how. Nor do you. It is a matter for the Gods.

"Therefore I say, let us give Mithras His full honor. Thereafter we can pray together for harmony in Heaven and a sign unto us.

"Hitherto I have carried out my sacral duties as King without regard to the times that are holy to Mithras. He's a soldier; He understands how men in the field can't always observe the pieties.

"But this year His birthday falls on the full moon.

"May I interrupt my Watch to celebrate it as it should be celebrated, in the Mithraeum here? If this assembly disallows that, I will not. My last desire is to provoke more trouble.

"However, think. Think how empty that rite of the Watch is, especially now, when I have not regained strength to answer a challenge. Think what it may mean—to the Gods, Whom we do not really know, and to our souls—if the Incarnation of Taranis takes one day out of three days and nights to do service to Mithras, Who is also a warrior. How can it harm? How might it help?

"I ask your leave to try."

Debate began. Gratillonius was surprised at its quietness. Most of the Suffetes thought the request reasonable. Of his chief opponents among them, Soren spoke against it, but briefly, in a tone of somber resignation, while Hannon sat huddled in eld. The Gallicenae had chosen no speaker—unprecedented—and Lanarvilis merely echoed Soren; Bodilis praised what might indeed be a seed of peace; the rest kept mute—Vindilis showed scorn, her remaining Sisters varying degrees of hope—until Dahut sprang to her feet and cried:

"Hear me! Who has a better right to choose? *I* say my father heard a voice from Beyond, and had the wisdom and courage to listen. Open your hearts. Grant him his wish." Tears gleamed across the waves of blood that made her flame with beauty. "After everything he's wrought for Ys, 't-t-tis little enough reward!"

The vote of agreement was close to unanimous.

—Gratillonius and Dahut had a moment by themselves, in the portico, as the adjourned meeting spilled forth into the early night. "Mithras forgive me," he blurted, "but today you've made me happier than ever He could in His Paradise."

"We've a long road before us," she replied. Her earnestness wavered between a child's and a woman's. "You're in the wrong, father, and I can but pray you'll make your way to the light. Best we not see each other, be together, as in olden days." Her voice caught. "'Twould hurt too much. For know, I love you still, my big, strong, lonely Grallon."

"Abide, darling." His words stumbled. "I'll yet find how to give you—not what you believe you want—but what you truly deserve."

She clutched his hand in both hers. The touch burned. "Meanwhile, father, you'll know those horrible whispers about me are false. You will?"

He could only hug her to him for an instant before they parted.

~ 6 ~

"Now say we our farewells," intoned Gratillonius. He lifted his arms. To the handful of worshippers whose feast had ended: "May the light of Ahura-Mazda, which is Truth, shine upon you. May the blessing of Mithras, which is Troth, descend upon you. May strength and purity dwell within you, and bring your souls at last to their home. Go in peace."

Thereafter he led them from the sanctuary. Sea-thunder growled faintly through the stonework, once they had climbed higher up onto the gloom. Torches guttered and smoked. It was like a liberation to come forth on top of the Raven Tower, though the chill cut and sundown was a sullen red streak above ocean.

Waves crashed on the wall below, an undertone to evening orisons. Gratillonius said his without quite hearing them. It was not that he had lost reverence. His mind was still in the crypt. How majestically had the service resounded, but how hollowly the echoes of it. There had been a sadness about it, a sense of goodbye, as if this were the last Birthday he would ever celebrate.

But that was nonsense, he told himself. The God upheld him. He was healing rapidly and entirely. Soon he would be able to cope with any new challenger—who was most unlikely to appear, given what had become of the others. While it might not be easy, he thought he could win the support of Stilicho, which meant the acquiescence of Rome. His opponents within the city were well-nigh powerless. More and more of them were coming back to his side, where the people of Ys had always been. The rift between him and the Gallicenae—some of the Gallicenae—must close in time, if only he was patient; for had not Dahut said she loved him? That alone kindled summer in his heart.

Then why this foreboding? Why had the noonday sun looked pale and shrunken? The blasphemy had crossed his mind that Mithras was defeated and in retreat. Gratillonius had stamped on it, as he had stamped on the face of Carsa, but it would no more go altogether away than would those memories.

The prayers ended. "Goodnight, men," he said in Latin. Replies muttered back. He tossed his ceremonial torch over the battlements. It streamed fire on the way to its drowning. From a guard he took the lantern he had left and used it to help him down the stairway and through the blindness that had fallen upon Ys.

Most of such folk as were yet in the streets recognized him, but few offered greetings, for he wore the vestments of his alien God. The guards at High Gate did salute him. Some of the workshops beyond were lighted and busy, but the clangor from them soon faded as he went on beyond, to Processional Way. Crossing the canal by the tiny bridge, he saw the water frozen over. Stars began to crowd heaven. Moon-glow above the hills was as cold as they and the ice were. He hastened his steps in spite of its making his ribs ache; footfalls rang loud through stillness. If he could reach the Wood before the moon rose into view, maybe he would not really have been absent on this midmost day of his Watch. But that idea was ridiculous, he told himself.

The grove loomed before him, blackness out of which fingers reached. Gleams from the house did not touch it, nor did he find much warmth of welcome when he entered. The strife between King and Gods naturally perturbed the staff more than it did an ordinary Ysan. Tambilis was on Sena.

Well, a man should be able to stand a little isolation. Gratillonius withdrew to the Roman-like part of the building. By lamplight he changed his sacred garments for a robe and settled down to read for a while. Good old Vergilius.

Wind woke him, a breath under the eaves. His candles burned low. Drowsily, he went to a window and looked out, blocking reflections off the panes with his body. Nothing but murk met his eyes. So clouds had blown up anew, had they? He stripped, killed the flamelets, crawled into bed and fell back into sleep.

—"Out with you! To your homes! You'll be told when you're wanted again. Out!"

Gratillonius sat up. For a moment he wondered what this dream was. Bedding bulged soft around him; air sheathed his torso in cold. He could just see the uncovered window, slightly less dark than the room. He had barely heard the voice through closed doors. Scurrying feet sounded louder and must have been what roused him. Oh, this was real. His scalp prickled. Should he take something that could serve as a weapon? The imperious tones had been a woman's. The heart jumped in his breast.

He groped about till he had come upon his robe and drawn it on. Then he advanced boldly enough. The years had made him familiar with the passage. When he flung open the door to the hall, coals glowed in the firepits and a few candles had been lighted from them. Through shadows he saw the attendants, hastily dressed, going elsewhere. Tall in a black cloak stood Forsquilis.

He halted. She heard his amazed oath. Her hair shimmered wild amidst the dark. "Hold," she commanded with the quietness that expects obedience.

When the last servant had gone, she beckoned. "Now we can talk," she said.

He approached her. The Athene face had turned gaunt in the past months; highlights wavered over arches of bone and lost themselves beneath. Somehow that made her twice beautiful, a night-nymph. "What brings you here?" he asked with deference.

"I went afar in my Sending," she answered. Her gaze smoldered upon him. "You cannot see through the clouds—Ys cannot, which is well for it—but the eagle owl flew above. The moon whitened her wings. That brightness dimmed, reddened, was nearly lost. The moon was in eclipse, Grallon."

"Nobody foresaw," he said numbly.

"Aye, nobody did, in Star House or wherever else my searching took me. I think Belisama withdraws the last of Her light from you, Grallon, for that you again affronted the Three on this day that is past."

He knotted his fists. "Then why did They hide the vision?" he snapped.

"You would deride it."

"At least I would say the eclipse would soon end, when the moon moves out from behind the earth. If the philosophers failed to predict this, 'tis hardly the first time they have."

Sorrow muted her words. "Aye, so you'd claim; and some in Ys would accept it and some would not, and thus the wounds in us would deepen. Better you hear from me. Mayhap you'll listen."

"Of course I will! But...I might not believe."

"You might not understand," she sighed. "You will not. You refuse."

"What is there for me to heed? That your Gods are angry with me?" He grinned. "That's no news."

She surprised him. "I came to warn you," she said, "not because They told me to. They did not. The sign was meant for me, to give to my Sisters, that unless we return to the Gods you make us forsake, They will forsake us. But I had to tell you first."

"Why?"

She leaned forward. "Because I love you, Grallon."

He gathered her to him.

—Sunrise was dull in the window when she rose from the bed and sought her clothes. "You are not going, are you?" he asked.

Fire had died away; her voice was ashen with weariness. "I must. Never tell anyone what happened between us."

He stirred, alarmed. "Why?"

She regarded him as if out of a cage where she was penned. "You will not yield," she said. "Last night I spoke falsely. I thought the darkened moon had told me to come to you, and after you had fallen asleep find a knife and slash your throat. Thus might Ys yet be saved.

But I could not. Now I must go and do what penance I can. Farewell, Grallon."

He scrambled toward her. She gestured him back, and somehow he could only obey and watch, helpless, while she clad herself. Almost, then, they kissed. She turned away in time and left him, never looking back.

XV

~ 1 ~

"Today I will go riding," said Dahut.

The chambermaid hesitated before replying timidly: "Again? My lady spends much time in the saddle." She did not venture to mention neglected sacral and secular tasks, but did add, "At least she should have an escort. There could be wicked men abroad, or an accident far from help."

Dahut tossed her head. "I know what I do. You tend to what you are supposed to understand."

The maid folded hands over breast and bowed low. Dahut brooked no interference from her hirelings. On succeeding to Fennalis's home, she had not only redecorated and refurnished it from top to bottom, she had replaced the entire staff. Tongue-lashings, cuffs to cheek or ear, summary dismissals soon won her a properly subservient household.

But they watched her, always they watched her, and when she was gone they talked.

She took her candlestick to the bathroom. Lamps burned there; perfume mingled with the mist-wraiths off the hot water. A long while she luxuriated in it, admiring and stroking her body, before she rose and called the chambermaid. Toweled dry, she returned to the bathroom and was, quite unnecessarily, assisted into the garments laid out—linen tunic, calfskin breeches, half-boots, purse and dagger belted at her waist. The attendant combed and braided her hair and wrapped the shining coils close around her head. She had taken to wearing it shorter than most women on Ys, only halfway down her back when loosened. That made it the more readily concealable.

She broke her fast lightly as always, with bread, butter, cheese, honey, milk. When nobody was with her, she slipped from the purse a vial, shook it over her palm, kissed and swallowed the ladygift. Thereupon she donned an outer coat of wool, whose thickness disguised curves of breast and hip. A cowled cloak did the rest. "Await me when I return," she said, and stepped forth into the winter dawn.

Seen from this height, the roofs of lower Ys had begun to glimmer forth out of darkness, while already the towers gleamed frosty. The headlands hulked above a livid sea. Air lay quiet and cold. Nobody else was on this street as yet. Once beyond view of her house, Dahut changed her gait to the loose-jointed walk she had practiced in secret. Boylike, she descended.

Often she did in fact seek the livery stables outside High Gate, since horses were not allowed to be kept within the city except by the King. It would never do for word to trickle back that she did not invariably do so. Today she took a circuitous route to Lowtown. As she went on, light strengthened and traffic increased.

About to cross Lir Way near Skippers' Market, she found that the square, generally deserted at this time of year, held a small crowd, with more folk streaming in by the minute and pushing on through the arch. She plucked the sleeve of a workman. "What's afoot?" she asked. Her voice she carefully deepened and roughened.

His glance saw little beneath her overshadowing hood. "An outland ship standing in, I hear," he told her. "Northmen of some kind."

Instantly eager to see, she mingled with the rest and passed onto the wharf. Falling tide had drawn the sea gate open. The vessel, which must have lain to until daylight when the crew could pick their way among the rocks, drew ever closer. Her eye as skilled in such matters as that of any Ysan, Dahut saw that this one was indeed from across the Germanic Sea, but not quite the same as a typical Saxon craft. The hull was about seventy feet long, wide-beamed, clinker-built, open save for thwarts on which twenty rowers sat. Stem- and sternposts curved high. A single steering oar was at the starboard. Mast, yardarm, and furled sail lay across trestles amidships. Paint whose flamboyant colors were faded and chipped bespoke much voyaging. The men numbered some forty, most of them big and blond. Their captain—she assumed—stood in the bows, helmed, ring-mailed, spear in hand, a splendid sight even at this distance.

"Pirates?" fretted someone.

"Nay," scoffed another. "Were they so mad as to cast a single ship against Ys, they couldn't've made it hither. Beware of brawls, though."

"Mayhap not," said a third. "When barbarians are on their good behavior, ofttimes they've better manners than most city folk. I'll be happy to hear whatever yarns they spin, if any of them can wield our speech."

Dahut cursed under her breath. She could not linger. Budic was free today. He would be waiting.

She slipped off and hurried to the edge of the Fishtail district. The legionary was there, in civil garb and also hooded. His glad call rang: "Oh, wonderful! I feared you'd been unable to come."

668

"Hush," she cautioned. The attention of passersby was unwanted. Approaching the door, she brushed against him, glidingly, while she took a key from her purse.

He had done well in finding her this place. The house was ancient, a block of eroded stone with interior walls almost as thick as the outer. It belonged to a widower, deaf, incurious, content to live and stay drunk on the small rentals paid by half a dozen roomers. They were a floating population of sailors, day laborers, hawkers, harlots, foreigners without much wealth, the kind of people who observed but did not pry. To them she was Cian, a Scotic lad lately arrived from Mumu to assist Tommaltach. Since that man's death, Cian had been errand boy to the caretaker the King appointed pending new arrangements with Conual Corcc when trade resumed in spring. Cian was often sent widely about, and therefore stayed here only occasionally. His Ysan being scant and broken, his Latin nil, he kept to himself, unless a friend visited.

From Tommaltach Dahut had learned the lilting accent and enough words to sound like a Hivernian.

Not for the first time, she took Budic past an entry and up a stair to the narrow corridor on which her chamber fronted. Unfastening the lock, she let them through and bolted the door from within. The room was small and meagerly furnished. Oiled cloth across the single window admitted dim light. Unkindled, a brazier gave no help against dankness and cold. However, the wine in a clay jug was of the best. Dahut poured into two wooden cups.

"I should fetch some fresh water for this, my lady," Budic said.

"Oh, that's a waste of these few hours we have," she replied. "Drink it pure, savor the taste. You're too solemn, my dear."

His mouth twisted. "I've reason enough." He gripped his cup hard and tossed off a deep draught.

Dahut barely sipped. "Aye, poor Budic," she murmured, "unhappy at home, tormented in spirit. You've been very kind to me regardless. Would that I could return to you a gift of peace."

"In Christ is peace," he grated.

"So you say. I strive to see how. Come, let us sit and talk. Nay, bring your stool next to mine." She dropped her cloak and removed the wool beneath. Abruptly he saw her bosom strain against thin linen.

He gulped. "Will you not be cold, my lady?"

"Not if you sit close and lay that fine big cloak of yours over both our shoulders," she laughed.

He flinched. "Best not, my lady."

She cocked her head. "Why?" she asked innocently.

Through the gloom she saw him redden to the roots of his fair hair. "Unseemly," he faltered. "And—forgive me—Satan's lures—"

"Oh, Budic, we are like brother and sister. Come." She took his hand. Defenseless, he obeyed her wish.

Staring straight before him, he inquired. "Have you prayed for insight?"

669

"Of course," she said. "Over and over. In vain." Not defiantly but sadly: "I cannot make sense of your faith. Try though I do, I cannot. *Why* did Christ die?"

"For you. For all mankind."

"How is that so different from other Gods Who die? They rise again and renew the earth."

"Christ died that He might redeem us from our sin and save us from the everlasting flames."

Dahut shivered. "That's a horrible thought, that we are born damned because of something that happened in the beginning. It chills me more deeply than this air does." She leaned against him. Her free hand sought his. "Must Ys burn for want of knowledge? Lir would only drown us."

"Ys can yet be saved. Let her heed the tidings."

"How? You've seen the very King, my father, forced to bow down before the Gods."

"Christ is stronger than Mithras."

"Aye, a Christian King—what might such a man do?"

"We've met in aid of your soul, yours alone," Budic said fast. "I am a clumsy preacher, but let me try." He looked upward. "O Spirit That came down to the Apostles, help my tongue!"

Dahut shifted closer still. "I listen," she breathed.

He spoke. She refilled his cup. He spoke, repeating what he had told her before and adding to it: of the Creation, the origin of evil, God's Covenant with His chosen people, from whom Christ was to spring. She asked him about those ancient Jews, but he knew little, apart from snatches of the Psalms. Rather he would seek to explain the mysteries of the Incarnation, the Redemption—ignoramus that he was, the subtleties escaped him too, but he *believed* and that sufficed— He talked on.

Dahut wondered aloud about Christ's laws concerning women. Was she right in her impression that many had found favor in His eyes, not simply His Mother, but the young bride at Cana, Maria and Martha of Bethany, aye even a woman taken in adultery? If He smiled on them, if He understood human needs and longings, why then should women be somehow unclean, why should celibacy be a sacrifice pleasing unto Him?

"We live for God, only for God," he rattled forth. "It is better to marry than to burn, but best is to become free of lust, of everything worldly."

"Does your God hate this world you say He made? Any good workman takes pride in his works. Taranis and Belisama are lovers, and They are in all who love. Look at me, Budic. I am a woman. Am I foul? Did God give me this body in order that I starve and torture it?"

He sprang from her, to his feet. "Stop!" he cried. "You know not what you do!"

She rose also and came to him, reached once more for his hands. Compassion glowed from her. "I'm sorry, dear man. I'd never wittingly hurt you. What is so dreadful?"

"I must go," he said. "Forgive me, I must."

"Why, we've talked a pair of hours at most. We thought to go out after food we could share, and be together this whole day."

"I cannot," he gasped. "Forgive me, my lady. You are not foul, nay, you are beautiful, too beautiful, and I—I must go pray for strength."

She smiled the least wistful bit. "As you will. I'll pray too. When can we meet again?"

"We should not. Your honor—"

"Budic," she said low, "I trust you more than any other living soul."

"I'll send you a message. Farewell!" He snatched his cloak and fled. The door slammed shut behind him.

Dahut stared at it. After a while, she kicked the stool he had been using across the floor. "Belisama, where were You?" she shrilled.

Suddenly she began to laugh. Long and loud she laughed, hands on hips, head turned to the ceiling, before she donned her outer garments and left.

The streets were now thronged, scarcely less busy than in summer, Ys getting on with its work while daylight lasted. But she had seen the many-colored spectacle all her life. Momentarily she walked toward High Gate and the stables—then turned and made for the harbor.

The strange ship lay docked between two high-hulled freighters idled for the winter. Onlookers had dispersed, for the crew was gone. City guards kept watch over every vessel. Dahut intercepted one on his beat. "Where's yon craft from?" she asked in her boy-voice.

"Britannia," he replied, "or so I heard."

"That's no Britannic hull."

"Well, her homeland is afar, but Germani come more and more to the east and southeast of yon island, raiding, trading, sometimes settling. I hear these fellows were visiting kinfolk there but grew restless and decided on a small venture to us, mainly to see what we're like. They unloaded some bales and boxes into a warehouse. Belike their chief will meet with merchants of ours."

"Where is he now?"

"What, you'd fain enlist with him, lad? Ha, ha! Hm, the Swan is the most respectable mariners' inn, but his sort more commonly seek the Crossed Anchors or Epona's Horse."

Dahut nodded and hurried off. At the second place, she learned that the barbarian skipper had taken a room to himself—surely with intent of having a woman for the night, said the landlord matter-of-factly—and wandered off a short while ago.

The Forum would be the logical place for him to aim at. There he could meet shipmates, if that had been agreed upon, and commence sightseeing. Dahut slipped and wove through the traffic up Lir Way.

671

Presently, inevitably, she saw him. He had changed his armor for a fur cap, tunic sable-trimmed and richly patterned, wadmal breeks, cross-garters, gold rings on brawny arms—no less grand a sight than before, with tawny mane and beard rearing above most heads, over the doorframe width of his shoulders. A bow wave and wake of stares, whispers, gestures eddied around him.

Dahut overtook. "Pray pardon, sir," she hailed.

He checked his stride for an instant, regarded her, shrugged, and indicated he did not know the language.

"Do you speak Latin, then, my lord?" she asked in it.

"Um. Not too good." The words resonated from his chest. "Vat you vant, hey?"

"Do wish a guide? I know Ys, everything to see, every opportunity, every pleasure. Let me show you, master."

His gaze sharpened in weather-beaten features. "Ho, I know your kind....No, vait a bit. You are not— Step you aside, ha, and we talk."

They found a spot under the sheer wall of a tower. "You are no boy," he said in his surf-rolling tones. "You are a girl. Vat for you dress like that?"

"To go about freely, sir, because I am *not* a whore. It is reckoned decent among us." Dahut smiled straight into his wariness. "You are observant, master. You'll want a guide who can lead you to what's worth finding—and get you the right female company too, if that's your wish, somebody warm, knowing, clean, and honest."

The seaman rumbled laughter. "Ho! Maybe ve try. Vat are your pay for this?"

"Whatever my noble lord thinks proper," Dahut purred. "Best will be if first I get to know him. Could we sit and talk?"

He assenting, she led him inside the tower. He gaped at the magnificence of the entrance, the corridor beyond, the shops opening onto it. One offered refreshments. They settled down to wine, bits of grilled marinated fish, garum sauce, cheese, dried fruits. The foreigner had no coin but produced a few small amber chunks. Dahut bargained deftly on his behalf.

"Who are you?" he asked.

She fluttered her lashes. "Call me Galith if you will, master—orphaned, making my way as best I can, rather than becoming a housewife or servant. But I am at *your* command. Tell me about yourself, I beg you. Your stories should be worth more to me than money."

Nothing loth, he obliged. He was Gunnung, son of Ivar, a Dane from Scandia. Of well-to-do family, he had already—still in his twenties —traveled about, trading north among the Finnaithae and south along the Germanic marches of the Empire. There he had picked up his Latin. A quarrel at home had led to a killing, the breaking of his betrothal, and his outlawry for three years. His father gave him a ship and he gathered friends to accompany him west for that term. After visiting among the Gallic shores, they turned to Britannia and thought to spend the winter in a village of Anglic laeti on the Icenian coast. They soon found it tedious. An overland journey to Londinium proved disappointing; it was both impoverished and hostile to barbarians. But Ys, fabulous Ys, they heard such tales of that as to resolve them on making the trip immediately, never mind the season.

Gunnung seemed not at all downcast by his situation. Rather, he was delighted to be in a fresh part of the world, snuffing about for every possible spoor of fortune. If he and his men did well, they might never return to Scandia.

"A strong man will certainly find many paths open to him here," Dahut agreed. "Shall we go look at a few?"

Throughout that day they roamed together. Watchful, she soon learned what interested him most, and led him to such things. By no means unappreciative of architectural wonders—especially towers, two of which they ascended—or wares displayed by jewelers and clothiers, he nonetheless cared more about fortifications, military engines, civil machinery, marketplaces, the working foundations of things. He listened closely to her tales of expeditions abroad, commerce, fights, discoveries, often asking that she explain something twice where his Latin had failed him. She exerted herself to charm as well, with anecdotes, japes, songs while they fared about.

The early evening closed in. They went back to his hostel. "See here," he exclaimed, "ve got more you can say me. Come in and ve eat. You are a girl like I never met before, Galith."

"Oh, I am not so strange," she murmured. "But I cannot sit in the taproom." At his surprised look: "I must needs take off this mantle and coat. The landlord would see I am female. He might well...recognize me...and that would be bad."

Gunnung forbore to ask why. "Come to my room, then," he suggested, "and I send after food."

"My captain is too kind." She kept his hugeness between her and everybody else.

In the cubicle, over bowls of stew and cups of ale, by the light of tallow candles, they laid plans for the morrow. Finally, Gunnung coughed out a laugh, stared at her, and said, "You have not done me vun thing, Galith. You promised you find me a voman."

Night filled the window. A brazier had added its warmth and closeness to the rank animal smell of the candles. "The hour is late," she replied demurely. "The girls downstairs are most likely taken by now. Do you want to go stumble around the streets?"

"Do I got to?"

For answer, she dropped glance and hands to her belt and slowly unfastened it. He whooped, rose, snatched her to him. She reached and felt with the same frankness.

His first lovemaking was neither exuberant and inventive like Tommaltach's nor half reverential like Carsa's. When he had the clothes off her he bore her down onto the bed and himself between her thighs and made her teeth clatter. He was not brutish, though, and the following times, which with her encouragement came soon after each other, were steady gallopings. She cried and moaned and told him he was superb.

Finally they slept. As the first gray appeared in the window, he roused, sought the chamber pot, came back and began to fondle her. She sat up. "Now, beloved, you shall know who I am," she said.

He blinked. "You are Galith—"

She shook her head and drew tangled tresses back from the red crescent. "Have you noticed this?"

"Yah, a scar, it don't make you not fair."

"It is the mark of the Goddess, Gunnung. This night She chose you to be the next King of Ys."

~ 2 ~

Snow fell in small dry flakes. Walking, Corentinus saw walls and roofs fade within a few yards, lost in the overall silvery-grayness. Air was almost warm and utterly silent, apart from the sound of his sandals on paving and a dream-faint pulse of sea.

Budic was among the guards at the palace gate. He lost his military bearing when the pastor loomed into sight. Corentinus halted before him and peered from beneath shaggy brows. Budic's eyes flicked to and fro like snared creatures. "We have not seen you lately at worship," Corentinus said.

"I have had...troubles," Budic muttered.

"Can you confide in me?"

"Not—not now. I pray. Believe me, I pray."

"Never cease that. My son, you are in worse danger than ever on the battlefield."

"I've done nothing wrong!" Budic said frantically. "I've not even seen—well, I haven't come near any temptation for days and days. And I didn't fall to it."

"Broody, he's been," said Guentius, the other legionary present.

"Let me alone!" Budic yelled.

Corentinus's shoulders sagged a little. Weariness dragged in his words. "Enough. I must see the King."

"How do you know he's here?" Guentius wondered. "He goes about so much, building back his strength now that his bones have knit."

"I know," replied Corentinus. "Pass me through."

One of the Ysan marines, who knew Latin, said with a touch of awe, "You are right. Surely he will receive you."

The tall man strode up the path and the stairs. A servant admitted him and took his snow-dusted paenula. He kept his staff, as if it were

674

a badge of authority. A second attendant sped off to inform Gratillonius, who arrived at once and said, "Welcome. Good to see you," then paused, looked, and added, "Maybe not."

"We must speak alone," the chorepiscopus declared.

Gratillonius nodded and led the way to his second-floor conference room. A servant carried a lamp to lighten its gloom and departed, shutting the door. "Be seated," Gratillonius invited.

"I'll stand," Corentinus answered. His host did likewise.

"What have you to say?" Gratillonius asked.

"Bad things, my son. I have heard certain rumors." (Gratillonius nodded again. Despite his calling and his ascetic ways, Corentinus learned more than most about what went on in Ys, and often earlier.) "I reproved those who whispered them, I told them to stop spreading malicious tattle that must be false. Nevertheless, when I inquired further I found that it has a basis of fact—nothing that proves wrongdoing, but a great deal that is unknown and unexplainable. So I prayed for a sign, not out of curiosity but out of fear for our beloved Ys. This past night it came to me in a dream."

"What faith can a man put in dreams?" Gratillonius challenged.

"Usually none. However, I know truth when it seeks me out; and you must admit that it has now and then. Nor is this anything I tell my old friend lightly or willingly."

Gratillonius girded himself. "Well?"

"Your daughter Dahut plots against you. She incited those two young men you fought. She will continue till you're killed."

Corentinus lurched. The lamplight showed him white to the lips. "No!"

"If you will not believe me, at least verify the facts that have brought the whispers on," said Corentinus with surgical relentlessness. "She disappears for hours on end, sometimes overnight. Less and less has she been telling the truth when she's claimed this was for a ride or a ramble. With passion she imagines her Gods have picked her to be the new Brennilis; but she skims over her religious duties or ignores them, as if there is something far more important for her. What can that be except becoming fully one of the Nine? Since you will not make her that, she must needs get another man to be her King."

Gratillonius shuddered. "Stop," he panted. "Be still."

"In the last ten days or so, she has been seen less than ever," Corentinus went on. "Nor has the giant Northman who led his crew here, exactly that long ago. They grumble that the proceeds of their trading are caroused away by now and he should take them back to Britannia. Why doesn't he? Were your man Rufinus on hand, he'd soon have tracked down what is going on. Set spies on those two yourself, King, before it's too late."

"You slander Dahilis's child?" Gratillonius shouted. "You foul-mouthed old swine! Out!"

675

"For your sake, for Ys," Corentinus beseeched. "If you discover I'm mistaken, what harm's been done? I'll abase myself before you. But you must open your eyes."

Gratillonius's fist shot forward. With the alertness of his roaming days, Corentinus swayed aside. The blow only took him on the left cheekbone. It was enough to resound. Blood welled from split flesh. Corentinus staggered. He recovered, brought his staff to battle position, lowered it. "Christ strengthen me to keep peace," he groaned.

"Spy on my daughter?" Gratillonius raged. "Oh, I'll have spies out, I will—watching you—and if you shit forth any more of your lies, if you look like you're doing any tiny thing that might be against her, I'll have your head rotting on a stake in a pigpen. Now go before I fetch my sword!"

"You're raving," Corentinus said. "Rome—"

Gratillonius had recovered himself. "I'll plan what to tell Rome," he replied. "If you behave, you can live. You aren't really worth the trouble that killing you would cause. But that's only if you keep your mouth shut. Get out. Don't come back."

"I spoke as a friend."

"You're not anymore. I'll talk with you again when you've come on your belly and admitted that that angel, or whatever it was your Christ sent you, is a liar. Now will you leave on your own feet or be tossed out like other rubbish?"

"You shall not keep me from praying for you, and for Dahut and Ys," Corentinus said. He turned, shuffled to the door, opened it, went out.

Gratillonius stayed behind. He paced, cast himself into a chair, sprang up to pace anew. His fist hammered the walls till cracks appeared in the Arcadian frescoes.

Eventually a servant appeared and dared announce, "Queen Tambilis has arrived, my lord."

"What? Oh, aye." Gratillonius stood a moment tensed, like a pugilist preparing against attack. He had expected her about this hour, after she had seen a female physician for something she had not identified to him. "Send her to me," he decided.

She entered radiant, saw him, and carefully closed the door. "What's happened, my darling?" she whispered.

Standing where he was, he gave her the story in a few jagged sentences.

"But that's horrible." She came to him. They held each other close.

"What can we do?" he asked in his despair.

Tambilis stepped back. "Can you talk with Dahut?"

"Nay. I think not. But she told me she...cares for me still."

"Of course she does. Well, I'll draw her aside and, as Sister to Sister, warn her to be more careful." Tambilis gathered courage. "Is it unthinkable that you mount an investigation? That should establish her innocence beyond question."

"It *is* beyond question," he rapped. "I'll not send dirty-minded little sneaks peering after her. They'd suppose I do have doubts, and they'd snigger and mutter and it would all be a worse besmirchment than a few idle speculations and the visions of a doddering crackpot."

"You may be unwise," she said low, "but I can see 'tis best to pursue this no further today."

"Aye." He cleared his throat. "What did the physician find?"

Happiness peeped through her distress like the first anemone through the last snow of springtime. "What I had hoped," she answered. "I am with child again, your new daughter, Grallon."

"What? I never knew—"

"Nay, not until I could be sure, lest I dash our hopes. For this is our sign of hope, our battle banner, which I raise for him who is the dearest of my whole world."

~ 3 ~

Weather turned bitingly cold and clear. When Dahut let herself into the widower's house, the murkiness almost blinded her. Vision returned as she made her way up the stairs.

A door stood open next to hers. A blowzy woman in a soiled gown, neckline down to her nipples, stepped out. "Hail, sweetling," she said with a leer.

Dahut barely knew her name and station: Mochta, an Osismian who had become a cheap whore. "I am no lover of yours," she responded coldly.

"Ah, the Scotic speech slipped there," laughed the woman.

Dahut stiffened and bit her lip. She had been preoccupied. "I learn," she said with the right intonation. "What would you of me?"

"Oh, naught, naught. For a surety, you're not about to hire me. Yet you might be thankful for my help."

Dahut dropped hand to knife. "What mean you?"

"Why, when you're too haughty to chat with the likes o' your fellow dwellers, you hear not what they say about you. That big man who's with you so much—they dislike boy-lovers in Ys. There was complaints to the landlord, there was. He'd've thrown you out, and asked for yon barbarians to be sent straightway from the city. But Mochta can see what's underneath clothes, or catch noises through a door to know what's going on. I told 'em you're no lad. Now they only laugh."

Dahut quivered where she stood.

"Why'd you go to such trouble?" the harlot gibed, grinning. "A fine lady, I'll be bound, a Suffete lady who wants to keep it quiet about her lovers. Handsome men too, both that I've watched. They could pleasure me aplenty, and *I* need the pay. Still, though you cut into my trade, I'm kind-hearted and done you this favor. Surely you'll be thankful to me?" she whined.

Dahut dug into her purse, flung a gold coin on the floor, and turned her back while she put key in lock. "Ah, good," Mochta exulted. "A very, very fine lady you must be. Who? 'Tis not for me to say your name, whatever 'tis, but a girl can't help wondering, can she? If ever you need more help, here I am."

Dahut entered and crashed her door shut.

Alone in the dimness, she yowled for fury and ripped at the fastenings of her garments. When they were off, she had regained self-possession.

Piecemeal she had smuggled luxurious female clothes to this place and stowed them in a chest. She chose a thick robe of tapestried silk and fur slippers, against the chill. Her hair she unbraided and shook down across her shoulders in glowing waves.

A knock thudded. She let Gunnung in. He reached to seize her, but she evaded him and glided back. "Not such haste," she said.

"Vy not?" he growled. "For two days I cool my heels and yawn, till you send me vord ve can meet." That had been by her principal male servitor, to whom the code phrase she used was meaningless. He had acted as her messenger on a number of occasions. She forbade him to talk about what she called secret and sacred business. At Gunnung's suggestion, she later hinted that it concerned the seals. Northmen knew more about those creatures than Ysans did, because Northmen hunted them—but could perhaps be induced to desist. "Vell, tomorrow you valk bowlegged!"

"That may be one thing Mochta noticed," Dahut murmured.

"Vat are this?" The Dane moved in on her.

She lifted a fending palm. "Hold." Such command rang in her voice that he halted and stared. "I waited because of caution. A Sister of mine warned me. Talk is going about. Even in this hovel, I've learned. You've dawdled too long, a fortnight or worse. No more."

He glowered. "You mean you vant I kill your father? Vat for a she-troll are you?"

"You vowed you would, that first morning."

"Yah, yah, but—"

Her eyes narrowed to blue ice-glints. "Gunnung," she said, "you have lain with a Queen of Ys. If word of that escapes, then hope the people tear you in shreds before my father's men take you, for he will put you to death in every slow way the Romans know."

He flushed and bristled. "You threaten? By Thor—"

"Lay violent hand on me, and I will cause it that you can never again in your life have a woman. I am of the Gallicenae."

Gunnung retreated a step. "Ve are lovers," he said hastily. "I did promise you."

Her smile thawed the entire chilly room. "Then make yourself King, my lover," she crooned. "Once you are King, you are safe; Ys is yours."

"More yours, I think," he answered, his tone going dry. "Vell, I vould yust remind you, first, it vere unvise to shallenge ven he is still mending. He can tell me to vait, and meanvile—"

"He has mended. Now he works to regain the strength he lost when he could do so little. Call him out before he finishes. He cannot refuse any longer. In good condition, he's a terrible foe." Dahut's speech softened. "I do not want you dead, Gunnung. I want you by my side, for many years to come."

"He might vin anyhow. And if he does not, there vill be others—" The Dane lifted his head. "But I am not afraid. I told you vy I vaited. A spae-voman told me vunce my luck vill alvays be best in fair veather. We have had snow and fog and high winds—"

"Until today. Tomorrow will likely be the same. Go to the Wood. I tell you, waiting longer is more dangerous than any fight."

He was quiet for a space, until: "I go tomorrow."

"Now!"

He shook his head. "Tomorrow morning early. Could be I fall."

"You won't." She undulated toward him.

"That lies vith the Norns," he answered. A smile eased the ruggedness of his countenance. "Vat I have here is hand-grippable—you, my strange lovely Norn. Give me heart for my battle."

"So be it," she yielded, and slid into his arms.

—She woke when a sunbeam struggled through the window cloth and touched her. That was well into the next day. She caught her breath. Gunnung was gone.

"Oo," she said when she tried to rise, and followed it with some of the curses she had overheard Maeloch use in her girlhood. Bruises were beginning to flower here and there on her. Straw stuck out from rips in the tick. Wincing, she got up and hobbled to the water jug. After she had filled and drained a cup, poured a basinful, swabbed herself, she could roughly secure her hair. Cian's garb lay on the floor. The costly robe she had dropped did not. With a cry, she opened her clothes chest. It was empty of fabrics, furs, and jewels.

She dressed herself and stumbled out into the street. Folk went about their business in ordinary wise. There should have been tumult. Gnawing her lip, Dahut made her painful way to the harbor.

The slip where the Danic vessel had lain was vacant. Half shut, the sea gate mocked her with a glimpse of unrestful brightness.

A patroller passed close. Dahut wailed at him: "Where are the Northmen?"

He stopped, gave her a stare, and asked, "Why d'you care, boy?"

"I do! *Where?*"

He shrugged. "Wherever they had in mind, I suppose. They left in almightly haste, before first light, when the doors were barely open. My mates and I thought perchance they'd gotten into an ill affair. But we'd received no orders to hold them, nor did they look like having been in a fight or carrying loot—only their baggage—save that the captain was as weary-acting a man as I've seen in years. I climbed the wall for a look as soon as there was light, and they were rowing like racers. They must be leagues off by now. What's your concern?"

Dahut screeched and turned from him.

—Astonished, Forsquilis regarded the unkempt figure that had hirpled to her door. Recognition came. "Follow me," she said. They went to her secretorium.

There she demanded sharply, "What mischief have you been in this time?"

"You must help me," Dahut said, hoarse-voiced. "You and I can raise a storm, can we not? Or a sea monster, or anything that will sink a shipful of treacherous wretches."

"Who? Why?"

"Those Scandians who've been in port."

"What have they done?"

"I want them dead," Dahut told her. "I want them down among the eels. May their souls drift naked in the depths forever."

"Why?"

Dahut stamped her foot. "I have been cruelly wronged. I, your Sister. Is that not enough?"

"It is not," Forsquilis replied, "all the more when 'tis unsure whether we can even command a breeze any longer. What happened?"

Tears of anger started forth. "Why should I tell you?" Dahut shouted. "I'll care for myself!"

She started to go. "Wait," Forsquilis urged. "Sit down, rest, take refreshment, and we'll talk."

"Nay. Never. Not ever again." Dahut went out. Forsquilis gazed after her for minutes.

—At home Dahut mumbled something about having sought the council of the Gods in a night vigil at Lost Castle. She had said the same thing before. Nobody responded, save to carry out her orders.

A long hot bath soothed much of the tenderness in her flesh. She emerged, was dressed, ate, drank. Thereafter she retired to her private room, barred the door, and settled down with writing materials—a brazier would consume any rejected bits—to compose the letter that would be carried, sealed, to Budic.

~ 4 ~

Once long ago, when he and the world were still young, Niall had walked forth from Temir on the eve of a holy feast, to have speech in confidence about a warfaring he intended abroad. But that was just before Beltene; the voyage would be open and splendid, against the Romans in Gallia; the men at his side were the druid Nemain maqq Aedo and the ollam poet Laidchenn maqq Barchedo. This morrow's day was Imbolc. Nemain was dead and Laidchenn had returned to

Mumu after his satires avenged the murder of his son. The deeds he was to do were unknown to Niall. He knew only that he must do them alone.

With his handfast captain, lean gray Uail maqq Carbri, he took the northward road between the Rath of Gráinne and the Sloping Trenches, and on downhill as of old. His four guards tramped behind, out of earshot. The day was late and dark, wind awhistle over dun meadows and leafless woods. Smoke blew tattered from the thatch of wide-strewn shielings. Where their doors stood open, firelight gleamed afar; this was to be a night of good cheer, when Brigit and Her white cow traveled the length and breadth of the land to bless it. Those glimpses made the walkers feel twice removed from the world.

"Then all is in readiness, darling?" Niall asked.

"It is," Uail told him. "The ship lies ready at Clón Tarui. A stout Saxon-built craft she is, and I myself have overseen the wrights as they made her perfect this winter. The crew will hasten there at once after the festivities; they should be on hand when yourself arrives. We are well provisioned, also with the gold you ordered. There remains only the kindness of Manandan and the merfolk, that we have a swift and safe passage."

Niall nodded. He had put the questions more to start talk going than because of any doubts. "The Gods shall have such sacrifices tomorrow as ought to put Them in the right mood," he said.

Uail could not refrain: "And yet I wish I knew why we go!"

"What men do not know, they cannot let slip," Niall answered sternly. "May the lot of you keep in your heads what I have been telling you over and over."

"We shall that, master."

"Repeat it."

"You are a chieftain who wants to explore what the outlook may be for you in the Gallic trade. Niall is a common enough name that it should arouse no wondering in the Romans, who know little about Ériu anyhow. We need but remember not to declare that you are Niall of the Nine Hostages, King and conqueror. We come to Gesocribate this early in the season so that we may be well ahead of any rivals. We wait there, living off the trade of our gold, while you go inland to ask among the tribespeople."

"It may take a month or more," Niall reminded. "Enjoy the time; but it is gess for you to say anything further, even among yourselves, no matter how drunk you get."

"I tell you again, dear lord, you should not wander off alone," Uail fretted. "It's dangerous. It's unbecoming your dignity."

"And I've told you before, if I tear off at the head of an armed band, the Romans will ask why. They may well forbid it and seize us for questioning. Whereas if I quietly drift away, that should lull them.

They'll take me for a barbarian simpleton, and imagine no real harm that a single traveler could do."

Uail sighed and shut his mouth. After all, Niall had once gone thus to meet him in Britannia. As for what harm the King intended, that must be against Ys; and a shuddery thing it was to think about.

They strode on. Twilight gathered. "Shall we be turning back now, master?" Uail asked.

"Not yet," Niall answered. "I hope for a sign."

Ahead of them gloomed an oakenshaw he well remembered. Suddenly upward from it flapped a bird. Niall halted. Knuckles whitened on his spearshaft, breath hissed between his teeth.

But this was no eagle owl such as had gone by on an unlucky eventide. This was a raven, eerily belated for one of its kind, and huge. Thrice its blackness circled above Niall's spearhead, before it wheeled and winged away south.

Niall shook his weapon aloft. "The sign indeed, indeed!" he roared. Joy carried him beyond himself. Uail and the guards made furtive signs against misfortune. Few men were glad to see the Mórrigu at the edge of night.

Niall turned about and ran the whole way back onto Temir hill. The rest had trouble keeping up.

Before the Feasting Hall he stopped, breathing deeply but easily, his ardor quenched like a newly forged blade. The building sheened great and white in the dusk, below its thundercloud of roof. Folk stood outside; the gold upon them kept the last brightness there was.

His younger Queen stepped forth. "We have been waiting for you, dear lord," she said.

"Mighty matters held me," Niall said. "Now we shall revel." He looked at the babe in her arms, fur-wrapped against the cold. He laughed aloud. "And do not give Laégare to his nurse. Bring him in that he may be at our feast, he who one day will be King."

~ 5 ~

Snow returned, this time on a wind from the sea that cast it nearly level through the streets of Ys and drowned vision in whiteness. The noise shrilled around Budic's knock when at last he had gotten the mettle to put knuckles to door.

Dahut let him in and retreated. His hands acted for him, closing and bolting the door without his awareness. Himself he could only look and be lost.

Warmth from the brazier, glow from clay lamps turned the drabness of the room into a snug little nest. He would never have cared, when she stood before him as she did. A belted robe of deep blue clung to her body, rose and fell with her bosom, where shadows played in the cleft under the red crescent. Loosened hair shimmered and billowed

682

down past widened eyes, quivering nostrils, parted lips. Arms lifted slightly toward him as if in appeal.

All at once tears broke free. She shuddered, sobbed, covered her face from him. "Princess," he cried in dismay, "what's wrong?"

"You came not and you came not," she wept.

"I *could* not." Step by step he rocked toward her. "Your father had us out on maneuvers these past several days. I never saw your letter till yesterday, and then— Oh, Dahut, what is it you need of me?"

"Your help. Your comfort. If you can give it, if you will, after you hear."

He stopped himself just short of embracing her. "What's happened? It must be something terrible. In Christ's name, tell me!"

"The worst. I fear I am doomed unless—" She gasped, gulped, overcame the convulsions. She hugged herself, and did not appear to notice that that drew further down the neckline of her robe. "I am cold," she said in a tiny voice. "The fire doesn't help. I grew so cold, waiting here for you after your word came to my house."

"Then speak," he begged.

"Now I know not if I dare. You'll cast me off. That would be more than I can bear."

"Never will I forsake you. I swear that."

"My father swore me the same oath once," she said with a serpent-lash of bitterness. Despair overtook her again. She lowered her head and looked at the floor. Her fingers clawed into the robe. "'Twas never my wish, Budic. Whatever you feel, never believe I willed it."

Blindly, he laid arms around her shoulders. She nestled into his bosom. "Oh, Budic, my love. I confess it. No shame is left me. I love you, Budic."

Almost, he fell. He came back from the cataract to feel her draw away from him and mourn, "Too late now. I am dead. This is a ghost who speaks to you."

"Tell me," he implored.

She looked at him, brushed away tears, blinked hard, tried thrice before she said, with forlorn gallantry:

"Oh, I was foolish, I brought it on myself by my heedlessness. Yet how should I foresee, I, a maiden, a girl who'd never known aught but love and honor—I who was the Luck of your legionaries, do you remember? 'Tis simple. You know a shipful of Northmen was in port for some while. Belike you saw them. Mayhap you drank in the same inn a time or two. Well, I was curious. Ever had I been eager to learn about the outside world, those wonderful realms that I shall never behold. In my boy's guise I struck up acquaintance with the captain, showed him about in Ys, listened to his tales of far ventures. 'Twas reckless of me, aye, but life had been so empty and he seemed an honorable man in his rough way. Also, I believed he did think me a boy. So there was no fear in me when he made a pretext to enter this room—he said he had a gift for me—but—"

She broke off and keened.

He screamed in his anguish. "Nay!"

"Yea," she said. "See." She lifted her arms, so that sleeves fell down from bruises still visible. "Over and over. 'Twas a nightmare I could not wake from, till at last I swooned. Then he went off and gathered his crew and sailed away."

"Did no one hear, and, and—did no one care?"

"I could not ask them. I beg you, do not talk with them either. Spare me that last rag of pride."

"Dahut—"

"Belike I should not have sent for you," she went on in the same flat tone. "But who else was there for me?"

"What can I *do*?"

She made a slight shrug and smile. "Flee if you will," she said wistfully. "I'll understand. You are pure. But if somehow you could find it in your heart to spend a very little time beside this ruin, I will have that to cherish through everything I must endure."

"What must you endure? Nobody knows but me. Torture will not wring it out of me."

"The Gods know. And I do, I whose dreams you haunt, Budic, I who have lost you forever. And...he will know who finally slays my father. Virgin must I come to his bed, I who am unwedded. When he learns— Well, of course I pray my father will reign for many years yet."

"You—oh, Dahut—did you think I, of all men, I would find you the less because...because that beast hurt you?" He hammered fist in palm. "Could I catch him and feed him inch by inch to the flames! But I, I can at least say I love you, Dahut."

They were embraced, they were kissing.

"Hang not back," she cried softly. "Hew me clean of him."

And again and again.

—Night drew in. Lamps guttered low.

"I will always remember this," she said, close beside him. "'Twill make my fate endurable. And I hope 'twill warm you too in your loneliness."

Alarm stirred him out of drowse. "What do you mean?"

She gave him a steady blue look. "Why, you must flee, you know." Calm pervaded the husky voice. "Seek elsewhere and never come back. 'Twere death for you to remain, after what has happened between us."

"Nobody need know."

The amber-golden locks brushed to and fro over his shoulder as she shook her head. "Impossible to keep it secret for long. Nor would I so sully a brave and beautiful thing. Oh, we could take a risk that no gossip about today will get out, but it is a risk—and you would die most hideously—and at best we would not dare meet again. Nay, fare you to a new life. I'll make sure that poor Keban is provided for."

"And I abandon you?" He sat straight. "God knows I am a weakling and a sinner, but a Judas I am not."

She raised herself likewise. Her clasp trembled on his knee. "What else can you do?" she whispered.

Resolution clanged. "I will make myself King of Ys, and you my Queen."

"My father!" Her tone was aghast. "Your centurion!"

"Aye," he said bleakly. "But Roman has warred on Roman erenow. You are more to me than him or the whole world and Heaven. And you would not be in this plight had he kept faith with you. Christ Himself taught that man and wife shall forsake all others."

"Christian King of Ys—"

His laugh rattled. "Nay, my dear. How long I've wrestled with this, sleepless on watch or in my cheerless bed. At last it is decided. Already I am blackened. What I shall do will damn me forever. Well, so be it. I will embrace the Gods of Ys as I do you, Dahut. Thus shall Corentinus's prophecy be fulfilled."

It flared in her. "Then you are the King who was foretold me!"

XVI

~ 1 ~

During the night snowfall ceased and freezing weather moved in. When day broke cloudless it saw what was rare in an Armorican winter, earth glittery white and a leafage of icicles aflash over the Wood of the King. The air was so cold that it felt liquid in the nostrils. Silence was so deep that it seemed to crackle, with any real sound barely skimming above.

At first Gratillonius could not see his challenger. The features were there, but they slid off his mind like raindrops off glass. Then he began to think: No, this is impossible, a nightmare or I've gone mad or a sorcerer is deceiving me. Yet he felt too clearly the chill on his face and the knocking in his breast, snow scrunchy underfoot, a sudden renewed ache in the ribs that had been snapped. He could count the rivets that held the metal rim and boss of Budic's shield, he noticed where the legionary emblem on it needed the paint touched up, a light and a heavy javelin rested in the man's left hand at just the angle that was Budic's wont, given his height, when he wasn't on parade, the woolen trews of winter wear sagged a bit over the top sandal straps, a small sloppiness for which the centurion had long since quit reprimanding an otherwise excellent soldier....It was the visage under the helmet that was different. The lineaments were the same, but a stranger looked out of them.

Gratillonius's tongue came to life. "What kind of jape is this?" it foolishly formed.

A machine might have replied. "None. I swung the Hammer in full sight of those men on the porch there. Go arm yourself."

"Have you forgotten what happens to mutineers?"

"The King of Ys will know how to deal with Rome."

It tumbled through Gratillonius that that might prove correct. Various officials would be glad enough to get rid of him that they would urge Stilicho to give his successor a chance. He said nothing, because it seemed unimportant beside the incomprehensible betrayal. Instead he let his body and its habits carry on for him.

Upon getting the news at the palace, without the name of the adversary, he had sent runners to inform the appropriate persons. Those were now arriving. Soren was as impassive as the sky. The marine guards tried to maintain the same control. The legionaries did too, with less success. They kept formation except for their eyes, which tracked Gratillonius whenever he stirred and swung slitted back to where Budic stood. Hands strained on spearshafts. Gratillonius heard his voice lay double stress on the usual command, that if he fell the men must be obedient to the victor until such time as they marched to Turonum and the tribune there.

"Let me 'elp yer make ready, sir," Adminius begged. Perhaps he was unaware of the tears that trickled down his cheeks, came to rest in the stubble on his lantern jaw, and gleamed in the sunlight while they waited to freeze.

Gratillonius nodded and led the way to the equipment shed. When the door closed, both were momentarily blind, after the brilliance outside. Gratillonius wondered if he was getting a foretaste of death. No matter. Adminius's words wavered: "Wot's got inter 'im, sir? 'E worshipped you, I know 'e did, second only ter Christ—and Christ'll cast 'im off for this, down inter 'ell, less'n a demon's took 'im, and 'ow could that 'appen ter a praying man like 'im? Oh, sir, you've got ter win this 'un, more'n any o' t' others. You can't leave us under a traitor an'—an' expect us not ter kill 'im!"

"You will follow the orders I gave you," Gratillonius clipped. "Is that clear, soldier? Shut your mouth and do your duty."

Adminius gulped, hiccoughed, fumbled his way to the rack and chest where the battle gear rested. It was the worn outfit that had fared with the centurion from Britannia and seen him through—how many combats at Ys? He'd had a shiny rig made for city and parade-ground use. Since challenge started coming on the heels of challenge, he had left the old one here; *it* didn't mind a few extra scrapes and nicks, and he felt obscurely that it brought him luck. The shield was new, of course, following the fight against Carsa. It hefted heavier than it should. Gratillonius had not yet rebuilt his muscles to their former solidity. When he stripped, cold lapped him around, and lingered beneath

686

the undergarments he donned. The metal almost seared him with frigidity. He took his helmet. A notion came to him that the luck drained out of it before he could put it on.

Adminius ran fingers over every joint and buckle. "You'll want the javelins, sir," he chattered. "'E's got 'is." Plume and vinestaff must stay behind. "Pardon me, sir, let me remind yer that casting is 'is main weakness. If 'e don't take special care, 'e 'ooks a bit ter the left, so by cocking yer shield after 'e lets fly—"

"Enough," Gratillonius interrupted. "It won't do to keep them waiting."

He stepped forth and was again blinded. Light bounced back off snow and flared in hard hues from icicles. Budic stood in a nimbus of radiance like some warrior God: incredible, how beautiful Dahut's bridegroom was.

Why need I live on? thought Gratillonius while the dazzlement danced around him. I did not know until this dawn what weariness had been in me. Some of the Queens and princesses will mourn—I dare believe Dahut among them—but they will take comfort from supposing that through my death the Gods of Ys renew the life of the world. And Dahut will no longer be torn, poor bewildered soul, between her father and her destiny. Whatever drove Budic to turn on me, he'll be kind to her. He loves her; that's been as easy to see on him as fresh blood, year after year. Oh, my death will solve many a problem. Also my own. I can lie down to rest, I can let this heartsickness fall off me and sleep, just sleep forever.

His eyes adapted. He trod at military pace to the oak where his two enemies were.

Side by side, he knelt on the frozen snow with Budic. Soren dipped the sprig of mistletoe in the chalice of water and signed first the King, then the man who would be King. Breath smoked from his lips as he intoned the Punic prayer. It came with a shock to Gratillonius that when he considered what dying would be like a few minutes ago, he quite forgot his spirit would go on pilgrimage toward Mithras. He tried to imagine that and desire it, but failed. He felt altogether empty of anything but tiredness and sorrow.

"Go forth," said the Speaker for Taranis, "and may the will of the God be done."

This time he refrained from adding more. His gaze followed the contestants while they departed. Everybody's did.

Though Gratillonius never looked back, he knew when he and his follower had passed out of sight. How well he knew, after all his prowlings among these huge dark boles. They enclosed him like the pillars of the Lodge, the pillars that were carved in the forms of Gods; but these had nothing of human or even beast about them, they bore forms much older and mightier. Their shadows turned the snow into a blue lake from which islands of brush lifted stiff, toning shrilly when a leg or a shield knocked ice off them. Here was a hall of ice. Its beams were hung with swords beyond naming; they shimmered and flashed in the light that came out of an unseen east and often struck sparks from them. Maybe death was like this, not a road to the stars nor a solitary night but hollowness within an ice labyrinth that reached endlessly onward.

Silent. Whatever else death was, surely it was silent. And he heard withes snicker, their ice tinkle, the snow creak beneath his feet.

He heard the footsteps behind him stop, then stamp. At the edge of an eye he glimpsed the movement.

His body had answered before he understood. He had flung himself aside, caught balance again, spun about. The thrust of the heavy javelin barely missed his neck.

He dropped his own spears and fell into single-combat stance, feet at right angles, knees tensed and slightly bent, shield ready between them and his chin. The sword flew free in his grasp. Budic had recovered too and withdrawn a couple of yards, clutching his light javelin.

For a space they stared into each other's eyes. A remote part of Gratillonius noticed that he still felt nothing, no fear or anger or surprise. It merely seemed incumbent on him to say, level-toned, "I should have expected that. However, I didn't know you for a coward as well as a traitor."

Budic likewise held his voice down, but unevenness crowded through it. "You'll die regardless. This way would have been kinder."

"Also to you, when you remembered afterward?"

The face that once remained so boyish was—not aged; beyond time. "No. You see, I'm damned whatever I do. It's sensible to win as easily as I can."

Puzzlement stirred faint in Gratillonius. "Why? What brought you to this?"

Budic edged backward between two trees. "It's best for everyone," he said. "For Ys, for Rome. I couldn't take the reins at once if I were badly hurt, and I must. You understand, don't you? I promise you burial according to the rites of your faith, and an honored memory."

Suddenly he brought his right arm up, back, forward. The javelin leaped.

Gratillonius had foreknown. Let that head bite into his shield, and the dragging shaft would make half his defense into a hindrance. He counted on Budic's tendency to hook. The lad couldn't be as calm as he pretended. There were only a couple of heartbeats' leeway, but Gratillonius was ready. He slanted the shield. The missile skittered over the curved surface and fell. Adminius would be proud of me, thought Gratillonius, and all at once that was funny; he barked a laugh.

Budic drew blade. He kept his place to see what his opponent would do. Gratillonius dismissed the idea of hurling a javelin back. As close as they were, Budic could be on him before he retrieved and

688

cast. Next he decided against moving ahead. The two of them were equally armed and armored now. Let Budic come to him.

Time stretched. Gratillonius settled down into waiting.

Budic's mask shattered. "Very well!" he snarled, and advanced. He kept to legionary style, though, which showed how dangerous he still was.

The distant part of Gratillonius noticed that he himself was making no gesture of surrender, in body or in mind. He meant to play the game out as well as he was able. It was something to do. The upshot didn't matter.

Just outside sword reach, Budic circled slowly in search of an opening. Gratillonius turned with him. They had scant room for maneuver here in the thick of the grove. Getting snagged by a bush or tripped by a fallen bough hidden under the snow could be fatal.

In a single motion, Budic stopped his sidewise course, made a step ahead, and stabbed at Gratillonius's right thigh. Gratillonius shifted shield to intercept and tried for Budic's bare forearm. Budic's blade curved about. Steel rang on steel and slithered back. Both men retreated. The circling resumed.

Budic passed close by a tree. Gratillonius saw when a limb would block him in bringing his shield leftward. Releasing tension on his right knee, Gratillonius pivoted on the left leg and struck at that side. Were he as young as Budic, he might have gotten around the edge. Budic was too quick for him, swung his whole body left and caught the point on his shield. It thudded into the wood. Budic stabbed at the arm. Gratillonius got clear barely in time. Blood oozed along a scratch from wrist to elbow.

"Hunh!" Budic grunted, and attacked. For a while they stood shield pressed against shield, thrust and cut, up, down, to, fro. Repeatedly, each tried the rim-catching trick, but the other was alert for it. They went on, stab, slash, defend, strike, a storm of iron.

When they broke off and paused, a few feet apart, Gratillonius was trembling. Air rattled in and out of a throat gone mummy-dry. Sweat drenched his garments; he felt it begin to chill. The ice cave pulsed, closed in on him, drew back into immensity, closed in anew.

Am I winded already? he wondered. Am I still this weak after my bones have knit? I thought I could do better.

He looked at the shadows of the ice-leaf trees and realized that the strife had gone on longer than he had counted.

Budic's breaths were deep but rhythmical. He smiled a curious, archaic smile. "You're going to die, old man," he said hoarsely. "Want to make it easy on yourself?"

Gratillonius shook his head. "Rather you."

Budic grew plaintive. "I hate this, you know. I have to kill you, but please let me do it clean and painless. Then we can be friends again when we meet in hell."

Once more, surprise stirred. "Do you really think you're sending yourself to Tartarus?" Gratillonius panted. "In God's name, any God's, why?"

Budic poised for a renewed assault. "Dahut is worth every price," he said.

"After you murdered her father?"

Budic's voice throbbed. "She's ready for me."

The rage that burst up through Gratillonius was like nothing else in his life. It froze all the world. Its white wind filled all space and time. It bore away humanness, mortality, the divine; nothing remained but ice, the crystalline logic of what to do.

The centurion took a military stride forward. "Soldier—*atten-TION!*" he shouted.

During the instant that habits and loyalties held Budic locked, Gratillonius reached him. Budic became aware. Gratillonius had slipped shield under shield edge. He threw his last strength into the motion that levered Budic's defense aside. Budic staggered. He smote. His weapon stopped on his foeman's mail. Gratillonius's point went into the throat.

He could do no more. He let go, dropped to his knees, rested his weight on his hands, and shuddered.

He had done enough. Blood spouted, a shout of red. Where it hit the snow, steam puffed. Budic lurched against a tree. The impact shook it. Icicles dropped. They made a brief bright knife-rain over Budic. He slid downward. Head and shoulders propped up by the bole, he sought Gratillonius with his eyes. His lips moved. He half raised his hands. Did he ask forgiveness? No telling, as fast as he died.

Too bad, thought Gratillonius. If I could've taken you alive, I'd have twisted out of you what you meant by that last obscenity.

Strength crept back, and a measure of compassion. At length he rose, went to the body, stood in the wildly colored pool where it lay. Dead, Budic looked very young. Gratillonius remembered marches, campfires, battles, parades, and stammered confidences.

He stooped, eased the corpse onto its back, closed eyes and jaw, secured them with sticks broken off a frosty shrub.

He didn't want to meet Corentinus, but he'd send a message bidding the pastor arrange Christian burial for this member of his flock.

And what had led the sheep astray? Gratillonius recovered his sword, wiped it clean on a section of his kilt onto which blood had not spurted, sheathed it. He also recovered the javelins before he trudged back to the Lodge. Good practice. Waste not, want not.

Something had gone hideously wrong. It had lured a man of his command to mutiny, death, damnation according to every faith Gratillonius knew about. He must find out what. Somehow it did involve Dahut. A shadow had fallen over the daughter of Dahilis. Well, her old Papa would bring her clear of it. That was plenty to live for. And his other girls, and Bodilis, Forsquilis, Tambilis—all the Queens, really,

690

with all Ys, his comrades, his men, everybody who trusted him. He'd be too busy for regrets.

Gratillonius straightened. His stride grew longer, onward through the winter wood.

~ 2 ~

Bodilis, Forsquilis, Tambilis, wisdom, knowledge, friendship. Thus Gratillonius thought of them as he entered and found them seated in expectation. Love went without saying, but here it bore three strangely different faces.

Well, they were three different people. He halted and returned their regard, their carefully formal greetings. Beneath the grayed waves of her hair, through the lines that time had plowed, he saw concern in Bodilis's countenance, and an underlying calm as strong as the bones. Forsquilis leaned back with the deceptive ease of a cat, the enigmatic expression of a Grecian idol. O Venus, she was beautiful, in the fullest ripeness of her womanhood; memory burned him. Tambilis perched nervous on the edge of her chair. Her pregnancy had just begun to show, early rounding out of belly and bosom, haggardness in visage. Like her two previous, it was causing her frequent discomfort. She had not sought his bed this past month or more, nor he hers; once she had whispered him hurried thanks for that, and a promise to make it up as soon as she felt better. With royal and military affairs cramming in on him, and daily exercises to the point of exhaustion in order that he get back in condition, he usually slept well anyhow.

Last night he had not.

"Be seated," Tambilis invited. Her gesture included a small table between their chairs and his, where wine, water, and cups waited.

"Thank you, I'd liefer stand for the present," Gratillonius replied. In fact, he started to pace, back and forth in front of them.

"I hope we can open up that cage you are in," said Bodilis.

He gave her half a smile. "I do myself. 'Tis no pleasant abode."

"Speak," said Forsquilis.

He cleared his throat and began. It was impossible for him to come straight to the point. He had prepared words that would lead toward it.

"In the three days since my last combat, I've been thinking and questioning much. 'Twas hard. So hard that hitherto I'd shied off. Nay, better said, I'd refused to believe there was aught that required asking about. Give Budic thanks of a sort, for that his...rebellion...shocked me into under- standing. I woke the next morning and found myself aware that some riddles must be resolved. To go on thence took all the courage I own.

"Why did Budic turn against me? Tommaltach and Carsa—well, they were young, headstrong. Ambition and, and lust seemed to account for their actions. Not that I'd imagined any such baseness in their metal. The betrayals hurt worse than the weapons. However, we're ofttimes surprised in this life.

"But Budic! My faithful soldier for almost twenty years. We stood on the Wall together. Together we came here and slowly learned that this was our home. His Christianity never divided us. If anything, devout as he was, it made him the more true to his oath. But then, without the least forewarning, he broke it, broke with everything he had been and believed in. *Why?*

"His messmates, his Ysan companions, everybody who knew him and whom I inquired of, are as amazed as me. None can explain it. I summoned his widow and interrogated her; she blubbered that she knew naught, but in the past two months he scarcely swapped a word with her."

"That pitiful creature," Bodilis murmured. "You were not harsh, were you?"

"Nay, no cause for that. I've seen to it that she'll get her pension. Folk do agree Budic grew moody and withdrawn at about that date. He'd absent himself for long whiles, and when he returned would tell nobody where he'd been. Some persons noticed him in Lowtown or out on the northern heights. Doubtless others saw him also but failed to recognize him, for he'd dress in plain clothes and keep his head covered. Something was gnawing in him."

"Have you spoken with Corentinus?" Forsquilis asked.

Gratillonius scowled, shook his head, quickened his pace. "Not yet. I did send him a note requesting he tell me aught he knew. He wrote back that he had no information save that Budic had quit seeking his guidance as of yore. We've neither of us any desire to meet."

Tambilis swallowed, ran tongue over lips, finally achieved saying, "Sisters, I've kept silence about this until today, but they quarreled... over Dahut."

"Aye," Gratillonius rasped. Now he could delay no more; but he was in motion, he could go ahead like a legionary quick-stepping toward the enemy line. "He claimed she'd poisoned the minds of Tommaltach and Carsa, that she wanted my death so my slayer would make her his Queen. Of course I threw him out. He's lucky I didn't kill him."

Forsquilis straightened. "He's far from the only one who's borne such thoughts," she said in a voice that stabbed. "He alone had the honesty to tell you them."

Gratillonius slammed to a stop. He reached for a carafe, pulled back his hand before he threw the vessel at her, and coughed, "You too?"

Tears stood in the eyes of Bodilis. "We must needs be blind and deaf not to have...wondered. Daily I've prayed the suspicion prove false. Belisama has not heeded me."

"*I* don't believe it!" Tambilis cried. "My own Sister!"

Gratillonius held his gaze on Forsquilis. "What of you, witch Queen?" he demanded.

Her look at him was unwavering. "You know what I told you in a certain dawn," she answered. "The Gods are at work. We are fated. I wish you had not asked me to be here this day."

"Do you, then, say we are helpless? I scorn that thought."

"Belike we can save something. What if you departed Ys and never came back? The strife might die away."

He bridled. "Desert my post? Abandon Dahut in her need?"

"I knew you'd refuse," Forsquilis sighed. "My one thin hope is that you may think further about this."

His indignation collapsed. "Dahut cannot be guilty," he groaned.

Abruptly the three women were at his side, embraced him, kissed him, stroked and murmured to him. He shivered and gulped.

After a while he could draw apart and tell them, flatly but resolvedly: "What I confront, much too late, is that those suspicions exist. They are hellish wrong, but they are not groundless. I must cease calling enemy anyone who feels them. Instead, I must get them done away with. I must uncover the truth beyond every possible doubt.

"How, though? I asked you to come, you, the three Gallicenae I can wholly rely on—come and give me your counsel, your help. For her sake."

His self-possession broke again. "What shall we do?" he pleaded.

"We awaited this," Bodilis told him. "Let us sit down, calm ourselves as best we may with a cupful, and think."

They did. Silence followed.

At last Tambilis inquired timidly, "Could you speak with her, Grallon?"

He grimaced. "I'm afraid to. She'd be so hurt that I could even utter the foul thing, and—and what could she do but swear she's innocent?" He paused. "You can better sound her out. Gain her confidence, till she tells you, shows you what it really is that she's been doing."

"I've tried already, darling." Tambilis's head drooped.

"She is indeed alienated," said Bodilis softly. "That's understandable. She was earnest in her worship when a child. Does she now go away to be alone with the Gods and seek Their mercy—on you, on Ys?"

"My arts have not availed to find it out," said Forsquilis. "However, there are folk who can follow a person unbeknownst."

Gratillonius's fists whitened on his knees. "You were always the one to speak the cruel thing.... Oh, 'twas necessary. I've made myself consider setting spies on her, though the idea gagged me. But who? Dirty little wretches from the Fishtail? They'd know how, as a decent man would not. I can see them leering through a window while she...undresses for bed....Could we trust their reports? Could they themselves know what it meant, whatever they glimpsed?"

Forsquilis nodded. "Aye. Suppose she danced before Taranis. 'Tis a rite forbidden men to witness. Or—other possibilities come to mind. And she could well grow aware of watchers. She has an awesome gift for sorcery, does Dahut. 'Tis ill to think what she might perchance wreak in revenge."

"But she'd never harm those who love her," Tambilis protested.

Gratillonius skinned his teeth. "If she struck the spy blind and palsied, 'twould suffice."

"She's only an apprentice witch," Forsquilis reminded them. "I myself could not cast such a spell. And yet—"

"Action is vital, true," Bodilis declared. "But let us move with the utmost caution. I know how you suffer under this, Gratillonius, beloved. Still, you can endure while we feel our way forward."

She sat quiet before continuing: "Suppose, first, I invite her and you two Sisters to dine. We can invent an occasion. We'll not force matters, we'll simply offer her comfort, after this latest ghastliness between her father and a friend. Comfort and, aye, gentle merriment. It may be we'll thaw her fears. In due course she may open her heart to us."

Tambilis brightened. Forsquilis went expressionless.

A knock resounded. "What the pox?" Gratillonius growled.

The knocking came again, and again, hard, a male hand behind it. Tambilis half rose, uncertainty on her face. Gratillonius waved her back and went to open the door.

Cynan stood outside, in the armor of guard duty. At his back was a tall blond man in Roman traveling garb.

The legionary saluted. "Beg pardon, sir," he said. "You told us you shouldn't be disturbed. But this courier has a letter from the praetorian prefect in Augusta Treverorum. We decided I'd better bring him straight to you."

The newcomer made a civilian's gesture of respect. "Quintus Flavius Sigo, sir, at your service," he announced in the same Latin. "Allow me to deliver a summons."

Gratillonius took the seal parchment proffered him. "I am called to Treverorum?" he asked slowly.

"You are, sir. Effective at once. Details in the letter. Allow me to hope you will not be unduly inconvenienced."

"I'll need a day or two to make ready."

"Sir—"

"I am prefect and King in Ys. I have my responsibilities. Cynan, take Sigo to the majordomo, who's to see that he gets proper quarters and whatever else he needs."

Gratillonius turned back to his wives. "I'm sorry," he said in Ysan. "But you knew I was expecting this, albeit not quite so soon."

Recently he had gotten a communication from Rufinus. The Gaul had reached Mediolanum and set about becoming a familiar at court. That took time, but he had won as far as being granted a brief audience with Stilicho, besides making himself a crony of numerous lesser officials. He reported that Stilicho was at present preoccupied with obtaining consulship and with preparations against Alaric the Visigothic King,

694

whose behavior grew ever more ominous. Nonetheless the half-Vandal Roman had appeared sympathetic to Rufinus's petition on behalf of Gratillonius, an impression that was reinforced by conversations with the underlings. Probably Stilicho was going to send orders north that the case be settled with dispatch, once for all.

Evidently Stilicho had done it.

Rufinus had expressed the hope—it shone through the sardonicism of his language—that the directive would require Gratillonius receive the benefit of any doubts. Gratillonius's own hopes were at the back of his mind, as he shifted the parchment around in his hands.

His immediate thought was that he'd be gone for more than a month, and investigation of Dahut must await his return. Good. Maybe the miserable business would resolve itself meanwhile. If not, well, in his absence no further evil could happen.

~ 3 ~

Guilvilis had Vigil on Sena. Gratillonius found that oddly saddening, in spite of his having sought her house the evening before. She had not ventured to offer him more than a kiss. It was shy and salt.

The rest of the Queens were here today, in the basilica of the Council. He had given the Suffete magnates much the same short speech as in the past when he was about to journey off: Necessity called him; nothing urgent was on the horizon; they should carry on the governance of Ys according to established law and usage; he ought to be back in ample time to take any initiatives that might be required. Thereafter he requested them to depart but the Gallicenae to remain. Soren surprised him by responding, "We all wish you well, O King. May the Gods fare with you," before his heavy form disappeared out the door.

Now Gratillonius stood on the dais before those Gods and his guards, looking down at the eight women on the first tier of seats. This morning was again lucent; light brimmed the great chamber. It made the white headdresses shine and the blue gowns glow.

One by one he regarded them. Tambilis; Bodilis; Forsquilis. Lanarvilis wrapped in aloofness. Innilis gazing wistfully from her place close to stern Vindilis. Maldunilis throwing him a smile that he knew was an invitation, come his return. Dahut—Dahut sat three or four feet beyond, alone. She likewise wore blue, which gave back the depths of her eyes, but—to cry out that she was not truly a high priestess—she was bareheaded. Her hair billowed loose past the face that was like her mother's. He thought he saw yearning upon her, as if she wished to spring into her father's arms but had not yet discovered how.

"I wanted privacy for us to say our farewells," he told them awkwardly.

"What is there to say, other than that word?" retorted Lanarvilis.

"Nay, Sister," Bodilis chided her, "we are more than Gratillonius's Queens. We are his wives, and his daughter. Let us send him off with our love."

"Oh, come home soon," Tambilis called low.

"Aye," said Vindilis grudgingly, "we must wish you success among the Romans."

"You'll win," Maldunilis insisted. "You will."

He barely heard Innilis: "And then can there be a healing?"

"I know this much," Forsquilis said, "that for better or worse, 'twill never again be as it was between us."

Gratillonius's gaze sought Dahut. Her lips moved the least bit, soundlessly, before she shook her head.

"Well," he said around a thickness in his throat, "abide in peace, my dears."

He took the Hammer from Adminius and led his soldiers out past the women. His last sight of the chamber showed him the eidolons of the Gods looming over it, and Dahut's head a blaze of gold beneath.

Folk hailed but did not accost him on his way through the streets to the palace. There he changed his robes for his centurion's outfit and left the Key in its coffer. Favonius awaited him, impatient, at the rear. He vaulted onto the stallion's back. Already mounted, by special permission, was the courier Sigo. They rode down to Lir Way and between the walls and images that lined it, among the people who thronged it, to High Gate. The twenty-three legionaries tramped after. They had made their own goodbyes.

Pack animals stood ready outside. The men took them over, assumed route formation, fell into the cadence of the road. Gratillonius led them toward Redonian Way. That was quicker than going through city traffic to Northbridge.

"Isn't this a rather late start, sir?" asked Sigo. "The days are still short. Julius Caesar never wasted daylight." He was a Treverian, his family long civilized, himself very given to showing off his Romanness in these times when barbarian Germani were everywhere on the move.

"We'll camp at a farm I know," Gratillonius snapped. "The next good site is a hard march beyond."

Briefly he wished he'd been less curt. Sigo was polite enough. No matter. He, Gratillonius, had too much else on his mind, in his breast. For no sound reason, he was glad to have shed the Key.

They crossed the canal and passed the turn off of Processional Way. The Wood of the King lay yonder. Against the snow it was as dark as clotted blood. They left it behind and came out on Point Vanis.

There Gratillonius drew rein. He and his men saluted the grave of Eppillus. The courier was startled but refrained from questions.

A moment longer Gratillonius lingered, to look back. The sea reached calm, like a steel mirror, save where it broke white across the reefs. In this clarity he could make out Sena afar, even the tower upon its lowness. The road swept down to where Ys stood athwart the cliffs of Cape Rach. The wall formed a ruddy ring from which the towers leaped agleam. Gulls flew around them, among them, hundreds of wings over Ys.

Keep Dahut safe, he told them. Guard her with your beauty.

Favonius snorted and pranced. Gratillonius curbed him, then loosened reins and rode on.

~ 4 ~

The cold spell ended. Snow began to melt. The canal gurgled engorged. Wind whooped, clashed breakers against rocks, shook trees, hounded cloud shadows across the land.

Soon trade would reawaken, as dirt roads grew passable. Occasional travelers were already arriving on the paved highways. For the most part they brought lumber, charcoal, furs, leather—winter produce. A few had come farther, pleasure seekers, negotiants, adventurers.

Mules drew three carts from the direction of Gesocribate, down to Aquilonian Way and there west. On the first of these a man sat atop its bales, strummed a harp and sang. The song was on an alien scale and in foreign words, but rollicked so that his companions listened with enjoyment. The sentinels above High Gate noticed and gave him special heed. They felt no misgivings. Ys stood open day and night to any peaceful person, and outlanders got an eager welcome. It was only that he was such a big, fine-looking man.

"Who goes there?" called a marine.

"You know me," the leader of the merchant party cried back from his horse, through the salt wind. "Audrenius the fuel dealer."

"I meant him with you."

"A Scotian who joined us on our journey. He's a good fellow."

"Niall is my name," shouted the stranger in accented but fluent Ysan. "I'm for seeing the wonders of your city."

The guard beckoned genially with his pike. Niall entered.

XVII

~ 1 ~

Rain mingled with sleet dashed down the streets of Ys. Wind clamored, Ocean roared. This had become a stormy year.

The taproom of the inn called Epona's Horse was a snug cave. A hypocaust beneath the tile floor warmed it. Though tallow candles and blubber lamps were rank to smell, their abundance brought forth vividly murals of beasts real and fabulous. Furniture was plain, heavy, well made. The landlord and his wife offered ample choice of drink and set a goodly table. Their four large sons maintained order and debarred thieves. Not a place for visiting dignitaries, who generally received Suffete hospitality, this was a favorite of modestly prosperous foreigners and Ysan commoners. Niall had taken a room.

He sat benched over ale. Across the board was a fisher captain, apparently of some consequence, named Maeloch. They had struck up a conversation when the latter, idled by today's weather, had come in for a stoup or three. A courtesan nearby, in thin sheer gown but well enough endowed to stay comfortable, sat with provocative posture and glances. The men were too engrossed to pay any immediate heed. At another table, a sailor and four artisans diced. Kitchen odors sweetened the flame-stench. The gale rattled shutters and hooted beneath eaves.

"What for d'ye concern yourself?" Maeloch growled. "Ye'll find more doings in town than a lifetime can hold. Why root about in filthy rumors?"

Niall shrugged. "I could not help but hear, could I, now?" he replied mildly. "My two days have passed in a bees' nest abuzz. And what else do you await, when the King's fought for his life thrice in four months, and is newly off to defend himself against charges the Romans have brought, the which seems to be on account of his saving Ys from a gang of Fomóri? Folk seek me out to gab of it. Mine's a new ear for them to unload their worries into. Some tell me one thing, some another. How shall I be knowing what to believe? 'Tis hoping I was that you might help. You look like a sensible lad."

Maeloch grinned ruefully and ran fingers through his grizzled black beard. "Me a lad?" His mouth tightened. "The yarn be long and fouled."

"And laying it out all neatly coiled will be thirsty work, I wager. Let me quench you, and myself too. Hoy-ah!" Niall called in the voice that had carried through battle and tempest. "A jug of this, with bread and cheese!"

"Thanks," said Maeloch. "Understand, I be nay in the councils of the high. But I ha' seen more and stranger things than most. Also, 'tis been my luck to be friends with Princess Dahut, her mother afore her and afterward the girl through her whole life. A humble friend, aye, nay what ye'd call close; still, I pride myself to say 'friend.' I'll try to set ye straight about such matters as I ken."

Niall did not quite hide the alertness that came over him. "Ah, the Queen who has no King."

Maeloch stiffened. His fist crashed down on the table. "Belay that! Watch your tongue, Scotian."

Niall reached for the sword he wasn't wearing. He stopped the motion and controlled his temper. "Let us not quarrel. I'll own to being ignorant. But do you be remembering I am a King."

Maeloch nodded, mollified. "I thought as much, the way ye bear yourself. Touchy of your honor, eh? Well, remember ye that I'll mean no offense, if none be given me. What tribe, and where?" He was taking for granted that Niall was the chief of some tuath.

"In Mide. I think ye'd not be recognizing any further names, mayhap not even this."

"Oh, I know about the Fifths of Ériu, at least, and more than that about Mumu. Man and boy, I've fought and traded with your folk, and can't reckon whether they gave us a harder time when we shattered their fleet these many years agone, or when since they've drove their bargains with us."

Niall coughed. It enabled him to turn his head and cover his face until he had regained color.

"Swallow down the wrong strait?" asked Maeloch. "Quick, drain your cup. Here comes what ye ordered."

Peace being restored, Niall said, "'Tis clear that you're in the half of the people who'll hear no ill of the lady Dahut."

Maeloch glowered. "They'd better be more than half." His tone softened. "That sweet, sore-beset lass. And yet I can't find blame in my heart for her father. We can but hope the Gods will somehow go easy, though I've scant belief that that's in Their nature."

"Tell me about her, then. The whole truth, everything you know."

Maeloch peered through the wavery flame-glow. "Why this curiosity, mate?"

Niall drew breath. "A feeling of mine. I've told how I'm in search of markets as well as marvels. Now I am a King, who trades in no lowly wares. Gold and the finest smithwork are mine, such as only your wealthy could buy. From what little I've heard of her, the lady Dahut is fond of splendor, or was till trouble fell upon her." He lifted a palm at Maeloch's parting lips. "Listen. I'm not the sort to hawk my goods, least of all before a royal person. My thought is that she might accept a gift or two of me. I've gold dust in my purse, but in my baggage things worthy of a Queen. If they please her, she may be so gracious as to bring me before other lofty folk. Also...a well-wrought bit of ornament might cheer her just a little in her distress."

Warmth stole into the rough countenance opposite him.

"But of course I must be knowing something about her first, right?" Niall went on. "Else I could make terrible mistakes. Why, I know not how to approach so grand a person."

"Oh, that be easy," Maeloch told him. "She's ever been gleeful to meet outlanders. Get a public scribe to write ye a letter asking for audience, and a public messenger to bring it her. I'll lay it ye'll have your invitation within the day."

"How then shall I behave?" Niall replied. "This is why I wish you'd be telling me more about her."

"Well spoken," gusted Maeloch. "Barbarian or nay, I've a notion ye may be exactly what she needs."

~ 2 ~

In a close-fitted dress of white silk, Dahut stood encompassed by the vermilion atrium of her house like a taper amidst a winter sunset, which lighted would deny the night that was to come. A necklace of amber smoldered around her throat, at its center a sea-green emerald resting between her breasts. From a chaplet of leaves in silver, her hair fell over shoulders bare almost to the arms. A vein showed blue, thistledown fine, through the fairness under her jaw.

She must not enthrall me, Niall thought. I will not let it happen.

He walked across the seals and dolphins that swam in the mosaic floor. Marmoreal pillars and ceiling with gilt trim seemed to stream their brightness down on her. Beneath a line of black spirals, inset panels bore pictures of the Gods. He made out stag-horned Cernunnos, Epona the Rider, the fearsome She of the Teeth Below. Others he was unsure of. There were some lovely nude maidens and youths among them, as well as cloaked and veiled women, beings part human and part beast, sacred animals. Unmistakable after what he had learned, Taranis of the Hammer and Belisama of the Evenstar flanked the inner door, while above its lintel brooded a many-armed sea monster that must stand for Lir.

It was as if the magnificence were meant to dwarf him, though not her. Likewise, sumptuous furnishings and a hint of incense proclaimed him a mere wild man. Yet her finely carven features had come to life as the maidservant let him in, and the eyes first widened, then grew intent as he neared.

Niall well knew how to show kingliness before men, and women. He moved neither shyly nor brashly, he neither minced nor swaggered; his pace flowed deliberate, the gait of a lynx in its forest. His head borne high, he smiled with mouth closed. The lightning blue of his gaze rested steady on the lapis lazuli of hers.

She saw a man of about her father's age. He might be several years older, but that showed mainly in the creases and crinkles of the weathered face. He was inches taller than Gratillonius, slenderer save in the upper torso, lithe as a boy. A straight nose led from broad brow to narrow chin. The primrose yellow of long hair, curling mustaches, pointed short beard had not greatly faded with age. He was clad in unabashed Scotic gaudiness: woolen cloak worked with roundels in seven colors, saffron tunic, green kilt that left bare the long muscular legs, kidskin shoes on surprisingly small feet, all trimmed with embroideries and furs, augmented with silver and bronze and chased leather. So might the veritable Taranis have advanced on her.

In his hands rested a tray covered by a fine cloth. He balanced it on his left fingers when he stopped and touched his brow to her, the reverential salute. The distance he kept between them was proper too. Still, he towered, she must look up.

"You are Niall of Hivernia?" she asked, needlessly and less than evenly.

He bowed his head. "I am that, and at the command of my lady Dahut, for whose kindness in bidding me hither I offer my highest thanks." His voice was deep, with a lilt in it like music.

"You are...very welcome. How brave of you to fare so far at this dangerous time of year."

His smile widened. The furrows that ran from it made it wonderfully lively. "Already the voyage shows a thousandfold profit." There was nothing unctuous about his speech, extravagance was natural to his race.

"You wrote that you are a trader?"

"I may become one, if Ys cares for my cargo. It lies now at Gesocribate, but how more glad I'd be to deal here! May I beg my lady accept a few tokens?"

He drew the cloth aside. Dahut caught her breath. A golden torc coiled on the tray, decorated with intertwined figures, granulations, and millefiori disks. On one side of it was a penannular brooch, the salmonlike grace of its silver a leap between twin giant pearls. On the other side, an intricately scaled snake seized its own tail to form a bronze buckle. "Oh! Why, they are, are sheer beauty!"

"The finest craftsmen in Ériu could not make them good enough."

"Come. Why are we standing? Let us be seated." Dahut gestured at a table laden with refreshments. "Carry that away," she ordered her servants. "Bring the best. The best, do you hear? Make haste!"

In her chair she examined the presents closely, with many remarks or queries; but her look kept straying to Niall. He met it with precisely sufficient reserve for decorum.

The wine arrived in advance of the delicacies. They tasted. "Ah, a noble draught, this," he said.

"From Aquitania," she replied. "Stay until eventide and sup. Nay, I insist. You'll savor the meal, I promise you, and I—want to hear your whole story, you who must have adventured from Thule to the islands of the West."

"Scarcely that wide about, my lady," he laughed.

"What you have seen and done—I watch the gulls soar off beyond sight, and my heart is nigh to bursting with the wish to follow them."

"Well, I have sailed and warred. And mayhap you'd like to hear somewhat of my homeland. She has her own enchantments."

Dahut leaned a little toward him. "I know you are a mighty man there. You cannot be aught else. It shines from you."

"I bear the name of King, my lady, but that means less...as yet...than it does here."

"They are the fiercest warriors in the world, the Scoti, are they not?"

"I've seen my share of battles."

"You shall tell me of them. I am no weakling."

"Not from what I've heard, my lady, with due respect. But Ys, now, your Ys is a miracle beyond telling. I came in that belief, and today I've found 'tis true."

Dahut flushed. She dropped her glance.

Raising it again, she said breathlessly, to low for her staff to overhear: "Would you like a guide? Someone to show you what you might never find for yourself. I could arrange that."

"My lady is too generous to a stranger with foreign clay still on his boots."

"Think me not wayward," Dahut adjured him. "Women in Ys have more freedom than in most lands. I'm told 'tis so among your folk too. Let us know each other, King Niall."

"That would be to me an honor, a delight, and the fulfillment of a dream," he answered.

~ 3 ~

Waxing close to full in a sky again clear, the moon brightened dusk, dappled streets, frosted towertops rearing against a sea argent and sable. It highlighted the gauntness of the man, whitened his beard and tonsured hair.

Forsquilis opened her door herself when he knocked. She nodded. "I looked for you to seek me," she said.

Corentinus gripped his staff hard. "How did you know?" he responded sharply. "Witchcraft does not cross the threshold of God's house."

"Mayhap. But I have had my visions and thought belike you would have more of your own, as we both did that night ere we met in the fog at the graves. Enter."

The atrium was warm, but cold air pursued them inside. No servants were in evidence. "Follow," she said, and took the lead.

She brought him to her secretorium. He had never been there before. Visibly, he braced himself against the pagan things that crowded around. The single lamp, fashioned from a cat's skull, gave more luminance than was natural through its eye sockets and out of the flame above. From shadows the yellow gleam picked an archaic, shamelessly female figurine; thunderstones found in dolmens of the Old Folk; bundles of dried herbs that gave the air an acrid undertone; animal bones engraved with mystical signs, age-mottled scrolls and codices; a couch bearing three cushions whose leather was branded with images of owl, serpent, dolphin; a rattle and a small drum such as wizards used in lands beyond the Suebian Sea; and more, from all of which he averted his face.

Forsquilis smiled without mirth. Singularly lovely she appeared, her slenderness sheathed in a black robe whose clinging and sheen mocked the shapeless coarseness of his, her tresses falling free around the pallid Pallas countenance. "Take a seat," she invited. "Would you like some wine?"

Corentinus shook his head. "Not here." Both remained standing.

"Do you fear defilement? I would drink in your place if you admitted me."

"It always has a welcome for those who seek its Master."

"Heard I a hopefulness there? Quell it, my friend." Her tone was kindly. "We do share a dwelling, this world of ours."

He too became gentle. "You are mistaken, dear. Earth has no roof or walls. It stands open to the infinite. We by ourselves have no defense against the business that walks in the dark."

Bleakness came upon her. "You have had forewarnings about Dahut," she said. "What were they?"

Corentinus clenched and unclenched a knobby, helpless fist. "I prayed for the soul of poor Budic. Over and over I prayed, hour after hour, until weariness overtook me and I fell asleep where I lay prostrated before the altar. Then in a dream, if it was a dream, I saw him. He wandered naked through an endless dark. I could not feel or hear the wind that tossed his hair, but its bitter cold struck to my bones. Faintly, as if across more leagues than there are stars, I heard him crying out. 'Dahut, Dahut, Dahut!' he howled, from his lips and from the mouth that the sword had made below them. He saw me not. It was as if I were not there, as if no one and nothing existed but himself, in that night where he drifted lost. But as I wakened and the world came back to me, methought I heard other voices weeping and wailing. And what they called was, *Alas, alas, that great city, wherein all grew rich who had ships at sea, from their gainful trade with her. In a single hour has destruction come upon her!*"

Forsquilis shivered. "It could have been a simple nightmare."

"You know not the book whence came those words."

Like a man hard-pressed in combat who retreats a step, Corentinus sprang over to Latin, not the carefully wrought language of a sermon but the vernacular of his mariner youth: "Well, whatever you think of the Woman who rides the Beast, if ever you've heard of her, storm signs are black enough around Dahut. Either a devil got into Budic or she did. And I don't mean it was just a hankering that swept him off, because I knew him too well till nearly the end. Likely she'd already egged on Carsa and that young Scotian. There, I've said it flat out, and I notice you haven't hit me."

Though she understood him, Forsquilis stayed with Ysan, as if its softer sounds could better carry sorrow. "I fear you are right."

"What's been revealed to you, and how?"

"You know of my night in the tomb," she said low. "It was chaos, save that throughout it went ringing the iron command that I must no

703

longer wield my arts in this web of woe; that if I did, not only would I be destroyed but Ys might suffer ruin."

Corentinus regarded her for a silent while. "You've obeyed?"

She bit her lip. "Almost."

"What may you tell me?"

"The unmagical things," she sighed. "Hints, traces, spoor not entirely covered over, such as you know of. Yester'en three of us—Bodilis, her daughter Tambilis, and I—supped with Dahut. She came unwillingly, I suppose because she had no ready excuse for refusal. Wine eased her a trifle. She would only talk of small things; her mind meanwhile went elsewhere." Forsquilis hesitated. "It went after a man. In a way beyond words, I knew that. Her eagerness filled the air like smoke off a fire."

Corentinus grimaced. "I believe it. We've got a lustful demon loose amongst us." In a jerky motion, he half turned from her. "I feel his power myself. Forgive me, Queen. You're too comely. Best I run from you."

"Think you I've no longings?" she exclaimed.

For another space they stood mute, aside from their breaths. Both trembled.

"I can do nothing," he said finally. "Gratillonius led off the Roman soldiers. Half my flock, the strong half. Nobody's left but a few women, children, and aged men. I'm aged too, and alone. I came to beg if you might have some way to cope with—with your Gods, before the true God gives Ys altogether into Their power."

Pain sawed in her throat. "I know what must happen. That much is clear to me. The King must die. Then They will be appeased, and Dahut become the new Brennilis."

"The Queen of her father's killer," Corentinus snarled. "Like you."

"I also. His hands on my breasts, his weight on my belly, his thrust into my loins." Forsquilis threw back her head and laughed. "'Tis very fitting. My punishment for my willfulness. The Gods gave me Their word one last time, in the dead of winter beneath a darkened moon. And I refused."

"What was that?" he demanded.

"Had I heeded, Grallon would now lie quiet," she shrilled. "The Suffetes would have gotten us a new King, as aforetime when the death happened otherwise than in sacred combat. Surely he'd have been a simpleton for Dahut to make into what she wanted. Surely the God would have absolved me, aye, blessed me, perchance even with death in the same dawn. But I denied Them."

Corentinus congealed in his stance. "Gratillonius's murder?" Slowly: "What if Dahut should die instead? It's horrible to say, but—"

Forsquilis shook her head violently. "Nay! Would you call plague down on Ys, or worse? Whatever comes to pass, the Gods want the blood of Grallon. And Dahut is that priestess of Theirs who shall bring to birth the new Age."

"So we can only wait for the victory of evil?"

"And endure what seeks us out afterward." She was lapsing into resignation. "Although you misspeak yourself. The Gods are beyond evil or good. They *are*."

"Christ is otherwise."

"How strong is He?"

"More than you can understand, my child." Corentinus took firmer hold of his staff. "I suppose we've said all we have to say. I'm going back to implore His mercy on Ys. Your name will be second on my tongue, straight after Dahut's."

"Goodnight." She stayed where she was, by the tall unwavering lamp flame, and let him find his own way out.

~ 4 ~

Clouds raced on a wild wind. Now and then stars glimmered among their tatters. The full moon seemed to flee above eastern hills. It cast hoar light over the edges of the clouds, light that blinked across the land beneath and turned the manes of waves into flying fire. When one stood at the bottom of a tower and looked up, it was as if the height were toppling.

A lantern bobbed in the right hand of a big man. His left arm was around the waist of a smaller companion, likewise in Scotic male garb. Wind flapped their cloaks and skirled around their footsteps.

"Did I not promise you we'd find merriment aplenty in Lowtown?" Dahut asked.

"You did that," Niall answered, "and you kept the promise, too. 'Tis sorry I am to part."

"Oh, we needn't yet. See, yonder's the widower's house. Come on to Cian's room and share a cup with your guide."

Niall's hold on her tightened. She leaned closer.

They made a game of tiptoeing upstairs. But after the door had closed on the shabby little chamber, they both grew abruptly solemn. He set the lantern down, turned to face her, took her by the shoulders. She gazed back with widened eyes and swelling lips.

He bent and kissed her, lightly, lingeringly. She threw herself against him. Her tongue sought between his teeth. Her hands quested about.

His were slower, searching with care. "Lass, lass," he murmured after a while, "be not in such haste. We've the night before us."

He began to undress her. She stood where she was, first mewing, then purring, while his lips and palms explored each revelation. When she was naked in the amber light, he quickly stripped himself. She gasped at the sight. He grinned, went to her, guided them both down onto the pallet. Still he caressed her, skillfully seeking what pleasured the most. She shuddered and moaned. When at last he took her, that also was like bringing a currach through the surf, until they mounted the crest of a comber and together flew free.

—Tides lulled. "Never erenow has it been like this," she whispered in his arms.

He smiled into the fragrance of her hair. "I told you the night's before us, darling. And many a night thereafter."

XVIII

~ 1 ~

"This'll be yer day, sir," Adminius said. "Go get 'em."

Gratillonius aimed a grin down at the snag-toothed face and jerked his thumb before he turned away. It was the least he could do, after his deputy had flouted both rules and Roman imperturbability to trudge from barracks to government hostel, ask how things went, and wish him well on behalf of all the men. Himself, Gratillonius had lower expectations than he arrived with.

Drawing his mantle together against chill, he sought the streets. As yet they were dusky between high walls, and scant traffic stirred. What wheels and hoofs went by seemed to make more than their share of noise, booming off the bricks. In a clear sky of early morning, the moon sank gnawed behind roofs. Entering Treverorum's massive west gate, he found little change after fifteen years. Or so it appeared at first; but then he had waited for several days until he got his summons. Now he thought the city was less busy and populous, more shabby and disorderly, than before. The countryside through which he traveled had also often looked poor, ill-tended, though that was harder to judge at this niggardly time of year.

The basilica was still enormous, of course, and it had pleased him to see how smart the guards were. Today he couldn't keep from wondering if they'd conduct him back to torture. When an underling took his cloak, he grew conscious that his tunic was old, in good repair but visibly old. He had given it no thought before, for he hardly ever wore Roman-style civil garb any longer. Well, Ysan array would have been impolitic. He'd gotten his hair cut short, too.

Activity made whispers along the corridors. Men passed by, officials, assistants, scribes, agents, flunkies. Retainers of the state, they were generally better nourished and clad than the ordinary person outside. But they were fewer than Gratillonius remembered; and a considerable part of them were weakly muscled, beardless, with high voices and powdery fine-wrinkled skins. Two such served as amanuenses for the hearing. Theodosius and, after him, Honorius had restored to the civil service those eunuchs imported from Persia whom Maximus had dismissed. Gratillonius understood the principle; without prospect of sons, such people ought not to harbor seditious dreams. He understood likewise that their condition was not of their own choosing. Nonetheless his guts squirmed at sight of them.

It was almost a relief to enter the chamber, salute the praetorian prefect, and stand attentive under the eyes of his enemies. He was over the slight shock of seeing who those were, and it no longer felt illogically strange that someone else should be on the throne where once Maximus sat.

"My regrets if you were kept waiting, sir," Gratillonius said. "This is the hour when I was told to report."

Septimus Cornelius Ardens nodded. "Correct," he replied. "I chose to start beforehand, with certain questions that occurred to me."

Questions put to Gratillonius's accusers, in his absence, the newcomer realized. Maybe now he would be allowed to respond. Or maybe not. He had reached Treverorum confident, but at yesterday's arraignment there had been no ghost of friendliness.

Quintus Domitius Bacca didn't seem pleased either. After coming the whole way from Turonum with his staff to prosecute in person the charges levied by his superior Glabrio, the procurator of Lugdunensis Tertia had been hauled out of bed this dawn and, apparently, suffered interrogation on a stomach that was still empty.

"May it please the praetorian prefect," he intoned from his seat, "I believe everything has been satisfactorily answered." He touched the papyruses before him. "It is documented here, in detail, that Gratillonius is a recalcitrant infidel who has made no effort whatsoever to bring his charges to the Faith. Rather, he has encouraged them to establish close relations with other, dangerous pagans beyond the frontiers; and this in turn has caused the Ysans to engage increasingly in illicit commerce, defiant of Imperial law and subversive of Imperial order. He organized and led an unprovoked attack on laeti, defenders of the Empire, which resulted in the deaths of many, the demoralization of the survivors, and thus a sharply decreased value of their services."

"Have done," Ardens commanded. "We've been through all that before. I told you I do not propose to squander time."

He was a lean man whose long skull, grizzled red hair, and pale eyes declared that any Roman blood of his ancestors had dissolved and been lost in the Germanic. Yet he sat in his antiquated purple-bordered senatorial toga with the straightness of a career soldier; his Latin was flawless; and without ever raising his voice, he conducted proceedings as if he were drilling recruits.

"With due respect, sir," Bacca persisted, "these are matters of law, basic matters. If he cannot even claim a mandate—"

Again Ardens cut him off. The wintry gaze swung to Gratillonius. "I do not propose to be chivvied into a hasty judgment either, like Pontius Pilatus," the praetorian prefect said. "There has been a number of letters and other documents to study. I adjourned the hearing yesterday in part because of wanting to weigh the evidence presented thus far." Harshly: "As well as because other affairs required attention, when the barbarians threaten Rome on every front. We shall not dawdle, cross-questioning each other. However, today Procurator Bacca brought forth an additional allegation. It develops that we do have a significant irregularity.

"Governor Glabrio's office made inquiries of Second Augusta headquarters in Britannia. Gratillonius, you would normally have received your discharge after twenty-five years of service. That period terminated for you last year. Procurator Bacca maintains that your commission as a centurion expired then, automatically; that you had no right thereafter to lead Roman soldiers; that you therefore stand self-condemned as a rebel and a bandit. You have made no mention of this, nor offered any indication that you tried to regularize your position, either as a military officer or as an appointee of the usurper Maximus. What have you to say?"

It was like a hammerblow. Suddenly the world was unreal. So much time since he enlisted? Why, they were mouthing gibberish at him. No, wait, he could count, season by season. The springtime was unreasonably, unmercifully beautiful when Una told him she must marry a toad—"a toad," she sobbed, before overcoming her tears—to save her family; and he, Gratillonius, whirled off to join the army. The year after that they'd been on joint maneuvers with the Twentieth across the mildly rolling Dobunnic country—it rained a lot—and the year after that the ominous news came through that down on the Continent the Visigoths had crossed the Danuvius—or was it the year following? Everything lay tangled together, also the years in Ys. Bodilis kept annals, she could sort his memories out for him, but she was unreasonably afar. Where had his life gone?

He could not tell.

Bacca smirked. "Obviously the accused has no answer," the scrawny man declared. "Since he has shown such complete absence of regard for law and regulations—"

Rage came awake. It ripped the dismay across. Gratillonius lifted a fist against him. "Be still before I stamp you under my foot, you cockroach!" Gratillonius yelled. A crushed face rose into his awareness. Well, Carsa had backed his words with his body, the way a man ought. Gratillonius gulped air and confronted Ardens again. "I'm sorry, sir," he mumbled.

Louder and clearer: "I lost my temper there. What this...person ...spews was too much for me. Oh, doubtless I did lose track. I forgot to write and ask. But nobody reminded me. And I was always too busy, trying to do my best for—Rome." He had almost said "for Ys." He folded his arms. "I thought I'd explained. I thought the facts would speak for me. What more can I add? Here I am."

"Silence," Ardens rapped.

They waited. Sunlight strengthened in the windows.

Ardens lifted his hand. "Hear the decision," he said. "Dispute it at your peril. I repeat, the Imperium has business more urgent than any one man's ambition, or his vanity."

If only that were true! rushed through Gratillonius.

"I find that the charges brought are essentially without merit," Ardens went on. "The accused has loyally carried out an assignment which was legitimate when given him and was never revoked. What errors he has made are small compared to the difficulties he must cope with, as well as his actual accomplishments. His conduct with regard to the Franks is *not* among the errors. Those men were attempting the life of the prefect of Rome. I would order punishment of them myself, had he not already inflicted it in full measure.

"Bacca, you will convey to Turonum a letter for Governor Glabrio. Know that it will require his cooperation with the King of Ys.

"As for the technicality advanced this day, it is ridiculous. I will instruct my own procurator to settle it. Meanwhile, by virtue of the authority vested in me, I will appoint you, Gaius Valerius Gratillonius, tribune, and return you to your duties in Ys."

For a bare moment, the armor came down. German and Briton looked at one another, antique Romans; and Ardens whispered, "It may be the last wise thing I ever can do."

~ 2 ~

"I love you," Dahut said. "Oh, I am drunk with love of you."

Seated on the pallet, arms wrapped around drawn-up knees, Niall regarded her but made no reply. Wind blustered outside. Cloud shadows came and went; the window cloth flickered between dimness and gloom. The brazier kept the room warm, though at cost of closeness and stench.

She knelt before him, her own arms wide, hands outheld open. Sweat from their latest encounter shimmered on her nakedness and made the unbound locks cling close, as if she were a nymph newly risen from the sea, seal-fluid, tinged with gold and azure and rose upon the white.

Tears glistened forth. "Do you believe this?" she asked. Her husky voice went thin with anxiety. "You must. Please, you must believe."

He bestowed a smile on her. "You have been eager enough," he drawled.

"Because of you. The men earlier—I pretended. They thought I found them wonderful. But only you, Niall, only you have awakened me."

He raised his brows. "Is that so, now? This is the first time you've been after telling me about them."

She lowered arms and head. "Surely you knew from the beginning I was no maiden," she said with difficulty. "How I wish I had been, for you."

His tone gentled. "That makes no matter to me, darling."

When he reached forth and stroked her hair, she moaned for joy and drew close. He shifted position until she leaned against him, weight supported on his right hand, his left arm around her.

She giggled and felt past his thigh. "How soon will you be ready again?"

"Have mercy, girl!" he laughed. "'Tis an old man you're asking."

"Old, foo!" Seriously: "What you are is a *man*. The rest were boys, or one was an animal. They did not know, they never understood."

"Why then did you take them?"

She flinched and glanced away. "Tell me," he persisted. "I know how dangerous a game it was for you. Why did you play it?"

Still she kept mute. He withdrew his embrace. "If you'll not be trusting me—" he said coldly.

Dahut's resistance broke. "Nay, please, please! 'Tis but that—I feared —I feared you'd be angry with me. That you'd leave me."

Niall embraced her anew, eased position onto buttocks, freed a hand to rove across her. Fingers played with her nipples. He had quickly discovered how much she enjoyed that. "I would never willingly do so, my dear," he murmured. "But you must see I need the whole truth. This Ys of yours is quite foreign to me. Would you be letting me blunder into my death?"

"Never. Leifer would I myself die."

Resolution hardened. She looked straight before her and spoke in rapid words, broken only by a slight writhing or purr when he sent a tingle through her:

"'Tis a story long and long, it goes back in time beyond my birth or my begetting. How I want to share it with you—my mother, my childhood, my loneliness and hoping—and we will share it, we will, because the rest of my life is yours, Niall. But for this day, when soon I shall have to go back to the prison where my father keeps me—

"Well, you've heard. Here between my breasts is the very Sign. I am Chosen but I am not taken. I am hallowed but I am not consecrated. I am the Queen who has no King.

"Niall, 'tis not ambition that drives me—that drove me; not vainglory; not even revengefulness. 'Tis that I know, I have known my whole life: The Gods have singled me out. I am the new Brennilis. As she saved Ys from the Romans and the sea, I am to save Ys from the Romans and Christ. I am the destined mother of the coming Age. But how shall I fulfill my fate without a husband, without a King? This my father denies me.

"He denies the Gods. Therefore he must die. Only by his death can Ys live. That I his daughter will weep for him, that is a small thing. Is it not?

"I caused those youths to go up against him for my sake. And he slew them.

"I had the same wish for you, Niall. That you would prevail and make me foremost among your Queens. See how much I love you, that I confess now it was not so from the beginning.

"It has become so. Niall, if you choose, I will flee with you to your homeland. We can escape ere anyone knows I am gone. Better your woman, among your tribespeople but in your hut, better that than Queen of Ys without you." She lifted her head. Her voice rang. "And let the Gods do Their worst!"

He was long quiet. His caresses went on, but softly, unprovocatively, almost as if he soothed a child. The wind yowled.

At last he said low, "Thank you, Dahut, darling. Your trust in me is a greater gift than gold or pearls or the lordship of all Ériu."

"I'm glad," she gulped.

"But what you offer me, dear, that I cannot take of you," he went on. "You are too fine a flower. You'd wither and die in our wild land. Besides, I fear those Gods of yours. Out at sea, I too have known the Dread of Lir. If you fail Them, Their vengeance will pursue you."

She shuddered. "And you. Nay, it mustn't be." Anguish: "Go, then. Go alone. I will live on my memories."

He kissed her bowed head. "There also you ask the impossible," he told her. "How could I forsake you—you—and ever again be more than the dry husk of a man? We are together, Dahut, till death, and mayhap beyond. Never leave me."

"Never." She lifted her lips. The kiss burned a long time.

Finally, calmly for a moment, Niall said: "Bear with an old warrior, sweetling. Over the years I've come into the way of thinking ahead. 'Tis the young who plunge forward unthinking, and too often fall. I owe you my old man's wisdom."

"You are *not* old—"

"Hark'ee. The course is clear before us, on to your destiny and my joy. I shall challenge Grallon when he returns and fell him." He grinned. "Indeed then you'll be Queen, true ruler of Ys, with a simple-witted barbarian like me for consort."

"Nay, we'll reign together!"

Her shout cracked apart. Terror snaked through. "Oh, but, Niall, he is younger, and he'll have his full strength back, and—and—Nay, of course you're the better man, I never doubt that, but he's a schooled soldier of Rome, and—without mercy—"

His composure was unshaken. "I told you I am forethoughtful. Sure, and that's half the Roman secret, as I learned in many a fight. I'll have time for thinking, learning, asking—asking, too, of the Gods Themselves, in ways we know at home—for how can They want anything other than your welfare, dearest Queen? Never fear; I'll find how to take Grallon."

"You will, you will!" she screamed, and swarmed into his arms. "You'll be King of Ys!"

—Twilight stole seaward. They lay side by side happily weary.

"You shall come live at my house," she said into his ear.

"What?" he asked, startled despite himself. "But that's recklessness, girl. You'll set the whole city against you."

"I think not." She nibbled his lobe. "Oh, we'll call you my guest. But 'tis wrong, wrong, that we must sneak into this kennel. Your own inn is wrong for you, you who belong in the palace. We'll be brave and proud. If the Gods are with us, who can be against us?"

~ 3 ~

A gale from the west drove an onslaught of rain before it. Never before had Gratillonius traveled in so much rain—since he left Treverorum, at a season which folk of northern Gallia reckoned as their driest —and this new attack, spears flung straight into eyes, was bringing his beasts to the end of their endurance. The men weren't far from that, either. Feet slipped and stumbled as badly as hoofs, on pavement unseen beneath inches of swirling brown water. He barely made out the wall ahead of him.

Formation was forgotten. The legionaries plodded however they were able, hunched down into garb as sodden as the earth. They had loaded onto the pack mules the armor they were too exhausted to wear. Gratillonius had finally done likewise. That was after he dismounted, less to spare Favonius, for the stallion alone seemed indefatigable, than to show his soldiers he was one of them, with them. Cynan led the horse on his left, Adminius walked on his right.

"Shelter, sir," the deputy said through the howl and roar. "'Bout time. Any'ow, there better be shelter."

"There will be," Cynan grumbled, "if we have to pitch people out of their beds."

Adminius leered through the bristles that had sprouted on his hollow countenance. "Right. All I'll want of any woman is the use of 'er bed, for about ten solid days and nights."

"None of that," Gratillonius ordered. "Get back and shape the troops up. We'll march in like Romans."

It behooved them on entering Cenabum. This was a place of importance, commanding as it did the routes between the valleys of the Sequana and the Liger. Now it seemed a necropolis, streets empty of everything but rain-streams, buildings crouched close within the fortifications. A man detached from gate guard led the newcomers to the principia. Gratillonius squelched into the presence of the military tribune and made himself stand erect.

"Well, we'll find space for you," the officer promised. "Rations may get short. Nothing's come in—no traffic's moved—for several days, and I don't expect it to for several more, at best. Amazing that you slogged on this far. You must be in one Satanic hurry."

"I've a commission to carry out," Gratillonius answered.

"Hm. The Imperial spirit, eh? Hold on, I'm not making fun of it, the way too many do. But resign yourself, centurion. You'll be here for a while."

"Why?"

"I lately got word. The river's overflowed its banks farther down the valley. Roads are impassable. You're bound for Armorica, you said? Well, you could swing north, nearly to the coast, and then west, but you'd add so many leagues I doubt you'd save any time—if your squadron could do it without a good rest beforehand, which I doubt just as much."

Gratillonius nodded heavily. He was not unprepared for that. When he crossed at Lutetia Parisiorum, the river there was lapping close under the bridges. He'd counted on making swift progress along the level highway by the Liger—maybe fast enough that he'd feel free to stop at Turonum, call on old Martinus and thank the bishop for his support —but evidently that was denied him. Any thought of traveling off the main roads, on unpaved secondaries, was merely ridiculous until they had dried somewhat.

"The weather may be as bad to north, or worse, anyway," he said. "It's been vile throughout, this year."

Arrangements completed, he went back into it, to his men where they waited in a portico, and led them to barracks. Afterward he could seek the hostel. Maybe tomorrow everyone could enjoy a hot bath, if the city baths had fuel.

"A shame, sir," Adminius said. "I know you wanted ter be back in Ys for the spring Council. Well, they'll manage, if I knows the Lady Bodilis."

Cynan gnawed his lip, said nothing, squinted into the blindness and chaos that lashed from the west. Gratillonius knew he thought of the Gods yonder, Who in his mind were creatures of Ahriman.

~ 4 ~

Suddenly came a quiet spell among the storms ramping over Armorica at that winter's close. Clouds still massed on the western horizon, but heaven above stood brilliant and the hinterland rolled flame-green. Ys gleamed as if stone, glass, metal were newly polished. Though breezes blew chill, migratory birds coming home filled them with wings and clamor.

As the sun drew downward behind Sena, the palace gates were opened. A few early guests, of the many bidden, had arrived. They were young, in garments and jewelry that flared like a promise of blossoms. Their chatter and laughter were just a little too loud. They avoided meeting the eyes of the marines who stood guard.

Those men snapped salute when a tall woman in a black mantle strode nigh. Vindilis nodded to them and passed on through, up the path and the stairs, between sculptures of boar and bear, to the portico and thus the main entrance.

In the atrium, candles glowed multitudinous from stands of fantastic shapes between the columns. Musicians on their dais played a lively drinking song in the Ionian mode. Thus far nobody danced. Winecups in hand, now and then a titbit picked off a tray which a servant proffered, the Suffete lads and lasses clustered before Dahut and the man at her side. Vindilis approached. They noticed. Their flatteries and fascinated questions stuttered to silence.

Dahut was quick to recover poise. She had outfitted herself with demure sumptuousness: samite gown, amber necklace, hair piled high within a silver coronet. Advancing, hand outheld, she smiled hard and exclaimed, "Why, what a surprise! I had not thought our revelry would be to your taste. But welcome, thrice welcome, dear Sister."

Vindilis ignored the hand. With eyes that seemed enormous in the gauntness of her face, she stared at the big man in tunic and kilt. "Since you would fain have your friends meet your guest, and commandeered your father's dwelling for this, it is right that at least one of the Nine greet him too," she said, calmly enough.

"Oh, but of course each of you shall—more privately, I expected," replied Dahut fast. "Niall, 'tis Queen Vindilis who honors us. But Niall does us honor of his own, Sister. He is a King in his homeland. He can become our, our ally. 'Twas but seemly that we show him respect, and...my royal father remains absent."

Niall's blue gaze never wavered from the darkness of Vindilis's. Smiling, he touched first his brow, then his breast: reverence for what she was, assertion that he was no less. "'Tis delighted I am, my lady," he said. "The fame of the Gallicenae lives in Ériu too. 'Tis a large part of what called me hither."

Vindilis astonished the others by returning the smile. "Word of you has gone about in Ys, of course," she said. "You're the cynosure of the hour: the more so because, I hear, you bear it with dignity."

"Thank you, my lady. Forgive me if ever I do show ill manners. Never willingly would I offend my gracious hosts."

Vindilis lowered her voice. "Your hostess. Unheard of that a Queen have a male guest in her house—save for the King of Ys."

The persons around struggled to appear at ease. Dahut whitened. "I do what I choose in my own home," she clipped. "Show me the law that forbids."

Niall made an almost imperceptible negative motion at her. To Vindilis he said, "Sure, and I fretted about my lady's good name, but

714

she would have her own way. In Ériu there would be no shame, and if any man spoke ill of her, he would soon be speaking never again."

Vindilis nodded. "Aye. No affront intended, King Niall. It must be weighty matters that brought you to us."

"I have more than trade in mind," he answered, "but that is best talked of elsewhere."

"True. I've no wish to mar your festivities, Dahut. Indulge me, though, for a few moments. I make no doubt these young people are as ardent as the Nine to know everything that our visitor cares to tell about himself."

The tension lightened. Perhaps only Dahut was aware of the undercurrent between priestess and seafarer. Niall's laugh seemed quite unforced.

"Now that would be a long tale, and not all of it fit for the hearing," he said. "We are barbarians in my country."

"Where in the Hivernian island does it lie?" Vindilis inquired.

He hesitated the barest bit. "Mide, if that conveys aught to you. Understand, I am indeed royal, but among us that has another meaning from here. You would call...most of our kings...mere war-chiefs of their tribes."

"And yet, I believe, sacral, as is the King of Ys," Vindilis murmured.

His tone stiffened. "We too uphold what is holy. We too give the wronged man justice and the murdered man vengeance."

"I see...How long will you favor us with your company?"

"As long as need be, my lady."

"We must talk further."

"Indeed we should. I am at my lady's service."

"But not at once," Vindilis decided. Again she smiled, this time at Dahut. "'Twould spoil your merriment to have an old raven croaking away at your friend. Goodnight, sea-child. Belisama watch over you."

She turned and departed. More people arrived. The celebration grew hectic. Throughout it, Niall stayed affable but ever inwardly aloof.

—Vindilis followed the crooked streets of Hightown down to Taranis Way. Little traffic was on it at this hour, and the city wall enveloped it in dusk. When she came out Aurochs Gate there was more light across headland and waters, but it too was fading. The sun was a flattened coal among purple-black cloud banks. Out on the end of Cape Rach, beyond the ancient graves, the pharos flame had been kindled; as yet it was nearly invisible against the greenish sky. Wind whined over grass and boulders. Vindilis sought the side road down the southern edge of land. Mired and gouged though it was, she never stumbled.

At the foot of the cliff, it gave on Ghost Quay. Two craft lay moored there. The rest awaited launching when it would be safe to make for the fishing grounds. This pair were kept against the next summons to the Ferriers of the Dead. She recognized *Osprey*, newly refurbished, replacing another vessel now in drydock. The tide was out, the rocks of the strands shone wet and kelp-strewn. Ocean growled. It was cold down here, rank with salty odors, windy, shadowy.

Vindilis picked her way along the trail to the row of rammed-earth cottages. While she had not visited them for many years, since girlhood, she knew which one she wanted. She made it her business to know things. Her knuckles rapped the door. In the chill, that barked them. She paid no heed.

The door opened. Maeloch's burliness filled its frame. He gaped. "My lady—my lady Vindilis! Be that truly ye? What's happened?"

She gestured. He stood quickly aside. She entered. He closed the door. The single room was lighted by a blubber lamp and the hearthfire over which his wife squatted, cooking the eventide's pottage. She gasped. Two young boys stared; two smaller children shrank back, obscurely frightened; an infant in a rude crib slept on. The place was warm, smoky, full of smells, cluttered with gear and the family's meager belongings.

"Let me take your cloak, Queen," Maeloch said. Vindilis nodded and he fumbled it off after she unfastened the brooch. Meanwhile self-possession returned to him. He *was* a free man, owner and captain of a taut little ship, and himself a familiar of certain beings and mysteries. "Be seated, pray." He indicated a stool. "I fear our wine's thin and sour till we can lay in more, and the ale not much better, but ye're very welcome; or my Betha brews a strong herbal cup."

"I will take that," Vindilis said, also accepting the seat. "But do not let your supper scorch." She beckoned. "Come and hearken. I'll be brief. Daylight is failing fast."

"Oh, I'll bring ye home, Queen, with a lantern—"

"No need, if you're as quick of understanding as repute has it."

Maeloch sat down on the clay floor at her feet. Betha whispered cookery instructions to the boys and started heating water.

"Have you heard of the Scotic stranger, Niall?" Vindilis asked.

Maeloch frowned. "Who has nay?"

"Have you seen him yourself?"

"From afar when I was up in town."

"Was Queen Dahut with him?"

Maeloch nodded reluctantly. "Methought it best nay to hail her."

"Then you must know he's now a guest in her house. 'Tis a byword through all Ys."

"Nay in my mouth. Yestre'en in a tavern, I loosened the teeth of a lout who dared snigger about her."

Vindilis gave the man a long look before saying, "Well, she is...defiant. Recklessly so. Would you wish a daughter of yours behaving thus?"

Maeloch sighed. "Our older girl be long since wedded. But—'tis nay for the likes of me to speak, but, aye, had the maiden asked me, my rede would ha' been dead against this."

"When her father comes back, he cannot shut his eyes to it, much though he might wish to."

"What's this to do with me, Queen?" Maeloch grated.

"You folk of Scot's Landing have dealt with those tribes for as long as history remembers. Often 'twas without knowledge of us in the city, who might have forbidden it."

"We've fought them when we had to."

"Granted. Today trade goes peacefully, for the most part. Conual Corcc in Mumu is amicable. Still, visiting Scoti usually mingle with ordinary Ysans like you. And sometimes, whether on purpose or because of being blown off course, you fishers call on them. So you know somewhat about them—it may well be, more than we disdainful Suffetes and royalty imagine."

Maeloch hunched his shoulders. "Ye want to hear what I can say about this Niall."

Vindilis nodded.

Maeloch tugged his beard. "'Tis scant, I fear. And I did ask around as well as ransacking my own mind, soon's the tales started flying about him and, and her. Niall be a common name amongst the Scoti. Mide be one of their kingdoms, tribes banded together. Its top King has made himself as mighty in the north of the island as Conual be in the south—nay, mightier yet, I hear. His name be Niall too. Niall of the Nine Hostages, they call him. He be so hostile to civilized folk that hardly a keel of ours has ventured nigh, and we have only third-hand yarns— My lady?"

Vindilis looked beyond him. "Niall of the Nine Hostages," she whispered. "Yea, we have heard. Gratillonius's man Rufinus could tell us more, for he fared into those parts....Niall." She shook her head. "Nay, scarcely possible."

"Mean ye we might have yon devil in our midst, seeking to snatch off yet another kingdom?" A laugh clanked from Maeloch.

Vindilis quirked a smile with still less mirth in it. "Scarcely possible, I said. A successful warlord like that must needs be mad to abandon his gains and come risk death in order to win, at best, exile among aliens. The King of Ys is the prisoner of Ys. This must be a lone adventurer, with his few followers left behind in Roman territory." She frowned. "Yet somehow that cannot be quite true either. He is more."

Maeloch pondered. "They've a strong pride and honor, the Scoti. They reckon it unmanly to lie. If Niall says that's his name—common enough, remember—and Mide's his home, I'd lay to it."

"But what has he left unsaid? What questions will he evade if they be put to him directly? He can always claim gess."

"Hoy?" Startled, Maeloch raised his head.

"Come, now." Vindilis's tone was impatient. "Because he is unlettered and has a stern code of behavior, a barbarian is not necessarily stupid, nor without wiliness. Too often have civilized people made that mistake."

She leaned forward. Her voice intensified. "This day I encountered Niall," she declared. "'Twas at a celebration Dahut gives for him, brazenly, in the very palace. She's lost in love. There's no missing it. Nor is the reason far to seek. He's handsome, virile, commanding, intelligent, and...utterly charming. I could count on my fingers the women of Ys who'd refuse him if he moved in on them."

"The Nine," Maeloch said, almost desperately.

"Of course. But Dahut is not—yet—in truth—one of the Gallicenae. Well! I sensed his pleasure as we exchanged our few words. We were sparring, and he had at once recognized a worthy opponent.

"He's fearless. Else he would never dare to do what he has already done. Yet he is no rash youth who does not comprehend his own mortality. He is a seasoned warrior and leader of men, coolly staking his life in a game whose rules are ice-clear to him.

"They are not to me. Why is he playing? How? And for what?"

"The Kingship of Ys," rumbled from deep in Maeloch's throat.

"Mayhap. I do wonder how he can escape a death-fight with Grallon. Yet he has not gone to the Wood and smitten the Shield. There is something else in his intent, something—even if he does win, even if he makes himself our new Lord—" Aghast, Maeloch saw her shiver. "Our magics fail us. Our Gods brood angry. What shall become of Ys?"

"If good King Grallon falls at his hands—" Maeloch sagged. "We'd be forbidden to avenge him, nay?"

"Someday he must fall," Vindilis reminded. "So is the law we live by. Let us be frank. Niall would do for Dahut what her father will not. It may be he would do for Ys what Grallon cannot. We are unknowing of what to await, what to hope for or to fear."

Maeloch sat a while in the flickery gloom. It was as if he saw through the wall, out to the sea whose noise forever enclosed him. Finally he said, "Ye'd have me fare to Ériu—Hivernia—without telling anybody besides my crew. Ye'll keep it secret also. In Ériu I'm to ask around about this Niall. Be that right, my lady?"

"It is," Vindilis replied. "If you dare. For the sake of your family here, and Ys, and yea, Dahut whom we love."

~ 5 ~

"In the name of Taranis, peace," chanted Soren Cartagi. "May His protection be upon us."

Lanarvilis, who this day led her colleagues, rose from among them. "In the name of Belisama, peace," she said. "May Her blessing be upon us."

She sat down again. Adruval Tyri, Sea Lord, helped Hannon Baltisi, Lir Captain, rise and stand. The aged man stared out of eyes going blind and quavered, "In the name of Lir, peace. May His wrath not be upon us," before crumpling back onto his bench.

Soren passed the Hammer to the leader of the marines who formed his honor guard. For a silent minute, he looked from the dais across the chamber, the high priestesses in their blue and white, the thirty-two officials and heads of Suffete clans in their variously colored robes—not a toga in sight anymore, when Ys lay wary and resentful of Rome.

He cleared his throat. "In the absence of the King, I, as speaker for Taranis, hereby open this Council of the vernal equinox," he began. "We have, as ever, numerous matters of public concern to deal with, some of long standing, some arisen during the past quarter year. However, I propose that we postpone consideration of them until tomorrow or the day after. None is vital, as are the questions I wish to raise first, questions of the terms on which Ys shall endure. Does this assembly concur?"

"The Gallicenae concur," Lanarvilis responded. Their glances crossed and she threw him a tiny smile. They had threshed this out beforehand, he and she and a few reliable councillors.

A sound of assent went along the tiers. Cothortin Rosmertai, Lord of Works, had a word of his own: "I trust those questions can be formulated with sufficient exactitude that we will have a solid basis for discussion." The plump little man was apt to pounce forth with shrewdness like that.

"I take it you mean we should eschew generalities," Soren said.

"And platitudes, sir."

Despite the weight on his spirit, Soren must chuckle. Then, grave again, he said slowly, "Were the issues clear-cut, we could indeed put them in plain language and examine the alternatives. However, as we are each aware, they are not. At best we can, and should, utter what has been skulking about in our minds; we should acknowledge the truth."

Well-nigh physically, he projected his massiveness over them. "We have lived with our succession crisis so long that 'tis come to seem well-nigh natural. But it is not. If the Gods have been forbearing, how terrible will the wrath be when at last Their patience comes to an end?" (Sight flickered over the tall images behind the dais and the guards, Man, Woman, Kraken.) "And what of lawfulness among mortals, what of rights denied and grief inflicted?" (Dahut's countenance flushed in twin flames across bloodlessness; the fists clenched in her lap; she sat spear-straight, head high.) "Yet the person of the King is inviolable to all save his challengers. And Grallon has prevailed against every one of those." He paused. "Thus far."

Tambilis broke procedure to cry, "Never did Ys have a better King! And now he's off to keep for us our freedom!" Bodilis, at her side, took her by the hand.

Surprisingly, Maldunilis added, "His Mithras is surely a strong God, when Grallon always wins." Guilvilis nodded with more vigor than might have been awaited from her wasted body.

Forsquilis stirred. "That may be," she said, "though I think His twilight is upon Him. But He is not *our* God. Nor is Christ." She returned to the withdrawal in which she had wrapped herself of late.

"Continue, Speaker," said Lanarvilis sharply.

"King Grallon has in truth been a strong and able leader," Soren said without warmth. "Whether he has always led us aright is—perchance not something for us to argue. Most Kings aforetime were content to leave the governance of Ys in hands that would abide after them." He lifted a finger. "This is what we have shied from voicing, lest we seem to wish evil on him. He is mortal. Late or early, the time will come when we lose him.

"We may already have lost him. He should have been back erenow. Granted, he may simply be delayed, from what we hear of storms and floods. But no messenger has gone ahead of him. He may have died —let's say in some meaningless misfortune. Or the Romans may have refused his petition, detained him, even struck off his head. At this hour, a legion may be hitherbound to impose a Roman governor on Ys."

Unease and anger rustled along the benches. Innilis took an unexpected initiative: "Nay. He told me the day ere he left, whatever else they might do, they lack manpower for that, when the Goths are so troublous down south." Vindilis cast her an inquiring glance. "'Twas at our Temple," she said. "He came in to pay the Goddess his brief respects, as the King should prior to departure. I chanced to have presiding duty. We talked a little."

"What I wish us to do is probe the contingencies," Soren resumed. "What if Grallon does not return? Or if he does, which seems the likelier event, what then?" He avoided looking at Dahut. "Because of the succession crisis, situations have arisen which he cannot ignore, as he has ignored so much else. Let us be silent about them here. The truth will come forth in its own time. But we might well think upon certain matters that go far deeper...such as what share the Queens—and the Suffetes, the Lords, the Great Houses—what their claims are as against the King. Then mayhap he will at last acknowledge what he has been doing unto Ys, and set it aright."

Dahut sprang up, parted her lips, caught her breath, lowered herself in the same haste.

"Did...the Queen...wish to speak?" Soren inquired.

Beneath all their eyes, she shook her head. It was plain to see that she could barely keep still.

He sighed. "Very well, let us get on with our thinking," he urged. "My lord Cothortin, behold how twisted and ambiguous are the questions before us. Yet confront them we must, somehow. Else it could be that this is the last Council of Suffetes ever to be held in Ys."

~ 6 ~

The night when Gratillonius and his men camped at Maedraeacum was the first clear one of their homeward journey.

After the stoppage they had suffered, they were pushing their hardest. If a town or hostel chanced to be at the end of a day's march, well

720

and good; but if they could make a few more miles, they left it behind and pitched camp at sunset, tents only. When their fire had heated their rations, everybody but a pair of sentries went straight to sleep.

The road bringing them into the Armorican peninsula was unpaved but Roman made, well graded and drained. Gratillonius had chosen it in preference to a more direct route through Condate Redonum because he had heard of flood damage there. Here the gradual rise of land toward the central plateau made for less mud than the squadron had struggled through earlier. Springtime burst forth in wildflowers, primrose, daisy, hyacinth, speedwell, borage, and more. Willows had leafed, buds were unfolding on oak and chestnut, blossoms whitened orchards. He remembered his first faring toward Ys.

That had been a lovely season, though, while this was raw. When clouds parted and the sun shone through, his troop raised a cheer. "Bloody near forgotten wot that looked like," Adminius muttered.

As it sank, they found themselves at a cluster of huts in the middle of plowland and pastures, with a shaw standing dark above tender green. Folk went coarsely clad, in and out of their thatch-roofed wattle-and-daub dwellings. Adults were deformed by toil. They watched the soldiers with dull wonder. Only their small children scampered up and shouted for joy at this break in dailiness. It was a village of serfs, such as could be found throughout the Empire.

Gratillonius formally requested what would not be denied, leave to stay in a meadow. When he thereafter asked the name of the community, the headman grunted, "Maedraeacum."

Memory jarred Gratillonius. Why, this must be—must have been—the latifundium that vengeful Rufinus and his Bacaudae destroyed... thirteen years ago, was it? He inquired about the family of—Sicorus, had that been the patrician's name?—but learned little. These people were too isolated. Their crops harvested, they brought to Redonum that large portion which was rent and taxes. From time to time bailiffs came to inspect the property. Occasionally men were conscripted for work on the roads or whatever else the masters they never saw wanted done. That was what they knew of the outside universe.

Obviously there had been no attempt to rebuild the manor house. Gratillonius wasn't sure whether that was because of fear, because it wouldn't have paid in these times of dwindled commerce and population, or because the heirs of Sicorus didn't care for rural life. A senator wasn't bound hand and foot to a trade or a place.

The headman pointed at a long, low mound in the offing. "Where the big house was," he said. Gratillonius went over but found no lesser trace. Tiles, glass, undestroyed goods and tools, everything of any use had been taken away. Doubtless the Duke's soldiers helped themselves first out of the ruins, then the new owner's agents removed whatever they wanted, then the serfs picked over the remnants, year after year. Even damaged furniture or scorched books would do for fuel.

The sun was on the horizon when Gratillonius got back to camp. A half moon stood wan overhead. Heaven was clear, air quiet and cold. He led his Mithraists in prayer. Those rejoined their fellows, who, with tents erected, stood around the fire waiting for the lentils and bacon to cook. Weary but cheerful, they cracked jokes which they had made a hundred times already. Gratillonius could have been there too. After close to twenty years, he could unbend among these men without undermining discipline. He found he wasn't in the mood, and wandered off.

Twilight deepened. The moon was barely enough to make the land ashy-dark; woods and hills were masses of blackness. Stars began to twinkle forth. Again he remembered his first journey toward Ys, when he was young and Dahilis awaited him, both of them unknowing. An eagle owl had passed above....

Forsquilis said the witchcraft had left her, the magical power was gone from all the Nine. Could that be true? Was the world itself growing old?

No, surely life remained, and would come winging to him out of the sky. He saw it yonder, low in the north, pale but brightening against the violet dusk.

He stopped.

The vision grew more clear minute by minute, as other light died away. It was a star in a silvery haze of its own glow. Easterly upward from it across a wide arc streamed a tail, vaporous white fire which at the end clove into three tongues.

The cries of his men reached Gratillonius as if from a vast distance, as if they were as far behind him as the comet was ahead, he alone in hollow space. He laid hold on his fear before it could take him. Better run back and calm the soldiers. Somebody among the serfs must have seen too and called the rest out, for he heard them howl in terror.

"You've spied a comet or two before," he'd tell his followers. "Didn't hurt you, did it? Brace up and carry on!" They would. But what prophecy was in those three tongues?

~ 7 ~

Foul weather returned, and worsened. Wind came mightily out of the west, scourging a ragged wrack of clouds before it, brawling and shrilling. Waves ran high. Spume blew bitter off their crests. Where they shocked upon rocks and reefs, fountains spouted.

Osprey plowed forward under oars, wallowed, shuddered, groaned in her timbers. Often a sheet of water burst over the prow, blinding the eyes painted there. They rose anew, streaming tears, and stared toward the streak that was Sena. Mainland lay as murky and vague aft; the towers of Ys had vanished into cloud and spindrift.

Bodilis huddled on a bench fixed below the mast, for what slight shelter it afforded. "Nay," she said, "the Council reached no decision, though it met a full four days, longer than ever in living memory. How could it—we—as divided as we are against ourselves? In the end, all we could do was swear together that we will die ere we yield our freedom up to Rome." The wind tattered her words.

"And meanwhile this storm got under way," Maeloch growled beside her. He had, in reverent wise, thrown a blanket over them both. They sat close, sharing warmth. "Why do ye go out? When the crossing be too dangerous for your barge of state, surely the Gods don't mean for ye to. That hairy star could be Their very warning."

"So my Sisters urged. But I think 'tis a last hope," Bodilis sighed. "I had a feeling, rightly or wrongly, there in the Council chamber when we took our oath—it felt to me as if They paid us no heed. Almost as if They had disowned us."

Maeloch tensed. "I'm sorry," Bodilis said, catching his glance and offering him a smile. "I spoke badly." She paused. "Yet truthfully. Well, mayhap if one of the Gallicenae goes forth to serve Them as of old, They will listen to her."

The skipper cast dread from him. "They'll have time enough," he said grimly. "Ye'll be weatherbound for days, unless I've mislaid my knowledge. By tomorrow I myself wouldn't dare try to fetch ye. How long? Who can foresee? Could be as much as a sennight. Lir brews a terrible brew this now, off in mid-Ocean."

Her calm was unbroken. "I can abide. You saw how I brought ample supplies." She smiled. "And writing materials, and my best loved books."

The lookout in the bows yelled. Maeloch excused himself, left her the blanket, went forward to peer. Water churned and roared. "Aye, Grampus Rock," he said. "We've drifted south off course." He hastened aft and took the steering oar from Usun.

Time passed. Rowing into the heavy seas, men were exhausted when they reached Sena, slipped in through the last treacheries, and made fast at the dock. Nonetheless they unloaded Queen Bodilis's baggage for her.

"I wish I could carry it up to the house, my lady," Maeloch said.

"You're sweet," she replied. "But 'tis only permitted me." Neither spoke of the night when Gratillonius went ashore in search of Dahilis, and cut Dahut free of her dead mother.

"Well, have a care," he rumbled awkwardly. His look sought the small, foursquare building of dry-laid stone, and its turret. "Stay inside if the wind rises much more. Remember, gales ha' been known to drive waves clear across this isle."

Anxiety touched her. "'Tis you and your friends who'll be imperilled. Should you really not go home at once, and wait till 'tis safe to leave for Hivernia?" She was among the few to whom Vindilis had confided the plan.

He shook his wool-draped head. "Nay. After this blows itself out, belike the waters 'ull be too roiled for days, amongst our reefs, for

723

setting forth from Ys. I'll give the lads an hour or two of rest here, then we'll snake free of the skerry ground and hoist sail. Once we've proper sea room, we can ride out whatever Lir may whistle up, and be on our way as soon as we can make any northing at all."

"You speak overboldly."

"No disrespect. Lir be Lir. But I be a man. He knows it."

"You are very brave, though, to hasten thus on your mission."

He seemed abashed. "'Tis important," he mumbled. "For Ys and, and your Sister, little Dahut."

"Go you, then, to learn what you can, for her sake," Bodilis said as quietly as the noise allowed. "And I will be praying for her."

He looked beyond, to the desolation of stone, harsh grass, distorted bushes, flung coils of kelp that stretched away at her back. "'Tis ye be the brave one," he said, "alone in the sea with the hairy star."

Bodilis gave him her hand. "Farewell, Maeloch."

"Fare ye ever well, my lady." He turned and stumped back to his vessel.

Bodilis carried her things piecemeal to the house and unpacked them. By the time she was through, *Osprey* had cast off. She stood watching the hull toil away northward until it was lost to sight.

XIX

~ 1 ~

Gratillonius drew rein at the grave of Eppillus, saluted, and looked ahead, down the long slope of Point Vanis to Ys.

It stood against the mass of Cape Rach like a dream. A haze of wind-blown spume and low-flying cloud grayed the wall, blurred roofs, made towertops shimmer and flicker as if they would be the pharos flame which could not burn tonight. Ocean raged, almost white save in the abyssal wave-troughs, crests so high that they did not break over most of the reefs, for it had buried them. It erupted against the mainland in bursts that climbed the cliffs, with shocks that Gratillonius thought he could feel through the earth. Wind was an elemental force out of the west. It thrust and clawed; to keep the saddle was a wrestling. The cry and the cold of it filled his bones.

This would be a night to house at home. His men were lucky to have arrived when they did. The blast had been strengthening throughout this day. Soon they would have had no choice but to take what shelter they could find and wait it out.

Gratillonius's gaze travelled left into the vale. The Wood of the King surged under the storm, a black lake foamed with early green. He supposed that was where he would be. This was the first of those three days when the moon was reckoned full. Having missed his last Watch, and afterward the equinoctial Council, he'd likely be wise to observe immediately the law by which he reigned.

No, first he had other, more real duties. He signalled the command that his legionaries could not have heard if he voiced it, and proceeded along Redonian Way. Wearily but happily, they took formation and followed him on the double. Their pack beasts lurched behind. Favonius snorted, curvetted, shied and then plunged, made wild by the weather. Barely could Gratillonius restrain him. What a grand animal he was!

It would have been quickest to enter at Northbridge, but spray was driving over it. Also, the King's first errand was to the palace, which lay nearer High Gate. Swinging around the eastern side, the travelers entered the lee of the city wall. Strong and ruddy it stood; Caesar's builder's had wrought well for Brennilis. But on the far side the old Gods, the angry Gods came riding from the sea.

Guards at the battlements had seen the party approach. Trumpets defied the wind. Men spilled out of barracks. The King of Ys entered between swords, pikes, and shouts uplifted in his honor.

It was quieter here, possible to talk without yelling, though air brawled and skirled while surf sent a deep drum-roll underneath. Gratillonius halted, brought the stallion around, signed to his legionaries. They clustered close, at ease, yet still bearing themselves in Roman wise. He smiled.

"Boys," he said, "we've had a tough trek, and I thank you for every mile. You are now relieved of duty. Take off your armor, go to your homes, and greet your families from me." He paused. "Your furlough will be permanent. You are overdue for discharge. I've been remiss about that, but your services were invaluable. In large part because of you, Ys is at peace, while prepared to deal with any future foes. Take your honorable retirement. Besides the usual veterans' benefits, we'll arrange a worthwhile bonus."

He was surprised to see Adminius, Cynan, several others stricken. "Sir, we don't want to quit," the deputy protested. "We'd sooner march with our centurion till our feet wear out."

Gratillonius's eyes stung. He swallowed. "You, you shouldn't nudge me like that," he said. "Let me think about this. At the very least, oh, those who want can continue in the honor guard on state occasions. I'll be proud of that. But you see, there's no longer any call for more. I don't think I'll be leading you away ever again."

He wheeled the horse and clattered off. At his back he heard, "Hail, centurion! Hail, centurion!" over and over.

The cheers died in the wind. Broken by walls, it whirled and leaped through streets, lanes, the crooked little alleys of Ys. Higher up, it streamed snarling around the towers. Air tasted of salt from the scud it bore along off the sea. The battering waves resounded louder as Gratillonius rode west.

Most folk had sought beneath their roofs. Nevertheless, Lir Way was not deserted. A fair number of people trudged toward the Forum, men, women, children. They were roughly though seldom poorly clad. Many carried bundles, some pushed barrows laden with simple goods. Gratillonius recognized certain among them. They were workers from the shops outside, countryfolk off the heights beyond, fishers out of Scot's Landing, and their households. They knew him in their turn, stared at the man with the white-shot auburn beard atop his tall steed, sometimes waved and shouted. "The King, the King, the King's come home!"

Gratillonius lifted an arm in acknowledgment. This was good to see. If the storm got much worse, they would have been in danger. The cottages under Cape Rach might actually be washed away. It had happened in the past. Somebody had had the foresight to organize evacuation of such persons into the city, and they were going to spread their pallets in public buildings. Who had the someone been? Bodilis— no, she'd have thought of the need, but lacked skill in leadership. Lanarvilis, likeliest, quite possibly assisted by Soren. If so, he must thank them. Could that, the concern for Ys they shared with him, begin a healing of the breach?

He left the avenue. As he climbed, the wind grabbed fiercer. His cloak flapped crazily, though he gripped it close. The city revealed itself as pinnacles in a cauldron of blown mist. Behind reddening, ragged clouds, the sun slipped close to worldedge. Its light glimmered off furious whiteness. Sena was hidden.

No guards stood at the palace gate. Well, it would have been useless cruelty to post them. Gratillonius dismounted, worked the bolt, led Favonius through and tethered the stallion to a tree. Its topiary was mangled. The garden lay a ruin, flowerbeds drowned, shrubbery twisted or flattened, shell scattered off paths. Gilt was stripped from the eagle on the dome. Gratillonius couldn't be sure in the waning light, but he thought a bronze wing had been wrenched out of shape.

Windows were shuttered. However, the staff must be inside. Gratillonius mounted the steps and banged the great knocker. Again and again and again...like a challenger at the Wood who did not know that the King lay dead.... They heard at last. The door opened. Light poured out into the wind.

"My lord!" exclaimed the majordomo. "'Tis you! Come in, sir, do. Welcome home." He forgot the dignity of his position and whooped: "The King is back!"

Gratillonius passed through. As the door shut, he found himself swaddled in warmth and brightness. The racket outside became an undertone. "I'm here to fetch the Key," he said, "then I go onward."

726

"But, my lord," the majordomo wailed, "you've had such a long journey, and my lady has been anxious—"

Gratillonius brushed past. The atrium spread before him, pillars and panels agleam in a star-field of candles. Across the charioteers in the floor sped Tambilis.

He could only stand and await her. She ran heavily, burdened with the unborn child. Her gown was plain gray wool, her feet merely slippered. The brown hair tumbled from a fillet of carved ivory which had more color than her face. She fell into his arms and wept.

He held her and murmured. "Be at ease, darling, at ease, I'm back safe and sound, everything went well, better than we hoped—" She clutched him painfully hard and shuddered.

After a while, under his strokings, she regained some control. Head still nestled in the curve of his left shoulder, she mumbled through sobs, "I've been so frightened...for you, Grallon. I had to w-w-warn you. Mother would have, but she's...on the island... praying for us all."

Alarm jangled through him. "What's this?" he snapped. "Why are you here?"

She disengaged herself. Her hands groped after his until he took them. Blinking, sniffling, she said in a small voice, "I moved hither a few days ago. I knew you'd seek the palace first, so belike I could tell you, put you on your guard, ere something bad happened. If n-n-naught else, while I was here, no more horrible feasts would be. What if you'd come home to one?"

His tone was flat in his hearing. "Well, tell me."

She gathered her will and cast the news forth: "A Scotic warrior dwells with Dahut. She gave a celebration in his honor, in this your house. They say 'twas as wild a revel as ever Ys has known. She and the man go freely about together. But she'll speak to none of us, her Sisters, nor does she seek the Temple or any of her duties. We know not what they intend, those two. Thus far he has kept from the Wood. They have claimed he's a chieftain who's searching out our markets, for trade. Or Dahut has. Niall japes and tells stories and sings songs but says never a meaningful thing. And he lives in her home."

Gratillonius had seen men smitten in combat stand moveless a while, trying to comprehend what had happened to them. Likewise did he respond: "Nay, this cannot be. Dahut could not defile herself. She is daughter to Dahilis."

"Oh, she's declared the Scotian has a room of his own. Her servants are silent. 'Tis plain to see they're terrified. She's taken lodgings for those that used to live in, and sends everybody off at the end of each day's work. Grallon, I have seen the looks she gives him."

Momentarily and vaguely, he thought that this was to be expected, that it might even be the answer for which he had yearned. Let the girl be happy with a man she loved. Her father the King could protect them, steer them between the reefs of the law, win her freedom from the Sign of Belisama.

He saw how impossible that was, realized Dahut must know this just as well, and remembered Tommaltach, Carsa, and Budic—Budic.

"What is this fellow like?" he asked in the same dull fashion.

"Tall, strong, beautiful," Tambilis replied. Steadiness was rising in her. "I think, though, he's older than you by some years."

"So if he challenges me, I might well take him? That would not end the trouble, my dear. Only if he took me."

Terror cried: "You'll not give in to him!"

Gratillonius shrugged. "Not purposely. I have a strong wish for his blood, I suppose. Still, what if he does not challenge? We shall have to think about this."

Tears ran anew down the cheeks of Tambilis, but quietly. "Oh, poor hurt beloved. Come with me. I'll pour you wine till you can rest the night. Tomorrow—"

He shook his head. "I must be on my way. I came only to fetch the Key."

"The sea gate is already locked. Men carried Lir Captain down. Sea Lord Adruval Tyri helped him close the lock."

"Good." Adruval had always been a trusty friend. "Nonetheless, I want to see for myself. Afterward I have my Watch to stand in the Wood, for the next three nights and what's left of their days. For I am the King."

"I'll meet you there," she said with a ghost of eagerness.

Once more he shook his head. "Nay, I'd liefer be alone." Sensing the pain in her, he added: "Tomorrow also. Besides, you ought not carry our little princess out into this weather. It should have slacked off by the third day. Come to me then."

She tried to laugh. "'Twould need the Gods Themselves to keep me away."

He kissed her, tasting salt, and went onward. The Key was in a casket in his bedroom. By the light of a candle he had brought along, he stared down at its iron length. Why was he taking it? The gate was properly shut.

But this was the emblem and embodiment of his Kingship. He hung it around his neck, letting it dangle from the chain on the breast of his Roman mail. It felt heavy as the world.

Tambilis stood mute, fists clenched, and watched him go out the door. Favonius whickered and stamped. The sun was set and dusk blowing in against the wind. Gratillonius loosened the tether and swung to the saddle. Hoofbeats clopped.

At a ring in the wall beneath the Raven Tower, he resecured his mount before he climbed those stairs. The storm screamed and smote. Surf bellowed. Here he could indeed feel its impact, up the stones and his body to the skull. Through a bitter haze of spindrift he made out the water, livid, and the western sky, the hue of a bruise.

Light gleamed weakly from a slit window. The sentries had taken refuge in the turret. Gratillonius passed by unseen, on along the top of the wall. War engine housings crouched, blurred to his sight, in the salt rain that drenched his clothes.

The harbor basin sheened uneasy. Metal-sheathed timber trembled to the battering of waves as he picked his way down the stair to the walk. Often he heard a boom louder yet, when a float dashed against the rampart. Yon spheres might want replacement later, he thought. The huge timber that was the bar creaked in its bracket. But the chain held it firm, and the lock held the chain. The sea gate of Ys stood fast.

Gratillonius wondered why he had come, when Tambilis had assured him there was no need. Something to fill an hour? He'd better be off. Darkness was deepening and the wind rising further.

On his return, a monster billow nearly came over the parapet. Water spurted across him. He stumbled, and recovered by slapping hands onto the tower. It too stood fast, above the crypt of Mithras. Should he descend and offer a prayer? No, if nothing else, that would be unkind to Favonius; and Mithras seemed remote, almost unreal, on this night.

Did Dahut sleep gladly at the side of her man?

Gratillonius hastened back to the pomoerium. He urged Favonius to a trot, and a gallop once they were on Lir Way. It was wholly deserted now. The buildings around the Forum loomed like giant dolmens—though did a window shine in the Christian church? The Fire Fountain brimmed with water, which the wind ruffled.

The moon had cleared the eastern hills. Towertop glass shone blank. Gratillonius fled on through the phantom city.

Out High Gate he went, onto Aquilonian Way, thence to Processional Way. The canal bridge rang beneath hoofs. The stream ran thickly, white with moonlight. The road bent eastward from the sea, toward the Wood. Nearing, Gratillonius heard boughs grind as the gale rushed among them. Like a second moon, the Shield swayed from the Challenge Oak, above dappled flagstones. It toned when the Hammer clashed on it.

Gratillonius dismounted and beat on the door of the Red Lodge till the staff roused. He himself led Favonius to the stable, unsaddled the stallion, rubbed him down; but he let the men bring hay, grain, and water. When they spoke of preparing a meal for him he said curtly that he wanted nothing but a crock of wine to take to his bedchamber.

There, after an hour alone, he could weep.

~ 2 ~

Still the wind mounted. By dawn it was like none that chronicles remembered. And still it mounted.

No one went forth. Even in the streets, air rammed to cast a man down, stun him with its roar as of the sky breaking asunder, choke and blind him in the spume that filled it. Glass and tiles fell from above, shattered, ripped loose, flung far before they struck. About the unseen noontide, upper levels of the tower called Polaris came apart. Metal, timbers, goods, and some human bodies flew hideously down to smash against whatever was below. The rest of the city endured, however strained and scarred. Oaken doors and shutters mostly clung to their hinges. Close-fitted dry masonry went unscathed. But the violence thrummed through, until every interior was a cavern of noise.

Northbridge Gate and Aurochs Gate were barred, for on those sides the sea thrust between rampart and headlands—higher yet, in those narrow clefts, than the billows from the west. Overrun again and again, the span on the north finally disintegrated. Water surged beneath the wall and broke into the canal, whose banks it gouged out to make a catchbasin for itself. The rock on the south side which shouldered against the wall of Ys was a barrier more solid, across which only the tops of the hugest breakers leaped. Nonetheless that portal also must stay shut; and because it had never been meant for this kind of attack, enough water got around it and under it that Goose Fair lay inches-deep submerged and Taranis Way became a shivering estuary for yards beyond.

Ebb brought scant relief, when the seas had such a wind behind them. At high tide, crests smashed just below the western battlements; jets sprang white above, like fingers crooked in agony; at once they shredded into spray and blew over Ys.

Yet the gate held.

Dahut and Niall were alone in her house. None of the servants she dismissed the evening before had dared return. It was cold; fires were out, and he cautioned against lighting any. It was dark; a single candle flame smoked in the bedchamber, where they had sought the refuge of blankets. It was drumful of tumult.

Dahut trembled close against the man. "Hold me," she begged. "If we must die, I want it to be in your arms."

He kissed her. "Be of good heart, darling," he said, his own voice level. "Your wall stands."

"For how long?"

"Long enough, I do believe. A wind like this cannot go on as a breeze might. It will soon be dropping, you mark my words."

"Will it die down at once?"

Niall frowned above her head. "It will not that, either. It will remain a gale through this night, surely. And the waves it has raised, they will be slower than it to dwindle. But if rath and doors have withstood thus far, they should last until the end."

"Thank you, beloved," Dahut breathed. She sat up, cast off the covers, knelt on the mattress. Her hair and her nakedness shone in the dimness. She looked to the niche where stood her Belisama image, the lustful huntress that she alone of the Nine cared to have watching over her. "And thank you, Maiden, Mother, and Witch," she called softly. "For Your mercies and Your promise that You will fulfill—through us twain here before You—our thanks, our prayers, our sacrifice."

She glanced at Niall, who had stayed reclining, pillow-propped against the headboard. "Won't you give thanks too?" she asked. "At least to Lir and Taranis."

Through the dusk she saw his visage grim. "For our deliverance? The Three have brought Grallon back just at this time. Is the tempest also Their work? Does Ys stand off the Gods Themselves?"

She lifted her hands. Horror keened: "Say never so! Ys does abide." She caught her breath. "And, and soon we'll restore the law. Soon you, the new King, will give Them Their honor. They foresee it. They must!"

He likewise got to his knees. His bulk loomed over her, blocking sight of the candle. "I have been thinking on that, and more than thinking," he told her slowly. "Dreams have I sought by night and omens by day. For I am fosterling of a poet, stepson of a witch, patron of druids, and myself descended from the Gods of Ériu. Much have I seen and much have I learned. Insights are mine that no lesser King may know. In me is fate."

She stared. "What? You n-never said this. Oh, beloved, I could feel in my heart you...were more than you pretended—But what are you?"

"I am Niall of the Nine Hostages, King at Temir, conqueror of half the Scoti, scourge of Rome, and he whom your father most bitterly wronged ere ever you were born."

Dahut cast herself down before him. "Glorious, glorious!" she cried brokenly. "Lir Himself brought you to me!"

Niall laid a hand on her head. "Now you have heard."

"It whelms me, lord of mine—oh—"

"It could be the death of me, did news get about too soon."

"My tongue is locked like the sea gate." Dahut rose to a crouch. Hair had tumbled over her eyes. She gazed through it, up at his massive murkiness. "But once you're King in Ys, we're safe, we're free." Joy stormed through her voice. "You'll be sacred! Together we'll beget the new Age—the Empire of the North—"

"Hold," he commanded.

Again she knelt, arms crossed over bosom against the cold, and waited. The wind wuthered, the sea thundered.

"Sure, and that's a vaunting vision," he said, stern as a centurion. "But ofttimes have the Gods given men their finest hopes, then dashed them to shards on the ground. Grallon follows his soldier God; and who shall foreknow whether Mithras proves stronger than the Mórrigu? Grallon is a Roman, living out of his proper time, a Roman of the old iron breed that carried its eagles from end to end of the world. He and his like cast me bloodily back at the Wall in Britannia. He and his schemes wrecked my fleet, slaughtered my men, and killed my son at the wall of Ys. Well could it happen that his sword fells myself in the Wood."

"Nay, Niall, heart of mine, nay!" She groped for him.

He pushed her back. "Your earlier lovers came to grief. Will you be sending me to the same?"

She flinched. He pursued: "You'll get no further chance after I am dead. You've made your desire all too clear. Grallon can be fond and foolish no longer. What do they do in Ys with unchaste Queens? Throw them off the cliffs?"

Dahut straightened. "But you will win! And then naught else will count. Because you'll be the King of Ys."

"Your wish spoke there," he said bleakly. "My insight has told me otherwise."

"Nay—"

He reached to lay a palm over her mouth. "Quiet, lass. I know what you'd say. If I despair, I can still escape. Sure, and 'tis dear of you. But could I be leaving my love to a cruel death, and name myself a man?

"Hark'ee. There is a hope. I have seen it in the flash of a blade, I have heard it in the croak of a raven, I have understood it in the depths of a dream.

"The King of Ys bears on his breast the Key of Ys. It is more than a sigil. It is the Kingship's very self. Behold how Heaven and Ocean cannot open the sea gate. That power lies with him."

"But Kings die," she quavered.

He nodded. "They do. And the power passes onward. It is mostly small. How often must the gate be barred and locked? A few times a year, for caution's sake. Sailors who ken wind and tide spend no great strength at their work. Nor do the Gods, keeping the world on its course—most of the time.

"Tonight, though, the sea beleaguers Ys. It hammers on the shield of the city. Power must needs blaze within the Key, the Key that stands for the life of your people.

"While this is true, the bearer is invincible. Were I or any man to go now against Grallon, he would prevail.

"Hush. Bide a moment. I cannot wait till the need is past and the power that is in the Key has faded. Tremendous seas will be crashing on wall and gate for days to come. Meanwhile the wind will have slacked and folk can move abroad. Grallon will seek me out. He must. Think. If I do not challenge him, he will challenge me. He is the King; he may do this, the more so if he claims he's exacting justice. And there will be no stopping him. For 'twill not be for his own peace or safety. 'Twill be on your account, Dahut, you, his daughter. He'll hope that having killed me, he can win clemency for you—blame the dead man for leading you astray—though because he is not really a fool, Dahut, never again will you have the liberty to work for his death.

"So it is."

She shook her head, bewildered. "The Sisters never taught me this."

"Did they teach you everything the Gods might ever reveal?"

She was mute, until: "What can we do?"

Teeth gleamed in the night-mask of his face. "If *I* bore the Key, the power would be mine. I could call him forth ere his Watch is ended, and slay him in the Wood."

"But—"

He leaned forward and took her by the shoulders. "You can do it for me, Dahut," he said. "You've told me how you can cast a sleep spell, how you did at the Red Lodge itself. This time you need not rouse him. Only steal in, lift the chain of the Key from off his neck, and carry the thing to me."

"Oh, nay," she pleaded.

"Would you liefer I die at his hands?"

"The Gallicenae have a second Key. They'll lend it to him."

Niall laughed. "Then at worst, we meet on equal ground, Grallon and I. Gladly will I that. Even so, puzzlement and surprise ought to have shaken him."

Dahut covered her face. "Sacrilege."

"When you are the Chosen of the Chosen?"

She cowered.

His sigh was as cold as the wind: "Very well. I thought you loved me, Emer to my Cú Culanni. I thought you had the faith and the courage to fare beside your man. Since you do not, I may honorably go from Ys in the morning. Meanwhile I shan't trouble you."

He swung his legs around and stood up.

"Niall, nay!" she screamed, and scrambled after him. He caught her before she went to the floor. "I will, I will!"

~ 3 ~

By sunset the wind had indeed lessened. It was still such as few could travel in, but along the Armorican seaboard it had wrought the harm of its full rage. There remained its malevolence.

Clouds blew thicker. Guards had resumed their posts, with frequent relief; but the moonlight was so fitful that the night watch did not see the two who slipped out through High Gate.

The going was treacherous at first. Workshops and stables beyond the wall had littered ruin over Aquilonian Way. Nails and splinters lurked for those who must climb across. More than once, Niall's strong hand saved Dahut from falling.

After they reached Processional Way they had a clear path save for torn-off boughs. The bridge across the canal survived. To the left, light flickered across water that chopped a foot or more deep under the rampart. It had not drained back into the sea, for even at ebb, waves boomed in through the gap between city and headland. On the right the amphitheater glimmered ghostly, the Wood of the King hulked altogether black. Farther on were gulfs of darkness. The moon hurtled among clouds which it touched with ice. When the road turned east and the walkers left the lee of Ys behind them, they felt the wind on their backs as an oncoming assault. It hooted and yammered. Louder, now, was the roar of Ocean.

Near the Wood, that sound was matched by the storm through the trees. Their groans were an undertone to its wails. Some along the edge lay uprooted, limbs clawing at heaven. Pieces broken off the Challenge Oak bestrewed the court. The Shield tolled insanely to the swinging of the Hammer. When a moonbeam reached earth, the metal shone dulled by the dents beaten into it.

Otherwise the Sacred Precinct had protection. The three buildings squatted intact, lightless. As Dahut came between them, a neigh burst from one, and again and again.

"Be quick ere that brute wakes the whole house," Niall snapped.

Dahut raised her arms. The moon saw her attired in the blue gown and high white headdress of the Gallicenae. Her chant cut through soughing and creaking. *"Ya Am-Ishtar, ya Baalim, ga'a vi khuwa—"*

Niall felt for the sword scabbarded across his back. At once aware of what he did, he dropped his hand. Its fingers closed on the haft of his knife.

"Aus-t ur-t-Mut-Resi, am 'm user-t—"

Niall made a wolf-grin.

"Belisama, Mother of Dreams, bring sleep unto them, send Your blind son to darken their minds and Your daughter whose feet are the feet of a cat to lead forth their spirits—"

The horse had fallen silent.

Presently Dahut did also. She turned to Niall. Moonlit, her face was as pale as the windings above it. He barely heard her amidst the noise: "They will slumber till dawn, unless powerfully roused. But come, best we be swift."

"We?" he answered. "Nay, go you in alone. I might blunder and make that awakening racket. You know your way about your father's lair."

She shivered, caught her lip between her teeth, but moved ahead. He accompanied her onto the porch. At the entrance he drew blade and took stance.

Dahut opened the door enough to get through. It was never barred, in token of the King's readiness to kill or be killed. She entered, closed it behind her, poised breathless.

Coals banked in the fire-trenches gave some warmth; shelter from the wind meant more. That sullen glow revealed little, but a lamp burned lonely. It had served two men slumped at a table, heads on arms. Other must already have been asleep on the benches along the walls. The light straggled forth, discovering among glooms only the ragged lower ends of battle banners, the scorn on two of the idol-pillars upholding the roof.

Dahut straightened and glided forward to the interior partition. Seeing its door ajar, she peered around the jamb. The corridor beyond was not quite a blindness. Windows were shuttered, and the moon would have given scant help anyhow, but a dim luminance, reflected off tile floor and plaster walls of this Roman half of the building, sufficed. She moved on, smoke-silent, though the storm would surely have covered any footfalls.

The door to Gratillonius's room stood open. Thence came the radiance of seven candles in a brass holder on a table at his bedside. He had been reading; a book lay on the blankets. She knew not whether her spell had ended that or he had earlier fallen into a sleep which she made profound. Between his grief at learning of her conduct—he must have heard, with Tambilis waiting meddlesome in the palace—and the tumult this day, he could have had scant rest or none until now.

Dahut stalked to the bedside and regarded him. She recognized his book. Bodilis had forced her to study it: the *Meditations* of Marcus Aurelius in Latin translation. An arm and both shoulders were bare outside the King's blankets. Doubtless he was naked, as he had been the night she came here to deceive him into making her his.

She sighed.

He did not appear helpless as most sleepers do. His features were too rugged. The mouth had not softened, nor the brow eased. But how weary he seemed, weary beyond uttering, furrows plowed deep, gray sprinkled over the ruddiness of his hair and streaked down his beard.

His neck remained a column smooth and thick, firmly rooted in heavy shoulders and barrel chest. Around it sparkled a fine golden chain. Blankets hid the lower part.

Dahut's breath quickened. She clenched fists and teeth.

Resolution returned. She bent above the King. Gently as a mother with a babe, she slipped a hand beneath his head and raised it off the pillow. Her other hand went under the covers, over the rising and falling shagginess to the iron shank. She slid the Key forth into her sight. The chain she passed above his head until it encircled her supporting arm. She lowered him back onto the pillow and waited tensely.

His eyes moved beneath the lids. His lips formed a whisper. He mumbled and stirred. Dahut waved her free hand over him. He quieted. She saw him breathe, but the wind smothered the sound.

She gave him a brief archaic smile and departed.

Through the hall she went, with a gait that grew confident until it was a stride. She passed out the door and shut it behind her as if she struck down an enemy. Niall backed off, startled in the gloom. She pursued, swung the Key, made it ring against his sword.

"You have it?" he asked hoarsely. "Let's away."

They stopped when they got to the road and could see better. The moon threw harried light upon them and the thing she reached to hang around his neck. Her arms followed.

He made her end the kiss. "Back we go, at once," he declared.

Dahut's laughter pealed. "Aye. Make haste. I'm afire!"

—In her bed, after their first fierce passage of love, she asked, "Tomorrow morning will you challenge him?"

"That might be shrewd," Niall said into the warmth and silkiness and musk of her.

"Catch him amazed, uncertain." She squirmed and burrowed against him. "Tomorrow night will be our wedding night."

"Grant me some hours of rest first," he requested with a leer.

"Not yet," she purred. Her lips and fingers moved greedily. "I want your weight on me again. I want to feel the Key cold between my breasts while you are a torch between my thighs. Oh, Niall, death itself cannot quench my wanting of you."

The wind keened, the sea rumbled.

~ **4** ~

Corentinus woke.

For a moment he lay motionless. His room was savagely cold. Through a smokehole knocked out of the wall under the ceiling for his cookfire, he heard the storm. A nightlight, tallow candle in a wooden holder, guttered and stank. He did not ordinarily keep such a thing, but at a time when woe might fall on his people without warning, he must be ready. It barely revealed his few rough articles of furniture. The depths of the chamber were lost in night. Once the temple treasury, it was much too big for a servant of Christ.

Corentinus's eyes bulged upward. Air went jagged between his teeth. It came back out in an animal moan.

"O dear God, no!" he begged. "Mercy, mercy! Let this be a nightmare. Let it be only Satan's work."

Decision came. He tossed off his one blanket and rose from his pallet on the floor. Snatching a robe from a peg, he pulled it over his lanky frame. Without pausing to bind on sandals, he took the candle, tucked his staff under an arm, and left.

The hallway led to the vestibule. Another small flame showed it crowded. Folk sprawled asleep, refugees from outside the city. Corentinus had admitted any who could not find better quarters, without inquiring as to their beliefs, and arranged for food and water and chamber pots. He made his way among the bodies to the inner door, opened it, and entered the sanctuary.

When he closed it off, he found himself in still more of an emptiness than his room. This section occupied a good half of what had been the temple of Mars, before Roman pressure brought conversion to the sole church in Ys. Little was in it other than the canopied altar block

736

and a couple of seats. The cross on the altar glimmered athwart shadows. The pagan reliefs along the walls were lost to sight.

Corentinus lowered candle and staff, raised his arms before the cross, and chanted the Lord's prayer. It echoed hollowly. He laid himself prostrate on the floor. "Almighty God," he said against its hardness, "forgive a thick-headed old sailor man. I wouldn't question Your word. Never. But was that dream from You? It was so terrible. And so darkling. I don't understand it, I honestly don't."

Here within the stone, silence abided.

Corentinus climbed back onto his feet. He lifted his arms anew. "Well, maybe You'll tell me more when I've obeyed Your first order," he said. "If it did come from You. A dunderhead like me can't be sure. But I'll do what the angel bade me, supposing it was a true angel. Doesn't seem too likely it was a devil like the one that tried to trick Bishop Martinus, because I don't see any real harm in this deed. Forgive me my wonderment, Lord. I'll do my best."

He gathered staff and candle. As he reached the door, he shuddered. With an effort, he opened it and re-entered the vestibule.

A woman had roused to nurse her infant. She saw the tall form and called softly, anxiously, "Is aught wrong, master?"

Corentinus halted.

"Please tell me, master," the woman said. "We don't serve your God, but we are in His house and ours are wrathful."

Thoughts tumbled through him. He could wake these people and bring them, at least, with him. But no. It wasn't that they were heathen, his small flock being scattered about the city. They were nonetheless God's wayward children. But they were the merest handful among unreachable thousands. Worse, he did not know what it was that would stalk them this night.

"Peace, my daughter," he said. "Calm your fears. You are the guest of Christ."

He blew his candle out. The wind would immediately have killed it. As poor as his congregation was, he economized wherever he could. He went out the main door, over the portico, down the stairs, across the Forum.

Wind still howled and smote. Air was still bitter with salt and cold. The gale had, though, dwindled enough that the crashing of the sea against the city wall came louder. Clouds flew low, blackening heaven, hooding towertops. The moon streamed just above western roofs. By its flickery pallor Corentinus hastened, up Lir Way toward High Gate and the Wood of the King.

~ 5 ~

After Dahut was sunken in sleep, Niall left her bed. Cautiously he put on the warm clothes he had worn earlier and flung aside when he and she returned here. The sword he hung across his back. At his left hip he belted a purse of coins, thinking wryly that it balanced the dagger on the right in more ways than one. Gesocribate was about two days distant for an active man afoot. Could he not buy food along the way he'd arrive hungry, unless he came upon a sheep or something like that and butchered it. However, if need be he could turn a deaf ear to the growls in his belly. There would be celebration at journey's end!

Or would there? His scheme might fail; he might himself perish— if the Gods of Ys were, in truth, less than death-angry with Their worshippers.

Niall bared teeth. Whatever came, *his* Gods would know he had ventured that which Cú Culanni might not have dared.

On an impulse he stepped to the bedside and looked down. Candle-light lost itself in the amber of Dahut's tousled hair. She lay on her back, arms widespread. A young breast rose out of the blankets. From the rosiness at its peak a vein ran blue, spiderweb-fine, down an ivory curve marred by a beginning bruise where he had caressed it too strongly. Wild, she had never noticed. Now the pulse at the base of her throat beat slow and gentle. Her lips were slightly parted. How long were the lashes reaching toward those high cheekbones. When he bent low, he sensed warmth radiating from her. She smelled of sweat and sweetness. The crescent of the Goddess glowed.

Almost, he kissed her. A stirring went through his loins. He pulled himself back barely in time, straightened, but did not go at once.

Gazing at her, he said very low in the tongue of Ériu:

"It's sad I am to be leaving you, my darling, for darling you were, a woman like none other, and you loved me as never I was loved before nor hope ever to be again. I think you will haunt me until I join you in death.

"But it must be, Dahut. I came here sworn to vengeance. I may not break my oath, nor would I; for Ys killed the son that Ethniu gave me, long and long ago. Yet sad I am that your Gods chose you for the instrument.

"How could you believe I would make myself King of Ys? Oh, it's mad with love you were, to believe that. I am the King at Temir, and I will go home to my own.

"Should I bind myself to this city I hate? Sure, and I would first have slain Grallon. But he was not alone in bringing doom on my good men. All Ys did, foremost its nine witch-Queens.

"Let me become its King, and I doubt such a chance as is mine tonight would ever wing its way back. In the end I too would fall, not grandly among my warriors, but alone in the Wood of slaughter; and from my blood Ys would suck new life. It shall not happen, not to me nor ever again to anyone else.

"I too will seek Grallon, where he lies in the slumber you cast upon him. I stayed my hand then, for you might have screamed. My first duty is against Ys. Afterward, if the Gods spare me—oh, it will go hard to kill a man in his sleep. I thought of waking him. But that would make a challenge fight, and though Ys be gone, what hold might its Gods yet keep on me? Let me go free.

"You wish to be my wife, Dahut. It's glorious you are; but so in her youth was Mongfind. Should I take for wife a woman who plotted the death of her father?

"As for the rest, two are also comely, though second and third behind you. But the second would bear a horror of me; when I embraced her, she would lie like a corpse and send her soul afar. The third is a sorceress who helped bring death to dear Breccan. Should I take to me the murderess of my son? So are the rest, apart from the cripple; and they are crones.

"Let them die, let the Sign come on fresh maidens, and still the Nine would be the only women I could have; and not a one of them would be giving me another son.

"Your Ys, all Ys is the enemy I am vowed to destroy. This night, the lady at my side is the Mórrigu.

"Farewell, Dahut."

He lifted the Key that hung on his breast and kissed its iron.

He departed.

Wind struck him with blades that sang. Seen from the doorway, the city was a well of blackness out of which lifted barely glimpsed spears, its towers. The horns of land hunched brutal. Beyond ramped the sea, white under the sinking, cloud-hunted moon.

When he loped downward, houses soon blocked that sight from him. He was a tracker, though, who had quickly learned every trail he wanted and had scant need of light.

The streets twisted to Lir Way. Crossing the empty Forum, he saw the Fire Fountain brimful of shivery water, flung off waves whose hammering resounded louder for each pace he took. He threw a gibe at the stately buildings of the Romans, at the church of Christ.

When he left the avenue, the streets grew more narrow and mazed than those where the wealthy dwelt. He was in Lowtown, ancestral Ys which Brennilis had saved. Behind the sheerness of a tower—clouds raced moon-tinged, making it seem to topple on him—he found the moldering houses of the Fishtail. The life that throbbed in them had drawn into itself, the quarter lay lightless, none save he and the wind ran through its lanes. He glimpsed a cat in a doorway. Its baleful gaze followed him out of sight.

Nearing the rampart, he entered a quarter likewise ancient and poor, but a place for working folk. Among these dwellings he came by the Shrine of Ishtar. Awed in spite of himself, he stopped for an instant and lifted the Key before the dolmenlike mass. Let Her within see that he went to wreak justice.

A little farther, he had the Cornmarket on his right. Its paving sheened wet. On his left a row of warehouses fronted on the harbor.

Between them he spied the basin. Ahead reared the city wall. Self-shadowed, the monstrous bulk stood like a piece cut out of heaven. Over and over, sheets of foam spurted to limn its battlements. The rush and crash trampled the sounds of gale.

Niall advanced. At the inside edge of the pomoerium stood the Temple of Lir, small, dark, deserted, but the rudeness and mass of its stones bespeaking a strength implacable. Again Niall halted and raised the Key. "Though this house of Yours fall, You will abide," he said into the roaring. "Come seek me in Ériu. You shall have Your honors in overflowing measure, blood, fire, wine, gold, praise; for we are kindred, You and I."

Just the same, he dared not enter the unlocked fane. Besides, he should hasten. Dawn was not far off.

Drawing his sword, knife in his left hand, he slipped up the staircase to the wall top. The Gull Tower reared ahead. Moonlight came and went over its battlements and the parapet beneath. Each time a wave broke against the rampart, spray sleeted; and the impact was deafening.

This was a guard point. Was a sentry outside, or did the whole watch shelter within the turret? Niall crouched low and padded forward.

Light shone from slit windows. The door was shut. In front of it did stand an Ysan marine. While the tower blocked off wind and water, he was drenched, chilled, miserable. He stood hunched into his cloak, helmeted head lowered, stiffened fingers of both hands clutching his pikeshaft.

He must die unbeknownst to his comrades.

Niall squatted under a merlon. The next great wave struck and flung its cloud. He leaped with it, out of the whiteness, and hewed.

Himself half blinded, he misgauged. His sword clanged and glided off the helmet. The young man whirled about. Before he could utter more than a croak, Niall was at him. The Scotian had let his sword fall. His right arm went under the guard's chin and snapped the head back. His left drove dagger into throat and slashed.

The pike clattered loose. Blood spouted. Niall shoved. The sentry toppled over the inner parapet, down to the basin. Night hid the splash. His armor would sink him.

Niall retrieved his sword. Had the rest heard?

They had not.

He wiped dagger on kilt, sheathed both weapons, and trotted onward. The sea showered him, washing away blood.

Above the northern edge of the gate, he stopped and looked. As if to aid him, for that instant the surf was lower and clouds parted from before the moon.

On his left gleamed, faintly, the arc of the harbor. Its water was troubled; he saw vessels chafe at their moorings along the wharf. Yet wall and gate kept it safe, as they had done these past four centuries.

Behind reached Ys, mostly a cave of night but its towers proud in the moonlight. Cape Rach, Point Vanis, the inland vale were dream-dim.

On his right heaved Ocean. Wind, still a howl and a spear, had in the fullness of its violence piled up seas which would not damp out for days; and as Niall stood above, the spring tide was at its height. Skerries lay drowned underneath, until time should resurrect them to destroy more ships. A few rocks thrust above the relentlessness out of the west. Each time a wave smote them, they vanished in chaos.

The sea was not black but white, white as the breasts of Dahut. A billow afar growled like the drums of an oncoming army. As it drew closer, gathered speed, lifted and lifted its smoking crest, the breaker's voice became such thunder as rolls across the vault of heaven. When it struck and shattered, the sound was as of doomsday.

Niall shaded his eyes and squinted. He sought for the floats that on ebb tide drew open the doors. There, he had found the nearer of them. It dashed to and fro at the end of its chain, often hurled against the wall. Had that battered the sphere out of shape? He could not tell in the tricky light, through the flying spindrift. But neither one had cracked open and filled. They were too stoutly made.

Now and then the sea recoiled on itself. Suddenly emptiness was underneath the floats. They dropped. Chains rattled over blocks in sculptured cat's heads till they snapped the great balls to a halt. It was a wonder they had not broken; but they likewise were well wrought of old. The waves climbed anew and again the globes whirled upon them.

Niall smiled. All was as it should be.

He started down the inner stair. Below the wall there was shielding against wind and water, save for what flew across. However, the stone was slippery and the moon hidden. He kept a hand on the rail and felt his way most carefully.

The stairs ended at a ledge. In the dark he stumbled against the capstan there and cursed. He should have remembered. He had kept every sense whetted when Dahut showed him the system, as her father once showed her.

Well, the machine had naught to do with him. It was for forcing the gate shut if need arose at low tide. He groped past a huge jamb to the walk that ran across this door.

Copper sheathing was cold and slick beneath his right hand. His left felt along the rail that kept him from falling into the chop of the basin. Whenever the surf hit, the door trembled and he heard a groaning beneath the crash. But it held, it held.

Distance between rail and metal suddenly widened. He was past the walk, onto the platform at the inner edge of the door. He turned to the right. His fingers touched iron, a tremendous bracket, and inside it the roughness of the beam that latched the gate.

They found the chain that secured the bar.

They found the lock that closed the chain.

They took the Key and felt after the hole.

It seemed like forever while he fumbled blind. A horror was in him, that he would drop the Key, that it would skitter off and be lost in the harbor which the gate guarded. He forced the fear aside and continued seeking.

The Key entered. He felt it engage. He turned it and felt the pins click.

He withdrew the Key, unclasped the lock, cast it from him to sink. A moment he stood moveless: then, with a yell, flung the Key after it.

The chain slithered through his grasp. The bar was free.

It would not likely rise of itself, however much it and the portal that it held shivered beneath blows. Niall was not finished yet.

He made his way onward. The south door had its own platform, butting against that of the north door at their juncture. There was another bracket. Beyond it was the pivot on which the beam turned.

A light cable ran from the north end of the bar, through a block high on the south door, and down. When Niall reached its cleat, he bayed laughter. He knew what to do, as fully as if he could see.

He hauled on the line. The effort was small, so craftsmanly counterweighted was the timber. Through wind and sea, did he hear it creak while it rose?

Soon he could pull in no more, and knew the beam rested entirely against the south door, that the gate of Ys stood unbarred. Niall cleated the cable fast.

He hurried back over platforms and catwalk, up stairs, to the top of the wall.

Wildness greeted him. Let the floats haul the doors open just once, just part of the way. The tide would rush in. Striking from both sides, waves would rip the barriers from their hinges. Dry-laid, the wall of the city might fall to pieces. Surely a flood as high as Hightown would ride into Ys.

A wave smashed home. Its crest cataracted over Niall of the Nine Hostages. He stood fast. After the salt rain was over, he cupped hands around mouth and shouted seaward: "I have done what was my will. Now do You do what is Yours!"

He turned and ran, to get clear while the time remained.

~ 6 ~

Gratillonius woke inch by inch. In half-awareness he felt himself struggle heavily against it. He sank back toward nothingness. Before he had escaped, the drag recalled him. It was as if he were a fish, huge and sluggish, hooked where he had lain at the bottom of the sea. That was a strong fisherman who pulled him nearer and nearer the light above.

He broke surface. Radiance ravaged him. He plunged. His captor played him, denied him the deeps, compelled him to breathe air under open sky. On his second rising, he saw the gray-bearded craggy face. The sea lured him with its peace. He went below. That was briefly and shallowly. Once more he must ascend, and now he came altogether out.

Corentinus's hands were bony and hard, shaking him. "Rouse, rouse, man!" the pastor barked. "What's got into the lot of you? Lying like dead folk—" He noticed eyes blink. Stingingly, he slapped the King's cheeks, left and right.

Gratillonius sat up. Astonishment and anger flared. The fish burned away, and he was on earth, himself. "You! By Hercules—"

Corentinus stepped back and straightened. "Use your wits," he said. "Shake off that torpor. Get dressed. Help me kick the men awake. You're in bad danger, my friend."

Gratillonius drew rein on his temper. This fellow wouldn't come here on a midnight whim.

Midnight? What hour was it? Wind yowled and rattled shutters. The room was musty-cold. His candles guttered, stubs. So a long while had passed since he dropped off—at last, at last—into blessed Lethe. Darkness outside must be nearing an end.

"Tell me," he said.

Corentinus took his staff, which he had leaned against the wall. He clung to it and let it bear his weight, stared before him and answered low: "A vision. I saw a mighty angel come down from Heaven, clothed with a cloud, and a rainbow was upon his head; and his face was like the sun and his feet like pillars of fire. And seven thunders resounded while he cried, 'Woe to the city! For it shall perish by the sea, whose queen it was; and the saints shall mourn. But go you, servant of God, make haste to the King of the city, and call him forth ere his foeman find him, that he may live; for the world shall have need of him. It is spoken.'

"I came to myself with the voice and the brightness bewildering me still. I didn't understand—"

Abrupt tears ran from beneath the tufted brows, across the leathery hide. "I did-didn't know what it meant," Corentinus stammered. "Could it be a demon in me? Would God really...let His innocents die by the thousands, unhallowed? I went and prayed for a sign. Nothing, nothing came. I thought, I grabbed after the hope, that God wouldn't destroy Ys. Wicked men might, the way they destroyed Jerusalem. You could forestall them. The command was to go and warn *you*."

He swallowed before he finished in a steadier tone: "Maybe this is a trick of Satan. Or maybe I'm in my dotage. Well, there didn't seem to be much harm in going to you. At worst, you'd boot me out. At best, you may untangle the thing and do whatever's needful. Me, I'll help any way I can. And—" he laid hand over heart— "I'll be praying for a clear sign, and for Ys."

Gratillonius had listened frozen. He recoiled from prophecies and Gods, to immediacies a man could seize. "It's senseless," he snapped. "The weather's easing off. We won't take any more damage from it. As for enemies, none could possibly come by sea, and the land's secure at least as far as Treverorum. I know; I just traveled through."

The same practicality responded: "No army bound here, no. But a band of sneak murderers could use the storm for cover. Who? Well, what about vengeful Franks? There are men who might well secretly have egged them on."

"I doubt that. The orders of the praetorian prefect were strict." Gratillonius ran fingers through his hair. "In any case, I am alert now."

"Your attendants aren't," Corentinus reminded him. "Not a man on watch. They're sleeping like drugged hogs. I say let's pummel them out of it, and all of you take arms. Might be a good idea to lead them to town. Forget your wretched vigil. Leave this house of death."

Remembrance came back of another night. Gratillonius gaped. He swung himself out of bed. "We'd better get going." His glance fell on the Christian's bare feet. They bled from a score of slashes. "What happened to you?"

"High Gate's choked with wreckage. I stopped and told the guards they ought to clear it, because we might have sudden need of the road. But I couldn't wait for that, of course."

Gratillonius nodded. It was a command such as he would have given, were he not confined to this kennel. Need he be?

He went after his clothes. Something was missing. What? He felt at his chest. He choked on an oath, sprang about, scrabbled frantically in the bedding.

The Key was gone.

Faintness closed in on him.

It receded. "What's the matter?" Corentinus asked. "I thought you were about to drop."

Gratillonius snatched for his garments. "You wake the men," he tossed over his shoulder. "Follow me— No, best you stay. They aren't trained fighters. But they should be able to stand off an attack on the Lodge, if things come to that."

"Where are you bound?"

"Yonder's a lantern. Light it for me."

Corentinus's voice reached him as if across the breadth of Ocean. He sounded appalled. "The Key of Ys! I should have seen, but you keep that devil's thing hidden—"

"It may well be a devil's thing—now. I'm going after it."

"No! God's word is to save you. If Ys is to fall—"

"I told you to light me my lantern."

A shadow wavered before Gratillonius in the dimness. He turned. Corentinus had raised his staff. Gratillonius snarled. "Would you club me? Stand aside before I kill you."

744

Not troubling with undergarments, he had drawn on breeks, tunic, boots. His sword hung on the wall, from a belt which also supported knife and purse. He took it and secured the buckle.

"In Christ's name, old friend," Corentinus quavered, "I beg you, think."

"I am thinking," Gratillonius replied.

"What?"

"I don't know what. But it's too ghastly to sit still with."

Gratillonius opened the lantern and lighted its candle himself off a stub. On his way out he took a cloak from its peg.

Wind squalled, whined, bit. Its passage through the Wood made a noise like surf. The Challenge Oak creaked, the Shield rang. Right, left, and behind, night crouched around the frantic yellow circle of his light. The wood and the meadow beyond were gray under the beams of a moon he could not see but which tinged the bellies of clouds flying low overhead.

Heedless of fire hazard, he carried the lantern into the stable and set it down. Warmth enfolded him, odors of hay and grain and manure. For an instant Gratillonius was a boy again on his father's land.

Glow sheened off the coat of Favonius. The stallion should have pricked up ears and whickered. Instead he stood legs locked, head hung, breath deep and slow—asleep. "Hoy!" Gratillonius entered the stall and slapped the soft muzzle. The beast snorted, twitched, slumbered on.

How long had the Key been missing?

Gratillonius had not meant to waste time on a saddle. He changed his mind. His foot helped him tighten the cinch to its utmost. The bridle went on despite the awkward position of the head, and the mouth did not resist the bit, but opened slackly when he put thumbs to corners. He donned his cloak and shut its clasp before he released the tether.

Leaving the stall, he led the reins over its top and kept them in his left hand. His right drew blade. "I'm sorry," he muttered, and reached between the rails. The flat of his sword smacked ballocks.

The stallion screamed. He plunged and kicked. Wood flew to flinders. Gratillonius jumped around in front, got a purchase on the reins, and clung with his whole weight.

Had the animal been disabled by pain or become unmanageable, Gratillonius would have left and run the whole way to Ys. Favonius traveled so much faster, though. "Easy, boy, easy, old chap, there, there."

Somehow the man gained control. He led the horse from the demolished stall. A last shying knocked the lantern over. Its cover fell off. Beneath it were wisps of straw scattered across the floor. The crib was full of hay. A tiny flame ran forth. Gratillonius gave it no heed. His task was to get the neighing, trembling beast outside.

He did. Wind tossed the long mane. He forgot about the lantern.

A shadow stumbled from the shadows. "I implore you, stay," cried the voice of Corentinus. "God needs you."

Gratillonius hoisted himself into the saddle. "Hoy-a, gallop!" he shouted, and struck heels to ribs.

"Lord have mercy," called the chorepiscopus at his back. "Christ have mercy. Lord have mercy."

Hoofs banged. Muscles surged. Gratillonius rode off.

<h2 style="text-align:center">~ 7 ~</h2>

Once on Processional Way, he had Ys before him. Most of the city was as black as the headlands which held it. Towertops shone iron-hued by the light of a moon too far down for him to see above the wall. Tears blurred vision though he squinted, for he raced straight into the gale. Mithras preserve Favonius from tripping and breaking a leg.

The road bent south. Hoofs racketed on the canal bridge. Water swirled just underneath, dense with soil. It made a restless pond, from crumbled banks to city wall and on around into the sea that besieged the cliffs of Point Vanis.

Processional Way ended at Aquilonian Way. Here the wind was largely of Gratillonius's own haste. He was well into the lee of Ys, but likewise into its shadow. Barely could he see the highway heaped with shards of buildings. He kept Favonius bound south a while, to get around. Drenched earth smothered hoofbeats. Or so he supposed, somewhere at the back of his mind. He could not tell in this din.

When it appeared safe, he reined the stallion to a trot and turned west over grass, shrubs, mud that had been gardens, until they two reached the wall. Northward along it they groped, to High Gate. Somebody hailed. Men were at work clearing debris as Corentinus had urged. Gratillonius thought they were a fair number. The officer of the watch must have summoned everybody in barracks.

"Who goes?" a voice challenged. Pikeheads lifted.

"The King," shouted Gratillonius. "Make way. Keep at your labor. We've need of that road!"

He walked Favonius past, not to trample anyone in the dark. Lir Way opened before him, empty between buildings and sphinxes. He smote heels for a fresh gallop.

Within the compass of the rampart, seeing was a little better. And he knew the way. After seventeen years, how well he knew it. Nothing obstructed it, either. The colonnades of the Forum passed by, specters under cloudy gravestones of towers. A few windows gleamed. They fell behind. He sped on, deeper into the roar of the sea.

The gate was his goal. Rather than stumble through tangled and lightless lanes, quickest would be to continue straight down the avenue to the harbor, speed over its wharf to the north end of the basin, turn left past the Temple of Lir to pomoerium and stairs, bound up to the

Gull Tower and summon the guards there to join him in defending the city.

Mithras, God of the Midnight, You have had our sacrifice. Here is my spirit before You, my heart beneath Your eyes. I call, who followed Your eagles since ever my life began: Mithras, also a soldier, keep now faith with Your man!

Skippers' Market sheened. Favonius's feet slipped from him on the wet flags. He skidded and staggered. Barely did Gratillonius hold saddle.

The stallion recovered. "On!" yelled Gratillonius, and flogged him with the reins. He neighed. The arch of triumph echoed to his passage.

They came between the waterfront buildings, out onto the dock. Its stone rang under the hoofs. Ahead, the basin flickered, full of a heavy chop. Ships swayed at their piers. Half-seen under moonlit, racing clouds, they might have been whales harpooned. The outer wall thrust bulk and battlements into heaven. Foam fountained above and blew away on the wind. The copper on the gate caught such light as to make it stand forth like a phantom. Surf sundered.

Favonius reared and screamed.

The doors opened. The moon shone through from the horizon. It frosted the combers that charged inward, rank upon rank upon rank. Ahead of them, below the wall, gaped a trough as deep as a valley. Amidst the wind that suddenly smote him with full force, Gratillonius heard a monstrous sucking noise. It was the basin spilling out into the depth. That rush of water flung the gate wide.

A crest advanced. As the ground shoaled between the headlands, it gathered speed and height. The sound of it made stone tremble. Yet when it reached Ys it seemed to stand there, taller than the rampart, under spindrift banners, a thing that would never break.

Favonius reared again. Panic had him—no, the Dread of Lir. Gratillonius fought to bring him back.

The wave toppled.

The gate had no time to close itself. The torrent broke past, into the basin, over ships and wharf. There it rebounded. The next wave met it. Between them, they tore the doors from the wall.

With the full strength of his shoulders, Gratillonius had gotten his horse turned around. Hoofs fled between buildings and under the arch. The sea hounded them. Pastern-deep, it churned across Skippers' Market, sprayed in sheets from the hasty legs, before it withdrew.

Up Lir Way! Gratillonius felt nothing but his duty to survive. The Key had turned in the Lock and the old Gods were riding into Ys. Let him save what he could.

A second billow overtook him, surged hock-deep. Wavelets ran across its back and flung spiteful gouts of foam. It would have peaked higher save that along the way it broke through windows, pounded down doors, and gushed into the homes of men.

When he crossed the Forum, Favonius swam. Against the turmoil around him, Gratillonius made out heads, arms, bodies. They struggled and went under. He could do naught to help them, he must seek toward where the need was greatest.

The avenue climbed. For a small space, he galloped over clear pavement. Clouds ripped apart and he had some light from above. A few stars fluttered yonder. The east was gray.

Favonius throbbed beneath him. The stallion had shed blind terror, or the tide had leached it from him. He heeded the reins. Gratillonius turned him left.

Rising narrow between Suffete houses, the side street brought him to a point where he saw widely around. Ahead, that jewel which was the Temple of Belisama shone pale behind Elven Gardens. Beyond, Point Vanis heaved its cliffs heavenward and cast back the legions of Ocean.

South of it they charged into Lowtown. The wall disintegrated before them. Glancing backward, Gratillonius saw the Raven Tower drop stone by stone into its drowned crypt. Through breaches ever wider, the waves marched ever stronger. They undercut their first highdweller's tower. It swayed, leaned, avalanched. The fall of its mass begot new, terrible upheavals. Its spire soared like a javelin into the flank of a neighbor, which lurched mortally wounded. From Northbridge to Aurochs Gate, the sea front rolled onward.

Gratillonius had not stopped while he looked. A glimpse into the wind, across what roofs remained, was enough. Already the flood seethed bare yards at his back. He galloped on through the gully of darkness, the noise of destruction.

Ahead on his left was the house of Dahut. Her alone could he hope to save.

It cracked wide. A wave engirdled it, hurled out of the spate that was Taranis Way. Stones and tiles became rubble. They slid into the water. It spouted, churned, and momentarily retreated.

Though the moon had gone down, light as well as wind streamed through the gap. Night still held out against day, but Gratillonius could see farther. He saw the daughter of Dahilis. She had escaped barely in time. Naked she fled up the street ahead of him. "Dahut! Wait for me!" The wind tattered his cry, the sea overran it. Her hair blew wild about her whiteness.

Favonius would catch her in a few more bounds.

The next surge caught Favonius. It boiled as high as his withers. Undertow hauled him back. He struggled to keep footing. The wave that followed swept around him and his rider. Right and left, buildings fell asunder. There was nothing but a waste of water and a scrap of road up which Dahut forever ran.

To Gratillonius, where he and his horse fought for their lives, came Corentinus. Somehow the holy man had reached Ys from the Wood as fast as hoofs had flown. Across the tops of the billows he came striding, staff in hand. Robe and gray beard flapped in the tumult. His voice tolled through it: "Gratillonius, abide! The angel of the Lord appeared to me before the heathen house. He bade me save you even now. Come with me before it is too late."

He pointed east along that street that led off this toward the mound where stood the Temple of Belisama.

Gratillonius whipped his mount. The wave pulled back, awaiting the higher one behind. Favonius broke free. His hoofs found pavement and he went on aloft as his master bade.

Corentinus paced him on the right. "No, you fool!" the pastor shouted. "Leave that bitch-devil to her fate!"

The new wave rushed uphill. Water whirled about the daughter of Dahilis, waist-high and rising.

Gratillonius drew alongside. She was on his left. He tightened the grip of his knees and leaned over. She saw. "Father!" she screamed. Never had he known such terror as was upon her. "Father, help me!"

They reached for each other. He caught her by a wrist.

"Take her with you, and the weight of her sins will drag you down to your death," Corentinus called. "Behold what she has wrought." He touched the end of his staff to the brow of Gratillonius.

Spirit left him. It soared like a night heron. High it rose into the wind that blew across space and the wind that blew through time. Against them it beat, above the passage taken by the Ferriers of the Dead. The moon rose in the west. The spirit swooped low.

Seas broke on Sena. The greatest of them poured clear across. They ramped through the house of the Gallicenae.

In the upper room of the turret, a single lamp burned in a niche before an image of Belisama. Carved in narwhal ivory, She stood hooded and stern, Her Daughter in Her arms, at a bier on which lay Her Mother. Though the window was shuttered, the flame wavered in wintry drafts. Shadows writhed and hunched. The voice of Bodilis was lost in the skirling around, the bellowing underneath. She stood arms folded, to face the Goddess. Her lips formed words: "No longer will I ask mercy. The Three do what They will. But let You remember, by that shall You be judged."

A crack jagged across plaster. Stones had shifted. The floor beams left their fittings. The planks tilted into the gap between them and the wall. Bodilis stumbled backward. She went into murk. The waters received her. She rose blinded, to gasp for air. The waters dashed her from side to side and against floating timbers. A broken red thing squirmed and yowled in the dark.

The whole house crumbled. Blocks slid over sand and rock to the inlet where the dock had been. The last human works left on Sena were the two menhirs the Old Folk had raised.

—Storm blew the heron back east. Behind him the moon sank. He came to the Raven Tower. Forsquilis stood on its roof, at the western

749

battlements. Wind strained her black dress around her, a ravishment she did not seem to feel. Her hair tossed like wings. The moon on the horizon showed her face whiter than herself or than the waves that rammed below. Pallas Athene had been less cold and remote. She watched the fury until it cast open the gate.

Then, swiftly, she passed through the trapdoor and down a ladder to the topmost chamber. There she had left kindled her lamp fashioned from a cat's skull. Taking it in both hands, she hastened along the descending stairs. Night and noise went beside her. Stones shivered and grated, began to move under the blows from both sides.

The guardroom was deserted, its keepers fled. Forsquilis set lamp on table and stepped forth for a look. Water plunged through the gateway and the gaps in the wall. As yet it was feet below the parapet, but soon it would reach this entrance and batter the door aside if she barred it. She did, reclaimed her lamp, and continued on into the depths. The bird followed invisible and unhearable.

At the bottom was the crypt, the Mithraeum. She entered, where never woman trod before. Between the Dadophori she passed, across the emblem of mysteries that floored the pronaos, and once more between the Torchbearers into the sanctum. Her flame made golden stars flicker in the ceiling, lion-headed Time stir as if in threat. Him too she went by, to the twin altars at the far end. Before her died the Bull at the hands of the Youth, that quickening might come into the world.

Forsquilis held out her lamp. "Now save Your worshippers if You can," she said. "My life for Ys."

Through the span of a wave-beat there was silence. Then she heard a mighty rushing. The sea had broken in. She set the lamp down, turned about, and from her belt drew a knife. The cataract spilled over the stairs, into the crypt. Before it reached her, she smiled at last. "Nor shall *You* have me," she said. Her hand with the blade knew the way to her heart.

The Raven Tower fell in on itself. The heron flew free.

—Ocean rolled inward across Lowtown. The heron saw Adminius asleep, exhausted, with wife and two children who had not left the nest. The incoming din woke them. Bewildered, half awake, they stumbled about in blindness. A wave burst the door. Flood poured through. Adminius drowned under his roof.

—Cynan shepherded his loves through a lane toward higher ground. Pressed between walls on either side, the pursuing water became itself a wall. The weight of it went over the family. Maybe it crushed their awareness before they died.

—The heron winged to the Forum and by a hypocaust entered the library. A few candles showed fugitives crowded in hallways, study rooms, the main chamber. Innilis went among the poor countryfolk and fisherfolk. Her garb of a high priestess was filthy and reeky, her face pinched and bloodless until it seemed a finely sculptured skull, but exaltation lived in her eyes. "Nay, be careful, dear," she said to a woman who scrambled erect by a shelf, heedless of the books thereon. "We must keep these, you know. They are our yesterdays and our tomorrows."

The woman held forth an infant. It whimpered. Fever flushed it. Innilis laid fingers on the tiny brow and murmured. Healing flowed.

Sound of wind and surf gave way to rumble and crash. Walls trembled. Shelves swayed. Books fell. Folk started out of their drowse, sprang from were they lay, gaped and gibbered. Water swirled and mounted across the floor. People howled, scrambled, made for the one exit. They filled it, a logjam of flesh that pummeled and clawed. A man knocked Innilis down in his mindless haste. Feet thudded over her. Ribs broke, hip bones, nose, jaw. The sea washed her and her blood in among desks and books.

Outside, it tumbled such persons about as had gotten clear of the buildings. Perishing, a few glimpsed a man on horseback, a-swim across the square.

—The heron circled over Hightown, where the great folk dwelt. Vindilis ran down the street from her home. Sometimes she slipped and fell on the wet cobbles. She rose bruised, bleeding, and staggered on. Her hair fell tangled over the nightgown that was her sole garb.

When she came out on Lir Way, crowds swarmed along it, fleeing for High Gate. She worked herself to the side, on toward the Forum.

Water raced to meet her. The avenue became a river. It caught Vindilis around her throat. She swam. The current was too powerful for her to breast. It swept her backward till she fetched against a stone lion. Long arms and legs scrabbled; she got onto the statue. Riding, she peered and cried westward. Still the stream rose. Vindilis clung. It went over her head.

—Soren sought his porch. Through wind and dark, he needed a while to understand what was happening. When he did, he went immediately back inside. To the servants clustered in the atrium, he said, "Ocean has entered. The city dies. Hold! No cowardice! You, you, you—" his finger stabbed about—"see to your mistress. Carry her if need be, out the east end. You three—" he pointed to his sturdiest men—"follow me. The rest of you stay together, help each other, and it may be you will live. Make haste."

Brushing past his wife, he met Lanarvilis bound from a guest chamber. She had thrown a cloak above her shift. He took both brown-spotted hands in his and said, "The Gods have ended the Pact. Well it is that you agreed to stay here till the danger was gone. Afterward, we shall see."

Shock stared, until the Queen rallied. Hand in hand, they went out into the night. Soren's wife caught a sob before she let the people assigned hustle her along.

The household stumbled downhill to Lir Way. They reached it quite near High Gate. The first false dawnlight made pallor within the opening.

On their left they saw the deluge approach from where the Forum had been. Behind that white chaos, yet another tower collapsed. It toppled straight eastward. The wooden upper works came apart. Fragments arced as if shot from a ballista. They seemed to travel infinitely slowly. Their impact filled no time whatsoever. Beams and planks slammed into the wall. They choked the gateway. A shard of glass hit Soren in the neck. Blood spurted. He fell. Lanarvilis knelt by him and shrieked, "Is this what I served You for?" The sea arrived and ground her into the barricade.

—Maldunilis's fat legs pumped. The flood chased her up her street. The sound of it was like chuckling and giggling. At first it moved no faster than she could run, for the way was very steep. Soon, though, she began to gasp and reel. "Help me, help me," rattled from her; but servants, neighbors, everybody had gone ahead.

She sagged downward, tried to rise, could not for lack of breath. The water advanced. She rolled onto her back and sprattled as a beetle does. "Bear me," she moaned. "Hold Your priestess." The water floated her. Around and around she drifted, among timbers, furnishings, cloths, bottles, food, rubbish. Sometimes brine sloshed over her nose. She emerged, choked, coughed, sneezed, grabbed one more lungful of air.

A man washed out of an alley and collided with her. He too was large; but he floated facedown. His limbs flopped and caught her. She tried to get free. That caused his head to turn. Eyes stared, mouth yawned. She flailed away from the corpse's kiss, went under, breathed water. Presently she drifted quiet.

—Her maidservant shook Guilvilis loose from nightmares and wailed the news. For a moment the Queen lay still. Then she ordered, soft-voiced. "Take Valeria with you. At once." That was her daughter at home.

The maid ran out with the candle she had carried. It left Guilvilis in the dark. She murmured a little at the pain in her hip when she crept out of bed. Bit by bit, she hobbled into the atrium. The three who attended her, and nine-year-old Valeria, were there. "Why have you not gone?" Guilvilis asked.

"I was about to come get you, my lady," the man answered.

"Nonsense! Don't dawdle. I can hardly crawl along. You can't carry me through a tide. Bring the princess to her father in the Wood." Guilvilis held out her arms. "Farewell, darling."

The girl was too terrified to respond. The man led her away. The women followed. Guilvilis must shut the door behind them.

They had lighted a pair of lamps. She sighed, found a chair, settled down, folded her hands. "I wish I could think of something to say," she murmured into the clamor. "I am so stupid. Forgive me, Gods, but I try to understand why You do this, and cannot."

After a while: "Should I forgive You? I'll try."

The sea came in.

—Valeria's party reached the pomoerium. There the flood trapped them beneath the wall of Ys.

—From the palace dome, just below the royal eagle, Tambilis had a wide view. Light from the east seeped upwind into night. By its wanness she saw waves roll everywhere around. To west, stumps of wall or tower reared foam-veiled out of them. Eastward remained more of the rampart and a few islets where ruins clung. North and south abided the horns of land; she made out the pharos, darkened at the end of Cape Rach.

"The tide is at its height," she said. "Soon it ebbs." Billows drummed, wind whined.

"We might have gotten ashore had we been quicker, my lady," Herun Taniti muttered at her side. The naval officer had put himself in charge of the guards detailed to her for the duration of the tempest.

She shook her head. "Nay, the thing happened so fast. I could see that. We'd have needed more luck than I believed the Gods would grant. Here we stand above and can wait."

"Well, aye, well, belike you're right. Yours are the Power and the Wisdom."

"If only—" She bit off her words "Grallon would scorn me did I lament." She covered her face. "But oh, Estar!"

Her home was the lowest-lying of the Gallicenae's. Her younger daughter had surely been without possibility of reaching safety.

Tambilis raised her head. Against the mass of Point Vanis gleamed the Temple of Belisama, on the highest ground in Ys. A part of that terrain extended some yards west, low as Sena. Surf bloomed about Elven Gardens. Her Semuramat was among those vestals who had had night duty yonder.

Herun tugged his ruddy beard. "Best we go down, my lady," he suggested. "They're frightened, your household. You give them heart."

Tambilis nodded and preceded him to the stairs. On the second level, floorboards quivered, plaster cracked and fell off in chunks, rooms reverberated. The ground level was flooded halfway to its ceilings.

That would be as high as ever the sea rose in this bay, were the weather calm. Still raving from the storm they remembered, waves rushed over that surface. They struck the palace walls, shuddered, fell back with a titanic whoosh for their next onslaught.

Tambilis looked about the corridor where she and Herun had emerged. Nobody else was in sight. The passage boomed dim and chill. "Poor dears, they must be hiding," she said. "Come, my friend, help me find them and comfort them." She straightened. "For I am a Queen of Ys."

A surge came enormous. Foundations gave way. Stone blocks tumbled. The dome broke, the eagle fell. As she went under, Tambilis closed herself around the child in her womb.

—Una, Sasai, Antonia, Camilla, Augustina—Forsquilis's Nemeta and Lanarvilis's Julia were at the Nymphaeum. The rest of Gratillonius's

753

daughters, quartered round about in Ys, Ocean engulfed. In like manner went most of the children of Wulfgar, Gaetulius, Lugaid, and Hoel, together with every work of those last Kings.

—The bird flew inland. A tall man with whitening golden hair ran along Processional Way. Before the Sacred Precinct, he slammed to a halt. The building on its west side, which held the stable, was afire. Wind-fanned, flames had already taken hold on the Lodge and spread to the Wood. They whirled, roared, hissed. Sparks streamed. Roofs caved in. Red and yellow flared over a courtyard where attendants milled about. They had snatched their weapons. The tall man howled. Before they should see and come after him, he left the road for the meadow and the heights northward.

—The night heron flew back to Ys.

Gratillonius glared around. The river that had been the street flowed swollen. Houses gave way like sand castles. Through the gaps they left, he saw how fast the eastern half-circle of rampart broke asunder. But the Temple of Belisama shone ahead.

"So are the Gods that Dahut did serve," knelled the voice of Corentinus.

For that moment, Gratillonius's fingers forgot her. The current tore her from him. Her shriek cut through the wind. He leaned almost out of the saddle to regain her. He was too slow. The waters bore her out of his sight.

Corentinus grasped the bridle and turned about. Favonius plowed after him, onto the ridge that the sea had not yet claimed. Corentinus let go.

A machine inside Gratillonius declared that it would be unmanly to surrender. He guided his mount over the neck of land, behind the striding shepherd. Waves crested fetlock deep. Spume blew. The Temple was vague in sight against the gray that stole from distant hills. They could shelter there and wait for ebb.

Bits of Elven Gardens lay heaped on its staircase or washed around beneath. Corentinus stopped, looked back, pointed his staff past the building. Dull startlement touched Gratillonius. "What?" The chorepiscopus walked on.

"I should follow you ashore?" Gratillonius mumbled. "No, that's too far through this water."

Corentinus beckoned, imperiously.

Gratillonius never knew whether he decided to heed—what matter if he died? How easy to go under—or whether ground slid and carried Favonius along. Suddenly they were swimming.

Corentinus walked ahead over the tops of the waves.

Around Gratillonius was salt violence, before him reefs of wall or tower, until the surf crashed in full force against land. A billow dashed across him, another, another. Glancing behind, he saw pillars topple. Flood had sapped earth. The Temple of Belisama fell into the sea.

Favonius swam on. Combers rocked the stallion toward gigantic whitenesses. Gratillonius left the saddle. They'd have to take this last stretch each for himself.

The breakers cast him about, up, down, around. Whenever his face was in air, he seized a breath, to hold when he went back under. Saving what strength remained, he made himself flotsam for Ocean to bear into the shallows.

He and the horse crept the last few feet.

That which upbore Corentinus left him after he had no more need of it. He waded to the new strand, where he stood leaning on his staff in the wind, gray head a-droop.

XX

By late morning, calm had fallen and the tide was out. Gratillonius dragged himself free of the half-sleep, half-daze that for a while had claimed him. He would go forth in search of something, whatever it might be—strength? peace? meaning?—before he returned to duty.

The room where he had been was dusky, its air warm and thick. Bodies huddled together, those few who had escaped the whelming: Suffete, sailor, servant, watchman, worker, trader, herder, widower, widow, orphan, all nameless now, wreckage that breathed, down in forgetfulness. No, somewhere a woman he could not see wept, quietly and unendingly.

Gratillonius trod forth. The amphitheater loomed at his back. Its arena was a mire, but storage chambers and the like lent shelter to such people as he had found, riding about after he won ashore. They could not linger, of course, without fire or food or even fresh water. Salt made the canal undrinkable as far as he had searched, and would be slow to rinse away. He must take them to where there was help. Surviving houses along the valley, whether abandoned or not, ought to hold some stores; and farther on were the Osismii.

First he required air, solitude, motion to work the rust from his bones, the sand from his head, so that he would be fit to lead his flock. The time seemed infinitely distant when he might acknowledge to himself that he was spent. Ys was gone; but he remained the tribune of Rome, a centurion of the Second.

The path brought him to Aquilonian Way. There he turned west.

The chill around him never stirred. Above reached a blank silver-gray. The world seemed likewise bled of color; bared soil, grass and shrubs hammered flat, murky puddles, trees felled or stripped, lichenous rocks, darkling cliffs, charred snags where the Wood had been. Ocean rolled and tossed, the hue of the sky. Horizons were lost in haze. Sound was his footfalls on paving stones, surf which farness softened, and mewing of gulls, whose wings made a snowstorm ahead.

He began to pass over that which the tide had left. For each step he took, thicker grew heaps of kelp, chunks of driftwood, marooned fish, broken shells. Among them he saw more and more work of hands: potsherds, glass, pieces of furnishings, forlornly bright rags, here a carpenter's adze, there a worshipper's idol, yonder a doll. Heavier objects lay closer to the water. What the gulls were after was those corpses that had come aground.

Gratillonius guessed the number as two or three hundred. More would doubtless wash in during the next several days; however, the sea kept most of its dead. He didn't go down to look. He belonged to the living. Maybe later he could give the bones decent burial.

He paused and gazed before him.

How empty it was between the headlands. Blocks lay everywhere disarrayed on the arc of the beach. Fragments of wall stood above the waves beyond. Reefs and holms were barnacled with ruins. He could not bring himself to guess what this thing might have been, or that. Everything was merely empty. He supposed that in time the currents would eat away what he saw, and only the skerries outside the bay abide.

It did not matter. Ys was gone.

Had Ys ever been?

Alone in the gray, Gratillonius wondered. It felt like a dream that glimmered from him as he woke—rampart, gate, ships, the towers tall above little shadow-blue alleys, watchfires and hearthfires, temples and taverns, philosophers and fools, witchcraft and wisdom, horror and hope, songs and stories that the world would hear no more, friends, foes, the Gods he denied and the God Who in the end denied him, and always the women, the women. How could this clay ever have kissed them or listened to the laughter of their daughters? Let Dahut be unreal!

Gratillonius shook his head. He would not hide from himself. Nor would he weep. Not yet, anyhow. He had work to do. Be it enough that Dahut was at peace.

Soon he must force his people to their feet and start the trek up the valley. But let them rest a bit longer. Gratillonius went on to the junction of Redonian Way and bore north. He would go out on Point Vanis, look down from above, then across the sea, and remember.

DOG AND WOLF

I

~ 1 ~

There was his hand, her father's strong hand, closing on the arm she raised toward him. The waters roared and rushed. Wind flung a haze of scud off their tops. Barely through salt blindness could she know it was he and sense the bulk of the horse he rode. Memory passed like a lightning flash: she had sworn she would never mount that horse again while her father lived. But he was hauling her up out of the sea that would have her.

There was then a shadow behind him in the murk and spume, a tall man who touched a staff to her father's head. His grip clamped the tighter, but he did not now draw her onward. Waves dashed her to and fro. Tide went in flows and bursts of force. The noise filled heaven and her skull.

It was as if she sensed the sudden anguish, like a current out of his body into hers. The fingers slackened. A surge tore her from them. She screamed. The flood flung a mouthful to choke her. She had a glimpse of him, saw him lean forth, reach after what he had lost. A torrent swept her away.

Terror vanished. Abruptly she was altogether calm and alert. No help remained but in herself. She must hoard her strength, breathe during those instants when the tumult cast her high and hold the breath while it dragged her back under, watch for something to cling to and try to reach it, slowly, carefully. Else she was going to drown.

The sea tumbled her about, an ice-cold ravisher. She whirled through depths that were yellow, green, gray, night-blue. Up in the spindrift she gasped its bitterness and glimpsed walls crumbling. The violence scraped her against them, over and over, but bore her off before she could seize fast. Waves thundered and burst. Wind shouted hollowly.

The snag of a tower passed by and was lost. She understood that the deluge had snatched her from high ground and undertow was bearing her to the deeps. Surf brawled white across the city rampart. Already it had battered stone from stone off the upper courses, made the work into reefs; and still it hammered them, and they slid asunder beneath those blows. Right and left the headlands loomed above the wreckage, darknesses in wildness. Beyond them ramped Ocean.

A shape heaved into view, timbers afloat, fragment of a ship. It lifted on crests, poised jagged against clouds and the first dim daylight, skidded down troughs, rose anew. The gap closed between it and her. She gauged how she must swim to meet it. For this chance she could spend what might was left her. With the skill of a seal, she struck out, joined herself to the waters, made them help her onward. Her fingertips touched the raft. A roller cloven by a rock sent it from her.

She was among the skerries. Fury swirled around them, fountained above them. Never could she reach one, unless as a broken corpse. Billows crashed over her head.

Dazed, the animal warmth sucked from her, she did not know the last of them for what it was. She was simply in the dark, the time went on and on, her lips parted and she breathed sea. The pain was far off and brief. She spun down endlessly through a whiteness that keened.

At the bottom of that throat was not nullity. She came forth into somewhere outside all bounds. Someone waited. Transfiguration began.

~ 2 ~

Fear knocked the breast of Gratillonius as he approached the Nymphaeum.

Around him dwelt peace. The stream that fed the sacred canal descended in a music of little waterfalls. Morning sunlight rang off it. This early in the year, the surrounding forest stood mostly bare to the blue overhead. The willows had unsheathed their blades, a green pale and clear if set beside the intensity of the pasturelands below, but oak and chestnut were still opening buds. Squirrels darted along boughs. Certain birds started to sing. A breeze drifted cool, full of damp odors.

What damage he saw was slight, broken branches, a tree half uprooted. The storm had wrought havoc in the valley; the hills sheltered their halidom.

Nothing whatsoever seemed to have touched the space into which he emerged. Swans floated on the pond, peacocks walked the lawn. The image of Belisama Mother stood on its pile of boulders, beneath the huge old linden, above the flowing spring. Earth of flowerbeds, gravel of paths, hedgerows and bowers led his gaze as ever before, to the colonnaded white building. The glass in its windows flashed him a welcome.

You did not let hoofs mar those grounds. A trail went around their edge to join one behind the Nymphaeum, which led on into the woods and so to the guardhouse and its stable. For the moment, he simply dismounted and tethered Favonius. The stallion snorted and stood quiet, head low. Despite having rested overnight at the last house they reached yesterday, man and beast remained exhausted. Recovery from what had happened would be slow, and then—Gratillonius thought—only in the body, not the spirit. Meanwhile he must plow onward without pause, lest he fall apart.

Corentinus joined him. The craggy gray man had refused the loan of a mount for himself and strode behind, tireless as the tides. He leaned on his staff and looked. Finally he sighed into silence: "Everything that was beautiful about Ys is gathered here."

Gratillonius remembered too much else to agree, but he also recalled that his companion had never before beheld this place, in all the years of his ministry. It must have smitten him doubly with wonder after the horrors of the whelming. Usually Corentinus was plainspoken, like the sailor he once had been. With faint surprise, Gratillonius realized that the other man had used Ysan.

He could not bring himself to reply, except for "Come" in Latin. Leading the way, his feet felt heavy. His head and eyelids were full of sand, his aches bone-deep. Doubtless that was a mercy. It kept the grief stunned.

But the fear was awake in him.

Female forms in blue and white appeared in the doorway and spread out onto the portico. Well might they stare. The men who neared them were unkempt, garments stained and wrinkled and in need of mending. Soon they were recognizable. Murmurs arose, and a single cry that sent doves aloft in alarm off the roof. The King, dressed like any gangrel. The Christian preacher!

They trudged up the stairs and jerked to a halt. Gratillonius stared beyond the minor priestess to the vestals whom she had in charge. His heart wavered at sight of his daughters.

Nemeta, child of Forsquilis; Julia, child of Lanarvilis. Them he had left to him. Una, Semuramat, Estar—no, he would not mourn the ten who were lost, not yet, he dared not.

He found himself counting. The number of persons on station varied. It happened now to be seven, or eight if he added the priestess. Besides his own pair there were four maidens ripening toward the eighteenth birthdays that would free them from service. He knew them, though not closely. All were grandchildren of King Hoel. One stemmed through Morvanalis, by an older sister of that Sasai who later became Gratillonius's Queen Guilvilis. One descended from Fennalis's daughter Amair, one each from Lanarvilis's Miraine and Boia. (Well, Lanarvilis had been dutifully fruitful in three different reigns; she deserved that her blood should live on.) Then there was a little girl of nine, too young for initiation but spending a while here as custom was, that she might become familiar with the sanctuary and serene in it. With her Gratillonius was better acquainted, for she was often in the house of Queen Bodilis, whose oldest daughter Talavair had married Arban Cartagi; the third child of that couple was this Korai.

He hauled his mind back from the past and addressed the priestess in Ysan: "Greeting, my lady. Prepare yourself. I bear dreadful tidings."

It might have been astonishing how steadily she looked back. Most often the house mother at the Nymphaeum was elderly, seasoned in dealing with people. Runa was in her mid-twenties. However, she was the daughter of Vindilis by Hoel. You would expect forcefulness, and persuasiveness too when she cared to employ it. He had never known her well, either, and as the rift widened between him and her mother, they met less and less. He knew that after she completed her vestalhood without the Sign coming upon her she married Tronan Sironai. The union was without issue and evidently not happy. Though she did not terminate it, she re-entered the Temple of Belisama and occupied herself mainly with the activities of an underpriestess.

"We have wondered," she said low. "We have prayed. Clear it is that the Gods are angry." At you, said her gaze.

Riding here, he had thought and thought how to tell what he must. Everything that had occurred to him had dropped out of his mind. He could merely rasp forth: "I am sorry. Ys is gone. Somehow the sea gate opened during the storm. Ocean came in and destroyed the city. The Gallicenae have perished. Most of the people have. I do not know that your husband, or any near kin of any among you, is alive. We must look to our survival—"

What followed was never afterward clear in his memory. Runa yowled and sprang at him. His left cheek bore the marks of her nails for days. He fended her off before she got to his eyes. She cursed him and turned to her vestals. One had swooned, others wailed or wept; but Gratillonius's Nemeta stood apart as if carven in ivory, while Gratillonius's Julia tried to give comfort. Likewise did Corentinus, in his rough fashion. Runa slapped faces, grabbed shoulders and shook them, demanded self-control. Gratillonius decided it was best he seek the guardhouse and the Ysan marines barracked there.

That was bad enough, though they refrained from blaming him. Three among them reviled the Gods, until their officer ordered them to be quiet. He, a burly, blond young man named Amreth Taniti, accompanied Gratillonius back to the Nymphaeum.

In the end, as memory again began clearly recording, those two sat with Corentinus and Runa in the priestess's room of governance. It was a chamber light and airy, furnished with a table, a few chairs such as were—had been common in Ys, and a shelf of books. Three walls bore sparse and delicate floral paintings. On the fourth the blossoms were in a grassy field where stood the Goddess in Her aspect of Maiden, a wreath on Her flowing locks, arms outspread, smile raised toward the sun that was Taranis's while at her back shone the sea that was Lir's. Beyond the windows, springtime went on about its business just as joyfully.

Runa stared long at Corentinus. Her knuckles whitened on the arms of her seat. At last she spat, "Why have *you* come?"

"Let me answer that," said Gratillonius. He had quelled weariness and despair for this while; he moved onward through what was necessary, step by step. So had he once led his men back from an ambush, through

wilderness aswarm with hostiles, north of the Wall in Britannia. "I
asked him to. We deal—I suppose we deal with Powers not human,
as well as our mortal troubles and enemies. You know I am a Father
in the cult of Mithras. Well, Corentinus is—a minister in the cult of
Christ. Between us—"

"Do you include me?" she demanded rather than asked.

"Of course. Now hear me, Runa. We need these voices of different
Gods so we can agree to set every God aside. Aye, later we can pray,
sacrifice, quarrel, try coming to terms with the thing that's happened.
But first we have the remnant of a folk to save."

Her glance raked him, the big frame, rugged features, grizzled auburn
hair and beard. "Then you deny that your deeds caused the Gods to
end the Pact," she said flatly.

He tautened. "I do. And be that as it may, 'tis not worth our fighting
about. Not yet."

"That's true, my lady," Amreth said almost timidly. "Bethink you
what danger we're in."

Corentinus raised a bony hand. "Hold, if you will." Somehow his
mildness commanded them. "Best we understand each other from the
outset. I shall say naught against your beliefs, my lady. However, grant
me a single question." He paused. She nodded, stiff-necked. "Ever
erenow, when a Queen died, a red crescent instantly appeared on the
bosom of some vestal. This marked her out as the next Chosen to be
one of the Gallicenae, bride of the King and high priestess of Belisama.
True? Well, the Nine are gone in a single night. Here are the last of
the dedicated maidens. Has the Sign come upon any of them?"

Runa sat straighter still. She passed tongue over lips. "Nay," she
whispered.

The knowledge had already seeped into Gratillonius, damping the
fear, but to become sure of it was like a sudden thaw.

"I utter no judgment concerning your Gods," Corentinus said quietly.
"Yet plain is to see that we have come to the end of an Age, and
everything is changed, and naught have we to cling to in this world
unless it be our duty toward our fellow mortals."

Visibly under the close-cropped beard, a muscle twitched at the
angle of Amreth's jaw. "Right that is, my lady," he said. "We marines
will stand by you and the vestals to the death. But this place was under
the ward of the Gods, and no raiders or bandits ever dared put us to
the test. Now...we number a bare dozen, my lady."

Runa sat back. She had gone expressionless. Gratillonius studied
her. She was tall; beneath the blue gown, her figure was wiry but, in
a subtle fashion, good. Her face was thin, aquiline, with a flawless
ivory complexion. The brows arched above dark eyes. Beneath her
wimple, he knew, was straight hair, lustrous black, which could fall
past the shoulders. Her voice was rather high but he had heard her
sing pleasingly.

She turned and locked stares with him. "What do you propose?" she asked.

Halfway through, he noticed that he had fallen into Latin. She followed him without difficulty. Amreth sat resigned.

"Ys is lost. Nothing left but a bay between the headlands, empty except for ruins." He forebore to speak of the dead who littered the beach and gulls ashriek in clouds around them. "Many people died who'd taken shelter there out of the hinterland. Very few escaped. Corentinus and I led them up the valley and billeted them in houses along the way. Those who don't succumb in the next several days ought to be safe for a while.

"Just a while, though. The granaries went with Ys. It's early spring. There's nothing to eat but flocks and seed corn, nothing to trade for food out of Osismia." He could certainly not make anyone go back and pick through the ghastliness in search of treasure. "Soon all will be starving. And the barbarians will hear of this, Saxons, Scoti, every kind of pirate. Ys was the keystone of defense for western Armorica. The Romans will have more than they can handle, keeping their own cities, without worrying about us. Most of their officials never liked us anyway. If we remain where we are, we're done.

"We have to get out, establish ourselves elsewhere. Corentinus and I are going on to search for a place. I am a tribune of Rome, and he's a minister of Christ, known to Bishop Martinus in Turonum, and— But meanwhile somebody has to give the people leadership, those we brought from the city and those who held on in the countryside. Somebody has to bind them together, calm and hearten them, ready them for the move. A couple of landholder Suffetes are already at it, but they need every help they can get. Will you give it, my lady?"

The woman sat withdrawn for a space before she said, "Aye," in Ysan. "Between us, I think, Amreth and I may suffice. But first we must talk, the four of us. Grant me this day. Surely you can stay that long." The hand trembled which she passed across her eyes. "You have so much to tell."

—Nonetheless, throughout words and plain meals and tearful interruptions from outside, she held herself steel-hard. As the hours wore on, the scheme took shape, and hers were two of the hands that formed it.

—At eventide, the vestal Julia led her father and Corentinus to adjacent guestrooms, mumbled goodnight, and left them. They stood mute in the gloom of the corridor. Each had been given a candle in a holder. The flames made hunchbacked shadows dance around them. Chill crept inward.

"Well," said Gratillonius at last, careful to keep it soft and in Latin, "we had to work for it, but we seem to have gained a strong ally."

Darkness ran through the gullies in Corentinus's face. "We may hope. Still, be wary of her, my son. Be wary of them all."

"Why?"

"A dog abandoned grows desperate. If it does not find a new master, it goes the way of the wolf. These poor souls have been abandoned by their Gods."

Gratillonius tried to smile. "You offer them another."

"Whom they will perhaps not accept, as long as the old smell haunts them."

"But the Gods of Ys are dead!" Gratillonius exclaimed. "They brought Their city down on Themselves—" down and down into the deeps of the sea.

Corentinus sighed. "I'm afraid it's not that easy. The Enemy never gives up, not till Judgment Day." He clapped his friend's shoulder. "Don't let him keep you awake, though. You need your rest. Goodnight."

—Gratillonius recognized the chamber assigned him. Here he and Dahilis had lodged when they came to ask a blessing on their unborn child, she who would become Dahut. He gasped, knotted his fists, and struggled not to weep. Only after he had surrendered did sleep come to him, full of fugitive dreams.

~ 3 ~

Southbound out of Gesocribate, Niall and his men passed within sight of the island Sena. Low it lay in the heaving seas, bare of everything but sere grass and brush, a pair of menhirs near the middle, and some stones of the building at the east end. Wind whistled as it drove smoke-gray clouds overhead. Waves ran murky, streaked with foam, bursting in white where they struck rocks. A few seals swam in them, following along with the ship at a distance as if keeping watch. Cormorants rode the surges, dived, took flight on midnight wings.

Niall nodded. "Lir was more wrathful that night than ever I knew," he said slowly.

A shiver passed through Uail maqq Carbri, and him a hardened man. "I do think the Goddess willed it too," he muttered. "That was Her house."

"Like the Ulati when they burned down Emain Macha before we could make it ours. Someday men will dare settle here again because of the fishing grounds. They will take those stones for their own use. Then the last trace of Ys on its holy isle will be gone. But I have seen the ruins. That is enough."

Uail's gaunt countenance drew into a squint as he peered at his lord. "Was it for your enjoyment you had us come this way?"

Niall straightened, taller than any of the crew, a tower topped with the silvering gold of his hair. "It was not," he said grimly. "Let no man gloat that Ys is fallen, for a wonder and a glory it was in the world. When we return home, I will be forbidding poet and bard to sing this one deed of mine."

Uail kept silence. The King had told how he destroyed Ys, then laid gess on further talk about it unless he spoke first. He could not thus keep the story from spreading, but it would take root more in humble dwellings than in high. Most likely after a few lifetimes it would be forgotten, or be a mere folktale with his name no longer in it.

Niall's eyes were like blue lightning. "I did what I did to avenge my son and my brave men, a sworn duty," he went on. "Else would that never have been my desire. As was, at the end I must...force myself." He gripped the rail and looked afar. The handsome visage was briefly twisted out of shape.

"You need not have this pain, dear," Uail ventured to say. "We could have gone directly back to Ériu."

Niall shook his head. "I must see what I wrought and make sure the vengeance is complete."

The ship toiled on eastward under oars. Ahead cruised her two attendant currachs, each with a pilot who had knowledge of these waters, picking a way among the reefs. The horns of land loomed ever more high and massive in view. Between their ruddy-dark cliffs there gleamed no longer the bulwark and the towers of Ys. Remnants thrust out of the bay, pieces of wall, heaps of stone, a few forlorn pillars. Waves chewed at them. The overturned carcass of a vessel swung about like a battering ram wielded by blind troops.

With care the crew worked their way toward Cape Rach. They saw the pharos on top, as lonely a sight as they had ever seen, and lost it as they passed along the south side. Flotsam became frequent, timbers, spars, but no other sign of man apart from a fragment of quay. The storm had swept away the fisher hamlet under the cliffs.

The beach was still Scot's Landing, laughed the men. They could go ashore. Their ship was no war galley capable of being grounded and easily relaunched; in accordance with their guise of peaceful traders, she was a round-bottomed merchantman. But they could drop the hook, leave three or four guards aboard, and ferry themselves in the currachs.

Niall led them up the path to the heights. It was slippery and had gaps, demanding care. Caution was also needful when foes not spied from the water might lurk above.

None did. Only the wind and mutter of surf had voice. Standing on the graveled road that ran the length of the cape, the men saw bleakness around, desolation below in the bay. Such homes as they glimpsed, tucked into the hills above the valley, seemed deserted. On their left were ancient tombs, beyond them the pharos, and beyond it nothing but sky. The air felt suddenly very cold.

Niall raised his spear and shook it. "Onward for a close look and maybe a heap of plunder, boys!" he cried. "It's glad the ghosts are of those who died here these many years agone."

That rallied their spirits. They cheered and trotted after him. His seven-colored cloak flapped in the wind like a battle banner.

A paved road brought them down to the bayshore. Part of the southern gateway rose there, a single turret, an arch agape, a stretch of wall which had irregularly lost its upper courses. Inland, on their right, the amphitheater appeared undamaged, or nearly so; but an oaken-shaw north of it had flamed away on the night Ys died, was blackness whence thrust a few charred trunks.

No matter that Niall of the Nine Hostages was their chief, the awe of a doom fell upon the men.

Waves rushed and growled over above the remains. Amidst and beyond the wreckage above the waterline lay strewn and heaped incredible rubbish. Waterlogged silk and brocade draped broken furniture. Silver plates and goblets corroded in torn-up kelp. Tools and toys were tumbled together with smashed glass and shattered tiles. Copper sheathing lay green, crumpled, beside the debris of cranes and artillery. Paint or gilt clung to battered wood. Calmly smiling, a small image of the goddess as Maiden nestled close to the headless, gelded statue of a man that might well have stood for the God. And skulls stared, bones gleamed yellowing in the damp, everywhere, everywhere.

Smells were of salt and tang, little if any stench. In the past few days, gulls at low tide and crabs at high had well-nigh picked the corpses clean, aside from what hair and clothing clung. Many birds walked the sands yet, scavenging scraps. They were slow to flee men who shouted or threw things at them. When they did, they flapped awkwardly, stuffed fat.

That was after the hush among the warriors broke. "Ho, see!" yelled on. He bent over, picked an object up, and flourished it: a pectoral of gold, amber, and garnets. Immediately his fellows were scrambling, scratching, casting bones away like offal, wild for treasure.

Niall stood apart, leaning on his spear. Uail did likewise. Presently the King said, distaste in his tone and on his face, "You too think this is unseemly?"

"It is that," Uail replied.

Niall seized his arm so hard that he winced. "I am not ashamed of what I did," hissed from him. "It was a mighty deed. But I must needs do it by stealth, and that will always be a wound in me. Do you understand, darling? Now we shall give Ys its honor, for the sake of our own."

Again he shook his spear in the wind. "Lay off that!" he cried. The sound went above the surf to the farther headland and back. Men froze and stared. "Leave these poor dead in peace," Niall ordered. "We'll go strip yon houses. The plunder should be better, too."

Whooping, they followed him inland.

—Toward sunset they returned to Cape Rach. Besides what they had taken from the mansions, they brought firewood off the wind-demolished, nearly dry buildings that had stood outside the main land

767

gate. Niall sent a currach party to relieve the watch on the ship, who were to bring camping gear for all with them. When they arrived, he gave them gifts to make up for the looting they had missed. "Will we do more tomorrow?" asked one hopefully.

The King frowned. "We might. I cannot promise, for it may be we shall have to withdraw fast. Soon the Romans are bound to come for a look, and they will sure have soldiers with them. But we shall see."

—He could not sleep.

The wind whispered, the sea murmured. More and more as the night grew older, he thought he heard a song in them. It was music that keened and cut, cold, vengeful, but lovely in the way of a hawk aloft or a killer whale adown when they strike their prey. The beauty of it reached fingers in between his ribs and played on his caged heart until at last he could endure no more. He rolled out of his kilt, stood up, and wrapped it back around him against the bleakness of the night.

Banked, the fire-coals glowed low. He could barely make out his crew stretched in the wan grass and the gleam on the spearhead of him who kept guard. That man moved to ask what might be amiss. "Hush," breathed Niall, and went from him.

Clouds had gone ragged. Eastward the moon frosted those nearby and seemed to fly among them. Time had gnawed it as the tides gnawed what was left of Ys. Dew shimmered on the paved road, wet and slick beneath his bare feet. Between the hulking masses of headland, argency flickered on the bay. As he came closer, walking entranced, wind shrilled louder, waves throbbed deeper.

He stopped on the sand at high water mark, near a shard of rampart and the survivor of those two towers which had been called the Brothers. Looking outward, he saw how ebb tide had bared acres of ruins. When last it did I was ransacking undefended houses, he thought in scorn of himself. By this dim uneasy light he discerned fountains, sculptures, Taranis Way running toward what had been the Forum. Across Lir Way, a particular heap had been the Temple of Belisama, and Dahut's house had stood nearby. A skull lay at his feet. He wondered if it had been in the head of anyone he knew, even— He shuddered. It was a man's. Hers would have the strong sharp delicacy of a brooch from the hand of an ollam craftsman in Ériu.

Unshod, he did not wish to go farther, through the fragments. He folded his arms, gazed at the white unrestfulness of the breakers, and waited for that which had called him.

The song strengthened. It was in and of the wind and the waves, but more than they, from somewhere beyond. It yearned and it challenged, a harp and a knife, laughter and pain, endlessly alone. Someone sported in the surf, white as itself, like a seal but long and lithe of limb, high in the breast, slim in the waist, round in the hips, plunged and rose again, danced with the sea like a seal, and sang to him. Vengeance, it sang, I am vengeance, and you shall serve me for the love I bear you.

768

By the power of that love, stronger than death, I lay gess on you, Niall, that you take no rest until the last of Ys lies drowned as I lay drowned. It is your honor price, King on Temir, that you owe her whom you betrayed; for never will her love let go of you.

Long and long he stood at the edge of the fallen city while the siren sang to him. He remembered how he had called Mongfind the witch from her grave, and knew now that once a man has let the Otherworld into his life, his feet are on a road that allows no turning back.

But he was Niall of the Nine Hostages. Fear and regret were unbecoming him. At the turn of the tide, she who sang fell silent and swam away out of his sight. He strode back to the camp, laid himself down, and dropped quickly into a sleep free of dreams.

—In the morning he ranked his followers before him. They saw the starkness and were duly quiet. "Hear me, my dears," he said.

"A vision, a thought, and a knowledge came over me in the night. You will not be liking this, but it is the will of the Gods.

"Ys, that murdered our kinsmen, must do more than die. Overthrown, she could yet be victorious over us. For folk will be coming back to these parts and settling. If they saw what we see, they would recall what we have heard, the tales and the ballads, the memory of splendor; and in their minds *we* would be the murderers. Shall they found a new city and name it Ys? Shall they praise and dream of Old Ys till heaven cracks open? Or shall, rather, the city of treachery die forever?

"Already, I have told you, I want no word of it bound to my own fame. Today I tell you that *nothing* of it may abide.

"Our time here is short. We cannot do the whole work at once. But this is my command, that we leave the valley houses be—others will clean them out soon enough—and start the razing of yonder lighthouse which once guided mariners to Ys."

—Dry-laid, it yielded more readily to strong men than might have been awaited from its stoutness. They cast the blocks over the cliff. When they set sail, half was gone. Niall thought of a raid in summer, during which the rest could be done away with. Of course, warriors would require booty. Well, much should remain around the hinterland, as well as in settlements on this whole coast.

He grinned. They might find a party of Gauls picking over the shards of Ys, and rob them. In the song of the siren had been promise as well as threat.

He sobered, and men who noticed slipped clear of his nearness. She had laid a word on him. Year by year, as he was able, he must obey. Untouched thus far on Cape Rach stood the necropolis. He must level it. First would be the tomb of Brennilis.

II

~ 1 ~

The sun was not yet down, but the single glazed window was grayed and dusk beginning to fill the room where Apuleius Vero had brought his guests. It was a lesser chamber of his house, well suited for private talk. Wall panels, painted with scenes from the Roman past, were now vague in vision. Clear as yet sheened the polished walnut of a table which bore writing materials, a pair of books, and modest refreshments. Other-wise the only furniture was the stools on which the three men sat.

The news had been brought, the shock and sorrow uttered, the poor little attempts at condolence made. It was time to speak of what might be done.

Apuleius leaned forward his slender form and regular features. "How many survivors?" he asked low.

Gratillonius remained hunched, staring at the hands clasped together in his lap. "I counted about fifty," he said in the same dull voice as before.

The tribune of Aquilo drew a sharp breath and once more signed himself. "Only half a hundred from that whole city and...and those from outside whom you say had taken refuge? Christ be with us. Christ have mercy."

"There may be two or three hundred more who stayed in the country-side, including the children. We've tried to get in touch with them."

Corentinus's fist knotted on his knee. Tears gleamed under the shaggy brows. "The children," he croaked. "The innocents."

"Most will starve if they don't soon get help," Gratillonius said. "Afterward the reavers will come."

Apuleius forced business into his tone. "But I gather you have leaders for them while you are off seeking that help. Where have you been?"

"Thus far, only Audiarna. The reception we got there decided me to come straight to you."

"What did they say?"

Gratillonius shrugged. Corentinus explained, harshly: "The tribune and the chorepiscopus both told us they had no space or food to spare. When I pressed them they finally cried that they could not, dared not take in a flock of pagans who were fleeing from the wrath of God. I saw it would be useless to argue. Also, they were doubtless right when

770

they said our people would be in actual danger from the dwellers. Ys is—was near Audiarna. The horror of what has happened, the terror of more to come, possesses them in a way you should be free of here at your remove."

Apuleius looked at Gratillonius and shook his head in pity. The centurion of the Second, the King of Ys had lacked strength to dispute with a couple of insignificant officials and must needs leave it to his clerical companion.

"We can take in your fifty at once, of course," Apuleius told them. "A trading town like this has a certain amount of spare lodging in the slack season. It is not a wealthy town, though. We can find simple fare, clothing, and the like for that many, but only temporarily. The rest shall have to stay behind until something has been worked out with the provincial authorities. I will dispatch letters about that in the morning."

"God will bless you," Corentinus promised.

Gratillonius stirred and glanced up. "I knew we could count on you, old friend," he said, with a slight stirring of life in his voice. "But as for the tribunes or even the governor—I've given thought to this, you understand. They never liked Ys, they endured it because they had to, and some of them hate me. Why should they bestir themselves for a band of alien fugitives?"

"Christ commands us to succor the poor," Apuleius answered.

"Pardon me, but I've never seen that order very well followed. Oh, Bishop Martinus will certainly do what he can, and I suppose several others too, but—"

"I'll remind them that people who become desperate become dangerous. Don't fret too much." With compassion: "It'll take time, resettling them, but remember Maximus's veterans. Armorica continues underpopulated, terribly short of hands for both work and war. We'll get your people homes."

"Scattered among strangers? After they've lost everything they ever had or ever were? Better dead, I think."

"Don't say that," Corentinus reproved. "God's left the road open for them to win free of the demons they worshipped."

Gratillonius stiffened. His gaze sought Apuleius and held fast. His speech was flat with weariness but firm: "Keep them together. Else the spirit will die in them and the flesh will follow it. You've been in Ys. You've seen what they can do, what they know. Think what you've gained from the veterans and, all right, those former outlaws who came to these parts. We're going to need those hands you spoke of more than ever, now Ys is gone. It was the keystone of defense of Armorica. How many troops does Rome keep in this entire peninsula—two thousand? And no navy worth mentioning; the Ysan fleet was the mainstay of that. The barbarians will be coming back. Trade will be ripped apart.

I offer you some good fighting men, and some more who can learn to be, and others who're skilled workmen or sailors or scribes or— Man, can you afford to waste them?"

He sagged. Twilight deepened in the room. Finally Apuleius murmured, "You propose to resettle the Ysans, your former subjects, rural as well as urban, in this neighborhood?"

Gratillonius was barely audible: "I don't know any better place. Do you?"

Corentinus took the word. "We've talked about it a little, we two, and I've given it thought of my own. I used to live hereabouts, you recall, and though that was years ago, the King's brought me the news every time he paid a visit. There's ample untilled land. There's iron ore to be gathered nearby, and unlimited timber, and a defensible site that fishers and merchantmen can use for their terminus." Apuleius opened his mouth. Corentinus checked him with a lifted palm. "Oh, I know, you wonder how so many can be fed in the year or more it'll take them to get established. Well, in part we'll have to draw on Imperial resources. I'm sure Bishop Martinus can and will help arrange that; his influence isn't small. The need won't be great or lasting, anyway. For one thing, the Ysan hinterland grazes sheep, geese, some cattle and swine. Their herders would far rather drive them here and see most eaten up than keep them for the barbarians. Then too, Ys was a seafaring nation. Many a man will soon be fishing again, if only in a coracle he's made for himself, or find work as a deckhand on a coastal trader." He paused. "Besides, the former soldiers and former Bacaudae who owe their homes to Gratillonius—I think most of them will be glad to help."

Apuleius gripped his chin, stared afar, sat long in thought. Outside, sounds of the town were dying away.

Finally the tribune smiled a bit and said, "Another advantage of this site is that *I* have some small influence and authority of my own. Permissions and the like must be arranged, you understand. That should be possible. The situation is not unprecedented. Emperors have let hard-pressed barbarian tribes settle in Roman territory; and Ys is— was—actually a foederate state. I have the power to admit you temporarily. Negotiating a permanent status for you will take time, since it must go through the Imperium itself. But the, alas, inevitable confusion and delay are to the good, for meanwhile you can root yourselves firmly and usefully in place. Why then should the state wish to expel you?

"Of course, first you require somewhere to live. While land may lie fallow, it is seldom unclaimed. Rome cannot let strangers squat anywhere they choose." —unless they have the numbers and weapons to force it, he left unspoken.

"Well?" asked Corentinus tensely.

"I have property. To be precise, my family does, but God has called most of the Apuleii away and this decision can be mine."

Gratillonius's breath went sharp between his lips.

Apuleius nodded, as if to himself, and continued methodically. "You remember, my friend, that holding which borders on the banks of the Odita and the Stegir where they meet, a short walk hence. On the north and east it's hemmed in by forest. Of late, cultivation has not gone so well. Three tenant families have farmed it for us, one also serving as caretakers of its manor house. They grow old, that couple, and should in charity be retired. As for the other two, one man has lately died without a son; I am seeing what can be done for his widow and daughters. The second man is hale and busy, but—I strongly suspect —would welcome different duties. God made him too lively for a serf. Can the Lord actually have been preparing us here for a new use of the land?"

"Hercules!" Gratillonius breathed. Realizing how inappropriate that was, he gulped hard and sat silent.

"Hold on," Apuleius cautioned. "It's not quite so simple. The law does not allow me to give away an estate as I might a coin. This grant of mine must employ some contorted technicalities, and at that will involve irregularities. We'll need all the political force we can muster, and no doubt certain...considerations...to certain persons, if it is to be approved. However, I'm not afraid to have the actual work of settlement commence beforehand. That in itself will be an argument for us to use."

"I *knew* I could count on you—" Abruptly Gratillonius wept, not with the racking sobs of a man but, in his exhaustion, almost the quietness of a woman.

Apuleius lifted a finger. "It will be hard work," he said, "and there are conditions. First and foremost, they were right as far as they went in Audiarna. We cannot allow a nest of pagans in our midst. You must renounce those Gods, Gratillonius."

The Briton blinked the tears off his lashes, tasted the salt on his mouth, and replied, "They were never mine."

Corentinus said, like a commander talking of an enemy who has been routed at terrible cost, "I don't think we'll have much trouble about that, sir. How many among the survivors can wish to carry on the old rites? Surely too few to matter, except for their own salvation. Let most hear the Word, and soon they will come to Christ."

"I pray so," Apuleius answered solemnly. "Then God may be pleased to forgive one or two of my own sins."

"Your donation will certainly bless you."

"And my family?" Apuleius whispered.

"They too shall have many prayers said for them."

Both men's glances went to Gratillonius. He evaded them. Silences thickened.

"It would be unwise to compel," Corentinus said at length.

The door opened. Light glowed. "Oh, pardon me, father," said the girl who bore the lamp. "It's growing so dark inside. I thought you might like to have this."

"Thank you, my dear," said Apuleius to his daughter.

Verania entered timidly. It seemed she had taken the bringing upon herself, before it occurred to her mother to send a slave. Gratillonius looked at her and caught her look on him. The lamp wavered in her hand. She had barely seen him when he arrived, then the womenfolk and young Salomon were dismissed from the atrium.

How old was she now, he wondered vaguely—fourteen, fifteen? Since last he saw her, she had filled out, ripening toward womanhood, though as yet she was withy-slim, small-bosomed, barely up to his shoulder if he rose. Light brown hair was piled above large hazel eyes and a face that—it twisted in him—was very like the face of Una, his daughter by Bodilis. She had changed her plain Gallic shift for a saffron gown in Roman style.

She passed as near to him as might be in the course of setting the lamp on the table. "You are grieved, Uncle Gaius," she murmured.

What, had she remembered his nickname from her childhood? Later Apuleius had made her and her brother be more formal with the distinguished visitor.

"I brought bad news," he said around a tightness in his gullet. "You'll hear."

"All must hear," Apuleius said. "First we should gather the household for prayer."

"If you will excuse me." Gratillonius climbed to his feet. "I need air. I'll take a walk."

Apuleius made as if to say something. Corentinus gestured negation at him. Gratillonius brushed past Verania.

Within the city wall, streets were shadowed and traffic scant. Gratillonius ignored what glances and hails he got, bound for the east gate. It stood open, unguarded. The times had been peaceful since Ys took the lead in defending Armorica. Watchposts down the valley sufficed. How much longer would that last?

Careless of the fact that he was unarmed, Gratillonius strode out the gate and onward. His legs worked mechanically, fast but with no sense of vigor. A shadowy part of him thought how strange it was that he could move like this, that he had been able to keep going at all—on the road, in council, at night alone.

The sun was on the horizon. Level light made western meadows and treetops golden, the rivers molten. Rooks winged homeward, distantly cawing, across chilly blue that eastward deepened and bore a first trembling star. Ahead loomed the long barricade of Mons Ferruginus, its heights still aglow but the wrinkles beneath purple with dusk.

He should turn around, raise his arms, and say his own evening prayer. He had not said any since the whelming of Ys. There had been no real chance to.

He did not halt but, blindly, sought upward. The rutted road gave way to a path that muffled foot-thuds. It wound steeply among wild shrubs and trees, occasional small orchards, cabins already huddling into themselves. Boughs above him were graven black. Ahead they were mingling with the night as it welled aloft.

He reached a high place and stopped. This was as far as he could go. He wanted in a dull fashion to trudge on, maybe forever, but he was too drained. It would be hard enough to stumble his way back down. Let him first rest a while. And say that prayer?

From here he looked widely west. A streak of red smoldered away. "Mithras, God of the sunset—" No, somehow he could not shape the words. Mithras, where were You when Ocean brought down Ys and her Queens, where were You when it tore Dahut from my hand?

He knew the question was empty. A true God, *the* true God was wholly beyond. Unless none existed, only the void. But to admit that would be to give up his hold on everything he had ever loved. But if the God was too exalted to hear him, what matter whether or not He lived outside of human dreams? A good officer listens to his men. Mithras, why have You forsaken me?

The sky darkened further. Slowly within it appeared the comet. It was a ghost, fading toward oblivion, its work done, whether that work had been of warning or of damnation. Who had sent it? Who now called it home?

The strength ran out of Gratillonius. He sank to the ground, drew knees toward chin, hugged himself to himself, and shivered beneath the encroaching stars.

~ 2 ~

A waning half moon rose above woodlands whose branches, budding or barely started leafing, reached toward it like empty hands. They hid the River of Tiamat, low at this season; among the stars that glimmered in the great silence went the Bears, the Dragon, the Virgin. Only water had voice, chirring and rustling from the spring of Ahes to a pool in the hollow just beneath and thence in a rivulet on down the hill, soon lost to sight under the trees. Moonlight flickered across it.

Nemeta came forth. Convolvulus vines between the surrounding boles crackled, still winter-dry, as she passed through. Her feet were bare, bruised and bleeding where she had stumbled against roots or rocks on the gloomy upward trail. First grass in the small open space of the hollow, then moss on the poolside soothed them a little. She stopped at the edge and stood a while catching her breath, fighting her fear.

The whiteness of her short kirtle was slashed by a belt which bore a sheathed knife. Unbound, tangled from her struggle with brush and twigs on a way seldom used, her hair fell past her shoulders. A garland of borage, early blooming in a sheltered spot despite the rawness of this springtime, circled her brows. In her left hand she carried a wicker cage. As she halted, a robin within flapped wings and cheeped briefly, anxiously.

She mustered courage and lifted her right palm. Nonetheless her words fluttered: "Nymph Ahes, I greet you, I...I call you, I, Nemeta, daughter of Forsquilis. She was—" The girl swallowed hard. Tears coursed forth. They stung. Vision blurred. "She was of the Gallicenae, the nine Queens of Ys. M-my father is Grallon, the King."

Water rippled.

"Ever were you kindly toward maidens, Ahes," Nemeta pleaded. "Ys is gone. You know that, don't you? Ys is gone. Her Gods grew angry and drowned her. But you abide. You must! Ahes, I am so alone."

After a moment she thought to say, "We all are, living or dead. What Gods have we now? Ahes, comfort us. Help us."

Still the spirit of the spring did not appear, did not answer.

"Are you afraid?" Nemeta whispered.

Something stirred in the forest, unless it was a trick of the wearily climbing moon.

"I am not," Nemeta lied. "If you will not seek the Gods for us, I will myself. See."

Hastily, before dread should overwhelm her, she set down the cage, unfastened her belt, drew the kirtle over her head and cast it aside. The night air clad her nakedness in chill. Taking up the knife, she held it against the stars. *"Cernunnos, Epona, Sucellus, almighty Lug!"* She shrilled her invocation of Them not in Ysan or sacerdotal Punic but in the language of the Osismii, who were half Celtic and half descendants of the Old Folk. When she slew the bird she did so awkwardly; it flopped and cried until she, weeping, got a firm enough hold on it to hack off its head. But her hands never hesitated when she gashed herself and stooped to press blood from her breasts to mingle in the pool with the blood of her sacrifice.

—False dawn dulled the moon and hid most stars. A few lingered above western ridges and the unseen wreck of Ys.

Nemeta crossed the lawn toward the Nymphaeum. Her steps left uneven tracks in the dew. She startled a peacock which had been asleep by a hedge. Its screech seemed shatteringly loud.

A woman in a hooded cloak trod out of the portico, down the stairs, and strode to a meeting. The girl stopped and gaped. Runa took stance before her. Now it was Nemeta's breathing that broke the silence. It puffed faint white.

"Follow me," said the priestess. "Quickly. Others will be rousing. They must not see you like this."

"Wh-wh-what?" mumbled the vestal.

"Worn out, disheveled, your garb muddy and torn and bloodstained," Runa snapped. "Come, I say." She took the other's arm and steered her aside. They went behind the great linden by the sacred pond. Hoarfrost whitened the idol that it shaded.

"What has found you tonight?" Runa demanded.

Nemeta shook her dazed head. "I kn-know not what you mean."

"Indeed you do, unless They stripped you of your wits for your recklessness." When she got only a blind stare in reply, the priestess continued:

"I've kept my heed on you. Had there been less call on me elsewhere—everywhere, in these days of woe—I'd have watched closer and wrung your scheme out of you erenow. It struck me strange that you never wailed aloud against fate, but locked your lips as none of the rest were able to. I misdoubted your tale that you snared a bird to be your pet; and tonight it was gone from your room together with yourself, nor have you brought it back. And you have crowned yourself with ladygift, the Herb of Belisama.

"I know you somewhat, Nemeta. I was nine years old when you were born; I have watched you grow. Well do I recall what blood is in you, your father's willfulness, your mother's witchiness. Each night after you went to bed, since the news came, I have looked in to be sure....Ah, you were aware of that, nay, sly one? You waited. But I slept ill this night, and looked in again, and then you were gone."

"Where? And what answer did you get? Who came to you?"

The girl shuddered. "Who?" she said tonelessly. "Mayhap none. I cannot remember. I was out of myself."

Runa peered long at her. Fifteen years of age, Nemeta was rangy, almost flat-chested. Her face bore high cheekbones, curved nose, big green eyes; the mane of hair grew straight and vividly red, the skin was fair and apt to freckle. Ordinarily she stood tall, but in this hour, drained of strength, she stooped.

"You sought the Gods," Runa said at last, very low.

Nemeta raised her glance. Life kindled in it. "Aye." Her voice, hoarse from shrieking, gained a measure of steadiness. "First just Ahes. I begged her to speak to Them for us. Not the Three of Ys, though I did make this wreath to—remind—the old Gods of the land. They might intercede or—or— When she held off—has she fled, has she died?—I summoned Them myself."

"Did any come?"

"I know not, I told you." Nemeta dropped her glance anew. Her fingers twisted and twined together. "It was as though I... blundered into dreams I can't remember— Did I see Him, antlered and male, two snakes in His grasp? Were there thunders? I woke cold and full of pain, and made my way back hither."

"Why did you do it?"

"What other hope have we?" Nemeta half screamed. "Yon pale Christ?"

"Our Gods have disowned us, child."

"Have They?" Fingers plucked at the priestess's sleeve. "Forever? At least the Gods of the land, They live. They must!"

Runa sighed. "Mayhap someday we shall learn, though I think that will be after we are dead, if then. Meanwhile we must endure...as best we can." Sternly: "You will never be so rash again. Do you hear me?"

Stubbornness stood behind bewilderment; but: "I p-promise I'll be careful."

"Good. Bide your time." Runa unfastened her brooch and took the cloak from her shoulders. "Wrap yourself in this, lest anyone spy your state. Come along to your room. I'll tell them you've been taken ill and should be left to sleep. 'Twould not do to have word get about, you understand—now that we shall be dealing with Christians."

As she guided the girl, she added: "If we hold to our purpose and are wise in our ways, we need not become slaves. We may even prevail." Bared to the sky, her countenance hardened.

~ 3 ~

When the warriors appeared, Maeloch spat a curse. "So nigh we were to getting clear. Balls of Taranis, arse of Belisama, what luck!" He swung about to his men. "Battle posts!"

All scrambled for their weapons, some into *Osprey* where the fishing smack lay beached. The tide was coming in, but would not be high enough to float her off for another two or three hours. With axes, billhooks, knives, slings, harpoons, a crossbow, they formed a line before the prow—fifteen men, brawny, bearded, roughly clad. That was almost half again as many as the craft carried while at work, but these were bound for strange and dangerous bournes. At their center, Maeloch the captain squinted against the morning sun to make out the approaching newcomers.

From this small inlet, land lifted boldly, green, starred with wildflowers, leaves already springing out on trees and shrubs. Here was no bleak tip of Armorica jutting into Ocean, but one of a cluster of islands off the Redonic coast of Gallia, well up that channel the Romans called the Britannic Sea. Fowl in their hundreds rode a fresh breeze which drove scraps of cloud across heaven and bore odors of growth into the salt and kelp smells along the strand. A rill trickled down from the woods decking the heights. The foreign men must have followed it. They continued to do so as they advanced.

Maeloch eased a bit. They numbered a mere half dozen. Unless more were lurking behind them, they could not intend hostilities. However, they were clearly not plain sailors like his crew, but fighters by trade—nay, he thought, by birth. It would cost lives to provoke them.

He shouldered his ax and paced forward, right arm raised in token of peace. They deployed, warily but skillfully, and let him come to them. He recognized them for Hivernians, though with differences from those in Mumu with whom Ys now had a growing traffic. Nor were they quite like those he had fought—seventeen years ago, was it?—after that gale the Nine raised had driven their fleet to doom. Here the patterns of kilts, cut of coats and breeks, style of emblems painted on shields were subtly unlike what he had seen before. But swords and spearheads blinked as brightly as anyone's.

Maeloch was no merchant. However, he had had his encounters when boats put in to Scot's Landing or chanced upon his over the fishing grounds. It behooved a skipper to speak for his men; he had set himself to gain a rough mastery of the Scotic tongue. "A good day to yuh," he greeted in it. "Yuh take...hospitality...of us? We...little for to give...beer, wine, shipboard food. Yuh welcome."

"Is it friendly you are, then?" responded the leader, a man stocky and snubnosed. "Subne maqq Dúnchado am I, sworn to Eochaid, son of King Éndae of the Lagini."

"Maeloch son of Innloch." The fisher captain had decided before he left home to give no more identification than he must. With phrases and gestures he indicated what was quite true, that *Osprey* had been blown east, far off course, by the gigantic storm several days ago. Once she had clawed her way around the peninsula, there was no possibility of making any port; she could only keep sea room, running before the wind, full-reefed sail as vital as the oars. When the fury dwindled, his vessel—seams sprung, spars and strakes strained, barely afloat because the crew spent their last flagging forces bailing her—must needs crawl to the nearest land. They grounded her at high tide, and after taking turns sleeping like liches, set about repairs.

Macloch refrained from adding that he had not simply chanced on the haven. He had never been so far east, but some of his followers had, and all heard about the Islands of Crows. That name had come on people's lips in the past hundred years, after the Romans withdrew a presence which had always been slight. Pirates and barbarians— seaborne robbers—soon discovered this was a handy place to lie over. With curses and a rope's end Maeloch had forced his men to gasp at the oars and the buckets till they found a secluded bay. He hoped to refit and set forth before anybody noticed them.

So much for that, he thought harshly. The island folk were a few herders, farmers, fishers. They had no choice but to stay in the good graces of their visitors, furnish food, labor, women...and information.

Doubtless a fellow ranging the woods up above had spied the camp and scuttled off to tell. Doubtless he got a reward.

"Scoti come far," Maeloch ventured. In truth it was surprising to find them here. They harried the western shores of Britannia and, in the past, Gallia. Eastern domains were the booty of rovers from across the Germanic Sea.

Subne tossed his head. "Our chief goes where he will."

"He do, he do." Maeloch nodded and smiled. "We poor men. Soon go home."

To his vast relief, Subne accepted that. Had the warriors searched *Osprey* they would have found hidden stores of fine wares, gold, silver, glass, fabric, gifts with which to proceed in Hivernia should necessity arise to shed his guise of a simple wanderer.

He was not yet free, though. "You will be coming with us," Subne ordered. "Himself wants to know more."

Maeloch stamped on a spark of dismay. "I glad," he replied. Turning to Usun, he said in swift Ysan: "They'd ha' me call on their leader. If I refused, we'd get the lot o' them down on us. Float the ship when ye can and stand by. Be I nay back by nightfall, start off. Ye should still have a fair wind for Britannia, where ye can finish refitting....Nay a word out o' ye! Our mission is for the Nine and the King."

Stark-faced, the mate grunted assent. Maeloch strode from him. "We go," he cried cheerily. The Scoti looked nonplussed. Belike they'd expected the whole crew to accompany him. But Maeloch's action changed their minds for them. Their moods were as fickle as a riptide. Also, he knew, they made a practice of taking hostages to bind an alliance or a surrender. To them, he was the pledge for his men.

He wondered if his spirit could find its way back to Ys, for the Ferrying out to Sena.

Game trails, now and then paths trodden by livestock, wound south from the brooklet, through woods and across meadows, down into glens and aloft onto hills, but generally upward. The warriors moved with the ease of those accustomed to wilderness. Maeloch's rolling gait, his awkwardness in underbrush or fords, slowed them. They bore with it. Warmth rose as morning advanced until sweat was pungent in his tunic.

After maybe an hour the party reached a cliff and started down a ravine that was a watercourse to the sizeable bay underneath. There men lounged around smoky fires. Below the height were several shelters of brushwood, turf, and stones. Some appeared to be years old. This must be a favored harbor for sea rovers.

Two galleys of the deckless Germanic kind lay drawn up on the beach, their masts unstepped. Leather currachs surrounded one. The other was by herself, three hundred feet away. She was longer and leaner, with rakish lines and trim that had once been gaudy. The sight jolted Maeloch. He felt sure he knew her aforetime.

Subne led him to the first. Those were two separate encampments. Such bands tried to keep peace, and mingled somewhat with each other, but had learned not to put much trust in their own tempers.

Scoti sprang to their feet, seized arms, calmed as they recognized comrades, and gathered around. They did not crowd or babble like city folk; their stares were keen and their speech lilted softly. Subne raised his voice: "Chieftain, we've brought you the captain of the outland ship."

A man bent to pass under the door of the largest hut nearby, trod forth, straightened his wide-shouldered leanness. Behind him a young woman peeked out, grimy and frightened. Maeloch saw a few more like her in the open, natives commandeered to char, cook, and be passed from man to man.

His attention went to the leader. Eochaid maqq Éndae, was that the name? The king's son was well dressed in woad-blue shirt, fur-trimmed leather coat, kilt, buskins, though the garments showed soot and wear. His age was hard to guess. Gait, thews, black locks and beard seemed youthful, but the blue eyes looked out of a face furrowed and somber. It would have been a handsome face apart from what weather had done to the light skin, had not three blotchy scars discolored it on cheeks and brow.

His gaze dwelt for a moment on Maeloch's grizzled darkness and bearlike build. When he spoke, it was in accented but reasonably good Redonic, not too unlike the Osismiic dialect: "If you come in honesty, have no fear. You shall be scatheless. Say forth your name and people."

He must have visited himself on these parts before and at length, Maeloch decided; and he was no witless animal. An outright lie would be foolhardy. The fisherman repeated what he told Subne, but in the Gallic language and adding that he was from Ys.

Eochaid raised brows. "Sure and it's early in the year for venturing forth."

"We carry a message. We're under...gess...not to tell any but him it's for."

"They know not gess in Ys. Well, if you gave an oath, I must respect it. Nonetheless—" Eochaid reached a swift decision, as appeared to be his way, and addressed a man who sped off. "We must talk further, Maeloch," he resumed in the Gallic tongue. "The Dani over there have lately been in Ys. I've sent for their captain. First you shall have a welcoming cup."

He settled himself cross-legged on the ground. Maeloch did likewise. The hut was unworthy of a chieftain entertaining a guest, at least in clear weather. Eochaid gestured. His wench scurried to bring two beakers—Roman silver, Roman wine, loot. A number of warriors hung about, watching and listening although few could have followed the

781

talk. Others drifted off to idle, gamble, sharpen their weapons, whatever they had been doing. All had grown restless, waiting on the island.

"You can better give me news of Ys than Gunnung," Eochaid said. "He was there two months agone; but a German would surely miss much and misunderstand much else." The marred visage contorted in a grin. "Beware of repeating that to him." His intent was obvious, playing Northman off against Armorican in hopes of getting a tale more full and truthful than either alone might yield.

Bluntness was Maeloch's wont. "What d'ye care, my lord? Foemen break their bones on the wall of Ys and go down to the eels in the skerries around."

For an instant he thought Eochaid had taken mortal offense, so taut did the countenance grow. Then, stiffly, the Scotian replied: "Every man in Ériu remembers how Niall maqq Echach won sorrow there. Will Ys seek to entrap the likes of me too? I should find out ere I again sail near."

Maeloch knew what was in his mind. Scoti had learned from the disaster and from the later strengthening of the Ysan navy to confine their raids to Britannia—until this new generation reached manhood. Would the city and her she-druid Queens avenge attacks on the rest of Gaul, as they would any on Armorica? Eochaid must be headlong, and belike driven by a murderousness he could only take out on aliens, to have ventured past it. Now, with his men turning homesick, he was having second thoughts.

His words reminded him of that which brought heat into his tones: "Not that I can ever really go back—never to my father's house. And this is the work of Niall. O man of Ys, in me you have no enemy. The foeman of my foeman is my friend. Might we someday, together, bring him low?"

A thrill rang through Maeloch. "Mayhap we do have things to say one to the other, my lord."

The runner returned with the foreign skipper. Eochaid lifted a knee in courtesy to the latter and beckoned both to sit. The wench brought more wine while namings went around.

Gunnung son of Ivar was a huge blond man, young, comely in a coarse fashion. His tunic and breeks were wadmal, but gold gleamed on his arms and was inlaid in his sword haft. A certain slyness glittered in his eyes and smoothed his rumbling voice.

Talk went haltingly, for he knew just a few Celtic words, Eochaid and Maeloch no more Germanic. The runner, a sharp-faced wight called Fogartach, could interpret a little. Moreover, Gunnung had a rough knowledge of Latin, picked up when he went adventuring along the Germanic frontier and in Britannia, while Maeloch had gained about as much over the years—though their accents were so unlike as to make different dialects.

Regardless, Gunnung was happy to brag. Not many of his kin had yet reached the West. It was Juti who were beginning to swarm in, together with Angli, Frisii, and Saxons. Hailing from Scandia, outlawed for three years because of a manslaying, he had gathered a shipful of lusty lads and plundered his way down the coasts of the Tungri and Continental Belgae. Finally they settled for the winter among some Germanic laeti in eastern Britannia, but found the country dull. Defying the season, they embarked for Ys, of which they had heard so much. Piracy there was out of the question, but they did a bit of trading and saw many wonders. "Of course, ve said ve vere alvays peaceful shapmen, ho, ho!"

Eochaid had been watching Maeloch. "Gunnung tells of strife in Ys," he said slowly.

The fisher scowled, searched for a way out—it was loathsome, opening family matters to strangers, let alone barbarians—and at length muttered, "The quarrel's more 'twixt Gods than men. The King has his, the Queens have theirs. 'Tis nay for us to judge."

"They've sent challengers against the King, I hear."

"And he's cut them down, each filthy hound o' them!" Maeloch flared. "When he comes back—" He broke off.

"Ah, he is away?"

"On business with the Romans." Maeloch swore at himself for letting this much slip out. "He may well ha' returned since I left. He'll set things right fast enough."

Gunnung growled a demand which Fogartach relayed, to know what was being said. Eochaid nodded and the interpreter served him.

The Dane guffawed, slapped his knee, and cried, "Tukhai!" Looking at Maeloch, he went on in his crude Latin, "Vill the King then throw his datter off the ness?" He leered. "That douses a hot fire. Better he put her in a whorehouse. She make him rish, by Freyja!"

Maeloch's belly muscles contracted. "What you mean?"

"You not hear? Vell, maybe nobody but they she got killed. For I think they also first yumped through her hoop." Gunnung sighed elaborately. "Ah, almost I vish I stayed and fighted too like she vant. Never I have a gallop like on her. But I do not vant for only nine vomen till I die, haw-aw!"

"Who...she?" grated out of Maeloch's throat.

"Aa, Dahut, who else? She vant I kill her father and make her Qveen. I am a man of honor, but a she-troll like that is right to fool, no?"

"Hold," interrupted Eochaid. He laid a hand on Maeloch's arm. "You're white and atremble. Slack off, man. I'll have no fighting under my roof," as if that were the sky.

"He lies about—a lady he's not fit to name," the Ysan snarled.

Gunnung sensed rage and clapped hand to hilt. Eochaid gestured him to hold still. "He's told me how a princess lay with him, hoping he would challenge her father and win," the Scotian said in Gallic. "Was it true, now?"

"It was nay, and I'll stop his mouth for him."

"Hold! I think the Gods were at work in this. You yourself said we must not judge. Dare you, then? If he lies, sure and They will be punishing him. If he does not lie—I know not what," Eochaid finished grimly. "But to me he has the look of a man who's luck has run out. Yet today he is my guest; and I will never spend my men on a bootless quarrel that is none of ours. Heed."

Maeloch stared around the circle of warriors. They too had winded wrath and drawn closer. Their spearheads sheened against the sun. Inch by inch, his fingers released the helve of the ax that lay beside him. "I hear," he said. To Gunnung, in Latin: "I be surprised. Hurt. You understand? Grallon be my King. Bad, bad, to know his daughter be wicked."

The Dane smiled more kindly than before. "Truth hurt. I tell truth." Wariness reawoke. "You no fight, ha?"

Maeloch waved a hand at the men. "How? If I want to. No fight."

"He's gloated about it," Eochaid said in Redonic. "That is ill done, and now here to your face. But you told me you have a task of your King's. Save your blood for that."

Maeloch nodded. He had gone impassive. "I will." He pondered. "Mayhap he can even help. There'd be rich reward."

"How?" asked Eochaid instantly.

Maeloch considered him. "Or mayhap ye can. Or both of ye. My oath binds me to say no more till I have yours. Whatever happens, whatever ye decide, ye must let my men and me go from this island."

"If I refuse?"

Maeloch drew down the neck of his tunic. White hairs curled amidst the black on his breast. "Here be my heart," he said. "My oath lies in it."

That was enough. Barbarians understood what Romans no longer did, save Grallon: a true man will die sooner than break his word. After a pause, Eochaid answered, "I swear you will go freely, unless you harm me or mine."

"Vat this?" Gunnung wanted uneasily to know.

"Scoti help me?" Maeloch replied. "You help me too? Gold. Scoti protect me."

"You no fisher?"

"I travel for the King of Ys. You not fought King. Not his enemy. You like to help? Gold."

"I listen."

Maeloch passed it on Eochaid. The four sitting men rose. Solemnly, the Scotic chief called his Gods and the spirits of this island to witness that no unprovoked hindrance should come to the Ysans from him.

"Now I can say this much," Maeloch told him. "We're bound for Hivernia...Ériu. The errand's about your enemy Niall and nay friendly to him. Our craft be just a fishing smack, damaged. We've nay yet got her rightly seaworthy, though we can sail in fair weather. This be a tricky season. We'd house at home were the business not pressing. An escort 'ud be a relief. We can pay well and...get ye past Ys without trouble."

Fogartach explained to Gunnung. "Haa!" the Dane bellowed in Latin. "You pay, you got us."

"It may be best that the men of Ériu guide you," Eochaid said.

"Yours and his together?" Maeloch suggested. "Well, settle that 'twixt yourselves. First ye'll want to see what we can offer ye." He paused. "Wisest might be that none but ye twain have that sight. Too often gold's drawn men to treachery."

Eochaid took a certain umbrage at that. Gunnung, however, nodded when it was rendered for him; he must know what ruffians fared under his banner. "He be not afraid to go alone with me," Maeloch stated in Gallic, leaving Eochaid no choice but to agree.

The Scotian did order a currach full of warriors rowed to the inlet to lie offshore—"in case we have a heavy burden to carry back," he explained. "This eventide all our seafarers shall be my guests at a feast."

He gave directions about preparing for that, sent word to the Dani, called for refilled wine goblets. When those had been drained to Lúg, Lir, and Thor, the three captains set off.

Forest took them into itself. Beneath a rustling of breeze, noon brooded warm and still. Branches latticed the sky and wove shadows where brush crouched and boles lifted out of dimness. Sight reached farther on the ridges, but presently nothing was to be seen from them either except tree crowns and a glittery blue sweep of sea. Nobody spoke.

The trail dipped down into a glade surrounded by the wood. Folk said that one like that lay near the middle of the grove outside Ys and was where the sacred combat most often took place. Maeloch, in the lead, stopped, wheeled about, and brought his ax up slantwise. "Draw sword, Gunnung," he said in Latin. "Here I kill you."

The big bright-haired man hooted outraged astonishment. Eochaid sensed trouble. He poised the spear he carried. Maeloch glanced at him and said in Gallic, "This be no man of yours. He befouls my King. Ye swore I'd be safe of ye. Stand aside while I take back my honor."

"It's breaking the peace you are," Eochaid declared.

Maeloch shook his head. "He and I swapped no oaths. Nor be there peace 'twixt Ys and Niall. Later I'll tell ye more."

Eochaid's mouth tightened. He withdrew to the edge of the grass.

"You die now, Gunnung," Maeloch said.

The Dane howled something. It might have meant that the other man would fall and his ghost be welcome to whimper its way back to the little slut he served. Sword hissed from the sheath.

The two stalked about, Gunnung in search of an opening, Maeloch turning in the smallest circle that would keep the confrontation. The Dane rushed. His blade blazed through air. Maeloch blocked it with his ax handle. Iron bit shallowly into seasoned wood. Maeloch twisted his weapon, forced the sword aside. Gunnung freed it. Before he could strike again, the heavy head clattered against it. He nearly lost his hold.

Maeloch pressed in, hewing right and left. His hands moved up and down the helve, well apart as he drew it back, closing together near the end as he swung. The sword sought to use its greater speed to get between those blows. A couple of times it drew blood, but only from scratches. Whenever it clashed on the ax, weight cast it aside. The next strike was weaker, slower.

Gunnung retreated. Maeloch advanced. The Dane got his back against a wall of brush. He saw another blow preparing and made ready to ward it off. As the ax began to move, Maeloch shifted grip. Suddenly he was smiting not from the right but the left. The edge smacked into a shoulder. Gunnung lurched. His blood welled forth around two ends of broken bone. The sword dropped from his hand. Maeloch gauged distances, swung once more, and split the skull of Gunnung.

A while he stood above the heap and the red puddle spreading around it. He breathed hard and wiped sweat off his face. Eochaid approached. Maeloch looked up and said, "Ye had right. His luck had run out."

"This is an evil thing, I think," Eochaid replied. "And unwise. Suppose he had slain you. What then of your task?"

"I have a trusty mate, and ye promised my crew should go free." Maeloch spat on the body. "This thing misused the name of Dahut, daughter of Queen Dahilis—or misused her, which is worse yet. The Gods wanted him scrubbed off the earth."

"That may be. But I must deal with his gang."

"Yours outnumbers them. And 'twasn't ye what killed him. Come with us to Ériu like ye said ye might."

"What is your errand there, Maeloch?"

"What be your grudge against King Niall?"

"This." As Eochaid spoke, it became like the hissing of an adder or a fire. "He entered my land, the Fifth of the Lagini, laid it waste, took from us the Bóruma tribute that is ruinous, made a hostage of me. And I was not kept in honor; he penned me like beast, year upon year. At last I escaped—with the help of a man from Ys—and took my revenge on that follower of his whose satire had so disfigured me that never can I be a king after my father. That man's father cursed my whole country, laid famine on it for a year. Oh, the women and children who starved to death because of worthless Tigernach! But he

786

was a poet, for which I am forever an exile. Do you wonder why I am the enemy of Niall?"

Maeloch whistled. "Nay. And I think he brews harm for us too."

"How?" Eochaid laid a hand over Maeloch's. "Speak without fear. I have not forgotten that man from Ys."

Maeloch stared down at the corpse. He gnawed his lip. "It goes hard to tell. But Dahut—she guests a stranger who admits he's from Niall's kingdom. They go everywhere about together. The Queens be... horrified...but she mocks them, and meanwhile the king be away. Has yon outlander bewitched her? His name is likewise Niall. I'm bound for Ériu to try and find out more."

Eochaid clutched his spear to him. "Another Niall?" he whispered. "Or else— It's always bold he was; and he has sworn vengeance on Ys. He lost his firstborn son there, in that fleet which came to grief long ago." Louder: "What does this Niall of yours look like?"

"A tall man, goodly to behold, yellow hair turning white."

"Could it truly be— Go home!" Eochaid shouted. "Warn them. Seize and bind yonder Niall. Wring the truth out of him!"

Maeloch gusted a sigh. "That be for her father the King. Besides, at worst, he, whoever he be, he can only be a spy. Let me fare on to his homeland and try to learn what he plans, ere he himself can return.... What ye say, though, bids me make haste. I'd meant going to friendly Mumu and asking my way for'ard piece by piece. But best I make straight for...Mide, be that the realm? We need to stop in Britannia first and finish our work on the ship. I'll send a man or two back to Ys from there—we'll buy a boat with word for King Grallon of what I've found out here."

Eochaid had calmed. "Well spoken that is. And indeed you should not bear home at once. When the Dani learn you've killed their chief, they'll scour the waters for you—along the coast, believing you've headed straight west. If you go north you'll shake them."

"Will ye come too? We could meet somewhere."

Eochaid sighed and shook his head. "They remember in Mide. This face of mine would give your game away." Bleakly: "We've thought we'll seek folk like ourselves, Scoti, where we may be making a new home; but that cannot be in green Ériu, not ever again."

Maeloch chopped his ax several times into the turf to clean the blood and brains off it. "I'll be on my way, then."

"I'll come with you to your ship, and sign to my own men that they return. Heave anchor when they're out of sight. I must let Gunnung's men know what happened to him, though I need not tell them more than that." Eochaid grinned. "Nor need I hurry along these trails. For it may be that in you is the beginning of my revenge."

787

III

~ 1 ~

Rovinda, wife of Apuleius, slipped into the darkened room. She left the door ajar behind her. "How are you, Gratillonius?" she murmured. "Sleeping?"

The man in the bed hardly stirred. "No, I've been lying awake." His words came flat.

She approached. "We shall eat shortly. Will you join us?"

"Thank you, but I'm not hungry."

She looked downward. By light that seeped in from the hallway and past the heavy curtain across the window she saw how gaunt and sallow he had grown. "You should. You've scarcely tasted food these past—how many days since you came to us?"

Gratillonius didn't answer. He couldn't remember. Six, seven, eight? It made no difference.

The woman gathered courage. "You must not continue like this."

"I am...worn out."

Her tone sharpened. "You fought your way out of the flood, and afterward exhausted what strength you had left for the sake of what people had survived. True. But that soldier's body of yours should have recovered in a day or two. Gratillonius, they still need you. We all do."

He stared up at her. Though no longer young, she was sightly: tall, brown-haired, blue-eyed, fine-featured, born to a well-off Osismiic family with ancient Roman connections. He recalled vaguely that she was even more quiet and mild than her husband, but even more apt to get her way in the end. He sighed. "I would if I could, Rovinda. Leave me in peace."

"It's no longer weariness that weighs you down. It's sorrow."

"No doubt. Leave me alone with it."

"Others have suffered bereavement before you. It is the lot of mortals." She said nothing about the children she had lost, year after year.

Two lived. Well, he thought, two of his did, Nemeta and Julia, together with little Korai, granddaughter of Bodilis. But the rest were gone. Dahut was gone, Dahilis's daughter, swept from him with foundering Ys, off into Ocean. Would her bones find her mother's down there?

"You should be man enough to carry on," Rovinda said. "Call on Christ. He will help you."

Gratillonius turned his face to the wall.

Rovinda hesitated before she bent above him and whispered, "Or call on what God or Gods you will. Your Mithras you've been so faithful to? Sometimes I—please keep this secret; it would hurt Apuleius too much—I am a Christian, of course, but sometimes in hours of grief I've stolen away and opened my heart to one of the old Goddesses. Shall I tell you about Her? She's small and kindly."

Gratillonius shook his head on the pillow.

Rovinda straightened. "I'll go, since you want me to. But I'll send in a bowl of soup, at least. Promise me you'll take that much."

He kept silent. She went out.

Gratillonius looked back toward the ceiling. Sluggishly, he wondered what did ail him. He should indeed have been up and about. The ache had drained from muscles and marrow. But what remained was utter slackness. It was as if a sorcerer had turned him to lead, no, a sack of meal. Where worms crawled. Most of his hours went in drowsing—never honest sleep, or so it seemed.

Well, why not? What else? The world was formless, colorless, empty of meaning. All Gods were gone from it. He wondered if They had ever cared, or ever existed. The question was as vain as any other. He felt an obscure restlessness, and supposed that in time it would force him to start doing things. They had better be dullard's tasks, though; he was fit for nothing more.

—Brightness roused him. He blinked at the slim form that rustled in carrying a bowl. Savory odors drifted out of it. "Here is your soup, Uncle Gaius," Verania greeted. "M-m-mother said I could bring it to you."

"I'm not hungry," he mumbled.

"Oh, please." The girl set it down on a small table which she drew to the bedside. She dared a smile. "Make us happy. Old Namma—the cook, you know—worked extra hard on it. She adores you."

Gratillonius decided it was easiest to oblige. He sat up. Verania beamed. "Ah, wonderful! Do you want me to feed it to you?"

That stung. He threw her a glare but encountered only innocence. "I'm not crippled," he growled, and reached for the spoon. After a few mouthfuls he put it back.

"Now you can eat more than that," she coaxed. "Just a little more. One for Namma. She does have good taste, doesn't she? In men, I mean— Oh!" She brought hand to lips. By the sunlight reflected off a corridor wall he saw her blush fiery.

Somehow that made him obey. And that encouraged her. She grew almost merry. "Fine. Take another for...for your horse Favonius. Poor dear, he misses you so....One for Hercules....One for Ulysses....One for, m-m, my brother. You promised Salomon you'd teach him sword- and shieldcraft when he was big enough, do you remember?...One for Julius Caesar. One for Augustus. One for TibÉrius. You don't have to take one for Caligula, but Claudius was nice, wasn't he?"

789

With a flicker of wish to argue, Gratillonius said, "He conquered Britannia."

"He made your people Romans, like mine. Give him his libation, do. Down your throat. Good." She clapped her hands.

Feet thudded in the hall. Verania squeaked. She and Gratillonius gaped at the tall gaunt man in the travel-stained rough robe who entered. He strode to the bedside and placed himself arms akimbo, glowering.

"I hear you're ill." His voice was harsher than before, as if he had lately shouted a great deal. "What's the matter? Rovinda says you have no fever."

"You're back," Gratillonius said.

Corentinus's gray beard waggled to his nod, as violent as that was. "Tell me more, O wise one. I've brought men for you. Now get out and use them, for I've reached the limit of what I can make those muleheads do."

"Sir, he *is* sick," Verania made bold to plead. "What do you want of him? Can't father take charge, or, or anybody?"

The pastor softened at sight of her face. Tears trembled on her lashes. "I fear not, child," he said. "To begin with, they are pagans, disinclined to heed me."

"From Ys—from what was Ys?"

He nodded. "We must start at once preparing a place for the survivors. The first few score have lodging here, but not for long; soon the traders will be coming, and Aquilo needs them too much to deny them their usual quarters. Besides, it could never take in all who are left in the countryside. They'll require shelter, defenses—homes. Your father has most Christianly granted a good-sized site, his farmland. Oh, you knew already? Well, first we should make a ditch and wall: for evildoers will hear of the disaster and come seeking to take advantage. I went back after able-bodied men. On the way, I thought they'd better include some who know how to fight."

He and Apuleius decided this, and he walked off...without me, Gratillonius thought. Inwardly he cringed. Aloud: "Who did you find?"

"I remembered that squad of marines at the Nymphaeum," Corentinus answered. "They refused to leave unless the women came too. They think it's their sacred duty to guard the women of the Temple. Well, that's manly of them. But I had a rocky time persuading the priestess in charge, that Runa, persuading her to leave immediately. At last she agreed. By then such a span had passed that I thought best we go straightaway. The marines could begin on the fortifications while I went after additional labor. But they will not. I stormed and swore, but couldn't shake them."

"Why?" wondered Gratillonius.

"In part their leader claims they must stay with their charges. I have to admit Runa's trying to convince them she and the others will be safe in Aquilo. But also, they say it's demeaning work. Furthermore, they don't know how to do it. Ha!"

Gratillonius tugged his beard. "There's truth in that," he said slowly. "It's more than just digging. Cutting turfs and laying them to make a firm wall is an art." After a moment: "An art never known in Ys because it was never needed, and pretty much lost in Gallia. I think we in the Britannia were the last of the real old legionaries. On the continent they've become cadres at best—the best not worth much—for peasant reserves and barbarian mercenaries."

The eagles of Rome fly no more. All at once the thought was not insignificant like everything mortal, nor saddening or frightening. It infuriated him.

"So stop malingering," Corentinus snapped. "Go show them."

"Oh!" wailed Verania, shocked and indignant.

"By Hercules, I will." Gratillonius swung himself out of the blankets onto the floor. He had forgotten his nakedness. Verania smothered a gasp and fled. His blunder lashed yet more life into him. He had to make it good. Flinging on tunic, hastily binding sandals, he stalked from the room, Corentinus at his heels.

Given directions, he found the party outside of town, at the western end of the bridge across the Odita. He must push through a crowd of curious local folk. They kept well aside, though, and he glimpsed some making furtive signs against witchcraft.

It was a clear afternoon. He felt a faint amazement at how bright the sunlight was. A blustery wind chased small clouds; a flight of storks passed overhead, as white as they. Light burned along the greenness that had bestormed fields and forest. The wind was sharp, with a taste of newly turned earth in it. Women's dresses, men's cloaks, stray locks of hair fluttered.

The vestals shared none of the wind's vigor. Their trip had been cruel to soft feet, though they took turns on the four horses and had overnighted in a charcoal burner's hut. They clutched their garments and stared with eyes full of fright—and Nemeta's an underlying defiance. Korai clung to Julia's hand like an infant. Runa did seem undaunted. Her lips were pressed thin in anger. She hailed Gratillonius coldly.

The dozen marines stood together, Amreth at their head. They bore the full gear of their corps: peaked helmets, flared shoulderpieces and greaves, loricated cuirasses engraved with abstract motifs, cloth blue or gray like the sea, laurel-leaf swords, hooked pikes. Gratillonius felt relief at seeing the metal was polished; but the outfits made them glaringly alien here.

He approached the leader and halted. Amreth gave him salute. He responded as was fitting among Ysans. "Greeting," he said in their tongue, "and welcome to your new home."

"We thank you, lord," Amreth answered with care.

791

"'Twill take work ere 'tis fit for the settling of our folk. What's this I hear about your refusing duty?"

Amreth braced himself. "Lord, I am of Suffete family. Most of us are. Pick-and-shovel work is for commoners."

"'Twas good enough for Rome's legionaries when Caesar met Brennilis. Sailors born to Suffetes toil side by side with their lowborn shipmates. Do you fear you lack the strength?"

Amreth reddened beneath his sunburn. "Nay, lord. We lack skill. Why not bring men off the farms?"

"They're plowing and sowing, lest everyone go hungry later. 'Twill be a lean year, with so many mouths. Be thankful Aquilo will share till we can take care of ourselves."

"Well, countryfolk who were your subjects are still back in the homeland. Fetch them, lord. Our duty is to these holy maidens."

"Aye. To make a proper place for them, not stand idle when they've ample protection waiting behind yonder rampart."

Amreth frowned. Gratillonius drew breath. "They who remain of Ys *are* my subjects," he said levelly. "I am the King. I broke the Scoti, I broke the Franks, and I slew every challenger who sought me in the Wood. If the Gods of Ys have forsaken my people, I have not. I will show you what to do and teach you how and cut the first turfs with these hands that have wielded my sword." He raised his voice. "Attention! Follow me."

For an instant he thought he had lost. Then Amreth said, "Aye, King," and beckoned to his men. They fell in behind Gratillonius.

"I will take them to the site, and barrack them later," he told Runa. "Let Corentinus lead you and the vestals to your quarters now, my lady."

She nodded. He marched off with the marines, over the bridge, through the town, out the east gate, northward along the river to the confluence. As yet he must compel himself, hold a shield up to hide the vacantness within; but already he felt it filling and knew he would become a man again. If nothing else, he had a man's work ahead of him.

It was odd how he kept thinking of Runa. Her look upon him had turned so thoughtful.

~ 2 ~

Most fruit trees were done with blooming, but a new loveliness dwelt in Liguria. From mountains north, south, and west, the plain around Mediolanum reached eastward beyond sight, orchards, fields marked off by rows of mulberry and poplar whose leaves danced in the breeze, tiny white villages. The air lulled blithe with birdsong. It was as if springtime would repay men for the harshness of the winter past, the brutality of the summer to come. Even slaves went about their work with a measure of happiness.

Rufinus and Dion rode back to the city. Sunlight slanted from low on their right. The horses plodded. They had covered a number of miles since leaving at dawn. In hills northward they had had hours of rest while their riders took the pleasures of the woodland, food and drink, lyre and song, frolic, love, ease in each other's nearness. But the return trip was long. When walls and towers became clear in their sight, the animals regained some briskness.

Rufinus laughed. "They're ready for the good old stable, they are! And what would you say to an hour or two in the baths?"

"Well," Dion replied with his usual diffidence, "it will be pleasant. And still—I wish this day did not have to end. If only we could have stayed where we were forever."

Rufinus's glance went fondly over him, from chestnut hair and tender countenance to the lissomeness of the sixteen-year-old body. "Be careful about wishes, dear. Sometimes they're granted. I've lived in forests, remember."

"Oh, but you were an outlaw then. You've been everything, haven't you? Naturally, I meant—"

"I know. You meant the Empire would bring us our wine and delicacies and fresh clothes, and keep bad men away, and be there for us to visit whenever the idyll grew a bit monotonous. Don't scoff at civilization. It's not just more safe and comfortable than barbarism, it's much more interesting."

"It did not do well by you when you were young. I hope those people who were cruel to you are burning in hell."

The scar that seamed Rufinus's right cheek turned his smile into a sneer. "I doubt it. Why should the Gods trouble Themselves about us?"

Dion's smooth cheeks flushed. "The true God cares."

"Maybe. I don't say that whatever Powers there are can never be bribed or flattered. Heaven knows you Christians try. I do ask whether it's worthwhile. All history shows Them to be incompetent at best, bloodthirsty and dishonest at worst. Supposing They exist, that is."

The Gaul saw distress rise in his servant. He made his smile warm, leaned over, squeezed the youth's hand. "I'm sorry," he said. "That was nothing but an opinion. Don't let it spoil things for you. I'm not bitter, truly I'm not. Since I became the sworn man of the King of Ys, my fate has generally been good. At last it brought me to you. That's why I praise civilization and call it worth defending as long as possible."

Large brown eyes searched the green of his. "As long as possible, did you say?" Dion's words wavered.

He was so vulnerable. But he needed to learn. His life had been sheltered: son of a Greek factor in Neapolis by a concubine native to that anciently Greek city, taught arts and graces as well as letters, apprenticed in the household of an Imperial courtier two years ago, assigned to Rufinus as a courtesy after the Gaul became a man whose goodwill was desirable, and by this new master initiated in the mysteries of Eros. "I do not want to make you unhappy, my sweet," Rufinus emphasized. "You have heard about the dangers afoot, both inside and outside the Empire. We needn't feel sorry for ourselves on their account. Coping with them is the grandest game in the world."

"*You* find it so," Dion breathed worshipfully. White with dread, he had watched Rufinus's hell-for-leather chariot racing and other such sports. The first time, Rufinus could only soothe him afterward by tuning a harp and singing him the gentlest of the songs that the envoy of Ys had brought from the North.

Rufinus blew a kiss. "Well, maybe the second grandest," he laughed.

His own happiness bubbled. Of course he longed for everything he had had to leave, but that was months agone and forebodings had faded. Here the newnesses, adventures, challenges, accomplishments —real victories won for Gratillonius and Ys—were endless, and now Dion had come to him. Oh, true, they must be discreet. However, that did not mean they must be furtive; those at court who guessed found it politic to keep winks and sniggers private, if indeed anyone especially cared. And this was no bestial grappling among the Bacaudae nor hurried encounter with a near stranger, it was an exploration day by day and night by night shared with beauty's self.

They left their horses at a livery stable and passed on foot through the city gate to a majestic street. Seat of the Emperors of the West for nearly a hundred years, Mediolanum had accumulated splendors and squalors which perhaps only Constantinople surpassed. Often Rufinus found the architecture heavy, even oppressive, when he thought of the slimnesses in Ys; sometimes the vulgarity ceased for a while to excite, the shrill contentions of the Christian sects to amuse, and he remembered a people who bore the pridefulness of cats; but this place was at the core of things, while Ys merely sought to hold herself aloof. This was where men laid snares for men, and his heart beat the higher for it.

Through workers, carters, vendors, beggars, housewives, whores, holy men, soldiers, slaves, thieves, mountebanks, provincials from end to end of the Empire, barbarians from beyond, through racket and chatter and fragrance and stench, he led the way to the home granted him. It was a small apartment, but in a respectable tenement and on the first floor. (In Ys he lived, by choice, up among winds and wings.) Dion would choose clean clothes for them both, they would seek the baths and luxuriate until they came back for a light supper the boy would prepare, and then—whatever they liked. Perhaps simply a little talk before sleep. Rufinus would do most of the conversing. He enjoyed the role of teacher.

A eunuch in palace livery sat on the hallway floor at the apartment entrance. He jumped to his feet when he saw them. "At last, sir!" he piped. "Quickly! I am bidden to bring you before Master of Soldiers Flavius Stilicho."

"What?" exclaimed Rufinus. He heard Dion gasp. "But nobody knew where I was or when I'd return."

"So I informed his gloriousness after I learned." The messenger's hairless, somehow powdery face drew into a web of lines. "He was most kind; he bade me go back and wait for you. Come, sir, let us make haste."

Rufinus nodded. "At once." With a grin: "He's an old campaigner, he won't mind dust and sweat on me."

"Oh, he has much else to occupy his attention, you know, sir. Doubtless you'll make an appointment with a deputy for tomorrow. But *come.*"

"Seek the baths yourself," Rufinus suggested to Dion.

"I'll wash here and have a meal ready for you," his companion answered, and gazed after him till he was gone from sight.

Hurrying along thoroughfares where traffic was diminishing, Rufinus tugged the short black forks of his beard and scowled in thought. What in the name of crazy Cernunnos might this be? Why should he be summoned by the dictator of the West? And of the East, too, they said, now that the Gothic general Gainas was in charge there; Gainas was Stilicho's creature, and Emperor Arcadius a weakling a few years older than his brother and colleague Honorius, who in turn was one year older than Dion....Rufinus had conveyed letters from the King of Ys, Bishop Martinus of Turonum, and others in the North. He had contrived excuses to linger while he made himself interesting or entertaining or useful in this way and that way to men of secondary importance at court, until by their favor his status was quasi-official. He could doubtless continue the balancing act till his term of exile ended and he went home. But how did he suddenly come to be of any fresh concern to Stilicho, so much that the great man wanted to see him in person?

Rufinus sketched a grin and swayed his head about snakewise. It might not be on its neck this time tomorrow.

Sunset flared off glass in upper stories of the palace compound. The eunuch's garb and password gave quick admittance through a succession of doors and guards. He left the Gaul in an anteroom while he went off to find the deputy he had mentioned. Rufinus sat down and tried to count the blessings of the day that had just ended. The garishness of the religious figures on the walls kept intruding.

The eunuch returned. Three more followed him. "You are honored, sir," he twittered. "The consul will see you at once."

Aye, thought Rufinus in Ysan, this year did also that title, of much pomp and scant meaning, come to the mighty Stilicho. Well, he had forced peacefulness on the Visigoths in the East (though 'twas strange that King Alaric received an actual Roman governorship in Illyricum) and had put down rebellion in Africa and two years agone had married his daughter to the Emperor Honorius....Precautions and deference were passed. The two men were alone.

Twilight was stealing into the austere room where Stilicho sat in a chair behind a table. Before him was a litter of papyruses he must have been going through, documents or dispatches or whatever they were, together with some joined thin slabs of wood whereon were inked words that Rufinus suspected meant vastly more. The general showed the Vandal side of his descent in height and the time-dulled blondness of hair and short beard. He wore a robe plain, rumpled, not overly clean, the sleeves drawn back from his hairy forearms.

Never himself a soldier, Rufinus had watched legionaries come to attention. He tried for a civilian version of it. Momentarily, Stilicho's lips quirked.

The smile blinked out, the look became somber. "You should have left word where you would be today," Stilicho rumbled.

"I'm sorry, uh, sir. I had no idea my presence would be wanted."

"Hm. Why not? You've been buzzing enough about the court and... elsewhere."

"The Master knows everything."

Stilicho's fist thudded on the table. "Stow that grease. By the end of each day, it drips off me. Speak plain. You're no straightforward courier for the King of Ys. You're at work on his behalf, aren't you?"

Rufinus answered with the promptitude he saw would be best for him. "I am that, sir. It's no secret. The Master knows Ys and its King—the tribune of Rome—are loyal. More than loyal; vital. But we have our enemies. We need a spokesman at the Imperium." He paused for three pulsebeats. "Rome needs one."

Stilicho nodded. "At ease. I don't question your motives. Your judgment—that may be another matter. Though you've shown a good deal of mother wit, from what I hear. As in finding that ring stolen from the lady Lavinia."

Without relaxing alertness, Rufinus let some of the tension out of his muscles. "That was nothing, sir. When I compared the stories told by members of the household, it was clear who the thief must be."

"Still, I don't know who else would have thought to go about it that way, and save a lot of time and torture." The general brooded for a moment. "You call Ys vital. So did the letters you brought, and the arguments were not badly deployed. But it's a slippery word. How vital was, say, the Teutoburg Forest? We don't know yet, four hundred years later. Sit down." He pointed at a stool. "I want to ask a few questions about Ys."

—Beeswax candles had the main room of the apartment aglow. Dion woke at Rufinus's footsteps and was on his own feet before the door had opened. "Oh, welcome!" he cried; and then, seeing the visage: "What's happened, my soul, what is it?"

Rufinus lurched across the floor. Dion hastened to close the door and meet him by the couch. "Stilicho told me at last," Rufinus mumbled. "He drew me out first, but he told me at last."

Dion caught the other's hands. "What is it?" he quavered.

"Oh, I can't blame Stilicho. I'd have done the same in his place. He needed my information calmly given, because he will never get it elsewhere, not ever again. Nobody will." Rufinus's long legs folded under him. He sank onto the seat and gaped at emptiness.

Dion sat down at his side and caressed him. "T-t-tell me when you w-want to. I can wait."

"A dispatch came today," said Rufinus. His words fell like stones, one by one. "Ys died last month. The sea came in and drowned it."

Dion wailed.

Rufinus rattled a laugh. "Be the first of the general public to know," he said. "Tomorrow the news will be all over town. It'll be a sensation for at least three days, if nothing juicier happens meanwhile."

Dion laid his head in Rufinus's lap and sobbed.

Presently Rufinus was able to stroke the curly hair and mutter, "There, now; good boy; you cry for me, of course, not for a city you never knew, but that's natural; you care."

Dion clung. "You are not forsaken!"

"No, not entirely. The King escaped, says the dispatch. Gratillonius lives. You've heard me speak of him aplenty. I'm going to him in the morning. Stilicho gave me leave. He's by no means an unkindly man, Stilicho."

Dion raised his face. "I am with you, Rufinus. Always."

The Gaul shook his head. "I'm afraid not, my dear," he replied almost absently, still staring before him. "I shall have to send you back to Quintilius. With a letter of praise for your service. I can do that much for you before I go—"

"No!" screamed Dion. He slipped from the couch and went on his knees, embracing the knees of Rufinus. "Don't leave me!"

"I must."

"You said—you said you love me."

"And you called yourself the Antinöus to my Hadrianus." Rufinus looked downward. "Well, you were young. You are yet, while I have suddenly become old. I could never have taken you along anyhow, much though I've wanted to. It would make an impossible situation."

"We can keep it secret," Dion implored.

Again Rufinus shook his head. "Too dangerous for you, lad, in the narrow-minded North. But worse than that, by itself it would destroy you. Because you see—" he searched for words, and when he had found them must force them forth—"my heart lies yonder. It's only the ghost of my heart that came down here. Now the ghost has to return from heaven to earth, and endure.

"Someday you'll understand, Dion," he said against the tears. "Someday when you too are old."

~ 3 ~

Osprey came to rest on a day of mist-fine rain, full of odors sweet and pungent from an awakening land. Maeloch had inquired along the way and learned that this was where the River Ruirthech met the sea, the country of the Lagini on its right and Mide, where Niall of the Nine Hostages was foremost among kings, to the left. He steered along the north side of the bay looking for a place to stop, and eventually found it. Through the gray loomed a great oblong house, white against brilliant grass. It stood a short distance from the water, at the meeting of two roads unpaved but well kept, one following the shore, one vanishing northwesterly. "Belike we can get hospitality here," he said. His voice boomed through the quiet. "Watch your tongues, the lot o' ye." Several of his men knew a Hivernian dialect or two, some of them better than he.

They made fast at a rude dock. By that time they had been seen, and folk had come from the house or its outbuildings. They were both men and women, without weapons other than their knives and a couple of spears. The compound was not enclosed by an earthen wall as most were. A portly red-bearded fellow trod forward. "Welcome to you, travelers, so be it you come in peace," he called. "This is the hostel of Cellach maqq Blathmaqqi. Fire is on the hearth, meat on the spit, and beds laid clean for the weary."

Such establishments were common throughout the island—endowed with land and livestock so that their keepers could lodge free all wayfarers, for the honor of the king or tribe and the furthering of trade. "Maeloch son of Innloch thanks yuh," he replied ritually. "We from Armorica." That much would be plain to any man who knew something of the outside world, as they surely did here.

"A long way you've come, then," said Cellach.

Maeloch beckoned to a crewman who had been on trading voyages to Mumu and could speak readily. "The storm at full moon blew us off course for the south of your country," that sailor explained. "Having made repairs afterward, and being where we were, we thought to do what had been in many minds and see if we could find a new market for our wares." That was true, as far as it went. To be caught in an outright lie would mean the contempt of the Scoti and end any chance of talking with them.

Cellach frowned. "Himself at Temir is no friend to the Romans or their allies." He brightened. "But his grudges are not mine, nor are they grudges of my tuath and our own king. Let us help you with your gear and bring you to our board."

"Yuh no afraid enemies?" asked Maeloch on the way up.

"We are not," Cellach replied. "Do you see rath or guards? True, the Lagini were close by, but they could never have come raiding without being spied in time for men to rally from the shielings around about. And Temir is some twenty leagues off; though the King there is often away, warriors aplenty would soon be avenging. Even in days when the hostel was founded, the Lagini left this strand alone. And now Niall has reaped their land with his sword, and afterward the poet Laidchenn called famine into it, till nobody dwells across from Clón Tarui. What my wife and I fear, so long as the sky does not fall, is only that we may fail to guest our visitors as grandly as did my mother, the widow Morigel, who had this place before me."

The main house was built of upright poles with wicker-work between, the whole chinked and whitewashed, the thatch of the roof intricately woven. Windows let in scant light, but lamps hung from the beams, which were upheld by pillars, and a fire burned in a central pit. The floor was strewn with fresh rushes. Furnishings were merely stools and low tables; however, hangings, albeit smoke-blackened, decorated the walls. One side of the cavernous space was filled by cubicles. Two wooden partitions, about eight feet high, marked off each; the third side stood open toward the east end of the hall, revealing a bed that could hold two or three. "You're few enough that you can sleep alone," laughed Cellach, "the which is not needful for those among you who are lucky."

True to his promise, when the mariners had shed their wet outer garments and shoes, he settled them at the small tables. Women brought ale and food. Scoti customarily took their main meal in the evening, but this midday serving was generous, beef, pork, salmon, bread, leeks, nuts, unstinted salt. The one who filled Maeloch's platter was young, buxom, auburn-haired and freckle-faced. She brushed against him more than once, and when he looked her way she returned a mischievous smile. "Ah, a daughter of mine, Áebell," said the landlord. He had joined the captain and Usun at their table. "It seems as though she favors you." Proudly: "If true, you are lucky indeed, indeed. She's unwed thus far, but not for lack of men. Why, King Niall beds her and none else when he honors this house."

The eyes narrowed in Usun's leathery countenance. "When was that last, may I ask?" he murmured.

"Och, only some eight or nine days agone, though long since the time before. He came here in a Saxon kind of ship, which his crew took onward while himself and a few warriors borrowed horses of me and rode straight to Temir in the morning. That was a wild night, I can tell you. They drank like whirlpools and swived like stallions. Something fateful had happened abroad for sure. But the King would not let them say what." Cellach shook his head and looked suddenly troubled. "I talk too much." He made a sign against misfortune.

Maeloch and Usun exchanged a glance. It was as if winter had stolen back upon them.

Nevertheless Maeloch donned a gruff heartiness when he sought out Áebell. She was easy to find, and free for a while. He invited her to come see his craft. Poor though his command of the language was, she listened eagerly as he hacked his way through it. He could follow her responses, and his skill grew with practice. While grimness underlay his spirit, it was lightsome, after a hard voyage, to boast before a girl. When she must go back to her household duties she kissed him hard and he cupped a breast, they two out of sight in the dim rain.

That night they left the drinking after supper hand in hand, earlier than most. A couple of her father's tenants uttered a cheer, a couple of sailors who did not have wenches at their sides groaned good-naturedly. In his cubicle she slipped her dress over her head and fumbled at the lacing of his tunic. His lust made her lovely; she glowed in the shadows. He bore her down on the bed and, both heedless of anyone who might hear, he rutted her.

When she had her breath again, she said in his ear, "Now that was mightily done. It's glad I'd be if all men were like you—"

"Soon I do more," he bragged.

"—or King Niall. Is it that the sea makes you strong?" She giggled. "Sure and he was a bull from out of the waves last time, in spite of brooding about Ys." She felt his frame go iron-hard. "Are you angered? I am not calling you the less, darling."

Still he lay without motion, save for the quick rise and fall of his breast above the slugging heart. "Were you ever in Ys?" she tried. "I hear it was magical. They say the Gods raised it and used to walk its lanes on moonlit nights."

He sat up and seized her. "What happen Ys?" he rasped.

"Ee-ai! You hurt me, let go!"

He unlocked his fingers. "I sorry. How Ys? Yuh know? Say."

"Is something wrong?" Cellach called from the fireside talk of those still up.

"Not, not," Maeloch shouted. To Áebell, low: "I beg, tell. I give gold, silver, fine things."

She peered through the gloom at the staring whiteness of eyeballs and teeth. "I kn-know nothing. He forbade they say. But they got drunk and, and words slipped free—" Rallying her wits, she crouched amidst the tumbled coverings and whispered, "Why do you care?"

"Ys great," he said hastily. "Rich. Make trade."

"M-m, well—" She nodded. "But I am just a little outland girl. I don't understand these man-things." She smiled and brought herself against him. "I only understand men. Hold me close, darling. You are so strong."

He obeyed; but no matter what she did, his flesh had no more will toward her. Finally she sighed, "Ah, you are worse tired from your travels than you knew, Maeloch, dear. Get a good night's rest, and tomorrow we'll make merry." She kissed him, rose, pulled the gown over her, and left.

After a while the last folk went to bed. A banked fire barely touched the darkness. Maeloch lay listening to the horrors in his head. Once he thought he heard hoofbeats go by.

In the morning, which was overcast but free of rain, he told Cellach he and his crew had better be off. "Now why would you be wanting to do that this soon?" the hostelkeeper replied. "You've talked with none but us here. You've shown us nothing of your goods nor asked what we in these parts might wish to trade for them. Take your ease, man. We want to hear much more. It's close-mouthed you've been, I must say."

Maeloch felt too weary after his sleepless night to press the matter. He sat dully on a bench outside and rebuffed Usun's anxious questions. Áebell was nowhere about. Had she sought another mate elsewhere, or was she simply staying from him till he could get over his failure? He cared naught. His wife and children, the first grandchild, those were encamped in him.

Áebell returned at midday. With her rode a troop of warriors. Their spearheads rose and fell to the onwardness of the horses, like wind-rippled grain. At their head was a tall man with golden hair and beard begun to turn frosty. A seven-colored cloak fluttered from his shoulders.

The household swarmed forth. The sailors drew together and advanced behind. Their weapons were in the hostel. "Lord Niall!" cried Cellach. "A thousand welcomes. What brings you to honor us again?"

The King's smile was bleak. "Your daughter, as you can see," he answered. "She rode through the night to tell me of men from Ys."

Some women gasped and some men gaped. Cellach held steady. "I felt the breath of such a thought myself, lord, that they are Ysans," he said. "But I was not sure. How could you be, Áebell mine?"

She tossed her head. "What else, the way he turned cold? And Ys was the enemy of Niall from before my birth." She edged her mount toward the tall man.

Aye, thought Maeloch, Scotic women were free, and therefore keen and bold, as Roman women were not. As women of Ys were, in their very different way. He should have remembered.

Niall looked over heads, pierced him with a lightning-blue stare, and said, "You are the captain."—in Ysan.

Maeloch stepped to the fore. The heaviness was gone from his limbs, the terrors from his heart. It was as if he stood outside his body and steered it. Thus had he been in combat or when close to shipwreck. "Aye," he said, "and ye too ha' lately fared from my city."

"I have that."

"What did ye there?"

Niall signed to his followers. They leaped off their horses and took battle stance. "Prepare yourself," he said quietly. "Ys is no more. On the night of storm, Lir came in."

At his back, Maeloch heard Usun croak like one being strangled, another man moan, a jagged animal noise from a third. "How wrought ye this?" he asked, well-nigh too low for anybody to hear.

Niall bit his lip. "Who are you to question me? Be glad I don't cut you down out of hand."

"Oh, ye'll get your chance. Come fight me, or forever bear the name of craven."

Niall shook his head. "The King at Temir is under gess to fight only in war." He nodded toward a giant in his band. "There is my champion, if you wish a duel." That man grinned and hefted his sword.

"'Tis ye that hell awaits," Maeloch stated.

"Hold your jaw!" Áebell shrilled furiously.

A chillier wrath congealed Niall's features. "My task is unfinished until naught whatsoever remains of Ys, the city that murdered my son and my good men. Your insolence has doomed you likewise."

"My lord!" Cellach thrust his mass in front of Maeloch. "These are my guests. On my land they have sanctuary. Heed the law."

For an instant Niall seemed about to draw blade and hew at him. Then Niall snapped a laugh. "As you will, for as long as you house them."

"That will be no longer than they need to take ship, lord." Cellach looked over his shoulder. "Be off with you," he spat. "It's lucky you are that there is no craft on hand for pursuing you."

"Nor harbor for you at journey's end," Niall gibed.

How fierce must his hatred be, that he stooped to mockery of helpless men? Or was it something deeper and still more troubling? Maeloch was as yet beyond all feelings, like a sword or a hammer; he knew remotely that later he must weep, but now his throat spoke for him:

"Aye, well may the memory of Ys glimmer away, for the Veil of Brennilis did ever ward her; but ye ha' gone it behind it yourself, and somehow this ill thing be your doing. Forgetfulness shall come over it also, and over everything else till folk unborn today wonder if Niall truly lived; but first we who do remember will bring ye to your death."

He turned to his crew. "Fetch your things," he ordered. "We can still catch the tide."

Behind him Áebell made fending signs against his curse. Niall reached over and touched her. She calmed immediately and smiled at the man she loved.

IV

~ 1 ~

Publius Flavius Drusus, old soldier, came in from his farm and took over as taskmaster in making wall and ditch for the new settlement. Work went fast, once the marines and the refugee laborers who presently joined them had gotten the knack.

"No, no," he explained to a man who had brought a turf; the spade wielders were beginning predictably to cut standard thirty-pound pieces out of the topsoil. "You lay it grass side *down*. That holds better, and we can smooth and level the dirt for the next course."

Amreth, who knew some Latin, translated for him and asked why the wall wasn't being raised more than breast high. A deeper or broader fosse would provide the material, together with added protection.

"We're doing this like an old-time legion setting up camp," Drusus answered. "We don't need anything else, at least not right away. Only two sides; we've got the rivers for the other two. The idea is simply to slow down an attack enough that men will have time to rouse, arm themselves, and take their stations. You see, meanwhile they'll have gotten their sleep, because they won't have needed but a few on sentry -go. They'll be fresh, ready for combat."

"What when the colony gets too big?"

"Well, we can lengthen this work. If the growth still keeps on, we'll build a proper wall, high, with timbers and stones in it. But first start begetting some youngsters, eh?"

Drusus's jape drew no smiles from those who heard and understood. Most had lost all but their own lives, mere days ago.

It was nevertheless fortunate that he could spare the time, as busy as Gratillonius became with shepherding people from the Ysan hinterland. At the outset he billeted them in Aquilo. When all free spaces there were filled, he must find shelter round about in the countryside.

After the first time he did this, he stopped at the confluence to inquire how things were progressing. Time pressed. Before long, trade goods would start arriving up the Odita and overland, and their conductors require those roofs in town that now covered his folk.

He found the defenses completed. They enclosed tents for workers and guards. Houses were going up, the wood for them taken from the nearby forest. They were rude Celtic shielings, but quickly built, sufficient to keep off the weather until something better was ready. Rustics should do well enough in them; Gratillonius wondered how survivors from the city would fare.

Somehow the labor had spared a stand of cornel between the wall and a brook that came from the north to meet the Odita. It was in bloom. He saw, and the frail whiteness stabbed him through. Tonight the moon would be full, as it had last been over the death of Ys.

He left at sundown, knowing he could not sleep, flinching from the thought of a room that would feel as black and narrow as the grave. First he should stable Favonius— No, a day's faring around did not seem to have worn the stallion out, given a while to rest and crop. "Would you like a ramble, old friend?" Gratillonius murmured. "Tomorrow you can take your ease in a pasture." He crushed the wish that he himself might someday enjoy the same peace. A man should not whine at the Fates.

They crossed the road and followed the river road east. Ultimately it would join the highway from Darioritum Venetorum, but that ran north of here on its way to Vorgium and Gesocribate. The great hill bulked darkling on his right; for a time gold lingered on the crowns of its uppermost trees, then died as the sky deepened and the first western stars blinked forth. He left it behind. The river turned north and the road went off more or less parallel to the Jecta stream though at a little distance from it and gradually climbing. High forest hid the tributary but the view south ran widely. Parts remained under cultivation—light gleamed yellow from a cluster of huts—while woods that were reclaiming the rest had not yet grown tall. Cornel, abundant in these parts, stood especially thick along the wayside. Sweetness breathed from it out of the shadows. There was hardly a sound but the clop of hoofs, occasional creak of leather, breath and heartbeat.

The moon rose, enormous at first, smaller and colder as it mounted. When Gratillonius looked at its ashen face his eyes were briefly dazzled. The light washed over the world like a sea. White blossoms caught it and shone like Dahut's hair, like her outreaching hands.

Something moved afar. Gratillonius strained to see. Another rider, hitherbound from the east. Welcome, whoever you are. Bring my soul back from the flowers and the moon. He clucked to Favonius. The stallion broke into a trot.

Nearing, he saw that the other horse was exhausted. Its man must have forced it unmercifully. Of course, you couldn't gallop all the time, and now the pace was down to a shambling walk, but—

Moonlight dappled a lean form, sharp features, fork beard that might have been snipped out of the night. Could it be? It was. "Rufinus!" yelled Gratillonius.

"Cernunnos! Is that you?" croaked the remembered voice. "Oh, at last."

Both sprang from their saddles. Favonius would not stray and Rufinus's poor beast could not. The men cast arms about each other.

"How did you know?" Gratillonius babbled. "How could you get here so soon?"

He felt Rufinus tremble and clutch him more tightly. That was distasteful, much though you had to allow for weariness and grief. Gratillonius disengaged himself and took a step backward. Rufinus stood for an instant alone before he mastered his shivering and teeth glinted in the old crooked grin.

"Word came to Mediolanum by special courier," he said. "Stilicho granted me postal privileges for my return. He didn't know I'd arrive at each relay point with my mount ready to drop and commandeer the next. In Venetorum I learned where you'd gone to. I didn't expect to meet you already, though. Don't tell me you had a vision or cast a horoscope."

"No, I was restless. Gods, man, how did you hold to that speed? You can't have slept more than half of any night."

Rufinus shrugged. "I was in a hurry."

His coolness broke apart. "O master, King, Ys is gone!" he cried. Moonlight runneled through tears. He stretched out his arms. "Who lives? Bodilis, the other Queens, your daughters, our friends, who's left?"

Gratillonius's words fell like thuds of a sledge hammer. "Two of my daughters and a grandchild of Bodilis. Maybe three hundred fugitives, nearly all rural. Otherwise none. Nothing."

"How did it happen? How could the Gods let it happen? Why?"

"Nobody knows, unless it be Corentinus, and he won't answer my question. I'm certain it was the work of an enemy. The Key was missing from my breast when Corentinus woke me that night—worst storm ever known—and the gate stood unlocked to the sea."

A wildcat might have screamed. "We'll find him! We'll get you your revenge! I will, I swear it!" Rufinus sank to his knees and embraced Gratillonius's. His sobs, raw and unpracticed, shook him as a hound shakes a fox it has caught. "Tell me how I can serve you, master. Only tell me."

~ 2 ~

Beneath wolf-gray heaven, wrack flew. The north wind drove it, clamoring shrill, fanged with cold. Spindrift hazed the waves. They roared in their wrinkled hordes, green-black where foam did not swirl, until they burst and fountained on rocks or against mainland cliffs. All birds were gone from sight. The skerries were empty of seals.

Osprey rolled, pitched, yawed, wallowed along on oars. Often the rowers missed a stroke. They kept looking shoreward. Nobody could tell if the salt that stung and blinded them was of scud or tears.

Maeloch stood in the bows, hunched into his leather jacket, legs braced wide. Now and then he signalled Usun, who had the helm. These waters were as ravenous of ships as always. Yet he too must glance over and over at the land, a league off. Within the hood, his face might have been cast in iron. The white-shot beard might have been too, as drenched as it hung.

Ys was gone. Naught but wreckage remained, snags of wall and pillar around which billows ramped. As he watched, a piece gave way. The splash when it fell was lost in surf. Even above the highwater mark, where King and Queens and the wealthy had dwelt, ruin littered a naked strand. He could see beyond to a few blackened spires; fire had consumed the royal grove. Mansions still clung to the hills, tiny at their distance, but surely their folk were dead or fled. The Gods of Ys had ended the Pact of Brennilis, and with it her city.

Out to Sena itself— He and his crew had descried a heap of stones at the eastern end of that island. There he had left Bodilis, dearest of the Queens since little Dahilis died so long ago. There, maybe, her bones abided. He had not risked putting in to search.

But how could it be that the pharos on Cape Rach was also broken, barely half of it left? Could Lir reach that high, or had Taranis cast His hammer in the hour of the whelming?

Maeloch knew he could not sanely seek answers today. He must go on to some unharmed haven, Audiarna or mayhap the Odita mouth and upriver to Aquilo. King Grallon had had friends in Aquilo.

Osprey struggled on south. Once she rounded the headland, wind and seas ought to be less wild. Maybe he could raise sail and let the men rest. If not, he'd have to pull far out and heave to, because they couldn't keep on like this much longer.

Easement or no, Maeloch dreaded that part of the passage. It would go by the place under the cliffs where Scot's Landing had been. And there would be emptiness. More than once, lesser storms than the one that drowned Ys had destroyed the fisher hamlet. But its dwellers had first taken refuge in the city and afterward returned to rebuild. Not ever again.

Faint through the wind, a shout came to him. He turned, saw a crewman point from his bench, bent his own gaze to the port quarter and squinted.

Well he knew that reef and the rocks around it. Waves crashed across them, fell back in monstrous whirls and rips, whitened the wind with spray through which death grinned black. Usun was steering well clear. What was it that lay on the back of stone, entangled with weed torn from the bottom, not yet altogether broken and strewn? A splintered curve rose across the sullenness of Cape Rach, up into the wind: the prow of a wreck. No man could live whose craft went yonder. Well, this was a cruel ground, where none but the mariners of Ys had ever been at home.

"Nay!" tore from Maeloch's throat. "'Tis *Betha!*"

He knew that high stempost, carved at the top into a Celtic spiral. Red paint still clung to clinker-laid strakes. It had been a fine, unusually shaped boat he bought while *Osprey* rested under repair on the Dumnoniic shore, and named for his wife, and sent off with four of his men to bring to Ys the tale of what he had learned in the Islands of Crows. Now the sea had reaved away both *Betha* and Betha.

"How?" he groaned. "Ye were bonny sailors, all o' ye. Why, Norom, ye were my own crewman. How often did I give ye the helm, Norom, aye, on crossings when we ferried the dead to Sena? How could ye go astray like this?" The wind snatched his words from him and scattered them over Ocean.

A sudden flaw of the air? But any Ysan pilot would give himself plenty of room. Did a gale threaten, too quickly for him to make harbor, he would beat out as far as he was able and cast a sea anchor. Fogs did sometimes rise to blind men. Maeloch himself had been thus trapped in the past, and once would have come to grief were it not for a certain seal. However, you could hear from afar where these rocks were, the brawling and hissing and grunting of the waters. Wherever else they blundered to, it should not have been here that a skilled crew perished.

They had come without warning upon the remnants of Ys. Had grief so greatly dazed them? Maeloch felt it rise anew in himself. He thought he had done with weeping, that night ashore in Hivernia on the way back; he and his men had howled like hounds. And mayhap that had been all the tears he would ever shed. What he felt now was the end of hope. There came to him dimly a memory of what Queen Bodilis had chanced to tell him one day, how the folk of distant Egypt used to ready their dead for the tomb before they were Christian. It seemed to him as though someone had lifted the heart and entrails out of him too. Hollow, he would soon blow away on the wind. Would it ever let go of him?

Something stirred on the reef by the wreck. He heard men cry aloud, they saw it themselves. White it glimmered amidst the spindrift. No seal sacred to Belisama—it stood upright, sweetly curved, clad in naught but fair hair that tossed banner-free around its beckoning to him.

"Thunder me down, 'tis a woman!"

A survivor? How? Or a spirit, or the Goddess herself, Our Lady of Mercy, calling Her sailors to Her? Come, come and be comforted, you who are weary and weighted. So had voices sung through dreams, such dreams as bring a man awake laughing in sunrise. She sang, she called, she promised and summoned.

Oh, you who must wander the wind-way and never
May rest by the woman who once was your bride,
Be gladdened by knowing it is not forever.
To you shall come peace with the turn of the tide.
You are not forsaken, but all that was taken
From you on the earth shall wing homeward to me.
Beloved and lonely, fear not. Here is only
An end to your sorrow, the gift of the sea.

The men bent to their sweeps. Usun put the helm over.

And Maeloch saw past her beauty to Ys that was dead, and back to the skerry whereon she stood with the waters furious at her feet; and he cast forth the joy that had begun to warm him within his breast. "Ha' done!" he shouted. "Would ye steer into yon rocks?"

Still the crew rowed, and Usun stood staring before him.

Maeloch whirled, bounded the length of the deck, smote fist into his mate's belly. Usun whoofed out his breath, doubled over, sagged to the planks. Maeloch seized the tiller. Usun scrabbled at his ankles and started to rise. Maeloch kicked him in the ribs. *Osprey* came around.

The rowers could have overridden the steering oar, but they were lost in their dream. "Stroke, stroke, stroke!" Maeloch bellowed, and, mindless, they heeded. A wave swept over the rail, cold dashed into their faces. Surf snarled close by. It fell aft as the vessel clawed off. Maeloch thought he heard a scream, as of a beast that had missed its prey. He cast a glance over his shoulder and saw no more than tumbling waters, the reef, and the wreck.

Usun clambered to his feet. "What got into me?" he choked. "Skipper, if 'twasn't for ye—"

The crewmen were likewise back in the mortal world. Bewildered, terrified, they rowed like lubbers; but they were safe for this while, till they got their full wits again. *Osprey* plowed on by the headland.

"A mermaid, who'd lure us to our deaths." Usun shuddered. "I've heard o' such, but off the shores o' witchy lands afar. I never thought to meet one."

"Ys stood guard athwart the gates of the Otherworld too," Maeloch said starkly.

"How did ye hold out, skipper? What gave ye the strength?"

"I know nay. Unless—unless 'twas remembering that we do yet have much to live for—if naught else, avenging Ys, and our kin, and poor little Dahut."

~ 3 ~

Seventeen persons crowded the atrium of the Apuleius home. They sat on what stools could be found, or on the floor, or stood. All stared toward Corentinus. Clad as ever in shabby robe and wayworn sandals, he loomed against the wall whereon was painted the Chi Rho. The symbol seemed to obscure delicate floral patterns elsewhere, as if giving back the darkness of a rainy day which filled the windows; and yet it was traced in gold.

"Thank you for coming," the chorepiscopus began in Ysan. "Well do I know what a hard time this is for you. Natheless we've reached a need that your folk consider their morrows; and I think you whom I asked hither are their natural leaders."

His look ranged across them. Most were men. Two women—no, a woman and a girl—sat in the front: Runa, priestess at the Nymphaeum when Ys perished, and the vestal Julia, daughter of Gratillonius and Queen Lanarvilis. The King's other daughter, Nemeta, by Forsquilis, had seemingly chosen to spurn the invitation. Well, she was a strange one, like her mother before her.

The rest of the vestals no longer had any special status. The sole additional person from the sanctuary was Amreth Taniti, captain of its small guard of marines. He stood behind Runa and Julia, arms folded, face dour.

Three more women were on hand. Two were widows of Suffete family who had been managing their late husbands' acres in the hinterland. The third, Tera, stout and sunburned, was a commoner and unwed, though she had had many lovers and commanded a certain awe among herdsmen; for she had been—not quite a priestess—ritemistress to their heathen God Cernunnos and His consorts.

The others were male: a few rich landholders, several small but once prosperous yeomen, some merchants and skippers, three who had belonged to the Council of Suffetes: Bomatin Kusuri for the mariners, Ramas Tyri for the artisans, Hilketh Eliuni for the overland transporters. They had all chanced to be in the countryside or, in four cases, to have escaped when Ys went under. Though he had no official standing, Maeloch should have been present too, once a Ferrier of the Dead—crucial to the old religion—and still surely a spokesman for his kind; also, he had just arrived from Hivernia and must have much to tell. But he and Gratillonius had gone off together, heedless of anyone or anything else.

Most here were drably or raggedly clad. A few bore a salvaged robe or jewel. Gone was the splendor of Ys. The pride lived on, though, in nearly every countenance that regarded him. Arrogant had Ys always been, sinful, worldly, until at last God gave her into the hands of those demons she had served for so long. Yet Corentinus could not but mourn for her and humbly offer his love to such of her children as remained.

Again and again the Suffete face met his eyes, the lean high-boned mask of lost Phoenicia. It had been uncommon in the city; too much blood of Egyptian, Babylonian, Greek, Roman, above all Celt had flowed in throughout her centuries. But it had been a sign of her being, as much as the towers agleam above clouds or the sea gate opened and shut by Ocean itself. Soon it must vanish, drowned in foreignness.

Maybe once or twice in generations hence it would be reborn, and parents wonder what had given an alien look to their offspring; but that would happen seldom, and finally never.

Already four of the clans were gone, destroyed entirely in the whelming: Demari, Adoni, Anati, Jezai. Each of the thirteen took its name from a month of the lunar calendar. Was it mere chance that those four were at the quarters of the year? God could thus be showing how the false Gods were fallen. The calendar that had set Their rites must give way and be forgotten before the calendar of Julius, like the pagan moon before the Sun of Christ.

"What have you to say to us, priest?" demanded Bomatin Kusuri in his blunt fashion.

Corentinus overlooked the incorrect title. He had business far more grave. "I wish less to speak at you than with you," he answered. "My power is only to give counsel and, yea, in certain matters, warning. You set your course for yourselves. My prayer is that it be the right one."

"The King should lead this meeting," Amreth said.

"He meant to," Corentinus explained, "but troublous tidings came suddenly upon him. We having already set the day, I felt it best to abide by it. Naught that is said will be binding on anyone."

"'Tis well he's absent anyhow," blurted Evirion Baltisi.

Attention sought him in surprise. He glared back, a large and powerfully built young man, dark-haired, bullet-headed, snub-featured. No matter his lack of the aristocratic lineaments, he was a grandson of Hannon Baltisi, who had been Lir Captain and bitterly hostile toward Christ. Like the old man in his younger days, Evirion was a seafarer, boldly trading and sometimes slave-raiding from Mumu to the Germanic coasts, beyond the Imperial bounds. It was rumored that he had also had dealings, not always peaceful, in places claimed by but no longer under any real protection of Rome.

"What mean you?" asked Runa sharply.

"That far from heeding Grallon, we should erenow have slain him and left him to the ravens for a traitor. Who else called the wrath of the Gods down on Ys?"

A whisper sibilated around the room, half appalled, half enraged—at whom?

Julia sprang to her feet. "That's not true!" she cried. Blood beat in her round young face. She struggled for breath. "My father, he upheld all of you. He saved more than anybody else could have."

Evirion slitted his look on her. "In those last months when King and Queens were sundered by his denial of her holy rights to Dahut —where were you, Julia? With your mother."

"Oh, but I—I—" The girl fell back onto her stool, bent head into hands, and wept. She was fifteen years old.

Evirion stood challenging the assembly with his glance. "Never did Grallon honor the Gods of Ys. His lips alone did, while he bowed down before his Mithras and made this agent of Christ his foremost counsellor. It was Grallon who finally broke the Pact and so brought doom. Then he led you to the Romans and their Church, as a bellwether leads sheep to the slaughterer."

"Why did you keep silent?" Hilketh inquired.

"None would have heeded, earlier. And certes we had necessity to bring survivors to safety and let them regain some strength of body and spirit. I did my share or more in that work. 'Tis time to exact justice and seek freedom."

"Where 'ud you seek it?" gibed Tera the shepherdess.

"Will you sink your neck under the yoke, you who knew the Stag-Horned One?" Evirion retorted.

"That's as may be. I've my brood to think of first. We'll see what Gods do best by 'em."

"The great Three are surely done with us," Runa said slowly, "or we with Them. Nor can we afford feuds among ourselves. Go back to our former lands if you will, Evirion, and wait for the barbarians."

The seaman scowled but kept still. Corentinus sensed a lessening of tension in the air. It had felt like the moments before a lightning storm breaks; now rain ran softly across the windowpanes. She was shrewd, that woman, and fearless, a leader born.

"You are founding a colony, a new community," reminded the chore-opiscopus in his most level tone. "Or may I say that we are, together? I have come over the years to feel myself one among you, a man of Ys. I grieve for Ys the beautiful even as you do. But we have our lives to live. We have children with us and children yet unborn. Tera has right, their welfare is our first earthly duty.

"Those who choose can in truth withdraw. Outlands are still pagan, wilderness is well-nigh unpeopled. But do you think you can thus preserve the ways of your fathers, or any memory of your city? Nay, in your waking hours you will grub for a bare living, while your sons grow up to be unlettered backwoodsmen and your daughters to be brood mares in huts they share with the pigs. Friends, in my time I've been sailor, vagabond, laborer, and hermit off in the woods. I know whereof I speak."

He had their entire heed. Quickly he went on: "Here at the confluence is the ground for a city—not a sleepy provincial town like Aquilo but a city real and great. The location is excellent. 'Twas mere accident of history that settlement began downstream of it, when ships can reach it on a flowing tide. The hinterland is rich, timber, iron ore, fertile soil. The neighbors are solid Osismiic tribesfolk leavened by Maximus's veterans, always admiring of Ys and ready to welcome everything you can bring to them. For above all you have yourselves. You bear the learning, the traditions, the loyalties; you are Ys. Keep well your heritage."

"Never will her towers rise anew," said old Ramas Tyri low.

"I fear you speak sooth." Corentinus looked toward Bomatin Kusuri. "But new ships can venture forth. Salt and surge were ever in Ysan blood. Let them now run in Armoricans for aye."

Again Runa took the word: "Ramas meant that whatever we build here, it cannot be like that which is lost."

Corentinus shook his head. "Nay, my lady, it cannot. If you would work upon Armorica, you must let Armorica—Rome—work upon you." He paused. "The city you build must be a city that avows Christ."

An ugly expression passed across Evirion and a few others. The rest seemed resigned or, some of them, half glad. Runa stayed impassive as she nodded and answered, "That is clear. What will you have us do?"

"Why, listen to the good news," Corentinus told them in a rush of happiness. "Open your hearts. He will dry your tears, heal your wounds, and welcome you into life eternal. In return He asks no more than your love."

"Then He wants everything," said a new voice.

Corentinus looked that way. A young man had spoken, shyly— slender, blond, blue-eyed, with thin straight features. The pastor recognized Cadoc Himilco, son of the learned landholder Taenus by a Gallic leman but raised like an heir. His father lay dying of a sickness in the lungs caught during the trek hither.

"I d-do not call this wrong," Cadoc went on. "We served the old Gods as our forebears did...because they did...but what were the Three, really? Nobody ever knew. Can you tell us about Christ?"

"With my whole heart." Corentinus refrained from pointing out how he had tried to, year after year, and ears were deaf until God had brought Ys into the abyss. The salvation of one soul was infinitely more important than any niggling resentment. There had been ample punishment.

There had been thousands drowned in their sins and error—that a few score be saved? He crossed himself as he veered from the forbidden question.

Forcing a smile: "Stand easy, brethren and sisters. Today you shall be free of sermons. Let us instead talk about the worldly matters around us and how to cope with them. Daily will I preach in my wonted spot for such as care to listen, and ever will I be ready to talk with anyone in private. Nor will I rant or scold. My Master awaits you, but His patience is without bounds."

Julia, who had sat head bowed, staring at the hands clenched together in her lap, glanced up. He thought that through the parching tears he saw a flash of hope.

~ 4 ~

While the meeting used his home, Apuleius had taken his family and slaves out to the farmstead he owned, on the edge of the land he had granted the colony. Toward evening Corentinus found him there in a room alone with Maecius, chorepiscopus at Aquilo. "I'm sorry, I didn't mean to intrude," Corentinus said. "Rovinda told me you were in here. I supposed she meant you were by yourself."

Apuleius smiled in the gathering dusk. "I was only taking the opportunity for prayer and spiritual counsel, on this day when nothing else is happening to me. The pastor was kind enough to come." His manner was unaffected, even cheerful; the growing devoutness of his later years left him as comfortable as before with his God. Sometimes Corentinus felt envy.

"How did the discussion go?" Apuleius continued. "Unless you want to keep that confidential."

Corentinus folded his lanky length onto a stool. "It went quite well, on the whole. We arrived at some practical plans. The flock should soon have a better notion of what to expect and what each member ought to do...or keep from doing."

"And did you win any to the Faith?" asked Maecius. He was aged, bald and dim of sight; the years when he, like Bishop Martinus, had made efforts to evangelize the countryside were long behind him.

Corentinus shrugged. "It'll take a while."

"Well, you are the man for that holy work. Proceed, surely with the saints at your side and the blessing of the Lord upon you."

"It's more difficult than that, Father," replied Corentinus, turning earnest. They said Maecius had always been too innocent; some said too simple.

Apuleius nodded. "M-hm. Language; how many of them know Latin? Folkways, customs, ideas of what is legal and moral. A tribe of foreigners, whom we can't properly assimilate while this generation is alive. They'll start marrying among our people, though. What then? Can we allow it?"

"If they confess Christ, of course we can." Doubt wavered in Maecius's voice.

"The means of that we must prepare, and soon," Corentinus told them. "A pastor who can serve their special needs. A church, not just a building—yours in Aquilo will be too small—but the whole underlying organization. Proper instruction. Baptism. In Ys I heard that much is changing in the Church these days; but away off there among pagans, I could not very well follow or understand it. Can you enlighten me?"

Maecius sighed. "At best, I was never a gifted teacher. And all these disputes about doctrine and liturgy— My poor wits might as well be at Babel."

"We need counsel and we need support." Corentinus regarded Apuleius. "Have I your leave to go seek them?"

"Where?" asked the tribune.

"Where else but to Bishop Martinus in Turonum?"

813

Apuleius nodded again. "The soldier of God." After a moment: "Make haste. He can't have much time left in this world. Who shall carry the light he has kindled?"

Darkness deepened. Rain stammered on the roof.

V

~ 1 ~

Titus Scribona Glabrio, civil governor of Lugdunensis Tertia, received Quintus Domitius Bacca, his procurator, in that room of the basilica of Caesarodunum Turonum which they generally employed for confidential meetings. Today not even an amanuensis was present.

"Ah, welcome. Come in, my dear fellow, and make yourself as comfortable as possible," Glabrio greeted. "Beastly weather, eh?" Outside, wind blustered cold, herding clouds and quick, hard rainshowers before it. Occasionally windowpanes flickered with a moment's sunlight, otherwise the saints and angels painted on the walls stared out of a gloom wherein their eyes seemed phosphorescent. "We'll have something hot and spiced to drink after our business is done."

Bacca folded his robe, which the walk here had rumpled, about his gaunt frame and took a stool opposite his superior's. "I get the impression the business itself will be of that nature," he said. A smile cut creases under his swordblade of a nose.

Glabrio nodded so vigorously that jowls and double chin wobbled. "A pleasure too long deferred. You have guessed what it is?"

"Considering what intelligence you've had me gather for you, and how quietly—"

"I have now digested the material."

Bacca glanced at Glabrio's paunch and raised the eyebrow the governor could not see.

"I took my time," Glabrio went on. "You know how prudent I am. Albeit God's vengeance has at last fallen on wicked Ys, the powers of evil may still have resources. I had to feel sure. But today we can begin planning in earnest. Our task is to complete God's work for Him and bring Gratillonius, whom surely none less than Satan rescued from the destruction—bring him low. Do you agree?"

"Well, it'll feel good," said Bacca in his desiccated fashion. He need not add: After he resisted and circumvented us for years, raised his power and honor in Armorica above ours and Rome's own, slew the Franks who were supposed to rid us of him and demoralized their survivors, met our charges before the praetorian prefect in Augusta Treverorum and not only got them dismissed but won elevation to tribune...indeed he has rankled in our flesh.

"It is right," Glabrio insisted. "It is vital. It is holy. Let this village he is founding grow, and the same evils will flourish afresh. Insubordination. A corrupting example before the entire province. Paganism. Black sorcery."

"Do you truly consider a few miserable fugitives such a threat?"

"Not in themselves, perhaps. But with Gratillonius as leader— No, we must make an end of his insolence."

Bacca stroked his chin. "That presumably means terminating the Ysan colony, the basis of whatever strength he may gain."

"I believe so. The people can then be redistributed."

"Scattered, you mean."

"That will be wisest, don't you think? Put them into their proper stations in life, teach them humility, save their souls. A holy work, I tell you."

Bacca frowned into the middle distance. "A difficult work, at least," he murmured. "Gratillonius has gotten himself rather firmly ensconced. He and his followers do have temporary permission to settle. Quite legal; Apuleius, the tribune of Aquilo, arranged it behind our backs, with the praetorian prefect Ardens. He's also a senator, Apuleius, you know, and has the ear of other important men, too. Application for permanent status is in train, and I doubt very much it can be blocked. My inquiries indicate Stilicho himself will be partial to the Ysans."

"How can that *be*?"

"Oh, all right, they're deluded, those men; Satan has whispered to them in their dreams; but the fact remains. Moreover, we'd better not forget a good many lowly people. Maximus's veterans, who owe Gratillonius their homes. Former Bacaudae, who could take up their old trade again if provoked. Osismiic tribesmen, who remember pirates and bandits kept off their necks, trade revived. We're going to have troubles enough without stirring up revolt...which could, among other things, cause the ImpÉrium to question *us*."

"I am no fool, thank you," huffed Glabrio. "I realize we shall have to proceed carefully. But we do have instruments to hand. Taxation—"

"The most obvious, because the most pervasive. As well I know."

"You should!"

"I do. My knowledge includes technique. A levy by itself may prove insufficient to destroy, or impossible to collect, or productive of the very resistance we wish to prevent. First we had better plan ways and means suited to the project. That includes making preparations for the next indiction, two years hence. We will want to have an influence on it."

Bacca's look speared the purple-veined face before him. "I anticipated this," he continued. "When you sent for me today I guessed why, and took the liberty of bringing a man of mine along. He's waiting in the anteroom. Shall I have him called?"

The governor flushed. "You take a good deal upon yourself, Procurator. Who is he?"

Bacca curbed impatience. "You remember Nagon Demari."

Glabrio reddened further. "The Ysan renegade last year? I certainly do. That disaster with the Franks was his fault. I thought afterward he fled."

"I deemed it discreet that he withdraw," Bacca explained coolly. "He and his family have been living on my fundus. A few days ago, foreseeing this summons of yours, I had him brought here and lodged in my town house." He gave the other no chance to use a mouth that opened and shut and opened again. "Your indignation was quite natural. But actually it's wrong to blame him for the scheme going awry. It was an excellent idea in itself...as you agreed at the time. No fallible mortal could have foreseen just how tough and ruthless Gratillonius would prove to be. Now, like it or not, Nagon is the single Ysan left for us to consult—to use; and he is eager. He knows those people, their ins and outs, as we never can. We need him for our principal advisor and later, I think, our agent. A wise man does not throw away his sword because a shield stopped it once; he keeps it for his next stroke. You are nothing if not a wise man, Governor."

"Well, well—" Glabrio fumed for a while but in the end agreed. He struck a small gong and bade the slave who entered fetch the outsider.

Almost, Nagon stamped through the door. He halted, his stocky frame half hunched as if for a fight, and glowered before he made himself give a proper salutation.

"You have much to answer for," said Glabrio in his sternest tone. "Be thankful to your kindly protector. He has persuaded me to grant you a second chance."

"I do thank you, sir," Nagon grated. His sandy hair stood abristle. Small eyes like glare ice never wavered in the flat countenance. "The procurator has informed me. Sir, I'm ready to do whatever is called for—anything at all—that'll bring yon Grallon to hell."

Glabrio bridged his fingers. Rings sparkled. "Really? You are quite vehement, considering what months you've had to cool off."

Nagon knotted fists that were once a laborer's. "I could wait till Judgment Day and never hate him the less."

"Ah, scarcely a Christian sentiment. True, he caused you to go into exile. But thereby he saved you and your family from perishing with Ys."

"No wish of his, that was!" Nagon barely kept from spitting on the floor. "And what brought Ys to ruin but him—he that made mock of the Gods—" After an instant: "Without owning the one true God." He swallowed. "Sir, I've asked about it. I've gone to the Aquilo neighborhood myself and talked with Osismii and such Ysans as I could come on in the woods. Ys is gone. My city, my folk, my clan. I am the last of the Demari Suffetes, do you know? I've only two children alive, both girls. The Demari die with me. What's left to live for?"

"Them and your wife," Bacca suggested. "Whatever career you can find among us."

"Oh, I'll provide for them, sir, of course. And I'll make my way as best I can. But if that could be by helping you against Grallon—" The breath staggered into Nagon and back out. "That'd be worth dying for."

"I hope we can arrange something better, including the satisfaction you want," Bacca soothed. "It does require patience."

"Say the word, and I'll catch him alone and kill him."

"He might very well kill you instead. Besides, that would be stupid, making a martyr of him, possibly angering the ImpÉrium. No, let us undermine him, discredit him, till he is powerless and disowned; and meanwhile, let him experience it happening."

"Bear in mind, my man, this is a preliminary conference," said Glabrio. "You will provide information. If in addition your opinion is occasionally asked, do not get above yourself. I have not forgotten the consequences of your last advice. Furthermore, everything that passes between us, today and later, is a secret of state. If you reveal a single word, you will rue it. Is that clear?"

Nagon was still for a space, so still that the noise of the wind outside flew alone through the room under the stares of the saints, before he said: "I understand."

"Good. You may be seated." Glabrio gestured at the floor. "We shall proceed."

A knock sounded at the door. "What the devil?" exclaimed Bacca. "Didn't you order we aren't to be interrupted?"

"Unless for something major," Glabrio told him nervously. "Enter!"

The slave obeyed, bowed, and announced, "I beg the governor's pardon and pray I have not erred or given offense. An emissary from the bishop has arrived and demands immediate audience."

"What? From Bishop Martinus? Why, he should be at his monastery—"

"I thought, rightly or wrongly, the governor would wish to know. Shall I admit him, or have him wait, or...send him on his way?"

"No, no." That last would be impolitic in the extreme. "I will see him."

The slave scuttled out. After a minute during which the wind gusted louder, a man came in. Young, lean, he was clad only in a rough dark robe and sandals. His fair hair was shaved off from the brow to the middle of the scalp, the tonsure of Martinus; weather had ruffled what was left into a halo against the dimness of the chamber.

"God's peace be upon you," he said evenly. "You will not remember me. I am of no consequence. But my name is Sucat." His Latin bore a curious accent, Britannic subtly altered by years of Hivernian captivity.

"I do, though," Glabrio answered in a relieved tone. "You are the bishop's kinsman. Welcome." He pointed to a vacant stool. "Will you be seated? Will you take refreshment?"

Sucat shook his head. "No, thank you. My message is soon conveyed. It is from Martinus, Bishop of Turonum. He commands you in the name of God that you show mercy to the poor survivors of Ys and afflict them no more than the Almighty has done; for that would be presumptuous, and un-Christian, and troublesome to the Church in her work among them."

Glabrio gaped. Nagon froze. Bacca stood up and spoke tautly: "May I ask why the bishop chooses...to advise the civil authorities?"

"Sir, it is not for me to question a holy man," Sucat replied, unshaken, almost cheerful, and beneath it implacable. "However, he did point out that there are souls to be saved; that their community may become the seed from which the Evangel will grow through a tribe still mostly pagan; but that first it needs protection and nurture."

"And exemption from the usual requirements?"

"The civil authorities can better decide such things than we religious. We simply appeal to their consciences. And, of course, to their hopes for their own salvation."

"Hm. How did you find us, Sucat?"

"The bishop bade me seek the basilica. He said the governor and yourself would be here, together with a third party who should also be reminded about charity. He said that if you want to discuss this with him, you are free to come out to the monastery; or you can arrange an appointment for sometime after he has attended to the suffering poor and conducted services in the city. Have I the governor's leave to depart? Good day, and God's blessing be upon you, His wisdom within you."

The young man strode out.

Glabrio dabbed at the sweat on his face, chilly though the room was. "That...puts a different...complexion on the matter, doesn't it?"

Nagon lifted hands with fingers crooked like claws. "You'll bow down to Martinus with never a word?" he shouted. "Him, so old and feeble he can barely totter into town once a sennight? What *right* has he got?"

"Be still," Bacca snapped.

He paced the floor, scowling into shadows, hands working against each other behind his back. "We've small choice, you know," he muttered at length. "Martinus may have no office in the government, but he stood up to Emperor Maximus, and with his influence he could break us apart and scatter the pieces. He would, too, if we made him angry enough."

"He could do worse than that." Glabrio's flesh rippled with his shudder. "He's driven demons from the altars where pagans worshipped them, and raised the dead, and talked with angels—he could bring all of them down on us— No, we'll heed him; we are good, obedient sons of the church."

A hiss went between Nagon's teeth.

Bacca stopped before the man, looked into his eyes, and said low: "Control yourself. Bide your time. Nothing forbids us to watch, and learn, and think, and wait. Our beloved bishop is in fact very old. Soon God will call him home to his reward. Then we shall see. We shall see."

~ 2 ~

Again Gratillonius sought privacy on the heights, but now it was with Rufinus. At first they walked in silence. The path climbed and curved amidst leaves whose brilliant green broke morning light into jewel-glints of color on raindrops that clung to them yet after the past several wet days. Cloudlets wandered on a breeze filled with fragrances. Birds a hundredfold rejoiced. Where the view opened downward, it was across a broad western sweep of land. The rivers gleamed through awakening acres; smoke rose from the hearths of Aquilo; northward the colony site at the confluence was half hidden by mists steaming out of its newly spaded earth, white against the forest beyond.

Finally Rufinus ventured, "You can unlock your throat here, master. You've kept too much inside for too long."

Gratillonius's close-trimmed beard only partly concealed how his mouth writhed. He stared before him as if blind. A minute or two passed while they walked on, until he said, "I wanted to speak alone with you." His voice sounded rusty.

Rufinus waited.

"You've been to Hivernia," Gratillonius continued presently. "You know them there."

Rufinus winced. The expression grew into one of pain as Gratillonius went unheeding on: "It's become pretty clear what happened, how Ys was murdered and who the murderer is. What we must figure out is how to get our revenge." Laughter barked. "How to exact justice, I mean to say...when Corentinus or Apuleius or their sort are listening. But probably it's best if they aren't."

"I've heard little," Rufinus said with care, "and what I have heard may well be unreliable."

"Maeloch— He came back from Hivernia himself, you know. After he...told me...what he'd learned— I thought of swearing him to silence. But of course it was already too late to gag the men who'd sailed with him. And others from Ys, they have their own stories to tell. Luckily, everyone's been too busy to think much about it. Except me."

Rufinus nodded. Of late, Gratillonius had often gone away by himself, riding or striding for leagues in the rain; and he was curt among people, and bore signs of sleeplessness.

"They'll also put two and two together eventually," Gratillonius said. "The story will be in every common mouth...throughout Armorica...for hundreds of years? Dahut's name—" He did not groan, he roared.

Both halted. Rufinus laid a hand on the massive shoulder beside him and squeezed until most men would have cried out. "Easy, sir," the Gaul breathed.

Gratillonius gazed past him. Fist beat in palm, over and over. "Dahut, whore to Niall the Scotian," rattled forth. "She stole the Key from me while I slept, for him. It must have been her. We all slept so heavily in the Red Lodge, in that wild night that should have kept us awake, and I know she could cast such spells, Forsquilis told me she had a gift for witchcraft like no princess—no Queen, since—since— And before that, oh, I closed my eyes and ears and who dared warn me? He can't have been her first lover, Niall. Why else did—Tommaltach, Carsa, those young men challenge me, make me who liked them cut them down in the Wood? And that Germanic pirate—Maeloch says he was lying, but I can't believe it and I don't think Maeloch really can either— Dahut! Dahilis, our daughter!"

"Are you quite sure?"

Gratillonius wrestled himself toward steadiness. "What else will account for everything we've discovered? And Corentinus, he knows. There at the end, he told me to let her go, let the sea have her, or...the weight of her sins would drag me down with her. Not that I cared, not that I did...willingly. The visions he gave me, of the Queens, how each of them died, it made me—I lost strength—" He snapped air. "Since then, he won't talk about the matter. When I've asked, he's said that's not for him to speak of, and gone straightaway to something else. Oh, he can find enough urgent business to steer me off this."

"Are you angry with him, then?"

Gratillonius shook his head. "Why? As well be angry with the messenger who brings bad news. And he did save my life, and other lives, and now when he's off to Turonum I realize through and through how much he's been doing for us here."

Suddenly, terrifyingly calm, he lifted his face to the blue overhead and declared: "No, this goes beyond the world. Gods have been at work. What else could have led my Dahut astray like that? The Gods of Ys, and that poor bewildered, lonely girl; They played on her like Pan playing on pipes made from a dead man's bones. And Mithras, Mithras was too careless or too afraid to stand by us. Dahut was left all alone with the Three, and They are demons. As for the God of the Christians—I don't know. I've asked Him for an honest answer, and gotten silence. So I don't know of anything except the demons. Maybe otherwise there's only emptiness."

Rufinus, who had entertained the same idea, shivered to hear it thus set forth. He waited a bit, while Gratillonius brought his gaze back to earth and across the lands afar, before he said low, "You want to avenge Dahut—and Ys—on Niall."

"Since I cannot reach the Gods," replied Gratillonius, flat-voiced, still looking into distance. "In any event, he needs killing."

Rufinus mustered courage. "First I do."

Startled out of grief, Gratillonius swung around to peer at him. "How's that?"

Rufinus stood straight, hands at side, and spoke fast. "Sir, I failed you. I may well have something to do with what happened. You remember my telling how I freed that prisoner of Niall's, Eochaid, the same man Maeloch found on the island. It seemed like a fine trick at the time. But it must have poured oil on Niall's fire against Ys. Certainly it made it impossible for us to send any mission to his kingdom, negotiate, try to engineer his overthrow. I was vain and reckless, I overreached, and Ys had to suffer for it."

A slow smile, with no mirth but considerable pity, lifted Gratillonius's lips. "Is that all? Nonsense. You should know the Scoti better than that. I do. They never forget what they think is any wrong done them, and anything that keeps them from having their way is a wrong. Blame me. I was the one who wrecked his fleet and his plans, all those years ago. And I don't feel guilty about that. It was a good job well done. As for you, why, you freed an enemy of his, who may yet become an ally of ours."

Rufinus hung his head. "Maybe. But I did go away, down south, just when the trouble was brewing. I should have stayed. I might have been able to warn you, or—or somehow head things off."

"You might have at that," said Gratillonius, "you, if any man alive could. I've wondered what made you go. It wasn't really necessary, and you didn't seem like simply wanting the adventure."

"I had...reasons," Rufinus croaked. "I thought it—might ease a conflict—I should have stayed, whatever it cost. All the way back from Italy, after the news came, I was feeling more and more certain the whelming couldn't have been an accident, it had to be some outcome of the evil I'd smelled everywhere around us."

"You did? You never let on."

Rufinus straightened, met his master's look, and grinned his grin that was half a sneer. "I'm good at putting a nice face on things." He slumped. "Now scourge me, kill me, anything to free me of this."

Gratillonius sighed. "All right, you made a mistake, but I was with you in it. I could have required you to stay, couldn't I? Are we magicians to foretell the future? I need your wits. Throw that remorse of yours on the dunghill, where it belongs. That is an order."

Rufinus's words seldom rang forth as they did: "At your command, sir! What do you want of me?"

"I told you. For the present, your thoughts. And your ways of dealing with people, seducing them into doing what you want and believing

821

it was their own idea. We'll have our hands full getting the colony established, dealing with Imperial officers, collecting intelligence about barbarian movements and making ready to meet them—everything." Gratillonius paused. "But it's not too soon to start thinking about Niall of the Nine Hostages." His tone had gone quiet as a winter night when waters freeze over. "I mean to wash Dahut's honor clean in his blood. Then my little girl can rest peaceful."

~ 3 ~

The day was so lovely that to sit in the murk and dinginess of Martinus's hut was itself a mortification. The door did sag on leather hinges, letting in a bit of sunlight and a glimpse of grass and river. Sounds also drifted through, from monks at their prayers—those who worked in the kitchen gardens stayed mute—all along the bottomland and up in the hillside caves which were the cells of most. But smells of loam and growth were lost in malodor; saintly men scorned scrubbing. The light picked out dust, cobwebs, mushrooms in the corners of the dirt floor. Two three-legged stools and a chest for books and documents were the only furniture.

The bishop's few remaining teeth gleamed amidst wrinkles and pallor as he smiled. "Do not pretend to virtues that are not yours, my son," he jested. "I refer to simplicity. You know perfectly well who should take leadership there. Yourself."

Corentinus bowed his head. That was never quite easy for him to do for a fellow mortal. "Father, I am not worthy."

Martinus turned serious. His dim eyes strained through the shadows, studying the visitor. "No man born of woman should ever dare imagine himself truly fit for the cure of souls. However, some are called, and must do the best they can. You are familiar with those people, and familiar to them. You get along well with their King—with him who was King. In fact, the two of you make a formidable team. Moreover, you are a man of the folk; you have known labor and hardship, shared the joys and sorrows of the humble. That includes the tribes round about. The effort to bring them into the fold has waned with Maecius's strength. You are still in your full vigor, never mind those gray hairs. Who better to take over the ministry?"

He sat still before adding, "This is more than my judgment, you understand. God has long marked you out. You are one of the miracle workers."

So lengthy a speech took its toll of him. He hunched, hugging himself against the chill despite the springtime mildness, regaining breath. Eyes closed in the snubnosed countenance.

They opened again when Corentinus protested hoarsely, "Father, that was nothing— No, I repent me; of course I must not demean His mercies. But that is what they were—the fish that kept me fed in my hermitage, the ability to heal or rescue, the rare vision of warning—mercies to a wretched sinner."

Martinus straightened. Something of the old soldierly manner rapped through his tone. "Enough. Humility is not a virtue natural to you either, Corentinus. Affecting it like this, false modesty, is nothing more than spiritual pride. You have your orders from Heaven. Obey them."

The tall man gulped. "I'm sorry." After a moment, his words wavering: "Let me confess it, I'm afraid. I don't know how to handle these powers. They were such small, comfortable miracles before. Now—"

"You confront the very Serpent." Martinus nodded. "I know. All too well do I know."

He leaned forward, intent. "The divine will is often hard to riddle. We make blunders which can bring disaster. And sometimes—oh, Satan works wonders of his own. I have seen what wore the semblance of Christ Himself—" He drew the Cross before him.

"But the Lord is always with us," he said, "even unto the end of the world. He will help us see through and win through, if only we ask. I recall a mistake—" Once more he must stop to breathe.

"Tell me, Father," Corentinus begged.

Abruptly Martinus seemed nearly at ease. He smiled anew. "Ah, no great thing. There was a shrine not far from here which my predecessor had consecrated as being of a martyr. But I could find no believable story about his passion; even his name was uncertain. Could members of my flock be calling on a false saint? I went to the grave and prayed for enlightenment. Night fell. A figure appeared before me, wrapped in a shroud black with clotted blood; for his head had been cut off and he must hold it to the stump of his neck. I bade him speak truth, and he confessed he was a brigand, put to death for his crimes. Afterward sheer confusion among the rustics—confusion with a former godling of theirs, I think—caused them to venerate him. I dismissed the ghost to his proper place, and next day made known the facts, and that was the end of that."

"You treat it so lightly," Corentinus whispered.

Martinus shrugged.

"But that which walked in the dark around Ys—" Corentinus went on, "that which I'm afraid still haunts the ruin It made—"

Martinus grew solemn anew. "We may have terrible things to deal with," he said. "Therefore we need a strong man."

Corentinus braced himself. "I'll do what I can, Father, since you want it."

"God wants it. In Him you will find strength boundless."

Then, in the practical way that was his as often as the pious, Martinus added: "A chorepiscopus at Aquilo is no longer enough, given the changed circumstances. We require a full bishop. We can't elevate you immediately. These are indeed deep waters. You and I shall have to talk, and think, and pray together, before we can hope for any idea of how to fare in them. Meanwhile, you need instruction. A great deal has happened, a great deal has changed, also in the Church, during those years you spent isolated in Ys. We have to make you ready for your ministry. It will be harder than most, my son, and perhaps mortally dangerous."

<h2 style="text-align:center">~ 4 ~</h2>

Returning from Mons Ferruginus, Gratillonius sought the house of Apuleius in Aquilo. His talk with Rufinus had vastly relieved him. The pain and rage were still there, but congealed, a core of ice at the center of his being. He could turn his thoughts from them. The day must come when he let them thaw and flood forth over Niall; meanwhile, he should get on with his work.

At the moment he had in mind to discuss the organization of defense, now that construction was progressing so well that soon his colony would be a tempting target. If only Imperial law did not limit the arming of populaces to peasant reservists—but it did, and Rufinus's woodsrangers were an illegality at which the authorities might soon cease winking, as they perforce had done while Ys was their bulwark....

Salomon bounded down the front steps to meet him. "Oh, sir, can we go?" he cried.

Gratillonius stopped. "What's this?"

"Why, you promised, sir, the first day the weather was dry you'd take me to your town and explain how it's guarded. I got my tutor to let me off, and I've been waiting, and—and—" The boyish voice stumbled. A tousled head drooped. "You can't?"

Gratillonius regarded him. At eleven years of age, Apuleius's son approached his father's height, though all legs and arms and eyes. Blue as his mother's, those eyes clouded over. He tried to keep his lip still. "Of course, sir, you're busy," he managed to say.

The man remembered. A promise was a promise, and this was a good lad, and he had no overwhelming urgency. "Why, no, I hadn't forgotten," he lied. "I was engaged earlier, but that's done with and I came to fetch you. Shall we go?"

Joy blazed. "Thank you, sir! Right away!"

If I had a son of my own—Gratillonius thought, and the old pang returned. But my Queens in Ys could bear nothing but daughters, and the same spell made me powerless with any woman other than them.

Am I still?

Too much else had filled him since the whelming. Desire was crowded out. He did awake erected from dreams, but the dreams always seemed to be of what he had lost, and he hastened to leave them behind him.

He started to turn around. A flash of white caught his glance. Verania had come out into the portico. "Must you leave at once?" she called softly.

"Why not?" demanded her brother.

"Oh, I have some small refreshments ready...if you have time, sir."

The wistfulness caught at Gratillonius. It would be unfair to make Salomon wait any longer. However— "Thank you, when we are finished," he blurted. "Uh, first, if you're free, would you like to come with us?"

Her radiance quite overran Salomon's disgruntlement. She skipped down to them with a gracefulness that recalled Dahilis, and Dahut (no). Hair, also light brown, blew free of its coiled braids in rebellious little curls. She had her father's big hazel eyes. The face hinted at Bodilis's daughter Una, and more and more the mind at Bodilis herself; pure chance, that, no relationship whatsoever to those two who lay drowned. His stare made her redden, plain to see under so fair a skin. The faintest dusting of freckles crossed a pert nose.... He hauled attention elsewhere and the three of them began walking.

Their way went opposite from the bustle at the dock, out the eastern gate and up the left bank of the Odita. To reach the section between the rivers without wading, it was necessary to take a wooden bridge just above their confluence. "We're going to put one across the Stegir," Gratillonius remarked. "Save time for carters and such, once our town begins drawing them from the west."

"Won't that be dangerous, sir?" Salomon asked. "I mean, you said the streams were two sides of your city wall."

"A shrewd question," Gratillonius approved. The stuff of leadership was certainly in this boy. He wasn't fond of book learning like his sister, nor as quick to master it, but he was no dullard either, and where it came to military subjects you might well call him brilliant. He shone in the exercises, too, or would when he had tamed the impulsiveness of his age. "It'll be a drawbridge, and flanked by a real wall."

"Will your city be grand like Ys?"

Verania sensed the wrenching within the man. "Nothing can ever be so beautiful again, can it?" she said. "But what you make, sir, it will be *yours*."

Somehow Gratillonius could chuckle. "Well, I expect the architects will have more to say about it than this old soldier. If we can ever afford them, that is. Confluentes won't become any Rome or Athens in my lifetime. I'll be satisfied if we get it beyond those cob and log shacks we're throwing up at first."

Verania shook her head. "Confluentes. Couldn't you find a prettier name?"

"It's fine," Salomon retorted. "It means what it is."—the juncture of the rivers.

"Serviceable, anyhow, same as we want the town itself to be," Gratillonius said. There had never been any formal decision about a name. It had simply grown from the mouths of soldiers and workmen.

The walk from Aquilo was short. Having crossed the bridge, the three found themselves looking at an expanse of open ground about a mile on a side, cut by a brook. The streams hemmed it in on the south and west, the woods on the north and east. Much of it was now mud churned by rain, boots, wheels, hoofs. Log pathways were crowded with traffic. Hammers banged, saws grided, frames lifted raw against heaven. The former tenant farms sheltered workers and their tools. Toward the northwest angle, beyond the fortification, the manor house of the Apuleii remained untouched. Dwindled by distance, its white walls and red roof, outbuildings, garden, orchard had a loneliness about them, like that of an old man who watches turmoil among strangers.

"We'll go around," Gratillonius said. "No sense in mucking up our feet." He led the way to the south end of the eastern earthworks and thence north.

Peaceful was the meadow outside the ditch, before the forest rose green and white. When he stopped and was about to describe the function of the barriers, he noticed Verania gazing yonder. Her lips moved. He barely heard: *"Now leaf the woodlands, now is the year at its fairest."*

It stirred a vague memory. "What's that?" he asked. She gave him a fawn's startled glance. "What you were reciting. Poetry, hm?"

She colored and nodded. "A line from the third Eclogue of Vergilius, sir. He w-would have loved this landscape."

He attempted humor. "Kind of cold and damp for an Italian, I should think."

"Oh, but—the cornel blossoming. That's what we ought to call your city," she exclaimed. "The Meeting of Rivers Where the Dogwood Grows."

Confluentes Cornuales, he rendered it in his mind. Not bad. He'd try using it and see if it caught on. The second part, at least, might well fit this entire country. Cornel was more than bonny. It supplied excellent wood for charcoal, skewers, handles, spokes, spearshafts: the needs of men.

Watch that! he reminded himself. You're not in a real country anymore. Ys is gone. You're in a province of the Empire.

VI

~ 1 ~

That was a chilly year, but toward midsummer a spell of heat set in and lasted a while. It brooded heavy on the day when Evirion met Nemeta. Forest leaves might have been cut out of sea-greened sheet copper. They roofed off the hard blue sky, save where beams struck through from the west to glance off boles and speckle shadows. No breeze moved, no animal scampered, no bird chirred. Silence stretched like a drumhead waiting for a storm to beat thunder from it.

A spring trickled to keep filled a pool. Insects hovered above its dark stillness. Sedge and osier choked the banks, held off only by the lichenous mass of a boulder. Nearby loomed a giant of a beech. Moss and fungus grew on its trunk and on boughs fallen to earth. Lightning had long ago blasted it, with fire hollowing a cavern higher than a man.

There stood the girl. The charred wood obscured her thin, drably clad body; face and mane sprang forth, snow and flame. She carried a stick as long as herself, around the top of which she had bound the coiling mummy of a snake.

Brush crackled. Evirion pushed his way through, saw her, stopped and wiped from his brow the sweat that stained his tunic and surrounded him with its reek. "At last!" he growled. "I thought I'd never find you. Why'd you pick this, of all meeting places?"

"Because no one else would be nigh," Nemeta answered. "They shun it, the fools. Power indwells here yet."

Evirion frowned. A hand dropped to the shortsword at his belt. "What do you mean? How do you know?"

Her eyes glowed cat-green. "When the Celts first came hither," she said low, "they piled the heads of slain foemen around this tree as an offering to their Gods. Long afterward, the Romans trapped seven fleeing druids beneath it, murdered them, and took the skulls away. Taranis killed it as you see. But spirits linger. I have felt them touch me and heard them whisper."

For all his size and strength, the young man must fight down unease. "We could have been quite alone in a mort of spots easier to reach."

"'Twas you asked for a secret talk about an enterprise you have in mind. It put me to some trouble, slipping away without rousing questions. I had a right to set my terms."

He considered her. Quiet but intense, she revealed nothing of the hoyden—mostly sullen and short-spoken, sometimes shrill in futile fury —that they knew at Aquilo and Confluentes. "There is more in you than I supposed," he murmured after a moment, "and already I understood you were the one whose help I should seek." He looked around him. The depths of the wood might have concealed anything. "Aye, you may well hope you can call on—whatever you call on—for a blessing or an omen or—what, Nemeta?"

"Say what you want of me."

"Come, shall we sit down?" he proposed. "I've brought wine." He gestured at a leather flask opposite his sword and lowered himself to the ground. Fallen stuff crackled faintly.

She shook her head. "We'll not water it from this spring. It too was once holy." Nevertheless she joined him, though hunkering and at a slight distance, as if prepared to bound away should he make a wrong move.

Evirion drank without dilution, passed a hand over his clean-shaven chin, and smiled. It livened his rugged good looks. "You are an astonishing lass. Fifteen years, is that your age? But then, you're the daughter of Forsquilis—" he turned somber— "and she was the last of the great witch-Queens in Ys."

"I'll never know what she knew." The girl's tone was stoic. "But I did learn a little from her ere the whelming. And others, like Tera— Give me the freedom to seek, and I may win back a small part of what went down with Ys." Abruptly she colored. The big eyes lowered before him. "That is my dream."

He seized the opening. "And what chance have you to make it real? What are you now, princess of Ys, but a scullion?"

"That's...unfair. Everybody must do whatever they're able. My father —we're his housekeepers, Julia and I. Not menials. He has no wife anymore—"

"Did his Queens go to market, cook, scrub, mend, weave, hold back in the presence of men, look forward to marrying a rustic lout and farrowing for him?" Evirion gibed. "How glad are you these days, Nemeta?"

"What of you?" she counterattacked.

"Why, I am wretched," he said without hesitation. "I, a Suffete born of the Baltisi, I who owned my ship and was her master on ventures from the Outer Isles to far Thule, since Ys drowned I've been a laborer. Oh, one who has some skill; I shape wood, rather than grub dirt or carry it in a hod; but I take my orders and swill my ration and at night lie on a clay floor in a wattle-and-daub hovel." Rage broke free. "I've been flogged! Like a common, mutinous cockroach of a sailor, I was flogged."

"I heard about that," Nemeta said carefully, "but 'twas in snippets mixed together, and I'm not supposed to ask."

"Aye, you're among Romans and Christians, who keep their women meek. Hear the tale. Cadoc Himilco—you know him, surely, the dog who comes sniffing around the skirts of your sister—"

"He and Julia...like each other."

"Well they might. *They're* not ill content, I imagine. A sanctimonious pair like that should fit well into the new order." Evirion tried to check his temper. "He and I were on the same task of building. He made a stupid botch. I reproved him. He struck me. Naturally I struck back, taught him a lesson. 'Twas three days till he was fit for work. And Grallon had me triced up and given three lashes. For defending myself!"

Nemeta tensed. "My father is, is a just man. Mostly. I heard Cadoc got one lash after he was well. You two shouldn't have fought when there's so much to do. Why did he hit you? 'Tisn't like him."

"I—ah, I do have a quick tongue. I called him a son of a pig."

"With his own father newly dead. And you disabled him for three days. I wonder how stupid his mistake truly was."

Evirion swallowed. Silence thickened. At last he said, "You defend your father more than I awaited."

"We—oh—we quarrel, everybody knows we do, and of course when the Nine broke with him because of Dahut—" The stick wavered which Nemeta gripped. She rallied and challenged: "Say forth what you came to say, or go."

"I've half a mind to do that, and leave you to your insolence and misery."

Her tone softened. "Nay, please, abide. Let's start afresh."

His anger subsided. Eagerness rose in its place. "Hark then. We've few skills that are of use anymore, we who stood high in Ys. The commoners with us, they can doubtless lose themselves and their names in the ruck. Must folk like you and me? How shall we escape the trap? Wealth would free us, but we've lost everything that was ours."

His voice dropped. He leaned close. *"It abides, Nemeta."*

She caught her breath.

He nodded. "Aye, in the ruins. Gold, silver, gems, coined money. The sea cannot have washed it all away—thus far—though it will erelong. Unless first we have courage to come reclaim our heritage."

She shivered and drew signs in the simmering air. "The Gods destroyed Ys. We're outcasts. 'Twould be death, or worse, to go back."

"Are you certain?" he pressed. "How do you know? Tell me that, and I'll let slip my hopes."

"Why, 'tis— Well, I—" She stared from side to side. The red hair bristled outward.

"You suppose so," he said. "Like everybody else. I think the dead there would welcome and aid whoever returned; for the aim is to keep alive some part of what they were. My thought is that I'll leave shortly after harvest. Then nobody will much care or heed that this pair of working hands is gone. Having won the means at Ys, I'll go on to Gesocribate and buy the best ship to be had. I'll get as many Ysans for crewmen as possible. We'll adventure forth again, our own masters again, and hell may have Rome!"

"Wha-what of me?"

"I'm not wholly reckless. I agree we know not what may haunt the desolation. I want a comrade who can sense, warn, do whatever is needful for our safety...amidst things of the Otherworld. This world I can handle myself."

She made a fending motion. "But I'm a child! I have no such powers."

"Mayhap you've more than you think, Nemeta. I've done my watching and my asking—more quietly, more patiently than most folk would believe me able to. You've guessed where lost objects were, and been right. Your dreams, such of them as you've spoken of, have a way of foreshadowing what happens. Ofttimes small objects fly through the air in houses where you are, though never a human hand cast them. When it seemed a prize cow of Apuleius's would die in calving, you touched her and muttered and at once the birth went easily. These and more—aye, small happenings, but they've already made you talked about, made some people look at you askance. They wonder what you do when you walk solitary in the woods. I wonder too."

"Naught, naught. I seek for Gods. M-my father lets me, he defends me in spite of—I've never really told him—" The girl straightened. "I won't help any foe of his."

"Still, you twain are not quite friends, eh? Well, he and I have been at odds, doubtless we shall be in future, but I wish him no ill."

Her gaze steadied and brooded. "Is that true? I hear you have blamed him for the fall of Ys."

He flushed. "I'll leave him alone if he'll do likewise for me. Let the Gods deal with him however he may deserve. Enough?"

Slowly, she nodded.

"Think of yourself," he urged. "Think what your share of our gains will mean to your life. Is that not worth any hazard? Afterward—aye, a woman has curbs upon her in this Roman world, but you'll have me for your friend, counsellor, partner if you wish. Or even more, Nemeta."

She tensed. Her words flew quick, not quite firm, yet underlaid with steeliness. "I am a maiden. No man shall own me, never. If I fare with you, first you must swear to honor that; and I will devise the oath you swear."

The least bit daunted by her manner, he hesitated an instant, then replied: "So be it. Indeed you are your mother's daughter. Now let us talk about how we may do this thing."

~ 2 ~

Work being finished that had needed every hand at the colony, and repairs upon her being completed, *Osprey* could again go fishing. She left Aquilo on the ebb tide, down the Odita to the sea.

For a while the river broadened. Farther on it narrowed and twisted through such a series of bends that the crew, when they first headed upstream, had sometimes wondered if they did not have the wrong part of the waterway and had entered a mere branch. Only on oars could a craft her size or larger keep from going aground. Twice she passed a merchantman at anchor, both waiting for the tide to turn so they could proceed. Boats full of rowers stood by to tow them.

There was scant other occupation in these parts. The banks were high and mostly wooded. Where the terrain sloped more easily one might see cleared land, farm or pasture. Much of this looked new but was not. It had been abandoned and had reverted to wilderness during the evil years, then reclaimed once peace came back. "I wonder how long 'twill last, now Ys and her navy be down," Maeloch said half aloud.

At the rivermouth a fisher hamlet huddled, and on the very edge of land the ruins of a Roman villa, sacked by pirates. Little of the buildings remained; folk of the neighborhood had quarried them for stone, tile, brick, glass. That was what became of nearly all the shells left behind when civilization receded.

Osprey put to sea. Wind was from the east. Sweeps came inboard, sail rattled aloft, and the smack ran over gray-green chop toward her old fishing grounds. First she must bear southerly, to round the peninsula. Maeloch kept her closer to shore than his men quite liked. These waters were less dangerous than those around Ys, but still had their share of rocks and shoals. Toward evening, he pointed to where hearth-smoke rose from the land and said, "We'll put in yonder for the night."

A couple of mariners groaned. "Why, that's daft, skipper," Usun protested. "We'll have moon enough to fare after dark. And we ken nay the approach."

"Just the same, we go in, me lads, as we will each darkfall that we can. 'Tis wise we make acquaintance with our fellows along this coast. They can tell us a mickle about it; and should we ever find ourselves in distress, why, we'll have their goodwill."

Usun shook his head. "In the time these calls 'ull take, we could make a second voyage. We've become poor men."

"With fewer mouths to feed than erstwhile," said Maeloch bleakly.

"Ye could at least ha' taken on a pilot who knows the way."

"That would be one more mouth to...talk. Helm over!"

Narrowed glances dwelt on the captain, but the crew obeyed. More than once had he issued strange orders; and thus far they had stayed alive.

It was slow work, crawling forward on oars, constantly heaving the lead. The sun had gone down behind western heights when *Osprey* arrived. The village was a mass of shadows, the men who waited to meet the strangers almost as murky. Maeloch sprang from the bows and advanced with hands open. In Osismiic he declared his name and port of departure. His dialect differed from what prevailed here, but was understandable. Suspicion dissolved. Everyone was delighted to meet newcomers, and they were invited to lodge overnight. As he had hoped, Maeloch ended in the headman's hut.

"Ye're kind to a wayfarer," he said as the wife set forth a belated meal of stockfish, leeks, and roots. "Let me offer somewhat." He had brought a jug of wine. Soon he and his host were on the best of terms.

Palaver went on long after dark. Maeloch led it toward pirates. That was easy. Nightmare memories were already astir. Even these dwellings had what drew barbarians—women to ravish, youngsters to take for slave markets, men to kill, and roofs to burn for the fun of it.

"They'll nay come back at once, the Saxons and Scoti," Maeloch said. "First they must hear o' what's happened, then make small, probing raids till they're sure the back of Armorica's sea defense be broken.

831

And the north shores be nearer them. 'Tis a long beat around the headlands where Ys was. Those who sail too nigh will likely sail no more." His rumbling voice lost steadiness for a moment. There had been that which sang on a reef. Boldly again: "But in time they'll reach ye, sure as death. Will ye be ready?"

Bitterness replied: "What can we be ready with? Fish spears and firewood axes—or our feet to carry us inland when we see the lean hulls."

"It could be more, my friend. Hark'ee. The Romans have nay the manpower to ward ye, yet will nay let ye arm yourselves and form a trained force, the kind that made the barbarians give Ys and her ships a wide berth. However, the Romans need nay know all that goes on in a quiet way."

The headman sat straight. "What d'ye aim at?"

"Ah, nay too fast. 'Quiet' be the word I used. But I be a man o' Grallon's, he who was King of Ys, and he did ask me to sound out those like yourself as I fared—"

~ 3 ~

The Sunday was clear, surely a good omen. Already at dawn, people began to gather in front of the cathedral. When Gratillonius arrived shortly after sunrise, the square was crowded. Mostly folk stood mute; those who talked did so in murmurs. The consecration of a bishop was an event of the highest solemnity.

The great building shadowed them. Brick, tile, and glass of its clerestory caught the early light, a brightness as cool as the air. Memory tugged Gratillonius's lips ruefully upward. When had he last attended a Christian service in Turonum, or anywhere else for that matter? Thirteen years ago? So little had he known then that he supposed the church was the only one in the city. Actually, the cathedral had been under repair after a fire. Today Corentinus would have setting worthy of him.

Apuleius waited at the head of the assembly, together with a few other men of secular importance from the territory. Gratillonius went to join them. Nobody said more to him than a greeting. He felt the constraint and tried to shrug it off his mind.

Beyond the columns of the porch, the doors opened. Darkness obscured the men who cried, "Come, all Christians! Come to worship!" They went down the three steps and across the pavement, calling their summons.

The people moved forward, upward, inward. Frescoes between the windows in aisles and clerestory were more plain to see than the picture of Christ the Lawgiver in the apse; but the light from the east that dazzled eyes was as a glory under His feet. At that end the floor was three steps higher, bearing altar, offertory table, and cupboard for holy things needful. Ranked in the apse were the clergy, wearing robes of white. Over these, priests had the dalmatic, bishops the chasuble, splashes of color against dusk. The bishops were three, Martinus in a carven chair flanked in lesser seats by the two colleagues whom the occasion required. Corentinus folded his long frame close to them. Priests used stools. The choir, double-ranked below them, seemed almost phantomlike. Candleflames glimmered.

The lay notables took stance behind a few benches set out for the aged and infirm. Several hundred commoners pressed in at their backs. The energumens had been led away. From the bema a deacon called for silence. The doorkeepers passed the command on to the overflow attendance in porch and square. Mumbling died out. For a minute the hush was enormous.

The deacon's voice trod forth: "Let us kneel."

Gratillonius felt a brief surprise. He was used to seeing those who prayed stand erect, arms raised in supplication. Was this a new practice, or had he forgotten, or was he still more ignorant of the Mass than he had supposed? Awkwardly, he lowered himself to the patterned stone floor.

A priest mounted the ambo on the north side and prayed, "—to God, Savior of the faithful, preserver of the believers, author of immortality—" The congregation's "Amen" sounded deep, and all stood up.

From the cupboard a subdeacon brought a volume of Jewish scripture to the first level of the ambo, read a passage, "—Better a poor man who walks in his integrity, than he who is false in his ways and rich...." and returned it. The people knelt while the priest read a second collect, and rose again. The first deacon called for silence. Another deacon brought a lavishly bound volume of the Apostles to the second level of the ambo, proclaimed the title, and read. Gratillonius thought Martinus must have chosen the shipwreck of Paulus in compliment to old sailor Corentinus. The deacon took the book back.

"Oh, all you works of the Lord, bless you the Lord," sang the choir. The response, "Praise Him and magnify Him forever," had not that soaring beauty, but force throbbed in it. Gratillonius kept silence. From the corner of an eye he saw how fervently Apuleius entered into the antiphony as it went on.

Meanwhile a subdeacon had lighted the incense in the censer. A rich odor wafted from it. The second deacon took the Gospel from the altar where it lay, the subdeacon censed it, and the deacon carried it to the third and highest level of the ambo. Resting it on the lectern, he announced the title, certain verses from holy Marcus. Seated clergy rose. "Glory to God Almighty," said the congregation.

The words welled: "And Lord Jesus told them: Pay Caesar what is Caesar's and God what is God's...."

The book was returned to the altar and the choir sang a brief anthem from the Psalms. Again the first deacon called for silence and the priest on the ambo made announcements. Gratillonius's mind wandered elsewhere. Another collect followed.

Gratillonius's attention awakened when Bishop Martinus trod to the top of the bema steps and gave his sermon. Drawing its text from the Gospel passage, it was characteristically short and pointed. Gratillonius half felt the preacher's eyes were on him. "—doing what Caesar requires, or just what is necessary to sustain life and common decency, is not enough. It can even become the subtlest of temptations. We do well to be honorable, unless we make so much of that that it turns into pride and causes us to neglect the far higher duty we owe to God—"

If he meant a reproach, he set it aside afterward, when his fellow bishops led Corentinus to him. Having signed themselves, they formally named the candidate and intoned together, "Reverend Father, the churches at Aquilo and Confluentes beg you to raise up this present chorepiscopus to the task of full bishop." Corentinus genuflected. Gratillonius's heartbeat quickened.

Martinus turned to the visiting leaders. "Speakers for those whose shepherd he shall be," he asked, "do you find this man worthy?"

Faith made no difference. A bishop must be acceptable to his entire community. When Gratillonius joined in replying, "He is worthy," he found himself stammering. Why? He had been instructed in everything that was to happen.

Martinus questioned Corentinus ritually and at length about his orthodoxy and intentions. Though equally stylized, the answers rang with sincerity. In the end, Martinus said, "May the Lord return these and other goods to you, and keep you safe, and strengthen you in all good."

A subdeacon brought a chasuble for Corentinus to don. Its rich blue, with glistening gold embroidery, looked out of place on his gauntness, but it was the work of loving hands at home. He knelt. Martinus prayed that he might prove a faithful and prudent servant over his family. The three bishops laid their hands on his head. "Receive the Holy Spirit," Martinus bade, "for the office and work of a bishop, now committed to you by the laying on of our hands; in the name of the Father, and of the Son, and of the Holy Spirit. Amen." Corentinus rose, hallowed.

The first deacon cried dismissal. It was time for catechumens, penitents, and infidels to leave. Gratillonius felt on his back the looks of Martinus, Corentinus, and Apuleius, about to enter the mystery that he denied. Its secrets were ill-kept, unlike those of Mithras, and he knew more or less what would take place; but for no sound reason, his exclusion hurt.

—However, those who stayed saw practices that had changed somewhat over the years. Offerings were now taken only from the baptized, while the choir sang. Thereupon the second deacon went to the top of the ambo and led a prayer for God's mercy on sinners and the ignorant. He then took a diptych, conjoined tables of cedarwood with heavy silver covers, and saying, "May you show mercy, Lord, on Your servant—" read out every name inscribed beginning with that of Emperor Honorius, continuing through bishops present and past, the martyr Symphorianus whose holy relics rested here, on to various living and departed members of the congregation whom there was special reason to name. At the altar Martinus prayed for God to bless them, free the souls of the dead from suffering, and let "this oblation converted to Christ's flesh and blood be effective." He ended with the words "through our Lord Jesus Christ," and the people answered, "Amen."

The gospel was taken to the cupboard and a linen cloth spread over the altar. On it were set the chalice and a ewer of water, while fresh incense went into the censer. A brief prayer proclaimed belief in the Trinity, confessed frailty, begged for forgiveness, and ended with the mutual "Amen."

A deacon took the chalice to the offertory table and half filled it with wine; another chose some of the bread donated and set it directly on the altar cloth. Martinus poured water into the wine. A deacon covered the Elements with a napkin. Words went to and fro: Let us greet one another. Peace be with you. And with your spirit.

Martinus kissed Corentinus, they both in turn kissed their brother bishops, these passed it on to the rest of the clergy and to the laity, who exchanged kisses. Meanwhile Martinus prayed aloud for mercy, remission of sins, and "that whosoever are joined in the kiss be more bound to each other and hold with affection in the breast that which is offered with the mouth."

Congregation: "Amen."

Martinus: "Let us lift up our hearts."

Congregation: "We have, to the Lord."

Martinus: "Let us return thanks to the Lord our God."

Congregation: "It is meet and just."

Martinus: "It is meet and just to give thanks to the Lord, Holy Father, Almighty Eternal God, Whose Son was born of a virgin, through the Holy Spirit; and being made man shrank not from the shame of a human beginning; and through conception, birth, and the cradle, and infant cries traversed the entire course of the reproach and humiliations of our nature. His humiliation is the ennobling of us, His reproach is our honor; that He as God should abide in our flesh is in turn a renewal of us from fleshly nature into God. In return for the affection of so vast a condescension, for which the angels praise Your majesty, the dominations adore it, the powers tremble before it, the heavens, the heavenly virtues, and blessed seraphim with a common jubilation glorify it, we beseech You that we may be admitted to join our humble voices with theirs, saying—"

All: "Holy, holy, holy, Lord God of Sabaoth. Heaven and earth are full of Your glory. Blessed are You through the ages."

While Martinus prayed onward, he and the other bishops each touched each piece of bread on the altar, and the chalice. "—This is the cup of the New Testament in My blood—" The prayers ended with the Lord's.

Martinus: "Free us from evil, Lord, free us from all evil, and establish us in every good work, You Who live and rule with the Father and the Holy Spirit forever and ever."

All: "Amen."

The choir sang an anthem as the four bishops broke up the loaves of bread. They took care that no crumbs fall on the floor; it was now Christ's body. Two subdeacons stood with peacock fans to keep away insects. The clergy took the Food and the Drink first, in order of rank, starting with Martinus; after them the choir, one at a time, while the rest sang antiphonally the Thirty-Fourth Psalm ("O taste, and see, how gracious the Lord is—"); last the other laity, ending with the doorkeepers. As a communicant came to the altar, he or she held out the right hand cupped in the left, and Corentinus placed a fragment of bread in it, saying, "Receive the body of Christ." The worshipper responded "Amen" and bowed head to take it. Thereafter he or she moved to the other end of the altar, where Martinus held out the chalice and said, "Receive the blood of Christ." Again the worshipper said, "Amen," bowed head, and sipped.

When everyone had finished, Martinus said, "Restored by Heavenly food, revived by the drinking cup of the Lord, we return praise and thanks to God the all-powerful Father through Our Lord Jesus Christ."

"Amen," they responded.

The chief deacon called on them to bow their heads once more. Martinus prayed for the hearing of prayers and for guidance. "Amen," they answered.

Martinus: "Peace be with you."

All: "And with your spirit."

Martinus: "Go, it is sent."

All: "Thanks be to God."

—Well, Gratillonius thought, his part was done. As soon as his friends were ready, he'd start home with them.

VII

~ 1 ~

Westward over Ocean, mists dimmed and reddened the sun-disc, brought the edge of sight ever closer to the headlands. Elsewhere the sky was gray, already darkening above eastern hills, and shadow filled the valley that ran out of them. Cliffs on either side of the bay hulked darkling. Wind eddied between, acrid with strand-smells. Though still some distance off, surf overwhelmed its whimpers.

"Once more," Evirion urged. "Only once, while the tide is out. Tomorrow morning we'll be off."

Nemeta shook her head. Locks blew rusty about the whiteness of her face, the hugeness of her eyes. She hugged her tunic to her against the chill. "Nay," she said thinly. "We have enough. And we've dared more than we should, in this world or the Other."

"A single great find, and we're not merely provided for, we're wealthy. Powerful. We can do whatever we will—for our people, Nemeta; for our Gods." Whoever They may be, Evirion did not add.

"But I feel the menace yonder. Sharper than this breeze. A wind out of the future." Nemeta waited until she had his look directly upon her. "You trusted me to find where treasures lay buried, and I did. Now trust me when I say Stop. Best would be if we departed on the instant." She gestured with her head at the amphitheater behind them. It had been their shelter these past three days and nights since they arrived at Ys. "We can sleep in one of the forsaken houses above the vale. If first we cover our tracks." That would not be quite simple, when they had two laden mules. Evirion had earned them by toiling for an Osismiic farmer; they were so aged and weak that that was possible for him in the time since he was released from labor for the community.

He laid hand to sword, a laurel-leaf blade of Ysan make. "What is it you dread?"

"I know not. I've a foreboding. It grew on me hour by hour today." She turned her gaze left, south, where Aquilonian Way climbed the steeps before bending east toward Audiarna.

He himself squinted west. The tide had in fact turned and was flowing in, though it would not lap at the ruins farthest inland for a few hours yet. Well before then, he gauged, everything would be shrouded in fog. If aught more was to be done there, it must be done soon—or on the morrow, but he had acceded to her and promised that then they would leave at first light.

That was a pledge readily given. The city he loved had become an uncanny place, a haunting ground. Several times he thought he glimpsed something white that danced more than swam in the waves among the rocks; fragments of song had frightened him with their allurement. He had said nothing to Nemeta about it, as uneasy as she was, and to himself insisted it must be mistake, illusion, dream giving half-life to wind and sea.

"I thought the danger all lay that way," he said. Indeed it was tricky to scramble over stones broken, tumbled, slippery with water and weed, where glass shards lurked, and to pry them apart and grope down-

837

ward—though worse was turning up a human bone or a skull to which the drenched hair still clung. Had you danced in those arms, traded kisses with that mouth?

But the gems and precious metals were there, the ransom of freedom. No single hoard yielded them as Evirion hoped; they were spread among what had been buildings, scattered by currents and the shifting of ruins as ground settled. Without the peculiar talent Nemeta had found herself to possess, the searchers would have needed a month to find what they amassed in days. As was, they bought every small gain with hurtful travail, hour by hour until darkness or waves made work impossible and they stumbled back to the amphitheater carrying their laden sacks, bolted cold food, and toppled into sleep through which walked nightmares.

Evirion came to think that it was as if the Gods mocked him: the Three of Ys, Taranis the Thunderer, Belisama the All-Mother, Lir of the Deeps, dethroned, homeless, become trolls. He denied it with every force he could summon, but it gnawed past his defenses like the sea undermining the foundations of the city. If not They, then Someone laired here and hated everything human.

Abrupt rage burned away doubt and fatigue. He would not surrender. If only by a gesture, he would declare his manhood.

"Well, stay behind and nurse your woman-fears," he snapped. "I'm bound on a last questing."

She stared at him, stricken. "Without me?"

"As you wish. I've no more use for your wand. Half the public coffers were in the basilica, and that's what I'll attempt."

He turned on his heel and stalked to the gateway outside which the tethered mules grazed. Within it were stored the boxes for loot—not that he used the word to himself—together with bags, spades, picks, crowbars. Grabbing up his tools, he strode down the broad path that led to Aquilonian Way. Grass had begun to thrust upward between its paving blocks.

Through wind and surf he heard feet patter. He glanced behind. Nemeta hurried after him. Her long bare legs glimmered in the dull light. She carried another bar in her left hand. Her right clutched the forked stick, graven with signs, that dipped in her grasp to show where they should dig.

"Are you coming after all?" he asked with a gladness that surprised him.

"I'd not...have you alone...out there," she answered unsteadily.

Or yourself alone ashore, he refrained from saying. "'Twill be quick, you know. Soon dark. Whether or not we've found anything, we'll come back and—and start a fire, enjoy hot food and our last wine, make celebration."

A slight smile trembled on her lips.

Desire stirred in him. She was attractive in her spare, half-grown fashion; so much life surged through her. On the coldest nights they had joined their bedrolls together, and he was hard put to honor his promise of chastity. Mayhap when they were safe—

Wreckage and remnants strewed the beach less thickly than at first. From the lack of valuables there, Evirion supposed that someone, possibly a gang or two of barbarian sailors, had picked it over. Since, bit by bit, spring tides reclaimed the debris. Doubtless the steepening of slopes helped. Without the wall for protection, the sandstone under Ys wore away as fragments rolled grinding across it. The caverns dug underneath had begun to collapse. Each time that happened, not only did whatever had rested on top fall into the hole, but earthquakelike shock brought low more of what had been standing elsewhere. The bottom dropped sharply toward depths of ten or twelve fathoms. Pieces of the dead city slid thither as currents tugged them, to be forever lost. A few decades from now, he guessed, nothing would be left save whatever was above extreme high water. Amphitheater, pharos, necropolis, the solitary headstone of Point Vanis—and even those? Somehow the lighthouse was half its olden height....

Man and girl clambered over the rubble that had been High Gate. Stumps of wall lifted on either side, like teeth in a jawbone. Lir Way was almost as choked. Courses of stone, pillars still upright, statues battered nearly into shapelessness, thrust forlornly above. The same chaos reached right, left, ahead, in some places mound-high, in others roughly leveled. Wetness sheened, kelp sprawled, three cormorants wheeled black overhead. The wind whistled.

The Forum had been sufficiently wide that parts of it remained clear, aside from shards. The lowest bowl of the Fire Fountain stood, filled with chunks of the upper ones and with seawater that the wind ruffled. On the northeast side, the basilica was recognizable. Several of its columns rose over the detritus in the portico. The roof had fallen in but the walls mostly survived, however scarred and weakened. Hitherto, given Nemeta's guidance, Evirion had sought easier unearthing. But it should be possible to clear the outer doorway leading to the treasury. With luck, in the time that was left them they might work part of the contents free.

Nemeta drew a ragged breath. "Hark. Do you hear?" she whispered.

He squinted westward as she pointed. Lowtown was a pit of gloom into which the waves were marching, forward, back, forward again and higher. He could not see them because of the fog bank, but he heard their roar and the rattle of loosened stones. And—a voice? A song? *O wearyfoot wanderer—*

"Nay!" he answered, louder than he had intended. "Wind, water, belike a seabird. Come. We must hasten."

He led her around to the side of the building that fronted on Taranis Way. They mounted the stairs. As he had noticed earlier, the bronze door there lay wrenched off its hinges. The space beyond was piled with refuse, but that was more broken tile than it was stone or roof beams, and only about three feet deep. Nemeta halted, laid down her bar, took the forked wand in both hands, closed her eyes, soundlessly moved her lips.

He had expected to see the end of the stick lift and point ahead, yet it fired his hopes. "To work!" he said, and attacked.

Nemeta cried out.

Evirion dropped his bar and turned. Around the corner of the building had come four men. Weapons lifted ugly in their hands.

The foremost gestured. "Hem 'em in," he rapped in harsh Latin. The rest jumped, one to his right, two to his left, making a semicircle under the stairs.

Evirion's vision pounced among them. Everything registered, noonday-stark in the fading light. They were tough, dirty, unkempt, clad in tunics and breeches that had seen much wear and little washing. Each belt bore a knife. The leader was an ursine blackbeard with a broken nose. He carried a short ax. His companions were slighter, never well nourished, but equally evil-looking. Their arms were a spear, a bill, and nail-studded club.

"Who are you?" Evirion called in their language. No need to ask their purpose, said his suddenly lightning-swift mind. He knew this breed, waterfront toughs without tribe or ethic.

The leader grinned. "Ullus of Audiarna, at your honor's service. And you, sir, and the young lady?"

"We are here by right. How dare you invade our home and profane our shrines? Be off before the Gods strike you!"

It was a belly sickness to hear Ullus laugh. His followers leered, uncomfortably but also unflinching. "Why, I guess we've as much right as anybody else to help ourselves," he said. "There'll be plenty more later on. We thought we'd got the idea first, but we found your tracks—your animals, your stores." Again his elation boomed. "Thanks for doing so much work for us."

Nemeta lifted her wand. It trembled as she did, and her voice: "I witch. Go. Or I curse."

The schoolchild Latin actually seemed to hearten the newcomers. Ullus licked his lips. "You'll feel different pretty soon," he told her. "Me and my boys know how to break a filly for riding, hey?"

Evirion drew sword. "I am a seaman of Ys," he stated. "You're from Audiarna, you said? That's a seaport. You know what I mean. Come any closer and you're dead."

Ullus's mirth gave way to rage. His ax chopped the air. "How I do know your kind, you! Or did, afore God brought you down in your pride and sins, like the preacher always told He would. Do *you* know how it is being poor all your life, dock walloper, deckhand, ordered around, worked till you drop, fed like nobody 'ud feed a pig, paid off in nummi, and the boot or the whip if we speak up? And meanwhile your ships from Ys 'ud swagger by, with you on deck in your gold and silk. Well, that's done with, fellow. The high are brought low and the low are brought high, like Christ promised. We're here to claim our share. Now drop that blade and come down slow. We may leave you your stinking life. But you got to behave yourself. Understand?"

Evirion did. They'd never let him past. They knew he might well outrun them, seize the mules, make off with the treasure. So at best, they'd hold him bound and vent their grudges on him till they were ready to leave. And then it would be safest for them to cut his throat and toss him out for the eels. As for Nemeta—

Trained in combat, he was more than a match for any of them. But they were four, two with pole weapons. Something like a plucked harpstring keened within him. He stood beyond himself and saw he was become an instrument whereon Belisama played, She in Her avatar the Wild Huntress.

He bent close to the girl. Her stare was blank, her face wet with more than mist; he heard the short breaths go in and out. "Listen well," he whispered in Ysan. "I'll attack them. You run to the left at once. Hide in this jumble. After dark, slip off to the hills. Do you hear?"

He might have been talking to a noosed hare. "You can't help me," he went on. "Go home. Tell them what happened. Cast a spell against these creatures if you like. Remember me, Nemeta. Go."

"Are you coming, or must we fetch you?" yelled a man.

"Easiest to throw rocks at him," said Ullus loudly.

"Ya-a-ah!" Evirion hallooed, and bounded downward.

He saw the broken visage gape open in surprise. He was there. He stabbed. Almost, he killed. Ullus's ax met his sword in midthrust and knocked it aside. He barely kept a grip on it. His speed carried him by. The bludgeon brushed his shoulder. That threw him spinning. He lurched a pair of yards, recovered, whirled about in a crouch.

Three men milled and howled in his direction. Beyond them, atop the stairs, he saw Nemeta dash off. So, said a remote voice, that's as it should be. Let me hold them for two or three minutes till she's safely away.

The spearman poised with his weapon and cast. It flew in a long arc, upward, directly before her shins. She fell over the shaft and toppled, step by step, a whirl of limbs and hair. He was off to meet her, ferret-swift. She rolled to a stop and picked herself up. He got there and flung arms around her. She screamed. He hooted.

"Good work, Timbro!" Ullus bellowed. "Keep 'er for us too!" He swung to advance on Evirion. The billman and the clubber hung back. "Move, you scuts! Hold him busy and I'll hit him from the rear."

They gathered courage. Evirion thought he saw the dawn of pleasure on them. Ullus was triumphant. He had no reason to hide his plan. It was clear and certain. He sidled across the avenue, around the Ysan.

To stand and fight would be to die, uselessly. The spearman had Nemeta down on the pavement. She struggled. His first struck her beneath the jaw. Her shrieks dropped to a thin wailing, her movements to feebleness. Between them and Evirion were the rest of the band.

He sheathed his sword, whipped about, dodged out onto the forum, and ran.

For a brief while he heard shouts and footfalls at his back. Then he was alone. None of them could match his fleetness; and even now, he had some knowledge of Ys. He zigzagged, climbed, slipped in and out among huge shattered remnants, until he had shaken pursuit. Still he kept on. He knew not why. It was as if the sea drew him.

Yet hard was the way he must fare. Down here the stones only saw sky when water was very low. Shells encrusted them, for hands and knees to flay themselves. Green weed wrapped them, slimy to make feet lose footing. Strange things grew, swam, scuttered in pools between. Fog swirled ever thicker and more cold. Through the blindness that it wove beat ever louder the rumble, rush, plash, smack, growl of waves. Evirion cast himself down at their verge.

He could dimly see a few feet in the wet smokiness. A rock lay fallen upon lesser ones. They were paving stones and building blocks; it was rudely hewn, if men had ever given it any of its shape—a megalith. He had come to Menhir Place, where Ys preserved a relic of an age ere ever the city was. What, had this first and last piety also been overthrown? Or was its raw mass the sign of a doom spoken at the founding of the world?

Evirion's panting faded into a sigh. He knew just that he too was broken. His emprise had enriched barbarians (aye, barbarians swarmed out of Rome as well as the wild lands; a carcass breeds maggots) and destroyed a girl. His strength had drained away with his hopes. The shoulder that the bludgeon had scraped throbbed with pain. The rent cloth around it hung sodden with blood. Water licked him, higher at every wave. The fog hooded his eyes, laid salt on his mouth, like tears.

Through the blood-beat in his skull he thought he heard a song again. Peace without end, love to enfold him as does the sea, all he need do was abide and she would come. Did the mists eddy together and form a wraith of her whiteness in the dusk? It was her lips that tasted of salt, her kiss.

Desire torrented upward. He rose, spread his arms, called into the deep noises, "Here I am. We'll go and snare the rest, won't we? I'll bring you their bones to play with out on the reefs."

A snarling gave answer, and a giggle in the wind.

The wind lifted. It blew him back shoreward. Or else he was the wind and the fog and the following sea. He flowed across rocks, poured along broken pillars, swept over tumbled roofs, a salmon bound upstream, an orca in the final shearing rush at a seal. The sword flared free.

In Taranis Way, the last man got up and belted his breeches. The red-haired girl sprawled at his feet. "Ready for another go, anybody?" he crowed. He was young, the fuzz thin across a face raddled with sores and pimples.

Nemeta stirred. Her eyes stayed shut, but she pulled at the hem of her tunic, trying to bring it down, while she squirmed about so as to lie curled tightly on her side.

"Nah," said Ullus. He cast an uneasy glance west across the Forum. Wind rumpled his beard and shrilled in his ears. Darkness advanced yonder, a wall of it from which gray tatters flew. "We've spent too much time with her as is. Might be sunset—who can tell through that stuff? Back to camp, their camp where the gold is, while we can still see what we're doing."

"Tomorrow'll be soon enough for work," agreed the spearman. He nudged the girl with his foot. "Up, you." When she merely shivered, he kicked.

"Hey, easy," said the youth. "Don't spoil that nice, tight thing. If she can't walk, gimme a hand with her."

"Ah, she can walk, all right." The clubber spat. "Stubborn bitch. I'll teach her better."

"Move!" rasped Ullus. "Never saw fog come in so fast or so heavy."

The boy and the pikeman dragged the girl half upright and shoved her along. She stumbled between them, eyes still closed. A bruise was starting to blossom on her jaw. Blood trickled down her thighs.

The vapors whirled around. Ullus swore. "Stick close. We'll have to feel our way. If anybody strays, he'll likely be lost till morning in this damned spook-hole—"

He with the sword sprang out of the brume. Steel smote. Ullus staggered, dropped his ax, clutched his belly, stared astounded at the red and the entrails that fell out between his fingers. "Why, why, can't be," he mumbled and went down on his face. There he threshed for a short while. The tall man with the sword was gone.

The three yelled fury and threats. They formed a triangle, back to back. The wind snickered and flung a deeper blanket over them.

The spearman shouted, "There!" and jabbed at a shadow. It was only a clot of mist. The tall man glided under the shaft and struck upward, into the throat. The club whirred at him but he was gone and it smote a toppled statue. That blow knocked a chip out of the sculptured mouth so that it no longer smiled but sneered.

Nemeta's eyes were open. The two who were left had none for her. They stood gaping into sightlessness. She slipped from them.

"We've got to keep moving," gasped the clubber. "You face right, I'll face left. Crabwise, got me?"

They advanced a few paces, reached a wall whose remnant top they could not see, moved along it. He with the sword leaped from above. He landed on the shoulders of the clubber, who went down with a

843

sound of breaking spine and ribs. The clubber lay where he had fallen, for he had no movement below the waist. He flailed his arms about and ululated. The spit bubbled red in his beard.

"No!" yammered the boy. "Please, please! I'm sorry!" He dropped his bill and fled. The tall man followed leisurely.

—Evirion found Nemeta halfway up Taranis Way, resting on a wing that had fallen off a stone gryphon. His blade dripped, but the hue was pale, fog settling on the steel and running down to carry the blood away. Surf noises sounded louder. The wind had died.

He stood and stared at her, barely able to see though the murk. "How are you?" he asked hoarsely.

She raised her head. "I live," she answered without tone. "I can travel if we go easily. And you?"

"Unhurt save for this shoulder, which isn't too bad." He left off mention of scrapes, cuts, and bruises from his scramble to the sea. "Tomorrow the carrion birds will make dung of those bandits."

"How did you do it?"

"I know not. Something other than my own spirit had me. Something that laughed as It bargained—four lives in exchange for our two."

She hugged herself, bit her lip, climbed painfully to her feet. "Then the deal is completed, and we'd best depart while we can," she said.

"Aye." He gave her his free arm to lean on. "Nor ever return. Unwise was I to come. The Gods I trusted are evil, or mad. Never can I make amends to you."

She looked before her, into the unrestful gloom through which they groped. "You did not compel me," she said wearily.

"At least," he vowed, "you shall have your full share of what we did win."

She shook her head. "I'll take none of it. Cast it from you."

"Hoy? After what 'tis cost us?" He overcame his shock. "And what it means to my life. How can you say that? What knowledge have you?"

"No more than you have of what happened this eventide—" All at once she could walk no farther. She swayed, her knees buckled. He caught her.

"Poor lass," he mumbled. "Poor hurt lass." He sheathed his sword and took her up. "Here, lay your arms around my neck. I'll carry you back. At dawn we'll leave. If you refuse the gold, well, you may always call on me for whatever else is in my gift. Always."

She nestled her head against him. "I'll remember that," she whispered.

~ 2 ~

Mons Ferruginus and the woods beyond the Odita blazed with autumn, red, russet, yellow under the earliest sun-rays. Dew glittered on grass, vapors curled white above the stream. It ran through an enormous silence, beneath blue spaciousness. Air lay chill but already full of earth odors.

No one else was about when Gratillonius left Aquilo. Folk were sleeping late after last night's festivities. Tables had been modestly spread, in this year when the neighborhood divided what it had with the survivors of Ys, but drink was plentiful and merriment, after a while, feverish. As early as manners allowed, he had retired to a bed in the Apuleius home. His own was too close to the noise.

Not that he begrudged the people their celebration. They had earned it. They were alive, safe, housed; more toil and hardship lay before them, but nothing they could not overcome. When Corentinus dedicated Confluentes, he simply gave utterance to the fact of the colony. It was built. Most of its inhabitants occupied their dwellings, the rest would as soon as they had finished whatever obligations they had assumed in the course of earning their keep. Well might they cheer for Gratillonius their tribune, Grallon their King.

Wryness twisted the man's mouth. He was neither, of course. If his appointment was not revoked, that was merely because no one in the Imperial administration had thought to do so. As for his throne, it was under the sea with the bones of his Queens.

He strode on. Gravel scrunched underfoot. He needed something to do, anything. Well, he had no lack. But decision, organization, leadership required others be present. He thought he'd seek the manor, where Favonius was stabled, saddle the stallion and ride into the forest. Take spear and bow along; he might have a chance at a deer or a boar. Afterward, the tension out of him, maybe he could start arranging the woodworking shop he wanted. The one in Ys had given him pleasure and, aye, peace.

Should he have become a carpenter? He might this day dwell quietly in Britannia with wife and...sons; oh, daughters too, the older ones married and giving him grandchildren. But he wasn't born to that station. Anyway, somebody had to keep guard over the carpenter's hearth.

At the upper bridge he lingered a few minutes. The air was so pure, the river so serene. How different from yesterday. Here Corentinus had stood and preached his sermon, while the bank and the harvested field beyond were packed solid with people, not simply those of Ys—of Confluentes but nearly everyone in Aquilo. After all, Corentinus was their bishop now, the first resident bishop they had ever had. Old Maecius had retired to the monastery at Turonum. You could sense a new order of things being born. Conversion of the pagan immigrants to the Faith would be just the beginning.

The rough voice echoed in Gratillonius's head: "—thanks to almighty God and His Son, our Lord and Savior Jesus Christ, for Their manifold mercies. May the Holy Spirit descend to sanctify and bless these homes—" Mainly, however, as usual, Corentinus had talked to the commoners like one of their own. "—'Love your neighbor' isn't any simpering bit of goody-goodyness, you know. It's as tough a commandment as was ever laid on a man. Often you'd like to bash your neighbor's head in, or at least kick him in the butt. You Aquilonians, and I include the surrounding tribesfolk, you've been mighty kind to these outcasts; and you Ysans have been brave, and mostly done your best to make some return; but I know of quarrels, or outright blows, wrongs done on both sides, and it could get worse instead of better as time wears on. Doesn't have to, though. We're none of us saints, but we can be honest and reasonably patient with the neighbor. We can all stand together against whatever troubles come on us, in this world where Satan always prowls on the lookout for souls he can snatch.—"

Gratillonius wondered why the words stayed with him. He'd heard their like aplenty during the years Corentinus was in Ys, and they'd never been anything startling in the first place. Was it their impact on Julia that drove them into him? Lanarvilis's daughter had stood unwontedly solemn, intent, listening. Most times she was calm, even cheerful; when the memory of what she had lost struck fully into her, she didn't weep or brood or get drunk like many survivors, she grew quiet and kept extra busy. Suddenly she had seemed beautiful to him. Before, she was merely a large girl, well filled out, roundfaced, snubnosed, blue-eyed, her best feature the wavy reddish-brown hair.

Well, if she was to find consolation in Christ, good for her. Likewise had Gratillonius's mother, for whom he named the child. He hoped the religion wouldn't estrange her from him. It was a glow near the middle of the cold and hardness in him that she, after the alienation of the final months in Ys, again gave him not bare filial obedience but, he thought, some love.

As Forsquilis's daughter Nemeta had not—secretive, rebellious, runaway Nemeta. Since her vanishment in late summer Gratillonius had had no heart for revelry. They were dancing on the ground outside the ditch, beneath torches lashed to poles, when he left. Julia and young Cadoc Himilco had looked very happy together. Let them savor it for whatever short while they could.

Gratillonius shook himself. No use moping here. He crossed the bridge. It was of wood, like the one above the Aquilonian waterfront, but smaller, meant for workers on the Apuleius estate and in the forest to convey their produce. Confluentes would bring more traffic than that; something better was necessary. He found refuge in thinking about ways and means.

On the opposite shore, three sentries paced back and forth between the Stegir and the south end of the eastern earthworks. Regulars, but local, they were not legionaries nor outfitted like legionaries; that was a thing of the past. However, they did wear helmets and coats with iron rings sewed to the leather, they did carry swords, spears, and small round shields. If their bearing and movements weren't soldierly by ancient standards, at least they were alert and reasonably smart; they had learned from Maximus's veterans. The nearest of them recognized Gratillonius and snapped to a halt, thudding his spear down in salute. No law entitled Gratillonius to that, but so men did in these parts. He made an acknowledging gesture and passed on.

Confluentes lay around him, the town he and Corentinus had brought into being. A visitor from a city would find it unimpressive. It amounted to less than a hundred buildings between two streams and a breastwork with ditch, in a corner of cleared land whereof the rest would now be devoted to subsistence agriculture. The buildings were wood and clay under thatch roofs. The largest, oblongs of coarsely squared timber, held three or four rooms and had windows covered with membrane; the rest were cylindrical wattle-and-daub shielings. Shops and worksteads were few, tiny, primitive. There was no marketplace, basilica, church, ornamentation; everything still centered in Aquilo. At this hour there was hardly a sign of life.

Nevertheless...the houses were well built, neatly kept. The streets ran in a Roman grid, with gravel on them. If men, women, children slept yet behind these walls, it was because yesterday they had rejoiced at what was done here and what might be done in years unborn.

He passed a house as long as any. It was for unmarried women, chief among them those who had been vestals of Ys. The door stood ajar. It opened, and Runa came out.

He stopped at her signal. For a moment they regarded each other. The daughter of Vindilis and Hoel wore a blue cloak over a plain gray gown. Its cowl was thrown back and the raven hair flowed free from under a headband, past the narrow face and the shoulders. "Well," she said at length, low and in Ysan.

"How are you?" he replied awkwardly, in Latin.

"Whither fare you this early?"

He shrugged.

"Restless, as often aforetime." From beneath the high arches of brow, her dark gaze probed him. The whiteness of her skin made that look appear doubly intense. "I too. May I walk along with you?"

He wondered if she had thought him likely to come by and had waited. "I'd in mind to go hunting," he said brusquely.

"You may change your mind after we've talked. A private hour is rare for us."

"Well—as you wish." He set off again. She accompanied him without effort. The long skirt billowed and rustled.

"They missed you after you left last eventide," she said presently. "They wanted their King among them. It was a hallowing, after all."

"The Kingship is dead. Those Gods indwell no longer." He observed in faint surprise that he had also gone over to the Ysan tongue.

"Are you altogether sure, Gratillonius?" She seldom shortened his name as most people did. "I stayed not late myself. Drinking and dancing are not to my taste. But I'd heard the regret. You cannot abdicate."

"What do you want of me?" he growled.

"Why must you suppose I have a petition?"

847

He grinned lopsidedly. "From you 'twould be a demand. Ever has it been. Oh, I understand and respect. We clash, but we work toward the same end, and you've been a strong help. Shrewd, too."

Especially had she done what neither he nor Corentinus could, taken chieftainship among the women, spoken for them, found places where they could work with a measure of dignity, pressed in her acid fashion for a little of the freedom they had enjoyed in Ys. The bounds now around them were high and strait.

Runa sighed. "That nears an end. One by one they settle in, marry or find service that will endure and is endurable. Aye, you can grant me something. But 'twill be for the colony as well."

"What?"

"I suppose you've heard that I won myself paid occupation."

He nodded. "I've seen some of what you've done. Apuleius showed me."

Skilled copyists were always in demand. Runa was not only literate, she could do calligraphy. Apuleius was eager to have duplicates of books on his shelves. He could trade them for volumes he did not possess—or, rather, trade the older editions and keep hers. She was well along with the *Metamorphoses* in spite of adding flourishes and figures that delighted the beholder.

"Corentinus admired it too when he returned," Gratillonius added. "I happened to be there. In fact, he asked whether you might replace the church's worn-out Gospel—I forget which one—after you've become a Christian."

"He takes much for granted, does he not, the holy man?" she murmured.

He threw her a startled glance. She gave him a look of—expectancy? "What would you of me?" he blurted.

"Apuleius has told me the family will no longer use the fundus. 'Twas never a profitable property; in the main, a retreat the children enjoyed, and they are growing up."

Gratillonius nodded. "Aye. The house lies outside the defense, you recall. Natheless, men have suggested I occupy it—for my palace? I'm content with my cabin in Confluentes. Still, I have thought—we'll hold occasional meetings, business concerning this community alone. The manor house our basilica? 'Twould be worthier than aught else we have."

"A good thought. In between, though, shall it stand deserted save for a caretaker? Nay, let me dwell there. I'll assemble a proper staff for its maintenance and for the reception of your...council. I'll have space and peace to carry on my work—which is more than copying books, Gratillonius."

Taken aback, he considered her proposal. It did look like having merit. True, tongues would wag. What of it? Females—widows, for instance—had commonly enough taken charge of places. "What more do you mean?" he inquired cautiously.

"Guidance," she said. "Counselling. I was a leader in Temple affairs. Let not my experience go to waste."

He harked back. After her vestalhood ended she had in fact made herself useful among the Queens until she married Tronan Sironai. Whatever happiness the pair had was brief. While no open breach occurred, most Suffetes knew she was soon ill content with the part of wife. She was much in company with the more intelligent young men of Ys; for them she put aside the dourness she bore at home. Rumor did not, though, make any of them her lovers. At last she took minor orders and busied herself in the Temple, where she handled her duties well. During the conflict between King and Queens she was wholly and bitterly of the latter party. However, since the whelming she had reconciled herself with Gratillonius. Sometimes, as today, she was outright amiable.

"Among females, I suppose," he ventured.

She frowned, parted her thin lips as if to retort to an insult, closed them again. When she spoke, it was stiffly. "Whoever may have need. 'Tis a cruel change we've all suffered. Many are worse wounded than you know." The tone softened. "Such as your child Nemeta."

He stopped in mid-stride and faced her. His heart stumbled and began to race. "You have news of her?"

Runa took his arm. "Walk onward. Folk will be astir. Best they see naught to make them wonder."

He fell into a mechanical gait. His throat felt engorged. "What can you tell me?" he demanded.

"First give me what information you have," she replied calmly.

"What? Why?"

"That I may know if any confidences remain for me to honor." After a moment she went on, against his outraged silence: "A girl can open her heart to an older woman as she cannot to her mother, or her father. Shall I betray her? Would you spill what a boy told you as he wept?"

He waged a struggle before he could answer: "Well, you recall I gave out she'd left to take a position offered her elsewhere, as nurse to the children of an honorable Gallic family. That was to shield her name."

"And yours," Runa said tartly. "Yet a clever story. With their educations, doubtless a number of well-born Ysan women will find themselves thus invited, once they're christened. Of course, Nemeta is fierce in her refusal to submit. What did she give you?"

"A scrawled note. I found it tucked into the sheath with my sword, days after Rufinus and his men were scouring the woods for any spoor of her."

"They were? I was unaware. Everybody was."

"You were meant to be. Rufinus is cunning." Gratillonius sighed. "The note said she would suffer no more humiliation but had gone off to a better fate. That was all. Since then, naught." His jaw clenched till it hurt. "Now, by Ahriman, tell me what you know ere I wring it out of you."

"I've lately had word from her," Runa said. "Ask me not who bore it. She'd fain come back, but it must be on her terms. No questions, ever. A house built on a site away from these towns, which she will choose. Freedom to make her own life. That's a freedom you must stand guaran-tor of, Gratillonius, because 'twill defy the Church. Oh, no whoredom, naught sordid; but what Gods she serves will be old ones."

"Where is she? I'll go speak to her."

Runa shook her head. "My faith is plighted."

Again he stopped. They had passed out of Confluentes, through a gap in the north wall and a ridge of shored-up earth that led across the ditch, onto the path beyond. The sentries there had also saluted him. The manor house gleamed from behind a callous loveliness of autumnal trees. He seized her by the upper arms. "Dare you stand between me and my daughter?" he snarled.

The grip was bruising, but she held firm. "Let me go," she said: a command.

He dropped his hand. "That's better," she told him. "Henceforward give me my due respect, if you'd have any good of me; and God knows you need all the good you can find in this world, Gratillonius. My counsel is that you give Nemeta what she wants. Else you've lost her forever."

They stood a long while under the climbing sun. Finally he muttered, "I pray your pardon."

She smiled in her prim fashion. "I grant it. You were overwrought. Come, shall we seek the house, look it over, mayhap take an early stoup of wine? You'll require a span of ease ere you can realize your happiness is coming home."

He stared at her. How stately she stood. Beneath that gown was a body lithe and strengthful—

No! he cried at the sudden tide of lust. My Queens not a year dead, and she the daughter of one of them!

But likewise was Tambilis, for whom I put her mother Bodilis aside.

But that was at the behest of the Gods of Ys, Whom I have disowned.

But the law I think of is the law of Mithras. But it was never clear about this matter. Besides, I have disowned Mithras too.

But I was bound for life to my Queens alone.

The chill in that thought helped him master himself. "Aye, let's do so," he said. "And thank you."

Where the River Vienna joined the Liger they made a broad stretch of water always peaceful. Forest enfolded it and a small human settlement. To this place came Bishop Martinus at the beginning of winter's pastoral rounds.

He loved these journeys. They were not long and arduous, with strangers at the far end, like many farings he perforce made, as far as the praetorian seat at Augusta Treverorum; then old bones ached and thin flesh shivered for weariness. They took him from the cares of his episcopate both in the city and the monastery. Those were heavy of late. Bricius, his disciple whom he had named to be his successor, now looked on him as a crazy dotard clinging to notions of poverty which might once have brought men nearer God but surely no longer served the needs of Mother Church and her princes. In the countryside harvest was ended, weather still mild, ordinary folk and the little children had leisure to meet him on his way, listen to him talk in language they understood, receive his blessing and mutely give him theirs.

But this year trouble pursued him even there. Word had come of a vicious quarrel in the presbytery where the rivers met. He would compose it if he could. With a few companions he set off down the Liger in his barge.

They arrived beneath a low gray sky. Trees raised bare arms from the banks. Water sheened dully. Fisher birds dived and bobbed back into sight. Their cries rang loud in the stillness. Martinus pointed. "Behold," he said. "The demons are like that, ravenous, never sated." He lifted his voice. "Begone!" Feeble though the shout was, they immediately took off, a racket of wings through the wet air. Once up they made a militarylike formation and flew out of the watchers' ken.

"A holy omen," breathed young Sucat.

The elders received the bishop with full reverence and took him uphill to lodge at the church. His attendants found pallets in their quarters or among humble families nearby. In the next pair of days, Martinus brought the factions to amity. "Put down your pride," he told them. "For your sake, Christ let Himself be mocked and scourged and nailed to the Cross between two thieves. The least you can do is humble yourselves before one another."

Even as he labored, fever was in him. When time came to go on, he could not. He lay burning hot, lips cracked, eyes stabbed by what faint light entered the room. He allowed none to touch him, and refused straw to lie on; he would keep with his wonted sackcloth, and ashes thereto.

It was not that he wished to die. Too much remained to do. Once those who held watch on him heard the quavered prayer: "Lord, if my people still have need of me, I am ready to go to work again. But Your will be done."

In the days that followed, as word got about, a swarm arrived, monks, nuns, grief-stricken common folk. Nearly all must needs do without a roof, bleak though the season was, and live on whatever crusts they had brought along. Yet they were determined they would follow their shepherd to his last resting place.

When the presbyters saw death nigh, they asked Martinus if he would like to be shifted to a more comfortable position. "No," he whispered. "Leave me looking toward Heaven."

Then his tone strengthened. Wrath called out: "Why are you standing there, you bloody fiend? You'll get nothing from me. I'm bound for Abraham's bosom. Go!"

He sank back. Breath rattled into silence. God's soldier departed, obedient to orders.

VIII

~ 1 ~

Axes rang in the forest, picks and spades grubbed at stumps, oxen hauled logs and bundles of brushwood south to Confluentes. Some land had been cleared during the summer, but that was for timber to make houses. Now men were readying a much wider ground to cultivate.

When nothing else claimed his attention, Gratillonius was there. In hard labor and rough comradeship lay healing of a sort. He did not lose prestige—Kings of Ys had been more like Ulysses or Romulus than today's Emperors—but rather gained admiration by strength, skill, and helpfulness. Besides, the faster the colony grew and began to export such things as lumber, the sooner his own position would be secure. At present he had scarcely a solidus to his name, nor any revenues to support himself in office and whatever public works might need undertaking. He could not continue much longer living on Apuleius's kindness. Indeed, the senator might find himself in trouble were it known that he put funds at the disposal of a man who had no clear Imperial standing.

Gratillonius cared little about that on his own account. The brash young centurion who had dreamed of becoming mighty and famous seemed altogether a stranger. What counted was his duty toward people who trusted him.

One day he happened to be the last homebound as the short period of winter light drew to an end. The gangs plodded quietly off, exhausted. Even Ysan commoners had never been accustomed to this kind of

852

work; their country was nearly treeless, open to the winds. Some among the loggers were of Suffete birth, too; there was scant other livelihood for them if they refused to become hirelings on established farms. Gauls bore the toil more easily, though it told on them also. Small groups of them had been arriving lately, piecemeal, not only Osismii but a few Veneti and Redones. They had heard tales of opportunities for a fresh start under leadership that bade fair to keep off the barbarian raids that Armorica once again dreaded.

Today, as Gratillonius was hewing, a man had appeared and asked that he come with him. Gratillonius recognized Vindolenus, a former Bacauda. Those who had followed Rufinus west and settled down as more or less law-abiding were generally still shy of the Roman authorities. They were apt to make their homesteads deep in the woods and well apart. There they worked tiny plots, hunted, fished, trapped, burned charcoal, to scratch out a living for themselves and whatever families they acquired. Despite their isolation, they formed a widely flung net which as King of Ys he had found invaluable for gathering information, transmitting messages he did not want to risk being intercepted, and keeping down banditry.

Thus he felt he could not deny this man's plea. "My oldest son, lord, he's deathly sick. If you'd bless him with your hands, he might live, you, the King."

"I wish that were so," Gratillonius sighed. "But whatever power of that kind ever was in Ys lay with its Queens. They're gone, the city is, and my Kingdom with them."

"No, my lord, begging your pardon, but I can't believe all the magic's left you, King Gradlon that drove off the Franks." Like most Gauls, Vindolenus softened Gratillonius's name differently from Ysans.

"Well, if it'll make you happier, I'll come, but I can promise nothing —unless, if I think a physician may help, to bring one tomorrow." At least the woodsrunners did not blame Gratillonius for the whelming of Ys and hold him accursed. That was doubtless thanks largely to Rufinus.

It was more than an hour's walk along twisted game trails to the hut. The woman and the rest of her brood greeted him with pitiful joy. He needed patience, but at last got from her an account of what she had tried, treatments and simples. They seemed as likely to avail as anything that anybody knew about in Aquilo. The boy lay twitching and muttering, eyes full of blankness. Gratillonius covered the burning forehead with his palm. "May health return here" was all he could think of to say.

"Won't you call on Belisama, lord?" asked Vindolenus. "She was the great Goddess of Ys, wasn't She?"

A nasty sensation passed through Gratillonius. "It was...not mine to serve Her, so I ought not invoke Her." These folk must have offered to Cernunnos, Banba, whatever ancient deities they knew; they might well have added Christ for good measure. "Mithras, God of men, grant that this youth grow to manhood in Your sight." That hurt him to say, as hollow as it sounded within his skull.

Afterward he must take a little refreshment, else he would hurt feelings and give a bad omen. By the time Vindolenus had guided him back and said farewell, the sun was down.

A streak of cloud glowed furnace red to southwest. It was the single sign of warmth. Elsewhere the sky ranged from ice-green to bruise-purple. The Stegir gleamed steely through naked fields. Confluentes ahead, Aquilo more distant, Mons Ferruginus beyond the Odita were hunchings of darkness touched by fugitive light-glimmers. Nearer was a yellow hint of comfort from the windows of the former manor house, but it too seemed to huddle under the vacant sky. A low chill gnawed in the quiet.

Gratillonius shifted his ax from right to left shoulder and started across the plowland toward the path that ran along the lesser river past the house and thence to the colony and his dwelling there. A flock of rooks passed overhead; their calls were peculiarly lonesome. Abruptly he stopped and peered.

Vague in the dusk, a horseman came from the northern verge of forest, off one of the tracks that snaked among its trees and brush, out into the open. He drew rein and appeared to look around, as if to get his bearings. Alone, though that seemed like an excellent mount he had— He wasn't far. Gratillonius broke into a trot. "Hail!" he called, first in Latin, then in Osismiic. "Wait for me. I'm friendly."

Whoever this was, he'd need a roof tonight, at least. It behooved the headman of Confluentes to offer it. And a newcomer with new tales to tell should be welcome in a season when few people travelled. Through Gratillonius's mind passed a line from the Christian scriptures he had several times heard Bishop Martinus use. "Be not forgetful to entertain strangers; for thereby some have entertained angels unawares." Odd how those words stayed with him. Well, they were solid counsel, like much else he'd heard from the same lips. Where now did old Martinus lodge?

As he drew close, he thought the rider tensed. It was hard to be sure. A voluminous cloak with the hood drawn up muffled what looked like a small, slender frame. Though a wan blur in vision, the face showed fine-boned and smooth. Was this a boy? Gratillonius put down his ax and advanced with hands widespread. Any traveler might well be skittish these days, meeting an armed man by twilight. Gratillonius himself was prepared to spring aside at the first hint of treachery.

He heard a broken scream, and halted. "Father!" wailed through the shadowiness, in Ysan. "Is that truly you?"

Lightning rived. Amidst the thunder that followed, Gratillonius called, "Aye. W-welcome, Nemeta. Welcome home."

He stumbled closer. She urged the horse aside. Something like choked sobs jerked from under the cowl. "Be not afraid," he begged. "I gave my promise. Why did the messenger, whoever that was—did he really take so long to reach you? Or did you linger? Why? I'll keep faith. You shouldn't have fared without an escort. But welcome."

Control regained, she lifted a hand. How frail it was. "Hold," she said unevenly. "I pray you, stand where you are. You've...surprised me. I was bound for the big house yonder. Runa is there, nay? She—she and I—I hoped she'd meet with you ere—I did."

He obeyed. His own hands dangled helpless. "I know Runa's been the go-between," he said dully. "But what have you to fear from me? I'll give you all you asked for. If I can't talk better sense into you. Do let me try, Nemeta. For your own sake. I plight you there'll be no scolding. Follow me to my house in Confluentes. We'll talk, unless you'd liefer go to bed when you've eaten. I've been in such a nightmare about you, but now you're home again. Naught else matters."

Starkness replied: "Your fears were well founded. Behold." She drew the cloak back. Enough hueless light was left for him to see the swelling under her tunic.

"Yea," she said, "thus it is. I fled in quest of freedom. Along the way I was caught and violated. I escaped, and in another place had a protector. He's an honorable man who never touched me save as brother might sister. After your answer to my message came, 'twas a while ere I could bring myself to leave, for by then I could no longer lie to myself about the state I was in. But at last 'twas clear that to bide where I was would be worse than my life here had been. I used some money given me to buy this horse, boy's guise, bedroll, provisions. Along byways, sleeping in thickets at night, I returned. Ask me no more—you promised—for this is everything I will ever tell."

Gratillonius had met the same glacial resolve in her mother Forsquilis. "I won't," he pledged, flat-voiced. "Of course I'm bound to wonder."

What had her hope been, the wild fancy of a girl in whom ran witch blood and soldier blood? Where had she gone? Who had forced her, and what had become of the creature? (Oh, to catch him, beat him flat, cut off his parts, gouge out his eyes, and—the Osismii knew what to do with their foulest criminals—set the hounds on him!) Where afterward had she wandered? Who was her benefactor—a Christian, maybe a cleric, hoping to win a convert or simply acting in the charity his faith enjoined? Had she any other friends?

"Seek not to find out!" she shrilled. "Leave what's happened in its grave!"

"If that be your wish." Gratillonius drew breath. "But come. All the more have we need to talk, to reason out how best we can provide for you and—" his throat thickened—"the child." My first grandchild, he thought. This.

He could barely see her head shake. "Nay. Let me go to Runa as I'd meant. Leave me a while in peace." She struck heels to the horse and cantered off. Night quickly reclaimed sight of her. He stood where he was a long time before he went onward.

—In Confluentes next day was much excitement. Evirion Baltisi came back. He was well outfitted and mounted, as were the several men hired to accompany him. In Gesocribate, he said, waited a ship he owned. Thence he had travelled around Armorica, assessing conditions and prospects. Here he would spend the winter, engaging and instructing crewmen. In spring they would go to the ship and take her on the first of many merchant ventures. Little more would he tell; but youth and eagerness blazed from him.

~ 2 ~

The new year might be more hopeful than the last. Weather grew springlike well before the vernal equinox. Corentinus took advantage of it, holding meetings outdoors whenever possible, beyond the colony wall. There he exorcised evil spirits, taught the Faith, and answered questions before large groups. Otherwise, lacking any building of size, he must needs see one or a few persons at a time, whenever it could be arranged—oftenest in their homes. He got little rest.

Rufinus perched himself atop the breastwork and observed such a gathering from that distance. When it ended and folk straggled back toward their occupations, he bounded down, across the ditch, over the field till he drew alongside Evirion. "Hail," he said in Latin, with his warmest smile. "How are you?"

The young man squinted at him. Their acquaintance was slight. "Why do you care?" he replied curtly, using the same tongue. Among the Romans he had gained full command of it.

"Oh, it's polite," said Rufinus. "However, I really would like to hear. I've been gone for some time."

Off on what errands? Maybe Gratillonius knew. "There are enough people to give you the gossip," Evirion snapped. "I'm healthy, thank you. I'm also busy."

Rufinus matched his stride. "Bear with me, please. I approached you for a reason. If you can spare an hour, I'd like to bring you to my house and pour you a cup of wine. It's decent stuff."

Evirion scowled. "You're Grallon's man."

"What, are you his enemy?"

"Well—" Evirion seized on an Ysan saying. "He and I are not surf and seal."

"Nor keel and reef," answered Rufinus likewise. Again in Latin: "Do come. You needn't respond to any questions you don't want to. And you could learn something."

Evirion considered, shrugged, nodded. Together they walked across the earthen way and through the portal. Evirion glanced at a sentry. "Why does Grallon insist on that absurd watch?" he grumbled. "If a foe was coming, we'd know in plenty of time to man the defenses."

"Not necessarily," Rufinus maintained. "Anyhow, it helps keep the men in training." They continued along the street. "I wish you'd put your hostility to him aside," he added. "What happened was not his fault."

"Whose, then?" Evirion's tone became less aggressive, as if he truly wanted to know.

"The Gods'? *I* want no part of beings that would destroy a city, Their worshippers, just because of some dispute over morals. It's worse than atrocious, it's stupid—or insane."

"I'll agree to that," said Evirion slowly.

"Me, though," Rufinus went on, "I'll put the blame where it belongs, on a ruthless man, a greedy little slut, and sheer bad luck. I notice you're turning from the Gods of Ys, like everyone else. In other words, you're ranging yourself with Gratillonius, where he always stood."

"No! I only—" Evirion's words turned into a grinding noise.

"You find it expedient to join the Christians. No offense." Rufinus squeezed the shoulder beside his. "I would too, if I had a reason like yours. What difference? We may as well bow down to one nothing as to another."

"Are you calling me a hypocrite?"

"Of course not. My humble apologies if I misspoke myself. Here we are." Rufinus opened the door of a wattle-and-daub hut and left it thus for light. As yet, no one in Confluentes possessed a lock, nor had any been needed.

Primitive, the dwelling was nonetheless soundly built. Already Rufinus was crowding it with a jackdaw collection of oddments—carvings, curiously shaped vessels, shells, pebbles, toys, a childish charcoal drawing on a wooden slab—as well as weapons, clothes, and utensils. If not quite neat, it was clean. Rushes covered the floor around a firepit. Furniture amounted to a pallet and two stools.

At a gesture, Evirion sat down. Rufinus poured from a jug into clay cups, gave him one, and joined him. "To your fortune," said the Gaul, and drank.

"What's that picture?" asked Evirion, to clear the air.

"By Korai. The little girl who was at the Nymphaeum, you know, granddaughter of Queen Bodilis. She comes visiting whenever she can. We're great friends. I'm her Uncle Rufinus."

Evirion cast a quizzical glance at this man who had never married, but inquired simply, "What do you want of me, out of all the rest?"

"News," said Rufinus. "You've been about in places and ways I haven't, couldn't."

"Are you simply curious?"

"Of course. Wouldn't you be? But I'm not so foolish as to try lying to you. The more I know, the better help I can give Gratillonius." Sudden pain twisted the lean face more than the scar ever did. "I was ignorant before, or blind, or cowardly, and— Disasters squat all around us, waiting to happen."

Evirion sensed a guard let down and attacked. "Would you turn Christian if he did?"

Mercurial, Rufinus recovered his lightness. "That's a moot point, seeing that he isn't doing so," he said with a grin. "He takes these matters far too seriously, as I've often told him." He drank, crossed his ankles as if lounging, and drawled, "Much the most of our people are willing to be baptized—glad, many of them, I suppose. They want something to cling to. But I daresay the feeling isn't unanimous. In your case, it's become necessary for your business."

Evirion stiffened. "I don't lick boots. Christ must be real, and strong. Look how He's winning everywhere. For me it's like—like being a barbarian warrior whose chief betrayed him. Another, more powerful chief offers me a berth. Very well, I'll take it, with thanks, and be loyal."

"I see. It's what I guessed about you. But others—the former priestess Runa, for instance. Tongues were clacking when I came back from the woods. She refuses, they say."

"M-m, not exactly," replied Evirion, mollified. "She's taking instruction. In fact, she's dived into what books the church has, and wrung Corentinus dry with her questions, till I heard him laugh she knows more—what's the word?—more theology than most priests. But she wants to stay a catechumen for a while longer."

"I thought that was the usual thing. I'm puzzled why you converts are to be baptized already this Easter."

"The custom has changed. Don't ask me why. The old idea, as I understood it, was that people needed time to make themselves ready. Runa says she does."

"Or less restriction than otherwise, less attention paid to her comings and goings?" Rufinus murmured. "She and Gratillonius's wayward daughter—"

"That's none of your affair!" Light from the doorway showed Evirion reddening.

"Agreed. Agreed." Rufinus raised his palm in token of peace. "Still, a fellow can't but wonder. I daresay Corentinus is unhappy about it."

"You'll find out what your master Grallon wants you to know, when he wants you to," Evirion fleered.

"He and Runa do seem to have become rather close....Look, I'm a mere backwoodsman, a landlouper. How can I say which tale is true and which a lie? I wish you'd give me some guidelines."

The mariner glowered. "What do you hear?"

"Rumors. Mistake me not. I don't spread them farther. But you aren't deaf either. You must have an inkling of these notions that you and Nemeta— No, hold on, nothing to your discredit. You'd have answered to Gratillonius before now if he imagined that. However, the two of you did disappear and return at about the same times. You're both close-mouthed. You visit Runa at the old manor—granted, quite a few people do, but mainly women, and Nemeta *is* staying with her. You've lent men of yours, prospective crew, to building her that house out in the forest her father's letting her have. At the least, might you be hopeful of a marriage, a way around the fact she's a pagan? That's the sort of thing I hear."

"Dogs yap. It means nothing." Evirion tossed off his wine. Before he could rise, Rufinus was up and pouring him more. With almost imperceptible pressure, the Gaul's free hand kept him seated.

He stared into the cup for a minute, grimaced, and muttered without raising his eyes. "Oh, you may as well hear from me what I've told others. Then they can't garble it for you. Nemeta and I both felt caged here. She knows certain secret things and...advised me. For that I'm grateful, and want to make some return. But it was a strange journey I went on. You're wrong, man, about there being no Gods—or demons, or whatever it is yonder....I got a pile of valuables for myself. They've asked me if I found it in Ys. If I did, what of it? Remember, though, Armorica is a very ancient land. Forgotten folk must have left hoards. Consider this a mystery I can't speak of."

"The Romans might not," Rufinus said.

Evirion looked up. "What d'you mean?"

"What do you suppose? There you arrived in—Gesocribate, right?— suddenly loaded with riches. You can't have bought your ship straight-forwardly. You're not born to the navicularius class; you're not even a Roman citizen. How many purses did you have to fill before local officialdom...obliged you? If the governor in Turonum gets wind of this, I can imagine him following the scent. You could be charged with banditry."

"I did no crime!"

"You'd have to prove that, my friend. Certainly your illegalities in the city would come to light. An investigation might also turn up gossip about Nemeta. She must have spent those months somewhere."

Evirion dropped his cup. Wine drained away into the rushes. He leaped to his feet. "You'd run to them with that story?" he shouted.

"Never." Rufinus sighed. "Can't you tell a warning from a threat? You've a way of charging ahead like a bull aurochs. I'm trying to do some of the thinking you should have done."

Evirion breathed hard. Rufinus smiled. "Let me talk to Gratillonius," he said. "The two of us alone. Then with you. It's in his interest to keep things quiet—but not to stop you in your course, because you can in fact help Confluentes prosper. We're on the same side. Confess it to yourself."

"You...want to think...for him too?"

"Well, I daresay these ideas have crossed his mind. But he's had so much else on it. He needs help. We all do, you not least. And we've nobody to give it but each other."

Evirion stared at his hands, which knotted together.

"Sit down," Rufinus coaxed him. "Have a fresh stoup. I know this is a heavy weight to dump on you in a single load. But we must plan ahead. Have you, for instance, have you given any thought to the matter of pirates? The Saxons and Scoti will be coming back, remember."

"That's a landlubber's question." Therefore it acted on Evirion like a tonic. "The ship's big and fast. Her crew will be large and well armed. I doubt whatever barbarians we may meet will care to do more than turn tail. They seldom attack at sea anyway. Land is where the best plunder and prey are."

"I see." Rufinus, who had been perfectly aware of it, nodded. "This gives me the ghost of a notion....But let that go for the time being. Do sit again. We'll drink and talk and drink some more. You never really know a man till you've gotten drunk with him."

~ 3 ~

Candlelight glowed warm, but the hue it cast over the girl in the bed was purulent, so white she was. Only her hair had color, red waves across the pillow, streaks of it sweat-plastered to a face where bones strained against skin. Reaching for her father's hand, her fingers were like straws, her elbows like spurs. The grip felt cold when his closed on it.

"I should go now and let you sleep," Gratillonius said in his power-lessness.

"Thank you for coming," Nemeta whispered.

"Of course I come whenever I can. Tomorrow again. Be better then." He attempted a smile. "That's an order, do you hear?"

"Aye." She glanced down toward the bulge beneath the sheet. "If it will let me."

"What?"

"Yon giant leech. Is it not yet bloated full?"

"Hush," he said, appalled. He must not let her speak hatred for this thing. Not among Christians. It was innocent. He must make himself accept his grandchild when it came.

Nemeta's head turned to and fro. "If I could have shed it—"

Across the bed from Gratillonius, Runa's tall black-clad form stooped. She laid her hand over the girl's lips. "Hush," she also said. "Rail not against...the Gods."

"Goodnight." The man bent likewise, to kiss the wet forehead. He released Nemeta, turned, and left with Runa. His daughter's gaze pursued them out the door. The woman shut it.

In the atrium, Gratillonius took his cloak from a serving maid whom Runa dismissed with a gesture. When they were alone he said in Latin, "She does seem to have mended a bit since I was here last."

The dark, hawk-sharp head nodded. "I think so. Small thanks to that dolt of a physician."

"Hm? I heard how you sent him away—"

"He wanted to bleed her, after the convulsion nearly cost her the babe. No, I've prescribed rest and nourishment, and predict she will soon be well."

Gratillonius's eyes met Runa's. "A miscarriage would have been a liberation," he said.

"It would have. I confess to hopes, for Nemeta's sake and...yours."

"She had been looking more and more sick. Almost since her return, do you agree?"

"Well, it wasn't fated. Now we must do whatever we can for them both. These are not olden times, when parents could expose an unwanted infant."

He hesitated. "You've been a true friend," he said at last. "I've often wondered why."

"Who else is there?"

"What do you mean?"

"You are still our King. In spite of everything, you are he without whom we are nothing, or we die." The least of smiles flitted across her thin lips. "Besides, you remain rather an attractive man."

Bemused, vaguely alarmed, he threw the cloak over his shoulders. "I'd better be off."

She grew serious. Her voice deepened. "This must be a cruel night for you. Would you like me to walk back to Confluentes with you?"

"Huh? Oh, no—no, thanks—no need— Hard for you too, I'm sure, but best we don't talk about it, eh? Goodnight. I'll look in tomorrow. Goodnight." He hastened out.

She can be an astonishing person, he thought. Cold and strict, but like a mother to my poor torn child, and then without warning she shows me this side of herself— Well, I do have to sleep.

His footfalls were loud on the path. Otherwise the single sound he heard was from the Stegir, purling and clucking along to his right. Some of the day's warmth lingered, but coolness rose beneath it and flowed into the breaths he drew, mingled with faint blossom odors.

Phantom white, the manor house dropped behind him. Ahead loomed the black masses of the colony town. Beyond the gleam upon the river, fields stretched wan out of sight. Eastward they ended at the forest, which was darkness dappled and wreathed with silver. A full moon

861

had just cleared those crowns. This low it appeared enormous, and its luminance drove surrounding stars from heaven.

Full moon, the first after the spring equinox. More than a solar year had gone since Ys died, but the Queens had reckoned their holy times by the moon, and tonight was the lunar anniversary of the death.

How still it was. Wind, racket, and sundering seas might never have been, might have been merely a nightmare; but then, so would all else be unreal, Dahilis, Bodilis, Forsquilis—Dahut, but he would not think of her, tormented and beguiled; he would call back to him her mother, Dahilis, to dance at his side in the moonlight or sing him a song across the years; he would not weep.

He clenched his fists till nails dug into calluses. Let him keep silence. Even rage against the Gods was unseemly for a man who had a man's work to do. Let him seek peace instead, let his lungs drink of it from the cornel flowers and in the quiet let him imagine he did hear her singing. She played on a small harp—

He stopped. Cold shocked up his backbone. Directly ahead, on the river side of the path, was a stand of dogwood. Its branches reached like snow beneath the moon. From under them rang the notes he heard, and a clear young voice.

Dahilis, I should not be afraid!

The music broke off. A gown billowed around hasty feet. As she came forth, loose hair rippled long, a net to snare moonlight. He recognized those delicate features. A tide of weakness passed through him. His knees buckled, he swayed where he stood.

But this was only Verania, Apuleius's daughter, she who used to call him Uncle Gaius. How like a woodland spirit she seemed, one of those that flitted on nights such as this around the sacred pool at the Nymphaeum. Only Verania, though. He caught hold of his strength and hauled it back into himself. "What are you doing here?" he nearly shouted.

She poised before him, gripping the harp to her breast as if it were a talisman. Yet her look never wavered from his. "I'm sorry if I startled you, sir." Her tone trembled a little. "I couldn't sleep."

"A devil of a thing, you, a maiden, wandering out alone after dark," he scolded.

"Oh, but it's safe, isn't it? You keep the country safe for us."

"Ha!" Nonetheless her words somehow softened the edges of pain. At least she gave him a task. "You're a fool. Disobedient, too. Your parents certainly don't know you've sneaked out."

She hung her head. Defenselessness could always touch him. He cleared his throat. "Well, I'll see you home," he said, "and if you can slip back in without waking anybody, they don't have to learn. But you've got to promise you'll never do anything like this again."

"I'm sorry," she repeated. He could barely hear. "I promise."

"Will you keep it?"

She raised a stricken glance. "I couldn't break a promise to you!"

"Ah. Um. Very good." It made no sense, but abruptly he didn't want to return. Not at once, to a cabin shut away from the moon. Besides, he'd be wise to soothe the lass first. "What was that you'd begun to sing?" he asked. "It sounded like nothing I've heard before."

She clutched the harp tighter. "A song...of mine. I make them up."

"You do?" He had known she was quite musical—her father sat proudly when at his request she sang for company—but not that she was creative in this as well as in her drawing and needlework. She was so shy. "Good for you." Gratillonius rubbed his chin. The beard made that like stroking a pet animal, a small added comfort against emptiness. "Where did you get the tune? It didn't sound Roman, nor like any Gallic I know of. Could almost be from Ys."

"It was meant to, sir."

"It was? Well, well." He saw no choice but to ask her for the whole. The words were Latin, he'd caught that much; a childish ditty shouldn't be unbearable; and anyhow, she had a lovely voice. "Would you sing it for me?"

"Do you want me to?" Anxiety tinged the words. "It's sad. It's what wouldn't let me sleep."

Afterward, when he had bidden her goodnight and lay in his own bed, he wondered if she had known where he was going and had waited for him to come back. He did straightaway sense that, afraid, she nonetheless wished keenly for him to hear it. "Go ahead," he urged. "Get it out of your system."

She edged off, took stance beneath the arching white cornel flowers where moonlight half reached her, and struck a shivery chord from the harpstrings. Low at first, her verses lifted as they went on, and for no understandable reason would hold him long awake.

"I remember Ys, though I have never seen her,
With her towers leaping gleaming to the sky,
For a ghost once walked beneath her mighty seawall
And along her twilit streets. That ghost was I.

"In my dreams I was a dweller in the city
Where I lived and loved and laughed aloud with you.
Now that Ys is overwhelmed and lost forever,
I must pray you give me leave to mourn her too.

"Here at sunrise, when I looked along the highways
I knew well the one our couriers took to Rome
And the fading path that led to Garomagus—
But the Ysan road flew off to magic's home.

"At the eventide, the time for storytelling,
There were many ancient tales of splendid Ys
That had risen from the seed of Tyre and Carthage
And that with her very Gods had sworn a lease.

"I will shed my tears for Ys the hundred-towered,
For the city facing west against the sea,
For the legend-haunting city, Ys the golden,
For the wondrous place where all once yearned to be.

"I'll remember Ys, though I shall never see her
Shining tall where only waves are left to grieve.
When we've given this new city to our children,
Will our ghosts return to Ys and never leave?"

~ 4 ~

Easter Eve was clear. Green misted the plowlands; leaves were bursting forth; the rivers sparkled on their way to the sea; everywhere sounded birdsong. Soberly clad was the throng that gathered at the church in Aquilo that day, but quietly joyful the spirits of many.

Julia, daughter of Gratillonius, hardly knew what she herself felt. Fasting had left her light-headed, for ordinarily her appetite was robust. Teachings, prayers, rites buzzed about in her head like swarming bees. The bodies packed close around her seemed from time to time to be at immense distances, their faces the faces of strangers.

The church, not meant to become a cathedral, could barely hold all the converts. There would have to be several celebrations of the Mass tomorrow, with worshippers taking their turns. On this occasion, those to be received were assembled in the street outside, with guards on the fringes to keep order. One by one they were summoned inside. First the children, next the men, last the women—it went on endlessly, Julia had stood here for centuries, nothing changed save that her feet ached worse and worse.

Then sunbeams, slanting richly out of the west and between houses, caught a blond head and came afire. Cadoc Himilco was mounting the steps to his christening. Faintness swept through Julia, and after it a rush of almost unbearable joy. Were angels aloft? Today was the day of her salvation.

Folk inched forward. She reached the front of the women. She heard her name called, saw the deaconess beckon. None of it was real. She stumbled, she floated, the angel wings whirred in her head.

Since returning as bishop, Corentinus had had a baptistry added to the stone building. It was wooden, little more than a lean-to at an end of the portico, but solidly made; he had worked on it himself in rare free moments. Likewise put together in some haste was the organization he needed, priests, deacons, a deaconess, brought in from among Martinus's people at Turonum or recruited here. He cherished plans for a new, properly enlarged church and Church—to be founded at Confluentes, where sites were still available—but this required first that by God's grace the colony flourish and grow.

Julia saw the dim little room as aflicker with rainbows. Its dankness smelled musty. For her the ceremony must be different from what Cadoc had known, she being a woman. Curtains had been drawn from wall to wall behind the font, lest the priest at the back of it see her naked. Nonetheless, as she disrobed with the help of the deaconess, she felt a sudden heat. It terrified. She needed no prompting to cry out thrice, "I renounce you, Satan!"

Thereafter she stepped down into the font. It was not a fine stone basin such as she had heard of, but a barrel-stave tub. The water was holy, though, deep enough to cover her waist. Motionless once the ripples she raised had died, it yet somehow licked at her loins. She drew her hair over her shoulders, tightly across her breasts, and kept her head lowered. In Ys you had not been ashamed of your body; Ys lay drowned.

The priest's voice tolled through a vast hollowness: "Do you believe in God the Father, almighty?"

"I do," she gasped. Oh, I do.

The deaconess dipped up the first bowlful of water, gave it to the priest, and guided his hands as he poured it over Julia. She remembered a brooklet falling across an edge in the hills behind the Nymphaeum, how it flashed and chimed, bound for the pool over which watched the image of Belisama.

"Do you believe in Jesus Christ, His only Son, Our Lord, Who was born and suffered for us?"

"I do." Forswear all heathen things. Forget them. Anew the water of redemption ran down her head and above her heart.

"Do you believe in the Holy Spirit, the holy Church, the forgiveness of sins, and the resurrection of the flesh?"

"I do." Forgive my sin, that I don't quite understand it. I believe. Let the water wash me clean.

A hand urged her forward. She went up the steps and stood dripping. At this point, the bishop would have anointed a man; but for modesty's sake, the deaconess simply embraced her—perfunctorily, being by now weary—and helped her on with the clean white robe that was Christ's welcoming gift.

Taking her former garments, she passed through a doorway knocked out of the stone wall, into the vestibule. This she knew; as a catechumen she had stood here listening to the services until the inner door was shut on those who were not initiated. Tonight she too would partake of the Mystery.

Corentinus waited just within the sanctum. "Bless you, my daughter," he said, and signed her with the seal of the Spirit. He held his post like an iron statue, though he must have been on his feet all day at least. Nonetheless she heard the wound within him, a hurried whisper: "Go home after we are done here and beseech your father that he come too. If you love him, do it."

The chamber was already packed. Lamps and candles burned everywhere. They, the incense, the bodies made the air chokingly thick. Julia felt dizzy, drunk. She feared she might fall or otherwise disgrace herself. What when she received the Bread and Wine?

Voices gabbled. Among the converts were a leaven of lifetime Christians, chosen for their calm tempers. They took the lead in kissing the new faithful, a tender hug and a quick brushing of lips.

But the converts were mingling with each other as well. Suddenly Julia found herself in the arms of Cadoc. The Light shone from his eyes. It burned when his mouth touched hers.

"Hoy, is't not sufficient, or a trifle more?" asked a sardonic voice in Ysan. The two disengaged. Evirion Baltisi stood hard by. "I also would fain greet my sister—chastely," he said. Cadoc flushed. The look he cast was less than charitable. Evirion returned it, with the slightest sneer. Then another woman came in, and another, and the milling of the expectant crowd pulled them apart.

~ 5 ~

Tera, who had kept sheep and led rites among those folk who sparsely dwelt in the hinterland of Ys, knew she would never know ease in Aquilo. Like most survivors, at first she found a place for herself and her four children on a farm. Unlike most, after the raising of Confluentes she did not move there, but remained where she was. That happened to be the freehold Drusus had hewn for himself out of the forest. The former soldier was a Christian, but easygoing; he saw no harm in keeping a person who knew how to get along with the ancient landwights. Besides, Tera was a good, sturdy worker, and her youngsters—two boys, two girls—did as much as could be expected at their small ages.

On Easter morning, they five were well-nigh alone. Apart from a pagan man who rode watchful about the acres, everyone else had gone into town for the postbaptismal services and the festivities that would follow.

The children dashed to her from their play and squealed that a traveler was coming. She left the bench outside the house on which she had sat half adoze, went around the wall, and peered southward. Snowpeaks of cloud brooded over fields where shoots thrust from furrows and paddocks where cattle grazed the new grass. At her back reared wilderness, a thousand bright hues of green decking cavernous shadows. The farmhouse and its outbuildings made the four defensible sides of a square with a well at its middle. They were long structures of cob, thick-walled, thatch-roofed, and whitewashed. Tera and her brood slept in the haymow, a territory she had claimed for herself and defended with threats—once, a pitchfork—against fellow underlings who shared quarters with the animals.

Aquilo was out of sight, miles to the southeast. Thence meandered roads, branching every which way, scarcely more than tracks worn by feet, hoofs, wheels. On the one that led to this place, a man was bound afoot. He was powerfully built, with gray-shot black hair and beard. His rolling gait he aided with a spear used like a staff; a knife was at his belt, a battle-ax slung across his shoulders. Yet the condition of breeks and tunic proclaimed him no outlaw; and the guard had let him by.

The hounds that Drusus kept, as most well-to-do Gallic landholders did, sensed the approach and gave tongue. Huge and savage, the half dozen were penned when someone who could command them was not there to order them back from tearing a newcomer apart. However, they had come to know Tera. At her word, the deep baying died away.

Recognition: "Maeloch!" She hurried to meet him and seized his free hand in both hers. "Why, what brings you hither, lad?"

"I felt restless," the seaman answered. "No haven for the likes o' me this day, Aquilo nor Confluentes. The King too, he went off aboard his stallion."

"But you'd call on a friend? Be welcome. I'm sure the master wouldn't grudge you a stoup of ale."

"'Twould lay the dust in this gullet. Ahoy, there." Maeloch grinned at the children. The two oldest pressed close, the younger pair looked from behind their mother's skirts. "Ye await a harbor fee, I'll be bound. Well, then, how be this?" His huge hand dipped into a pouch and came forth full of sweetmeats.

"You've a chiefly way about you," Tera said.

Maeloch scowled. "A chief 'ud give gold. The day may come—"

And in the clay-floored kitchen, he said over his cup: "I've somewhat to talk about with ye."

"I thought so," Tera replied. "If your legs are not worn down, let's go walk in the woods. No ears yonder to hear us, unless they be on the elves."

He gave her a close regard. She stood before him in an oft-mended linsey-woolsey shift, on her bare feet, stocky, strong, and returned look for look. A shock of hair, sun-bleached flaxen, bonneted a round, pug-nosed face from which not quite all the youth had weathered away. Her eyes were small but a very bright blue. You would not have guessed she was familiar with spells, spooks, fayfolk, and maybe even the old Gods of the land.

"Aye, ye'd know," he said. "It be a thing I mean to ask about."

He drained his drink, she gave orders to her older boy, and they set forth. "I've scant wisdom or might," she warned. "Naught like what the Queens of Ys did; and their powers were far on the wane in our last years. I made my offerings, cast my sticks, dreamed my dreams, and sometimes it worked out aright and sometimes not."

"I know. Ye've done naught like that since the whelming, ha' ye?"

"Nay. Only a muttered word, a lucky charm, a sign seen in wind or water or stars. What else can I? What dare I, any longer?"

They left cleared land behind and were in among trees. The trail, leading to the Stegir, was packed hard by use, yet it seemed as though that use were on sufferance, perforce around great roots and mossy boulders. Brush hedged the path, boughs roofed it, boles loomed in a dimness speckled with sun-flecks. Air hung heavy. Through silence drifted the moaning of doves; now and then a cuckoo call rang forth.

"Nemeta will dare, I think," said Maeloch after a while.

"The King's wild daughter? I've heard a little."

"They're building her a house in these woods. Her wish, which Grallon grants. Scant more than that will he say about it, to me or anybody."

Tera caught his hand. Compassion gentled the hoarseness of her voice. "You fret for him—because of him, nay?"

"He be my King. And yours...Look after her, will ye?"

"How can I?"

"Ye'll find ways. How many women amongst us ha' had strength to hold out against Corentinus?"

They wandered on.

"Why do ye?" he asked at length. "How can ye?"

She stared before her. "I've not wondered much about it," she answered low. "It felt like—being herded. Oh, he's a kindly herdsman, I suppose, but I was born free."

"With a God your father? I've heard that said."

She laughed. "My father can have been any man my mother liked. Same for my brats. I can guess, of course." Sobering: "Thrice I've seen Cernunnos, his antlers athwart the moon, and once—but that may have been a dream after I'd breathed too much of the hemp smoke." Forlornness touched her. "They're ghosts of what They were, the Gods are. For sure, my children will go to Christ. Else their age-mates'll mock them, and why should they suffer?"

"But ye'll abide?"

"I hope I will."

"It be a terrible thing to be old alone."

They reached the riverbank and stopped. The water rilled so clear that they could see stones on the bottom and fish darting across. Years ago, a tree had fallen. Moldering away to punkwood, it had spread a place for moss to grow thickly alongside the stream. Maeloch and Tera sat down on what remained of the trunk. It too bore a padding soft and cool.

"You risk the same, lad," she said. "For Grallon's sake?"

He tugged his beard. "N-nay. His God and mine never came betwixt us."

"But you serve yet the Three of Ys?"

He heard the scorn slice through her tone, and shook his head. "Nay after what They did."

"Nor I. But to inlanders like me, who just came to the city on market days, They were something afar. We lived with the wights that had always been of our land; and what Gods we called on were of the Gauls, or the Old Folk before them. Now you—"

"I have none left me," he said, forcing the words out. "I might well seek to Christ—save that that 'ud mean forsaking the spirits in the sea. D'ye understand? Those I ferried across to Sena. Where be they now? Who'll remember little Queen Dahilis, her happy laugh and dancing feet—who'll kindle a torch on the eve of Hunter's Moon, so our dead can find their way back to them they loved—save it be me?"

She caught his arm. "Me too, if you'll allow. And I've Gods for us both."

He turned his face and body to hers. "I had thoughts about that, lass," he growled.

"Me too," she said again. "'Tis been a lonely while."

The moss made them welcome.

IX

~ 1 ~

Immediately after Easter, Evirion Baltisi travelled overland with his crewmen to Gesocribate to claim the ship he had waiting for him there. Rufinus came along. He said it should be amusing, he might collect a grain or two of information, perhaps he would even have an idea or two to offer. Aquilonian men muttered that a pagan aboard was bad luck, but the Ysans, who outnumbered them, put a stop to that. Newly Christian themselves, they yet remembered how their city had been the queen of the sea.

Evirion had left the craft drydocked, which meant that upon his arrival, a couple of days went to launching and fitting. None of the company minded. This city offered inns, stews, and other entertainments such as Aquilo lacked. Rufinus disappeared into haunts he knew until they were ready to sail.

Nevertheless Evirion departed furious. He had understood beforehand that he would be unable to take on a cargo here. The guilds and authorities had barely been persuaded—bribed—to let an outsider acquire a ship. Now an official wanted to detain vessel and captain while he sent notice to the procurator of what appeared to be an illegal

869

transaction. The tribune put pressure on him to let the matter pass, but expected compensation for the service. When he heard what sums Evirion had laid out earlier as well as this time, Rufinus whistled. "They led you by the nose," he said. "You shouldn't have paid more than half this much." It did nothing to mend Evirion's temper.

Still, he had his ship, and his hopes for the future. A beauty she was, Britannic built, her keel laid years ago but abidingly sound. He had had her worked over from stem to stern, under his own eyes, until she suited his manifold purposes. She was slenderer than a Southern merchantman, her stern less high, though the castle did enclose a small cabin. A lifeboat was lashed fast amidships. At the bow was a projecting forefoot; at need, he could safely drive the vessel onto a beach. Stepped well forward, the mast carried a sprit rig. It drew less strongly than a square sail, but gave greater maneuverability, and wind was seldom lacking in Northern waters. The bowsprit bearing the artemon terminated in a carven scroll; the sternpost was shaped like the head of an enormous horse, facing forward, painted blue. The hull was black with a red stripe. Defiantly, he had named her *Brennilis*.

When he stood out from Gesocribate harbor, his intent was to proceed back to Aquilo. There he would take products of the land, with such manufactured goods from elsewhere in Gallia as were available—on consignment, since he lacked the means to buy them and could not raise a loan until he was better established. Then he would make for southern Hivernia. Dominated by King Conual, who had been friendly toward Ys, the folk of Mumu would likely give him profitable exchange. Two or three such voyages this year ought to shake ship and crew down for longer, more adventurous journeys later, to Germanic lands in quest of amber, furs, and slaves.

Evirion had meant to steer well out west into Ocean before turning south and then east. He had no wish to come anywhere near the ruins of Ys. Warnings given him should have reinforced his intent. Reports had arrived of Scoti in that bight north of the Gobaean Promontory which the Ysans called Roman Bay. They were too few to be a serious threat, save to such isolated persons as they came upon. "I suspect they've been sent to probe, to find out what strength the empire has hereabouts these days," said Rufinus. "Where they see a defenseless village or homestead, they'll plunder it."

"Too many of those," Evirion spat, "thanks be to the Empire." The network of coastal patrols that Gratillonius wove had fallen apart as soon as Ys perished.

"*We* have defenses," said Rufinus.

Evirion stared. "What do you sniff at now, fox?"

"Given a large hull and well-armed men, we can rather safely go take a look for ourselves. Who knows what we may gain?"

Evirion was usually ready for a daring venture. In his present mood he leaped at the suggestion.

Brennilis spent her first night anchored off Goat Foreland. In the morning, after giving herself ample sea room, she wore east on a breeze out of Ocean, into the bay. The weather was bright and gusty. Whitecaps surged over blue. Achingly remembered cliffs showed on the starboard horizon. For the most part men chose to look ahead, where hour by hour green hills swelled out of the water. At last someone shouted, and curses went the length of the hull. Smoke was rising to stain the sky.

"We'll see about revenge," Evirion promised.

After a while they spied seven lean leather boats. Spearheads blinked where the kilted, fair-skinned men went alert on sight of the stranger. Evirion sought the bows, gauged wind, currents, distances, speeds, and signalled the helmsman. *Brennilis* surged forward, a bone between her teeth.

The Scotic craft scattered. Their crews would have no chance in a fight against this ship, with her high freeboard and mail-clad sailors. Evirion chose one on which he had the weather gauge and bore down. Under sail *Brennilis* was faster. The Scoti caught his intent and began to strike their mast. Using oars alone, theirs would be the more nimble craft. Crossbows thumped on the merchantman. Two warriors fell. Thus hampered, the rest were too slow at their work. *Brennilis* struck. Her forefoot stove in the slight hull and capsized it.

"Hard over!" Evirion roared.

Sail cracked, yard slatted, the ship came to rest. Crewmen tossed lines to the swimming barbarians. Anguished, the others circled in their boats at a distance. "Best not let them make an attack," Rufinus advised. "They'd die, but we'd lose too."

Reluctantly, Evirion agreed. As soon as the half dozen Scoti were on board, he put around and beat outward toward Ocean. The currachs followed for a while, but fell behind and finally turned south. That far off, they seemed like cormorants skimming the waves.

Pikes and bows held the dripping captives close to the poop. Rufinus approached them. "It's binding you we must be," he said in their language, "but if you behave yourselves you'll live."

A big red-haired man, who seemed to be the skipper, returned a wolfish grin. "That wouldn't matter, could we take some of you down with us," he replied. "But as is, well, maybe later we'll get the chance." He glanced upward. "We've fed your birds, Mórrigu. I hope you'll not forget."

"Bold fellow," said Rufinus. "The Latin word would be 'insolent.' May I ask your name?"

"Lorccan maqq Flandi of tuath Findgeni," rang forth.

"That would be near Temir, would it not?" Rufinus recognized the dialect and had recollections from his visit to those parts.

"It would. A sworn man of King Niall of the Nine Hostages am I."

"Well, well. Now if you will hold out your arms— These are honorable bonds, and yourselves hostages."

The prisoners submitted, scowling. When Lorccan's wrists were lashed together and his ankles hobbled, Rufinus drew him aside and offered his own name. "I have been in your beautiful country," he added. "Sure and I understand how already you must long homeward. Let's try between us to make that possible."

They stood at the lee rail, talking quietly; the wind blew their words away. "None less than King Niall must have sent such men as you," Rufinus insinuated.

"We had meant to fare," answered pride. "But himself did speak to me and my companion leaders before we left. He must go north to put down rebellion among the Ulati, else he would have come, and today it would be you with ropes on you, unless you lay dead. Your turn will come."

"And what raiders like you have to tell will be helpful to him." Rufinus stroked his beard, twined the forks of it together, gazed afar, and after a short span said absently, "You have been to Ys, I see."

Lorccan started. "How do you know?"

Rufinus smiled. "Not by witchcraft. Around your neck is a pendant of gold and pearl, Ysan workmanship. Somehow I doubt you came by it in trade."

"I did not," Lorccan replied, turning grim. "I found it there."

"Among the ruins? I hear they are dangerous, a haunt of evil spirits. You are either a brave man or a foolish one."

"I won it doing the work of my King."

"Oh? Rumor is the whelming of the city was his deed. Is he not satisfied?"

"He is not. He laid on us what he says he will lay on all who rove this way, that we tear down some of what remains. I found this in...a tomb." Lorccan grimaced. He could not be entirely easy about it, however bold a face he showed.

"The rocks thereabouts are hungry."

"My party went afoot, from older ruins where we were camped."

"Ah, Garomagus. And I take it you had satisfactory pickings thereabouts?"

"Some." Lorccan stiffened. "You wield a sly tongue. In grief for friends lost, I have spoken too much. You won't be learning from me where the booty was stowed."

"It can buy you your freedom."

"And what of my shipmates?"

"We can bargain about that. Otherwise we'll take the lot of you to Venetorum for sale. They know there how to gentle slaves. Think." Rufinus walked off.

When the Scoti had been herded below and secured, he went to Evirion. The captain was back in high good humor. "We're done well," Rufinus agreed. "However, the real treasure we've gained won't go onto any scale pan."

872

"What's that?" asked Evirion.

"Knowledge," said Rufinus softly, "that my King will be glad to have."

~ 2 ~

Trees groaned in the wind that roared raw about them. Rain made a mighty rushing noise through their crowns. Where unhindered it struck the Stegir, the river foamed at its force. Blackness drowned the forest, until lightning flared. Then again and again each leaf, twig, droplet stood luridly in the glare. Thunder rolled after on wheels of night.

In her house, Nemeta screamed. "Hush, child," Tera said. Her voice barely made its way against the racket outside. She laid a hand on the sweat-cold forehead. "Easy. Rest between the pangs."

"Out, you damned thing!" The voice was worn to a rasp by hours of shrieks and curses. "Out and die!"

Tera fingered the charm bag hung at her throat, as often before. For a mother to hate the life she was bringing forth boded ill. "Cernunnos, give strength," the woman muttered wearily. "Epona, ease her. All kindly landwights, be with us."

Flames guttered and smoked in earthen lamps. They cast misshapen, unrestful shadows which filled every corner of the room. Nemeta's face jutted from the darkness. Pain had whittled it close down around the bones. Teeth glimmered as if her skeleton strove to break free. Her eyeballs rolled yellow in the niggard light. The straw tick beneath her was drenched and red-smeared.

Her belly heaved anew. "Sit up and bear down," Tera said, and lent her arms to help. She had forgotten how often she had done this. Would the labor never end? "Not two, but three bulls to You, Cernunnos, if they both live," she bargained. "I'm sure King Grallon will give them. Epona, to whatever else I promised I lay—aye, my man Maeloch will carve Your form in walrus ivory, I can make him do that, and 'twill be there at Your rites always after. Elves, nymphs, ghosts, every dweller in woods and waters—ha, d'you want me to lead the Christian wizard to your lairs? He'll ban you, he will, he'll give your haunts to his saints, 'less you help us this night."

Lightning burst. Through cracks between shutters, it seemed to set afire the membranes that covered the windows. Thunder grabbed the cabin and shook it. Wind boomed and clamored. Between the thighs of Nemeta, a head thrust forth.

"He comes." Tera was too exhausted to rejoice. Her hands worked of themselves.

"Aye, he, a boy, the King's grandson." She lifted the sprattling form and slapped its backside. The storm overrode the first wail.

There was the cord to cut and tie, there were washcloth and towel and blanket, there was the afterbirth, and then Tera could care for the mother. She cleansed the thin naked frame, helped it stagger from the pallet on the floor to the fresh bed that waited, got a gown around the limbs where they flopped loose, combed the matted ruddy locks. "We've soup in the kettle, dear," Tera said, "but here, hold your wee one for a while. You've earned the right, so hard you fought."

Nemeta made fending motions. "Nay, take it away," she whispered. "I've cast it from me. What do I want with it?"

Tera turned, hiding the trouble on her countenance. Nemeta fell into sleep, or a swoon. The infant cried.

—Morning was cool and bright. The ground lay sodden under torn-off boughs and bushes, but drops of water glinted like jewels. A messenger arrived from Gratillonius, as one had done daily since Tera came to look after his daughter. Nemeta had said she did not wish to see anyone but a midwife, nor have any who was Christian. Gratillonius masked his hurt and spoke to Maeloch. Tera and her children now lived with the fisher captain in his house in Confluentes.

"Aye, at last," she told the runner. "A boy. Sound, though 'twas a cruel birthing. Tell my man I'll be here a few days yet, till she's on her feet." She added a recital of supplies she wanted brought on the morrow.

Alone again, the two women could rest. Tera had little to do but keep house and fire, cook, wash, tend mother and babe. Those both did as well as could be awaited; the blood of the King ran in them, and they were properly sheltered.

Nemeta's cabin was no hovel. It was stoutly built of logs, moss-chinked, with clay floor, stone hearth, sod roof, a brown-green-gray oblong nested close to a huge old guardian oak. Close by flowed the Stegir. Forest crowded around, full of life and sun-speckled shadows, while a beaten path wound toward humankind. Nemeta chose the site because it was immemorially holy, a place where folk had come seeking the help of the spirits since the menhirs first arose. Years ago, a Christian hermit actually settled here. Her workmen had heaped up the rotted remnants of his shack, and she kindled them to burn an offering.

That day passed mutely on the whole. Most sound within the walls came from the babe. "You must soon take him to your breast, you know," Tera said in the afternoon.

"Aye," Nemeta sighed from her pillow. "Nine months it sucked my blood. It may as well have my milk."

Seated on a stool at the bedside, fingers twined together in her lap, Tera said slowly, "I'm disquieted about you, lass. You've been dumb throughout, save when bearing. You stare like one blind. But at what?"

The young woman's lip flicked upward. "You told me not to waste strength crying out while the thing happened. I strike a balance, nay?"

"You do wrong if you blame the child."

"Do I? Four beasts begot it; and it would not go away."

Tera regarded her a while. "You sought to be rid of it, then."

"Of course."

"How?"

"I tried—oh, what I hoped might serve, whatever I could think of. But what did I know, I a stranger in the Roman city? Afterward—" Nemeta's voice halted.

"Afterward," Tera followed, "you stayed with Princess Runa."

Nemeta compressed her mouth.

"Trust me." Tera reached for a hand lax on the coverlet and cradled it in hers. "Think you yours is the first woe like this that ever I kenned? I'll keep silence. But sometimes yon leechdoms wreak lasting harm. If you'll tell me what you tried, I'll better know how to help you."

Nemeta considered. When she spoke, her tone was hard with resolution. "Do you swear secrecy? That without my leave you'll utter no breath of whatever I may say here?"

"I promise."

"Nay, you must give oath. Silence about every single thing you heard or saw in the whole while you've been with me."

Tera grimaced. "That's a heavy load. But— Aye." She took a knife that hung at the cord around her waist, nicked her thumb, squeezed a drop onto the floor. "Hark. If I break faith with you, let the Wild Hunt find me, let its hounds lick my blood, let my ghost stray homeless between the worlds. Cernunnos, You have heard."

Nemeta sat up in bed. She shivered with sudden ardor. "You know the old lore, then. Teach me!"

Tera shook her head. "I know just enough to fear how spells can turn on us. Lie back down. Tell me what I asked."

Grudgingly, Nemeta obeyed. She spoke of bitter or nauseating herbs she had taken, of casting herself belly first on the ground, of searches for a witch or wizard or renegade physician. Nothing availed. Outsider, pagan, therefore object of suspicion despite the money Evirion left her after he departed, she dared not inquire forthrightly, even among the poor of Gesocribate. Christian law forbade doing away with the unborn as well as the newborn.

"Runa gave me sapa to drink," she finished. "It only made me weak and ill. At last she said I'd best stop. Presently I felt better. But I was being kicked within my body. As a rider kicks his animal."

Tera frowned. "Sapa?"

"A Roman brew, Runa said. They make it by boiling grape juice in a lead vessel. 'Tis thick, sweet, commonly added to their wines. I took it pure."

"Hm. In Ys they thought lead a slow poison. Belike that's soothfast."

Nemeta raised her eyes. "Runa told me Roman whores are wont to drink sapa. It whitens their skins. Ofttimes it sloughs out their unwanted

875

young. How right, I thought, if I drink a whore's potion against this maggot in me. But it failed."

Tera sat silent before she answered, "Well, keep the child till we find him a foster home, your father and I."

"Does *he* want it?"

"I've a feeling he'd be happier had it died in the womb. And yet...'tis his grandchild, and Queen Forsquilis's. I think he cared for her as much as he did for any of the Nine, aside from Dahilis the mother of Dahut. But Dahilis left us ere I was grown. I knew her just by hearsay. I've seen Forsquilis, though, beautiful, strong, and strange. Aye, Grallon will do whatever he can for the grandchild."

"I will endure, then," Nemeta mumbled. When Tera brought the infant over, she bared her breast and held him close. He suckled with savage eagerness.

—In the time that followed, she showed him neither love nor cruelty. Nursing him, learning from Tera how to care for him, were things she did. Otherwise she gazed afar, spoke little and distantly, fingered the magical objects she was collecting. As strength returned, she first paced the cabin like a cat in a cage, later went off by herself to walk in the woods and bathe in the river.

Those were brief whiles, but increased rapidly. On the third day, Tera said, "Well, I can leave you and go tell your father you're up and about. He'll be glad. When can he come see you, or you come to him?"

Nemeta's answer was low and cold. "I'll send word."

"Men of his will still look in on you daily for a span." Tera's tone softened. "Keep him not waiting much longer. He's laden and lonely."

"He shall hear. Thank you for your help."

Tera drew a sign in the air. "May They be with you, dear."

—When the woman was gone Nemeta began to tremble. It worsened till she crouched in a corner hugging herself while the teeth clattered in her jaws. The babe cried. She threw a curse at him. It drowned the noise he made. She howled aloud for a long time.

Thereafter she had mastery of her flesh. Rising, she busied herself. There were things to pack together—knife, a stake she carved, the scribed shoulder blade of an aurochs, flint and steel, tinder, bundle of kindling wood—and a distance to go while daylight wore away toward sunset. As she worked, she muttered, sometimes prayers she had learned as a vestal, sometimes scraps of what she had heard were spells. It helped curb rage at the clamorous creature. She would have gotten silence by nursing him, as well as relief from an ache in swollen breasts, but she could not quite bring herself to that.

At last she donned a clean white shift and hung her filled sack across her back. Quickly, she stooped to lift the infant from the basket Tera had brought to be his crib. He struggled before she got him firmly held on her left hip. With her right hand she took the staff twined with a snake's mummy; and she set forth.

Heat, stillness, odors of wet mold hung over the game trails down which she padded. The babe's yells dropped to a whimper and to naught; rocked by her pace, he slept within the bulwark of her arm. Now and then she heard wings whirr or a cuckoo call. Through the few gaps between boles, sunbeams slanted ever more long and deeply yellow. Finally they went out and shadows closed on her.

She reached the place that people shunned. Here too was a narrow opening in the forest, looking west. Heaven smoldered red where Ys had been. Overhead it arched wan behind leaves; eastward, night filled all spaces. The pool burned with sunset. Swifts darted noiseless in pursuit of mosquitoes that swarmed above it. Chill seeped from the earth below the fallen leaves. They rustled and scratched at her bare feet.

She set her loads before the boulder at the water's edge. It bulked high as her waist, black athwart sundown. The babe started crying again, a sound that sawed the air. Nemeta scuttled about gathering deadwood dry enough to burn. She must lay and light her fire while she could see what she did.

It was never an easy task, making needfire, but she had skill. Her father had taught her. He had taught her whatever he could that she wanted to learn when she was a little girl, ere the rift between him and his Queens denied him to her. How she had missed the big man with the knowing hands.

Her child screamed on and on. "Be quiet," she snarled. "Oh, soon you shall be very quiet."

The fire flickered up. She made sure it would burn untended for a space. The western embers were turning to ash.

She stood, lifted arms, spoke aloud: "Ishtar-Isis-Belisama, I am here. I call on You, Maiden, Mother, and Hag; Lady of Life and Death; Comforter and Avenger. See, I make myself pure before You."

She stripped off her garment and waded into the pool. Withes caught at her. Slipping along her nakedness, they lashed and stung. Roots made her stumble and bruise her feet. She went on until she stood at the middle, ooze cool around her ankles, water to her waist. Thrice she scooped a double handful and poured it over her head. "Taranis," she called and she did, and "Lir," and "Belisama."

The fire sputtered low when she returned. She squatted to build it anew, feeding it until the glow quivered as far as the lightning-blasted beech nearby. A burning brand in her left hand, the knife in her right, she danced slowly three times around the great dead trunk while she named her Gods.

The babe wailed, kicked, reached arms up from the blanket whereon he lay. Nemeta came back to stand above him. For an instant she found herself moveless, muscles locked together. With a gasp and a shudder she broke free. She plunged the torch into the soil; its flame went out. Her left hand caught the child by a leg and lifted him. He was so small, he weighed scarcely anything.

She took him to the boulder and stretched him on its flat top. He writhed. His cries had grown thin. She held him down and looked aloft. Day was altogether gone. Stars blinked.

Her words rushed forth, half-formed, falling over each other. "Taranis, Lir, Belisama, behold the last of Your worshippers. Men fled in terror of Your wrath, sought a home with the new God of the Romans or the doddering old Gods of the Gauls. I, Nemeta born to the King of Ys by Your Queen Forsquilis, I alone keep faith with You. Hear me!"

The knife gleamed in her right hand. It was big, heavy bladed, almost a sword. She had bought it in Gesocribate from a shopkeeper who said it had, long ago, made pagan sacrifices.

"Ys lies drowned," Nemeta yowled. "The Wood of the King has burned. Take what I give you!"

The knife flashed and struck. The cries ceased.

Nemeta lifted the dripping tiny head alongside the blade. "Blood of my blood I give You, flesh of my flesh, I Your worshipper. Now give me what I want!"

Her voice sank to a rasping purr. The flames snapped louder at their back. Their light turned the smoke to a living presence.

"Lir: May those four who made prey of me beside Your sea never win free of it. Let her who haunts the ruins torture their souls forever.

"Taranis: May their kin, in the city Audiarna, perish like vermin. Let this blood of theirs which I have shed to You drain wholly out of Your earth.

"Belisama: May I gain the powers that belonged to my mother, Queen Forsquilis. Let me never again be captive and helpless, but witch-priestess unto You.

"It is spoken."

The fire sank. By its uneasiness she found her way back to the pool, wherein she cast the body, and to the tree, in whose charred cavern she laid the head and pegged it fast.

She prostrated herself, got to her knees, rose to her feet, arms uplifted. "Be always with me," she implored.

Having gathered her things, she set off homeward. It would be impossible to find her way through the dark, but how could she linger here? She would come on a glade where she could see the stars and take shelter there. At dawn she would seek the cabin, wash herself clean in the river, dispose of the bloodied shift. When Gratillonius's man arrived she would have her tears ready. "I went out after berries. I came back and the door stood open and the crib lay empty. Did a wolf steal my babe, or the elves, or, oh, what has become of him?" Her father would believe, he must believe, and console her as best he was able.

3

The feast of St. Johannes had taken unto itself the ancient rites of Midsummer, but otherwise they had changed little. Even many Aquilonians left the city on the eve to dance around bonfires such as blazed from end to end of Europe, or leap across them, or cast the wreaths they had worn and pebbles they had gathered into them. Burning wheels rolled down hills while besoms, set alight and waved around, showered the night with sparks. Wild revelry followed, and hasty marriages during the next few months. Relics, partly burned sticks and the like, were kept till the following summer as charms against misfortune. Brotherhoods and sisterhoods existed to prepare for these gatherings, lead them, and dispose of the remnants lest those fall into the hands of sorcerers.

Bishop Corentinus could not have stopped this, nor did he wish to. Rather than hold the Church aloof from something that dear to her children, he would bring her into it. His priests went about blessing the piled logs before they were lit and conducting prayers for a good harvest. Everyone who possibly could was supposed to attend Mass the day after; confession was encouraged. As for misbehavior, he must hope that in the course of generations it would die out. His duty, and vital, was to purge the observances of their openly pagan elements.

In this one year, however, he saw an opportunity to reinforce the Christian aspect. Among the Confluentians was a large and growing proportion of wedded couples. In some cases man and wife together had escaped the destruction; in other cases they mated with fellow Ysans or with Osismii after reaching these parts. Such knots had generally been tied in heathen wise, if there was any sanctification at all. As yet, rather few members of the widespread tribe had been converted. Corentinus meant to imitate his mentor, holy Martinus, and evangelize the countryside. While any union honestly entered into was doubtless only venially sinful, God's ministers alone could make it truly valid, eternally secure. If it be done at the very Midsummer, it would help the folk understand whose day that truly was. This in turn should give the unbaptized cause for thought and thus guidance toward the Light.

Accordingly, the bishop occupied himself for a pair of months in advance, persuading and arranging. The occasion was a triumph crowned by Julia, daughter of the leader Gratillonius, and Cadoc Himilco, scion of Suffetes, when they joined in Christian wedlock.

They had gone side by side beforehand to make their intention known to her father. He had consented, with a brevity and reserve that slightly diminished her joy, and asked the young man to see him alone later at his house.

It was a simple, white-painted building of squared timbers with a few utilitarian rooms, though it did posses glazed windows and a tile roof. The main chamber, which could scarcely be called an atrium, was for receiving guests. It held little more than some articles of furniture.

The plaster of the walls was undecorated and the floor, clay, covered merely with rushes. Gratillonius gestured Cadoc to a stool, gave him a cup of wine, took one for himself, and sat down too.

For a space they took each other's measure. Cadoc saw a burly man, plainly clad in Gallic shirt and breeches, grizzled auburn hair and beard close-cropped after the Roman style, face weathered and, of late, heavily graven around the gray eyes and high-arched nose. Gratillonius noted features also darkened by the sun that had bleached blond locks, but still smooth, clean-shaven; the shabby clothes decked litheness.

"Well," he said at length, in Latin, raising his cup. "Your health. You'll need it."

"Thank you, sir." The reply was deferential without being servile.

"On the whole, I'm pleased," Gratillonius said. "You come of good stock. Your father was a fine man, and my friend."

"I'll try to be worthy of your kinship, sir."

Gratillonius regarded Cadoc over the rim of his goblet. "That's what I want to talk about. This is not much of a surprise, you know."

The visitor smiled. "Julia warned me you observe more than you let on."

"I keep my thoughts to myself till they're wanted. How do you propose to support a family?"

Startled, Cadoc said, "I have em-em-employment, sir."

"As a carpenter. Not a gifted one. And the demand is dropping as we fill our most urgent needs. What else can you do?"

Cadoc bit his lip. "I've considered that, believe me, sir. I am educated, can read, write, figure, have knowledge of literature, history, philosophy. In Ys I w-was acclaimed for...horsemanship. I brought down game in Osismiic woods—"

"You learned what it became a Suffete of Ys to learn," Gratillonius interrupted. "That didn't have much to do with what concerns Rome. Nor was it in any way unusual. Confluentes has a glut of people who could be scribes or tutors. The best of them might make fair-to-middling amanuenses, but Apuleius and Corentinus already have theirs, and who else hereabouts wants any?"

Cadoc flushed at the bluntness. "I'll earn my keep."

"Evirion Baltisi's venture bids fair to prosper. Maybe he'd take you on."

"No!" snapped anger. Then: "I'm sorry, sir. Y-you may not be aware there's bad blood—no, not that, I suppose—call it, uh, ill feeling—between him and me. I'm willing to forgive, b-but will he accept?"

"He may think the forgiveness is owing him," said Gratillonius dryly. "I was aware, and only probing you. I have thought of something, but it calls for wit, strength, and boldness."

Cadoc's countenance brightened. "What, sir? Please!"

Gratillonius rose, set his cup on a table, paced to and fro with hands behind his back. "Exploring and surveying. See here. Aside from a few Roman cities, Gallic settlements, the croplands and meadows around, the roads between, most of middle Armorica is wilderness. Hunters, charcoal burners, and so forth, they know their own parts of it, but nobody knows the whole. To all intents and purposes, it's impassable. If you wanted to go from, say, Venetorum to Fanum Martis, you'd have to travel around through Vorgium or Redonum, adding days you could maybe ill afford. It didn't matter when Rome guarded the coastline and you could go by sea, but that's past. The barbarians ravage one section and are off before soldiers can arrive from another. For a while I got Ys to take the lead, and a naval force kept our waters safe, but now that's gone too. Besides, the Germani are pressing on Rome's eastern land frontiers. Again and again they break through. Before many more years, they may well be spilling this far west.

"Whatever defense we can raise—I'm looking into the matter—it's got to have mobility, interior lines of communication and transport, or it's no real use. What I have in mind is ways through the forests and over the heaths. No proper roads, we haven't the manpower to build them; just trails, but suitable for men, horses, maybe light carts on some. First we have to learn the country and decide what the practical routes are. Then we clear, grade, bridge where there isn't a ford, maintain— You follow me?"

Cadoc stood. "Oh, wonderful! I am to pioneer this?"

"We'll try you out. It'll be a trial of the whole idea. I'll teach you the basics of surveying, requirements of terrain, and so forth. Rufinus and his men will give you some companionship and guidance, but that's necessarily limited. You'll be largely on your own. Not the same as roving afoot in search of small game, as I know you've done hereabouts when you had free time. Deeper in are outlaws, woods dwellers hostile to strangers, wild beasts—trolls and spooks, for all I know—as well as nature's traps, swamps, streams, storms, sickness. You can easily die, and your body never recovered. You'll get no glory, because we have to do this quietly; the ImpÉrium won't, and doesn't like being bypassed. I wouldn't have told you about it if I didn't have reason to think you can keep your mouth shut. On the other hand, you'll be pretty well paid, in honest money, out of the Aquilonian treasury. I've settled that with Apuleius. You'll be helping secure your family's future. What say? Are you interested?"

"Of course!" Impulsively, Cadoc embraced Gratillonius. "Thank you, thank you!"

The older man smiled a bit. "Save your gratitude till you come home from your first field trip. You may find it in short supply then."

"I won't. I know I won't. And—I'll be meeting those backwoods folk—I can bring them the Word."

"What?"

"The good news. Tell them about Christ. N-not that I'm an apostle or anything like that, I'm not worthy, but if God wills, I can open a way for those who are."

"Hm." Gratillonius frowned, shrugged, and grunted, "If it doesn't antagonize the natives, or otherwise hinder your work, all right."

"Oh, I wouldn't let it do that." Cadoc beamed. "I'll have my Julia to care for, and our children. Your grandchildren, sir." He saw the other visage freeze and exclaimed, "I'm sorry. I d-didn't mean—it was tragic what happened."

"Not altogether," Gratillonius answered curtly. "Sit down and I'll tell you more about what I'll expect of you."

—Midsummer noontide was warm and clear. Fragrances from the forest breathed over fields where grain ripened. A lark caroled on high. Finches twittered near the ground. From Aquilo's eastern gate streamed and chattered Confluentians, homeward bound for festivities after the mass avowal and service at the church. Breasting their tide, Gratillonius entered the city and made his way among people equally cheerful. It was a day for rejoicing. Apuleius had invited him to a banquet in honor of his daughter and her new husband. The last thing she had done for him was to wash and pipe-clay a tunic, mend his one colorful cloak, and wax his best sandals, that he might make a little of the showing she told him he deserved.

Citizens hailed him respectfully and tried to give way, but inevitably he was sometimes jostled. Passing the church, he felt a contact and ignored it until that person took his arm. Looking around, he saw Runa, clad in a dark green gown that set off the fair skin and raven hair. "Why, greeting," he said.

"Hail." She smiled. "Shame on you, that were not here for the wedding."

"I am not Christian."

"You could have been with the catechumens like me, to watch ere the Mysteries commenced."

He wondered why she had hung around after the door to the sanctum was closed, and then after the service was over. With some difficulty, he explained: "I thought best not remind Julia of what I am, on this day of her days. It distresses her."

"Yet you come to the feast."

"That's different. You too?"

She nodded. Light shimmered in the tortoiseshell comb that held her locks coiled and piled. The gesture presented him with a view of her throat, swanlike, perhaps her best feature. "The senator was kind enough. He likes my work for him."

He could think of no more conversation.

"But it grows wearisome," she went on as he failed to respond. "When 'tis done— Mayhap you'll put in a word for me. I know I can stir his interest myself. Yet he may feel shy of maintaining me for what

I propose, when there are so many demands on the city's coffers and his own purse."

Gratillonius sympathized. He could imagine few tasks more dismal than copying books. "What is it?"

"A history of Ys, from the founding to the end. They should be remembered, those splendors and great deeds."

He wondered at the vividness with which there came back to him a girl who sang beneath the moon. *"I remember Ys, though I have never seen her—"*

"Should they not?" Runa persisted into his silence.

He shook himself. "Aye. And you ought to find the work interesting."

"We can hope for the bishop's approval, I believe. He may even be willing to underwrite it. The fall of the proud city holds a powerful moral lesson." She sensed his distaste and hurried on: "But really, what I want is to keep what we loved alive in the minds of men. Save our dear lost ones from oblivion."

"A vast undertaking."

"'Twill require years. First I must talk with every survivor, and whoever else has recollections—soon, lest death hush them. You foremost, Gratillonius. Though I pray you'll long abide to ward us."

He winced. "Speaking of that...will be hard."

"But you owe your Ys, your Queens, children, friends their memorial. I'll go gently. We can do it a little at a time."

He sighed, looked straight before him, and said, "First get Apuleius's agreement."

"You will help me win that? We've worked well together, you and I. We can again. Say you will."

He nodded. "Aye. Though best wait till the hour is right for broaching it."

"Certes. And by then your wounds may have healed more. Gratillonius," she said softly, "you must not remain fast bound in misery. You have a life before you."

"I have my work."

"And happiness to regain." Her fingers tightened the least bit on his arm.

They reached the tribune's house. Skirts flew white around slenderness as Verania, heedless of propriety, darted forth onto the portico. "Oh, you're here!" she cried. "I'd begun to fear you were sick or, or something."

"Why, your father told me to come about noon," he replied, smiling. A chill within him seemed to thaw.

The maiden flushed. "It felt later," she whispered. "I haven't seen you for so long." Confused by her own forwardness, she stood in his path on the stairs. He halted before her.

"I've been busy," he said. "Today—"

"Your host and hostess await you," said Runa firmly, and guided him on past.

X

~ 1 ~

Late on a drizzly day, Bannon of Dochaldun reached the cabin. Beyond its guardian oak the forest faded off into grayness. Amidst that quiet, the Stegir seemed to run loud past reeds and over stones; yet the sound came somehow muffled. Bannon shivered a bit in the dank chill. Water dripped from leaves, the bridle of his horse, the ends of his mustache. His clothes hung heavy.

Dismounting, he knocked. At first he thought the one who opened the door was a boy, gracile in tunic and breeks; then he looked into the thin face and at the hair that tumbled past the shoulders, the hue of flame, like a shout through the gloom all around. Why should a witch who lived by herself not dress like a male, at least for getting about in the woods? he thought. It was better than skirts....Behind her glowed a couple of lamps and a fire banked on the hearthstone.

"Greeting," he said awkwardly, and named himself. "You're Nemeta, daughter of King Gradlon?"

"I am," she replied in his own Osismiic. "If you come in peace, enter. If not, go." She touched a leather bag on a thong around her neck. It must hold charmstuffs. To its outside was sewn the skull of a vole.

"Peace, peace, lady," Bannon said in haste. "Let me but care for my beasts." He had been leading a remount.

"I must have a shelter put up for their kind," Nemeta remarked. "You are the first to arrive riding. Bring your gear in where 'tis dry."

Bannon tethered the horses at a spot with grazing and entered the cabin. It was snug but murky. He glimpsed household wares and stores at the rear, food hung from crossbeams, an ale keg. Closer by was a shelf whereon stood objects from which he averted his glance; staring at sign-carved sticks and bones or at queerly shaped clay vessels was not for the likes of him. He hung cloak and coat on a peg and, at her gesture, took a stool by the fire. "Ah-h," he said, and held hands to the warmth. Smoke stung his eyes before it drifted sullenly out of the roofed vent above.

"Drink," invited Nemeta, and dipped him a wooden cup of ale. She perched herself opposite. The big green eyes caught what light there was and glimmered. He thought of a cat watchful at a mousehole.

A draught or two cleared his throat. "I am the headman of my village," he began.

"I know," she said.

Had she heard? Dochaldun was a mere cluster of dwellings, off by itself in some acres cleared around a hill, a long day's ride from Aquilo. Its folk mainly kept pigs, which mainly lived on mast, though they also had cows and poultry and raised oats. They seldom went anywhere, save at certain times of year to the gatherings of several communities like their own. A person come from magical Ys less than two years ago seemed unlikely to remember even the name, if it had happened to cross her ears.

"They say you know much," Bannon ventured.

"Your kine are falling sick," Nemeta declared coolly. "You wish me to cure them, as I did for the herds at Vindoval and Stag Run."

He could not tell whether fear or gladness made his heart rattle. Sure it was that a chill pringled through his backbone and out into his fingertips. "You are indeed a witch," he breathed.

Her smile was wry. "I may have guessed. Murrains go about. I am not all-wise. How did you learn of me?"

He summoned courage. If the stories were true, she had wrought well and harmed nobody. They told of each animal led to a fire into which she had cast several herbs; the touch of a wand; a snippet of hair cut off and burnt while she spoke in an unknown tongue; within a day the creature recovering, and those that were healthy staying so.

"'Twas a rumor," Bannon explained. "I had a son of mine track it down. Along the way he heard of lesser deeds you've done. You'll soon be famous, lady."

"Are you Christians yonder?" she asked.

"We are not," he answered, taken aback. "Would you have us be?"

She snickered. "'Tis easier when you're not, though it hasn't barred some from seeking my help."

"They know you for King Gradlon's daughter—"

"I'm done with that," she cut him off. "I take no more alms of anyone."

Her tone became crisp: "Well, now, these are my terms. For coming to your kine and treating them, you shall send back with me a barrel of well-ground oats, sufficient for a year. If the herd grows well, and it will, each month for thirteen months you shall send me a large ham or the same weight in smoked chops. Have I your pledge?"

"That is...much to pay," he demurred.

She grinned. "From elsewhere am I already supplied with wheat flour, butter, and cheese, besides small things for small services. As yet, I have need of more clothing and other woven goods. You may give me those if you'd liefer, but it must be to the same value. I do not haggle. Agree or take your leave."

He had had enough forewarning to sigh, "Be it so. The oats and meat. By my honor."

He had half feared she would require a stronger plighting, but she accepted his word, as well she might. "Good. We'll be off in the morning. I see you meant to guide me back—no magic; you brought a second horse. But take your ease. I'll soon have a meal ready."

With deft hands she fetched a skinned and drawn hare from her larder, cut it in pieces which she rubbed with fat and salt, roasted it on a spit. He wondered whether she had snared it in the ordinary way or sung it to her knife. Also on his trencher went a boiled egg, leeks, roots, and hardtack, while she kept his cup filled. It was strange, having a princess and witch serve him as any housewife might. His head began to buzz in the smoky air.

She kept mostly silent until at the end she said, "You will clean the things tomorrow ere we leave."

Briefly he was astounded, he reached for his dagger, then the meaning of it went into him and he laughed. "Very well, she-chieftain!"

"Your saddle blanket isn't rightly dry," she said, "but I'll lend you covering. Wait here."

She went out. When she came back he took his turn, letting his water in the dark and the rain. As he reentered, he saw her beside the narrow bed, naked. Light flowed tawny over small breasts and subtly rounded flanks.

Desire upwelled. "Lady—" He moved toward her.

She raised a hand. "We will sleep." A drawn sword might have spoken. "Step no nearer, or you will weep for it throughout the rest of your days."

Terror smote. "I'm sorry. You're b-beautiful, and—I'm sorry."

"Blow out the lamps when you've undressed," she said indifferently. With a nod at his bedroll on the floor; "You shall sleep soundly tonight, Bannon."

To his astonishment, he did, quickly drifting off into dreams. Weird, full of music, afterward half remembered, they haunted him until next the moon was new.

~ 2 ~

That summer was cruel to sandy Audiarna. An outbreak of the Egyptian malady wasted it, especially among its poor. Victims turned feverish and strengthless; they grew leathery membranes in mouth and throat, could scarcely swallow, and were apt to bleed heavily from the nose; pulse was weak and rapid, the neck swollen, the face waxy. Most died within a few days, while those who recovered took long to regain full health and in the meantime often suffered paralytic attacks.

This caused ships and overland traders to stay away, thus cutting tax revenues when they were most needed. Hinterland peasants must feed a city which they entered reluctantly. Then at harvest season a new terror struck them.

Gratillonius heard about it from Apuleius, to whom the tribune of Audiarna had sent an appeal for help. The two men discussed it at the senator's house. "A great beast of unknown sort prowling about," Apuleius reported from the letter received. "It's killed and devoured not only livestock, but lately men—twice. When they didn't come home from outlying fields, searchers found their broken, scattered bones. There's a talk of pugmarks like a lynx's, and sight in twilight of a shape that seemed feline—but enormous. They fear it's a creature from hell, loosed on them for their sins, and huddle in their hamlets with the crops left untended, waiting for the first heavy rains to ruin the harvest."

"Hm...a bear?" Gratillonius wondered. "No, not with such a track. Nor've I ever heard of bears behaving that way....Are all men in the city too sick to go after the thing?"

"Or too demoralized. Their prayers and the prayers of their clergy have availed nothing. They ask the spiritual help of Bishop Corentinus and the temporal help of those whom God has spared."

Gratillonius nodded. "They remember how the King of Ys brought former Bacaudae into these parts to keep the woods safe."

Apuleius looked closely at his friend. "I can understand your bitterness toward the Audiarnans, after they denied a place to your fugitives last year," he murmured. "But in the name of charity—"

Gratillonius laughed. "Oh, never fear. I'll have Rufinus whistle up a gang of huntsmen in short order. And I'll lead them myself."

"What? No, you can't be serious. This may truly be a demon. And whether or not, your life is too valuable to risk."

Gratillonius uttered a rude soldier's word. "I've been dealing with one petty squabble after another, or scarcities or regulations or— It's like wading through a bog of glue. By Hercules, here's a chance to get out and do something real! I'm bound away as soon as I have my men, and that's that."

A small cry brought his attention around. Verania had entered. "No, please!" she begged. "Not you!"

"And why not, my dear?" asked Gratillonius with a smile.

"I've tried to tell him why not," sighed Apuleius. "Well, I daresay you came in to announce dinner."

She nodded. Her lip quivered. Gratillonius rose with her father. He wanted to pat her on the head, or better hug her, and speak reassurances. Of course, decency forbade. "I don't send men out on hazardous duty I wouldn't take myself," he said to her. "Though I hardly think this compares with a war. It's just a hunt, Verania."

"Adonis w-w-went hunting," she stammered, and fled the room.

Perforce she waited in the triclinium, beside Rovinda and Salomon. She had blinked back tears, but Gratillonius still wanted to console her. Having a pretty girl fret about him felt so warm. The best that occurred to him was to say to her brother, "You've heard too? I'm off after the beast that's been preying around Audiarna. Shall I bring you its tail?"

Worship looked back at him.

~ 3 ~

The devil was elusive. Gratillonius, Rufinus, and their ten followers quested for three days. They found the merest traces, and trails too cold for their hounds.

Each morning they went forth in groups of three, each evening returned to camp. Gratillonius had had the tents pitched upstream from Audiarna, well out of sight and contagion. Fields greened deserted, silent but for the cawing of crows that unhindered robbed them. Forest hemmed and darkened the northern horizon. Likely that was where the brute laired, and the men coursed its tracklessness daily. However, Gratillonius chose to base himself in the open; there a sentry could see whatever was coming. Also, that was the way the creature must fare if it would again have human flesh.

Ranging about or idled at night beside the fire, Gratillonius found his thoughts slipping their moorings. They would not abide by the question of what the thing was that he hunted or how to slay it. Instead, against his will they drifted to his own fate. No longer could he keep himself busy enough in his waking hours that sleep fell straightaway upon him. What did he hope for? Chief of a colony founded in desperation, he lacked any vision of its future by which to guide it. Ninefold widowed, he lacked any son to carry on his name, and of his two living daughters, one had made herself an outcast. Celibate as Corentinus, he lacked any God Whom the sacrifice might please. Among men he found companionship, and two or three good friends, but always some barrier, faith or purpose or something less clear, between their hearts and his. Among women—

He needed a hand-graspable achievement.

Rufinus's sardonic wit and the banter of the company provided a little distraction. They had been chosen for cockiness in the face of man, magic, or mystery. Gratillonius wished he could join in their japes, as once he did with his legionaries, but his mood was too heavy.

The end of the search came in a rush. He, Rufinus, and a woodsman named Ogotorig were on their way back from yet another sweep. Leaving the forest, they started toward the river, careless of trampled grain. At the water they would drink before following it on south to camp. Wearisome hours lay behind them—endless trees, brushwood that fought, flies, mosquitoes, stinging ants, heat, thirst, silence broken only by their curses or the mockery of a cuckoo—and they plodded mute, their dogs droop-tailed behind them. Going in deeper than before, they had emerged late. The sun was down. Dusk drifted westward through coolness that still smelled green. The stalks rustled softly. Swifts darted half-seen across violet-gray heaven.

Suddenly a hound growled, then gave tongue. At once the rest were clamorous. They darted forward, fast lost to sight. "Ha!" Rufinus exclaimed. "Has he stumbled on us?" He broke into a lope. Gratillonius pounded alongside. Their boar spears bobbed to their haste. Ogotorig stopped to string his bow and nock an arrow.

A deep growl coughed through the baying of the hounds. A yell tore loose, ended in a rattle, the voice of death. The dogs barked, shrill and afraid. Gratillonius heard how they milled about. What a damnable time and place to meet the quarry. How could you see where it was, what it did?

He tripped over the ripped body of a hound. The blow that killed it had flung it yards off. "'Ware charge!" Rufinus called. Gratillonius saw the grain wave before him, like water when an orca attacks from beneath. Rufinus had moved to get between him and it, but the onslaught was quicker. Gratillonius barely had time to ground his spear.

The thing that rushed at him was dim in the gloaming, huge, he felt the soil shiver beneath its weight. He had a glimpse of shagginess, a mane, eyes agleam and cat-gape open. The shock came.

It knocked him down. The beast had not plunged at him like a boar, but veered. A clawed paw slashed air as he fell. It could have shattered his skull. Rolling over, he bounced to his feet and drew sword.

Blood ran black where his spearpoint had furrowed. That was a flesh wound, and the brute had turned on Rufinus. The man danced aside, jabbing. Did he laugh into the snarls and the brief, thunderlike roar? Gratillonius heard him: "Back, Grallon! Stay clear! Give the archer a shot!"

Ogotorig's bow twanged. A shaft smote; another, another. The monster retreated. Wrath rolled in its throat, but it swung about. Making for the wood, it went slowly, the off hind leg lame. "After it," Gratillonius bawled, and took the lead.

Exultance leaped in his breast. He never thought how readily he could die. He stayed wary, though, senses alert until the fading light could have been noontide. To breathe the rank smell was to drink wine.

In—thrust home—the blade grates past a rib, meets heaviness beyond, twists back out—spring aside—blood pours off steel—emboldened, the hounds bay, rush in, tear at legs and flanks—the tormented giant shakes itself, drops fly like slingstones from its gashes, and turns around again to do battle—Rufinus drives his spear in from behind and cackles laughter as he shoves deeper—Gratillonius stabs near a shoulder—the beast sinks to earth, the hounds are upon it, it smashes one and maims another before the men can drive them off—Ogotorig looses arrow after arrow—the creature shudders, blood bubbles around a snarl—Gratillonius steps reckless close, looks into the dimming eyes, and gives the mercy thrust, for this has been a valiant foe. Nonetheless, it—no, he—takes a while to die.

The wrecked hound yammered till Rufinus ended its pain, the last hale one flopped down and panted. The men stood amidst flattened stalks and peered through the darkness that rose and rose. Early stars were out.

"What *is* it?" whispered Ogotorig.

"A lion." Awe hushed Gratillonius's tone.

"First I've seen, aside from statues and pictures," Rufinus said.

"Same for me," Gratillonius answered. "But he's a sign of strength and courage, you know."

"How on earth did he get here?"

"I don't suppose we'll ever know. Escaped from a cage somewhere. I've heard that rich patrons in big cities can get animals from afar for the games, though not often anymore. Maybe this one was bound for Treverorum after being shipped through Portus Namnetum when he got free and wandered this way."

"He limped, did you notice? From a fight with a bear or what? Anyhow, not fit to live off deer. When he started taking cows and sheep, the peasants drove their stock into byres or pens. No wonder he snatched a couple of men when they happened by. Poor creature. Poor lost, lonely, unsurrendering lion."

In the exhaustion that now welled up within him, Gratillonius had dropped into Latin, and Rufinus had responded likewise. "What do you speak of?" Ogotorig asked in his native language. "How on earth did he get here, you wondered." He bent, smeared a little of the spilled blood on his forefinger, daubed his breast with it. "How off earth, I'd say. Wizardry at work. Cernunnos, hunter God, keep us from harm."

The man could be right, Gratillonius thought. What had come was freakish: first pestilence in the city, then this in the hinterland. It was as if a vengeful spell were cast on Audiarna.

~ 4 ~

The bridge boomed underhoof, triumphal drums, and Gratillonius rode through the gate into Aquilo. Sunlight slanted along the road behind him and made a glory of his tousled hair. Soon enclosing houses had him and his followers in shade, but women and children spilled out of them to mingle with their men in the streets. The cheers surfed around, before, everywhere through town. "He's won, he slew the demon, God be praised!" For riding at his back came Rufinus, who bore on a spearshaft the clean-boiled skull of the lion.

Thus Verania saw him from the portico of her father's home. She had dashed out at the sounds of jubilation and nearly fell. Salomon caught her in time. She squeezed her hands together above her bosom

890

and erupted into tears. He must swallow hard before he could stand in manly wise.

There Gratillonius drew rein. Apuleius and Rovinda came forth. Gratillonius waved. "It's done," he called. "We made an end of the manslayer." When had such joy last fountained in him? At the overcoming of the Franks? No, that had already lain beneath the shadow of strife in Ys. This was wholly clean and brave.

Apuleius barely curbed a whoop. Wrapping himself in Roman gravity, he walked down the stairs. "A marvelous deed," he said through the din. "Yet we of this household will give the most thanks that you have returned unharmed. Enter, you and your band."

Such of the woodsmen as understood looked abashed, except for Rufinus. They were strangers to life among the prosperous. Their chief grinned, though, and licked his lips. "They set a grand table," he said in Gallic.

"Thanks, but we're dirty and sweaty from traveling," Gratillonius replied. "We wanted to relieve any anxiety, but what say we go on to Confluentes—tell the people there, make ourselves presentable, and then come back?"

His glance fell on Verania. "Ho, little lady," he called on impulse. "What are you weeping about?"

"I am, am, am so happy," she stammered.

The brightness waxed within him. "Salomon," he shouted across the hubbub to her brother, "you'll get the tail I promised you. Verania, how'd you like the skin for a rug when it's cured?"

Apuleius reached his foot and looked upward. The countenance, lined and graying but still handsome, had gone grave. "No, best give that to the church in thanks for God's help and mercy," he said. Before Gratillonius could protest: "As for Confluentes, I'll send word. Please don't spoil your well-earned pleasure at once, but wash and borrow clean garments from us, enjoy the best meal Rovinda can provide on short notice, tell us your tale over wine, and take a good night's rest. Trouble can wait."

It was as if a knife stabbed. Gratillonius felt muscles grow taut. At the abrupt pressure of his knees, Favonius whickered and curvetted. He needed a moment to quiet the stallion. The people jamming the street seemed also touched by sudden unease. The chatter ebbed from them and they stood staring.

"What's this?" Gratillonius barked. An inward groan: What now?

"No immediate business," Apuleius said. "It can wait." Distress flitted over his features. "I should have kept silent till tomorrow. Truly, your safety, what you've done, overweighs entirely this other thing. It was inevitable, anyhow."

Gratillonius bit back a curse. "Will you kindly tell me what the devil it is, or must I go ask them yonder?"

Apuleius sighed. "Very well. The procurator has appointed a new agent for this region. He came while you were gone. A former Ysan himself—one Nagon Demari—ah, you remember?—become a Roman citizen. He went about looking at all persons and property, and estimating assessments. We can pay what we must in Aquilo; I've always been careful about keeping reserves and persuading my populace to do likewise. But Confluentes and its dwellers have never been on the tax rolls, of course—"

A surf roared through Gratillonius. He seemed to swim in it, barely keeping above, while it whelmed everything else. Whenever he broke above a wave, his mouth full of its bitterness, he would hear amidst the noise:

"—land tax—" How many husbandmen had it dragged from their homes, down into serfdom? "—quinquennial—" The levy each five years, less in amount but in its working worse yet, for it emptied the coffers of artisan and merchant alike, crippling where it did not bankrupt. "—indiction next year—" The Imperial decree every fifteen years which set the rates on property and polls; and Confluentes had no record of past payments from which to argue for moderation. "—naming of your curials—" His father had been made into such a beast of burden.

"—irregularities and outright illegalities—" They had no designated overlords in Confluentes. There had been exemptions for Maximus's old soldiers, because they were veterans, but abruptly their right to have land in freehold or to engage in trade was questioned, in view of the fact that it was a usurper under whom they last served. The folk from Ys were not even citizens.

"—fines and other penalties—" Ruin; bondage.

"—compounding—" Besides overt payment to the state, bribes with no limit other than what the officials decided was obtainable, nor any warranty that in after years someone else would not smell out the transactions and demand his own price, unless in zeal he denounced the whole thing to the Imperium itself.

"—suggestion that children have market value—" Gratillonius remembered a young girl who reached between bars to lay her hands in his and ask if he could take her home.

He grew aware that Apuleius was tugging at his ankle. From the portico above, Rovinda and her children watched with horror on them. People began to slip out of the crowd and go elsewhere. The huntsmen glared around. "Gratillonius," the senator called across the surf. "In God's name, man! You look like a Saxon about to start off on a killing spree. Calm down!"

Gratillonius stared at the sword he had drawn. Its blade gleamed dully through evening shades. The tide within him ebbed away. What it left was as cold and sharp as the steel.

"Dismount, come inside, have a beaker, calm down," Apuleius pleaded. "He's gone, I tell you. Nothing has happened yet. I interposed my authority—kept a few armed men at his side to forestall violence; that would have been disastrous—bad enough, the taunts your Ysans flung at him— But he was not actually here to collect anything. Corentinus and I sent him off with a flea in his ear. He'll be back, we can't stop that, but we do have time for appeals to higher authority, time we can stretch into months, I think, if need be. Come, old friend, let's consider how we can work together."

Gratillonius looked toward Rufinus. "Ride ahead, you and the boys," he ordered. "Tell them in Confluentes to meet outside the basilica—the manor house, you know. I'll be there shortly and speak to them."

His henchman dipped the shafted skull and raised it again, as a cavalry trooper might salute with a battle standard. "Aye, my lord," he answered in Ysan. The lean visage had gone wolflike. "After me!" he shouted in Gallic, and clattered away at the head of his hunters.

"I've done what I can to reassure them," Apuleius said. "They're still terrified; no, I believe some are furious, though they don't confide in me, the Roman. You can do better. But plan what you'll say. This was by no means unanticipated, you recall. We knew there would be problems with the government."

Gratillonius remembered vaguely. Later he could summon up those talks between him and the Aquilonian tribune. They might be less than clear to him. He hadn't given them the attention they rated, with everything else he had on his mind. Well, Apuleius could repeat, add detail, stand true as Apuleius had done throughout the years. First, though— "I didn't expect it would be this bad," Gratillonius retorted.

Apuleius shook his head. "We are not alone. I fear it will be difficult for all Armorica."

"Well...we'll get together later. Tomorrow?" Gratillonius breathed deeply. "I must go and meet with them. It can't wait. They are my people."

He touched heels to Favonius. The horse stamped eagerly, wheeled, and broke into a trot. Gratillonius glanced back. Dismay was gone. His will had hardened and he was off again to battle, for the family at his back as much as for anyone. He waved. "Goodnight!" he called. When he smiled, he was looking at Verania. She straightened and waved too.

He forced himself to keep an easy pace, also after he had passed through the east gate and was bound up the river road. The sun stood on the horizon. Fields reached dim, but water and the crowns of trees glowed golden beneath a sky where light would prevail for an hour. Birds flocked homeward. The stream made a cool music around hoofbeats. Leather creaked. The odor of the stallion was warm and sweet. He touched the sheathed sword. This was his land. He lived to nurture and defend it, that his blood might have it in heritage.

Give Rufinus's crew time to halloo around in the colony and the dwellers time to assemble. Meanwhile he would seek his house—care for Favonius, of course—scrub and groom himself—aye, put on the armor Apuleius had had made for him, because tonight he must be warmaster of this tribe.

~ 5 ~

Twilight deepened, the same dusk as at his victory over the lion. Westward a planet shone like a lamp against royal blue. Beyond the manor and off to the east, forest raised a battlemented wall. Stars glimmered there, and a curve of moon aloft. From the steps of the house, Gratillonius saw his Ysans in a mass, shadowed, become one great expectant animal; but above them a few rushlights lashed to poles flamed defiance. He would have been well-nigh invisible, save that Runa had set lanterns on stools right and left of him. Their luminance sheened off his coat of mail, helmet with centurion's crest, sword once more in his hand. He caught the hot scent of their burning. She stood in the gloom behind.

"—hold fast." His voice rolled out and out across the darkening world. "To those who would break us, we answer Nay. We bid them be off and let us get on with our lives. Best for them if they heed!

"I promise no swift end of troubles. Surely we shall have to make accommodation with the Roman law; and it is proper that we pay our fair share of costs for the state, Rome who is now your mother also. It will not be easy, getting our rights. But we shall, and while the fight is fought, your best service is to go on about your daily business, unafraid.

"Unafraid. Hearken. You've heard talk of men and women made chattels, aye, parents forced to sell their children into hopeless toil or what is worse. I've seen it happen. But I say to you, it shall not happen again...while we stand fast. Those things are limited by Roman law.

"Now we may or may not be wise to seek citizenship for ourselves. As foederates, clearly recognized by treaty, we would be better protected in some ways. On the other hand, we have little to bargain with. I will get counsel about this. But while these questions are before the Imperium, we can hold all else in abeyance. That, and everything that follows, needs the guidance of men wise and strong. Else it will fail. But we have such men on our side: Apuleius, senator and tribune; Bishop Corentinus, prince of the Church. Trust them."

"You too, Grallon!" rang from the gathering.

He chuckled. "Nay, I'm naught but an old soldier." His tone deepened as the sword rose. "But I do myself still hold tribune's rank. Mine is the right to speak directly for you—to the praetorian prefect Ardens in Augusta Treverorum, who is friendly toward me and surely toward you; above him, to the Imperial counsellor, consul and Master of Soldiers, Stilicho, who must know what it means to Rome, a strong folk bulwarking this far end of her realm. I stand to ward you.

"For I am the King of Ys."

Tumult hailed him, cheers, laughter, and tears.

—The tall torches swayed away through night. Stillness descended. There were many stars.

Runa came to him. She had thrown aside the black cloak that hid her. A silken gown flowed close about her stride, like the hair down past her shoulders, and shone in the lantern light, like her eyes. She reached forth both hands. He took them before he thought. Thinking was beyond him anyhow. The power of what he had done throbbed through his body and radiated into the air around.

"You *are* the King," she said. Her voice shook.

The narrow face seemed to float before him, a cameo. How fair was her skin. "Once I'd have told myself, aye, he is Taranis on earth," he heard. "That's forbidden, and you'd deny. But you were more than mortal this evening, Gratillonius."

He shook his head, blindly. "I did but hearten them."

"Such power comes from outside the world. You cannot at once return to mortality. 'Tis too far below. You are a God...a demigod, a hero. Your will be done. Abide the night."

She pressed close, she was in his arms, their mouths strained together. The high tide roared back, but upbearing him on its arrogance.

For an instant, a freezing current passed. "The Queens," he mumbled into the fragrance of her locks.

"You've left the Gods of Ys. They've lost all hold on you. Come."

The surge carried him forward.

—In her bedroom, she barely set aside the lantern she had carried along before he seized her. "Nay, wait," she began. He bore her down onto the blankets and hauled up her skirts. The light slipped smoothly over slender legs, rounded thighs and haunches, till it dived into the sable between. She smiled. "I said, your will be done, King."

Almost, he cast himself on her then and there. His mail rustled. Fleetingly he remembered how she had caught her breath as he drew her against it. That must have hurt. He unbuckled his helmet and threw it clanging to the floor. His sword belt dropped on top. The coif came off with the chain links he pulled over his head. Breeches next! She spread her legs and reached to embrace him.

—Afterward he said, "That was too hasty. I'm sorry."

She ruffled his hair. "'Twas a long time alone for both of us. We have the night."

"Aye." He roused from the peacefulness of release and they undressed entirely, helping each other. Her breasts were small but firm, with brown nipples already again rising. "What pleasures you?" she asked.

"Whatever you like." As yet he felt shy about telling her what he had enjoyed with—Forsquilis, and Tambilis, and—the manifold ways of his Gallicenae. Nor did he dare call them back to him.

She kissed him savoringly. "Well, let's seek the bed and— You've had no supper. Are you hungry?"

"Not for food," he laughed.

"We'll wake Cata later and have her feed us. She can scarcely be more shocked than she already is. It does the complacent old biddy good. But this hour belongs to us and none else."

~ 6 ~

They went afoot to Aquilo. Noontide brimmed with sun, warmth, and harvest odors. Bees buzzed in clover. The view over the Odita was of men, women, and animals busy across the fields, children following to glean. "They gather more briskly than they did yesterday," Runa said.

"They've hope 'tis for themselves they do, Ysans and Gauls alike," Gratillonius answered.

She closed fingers on his arm. "Your work, man of mine."

Somehow those words wakened a misgiving in him, but it was faint and he sent it away.

They entered the town. Clad as befitted dignitaries going to conference, they stood doubly out among ordinary people bound on ordinary occupations. The whole place felt alien to Gratillonius, half a dream. Most of his mind tarried in the night before.

Realizing that, he hauled it back and gave it marching orders. Urgent business was on hand, the initial discussion of strategy and tactics with Apuleius. Simply composing a letter to the praetorian prefect would require much thought; and it must be on its way soon, by the fastest of couriers.

A slave admitted them to the senator's house. He met them in the atrium. Brightness filled it too, shining from the purity of walls and their delicate murals. Apuleius wore a white robe worked with gold thread; Gratillonius thought of a lighted candle. Brows lifted slightly. "Hail," said the gentle voice. "I had begun to fear something was amiss."

"I'm sorry I'm late," Gratillonius replied. "Overslept." A luxurious looseness perfused him.

Apuleius smiled. "Well, you earned the right. I've heard about your speech. We've held the meal for you." He inclined his head toward Runa. "You give us a pleasant surprise, my lady, but you are very welcome to join us."

Verania flitted in from the rear of the house. Joy sparkled from her. "You're here!" she said to Gratillonius. "I have something special for you on the table."

Apuleius frowned indulgently. "Quiet, girl. Mind your manners."

She halted at the inner door, spirits undampened. Gratillonius smiled at her and raised his hand. Her lashes fluttered down and back up again. Rosiness came and went in her cheeks.

"I brought the lady Runa along," Gratillonius told Apuleius, "because her advice should be valuable. She knows, understands things about the Ysans that, well, a man, an outsider like me never really could."

"Subtleties." Apuleius nodded. Immediately he turned solemn. "I wonder, though, if that isn't premature. And...the bishop will arrive later today."

"I'll absent myself," Runa offered with a meekness new to her listeners.

"Oh, he's no woman hater," Gratillonius said.

"But he would doubtless feel...awkward....especially given the circumstances," she pointed out.

Apuleius's glance went from one to the other and back. Runa drew close beside Gratillonius and took his arm. Together they returned the look.

The Roman became expressionless. "Well, well," he said low. "It appears you two have an understanding."

"We do," Gratillonius declared. Glee broke forth. "In all honesty, I brought her because I wanted you to know right away, my friend."

In the doorway, breath tore across. Verania covered her mouth. Her eyes widened till they seemed to fill her whole face. Apuleius turned his head. "Why, daughter, what's wrong?" he asked. Concern dissolved the reserve he had clamped on himself. "You're white as a toga. Are you ill?"

"F-f-forgive me," she choked. "I can't dine—today—" She whirled. They heard her footfalls stumble down the corridor beyond.

~ 7 ~

Autumn blew gray from the north. Wind bit. White-capped, iron-hued seas trampled its shrillness beneath their rush and rumble. The air was full of salt mist. It hid the tops of the mountains behind the firth. They lifted stark, ling-clad, with a few gnarly dwarf trees clinging amidst boulders; streams plunged toward the sea. Eochaid had heard that those heights sheltered deep glens and mild vales, but at the prow of his ship he saw none of it. There was haven here, though, and smoke in tatters from a great rath ahead.

Rowers put out a last burst of strength to drive their galley boldly forward. Currachs accompanying her skimmed like gulls. Eochaid had donned a cloak he otherwise kept locked away from weather, of the six bright colors which he as a king's son might wear. It took eyes off the faded and mended shirt, sea-stained kilt, worn-out shoes.

Spearheads glimmered in front of the earthen wall. Men of the rath had come out to see what strangers drew nigh. "A goodly muster," said Subne at his captain's ear, "and, for sure, more of them alert inside. I think we've found the king where he will be spending this Samhain tide."

"May we be finding what else we seek," Eochaid said, more to Manandan maqq Léri and whatever other Gods were listening than to any man. He had already promised sacrifices if They were kindly.

Approaching, he raised hands and cried peace. The warriors ashore stood warily while galley and currachs ran onto the strand. When the crews jumped out to secure them, clearly not hostile, the watchers let weapons droop and smiles arise. Their leader advanced to greet Eochaid in the name of Aryagalatis maqq Irgalato, his king.

His speech had the burr of the Ulati. This Dál Riata was a settlement from the land of that same name in northern Ériu. Nonetheless, it was the language of the home island the wayfarers heard, after three years of roving. More than the wind stung tears from their eyes.

Yet Eochaid must enter not as a gangrel but as a chieftain in his own right. Proudly he walked, and behind him his men bearing gifts of Roman gold, silver, jewelry, cloth, the choicest of their plunder.

The ringwall enclosed a number of buildings: barn, stable, workshops, storehouses, cookhouses, lesser dwellings, and the royal hall. Nothing was nearly as grand as Eochaid remembered of his father's holdings in Qóiqet Lagini, let alone what Niall of Mide and his sons possessed. This house was long but low, poles and daub weathered, thatch overrun by moss. However it was the present seat of a king, and he a man with many spears at his beck.

A runner had told Aryagalatis who was coming. He lifted the knee in salutation and bade Eochaid take a stool before him, Eochaid's followers to settle themselves where they could find places in the smoke and dimness. He was a stoutly built, rugged-featured man with a black bush of hair and beard. His clothes were more for warmth than show, but gold shone on his breast.

Women brought ale for the warriors, hoarded wine for him and Eochaid. Much seemly talk passed on both sides, giving honor, mentioning forebears and kin, exchanging news. When he received his gifts, Aryagalatis could do no less than offer lodging for as long as his guests wished. His chief poet made verses in praise of Eochaid. They lacked the polish heard among the high ones of Ériu, but hallowed fellowship equally well.

"I will speak openly, lord," Eochaid said at last. "You know what misfortune has made me homeless."

Aryagalatis looked hard through the firelight at the marred, once beautiful face. "I do," he answered carefully. "Your deed will keep you from your motherland forever."

Eochaid held his voice steady. "Injustice and mistreatment drove me mad. It is not the first time such has happened to a hero. Myself and these loyal men have proven on the Romans that we keep the goodwill of the Gods."

"I think that may be true. But say on."

"We are weary of wandering. Thin is the comfort in a camp on an islet or with a woman wrenched from her home. We have homes of our own to make, wives to wed, sons to beget and rear. It is land we ask of you and troth we will give you, Aryagalatis."

898

The king nodded. "Sure and that comes as no surprise. Well, Alba has land aplenty, once the Cruthini are cleared from it. And since they do often come back, we have always need of fighting men. Let us talk more about this during the winter, Eochaid maqq Éndae."

A sigh as of a wave went through the house.

The exile doubled a fist on his thigh. "You may well also want all the spears you can find," he said, "when Niall of the Nine Hostages attacks your folk across the water. He may not stop there—though surely you will be crossing over to give help and take revenge."

Aryagalatis frowned. "This we will not talk of. That could be bad luck. I know he is your enemy; but while you bide among us, you and your men, you will not be provoking his wrath. Do you understand?"

"I do." Eochaid forced sullenness from his voice. "You will find me grateful, lord. Then, if ever the time does come— But now we want only to wish for your good fortune. May you feed fat the ravens of the Mórrigu!"

XI

~ 1 ~

Midwinter's early darkness had fallen before Gratillonius got his horse properly stabled. Under a thick overcast, Confluentes was a still deeper huddle of black. Though he knew every house, street, lane, almost every rut, he stumbled often enough to make him swear at himself for not bringing along a groom with a lantern. There was too much night within him as well as without.

At last he found his own door and passed through into light of a sort. Tallow candles in wooden holders burned around the main room. They mingled their reek with the closeness that a couple of charcoal braziers laid in the air. Nonetheless a tinge of dank chill persisted. Summer felt ages agone.

His manservant took cloak and coat from him and said the maid, who was actually a middle-aged widow, would set forth a meal as soon as might be. Not knowing when to expect his return, she had perforce let preparation wait. "Bring me a stoup of wine," Gratillonius said. "Nay, mead." If wine was worth drinking, it had gotten sufficiently scarce in these parts and at this season—what with piracy, banditry, and the fear of them cutting away at commerce—that he'd rather save it for happier occasions.

Runa entered from the inner house. She wore a shapeless dress of brown wool, thick socks beneath sandals, and a wimple, under which he knew her hair was coiled in tight braids. "Well, you've come," she said. They had taken to speaking Latin in the presence of his servants, who were Ysan countryfolk with scant grasp of the language. Neither of them liked having words of theirs bandied about. "Where were you?"

"I went riding."

Her arched brows lifted higher still. "Indeed? All day, when you've been telling me you haven't half the hours you need for guiding your people?"

He checked an angry retort. That was not what he had declared, and well she knew it. Crises, most of them petty but important to those concerned, had a way of springing up in bunches, like weeds. Otherwise he had undertakings to supervise, military instruction and drill to maintain, dickerings with Osismii and Aquilonians to carry out. But much of his time he spent standing by, passing it with wood and leather in his little workshop.

"A day is very short, these months," he said. "I needed to get out by myself." —use his muscles, gallop along empty roads, range afoot into leafless woods.

"You might have had the goodness to stop at the basilica and tell me you'd be late." She spent her own days in the former manor house. Sometimes she visited the homes of settlers, gathering their memories of Ys and its history, but oftenest she summoned them to her. The habit of deference to a priestess remained in them.

His patience ruptured. "Damnation, must I always be spoke to your hub?"

The manservant brought his goblet. He raised it and swallowed. The mead was well brewed, dry, flavored with woodruff, a pungency recalling meadow margins where cornel bloomed. His mood mildened. This was no easy life for her either. "Well, I should have told you," he admitted, "but the news I'd gotten—Apuleius had the letter passed on to me at sunrise—that drove everything else out of my head." It flitted through him that formerly Apuleius would have come in person, or invited him to Aquilo, and they would have talked.

"Oh." She also gentled. Somehow that made him aware of her pallor, even in this dull light. She had been ill for several days of late, keeping to herself in the manor house as if too proud to let him see her thus. Recovery advanced, but as yet she didn't quite have her full strength back. "Bad. From the South?"

He nodded. She came to him, took his elbow, guided him to a bench built against the wall. They sat down together. Straw ticking rustled beneath them.

He gestured an order that the servant bring drink for her, and stared into his as he dragged forth: "The Visigoths broke down every defense. They're looting and burning all through northern Italy."

It was a minor wonder, perhaps, that couriers had brought the word this far, this soon. Only last month had King Alaric invaded. The war was not much older than that, it had broken out with such stunning swiftness and ferocity. Before, Emperors Arcadius in the East and Honorius in the West—rather, their ministers—seemed to have made peace with those warriors. Alaric had become Master of Soldiers in eastern Illyricum. The thought was like poison in Gratillonius, that quite possibly Constantinople had then secretly persuaded him to fall on Rome.

Be that as it may, "The Imperium has to call in reinforcements," he said. "The letter mentioned troops on their way from the Rhenus. Come sailing weather, if the war is still going on, I wouldn't be surprised but what they're hailed out of Britannia too. And then what about the barbarians along those frontiers?"

"Horrible." Runa's tone stayed level and she did not reach for his hand as Tambilis, say, would have. "But what can we do except continue in those tasks God has set us?"

He grimaced. "Mine is to hurry up the reconstruction of our defenses. If only those sh—those donkeys in Turonum would so much as answer my letters about it!"

"Don't start pacing again. You know how I dislike that. In a year's time, ten years, a hundred, this will be past."

"Like Ys," he said bitterly.

"Well, Ys had its woes too, century after century. Just the same, what I am writing will be glorious as long as the world endures."

The man brought her mead. She sipped as she talked on about her book. It could not simply be written from beginning to end. Her education came back to her in pieces, suddenly she would remember something that happened generations ago, and record it before she forgot again. The other survivors had minds less orderly. "And you must be more forthcoming yourself, Gratillonius. I really must insist you tell me things, tell me in full. I know it hurts you, but you should have the manhood to do it, considering what this means. Oh, and if you'd only trouble yourself to make notes, how much toil you'd spare me, instead of puttering at your bench like a common carpenter."

He refrained from remarks about duties—promises, at least—owed on her part. When Apuleius and Corentinus agreed to jointly sponsor her history, it had been with the understanding that she would continue copying books as well, but thus far she had not again touched that task. When Gratillonius once brought the matter up, she flared that the work was fit for any slave who had had a year's schooling.

Tribune and bishop abstained from reproaches. Indeed the latter had said little to her and nothing to Gratillonius about their unblessed union. She was just a catechumen, her man an unbeliever. Yet he hated to suppose Corentinus and Apuleius had dismissed them from their hearts. He hoped they hoped the pair would repent and reform. However that was, he rarely saw the churchman these days.

901

"—scrawling on wretched wooden slabs. When will you get me a proper supply of papyrus? Or parchment. You said you would."

"It's not that easy," Gratillonius told her. How many times already had he done so? "Traffic from the South goes by fits and starts. Skins have more urgent uses. Besides, scraping them and the rest of the preparation, that's long labor."

"You can find idle hands aplenty to train. Let your hunters bring in deer to replace the sheepskins. Talk to Apuleius. He can arrange such things. He'll scarcely give me a civil word."

No, thought Gratillonius, that family had likewise drifted apart from him. Not that there was a breach, anything like that. He and the senator continued to meet, confer, work as a team. Sometimes when they had been at it till late he stayed for supper. But the conversations didn't range around as they used to, and he didn't get invitations simply for pleasure, and he seldom encountered Rovinda or the children.

Had he given offense? That wasn't reasonable. They had taken him for what he was before, the nine times wedded King of Ys. He did nothing now that they wouldn't expect of such a man, or of many a Christian. Now and then he thought he glimpsed sorrow in the eyes of Apuleius or Corentinus. Of course, in those eyes he was debauching Runa, the convert....Whatever the cause, a constraint had come upon them, and begotten its like in him. Not knowing what to say or do, he kept as withdrawn as possible.

"—if we moved to a city, a real city, Treverorum or Lugdunum or Burdigala, someplace with intelligent people, books, supplies."

"I have my duty here," he snapped. And no wish whatsoever to become one more drop in a bucket.

"A decent house, at the absolute least!"

That had ignited their first quarrel, and others afterward. She refused to leave the manorial one. True, she could far better work in its well-lighted and hypocaust-heated rooms. But for his part, he would not move in with her. He declared that his proper station was inside Confluentes, readily accessible to his people, quickly able to reach any trouble. His private self knew it would feel wrong, like some sly betrayal. They settled on her spending her days there, most of her nights here; but she hated these rough quarters and kept trying to change his mind.

"My lord and lady, your meal awaits you." The servant came as a deliverer, Gratillonius thought wryly.

His mood grew mellower as he went in with Runa, sat across from her—in the other place they would have reclined side by side, Roman style—and shared food and drink. She too seemed glad to have escaped a fight and anxious to let the newest scratches heal. They could converse interestingly, as he could with few men. This evening she asked him to tell her what he knew about the Goths.

That was not a great deal. Their tribes were divided between a western and an eastern branch. Wandering down from Germanic lands, they had settled in regions north of the Danuvius and the Euxinus. Later the thrust of a wholly wild and terrible breed, the Huns, caused them to seek refuge among the Romans. They proved to be formidable soldiers, especially as cavalrymen, but untrustworthy subjects, apt to rebel. Most became Christian, though of the Arian persuasion....This led on to Gratillonius's experiences with other barbarians, Scoti and Picti, in Britannia, and thus to recollections of his boyhood.

Aye, he thought in Ysan, I ought to stand grateful for the good she does. 'Twas not only loosing me from the dread of the King's ancient captivity. However, that was wonder enough, and— She's fair to behold, like a dark-eyed ivory hawk; and if she lacks such ardor as certain of the Queens gave me, still, she is a woman.

At the end, he smiled and asked, "Shall we to our rest? The hour is indeed late, and I'd liefest not be overwearied."

She looked away. "I'm sorry," she replied in Latin. "The moon forbids."

He sat straight up on his bench. "No, wait. That was—a dozen days ago, I think."

"You know what I mean," she said.

He did. She wanted no child to weigh her down, endanger her life, and burden her for years afterward. So she had told him, one night during which his anger grew flame-hot and hers snow-cold.

Resentment lifted afresh. "Go back to the manor, then. I'll send Udach along with a light for you."

She met his look almost calmly. "Not that either," she murmured.

We draw too near the edge, too often, Gratillonius thought, and accompanied her to their bedroom.

She set down the candle she had borne from the dining table and turned around toward him. Has she decided otherwise? he wondered. Gladness came to a glow. He stepped closer. "Earlier I talked of being spoke to your hub," he laughed. "Suddenly I see how right that was."

She raised a palm. "No. Not thus." The thin lips curved. "But I do want you to be happy."

He could have forced her. That would doubtless have been the end of their association. Ysan women were seldom submissive. He stopped and let her approach him.

What followed slaked the flesh but left him feeling unfulfilled. He slept lightly, several times waking from dreams where someone kept calling him.

—The slightest wan glimmer showed through a crack in a shutter. He knew he would sleep no further. Runa did, and for a little while he lay by the warmth of her, but restlessness drove him to his feet. Fumbling in murk, he found his tunic on its peg and slipped it over his head against the chill. Knee-length, it would serve. He wanted fresh air.

Beyond the door he saw houses nearly formless among shadows. The east had barely lightened. No sunrise could break through such

cloud cover. It was the Birthday of Mithras. Gratillonius rarely saw a
calendar, but everybody knew when solstice happened, and from that
he could reckon this day.

How leaden it was. Not that that mattered. He had forsaken Mithras
as Mithras had forsaken him. Yet his mind flew off across years, to a
young man on the Wall, and another who hailed the same dawn and
met him at sunset for prayers. O Parnesius, comrade of the heather,
it's been so long. Where are you now? Are you now, any more?

~ 2 ~

Spring cast green over the low land around Deva. Trees budded
and bloomed, sudden amazing whiteness, as if bits of the clouds that
wandered overhead had drifted to earth. Birdflocks were returning.
Showers left rainbows, sparkles, and clean new smells.

On a small and sparsely wooded hill, men fought. Shouts, yells,
footfalls, blasts on horns, rattle and clash of metal, hiss of arrows, thud
of slingstones frightened robins and finches from their nests. Carrion
crows flapped watchful. A mile away, the city walls mirrored their rose
hue in the river gliding past them. Round about, smoke stained heaven
where villages lately sacked and torched still smoldered.

Far outnumbered, the Romans made the hill a strongpoint whence
they cast back wave after Scotic wave. They made the trees their fellows
in the shield-rank, as if they had grown roots of their own. When a
man sank, one behind dragged him dead or alive inside the square
and took his place. Mail-clad bodies nonetheless sprawled or, hideously,
moved and moaned on the torn sod farther down. Most of the fallen
wore much less, coat and breeches or only the kilt, some among them
naked. Blood seemed twice red on their lily skins. Sweat and death
bestank the air.

Again Niall shouted to his warriors and led them in a rush. Bones
broke under his feet. Once a loop of gut from an opened belly wrapped
around his ankle. He kicked it off without slowing. Helmets gleamed
ahead. His blade leaped up, down, right, left. A hostile point struck
into his targe. Before the hand behind could pull it free, that hand
dangled from a wrist cut halfway through. Niall drove the screaming
creature before him, onto its back. He was into the Roman line. A
banner on a pole hung before his eyes. He would hew his way there
and cast it down.

Shields pressed against him. Swords reached from around them.
The sheer weight forced him off. The line closed anew. Breath quick
and harsh in his throat, he backed down the slope. The men of Ériu
washed past him.

They rallied as before in the swale below, killed accessible enemy
wounded, did what they could for their own, clustered around their
tuathal chiefs. A certain quiet fell. Their will and courage stayed high,

but again they had taken hurts and losses without victory, and needed a rest. They sat or lay widespread on the damp ground. Waterskins went among them.

"I got a look this time," said Uail maqq Carbri. "They haven't much left to call on. A few more charges, and we'll open gaps they can't fill."

"Those will be costly, darling," Niall warned, "and may take us past nightfall." He scowled at the westering sun. No moon would rise until a sliver did shortly before daybreak. He would be unwise if he made any assault in the dark. It would give the Romans, who worked together like arms and legs on a single man, too much advantage. Moreover, the bravest among his lads was prone to terror at night, when anything might stalk abroad. Let fear take hold of the host, and at best they would stumble over each other as they fled wailing back to camp. At worst they would scatter blindly and morning would find most of them alone, ready prey for the Britons.

Was it mere bad luck that had brought that troop here? The word from his spies had seemed a promise from the Gods. The legion that, time out of mind, had lived in yonder city was to leave. As soon as the season allowed, it would march out, across Britannia to a southern seaport, and embark for war across the Channel. Already depleted, the two that stayed behind could hardly garrison Deva too. Until the Romans got together a new force, if they were able, that whole rich countryside, hitherto almost untouched because of the legion, lay like a virgin defenseless. Niall would be the first man there.

And so he had been, with hundreds at his back. Daring the treacherous tides and sands at the rivermouth, they brought their currachs upstream. From the tents they pitched they ranged forth, raping and reaping. Horsemen with bows and spears slowed them, but they drove those off and had not seen any for a pair of days. Niall cherished thoughts of taking the city itself, which seemed as weakly held as you might hope. But then the soldiers came down the highway from the east.

Uail's voice broke in on him: "See! I do think they are sending out a herald."

The man who trod from the enemy line wore no proper garb for that holy office, nor did he carry the white wand in his right hand and sword in his left. However, he walked slowly, mail-clad but weaponless, arms lifted. Behind him, two others winded long horns to show this was not flight or stealth.

The Scoti stared. Such of them as had snatched bow and spear let it drop. Yet those were three bold men. Where the slope began to level off they stopped and waited.

"I will speak to them," said Uail, who knew Latin well. He took time to cut and peel a branch for carrying along. A hornet buzz of voices followed him.

The exchange was brief. Uail sought back to the King and told that the Roman captain did indeed ask for a talk. Niall's heart thumped.

He kept his dignity, striding unhurried over the grass, ahead of his henchman, until he met the one newly arriving from among the foe. His torn, grimed clothing, stiff with dried blood and sweat, might have been sacral raiment.

The defender was, at least, just as smelly—and as uncowed. For a few slow breaths the two stood silent, look against look. The soldier was a strongly built, medium-tall man of about forty. His face was square and somewhat hooknosed, brown-eyed, stubble black on the big chin. Niall recognized the vinestaff and sidewise crest of a centurion. Chased with silver, the lamellar cuirass told of senior rank.

His voice was hoarse from the day's fighting, but resonant: "Hail. Shall we give oaths that whatever comes of this, both parties return unharmed?"

Niall could follow the Latin in part, though he was glad to have Uail's help. He showed more anger than he really felt. "Do you suppose I would be violating the truce of heralds? That gives me small cause to believe *you* will keep faith."

When Uail had made the response clear, the officer flashed a grim grin and said, largely through the interpreter, "Very well. We'll trust each other that far. I command the vexillation. My name is Flavius Claudius Constantinus." He uttered it in full, which Romans seldom did, as if it meant something special.

Since he gave his foeman due honor, agreement might be possible. "I am Niall maqq Echach, called he of the Nine Hostages, King at Temir in Mide, lord over my northern conquests in Ériu."

Thick brows rose. "That man? We know your name, all too well. I'd give much gold and many prayers to bring you down. Maybe I should cut the parley short and start the battle over, in hopes."

Pleased by the recognition, Niall answered, "You are free to do that. But it's we who will overrun you, and I who'll take your head home with me."

Constantinus barked a laugh. "Insolent rogue!...Render that 'Proud swordsman,' translator, or we'll get nowhere....How battle goes is in the hands of God. He's more than once cast down the high and raised up the low. But I have my men to think about. And you have yours, King Niall."

"Men of mine scoff at death."

"No doubt. However, wouldn't you rather bring them back whole, with their gains, bring them back to fight another day and breed sons for your sons to lead to other battles—rather that than leave all your bones here for the crows? That's the choice I offer you."

"Say on."

Constantinus's mouth tightened. "Ah, you're no witless animal, worse luck. Well." He put on ease, tucked staff under arm, hooked thumbs in belt, and drawled, "I'll explain. We're not such fools either. When orders came for the Twentieth to pull out, we knew pretty much what

906

would happen shortly after it did, and prepared as best we could. That included keeping our hillman allies ready. You've bounced off them before, you Scoti. Their king, Cunedag, with his cadre of Votadini, he threw your settlers out of that country once, and those who've since returned haven't done it anywhere close to him. Now he lives near Deva—d'you understand?

"The Second Legion is away south at Isca Silurum, and has that whole territory to guard. But my Sixth is at Eburacum, on the eastern side of the island. We've got our own watch to keep, against Saxons and Picti, but we can spare this many men. When we heard of your arrival, we sent to Cunedag at once. Not that he wouldn't have heard too, but we let him know we were ready to work with him. While he raised his warriors, we dispatched cavalry to harass you, and I led my infantry here by forced marches. The legions may be shrunken and weak everywhere else, but by God, we Britons can yet soldier like Romans!

"Well, here we are, our two forces. While you fight me, you're pinned down; and the Votadini and Ordovices are on their way. I expect them any hour. You can grind us down *almost* to the last man, but you'll pay for it, and what's left of you will be staggering half asleep when our foederates strike.

"Or you can withdraw, pack up your plunder, and escape. The choice, I've said, is yours."

Niall stood silent after Uail had rendered the last of the speech for him. A breeze ruffled and cooled his hair. It brought him the noises of the crippled and dying where they lay.

Did Constantinus lie? Niall thought not. He had known a greater host than his would come from the uplands with much of its own to avenge. He meant to be gone before then. He had not awaited it this soon. Yet if it were not so, why would the Romans have squandered soldiers they could ill afford? The only reason must be to keep the men of Ériu engaged until the reinforcements appeared.

A question remained. "Why have you warned us?" Niall asked. "Had you kept silent and stood fast, the net would have closed on me."

Constantinus's iron smile passed again over his face. "If I'd known beforehand whom I dealt with, I might well have chosen that," he answered. "The news took me by surprise. Too late now. And we have carried out our orders, limited the harm you did. It's not our fault Cunedag's been slower than we hoped. He's growing old. In any case, my orders also were to spare as many of my command as possible. Rome has need of them. How do you feel about yours?"

He could take that head, Niall thought. Maybe he should. Power was in this man, a smell of fate about him; if he lived, many a woman would weep. But so would they keen in Ériu for their men whom Niall had led to death afar.

907

Across twenty years, the King remembered the onslaught on the Wall in the North and what that had cost. With the ashenness in his hair had come a measure of ash-cold wisdom to his soul. And this was nothing but a raid. The plan from the first had been to depart when the Britons brought too much strength. Let the Scoti carry off honor and a goodly load of booty.

"You will have fame after this day, Constantinus," Niall said. "Maybe we shall be meeting again."

Meanwhile his fleet could harry farther up the coast. Then he must turn back and quell unrest at home. Throughout, he must stay bold but never reckless. He felt his own fate, whatever it might be, still upon him, still to be lived out. Next year— More and more, a song haunted his dreams. He had been too long away from Ys.

~ 3 ~

Governor Glabrio summoned Procurator Bacca to a private meeting. There he gave him the news that had arrived by special courier. The Visigoths were leaving Italy. After the Imperial relief of besieged Mediolanum and a drawn battle fought on Easter Sunday, they had retreated into Etruria. The Romans continued to press them and now, with members of his family captured, Alaric had made terms and his army was bound back toward Histria.

"You must confer with Bishop Bricius about arrangements for a suitable thanksgiving," said Glabrio. "The festivities that follow should emphasize the enduring power of the Roman state, under God."

"No doubt," replied Bacca. "It would be unkind to make any mention of the loose ends."

Glabrio showed irritation, as he often did at remarks by this man. "Oh? Just what do you mean by that, pray tell?"

"Why, it's obvious...to one of your perspicacity."

"I prefer frankness. Openness. Fewer of your equivocations, *if* you will be so kind."

Bacca shrugged. "The letter says nothing about the barbarians returning their loot, let alone paying reparations for their ravages. They withdraw in peace, probably not very far, to live off the country and wait for—what? One should think the redoubtable Stilicho would handle them somewhat more vigorously."

"Ah, I daresay, ah, the Master of Soldiers has his reasons."

Bacca nodded. "This isn't the first time, you recall, when he might have crushed Alaric and didn't. Does he nurse a deep plan for the longer term, in which the Visigoths are to be his allies? He's always shown a partiality to barbarian foederates that some Romans find disquieting. Of course, considering his ancestry— Another conceivable explanation is that he vacillates and cobbles together hasty improvisations, like most mortals. His preoccupation with the Ostrogothic threat in Rhaetia seems to have been what allowed Alaric to enter Italy in the first place."

"Have a care." Glabrio lifted a finger. "Indiscretion can prove costly. I will not be party to subversive talk."

"Too much discretion can be even more dangerous," Bacca said. "Men who value their necks should try to see situations as they are, not as one would prefer them to be. And," he added on a proper note of solemnity, "as a patriot one necessarily considers where the best, the strongest governance of the state may be found."

Glabrio's jowls flushed. "You speak of decisiveness. You are very fond of speaking of it. But where is yours? I must say, I expected you would join me in rejoicing and prayers—this great deliverance—not sit there with your sour naysaying. Have a care. I cannot continue indefinitely, weighted and obstructed by persons—persons who are—I refrain from calling them timid. No, they are too proud of their cleverness. They are too clever by half."

"Oh, but I share your elation, Governor. Pardon me if I gave the wrong impression. You know I am not a demonstrative man by nature." Bacca smiled. "If I keep silent while hosannahs are sung, it's because I cannot carry a tune. My station in life lies with the grubby details, none of them singly worth the attention of a leader, but collectively adding up to mountains in his path. I can then show where the passes over those mountains are, and offer suggestions as to how and when it is most expeditious to proceed. But the decision is always the leader's."

Glabrio grunted in the way that showed he was mollified. "You have something to propose," he said. "I know you."

"As a matter of fact, I do," replied the procurator. "It concerns this colony of Ysans at Aquilo." He saw fresh vexation rising, and hurried on: "Hear me out, I beg you. You've been after me to move—"

"High time. It's been two years now since I told you something must be done. And how long—more than half a year since the agent *you* chose went there and returned empty-handed."

"He was not sent as a collector," Bacca reminded. "The curials at Aquilo have been rendering the normal amounts, in both money and kind, on schedule. So the situation is ambiguous, and this is what frustrates us.

"I acknowledge, Governor, you've been a saint in your patience, especially compared to Nagon Demari. He drips venom like a viper. I've all I can do sometimes, restraining him from rash, even violent action. You understand what that could bring on. Gratillonius does have powerful...friends? At any rate, men who think they see value in him, potential usefulness. If nothing else, they want to wait and see what the decisions are on the highest level."

"None!" fumed Glabrio.

"The Imperium has other things on its mind."

"Nevertheless— Well, I should not have entrusted you with the business. You phrased your letters far too weakly. They conveyed no sense of the urgency and importance of it. Meanwhile Gratillonius does whatever he chooses, without regard to the law, like—like a foederate. An uncurbed foederate. An Alaric. How long must I endure it? Not much longer, I tell you. I will not."

"You need not, God willing," said Bacca fast. "As I've tried to explain before, I've gone ahead cautiously because of the possible consequences, should some mistake occur among all the incalculables. Despite this, I instructed Nagon to be harsh and menacing at Confluentes. That did drive the people there closer than ever to Gratillonius. He seems their only hope. But we need not fear a rebellion, like the Gothic uprising against Valens. Confluentes is a mere village. We can bide our time.

"Today, I believe, that time has come. I've been thinking hard about the matter, throughout the months when you supposed I was neglecting it. I have talked quietly with various people, such as our new bishop, and corresponded with others, and in general laid a foundation. What I waited for was an opportune moment—this moment."

Glabrio's eyes bulged. "What do you propose? When?"

Bacca made a soothing gesture. "A little more waiting, Governor, a little more patience. Today's news means that the situation will shortly be propitious for us. Stilicho will be ready, anxious, to look at countless questions he and his subordinates have perforce postponed. That includes preparing the indiction, this being the year for it. We control the local census takers; and in our report, we can make recommendations.

"The Emperor Honorius, too, will want to follow *his* victory over the Goths by a show of other actions, preferably benevolent. But as I suggested earlier, Stilicho can scarcely feel himself omnipotent. His enemies at court must be raising the same arguments I did, with far more force. He will want allies. He will be prone to agree with the proposals of important men—such as the governor of Lugdunensis Tertia. He will not examine them too closely.

"Let us compose letters to the appropriate persons. Stilicho will be among them, but we don't want anyone to feel slighted. Let us state that the Confluentian question really must be resolved. No hostility toward the good Gratillonius or his unfortunate people. None. On the contrary, we recommend an immediate grant of citizenship."

Glabrio opened his mouth to object. Bacca headed him off: "The more they depend on him, the more helpless they'll be when we break him loose from them. Because you see, the decree we request from the Emperor will include certain details, each single one entirely legal and reasonable—"

4

They were making a furnace at the top of Mons Ferruginus, where winds could blow free to help charcoal burn the fiercer, and Gratillonius was up there as often as the claims on him allowed. It was a chance to work with his hands—things were so much more forgiving than men and women—as well as to see a hope abuilding.

Iron ore was not far to seek, but no one since the Roman conquest had gone after it. Purchase from slave-manned works elsewhere was easier, cheaper. Now you could rely on importation no more, unless by yourself. Best would be to make your own, and trade off the surplus at a profit. Olath Cartagi, who had been apprenticed to a dealer in metals in Ys, got the idea. He found a man who knew the art to be his partner. Apuleius lent them money and Gratillonius gave all the support he was able.

This went beyond a single enterprise, Gratillonius knew. A ready supply of iron would call up blacksmiths, whom Confluentes needed. Their products would serve other new industries. The colony would in time become a city—not mere inhabitants herded together.

He supposed sufficient ground had been broken to feed them, clothe them after a rough fashion, buy minimal necessities and pay taxes in kind. But with nothing else, it meant a peasant's existence, presently a serf's, never better than an animal's and ofttimes worse. Into oblivion would go every skill, dream, memory, freedom that had formed the soul of Ys. And Julia's first child was swelling within her, his grandchild that he could dare to love.

Take hands off ards, spades, sickles, aye, women's hands too when the power of creation dwelt within them. Do it before toil irreparably thickened fingers and blunted minds. Coppersmiths, goldsmiths, jewelers—masons, sculptors, glassworkers—weavers, dyers—merchants, shippers, seamen, fresh growth in the trade Aquilo already did—civilization, and the strength to ward it!

Here on this height was a beginning.

Olath straightened, rubbed the small of his back, blew out breath like a weary horse. "Enough for today," he said.

Gratillonius nodded. With surrounding trees cleared away, he had a view down wooded hillside whose green glowed transient gold, across the flat strip along the Odita, over the burnished surface of that water and croplands beyond. After a warm day, mistiness obscured the western horizon and turned the sun into a huge ruddy shield. Air cooled fast; sweaty garments clung clammy. Smoke from fires smothered their acridness, though, and muscles, relaxing, felt less exhausted than sated. It had been a good day's work.

Olath waved and shouted: "Pack it away!"

The gang grinned and busied themselves preparing the site for abandonment till tomorrow. Most of them had been engaged in the various jobs of cleaving and dressing stone to line the smelting pit and its drains. Earlier they had hauled the raw material in, a couple of menhirs which had stood nearby since ages that myth had forgotten. At first such disregard for the Old Folk shocked Gratillonius, then he realized how his years in Ys had wrought on him. The claims of the living outweighed any by the dead. Confluentes would need stone too as it burgeoned, for pavement, better buildings, stouter defenses, the cathedral church that Corentinus planned.

"I should stay and help," Gratillonius said, "but must go bathe and change clothes ere dark. Maeloch's leading several headmen on the tide, from fisher villages. He sent a runner this morning. We're to speak of joint undertakings, in work as well as patrol against pirates. 'Twill keep me occupied a day or two."

"You honor me in explaining, lord King," said Olath, "but 'tis needless. You're no common laborer."

"He has the shoulders for it, he does," laughed another Ysan who overheard.

Gratillonius smiled and started down the trail. How splendid that such a man, after everything he had lost and endured, could again crack a joke.

His mind ran ahead of him. Food, drink, lodging for the guests—the better he entertained them, the more willingness he could hope for. As yet, Confluentes could not carry a full share of the load he wanted borne; and Apuleius was not free to commit Aquilo even to so loose an alliance. Well, sailors should be content with heartiness at a feast. It was doubtless for the best that Runa refused to take part. ("Shall I be matron—head servant—to a pack of stinking tribesmen?") Julia had stepped in, dear dutiful Julia.

Gratillonius sighed. More and more he wondered why he continued the union. A woman in his bed; lively conversation sometimes, when otherwise he would be lonely or among dullards, but only sometimes; counsel that might prove worth heeding, but when he deemed it was not, he got an icy tirade and days of sulking. She'd resigned herself to the manual work he did; at least, she'd stopped saying it demeaned her, or anything at all about it.

He came down to the riverside and the road toward Confluentes bridge. Half a dozen men were walking the other way. They were strangers, Celts by the look of them, dusty, shabby, wayworn. For an instant he wished he had a sword rather than an everyday knife. But no, the horrors that prowled these years were still remote. Watchers along the routes satisfied themselves that travelers were harmless before allowing them to go on. Thus far Apuleius had turned aside complaints about it from Turonum.

"Hail," said Gratillonius politely as the newcomers drew near.

"Hail," replied a man who seemed to be the leader. He peered through the sunset light. "Uh, by your leave." His Gallic dialect was

912

of the Redones. "We seek the King of Ys. They told us at the bridge he was yonder. You'd not be him, maybe, your honor?"

"Ys is gone." That hurt to say, and always would. "I am Gratillonius, tribune of those who live." Everybody halted. "What would you with me?"

They made gestures of respect which were clumsy except on the part of a blond young fellow. With a sudden thrill, Gratillonius recognized that particular salute—and the cut of the tunic, the faded patterns in the wool—this was a Durotrigian, from Britannia, neighbor to his Belgae!

"Vellano son of Drach," the leader introduced himself. He named the rest. The Briton was Riwal. "Honored to meet you, my lord."

"I've small time this evening," Gratillonius warned. "Say what you want."

"Why, leave to be your men, lord. We'd serve you faithfully, we and our kin who'll come join us. See, we're strong, healthy, we can show you our skills, and we can each of us fight also, if need be. We ask for a home, lord. For that we'll give you our oaths."

"What, have you no roofs of your own?"

He had heard the story before and learned how to draw it out. Not that he inquired too closely. Displaced farmers and unemployed artisans or laborers were one thing. They weren't supposed to move without permission which was hard to get, but when they did, quietly, as a rule the authorities mounted no search. Those who survived usually ended in servitude, which was preferable to their remaining restive, occasionally riotous freemen. Or else they became Bacaudae, altogether out of reach.

Runaway serfs and slaves were another matter. Gratillonius didn't ask, and had his ways of steering them from telling him. As yet, no census taker had visited his community.

These travelers seemed to be just what they claimed. "However, I shall have to talk further with you ere I decide," Gratillonius told them. "You understand we can't let in thieves, murderers, lepers, any such folk."

"We're none like that, lord."

"For your part, you must know clearly beforehand what's expected of you. This is not a nest of barbarians."

"We know that, sir," said Riwal the Briton. "'Tis why we've come our long, hard way."

"Longest for you." Gratillonius considered the weathered, hunger-gaunted face. "What drove you from your tribe?"

"The Scoti," Riwal said roughly. "One legion's gone, the other two spread thin and undermanned. When raiders from the sea sacked and burned Vindovaria, we wondered in our own village who'd be next. I vowed my wife and youngsters should not sit and wait our turn. We'd heard tales about safe havens in Armorica. The Gods blew a fisher from there off course and brought her, short of crew, to our little bight. I got a berth on her."

Gratillonius wondered if the man, once among the Redones, had inspired his companions to seek here or had chanced to learn of their plans and persuaded them to let him join. It seemed impossible that the fame of tiny Confluentes had drifted on the winds as far as Britannia.

No, but wait; tales of Ys; and after the city foundered, people would ask whether there had been any survivors, and pass the story—

Gratillonius would find out. Hercules! To talk with a Briton again! This was not the first one to seek refuge in Armorica. There were even some small settlements of them. But this was the first such immigrant he had met. Why, Riwal might know what had become of the Gratillonius estate back there, the Gratillonius blood. It was hard holding that blood cool, it leaped so in his veins.

"I'll get you a place for the night," the tribune said, "and somewhat to eat on the morrow. Barn straw and beggar's fare; but later we'll see what more can be done. Come with me."

~ 5 ~

Having returned from a voyage to Hivernia where he did a profitable trade along the southern shores, Evirion borrowed a horse and rode off to call on Nemeta. It was a relief to arrive at her cabin after a few hours and find no one else there. More and more folk were seeking aid of her.

Summer weighed heavy on the land. Rainfall the day before had not eased its heat, only thickened the air. Leaves hung listless, their green dulled, beneath a stone-blue sky. New clouds were massing in the west and thunder muttered afar. Muddy smells and thin haze smoked above the river, whose purling was almost the single sound going in or out of forest shadows. Garments clung to skin dank and rank with unshed sweat. Flies pestered the mount, mosquitoes the man.

Nemeta's hair seemed to burn the sullenness out of the day. Evirion sprang from the saddle as she came forth and strode to take both her hands in his. "How have you fared?" he exclaimed.

"Well enough." She looked upward into his eyes. Crinkles radiated from them; they had squinted against many weathers. "But you?"

"I likewise. No troubles, though we heard rumors of marshalling to the north. How good to see you again."

She smiled in her way, which always held something back. "The pleasure is mine. You're kindly, that you come so often."

"What else could I? You must be lonely. Will you never heed your father or me and move back into town?"

Nemeta shook her head. The unbound locks rippled over her tunic. "Nay. I have my companions here."

Once more he wondered what those were. Surely not human. While she received visitors and might go off to their homes to cast a needed spell, every tale told about her buttressed his belief that he was the nearest thing to a friend that she had among mortals. Formerly there

914

had been Runa, but she was now leman to the King of Ys, above consorting with a little woodland witch. Briefly, Evirion's lip lifted.

"What matters most, I have my freedom," Nemeta went on. When he had tethered the horse, she took his arm. "Come, let's go within where 'tis cooler. I've lately earned a cask of very good mead. Can you stay a while?"

Her slenderness, bowstring-taut, filled his vision. "As long as you will have me," he said, and felt the blood beat in his face.

She stopped, regarded him carefully, at last sighed, "I meant for hours. Best you start home ere sunset."

"Home?" broke from him. "That hovel?"

With a slight pressure, she moved him onward. "You do your house an injustice," she said, forcing a bit of merriment. "'Tis larger than this. And soon you'll be able to afford a Roman mansion."

"Why should I want one?"

They entered the cabin. Its darkishness embraced them. She gestured him to take a stool and herself flitted to the storage end of the room. "Why, you ought to be marrying and starting a family," she replied with continued cheer. "Already, I daresay, the maidens of Aquilo day-dream about you and their mothers think what a fine catch you'd be."

He tried to match her mood, or at least her pretense. "Oh, I'm too much away. We'll be gone again, my crew and I, after we've refitted *Brennilis*. And 'twill be a longer faring this time. We may have to winter abroad."

She twisted on her heel and looked wide-eyed at him. "Whither?"

"Across the German Sea, to the Cimbrian peninsula and thence, I think, up toward Thule. Amber, furs, slaves, walrus and narwhal ivory. I went there before, you recall. 'Tis a well-rewarded venture if one outlives it."

She hung her head. "But the dangers—"

He shrugged in his manliest wise. "The gains. For Confluentes too. I've talked with curials of Aquilo. They think I can sell most of what cargo I bring home, mayhap all, here. Outsiders will be drawn by it, and so we build up an emporium."

"You are...a patriot, is that the Latin word? I will try...what I can do." Hastily, Nemeta filled two cups and carried them back. "Now tell me about your newest adventures," she said with great sprightliness.

He had begun when footsteps sounded outside and a form filled the open doorway. Both of them rose. "Is it you?" Nemeta called, and made a mouth.

Cadoc Himilco entered. He was clad in Gallic style—shirt, coat, breeches of sturdy material dyed green, low boots, pack on shoulders—and armed with spear, shortsword, and bow: the outfit of a ranger in the wilderness, such as Gratillonius was making him into. "Hail," he greeted. Recognizing Evirion, he stiffened. "What do you want?"

The seaman showed the same dislike. His height and breadth hulked against the newcomer's slim frame. "Or you?" he challenged. "Help in finding your arse without a periplus?"

"Hush!" said the woman. "You're both guests. You've each visited me erenow. Sit down and we'll drink together."

Neither listened. "I am her friend," Evirion growled. "Like a brother, d'you understand? But what are you? Or what do you hope to be, your wife not knowing?"

Thinly sculptured features flushed beneath the freckles the sun had laid over them. "Curb your tongue," Cadoc snapped. "Julia d-does know. She's half-sister to this poor lost soul, after all. She'd come herself, were she able."

"Cadoc wants to win me from heathendom," Nemeta explained. "He's thrice preached Christ, these past months."

"Would that I'd oftener been free to do so," Cadoc said.

Nemeta tossed her head. "Thanks be you weren't! I've suffered it for old times' sake, but frankly, now, you've become a nuisance. Sit, and we'll talk of better things."

"Naught is better than Heaven." Cadoc turned back to Evirion. "I asked you wh-wh-what you seek here."

"And I command you stop your prying," the other man answered. His fists doubled. "Or do you want a dunk in the privy?"

Cadoc stood straighter yet. His weather-bleached hair shone like a pale lamp in the gloom. "Aye, you've the s-s-strength of body to beat me as you did aforetime. But you're soft in the spirit, Evirion Baltisi, too weak for the Faith. Else why would you bid for the help of d-demons?"

"I do not—" The mariner choked on his words. Nemeta had in fact chanted charms for him in advance of his voyages. He had expected she would again. He didn't believe they had much power, but there was a certain comfort in them, as there was in any lucky token. And it was a gift she gave him.

"I am her friend," he declared. "She's glad to see me. She's not glad to see you. Be off."

"N-n-nay. You're the one m-must go."

"What?"

Nemeta laid a hand on Evirion's arm. He stood shivering with rage.

An anger more cold, an indignation, rang through Cadoc's words and drove the stutter from them: "We know ignorant peasants come here. We pity them and mean to guide them toward the Light. What sort of example is it when you—baptized, educated, a man of means—do like them and seek out a pagan sorceress? You're derelict in your duty. Were it your soul alone in danger, I'd be tempted to turn a blind eye, Christ forgive me. But you're leading others to Satan. This must end. Now."

"And if not?" rumbled from Evirion's gullet.

"Then I've no choice but to inform the authorities. You'll be excommunicated. No Christian may have dealings with you. Think upon that, if your salvation is of no concern to you."

"Evirion, hold!" Nemeta cried. "Don't stir!"

Cadoc looked at them both. "I'm t-truly sorry," he told them, and it was in his tone and gleamed on his eyelids. "Believe me, I've no wish to p-play spy, nor any ill will. Oh, Nemeta, would you but hearken and understand, how joyfully we'd welcome you home! And you, Evirion—we've quarreled, but you are a good man at heart, and I pray you be saved from doing evil."

"Go," the seaman rasped, "ere I kill you."

"Very well. N-n-not in fear, but to keep the peace. I'll hold my lips shut too. None shall learn from me where you've been. If you come here no longer. Don't!" Cadoc pleaded, and stumbled from them.

As the sound of him died away, Evirion drained the vessel he had been gripping like a weapon. "Arrgh!" he snarled. "Give me more, lass, or I must needs smash something."

Nemeta hastened to serve him. He gulped that as well, and shuddered toward self-control.

Glowering into a shadowy corner, he said in a voice gone colorless, "The main question is where and how to kill yon insect."

"Nay, you speak madness," she protested.

"What? You'd have me obey him?"

"Not that either. My friend, dear friend, my—my brother—" She clutched his free hand. "Only be careful. And stay your wrath, I beg you. For your own sake and aye, for Julia's and my father's. And even mine."

He set the cup down and fingered his knife. "Hur-r, I suppose I can come afoot and see you unbeknownst. 'Tis a short while till I leave, anyway. But how 'twill gall!"

She nodded. "I'm angry myself. I'll be casting the wands to see whether— Yet because of those others, and simple prudence, we'll do naught harmful, either of us. Will you swear to that?"

He shook his head. "I'll give you my word for this span of time. After I return, what I do will hang on what happens. If that sniveler stays in my way, I'll smash him."

"Or I will make an end of him myself, should he force me to it," she said, a hiss in the words.

XII

~ 1 ~

"You are most hospitable, Senator," said Q. Domitius Bacca. "It encourages. In all candor, the governor and I had feared a certain amount of...reluctance. But clearly everyone present has the interests of Rome paramount in his heart—or hers, my lady. Excellent. They are the interests of civilization itself, you know."

Wind hooted and dashed rain across roof tiles. Though the hour was at midafternoon, murkiness filled windows and sneaked around the flicker of wax candles. The hypocaust in Apuleius's house had overheated the triclinium. Gratillonius longed to be outside, alone with the honest harshness of autumn.

Shadows deepened the lines in Bacca's gaunt visage. His glance went to and fro around the party reclining, antique fashion, at the dining table: Apuleius, neat gray man nearsightedly squinting; Corentinus, whose rawboned length fitted ill into a gold-trimmed robe suitable for this occasion; Gratillonius, who looked trapped in his own best garb; Runa, modestly clad and given to fluttering her lashes downward, but with hair upswept in such wise at to show off swan throat and ivory complexion, the blue-blackness of it caught by a shell comb inlaid with nacre.

"We are delighted ourselves," said Apuleius without warmth, "that the procurator has deigned to visit us in person."

"Ah, but you deserve the favor." Bacca took a sip of wine. "Aquilo is by no means insignificant; and after the tragedy of Ys, Christian charity requires that the government take Confluentes under its special, loving ward."

Corentinus cleared his throat. Gratillonius suspected that was to head off an oath from his seafaring days. "The Church might best judge what's charity and what isn't," said the bishop. "Suppose we get straight to business."

Bacca raised his brows. "At our meal? That scarcely shows respect for the tribune's generous welcome." He smiled and nodded toward Runa. "Nor for our lady."

In this light it was hard to tell whether she flushed or not. Gratillonius knew how she resented being patronized, and admired the restraint of her reply: "Since the procurator has done me the honor of requesting my presence, as if I were a man, I should take whatever my share

918

may be in the discussion—though God forbid I go beyond what beseems a woman."

Maybe he didn't admire, Gratillonius thought. This was no time to toady. What had become of the independence she claimed so often from him? Anger boiled acrid in his belly.

"Well, perhaps I should make my reasons for that quite clear," Bacca said. "The word I bring—the Imperial decree concerning Confluentes, and the governor's intended measures for carrying it out—it means great and sudden changes in people's lives. You leaders must guide them, keep them in paths of virtue and obedience. This will admittedly be difficult. I have come to explain, aid, and oversee the beginnings. Ysans were used to consulting with their wives, and believed their Queens had supernatural powers. Now, of course, they know the truth. But old habits die hard; and I am sure the women do have counsel as well as influence to lend us. My information is that you, my lady, stand highest among them in both rank and regard. Therefore we need your help."

Apuleius cast a glance at Gratillonius. "Two others were princesses," he reminded.

"I know," said Bacca. "But—correct me if I am wrong—my understanding is that one of them is very near her time. If nothing else, it would be unkind to make demands on her beyond the holy ones of motherhood. The second is...unavailable. Is that right, Gratillonius?"

How much have his spies told him? swept through Nemeta's father. Too damned much, for certain. If I could run a sword through that slippery windpipe!

It would be useless. Worse than useless. Gratillonius sagged onto his elbow. He made his head nod.

"Well, then," Bacca continued, geniality undiminished, "I think a preliminary conference between myself and you, the key persons in these little communities, is desirable. I can spell out the terms of the decree and answer questions. Together we can plan how to proceed. For it will, I repeat, be difficult at first. Beneficent in the long run, as the Emperor in his wisdom well knew; but in the early stages, a test of your capabilities and, may I say, your loyalty." He found his target across the table. "Yours especially, Gratillonius."

~ 2 ~

Once, beyond the Wall of Hadrianus, a detachment he had led forth on a scouting mission marched into ambush. The Romans fought their way to a hillcrest and formed up, but the wild men were many and the centurion could hope for no more than to take a number of them with him. While the enemy swirled and howled about, gathering for a rush, he looked through rain at the painted bodies and wet iron and wondered where the years of his life were gone.

Providentially a larger band from the Sixth, under Drusus, heard the racket and quick-stepped toward it. All of a sudden a Roman standard blew brilliant above the heather, a tuba sounded, and the javelins flew. Gratillonius took his men back down, and the squadrons cut themselves free.

Now he stood on another high place and yonder stood Drusus, but there could be no rescue, not for either of them, ever again. They had not even any foes they could kill. And where had the years gone?

This market day shone bright. Clouds scudded over the blue, wavelets ran upon rain puddles, the woods tossed and distantly roared as the wind bit into them, leaves broke free of yonder red-brown-yellow minglement and scrittled across fields, the last migratory birds trekked aloft with cries ringing as cold as the air, all the world seemed to be in departure. That, at least, was right, thought Gratillonius.

From the top step of the old manor house, his basilica that had been, he saw his people that had been. Here and there a face leaped from the crowd into his vision, like a blow on the shield he no longer carried.

Those were Suffete Councillors of his in Ys—Ramas Tyri, who spoke for the artisans; Hilketh Eliuni of the carters; master mariner Bomatin Kusuri, he of the Celtic tattoos and sweeping mustaches, who had fared overland with his King. Close to them was Amreth Taniti, captain of marines, lately grubbing the soil and the bitterness of it eating him away. Olath Cartagi, ironmaker, nourished a cheerfulness that was about to be taken from him. Maeloch and his woman Tera had elbowed to the front, as near Gratillonius as they could get. Cadoc Himilco was at their side, forgetful of status, half of him off with Julia where she lay in labor.

They trusted their King. And so did others. He made out new settlers, Vellano of the Redones, Riwal from Britannia, and more. He recognized Bannon, headman of Dochaldun, with fellow Osismii who had heard that this day's market would deal in omens. Even the numerous Aquilonians stared expectant.

Some persons were missing. Gratillonius didn't know whether he wished they were here or not. Nemeta, off in her pagan hermitage. Evirion Baltisi, supposedly among the Northmen if he lived. Rufinus, whom Maeloch had ferried to Mumu in Hivernia, where he would spend the next months gleaning intelligence on Niall of the Nine Hostages—for whatever good that might do now—

Bacca leaned slightly toward Gratillonius and said in his ear, "I suggest you commence." The latter forced a nod. Bacca assumed an erect stance. In his toga he was like a marble pillar. Did Runa watch from within the house? No doubt. She'd been so gracious to the procurator, so attentive to his every word. Gratillonius had gone riding, chopped firewood, busied himself in his workshop.

Well, get it over with. He raised his right arm. The buzz and stir before him died out. His voice rolled forth.

Surprised, he found it hurt less than the rehearsals in his mind. He felt himself almost outside the thing that spoke.

"People of Confluentes—" He must use Latin while Bacca listened, who had no Ysan nor, likely, Gallic; for Bacca would report. "—of the whole municipality of Aquilo—" How far did those bounds go? The Imperial will was that this entire region come under close control. "I have the honor to present to you the procurator of your province—" That was the proper form, wasn't it, for a lord of state? "—decided I should give you the news, rather than one of your officials, because you're most familiar with me—" They must hear it from his mouth, which had made such brave noises earlier, that he surrendered.

"Rejoice! In his wisdom and compassion, the Emperor Honorius has been pleased to receive us wholly among the Romans. By his decree, we are all of us, men, women, and children, formerly mere foederates from Ys—we are full citizens of Rome."

Shouts. Groans. A few cheers. Much stunned silence. Hurry on, hold their attention, keep them in hand.

"—I am dismissed as tribune. That title has become meaningless—" Not really.

"Nor, of course, can I or any citizen be King, in this great Republic. You may no longer call me that. Please don't embarrass me and break the law—" Maeloch spat on the ground in plain sight of Bacca.

"—I am a curial of Aquilo, by appointment. My special responsibility is to those citizens who were once Ysan subjects. Under the tribune Apuleius, as directed by our Governor Glabrio in Turonum, I have many duties for your well-being—

"—collect the taxes—

"—maintenance of public order and legality—

"—runaway serfs and slaves identified and returned to their proper places—

"—no more illicit relationships with outlaws in the wilderness. The government intends to rid Armorica of them. We must do our part—"

Bomatin folded arms and glared at his old friend. Bannon clutched the haft of his knife; he had spears at home.

Gratillonius stretched a smile across his face. "Now none of this can happen fast," he said, and heard his tone grow nearly natural. "Go on about your daily lives. Thanks to the Emperor, you have a security you didn't before. True, the taxes are high, but the needs of the state are pressing. Senator Apuleius, Bishop Corentinus, and I, we'll see to it that nobody is destroyed. We'll arrange terms, grant loans, that sort of thing. You know us; you know we'll look after you. We don't plan to make any immediate arrests, either. Everybody who wants to square himself with the law will have his chance. Stay calm. You're Romans, with the rights of Romans."

921

He cast a glance at Bacca. The man remained impassive. Gratillonius had won permission to add this slight comfort to his speech—he never would have if Corentinus and Apuleius hadn't thrown their weight on his side—but he'd departed from the prepared text, because he felt sure it would have driven the wedge between him and the people deeper yet. Not that he'd said anything forbidden, but Bacca might object to how he said it.

He caught no hint either way. Looking back to the assembly, he finished, "That's all. I'll hear whatever you want to tell me in future, and if you have a legitimate complaint I'll try to do something about it, but for now, this is all. Hail and farewell." The wind scattered his words with the dead leaves.

~ 3 ~

He shut it out when he closed the door of Cadoc's house behind him. His son-in-law was already in the foreroom, having sped there immediately after the meeting. Fine raiment, though rumpled and sweat-stained, was garish amidst rush-strewn clay floor, roughly plastered walls, thatch above ceilingless rafters. Tallow candles guttered against twilight seeping in through the membranes across windows. A charcoal brazier gave some warmth but strengthened the stench.

Cadoc sprang from his stool. "Welcome, sir," he greeted unevenly, in Latin. "G-good of you to come."

"She's my daughter," Gratillonius answered in Ysan. "How fares she?"

"It goes, the midwife said, it goes." Cadoc smote fist in palm. "But so slowly!"

"No more than usual for a first birthing," Gratillonius told him, and hoped he spoke truth. "She's a healthy lass."

"I've been praying. I've made vows to the saints." Cadoc mustered determination. "If you did likewise—"

Gratillonius shrugged. "Would the saints heed an outsider? It might turn them hostile."

Cadoc shuddered.

"Be at ease," Gratillonius counselled. "Men perforce abide these times." He grinned a bit. "Well do I know."

The stare he got made him realize his mistake. "See here," he continued at speed, "You should take your mind off what you can't help, and we've this moment alone. I'd have come sooner, but folk thrust around me, plucked my sleeve, gabbled and sobbed and yelled. 'Twas like being a wisent set on by a pack of hounds."

Cadoc ran tongue over lips. "They w-were wrathful, then?"

"Not at me. I misspoke myself. I meant that they...clung." Through Gratillonius's head growled Maeloch's voice, *"By every God there may be, ye be still the King of Ys."* And Maeloch's Tera had flung her stout arms about him and quickly, savagely kissed him on the mouth. He

922

gusted a sigh. "How can I make them wary? We're off on a foreign road."

"The road of Rome," said Cadoc slowly. "I understand. They must learn the way to walk it, and...you must be their teacher."

"If I can." Gratillonius began pacing, side to side, fingers clenched against each other at his back. Footfalls thudded, rushes rustled. "I fear that what Rome orders me to do will slay what faith most of them seem yet to have in me—a faith I suspect surprised Bacca, and one he will seek to make me destroy."

"You have experience, sir, in...in balancing demands against each other—you, the K-k-king of Ys."

"No more. And that was different. We were sovereign, the Nine and I. Oh, we must take Rome into account, most carefully into account; and of course I bore my duty toward her, I, an officer, a son of hers. But still, we were free in Ys. How do they handle it here?"

"They do as their superiors bid. Nay?"

Gratillonius barked a laugh. "I know better than *that*." His small levity flickered out. "Well, we can't allow rebellion."

"What would you have me do?" Cadoc asked.

Gratillonius stopped before him. Out of turmoil, decision crystallized. "Why, carry on your survey, along with such other rangers as we can trust to be quiet about it. Naught unlawful there. However, we'd liefer they don't hear of it in Turonum, eh?"

Cadoc opened and shut his mouth before he could reply, "Then you mean to g-go on weaving your net of defense? But you can't! It calls for the outlaws in the wilderness, and—and you, we, we're to hunt them down."

"I have no plan," Gratillonius snapped. "Everything may well come to naught. But I said we're not forbidden to keep exploring the woodlands. Nor are we yet commanded to take positive action against their free dwellers, and I doubt any such orders will be forthcoming soon." Memory of army days bobbed from the depths. He seized on it as a man overboard might grab a plank. "If they do, well, belike I'll find myself unable to execute them fast or thoroughly. Meanwhile, soldiers at war may parley. I'll be talking with those old bandits—through Rufinus, when he gets back— Ere then, I can only sit still. Agreed?"

Cadoc traced a cross in the air. "You run a terrible risk, sir."

"Blind obedience holds a worse one. Think. You know what's begun happening again along our coasts. Nay, you don't really, you've not seen it—I have in the past—but you've heard tell. Unless we ready ourselves, one day barbarians will come up this river too. What then of your wife and children, aye, your precious church? Are you with me?"

"I'm not afraid."

Gratillonius heard the offendedness and admitted it was justified. Cadoc had totalled months, oftenest by himself, in the country of wolves.

923

"B-but prudence, sir," the young men went on. "God's will. Th-those men He has chosen to set above us—"

The inner door opened. The midwife entered. Her hands were washed but her apron speckled with red, that looked black in the candle-light. At her bosom she carried a swaddled bundle.

"Christ help us!" Cadoc beseeched.

From the burden lifted a tiny wail. The woman smiled. "Here's your son," she said in Ysan. "A fine boy. His mother is well."

The men crowded close. Ruddy and wrinkled, the infant sprattled arms outward. His hands were like starfish.

"God be praised," Cadoc moaned.

"Go see her if you will," said the midwife. "Be not affrighted by the blood. 'Tis no more than you'd await. I'll cleanse and make the bed fresh and she can rest till she's ready to nurse. A brave girl, she, hardly ever cried out, aye, true daughter to the King of Ys—"

The men scarcely heard, being already on their way inside.

The bedchamber was a cubicle set off from the main room by walls, or curtains, of wickerwork in the rudest Celtic manner. It stank from the hours of labor. Shadows fell thick over Julia where she lay, but sweat gave her face a sheen. Reddish-blond hair was plastered lank across it. Her eyes were half shut. Cadoc bent above. "Darling," he breathed. "I'm s-s-so happy. I'll make devotions for us both and, when you're churched, we'll hold a feast of thanksgiving."

Gratillonius stood aside. He didn't think he quite belonged here. But her gaze found him and she gave him a drowsy smile.

The midwife bustled in. "Now, out, out," she fussed, "and let me care for the poor dear. Go admire your get. But handle him not, d'you hear, till I've shown you how....Oh, but my lord, you'll know. I'm sorry."

Back in the main room, Cadoc leaned over the infant. "My son," he murmured. That had been forever denied the King of Ys. He straightened. "Your grandson, sir."

"Aye, so he is," Gratillonius said. Because he must say something.

"I shall give thinks. Many thanks to Heaven. Would you—" The question trailed off.

"Nay, I'd best be on my way. I'll call tomorrow. When you find time, think upon what we've spoken off. Goodnight."

It was a relief to step out into the cold and the wind of dusk. The lanes between houses were blessedly empty. Gratillonius started toward his dwelling.

How wonderful that Julia had come through her battle unscathed—though you were never certain till days afterward—and she had known her father and smiled at him. She always was a sweet child. He'd done well to name her after his mother. Did that Julia look down this night from the Christian Paradise she'd yearned for, and reach a hand in blessing above her son's grandchild?

924

The parents were going to christen him Johannes, weren't they? Aye, Julia had told Gratillonius that a while ago, awkwardly. "If 'tis a boy, we'll call him after the Baptist. His day was our wedding day, you know." Gratillonius had silently hoped for a Marcus, his own father's name. He doubted the reason for the couple's choice was pure sentiment. Julia would have made that up after the fact. Cadoc simply wanted a powerful patron. Or so Gratillonius believed.

A grandson, honestly begotten, appearing sound in every way. Rejoice. Gratillonius couldn't. Aside from being glad, in an exhausted fashion, that his daughter lived, he felt vacant. Well, he'd seldom had a worse day Later his heart might awaken. Although, in full frankness with himself and nobody else, he didn't quite like his son-in-law. Cadoc meant well, he was a kind and faithful husband, a brave and able man, but that super-piety of his— We'll see how the kid turns out, Gratillonius thought.

Light glimmered dull from his house—the front room only, one or two candles his servant had kindled. Runa was at the manorial building. She'd spent her nights there since word first arrived that the procurator and his entourage would come in person. "We must have the place worthy of him," she said. "We cannot let him think us barbarians or peasants." Gratillonius had swallowed the implication that that was how he lived. It didn't matter. He'd be too busy himself to pay her the attention she considered her due.

A man got up from the wall bench as he entered. "Good evening to you, your honor," he said in Osismiic. "God grant all is well."

Gratillonius nodded. "It is that, we think. A boy."

"A boy, is it? God be praised. May the angels watch over his crib."

Gratillonius looked into the weathered face. This was one of the deacons Corentinus had chosen, a trusty fellow who otherwise was a boatman on the Odita. "What brings you here, Goban?"

"The bishop sent me. He'd like you to come talk with him—confidentially, you know, if your honor's not too tired."

A thrill tingled some of the grayness out of Gratillonius. He understood what this meant. Corentinus and Apuleius had both absented themselves from the assembly. Bacca had as much as told them to. "This is a matter for common workers and tribesmen. I must be on hand to impress them with the seriousness of it, but your dignity could be compromised." —and their presence could be taken as moral support of the speaker. When guests were leaving the senator that day, Corentinus had found a chance to draw Gratillonius aside and mutter, "We'll discuss this after you've endured it, we twain," in Ysan.

"I'm ready," Gratillonius said.

"He told me the hour don't matter, and he'll have a bit of supper waiting. I'll head back to my lodgings, if it please your honor." Goban winked. "Just so nobody sees us together and gets the wrong idea, right, sir?"

925

Right, Gratillonius thought as he went forth again. Not that any conspiracy was afoot. Corentinus merely wanted Bacca's nose out of it. Therefore Apuleius, who was hosting the procurator, couldn't be on hand. However, no doubt senator and bishop had gone into the matter today in private.

How to cope with the new order of things. First and foremost, Gratillonius supposed, how to keep the taxes from grinding Confluentes away. The rates Bacca brought were out of all proportion to what the colony was as yet able to produce. Apuleius could stave off ruin for a space—appeals which wouldn't be granted but which would consume time, loans from the Aquilonian treasury or his own purse, lean though both were getting—but sooner or later, one way or another, payment must be dug up. And he, Gratillonius, the curial, must do the digging. From the land and flesh of his people? No, he was their leader, their defender; but the state had forbidden him to work for their defense; but somehow—

Wind flapped the edges of his cloak and streamed chill over his skin. It brawled in trees along the river road. The water ran darkling. Light flickered across it, cast by the near-half moon that fled between rags of cloud above the western fields. Shelter waited in the bishop's house. Corentinus would surely start by asking after Julia. He'd give thanks for the safe birth, but in a few words, man to man with the saints; then he'd lead the way to his table, rough fare but hearty, and fill the mead cups, or maybe wine for celebration and defiance. It might be like old days in Ys, or at least like the time afterward when they'd worked together for the survival of the folk, before this miserable breach opened between them.

The gate of Aquilo stood wide as usual. Bacca had tut-tutted at that, the first night. Gratillonius explained there was nothing to fear, so far. Bacca made remarks about not allowing people to go in and out freely after dark, lest they be tempted to lawlessness.

The streets were, in fact, deserted save for the wind. Gratillonius passed Apuleius's home. Every pane was aglow. Nothing too good for the procurator. Runa meant to give him a banquet herself before he left. Gratillonius had been inventing excuses for not attending.

A white form flitted out of the portico shadows and down the stairs. For an instant his heart recoiled from ghosts, then he told himself sharply that no matter how weary he was, he had no business being a fool, and then she reached him and he saw, barely, by what light the moon and the windows cast, that it was Verania.

"How, what's this?" he exclaimed.

Tears glistened. "I waited," she gasped. He saw how she trembled in her mere gown, how her hair was gone disheveled. She had not dared take a cloak. Somebody might have noticed.

"Whatever for?" When had they last met, except in passing on his infrequent visits?

"T-to tell you—Gratillonius—"

How had she known he'd come by tonight? She must have overheard her father and Corentinus. Or had she listened beyond the door?

"You're *still* the King of Ys!" she cried, and whirled and ran back. He heard the weeping break loose.

Bewildered, he stood where he was. The house took her into itself and closed up again.

What a girl, he thought after a moment. Something wild dwelt within that quietness. But no, not a girl any longer, a young woman, and fair to see. What was her age now—sixteen, seventeen? More or less the same as Dahilis's when Gratillonius came to her.

Or Dahut's when she died.

It was as if the wind blew between his ribs. He hastened onward.

~ 4 ~

"You humiliated me," Runa said. "You disgraced yourself. Begging off from my feast for the procurator— You might at least have considered how that damages your position with the state. You claim so much concern for my people. But no, nothing counted besides your own wishes."

Because she had chosen to speak in Latin, Gratillonius did likewise. "I tell you again, it was urgent I go reassure those two important headmen who weren't at the assembly."

"You lie." She kept the same monotone, colder than the rain which roared outside and made blindness in the windowpanes of the old manor house. "It could have waited until he was gone."

It could have. Gratillonius had flat-out judged he'd be unable to spend any more hours deferring to Bacca. A fight would have spelled disaster.

"You simply didn't care," Runa said. "Not about me or the people or anything other than getting back among the oafs you feel comfortable with."

Despite lamps, the room was gloomy. A saint on a wall panel—big-eyed, elongated, stiff, centuries and a world removed from ancestral Rome—stared through shadows whose dance in the draft made him seem to move also, as if pronouncing an anathema. The hypocaust kept floor tiles warm, but cold air slunk around ankles and even at head level you breathed dankness.

Today Runa resembled the saint, narrow face, upright stance, implacable righteousness. "I have borne with you," she said. "I have suffered your arrogance, your brutishness, your utter lack of any consideration, hoping God would unseal your eyes as He was pleased to unseal mine. But no. You keep them shut, willfully. All that matters to you is yourself."

Gratillonius looked down at his hands and sought to curb his temper. He could slap her, but what was the use? "You're not like your mother,"

927

he told her. "She consigned me to hell in a few words. How long do you mean to go on?"

"Oh! Now you insult my mother! Well, knowing you, I shouldn't be surprised."

Somehow he felt a sudden tug of pity. We were quite close, he thought while he said the same words aloud. "Have you really turned altogether against me?" he added.

She brought fingers to bosom. "It hurts me, it hurts me more than you can possibly know. But you have already given me so many wounds. This has only been the latest of them. The last, God willing."

"Then you're breaking with me." He was about to voice the hope that they could still work in tandem.

"I am leaving this wretched place," she said.

He gaped. "Huh? How—where—"

"Procurator Bacca has most kindly invited me to accompany him to Turonum."

"What?" To taken aback for thought, he heard his tongue: "How's he in bed? I'd guess he spends the whole night explaining this will be good for the state."

She reached claws toward him, withdrew them, and clipped, "That will do. For your information, I'm finished with sin. In Turonum I'll be baptized and join the community of holy women."

Gratillonius recalled vaguely that Martinus had founded such a thing, corresponding to the monastery.

"And I shall be with civilized persons."

Aye, the tale was that Martinus's successor Bricius held that total austerity was outmoded; it became a master of the Church to live somewhat like the masters of the world with whom he dealt. Runa should do well enough—she wasn't addicted to luxury—and find congenial company in the magnates, especially as she rose to a commanding position among her women. She'd do that, he felt sure.

"The celibacy oughtn't to be any hardship," he said. That might be unfair, though in fact she had responded less and less to his attentions as time went on, and found more and more occasions to avoid them.

Color tinged those sharp cheekbones. "It is a sacrifice I pray will be acceptable to God. I have so much to atone for. Satan was everywhere. Heathendom—fornication, outright incest, with you—lending your daughter my agreement to her running off, with everything that that led to—seeking of the death of her unborn child for her—and doing away with yours, Gratillonius!"

Her look challenged him. She strained arms back and breasts forward, like a Trojan woman before an Achaean sword.

Maybe later he'd be appalled. In this hour he felt nothing beyond...a vague sense of release? "I suspected," he said tonelessly. "But I never pursued the thought, I let it skulk aside, because you were my mate and I'd cause to be thankful to you, most of all that you freed me from the ghosts of the Nine, but for other things as well."

"And you didn't care," she said after a minute. "You wouldn't. You can't. I wonder if you haven't been a penance God set me."

Derision: Is that sound Christian doctrine? Doesn't baptism wash every past sin away? It's the ones afterward that count.

"I will try hard to forgive what you've done to me," she said. "I will pray for your salvation. But I'll pray more that God not allow you to lead others astray."

"Goodbye." He turned and walked out.

He heard her follow. "What?" she yelled. "You depart like that? You haven't the simple courtesy to listen?"

"The law doesn't require it," he replied over this shoulder.

"You haven't the courage, that's what! You don't dare hear about the hurt you've done me."

I am afraid, he refrained from saying. If I stayed longer I might well strike you, and that could break your neck.

The first breath of regret touched him. "I wish things had ended differently," he confessed.

Still he didn't look behind. In the entry he retrieved his drenched paenula and pulled it over his head. The wind caught at the door as he opened it. He pushed it back shut and went off through the storm toward Confluentes.

XIII

~ 1 ~

Winter heaven hung featureless gray. Trees could well-nigh snag it in their twigs. Mists drifted through raw air. The drip off boughs was the only sound there was, save when dead leaves stirred soddenly underfoot.

Then Bannon said, "Here it is."

He did not call Gratillonius "lord" as aforetime, but it was Gratillonius whom he had sought. "I came to you myself, 'stead of sending the hunter who found the thing, because 'tis a matter for chiefs," he had related in the house. "You know about the outside world, what the Romans might make of this if they hear, maybe even who could have done it—for surely no Osismiic man would, unless he be mad." The pair of them had gone off into the forest without telling anyone else.

929

Folk shunned the spot they came to, believing it a haunt of vengeful wraiths and what was worse yet. The man from Dochaldun had only dared them, by daylight, when helping to search the woods for two children missing from the village. What he saw sent him running home while he clutched his lucky piece and babbled charms against horror.

Amidst osier and sedge crowding a pool, a boulder that looked like an altar for trolls heaved up its mass. Nearby stood a great beech. Lightning had blasted it long ago, and fire gouged out a hollow. Gratillonius squatted to peer inside. He spent a few heartbeats finding what Bannon pointed at, for it was very small, discolored nearly as dark as the char, and begrown with some of the fungus that clustered on the bark outside. In a few more years it would molder quite to nothing.

He stared into the eye sockets. "This is naught of the little ones you've lost," he said low. "They were old enough to walk. This is the skull of a suckling babe, maybe a newborn. And 'tis been here a while."

"It has that," Bannon answered firmly, "for 'tis pegged in place. No wolf does such a thing."

Gratillonius saw and felt for himself, nodded, and rose. "A human sacrifice."

"Not by any of us, I tell you!"

"Of course." Stories of bloody rites in olden times might or might not be true, but the Romans had certainly exterminated the druids in Gallia. The pagan Gods whom most rustic Armoricans still worshipped were content with fruits of the earth, the mightiest of Them with an animal on Their high holy days.

"Some madman in the past, or a stray barbarian, or who knows what?" Gratillonius said. "I'll see to the burial of this poor shard if you wish. Why should you care?"

"The children we've lost—"

"Children are forever wandering off, and not always found again. I'm sorry, but so 'tis. It has naught to do with this."

Bannon seized Gratillonius by the wrist. "*Does* it? Can you swear no black wizard goes abroad, stealing our young for his cauldron? My thorp will be wanting more than words."

Gratillonius understood. The knowledge was heavy as the sky. "You'd fain talk to Nemeta," he said.

Bannon nodded. "I'd not be recklessly accusing of her. She's done well by us in the woods." His features tightened. "But we must make sure."

"And I—"

"If she's guiltless, maybe she can find out the truth. We've hardly anything to pay her with at this season, though. I asked you along also for coming with me to her. It may help. You are a just man. We have few just men anymore."

Unspoken was the likelihood that, if the tribesmen thought she was a murderess after all and her father was trying to shield her, they would kill both.

—Flames flickered in lamps. Brightest burned a Roman one. The bronze and oil were witch-wage lately earned. Darkness had fallen as the two men reached the oak by the Stegir which Gratillonius remembered so well. Nemeta bade them come inside her cabin and spend the night before starting back.

Seated on stools, wooden cups of mead in their hands, they looked up at her where she stood. Barefoot despite the chill, she nonetheless wore a gown of finely woven wool, close-fitted to her litheness. The red hair smoldered, the green eyes gleamed through shifting shadow. It came to Gratillonius that his scrawny girl had become a woman to kindle desire; but the beauty was somehow more hawk or vixen than it was human.

"Epona hunt me through hell if I lie." Her voice moved cat-soft around the things that hung on the walls. "Never have I harmed child of yours or of any living man."

Bannon looked toward Gratillonius. Someone must say it. Gratillonius lifted the load, he felt as if it were about to break his bones, and answered, "Your own was lost, a year and a half agone."

Her gaze scorned him. "It was. Would you make trial of me? I will meet the hounds, or whatever ordeal you name, and the Gods will uphold me."

"Nay, I meant not that!" he croaked in Ysan.

"You are a witch—" Bannon stopped short. Nemeta played her glance over him and fleetingly grinned. Unless a Power intervened, she would be safe in any test that called on the World Beyond.

The chief cleared his throat. "None of us want to blame you," he said. "'Twould be ill for us too." Again she grinned. If the Romans heard of manslayings to pagan Gods, they might well send soldiers to strike down men and burn down homes. "But must we go in dread this'll happen afresh, or has happened? Can you find our little ones for us, wisewoman?"

Nemeta shook her head. In the uneasy light, Gratillonius could not make out whether compassion crossed her face. "I've been asked the same erenow," she said. "Maybe in later years; but as yet my arts are slight, and—the forest Gods keep the secrets of Their beasts."

"The killer, then. Can you track him for us, that we may make an end of him?"

She stood still a while. Through the shutters they heard an owl hoot, once, twice, thrice.

"He's a dangerous one to deal with," she said slowly, "for an offering like that, if made aright, feeds strange strengths. I've doubt I can cast a net over such a man. Yet surely we should rid the land of him. And soon, ere his might grows more."

931

Gratillonius read meaning in her tone. Fear stabbed. Bannon understood too, in fierce joy, and exclaimed, "You know who he is?"

"I do not," Nemeta answered. "I only know who he might be, and I could be mistaken."

"Who?"

"Cadoc Himilco, the trailmaker from Confluentes."

Gratillonius dropped his cup and leaped to his feet. "Nay, this is moonstruck!" he roared in Ysan. "Have done!"

Bannon rose beside him, to say with hand on knife, "Let her speak."

"But he—I know him, you do yourself, Nemeta, your own sister's husband," Gratillonius stammered. "And a Christian."

"He has indeed plagued us with his Christ, has he not?" Nemeta said to Bannon.

The Gaul nodded. "He has. A pest. A threat, maybe, he talks of overthrowing the shrines. But—"

"Men have lied about their faith often enough," Nemeta said. "Some did out of fear, others—well, Cadoc does range the wilderness wherever he likes. Who knows what he does there, or why? I've had feelings about him that crawled within me."

"Why, you need only talk with him to know him sinless," Gratillonius protested.

"Unless you are Nemeta and have witch-sight?" Bannon growled.

She lifted a hand as if to ward her father off. "I say naught for certain," she reminded. "He may be harmless. You should hear him out."

"He's away." Sickness caught Gratillonius by the throat. "We run the survey in all seasons."

"When he returns, we will ask of him," vowed Bannon.

Nemeta smiled. "Meanwhile, best keep silence about this," she proposed.

Gratillonius knew that would be impossible, once Bannon brought home the tidings.

~ 2 ~

Daily the rumor grew. Gratillonius became fully aware of it when Julia came to him weeping, half crazed. "They mutter those things about Cadoc—one loyal maid warned me, one—I listened when they knew not I was nigh— What will become of him? Of our Johannes? Oh, father—"

He held her close, consoled her to the pitiful degree he was able, at least got her quieted by his promises, then went to Corentinus.

"I've heard," the bishop said. He had ears in many places. "Of course it's baseless. Those children simply fell prey to misfortune, and as for the babe that was sacrificed, Christ Himself would testify to Cadoc's innocence. But pagans live without His comfort, you know.

They're all too apt to see magic and malice at work when anything goes wrong. These endless winter nights drive everybody a bit crazy, too. Hatred is easier to live with than fear; it gives you someone to attack. And...I'm afraid Cadoc has made himself disliked among the backwoodsmen. He's been too zealous. Evangelism isn't his proper calling. I'll speak to him about that."

"If you get the chance," Gratillonius replied. "How can we even protect him, let alone clear his name?"

Corentinus sighed. "I myself have hardly any voice among the pagans. What you could do—" The eyes beneath the tufted brows pierced. "You could search out the true guilty party, hiding nothing. If you will."

Gratillonius left as soon after that as possible, and turned to Apuleius. The senator received him kindly enough, though somewhat abstractedly. The latest news received was of still another setback in his effort to have the taxes on the Confluentians lowered. The Germanic menace smothered it. Official alarm had redoubled since Emperor Honorius, after the Visigothic invasion of Italy, moved his capital from Mediolanum to Ravenna, where landward marshes gave added security and the sea offered ready escape to Constantinople. Not but what the danger wasn't real. With the defenses of the Rhenic frontier weakened and the tribes beyond it ever more restless, the praetorian prefect had grown impatient with lesser claims on his attention.

"My heart goes out to your daughter," Apuleius said. "And her husband, when he returns to this grisly business. But what can I do? Keep him under guard, day and night? We haven't the guards to spare, you know. Best we send him, them, to live elsewhere. I can try to arrange that."

"If he isn't murdered in the woods on his way back," Gratillonius said.

"God forbid. I'll pray. If you would also—"

Again Gratillonius made an early farewell. Since Runa departed, constraint had diminished between him and the other two men, but the old cordiality had not risen from its grave. It would be hard having Julia move away. Hard on her too. What roots she had left were in Confluentes. And what kind of living could Cadoc make, out among the Romans? Lacking status, money, or skills that anybody wanted to hire, he might well end by selling himself and his family into slavery.

If only Rufinus were here. How sharply Gratillonius missed the rascal. There was a barrier there too. Somehow, in spite of all they had been through together, they were never really near each other in the way in the way that Gratillonius and Parnesius had been. It was as if Rufinus somehow feared complete openness. Because he felt guilt about the catastrophe of Ys? Gratillonius had told him over and over to forget that. Maybe he couldn't. Or maybe what happened to him in his early youth had forever scarred his heart.

933

He was always ready with counsel, though. He'd find some fox-trail out of this trap, if anybody could. But what?

My mind is so slow, Gratillonius thought. Well, if it keeps plodding along, it may finally get somewhere. Up on your feet, soldier.

That night he lay awake till the east whitened, and this was around midwinter. Back and forth he trudged through the blindness, about and about, to and fro, from thing to thing, and found no answer. A couple of times he wished Runa were at his side, or any woman, that he might lose himself in her and afterward sleep. Otherwise he had decided he didn't miss her. And he had no right to go rutting indiscriminately like a common roadpounder on furlough. He was on duty, he the centurion....

When he woke from a doze, at midday, he had no revelation. He merely opened his eyes and saw something that might work. He mulled it over while he made his preparations by what sunlight was left, and then got a good night's rest. Stars were still brilliant overhead as he left Confluentes.

He would rather have ridden Favonius, but his way led him by paths that were often barely useable by a man on foot, into the forest. Darkness was grizzled when he reached the hut of Vindolenus.

The former Bacauda and his wife made the visitor welcome. They brought forth the best food and drink their meager stores held. A couple of years ago they'd begged the King of Ys to lay hands on their oldest son, and the boy had indeed recovered from his fever. Gratillonius doubted his blessing had anything to do with that. Nevertheless, now he called in the debt.

"You've heard the tale about my son-in-law being a sorcerer who steals children and offers them to his demons?" he asked.

The backwoods dweller reached uneasily for a small thunderstone, spearhead-shaped, such as folk sometimes found and believed to be lucky. He rubbed it. "I've heard a little, lord," he mumbled.

"It's false. Do you hear? I, the King of Ys, swear it's false."

"Well, if you do, lord, then surely it is."

"He should be on his way home from his latest scouting. I must find him ere anybody else, bring him to safety, and show the folk he's blameless. Can you guide me?"

"M-m-m." The lean countenance drew into lines of thoughtfulness, the faded eyes looked afar. "If you've a notion whereabouts he may be, north or west or east o' here—m-m-m, the trails, the streams—" Cautiously flickered the eagerness of a hunter. "I can try, lord."

"And afterward keep silence, you, your woman, your children. By the Gods of the land and the Gods of hell, you shall."

Vindolenus seemed almost affronted. "Lord, I learned from the Romans how to hold my tongue, and I've taught my household. Think you we'd blab to a herd of scruffy tribesfolk?"

Gratillonius saw no reason to tell how much he himself needed secrecy. He was dealing with one of the men whom Rome commanded him to hunt down. His hope had been that thus far they didn't expect he would. Must he in fact, later, break faith with them?

~ 3 ~

His hounds roused Drusus in the middle of the night. They bayed, deep ringing threat, and strained against the staves of their pen. He took his old military sword from the wall, a tallow candle in his left hand, and went forth into the drizzing dark. Men of his had already surrounded the newcomer. Their weapons were lowered. Drusus saw why. "Gratillonius!" he exclaimed. "What the devil are you doing here at this hour? Where've you been, anyway? I heard you were gone from town these past ten days."

"That long?" said the unkempt, travel-stained man. "I wasn't counting. No matter. I came out of the woods not far from here and thought my friend would give me a doss till tomorrow."

"Of course, of course. Come on in. We'll heat up some wine, how about that? And talk, if you're not too tired. Plenty of night to sleep in afterward, this time of year, eh?"

—In the morning Drusus told his wife that he and their guest would take a few hours' walk into the forest as far as the Stegir. While on his errands, Gratillonius had seen spoor that looked promising of big game. They'd bring two hounds, otherwise go alone.

After they returned, Drusus said that he had been shown traces of wisent. The beasts had long since grown rare and, in spite of their size, shy. He didn't want people hallooing around scaring these two or three off. "Stay out of the woods for now, everybody, you hear? I'll go by myself during the next few days and see whether the dogs turn up anything. No grumbling. You heard me. If the buffalo really are still hereabouts, we'll get up a hunt."

Gratillonius returned to Confluentes next morning on a horse lent him. When he was gone, Drusus told his wife: "He didn't want to talk about it much, but the reason he went off alone like that was this business of the child killings. He couldn't stand any longer hearing—no, not hearing, but knowing about the whispers. His daughter's husband!"

"It is horrible," she said. "Do you think Cadoc is guilty?"

"I hate to suppose so, but—well, where there's smoke, there's fire, eh?" Drusus shook a fist. "Body of Christ! Whoever the murderer is, I'd feed him to my hounds!"

"But if he is a magician as they say, can't he stop them?"

"Not when God binds him and his spells. We'll do this like Christians."

In the following several days Drusus said more in the same vein to the household, the neighbors, and on a visit to town. His vehemence surprised those who had known him as easygoing in matters of faith.

Well, naturally, black witchcraft was a different thing; and Drusus had children of his own, two of them quite young.... Otherwise he continued his searches for the wisents, trying a different brace of hounds each time, until at length he sighed that they had evidently left the area.

Any word concerning Cadoc spread far and fast, as tensely as everyone awaited his homecoming. Pagans found themselves as ready as Christians to accept a trial by ordeal, an idea that somehow came into circulation. Their Gods no more drank human blood than did Christ. If properly asked, They would surely not let such an evildoer work defensive sorcery. Many muttered that Gradlon was bound to protect his son-in-law and whisk him beyond the reach of justice. Best would be if right-minded men found Cadoc first, alone in the wilderness. Yet magic, unchecked by religious rites, might wilt a sword before it could strike. Terror closed in like the winter nights.

Thus astonishment was twofold at the next word that went forth. The suspected one had appeared in Confluentes. Not a single hunter had glimpsed him on his way. Had he flown through the air? But he met no welcome. The tribune immediately ordered his arrest on charges of murder and diabolism. The penalty was death.

Aquilo seethed at the news. Cadoc had pleaded his innocence. There were no witnesses. Sent to a Roman court, he would most likely get off. But Apuleius and Bishop Corentinus had too much care for their people. They would let their God—or the Gods—judge this case, that doubts might once for all be laid to rest.

Julia and her infant had moved in with her father. The three stayed in seclusion.

They emerged for the trial. It took place outside the wall of Confluentes. The day was bleakly bright. Ground had frozen hard and trees bore a thin, glittery leafage of icicles. Breath smoked startlingly white under the blueness above. Townsfolk, farmfolk, woodsfolk ringed the field in. They had been required to leave their weapons, and guardsmen stood about to keep order. Low in the south, the sun cast a sheen over helmets, mail, and uplifted pikes.

A shout arose. Solemnly, Bishop Corentinus led his priests out into the middle of the space. Mass had already been offered at the church; now they called on God beneath His heaven. On this day, it had been announced, pagans might also invoke their deities here, if they did so inconspicuously.

The clergymen withdrew. Apuleius conducted Cadoc forth under guard. The young man wore a peasant's smock frock, whose brown made his hair seem to glow silver-gold. He stood straight and agreed fearlessly that he would submit to the test. Senator and soldiers left him standing alone.

A breath went like a wind through the crowd. From a tent pitched by the wall, Drusus paced. He wore his legionary armor, the first time that most who were there had seen it, a vision out of the mighty past.

His right hand gripped tight a leash which held his lead hound. The rest of the pack came after, brindled gaunt beasts larger than wolves. The setting had put them on edge; they growled, snarled, snapped air as if it were prey.

Julia gripped Gratillonius's hand. The nails dug deep. He stayed mute.

Drusus slipped the leash. His call ripped aloud! "Halloo! Kill!" He pointed at the solitary figure of Cadoc.

The hounds clamored and bounded forward. Cadoc waited.

The hounds reached him. They slowed, stopped, walked around. Several whined in puzzlement. The chief of the pack licked his hand. He bowed and ruffled the terrible head before he prostrated himself in prayer.

Like a breaking wave, a shout rose from the watchers. They sought to storm into the place of the miracle. Pikeshafts held them back. That was as well, for the hounds had lost no ferocity. A man who slipped by the cordon was badly slashed before Drusus, with whip and ungodly words, got them under control. Cadoc remained lying.

The crowd surged off toward Corentinus, Apuleius, Gratillonius. Men wept side by side with their women, or laughed or cheered or sang. A few begged for baptism.

Julia fell into her father's arms. Headmen and tribesmen pushed through the Confluentians who milled about him and cried for his touch, for his wonderworking heed, he, their lord, the King of Ys.

~ 4 ~

A light snow fell. Against the blanket it laid, trees looked black. Sight soon lost them in the sifting gray-white. Murmur and gurgle of the Stegir made an undertone to silence. The air had turned almost warm. It was as if the year had finally begun to await spring.

Nemeta had swung window shutters aside and left her door open, so the stenches of the night could leave her cabin. That let in the dove-hued day. Its softness washed shadows from corners and made the instruments of witchcraft into simple, rudely fashioned things of wood, stone, skin, bone.

She and Gratillonius sat on stools opposite each other. Between them glowed a brazier to which they held their hands.

"I know what you did," she said in Ysan.

"You would," he replied as quietly.

She shook her head. "Nay. Not by magic. Mere reason. What must have happened."

"Tell me."

"You got a man of Rufinus's to help you find Cadoc. You left the two of them in a brushwood shelter not far from Drusus's farm and went to seek his help. He's your old soldier comrade, you got him his home, he'd never refuse you. Together you planted the seed of the

937

thought that Cadoc be tried by ordeal—by having the hounds set on him, as the Osismii do to the worst of their criminals—and those hounds would be Drusus's. Meanwhile he brought them piecemeal to Cadoc and taught them this was a person they must not attack. When that was done, Cadoc took down the shelter and Drusus smuggled him into Confluentes. Corentinus and Apuleius already knew what parts were theirs to play. That is how it went."

"You are a clever girl."

"Not truly. What I cannot understand is why anybody would swallow the claim of a miracle. Why did they not reason too?"

"They wanted to believe. Folk are not logical about matters that touch them deeply. You should be more among them, child. 'Tis ill to live alone."

A thrust of bitterness: "I thought Corentinus and Apuleius were honest."

"The bishop says merely that God's will was done. The three of us, with Drusus and Vindolenus, did what we deemed necessary."

"To save yon ranting pest— Forgive me, father. But to me and the tribesfolk, he is."

"He's learned his lesson. He'll stop trying to push others about in their lives." Sternly: "Therefore put down your malice against him."

"If he does leave me in peace...But 'twas a risky thing you did. It could have gone awry, and he'd have died. Why didn't you just send him afar?"

"That would have been cruel for him and his. But mainly, I think, I hope, mainly we had the people in mind, Corentinus and Apuleius and I."

"How?"

"By letting the frenzy about Cadoc grow unchecked, we choked off wonderment about who else might have slain the babe. That could have riven kindred asunder. Then by...showing him innocent in a remarkable way, we emptied the fury out of them. It will not return. They accept, now, that their own children were lost in ordinary sad wise."

She stared long across the coals at him. "You *are* the King," she finally whispered.

He sighed. "I must not be." Starkness came back upon him. "But I do command you, master your spite. Keep silence about what we have spoken of this day. Let memory of that dead infant fade away with his little ghost. Else it could prove the worse for you, Nemeta."

She caught a sharp breath. "Do you believe I—"

He lifted a hand. "I don't want to hear more. But beware those Gods you serve."

Forlorn defiance: "You have none."

"I know."

"Oh, father," she cried, "you are the one of us that's all alone!"

She jumped to her feet and came around the smoldering fire. He rose to meet her. She laid her face against his breast and held him tightly while she shivered. He embraced her, stroked her hair, and made noises, the meaningless noises of love he had crooned above her cradle.

~ 5 ~

Willows had leaved, oak and chestnut were beginning to, plum trees bedecked themselves in blossom. Other petals colored the sudden vividness of grass, among them borage like small pieces of sky. Migratory birds were coming home.

Rufinus was back. It had been a hard journey for him, by currach from Mumu to Abonae, by ship from Dubris to Gesoriacum, and haste overland across both Britannia and Gallia. But he had not chosen to wait till later in the season when skippers would venture a passage straight over Ocean. He would bring the news to his master as early as might be.

They walked east on the river road, a place to talk unheard; and still they used Latin. On their left the Odita gleamed on its way toward Confluentes, Aquilo, and the sea. Forest rose greening beyond. On their right stretched fields also coming to life, men and oxen at work in the distance, a sight sometimes veiled by flowering dogwood. A lark piped above.

"I've adventures aplenty to relate from this winter, especially when I slipped into Niall's country. Some of them could be true," laughed Rufinus. "But they can wait. What matters is that he will most certainly be back among us this year."

Later Gratillonius would ask precisely what his man had heard and seen. However, it was clear that no barbarian king could ready a campaign in secret. Niall must have made his will known months ago and bidden warriors be ready. A chill tingle went along Gratillonius's spine. "When?" he asked.

"They'll set out very shortly after Beltene. That's what they call their spring festival, do you remember?" Rufinus's humor dropped from him, his voice harshened. "His intent is to ravage northwestern Armorica. Not that he'll have a huge fleet—nothing like the one I've heard about, that you broke—but picked crews. They'll strike and be off elsewhere on the same day. I'm sorry, but I couldn't learn much more than that. His kind generally make up their plans as they go along."

Everything we got restored during those years at Ys, thought Gratillonius. Pain twisted. "We'll warn the Duke, of course," he said with the same roughness. "Maybe he'll pay attention, though all the authorities in Turonum dislike and distrust me. It won't make any great difference, what with the condition of defenses these days."

"Wait. I do have this," Rufinus told him. "The end point of the Scotic raid will be Ys."

The pain became a sharp thrilling in the blood. "Why? To loot?"

"Mainly to destroy. The whelming didn't drown his hatred of the city. He's vowed to bring down the last stone if he can. Pirates and even traders of the clans he rules over, they have standing orders to put in whenever they come by and do some more demolishing. He himself— We can make a fair guess at when he'll arrive there."

Gratillonius nodded. "You confirm what I already thought. Tales scuttle around. You, though, you've brought the information we need about the one man we want. Good work."

"Will you tell the Romans?" Reluctance was in Rufinus's question.

Gratillonius shook his head. "Not about this. You keep your mouth shut too, so word can't drift to them. They wouldn't dare tie soldiers down, waiting to spring a trap. From their viewpoint, they'd be right. Also, Ys is nothing to them, or worse than nothing. They'd consider it a favor, getting rid of that reminder on these shores."

Rufinus waited. Gravel scrunched beneath hobnails.

"Besides," Gratillonius finished, "if they knew what I have in mind, they'd forbid it. In fact, it could give them the excuse they want to haul me off on charges of treason and behead me. Military action is reserved to the army, you know. For ordinary people to band together against their enemies, that's prohibited. I'll be calling on tribesfolk, and such Ysans as I can trust, and especially on your men, Rufinus, who are now outlaws again."

On which account he must dissemble before Apuleius and, he supposed, Corentinus. That hurt as badly as anything else. Since their conspiracy with him on behalf of Cadoc, they had quite put aside the matter of Runa. She was saved; he was not, but they could cherish hopes and meanwhile, day by day, like the land itself, friendship came back to life.

They might well admit his cause was worthy. But he could not put Verania's father at hazard.

She loved the springtime so, he recalled. After the Black Months, she broke free into joy with the dogwood and the larks. How clouded it would become if she knew what he intended. He must not let on when they saw each other, which was pretty often. That would make him gruff, for he lacked Rufinus's gift for masking himself with mirth, and she would be wounded and wish she knew what was troubling him.

He squared his shoulders. This wasn't really the wrong kind of day wherein to plan bloodshed. It was the exact same time of year, back when Verania was in her mother's womb, that he had slain the King in the Wood.

XIV

~ 1 ~

Strange it was to be again at Ys. Three years had not diminished the longing for what was lost, nor had three days hardened the heart. Standing atop what had been the amphitheater, Gratillonius found he must once more punish himself with a westward look.

The sun was low, dulled by haze, but cast a steel-gray glimmer across the waters. Cold and salt from the south, a breeze had lately stiffened and begun to raise whitecaps on them. They drummed afar, an incoming tide that burst and spouted over the rocks, surfed against cliffs, roiled about the ruins. The mist should have scattered but somehow it lingered, even thickened. Sena lay hidden beyond the vague worldedge it made. The horns of land bulked murky, decked with pale grass that rippled to the wind. A few seabirds cruised above.

The watchman who had sent after him touched his arm. "They *are* the enemy, lord! They must be!" His voice cracked apart. He was a stripling, a backwoods Osismian clad only in a piece of wool, armed only with a spear. You took whom you could get and believed you could trust, if you would make war on barbarians.

Gratillonius started out of his moment's trance and brought his gaze around. It left Cape Rach, where nothing remained of the pharos and little but tumbled stones of the tombs. The road out to them was nearly obliterated, gravel washed away by rains, bed invaded by weeds. Vision swept across the bight where Ys once stood. What pieces of the city had survived at first were mostly gone, collapsed and rolled off down the sloping sea bottom; against the sun, he glimpsed only formless blacknesses. Waves and scavengers had long since picked the beach clean. The canal which bore the sacred water from a Nymphaeum lately burned to the ground (by chance, Christian torch, thunderbolt of a God?) had silted and fallen in on itself. Without that drainage, the low ground of the amphitheater was becoming a marsh. Sight flew onward—a shadow tracing where Redonian Way had run; the end of Point Vanis, where somebody had dug up old Eppillus's headstone and carted it off or cast it into the sea; gutted hillside mansion with window-frames empty as a skull; beneath, brush reclaiming those charred acres which had been the Wood of the King.

The heights blocked view of Lost Castle. Gratillonius had seen that the Celtic fortress remained untouched save by weather. Older than

Ys, it would endure uncounted centuries longer. He stared past, north-ward over the great sweep of Roman Bay.

Aye, a fleet. What the boy and his fellows on the wall barely glimpsed through the blurry air had drawn close enough to be unmistakable. He could not yet be sure how many leather boats coursed the waves—about a score—but two galleys of the Germanic kind walked on their oars amidst the pack. Standing well out, it beat west along the Gobaean Promontory; and around the shores behind it were surely wreckage, misery, and death.

At that instant Gratillonius felt simply a liberation. All was done with, the furtive preparations, the fears and squabbles and things going wrong, the wait here as men chafed and groused and neared mutiny, the wrench whenever a beacon flared on the horizon or a courier sped in to gasp that the pirates had landed again. He had awakened from his slow nightmare, he had come through the swamp of glue to firm ground, and the freedom to fight was his.

"The Scoti," he said. "Stand fast, lad. We still need eyes aloft."

He remembered to stride, not run, as befitted the commander—over the wall, past the crude platform on it that held the pyre of his own beacon, down the inside stair. Level by level, the signs of destruction thickened, a statue wantonly smashed, an inlay pried out, an upper tier broken and lower bench scarred by stones thrown down them, the spina gone from the arena and that ground turned to mud under inches of stagnant water. Apuleius had learned that Governor Glabrio actively encouraged the plundering of Ys. Its remoteness, the stories about what haunted it, the danger of brigands did not hold off everyone who wanted fine construction material. Looted of treasures, the remnants were a quarry.

Nonetheless Gratillonius wondered at how fast the demolishment by both man and nature went. Did the Veil of Brennilis reach out beyond the grave? Did Lir, Taranis, and Belisama pursue Their vengefulness yet?

He forced the mystery from him. This was the day of battle. Mithras grant—fate, or whatever ruled the world, grant the revenge he himself wanted, for Dahut.

Shadows filled the bowl of the amphitheater with dusk. Men dashed about like the sea in the bight. They shouted and swore, they clashed metal together, their feet thudded on the benches, echoes flew. Gratillonius saw Drusus across yards. The veteran was assembling those like him who had joined the force. They were aging, their armor didn't fit so well anymore, but they would be steady, the core of strength.

Amreth yelled at men from Confluentes. His marines were a cadre among them, but few. Most had no knowledge of warfare nor any but the barest gear for it—some merely sickles, woodman's axes, sledge hammers, pruning hooks. Yet a ray of wan light through a hole broken in the wall showed a kind of joy on Amreth's face. No longer was he a peasant.

Bannon and a couple of other headsmen herded their Osismii together. Those knew a little about fighting, not much but a little. They lacked discipline but probably wouldn't panic unless others did first.

Rufinus and his outlaws crouched in a group. Ill clad, disheveled, armed as each saw fit, insolent as wolves, they would be the deadliest part of Gratillonius's ragtag legion.

He made his way around to the box that had been for the King and the Nine, and entered. It had been savaged worst of all. Marble splinters crunched beneath his feet. From this location a speaker could make himself heard throughout the space around. He must not remember games and gaiety, music, dance, the flash and the long human roar as racing chariots rounded the spina, most especially the women with him, the mothers of his daughters. He must fill his lungs and bellow:

"Hear me! Silence! Listen! Your commander has your orders for you.

"Those are the Scotic raiders. They're headed by Point Vanis. They should cross the mouth of the bay and reach Scot's Landing in another hour. Make ready! Meet outside in your different units. You know what to do. You know what we will do." It took repetitions to get their full heed. Then: "Death to the barbarians! Vengeance and victory!"

He pushed through the ruckus toward the cubicle he had occupied, to arm himself.

~ 2 ~

The galleys dropped anchor. They had grounded on many a strand this springtime; but heavy with booty, they would be in peril here. Cobbles covered a strip which the tide made even narrower, beneath red-brown ramparts of cliff, while the rising south wind churned water about the remnants of Ghost Quay and sought to drive hulls hard against it. Currachs could ferry the crews ashore. The bit of beach having room for few, most boats would thereafter lie empty, tethered to the ships or each other, watched by a few men left aboard the vessels under captaincy of Uail maqq Carbri.

Calls and laughter rang through the sea noise. Too loudly, he thought, too merrily. They denied forebodings about this sinister shore where nothing further was to be gained, gold or silver or fine and wonderful weapons, only the toil of breaking stone from its seat and dragging it off to push from the heights into Ocean. Well, they knew when they embarked that the King would require it of them, and had he not led them first to riches and glory? He would not keep them long, just tomorrow and the next day, then ho for home; and there he would reward them from his own share of the plunder as richly as beseemed the high King at Temir.

943

Three nights to walk from camp to the dead city and be with her who sang. If she came. He believed she would. Foreknowledge must be hers. Ranging through the depths and across the waves, she could have spied him, followed him. On one night, which they spent at sea, he had had glimpses....The moon was gibbous. It would be there after dark for him to see by—see what?

He felt a thrill of dread that was half rapture. It was not fear for himself. She had plighted him her troth if he paid her the honor price she wanted, and he had been doing that. His sense was of going beyond the world. It was like when he had been a boy about to have his first woman, a youth right before his first battle, a man abroad on the night of Samain Eve; but it went deeper than any of those, flowed through him quieter but stronger. He knew not what would become of him, and that was daunting, yet he could not wait for the meeting.

"I've been away from you too long, I have," he whispered down the wind.

The eagerness was real with which he sprang into the lead currach and stood erect as the oarsmen brought it bounding to shore. To hearten his men—and, breathed an inner voice, himself—he wore his bravest garb, helmet ablaze with gilt on locks that were formerly as bright, seven-colored cloak flapping like wings about red tunic and plaid kilt, spear on high and shield faced with polished bronze. Everybody was outfitted for combat, but none to match him.

Not that he looked for trouble. Last year a Scotic wrecking crew had found a band of Gauls come after building stone, subdued them without loss, and borne the survivors off for slaves. Niall counted on no such luck. It didn't matter. Tonight, pulsed within him, tonight, he waves and the moon and the white one who sings.

The ledge on which the fisher houses had clustered was largely tumbled, the upward trail a bare trace. Niall led the way. Supple as of his followers, he skipped from rock to niche to treacherous e. Gulls dipped and soared about him. He made the last leap to op so as to land in a crouch, ready for battle.

The headland stretched empty. Its grass tossed wan under the wind. the heights that reached eastward and the valley between were a dwe d shades of green. Little sign of man abided—the amphitheater, and s half hidden by the growth that was overrunning them, marks scudd s of roadway. The moon stood pale above distant hills. Clouds behind There were no shadows, because the sun was low in the west and ske stiness that despite the wind was encroaching on the rocks outside of Ys.

Niall an advance slantwise across Point Vanis. He would camp near the ient tombs, or what remained of them. Not much did. His warrior night well finish them, with time left to break down shells of homes an et fire to whatever would burn. He needn't be impatient about that, ho ever. The years—weather, roots, rot, humans who enjoyed destruction or wanted to clear the sites for themselves—would more slowly wipe them away. But he should not make her wait for that if he could help it.

He had heard Ys itself was gone beyond ruination by mortal hands. The city hove in sight. He stopped to look. His sailors had spoken truly. Ragged snags of wall or tower still rose above the water, farther out than a work party could wade even at low tide, but they had become very few. Most of what showed were formless rubbleheaps, not yet brought down below sea level. Things closer inshore, some beyond high water mark, had taken less battering; yet they too were almost all down. Men had smashed at them for the stone or in hopes of finding treasure. Storms, unhindered by a city rampart, cast monstrous billows at them. The earth slid from under their foundations as the soft sandstone at the bottom of the bay came apart. Niall could barely recognize that which had been the gate of the Brothers.

I did this, he thought. I let the sea in over Ys.

I believed that would be the end. I would turn home with my vengeance taken, the ghosts of Breccan and my men who died here set at peace. But the strife wears on. She will not let me go free.

A horn sounded, so faint at its distance and against the wind that he might never have been aware. His eyes told his ears of it. Tiny at their remove, men swarmed from behind the amphitheater. Blink of metal bespoke others hurrying down from the houses where they had laired.

Ambush.

The warriors saw too. They milled about and shouted. Niall's glance swung past them. They'd be outnumbered. Retreat to the currachs— deadly slow. The enemy would arrive before more than a handful could escape, and trap the rest on the cliff edge. He raised his spear for war, his shield for silence. "We'll hold fast where we are, lads, and reap them as they come!" he cried. Smoke rose thick from the amphitheater wall. His illwishers had kindled a beacon.

~ 3 ~

Six or seven miles thence, a watcher on a hilltop spied the signal. Wind tattered it, but surely yonder fire burned for a single reason. Shouting, he sped down the path that twisted among trees, to his village.

It was half a dozen huts on a tiny inlet where a stream ran into the sea. Its boats were gone. Men were out fishing. They would not return till sundown, if then. War or no, they had a living to haul out of the water.

Yet several craft like theirs lay drawn ashore. On the cove a larger smack rode at anchor, eyes painted forward on the black hull. Farther out was a merchantman, magnificent and awesome to simple folk.

The boy yelled and pounded on doors. Men came forth. Others stirred from boats or beach where they had idled away their days. Weathered countenances worked. Oaths rattled. "At last, at last...Is it true, now?... Lir, I promise You the best of my every catch for a year..."

"Avast!" bawled Maeloch. "We'll go see!"

A number pounded after him up the hill. "Aye," he panted, "no mistaking that. The King's fighting. Quick and go to him!"

When they got back, Evirion Baltisi had had himself rowed in from his ship. He had spent the weary time of waiting there, often wishing he had stayed longer in Thule and come home too late for this. Better a bunk aboard than a smoky hut so crammed with visitors that a man couldn't leave at night for a piss without stepping on them. Now eagerness blazed in him.

Maeloch was more matter-of-fact. They conferred briefly while the crews gathered whatever weapons they owned, launched their boats, hastened out. Women and children watched from the village. Most stood mute. Some waved, farewell, farewell, luck fare with you.

Evirion's boat took Maeloch to *Osprey*. Her crew numbered more than the fishermen of old. She carried as many fighters as had been willing to ride with the skipper. Hence rations had grown short, tempers vicious, while yonder summons tarried. He'd begun to wonder if the damned Scoti would ever arrive. Staying here like this would hardly have been possible if it weren't in territory which had been Ysan. To these uncouth and impoverished folk also, the city was their life. These days they hoped for protection by Audiarna; but they remembered.

The vessels stood out to sea and started west. They scarcely made a fleet, nine boats with five or six men apiece, *Osprey* with a score, and *Brennilis*. The ship was good-sized, her crew trained in arms, and a number of landsmen had joined them. As they travelled, two more boats slanted in to take part—fishers from the village who happened to see. It was their war too. Still, the force seemed a puny thing to throw at Niall of the Nine Hostages.

"A single slingstone 'ull do for bringing any wolf down," Maeloch growled into his beard.

He stood in the bows, watchful. Waves chopped leaden, streaked and crested with white. The smack rolled, plunged, groaned to their thud and splash against her. Oars creaked on thole pins. Wind thrummed mast stays. It was a south wind, but bitter and steadily rising. Starboard the land loomed dark and ever more sheer. Surf foamed at its feet. Mist ahead, which should not be in air like this, dimmed sight of its western end. The sun had become a sallow shield low above an unseen horizon. Cormorants wheeled in hueless heaven, blackness aflight. With only sail, *Brennilis* kept well out, lest she be driven around. Seeing her thus dwindled was a lonely thing.

"We'll do it, regardless," Maeloch muttered. "Don't s'pose I can bring ye Niall's head, but how'd ye like a gold ring off his arm, Tera?"—

Tera, who after two years was fruitful with their child, first of his children since Betha and all theirs drowned with Ys. "Ye'll have your revenge, little Princess Dahut, we'll give ye your honor back."

~ 4 ~

Dusk fell early in the forest. The sun was beyond the trees and the moon had not yet risen above them. Heaven reached gray-blue over the stealthily flowing Stegir, but beneath the king oak gloom deepened.

Within the cabin was nearly full night. Nemeta put aside the bowl into which she had stared unwavering for hours. She could no longer make out the water within it drawn from the witch-pool and tinged by drops of her own blood. Whatever visions had drifted there must now form themselves from the half-shapes behind shut eyes. She did not think they would be any more clear.

Wind soughed outside, a noise as of the sea. Two boughs rattled together like clashing swords.

She rose from her cross-legged position on the floor. It had left her joints stiff and painful. Chill wrapped around her nakedness. Well though she knew this room, she must fumble a while before she found her snake staff.

She stretched herself on her narrow bed, hands crossed over the pole. Its top rested at her throat, the mummified head on her small breasts, the scales down her belly, the rest of the wood against her groin and between her legs. Staring into blindness, she whispered in Ysan, "Mother, I've cast what few, weak spells I know. Help me. Come to me, mother, from wherever you have wandered, come lend me the wings that once were yours. I will fly to my father."

~ 5 ~

Gratillonius knew that battle would be chaos. Combats never obeyed any man's plan; and here he led no soldiers, but a gathering of colonists, rustics, outlaws, barely leavened by some aging veterans and former marines. Working as a whole was beyond their grasp. And they must take the offensive, cast their bodies against sharpened metal, hold down the fear that even legionaries always felt, that told a man to use his common sense and run away. Gratillonius could only form squads of those who knew each other and hope they would hang together and so keep heart in the rest.

The Scoti were warriors by trade, skilled, well armed, contemptuous of death. They lacked Roman discipline but could keep an eye on the chieftain's standard and each ward a comrade as well as himself. They numbered about two hundred, Gratillonius fleetingly gauged. Against them he had almost twice as many, who fought for their homes—though the enemy fought for life— That was his solitary advantage.

947

Since he could not oversee and try to guide operations like Julius Caesar, he took sword and shield himself. He went with the old legionaries. While waiting for this day they had drilled, a little of the craft had come back to them from their youth, they tramped side by side and struck the Scotic flank like a single engine. Drusus was their actual officer. Gratillonius pressed forward on his left but held ready to go elsewhere as necessary. On Gratillonius's left, a step behind him, his fellow Briton Riwal carried the banner that marked the commander's place. It was blue, with an eagle embroidered in gold. Julia had made it for him. Her eyes had sometimes been red, but she sewed on and kept silence.

Her man Cadoc was with Amreth and the other Ysans. Nearly all of them untrained and poorly equipped, they were less a unit than a gang of individual men who tried by ones or twos to bring down individual foes. The marines gave a small core of steadiness, though they themselves had scant experience. Still more did the fear of shaming oneself before a neighbor stiffen the will to fight.

Much the same was true of the Osismii. Pacified these past four hundred years, they were brave—no timid man had answered the call that went secretly over the forest trails—but knew nothing of affrays except for private brawls that seldom ended in death. They too rushed, slashed and hacked, fell down or fell back, tried again in the same man-to-man awkwardness, or dithered about dismayed by lifetime friends who lay gruesomely dead or shrieked for pain in the clutter and stink of entrails.

Rufinus and his wolves were the appalling manslayers, murder made flesh. They skulked about, watched for a chance, leaped in with a snap of weapons like jaws, were gone before a return stroke could reach, harried and hooted and grinned. From the sides their archers and slingers coolly waited for a clear target, then let fly and hit as often as they missed. When a band of Scoti made a desperate rush after them, they laughed and faded off on dancing feet.

Once the Confluentians collided with such a sallying party, away from its main group, and cut it to pieces at whatever cost to themselves. The sight brought Gauls to blood lust and they attacked in a mass that almost reached the barbarian lord. His guards drove it back in confusion, and its losses were hideous, but many a Scotian sprawled gaping at the sky. Every islander harvested was a loss Niall could ill afford.

Thus Gratillonius saw the struggle, whenever a respite allowed. A part of him weighed what he learned, gauged how the work went, told him to push onward. Then he must rejoin Drusus's troop, and for the next while forget all reason, all self. It was cut, thrust, parry, feel the shock of a blow given or taken through metal and bone to the marrow, glimpse an opponent's face contorted into a Medusa mask, engage an arm whose owner was a blur behind a shield, let sweat sting eyes and salten lips and make underpadding sodden and hilt slippery, haul air

948

down a dry fire of a throat, shake at the knees and know he was not a young man any longer. Clash, clang, thud, scream, gasp filled the universe. He lost footing on soaked ground and lived because Drusus covered him while he got back up. He recollected vaguely how he himself had saved Riwal when a giant of a Scotian broke through the Roman line. He fought.

Betweenwhiles he would catch sight of his goal. Niall reared high in the tumult, helmet like a sun, cloak like a rainbow, unmistakable. His sword and his voice rang. Surely he had suffered injuries, but nothing showed, no stone or arrow found him, he seemed as far beyond fatigue as Mithras at war. How could his sworn men do other than die at his feet?

Suddenly timelessness tore across and time was again. Gratillonius stood on Point Vanis with only the wind and the plaints of the wounded about him. A blackness swept across his eyes, a whirling, he nearly fell. Riwal caught his arm. Steadiness returned and he looked around.

A remnant of Scoti had rallied and hewn their way out of the trap. The cliff trail being denied them, they were headed the other way, toward Ys. They moved in a band, less than a hundred, ragged, reddened, stiff with hurts and weariness, steel dimmed by blood, but together and defiant. At their head, under his own flamboyant flag, blazed the helmet of Niall.

The battlefield was heaped and strewn with dead men, crippled men—hard to tell which grimaced the more horribly—and shields, arrows, spears, slingstones, swords, axes, daggers, bills, sickles, hammers, clubs, some broken, some bent or blunted, some ready to kill afresh. Blood dripped, steamed, glared bright or darkened with early clotting. Brains, guts, pieces of people littered the grass. Gulls had begun to crowd overhead. Their mewing grew loud, impatient.

Gauls and Ysans, such as could, lay or sat or stood droop-shouldered, exhausted. Gratillonius saw a couple of them vomit; doubtless more had already. A number had shit in their breeks. The veterans rested more calmly about Drusus. Gratillonius felt a rush of relief when he found Cadoc nearby, arms lifted in prayer. Rufinus's woodsrunners were the coolest. Several of them still had vigor to go about cutting the throats of Scoti and trying to do something for casualties of their own side.

That outfit had suffered the least, though its losses were severe enough. Gratillonius tried to count. He couldn't, really, but he estimated he'd spent a hundred men. That much out of four hundred would have cost him his command in any proper army. But he didn't have one, of course. The Scoti had died in equal numbers merely because each man of them had two against him.

And the chief devil among them was still alive.

Rufinus approached. "We're not finished yet," he said.

Gratillonius's gaze followed his finger. They happened to be in view of Scot's Landing. The reinforcements had arrived. Gratillonius recognized Evirion's ship, anchored at a safe distance, and *Osprey* closer in. Smaller craft plied to and fro, bringing fighters ashore. The first were now bound up the trail. Several were aboard the Scotic galleys. Apparently those had been captured without bloodshed.

Rufinus guessed Gratillonius's thought. "No, the enemy didn't try to hold out on the water," he said. "They understood right away it was hopeless and made off. Yonder."

The sun was very low, dull red and deformed behind the mists. Had the battle taken so long? Or, rather, had it taken no longer than this? Things were hard to make out on the heaving gray of the waves. Gratillonius shaded his eyes and squinted. Most of the leather boats were loose. The Scoti must have manned them with skeleton crews and fled as fast as possible. They were bound west along the point. Oars sent the light craft skimming, graceful as flying fish. *Osprey* threshed in pursuit, but heavier, with more freeboard to catch the south wind, had no chance of interception before the fugitives were past the headland. Through Gratillonius flitted an image of Maeloch roaring at his rowers and his Gods.

"Let 'em go," he said mechanically. "They'll carry the tale home."

"No," Rufinus answered. "That kind don't run to save themselves. They'll make for the bay, with the idea of landing and joining what's left of Niall's troop. What they'll actually do is take them off."

Gratillonius stared into the spare, fork-bearded visage. "By Hercules, you're right!"

Rufinus yelped a laugh. "I needn't be. Here's extra men for us, all fresh and hot. We'll corner Niall, and with any luck we'll bag the currach crews as well."

Lightning sizzled through Gratillonius. It flashed the numbness and every hurt out of him. He went about calling for volunteers. "If you think you can fight one more fight, come with me. You'll get a double share of booty. But if you can't, stay here, and no disgrace to you. We're mortal. No sense in dying, if you're too tired to send a Scotian to hell. Look after your wounded friends. Pray for our victory." That last was hypocritical, he could well imagine Rufinus's lip twitch in amusement, but they expected it.

Evirion had debarked, fully armored, at the head of a formidable team of mariners. Cadoc insisted he was able to carry on. Was that a good omen, those two who had quarreled so much now side by side? The fishers newly come were at least a tough lot. Drusus, Bannon, men of theirs; Rufinus, and those of his who survived— About three to two this time, Gratillonius reckoned; but a fair part of his force was unbloodied, whereas the Scoti staggered along.

"You'd better stay, sir," Rufinus said.

"No," Gratillonius snapped. "What do you take me for?"

"You've fought as well as anybody. We need you alive."

"I am damn well going to be in at the kill." There to avenge Ys and Dahut. The eagle banner rippled on Riwal's staff as Gratillonius led his troops downward.

Point Vanis shouldered off the wind. Mist eddied and smoked over the bay. It was cold and smelled of the deeps. The sun was a red smear out in the formlessness that crept across the skerries. Ruins and rubble hunched nearly as dark as the cliffs on either side. Waves tumbled and clashed. When they flowed off the beach, it gleamed wet until they assailed it again, higher each time. Eastward, night drained into the valley. That part of the sky was clear, purplish, moon ashy above the hills.

The Scoti had formed rank on the strand, as if hoping the sea would guard their backs for them. They were an indistinct mass where swords and spearheads glimmered. In fact, no vessel but their own nimble kind could reach them through the wreckage in the bay. However, a man could wade in the shallows.

Gratillonius stopped his followers out of earshot. "I'll lead our main body at the center," he said. "Let us get well engaged with them. Then you, Evirion, on the right, and you, Rufinus, on the left, take your men around and hit them on the flanks, and from behind if you can. We should be done before those boats get here. I daresay they'll turn tail when they see, but we can try to grab some. Is this clear? Forward."

He strode ahead at the Roman pace, sword in hand, shield held just below nose. His sandals smote earth. Grass brushed past his greaves. Mail rustled. Sweat chilled him as it dried, but he'd soon be back in action and warm. A vast calm had taken hold. It was his fate toward which he walked.

Something passed at the corner of vision. He heard a man at his back exclaim, and looked. His stride broke. His heart stumbled. Wings ghosted overhead. Great eyes caught the last daylight. It was a bird, an owl, an eagle owl.

No, Forsquilis was dead, she died with Ys, here was nothing more than a stray! Gratillonius told himself to be at ease. If this meant anything whatsoever, it betokened well, because Forsquilis had loved him. His spirit refused obedience. He went on with a high thin keening in his head.

But he must never show fear or doubt. His was to lead the attack. He might even have the unbelievable luck that his was the sword to strike down Niall of the Nine Hostages.

The gilt helmet sheened through the twilight. He choked off an impulse to charge and continued at the drumbeat Roman pace.

A cry like a wildcat's ripped from among the Scoti. Others took it up till it outrode the rushing of near waters, the booming of surf more distant. Steel shook against heaven.

Gratillonius and his men met it. Shield smashed on shield. He laid his weight behind, leaned against his enemy while his blade searched. A blade gonged off his helmet, skittered across his mail on the right side. He cut. He felt the bone give beneath the edge. The barbarian yowled and lurched back. Gratillonius pressed inward. They were everywhere around him. No, here was a mailcoat, a man of his who grunted and thrust; there was another, near naked, but wielding a blacksmith's hammer, and a skull split before it like a melon. He was in the water, everybody was, the tide lapped around his knees. The flanking assault had worked, the Scotic line was crumpled and crumbled. Niall's banner went down. Rome's hung over Gratillonius. The colors were lost in mist and murk, but men knew it for what it was.

The melee opened up. He spied Niall himself, waist deep. The foeman lord was alone, his nearest warriors slain, the rest swept from him into a millrace of slaughter. Two ragged shapes—Gauls, were they Osismii, were they Bacaudae?—closed in on him. He shouted. His sword leaped. A man was no more. The second tried to slip aside. Niall made a step through the tide and clove him.

"After me!" Gratillonius called. He slogged outward. The bottom was lumpy and shifty, the water surged and sucked, but he pushed on to meet Niall, and behind him was a score of avengers.

A curve of white, a drift of gold sprang in the waves. Even by this half-light, he knew that hair was gold, was amber, was a challenge to the sun that would turn it fragrant. Naked she swam, orca-swift, seal-beautiful, and her laughter lilted as he remembered it. She came about in a surge of foam, stood with her breasts bare—rosiness had left their tips, they were moon-pallid—and held out her arms to him. Her face was heart-shaped, delicately sculptured, with full mouth and short nose and eyes enormous under blond brows. "Father," she sang, "welcome home, father."

The sword fell from his hand. The shield slatted loose on its shoulder strap. "Dahut," he uttered amidst a roar throughout his world.

"Father, follow me, I love you."

She kicked free of the bottom, straightened her slenderness, swam like a moonglade before him. He groped after her. "Dahut, wait!" he howled. This could not be. How had she outlived Ys? Yet every dear shape was there, head, smile, the little hands that had lain in his. "Dahut, come back!"

He did not see how the men behind him recoiled, stopped where they were, gaped and shivered. He fought his way on into the deepening water. She frolicked close by Niall. The Scotian hefted sword and went to meet the Roman.

It is Dahut, flew through Niall, it was always Dahut. I knew but down underneath I dared not name her.

She streamed by him, supple as the water, white in the twilight. Her speed left a wake in the waves. The wet hair trailed like seaweed, but heavy and clinging to the back that once arched against his weight. Her glance crossed his. It smote him. The bloodless lips parted in laughter. She rolled over. Light washed across her belly. Legs and one arm drove her onward. The uplifted arm beckoned to the man who raved behind.

She plunged and vanished. Niall wrenched his neck around. Yonder foe who had lost his wits wallowed about yet, wailing for her. He'd let go his weapon. She had chosen this prey, Niall thought awhirl. He knew not why, but it was her will, and here in Ys that they had slain together he was her slave. And a new killing should bring him back to himself, make him able to save his last few men—somehow, with her aid.

He hefted his sword and went to meet the Roman.

Wings beat, soundless above the sounding breakers. He looked up. The span was great, an eagle owl's. He glimpsed hooked beak and cruel claws. The eyes were glass bowls full of venom. The bird glided straight at him. It could flay his face and gouge his own eyes out.

Witchcraft was abroad. Niall took firmer grasp on his shield. As the owl swooped near, his blade swung.

He should have struck and flung down a bloody carcass. The iron bit into water. The owl veered. Feathers brushed him and he felt just spray off the waves. The owl swept around and came back. He saw the sword pass through. It was slashing fog. The owl hit him. Nothing tore, but he was blinded. He dropped his shield and with his left hand batted uselessly at the thing that flapped about his head.

It was a wisp, a ghost. It could not strike him nor he it. But it could hold him here, harry him if he fled, keep him fumbling helpless till an enemy found him. "Dahut!" he cried.

She rose from below. The blindness slipped aside. He saw that she had caught the owl by the right wing. It struggled. Maybe it screamed unheard. Claws raked, beak slashed, left wing buffeted. No mark appeared on her white arms. She clung, her strength against its, and dragged it downward toward drowning.

Niall never thought to stand aside, until afterward. You helped a comrade in combat. He lunged. His foot caught on a submerged fragment of Ys. He tripped, splashed, went under. His body collided with Dahut's. It was as solid as his, but even in the water he felt how cold.

Rising, he saw that the impact had jarred her and she had lost hold of the wing. Yet she had broken it. The lamed owl fluttered wildly athwart the moon, fell, was gone. He should have seen it sink, but didn't. He thought it faded, thinned, became a drift of mist, and was there no more.

For an instant, Niall and Dahut confronted each other. Amazement shook him. Real, no trick of the eye but moving flesh, she nonetheless had power to seize a phantom. Half ghost herself, she was.

Sharp teeth gleamed in a snarl that mocked a smile. She kissed him on the mouth. The cold of it burned. She dived. He had a glimpse of her writhing away like an eel.

Dazedly, he looked about him. The Roman soldier had vanished too. Maybe he'd come to his senses and returned to the men of his who roiled in the shallows. The sky was still pale overhead, Niall could see for many yards, well enough to know friend from foe. The enemy had broken ranks, withdrawn one by one from battle into bewilderment. The Mide men were farther out, in disarray but together.

Niall grew aware of shapes slipping inward from between stumps of wall where billows surged and broke. For a skipped heartbeat he supposed them a pack of sea demons. Then he recognized, and gladness lifted stark. Those were currachs of Ériu.

He had lost his shield but never his sword. He raised it on high. His voice crashed through the surf: "To me, lads! To your King! We're going home!"

~ 7 ~

Rufinus guided his master shoreward. Gratillonius lurched as if blind. Rufinus held him tightly by the arm.

"Dahut," Gratillonius sobbed. "The owl, what became of the owl?"

"Easy now, sir, we're almost there," Rufinus said.

Leaderless, terrified by what some of them had seen, the Armoricans milled on the beach in clumps or flattened themselves and moaned out prayers. The Hivernians could have taken advantage of it, but they were few, worn out, most likely also shaken by sight of a mermaid who fought with a bird of prey. Besides, leather boats were arriving to bear them off. The lean hulls rocked as warriors crawled aboard. Most needed help.

"It was Dahut," said Gratillonius numbly. "But who was the owl?"

The tide washed dead men onto the strand.

~ 8 ~

Outside the bay, wind blew hard and waves ran mighty. Their dash around the headland, following a long day's travel, had wearied rowers. Their craft overloaded with fugitives who could only stare emptily at sea and sky, they could not buck against the weather. At best they could keep a northwesterly heading. It bore them to the skerry grounds. Billows crashed and spurted across reefs. Rocks loomed. Riptides swirled

954

between. The last daylight was fading, the moon was less than full, and the mistiness that had already swallowed sight of distances was here thickening from haze to fog.

Niall crouched in the bows of the lead currach and peered ahead. Wind whined, water brawled and hissed, spindrift blew sharp. His whole body ached and throbbed. "Sure and it was a bad thing that we came," he confessed under his breath to his Gods. "There will be keening aplenty in Mide. I'm sorry, Lir. I should have left Ys to You."

Something gleamed in the froth. A slim shape with a wondrous roundedness of breast and hip swam before him. She waved, she summoned, her song mingled with the wind. Follow me, follow me.

"You will guide us?" he whispered out of the maze wherein he wandered.

Follow me, follow me.

Fresh joy leaped forth. He rose, balanced himself against roll and pitch and yaw, gave his tattered cloak to the nearest man and said, "Lash this to a spear for my banner." His helmet, too, caught the last wan light. He would be the beacon for his handful of boats, while Dahut led them through rocks and shoals to open sea. "Follow me, follow me!" he shouted.

A vessel hove in view from behind Point Vanis. She was plank-built, bigger than any currach, an Ysan fisherman. Steel agleam crowded her deck. The black hull swung about on oars till the eyes at the prow found the wayfarers from Ériu. A sail flapped up on her yard, filled, and drove her swiftly ahead.

~ 9 ~

"Skipper, ye're daft!" Usun protested. "Into yon hell, strong wind, high tide, night falling and fog rolling in 'gainst every law o' nature—nay!"

"Aye," said Maeloch. "Daft 'ud be to let him go free and work more harm on our folk."

"How can ye tell he be there?"

Maeloch pointed. Through the dusk and brume, across half a mile, a helmet glinted like a star. "Who else? From what we've heard, he'd be the last o' the lot to fall, and 'twould be on a heap o' slain. But the pirates ha' taken off such as lived at the bay. He'd be in the lead, cutting his way through and bringing them back to their lairs. Sure as death he would."

"But—"

Maeloch slapped Usun's back. "Brace up, man. We can overhaul them well ere full dark. The moon'll help. They'll nay be far inside the skerry grounds—which we know like the way to our women's beds, and they nay at all. I think the rocks will catch most ere ever we can. As for the rest, we've bowmen and slingers, we've a good stout forefoot to ram with, and our rail's too high for them to beswarm. Ha, they've been given into our hands. Ye wouldn't scorn the gift, would ye?"

His voice trumpeted: "Revenge for Ys! Kill yon sharks or they'll be back for your wives and kids! Haul away, ye scuts!"

The men howled answer. They too were become hunters. Blood was on the wind. Usun shrugged and went aft to take over the helm. Oars poised ready to help. Rigging sang, timbers creaked. *Osprey* dashed forward with a bone between her teeth.

Maeloch took stance in the forepeak. He gripped his battle-ax hard, though odds were that he'd have no need of it. Despite the furiousness in him, he strained to see, he loosed every sense to keep watch. Better let the barbarians escape than suffer shipwreck. But he didn't think either would happen. Aye, there was Torric's Reef and there towered the Carline, passage between them was tricky but if you kept alert for surges—"Right oars, pull!"—you could slide straight through instead of going around—"Up oars! Port the yard a tad...so....Make fast."

The gap closed. He saw that the tall man in the golden helmet now had a flag of sorts. It fluttered in the wind like a bird caught by one wing.

Ahead, seas raged around the Wolf and her three Cubs. Steer wide, starboard. Close beyond were the currachs.

"Little Princess Dahut, tonight ye'll sleep sound," Maeloch said.

Whiter than foam a shape darted from under the prow. He had barely time to see an arm lift, a hand crook fingers in summons.

Portside aft, fog rivered out of the bank that hid Sena. Suddenly it was there, Maeloch blind on his deck. He heard men yell, oars rattle. Wind dropped nearly to nothing. The sail slatted and banged.

With the speed she still had, *Osprey* drifted across the tide and struck.

It was a monstrous blow. Maeloch fell and rolled. He caught the rail and heaved himself to all fours. The hull slanted crazily. Again and again billows drove it onto stone. Timbers broke with a crack like thunder. The sea came aboard.

Maeloch saw a man reel past, and reached to catch him. The weight was too much. The man wore iron rings sewn to a leather jacket. He went over the side and straight down.

Wind sprang forth anew. It battered *Osprey* as the waves did. She broke apart.

Maeloch found himself swimming. The water trumbled him about. Whenever he got mouth in air, he snatched a breath. Then he was back in swirling darkness. He swam on. Fear was forgotten. He stood outside himself, watched the struggle, gave redes which his body tried to obey. Meanwhile he remembered Betha, their children, Tera, the child of his that she bore. By every God there was, will They or nill They, he was coming home to them.

Stone scraped him flensingly. He caught hold, clung, crawled.

When he got up onto hardness, the fog had blown away. Early stars flickered in the wind. The moon tinged the breakers that brawled around. Strakes and spars dashed among the rocks. He saw nobody else.

Well, he'd hang on. Save in storms, the Wolf was never quite under water. Tomorrow boats would arrive in search. He beat arms across his chest. That might flog some warmth into him. Oh, Usun, old shipmate...

The woman rose. She mounted the reef and walked toward him. Naked she was, dead white but for the deep hair, and smiling. She held out her hands.

He knew her. He was in a nightmare, he must wake, he stumbled back. "Dahut, nay!" he screamed.

At the water's edge he could flee no farther. She reached him and embraced him. Her strength made naught of his. Her flesh was more cold than the sea. She bore him backward and downward. The last thing he saw before he went under was her smile.

Presently she rose anew and swam toward the currachs, to guide them on until they were safely out into Ocean.

XV

~ 1 ~

The bishop's house in Aquilo was modest, and under Corentinus had become austerely if not ascetically furnished. One room in it, small, whitewashed except for a Chi Rho on a wall, held a few things that were his own, mostly gifts of love given him over the years—a ship model, a conch shell, a glass goblet, a flower vase, the doll of a little girl who had died—as if to lend him comfort. It was a room that heard much pain.

Gratillonius leaned forward on his stool. It was low; he sat hunched above lifted knees. The fists on them opened up beseechingly. "What have I done?" His words were thick with unshed tears.

Face-to-face with him, Corentinus answered gently, "You did what was right. Thank God you were able to do it."

"But the cost. Maeloch; every man there who trusted me and died."

"It was heavy. Not your fault. You didn't have the proper professional force you needed."

"Just the same—"

"Just the same, think what you have gained for us." Corentinus counted off on knobbly fingers. "A loss to the barbarians at least as great. We may hope they take the lesson to heart and don't come back here soon. That means, even in homes now grieving, a better life ahead. Also because of this, that you brought about, the people have a new sense of their own worth. Under you, *they* broke the wild men. I don't believe Our Lord frowns on that kind of pride. And the booty. Since there's no way to return it to its former owners, most of whom must be dead or fled anyway, you're making a righteous division. Men, or their widows—good of you to remember the widows—have hard need of some money; and those who share with the truly poor will have boundless reward in Heaven. As for the bulk of it, you said something about your intentions before your misery crushed you." He leaned over and clasped Gratillonius's shoulder. The seamed and craggy visage softened. "They're worthy of a Maccabaeus."

The other man dropped his gaze to the floor. "That may be. Though I wonder if the gold isn't cursed." A shudder racked him. "The horror we met—"

Corentinus tightened his grasp. "That's what's shaken you so badly. You've only told me so far that a terrible thing happened at the end. What was it?"

Gratillonius fought for breath.

"Speak," Corentinus urged. "You've already met the thing itself. Today you only have to name it."

Still Gratillonius panted.

Corentinus laid both arms about him. "I'll find out from others, you know," he said quietly. "Better straight from you. What, old friend?"

Into the beard and the coarse robe, Gratillonius coughed. "It was, it was, it was Dahut. My lost daughter Dahut there in the sea. She called me. She led me toward her lover Niall, who murdered Ys. An owl tried to stop him, she rose from the water and tried to drag it down, I don't know any more myself, but, but, but Niall couldn't have escaped, Maeloch couldn't have been wrecked—w-w-without her—could they?" He clung tight.

Corentinus stroked his hair. "We've heard evil rumors," he said. "This confirms them, I suppose. Except that the truth is worse. You've got to bear it, man. You can, soldier."

"What can I *do*?"

"I think you have done it already. Won a victory for your people. Now hold your spirit fast."

After a while Corentinus could let go. He got up, poured two cups of diluted rough wine from a jug—this was a room that heard much pain—and brought them back. Gratillonius clasped his almost hard enough to splinter the wood. "Drink," said Corentinus. "Our Lord did, the evening before His agony began. You are in yours."

Gratillonius obeyed. Having taken a couple of swallows, he said dully, staring before him, "Dahut. She was a dear child. Like her mother."

Standing above him, Corentinus shook his head and signed himself, unseen.

"How could it happen to her?" Gratillonius wondered. "How was it possible she could turn into this? Why?"

"That is a mystery," Corentinus replied, "perhaps the darkest mystery of all."

Gratillonius looked up, startled. "What is?"

"Evil. How it can be. Why God allows it."

"Mithras—" Gratillonius stopped at the word.

"I know the Mithraic belief. It gives no real answer either. Oh, it claims to, the cosmic struggle between Ahura-Mazda and Ahriman. But that doesn't really make sense, does it?"

"I left Mithras when Ys foundered."

Corentinus smiled very slightly. "You did the right thing for the wrong reason, my son. Who are we men, that we should hold the Almighty to account? And why *should* we understand such things as evil? The Christian faith is honest about it: we don't and we can't."

"Then what?"

"You've heard, but refused to listen. What we do know is that in Christ is rescue from evil, and only in Christ. Not in this world, unless it be inside us, but the promise of salvation for us all."

"All?" whispered Gratillonius.

"Who will accept it," Corentinus finished for him.

Gratillonius rose. "Dahut also?"

For a moment Corentinus was caught off guard. He looked well-nigh daunted. Then he answered as mutedly, "I don't know. I can't see— But how could I dare set limits on God's mercy? I'll pray for her too if you truly wish."

"I do," Gratillonius said. "And...will you teach me more?"

~ 2 ~

Nobody now forbade that Evirion visit Nemeta.

The day was bright and the forest rejoiced. In green depths, sunlight speckled shadow and sweetnesses drifted. Doves cooed like a mother above a cradle. Swollen by recent rains, the Stegir rang and gleamed on its way to the Odita. Swallows and dragonflies darted lightning-blue above it.

He drew rein at the old oak and dismounted. She came out of her cabin. The fieriness of her hair set off how haggard her face had grown. She walked draggingly to meet him.

In his glee he did not notice until he hugged her. She responded with a slight pressure of her left arm. Stepping back, he saw how the right dangled. "What's wrong?" he asked. "Did you hurt yourself?"

She twisted a grin. "In a way."

"But this—" He pointed. "What did it?"

"A might greater than mine," she said. "Never again will I fly."

He did not understand at that moment. Later he would recall tales that had gone about concerning the battle of the bay, happenings he had been too busy fighting to witness. "Oh, poor darling!" Tears blurred sight of her. Men in Ys had not thought that unmanly. He blinked hard and reached to take her left hand between both his. "How can I help you? You've but to tell me."

"Thank you," she replied in the same monotone, "but I've no need. My father offered too, when he heard of this lameness."

"You refused?"

She shrugged her left shoulder. "I'd have had to move back to Confluentes. What use, there, is a one-armed woman? Here I'm at least a small wood-witch. Men will come do what work I can't myself, in return for my craft."

He was always impetuous, but felt no surprise at his next words. They had been within him for some time. "Wed me! You'll be a fine lady, with servants and, and my love."

She smiled and shook her head. The green gaze mildened. "Nay. You're kind and true, but you're a Christian and I'd have to make pretense of that. Better to keep what freedom is mine."

"Well, the devil with marriage, then. Come live with me."

"What of your standing in the city?"

He let go her hand and raised a fist. "That for the neighbors!" After a space, levelly: "They need me too much, the trade I bring them, for meddling in my affairs."

"You're away more than half the time."

"Aye, your life could become wretched meanwhile. Sail with me."

The idea would have shocked a Roman woman. Hope sparked in him when she regarded him quite calmly. It died out at her sadness: "I have lost all desire for men. Nor would I so fare, did I wish it. You'd have the worst of luck."

"I can't believe that. Why do you say it?"

"My Gods are angry with me. I told you I've crossed a power beyond aught I'll ever command. They bestowed it. She who bears it would know and come after me."

Rage flared. "And yet you serve those Gods!"

"I'll make terms with Them if I can," she said. Her look upon him turned hard. "By Them I keep my freedom. So They are still my Gods."

Again he was silent a while. "And you are still your father's daughter," he said at last.

~ 3 ~

Window glass made greenish and somewhat dimmed the daylight in the room to which Apuleius took Gratillonius. It was like a patina of age on the wall panel paintings, and in fact they went back generations, to the building of this house—the formal woodlands and meadows,

960

decorous fauns and dryads, cheerful shepherds and milkmaids. The air was grotto-cool and quiet.

Gratillonius had excused himself from sitting down— "I'm too restless" —so Apuleius courteously kept his own feet as the other man prowled. He had already had an account of the fight, heartily approved, softly offered sympathy at the way it ended. Today they both had work on hand.

"You're right, we must move fast," Apuleius said. "I can find three or four reliable agents; can you name one or two more?...Good. The captured galleys, I think we'd better resign ourselves to selling dirt cheap in Gesocribate."

"No, I want to keep them," Gratillonius answered. "I've a notion they may come in useful."

"Hm? Well, as you like. But leave them in some obscure place, a cove or stream or whatever, well away from here. We don't want to be found in possession of them. Those few Scoti you took alive are less urgent, since they don't speak Latin or Osismiic. I know a dealer who'll take them on consignment. Don't expect to get rich from that sale, either. The breed is considered too fierce for domestic service."

"I wasn't counting on much there," Gratillonius said impatiently. "What about the gold and silver, though? Coins, jewelry, plate. We found expensive cloth stuff too, and spices and wine and that sort of thing."

"It can be stowed in private places. We want to move it rather slowly, piecemeal, so as not to attract attention."

"But damnation, we need the money! I've given the men or their heirs their parts."

"I know. That's all right, because it's thinly spread among unnotable persons. If their lot suddenly betters a little, who's to notice?"

"The Imperium has its eyes. Postal couriers, for instance."

Apuleius stroked his chin and smiled. "Of course. But our local observers report first to me. Over the years, I've seen to it that their stations are filled by...trustworthy men. An elementary precaution, commonly taken."

Gratillonius held to his purpose. "You and I can't help being noticed. And we've expenses we've got to meet. First and foremost, the fu—the bloody taxes. Half the reason I organized that operation was the hope of getting the means to pay them for the next several years."

"Oh, we will, never fear. It's simply that we can't hand over a bag of solidi. That would raise questions, especially since the assessments are normally paid in kind. We'll dispatch Evirion down the coast—Portus Namnetum comes to mind—where he'll buy what's required. It will surprise them in Turonum. However, they'll have no way of proving the Confluentians didn't grow most of it themselves and that a wealthy wellwisher who prefers to remain anonymous—God does not like us to make a show of our charities—came up with the shortfall."

An oath escaped Gratillonius's teeth. "All this to go through, because we dared fight a pack of barbarian robbers!"

Apuleius signed. "So it is. We must be most careful, you and I, about what we admit to. The fact of the battle cannot be concealed. There must be no evidence that you planned and organized the movement."

"Certainly not."

"How have you meant to protect yourself and your men from charges of forming a local militia?"

"Well, you see, it wasn't; it isn't; not really. The ordinary man who was there—if the authorities interrogate him, all he knows is that the word went around that something must be done about those pirates, and he decided to join in. As for me, I'll say that when I learned this was afoot, I thought I'd better provide leadership, or the fellows would be slaughtered."

"A weak story."

Gratillonius halted in his tracks and glared. "Well, what would you say?"

"I would obfuscate." Apuleius smiled afresh. "Let me be your mentor and generally your spokesman. A man in my position learns how to misdirect unwelcome attentions and bog down unwanted proceedings. You needn't pack for flight nor lose any sleep. Whatever investigation takes place will be undermanned and perfunctory, because in fact there is nothing clear-cut to find. People were desperate; you stepped in to mitigate the emergency; you have not subsequently maintained any kind of private army. Believe me, Glabrio won't complain to the praetorian prefect. The risk is too high that he would be reprimanded, perhaps demoted, for letting the things happen that did. However, preserving you depends on keeping the details of actual events vague. Don't talk about it more than you absolutely must, not even to your Ysans. Above all, don't boast."

"I've no wish to do that," said Gratillonius grimly.

Relief and thankfulness burst through. He held out his hand. "By Hercules, Apuleius, I thought I could count on you, but this—you're a *friend!*"

The senator took his arm in the old Roman manner and murmured, "What else? Praise God I can again be what I've longed to be."

"We'll work out details. But right now, it's like...coming home from exile." Horror and grief came along, but hushedly, things he could set aside most of the time as a man sets aside the pain of an unhealable wound while he goes about his proper business and daily life the best way he is able.

"It's grand of you— Oh, I understand how it must hurt, playing this kind of tricks with the law you've always honored," Gratillonius said awkwardly.

The response was grave: "That law conflicts with a higher one."

962

Gratillonius nodded. "The Church's. Christ's. It is...better, surely, than the state's. So it must be higher."

Apuleius caught his breath. "I expected you'd talk only of honor."

"Where does honor spring from? I've asked Corentinus to explain. This time I'll listen."

"Oh, my beloved friend. My brother." Apuleius embraced Gratillonius, who returned the clasp.

Presently they left the room to get a bit of food and a stoup of the best wine in the house. They joked and laughed a great deal, nothing maudlin about them! Verania entered the triclinium just when they did. It was as if she brought the summer day inside with her.

~ 4 ~

News from the South that year had people back on the hook. Once more Alaric and his Visigoths invaded Italy. At Verona they took a resounding defeat and withdrew. Once more Stilicho failed to follow up his victory and do away with them. Instead he arranged for their settlement in the Savus Valley, astride the border of Dalmatia and Pannonia. Emperor Honorius gave himself a triumph in Rome, the first that that city had witnessed in more than a century.

Procurator Bacca secretly called his agent Nagon Demari to his house in Turonum. They met alone at night. Without Glabrio they could sit over drink and talk more or less freely.

"An interesting communication has arrived," Bacca said. Candlelight filled the hollows of his face with darkness.

Nagon leaned over the table. "What?" he rasped.

"Tribune Apuleius of Aquilo writes, largely on behalf of his associate, the curial Gratillonius, that we should cancel confiscation proceedings. The taxes from Confluentes will be paid in full."

The stocky man sat back, aghast. "Name of God! How?"

"You'll try to find that out when you go to collect, of course. I doubt you'll learn much or that the source will be anything we can lay hands on. It will be the same as with identifying runaways who've settled there or going after the Bacaudae in the woods. Nobody is disobedient, but nobody is competent either, or able to attend to the matter at this moment, and so nothing gets done. I'll pass on to you what little I've discovered."

Nagon smote the tabletop. "Is Satan at work?"

"Shrewd minds are, at least. Backed by strong arms. And...I hear the natives thereabouts are feeling their oats since the Scoti were trounced. Be very polite and circumspect when you call on them. We don't want to stir them up further. Besides, I'd be sorry to lose you."

Nagon gnawed his lip and ran fingers through his sandy-gray hair.

"Not that I propose to leave them in their contumacy," Bacca went on. "We both know that Confluentes is a tumor that must be excised

963

for the health of the state. Unfortunately, certain highly placed men have not seen this for themselves. They would deny our diagnosis and refuse to allow the surgery."

Nagon caught the other's drift. He straightened on his bench and thrust out his jaw. "I am ready, sir."

Bacca smiled. "I knew you would be. Careful, though. Discretion is of the essence. I have a tentative plan. While you are there, you will study the layout, the whole situation, from the viewpoint of how feasible my idea may be. Report back fully and frankly. It would not do to go ahead with a procedure that is likely to fail and possibly bring grave consequences on us. Nor to rush. If you find it worth attempting, we shall have to wait for the season when it will have maximum effect." He put elbows on table and fingertips together. "Surgery requires both neatness and proper timing, you know; and the surgeon must hold himself deaf to the screams of the patient."

~ 5 ~

Rain fell in serried silver. Wind dashed it against walls and window-panes. The first breath of autumn was in it. Gloom and chill filled the bishop's house, for he scorned such worldly comforts as hypocausts; but candleglow made his private room a cave of light.

"You tell me Christ walked the earth as a man," Gratillonius said. "I've been thinking what manhood was His, to die on the Cross when He could have called the legions of Heaven down to save and avenge Him."

Corentinus smiled. "We each of us see our own Christ," he replied.

Gratillonius pushed on toward that over which he lain wakeful. "He stood by His vows and by those He loved. Would He want me to do less?"

Corentinus looked hard from beneath his brows. "What do you mean?"

Gratillonius shifted on his stool, swallowed, and blurted. "You know. My daughter Nemeta. You've warned me I've got to give up, forswear, heathen things. But she will not. And there she is, alone with her withered arm."

"God may well have smitten her," said the stern voice. "Yet still she won't heed."

"She can't. Nor can I forsake her."

"Not even for your salvation?"

"No." Gratillonius sighed. "Am I beyond hope? I'll go."

"Stay!" rapped Corentinus. He made as if to seize his visitor, drew his hand back, and spoke quickly, in a milder tone: "Surely you didn't suppose I meant you could have nothing to do with pagans. That's nonsense. We have to deal with them all the time. There's nothing wrong with feeling friendship. Our Lord Himself did. Or love—it is commanded. I meant ungodly rites, that sort of thing."

964

"Of course. I understood that. But she...practices them. Her house holds a store of witchy tools."

"I know. Certainly I could never forbid you to call on her, as long as you don't take part in any abominations. But can't you bring her the truth?"

"I tried. She came near showing me the door. I won't try again."

"Ah, well." Corentinus sighed like wind spilling from a sail. "I'll pray for her. And you do the Lord's work anyway."

"Hm?"

"A man as widely admired as you. You must be aware. Salutary example. More and more pagans come to hear me when I preach, or make welcome the priests I send out to evangelize. Some have already asked for baptism."

Gratillonius frowned, hesitated, finally said, "I don't think I should myself, yet. I couldn't live up to it."

"None but a saint can, my son."

"I, though, I can't try as hard as I ought. I can't even wish I could. Too much anger in me."

"Vengefulness. But also honesty."

"I've been wondering what I should do. Look, I can't go off for forty days and pray, anything like that. Too bloody much work here."

Another smile flickered through Corentinus's beard. "After these sessions we've had—" He donned solemnity. "Well, answer this truthfully. Do you believe in—no, I won't throw the formula at you. Do you believe in the one God, Who sent His only begotten Son to earth—the Son Who with the Holy Spirit is Himself—that we might be saved from our sins and live forever with Him?"

"I do." I must. I think I must.

"Then you would call yourself a Christian, Gratillonius?"

"I'd...like to."

"That will do for now. Frankly, I have my doubts whether this new style of early baptism is always a good idea. Be that as it may, what you have just said makes that brand of Mithras on your brow no more forever than another scar. You are a catechumen, my son, not ready to take part in the Mystery, but a brother in the sight of God."

"A Christian." Gratillonius shook his head in bemusement. "It feels strange, and yet it doesn't. I've come to this so gradually, after all."

"If the job went slowly, may it prove the sounder for that. I expect it will."

Gratillonius was silent for a space, until, in a rush: "Could I, as I am, could I marry a baptized Christian?"

Laughter gusted from Corentinus. "Ho, thought you'd surprise me, did you? I've only wondered when you would. You sluggard, Verania's already gotten up the pluck to ask me the same."

"Here we are," said Cadoc harshly. "Why did you want me to come?"

Rufinus's house in Confluentes made him uneasy, not because it was small and rudely made, but because of its owner. Worse than a pagan, he professed complete unfaith; his friends were mainly former Bacaudae like himself, out in the woods; his secretiveness, beneath the genial mask, gave rise to uncanny rumors. This dark space, crowded with oddments, hardly reassured. Cloud shadows made the window membranes flicker as they came and went. The wuthering of the wind recalled tides around a skerry, such as two shipwrecked men might be alone on.

Rufinus's teeth glistened in the fork beard with his quick, disturbing smile. "I've been bracing different men," he said in Latin. "Today it's your turn." He gestured at a stool. "Won't you sit down? I can offer wine, ale, mead. The mead is far and away the best."

Cadoc ignored both invitations. "Why do you do it?"

"Why invite you, do you mean? Well, you showed courage at the battle, but naturally, that by itself isn't enough. It might be a disqualifier if not coupled with a measure of wits. Gratillonius is your father-in-law and, lately, your fellow Christian. You've been working to further his plans, what with surveying the wilderness for future roadways—oh, of course I know what you're at. I would have known even if Gratillonius hadn't told me. What I'm trying to get together, very quietly, is a syndicate to start making those notions of his come real."

"Hold on!" exclaimed Cadoc, alarmed. "I don't— There's n-n-nothing illegal about exploration. I don't want to flirt with...with outlawry."

Rufinus raised a brow. "Like me?"

"You said it."

"You're not afraid to hear me out, are you?"

"Go on," Cadoc snapped.

Rufinus went into a corner, squatted, took forth a jug, opened it, and poured into two cups. Meanwhile he talked. His tone was even but unwontedly earnest. "Rome or no Rome, we've got to organize some kind of defense. We can't rely on the army. You must know that. The Scoti would have gobbled our local garrison and reserves up and picked their teeth with the shinbones if they'd come up the Odita instead of along the coast. Gratillonius raised a force—between us two, we can say right out that he raised it—and gave them a drubbing. But at what a cost! Nothing like that can work again. The ordinary man who was there or who's heard about it is glad of the victory. However, if he's not a fool, he now sees what sort of casualties untrained, undisciplined clutters of people are bound to take. He'll see that this one survived only because of special circumstances that won't repeat themselves for his benefit. Come the next menace, he'll do the sensible thing and hotfoot it for the timber. I would myself. Wouldn't you?"

He returned with the cups full and pressed one into Cadoc's hand. "We must accept what God sends us," the visitor argued.

"Did He send us the Scoti?" sneered Rufinus. "The Saxons? You were a man of Ys once. You remember those Franks. What if Gratillonius had meekly yielded to them?"

"But we can't—set ourselves in defiance of Rome— W-we'd simply have two sets of enemies."

"We'll find ways," Rufinus said in a more amicable wise. "Today I only want your agreement in principle."

"Why isn't Gratillonius asking it?" Cadoc demanded.

"He can't so well. Still too much under the Roman eye. Nor does he have a gift for this sort of thing. He foresaw the need, but not the nasty little difficulties." Rufinus laughed. "Besides, these days he's preoccupied."

"With his betrothal?"

"What else? Let the poor man have what enjoyment he can. He hadn't gotten much, these past several years."

Relaxing a trifle, Cadoc drank. It was a good mead, dry, pungent with thyme and rosemary. "She is a sweet girl," he said, "and pious."

"With steel underneath, I think. Rejoice for him."

"Do you?"

"Why, of course," said Rufinus, surprised. "It isn't right for a man to live alone, the way he mostly has since the whelming."

"You do," said Cadoc slowly, gaze fixed on him, "and not because of holiness."

Rufinus scowled. The scar on his cheek writhed. "That's my business. Better for you to think of your own wife and child. If the barbarians come, no doubt you'll die heroically defending them, after which they'll gang-rape her and toss the kid around on their spears. Wouldn't you rather keep them off in the first place?"

"What *are* you getting at?" Cadoc curbed his temper. "W-we could try to have more men enlist."

"Ha! A whole extra ten or twenty? I'd guess that's about the number the army could and would accept out of this entire region. If you don't know how such things work, I suggest you learn."

"Then what do you propose?"

"It isn't clear yet," Rufinus admitted. "I told you, all I'm after is agreement in principle. I've been thinking, however. Gratillonius and I have had a couple of talks since the battle, too. It did give us some experience, something to base our thinking on. The rough units we formed, townsmen, tribesmen, seamen, woodsmen, were natural ones, that we seized on in our haste. But by that same token, they look promising as the kernels of a future standby force. You're right, we can't organize an actual army. What we can do, I suspect, is form associations within those groups—brotherhoods, benefit societies, whatever names they want. The avowed idea will be to foster cooperation

967

in a number of matters, among them the maintenance of law and order. This will obviously require training in weapons, formations, maneuvers, and so on. Everything quite loose, each brotherhood independent of the rest. But the amount and quality of training and the kind of weapons, as least among those who live off the highways, needn't be publicized. Such people don't circulate so much that gossip would likely to come to the ears of the mighty in Turonum or wherever. Besides, it wouldn't be actual soldierly drill or equipment. Just hunters honing their skills, say, or sailors practicing to contend with pirates. Nothing to alarm any Roman. But...the leaders of the groups would know each other, and meet from time to time. In the event of an emergency, they could quickly assemble a mixed but pretty effective collection of fighters."

He had taken sips as he talked. Now he drained his cup.

Cadoc had listened with increasing attention. "Conspiracies are apt to leak, aren't they?" he warned.

Rufinus grinned. "You're not altogether the dewy infant you sometimes act. Correct. But this isn't really a conspiracy either. Let's call it discreet. If we can form a club of men who're possible leaders, and it agrees on a general plan, then we can approach Gratillonius. That'd make a nice present for him, wouldn't it?"

"We'd still be taking a chance," Cadoc persisted. "And, and the cost is certain, time and effort we need for other things. Would the force you're imagining—could it become good enough t-to warrant this?"

"Absolutely. Because the risk and the cost of doing nothing are sky-high more."

"And of failure? We failed at Ys, you know. We won booty and lost lives, but we failed in what was Gratillonius's main purpose. He told me about it. The Scotic King Niall remains alive and...free to work fresh deviltries."

"He won't for much longer," said Rufinus, abruptly stark. "I swear it. After what he did to Gratillonius—to Ys, he shall not live."

Cadoc looked closely at him before murmuring, "You're very concerned for Gratillonius, aren't you? As if that was the foremost thing in your life."

"He's my master," said Rufinus. Briskly: "Well, what about the idea? I don't expect you to decide at once. But offhand, how does it seem to you?"

Cadoc shook his head and stared afar. "It may be the only hope we have," he answered low, "God help us."

~ 7 ~

After the swearing to the marriage contract—on the porch of Apuleius' and Rovinda's home, that everyone in the crowd taking holiday for this might be witness—the wedding party proceeded to the church. There Bishop Martinus blessed the union and held a Mass to celebrate and consecrate it. Gratillonius must wait in the vestry when the door closed behind communicants in the Mystery, and he knew this hurt Verania, but she came forth to him radiant.

Thence the numerous invited guests walked to the old manor house outside Confluentes. They let the bridal pair go first, and themselves bore torches. Most of both populations followed behind. Song rose, sound of harp and horn, mingled with laughter. It was a brilliant day, fire well-nigh lost in its light. Leaves blazed with red, russet, gold, the reminding hue of evergreens. Many birds had departed, but blackbirds, crows, sparrows flew from the din in their sober garb, while a hawk aloft caught splendor on its wings. They were no brighter than Verania's hair, a lock or two fluttering from beneath a garland of autumn crocus and the veil, with the color and vividness of a maple leaf, that she had now drawn back from her face. She held Gratillonius's arm tightly.

Trestle tables had been set up in a nearby field, well laden so common folk could make merry too and drink to the couple's good fortune. For the wedding party, the manor house was swept and garnished. If flowers were scarce, there was abundance of juniper boughs, fiery rowan berries, clustered nuts.

Gratillonius thought briefly that it was as if the place denied every memory of Runa, poor Runa. And today it was not a basilica either, it was an ancestral home of the Apuleii, biding him welcome into the family.

The feast was not lavish, which would have been beyond the father's and bridegroom's thin-stretched means, but it was excellent, served forth on snowy linen and fine ancient ware. Polite, the company was also in a mood for enjoyment. Afterward musicians played, men and women talked, watched a performance of classical dances, talked, mingled, talked, helped themselves to refreshments, talked, while the atrium grew hot and the newlyweds waited.

Everyone offered Gratillonius congratulations. He'd already gotten those that meant most to him, from persons who were outside or not here at all, Rufinus, woodsrunners, tribesmen, sailors, their wives.... Well, the prosperous husbandman Drusus was present; and then Rovinda whispered to him, "How glad I am, how thankful to the kind saints"; and later Apuleius, a trifle in his cups, therefore extremely dignified and honest, said, "I've waited a long time for this, you know."

And finally the sun set and the guests made their farewells. It was maddening how often they lingered at the exit, talking, but the last of them did finally go. They left behind Gratillonius, Verania, her brother, her parents, and household slaves. Also, Drusus had posted several armed men around the walls for the night. Nobody would make a disturbance.

Bearing candles, the few went down the corridor to the bridal chamber. At its door, Salomon uttered with the enormous gravity of youth, "God be with you, my new brother," fell into flame-faced confusion, and shuffled his feet. The slaves said no more than, "Goodnight," though tenderly, for they had always been kindly treated. Nor did Apuleius and Rovinda, but they two each kissed Verania and Gratillonius on the cheek.

The groom stooped, gathered the bride in his arms, lifted her. How slender, firm, warm she was. He carried her past the open door. Rovinda shut it. Gratillonius set Verania down. She did not let go of his neck until she was standing.

Here the air was fresh and rather cold, sweet with arrays of juniper. On one wall hung a tapestry—Ulysses and Penelope when she first knew him on his return—that was traditionally brought forth for nights such as this. Multitudinous candles burned. Drapes did not entirely cover the windows, whose glass reflected the light like big stars.

For a while the pair stood looking at each other. He thought that in her saffron gown she was like a candle herself, aglow above, holding darkness at bay. His heart thudded.

Her smile trembled to a sigh. "I am so happy," she said at last.

"Me too," he answered in his clumsiness. He could not have gotten a lass more dear. How long Dahilis had rested under the sea. But Dahilis would not want him dwelling on that. If her ghost could come tonight from wherever such as she went, she would bless them.

"I waited many years for this," Verania said, while the color ebbed and flowed in her face. She hadn't been in hearing when her father gave Gratillonius the like words. "I think it's been as long as I can remember."

"Oh, now," he mumbled.

"You came riding and striding so gallantly. You were like a wind fresh off the waves that I'd never yet seen."

"Ordinary soldier man. I don't deserve this."

Suddenly her laughter trilled. "What, shall we contend in humility? Haven't we better things to do?"

It sang through his blood. He made a step toward her.

She lifted a small hand. "Hold, please," she said in quickly descending seriousness. "Before we—I should offer thanks, if I may."

His own hands dropped to his sides. "Of course. I was forgetting."

She went to stand by the richly covered bed, lifted arms and eyes upward as if there were no ceiling, and crooned in a voice not quite steady, "Our Father, Who are in Heaven—"

Blindingly came back to him his wedding night with Tambilis. He stood for a moment at the bottom of Ocean among his dead.

He thrust himself from it, all of that from him, and joined Verania. "I should offer thanks too," he said. The glance she cast him was ecstatic.

The formula pattered from his lips. He thought that now if any time he ought to feel what he was speaking. But no awe arose, no sense of Presence, nothing like that which had come over him when he was consecrated a Mithraic Father. Did Christ not care to hear him?

Help me, blessed Virgin, he found himself appealing. Maria, Mother of God, lead me to Him.

Somehow that brought peace to his breast.

Verania took his hand. Her lashes dropped, till she forced herself to level those hazel eyes at him and say, "We've paid our thanks. Shall we...take the gift?"

She's braver than I am! he thought. Joy rushed free. He drew her to him.

In Ys they would have left the candles burning through the night. Verania went around gently blowing them out. After that, though, she held nothing back; and enough moonlight stole in to bewilder him with beauty.

~ 8 ~

In the dark of the moon before winter solstice, Confluentes burned.

Verania sensed the first smoke and crackle in her sleep. She roused and shook Gratillonius. He opened his eyes on thick night and sat up, instantly ready for battle. "Darling, I think we have a fire," she said, almost calm. Even as his nostrils drank the acrid whiff, he was aware of her warmth and woman-fragrance close against him.

"Out!" He swung his legs around, got feet on floor—its covering shifted and rustled—and surged erect. Familiar with the layout of his dwelling, he found the door, unbarred and opened it. His first sight was of stars, numberless in crystalline black above roofs and lanes. A thin hoarfrost shimmered over earthly things. His breath steamed before him. Shouts from elsewhere reached his ears. They swelled to a clamor.

Verania appeared. She had fumbled her way to the clothes pegs and taken a tunic for him, a shift for herself, to throw across their nakedness. He ignored them while he jumped forth and stared at the house from outside. Flames crawled yellow and blue at a corner below the eaves. A breeze from the north fanned them. Feeding on dried turf, they were quick to gain size and strength.

He looked around. In moments, other fires leaped tall; those roofs were thatch. He saw them each way he gazed. "Out!" he said again. Verania hesitated. He stepped back, seized her wrist, hauled her from the doorway. "Come along. I've got to take charge, if I can."

She handed him the tunic. Laughter broke against his teeth. What a time for modesty. But no, she was right, it was bitterly cold. "Hang on," he said and, while she was pulling the gown over her head, ducked back inside.

"Gaius!" he heard her scream, and roared: "Stay where you are. You're carrying more than yourself." Just a few days ago she had joy-deliriously told him of reasons to believe she was with child. He found sandals for them both and returned.

Garbed and shod, they started off hand in hand. He cried to everyone he saw—dashing in and out with ridiculous little possessions, moaning and stumbling along in blind funk, standing stupefied— "Leave off that! Go straight to the rivers. Pass the word." If obedience was not immediate, he added, "I order you, I, the King of Ys." That usually worked.

Somewhere a roof fell in. Sparks and embers fountained above the black outlines of its neighbors and splashed on them. They caught fire too. A growling as of an angry surf waxed; above it went a sizzling, spitting, and whistling; Confluentes keened for its own death. Red flickered in smoke. Where it did not hide them, the stars watched indifferent.

Gratillonius and Verania came out in the open close to the meeting of the streams. Water sheened darkly through gray-white reaches. Beyond the Odita, Mons Ferruginus hunched into heaven. People were gathering, more of them by the minute. He dared hope everyone had escaped. They milled around, wept, cursed, prayed, implored, babbled. "Keep them off me, will you?" he requested of Verania. Young though she was, she had an inborn dower of giving heart and solace.

"Can we fight this, sir?" asked a guard. "I've seen a few men with buckets."

Gratillonius shook his head. "Good for them, that they thought of it. But no. Look. It's not a single fire, it's a score or worse. More every minute. Let's get the crowd to shelter."

Rufinus appeared. He spent the winters in town, except when he went off on one of his solitary and unannounced, unexplained long rambles. In the uneasy red light, he might have been a demon from hell. "This isn't accidental," he said. "It was set. Somebody crossed the ditch and the wall—about the middle of the east side, I'd guess—and went around with a torch."

Verania heard. Anguish wrenched her mouth out of shape. "Why?" she wailed. "Who would do such a thing? A man possessed?"

"I suspect not," said Rufinus bleakly. "Sir, may I take a party to try tracking him down?"

Gratillonius nodded. "Go." He thought Rufinus must share his guess as to who had sent the arsonist.

He had more urgent business. With those men and women who showed themselves capable of it, he pushed his way into the throng, bullied, cajoled, bit by bit imposed a ragged sort of order.

People in Aquilo were aware; their own watchmen had seen and called them. Several arrived to offer help. Gratillonius got most of his homeless across the bridge and onto the road leading there. A number of able-bodied men he kept. The basilica manor house and its outbuildings could shelter them. Once again those stood vacant except for caretakers. Verania might have lived there with her husband in much more comfort than his dwelling afforded, but had said of her own accord that his place was among his Ysans and hers at his side.

He set about roughly organizing his gang. "We'll try to save what can be saved," he told them. "We won't get reckless; nothing is worth a life. But it'll mean a lot if we can keep the town granary from burning, for instance, and I think maybe we can."

Verania caught his arm. "You *will* be careful?" she pleaded.

Even then, he could smile down at her. "Certainly. I want to meet my son, you know."

"That manuscript—I forgot it, God forgive me, but could you possibly —not to take any chances, oh, no, but it is a precious thing—"

He had forgotten too. Memory jolted him. She had lately carried from the basilica what there was of Runa's Ysan history, mostly notes, to study at home in her rare moments of leisure. Otherwise she never mentioned Runa, nor did he. At that time, though, she had said, "I have her to thank for all this about your city. Maybe we can find someone who'll carry on the work."

By flamelight and starlight, he shook his head. "I'm sorry. That's bound to be impossible."

And it drummed within him: The Veil of Brennilis, the revenge of the Gods, whatever it is, casts it shadow yet, and always shall, until Ys is wholly lost and forgotten. We'll never find time to write that chronicle, nor will anyone else. The story of Ys will die with the last of us who lived the last days of it; and our city will glimmer away into legend.

He turned to his men. "Let's go," he said.

—Rufinus came back about dawn. Gratillonius was awake in the basilica. The sleep of exhaustion held the others. They had kept the blaze from spreading to granary and warehouse. Those Gratillonius had originally directed to be built near the Stegir, with space between them and adjacent structures. Some houses had survived as well, some valuables were pulled out of others before they caught fire. It was not a great victory.

Under the pale east, Confluentes was ash heaps. Dwindling flames gnawed at charred timbers. Most walls had collapsed as the wood weakened too much to hold clay. A few stood black, like boles after a forest has burned. Smoke lay in a stinging, stinking haze.

"We found tracks in the frost, a couple of fellows and I," Rufinus reported. "Three sets. They'd sneaked out of the woods and returned. There they dispersed. We couldn't follow two. They'd taken care to leave no trail we could see by night once they reached the trees and brush. The third was a dunderhead. He'd actually made a campfire and rolled out a blanket for a rest before daybreak." His curtness dissolved in a sigh. "Unfortunately, when we appeared he panicked and bolted. Before we could run him down, one of us put an arrow through him. I'd rather not say who. He's young, hotheaded; the damage is done, and he's loyal and promising. When I dressed him down, he cried and asked to be whipped. A month's worth of the silent treatment will drive the lesson home better than that."

He must be an adorer of yours, Rufinus, thought Gratillonius. Aloud: "Are you sure the party you found was guilty?"

"His clothes were freshly stained with oil. How'd that happen, except when he was pouring it out of a jug onto the wood he was going to set alight? Good clothes, too; he was well fed, and barbered within the past few days; so, no landlouper. What else would he be doing in the wilderness at night in the dead of winter?" Rufinus studied Gratillonius. "Do you want to come with me for a look at the corpse? We'd better cover it up, just in case, but it might be somebody you'd recognize. Somebody who—let's say—was with tax agent Nagon Demari on his last visit to us."

"I think likelier not," Gratillonius replied. "They aren't stupid, those who ordered this thing. They'd guard against the chance of their bully boys getting caught at it."

"And mine wringing the truth out. M-hm. A middleman hired them." Rufinus pondered. "Not common alley lice. You couldn't rely on that sort, especially to get through the forest. Maybe the middleman paid their gambling debts and told them he had a long-standing grudge against Ys. If we'd gone to Turonum with his name, we'd have found he'd left for the far South, leaving no address, and no underling of the governor's had any knowledge of him."

"It doesn't matter," said Gratillonius.

Weariness overwhelmed Rufinus. "No, it doesn't, does it?" he croaked. "Confluentes, your colony, your hopes, they're gone."

Gratillonius put a hand on his man's shoulder and tightened the grip till Rufinus met his eyes. The windows in the atrium came awake with the first wan light of day. "Wrong," Gratillonius told him. "We have that treasure Apuleius is keeping for us. We have friends who'll help us again, more willingly this time when they know what we're worth. We have ourselves.

"Those maggots won't eat us away. We're going to build Confluentes over; and we'll make it too strong for them."

XVI

~ 1 ~

Springtime dusk. The air was soft, odors of greening and blossoming not yet cooled out of it. A moon close to fullness had cleared Mons Ferruginus. It looked like old silver afloat in an ever deeper blue sea. The earliest stars trembled forth. Sunset's ghost still lightened the western sky. After the tumult of day—hoofs, boots, wheels, hammer, saw, chisel, trowel, shovel, hod, shout, grunt, oath, banter, the trudging off at the day's end—quietude rested enormous over the land. Through it drifted little save belated bird-cries, ripple of the Odita, occasional tiny splash when a fish leaped, footfalls on the river road.

Gratillonius had been gone half a month, travelling about to make his arrangements. He wanted to see how the work had fared meanwhile. At this hour he could get an overview; tomorrow he would watch it in progress. His wife accompanied him from her parents' home in Aquilo, where they were living until their new dwelling was ready. The manor house was full of engineers and other directors. Mostly hired from elsewhere, they naturally expected better quarters than the shacks and tents that served common laborers.

Verania's brother Salomon had asked if he could accompany her and her man. They gave leave, for they had talked about him earlier, when they were alone and after they were at peace with nature.

He pointed. "See," he said importantly, "they've begun on the new wharf."

Gratillonius made out pilings planted just above the juncture of the rivers. The ground beyond was trampled, muddied, heaped and littered with lumber, equipment, scraps, trash. In the end this was supposed to become facilities for ships. Then the bridge at Aquilo would be demolished, so they could come here to the actual head of navigation, a better site in every respect.

A new bridge would span the Odita at Confluentes, stone, with towers at either end for its defense. "Wait," requested Verania, halfway over the old wooden one. "The evening is so beautiful." They lingered a few minutes, watching light shiver and fade on the stream, before they continued.

The same light touched the pike of a guard on the opposite side. A number paced their rounds, for the legionary embankment had been leveled, the ditch filled in. Stakes marked where a real wall of the Gallic sort was to be. It would make a complete circuit, east of the Stegir and north of the Odita. That would give room for proper streets and large buildings, as well as a population growth Gratillonius hoped would prove rapid.

The sentry challenged the newcomers. When he recognized the man among them, he snapped a Roman salute. It was crisp, though his outfit was homemade. Drusus and his veterans had long since stopped counselling the local reservists—that came to be frowned on in Turonum—but they were instructing Osismii who had formed an athletic association.

"How goes it?" Gratillonius asked.

"Right well, my lord," replied the guard.

"He speaks truth," said Salomon as the three walked on. "It really does go apace, now when rain and darkness don't hamper us so much. There's no trouble to speak of with thieves. Rufinus's scouts stop any that try to sneak here from outside, and we inspect outbound loads for stolen goods."

"We?" teased Verania. She had been bubblingly lighthearted since Gratillonius returned; but he sensed that it cost her an effort.

"Aw, well," muttered Salomon, abashed. He had grown taller than she, close to the height of Gratillonius, but was as yet reed-thin; under a shock of brown hair, his face continued, for days after he had been shaved, as smooth as hers.

Gratillonius took pity. "He worships you, not far short of idolatry," Verania had told him. "Well he might."

"You stick by your studies," Gratillonius said. "That's your share of the work, making ready for when we'll call on you."

Dim in twilight, Salomon nonetheless glowed.

They wandered about. Order had begun to emerge from confusion and ugliness. Scaffolding and cranes loomed where masonry climbed. Elsewhere were only sites marked off or foundations partly dug, but space and ambition prevailed—for a real basilica, for the big church that Corentinus would make his cathedral, for workshops and storehouses and homes, for a town whose bones were not clay and turf but brick and stone—a *city*.

Northward and eastward, greenwood no longer crowded close. Axes had slain trees across a mile or more in either direction, to make room and timber. Cookfires glimmered yonder, throughout the encampment of the workers. It was a huddle of the rudest shelters, hog-filthy, brawling, drunken, whorish. Dwellers in the neighborhood were too few, and generally bound down by their own occupations. Gratillonius's agents had ranged from end to end of Armorica during the winter, recruiting muscle where they found it. Many of the hirelings were doubtless runaways, claiming to be laborers with a right to take jobs elsewhere. As word spread, no few barbarians who had wandered into Roman territory joined the force. But stiffened by armed men at their beck, the supervisors kept it disciplined in the workplace, without strength left at day's end for much riotousness. And...there was life in the camp, a gusty promise as in an equinoctial storm. The new Confluentes would remember.

Not that Gratillonius meant to keep that lot of boors here. For those who proved themselves desirable and wanted to stay, he'd make what arrangements he was able. The rest must go, once the basic task was finished. It might be hard to get rid of some, he might have to bloody heads, but he wasn't going to allow more rabble than he could help. The immigrants he hoped to attract were steady, civilized men, seeking a chance to build a better life for their families. Gallia must hold many such, who would find ways to reach him. And more were in beleaguered Britannia. If he sent word across the channel—

That was a thing to think seriously about, and maybe do, in years unborn. Tonight he walked in peace with his wife, who carried their child within her, and the boy to whom he was like a second father. Distance dwindled noise from the camp to a bare murmur beneath the hush. A bat swooped by. The last light from the west shone through its wings. "Look," Verania said. "Like an angel flying."

"A sign unto us?" marveled Salomon. He gestured at the murky heaps around. "How splendid this will soon be."

Gratillonius smiled. "Easy, there," he cautioned. "It'll take a while."

"The work goes fast."

"Because we're pushing with everything we've got. The city has to be habitable and defensible before winter. But afterward things will slow down. It'll be mostly up to individual people, and they will have their livings to make. We'll have spent every last nummus in our present treasury."

Verania sighed. "The cost—" She checked her voice. He heard a gulp, and laid his left hand over hers, which rested on his right arm. Gently, he pressed it.

"You know how we'll meet that," he said.

Since he revealed his plans to her, secretly, last month, she had been fighting desperation. She did so wordlessly, but he knew, and wished he could find reassurances that wouldn't sharpen her fears. They burst through for an instant: "You can't change it?"

He shook his head. "No. That'd break faith with a good many men. With the whole people."

She tensed her clasp on him. "God watch over you, then."

They had stopped in their tracks. "With you to pray for me, what have I got to worry about?" he responded, the weak best he could think of.

"What's this?" asked Salomon.

Gratillonius drew breath. "We've been meaning to tell you," he said. "Here we're safe from eavesdroppers. Your father and your sister both believe we can trust you to keep silence, absolute silence."

The skinny frame quivered and grew taut. "I s-swear. By God and all the saints, I do."

Verania too was relieved a little by speaking forth. "You've heard the talk about Gratillonius going along when Evirion Baltisi makes his first voyage of the season, soon after Easter," she said.

"Of course. To look for markets. Oh, sir, I've asked you before. Take me! I'll earn my keep, I promise I will."

"I'm sorry," Gratillonius answered. "An ordinary trading trip would be risky enough these days. This won't be one."

"What will it be, sir? What?"

Gratillonius held hands with Verania while he spoke in his most carefully measured tones: "We're building Confluentes again, and building it right. That's a huge and expensive job. Doing it in a hurry makes it more expensive yet." Finish before Glabrio and Bacca hit on some means of forestalling it. Apuleius was already contending with their objections and legalisms. "We're employing as many Ysans and Osismii as we possibly can, you know. That means farms and other businesses neglected. We'll have to bring in food, most necessities. By autumn, when we've paid off the outside experts, contractors, laborers, we'll have emptied the treasury of Confluentes, everything we took from the Scoti. How then can we go on with what remains to be done? And the city will have to keep paying the people's taxes for them, for the next several years, till farms and industries are solidly on their feet. How?"

"I don't know," Salomon admitted with a humility rare in him. "I should have thought about it."

"Well, nobody gave you any figures," said Gratillonius, smiling at him through the dusk. "We keep such things confidential. I don't want to discuss why, though I think probably you can guess."

"He's bound forth to get what we need." Pride and dread warred in Verania's voice. "I've begged him—he shouldn't go himself—but—"

"But without me, it'll fail," Gratillonius said flatly. "A matter of leadership."

"Yours," breathed Salomon.

Gratillonius turned his gaze back on him and continued: "Evirion and I will rendezvous up the coast with picked men. They'll fill his ship and those two galleys we captured last year. We'll make for the Islands of Crows. You've heard of them, pirate haunts off the Redonic coast. Barbarians often spend the winters there, so they can start raiding again as soon as weather allows. Scoti, Saxons, renegade Romans, every kind of two-legged animal, in lairs stuffed with loot. Rufinus has had his spies out, he's heard a great deal on his missions to Hivernia, he knows where the big hoards are likeliest to be. We'll strike, cut the scum down or scatter them, and bring the treasure back."

No wisp of a thought of danger was in the cry: "Oh, sir, I've got to go!"

"You do not," said Gratillonius. "You're far too young."

Salomon doubled his fists. Did a trembling lower lip stick out? "I'm f-f-fifteen years old."

"You will be later this year," said Verania sharply.

Gratillonius let go her hand and laid both his on the youth's shoulders. He looked into the tearful eyes and said, "You'll have your test of manhood, I promise. It will be harder than you know, keeping silence."

"I w-w-will. I've sworn. But I can fight too."

"Carry out your orders, soldier. I told you already, you've got your share of duty and then some. I'm afraid you'll see plenty of fighting later on. Meanwhile, we can't squander you on a simple raid."

Salomon gulped. "I don't understand, sir," he pleaded.

"I believe you are the future leader of our people—of all Dogwood Land, maybe all Armorica. Your father is beloved; they'll be ready to follow his son, come the day. You've done well in your studies, I hear, and very well in the lessons about soldiering you got me to give you. You have the fire. I won't let some stupid encounter blow it out."

"No, you, sir, you're the King."

Gratillonius released his hold. "There's too much of the uncanny—of Ys—about me," he said. "Those who haven't known me before, they'd never feel the way they must about their leader, the way I think they will feel about you. But I'll be at your side as long as I'm on this earth."

Overwhelmed, Salomon sank down on a baulk of timber and stared before him at the stars above Mons Ferruginus, beneath the moon that rose and waxed toward Easter.

Verania drew Gratillonius aside. She held him close and whispered in his ear, "Come back to us, beloved."

"To you," he replied as low; and, since nobody watched, he kissed her. She returned that with a passion he well knew, and only he.

Like the bat at sunset there flitted through him: She's not Dahilis. Nobody could ever be. But she is mine, and here are no heathen Gods to break us from each other.

~ 2 ~

The men from the currach reached holy Temir a few days after Beltene. They had heard King Niall was there yet.

Their captain and spokesman Anmureg maqq Cerballi stood before him to say: "The Romans took us unawares. They must have gotten pilots, islanders who knew those waters and shores even better than we do. Suddenly, there they were, two Saxon galleys out of the fog and onto the beach. Men jumped from them and started hewing. It was butchery. Oh, sure, brave lads rallied and I think must have taken some foes with them, while others among us escaped inland, but most died and we lost everything, all we had won in two years of work."

Rain roared on the thatch of the King's House. Wind shrilled. Cold and darkness gnawed against the fires inside. It was wrong weather for this festival time.

Nonetheless Niall sat benched in state, with his warriors well clad around the walls, their shields catching the flamelight above them. Servants scurried over fresh sweet rushes to keep filled the cups of mead or ale or, for the greatest, outland wine. Smoke thickened the air and stung eyes, but soon it would be full of savory smells, when the tables were set up and the meat brought in from the cookhouse.

Niall leaned forward. The light limned his face athwart shadow, broad brow, straight nose, narrow chin. It showed little of the ashiness in locks and beard that once were primrose yellow, nor of the scars and creases or how the blue of the eyes had faded. In richness of fur, brightly dyed wool, gold and amber, his body now verged on gauntness; but the thews had not shrunk, the movements remained steady and deft. "Why do you call them Romans?" he asked.

"Some were so outfitted, lord," Anmureg replied. "Others appeared to be Gauls, though from elsewhere than Redonia. We heard Latin as well as their own language, when their chiefs were egging them on against us. Then when my crew was at sea—we happened to be together near our currach, making a small repair, the only ones, for the which we have promised Manandan sacrifices—the fog thinned and we saw a ship of the Roman sort anchored offshore, and one of the galleys drawing close to her in peaceful wise."

Another of the men who stood there dripping from the rain said slowly, "She looked much like what I'd seen earlier, King, that galley did."

Niall held himself unmoving. "How was that?" he inquired. Beneath the crackle in the firepit, stillness deepened around the hall.

"You bought a Saxon galley for yourself, King, shortly before I went off a-roving. Black she was, with a yellow stripe, twenty oars, the sternpost high and spiralled at the top and gilt."

"Such as you lost at Ys," declared Cael maqq Eriai. He, an ollam poet, could dare.

"Did you see the other your enemies had?" Niall asked, his voice deadly quiet.

"Not really well, any of us," Anmureg said. "Yourself will understand what wildness ruled on that beach. We here barely stood off an attack till we had our currach launched. Better, we thought, come back and tell your honor about this, than leave our bones there unavenged. The Gauls call those islands the Islands of Crows."

"You did leave two ships behind at Ys," said Cael.

"Ys-s-s," hissed from Niall. "Forever Ys."

"The men who took them may have sold them off," suggested a brithem judge nearby.

Niall shook his head. "They would not," he said; a gust of wind keened at the words. "Over the years I have gathered knowledge of the King of Ys, that Grallon. His city is fallen but he will not rest in the grave where he belongs. This latest is his work too."

"It is that," the druid Étain told him. "A fate binds you two together, though you have never met and never shall. It has not yet run to its end." Because of her calling, she was the sole woman there. Save at Brigit's Imbolc, usage on Temir was that a Queen entertain female guests in her own house. Étain's long white dress made her a ghostly sight among the shadows.

Cael saw how much heartening everybody needed. He stood up, jingled the metal that hung on his staff, reached for the harp he had tuned beforehand. Rain drummed to the strings. Created as he uttered them, the words rang forth:

"Valiant lord of victories,
Avenge your fallen men!
Heroes rise throughout your hall,
Hailing you their King.

"Goddesses whose birds you've gorged,
Grant that you may fare
Windborne, fireborne, laying waste
Widely, Roman land.

"Sail upon the southbound wind.
Set your foot ashore,
Letting slip from off his leash
The lean white hound named Fear.

"Swords will reap when they have soared
Singing from the sheath
Heavy may your harvest be
Of heads and wealth and fame."

Shouts drowned out the weather. Men pounded fists on benches and feet on floor. Niall climbed erect, raised his arms for silence, loomed above the company, and cried:

"Thanks be to you, poet, and good reward shall you have. You too, warriors who bore us this tale—first, dry clothes, full bellies, and lodging in brotherhood; later, your share in the revenge we will take. I swear by Lug and Lir and the threefold Mórrigu, for what you and your comrades have suffered, Rome shall weep!"

—But that evening he walked from Temir, and with him only the female druid Étain. Four guards followed, well out of earshot, the least number the King could take and not demean his name.

The storm had blown over. Grass lay rain-weighted, air nearly as wet. Clouds ringed the horizon. Eastward they towered in murky masses, off which whiteness had calved into the deepening blue. Westward they glowed with sundown, molten copper and gold run together across that whole quarter of the sky. Hush and a soft sort of chill lapped earth.

Niall made his way down from the heights of Temir and up again to the ancient hill-fort sacred to Medb. It was empty of men, because he had enough in this train for any trouble. So there he could speak freely, and maybe likewise Those Who brooded over it. Étain came along in shared muteness. She was a woman tall and thin though sightly, her hair thick and red and the first frost of her years in it.

Atop the ringwall they looked vastly over the western plain, the forest and Boand's River to the north. Niall kept his gaze yonder while he leaned on his spear and said, "I wish your counsel."

"You do not," replied the druid. "You wish my comfort."

He cast her a glance and a troubled grin. "Well, have you any for me?"

"That is for you to know."

I felt easier with old Nemain, he thought. And Laidchenn's poems had wings, where Cael's walk. Well, time slips through our fingers till at last we hold no more of it.

"A name can abide," she told him.

Startled at being answered, he said in his turn as steadily as he was able, "I would have mine stand always with its honor."

She nodded. "Will you or nill you, that is so. Else power must also fall from it."

"That will surely outlive me. Sons of mine are now kings across the breadth of Ériu."

"But the one of them who is to have Temir and Mide from you—and he will, after your tanist falls—is a little child still. To his heritage you must add terror among his enemies; and for that, you must redeem what happened last year, against which today's news was no more than a spark on fuel. Say how you mean to do it."

He looked again at her, and now did not look back away. Sunset colors welled up behind her. "I think you already know," he murmured; "yet the speaking may help me.

"One-and-twenty years ago, while Rome writhed at war with itself, I gathered a fleet and the finest of my warriors. We set course for the River Liger that flows to the sea through rich lands and past gleaming cities. Boundless could our winnings have been. But the witch-Queens of Ys raised a gale that drove us onto the rocks; and their King slew most of us who made it ashore."

He drew breath to quell an undying pain and went on: "Well, Ys is no more, and yonder stream flows as of old. From travellers and scouts I know how stripped are the garrisons that hold Gallia, with the lower end of the river in the hands of strangers. Soon I will make known my intent, the which is to fare with the same strength to the same hunting ground. Men who follow me will win booty, glory, and revenge for their fathers. Afar in Rome, its King shall bewail his loss, and until the heavens fall they will remember us."

His lifting bravado sank when she asked, "You will not be calling at Ys, though, will you, now?"

"I must steer wide of it," he said harshly, "or the men would cast me overboard to her who haunts that water."

"It is you that she haunts, and after you, him whom she also loved."

"What do you then see for us?" he whispered.

"In the end, you shall not go down to her. That fate is for him."

He scowled. "You speak darkling words."

"As the Gods do to me." Étain reached to stroke his cheek. There was sadness in her smile, but it was undaunted. "Come to my house, darling," she said, "and I will give you the best comfort that is mine; for it is what any mortal woman has power to give."

~ 3 ~

Laden with plunder, *Brennilis* and her companion ships—*Wolf* and *Eagle*, for the emblem creatures of Rome—left the Islands of Crows and steered for Hivernia. There, in Mumu, they set Rufinus off. Once more he would range about gathering intelligence on King Niall, returning to Gallia by some fisher or merchantman making that passage late in the season. "Have no fears for me," he laughed. "I've become an old Ériu hand."

A hand to strike down the enemy, Gratillonius hoped.

Homebound, the ships stood well out to sea. Not only were the waters around Ys dangerous, sight of that land was almost unbearable for some aboard. When they felt sure they were to the south of it they would turn east. That would doubtless mean doubling back along the Armorican coast to the Odita mouth, but was amply worth the added time and effort.

On their second day from Hivernia, a west wind sprang up. Rainsqualls and driving clouds hid every star or scrap of moon that night; in the morning, the position of the sun was a matter of guesswork. With the sky went knowledge of bearings. The ships wallowed on through ever heavier seas, through wet and cold and clamor.

"What foul luck," growled Gratillonius when the next day brought no surcease.

"I wonder if luck is all it is," replied Evirion.

"You've said what I did not want to say."

Late that afternoon they saw white spouts and sheets to port. Evirion nodded. "The Bridge of Sena," he reminded landsman Gratillonius— rocks and reefs strung out for miles west of the island. "We should clear them, going close-hauled, but 'twill be a near thing. The galleys will need hard rowing."

Gratillonius snorted a laugh of sorts. "Naught like yonder kind of sight to put force in a man's arms." A jape was a shield.

Wind raved. Spindrift flew bitter. Pushed near the grounds, the farers saw billows crash on skerries and churn between them, foam turning their gray backs into snow-swirls. Spray dimmed sight, a flung-up fog under the hastening smoky clouds. It roared, snarled, hissed, as if dragons ramped within.

And yet the ships clawed off. Beneath strained sail or on straining oars, they lurched and pitched their way south. The dread that had grown within him began to loose its hold on Gratillonius's heart. Soon, he thought, sometime in the endless hours before dark, they'd be past the trap.

Evirion cried out. The galleys were port of the large ship. Shallower of draught and lower of freeboard, they let their crews see rocks that the waves half hid, in time to veer off and thus warn *Brennilis*. The one farthest in, *Wolf*, had abruptly turned east. She was bound straight for the surf.

"What in Lir's name are they doing?" Evirion yelled. "Come back, you clodheads! Come back, Taranis thunder you!" The wind shredded his call, the breakers trampled it underhoof.

Eagle swung about and bore west. Her oars flailed the water. Whatever they'd seen or heard aboard *Wolf*, the other crew had caught just enough of it to make them flee.

Gratillonius remembered what Maeloch had told him, and later Nemeta. He remembered the fight in the bay at dusk. For an instant horror stopped his heart. Then he was again the commanding officer of his men. Amreth Taniti, the whole squad of marines from Ys, was in *Wolf*.

He grabbed Evirion's arm. "They've been lured," he said above the skirl and thunder. "If we let them go, they'll drown." And with them a goodly part of the treasure that could save their people—but it was the men, the men who filled his head.

"Christ have mercy," the captain groaned. "What can we do?"

"Get me rowers for the lifeboat. Launch it. I'm going after them."

Evirion gaped. "Have you gone mad too?"

"God damn it, don't piss away what little time we've got!" Gratillonius snapped in Latin. "Jump to it, if you haven't lost your balls overboard!"

Evirion's face darkened. Gratillonius knew it was touch and go whether the young man would strike him or obey him.

Evirion was off along the deck, shouting into the wind.

Gratillonius came after, likewise bawling forth words. "Eight men for the rescue! Eight brave Christian men! You scuts, will you let that demon have your mates? Christ'll ride with us!"

He was not at all sure of that. But Dahut, Dahut—when she was little he'd kept her from games that might be dangerous—she must not play at the bottom of the sea with the bones of men she murdered, because that could become her doom forever.

The eight were there. Gratillonius recognized a couple of pagans among them. Did they want to show they were as bold as anybody else? No matter. Unlash the boat, drag it over a wildly rolling deck, tilt it across the rail, lower it when that side swings toward the waves, slide down a rope into a hull awash, fend off, bail while the rowers took their oars and threw the strength of their backs against the sea.

Gratillonius emptied out a last bucketful, crawled over the thwarts to the forepeak, braced himself and stood half crouched, peering ahead. Wind savaged him and his waterlogged garments. Waves loomed wrinkled and clifflike on both sides, rumbled past, became surges up which the boat climbed till it poised in spume and shriek before plunging into the next trough. The galley grew in sight. Her crew had shipped their oars. He saw them dimly through the spray, crowded forward, while the wind chivvied *Wolf* toward the breakers. Those were a tangle of mist and violence. Were the men blind, deaf? What gripped them?

Through the noise, a voice; through the chaos, a vision. Somehow the ghastliest of everything was a sunbeam that struck through, blinked out, struck through to gleam on her wet whiteness. Naked she was, save for wildly blowing long hair and the same gold aglow at her loins, white and slender and entrancingly rounded; aye, her beauty had blinded them, and she held out her arms and sang to them. Unhearable in the fury around, the song's clarity streamed forth to encoil the spirit; and what it promised no man but a saint could flee.

Desire came ablaze in the blood. Gratillonius's member leaped to throbbing stiffness. She was Belisama, she was Dahilis, she was there and he'd have her!

No, she was Dahut, and the vessel that he neared was drifting to shipwreck.

Had he watched and listened an instant longer, she would have caught him. To break free was like ripping his manhood out. His rowers had their backs to her, they had not seen, but they faltered. "Row!" he bellowed. "Row, you scoundrels! Stroke, stroke, stroke!" He drew his knife, wedged himself between the nearest, slashed whenever a head turned around. Twice he bloodied a cheek. Meanwhile he hurled noise out of his lungs, commands, oaths, snatches of prayer, lines from a marching song—"Again the tuba, the tuba calling: 'Come, legionary, get off your duff!'"—anything to ram between that song and his men.

The boat thudded against the galley. He seized a rail and sprang across. Inboard, he stumbled over the benches to the crew. They stared before them. At the very bow was Amreth. The marine captain leaned far out, strained toward her who beckoned and sang.

Where the foam runs white on my breasts,
> *White, sparkling, beloved,*
>> *Your kisses course hot—*
Where the sun strikes up to your eyes,
> *Blue, sea-flung, beloved,*
>> *My gaze clings with joy—*

Come you here, as the sun joins the foam,
> *In all splendor, beloved,*
>> *Come cleave to me now—*
Let kissing join gazing, join splendor
With all that's most fierce and most tender
Until our joined souls we both render
> *To Lir in His deep.*

Gratillonius shouted. He struck with fists, feet, knees, brutally hard, whatever might shock them out of their daze. When he cast them down onto the benches, they sat hunched, shaking their heads. He wrestled oars back into place, clamped hands about them, hallooed deafening into ears: "Row! Row! Row!"

Did the song ring with victory? The galley sprang toward it. Gratillonius bounded aft. He seized the tiller and put it over. He should have had rowers on one side only, to make the turnaround fast. He dared not give the order. The men were stunned. They worked like oxen at a millstone. He must not risk them coming fully aware. The slowness raked him.

But then *Wolf* was headed back out. Gratillonius's bulk blocked off sight of the one on the reef. "Stroke, stroke, stroke!"

In the bows, Amreth howled. He sprang. A wave bore him past the stern, toward Dahut.

"Stroke, stroke, stroke!" Gratillonius glared right and left. The lifeboat was also bound for safety. He hazarded a glance behind. Did he catch a last sight of him who swam, or was it seaweed or a piece of wreckage? No more sunlight kindled the foam-haze. There were only rocks and breakers.

The rhythm of the oars clattered to naught. Men gaped at each other. Emptiness in their eyes gave way to bewilderment. "What happened?" Gratillonius heard in tatters through the wind. "What came over me? A dream...I can't rightly remember—"

Eagle coursed to join her sister and give help. *Brennilis* sailed on. Men crowded her port rail to cheer.

Gratillonius sagged at the rudder. He could let go of himself now.

Christ, if it was You Who stood by us, thank You. I wish I could honestly say more than that. Maybe later. I'm so tired, so wet, so wrung. All I want to do is crawl off and sleep. If I can. Maybe first, once I'm alone, I'll weep. Forgive me, if You please, when I don't weep for those we lost fighting in the islands or for Amreth my friend, but for Dahut.

~ 4 ~

"No doubt of it, sir," Nagon Demari said.

Bacca raised his brows. "Oh? Just what are your sources?" he inquired. "You can't be exactly beloved in those parts."

Taken aback when the procurator did not at once hang on what he had to relate, Nagon answered sullenly, "I've got my ways."

"Of course. In a position like yours, one must. But what do you yourself employ?"

Nagon stood before the seated man with his legs planted apart, shoulders hunched, head thrust forward, as if under a load. "Well, a couple of fellows who escaped from Ys, common dock workers they were, they've not forgotten what I once did for them and their kind. The great Grallon isn't so wonderful in their eyes. For a little money, they're glad to tell me things. Others—really need money, or they've got a grudge, or I've learned something about them they'd rather nobody knows."

"The usual methods. You had experience in Ys. What is this latest news?"

"Not mere rumors. I went myself when I first heard those, and asked around. Not into town, you understand. The farms, the villages, places where they don't always know who I am."

"Nor are rustics apt to have much firsthand political knowledge of any kind. But what did you find them abuzz over?"

"Grallon's back with another load of loot. This time he went and took it off pirates in—seems to've been the Britannic Sea."

Bacca's lips shaped a soundless whistle. "Indeed?"

"That's the word, sir." Exultation danced in the flat face, the small pale eyes. "You've got him! He's finally overreached himself. Deliberately organized a military expedition, a civilian armed force. You can behead him!"

Bacca sat still for a minute or two. Nagon dithered.

The procurator sighed. "I'm afraid not," he said. "You can't have heard from anybody who took an actual part."

"No, but word's leaked out like through a sieve."

"He's known it would, and allowed for it."

"Arrest a few men who did go, interrogate them under torture—"

"You're an able man in your fashion," Bacca said, "but statecraft is beyond you. Think, however. If we moved openly against Gratillonius, at this hour when he's come home as a savior, why, we would quite likely have a rebellion on our hands. Do *you* want to explain that to the praetorian prefect? Do you imagine the lord Stilicho would praise our handling of the case? Meanwhile, Gratillonius and his worst trouble-makers will have slipped off into the wilderness; and his friends the tribune and the bishop will insist this is all an unfortunate misunderstanding.

"No, we cannot act on a basis of gossip, no matter how well founded it appears to be. You will speak no further of this to anyone whatsoever. Is that clear?"

Nagon's countenance purpled. He lifted fists in air. "Was my work for nothing?" he cried. "Is that devil going to keep on his merry way and, and make a joke of us? Can't you get it into your head, he's *dangerous?*"

Bacca held up a palm. "Softly. Watch your tongue, especially in the presence of your superiors."

Nagon slumped. "I'm sorry, sir," he got out.

"That's better." Bacca rubbed his nose and stared long at the opposite wall. Finally he said, "I do appreciate your efforts, and they do have value. I would have gotten wind of this one way or another, but belatedly and in much less detail than I imagine you can supply. What's important, I think, is the knowledge that Gratillonius does now have at his beck a force capable of carrying out such an operation. Thus far it must be small. Being warned, we can take steps to prevent its further growth, until such time as we are ready to eradicate it.... Success like his feeds on itself. We must insure that there are no more successes—no more missions for him and his irregulars. This requires—m-m, some very tactful discussion with...the Duke of the Armorican Tract....Not to provoke him into ill-advised action against Confluentes. But to make clear to him that the help of such people is more to be feared than the onslaught of the barbarians....Courage, Nagon. You've done well. Sit down, give me your full report. In due course you shall have an appropriate reward."

~ 5 ~

Harvest brought wholeness.

"I'm not sleepy yet," Gratillonius said. "I'll go for a walk first."

Verania yawned. She always did so in a way that made him think of a kitten. "Well, I'm quite ready for bed," she admitted.

He chucked her under the chin. "I won't be gone long. As soon as you're healed, I won't be gone at all."

She gave him a heavy-lidded glance. "Speed the day."

They kissed, less strongly or lingeringly than they desired. She was warm and supple against him. Memories of a skerry glimmered away for this while. "I'll leave a light burning, of course," she said. "Enjoy your walk. It is a beautiful evening."

He stooped above the tiny, homely miracle in the crib. "Goodnight, Marcus." He looked over his shoulder. "Ungracious rascal. I do believe he snored at me."

She wrinkled her nose. "Takes after his father, he does." In haste: "Not really. Not in that way. You don't often."

His son, he thought. Bearer of the name. Her parents had supposed he chose "Marcus" for the Evangelist, and were pleased. Except for Verania, who went cheerfully along with the conspiracy, he wouldn't disenchant them. His father in Britannia had been Marcus. Strange how this new life strengthened its own wellsprings, even those that had long since flowed into quietness.

He took his cloak and went from the bedroom, down the corridor, out the atrium and front door of Apuleius's house. A few months hence, he and Verania would have their own home; and it wouldn't be a cob-and-turf hovel. In the meantime, the older couple couldn't be kinder. Salomon sometimes got brash, but the boy meant well and... already, as easily and naturally as a seed becomes a sapling, was the leader of his age contingent in Aquilo.

May the sapling grow to a mighty oak.

Not far past full, the moon lifted above Mons Ferruginus.

Light speckled streets and frosted roofs. Air was still warm and full of earth odors, once Gratillonius had left the city behind. He found a path leading to the heights. Along it he was frequently in darkness cast by trees or by the hill itself, but his feet knew the way.

Years ago, he thought as his tread whispered upward, a few days after the whelming of Ys, he had climbed this same track, in flight from emptiness. It ran him down and brought him to the ground. Or, rather, he had borne it with him while he fled it. Why was tonight otherwise? Why should he dare be happy?

The last of his people were striking new roots, but Rome could well rip them out again. The East might stand firm—he couldn't tell from what confused and fragmentary accounts reached this far—but the walls of the West crumbled before the wild men. Christ was strong; Christ was strange. Nemeta dwelt alone and crippled. What loneliness was Dahut's?

Verania had given him a son.

He reached the top, near the iron smelter where wood had been cleared away, and looked across the land. Fields were hoar, forest crowns dappled, rivers atremble with moonlight. Stars glinted in violet-blue.

Gratillonius raised his hand. This will be yours, Marcus, he vowed. Nobody shall take it from you, ever.

Aloud into the huge silence: "For your sake also, I am going to make Niall dead. Christ be my witness."

XVII

~ 1 ~

"—duly noted.

"Your interest, if sincere, is commendable. However, the value of your report is questionable at best. Your alleged agent in Hivernia has provided nothing more than his own word about what rumors and boasts he heard. The fickleness of barbarian will is notorious. This story of a seaborne raid on the scale of an invasion is in all likelihood some petty chieftain's fantasy.

"Defense is adequate around the Liger estuary. Your recommendation that the Saxon laeti there be reinforced, implying as it does that Christian soldiers go under pagan command, approaches profanation. To strengthen the garrisons upstream, as you also propose, shows you are quite ignorant of the peril at the Germanic frontier, not to mention policy considerations that require maximum troop strength in the South and East.

"Your scheme of raising native forces is totally unacceptable. Law forbids, and this office is not so foolish as to request an exception be made. We have received accounts of such activities on your part, and hereby warn you in the strongest terms that they must stop at once. Otherwise the consequences will be grave for everyone concerned in any violations. Most certainly, the appearance of armed and organized

civilians in the Liger Valley will constitute insurrection. Claims of emergency will not excuse it, and punishment will be condign.

"Your obedience to the Imperial decree and your cooperation in suppressing rash attempts at action are required. Copies of this letter are being sent to—"

Gratillonius tossed it down. He had been reading it aloud. "Never mind," he said dully. "There's more, but I'm about to gag."

"What can Apuleius do?" asked Rufinus.

"Nothing. Understand, this is directly from the Duke of the Armorican Tract."

"The man in command of all our defenses. So Glabrio's finally gotten to him. And he in his turn to whoever's in charge among the Namnetes and Turones." Rufinus tugged his beard. "M-m, it's not quite that simple, I suppose." A grin flickered over the vulpine face. "Rome has reasons to keep weapons from its citizens."

"In God's name!" groaned Gratillonius. "What do they imagine we're plotting? We only want to help."

Winter's rain brawled on the roof and sluiced down window glass. For all its newness and bright paint, the atrium of his house was full of the day's gloom and chill. One could barely see a wall panel that Verania was decorating in her scant spare time. It would show sprays of tall flowers. At first she had intended a picture of Ys, but he replied that the city should rest in its grave, after which she sought to kiss away the pain she heard.

"Well, they distrust us, and we'll have to lie low," Rufinus said. "Maybe after the Scoti have struck—because they will, as surely as fire will burn you—then the lords of state will listen."

"I wonder about that. And anyway—the whole valley sacked? Dead men in windrows, cities torched, Gallia slashed open right through its heart. How long can *we* survive that?"

"I know, master. Your hands are tied." Rufinus straightened. "But mine aren't."

Gratillonius stared at the lean, leather-clad form. "What do you mean?"

"Give me a ship and crew in early spring. Niall won't leave till after Beltene. I'll have time to brew up something."

Gratillonius's heart slugged. "By yourself? Are you out of your head?"

"No more than usual," laughed Rufinus. Soberly: "I can't promise a thing, of course, except that I'll try. I've been half expecting something like this letter, and thinking, but it's vague in my mind. Has to be, what with every single piece in the game a shadow—a shadow thrown by a guttering lamp....No, I shouldn't say more, even to you. Please don't ask me. Just let me try."

Gratillonius reached an unsteady hand toward him. "By Hercules, old friend, you are a man."

Rufinus barely clasped the arm. He turned on his heel. "I have to go now," he said to the one at his back.

"No, wait, stay for dinner, at least."

"Sorry, but I have—things to do—out in the woods. I'll likely be gone several days. Have it well, master." Rufinus strode from the room.

~ 2 ~

Eochaid maqq Éndae held an islet in a narrow bay of the Alban Dál Riata coast. Skies were low when the galley from Armorica arrived; underneath their gray, mists held the tops of the mainland mountains. A cold breeze ruffled the water. Its murkiness made rock, sand, and gnarly dwarf trees on the holm doubly drear. Smoke blew ragged from hearthfires inside a rath. A shed ashore, near a wooden dock, must hold a small ship, and several currachs lay above high-tide mark.

Warriors had hastened out of the stronghold and formed a line before it. Rufinus's rowers brought his vessel to the pier without showing any weapons, and he himself sprang forth, his hands lifted empty. He had donned fine clothes, red cloak above saffron-dyed wool tunic, breeches of blue linen, kid boots. An ornate baldric held his longsword, a belt studded with amber and garnets his knife and pouch. "Peace!" he cried in the tongue of Ériu. "A friend of your chieftain seeks him."

Eochaid stepped from the rank, his own blade lowered. He was coarsely clad. Winter indoors had paled him, so that the three blotchy scars marring his face stood forth in full ugliness. "Who is this?" he asked; and then, looking closer: "Is it you, truly you?" He dropped his sword and ran to embrace the newcomer. "A thousand welcomes, my heart, a thousand thousand!"

Rufinus returned the gesture. Eochaid released him and called to his men, "Here is himself who got me free of Niall's bonds—six years ago, has it been? Were it six hundred, I'd remember him. All that I have is yours, Rufinus."

"I thank you," said the Gaul, "my crew thanks you, my King afar thanks you."

"Come, disembark, come inside. What God has brought you to me, darling?"

"Whichever deals in vengeance," Rufinus answered low. "We've much to talk about alone, you and I."

—Within the earthen wall were houses, byres, cribs, pens, everything meager and crowded together. It was no great estate that King Aryagalatis had bestowed on the fugitive prince. He and his followers might have done better inland; but that, he explained, would mean endless trouble with the displaced Cruthini, and keep him from the sea. "Here we fish, trade, sometimes make a raid southward, otherwise keep our bit of livestock, and always bide our chance," he said. "The day will come for us. It must."

His dwelling was the largest, of the same turf and dry-laid raw stone as the rest but fitted inside with things of gold, silver, and glass.

Like most of his men, he had acquired a staff of workers, male and female, generally slaves though a couple of them hirelings from poor families of the nearest tuath. The showpiece was a woman captured from the Brigantes; she knew Latin and was still comely in spite of the hard life and bearing him two children thus far, neither of whom lived long. He offered Rufinus the use of her, or any other of his household.

The guest declined gracefully. "This voyage of mine, seeking you out, my dear, is so important that I took a gess as part of the price for its good outcome. While the feast is being made ready and my men settling in amongst yours, could we go off by ourselves?"

"We can that, if it be your wish." Eagerness quivered in Eochaid's voice. "The boatshed is at least shelter from the wind, and I'll have a cask of mead brought us. I've slept in there twice, when I sought presaging dreams; and they came to me, though double-tongued as sendings from the Gods so often are."

Within were dank dimness and a smell of tar from the galley filling most of the space. The two men sat down with cloaks between them and the ground. They broached the cask and drank from Roman goblets.

"I have heard tales of you," said Rufinus: "how, after you got away from Niall, misfortune still dogged you—"

"It has that," Eochaid declared grimly.

"—but you won through to this."

"Little enough for a son of King Éndae."

"Great enough for me to hear about, and ask my way till I found it."

"Even here, Niall reaches." Eochaid tossed off his cupful and dipped another.

Rufinus nodded. "I know. He readies for a mighty faring south, and calls on every king who is under him or allied to him. But how does he command Aryagalatis?"

"Through the motherland, Dál Riata in Ériu. A son of his has wrung tribute, obedience, from that far corner of Qóiqet nUlat. Agreement was better than invasion."

"M-m-m.... I've heard tell that Aryagalatis is by no means unwilling."

Eochaid bared teeth. "He is not. The loot and glory bedazzle him as they do everybody."

"Other than yourself."

"What do you think I am?" Eochaid flared. "Never would I follow Niall maqq Echach! May pigs devour my corpse if ever I do!" He drank again and calmed a little. "Aryagalatis understands. I am free to stay behind."

"You chafe, though."

Eochaid sighed. "This is a cheerless place."

"I've come to tell you," said Rufinus weightily, "that you can indeed follow Niall to his war."

The marks stood lurid on Eochaid's skin. "You are my guest, but have a care."

Rufinus smiled. "Sure and you don't think I'd be insulting of you, my heart, do you?" he purred. "A hunter follows an elk that he may bring it down."

Eochaid's hand jerked. Mead slopped from his goblet. "What's this?"

"Listen, please. It's what I've sought you out for, and a weary voyage that was." Rufinus waited until the Scotian was thrummingly still, then said:

"If you tell King Aryagalatis you would like to come along after all, as it might be out of loyalty to him your befriender—as well as for a share in the gains—it's glad he'll be, I'll wager. You and your men are proven warriors. At the same time, he should heed your wish that he say nothing about it to Niall. That could only bring trouble."

"How shall Niall stay unaware?"

"Why, if Aryagalatis makes no mention of it—and Aryagalatis will see very little of him—then talk between crews will scarcely come to the ears of the great King. He'll have so much else to think about and do. I daresay he's well-nigh forgotten you. True, you plundered about in his country once, and later killed the son of his chief poet, but both were avenged in dreadful ways, and—saving your honor—you will be just one small skipper in a fleet from much of Ériu."

Eochaid gripped his dagger. Knuckles stood white above the hilt. "I am no more than that," he said hoarsely. "I, a son of the Laginach King, because of Niall maqq Echach."

"Then make his sons grieve for it."

"How?"

"We shall see. I will travel with you." Rufinus poured and drank before he locked eyes with his host and said: "This is needful. It's why I've sought you out. Going by my own ship, I'd be a marked man. Everybody would ask who I was and where I hailed from. In your crew I'll be hidden. As far as they know, I'm simply your outland friend who's joined you for the adventure. There must be many such in so big a band. Word of me will be lost in the racket of weapons."

Eochaid gave him stare for stare. "Why do you do this?" he asked, deep in his throat.

"I am a man of King Grallon's," Rufinus answered. "And he too has much to avenge on Niall. Oh, endlessly much."

"The King of Ys." Awe shook the words. "What is your plan, man of his?"

"I told you, none. We must wait for our chance. In the welter of such an expedition, it's bound to come, the more so when there are two of us to watch for it and seize it."

Eochaid looked away, into darkness. "This is no real home for me," rustled from him, like dead leaves blowing. "If I must become a roofless wanderer again, or die, after striking Niall down, why, it's joyous I'd go to my doom." He shook himself. "But the hope is so farfetched. We could die for naught, we two."

Rufinus reached in his pouch. "At the feast this evening we'll exchange such gifts as befits our honor," he said; "But here is one I've brought to give you in secret, and the most precious of the lot."

He undid protective wrappings and held out his hand. Eochaid took the thing he offered and brought it close, the better to see in the cold dimness. It was the skull of a falcon, held together by sinew cords. Graven in the bone was an arrow.

"This winter past, I went to a witch who dwells in the forest," Rufinus told him. "I asked her help. She cast what spells she was able, and made this, though she had the use of but one arm. She said it ought to bring you luck."

Uneasily, Eochaid turned the charm over and over. "What did you give her?"

"Nothing," Rufinus answered, forgetting his tale of the gess. "She thanked me. She also has Ys to avenge and...and Grallon to love."

~ 3 ~

That year Beltene in Mide was the greatest and most magnificent ever heard of since the Children of Danu held Ériu. To Temir swarmed men who would fare south with Niall after the rites and the three days of celebration that were to follow. Their tents and booths overran the land round about, a sudden bloom of colors and banners and blinking metal. Their tuathal kings and the wives of these packed the houses on the sacred hill.

Guests were all the more crowded because they must yield place to the mightiest yet seen here, other than Niall himself—Conual Corcc, up from Mumu to keep the feast with his foster-kinsman. Beautiful and terrible were the warriors who accompanied their lord. Chariots rumbled, riders galloped and reared their horses, spears rippled to the march like grain ripe beneath the wind, shields flashed, horns roared when that company appeared; and most wonderful was that it came in peace.

Disquieting to thoughtful folk was that it would depart in peace likewise. King Conual had no wish to sail against the Romans. Rather, he had come in hopes of stopping the venture, the tale of which rang from shore to shore of Ériu.

In this he failed. "I feared my words would be useless," he admitted at the end. "But for the sake of the old bonds between us, I must in honor speak them."

"I thank you for your care of me," said Niall; "but better would be if you laid your strength to mine."

They were side by side in the Feasting Hall on the last night before men went home or went to war. The meat was eaten, the tables cleared away, now servers flitted about refilling cups. A savor lingered in the smoke which firepit and lamps tinged pale red. Elsewhere throughout that cavernous space it gleamed off hanging shields and the gold, silver, bronze, amber, gems upon the men benched around the walls. Talk and laughter boomed between. There was an edge to its roughness, for omens had been unclear and word of that had gotten about. Everyone worked hard to keep good cheer alive. Close by the two great Kings they sat quiet, listening.

"I have my own land to think of," said Conual. "We prosper by trade with the Romans."

"As you did with the Ysans—" Niall stopped short. "I would never be calling you afraid, darling."

Conual lifted his head. The locks were still flame-hued. "I try to be wise," he said. "Why should I offend the Romans and their God? He has ever more followers in Mumu."

"And this makes you hang behind?" Niall's sneer was meaningless, as he himself well knew. They had been over and over the grounds for Conual's counsel against the expedition—recklessness, the gains not worth the risk—and Niall's for going ahead—glory, wealth, binding closer to him his allies here at home, the fact that he had uttered his intention and could not now back down.

"It does not," said Conual evenly, "as you know. However, I think the morrow is His. I will go to the Gods of my fathers, but it may well be that after me the Rock of Cassel upbears His Cross."

Niall cast a glance at the druid Étain, the sole woman present. Her face remained shut and she said nothing. Thus had it been since she cast ogamm wands and kept silence about what she read.

In sudden cold fury, Niall spat, "He'll have a harder time in Mide!" He turned and beckoned to Laégare, youngest of his living sons, heir to this Kingship; so the tanist Nath Í had sworn beside the Phallus. At six years of age, the boy was reckoned ready to join men at their board. He had sat quietly, for he was of such a nature, though fierce enough in sports and battle practice to gladden his father.

"Come here, my son." Niall bade.

Laégare obeyed. Straight he stood, his hair a brightness amidst leaping shadows. Niall leaned forward and laid hands on his shoulders. "Tomor- row I go from you," Niall said. A hush spread like ripples from a stone thrown into a pool, as others heard.

"If only I could too!" Laégare cried.

Niall smiled. "You're a wee bit young for that, my dear." He grew somber. "But I will take an oath of you, here and now."

Laégare's voice barely trembled. "Whatever it is, father, I swear."

"This: that never in your life you make sacrifice or give pledge to the God of the Romans."

"That is a heavy gess to lay on a King," said Conual, troubled. "Who knows what will come to him and his people?"

"At least he shall keep the pride of old Ériu," Niall told them all. "Do you take this last command of mine, my son?"

"I do that," Laégare replied. His voice was still childish, but it rang.

~ 4 ~

As Niall rode toward the sea, a hare darted across his path and a fox in pursuit of it. At once he called to him those men nearby who had seen and ordered silence about this. "Many would lose heart if they heard of such a sign," he reminded them. His head lifted against heaven. "I go where the Mórrigu wants me."

His old henchman Uail maqq Carbri said nothing to that, but bleakness took hold of the gaunt face.

A generation ago, the mouth of Boand's River had seen as great a fleet as was gathered there now. Currachs drawn up ashore or bobbing in the water seemed beyond counting, as did the warriors who milled around them. At anchor in the shallows lay over a dozen Saxon-built galleys. Once more Niall's bore a Roman skull nailed to the stempost; but this hull was painted red, for blood and fire.

The day was cloudless. Light flared on weapons aloft as men shouted greeting to the King. Color on shirts, kilts, cloaks, shields made a whirlpool rainbow. Gulls soared a hundredfold, a snowstorm of wings. Niall sprang from his chariot and strode toward his ship.

Uail squinted upward, shook his head, and muttered to Cathual, the royal charioteer, "The last time, you remember, a raven came down and perched on his shield. What have we today?"

"I fear I shall never be driving him again," said Cathual. Hastily: "Because I am not the lightfoot youth I was. It was kind of him to let me hold the reins on this final trip of his." He winced. Somehow he seemed unable to speak his meaning; the words came out unlucky.

He was not alone in his forebodings. Things had been happening for months which betokened trouble. They could be as slight as a cuckoo heard on the left or as terrifying as groans from the graves at Tallten on Beltene Eve. Old wives wove amulets for their sons to carry. Druids made divinations and shook their heads.

Yet somehow there was no portent of utter disaster, of anything like the ruin suffered at Ys. The feeling in the air was more akin to a sorrow, though none could name that from which it welled. Niall, conqueror of the North, showed no trace of sharing it. Warriors must therefore deny it in themselves and follow him with good cheer. They dared not open their hearts to each other about it. Thus nobody knew how widely and deeply the cold current ran. The clamor at his back was as of wolves and wildcats.

He waded out to his ship, laid hand on the rail, and boarded in a single leap. Tall he stood at the prow. The light touched his hair with a ghost of the former gold. To Manandan son of Lir he offered a red cock, slashing its head off with his sword and laving the skull with its

996

blood. "And white oxen shall You have when I bring home my victories!" he cried.

Men went to their craft. Oars rattled into place. They bit the ebb tide, and the fleet walked out over the sea.

Never did Niall look back at his country.

He passed it on that first day and made camp for the night south of the Ruirthech outflow, in Qóiqet Lagini. No fighters came to trouble them, nor did they find cattle or sheep to take. The coast stretched desolate. Not yet had the Lagini recovered from the woe that Laidchenn's satire brought on them. When they did, Niall knew, vengefulness must kindle the marches. Well, he would deal with that then; Nath Í would after him; Laégare would when his day came; such was the fate of a King.

At dawn the camp roused and the voyage went on. Weather stayed fine in the next days while the vessels worked their way down the side of Ériu. Their last evening on it, Niall called the tuathal leaders together at his fire. They were many, as diverse as their homelands, some fair as he, some dark, some red-haired, some gray, clad in linen or wool, or skins, a few with hair drawn into horsetails like Gauls or with tattoos like Cruthini—subjects, allies, all the way from Condacht's western cliffs to Dál Riata's colony beyond the Roman Wall.

"You see how the Gods are with us," he said; "but they only want us to run mad in battle. First we must get there, the which will take both cunning and patience." While they knew more or less what he intended, he now laid it out at length and answered questions with unexpected mildness.

They would not cross over to the Dumnonic tip of Britannia. The Romans must have gotten at least a breath of what he had afoot. They would look for such a layover. Weakened though their forces were, they, with help from the fierce hillmen north of the Sabrina, might had readied an ambush. "We could doubtless fight them off and get away, but we'd take losses without any gain of booty," Niall said. "Don't belittle them." His mind harked back to a combat near Deva, three years ago, and the strangely impressive centurion with whom he spoke. "Rome is an aged beast, but she still has fangs. We'll get enough of her at the Liger."

He would go on without further stops. That was a long way across open sea; and he would make it longer still by steering very wide of the headlands where Ys had been and the hungry skerries were yet. The Scoti must keep together. Let fog or storm scatter them, and they were foredone. "It is for us to dare," Niall finished, "and undying will be the honor we win."

He overbore objections. They were scant. Everybody knew that their lives were his, and his alone. It seemed to them that he had taken power over wind and wave as well as war; or so they must needs believe.

Therefore, at sunrise they departed due south. This day was also bright. A favoring wind raised whitecaps on the glittery sea, and sails blossomed. Unutterably green astern lay Ériu. To watch it fall from sight was like waking from a dream of someone beloved.

Niall did not. Always he looked ahead.

Sunset smoldered on the rim of vast loneliness and went out. The night was moonless. He had planned things thus. The Romans would reckon on a force like his waiting till it had light after dark, for skippers to keep track of each other. To catch the enemy unawares, he had his galleys spaced well apart, lanterns burning at their rails. By these beacons the currachs would steer.

The wind continued friendly. It filled the sail and yet did not much chill the flesh; it lulled through the undertone of the seas, the seething at the prow, the slight creak of timbers and tackle as the ship rolled onward. Gentle as it was, it did not make the stars gutter. They glinted uncountable around the frosty River of Heaven, almost drowning out the pictures they made, Lúg's Chariot, the Salmon, the Sickle—but high astern stood the Lampflame by which men know the north; and as it sank night by night, it would tell him when to turn east for his goal. Yellow gleams swayed in strings out on Ocean's unbounded night, the riding lights of the galleys.

Niall stood by himself in the bows of his ship. Save for the steersman and two on watch at the waist, sleep filled her hull. With his back to the lanterns he had some vision of mysterious shimmers and foam-swirls under the stars. The skull nodded gray above him.

I am bound for that which I was robbed of, these many years agone, he thought.

It was a quiet thought. He felt beyond hope or anger; his mind was like the wind, steadily bearing south. I am going at last to my luck.

A surge passed through the water. A white and rounded slenderness lifted half out of the bow wave. It swam alongside, or it flew or it was borne, softly and easily as the wind. He saw how the heavy hair streamed behind. She turned toward him, raising her right arm—to greet, to beckon?—and he saw starlight wash over the wet breasts. Her face was ice-pale, her eyes two nights with each its own tiny star.

"Manandan abide!" he choked. Somehow the men on watch did not hear. Was the cold that flowed over him from her or from within himself?

She smiled. Her teeth were the hue of bleached bone. In a way unknown to him he heard: I have said that never will my love let go of you, nor will it ever, Niall, my Niall.

Dahut—But we are so far from Ys where you died.

Across the width of the world can I hear your name, Niall, my lover. It has flown on the wind and the wings of the gulls. Tide had carried it along, and the secret rivers of Ocean, and the whispering of dead men in the deeps. The Gods Whose vengeance I am have told me. Your name was a song and a longing. I followed it, blind with my need; and now again I behold you.

His desire terrified him. —Why can you not rest peaceful?

That which we did in Ys, the work of the wrathful Gods, binds us together and always will. My doom is to love you.

That dooms me too.

Fear not. For you I am the blessing of the sea. I give you fair winds, sweet skies, starlight and moonlight and radiant days. I guide you past rocks and shoals, I bid the storm swing wide of you, I bring you to safe harbor. I wreck the ships of your foemen, I drag them down below, I cast what the eels have left of them ashore for their widows to find. I am your Dahut.

But you cannot free me from the dread of what you are, nor from the sorrow of it, that this is because of me.

Aye, you betrayed me then, and left me alone. You shall betray me again, and leave me alone.

Not willingly, haunter of mine.

Nay. But by dying, as all men must. Unless your death be at sea— Niall shuddered.

She reached toward him. Her fingers brushed his, which clutched the rail. Cold stabbed through. She lowered herself back into the starlit water and told him sadly:

I cannot bring that about. I can only wish for it, while I strive to make your years on earth as long as may be and your death as happy as may be, old and honored among your own kindred; for I love you. Let me fare by your side, Niall. Your men shall not know. They shall merely wonder how easy a voyage is theirs. By day I will look at you from the covert of the foam. By night—all I ask is that you stand like this a little while before you seek your rest, that I may feel your gaze upon me and smile at you. You will hear my songs in your dreams.

The fear left him. There grew in its stead a gentleness toward her yearning, and a sense of the strength that coursed in his blood, and a sly hankering for King Grallon to learn of everything. "I give you that, Dahut," he said.

~ 5 ~

Mightily swept the Liger to the sea. Where Corbilo guarded it on the right bank, its mouth gaped more than a league from shore to marshy shore. Sandbars in late summer, swollenness in late winter made navigation tricky; and at every season the Saxon laeti of that neighborhood were ready to fight for their new homes.

Sight of the Scotic fleet sent the few ships they had on patrol rowing back at full speed. More would be marshalled at Corbilo, and warriors flocking in from the countryside. The city was a husk of its ancient self, inside walls hastily and clumsily raised, but the only sure way to go past it was to take it first, and that meant a hard battle.

Beyond it, though, were nothing but Gallic reservists and legionary garrisons too depleted to put any stiffness in them. The valley lay open for ravishing.

Niall's achievements stemmed from his ever having been more than the ablest and boldest among fighters; as much as the wildness of his followers allowed, he gathered knowledge and laid careful plans beforehand. According to orders, galleys and currachs made landing just north of the estuary, in a sheltered bay which spies had come to know very well during the year that was past. There he would establish himself unassailably before taking the bulk of his forces on foot against the city.

A Roman road led to it through lands that had otherwise largely gone back to forest in the past century or two. A couple of fisher hamlets and a nearby farmstead stood empty, their dwellers fled. Aside from some livestock they had nothing worth reaving and were soon burnt. The smoke of them blotted the sunlight streaming from the west.

Vessels necessarily put in over a lengthy stretch of that shoreline. In case of an alarm, skeleton crews were to take them off the beach while most men ran to the King's encampment and formed a war-host. Eochaid's small galley had kept near the tail of the fleet throughout the journey. He brought her to rest farthest north of any, along with her accompanying boats. "Make things ready here," he ordered Subne. "Rufinus and I will go scouting a while."

His henchman peered into the marred face. He saw how tightly it was drawn and how the lips quivered within the beard. "You have been strange on this faring, my heart," said Subne; "and the strangest is that you came at all. Is it wise what you are thinking, whatever that may be?"

"It is what I have thought for these long years," Eochaid answered.

Subne sighed. "Come what may, I will keep faith with you." He glanced around. The crew were abustle unloading, seeking firewood, shouting to other gangs on the strand. "I cannot speak for every man here. Some could remember too well that they have women and little ones in Dál Riata."

"You borrow trouble, my friend," said Rufinus smoothly. "We're just off for a look around, this lovely evening."

Naturally they went armed. He wore his woodsman's leather with knife and short sword, sling tucked into belt, spear in hand. Among the stones in his pouch he had, unobserved, put some coins. Eochaid's litheness was in kilt of somber green, a sheathed dagger tucked into it. On his back were a longsword and quiver. He carried a hunting bow.

They left the tumult and went in among the trees. "Likely we *are* only scouting," said Rufinus. "Don't get rash, my dear."

"Nor dither and dawdle," Eochaid grated. "Now, while all is in turmoil—" He snapped his jaws shut.

Brush rustled about legs, old leaves beneath feet. These woods were not yet high or thick. Between the boles was a sight of Ocean, still and burnished-bright. A faint sound of waves mingled with the silence here, a tang of salt with the warm odors. Leaves glowed golden overhead. Rays streamed through to cleave the shadows around.

Having gone a ways inland, the companions turned and went south. Presently Rufinus gestured and moved right. He had taken note of landmarks, a beech standing above its neighbors, a coppice of dogwood likewise visible from the water. They gave him his bearings. Noise waxed as he neared the strand. He stopped, laid finger to mouth, squinted against a sunbeam, finally drew Eochaid aside into the cornel.

From its shade and densely growing stems they looked upon the King's ground. Drawn up where wavelets lapped shore was the red galley. The Roman skull grinned above a pack of currachs nestled on either flank. At hover on Ocean's rim, the sun cast their shadows long upon Gallia. Men scuttered and bawled, making ready for night. They had pitched a tent and started a cookfire, now they claimed places for themselves and sought the best spots to post guards. Spearheads and axes blinked athwart the shining reach of the bay. Banners fluttered brave in a light breeze. Shouts, laughter, lusty song flew with the seabirds on high.

Rufinus heard the breath hiss between Eochaid's teeth. His gaze followed the other's. A man had come into sight from the left, where he must have been talking with chieftains. Like the beech in the wood, he towered over the rest. His powerful frame was as roughly clad as any, but across his shoulders he had pinned a cloak of seven colors. The sunset light passed by it and made a golden torch of his head.

"Niall," Rufinus heard, both name and curse.

How beautiful he is! the Gaul thought.

Movement drew his heed away. At his side, Eochaid strung the bow. Rufinus grabbed the Scotian's arm. "Wait, you," he warned.

Eochaid shook the grasp off. "I've waited too long already," he snarled. "May he choke on the blood he has shed."

Rufinus stood motionless. Any struggle would give them away.

Eochaid finished stringing the bow and reached for an arrow. "May the winds of winter toss his homeless soul for a thousand years." He nocked the shaft, raised up the bow, drew the string to his ear. Niall had stopped by the galley. He waved aside a man who wanted to speak to him and looked out across Ocean as if in search of something. "May he be reborn a stag that hounds bring down, a salmon on the hook of a woman, a child caught in a burning house where its father and mother lie slain." The bow twanged.

Niall flung his arms aloft, staggered, fell down on his face, feet in the sea, head beneath the skullpost. Red poured out into the water.

Rufinus seized Eochaid's arm again and yanked the man around. "Quick!" he said through the sudden uproar. "Go how I tell you! Else we're dead—" And, unless they were lucky, not soon dead.

You couldn't run through these thickets. At first Eochaid lurched ahead like a sleepwalker. Rufinus followed, giving orders that got awkward obedience, covering the trail as best he was able. It would have been much easier and safer to make off by himself. If necessary, he would. Gratillonius needed him, and this tool had served its purpose. Yet he'd rather not toss Eochaid aside and forget him.

Whatever pursuit there was came to naught. The Scoti could not tell just where the shot had come from; they were witless with grief and rage; Eochaid regained his share of the woodcraft of which Rufinus was a master. Dusk veiled them.

—Eochaid sank to the ground. It was chill and wet beneath him, the verge of marshland. Rufinus remained standing. Trees gloomed around them; they could barely see one another. Between the leaves above, blue deepened slowly toward black. A star or two shivered forth.

"Well, this will be a comfortless camp," said Rufinus, "but we should be in the way of getting a little rest before morning."

"What then?" asked Eochaid.

"Why, I'll be off home, reporting to my lord, and I counsel you do the same. Sure and it's a grand welcome your father ought to give the man who rid the world of the old bucko."

Eochaid shook his head, which hung heavy as a stone. "I cannot be forsaking my men. Nor is it to my honor that I sneak from my deeds like a thief."

Rufinus sighed. "I was afraid of this. You're a mortal danger to those men, once word gets about—and it will, whether or not you speak, because people know you were Niall's foe and out of sight when he fell. Of course, you are free to blame me. I'll not mind that."

"Never, and I wish you had not said it."

"Well, steal back there if you must, then flee before dawn with such of them as may still call themselves yours. Niall's sons will be scouring the seas and every land they can reach, in quest of revenge. I forbid myself the risk of being your guide, but if you can get to Confluentes I'll find a place for you among my foresters."

"Nor that, though I suppose I should be thankful to you," said Eochaid dully. "I won't be calling you a man without honor, but whatever you have of it is something unknowable to me. This that you've brought about—I thought my vengeance would be a flame of glory, but I shot him unseen and they will only remember me as his murderer. Go away, Rufinus. You freed me once, but now leave me alone."

The Gaul was silent a while before he murmured, "I freed you because it was wrong to keep a proud and splendid animal caged. Afterward I took you hunting with me. Well, things change, and this is the hour between dog and wolf. Goodbye." He slipped off into the twilight.

There was not enough dry wood in these parts for a balefire worthy of Niall of the Nine Hostages. Those of his sons who had come along ordered his ship dragged fully ashore and set alight. He lay before it on a heap of green boughs. They had taken the arrow from his breast, washed him, dressed him in his finest, combed his hair, closed his eyes, folded his hands over a drawn sword.

High roared the flames, white where they devoured, blue and red and yellow above, streaming away starward in sparks. The water seemed ablaze too. Night leaped in and out but never quite reached the King. The steel in his clasp outshone the gold on his arms, at his throat, around his brows. Spears fenced him in flashing fire, held by the tuathal kings of Ériu who stood around garbed for a battle they could never fight. Beyond them, the length of the beach, darkness prowled between torches lifted throughout the host of warriors. Ocean whispered underneath their weeping.

Éogan maqq Néill, eldest of the sons who were there, trod forth. He carried the arrow. So close he came to the burning ship that it scorched his hair while he cast the shaft in and cursed him who had sent it.

He withdrew, and Uail maqq Carbri left the ranks and went to stand by the King. He was no poet—there would be many of them to make laments, the foremost Torna Éces himself—but this gray man had been handfast to Niall since they both were boys, and the sons gave him the right to speak for all.

"Ochón," he wailed, "Niall is gone! The stag whose antlers touched heaven, the salmon whose leap was silver in the cataract, the child whose laughter filled earth with music, has left hollowness in our hearts.

"Ochón, Niall is fallen! The hazel whose boughs were a snare for sunlight, the rowan whose berries were fiery as love, the yew whose wood was strong for bows and spearshafts, has left emptiness on our horizon.

"Ochón, Niall is dead! The warrior whose blade sang terror, the King whose judgments were just, the friend whose hand was open, has left ashes on our hearths.

"Niall, you were our strength. Niall, you were our hope. Niall, you were our soul. Farewell forever. Ochón for Mother Ériu, ochón for—"

He faltered, stared down and then around, stammered, "For-forgive me, I can't go on," and stumbled off with head in hands and shoulders shaking.

The host howled their sorrow to the fire and the stars. From the sea beyond the light rose a sound more shrill, as of a winter wind although the air lay moveless. Someone out yonder was keening too.

—In the morning, the chieftains held council, soon ended. None cared to go on. After what had happened, and upon remembrance of warnings over the months, it seemed clear that this faring was doomed.

Craftsmen made a long box for the body of Niall and put it aboard Éogan's ship. The fleet set homeward.

Weather stayed gentle. Breezes from the south kept sails filled. Strangest, maybe, was how no stench rose from the coffin. Sometimes at night men glimpsed a whiteness alongside. It seemed to be showing them the way.

Their grief remained boundless. When they came back at last, they buried their King not where lesser ones rested, but in earth of his own. They called it Ochain, the Place of Mourning.

~ 7 ~

Rufinus could not sleep.

Hour by hour his bed had narrowed, like the soil of a grave settling inward. When he twisted about, the sheet tightened around him. Windowpanes were blank with moonlight. It hazed the blackness and dappled the floor. The air hung dead. He heard a faint sharp singing at the middle of its silence and knew this was from himself, a night-wasp he had hatched. Pieces of dream drifted by. They were gone before he saw their faces.

He should be at ease. The Lord, or the Gods, or Whoever, knew he'd drunk enough. Gratillonius had been in such a gusty mood. He often was, ever since Rufinus brought the news. "Not that everything's over with," he said, a little slurrily, when the candles were burning short. "The Scoti'll be back. You've bought us some years, though, some years, at least. We'll make ready. And now Ys can rest. Can't it? And Dahut, if that wasn't an evil spirit in her shape haunting the rocks, surely now Dahut too—I'll ask Corentinus. When he returns. He's off in Turonum, arguing with Bishop Bricius. Swears, if need be, he'll carry the matter as far as Rome. Our right here to grant asylum— Oh, I've told you before, haven't I? Well, here's to you, old buddy. Best investment I ever made, leaving you your life there in the Wood. Paid me a hundred times over, you have. A thousand, if Dahut's free. Here's to you."

His beaker clashed against Rufinus's. How those gray eyes shone! The drinkers had gotten merry and bawled out a couple of songs and at last hugged each other goodnight.

Rufinus remembered the arms, beard rough against his cheek, winebreath and also the sweat-smell, which had the cleanness of a man's who is much outdoors.

Moonlight inched across the floor.

"Oh, hell take this," ripped through him. He sat up and swung his legs out of bed in a single sweep. Tiles were hard and cool underfoot. He rose, stretched, shook nightmare off.

No reason to fumble with striking fire for a candle. He knew his way around this room as well as did the house cat, and it was her favorite in the house. He spoiled her rotten, as he doubtless would young Marcus. His hands knew how to fetch ranger's garb from the chest and slip it over his body. Weapons, bedroll, pack of provisions he always kept ready. He made them fast and opened the door.

The corridor beyond was a tunnel where he was blind. Fingertips brushed a wall which by day would look pretty; Verania was well along with decorating it. Rufinus missed the freedom and casual clutter of his own house, but he'd been too much gone, and too indolent in town, to see about replacing it; you couldn't put up another wattle-and-daub shack in phoenix Confluentes. Someday he'd take care of the matter. Meanwhile it was kind of Gratillonius and Verania to give him a room in their home.

And they didn't meddle. When they found him missing, they'd simply smile. "Off on another of his rambles, is he?"

He passed through the atrium and entry and out the unbarred front door. It gave directly on the street; luxuries like a portico were for years to come, if ever. The wall reared sheer at his back, white with moonlight. How the moon shone, and it still a day short of being full. He wished he could have bidden Gratillonius—and Verania—farewell, with thanks; but of course they were asleep.

His sandals padded over cobblestones. Confluentes might never boast Roman paving blocks. Well, only cities old and rich had ever had them, and this was certainly better than dirt lanes. Rufinus dodged around horse dung and offal heaps. Though Gratillonius fumed about it, there was likely no hope of enforcing such cleanliness as had been on the streets of Ys.

Nor would such towers again soar above the sea. Rufinus hastened on between shadowing houses.

The pomoerium opened before him. It was unpaved, hard-packed, its dustiness pale beneath the moon. He had followed Principal Way and ahead of him lifted the earthen wall, moss upon it full of dew, wooden towers squat above the south gate. It stood ajar; he saw the bridge and river beyond. The moon sailed high. To him the markings upon it had always looked like an old woman who grieved. But elsewhere stars glinted, and a breeze wandered through the gate bearing a scent of wild thyme.

Rufinus drank it. He would go hence into that land from which it blew.

He started across the open space. "Hold!" cried a sentry on the north tower. "Who's there?" The sound was lonesome in the night.

"Friend," gibed Rufinus. "Enemies come the other way, have you heard?"

"Ha, you," laughed the man aloft. "The moon-cat. Well, go with God, wherever you're bound."

I'd liefer not, thought Rufinus as he passed between the massive iron-bound timbers of the doors. Or He'd liefer not. Shall we agree on it, You and I?

Moonlight flowed with the river. Past the bridge, plowland stretched dim toward the sea. On the left, though, a ribbon of road followed the stream, toward the highway to Venetorum. Striding along it, gravel acrunch, he would soon find woodland; and soon after that, a trail which most travelers never noticed led into its depths.

He started across the bridge. The planks felt somehow soft. Perhaps that was because on his right was the new one, half-finished masonry, and behind it a sprawl of docks still under construction. The night blurred shapes. Water clucked and purled, sliding past stone.

In the forest lived one who loved him—too humbly, maybe, but Rufinus hoped to teach him pride. His hut lay within a sunrise's reach. Afterward they could sleep late, and then range the woods for days.

And I will raise your image before me, Grallon, thought Rufinus. He smiled with half his mouth. Poor old fellow, you'd be so shocked if you knew, wouldn't you?

She came from downstream up a pier onto the bridge. Small and cold on high, the moon made shimmer the water that ran off her nakedness.

Rufinus halted. He stood wholly alone with her. The shout of the guard, who saw, might have been in a dream or from the Otherworld.

She grinned. Her teeth were shark-white. Did you think I would let *you* go free? he heard.

She glided close. He drew his Roman sword and stabbed. It would not bite, it slid off and fell from his hand. She laid arms around him. They were freezingly cold.

"Oh, Dahut—" Rufinus had no strength to break loose. Locked together, he and she toppled into the river. He caught a taste of the incoming tide. Her lips and her tongue forced him open to her kiss.

XVIII

~ 1 ~

Clouds drifted low, heavy with rain. The breeze rustled leaves. They cast no shadows today, but dimness under their arches grew purple-black as vision ranged into the forest. No birds were calling. The Stegir mumbled lusterless.

Gratillonius halted at the oak and dismounted. Favonius nickered. He secured the stallion. Nemeta must have heard, for she came out of her dwelling. Her hair bore the only bright color in the landscape. She stopped before Gratillonius and regarded him silently. It was as if neither quite dared speak.

"How are you?" he asked at last in Ysan. They had not met for months. Summer freckles spread healthily over her arched nose, but she seemed thinner than ever. The sleeves of her plain gray shift were a trifle short; he saw that her right arm had shriveled nearly to the bone.

Her brusqueness told him that she remained herself: "I know why you've come."

It boded ill, though. "I thought you would," he replied. "But how?"

She chuckled without mirth. "Not by any spell. I do get the news here." The frigidity broke open. She blinked against tears, shivered, abruptly cast herself against him. "Oh, father!"

He held her close, stroked her mane, let her burrow into his bosom. Her breath rattled. "You liked Rufinus too, did you not?" he murmured.

"Aye, he w-was kind and jolly—when I was a little girl—and—and he was good to you, when all the rest of us had turned on you—" She wrenched free. Her left hand swiped angrily at her eyes.

He could no longer hold his question inside him; yet it resisted coming forth. "Was it, then— The sentry isn't clear about what he saw. It seemed him 'twas a woman, moon-white, but— We know not. We've searched the shores and dragged the river, but haven't found the body."

Nemeta had mastered herself. "You never will," she said in a cold small voice. "'Twas borne to the sea."

"You've gone into these matters. Can you tell what—what was that thing?"

"Dahut."

"A demon in her shape?"

"Herself. She drowned with Ys, but They would not let her stay dead."

He had awaited this, and prayed it not be, and now that it was he must fight it still. "Who are They?" he challenged.

"The Three. She is Their vengeance on the city."

"You can't be sure! How do you know?"

"By my dreams. By the wands I have cast. By things half seen in a pool and in the smoke of a sacrificial fire."

"You could be mistaken. You could be crazed, huddling alone for years."

Pain shook her tones. "Would you have sought me if you didn't believe I could tell you the truth? Father, I know those Gods. I am the last of Their worshippers."

His throat thickened and burned. "Gods like that—you serve, you whose mother They killed—why?"

She made a faint, one-sided shrug. They had been over this ground before. "There are none other for me. Epona and the rest are shrunk to sprites, phantoms; nor do I think they would heed me if I called, as far as I have gone from Their ways. Wotan and His war-band are aliens. I must have some few powers if I am to live as anything better than a slave. From Lir, Taranis, and Belisama I have them."

"Christ has more."

She stiffened. "He'd deny me my freedom."

Hatred sank within him. In its place came sorrow for her, and a weariness he could feel to his marrow. "I've heard this too often," he said. "For the dozenth time I beg, bethink you. Is Verania a slave? Come back with me. She'll be like a sister to you, and I—while I live, you'll be your own woman. And afterward too, if God lets me build what I'm trying to build. Come home, Nemeta, daughter of my Forsquilis whom I loved."

The sudden fear he saw on her slashed through him. Her eyes widened till white ringed the green. Her left hand made a fending gesture. "Nay," she whispered. "Dahut would find me."

"What, you?"

"I counselled and helped Rufinus on his mission to get Niall killed."

For my sake, he understood, and wanted to hold her again but seemed unable to stir.

"'Tis become Niall that she chiefly exists to avenge. And she knows where they are who were his bane." Nemeta clutched at her breast. She turned her head to and fro, looking. The violence of the motion made her useless arm swing. "I don't think she can swim this far up the Stegir. No tidewater here. She's wholly of the sea now. I dare never go near the sea again. But she can follow the tide through the Odita to Confluentes."

She steadied. He groped in the dark after common sense. "Rufinus was a pagan; nay, he held by no Gods whatsoever. You—Christ will protect you."

"If I accept Him." The red head shook. "That's not in my heart."

Somewhere at the back of his soul, he wondered about his own faith. Why had he sought Christ? Was it merely for power against evil—at best, because He stood between the world and chaos, like a centurion between Rome and the barbarians? Gratillonius knew Christ lived, but in the same way that he knew the Emperor did. He had never met either. He admired Christ; but did he love Him?

"He will accept you if you ask," Gratillonius said.

The brief pridefulness crumbled. Nemeta looked away, into the dusk of the forest. "Will he ever?" he barely heard. "Can He? Father, you know not the things I have done."

The grimness that that awakened was somehow strengthening. "I may know more than you think," Gratillonius told her. "His waters wash every sin from us." And that is why I haven't yet dared be baptized.

"Well, talk to your bishop—about Dahut," she said in forlorn defiance. "I've told you all I've learned."

"Nemeta," he pleaded, "you mustn't suffer this any more, loneliness, poverty, fear. Let those who love you help you."

Her courage lifted anew. "Oh, now, in truth 'tis not so bad. I have my house, my cats—" She even smiled. "You've not met them. They're inside. Three kittens. And I do have my freedom, and these deep woods—" The mood broke. "Father, 'tis you I sometimes weep for."

Wind moaned in the trees. The first raindrops fell down it.

~ 2 ~

Gratillonius was at work several miles from Confluentes when Salomon found him. A man must work, no matter how hollow he felt within.

A curial, responsible for the lives of many, required a suitable livelihood. You couldn't forever spend pirate gold; besides, it was earmarked for public purposes. Since his marriage he had gone into partnership with Apuleius. Without talent for the management of land, the latter had never been able to make the fundus pay, and Confluentes had taken over that ground. Broad new acres being cleared and claimed, the senator financed operations which Gratillonius—farm boy, soldier, ruler—knew how to run. Sharecroppers were established and this year producing their first, excellent harvest. Meanwhile Gratillonius was properly organizing the horsebreeding Apuleius had begun. Favonius would be the prize stud, but he meant to get more, for the servicing of the finest brood mares he could find. There ought to be a boundless market. Rome needed cavalry.

On this day he was overseeing the fencing of a meadow, taking a hand himself. He didn't enjoy that as erstwhile, he no longer enjoyed anything, but at least it got the cramp out of his muscles. Salomon rode up at his usual breakneck pace, reined in his mount and made it curvet. "Hail!" he shouted.

Gratillonius squinted against the sun, which haloed those locks the hue of Verania's. At sixteen, Salomon was still smooth-cheeked but otherwise a young man, tall, his gangliness filled out and become both hard and supple. His tunic and breeks were striped in the gaudiest Gallic style. "What brings you?" Gratillonius grunted.

Salomon winced a bit. He had, though, resigned himself to his brother-in-law's recent curtness. "You wanted to know when Corentinus returned. Well, he has."

It gave an excuse for a gallop, Gratillonius thought. However, the announcement let him meet with the bishop today rather than tomorrow. That might or might not prove a kindness. "Thanks," Gratillonius remembered to say. He left instructions with his foreman and got onto Favonius.

Radiance poured from above. The clover sown this year bloomed white. Bees droned about, gathering its riches. A stand of wild carrot filled the warmth with pungency. Its filigree was like sea foam.... What was the weather at Ys? He imagined fog, the breakers crashing unseen on rocks and remnants. Evil creatures hated sunlight, didn't they? It hurt them.

At the grassy wall of Confluentes, Salomon bade him goodbye and went off, doubtless in search of company more cheerful. Gratillonius continued around. The church there was still abuilding. Corentinus hoped to dedicate it as his cathedral before winter. Enlargement and beautification might continue for generations. That had been an idea strange to Gratillonius; but the world was moving into a different age.

He found the bishop at home in Aquilo. Corentinus met him in the doorway. A minute passed, during which the street traffic seemed remote, while eyes beneath shaggy brows ransacked the visitor. Finally Corentinus said gently, "Welcome, my son. Come in where we can talk."

Gratillonius followed him to the room in which secrets were safe. Corentinus gestured at a stool. Gratillonius slumped onto it. Corentinus mixed water and wine in two cups.

"How did it go?" asked Gratillonius. His words were flat.

"Unseemly strife," Corentinus answered. "I had to get mightily stiff-necked. Not so much with Bricius. He only thought he had more authority than me. I set that straight in short order. But he clung like a limpet to Glabrio's arguments when we carried the matter before the governor."

"I don't understand."

"Really? I'd supposed you did. The question is what right of sanctuary the Church—any church—has. You probably weren't aware of it at the time, and Heaven knows you've had plenty else on your mind since, but seven years ago the Emperor actually abolished the right of sanctuary. That provoked such resistance that he restored it a year later."

Honorius! thought Gratillonius. Had that half-wit any constancy at all? Last year he'd closed the Colosseum, banned gladiatorial games: undeniably a good deed, but why had he let them go on until then, until he'd given himself a triumph in Rome for the victory Stilicho won?

It didn't matter.

"The law is unclear," Corentinus continued. "It can be read as limiting the right in many ways. What kind of fugitives can we take in? Must they be Christians?" He offered his guest a cup.

Gratillonius drank without noticing the taste. "I remember now," he mumbled. "Pardon me. My head is fuzzy these days. You want freedom to use your own judgment in every case, is that it?"

"Exactly." Corentinus stayed erect, looming above the man who sat hunched. "The governor doesn't like that any more than the Emperor ever did. It sets the Church above the state: as is fit and proper, of course." He tossed off a hefty draught. "Matters came to a head like this because it was me involved—meaning you. Confluentes is drawing new people from as far as Britannia. They don't knuckle under easily. Having the Church to appeal to encourages this. Well, I upheld my sovereignty, but I and those clergy who think the same have a long struggle before us. Clear to the Pope in Rome, I'm sure, and to the Emperor, whoever and wherever he is then."

Wherever indeed, Gratillonius thought. Honorius had his seat in Ravenna, from which escape by sea to Constantinople was easy. Stilicho had lately moved the prefectural capital of Gallia from Augusta Treverorum, south to Arelate, also near the sea. It was as if the frontiers were closing in. Or falling in?

"But you didn't come about that, Gratillonius," he heard.

"No." He stared into the cup between his knees. "Have you gotten the news yet?"

"Certainly. Poor Rufinus. A ghastly ending. I'll pray for him. He just may have had time to see the Light. Or, anyhow— Well, we can ask there be mercy for him, if possible. We owe him that much."

Gratillonius barely had strength to force out: "It was Dahut that killed him."

Corentinus reached down to grasp his shoulder. "You've feared something of the kind since your battle at Ys. I have too. But it could be...a demon, or sorcerer's work, or...*creature*."

Gratillonius shook his head. "I know now. It's Dahut."

Corentinus was silent for a space. "I won't ask you how you know," he said at length, heavily. "I'm afraid you're right. Satan is aprowl in Armorica."

"She—" Gratillonius couldn't go on.

"Is surely lost," Corentinus finished.

Gratillonius looked up at him. It was like looking up at an ancient oak behung with gray ivy. "Can't we, can't you do anything?"

"We are free to pray for a miracle," said the compassionate, implacable voice. "Otherwise— It's not simple demonic possession. Exorcism —I can only guess, but I think an exorcism would have to be done in her presence. And she can steer clear of the Cross, or flee it and jeer from afar."

Gratillonius jumped to his feet. The stool clattered one way, the wine cup spilled its redness another. "But we can't forsake her!" he yelled.

Corentinus spread his big sailor's hands. "What would you have me do, if I could? An exorcism will cast her down into hell, eternal torment."

"Oh, no, no. Can't she be saved?"

Corentinus seemed, all at once, aged. "I don't see how. At least now she isn't burning. She's taken her revenge. She may in future be content to haunt Ys. Leave her alone with the sharks, and with God."

"That's...hard to do."

Corentinus embraced and held him, much as Gratillonius had embraced and held Nemeta. "I understand. But you've got to stop brooding over this. You're man enough to stare it down and get on with life; or else I've terribly misjudged you."

1011

"I've tried," said Gratillonius into the coarse cloth.

"Try harder. You must. My son, my friend, you are not the first father in the world whose little girl turned wicked, nor will you be the last. It gives you no right to pull away from those who need you, who are worthy of your love.

"Let's pray together. In Christ is help."

And afterward: "In Christ is joy. And so there is in your darlings. Go home to them."

—At his house Verania met him, their son beside her.

~ 3 ~

On a day in autumn when the wind went loud and sharp over stubblefields and sent leaves whirling off trees in little scraps of color, folk at Drusus's farm were surprised to see a big man ride up. This was a busy season, as they readied for winter. "The master is in town, sir, the cattle market," said the steward. "He'll not be back for another day or two."

"I know," replied Evirion Baltisi. "I met him there, and he gave me some news that's brought me here."

He dismounted, went inside, paid his respects to the lady of the house. She made him welcome, but had such work on her own hands that she was soon glad to direct him to Tera, who had been the woman of his fellow skipper Maeloch; and it was Tera whom he had come to see.

He found her in the cottage she occupied with her children. Newly built, simple but snug, it stood at some distance from the other buildings, behind it a kitchen garden and pigpen. Fowl wandered about. She was indoors, pickling flesh; the very air in the single room tasted of vinegar. Her youngest offspring played in a corner, the rest were at tasks of their own on the farm itself. "Why, Cap'n, how wonderful!" she cried when he trod in. "What brings you this far from the water?"

"To learn how you fare," he answered.

"What, me? Quite well, thank'ee. And you?"

"I'm home again," he snapped. "'Twas a long voyage." Mildening: "Yesterday I heard you'd sold Maeloch's house—your house in Confluentes, and moved back hither. Is aught wrong? He was my comrade. I'd fain do what I can for his widow."

She laughed. "Good of you to give me that name. Sit down." She waved at her two stools, set her things aside, wiped her hands, dipped wooden cups full of mead from a small cask, and joined him. Meanwhile she explained: "You're sweet, but fear not for me. 'Twas in town I grew unhappy after Maeloch was gone, me now a nobody, unchristened, offered naught but the meanest of jobs. Here I am free again, with the woods and their landwights not too far off to walk to when there's a break in the work."

"You're not a hireling of Drusus's?"

"Nay, more like a tenant. The kids and I could not go live alone. That would be unsafe, when Ys is no more."

Evirion looked abruptly grim, then thrust his thoughts aside and made admiring noises about the boy, Maeloch's son, as the mother expected. "How was all this arranged?" he inquired after a time.

"Through King Grallon," said Tera. "I turned to him when the narrowness of streets and spite of neighbors got more than I could bear. Should have done it earlier. He made a deal for me. Drusus took the house, to sell or rent. In return, he built me this dwelling and gives me the use of this plot. Mostly we work for him, me and the kids, getting paid in kind and in protection." She sighed, not unhappily. "Also in open skies and leave to be myself. Oh, I've cause to make my small spells for the welfare of Grallon and Drusus, but don't you be telling them that. It can do no harm, can it? Mayhap a wee bit of help to them. And Grallon, at least, that overburdened man, needs all the help he can get."

"Know you how he is these days?" Evirion asked anxiously. "What I've heard since I came back has been scant and confused. He chancing to be away, I could not call and see for myself."

"He was gruesome downcast after his man Rufinus perished. The rumors about that are eldritch, nay? 'Tis no wonder he grew so forbidding at any talk about it, but thus he only drove the mutterings into corners."

Evirion nodded. "'Twas a bad business, whatever it was. Aye, when we put to sea I was troubled about him."

"Ease your mind. Over the months, he's gained back heart. Not that I was watching over him, but word gets about—and I've overheard Drusus and his wife speaking of him, they care too—and I've had my whispers from the landwights.... Thanks be mostly, I think, to his Verania, he is himself again. There's a lass!"

"Good!" gusted from Evirion.

Tera cocked her head at him. "I recall you as being less than his friend."

"That was straight after the whelming. Later—above all, since the battle at Ys—well, we need him."

"And you've grown inchmeal fond of him to boot, I daresay." A teasing note: "Him and his pretty, unwedded daughter."

At once Tera saw she had gone too far, and went on in haste, "But how has your life been? A long journey, you said. Whither? What happened?"

Evirion's mood stayed darker than before. "Niall being fallen, I reckoned the sea lanes he'd plagued would be clear. And so they were, for a span. We did fine business in southern Hivernia, western Alba, and Britannia. But then, as we were homebound, though 'twas uncommonly late in the sailing season, we met Saxons on the water—twice—good-sized packs of their galleys that set after us. For all the size and armament of *Brennilis*, naught saved us but speed. Had the winds been otherwise, I'd lie this day on the bottom. I think a great movement of wolves is again getting under way, and next year we'll hear them howling at our thresholds."

Tera gripped her cup hard. "Despite what befell this spring?"

"Oh, we'll not have Scoti and Saxons together," said Evirion. "Maeloch helped see to that."

Tera looked long into his eyes before she asked low, "Did he? Niall fell not at Ys, but this year. We've all heard tales of it, no two the same. So what did Maeloch really do? What did he die for?"

Evirion chose to misunderstand her. "He was pursuing the Scotic boats, as well you know. Surely Niall was in one of them. Maeloch well-nigh had him overhauled. But a flaw of wind and fog—the weather was very strange that twilight."

"Strange indeed." Her gaze went beyond him. "I've cast my spells, hearkened to my omens, trying and trying to know what went on there at the end. But naught will come to me. Alone, I am helpless against... whatever it was." She straightened. "Well," she said almost briskly, "what use in fretting? Each gladsome day we have lived is the one treasure that nobody can rob us of."

~ 4 ~

The Black Months need not be dark. Rather, they could fill with ease and pleasure. Summer's labor was over and winter's was mostly light. Small festivities twinkled before and after the great celebrations at solstice. Occasionally Gratillonius and Verania shocked their servants by staying in bed till the late sunrise.

A pair of candles burned soft, an Ysan practice she had learned from him. The chamber lacked a brazier, but it was not very cold outside and the house was solidly built. Her sweet sweat had anointed the air.

She sat up amidst rumpled blankets, reached for a cake of wheat and raisins on a table, broke a piece off and handed it to him. "Here," she said.

"Thanks," he replied, "but I'm not hungry yet."

"Eat this anyhow. Maintain your strength. You'll need it."

He nibbled from her fingers. "Already again?" he marveled. "And everybody says how demure you are."

She wrinkled her nose. "Ha! You don't know women as well as you think you do. I'm the envy of Armorica, I am."

She leaned over his pillow. Her hair fell in a tent around him. The candlelight glowed along her arm, illuminating the fine down. He reached, cupped a breast, felt milk start forth across its fullness. It was astonishing how one so slender could still nurse a child as lusty as Marcus. Maybe that was why she hadn't conceived anew, more than a year after the birth. They both hoped that was why. It wasn't for lack of trying, once he had put grief behind him.

Her free hand roved impudently. "Well, well," she laughed.

"Oh, give me a while longer."

She raised her brows. "If you're tired, you can keep lying there and—"

"No, no. How could I feel tired with somebody like you, till the moment I collapse in a cloud of dust? It's only that we were in such a hurry at first." He laid hold of her at the delicate shoulder blades and drew her downward.

"And what would everybody say if they knew how the rough, tough Gratillonius likes to cuddle, and how well he does it, too? Fortunately, I like it myself."

"And do it superbly."

She laid her mouth to his. "R-r-r," she purred.

It racketed at the door. "What the devil?" he growled. The knocking was frantic. None of the staff would interrupt without urgency. "Coming!" he called. His feeling was mainly anger at the wretched mischance, whatever it might be.

Verania drew blankets to chin. Gratillonius didn't trouble to throw anything over himself. That was a man yonder, as hard as he'd struck. Gratillonius opened the door.

Salomon stood there. He wore merely a tunic, hadn't stopped to bind on sandals, must have kicked off indoor slippers and set forth at his full long-legged speed. He still panted. It was in deep, shuddering sobs. Tears coursed from his eyes.

"Father is dead," he reported.

—The sky arched clear, magnificent with stars. The lantern Salomon now carried—he hadn't thought to bring one, and his feet were bruised where he had stubbed them—brought hoarfrost into sight. Here and there a window shone or a man walked, but after the three left Confluentes they were wholly alone. The sound of their stumbling stride rang loud above the river's susurrus.

"We'd finished breakfast," Salomon said. His voice had gone empty. Breath puffed spectral. "A courier had arrived yesterday before dark, but father was keeping a vigil at the church. Mother and I were asleep when he got back, and nobody else thought to tell him. He sent at once when he heard this morning." Of course, Gratillonius realized. Apuleius was an early riser and immediately with his duties. "The man wasn't at the hostel, he'd chosen to stay with somebody he knows here and it took a while to find him. Father was fuming a little. You know how he is—was when he got angry, soft-spoken as ever but the words came out clipped. It didn't seem worth a fuss to me. He'd been feeling poorly the last couple of days, though; didn't say much, but when he mentioned pains you always knew they were real. Well, the courier finally brought him a letter from the governor in Turonum. Father opened it and stood there reading. I saw him frown, purse his lips—then, oh, God, he buckled at the knees and fell. Just like that. He hit his head, not too hard, it barely bled, but he lay there gasping—quick wheezes, and in between them he didn't breathe at all—and his eyes, his eyes were rolled back, blank. I saw the pulse in his throat. It was going like a hailstorm. We gathered around, tried to help, wanted to get him to bed. Mother sent a boy off after the physician, and then suddenly he didn't breathe and his pulse didn't beat and he was dead."

"What was in that letter?" asked Gratillonius, the single thing he could think of to ask.

"Who cares?" Salomon cried. "Father's dead!"

Verania clutched her man's hand very tightly.

—Lamps and candles burned everywhere in the house in Aquilo. Rovinda had gotten Apuleius lifted to a couch and a blanket laid over the foulness of death. She had herself closed his eyes and cleansed the froth from his mouth. As Verania came in with Gratillonius and Salomon, Rovinda quickly drew the blanket across his face.

"Mother, can't I see him?" Verania sounded like a bewildered child.

"Wait a while, dear," the woman answered.

Wait till the grimace has smoothed out and he's expressionless, Gratillonius thought; but not till the corpse-bruises begin to show.

Verania went to Rovinda's arms. Salomon stood numbly aside. Slaves gaped in the background. The physician plucked Gratillonius's sleeve. They withdrew to a corner.

"God must love him," said the physician low, "as well He might. I doubt that he felt or knew of his dying."

"It's cruel for his family," Gratillonius replied in the same undertone. "No warning. Struck down, senselessly; the end of their world, like *that*."

"God's will—"

Gratillonius's hand chopped air. Then he remembered he must not brush the saying aside. Who was he to accuse the Lord? Apuleius was wanted in Heaven. His kin and friends should be happy. Why was that never possible?

"I'll take over," Gratillonius said. "Thanks for your concern. Rovinda's brave, she'll bear up."

She and Verania were murmuring between themselves. The mother beckoned Salomon over. Gratillonius felt hurt. Verania cast him a glance and it was healed. Naturally they needed a little time to themselves.

His gaze drifted about. It caught a pair of wax tablets bound together, which somebody had picked up and put on a table. The dispatch. Gratillonius stepped over to read it. He saw terror on Verania as she observed, and cast her a reassuring smile. Ill-omened though the thing was, it could not be what had slain Apuleius.

The message stood clear in shadows and highlights. It was a communication such as the governor's office sent in multiple copies to local officials when important news had been received.

A fresh horde of Germani was on the move. They were chiefly Ostrogoths out of those lands at the Danastris into which the Huns were pressing. At their head was the infamous warlord Radagaisus. They had crossed the Danuvius. Terrified swarms fled before them as they advanced on Italy.

~ 5 ~

In perfectly chaste wise, Procurator Bacca and the lady Runa had become well acquainted. He enjoyed her conversation and she his: much superior to any else in this provincial city. She was often a guest at his home, and he sometimes visited her to look at her work, calligraphic copying varied by desultory efforts to compile the annals of the Turones.

After all, she was a lay sister among the nuns; furthermore, under Bishop Bricius the rules were considerably relaxed for both male and female religious communities. Runa lived comfortably enough for a person of her tastes, which had never run to sensuousness.

"I asked you over this evening because I need your advice," Bacca said after they had dined and gone to his scriptorium. They left the door open for propriety's sake, but everybody knew better than to pass near. The room within was more plain than might have been awaited. Its only special contents were several handsome books, writings of Aristophanes, Ovidius, Catullus. Rain brawled through the murk outside.

"Oh?" murmured Runa. Seated on a cushioned bench, she smoothed her skirts. The gown was simple and modestly cut, as became a woman of her dedicated standing, but its rich dark material set off her white skin and complemented the high-piled raven hair. "I am honored. What is this about?"

Bacca lowered his lankness to a stool facing her. "About the counsel I'll give Governor Glabrio and, I trust, make him heed."

Runa kept an expectant look on him.

"Have you heard?" he said. "Apuleius Vero, the tribune at Aquilo, has died."

"Really? Well, he was getting on in years, wasn't he?" She inquired no further, though she added, "God have mercy on his soul."

"The question is, who should his successor be?"

She flushed faintly. Her nostrils dilated. "A strong man, in that nest of troublemakers."

"Precisely. What would you say to Gaius ValÉrius Gratillonius?"

"You joke!" she exclaimed, astounded.

"For once, I do nothing of the sort," he replied gravely. "See here. In view of the situation there, the mingled peoples, relationships, tensions, grudges, and factors unknown to us—wouldn't any man of ours find himself in an impossible position? *I* wouldn't want the job."

"Make them obey. Apuleius was always on Gratillonius's side. A new tribune wouldn't delay, argue, obstruct. If necessary, he'd call in troops."

Bacca sighed. "It isn't that easy. Aquilo—Confluentes—is more important than you may realize."

"Because Gratillonius has made it a thorn in your side."

"That. But also because, in spite of everything we've done—I say this candidly, confidentially—he's made it flourish. It grows. It's a magnet for industrious immigrants; one way or another, legally or illegally, they're coming in, and won't meekly let themselves be displaced. A thorn? It should be a bulwark. God knows we need that."

She scowled and bit her lip.

"He preserved us from the Scoti this past summer," Bacca said; "but now the Ostrogoths are ravaging into Italy, and I wonder if He will vouchsafe us another miracle. He may have taken Apuleius away—without warning, I gather—as a sign that He won't."

"Would you trust Gratillonius?" Runa demanded. "Dare you?"

"What do you think? You've...known him well." She dropped her glance and doubled her fists. "Set grievances aside," Bacca urged. "Give me a totally honest opinion, no matter how it tastes in your mouth. This is for Rome."

She looked back at him. "How earnest you've become."

"Not a comedian tonight, my lady. Rome is my Mother. Is she still his?"

Runa sat silent, as if listening to the rainstorm, until, grudgingly, she said, "He never caused me to think otherwise."

Bacca offered a flicker of a smile. "Thank you. I thought so myself, but wanted your confirmation."

"He's...too stubborn. Utterly self-willed."

Bacca nodded. "It's led him to the verge of insubordination, or beyond, over and over. But outright rebelliousness? Among his merits, set this lack of political experience and subtlety. He wouldn't conspire against us, would he?"

"No," she fleered. "He isn't that bright."

Bacca stared at the rain on the windowglass. It made the reflected lamplight shimmer. "I almost wish he would. What an Emperor he'd be."

She drew back on her seat. "Are you serious?"

"Perhaps. Consider what he accomplished in Ys, and is accomplishing in Confluentes. I suspect that if he tried for the purple, I'd support him."

She peered at the door. Nobody stood in the corridor. Nevertheless she leaned forward and dropped her voice. "This is dreadfully dangerous talk."

"I trust you," he said.

Touched, she could only gulp and tell him, "Thank you."

Bacca's fingers twitched. "We desperately need a leader strong, able, and—honest. Stilicho's double games with the barbarians

1018

aren't working." He straightened. "Well," he asked, "do you then think we can get along with Gratillonius as our tribune?"

"It would be difficult at best," she warned. "You'd have to make concessions to him."

"That's clear. In fact, we'll have to give up our efforts to destroy him, and instead try convincing him we aren't actually such bad fellows." Bacca laughed. "I hope Nagon Demari won't be too disappointed."

XIX

~ 1 ~

Spring returned, made green the graves of winter and strewed them with flowers. Days grew longer than nights. Migratory birds trekked home.

The Ostrogoths and their allies were devastating Italy. Where they did not reach, the fear of them did. Imperial agents went through the provinces, frantically seeking military recruits. They offered a bounty of ten solidi, three on enrollment, the balance on discharge after the peril was quelled—if it could be. Slaves got two solidi and their freedom.

Few accepted in northern Gallia. Their own homelands were under attack. Saxon fleets swarmed oversea to loot and burn along the coasts; many crews went deep inland, and some began work on strongholds where they could stay through the year or beyond. The Picti and Scoti harried Britannia. Fugitives who got to Armorica said that King Niall's successor stood high among the latter. Otherwise hardly any civilized ships stirred from port. Even fishermen dared not venture far; their poor catches joined with lost crops to spread hunger.

A while after Easter, Nagon Demari arrived at Confluentes.

Gratillonius ordinarily received visitors at home. It made for a congenial atmosphere as he talked with Osismiic chiefs, travelers from outside, or common folk who had problems. Besides, the large new basilica in Confluentes was only partly built. He thought it too risky to continue using the manor house outside the wall, no matter that nothing within approached its graciousness. As for the basilica in Aquilo, it was full of the homeless and the orphaned. Corentinus supported him in the idea that their needs outweighed the government's.

"I will not have that man in my house," Verania said. She could be immovably decisive when she chose—occasions rare enough to warrant respect. Moreover, Gratillonius shared her feelings. He ignored her possessive pronoun. Between them such questions were meaningless.

1019

Thus he sent a message to the hostel. It was written, not verbal, so he could be sure it carried his exact words. "You will meet me in the basilica of Confluentes at noon."

Sounds of ongoing construction racketed in the room he employed. It was starkly whitewashed, with a concrete floor that was supposed to be tiled sometime. Its furnishings were a table with writing materials—wooden slabs, ink and quills, wax tablets, styluses—and a few stools. He did not rise when Nagon entered, and waited for the other man to give the first "Hail." Thereafter he gestured at a seat.

Nagon took it. Rage mottled his flat face. "Is this how you receive an officer of the Imperium?" he rasped.

Gratillonius grinned. "You see for yourself that it is."

"Have a care. Be very careful."

"Watch your language. As tribune, I outrank you by quite a bit."

"That can be changed."

"Not by an errand boy. I won't warn you again about curbing your tongue. What do you want?"

Nagon's lips moved and his Adam's apple bobbed several times before he said, trembling, "I'm here about the taxes, of course."

"They'll be paid."

"In the proper kind and amount, I *trust*."

Gratillonius had expected something like this. "In gold of, uh, equivalent value, as we've been doing in part."

"Oh, no. No, sir! You've gotten too much leniency already. The basic payments are to be in kind as the law requires."

"The procurator's office knows we aren't yet prepared to spare that much food and manufactured goods. We can't import them this year as we have done, when pirates bedevil the sea lanes and supply is short everywhere. It was a silly exercise anyway. What with the refugees we're getting, we'll skirt the edge of famine ourselves."

Glee glittered in the little pale eyes. "No excuse. The army can't eat your gold. If you do not tender your lawful share, I shall have to institute collection proceedings."

"Such as rounding up children for the slave market? Will the army eat them?"

"That's enough."

"It certainly is. Now listen to me. Where are the solidi coming from to pay those enlistees the Imperium is trying to attract? We can help substantially with that. As a matter of fact, I mean to order an extra contribution from our treasury, if the procurator will accept the tax in money. You wouldn't understand patriotism, Nagon. I can't say whether your superiors do or not, but they understand business. They'll agree. If the poison in you hasn't addled your wits, you must know they won't let you do your viper's work among us. What did you come here hoping for? To scare a few women and children? To provoke men into rashness?

You can't. I'll write to Turonum this afternoon, but I won't trust you with the letter. Go away."

Nagon sprang up. Gratillonius rose too and bulked over him.

"I'll go," Nagon chattered. "You're happy, aren't you? Oh, you're enjoying yourself, persecuting me. You want to take my livelihood from me, don't you, and laugh when my family starves. You want to drive me out of the world like you drove me out of Ys."

"Too bad I succeeded in that," Gratillonius drawled. "You'd have gone down with the city."

Tears came forth. Nagon waved his fists. He shuddered and sobbed. "I'll go. And Glabrio will scorn me and Bacca will patronize me and I'll be a whipped dog. But not for long. Not for long. I'll return, Gratillonius. And when I do, it will be your turn to howl. You'll be sorry for your cruelty, but it will be too late. I'm not stupid, you know. I have a great deal of information about you and your friends. You'll be helpless, Gratillonius. The whip will be across your heart then. Think about it—till I return." He stormed from the room.

~ 2 ~

Flavius Vortivir, tribune at Darioritum Venetorum, was a hard man but righteous in his fashion. It had been said that he and Apuleius were the only senators in Armorica not corrupt; but Armorica didn't have many. Though Gratillonius was only a curial, Vortivir received him on equal terms. He spoke for Confluentes and Aquilo, communities growing when others were shrinking, the see of one of Armorica's few bishops.

"We can set aside the old rivalries, I hope,"—those between the Osismii and the Veneti—said Gratillonius with a smile.

"The newer ones are more difficult," replied Vortivir with his usual lack of humor.

Because it was a beautiful day in a year that was turning out generally cold and wet, they sat on the portico of his house. It was high enough on its hill to look over roofs, the southern city wall, and a mile to the landlocked, island-studded gulf into which the river emptied. Haze gave that water a mysterious shimmer, like a lake in a dream. Tales and songs among the tribespeople told how this had been dry land once, back when the Old Folk raised those avenues of tall stones which still brooded near here. But the sea had broken in....Gratillonius strove not to remember Ys too keenly.

"What do you mean?" he asked.

"You lure commerce and—worse, much worse—men away from us, when they are sorely needed."

Gratillonius picked his words with care. "Sir, we do not lure. Whoever comes to us does it of his own choice."

"Not a choice the law always allows."

"We're accused of harboring runaways. All I can reply is that we aren't magicians, to hear men's inner thoughts. Idlers, thieves, and ruffians don't get leave to stay. If someone believes he can identify a person among us who belongs elsewhere, he is free to come try."

"Ha, I know how likely that is. A hard trip, considerable expense, and the man in question will have disappeared...till the searcher leaves, having met a hedge of pretended ignorance and a quagmire of pretended incompetence. You can uphold the law better than that."

"I have more urgent business than looking into private lives, and damned little staff to handle any of it for me. I admit we are taking in outsiders, refugees."

Vortivir nodded. "True. That much is well done of you. I'm not seeking a quarrel, Gratillonius. You are my guest, and your letter said you wanted to discuss a matter of public concern."

"I do. It touches on a big reason why we seem to be lucky in Confluentes, and so draw settlers. That's not happenstance."

"Your enlightened administration?" asked Vortivir, not quite sarcastically.

"I make no claims about that. Also, please remember I've been the tribune for less than half a year. It's longer than that since any raiders hit Osismia. Even the plague of them Rome's now got hasn't reached us yet."

Vortivir's look grew somber. The Veneti had suffered. "Do you think that setback they took at your hands—four years ago, was it?—frightened them off for good? That's not their way."

"Of course not. However, it's given them a healthy respect for us. Saxons too; they heard what happened to the Scoti. Why should they walk into a bear's den, when the rest of the Empire is easy pickings?"

Vortivir studied Gratillonius for a space before he said, "They're bound to test you again. Will the same...spontaneous gathering of wildly diverse groups...meet them?"

"It could," Gratillonius answered.

"The law keeps the tribes disarmed. It has to, or they'd soon cut the Empire apart, feuding with it and each other."

"A citizen has a right to defend himself against a robber. I see nothing wrong with encouraging him to learn how to do it."

"That depends." Abruptly Vortivir spat off the portico, turned squarely to the other, and snapped, "How long shall we chop words? It's obvious why you're here. You've sounded me out in the past, and inquired about me, same as you have everybody else you approached or will be approaching."

"I wouldn't want...to speak sedition sir. Nor tempt anyone to."

"Well, I'm not the kind who'd tempt you! I'll state the facts myself. You have these irregular reserves, or whatever you call them. It's debatable whether their existence quite violates the law, and if so, how much. But the question had better not come before the Imperium.

1022

Their activities have spread well into the rest of Armorica, mostly the back country but also a number of small coastal settlements. You want to weave men of all the tribes into this loose network of yours. You hope for my sanction, or at least for my blind eye turned your way. Correct?"

"Correct, sir. The aim is purely defensive. That includes suppression of domestic banditry. Together the tribes can do what none can do separately. For instance, you Veneti are a race of seamen." (As the Ysans were.) "You've got boats to keep watch well offshore and carry back warning. You've got ships to bring help to where it's needed. Most of that help could come from inland. For instance, if you were in touch with Redonic members of the association—"

Vortivir lifted a hand. "That's clear. Let's spare the time it takes. There will be plenty of details that are not clear. This doesn't come as any staggering surprise to me, you know. I keep reasonably well informed about events, and about the men who make them happen. If anything, I'm a little surprised you haven't seen me earlier."

"There was a dispute with a couple of Namnetic headmen—"

"Never mind. Tell me about it later. For the moment: Gratillonius, you not only have my sanction. Provided you can settle a few remaining doubts in my mind, and I'm pretty sure you can, you will have my active cooperation."

Gratillonius's hard-held breath burst from him. "Sir, this, this is wonderful!"

"I regard it as my duty," Vortivir said. "That law about armament tamed the old savages. Today it's letting new savages at the throat of Rome."

~ 3 ~

A Saxon flotilla forced the passage of the bay where Gesocribate stood. The barbarians overwhelmed the garrison, scaled the walls, looted, raped, killed for two days, finally set fire to the city and vanished back up the Britannic Sea.

There was nothing the Osismii could do except tender help afterward. A seaport populated largely by mariners who came and went, therefore under closer than ordinary official surveillance, Gesocribate had been outside the native defense movement; and it lay alone at the far end of the peninsula. Its example did jolt many Armoricans into joining the brotherhoods, and these grew more openly militant.

In Confluentes, Evirion raged. It was bad enough that he was penned there, his ship idled, himself likewise as well as tortured equally by boredom and by fretting over the future of his business. What had now happened was a blow to one of his most important harborages and marts. If the home guard could have been there! If he could have been in the front line, splitting enemy skulls!

Occasional paramilitary drills gave him something to do, but redoubled his frustration. He could find no work unless it be as a common laborer, and he would not stoop to that. Nor could he, without fatal damage to his authority over his crew, should *Brennilis* ever put to sea again. He drank too much, got into fights, consorted with whores, lay hours in his own bed staring at the ceiling, slouched sullenly around the towns or along the roads. For reasons obscure to himself he shunned the forest. Yet that was at last where he went.

Summer was then well along, a bleak one this year, chill rains and fleeting pale sunshine. However, for a time it grew hot. Through several days the weather smoldered with never a cloud; folk at night tossed sweating under the weight of air, while crickets outside shrilled mockery. Finally thunderheads massed in the south. Their bases were caverns of purple darkness, their heads noonday white until the sky dimmed. Slowly the overcast thickened. As yet no wind stirred on earth. In heat and silence, the land lay waiting.

Four mounted men rode past Aquilo and up the river road to Confluentes. They led one horse whose saddle was empty. Hoofs clattered on the new stone bridge. They did not enter the city, but passed around and took the dirt road along the Stegir.

That drew remark from onlookers. Their hails got no response. The party trotted onward from the northwest tower, by the old manor and its orchard, through the lately cleared fields beyond, until they reached the present edge of the woods in that direction and disappeared within.

A man came into a tavern, excited, and told his friends what he had seen. The place was tiny, a room in the owner's home; everybody heard. "Two soldiers they were, armored, and two civilians, one of them pretty well dressed, the other a monk or something. Been traveling hard, from the look of them. What could they want?"

"Government business?" wondered a drinker. "But why didn't they stop off at the hostel in Aquilo? My brother works there, and he was telling me this very morning how they haven't had anybody except postal couriers for—I forget how long. So those fellows just got here, and if you saw aright, they didn't even stop to freshen up."

"Ah, these be strange times," muttered a third man. "Holy Martinus, watch over us."

Evirion put down his half-emptied cup, left his bench, and hurried out. "Hoy, what the devil?" sounded at his back, but he simply broke into a run when he reached the door.

At his house he shooed away the servant who was cleaning it. Once alone, he took from a chest a pair of knives, his sword, a crossbow such as mariners favored, and a case of bolts for it. A long cloak concealed them while he thrust his way through traffic. A wake of indignation and profanity roiled behind him.

Outside the east gate clustered a number of shops denied space within because they were noisy or smelly or the owners could not afford it. Among them was a livery stable. Evirion selected what he deemed was the least jaded of its three horses, and did not haggle but paid over at once the asking price of a day's rent, in coin. "That should make you outfit her fast," he told the groom. "Failing it, I have the toe of my boot."

If he pushed the sorry nag hard, she might well founder on him. He made the best speed that prudence, not mercy, allowed. It was some slight help for the seething in him that the Romans wouldn't expect pursuit. You couldn't generally gallop along the woodland trails anyway. Their gloom was dense this day, except where the twisting course brought him near the Stegir.

~ 4 ~

Thunder rolled down the sky. Cold gusts went like surf through the treetops. Clouds decked the sun with darkness, but a weird brass-yellow light came through, pervasive as if without any one source, and sheened on the river.

Nemeta stepped from her cabin as the men drew rein. For an instant she surveyed them, and they her. Two were soldiers, cavalry, though not heavy lancers. Helmets and coats of ringmail shone hard above leather breeches and boots. Their swords were long. Axes were sheathed under their saddlebows and shields hung at their horses' breechings. One led a riderless animal.

On their left a lean man with an undershot jaw sat awkwardly, not used to riding and sore from it. He too was trousered, in cloth, but had sandals on bare feet and a brown robe that must be his only everyday garment, pulled up past his knees. Above a short beard, the front half of his scalp was shaven, the hair making a ruff behind. He pressed a small casket close against his side.

The fourth, on the right and somewhat in the lead, wearing blue linen beneath a fine tunic, unarmed aside from a knife—

"Nagon Demari," she said. Dismay shook her voice.

The stocky man skewered her with his gaze. "You are Nemeta, daughter of Gratillonius," he snapped.

"Aye," she replied unthinkingly in Ysan. "What would you of me?"

"Answer me, in Latin."

She braced her thin frame. "Why should I?"

"Obduracy will make matters worse for you," he told her, unrelenting as the thunder. "Name yourself to these men."

She moistened her lips before she uttered, "I am...Nemeta," in their language.

"Bear witness," Nagon ordered his band.

Nemeta half raised her useable hand. The wind tossed stray red locks around the white face. "What is this?" she cried. "How do you know me, Nagon? I was a young girl when—when—" She faltered.

He smiled with compressed lips. "You know *me*."

"All Ys knew you. And since then—"

"I have gathered information, piece by piece in these past years. I am a patient man when there is need to be."

"What do you want?"

They stared and stared at her. Nagon squared his shoulders, drew breath, and intoned against the wind: "Nemeta, daughter of Gratillonius, you are a pagan and a witch. Your unholy rites are banned by the law. Your diabolical practices have endangered souls for far too long. Some may already be in hell because of you. By authority of the governor of this province, I arrest you, for conveyance to trial at Caesarodunum Turonum." Thunder followed, louder and nearer.

She took a step back, halted, stiffened, and stammered, "This, this is...preposterous. I am the daughter of the King—of the tribune."

A laugh slapped at her. "He has indeed been negligent." Sternly: "Make no more trouble for him and yourself. Come. Here is a horse for you. Will you need help in mounting?"

"Hard rain any minute now, sir," a soldier said. "Why don't we wait it out in the cabin?"

His companion flinched and exclaimed, "Not in a witch's house!"

"We go straight back," Nagon commanded. "We are on the Lord's business. Come, woman."

"No, I won't!" Nemeta yelled. She forked the three middle fingers of her hand and thrust it at them. "I *am* a witch! Begone, or I'll strike you down! Belisama, Lir, and Taranis, hear!"

"Witness," Nagon told the others. His voice crackled with exultation. The soldiers stirred uneasily in their seats. He turned to the fourth member of the group. "Brother Philippus."

"I am a priest, my child," said the tonsured men to Nemeta. It was hard to hear him through the rising storm. "An exorcist." He opened the casket and took forth a scroll. Without a grasp on its reins, his horse stamped and tossed its head. "Your poor wickedness has no power against the Lord God and this, His holy word. Attempt no spells. They can only bring a punishment more severe."

Nemeta whirled and sprinted aside. "After her!" Nagon shouted.

The soldiers spurred their mounts. Before she reached the brake, they were on either side of her. She was lost between cliffs of height. One man nudged her roughly with his foot. She stumbled back from between them. Nagon and Philippus closed in too.

She slumped. "Again, four of you," she whispered. Her head sank till they saw just the fiery hair.

"Resist no more," said the priest, "and none shall harm you."

"That is for her judge to decide," Nagon crooned.

Lightning flared. Hoofbeats answered thunder. A horse came around the bend of the trail, lathered and lurching. When its rider yanked on

1026

the reins, it halted at once and stood with head a-droop. Breath wheezed in froth.

"Hold on, there!" bellowed he who sat it.

They gaped. Nemeta raised her eyes and gave a kind of moan. "What is this?" Nagon demanded.

"They're...taking me away." Nemeta's words blew frail on the wind.

"Oh, no, you don't," said Evirion. He brought up the crossbow he had had on his left arm, cocked and loaded. "Stop right there."

A soldier cursed. Philippus called on God. Nagon reddened and whitened with fury. "Are you crazy?" he choked. "We're agents of the state."

"Has she summoned a demon to possess you?" quavered the exorcist.

Nemeta reached resolve. She took a pair of steps from her captors toward the mariner, stopped, and said almost quietly, "Evirion, don't. Go. You can't help me this time."

Death was on his countenance. "The hell I can't. Come here, woman. You others stay back. The first of you that moves, I'll drop."

Nagon grinned his hatred. "And what about the next?" he challenged.

"Please, Evirion," Nemeta begged. "I don't want you beheaded too."

"It could be worse than that, from what I've heard," the big man said. "Come here."

She shook her head.

"All right," Evirion snarled. "I'm coming after you."

He sprang from his horse and advanced on her.

"Get him!" Nagon screamed.

The cavalrymen drew blade. A charger neighed. Both boomed past the prisoner and down on the seaman.

Evirion pulled trigger. The bow rang and thumped, the bolt whistled through the wind. The man on the left let go of his sword and toppled. He struck soddenly and lay still in an outwelling of blood. Lightning made his mail shimmer. His horse galloped on, crashed into the brush, was gone.

The second was already at Evirion. A stout crossbow could put a shaft through armor, but took time to load and set. Even to a trained infantryman, a mounted attack was a terrifying sight. Evirion barely dodged aside. He threw his bow. The heavy stock struck in the midriff. The rider did not fall. For a moment, though, he lost control. Instead of taking the chance to run, Evirion darted in. His sword hissed free. A hoof nearly smote him. He got behind and swung.

Hamstrung, the horse screamed, kicked air, plunged and scrabbled. "You swine!" its master shrieked, and threw himself off to the ground. The horse reeled aside, fell, lay thrashing and screaming. Its rider had kept hold of his sword. Evirion pounced like a cat before his opponent was afoot. They went down together. The heel of Evirion's left hand smashed the soldiers's nose from beneath. Suddenly that face was a red ruin. The man jerked once and died.

Evirion bounced to a crouch. The encounter had passed in a whirl. The priest clung to the neck of his panicky, rearing mount. Nagon was in little better case. His eyes darted, found Nemeta still frozen. He writhed from the saddle, thumped to earth in a heap, was immediately up and on the run, toward the woman. His knife gleamed forth.

"Nemeta!" Evirion roared, and plunged toward her. She came aware and leaped. Nagon was almost there. He meant to take her hostage or kill her, Evirion knew; no matter which. Nagon's left hand snatched out and caught her by the hair. She jerked to a halt. With a whoop, he pulled her into stabbing distance. She caught that wrist in the crook of her left arm and her teeth. She fell, dragged it down. Her skeleton right arm flopped at his ankles.

Evirion arrived. His sword sang below the lightning. It thwacked as it bit into the neck. Blood spouted. Nagon went to his knees. "Oh, Lydris," bubbled from his mouth—the name of his wife. He crumpled on his face and scrabbled weakly for a while. Blood flowed from him slower and slower, out into an enormous puddle whose red caught the lightning-light.

Evirion knelt and held Nemeta close. The blood that had gushed over her smeared across him. "Fare you well?" he asked frantically in Ysan. "Are you hale, my darling?"

"Aye." The answer came faint. "Not hurt. But you?" Her eyes found his.

"I was the quickest of them." He helped her to rise. She leaned on him, tottered, and sank down once they were out of the pool.

"I'm well, but—but my head swims—" She lowered it between her knees.

The exorcist's horse had thrown him. Dazed more by horror than impact, he groped backward from the red-painted man who turned his way. He lifted his arms as if in prayer. "Please, no," he begged. "I belong to the Church."

Evirion pointed. "Go," he said. "Upstream. Don't turn around till...till sundown."

"No, not alone at night in the wilderness!"

"'Twon't hurt you. Use this house if you like." Evirion's laugh clanked. "You shouldn't fear witchcraft, should you, priest? But I don't want you here before dark. Tomorrow, if you can't remember the trails, follow the river to Confluentes. Go!" He made one threatening stride. Philippus whimpered and scuttled off.

Evirion went about securing things. His jade had stood numbly throughout. He cut the throat of the crippled charger. The priest's gelding and the remount were still close by, somewhat calmed. They shied from him, but he caught the reins of first one, then the other, as thickets slowed their escape, and they let him tie them to branches. He collected weapons, washed them in the river, bundled everything in his cloak. The wind blew still stronger and louder. Lightning went in flares and sheets, thunder crashed, a deeper rushing noise told of rain oncoming.

By the time he was through, Nemeta had recovered. She went to him and laid her cheek against his breast. His arms enclosed her. "Evirion, what now?" Her tone still shook. "My father—"

"He's gone on one of his trips," the man told her. "I'd guess Nagon knew he would be, and timed himself for it."

A ghost of joy lilted. "Well do the Gods stand by us! Nobody can accuse my father of aught."

"They'll be after you and me. Let's begone. Here we've two good steeds."

"Whither?"

"I know not. The forest?"

She looked up. A steadiness to match his came into her. "Nay, not at once. We needn't blindly bolt. In Confluentes may be some help. At least, he—my father has the need and right to learn what truly happened."

"Hm— Aye. A sound thought. Well, come, then. 'Tis a long ride, and the earlier we begin, the better."

She disengaged from him, moved toward the horses, stopped. "My cats!"

He blinked. "What?"

"I cannot leave my three cats behind. Who'd care for them?"

Laughter cataracted from him. When its wildness was past, he knuckled his eyes and said, "Very well, fetch them along. I should in honor return this Pegasus I hired, too."

She went to her dwelling. "I'll take them in a basket, to shield them from the rain."

"What about us?"

At her door, she looked back, across the sprawled dead men. "It will wash us clean."

~ 5 ~

The storm passed over. Eventide rested mellow. It tinted the battlements of Confluentes with gold. Swallows darted along the Odita.

Having brought them to Gratillonius's private room, Verania regarded her two drenched, hollow-eyed visitors and asked softly, "What is this?"

"A terrible story," Evirion said. "Best we tell your brother Salomon."

"It happens he's here. I'll go for him if you like. But—Nemeta, dear, we haven't seen you in years. Be welcome. We'll have a bath and a bed for you—oh, and supper, of course. Can you stay till your father returns? He'll be so happy."

Nemeta shook her head. "I must be off." Her glance went fearfully to the window. Low light made its glass shine sea-green. "Never can I spend a night here." The cats she had released from the basket

1029

ceased sniffing about the room and sought her. "But can you take these from me?" she requested. "They're housebroken and sweet."

"If you wish it, certainly. I'll call Salomon." Skirts rustled as Verania went out. Nemeta squatted down to stroke and reassure her pets. Evirion prowled.

Verania re-entered. "He'll be here shortly," she explained. "He was asleep. He stays with me when my husband is away. Not that I need be afraid of anything. Gratillonius wants to mark him out as—an heir to leadership. Our mother agrees." Proudly: "People have started bringing disputes before him, and he's active in the guard. But today he went hunting, the weather caught him, he came back exhausted."

"Thank you, my lady," said Evirion. "Maybe you'd best withdraw."

Verania looked at him. "Nemeta will stay, won't she?" When he nodded: "Then it shouldn't be talk unfit for a woman to hear."

"It's dangerous to know."

She flushed. "Do you suppose I won't share any danger that touches my man? We're close, he and I. Let me stay."

"Or she'll have to get it from her brother," Nemeta divined. "I'm sorry, Verania. We can certainly use your counsel."

Salomon appeared, hastily tunicked, hair uncombed and fuzz on his cheeks. But his youth had shrugged fatigue off and he was alert. "Nemeta! Evirion!" he cheered. "Why, this is splendid." He paused. "No, it isn't, is it?"

"Close the door," his sister told him.

They heard the story. Never did they call the deed a crime.

"Holy Georgios, help us," Salomon prayed.

"That horrible creature, Nagon," sighed Verania. "Sick with his own venom."

"He was that, I suppose," Evirion said. "He should have escaped while he could. But he went after Nemeta, and naturally I chopped him."

"God help me, I don't think I can pray for him."

Salomon folded his arms and stared downward. "Never mind that now," he said. "What should *we* do?"

"We, Nemeta and I, we won't stay," Evirion promised. "Whether or not that fool priest makes it back, and he will, they'll soon have a pretty good idea in Turonum of what went awry. We mustn't get you fouled in their net. Give us a rest, a bite to eat, dry clothes, some provisions we can carry, and we'll be off as soon as it's dark."

"Nobody will know we were here," Nemeta added. "We were two more wet people among the few in the streets. Your doorkeeper didn't get a good look at me, and never met me before anyway." She had, after all, brought a cloak for herself, and used the cowl to screen her face and distinctive hair. "Who'll think to question him? I suppose he knows Evirion a little, but why should he remember what day he last saw him?"

"Besides, he's loyal," Verania said. "My family's treated its slaves like fellow children of God....But into the wildwood, you two?"

Salomon lifted his head. "Give Gratillonius time, and he may be able to negotiate a pardon," he declared. "In any case, you've got shelter where the state can never find you."

"Where?" coughed Evirion.

"With one of our brotherhoods. Rufinus's old Bacaudae. They'll be glad to take you in."

"How can you be sure?"

"I've been among them enough. Gratillonius wants everybody to get to know me, and me to know them. Come night, I'll guide you."

XX

~ 1 ~

"You know why I'm here," said Gratillonius. "Let's get on with it."

"By all means," replied Bacca cordially.

They sat alone in his room of erotic books in Turonum. Outside, wind blustered. Glass panes flickered with cloud shadows.

"My daughter—"

"And her murderous accomplice."

Gratillonius's eyes stung. "It never had to happen. She harmed nobody. I think she helped many. The country's full of good little witches like her."

Bacca's gaunt visage assumed sternness. "Your duty is to put a stop to that."

"Then every Roman official is derelict," Gratillonius retorted. "I could find witches within five miles of here. So could you, if you'd take the trouble."

"We have more pressing concerns."

"Me too. I thought you wanted my goodwill."

"We did. I still do." Bacca sighed. "Let me give you the background. Nagon was clever. He waited till I was out of the city, then approached the governor. Glabrio has never liked or trusted you."

How true, thought Gratillonius. That was why he had sought audience with the procurator instead. Not that Bacca was a friend either, but he seemed reasonable in his rascality.

"He was quite willing to be persuaded," the smooth voice continued. "One can imagine Nagon's exhortation. 'End the scandal of paganism and sorcery in the very family of a Roman tribune. It's not only his flouting of law and religion, it's his intransigence. Give him a sharp reminder that he must mend his ways. Humble him. Undermine him.'

"They didn't tell me about the decision. Glabrio says he wanted to avoid a futile dispute when his mind was made up. Confidentially, I suspect he was afraid I'd change it for him.'"

That also sounded true, Gratillonius thought. Glabrio had spite of his own to vent. Weak men are often vicious.

"Once Nagon brought her back, publicly accused, it would be too late," Bacca finished. "We would have no choice but to proceed against her. It was a poor return Nagon made me for my protection, I grant you."

Gratillonius's heart thumped. "Well, how about repairing the damage?" he pressed. "Issue a civil pardon. Bishop Corentinus is ready to give absolution."

Bacca's lips pinched together before he answered, "Impossible. That man murdered two soldiers and an officer of the state."

"She was innocent, helpless." Heavily: "Let him stay outlawed." It hurt Gratillonius to the point of nausea, but he had cherished no real hope for Evirion.

"You have not been precisely zealous in organizing pursuit of him," said Bacca.

"How can I ransack the wilderness?"

"You have men who live in it."

Gratillonius shook his head. "No, I don't," he declared with a slight, malicious pleasure. "I'm not allowed to, remember? I have been given no authority over those squatters."

"Very good!" laughed Bacca. "Then why are you so sure the girl is even alive?"

"Let's say I'm confident of God's mercy and justice."

Gaze met gaze. Gratillonius knew that Bacca knew he got word from the forest. For the procurator to state it forthrightly would mean scrapping the policy he had been at pains to get adopted.

Bacca's wry smile faded. "Corentinus cannot reconcile a pagan with Him," he pointed out.

"She would accept baptism."

"I suppose she would, as a matter of expediency. Later—who knows?—his grace might touch her. But it cannot be. She would have to appear in public. Otherwise, what practical difference would these maneuvers make? When she did, we would have to seize her. The case is that notorious. There is much rebelliousness in Armorican hearts these days. Sparing her would feed it like nothing else. No, reprieve is a political impossibility."

Gratillonius bent forward, elbows on thighs, hands clasped between knees, head low. "I was afraid of that. But I had to come try."

"I understand," said Bacca gently. "Courage. Perhaps in a few years, when the sensation has died down, if things in general look less precarious, perhaps then—" He let the words die away.

1032

Gratillonius straightened. "You dangle that bait before me?"

"It may be honest. We shall have to wait and see. At the moment, I cannot give you any promises other than—taking the pressure off you about this business...provided you cause no further questions about your loyalty to be raised."

"I won't." Gratillonius could not quite swallow the insult. "You snake, this is extortion."

Bacca seemed unoffended. "It's for Rome," he replied.

~ 2 ~

Autumn weather came earliest to the high midland of Armorica. First the birches grew sallow and their leaves departed on chilly winds, then red and brown and yellow rustled all over the hills. Ducks left the meres and the reeds around them brittled. The rivers seemed to run louder through gorges filling with shadow. Clear nights were crowded with stars; the Swan soared over the evenings and Orion strode up before dawn.

Nemeta thanked Vindolenus and left him to get a bit of food and some rest in Catualorig's house. It was a thirty-league trek the dour old Bacauda had made from the Confluentes neighborhood—thirty leagues for a bird, two or three times that on twisting trails or through tracklessness. Only once earlier had he been able to do it, carrying gifts and a message. He had his living to make; and Gratillonius did not share out the secret of where his daughter was. Vindolenus had taken her and Evirion there in the first instance, after Salomon brought them to him and asked they be given a refuge safely remote. In Roman eyes, men like this were still felons, unwise if they made themselves conspicuous. Some had scattered very widely, founding homesteads where no Armorican tribe would dispute it; but they kept in touch.

Nemeta carried the letter outside. It was a day of pale sunlight and nipping breeze. Fallen leaves rattled over the clearing around the rude, sod-roofed cabin. Its pair of outbuildings crowded close, dwarfish. Rails marked off a fold. Chickens scratched in the dust. A rivulet gurgled and gleamed. Catualorig's daughter returned sulkily from the excitement of the arrival to scrub clothes on the stones in its bed. From behind the cabin an ax thudded as her mother chopped firewood. The man and his two sons were about their tasks in the forest. It hemmed in the dwelling place and a tiny, hand-cultivated field. Height and hues cloaked the ruggedness of terrain, but the northward upslope was unmistakable.

Nemeta found a log at the edge of the plot, sat down, untied the tablets, and spread them on her lap. She had become quite adept in the use of a single hand and bare toes. Words pressed into wax were necessarily spare, and Gratillonius's writing style was less than eloquent. Yet she read over and over:

"My dear daughter, we are all well. Food is short but nobody hungers too much. The barbarians are still bad but have not touched us here. Good news too. In August the Romans broke the invaders of Italy at last. Stilicho had collected many recruits, also Alan and Hun allies from beyond the Danuvius. He cut the barbarian supply lines then killed them group by group. At last Radagaisus was captured and beheaded. We miss you and hope you are well. Your father."

A finer imprint continued, news of people she knew and of everyday things. It ended: "We love you. God willing we will yet bring you home. Greet Evirion. Verania."

Nemeta rose, tucked the tablets close to her, and hurried off upstream. Somberness had left her face. She hummed a song children in Ys once sang when at play. Along the trail she spied the younger boy, herding the swine, and gave him a hail whose cheeriness astonished him.

Shortly she heard the blunt noise of a mallet on wood. Another clearing opened before her. This one was minute, made where a brookside stand of shrubs could readily be removed. An uncompleted building occupied it. It too was small, of the primitive round form, though it would eventually boast a couple of windows with membranes and shutters. The soil was poor for wattle-and-daub, and Evirion built with stout poles, carefully chinked. The roof would be of turf, smokehole louvered; he was no thatcher, and besides, this would diminish the fire hazard. He stood on a ladder—a length of fir with the branches lopped to stubs, leaned against the wall—and pegged a rafter to a crossbeam. Like her, he wore a single garment of coarse wool, for him a kilt. Muscles coiled in view. His beard had grown out and his hair was a hayrick.

"Evirion!" she cried. "A message—Vindolenus again—this time he brought us warm clothes and, and come read for yourself. 'Tis the most wonderful news."

"Hold," he said, and finished securing the roughly shaped timber. Only then did he drop the hammer and climb down. "Well, well. So there is still a world out there. Ofttimes I've felt unsure."

"Take it. Read." She thrust the tablets into his hands.

He scanned them, laid them on the ground, and muttered, "Italy saved. Doubtless a fine thing, but much of it must lie in wreck by now."

"You don't rejoice," she said, crestfallen.

He shrugged. "Why do you? We remain exiles."

"Oh—my father—"

"Aye. You're glad because this word gave him a little happiness." Evirion smiled. "So should I be. He's a good man—the best. Nor should I whine at my own fate."

Warmth swelled in her tones. "You never do. You're too strong for that."

"In some ways. In others— Well, brooding on such things weakens a man by itself."

She waved at the house. "Behold what you've done. And in all weathers, too, this harsh year."

"Ha, I'd better. Winter draws nigh."

"You'll outpace it. Once begun, you've raced ahead like wildfire." He could accomplish little until Vindolenus had brought the tools he requested from Gratillonius. Catualorig's were few, crude, and often needed by him. The settler and his sons lent a hand when necessary, but for the most part had no time to spare for it. They likewise must prepare for winter.

"Aye, 'twill be ready within another month, if my luck holds," he said. "But I'd fain also make it a little comfortable."

"That can come later. I can scarce wait to move in."

They shared the cabin with the family and, at one end of it, two cows. The dwellers were friendly enough but had no conversation in them. After dark, they snuffed the tallow candles and went to bed on skins spread over juniper boughs on the earthen floor. Then the only light was from coals in the banked firepit. Air was thick with smells of smoke, grease, dung, beast, man. When Catualorig mounted his wife, nobody could sleep till he was done, though that didn't take long. The daughter was apt to giggle at those sounds.

Nemeta and Evirion had quickly decided they didn't want to be immediate neighbors. Fortunately, the yard lacked much space for another structure. It would have been ill done to offend people who were so kindly and who loved Gratillonius themselves.

"'Twill never be like what you had in Ys, nor even later by the Stegir," Evirion said, "but let me give you something better than a cave."

"Could I but help!" Her pleasure blew away on the wind that soughed around. "It hurts being useless."

"You're not."

"With this arm? And none of my arts?" She dared not practice her small witcheries. Thinly populated though the hills were, word of it would spread, and in time get to Roman ears. Her whereabouts betrayed, she might flee onward, but Gratillonius would be destroyed, with all that he had labored for. Nemeta had not offered the Three as much as a chant. That could have disturbed the inhabitants, who sacrificed to spirits of wood and water and to whom Ys was a tale of doom.

"You are *not* useless," Evirion told her. "You do well with your single hand. They have gain of your aid. You lighten their lives with your stories and poems. You bring me my midday food as I work, and talk and sing to me. Without that cheer, I'd lag far behind."

"The most I can tender you," she answered sadly, "who lost everything because of me."

"That's just as false," he blurted. "You're enough, and more."

"Oh, Evirion—"

He moved to hug her. It would have been chaste, but she slipped aside. His arms fell.

"I'm sorry," he said dully. "I forgot. The curse of what happened that day by the sea."

She hung her head and dug a toe into the earth. "The Gods have not healed me of it," she whispered.

"Those Gods?" He curbed his scorn and attempted gaiety. "Well, anyhow, soon you'll have your own house."

She looked up, half alarmed. "Nay, ours."

He let the mask drop from him. Pain roughened his voice. "So I believed too. but I've thought more, and, and may as well tell you now. This hut— Belike 'twould be too much for my strength, living with you as a brother and sister in a palace. In a single space, impossible. This shall be yours alone."

"But what will you do?" she wailed.

He forced a grin. "I'll fettle me. Our present lodging can easily become a merry place."

She stared.

"That's a sprightly young chick Catualorig's fathered," he said, "and she's been giving me a twinklesome eye, and he's already hinted he'd liefer have me than a ruck of woodland louts beget his grandchildren."

"What?"

He heard and saw she was appalled. Hastily, he said, "Ah, I tease you," then could not resist adding, "Mayhap."

Nemeta tightened her left fist, gulped, finally uttered, "Oh, I've no right—" A yell: "Nay, you're too good for an unwashed hussy like that!"

"Weep not," he begged, contrite. "Please. I was jesting."

She blinked hard. "W-were you?"

"Not altogether," he admitted wryly. "The desire does wax in me day by day, and there she is. But if naught else, 'twould be cruel of me, when I'm bound to forsake her."

"You are? Where can you go?"

"Anywhere else." Bitterness broke through. "You've called yourself useless, wrongly. But what am I? Once this thing is done, what's for my hands? I'm a blunderer in the hunt. I doubt I could dig a straight furrow or make aught grow save weeds. Nor do I care to. This is no life for a seaman. Come spring, if we're here yet, I'm off."

The green eyes were enormous in a face drained of color. "What will you do?"

"Make my way south." He gained heart as he spoke. "Who'll know me, once I've changed my name? Surely I can find a berth as a deckhand. Any skipper so bold as to sail nowadays must reck little of guilds and laws. I think of earning me a passage to Britannia. 'Tis in turmoil, but that means opportunities."

She reached out her hand. "Nay, Evirion," she pleaded. "Leave me not."

"Be of good cheer. You'll be quite safe. Catualorig will keep y
fed and fuelled. 'Tis no great strain on him. Game is plentiful and he
a master huntsman, besides having his livestock."

"But reavers, barbarians—"

"They've never come this far inland. Naught worth their stealing.
And no man of these parts will dare lay a finger on you. Gratillonius's
vengeance would be swift and sure. Moreover, though you've put your
arts aside, they've some idea of what you can do at need. Fear not.
Bide your time."

"'Tis you I fear for! Out in yon ongoing slaughter—"

"I'll live. Or if I die, the foe will rue the price. At worst, 'twill be
happier than this—this—" He stopped.

"What? Speak it."

He yielded. "This emptiness. Endless yearning."

She stood a long while silent. The wind ruffled her hair, like flames
dancing. Finally she drew breath and said, "We can end it."

"How?"

She looked straight at him. "I love you, Evirion."

He had no words.

"I dared not say it." She spoke almost calmly. "Now I must. I will
be yours. What, shall you not embrace me?"

He reeled to her and gathered her in arms that shivered. "I'd never
...willingly...hurt you," he croaked.

"I know you'll be gentle. I think, if you're patient, I think you can
teach me. Can give me back what I lost."

He brought his lips down. Hers were shy at first, then clumsy, then
eager.

"Come," she said amidst laughter and tears. She tugged at his wrist.
"Now, at once. Spread your kilt under me. Away from the wind, inside
these walls of ours."

~ 3 ~

A sharp summer was followed by a hard winter. Snowfalls, rarely
seen in Armorica, warmed air a little for a short while, then soon a
ringing frost would set in. Against the whitened steeps where Gesocribate
had nestled, its burnt-over shell seemed doubly black.

Brick and tile, the house of Septimius Rullus was among those that
had escaped conflagration. It was sacked; the rooms echoed hollowly.
Cleaning had removed the shards of beautiful things and the filth, but
could do nothing for murals smoke-stained and hacked, mosaic floor
wantonly chipped and pried at. The curial survived because he left
the city when the Saxons first hove in view. That was not cowardice.
Old, a widower, he could only have gotten in the way of the defenders
and consumed supplies they needed if the combat turned into a siege.
He had taken with him as many of the helpless as he was able to lead,

spirits from breaking while they fled across the hinterland
in whatever shelter they found, brought them back to
here among the ruins.

here had avoided the general massacre in various ways.
barians had also overlooked food stores sufficient to last this
ant population a few months, if miserly doled out. Manufacturies
sumed on a small scale, producing goods to trade for necessities.
The nearest thing to a tribune that ghost Gesocribate had, Rullus got
all this effort started and held it together. Therefore Gratillonius, who
had heard the story, sought him out.

They sat on stools hastily made and held their hands close to a
single brazier, in lieu of a hypocaust for which there was not enough
firewood. Its glow and a couple of tallow candles stuck to a battered
table gave feeble light. Outside was day, but panes had been shattered
and windows were stuffed with rags. It was just as well, perhaps; the
chamber was no longer a pretty sight. A slave had brought in bread,
cheese, and ale. The farm-brewed drink was in two goblets of exquisite
glass and a silver decanter; the raiders had not found absolutely everything. Rullus had remarked that he would sell the pieces when he
found a buyer who could pay what they were worth. "My son and
son-in-law were both killed," he added stoically. "Their wives and
children have more need of money than of heirlooms."

A handsome graybeard with a scholarly manner of speech, he reminded Gratillonius of Apuleius, or of Ausonius. (Christ have mercy,
how many years was it since Gratillonius met the poet?) Breath puffed
white in the gloom as he said, "This is a poor welcome for you."

"Who can offer more than the best he has?" replied Gratillonius.
It had been a saying of his father's.

"Well, you of all men must realize what it means to come down in
the world. It was rather different for us, of course. This city flourished
when I was a boy. But trade shriveled year by year—revived for a
while, then Ys fell—and so our catastrophe has cost humanity less
than yours."

"Do you think you can rebuild?"

"Not as it was. Under certain unlikely conditions, we could resurrect
something. But only Our Lord had power to bring Lazarus entirely
back to life."

"What do you need?"

"Basically, a measure of assurance that it won't be for nothing. Thus,
a defense we can rely on."

"That's what I've come about."

Rullus studied the shadows and highlights of his guest's face. "I
thought so. One hears, shall we say, rumors."

"They may have been misleading. I do not propose breaking laws."
The hell I don't, Gratillonius thought. The risk be damned. We've got
to take it. Gesocribate be my witness. "Men of the city and its environs

1038

can be taught to defend themselves until...military reinforcem
arrive."

Rullus lifted his brows. "Suppose they don't."

"Well, given a proper understanding between you people and the
rest of us, we can jointly set up a line of communications—beacons,
runners—so men from farther inland can arrive in time to help."

"In a strictly civilian capacity, of course."

"Of course." Gratillonius's tone was equally dry.

Rullus sighed. "A beautiful fantasy."

"It's become real."

"I know. The deadly surprise the Scoti got at the Gobaean Promontory. Other incidents subsequently." Rullus shook his head. "But you
see, Gesocribate can't meet the conditions. You presuppose a viable
city, worth saving, able to take a share in the common defense."

"It can be built. Meanwhile, for the sake of the future, we'll mount
guard over it. You can have a going concern again in a year or two,
I'd guess. I can find some of the necessary manpower for you."

Rullus lifted a finger. "Ah, but the defense you are thinking of will
be insufficient."

"I tell you, we can hold off the barbarians."

"I mean the tax collector." Rullus's voice became bleak. "There is
no prospect of remission, merely because we've had a disaster. The
government is insensately desperate for resources, like a starving man
who eats the seed corn. When payment falls due next year, I shall be
wiped out, together with every so-called free man down to the lowliest
fisher."

"Appeal to Arelate. If need be, to Rome—Ravenna. I can help. I've
gotten a few influential associates."

Rullus remained skeptical. "I fear the chance of success is negligible.
And imagining we do get a little leniency, why should we rebuild? As
soon as we have anything again, we'll be wrung dry of it. Better to
seek some great landholder's protection. Not that I'd make a serf he'd
want, but the monks at Turonum may take me in....No matter. These
are not times when we should pity the aged. It's the young we must
weep for."

"Hold on!" exclaimed Gratillonius. "I've considered this too. If nothing else works, well, Confluentes can spare Gesocribate enough out
of its treasury to keep you afloat till you're back on your feet." And
what would Ausonius have thought of that figure of speech? flickered
through him.

Rullus was silent a minute before he said slowly, "This—is a rather
overwhelming charitableness."

Gratillonius smiled. "We have our selfish reasons. Armorica, which
includes Confluentes, needs your port. It's been a main link with
Britannia."

"Would that be of any use anymore?" asked Rullus, puzzled.

you mean? Of course it would. Trade, mutual defense—"
't heard?"

deep, as if the cold around had turned into a single
...on the road spell. Tribal chiefs to see along the way."
lus nodded. "We got the news three days ago, from yet
boatload of people hoping for a better life in Armorica. The
s have gone home or into winter quarters, and— These waifs put
here because they knew it was the nearest safe anchorage, if no
longer a real harbor."

"Hercules, man! Don't torture me. What'd they have to tell?"

"I'm sorry. It's so painful. The legions in Britannia, what's left of
them, have risen. They've deposed the diocesan government and proclaimed a man of theirs, one Marcus, Emperor."

"Marcus," Gratillonius whispered. In that stunned moment he could
only think: The name of my father, the name of my son.

"So the immigrants may discover they were unwise," Rullus continued. "When Marcus crosses over to Gallia, we'll have a new civil
war."

~ 4 ~

As the year spun down to solstice, cold deepened. The Odita and
Stegir lay frozen between banks where the snow glittered rock-hard.
Icicles hung from naked boughs, eaves, battlements, like spears turned
downward. When a man had been outdoors a while, his mustache was
rimed. Skies were cloudless, the sun a wan disc briefly seen low in
the south, the nights bitterly brilliant. The occasional traveler from the
east related that it was thus over the whole breadth of northern Gallia,
and beyond.

After the meager harvest, midwinter festivities were lean. In Confluentes and its region they had, though, a hectic exuberance, as bright
and loud and dancing as the bonfires lit to call the sun back home.
Folk had outlived that spring, summer, autumn. They had enough to
see them through the winter if they husbanded it. The Saxons had
steered wide of them and ought not to be a danger again till after the
thaws. They and those they loved could draw into their snug little dens
and be at ease, at peace.

Gratillonius and his family had moved back to the house in Aquilo,
and meant to abide there till about equinox. It had a hypocaust, whereas
they feared what their own place, ill heated by open fires, might do
to Marcus, *their* Marcus. Rovinda and Salomon received them happily.
They had a bedroom to themselves; the child slept with his nurse.

One evening about a score of days after the solstice, father and son
were romping as usual, until Verania said, also as usual, that that was
ample ride-horsey and a certain young man was much overdue for his
rest. Gratillonius went along and sang over his crib, which had become
another of his customs. This time it was the three or four decent stanzas

in an old legionary marching song. He had explained that all too soon small children developed a sense for music and, like their elders, requested him to stop.

He returned laughing to the atrium. "That boy's going to be a great cavalryman!" he said. "Did you see how he sits? Might almost have grown out of my back. Any time, now, I expect he'll reach down and make reins of my ears."

Verania smiled at him from the stool where she sat embroidering. A five-branched brass candelabrum, on a table beside her, gave adequate light. Tapers elsewhere kept the rest of the room bright and brought out the soft hues of its murals. The household could afford clean-burning wax; this area was rich in honeybees. The light caressed her as Jupiter had caressed Danae, golden in hair and on cheeks and along the slight fullness that had begun proclaiming to the world that she was with child anew. The air was warm, but because he liked it she had had a small amount of charcoal kindled in a brazier and laid a pine cone there. Its smoke was like vanished summers.

Rovinda was the sole other person present, seated nearby with distaff and spindle. Apuleius had taught that work with the hands beseemed patricians—Ulysses, Cincinnatus, not to mention the Savior—though he himself was manually awkward. Salomon was out carousing. At his age you couldn't be forever serious, and he never let it get the better of him. The slaves had been dismissed for the night.

Trouble touched the older woman's face. She was, still, often hard put to maintain serenity. "Must he become a soldier?" she asked mutedly.

"Oh, perhaps a merchant or landholder," Verania said.

Gratillonius didn't feel like sitting down yet. He stood before them, several feet off so they needn't crane their necks up, folded his arms, and replied, "I'm afraid he'll have to know his weapons whatever he becomes."

"Not if it's a churchman," Rovinda pointed out. She sounded wistful. Since her husband's death she had turned extremely pious, as if to make amends for past religious lapses and earn hope of rejoining him in Paradise.

The idea quenched Gratillonius's already dampened mirth. Nothing really wrong with the clergy, no, no; in fact, Corentinus was a fine fellow, and Martinus had been admirable in his odd fashion; an able man could rise to bishop, even Pope, and make his mark on history; nevertheless, his firstborn son—

Verania read the distaste on him and told her mother, "No, I don't think that's in Marcus's blood. He's such a lively little scamp. Maybe our next will be more the sort."

"Then the future is his," Rovinda said.

"M-m, it could as well be a girl, you know."

"And as welcome," said Gratillonius. He wanted strong sons, but a couple of new Veranias would certainly lend sparkle to his days. She cast him a fond look, which he sent back.

Rovinda's spindle twirled to a stop. She stared away, as if through the wall into the darkness outside. "God forgive me, I almost hope not," she murmured. "Women are too weak."

"I wouldn't say that," Verania answered. "Each time we go in childbed, we do battle."

Across the years, his Queens and their daughters in Ys rose before Gratillonius; and Julia; and Nemeta, Nemeta. How fared Nemeta this cruel night?

"We haven't the strength to wield swords nor the right to be priests," Rovinda said.

Gratillonius cleared his throat. "Any girl of ours will marry a man who can protect her," he declared loudly.

Verania smiled. "I did."

Gratillonius felt soothed. "I try."

That quick fierceness which she mostly kept asleep flashed through Verania. "We'll hold what is ours."

"God has been good to us," Rovinda said, "but by the same token, we have much to lose. Be not proud. In Heaven alone is sureness."

Gratillonius could not let that go by. "Therefore, here on earth we need cavalrymen."

Rovinda shook her graying head. "If only we didn't. These are terrible times we live in."

Verania turned grave. "The hour between dog and wolf," she said low.

"What?" asked Gratillonius. Recollection came; it was a Gallic phrase for the twilight. "Oh. Right. They are wolves, the barbarians, two-legged wolves. I could have put it that what we need is watchdogs. Hounds for hunting, too."

"It isn't that simple, dear," Verania told him with her father's earnestness and love of discourse.

"Why not?" He spread his hands. "Look, I don't want to spoil the evening. We've gotten way too serious all of a sudden. But I've seen the work of the barbarians, and the single thing to do with them is kill them, hunt them down, till the last few skulk back to the wilderness that bred them. Stilicho thought he could tame them. I pray he's finally learned better, because Mother Rome has!"

"They are human beings," Verania argued. Not for the first time, it crossed his mind how bored he would be with a wife who never did. "Each king of theirs is a hero to his people. He surely thinks of himself as responsible for their well-being, their lives."

"Ha! He thinks of his own glory and how much he can rob."

Verania took her man aback: "Are civilized rulers different? In any event, our ancestors were wild Celts. Or Homer's Achaeans—how did the Trojans see them?"

"Are you telling me we're all the same?"

"We are all of us sinners," Rovinda said.

"No, there is a difference, a very real difference," Verania granted. "But it's not in the blood. It is—hard to put into words. I tried, four years ago when you went off to war against the Scoti, and in the end found I'd only made a verse."

"Let's hear it," Gratillonius said, interested.

A certain shyness brought Verania's lashes fluttering downward. "Oh, it's nothing. Just a few lines. You see, I was trying to understand *why* you were out there, you, the one I loved, setting your life at stake."

"Let's hear it," Gratillonius repeated. "Please."

"Well, it's— If you insist. Let me think....*Would you know the dog from the wolf? You—*"

A banging resounded. "Hold," Gratillonius said. "Somebody at our knocker." He strode across the room to the entry and the front door. Unease prickled his skin. Who could this be? It wasn't barred till the last person went to bed. If Salomon for some reason came home earlier, he'd simply walk in. If later, as was likely, he'd thunder the porter awake, unless it was when the house was again astir before dawn. The aged slave was yawning and creaking out of the alcove where he slept.

Gratillonius opened the door. Keen air flowed in across him. A full moon had cleared rooftops and made the snow on them gleam, more radiance than what trickled into the entry from the atrium. A man wearing breeches, boots, heavy tunic, cowled cloak stood in the portico. He was short, with bow legs bespeaking a life on horseback. "Imperial courier," he said wearily. "I have a dispatch for the tribune Gratillonius. They told me at the hostel he's here."

"Come in," Gratillonius invited, and led the way back to the atrium. The porter closed the door behind them. "I am the tribune. You've ridden hard."

"We all did, sir. Epona be thanked for the clear nights. I understand this message is from the frontier."

It would have gone first to Turonum, while other copies were galloped in relays to Arelate, Ravenna, wherever they must get the bad news as fast as possible. It could only be bad news. At Turonum, more copies were made and directed to regional authorities. It could only be bad news that concerned all Armorica, urgently.

"Can you get this man something hot to drink, or at least a cup of wine?" Gratillonius asked the women. They had risen and stood stricken, waiting. "Let's have the letter, fellow."

He brought it to the candelabrum where Verania had been embroidering, untied it, and read. Considering distances and road conditions, he decided the information was about ten days old.

A horde of barbarians had crossed the ice on the Rhenus, uncounted thousands of them. It was as though entire Germanic nations were on the move together; scouts had certainly recognized the standards of Alamanni, Suevi, Vandals, Burgundians, with Alani whose fathers had migrated from Scythian reaches where now prowled the Huns. Moguntiacum had fallen to them almost at once, stood plundered and ablaze, while their tide rolled unstoppable, strewing to their death-Gods any feeble opposition that it met, over the snow into the lands of Rome.

Gratillonius stood a long while unmoving. His silence spread outward from him till it brimmed the house. Deep within it he thought—scarcely felt; no shock or horror; those could cry out in him later but at this moment he was entirely watchfulness and thought. The thing that was happening was foreordained, not by God or the stars but by the blindness of men, since he lay in his mother's womb. His response to it was equally ineluctable.

"We must call up the brotherhoods," he said.

XXI

~ 1 ~

Augusta Treverorum, the splendor of the Roman North, seethed with looters, murderers, rapists, like a corpse with maggots. That news reached Confluentes as Gratillonius was about to ride forth. It redoubled the urgency with which he and his companions hastened to Vorgium.

There, near the middle of the Armorican peninsula, the leaders met. They were poorly housed and ill fed. The city had dwindled to an impoverished village amidst the wreckage that repeated sacks a generation or more ago had left. It was needful to clear from the council chamber of the basilica those people who slept there. Straw from their pallets littered the floor, smoke from their fires blackened walls and ceiling. Windows were rudely boarded up, choking the space with gloom as well as rime-frosting chill. Handy men among the delegates got pine torches started, lashed to improvised holders. Fixed stone benches provided seating, if you didn't mind dirt and a numb butt.

Corentinus and Gratillonius mounted the dais. While the bishop gave an invocation, Gratillonius's gaze probed the uneasy murk. They were a mixed fifty-odd who confronted him, city dwellers with cloaks drawn tight around riding garb, tribal headmen in thick woolen tunics with breeches or kilts, wilder-looking backwoodsmen wearing mostly leather and pelts, farmers, herders, fishers, artisans—and in the front row, pipe-clayed white and purple-bordered, the archaic senatorial toga in which Flavius Vortivir had arrayed himself. Eyeballs glistened, breath sounded harsh in the echoful emptiness. Memory of the Council of Suffetes in Ys was suddenly almost unbearable.

He forced it from him and trod forward as Corentinus finished and stood aside. Raising his right arm, he said: "Greeting. We know why we are here," at this place, which he had chosen partly for its location and partly for its reminding ruins. "It was short notice, and I thank you for arriving within the days I allowed you. Now let's waste no further time. If nothing else, the inhabitants need their room back by nightfall."

Corentinus rendered it into Gallic for such as had little or no Latin. The dialects of Armorica were mutually comprehensible.

Vortivir signalled for attention and Gratillonius acknowledged him. "Nevertheless, it is necessary to spell things out," said the tribune of Venetorum. "We are no gaggle of tribesmen, to go honking off at the first noise we hear." Several Gauls showed offense, and Corentinus gave a translation more tactful. Vortivir, who knew both languages, registered displeasure of his own. Gratillonius frowned at him, but needed him too much to reply with other than:

"Please state our meaning, sir. Maybe we'd better thresh this out between us, and then the bishop can render the gist of it."

"Undeniably," said Vortivir in measured tones, "we face a terrible threat. By all accounts, this irruption is the largest and worst yet visited on Gallia. However, it is still a good three hundred leagues from here."

"Less from the edge of Armorica," interrupted the old mariner Bomatin Kusuri, who spoke for the Ysans. "And moving west."

"We have our garrisons and their local reservists," Vortivir answered.

Gratillonius could not entirely hold back the bitterness: "We know what those are worth. Look around you. Vorgium was once the first city in Armorica."

"After Ys," said Bomatin in his mustache.

The veteran Drusus gestured, got the nod, and added: "Or think of the cities that fell this month. They had their garrisons and reserves, with catapults on high walls to boot."

"If we stay as we are, the barbarians will devour us piecemeal," Gratillonius said.

Vortivir: "You want to assemble those irregular guard units— 'societies,' 'confraternities,' 'sport and exercise clubs'—that you've gotten formed, and try to hold the line."

Gratillonius shook his head. "No, sir. We have to be mobile. We can't maintain an army" (there, he thought, I've said it) "like that for more than ten or fifteen days. We lack the organization. Every man will have to bring his own rations and bedroll and whatever else he'll need. If we let him forage, our force will be just a gang of bandits. You and I and others like us can do something about extra supplies, baggage animals, maybe a few wagons—surgeons—a commissariat of sorts that can *pay* for what food and stuff we requisition—such things, if we're lucky; but it'll be strictly limited.

"No use waiting in a stronghold till we starve. The barbarians could easily bypass us. The brothers will know this. They aren't stupid; they can figure it out for themselves. They won't come in the first place. Better stay home, prepared to flee with their families. I would myself.

"No, we have got to show that the force will be effective."

Vortivir: "Also, since your army's action, its very existence, will be illegal, it must do whatever it does quickly and disband, melt back into the general population, before the government sends troops against it."

Gratillonius nodded at Corentinus. This appeared a strategic moment for a summary. The bishop's was concise.

Bannon, headman of Dochaldun, lifted a fist. "That shows you what Rome is worth!" he roared in Osismiic.

Doranius, a young man from Gesocribate who represented aged Rullus, spoke in Latin: "That is what we pay our taxes for."

Gratillonius: "Wait, wait. I'll have nothing to do with rebellion. Bad enough, what's going on in Britannia."

Vortivir: "You are already in rebellion, sir. I am merely calling the fact to everyone's attention. Let us clearly understand what it is we propose to do before we go ahead with it. Otherwise we'll reap panic and disaster."

Doranius: "What is it, then? We meet somewhere—oh, Gesocribate still has a few hale men—and march against the horde? Is that really your intent, Gratillonius? We'll be annihilated."

Vindolenus, former Bacauda, who knew Latin: "We'll take plenty of them along to serve us in hell."

Bannon, who had gotten the drift: "We'd never get that far before we ran out of food and starved. Not that the lads would go much beyond Armorica. They want to defend their homes, not a lot of fat Romans." A growl of assent went among the native chieftains.

Gratillonius: "Hold on. Of course I know our limitations. I don't imagine we can mount an expedition. But remember, those Germani aren't a single army like a Roman force. They can't be; not their nature. They're a swarm of war bands, each following one of several score, maybe two or three hundred, lords. I'll bet fights break out every day between groups, and men get killed, and this brings on more fights. The Germani must be dispersed and their coordination ramshackle. Some are surely going to feel squeezed out by others more powerful, and scatter west to pick up what they can. A part of them, travelling fast, going by cities they haven't the manpower to take, could get as far as Armorica. That wouldn't be a full-scale invasion of us, no. But it'd leave desolation where it came, and might well give the rest the idea of ravaging their way in the same direction.

"My hope is that if we—taking advantage of scouts, couriers, beacons —if we find such a band or two, we'll cut them up. If we don't meet any, well, then we haven't lost much except our time, and gained experience I believe will be invaluable in future. If we do, if we encounter Germani and win, word will get back east. It may decide those kings, in their gravelly little brains, to sheer off from the far West. They'll

1046

see it would be costly; it'd give the Romans added time to mobilize against them; they could find themselves boxed in this peninsula; and Armorica is poor country compared to the South."

Doranius: "Especially after what barbarians have already done to it, in this past century."

Bomatin: "Thanks to Rome, that was supposed to protect it."

Gratillonius: "I said no seditious talk! By Hercules, the next man speaks any such word, I'll gag him with his own teeth."

Corentinus: "Peace, brothers. In God's name, don't go off on side paths."

Vortivir: "Yet you, Gratillonius, are the one who called this meeting—who begot the brotherhoods themselves."

Gratillonius: "Of necessity." It began so gradually, when I was King of Ys. I didn't really see what was happening or where it was headed. Do I now? "Later I'll put our case before Stilicho—before the Emperor." He had reached the resolve on his winter journey here: "He can behead me if he will."

Vortivir: "Oh, no. We need you far too much, my friend."

Corentinus: "It is God's ship you steer. You may not take your hand from the helm." Into the rising hubbub he again reported in Gallic.

Uproar followed. I am committed, Gratillonius thought. There's no way back. But where is it we're bound?

Corentinus got the turmoil quieted. Then Vortivir's voice carried sharp: "I spoke as I did because we must consider the aftermath before we act. I was not speaking against the action itself. It has my full endorsement."

Drusus: "And we won't all be rank amateurs, sir. I know a good many reservists will join us, once they see what we're up to."

Vortivir: "I have been looking into that myself. Most of mine will."

More cries rang out.

"Quiet!" ordered Gratillonius. "Very well, the senator has made an excellent point and we must reach a decision about it. First, though, we have to talk war."

~ 2 ~

Skies hung heavy, low above old snow and skeleton trees, a world of grays and whites. The hues men brought into it were dulled; banners hung listless in the cold.

"Will they never come?" Salomon fretted. "We could freeze to death, waiting like this."

"Most of a soldier's life goes in waiting," Gratillonius told him.

They sat their horses before such other men as rode this day, on the crest of a long hill. It dropped ahead of them into a broad trough between it and another ridge. A dirt road ran through, over one, down into the dell, up the next, and beyond. On their left was a wood, tangled second growth on abandoned farmland. From where the hill slanted downward in that direction, across the road, and onward to the right, the country opened up, except for hurdles and rail fences. In the distance that way, a village squatted under its thatch. No smoke rose; the people had fled, driving livestock along. This was the ground Gratillonius had chosen for his battle.

Scouts had brought news of the enemy; skirmishers had gone forth to draw him; now it was to wait. Not to hope, unless you were young like Salomon, nor to fear: only to wait, composing your soul because that helped conserve your strength.

Gratillonius sighed, with a rueful smile. "What is it, sir?" asked Salomon. Since first they fared off, he had set intimacy aside and striven to be military.

"Nothing. A stray thought." A remembrance that he, Gratillonius, approached the half-century mark. It seldom entered his awareness. He still had most of his teeth and the skill in his hands. Speed and wind weren't what they had been, but they were there and sufficient when he called on them, and the mail coat rested lightly. While things extremely close got blurred, his vision was otherwise keen. Even in this weather, he suffered no aches or coughs. But—Verania had contracted for a long widowhood. It might begin today.

Favonius snorted and stamped. "Easy, boy." Gratillonius reached past the dear coarseness of the mane to stroke the warm neck.

Presently he'd learn how well the stallion did in combat. They had practiced together, as had the men and horses at their back, but it was unschooled and restricted. A real cavalry mount required raising to it from colthood. Likewise did its rider. The best that might be awaited of these was that they wouldn't balk or bolt—most of them.

In front, about halfway down the hill, were the foot, the vast majority, about three thousand, as motley as their captains. The line, four deep, was rough. Men shifted position, hunkered down, trotted in place to keep warm, talked, altogether unsoldierly. The best outfitted had a cap and breastplate of boiled leather. In rare cases, pieces of iron had been sewn to especially vulnerable spots. Many had nothing but the clothes of workaday life, greasy and stenchful after these past days, with perhaps a wooden shield. However, axes and spears were bright, as would be blades when unsheathed. Bows and slings rested ready.

And those troops were better organized than they looked, not as a single army but as brotherhoods of neighbors, each man known to his comrades and his leader. They had come from their widely scattered homes to rendezvous a little east of Condate Redonum in orderly wise and with various answers to the problems of provisions—parched or smoked food, mules, noncombatant bearers, light carts, or whatever. A few units, arriving belatedly, had quickened their steps and caught up with the rest. The standards were of every size, shape, and material, but each bore an emblem that meant much, embroidered tree or fish or horse or Cross or the like, unless it was a bundle of evergreen boughs or a pair of aurochs horns on a pole.... The local reservists who had joined them should help provide stiffness.

A block of men stood separately on the far right at the bottom of the hill. They were those Gratillonius deemed his best, Drusus and whatever other of Maximus's veterans were able to campaign, the Ysan marines, the much larger number of younger fighters trained by these, and a band of Frankish laeti from Redonum who had gotten wind of the enterprise and, astoundingly, showed up to join. Well, if they could lay old grudges aside in the face of a common danger, Gratillonius could too. He didn't have to like them.

Hidden in the woods on the left were the foresters Rufinus had shaped into a force. (God, how he missed Rufinus, and Maeloch, and Amreth, and more and more gone down before him into the dark!) Also hidden, by the bulk of the hill, were the supplies, wagons, animals, traces of encampment. He hadn't left a guard there. He didn't expect the barbarians would flank him and take possession. If they did, small difference. The army had pretty well used up its rations, and could not keep the field more than a few days past this. At that, the trek home would be a hungry one.

Gratillonius and those who met with him in Vorgium had given themselves a month prior to rendezvous. He reckoned it would take any invaders longer than that to reach Armorica. They'd have a lot of miles to cross, pillaging as they went, maybe once in a while overrunning some pathetic attempt at resistance while bypassing any real strongpoints— whose garrisons wouldn't dare try taking them in the rear. Since the time available to his troops would be short, they shouldn't start off until the earliest date at which it was reasonable to look for an incursion. Besides, a month gave opportunity to accumulate additional stuff, get together a small baggage train, recruit a few physicians and such.

Of course, it also gave opportunity for Glabrio to learn what was going on and take measures. You had to keep things as quiet as possible, and nevertheless rumors were bound to reach Turonum. Inquiries went off to him. He stalled them. It helped that governor and Duke had other worries to occupy them. In Britannia the legions had cast down the Marcus they raised, killed him, and proclaimed one Gratianus Emperor. Ill-omened name, that....

Then the hour came when Gratillonius sent forth his summons, and after that it was too late for anybody to stop anything.

Horns lowed, shouts ripped, faint across distance but growing. On the crest of the opposite hill, men appeared. A kind of sigh went through the Armoricans. Here came the battle.

The die is cast, Caesar said. Gratillonius knew that for him it had been cast earlier—but when? At the departure from Redonum, an open and irreparable breach of Imperial law; at the meeting in Vorgium, when the decision was made; at the moment in Confluentes when he resolved to call that meeting; or earlier, out on the Gobaean Promontory, or far back when he reigned in Ys, or when he marched off at the behest of Maximus, or— No matter. He had these Germani to deal with, and later those Romans.

He'd hoped more than he'd feared that there would be no action after all. The men grumbled at tramping about in winter between comfortless bivouacs, but they'd have returned home alive. Bacca might thereupon have agreed, and gotten Glabrio and the Duke to agree, that this episode was best smoothed over, that it could actually prove useful toward convincing the Armoricans of their folly. There would be no way to overlook an armed engagement, not small and off at the end of the peninsula, but major and in the heart of Lugdunensis Tertia.

Well, Gratillonius thought, I've been spared the worst horror, that we went back and *then* the barbarians arrived.

His skirmishers were running down to the bottomland. They'd taken bad losses, he saw, and now fled helter-skelter; but they'd done their job.

"Shall I go?" cried Salomon. His mount sensed his impatience and whinnied. That made Favonius curvet.

"No, I told you I want you here with me where you can see what's happening," Gratillonius snapped. "You may learn something. You owe that to the men you'll lead."

"Sir." The tone, half mutinous, became a gasp and a shout: "There they are!"

The Germani poured over the crest. They weren't dashing, but went along at a steady, mile-eating wolf-lope which would in the end have overtaken their quarry. When those in front saw what awaited them across the dell, they checked for an instant, and the surge flowed back through them as it does through a breaker striking a reef. Horns winded, yells lifted, spears tossed in the air like stalks in a storm. Yet they must have known that those men who harassed them came from some larger company; and however that might be, their hearts were always battle-ready.

"If they stop and hold their hill, we're in trouble," Gratillonius told Salomon. "A charge is about the hardest thing in war even for seasoned troops. But I don't expect— Ah, no, they're moving again."

In a spindrift of roars and howls, the wave rolled on. They were mostly big, fair men with long mustaches and braided hair. Many wore coats of mail, many more at least had iron helmets. Some in the van had been on shaggy little horses—the riders' feet nearly touched the ground—but sprang off and let their mounts go or turned them over to boys who'd run alongside. Only the Goths among Germani were cavalrymen.

"Pay attention," Gratillonius instructed. "That advance isn't as pell-mell as it looks. They train from childhood. Notice the standards," as varied as the Armorican. "See how they're spaced. See how the whole is shaping into a kind of wedge as it proceeds. The usual Germanic formation. They can't coordinate themselves any better than that, though." Not that he had much personal experience with this race; but he had learned from men such as Drusus, who did.

Salomon leaned forward in the saddle as if straining toward the dark mass. "How many are they?" he wondered. "Countless. I feel the ground shake under them."

"A common bit of imagination. As for their number, m-m, I make it about two thousand, possibly a bit more. We have the advantage there. It may or may not outweigh armor and practice. Don't underestimate their leadership. That petty king—I suppose that's what he is—had to have a certain amount of shrewdness as well as boldness, and a firm hold on his followers, to get this far."

An ambitious fellow, no doubt, who struck off to scoop up the easy cream ahead of the rest. Somewhere he'd call halt, establish a base, stake out as large a territory as he thought he could hold against the Romans and the later-arriving Germani. Likeliest he did not intend to settle down there. It was for the widest and most thorough spoliation, the utter ruining of the land round about, before he moved on.

Behind his warriors would be stolen animals—horses and mules, no cumbersome wagons—laden with plunder and maybe with food. The food would be particularly welcome, supposing the Armoricans won.

"Take your shield, Salomon. Up across your face; look over the top. They're getting into arrow range."

A command rapped. With a monstrous whistle, Gratillonius's archers loosed their volley. And their next, and their next. On higher ground slings whipped and spat.

Attacking, the barbarians could but slightly reply in kind. Some missiles flew from the sides of their wedge. Gratillonius saw a couple of his men drop. Neither was killed, both were taken off, their comrades stood firm. Good; the first river had been waded. The others that must be crossed would be in furious spate. But quite a few Germani fell, and were trampled under onrushing feet.

"Hold steady," Gratillonius ordered Salomon. "Control your mount. Stay calm. Watch close, and *think* about it."

He signalled. That evoked more commands. Pikemen lowered their weapons.

The enemy struck.

Thunder and earthquake erupted. The Germanic host turned into a roil of creatures that snarled, yelped, struggled to get at the defenders, got there, smote, died, sank under those behind. Four deep, the Armorican line held firm. When one of its front rankers went down, the man at his back took his place. Swords, axes, knives, spears, clubs hewed, sliced, thrust, hammered. Shield thumped against shield, weight strained against weight. A man stared into the eyes of a stranger and strove to kill him. It was as though a mist of blood and sweat blurred the hillside.

If the enemy broke through, that was the end. Make him commit himself beyond retreat; yet watch for the time when your own line began to waver and buckle. It would. These were not lifetime fighters, they were simply men defending their hearths. Gauge the right moment—

Gratillonius turned to a lad on a pony. "Go tell them to come out of the woods," he said. The boy sketched a salute and trotted off, wide of the combat.

Gratillonius bit back terror and said calmly to Salomon, no louder than needful to carry through the hell's clatter and clamor below: "All right, son, be on your way. But do not attack till you hear the trumpet. Understand? When you hear the trumpet." He clapped the young shoulder. "God be with you."

"And you, Gradlon." There was no solemnity in Salomon's response. Eagerness flamed. He spurred his horse and cantered off to the right and downhill. Beside him rode his standard bearer, carrying on a pole the insigne Rovinda and Verania had made for him: upon blue silk, a golden A, for Aquilo and Apuleius and a new beginning.

Salomon's cloak fluttered red from his mail. On his helmet tossed a white plume. The shield in his left hand was blue, a gold Cross upon it. Like Favonius and the few other horses meant for combat, his bore chamfron and a pectoral of leather. A youthful God he might have been, Apollo's lyre singing him onward. But, oh, Christ, how easily made into a twisted, gaping, discolored corpse!

The danger had to be. He would have it so himself. His need was to learn warfare, leadership, and to gain a name that kindled fire in men. It was the need of his people.

The Armorican line had gone ragged, in places seemingly melted together with the foe, in places only a single man deep. Reserves came down from the rear, but those were untrained, the unstrong, doomed if they were in action very long, unless they panicked and thereby dissolved their whole army.

Salomon joined the veterans in the plowland on the right. Their square had sent assaults reeling back. At the feet of those soldiers dead men sprawled and the snow thawed red, smoky from blood-heat. They had resisted the temptation to pursue and held fast as ordered. The barbarians gave up on them for the time being and pressed wholly forward, except for a contingent that glowered watchful some yards distant. The newcome riders and banner now gleamed above their heads.

Out of the woods sped the foresters, old Bacaudae, their elder sons, hunters, trappers, loggers, charcoal burners, solitaries. At their front, brightly armored, trotted Cadoc. They formed a wedge of their own and pierced the Germanic one in flank and rear. Men mingled, a whirlpool of slaughter that chewed its way inward.

"Sound the charge," Gratillonius told his trumpeter. The brazen calls lashed through voices, thuds, clash, dunting of horns. Salomon

1052

and his standard bearer led the soldiers against the barbarian left. Briefly, faintly, there came to Gratillonius their shout, "Salaun, Salaun!" It was the Gallic softening of their new leader's name.

War receded from the hill, not at once but in waves, eddies, retreats, rallies, retreats, vast hollow roars, like ebb tide in the bay of Ys. Man by man the Germani grew aware of the onslaughts and went confusedly to meet them. The Armorican infantry stood, or flung themselves to the ground, behind windrows of killed and wounded. They gasped for air. That sound was lost in the noises from the hurt.

Gratillonius clucked to Favonius. To and fro he rode along the line. "Good lads," he called in their language, "brave lads, it's grandly you've done. A last great push, now, and we'll take them, we'll have them and reap them. In Christ's name, by Lúg and Epona and Cernunnos and Hercules, we go!"

And finally, when he had them marshalled and a direction chosen, he went to the van with his fellow riders. His standard bearer lifted his banner. It was Verania's work, black on gold with a red border. At first he had wanted an eagle, Rome's bird, but they decided that was impolitic and he bore a wolf, the She-Wolf who nurtured the founder of the City.

He drew sword, raised it, brought it down, and touched spurs to sides, most gently. Favonius trotted, cantered, drummed in gallop. The other horsemen came on his right and left. A few had made modern lances and taught themselves the use, but most wielded blades. It would take long for Armorica to breed cataphracts. Those were a handful, mere captains and symbols and terrifying sight; but at their backs the men of Armorica paced down to battle.

They struck.

After that everything was chaos, riot, no more plans, no more formations, man against man, a blow taken, a blow given, then somebody else there, slash, guard, stab, keep your saddle or lose it, keep your feet or die. Gratillonius stayed mounted. Favonius did not go runaway like some, but he went mad, screaming, lashing with hoofs, slashing with teeth, havoc made flesh. Gratillonius kept him well clear of friends. Foes were plentiful enough.

And then they weren't. They were slain or crippled or broken apart. Survivors dashed singly over the field in chase of their lives. A few formed into desperate little knots. The Armorican archers and slingers collected missiles off the bloodied snow and butchered them at leisure. Armorican foot and horse bayed in pursuit of the fleeing, caught them, chopped them down, glared round and went after the next nearest. The corpses were many before the hunters quit, exhausted, and turned back.

From a rough count, Gratillonius estimated later that perhaps a hundred Germani won free. Scattered as they were amidst a revengeful populace, most would surely die. Knives, wood axes, pruning hooks, sickles, flails, cudgels, flung stones were peasant weapons, and town garrisons would sally forth in search of any stragglers reported. A very few would bring to the horde the tale of what they had met in the West.

~ 3 ~

Twilight deepened fast. The world had fallen quiet. Germanic wounded had been silenced and left with the already slain for the crows. Armorican wounded had been cared for as well as might be and rested, slept, or sank into stupors from which they would not awaken. Words mumbled and flames crackled across spaces where the torn, drenched soil was freezing hard. Some brotherbands had collected firewood; others, less lucky or more weary, had merely settled down together. Now and then an abandoned dog howled on a farmstead. It sounded much like a wolf.

The dispersal was rotten military practice, but hardly any of the men were real soldiers, all were bone-tired, and nothing would attack them during the night. Guards stood posted around a shadowiness which was the gathered Armorican dead, awaiting burial in the morning before the living turned home.

Salomon, Cadoc, Drusus, and several more from their area sat around one fire. Bomatin Kusuri was missing; he lay in yonder ring of spears. Cadoc's left hand was wrapped, the little finger lost after his shield got knocked from his grasp, but it hadn't bled too badly and he remained alert in a glassy-eyed fashion. Salomon wore a dressing on his right forearm, over a minor cut—nothing worse, though he had ramped among the enemy till his mount was disabled and his standard bearer pierced, then taken to the ground and continued hewing while the banner swayed and fluttered in his grasp.

Exuberance left no room in him for fatigue. He gesticulated wildly. "I tell you, their baggage is cram full of gold and silver and gems!" he gloated. "Every man of ours can bring back a good year's pay, and we'll have a hoard left over for the public treasury."

"Think of those from whom it was robbed, in churches and storehouses and homes," Cadoc mumbled.

Salomon bit his lip, a brief gleam of teeth in the wavering ruddy light. "Oh, true, but done is done, we can't ever find the rightful owners if they're even alive, and this gives our men a share of the victory, solid in their hands."

"It'll help morale, sure," grunted Drusus. "What'll help more is the armor and weapons we collected. Next time we won't take near the casualties we did here."

Cadoc covered his face. "Christ have mercy, shall there be a next time?" Quickly, he looked up. "Understand, I'll be there. What were our loses?"

Gratillonius trod out of the dusk. "I've been going the rounds getting information about that," he said. His voice was hoarse and without timbre. "About three hundred dead or seriously hurt." He sat down, crossed his legs, held his palms toward the fire. Like the rest, he wore leather breeches that wouldn't take up too much wet or cold before he rolled into his cloak for the night. "Bad. Under normal conditions, Pyrrhic. But no worse than I expected, frankly. And we gave so much better than we got that I don't think many among us have lost heart, if any have. Instead, most ought to have learned the lesson."

"What lesson, Gradlon?" asked Salomon. He and Verania were slipping into the Armorican usage for his name; it made a kind of endearment.

"The need for better organization, training, and discipline. We only prevailed today because we had some of that, together with terrain and other circumstances favorable for the tactics I picked. At the same time, our men have now been blooded, and taken it well, and that means a great deal. It works both ways, naturally. I, our officers, we've gotten a lot to mull over, about how to handle an army of this kind. And it'll be our responsibility to build the organization and do the teaching."

"We'll never build a legion, though," Drusus said.

"No," Gratillonius sighed. "The time for that is past. We don't live in the same world anymore."

"I understand, sir. Just the same, it's too bad we can't hold—oh, not a triumph for you, I suppose, but at least a parade. Come home together, in formation, standards high, before the women and kids and everybody. That always did wonders for our spirits...in the old days."

Gratillonius smiled, a wolfish withdrawal of lips from teeth. "As a matter of fact, I mean to offer a fair-sized body of picked men exactly that chance to show themselves off. You're invited."

They stared. "What, sir?" asked Drusus.

"They'll follow me when I report to the authorities in Turonum."

~ 4 ~

No Roman could be sure why the barbarians did as they did. Perhaps they themselves did not know, perhaps they were more a natural force than a human thing, their impulses as blind as a storm.

They sacked Durocotorum and Samarobriva. That was as far west as the bulk of them got. From there they lumbered northeast, laying waste Nemetacum and Turnacum, with the hinterlands of those cities. That entire corner of Gallia was desolation.

They had stripped and burnt it bare. It could no longer support them, nor anyone else. But why did they not bear southwest, till they found the rich valley of the Liger and raged down it to the sea? Had something that way given them pause?

Rome knew only that from Turnacum the horde moved almost due south toward Aquitania.

~ 5 ~

They were three who sat behind a long table in a room of the basilica: the Duke of the Armorican Tract, the governor of Lúgdunensis Tertia, and his procurator. Gratillonius stood before them, alone. None desired witnesses to this meeting. That would have made impossible the saying of certain things.

The room was still for a while. Outside, the wind wuthered across brown fields and piped between city walls. Clouds scudded. Earth drank warmth from the sun, and snowdrops blossomed under newly budding willows.

Flaminius Murena, the Duke, cleared his throat. He was a large man, as Gallic in his blood as Gratillonius was Britannic, but from the darker tribes of the South. Like Bacca, he wore a robe. Glabrio affected a toga. Gratillonius was in his riding clothes.

"So," Murena said, "you raised your own army after all. Now you've come here with an armed force capable of overwhelming our garrison. Are you about to reach for the purple?"

"No, sir," Gratillonius replied levelly. "I am not."

Glabrio showed purple himself, on his jowls. "It isn't even a proper military unit," he fumed. "A rabble, a rabble in arms!"

Bacca's tone remained soft. "This is the most alarming prospect," he said. "Gratianus in Britannia could conceivably turn into another Constantinus. But you have raised the Bacaudae against Rome."

"I have not," Gratillonius said, "and my followers are nothing of the sort. They are decent, hardworking, ordinary folk who ask nothing except to be left in peace." Never mind what leather-clad woodsmen and shaggy tribesmen slouched about among those fighters who occupied the streets of Turonum and, without making it totally blatant, surrounded the basilica. "The Germani wouldn't give them that; and the Romans couldn't stop the Germani...by themselves." To Murena: "Sir, what we did was save this military district of yours for you."

"And what do you mean to do next?" the Duke demanded.

Gratillonius shrugged. "Go back to our everyday lives. Stand by to come to your side again whenever need be. No, I have no intention of rebelling. Let Gratianus cross over from Britannia and he'll have us to deal with."

Bacca stroked his chin. "Since you have such respect for the law and our Emperor," he purred, "it's curious how you kept his ministers waiting this long until you condescended to visit them."

Glabrio: "Outrageous. Repeated refusals to obey my summons. Unheard of."

Gratillonius: "My replies explained the reasons, over and over. First we had to go home, care for the injured, let our men pick their lives back up. Then it was time to start working the farms. It still is. I have my own, as well as everything that's had to be postponed in my tribuneship."

Glabrio: "Tribuneship! You arrive with that pack of bandits and dare call yourself an officer of the state?"

Gratillonius: "I did it for your sakes, sir."

Glabrio: *"What?"*

Murena: "Easy, Glabrio. Say on, Gratillonius."

Gratillonius: "If anything untoward should happen to me, that would be unfortunate. It could well unleash the selfsame revolt you fear. I thought that bringing a bodyguard was a sensible precaution."

Bacca: "Against hotheads?"

Gratillonius: "I'm sure the procurator is not among them."

Bacca: "What do you propose?"

Gratillonius: "I told you, I'll go quietly home and take up my work and my public duties." Slowly: "But the men who saved Armorica—all of them, everywhere, serfs, reservists, everybody, they must have amnesty. No harm shall come to a single soul of them. Otherwise I can't answer for the consequences."

Bacca: "I daresay you'd quickly learn about any...incidents."

Gratillonius: *"They* will. The brotherhoods."

Murena: "You refuse to disband them, then?"

Gratillonius: "Sir, I couldn't. Men are flocking to join. Isn't the only sensible thing to allow this, encourage it, help improve it, and so keep it at the service of Rome?"

Murena: "Under you."

Gratillonius: "I offer my counsel."

Bacca: "You mean your good offices."

Glabrio: "Offices? Impossible! Absurd! Your commission was revoked the moment I learned of your deeds."

Gratillonius: "That's in the governor's power, but please remember that my petition is on its way to the Emperor. Not for myself, but for the people of Armorica, asking for a rescript granting us the right to defend ourselves. Meanwhile, if the governor chooses to replace me as tribune, I'll cooperate with the new man to the best of my ability."

Murena: "Ha! Glabrio, don't waste anybody on that nest of vipers."

Gratillonius: "If we have to govern ourselves in Aquilo and Confluentes, we will. We'll maintain law and order. The taxes will be paid on schedule."

Glabrio: "And when your petition is denied, when the order comes from Ravenna for your arrest and execution, what then?"

Gratillonius: "I'm not sure that it will, sir. Lord Stilicho may well advise his Imperial Majesty that what we have in Armorica is the foundation of a Roman fortress."

Bacca: "If he does that, then, bluntly put, he's a fool who can't see past the end of his Vandal snout. The precedent—"

Gratillonius: "Times change, sir."

Bacca: "And Stilicho...is given to improvising."

There was another silence. The wind blustered.

At length Murena asked, "Has anyone anything else to say?" Throttled fury trembled in the words.

"Just putting our agreement in plain language that none of us can forget or misunderstand," Gratillonius answered.

"Because it can't very well be recorded, can it? We must connive with you at gross illegality to avoid what is worse." The smile on Bacca's lips was a grimace as of a man in great pain. "You're right, times do change. A strong Emperor with some sense of statecraft— But let us get on with our distasteful business."

"Then I'll go home," said Gratillonius.

~ 6 ~

"Hail, Caesar!" boomed the deep young voices.

From the towertop where he stood, Constantinus saw widely over those domains that were his. The river sheened beneath soft heaven and brilliant sun. On its opposite bank reached the roofs of the civilian city, red tile, neat thatch, and beyond them a landscape of hills and vales grown vividly green, white where fruit trees and hawthorn blossomed, the breeze from it laden with odors of earth and flower. So had the springtime been five years ago, at Deva on the far side of Britannia, that day when he turned back the mighty barbarian Niall.

"Hail, Caesar!"

His gaze dropped between the walls of the fortress. So had they stood for centuries. Here had come the Emperor Hadrianus, who built the Wall; here had died the Emperors Severus and Constantinus; here the legions had proclaimed that man's son, another Constantinus, their Augustus, he who first conquered in the sign of Christ. This countryside had prospered peaceful throughout the wars that tore the Empire, lifetime after lifetime, because Eboracum abided as the home of the Sixth Victrix. Strange to think that he, Flavius Claudius Constantinus, would end its long watch.

"Hail, Caesar!"

The cry was antiquated. Caesar had come to mean simply the Imperial associate and heir apparent. The troops were making him supreme Augustus. They would march and sail and march at his beck to enforce it—or, if he failed to lead them, kill him and name another. Below, at the front of the armored men massed and shouting, the head of Gratianus gaped on a spear.

Constantinus lifted an arm. Across the shoulders of his own mail he had thrown a purple cloak. His brows bore a laurel wreath. Swords drawn, his elder son Constans stood proud on his right, his younger son Julianus on his left.

Stillness fell, till he heard the murmur of the breeze and a lark song on high. Faces and faces and faces stared upward. Sunlight gleamed on their eagles. Elsewhere in the world, horsemen had become lords of the battlefield. Only in Britannia did something remain of that unbreakable fighting machine which had carried the power of Rome from Caledonia to Egypt. Oh, the machine had corroded, he'd need plenty of cavalry himself, but the Sixth and Second, the Britannic infantry, set down in Gallic soil, would be the dragon's teeth from which his armies grew.

He filled his lungs. When he spoke, it rolled forth over the ranks. He'd learned how to do that, as common soldier, centurion, senior centurion. Thence he went to camp prefect, but that was a short service. Already the troops were ill pleased with Gratianus, who was doing nothing, like Marcus before him. Constantinus had known how to steer that discontent....

"Hail, my legionaries! Great beyond all measure is this honor you have done me. Next after God, I thank you for it. Under Him, I will prove myself worthy of it.

"You are soldiers. I am a soldier, one among you. I too have marched and fought, endured rain and snow, hunger and weariness and the loss of dear comrades. I too have eaten bitterness as barbarians pillaged and burned along our shores, killed our men, ravished our women, dashed the brains of our little children out against walls that our fore-fathers raised. And Britannia is not alone in her wretchedness. Again and again, Goths break into the Southern lands, even into Italy. How long till Rome herself burns? And now the Germani spill across Gallia, right there over the narrow sea. And a weakling Emperor with a witling councillor lies idle.

"The time is overpast for action. Rome needs a strong man, a fighting man, an Emperor who sits less on the throne than in the saddle. If God will give us such leadership, we shall yet prevail. We will crush the heathen; but first we will crush the fools and traitors who let them in.

"This I promise you. I promise it by Christ Jesus, Our Lord and Savior. I promise it by my great namesake Constantinus, whom your forebears hailed within this very stronghold, and who went forth to restore the empire and establish the Faith. I promise it by my kinsman Magnus Maximus, who likewise went from here to redeem; he fell, but his spirit lives on, immortal. By my own soul and hope of salvation, I promise you victory!"

He paused for cheers.

~ 7 ~

The sun drew nigh to midsummer. This was a beautiful year, as if to atone for last. Croplands burgeoned, kine sleekened in lush pastures, forests teemed with game and rivers with fish. Armoricans kept watch over their coasts, but seaborne raiders were few and all were beaten off. It was as though Saxon and Scotian bided their time until a certain word should reach them. Meanwhile folk made ready for the solstice festival.

In a private room of the basilica in Turonum, Duke Murena stood before seated Governor Glabrio and Procurator Bacca. A letter was in his hand, hastily scrawled on a wooden slab. His phrases fell like stones. "That is the news."

Glabrio ran tongue over lips. His features hung tallow-white. "Nothing more?"

"Not yet," Murena said. "Weren't you listening? He was in the process of landing when this went off to me. I'll expect he'll guard every road out of Gesoriacum, take control of communications, while his Britons finish crossing and his Gallic allies gather."

"Which way will he move, then?" The question quavered.

"South, surely." Impatience edged Murena's heavy tones.

"Those Germani—"

"They're down that way, but more to the west. If I were Constantinus, I'd strike for Arelate. Of course, before venturing that far, he's got to consolidate his position in the North."

Bacca rose. "A new Constantinus, come from Britannia," he said low. "A new age?" Wonder transformed the sunken countenance.

"What shall we do?" Glabrio cried.

Murena shrugged. "Whatever seems advisable."

"Could we stay neutral?"

"That may prove inadvisable."

"Armorica did wh-when Maximus struck."

Bacca's tartness returned. "This isn't Armorica," he pointed out. "Turonum was as involved with Maximus's campaign as any place was, and afterward fully under his rule. Besides, Armorican aloofness was largely the work of Gratillonius, who had Ys for his tool kit, and he did the job on behalf of Maximus."

Color mottled Glabrio's skin. Fury elbowed fear aside. "Gratillonius! Will he declare for this usurper too?"

"I rather think not," replied Bacca. "He denied any such intention to us, and he is a man of his word. I made a mistake when I recommended him for tribune—though an inevitable mistake, mind you—but that much I'm still certain of. Also, I know, he grew disillusioned with Maximus."

"And today he's no King of Ys," Murena growled. "Nothing but a mutinous scoundrel with a lot of Bacaudae on call."

"And a much larger lot of ordinary Armoricans," Bacca said. "They won't likely want any part of this new quarrel."

"Gratillonius, Gratillonius!" puffed Glabrio. He pounded a knee. "Must he forever obsess us? Armorica's only a military district, an outlying part of my province. I have my whole province to think of."

"And Rome," added Bacca, quietly again.

Glabrio blinked up at him. "Well, of course, but—"

"If you mean that sincerely, then you'll declare for Constantinus."

Glabrio swallowed. "Would that be...prudent?"

Murena paced a turn around the room. "My guess is that we won't dare not, unless we start for Hispania tomorrow morning," he said. "I've been keeping track of events in Britannia as best I could, you know. It's hard to see what can stop him this side of the Pyrenaei Mountains. Stilicho stripped Gallia of regular troops, as well as volunteers, to meet the Goths. Those that've come back—and my intelligence of such things is good—they mostly feel disgusted. They think their absence was what invited the barbarians into their homeland. No matter that they'd returned by then, this is how they feel. And there is some justice to it. Their losses were heavy, and the Gallic military has been disorganized ever since. Meanwhile Italy is a wreck and Stilicho spars with the East. No, I think pretty soon men of Constantinus's will be here in Turonum, and soldiers everywhere in western Gallia going over to him."

Bacca pounced. "Therefore we should declare for him at once. Win the favor of our future Augustus."

"That—is an unnecessary risk?" Glabrio's indignation had faltered. He plucked at this robe. "Constantinus may fail. In that case, we must be able to show we had no choice."

"And afterward be political eunuchs," Bacca retorted scornfully. Ardor followed: "Whereas if we join the cause early—the cause of him who does look like the man with the power, the mission, to save Rome— God Himself will smile on us."

"You speak more surely of Him than is usual for you," Murena gibed.

"I speak from the heart."

"M-m—"

"Consider also this matter of Armorica."

"What of it?"

"Insubordinate. Defiant. Here we have an opportunity sent from Heaven."

Glabrio straightened his bulk. "How?" he piped.

Bacca waited, making attention come full upon him, before he said: "Without special incentive, Constantinus will pass Armorica by, won't he? It's just a thinly populated peninsula. If he doesn't expect it'll menace his rear, he'll ignore it till later. Maximus did—because Gratillonius made it safe for him."

Murena scowled. "Do you think Gratillonius would incite the Armoricans to fight for Honorius?"

"Scarcely," answered Bacca. "I don't believe he could if he wanted to, nor do I believe he does want to." He raised a forefinger. "What I do think is that we, as Constantinus's early friends, can show him the advantages of making Armorica positively his. Immediately, for manpower and revenue, both of which he'll be wanting in quantities as vast as possible. In the longer and more important run, to eliminate this armed peasantry, this cancer in the state, before it spreads further. That alone will make the magnates throughout the Empire see him for what he is, the deliverer, the guarantor. And the demonstration, at the very beginning, of his determination to rule—that will bring submission and support like nothing else."

"Can he spare the troops?" Murena asked doubtfully.

"It won't take but a handful. Not barbarian wolves, Roman soldiers: *Roman*, protecting Imperial officers in the performance of their duties. I suspect they'll only need to occupy Confluentes. Then everything falls apart for Gratillonius, and soon Armorica is ours."

Glabrio stared at a vision of glory. "To break Gratillonius," he crooned. "To destroy Gratillonius."

XXII

~ 1 ~

To Gratillonius it was like a storm he had seen afar, gigantic bruise-dark cloud masses thundering and lightening over the hills toward the ridge where he stood. Yet he was surprised when at last it broke over him—at how quietly the thing went, and how its bolt did not strike at him but into his heart.

Light spilled from a sky where only scraps of fleece drifted above thousandfold wings. Summer brooded in majesty on ripening grain and fragrance-heavy forests. There often the only sounds were bees at work in clover and the call of a cuckoo. Air lay mild over earth, as might a benediction or a woman's hand.

He was out among his mares and stallions when a boy galloped up with word from Salomon. At once Gratillonius resaddled Favonius and made racetrack speed back to Confluentes. At the south gate he saw the strangers across the Odita on his left, coming along the road from Venetorum. For an instant a surf of darkness went through him. It was as if he were again at the whelming of Ys.

"Romans," the boy had said; and across the fields and down the woodland trails, word had already scuttered to him of squadrons out of the east. Closer than that it did not speak of them, for the time was long and long since Armorica had seen anything of quite this kind.

Two men rode at the head. One wore civil garb. The other was helmeted, beneath the transverse red crest of a centurion. Behind them

1062

tramped thirty-two afoot. Sunlight gleamed fierce off mail, shields, javelin points. At their rear, three led the pack horses. At their front, one had a bearskin over his armor, and from the staff in his hand rippled an eagle banner.

Legionaries as of old, as of Caesar or Hadrianus, as of Gratillonius's youth when Britannia still bred them, not mounted lancers nor barbarian auxiliaries nor peasant levies but Romans of the legion; O God, he knew that emblem!

The dizziness passed. He grew aware of those who trailed, a hundred yards or more to the rear, Osismiic men, perhaps fifty, a sullen, wary pack, their clothes gray with grime but spears and bills slanting forward, axes and bows on shoulders. And he knew without seeing that shadowy forms had flitted along through the woods and now waited at the edge of cultivation. And city dwellers were on the walls at his back, beswarming the pomoerium, choking the gateway. He heard them mutter and mumble.

The soldiers never looked right or left or rearward. A single proud being, they advanced on Confluentes. Dust flew up to the drumbeat rhythm of their hobnails. Their centurion held his mount to the same rate, the Roman marching pace that once carried the eagles across half a world. So had Gratillonius led his vexillation to Ys, four-and-twenty years ago.

A pair of his guards kept uneasy watch at the far end of the bridge. Gratillonius rode across. Hoofs thudded on stone. "Get back there," he instructed the men. "Call the sentries down from the wall. I want that gateway and the street cleared. I want everybody orderly. Go!"

Relief washed over them. They had something to do; he had abolished formlessness. They hastened in obedience. He cantered on.

Nearing, he made out faces. Family faces, not of anybody he knew but unmistakable. Some twenty of them could only be Britannic. The insignia grew clear in his sight. They were of the Second Augusta. His legion.

Their ranks came on against him. He lifted his right arm in Roman salute. A strange figure he must be to them, he thought, a big man with gray-shot auburn hair and beard, in rough Gallic tunic and breeches that smelled of sweat, smoke, horse, but riding a superb animal and at his hip not a long Gallic sword but one like their own.

The centurion returned the gesture. Gratillonius reined his stallion in, wheeled, and drew alongside, so that he and the centurion rode almost knee to knee. A small, homely squeak of saddle leather wove itself through the footfalls at their backs. The centurion was lean and dark-haired, but with skin that would have been fair if less weather-beaten. The civilian on his farther hand was gangly and blond, well clad for travel, bearing somehow the look of a city man though obviously fit for a journey like this.

"Hail," Gratillonius said, "and welcome to Confluentes."

"Hail," the centurion replied brusquely. Both men gazed hard at the newcomer.

"I am Valerius Gratillonius. You might call me...the headman here. When I heard of your approach I hurried to meet you."

"You, Gratillonius?" exclaimed the civilian. He collected his wits. "This is unexpected, I must say."

"I'm sure you're aware the situation here is, hm, peculiar in many ways."

"Starting with that weapon of yours," the centurion said.

"These are dangerous times. Most men go armed."

"I've noticed. That's part of what we've come about."

The pain of it jagged through Gratillonius. *My brother of the legion, our legion, do we have to spar like this? Why? How have they fared all these years in Isca Silurum? Do you know if my father's house still stands and who holds the land that was his? What has it meant to you, bearing your eagle from Britannia after four hundred years? Couldn't we sit down over a cup or twenty of wine—I have a little of Apuleius's Burdigalan left, I'd gladly break it out for you, Centurion—and tell each other how it's been, how it is?*

"On behalf of Constantinus," he said coldly.

"The Augustus," replied the civilian.

"Let's try not to quarrel," said Gratillonius. "May I ask your names?"

"Valerius Einiaunus," the civilian answered, "tribune of the Emperor for affairs in this part of Armorica."

My gens, Gratillonius thought. *It doesn't mean anything, of course, hasn't for centuries, except—except when Romans were newly settling into Britannia, a man of the Valerii became the patron of our ancestors; and both their houses bore his name ever afterward, along with Belgic names they tried to make Latin; and now we have both forsaken Britannia.*

"Cynan," the centurion introduced himself, and blinked. "What's wrong?"

"Nothing." Gratillonius brushed air with his hand and stared elsewhere. "Surprise. I used to know somebody of that name. Are you by any chance a Demetan?"

"I am." *As Cynan who marched to Ys and died there had been.*

Gratillonius forced himself to meet the blue gaze. "What's your cohort, Centurion?"

"The seventh."

It would be. My own. It would be.

"Well, I've had reports of your vexillation for a while," Gratillonius said. "You've not met much friendliness, have you? It's a touchy business. I'll do my best for you, and hope we can talk frankly and reach agreement."

Cynan jerked a thumb backward. "Rustics like them have dogged us since we left Redonum," he said. "They turn back at the next village, but always there's a fresh bunch of louts, and nothing but surliness from anybody. Often jeers, pretty nasty ones, and even rocks and offal thrown at us. It's been a job, keeping my men from retaliating."

Einiaunus's look lingered on Gratillonius. "They're as many as the Emperor felt he could spare for this mission," he said. "If necessary, they should be enough to cut their way back to him."

"I wouldn't count on that," Gratillonius replied around the fist inside his throat. "The Armoricans— But we'll talk." He regained fluency. "First let's get you settled in. I'm sorry I can't offer you hospitality myself, but my wife is very near her time, and besides, it's better that all of you keep close together. That strikes out the hostel in Aquilo too, I think. It couldn't hold near this many and there's no campground nearby. I've arranged for you as best I could, and—if you don't mind— we'll improvise quarters in the basilica of Confluentes. It's unfinished, but a solid block. I've had boughs brought in for men to sleep on, and a couple of real beds in rooms of their own. As soon as you're ready, we'll talk."

"You seem more reasonable than I'd been led to expect," Einiaunus said. "That augurs well for everybody."

Abruptly Gratillonius could no longer keep up the pretense. He snapped off a laugh. "Put down your hopes," he said. "I mean to tell you the truth."

~ 2 ~

The long day of Armorican summer wore on. Men and women of Confluentes went about their work. The crowd that gathered around the basilica was mostly from outside, yeomen, tenants, tribesmen, a number of forest dwellers. They stood, or sat on the cobbles, or wandered about, hour after hour. They spoke mutedly among themselves, ate and drank what city folk brought them, sometimes tossed dice or arm wrestled or listened to someone who made music. As their toil ended, more and more Confluentians and Aquilonians joined them, and seemed to take from them the same implacable earthy patience. The westering sun cast beams that flared off weapons.

In the monastically austere room that Gratillonius used for private conferences, Einiaunus met with him, Bishop Corentinus, and youthful Salomon Vero. Cynan was there because Gratillonius insisted. At the same time Gratillonius had declined a suggestion that he and Einiaunus speak alone. Though the western window was blank with radiance, twilight crept up over them.

Einiaunus straightened. "The documents, the decree, I have brought for you to inspect," he said. "But since you asked, I'll first deliver the message orally. That won't be hard. The requirements of the Augustus are simple and just."

Blood throbbed in Salomon's countenance. "Merely that we take a hand in his usurpation," he sneered.

Einiaunus and Cynan bridled. "Hush, my son," admonished Corentinus.

Einiaunus eased a little. "Thank you, your reverence," he said. After drawing breath: "For you Armoricans, obedience is only prudent. In fact, this is such an opportunity that you should be filling your churches to thank a generous God. You'll gain pardon for past offenses and be at the forefront of glory." Into skepticism: "Everywhere Constantinus is victorious. As I left Turonum to come here, he and his main body were departing for Lemovicium. The garrison there, that far ahead of his advance, it had already expelled Honorius's government and called on him to reign."

Corentinus shook his shaggy head like an old bull. The shaven brow glimmered among shadows. "We saw Maximus come and go," he sighed, "and before him Magnentius, and—God alone knows what the outcome of this will be. But I cannot believe He looks kindly on the warfare of brother against brother."

"It is not!" Einiaunus denied. "It's to raise up the one man who can save Rome."

"And therefore he pulled the last legions out of Britannia," Gratillonius said. The words coughed forth like vomit, and as bitter. "Therefore he left his homeland, and yours, and mine, naked to the wolves."

"The legions will return, redoubled in strength," Einiaunus vowed.

"I think not. The Twentieth never did. It's the Saxons who'll return, the Picti, the Scoti, the darkness."

"Enough of your nightmares. Let me state my message."

"Hear him," Corentinus said.

Encouraged, Einiaunus smoothed his tone: "You especially should be grateful, Gratillonius. When the governor of Lúgdunensis Tertia exchanged letters with the Augustus, and later when they met in Turonum, what he urged was your arrest and execution as a rebel."

Gratillonius snorted contempt. "And he got disappointed."

Corentinus frowned and made a warning gesture.

"The Emperor was merciful," Einiaunus persisted. "He was prepared to believe you were driven to desperate measures by the failure of Honorius and Stilicho to protect Armorica—precisely the failure that Constantinus Augustus will correct. He's willing to grant you and those who follow you complete amnesty."

"And in return," Gratillonius growled, "I give over to him our treasury, and disband the brotherhoods, and order the Armoricans to go along with his conscription of them for his war."

Einiaunus showed surprise. "How can you know this?"

"Word reaches me. Constantinus has sent out a few parties like yours to other ares. Smaller and less well armed, to be sure."

"The Armoricans blocked the roads as soon as they knew, and turned them back," Salomon exulted. "One party that refused to go away is dead."

Einiaunus and Cynan sat speechless.

"You see," Gratillonius hammered, "our men don't want to leave their country unguarded, like Britannia, while they fight on alien soil for a usurper, like you."

Cynan opened his mouth and snapped it shut again.

"I hoped you could bring them to reason," Einiaunus said slowly.

"To submission, you mean," Gratillonius answered. "Well, if I wanted to I couldn't. Not anymore. They've had their fill. And I don't want to. I've had my fill."

Corentinus leaned forward. "Has it occurred to you, Einiaunus," he asked softly, "that Governor Glabrio knew this is how things are, and misled your Emperor?"

"Why on earth would he?" the tribune retorted.

"For revenge on us in Confluentes."

"—Maybe." The tone crispened. "But you are in a state of insurrection here, you and your Bacauda army. Constantinus can no more tolerate that than Honorius can. And Constantinus is stronger."

"He is not," Gratillonius said.

Einiaunus stared. Cynan sucked in a breath, narrowed his eyes, leaned forward.

"You came with your legionaries in the hope you'd frighten us into submission," Gratillonius began to explain.

"Or shame you into it," Einiaunus interrupted.

"God will judge where the most shame ought to lie," Corentinus said. "But did I hear you forcing that indignation into your voice, my son?"

Gratillonius decided to ignore the exchange. He went on: "Glabrio and Bacca suppose that we, in this community they suppose is a backwater, don't understand the true situation. They expect the appearance of a legionary vexillation will overawe us." My legion, twisted within him. It was my legion once. "Well, they're mistaken. We're quite adequately informed."

"How?" asked Cynan. Did the sound betray pain of his own?

Gratillonius spoke starkly. "Armorica is still attached to the rest of Gallia, and Gallia to the rest of the world. People still go to and fro, traders, couriers, ordinary folk on their private affairs, and others less respectable. They're apt to observe more, and with more shrewdness, than their overlords imagine. Over the years, I've made my connections among them." Mostly, Rufinus made them for me. "And then there is the Church, a network from end to end of the Empire. We have our friends in the Church, we Armoricans.

"So we know what maybe Constantinus himself doesn't really know, that he isn't an advancing conqueror, he's a reckless gambler. Only look at everything he has to take into account, prepare for, try to cope with as he meets it.

"The Germani are in Gallia, in huge and growing numbers. We've turned them southward, but that just makes matters worse for anybody whose fate depends on controlling what happens. Constantinus has got to maintain strength against them. He has got to come to some kind of terms with them. That alone will take half or more of his attention, his resources.

"Arcadius in Constantinople is a sluggard, a fool, and an invalid who's not likely to live much longer. His Empress—daughter of a Frankish general—supplied the backbone, but she's dead now and he's the puppet of his praetorian prefect, who hasn't got Stilicho's forcefulness. Stilicho hasn't dropped his old ambitions. He's negotiating with the Goths again, and my sources don't believe it's anything straightforward. My guess is that he wants them to occupy Greece while he invades the Eastern Empire farther north. What will come of that, if it happens, God alone can foretell. Constantinus certainly can't. But he'll face the consequences.

"And will Stilicho forever continue the fiction that he acts on behalf of Honorius? Rumors fly that he means to seize the throne of the West—the thrones of West and East both—in the name of his son. If he does, Constantinus will have that problem. If he does not, or if his enemies at court bring him down, Constantinus will have a different but equally dangerous problem.

"No, your self-proclaimed Emperor has far too much else on his hands to pursue this matter of Armorica's denying him. You were sent with the idea that we don't know this and you could take charge here. You've already seen how the mass of the people feel about that. Now I've told you what we, their leaders, know, and what we intend to do and not do.

"Take your soldiers back, Einiaunus. You'd have had to quite soon anyway. Your Constantinus needs every man he can scrape up."

Gratillonius's throat felt rough, his mouth dry. His heart thudded. He longed for a strong gulp of wine. But he must keep his Roman stoicism until he could be by himself.

Einiaunus had turned white. "You forget one thing," he thrust forth. "Law. Over and above any single Emperor, the state. I call on you in the name of the law, at least to lay down your arms."

Corentinus cast a glance at Gratillonius and replied for him, "Let us not waste time disputing which party is in the worst violation. Without righteousness, justice, the law has lost its soul. It's no more than a walking corpse."

Gratillonius rallied. "Never mind catchwords," he said. "The fact is that this last demand has broken us of tameness. We *will not* give up our right of self-defense. We *will not* take part in your damned civil war."

"Then you support Honorius."

"Call it what you like," Gratillonius said, suddenly weary.

Corentinus lifted a hand. "Our trust is that we support Rome, and Christendom," he said.

"You and your pagans?" Einiaunus gibed in his despair.

1068

"Let's have done," said Gratillonius. "Go home....No, go back, back to your Emperor. You've left your home to the barbarians."

Cynan stirred. "Watch your tongue, fellow," he rasped.

Gratillonius cast him half a smile. "I'm sorry," he murmured. "This isn't so easy for you, is it?"

"I have my duty, sir."

"And I have mine....I'll go, now, and talk to the people outside, and have rations brought you. Tomorrow you start back. I'll give you an escort as far as Redonum, one that ought to act as a safe conduct. Salomon."

"Sir?" said the young man.

"You collect a squadron for this and lead it. Show your standard in the van, every mile you go."

Reluctance: "That's hard duty, sir. Not the danger, I don't suppose there will be any, but—"

"You have your orders," Gratillonius declared. "It's part of learning to be a King."

~ 3 ~

That night Verania was delivered of a daughter. Her husband kept watch at her door till he heard it was well with them, then went in and kissed her.

He returned a few hours past sunrise. This year workmen had completed the addition of a solarium to their house. Glass had become costly, but the gift rejoiced her, she who was so much a child of light. Gratillonius found her there, resting in a chair with arms and reclined back and soft upholstery which he had made for her himself. He had also made the crib beside her, and carved it with birds and flowers. A maid sat in attendance, spinning yarn. Marcus was outdoors playing, as beseemed a healthy three-year-old.

Verania had a book on her lap, her beloved *Georgics* of Vergilius; she had inherited her father's library. The brightness of the small airy room found its center in her hair. She hadn't yet gotten it done up in matronly wise, it was damp from washing and flowed like a maiden's across her white gown. When Gratillonius entered she laid the book down and smiled as had the little girl who skipped forth to meet him, he riding from Ys.

He bent low till hazel eyes blurred in his vision and the sweetness of her filled his nostrils. Lips brushed across lips. Standing back, he asked, "How are you?"

"Most wonderfully well," she answered.

He studied pallor in cheeks, dark smudges beneath lids. "You would say that."

"She speaks truth, lord," ventured the maid. "This wee slip of a thing, she's tougher than most peasant women."

"Nevertheless you ought to be in bed," Gratillonius fretted.

"I'll go back soon," Verania promised. "But the weather's lovely, and I felt quite able to walk this far and sit."

Somehow she always got her way, and he had decided that that led to the best for him too. He stooped above the crib. The newborn slept, a wrinkled red miracle, incredibly tiny. "Maria," he murmured. Verania had wanted that name, should it be a girl, to honor God's Mother. He agreed, feeling inwardly that it honored every mother.

Verania's gaze dwelt on him. "You're the one to have a care about," she said. "Have you slept at all? You're emptied out, poor darling."

He shrugged. "It's a busy time."

"What's happened since yesterday evening?"

He lowered himself to a stool facing her. "I've just sent the Romans off, with Salomon for escort." The last of my legion.

Gladness had yielded to concern in her. Now something else took possession. So quiet was it that he could not tell whether it was dread or sorrow. "You have cast the die," she said slowly.

He grimaced. "It was cast for me. Again and again and again, always coming up the same. When Constantinus landed in Gallia, that was the final throw."

"You play on."

"It's become a different game."

"And Salomon also a marked man."

Though he heard nothing of reproach in her tone, he must plead, "How could I have stopped him? And we need him. I've told you before. Everybody loved Apuleius and remembers him. They'll rally around his son as they would around nobody else."

Pride suddenly pulsed: "Except you."

"I won't be here forever." He saw her stricken, jumped to his feet, laid hands on her shoulders. "Easy there, sweetheart. I intend to last for many years yet, annoying the devil out of those who'd prefer it otherwise." A smile trembled briefly on her mouth.

He straightened, turned, paced to and fro before her. "But I've got to think beyond," he said. "Come my time, Marcus will still be too young. Not that I could ever be King, or leave the kingdom to my son. Too much of Ys clings to me."

Her eyes widened. She brought hand to lips. Her whisper came appalled. "King—!"

Trying to explain, knowing how awkwardly he did it but unable to find any better words, he plowed on. "What I can do is take the immediate leadership. Forge the sword. Lay the foundation. The rest will be for Salomon after me."

"Do you really mean to break from Rome?" The voice shuddered. "You, my husband? He, my brother?"

Aghast, he could only halt and stammer, " Oh, darling, the pain in you!"

She steadied. "I hear it worse in you," she told him sadly.

"I don't necessarily mean we rebel," he said. "Except against this rebellion, this Constantinus who deserted Britannia for his own ambition. I was wrong about Maximus, long ago when I was young. I can't make the same mistake twice, can I? Afterward, when Armorica has the strength to bargain, then maybe—" He didn't know what then.

She nodded. Her calm deepened. "I see. You say 'King' as a short word for something infinitely complex and changeable."

"It may come to real kingship in the end," he confessed. "I can't foresee. Pray for a good tomorrow. God will hear you more willingly than me."

"He hears all who speak to Him." She looked away for a while, out at sunlight and sky. He stood silent. The spindle whirred at his back.

Verania returned herself to him. "No, I don't imagine you could have done anything but what you are doing," she said.

He spread his hands, closed them into fists, dropped them slack at his sides. "I thought about it. My thoughts ran around and leaped and dashed themselves against walls like a wolf in a pitfall. Should I take you, Marcus, Maria, and run? Where to? No place in the Empire. Changing our names wouldn't help. What work could a masterless man my age find, among those guilds and laws, unless as a field hand, serf, or slave? Settle in the wilderness, or with the barbarians? What sort of life would that be for you and our children?" Unconsciously, he came to military attention. "No, Verania, we'll live and die as Romans."

Her voice caressed him. "I understand. The chiefs, the people will rise regardless. That can only bring ruin on them—without you and Salomon. You can make things better rather than let them go on getting worse. Do what you must, with my blessing. And I think with God's,"— her smile flowered—"my dear old watchdog."

She reached out and took his head between her hands as he bent down to kiss her. A wave of healing went through him. And yet below it, like an undertow, passed memory of her poem. *"Would you know the dog from the wolf?—"*

He stood up. "Thank you," he said. "I will go get a little sleep."

"And then?"

"Send out my summons. Also to Nemeta and Evirion. They can come home now."

And also, he thought, seek out a certain smith, the best in Osismia, perhaps in all Armorica. Confluentes had drawn men like that. He would bid him lay other work aside and make a sword befitting a king.

~ 4 ~

Rain came, not cruelly slashing as in last year but a mildness that swelled the crops to full ripening. It made earth a shadowless cool gray haunted by its whisper on the leaves. When the sun broke through, mists curled beneath spiderwebs turned to jewelry strung with stars.

1071

Dwellers in a land always wet, the Armoricans paid these showers scant heed while they went about their labors. Earlier they had joked that seven clear days in a row were a dangerous drought; the moss on them was dying.

One afternoon a cry from Verania brought Gratillonius out of the workshop in a rearward room where he had been releasing some of the tension in him through his hands. He found her and a gaggle of chattering servants in the atrium. The front door stood open on dim silver. The air that drifted through it mingled with city odors of smoke and horse dung the richer scents from beyond, of soil and growth. Two had entered, man and woman. Water dripped off them and puddled on the floor.

Coarsely garbed as they were, in wool stiff with grease and smelling in this weather like a sheepfold, for an instant he thought them woodfolk of the most primitive sort. The man was big, shock-headed, full-bearded; he was ferociously armed, bearing knives, sword, crossbow, and a staff with a fire-hardened point on top. The woman was wrapped in a cowled cloak, but the ankles above her deerhide shoes showed her to be fine-boned.

Then Verania sped to embrace her, and the hood fell back and unkempt locks made a flame in the chamber. "Nemeta!" Gratillonius bellowed, and plunged to take her for himself.

How thin she was. He thought he could feel the arch of every rib, and her poor dead arm dangled loose though the left clung hard and dug fingers into his back. But when he stepped away he saw skin clear, eyes cat-green, and after her trek she stood firm-footed beside Evirion.

"Welcome, welcome, welcome," Gratillonius babbled, foolish with delight. "A long, hard walk, wasn't it? But here you are. How we'll feast!"

Nemeta looked from him toward Evirion, and edged nearer the young man. He let his shaft clatter to the tiles and took hold of her searching hand. "Damp days, and pretty hungry." Why did he sound so gruff? "Vindolenus wanted to hunt, but we made him push on. We lived on cheese and hardtack we'd packed, and berries, and whatever his hook or traps caught overnight."

"You must be ravenous," Verania said. "Which do you want first, a bite to eat or a bath and dry clothes?"

They ignored the question. "How fares it?" Evirion asked Gratillonius, remembered the wife, and inquired again in Latin.

"You're barely in time," Gratillonius told him. "Day after tomorrow, Salomon and I are off to Vorgium. Come along if you're able. You'll be important to us in the time ahead. Did I write to you that you still have your house and ship? Everything was confiscated, sold for the public treasury, but...Salomon was the only bidder."

Evirion blinked, smacked his thigh, whooped a laugh.

"And you, Nemeta, must stay with us," Verania said. "We've ample space."

The red head shook. "I thank you, no."

"She's with me," Evirion stated half defiantly.

Gratillonius felt less jarred than he might have expected. They'd been a year alone in the wilds, those two—the settler and his family could not have counted for much—and both were young, attractive, bound together by the same danger and thus, at last, by the same need.

"We are going to be married," Evirion said.

Verania clapped her hands. "Oh, Nemeta, wonderful! And you, Evirion. Everybody will be overjoyed for you—" Happiness faded. "No. I'm afraid—the bishop says—"

Nemeta lifted her head to look straight at her father and stepmother. "I am a Christian now," she told them. It rang like a challenge. "As soon as Corentinus will baptize me, he may."

Verania broke into tears and hugged her all over again. Gratillonius barked clumsy good wishes until he turned about, seized Evirion's hand, and choked, "Thank you. You've g-given me back my daughter."

The other's grin masked a diffidence which his voice betrayed. "'Twasn't easy, sir. I'm no missionary. It's just that, well, there we were, the Black Months holding us, talking and talking and— She wanted to learn about me, my life, everything. I the same for her, of course, but hers had been so terrible." His words dropped low. "She was afraid. Not in any cowardly way, nobody's braver than Nemeta, but deep inside, as dreadfully as she'd been hurt and, and the things that'd caused her to do. But the hurting started to go away and she began to understand she'd be *welcome*."

"And the Gods of Ys lost Their last worshipper," said Gratillonius in a rush of savage glee.

"Well, I'm no holy man, sir, but it is true that baptism washes out every sin, isn't it?" The question was not humble. Evirion stood with hand on sword haft as if to say it had better be true.

Gratillonius nodded. "The bishop tells me that pretty often. He wants me baptized. And I will be, but I don't yet feel quite right about it. Nemeta, though—" Eyes met eyes. An undertone: "The sooner the better. You know why, I suppose. Corentinus will have to know also, if the old fox doesn't already. Nobody else need ever."

His daughter's lover gripped him by the arm. They stood a minute thus.

Verania had let go, and Nemeta was saying in reply to her. "We can't. I'm sorry, we must leave at once."

"For where?" asked Verania, shocked.

"My old cabin in the woods, if it remains. That's a long way. We can't reach it till after nightfall. Could we borrow lanterns, or even a pair of horses?"

"In God's name, why?"

1073

"Not for witchcraft. I'll cleanse it of that, I swear. But—" Nemeta gathered courage. Her gaze locked with her father's. "You know," she said.

Memory stooped on him—a day in the forest outside that dwelling —and struck. The talons broke his joy apart. Little feathers and blood drops of it rained around him. "Dahut," he uttered.

"I dare not linger near tidewater," Nemeta told Verania. The listening servants shrank from her and made signs against evil. "She came this far upstream for revenge on Rufinus, who got Niall killed. I helped him in that. She'll know I'm here—already she knows—and she'll come after me too."

"She hasn't shown herself to me in these parts," Gratillonius said out of hopefulness.

"I don't know why," answered the unmerciful terror. "I can only guess. You weren't directly part of the death. Or else it is that—that— No. I don't know why."

"Or else it is that I am her father."

"But this is horrible!" Verania nearly screamed. "That you have to go in fear of that, that unclean thing—" She saw the look on Gratillonius, went to him, laid her face to his breast and wept. He consoled her as best he might.

"I've wondered if the bishop could protect her," Evirion said.

Gratillonius shook his head above his wife's tears. "No," he replied. "I don't see how. Not without exorcising Dahut. He's moved here to Confluentes, but—well, we don't know how far she can come up on land, but he has to be out of his house most of the time, and anyway, you two couldn't simply cower in there." A dreary chuckle. "He can't allow carnal relations under his roof, can he?"

"We've got to be on our way soon."

"*You* can't hide in the woods anymore. We need you! I'll explain why in a minute. And, and haven't you had enough of that? I'm surprised you stood it this long."

"I couldn't have without Nemeta."

An idea bobbed up, like flotsam from a sunken ship. "Wait. You can stay closer. I've built a house out by my horse pastures, less than three leagues from here. It's only a shieling for the watchman and whoever else may have to spend a night there, but it's warm and tight and we can bring some things along for you. You may as well keep guard; he'll be glad of a chance to come to town. Later we'll see what better we can do."

"Water," said Nemeta. Her eyes stood huge in the white face.

"A burn. It feeds a pool where the horses drink, then runs on to the Stegir, a league or so away. No trace of salt." Gratillonius ordered up a laugh. "I repeat, the place is nothing much, but surely a palace compared to where you've been. You can make of it whatever you like."

Verania disengaged from him. She gulped and dabbed at her eyes, but it lifted from her: "Why, that's right, Gradlon. Of course."

"Meanwhile," he reminded them, "we have plenty of daylight left for celebrating in."

His cheer was a lie. Before him wavered Dahut—strangely, not as he had last seen her, a swimmer in bloodied surf around the ruins, but the living girl who cried for his help while the sea swept her from him in sundering Ys.

~ 5 ~

A pair of candles and a banked hearthfire brought Nemeta and Evirion out of the night for each other, highlights on countenances, along the angles of his body and the delicate curves of hers. The air smelled of smoke and lovemaking. Rain chuckled at the eaves of the shieling.

He raised himself to an elbow and looked down at her. The straw in their pallet rustled beneath him. She reached up her good hand to stroke his newly smooth cheek. He caught the wine scent on her breath, wild and sweet.

She smiled at him and said drowsily, "There will be no more witchcraft."

"What?" he asked in gentle startlement. "I thought you—"

"Oh, I forswore it when I gave myself the name of Christian. And yet...'twould have been unwise for me to become fruitful, nay? Off in the wilderness, with naught of knowing what would befall us or when we must flee onward. I cast certain small spells at certain times between moon and moon, and they seem to have worked as I hoped. No more than that, I swear, beloved. And now not even that. We are come home. Tonight I have opened my womb for you."

~ 6 ~

That year they kept the Feast of Lúg in Armorica without their chiefs. They held what fairs and festivals a tribe could afford in this troubled time, they plucked flowers and herbs on grounds that were anciently holy, they met on hills and by streams and springs and sought with apprehension to divine the future. In churches the Mass was more than commonly prayerful.

Most leaders were at Vorgium, those who had been there earlier and the many who came freshly, hammering out the compact by which they would live or die. As the full moon rose, they went forth from the ruined city to swear to it.

One man, and a Christian priest he was, had garlanded a menhir beyond the walls: as his forbears had done at the Feast of Lúg since first the Celts rolled their chariots into Armorica, and maybe the Old

Folk before them. Nearby hulked a dolmen. They had kindled needfire between, and built it up to a tall, booming blaze. Under the moon, first with mistletoe, second with drawn blades, last with blood from themselves, by Lúg and Christ and the threefold Mother, they plighted their faith.

Standing above them on the capstone of the dolmen, hands resting across the pommel of a naked Gallic sword, Gratillonius wondered what the civilized men present—and those were not few—thought of this. Were any repelled, did most hold it a necessary concession to allies, might it catch some by their hearts? Flamelight cast iron, clan emblems, wild faces in and out of shadow. The moon limned treetops ghostly against a sky where the Dragon coiled far aloft around the Pole Star. Its light upon dew beyond the fire's dominion made a phantom also of the open land, fields gone back to grass and brambles which lapped around broken walls he could no longer descry. When the shouts rang away into silence, he heard an owl calling. Rome of the law that he would fain uphold seemed as remote as yonder stars, Rome that he had never seen nor ever would.

The gathering waited for his word.

He lifted the sword before him, kissed the blade, brought it around and sent it hissing into the sheath. "I thank you," he said in the cadenced tones of a centurion addressing his men; but tonight his language was the language of Armorica. "I thank you for the honor you have given me, and the patience you have shown,"—he would not say anything about endless wrangling, pettiness, anger, bloodshed barely averted a couple of times—"and above all for your loyalty to the people and the law. With everything that is in me, everything I am, I will strive to be worthy of your trust."

He couldn't help it, he was no orator, his words turned plain and hard. "You've chosen me to be your lord, your duke. My charge is nothing more or less than to see that you, your wives, your children, the old and the young and those not yet born, shall be free to get on with their lives untroubled by robbers, murderers, slavers, within and without. For that we'll have to fight. I was a soldier once. I'm taking up my trade again. You must be soldiers too. I'll have work out of you and your followers, sweat, long dull days where nothing happens, wounds and death when we need to spend men. You will carry out orders with no back talk. I'll be free with my punishments, and as for rewards—as for rewards—why, those will be your wives and children and the roofs above them. Is that clear?"

They shouted. Nonetheless, he knew, this night called for something that was not in him to give, he, rough old roadpounder. They wanted one who could not so much speak as sing to them, a young God, a dream become flesh.

"I am only the duke," he said. "I'm your leader for now, but just a soldier. Not your King. Here we can't name any such man. There's no foreknowing what will happen, what will be wise. All we can do for years ahead is defend our hearths. But you have a right to hail my deputy—him who'll take my place if God or the luck of battle calls me away—who after I've stepped down, if I live, will carry on— Salomon Vero."

It was no surprise. Everyone had understood beforehand. Yet blades flashed and shouts crashed until birds of day flew crying from their nests. "Salaun! Salaun! Salaun!"

The son of Apuleius swung lithely onto the dolmen and trod into firelight. Gratillonius knelt, picked up what had rested at his feet, unwrapped it. Steel shimmered like rippling water. Bronze plated the guard, silver coiled in the haft, and on the pommel smoldered a ruby, for the star of Mars. He lifted the weapon on high. "Take the sword of Armorica," he called, and laid it in Salomon's hands.

XXIII

~ 1 ~

Harvest was done, the last sheaf consecrated as the Maiden, the wether chosen as Wolf of the Fold sacrificed, a branch hung with ears of grain brought into house or barn. Much remained to do, but the wise-women said this glorious weather would hold for another month or better, and the chiefs said that meanwhile more urgent was the business of war.

Suddenly, there the host was, down out of Redonum to Portus Namnetum and its neighbor Condevincum. Badly outnumbered, threatened by uprising between the walls and dissension in their own ranks, the garrisons yielded without a fight. Gratillonius left a force sufficient to hold the gains, under Vortivir, who understood how to govern a city and make warriors respect pledges of no looting or violence. The bulk of his men started up the Liger Valley, commanded by Drusus. Gratillonius himself led a picked detachment rapidly ahead on horseback, with remounts. Most of them lacked the art of fighting in the saddle, but that didn't matter now. As formidable as they were, the troops at Juliomagus made no move when they passed, nor did anyone disturb them at night.

On the third morning they clattered by the monastery across the river—the brothers scarcely had time to call on God and holy Martinus before the armed men were again out of view—and reached Caesaro-dunum Turonum.

To watchers on the ramparts, they were a dismaying sight. The stones of the bridge rang under the hoofs of their horses. Standards rippled to their speed until they drew rein; on the foremost banner grinned a she-wolf. Spears swayed like stalks before a rising wind. Sunlight flashed darkly over helmets and mailcoats, most taken off slain Germani. Barbarically bright were many cloaks or Gallic breeches; but it was the wilderness that had yielded those furs and lowing aurochs horns.

Three hundred strong, they massed on the riverside just out of ready bowshot. One cantered from among them holding up a green bough. Stentor-voiced, he called for truce and parley. Duke Gratillonius—surely the big man of middle age, outfitted like a centurion, who dispatched him—wished no harm on the city. If he must, he would take it. This company alone could get over its weakly manned defenses. However, he would wait for his army. The Romans were free to send riders under safe conduct who could verify its strength. If caused to spend added days away from home, where it was needed both for warding against barbarians and for help with the winnowing and other vital tasks, it would be an angry pack of men. Duke Gratillonius would still forbid a sack, but he could not warrant that any of the garrison would survive. Better that the Imperials promptly negotiate terms.

—In the event, Bacca and Bricius were the delegates who came forth, accompanied by half a dozen scribes and assistants. Gratillonius received them in a large tent he had had pitched. Camp life brawled around it, rough tones and laughter, fire-crackle, footfalls, clash of iron, occasional shout or neigh or snatch of a song old when Caesar came and went through Armorica. The blue-and-white sailcloth gave shade but scant shelter.

Gratillonius, armored yet, said, "Hail!" and gestured at some saddles. "I'm afraid that's the best I can offer you to sit on," he told the guests, "and river water the best drink. We've travelled light, so as to travel fast."

Bricius, his portly form attired in a red silk robe, a golden cross hung on his breast, puffed indignantly, "I will not demean my sacred office by squatting down like a savage."

Bacca's smile was wry. "We may as well stand," he said. "I doubt this will take long. What do you want, Gratillonius?"

A gem glittered as the bishop lifted a forefinger. "Beware," he warned. "You rebel against God's anointed. Satan makes ready a place for you."

Bacca dissolved the scowl on Gratillonius by remarking, "There are some who consider God's anointed to be Honorius."

"Mother Church takes no side in earthly quarrels between her children," Bricius said hastily. "She can but sorrow, that they are proud and hard of heart. God will give victory to the righteous. You, though, Gratillonius, defy any and all authority. I say to you that unless you repent and make amends for the damage you have done, God will cast you down, and your torment shall be eternal."

"Bishop Corentinus tells me differently," the leader snapped. "If Christians can't even agree on what they believe, the Church has no business in their worldly affairs."

"I have the impression that Bishop Corentinus does not quite accept that proposition either," Bacca said, crumpling his cheeks with a second lip-shut smile.

"Well, I'll take my ghostly counsel from the man I know to be honest," Gratillonius said. "You've wasted your time coming out, your reverence. Please don't waste ours too."

"Oh, the insolence!" Bricius groaned. "Scribes, are you noting this down in full?"

"It won't be much use to anybody. Naturally, your reverence and the monks, all clergy, can stay. No one will lay a hand on you or anything of yours, and we'll maintain order and allow trade as usual, so that the city needn't suffer either." Gratillonius turned to Bacca. "But the officials of the state—Governor Glabrio, Duke Murena, and you, Procurator, together with your underlings—you shall go. Officers of the garrison likewise, unless they swear obedience to those we'll put in charge. Same for ordinary soldiers; but I expect, since they're almost entirely local lads, they'll choose to stay. That happened at Namnetum."

Bricius gobbled in dismay. Bacca regarded Gratillonius coolly and said, "We weren't sure, but the cutoff of communications suggested you'd occupied the port. What else?"

"We'll do the same at Juliomagus, but that's a minor job. I wanted to secure Turonum first."

"Expelling the Imperium, as you've done throughout Armorica. But you're a considerable way from Armorica, my friend."

"Listen." Gratillonius softened his tone. "I remind you that when we sent those people packing, it was bloodless." Well, almost. Despite his orders, some grudges got paid off. He couldn't be everywhere, but must rely on the patchwork confraternities and on tribal bands awakened to remembrance of the fact that their forefathers had been warriors. "They've mostly come to you, including such officers and troops as refused to join us. Those aren't many. Armorica has never been well defended, which is a main reason she's in revolt today. Murena's been trying to make those soldiers a kernel for a force that will retake our country. He's written to Constantinus, asking for reinforcements. Don't deny it. We've intercepted a letter. This countryside is also full of disaffected folk, and I've had agents among them for a long time." Rufinus accomplished that. "Murena has doubtless sent appeals that did get through. We cannot allow such a threat to be built up, six easy days' march from Redonum."

Bacca lifted his brows. "Ah, but can your impetuous Gauls hold a position six days' march distant from Redonum?"

Gratillonius chuckled. "You're a shrewd devil, you are. Care to join my staff? I promise you an interesting life."

"Were I young, I might consider it. But I fear I value my comfort, books, conversations, correspondence too much. My hope was, and perforce continues to be, that Constantinus will guarantee them. Are you not the least bit afraid of his vengeance?"

"He's busy in the South, Romans ahead of him, Germani on his flank. If we neutralize the lower Liger Valley and make accommodation with the Saxons at the estuary—that's in train—then he'll have no base here. He won't send troops to bog themselves down in a war that serves no strategic purpose. I credit him with better sense than that. Supposing he does win out at last over his present enemies and gets things well enough in hand in the South that he can turn his attention back to the North—that can't be for years, and meanwhile we'll have been making ready."

"You do not actually propose to hold the valley, then?"

"We might hang on to Namenetum. I'd like to, but it depends on how the next several months go and what arrangement we finally make with the Saxons at Corbilo. Otherwise, once you officials are out, we'll simply keep an eye on Juliomagus and Turonum. It'll be in everybody's interest to leave them in peace. Tell Constantinus that."

"You assume I will...be seeing the Augustus again soon."

"What choice have you? Listen, I am not going to dicker with you, or Glabrio, or Murena, or anybody, about anything except the practical details of how to start you headed south. I want it to happen fast. Understood?"

"In short, you demand capitulation. Have you thought that this might put, say, Murena on his honor to refuse?"

"I'll leave you to handle Murena's honor," Gratillonius drawled.

The procurator laughed. "You're a fairly shrewd fellow yourself, in your fashion. Damn, I wish we could have worked together. I'm actually going to miss you. Well, let's get busy."

Bricius had smoothed himself and maintained a polite silence.

~ 2 ~

Next morning the Emperor's men departed. With them travelled their families, sympathizers, most paid subordinates, and some slaves. Others refused obedience and stayed behind, expecting to become free. Gratillonius hoped that wouldn't bring undue grief on them or on innocent civilians. He could not take up their cause, or any but Armorica's.

The Romans showed nervousness at first, unsure what the Gauls who lined both sides of the highway would do. The soldiers among them surrounded a richly curtained litter which doubtless carried Governor Glabrio. The Duke of the Armorican Tract rode in armor, astride a tall horse, at their head, looking straight before him, his face locked into fury. More horses and mules followed, carrying people or possessions. Oxcarts creaked heavy-laden; here and there a gleam from below the canvases or within the tilts showed how much treasure was loaded aboard. Gratillonius had advised against that. Well, what escort the caravan had could probably discourage bandits; it was only sixty or seventy miles to Pictavum, the nearest substantial city.

The Armoricans neither molested nor mocked. They watched, swapping occasional soft words, perhaps a little awed by what they had so easily done, perhaps a little frightened at seeing empire ebb away like this.

From his saddle Gratillonius spied Bacca on an easy-paced gelding, quite self-possessed. Beside him trundled a canopied cart in which sat a plump woman, well gowned, with two half-grown children. The driver was a youth slightly older. Gratillonius realized in vague surprise that he had never thought of the procurator as having a family.

Several yards farther in the dismal parade, another woman came alone. She sat lightly on a gray palfrey. The breeze fluttered a cowled black cloak away from an enveloping dress of good brown material and a small pectoral cross. Again Gratillonius felt surprise brush him. Did Roman women ride horses, even sidesaddle? He'd seen ladies do it in Britannia when he was young, but they were provincials, and not among the wealthier ones.

Recognition shocked.

"Stay where you are," he told his guards, and trotted Favonius out onto the pavement. Eddies of alarm swerved some outcasts in their course. He heard gasps, mumbles, a squeal. Ignoring them he drew next to the woman. She had glanced about, seen him, and at once looked forward, as stiffly as Murena.

"Runa," he said in Ysan, "Runa, I awaited not this. Methought you dwelt among the religious women. They'll take no harm, I swear."

She held her vision to the south. His travelled over the sharp profile and ivory skin, down to the slender hands. They had held him close once, those hands. Veins made a faint blue tracery on them, and he had never seen any other fingers or nails as finely formed as theirs. They had wrought much beauty on parchment and papyrus, those hands.

"Have you fared so ill here that you would liefer hazard a journey into war?" he asked. "Come back with me then to Confluentes. You shall have a decent home and due respect. Aye, you'll have friendship. We who remember Ys—"

"I'm going to civilization," she interrupted in Latin, still keeping her face from him. "You've destroyed it here."

"Now, wait!" he protested in the same language. "We're behaving ourselves a sight better than Romans do when they take a city—no, their barbarian hirelings and allies. Turonum could well be an ash heap if we hadn't stopped the Germani in Lúgdunensis Tertia. It wasn't

1081

me who ordered away the last defenders of Britannia to fight against fellow Romans. Destroy civilization? All we want is a chance to save it!"

She did finally give him a steadfast glare. Words ran forth, cold as a river in winter spate. "Oh, you're quick with your excuses. You always have your noble-sounding plans for the public benefit. It frees you to ride roughshod over mere human beings, doesn't it? Not that you dismiss their cries. You don't hear them. You never hear anything you don't want to hear. Nor see, nor feel. You don't suppose you ever hurt me, because you cannot imagine how you might ever. You're more alien than the bloodiest barbarian. At least he has a heart, though it be a wolf's, where you have a stone. Go back to that simpering little wife I hear you've taken. Poor creature, I hope she likes pain; I hope she is very happy with you. Go back—"

"Thank you, I will," he said, and rode off.

She wouldn't be pleased if she learned that his sole feeling was of relief. She'd closed a wound in his conscience which had sometimes bothered him, and he need give her no further thought.

~ 3 ~

Salomon was at Confluentes, in charge while Gratillonius took the army away, when a boy on a spent horse galloped in from the west. Morning was young, shadows long across meadows where dew still sparkled and heaven startlingly blue over city roofs. The prince, as Latin speakers were already calling him, had just come up from Aquilo to his matutinal duties at the basilica: conferences, mediations, judgments. He found most of the work unspeakably tedious, but Gratillonius insisted it was part of being a ruler. Later he'd go hawking.

Hoofs stumbled over cobblestones and stopped his feet on the stairs. Men stared at the desperate lad on the lathered animal. His cry seemed to echo through an immediate silence. "Help, the Scoti are at Audiarna, they're enough to overrun us, in God's name help!"

Salomon ran down to meet the messenger and conduct him inside. Gratillonius had instituted the practice of posting two sentries at the basilica during the hours it was open. Salomon told them to keep the gathering crowd orderly and as calm as possible. He led the boy on into the private room, sat him down, sent a housekeeper off for mead, and said with a control that amazed himself: "All right, you reached us, you're safe. Catch your breath and cool off a bit first."

The slight frame shuddered. A wrist rubbed eyes that stung from sweat. "Sir, they, they—Scoti, hundreds and hundreds—at Audiarna—"

Eeriness thrilled through Salomon. He had gotten no hint of pirates anywhere closer than the north coast, off toward Fanum Martis and Saxons at that. Fishers who spied strange ships on the horizon would promptly have put in and delivered a warning. Gratillonius's network of beacons, runners, riders would carry the news to him before the crew got ashore.

1082

The servant brought the mead. A long draught brought balance. "They came up the river about moonset, when dawn was barely in the sky. By the time the watch had seen and roused us, they landed and were spilling around our walls. We counted forty leather boats. The commander ordered a sally just to get me through them and away. I heard the roaring and screaming for a long while afterward. That was...more than an hour ago? How has the battle gone? Sir, can you help us?"

Forty Scotic vessels. Salomon's reckoning went meteor-swift. If they were large, that meant some four hundred barbarians, maybe even five hundred. Gratillonius had not stripped Armorica of fighters for his expedition—by no means—but he had taken the best of them, or nearly so. There remained a great many members of the different brotherhoods, scattered in their daily occupations, plus a leavening of crack troops left behind against contingencies, that had seemed unlikely.

Now that ordinary men were openly taken into the guard and drilled, Audiarna might give a better account of itself than the Scoti expected. On the other hand, those men were, as yet, largely raw recruits; and the city had never regained the population it lost to the epidemic six years ago. The Scoti had no skill at siegecraft; they would take the place by storm or not at all. Whatever happened, tomorrow morning at latest would see it finished.

Salomon beckoned. "Come," he said, and led the messenger to the council chamber. People waited there, impatient at his delayed arrival, a couple of chiefs, various yeomen, artisans, merchants, sailors, woodsmen, three women such as Gratillonius encouraged to bring their grievances before him. They grew quite still when they saw the face of Salomon. He mounted the dais. "Put your business aside and hear this boy," he told them. "Meanwhile bring me my couriers."

—Evirion answered the summons at a dead run from his home in the pastures. He still gulped for air as Salomon drew him aside and described the situation. That rekindled him. "Michael and Heavenly host!" he exclaimed. "What would you have me do?"

"How quickly can you take your ship to Audiarna?" the prince asked.

Evirion started, recovered, moved his lips in calculation. "No pledge, of course," he said. "I can board my crew in time to catch this outgoing tide, but travel's always slow on the river. If you can provide plenty of strong backs for the towboats— You can? Good. Once we've cleared the bar, the wind is anybody's guess, but mine is for a rather light, steady sea breeze. We'll have to work well southwest, which'll also be slow, but then we should have a run almost straight downwind. Before sunset is about the best I can say, and when we get there we'll have the tide against us."

"God grant you better luck. Your cargo will be the keenest men from these garrisons."

"I never bore any more gladly." Evirion looked beyond the walls. "Grallon was right. My seamen and I chafed when he made us stay behind, but he was right. We careened *Brennilis*, you know, cleaned her bottom, made everything shipshape, and became a crew again after that long year on the beach. Did he foresee this need?"

"Hardly, or he'd have left us more strength," Salomon replied. "But—the way he puts it—he hedges his bets."

That was not in the nature of a young man afire to go fight. Salomon hoped fleetingly that in the years to come he would learn. If those years be granted him and his mentor.

—They were not a real cavalry force whom he led west, though all went mounted. Some had mastered the lance, more could strike from the saddle without risk of losing their seats or having their steeds panic, a few had trained themselves into horse archers. The choicest such were afar in the Liger Valley. Most of Salomon's were fighters afoot, who rode in order to reach the scene quickly. He made them, too, vary the pace, spare the animals. A long afternoon lay ahead in which to spend four-legged strength.

~ 4 ~

Smoke and soot drifted from burnt-out farmsteads. Thrice had the Scoti hurled themselves at the city. Thrice had men on the walls sent them back, but at a cost to their own ranks that they could ill afford. Each wave came higher than the last.

A cheer lifted thin when the oncoming armor blinked into view. The attackers abandoned their improvised scaling ladders and swarmed snarling, yelping, turbulent, to meet the newcomers.

Salomon leveled spear. The standard of blue and gold flapped furiously in the van of his charge. A warrior stood before him, half naked, sword awhirl over a face contorted by a wildcat scream. Salomon's point went in with a dull impact. The man stumbled against another. Blood spouted from his belly. Salomon hauled the lance out. Loops of gut snagged it. He shook them free while he clubbed the next enemy with the shaft. A tug on the reins, a nudge of the spurs, and his horse reared, appallingly tall, blotting out the sun. Bones splintered under descending hoofs. Salomon pressed inward. An ax chopped his spear half across. He dropped it, grabbed sword, hewed around him.

Not very far in, though. The Scoti were too many. His riders could drown in the whirlpool of them. He signalled the trumpet at his back to sound retreat. The troopers beat their way out of the crowd. They rejoined the larger number of comrades who had jumped to earth and fought as infantry—a barely organized infantry, armed and outfitted in wildly diverse fashion, but stark in its determination.

The barbarians fell away, disordered. They rallied fifty yards off, shouted and glowered and threatened, but made no move at once to counterattack. The dead who sprawled and the wounded who writhed on the red sod between held far more of them than of Armoricans.

Their living remained vastly the superior. A concerted rush would drag down Salomon's band as hounds drag down an elk. The price would be high, though, even to men who disdained death. It could well end any hope of capturing the city. Salomon saw a lean gray wight lifted on a shield in the ancient Celtic manner. He seemed less to harangue the war party than address it. There followed lengthy, often florid argument, also in the ancient Celtic manner. Excellent, Salomon thought. Every minute that passed was a minute in which to rest, a minute wherein friends drew a bit nearer.

The sun trudged down the sky. Decision came. The mass of the foe turned back to Audiarna, leaving about a hundred to deal with the Armorican reinforcements.

That was as Salomon had hoped. The Scoti evidently didn't know how many more he had on call. Unless sheer thirst for blood and glory made them indifferent. You never really knew what went on in those wild heads. What he must fight was a delaying action.

His immediate opponents howled and attacked. They had the numbers but he had the horses and, in his foot, at least the seed corn of legionary discipline. Those men closed ranks and held fast. His riders harried flanks and rear. The charge broke up, bloodily.

After that the battle became a series of skirmishes. Salomon's command beat off assault after assault. In between, it struck at the main body of the Scoti, now here, now there. The tactics were simply to reap and retreat. That alone was confusing to warriors who knew of nothing but headlong advance, except when "the dread of the Mórrigu" stampeded them altogether. It blunted their onslaughts against walls to which a heartened garrison clung tighter than before.

Though the Armoricans took losses, their count swelled. Osismii who had gotten the word arrived in groups, hour after hour, to join the blue standard. At last the core of the Confluentians appeared. They were not fresh, after their forced march; but by then, neither was anyone else on the field.

The Scoti left the walls. They collected into a single huge pack and moved toward their foe to tear his throat out. Quite likely they could do that much, a consolation to them for the survival of a city they would thereafter be in no condition to take. "We are in the hands of God," Salomon called to his troops. "Know that and keep your hearts high. Let our battle cry be—" not religious, with all the pagans here— *"Armorica and freedom."*

Should he have said "Osismia" instead? The idea of Armorica as a nation was barely in embryo....No, let him nurture it, let him feed it with his blood.

A shout lifted. Among the enemy it turned into a screech, wail, death-dirge.

Up from the sea and into the river mouth came a ship. Her sail spread like a wing on the evening wind that drove her majestic against the tide. Black with a red stripe, her hull flaunted a scrolled bowsprit whose gilt blazed in the long sunbeams. From her stern reared the head of a gigantic horse, as if Roman cavalry also rode over the waves. Yet somehow she was not of Rome. She might have been a ship of Ys risen from that drowned harbor to carry Nemesis hither.

Her deck pulsed with men armed and armored. She grounded among the boats, crushing two of them under her forefoot. A catapult near the prow throbbed. Its bolt skewered three men of Hivernia. The crew sprang out or slid down ropes, waded ashore, formed and moved forward, a walking thicket of pikes. A few stayed behind and began demolishing the rest of the boats.

That broke the Scotic will. Warriors turned into a shrieking blind torrent. It gushed past the city, down to the riverbank, to get at those craft and away before every man of it was trapped into exile. The Armoricans pursued, smiting.

Their harvest was large. It cost them. Even demoralized, a barbarian was a dangerous beast. The wrecking gang must scramble clear, and several were too slow. The squadron from the ship barely held its ground while the escapers poured around it. The sailors left aboard were hard put to fend off valiant savages who tried to climb the sides. In the end, perhaps two-thirds of the Scoti crowded into what boats were left, bent to their oars, and vanished seaward.

Well, Salomon thought, they would bring back a tale that should give pause to future pirates. And Audiarna had been saved. The story his followers told would be of hope reborn. He wiped and sheathed his sword, lifted his hands aloft, and from the saddle gave thanks to the Lord God of Hosts.

~ 5 ~

Clouds had risen on the rim of Ocean and a vast sunset filled the west, layered flame and molten gold, smoky purple slowly spreading as night moved out of the east. The moon lifted enormous above trees as black as the battlements close by. Heaven overhead preserved for a while a greenish clarity. Across it winged a flight of cormorants, homeward bound to the skerries outside Ys. Waves and the river went *hush-hush-hush*. Wind had lain down to rest in the cool.

Before he sought his own sleep behind yonder gates, Salomon had much to do. He must see to quartering and feeding his men, as well as what horses they had left; the badly wounded required special conveyance into town; the dead wanted care too. Fallen Scoti could wait where they were for a mass grave in the morning, but the Armoricans should rest together under reverent guard until their brethren bore them home.

There were words to speak, praise, encouragement, condolence, shared prayer. Finally there were words to exchange with the enemy. Those maimed lay still, knife-stuck; but a dozen or so had been captured, hale enough to seem worth binding. They sat on the trampled grass near the stream, hobbled, wrists lashed behind backs, in a dumb defiance. Equally weary, their keepers leaned on spears whose heads glimmered in the dying light. The hull of *Brennilis* made a cliff blocking off the sea.

Salomon approached with Evirion, who understood the Scotic language. "I don't know what information, if any, we can get out of them," the prince explained, "nor what use, if any, it may be. However, Gratillonius believes in gathering all the intelligence he can."

Hardly had the skipper begun to say that this was their conqueror who had come, than one among them crawled to his feet. He was aged for a warfarer, the gray hair sparse on his head, beard nearly white. Scars won long ago intertwined with gashes and clotted smears from today. His tunic hung a rag on the gaunt body. Yet gold shone on neck and arms, and his look made Salomon think of a hawk newly taken from the wild.

"Sure and is it himself you've brought?" he said in Latin. Hivernian lilt and turn of phrase made music of it. "Ill met, your honor." He smiled around the teeth left to him. "But 'twas a grand fight you gave us. No shame in defeat at hands like yours."

Astonished, Salomon blurted, "Who are you?"

The seamed visage registered offense. "It is unworthy to mock a man in his grief. The Gods mislike that."

Verania had said barbarians were more than witless animals. Someday such as these might be brought to Christ. "I'm sorry," Salomon replied. "You've worn me out, and I forgot myself."

The man laughed, a clear sound, like a boy. His friends raised their heads to behold him athwart the sky. "Ah, that's better. I am Uail maqq Carbri of tuath Caelchon in Mide, and fortunate you are, for I it was who led this journeying from Ériu."

"What?" Incredible luck, maybe. No, likely not; his people would never disgrace him by offering ransom. Just the same—"I command the Armoricans here, Salomon, son of Apuleius. Our lord, uh, our lord Gratillonius is away or he would have met you himself."

"I knew that," said Uail. "It was a reason why we came. We did not await the young wolf fighting as stoutly as the old, saving your honor."

"You knew? How, in God's name—by what sorcery?"

Uail's smile grew sly. "Ah, that would be telling."

"Tell you will!" Evirion snarled.

Uail gave him look for look and said quietly, "Your Roman tortures would only close our mouths the harder." To Salomon: "But you and I might strike a bargain, chieftain with chieftain."

His face was blurring as dusk closed in. "Go on," Salomon urged, and felt how suddenly the eventide was chilling off.

"I will answer your questions, so be it they touch not my honor or the honor of my King, until—" Uail glanced east. "Until seven stars are in the sky. That is generous of me, for the moon will make the little ones slow tonight. Then you will strike the heads off us you have bound."

"Are you mad?" Or a barbarian.

"I am not, and I know I speak on behalf of these lads with me, young though they are while I am long past my time, I who outlived my king. You will make slaves of us otherwise, will you not? You will put us to digging in your fields and turning your millstones. Because our owners fear us, they may first blind us—or geld, and we may be so unlucky as not to die of that. I bid you my answers in return for our freedom. We shall swear to it by each his Gods and his honor. Is this not fair?"

"Make the deal," Evirion whispered in Salomon's ear. "It's the best we can do. But don't let him blather on till the time's run out."

Salomon swallowed a lump of dryness. His pulse thuttered. "It is fair, Uail," he said. "I swear by Christ Jesus, my hope of salvation, and, and my honor."

"And I by the heads of my forefathers, the threefold Mórrigu, and my honor, the which is the honor of my King Niall."

"Niall!" exclaimed Salomon.

Uail's voice rang. "I was his handfast man these many years. He was my King, my father, my dearest brother. It was for the avenging of him that I called the young men to sail with me: not for plunder or fame, though that lured them, but for vengeance upon his murderers. Ochón, that we failed! Ochón for the dead! Ochón for the righting of the wrong, now when none abide who remember Niall as does this old head soon to fall! But we gave him a pretty booty of newly uprooted souls, did we not?"

"But Niall died—south of us—at the hand of another Scotian."

Hatred flickered. "Ah, you would be knowing of that, wouldn't you?" After a breath, Uail spoke half amicably. "Well, I do not believe you, Salomon, with your honest face and all, had any part of that work of infamy. Nor quite did your King Grallon, though the Gods know he had much of his own to avenge and I do not think he forbade—"

"How did you reach us like this?" Evirion interrupted. "Nobody saw you before dawn."

"Ah, we stepped masts and sailed straight across," Uail said blandly. "By day and by night the wind was fair for us, the waves gentle, and we unafraid though everywhere around us was only Lir's Ocean. I knew that our course held true, and from me the lads took courage—"

"None of your damned talking the time away!" Evirion broke in again. "Where did you make landfall?"

"Why, just where we wished, at the headlands of Ys. In among the rocks we threaded, cat-sure, never endangered, and there we took the first small part of Niall's revenge for him. Men were at work ashore, breaking what still stood. We put in and ran them down, like foxes after hares, and laughed as we slew them. You may go find their bones and the bones of their oxen above Ys. The oxen we roasted and ate; the gulls will have feasted on the men."

Salomon remembered sickly that despite the terror that misted yonder bay, bold scavengers made forays yet. The gold and gems were gone, but dressed stones remained. They called to need more than greed. Folk built houses, often where raiders had destroyed wooden ones; they decked paths against winter's mire; they raised shrines or chapel—Gesocribate required much building material to repair and heighten its shattered defenses—

"Then you rowed by moonlight to Audiarna," Evirion was saying. "What would you have done if you'd taken it?"

"Why, looted, killed, and left a waste, a memorial pyre to Niall," Uail said. "After that, ah, well, that would have been as the Gods willed, and a fickle lot They are, as every sailor and warrior well knows. We bore hopes of going on upstream, not this river but your Odita, as I understand you call it, to scize Grallon's very rath, and him returning to no more than what Niall found at Emain Macha. We might not have chosen this attempt, for I am not as rash as you may be thinking, but if not, then we would have raged up and down your coast until—"

"Hold!" Salomon cried. Twilight deepened. Moonlight tinged the grass and the dead. The cold was within himself, he knew, and shuddered with it. "Who told you Gratillonius was away?"

"She did," Uail answered. "She rose from the sea and sang to me while I walked by night mourning for my King. That was where the Ruirthech flows into its great bight, and across it the land of the Lagini to whom he gave so much sorrow, but who in the end—"

Salomon seized the ripped tunic in both fists. His knuckles knocked on the breast behind. "Who is she?" he yelled.

"The White One," Uail said, "she who swam before our prows to guide us and—" He looked over his shoulder at the night-blue east, beyond the moon, and finished triumphant: "And now, your honor, behold the seven stars."

XXIV

~ 1 ~

There was a man named Catto who was a fisher at Whalestrand, a hamlet clinging to the shore near the eastern edge of the territory that belonged to Ys. After the city foundered, the Whalestrand folk allied themselves with the nearest clan of Osismii and brought their catches to Audiarna. There Catto, embittered at the Gods of Ys, soon learned to call on Christ.

He saved what he could, and was at last able to get a small vessel of his own, which he named the *Tern* and worked with his grown sons Esun and Surach. Their affairs prospered in the meager fashion of their kind. They were ashamed when they learned the Scotic raiders had gotten past their watchfulness, though that was at night; but first they had rejoiced to see currachs full of wild men fleeing scattered back oversea.

Once sure that the danger was past, Catto hoisted sail and left home behind him again. The season grew late; fishers must toil until storms and vast nights put an end to it, if they were to have enough to last them through the winter. *Tern* was not a boat for venturing out far and staying long, but her sailors knew the shoals around Sena. There the nets often gathered richly, and few others cared to go near that haunted island.

The vessel had just passed Cape Rach when a fog bank to the south rolled on a suddenly changing wind over her—whereupon the wind died away and left her becalmed. For hours she floated blind. The gray swirled and smoked so her crew could barely see past the rail to slow, oily-looking swells that rocked her before them with hardly a whisper. The sound of water dripping off yard and stays was almost the loudest in the world. Cold and dankness seeped through to men's bones.

Then, blurred by faintness but ever stronger as time crawled along, came the rush and boom of surf. "We're in a bad way, lads," Catto told his sons. "The Race of Sena is bearing us where it will, but never did I know it to flow just like this." He peered out of his hood, forward from the steering oars whose useless tiller he gripped, into the brume. "Pray God—nay. He'll ha' no ear for the likes of us—ask holy Martinus if he'll bring us in safe, for 'tis out of our hands now."

"Can he see where we are, or walk over the water to us?" Surach wondered.

"There's them that could," Esun said, and shivered.

Darkness thickened, but they made out a reef that they passed, a lean black length around which the waves grunted and sucked.

"I'll give the Powers whatever they want for our lives," Catto said.

He thought those might be unlucky words, and fumbled after better. All at once a breeze sprang up, sharp and salt on his lips. The mist streamed away before it, lightening around the boat though low and murkful yet overhead. To starboard and port the noise of breakers deepened but also steadied. Among the vapors, dim and mighty shapes began to appear. Closer by, lesser ones lifted jagged, turbulence afoam at their feet.

"Christ ha' mercy, 'tis the bay of Ys," Catto cried. "We've drifted this far and the wind's blowing us in."

"What'll we do?" Esun called back through the roiled gray. Surach clutched an amulet of sea bone hung from his neck and mouthed half-remembered spells.

"Steer on," Catto answered grimly. "Stand by to fend off, ye twain."

Both younger men fell to. Soaked and heavy, airs slight to belly it out, the sail gave *Tern* little more than steerage way, about the same as Esun and Surach had they been at the sweeps. Thus they could wield boathooks when she was about to collide or scrape, while their father kept the helm. Here the rocks were not natural, but remnants of what human hands once wrought. Several years had brought most low and eroded the sandstone of what still reached above water. Nonetheless they could tell what tower yonder snag had been, see a piece of wall below which they used to walk, glimpse a broken pillar drunkenly leaning, stare into a sculptured face trapped in a skerry of tumbled marble blocks. Not labor alone made the breath sob in their throats.

The tide was in flood, close to full, but this evening its violence was at the cliffs and it went up the beach almost gently. Ground grated under forefoot and keel. "Heave anchor!" Catto ordered. His shout was muffled in the emptiness around.

"We'll camp ashore," he told his sons. "There'll be another high in the morning to float her." They were glad of that. Here a night aboard would have been cheerless indeed. The three waded up through the shallows carrying food, gear, and a line for making their craft doubly secure and aiding them back.

Wind strengthened. It shredded fog and drove clouds over the headlands that gloomed right and left. Westward past the ruins and the rising restlessness beyond, sunset glowered sullen red and went out. Eastward the valley filled with a night which had already engulfed the hills at its end. The wind whined and flung briny cold at the men. "'Tis swinging north," Catto said. "If it stays like that, Point Vanis 'ull break it for us tomorrow and we can row till we're clear and then catch it for a run to our fishing grounds. Thank ye, holy Martinus."

"If 'twas him," Surach muttered.

They ventured not to whatever shelter the partly demolished amphitheater afforded. Ghosts might house within. However, while some brown light lingered they sought among the grasses and bits of pavement that way, and made a find. Bones of oxen lay strewn about ashes of the fires that had cooked them. The wagons those animals drew had mostly been hacked up for burning, but fragments were left.

"Scotic work," Catto thought aloud. "I suppose Prince Salomon sent a party to fetch the slain drivers for rightful burial. Well, poor fellows, they'll nay grudge us what warmth we get from this." He and his sons filled their arms with wood and carried it back to the beach, where they had hitched their line to a rock above high water mark. Such nearness to their boat gave a little comfort. By the last of the dusk, Catto used flint, steel, and tinder on what Esun and Surach split for him. Flames licked up to flap yellow on the wind.

The men spread their bedrolls and hunkered by the fire with hardtack, cheese, dried fish, water jug. Its light brought leathery faces flickery into sight. Night prowled, whistled, mumbled close around. "Aye, an eldritch haven," Catto said, "but we'll gi' thanks for it natheless, and tomorrow 'ull see us where we ought to've been."

Laughter sang in the dark. The food dropped from their hands. They leaped to their feet and stared outward. The high, sweet music jeered:

"Fishers who would fain put forth
As the wind is shifting,
Spindrift-bitter, to the north,
Where will you be drifting?
Low beyond this loom of land,

Rock and reef await you.
Wives at home shall understand
That the congers ate you."

Catto lifted his arms against the blowing blackness. "Holy Martinus, help us, help us," he groaned.

The song danced nearer.

"Thunder-heavy in His wrath,
God Whom you've forsaken,
Lord Taranis walks your path,
And the seas awaken.
Where His graybeard combers break
While the rigging ices,
As of old, comes Lir to take
Ancient sacrifices."

They saw her at the edge of sight, the White One risen out of Ys, and whirled and fled inland. The song pursued. It seemed to ring from Cape Rach to Point Vanis and back again, up the valley between the hills under the wrack, it filled the world and their skulls, it echoed within their ribs.

"Belisama leads Her Wild
Hunt of unforgiving
Women once abed with child,
Torn away from living.
Vengeance winds you in your flight.
Hounds of Hers will follow,
Howls resounding through the night,
Hollow, hollow, hollow."

—They ran until they dropped beneath the weight of dread and their senses whirled from them. So did they lie when day broke. Unbelieving, they blinked at each other, crept painfully to their feet, limped off in search of humanity.

Later they returned with some reckless young companions they had found, they themselves unsure what had happened, save that it had been horror beyond anything the priests had to say of hell. After all, *Tern* was their livelihood. But she was gone. Nobody who fished those waters ever saw her adrift.

They plodded back to Whalestrands. By that time Catto had a fever. He raved on his bed in their hut till the tide of thick fluid in his lungs drowned him. Esun got work as a deckhand but Surach must become a dock walloper in Audiarna at starvation wages.

Word flew around. After they heard, no more fishers put to sea that season, and many talked of staying ashore next year. It would mean suffering for a land that depended heavily on their catches, and desperation for them, but they feared Dahut more.

~ 2 ~

The storks had long since departed, and now skies were full of other wings trekking south. Through nights when hoarfrost settled on stones and on grass going sallow, cries rang, plover, dunlin, lapwing, swan, wild goose and duck. Birch leaves turned pale gold and drifted to earth. Stags in forests made ready their antlers. Huntsmen's horns bayed through wet reaches where green had begun to fade. Rowan berries flamed. Apples fell with a sound as of someone knocking on the door of the year.

Gratillonius walked with Evirion and Nemeta from their hut in his pastures. It was a cool day, windless, diamond-clear. Down its quietness drifted the call of the geese passing over in their long spearheads. Low above woodlands outside the rail fence, the sun washed with light an eagle at hover. Horses grazed, lifted their heads as the three came near, sometimes broke into a gallop across the broad spaces he had given them, manes and tails flying.

He had found it impossible to say what he must in the smoke and gloom of the shieling. His words were for Evirion, but as close as Nemeta was to them both, she went along. They followed a footpath by the rails. It had width only for him, so Evirion paced on his left and Nemeta beyond, the forage dampening the men's breeks and the woman's bare feet and ankles.

"A late time for sailing, I know," Gratillonius said. "But we're barely past equinox, and can reasonably hope the autumn will be as mild as spring and summer were. You're a crack mariner and command a well-found ship. Salomon's chastened the Scoti for a while; news of what he dealt out will have reached other tribes of theirs. The Saxons have gone home or into winter quarters from which they won't range far if at all. Besides past experience, I've some confirmation of that from the king of those at Corbilo. He's become fairly friendly to us, but keeps in touch with his kinfolk elsewhere. I wouldn't ask this of you if I didn't believe you'll be safe." He hesitated. "Or as safe as most men these days, which I admit isn't saying much."

Evirion's blunt features showed still less doubt. "To Britannia, eh?" he replied. "What for?"

"I've an idea we can reach agreement with several leaders in the West. Think what it's meant to them, Constantinus pulling out the last legions. Oh, he left skeleton garrisons behind, but from what I've learned, they are exactly as useful as any skeleton. Some Britons must be in despair; some may still cling to belief in his promises; but surely some are furious. They'll feel as betrayed as we in Armorica, and mightily interested in what we're doing about it. God knows we need every ally we can get."

"What help can they give us?"

"That, we'll have to explore. I can imagine things like joint patrols at sea and even joint expeditions to clean out the ugliest barbarian infestations there and here. It will take time to organize, prepare—years, most likely. But the sooner we start, the better. We have the advantage for a while that Rome's whole attention is off us. That may not last."

"Well, I have some acquaintance with people in those parts. I can try sounding them out."

"That's the purpose of this trip. I'll give you letters to several leading men who look like good prospects, and you'll have Riwal and a couple of other reliable natives along to advise and assist."

"How long will this take?" asked Nemeta. Her voice was small.

"Not too long, I trust," Gratillonius reassured her. "This isn't really a diplomatic mission or anything like that. Unless he gets weatherbound, you should have him back well before solstice."

"I can trade," said Evirion eagerly. "That'll give me a cover, and be worthwhile in its own right. Wares have been piling up in our dealers' storehouses, what with trouble and fear emptying the sea lanes. I'll bring you home a healthy profit, darling. We'll build us a proper house."

"Right," said Gratillonius. "How soon can you go?"

"A very few days. My men are as impatient as I for a whiff of salt water and a sight of new shores."

"Dahut."

The name from Nemeta stopped them in their tracks. They turned to look at her. She stared past them, beyond meadow and horses and forest, to that which distance hid in the west. Fiery hair and jade eyes were like autumn colors above early fallen snow. The bones in her face stood forth well-nigh as sharp as those in her dead arm.

"You'll be rounding Sena." Her whisper trembled in Ysan. "She will know."

Evirion took her left hand in both his. "Now, beloved, be of brave heart," he urged loudly in the same tongue. "We'll stand far out to sea."

"She can swim wheresoever she lists that the tides flow. Wherever she scents ruin to be wreaked."

He scowled. "Aye, she has strength, strength enough for dragging men under to their deaths. But 'tis not such as would avail against a ship, nor drive her through the waves swifter than a dolphin."

"The fishers—"

"They've let themselves be terrorized. What really happened that night at Ys? Had yon men stood fast, she'd have slunk back to her eels and sunken wrecks. My crew helped choke her on her malice at Audiarna. We'd welcome a fight against her own self!"

Remembrance came to them both of who stood at their side. The look on Gratillonius struck them mute.

The older man swayed a little on his feet. Fists clamped together as if he would strangle the air. Words grated out of him: "I've not forgotten her. Evirion must be right about her powers. Else would she have slain us all when we fought her Niall at Ys, her lair. She does have other might than of the body—"

Evirion drew Nemeta close to him.

"But that too must lie within bounds," Gratillonius went on. "A certain command of the weather, meseems. Yet if you do indeed steer very wide of Sena, no storm can force you onto the skerries. Can it? Are you of a mind yet to fare, Evirion?"

"I am," said the captain.

"Good. We will talk...more...later. I leave you now. You twain will have your...farewells to say."

Gratillonius stumbled off alone, back toward the place where Favonius was tethered. His daughter and her man moved to follow, then stayed where they were, holding each other, watching him leave them. A new flock of wild geese cried overhead on its way south.

~ 3 ~

Salomon dispatched a note to Verania requesting she pay him a discreet visit at his and their mother's home in Aquilo. She left the children in care of their nurse and walked. That day was cold and gusty after a night of rainshowers. Clouds smoked in haste above tossing, soughing treetops. Wind ruffled the steely-gleaming Odita. Crows in the fields flattened their wings before it like hens before a cock. The first fallen leaves scrittled across the land.

Rovinda was attending Mass, which she did whenever possible. Salomon received his sister at the door, helped her remove her cloak, led her to the room where their father used to read his books and write his letters. The walls bore the same gentle, slightly faded pastoral frescoes, but instead of codices and papyrus the table held the sword of mastery in its sheath, while behind it a staff on a pedestal displayed the battle banner.

"Have a seat," Salomon invited. "What refreshment would you like?"

"Nothing, thank you," she replied, and remained standing. He did likewise.

Silence fell, except for the wind's bluster outside, until he said awkwardly, "I want to ask you—about Gradlon."

"I thought so." Her look upon him steadied.

"Why is he doing this?" broke from him.

"You should know better than I," she answered as softly as before. "The newest revolt—"

"Certainly I know!" he snapped. For a moment his weather-darkened countenance flushed red. The thought rang between them: The western Caletes taking fire from us and declaring themselves also free of Rome. Northern Gallia broken out of the Empire between the mouths of the Liger and the Sequana. Salomon checked his temper and said with care, "I realize he must go there and show himself, his best troops, tell them what we've done here and that they can do likewise but only if they'll work with us. Of course. This soon, though?"

"It is a short time. Hardly more than, m-m, ten days since he returned from Turonum."

"And the news didn't reach us till after that."

Verania sighed. "I confess it's hard to bear. But I must, because he must."

"What do you mean?" Salomon demanded. "I asked you, This soon? Why? It's insane. He's like a whirlwind. Evirion left for Britannia only the other day. Can't Gradlon be satisfied with that for a while? The men he's taking—I tell you, they're not happy at being hauled off again at once from their firesides, for another two or three months on the road."

Verania's hazel gaze widened. "Didn't he explain the reason to you, of all people? Those are Celts too. Even in an important city like Rotomagus, they're still Celts. If he doesn't get them bound together—by persuading, wheedling, bargaining, bullying, till he has their sacred oaths—they'll soon be at each other's throats. Some will pledge Pseudo-Constantinus allegiance if he'll help them against their neighbors. There goes any hope of holding him off after he's through in the South."

Salomon whistled. "Pseudo-Constantinus! Sister, you do have our old man's gift for phrases." It diverted indignation and he continued levelly. "Of course Gradlon's explained to me. We talked about it already before he went to the Liger Valley, because he thought other secessions were likely. But he never said his part in it would be this urgent. Surely it can wait till, oh, Beltane. The tribes, the clans won't stir during the Black Months. Why must he?"

"Why are you so concerned?" she responded. "What harm if he does it early rather than late?"

His glance went around, to the window, the wall, the sword, back to her, like a newly caged bird. "It's...everything." His tongue moved heavily. "I fear for him. Something's gone terribly wrong. He arrived home so cheerful. He'd done so much, and talked about our getting a well-earned rest, and— Not that I ever imagined him sitting idle. But he has a pile of matters needing attention here, and—and his own family!"

She smiled the least bit. "Well, you know him. Old duty horse."

"This isn't duty," Salomon maintained. "He's driven. Almost since he came back, he's been caught in a pit of gloom. He tries to hide it, but, well, when he suddenly grows short-spoken, or outright unmannerly—when he goes off on those long gallops—and this, this demonic haste—" Fear shivered. "Could it be a demon?"

"It is," Verania said low.

"What?" he croaked.

"Oh, not as you suppose. Not possessing him. But it's why he must go. He hasn't told me; I don't believe he can tell anyone. But I know. In work is his hope of healing, work from the moment he wakes till the moment he drops, so he can sleep through some of the night."

Salomon braced himself. "Tell me."

She must summon will of her own. "Dahut. This evildoing of hers. He shoved it aside at first, wouldn't think of it, or anyhow didn't speak of it, but in the end—he'd just broached his plan to Evirion—she, Dahut, broke through the wall he'd raised. Now he has to escape her."

"I see...." Salomon breathed.

Verania struggled against tears. "His daughter. The child of his Dahilis, whom he never stopped loving." She seized both her brother's hands and hurried on: "No, no, he's happy with me—he has been—and I'm the mother of two children he adores, but there will never be another Dahilis. It's all right. I am content. I simply pray that someday he'll be free of Dahut."

Salomon stared before him. "He thought after Niall died and...she avenged him...she'd only brood over the sunken ruins of Ys. Instead—"

Vigor came back to Verania's tone. "Instead, her malignancy hounds us. It's too much to ask that he face at once. Let him go off and be among men, ride hard, meet challenges, risk his life if need be. A good farewell is the single gift we can give him, you and I."

"And a glad meeting when he returns."

"Pray God he does, heartened."

He stood for a space quiet, until he shook himself and said with half a smile, "I think, before he leaves, I can jolly his men somewhat. They are the best we have, our chosen few. I'll remind them of that— Celts do love flattery—and speak of new places they'll see, adventures, celebrations, willing girls—it'll help Gradlon's spirits, having theirs high."

"God bless you," Verania murmured.

He turned grave. "And you, sister mine. Thank you for this."

—When he reached the parade ground north of Confluentes, near his family's old manor house, a squadron of infantry was at drill. To and fro they marched, wheeled, countermarched. Their boots struck earth together, dust flew and thud racketed up into the wind. Each man was outfitted however he or his kin could provide, a wildness of mail, leather, kilts dyed in gaudy clan hues; but a ripple as through a ripening wheatfield went in the pikes that flashed aloft, and the officer who watched from horseback had no reason to shout commands. It was they who set their cadence, singing together, one of the many new songs that went about the country; and while the tune had been old among the legions, the language today was not Latin.

"When the Scoti come a-raiding, or the Saxons or the Franks,
It's the horn of Gradlon calls us—Take your weapons! Form your ranks!

"Pound the road to Audiarna, sail Odita to the sea,
Be a tribe what you may name it, all Armorican are we.

"For we're done with belly-crawling to beseech the lords of state
That they please defend the people from the reaver at the gate.

"Where were all the mercenaries when the Vandals ran in rout?
In the barracks gulping senseless till they spewed the wine-juice out.

"Where were all the tax collectors when we saved them from the sack?
In the privy shitting rivers, thinking how much gold to pack.

"Let the legions make their Caesars. We must guard the fields of home.
We will follow good King Gradlon and we'll stand no more with Rome."

~ 4 ~

Sunset smoldered among the ragged dark clouds. For a while it reddened wave-crests, to bridge the waste between worldedge and *Brennilis*, but Ocean kept shattering the work. Then it died out and the west deepened from ice-green toward purple and thence black. Eastward the waves took a sheen more pale, also broken and fugitive, off a hunchbacked moon three days short of the full. Clouds yonder made it seem to fly, yet it stayed over the starboard rail, as if the ship too were rushing at windspeed across endlessness.

The clouds were merely a wrack, fleet moon-tinged scraps. The brighter stars flickered visible, Eagle, Swan, Lyre, Dragon, a glimpse of the Bears sufficient to mark Polaris, by which Evirion steered. He fared thus through night, twenty miles or more from any land, not in recklessness but because the fortunes of wind and current brought him abeam of Ys, as nearly as he could gauge, at this chosen time.

Every man agreed that the only wisdom was to pass those evil headlands as soon as might be.

Sharply heeled, *Brennilis* creaked; her forefoot hissed and smacked, cleaving water; lines aloft thrummed to the skirl of air; sometimes the leach of the straining spritsail snapped or its spar shifted about and boomed against the mast. The seas had a thousand voices of their own, deep drumroll, torrent, splash, whirr, growl, while their surges pitched the hull that rode them. Spray off their manes fell bitter on lips. The cold of them was a live thing that coiled and tugged and bit.

The wind was from the moon, though, not the sunset as men had dreaded. It thrust the ship off the reach of rocks beyond Sena, out onto the deeps where there were simply billows to do them harm. Powerful, it was not too much to beat across, holding a course that ought to make landfall somewhere on the west coast of Britannia. That was another reason Evirion had decided to sail on in the dark.

Standing lookout at the prow, Riwal the Durotrigian gazed homeward. He saw little more than the vague gray of the artemon, until across murk his vision met stars; but yonder lay the country of his birth, the fields and folk of his tribe, an upwelling of memories...the downs shouldering into a vast summer sky, chalk cliffs tumbling to water utterly blue, himself small and gorging on blackberries (the prickliness was part of the joy) with honeybees abuzz around him....No. Home was no longer there. In five years since he made his way to Armorica, and saved earnings till he could send after wife and children, they had struck new roots; and it was in a better place, in the lee of Gradlon, safer than most from the storms that savaged the world. Yet maybe his sons would remember together with him, maybe they would keep the dear music of the old speech and something of the old ways. For more and more Britons came over in search of refuge.

Nevertheless—

He felt mass betread the deck behind him. Turning his head, he recognized Evirion's tall form. "How goes it?" asked the captain.

"All's well, sir," Riwal said. "I thought you were asleep."

"I'll sleep in the morning, when I know we're clear of the Gobaean. We can't hope to pass West Island by then, but any dangers will be natural ones."

Riwal wiped his drenched mustache, cleared his throat, and ventured, "I've been wondering, sir. This isn't too late in the year, but if we aren't so lucky with the weather when our business is done and have to winter in Britannia—"

"We won't," Evirion vowed. "I'm going home—" He peered starboard. "Hoy, what's that?" And in a roar: "Sheer off, you! Helmsman hard a-lee!"

Riwal barely saw what came out of the night. A large fishing boat, sail filled with the wind that drove her straight at *Brennilis*, a last great

1099

leap, he had not quite understood when stem smote strakes and the doomsday crash hurled him backward.

He struck the port bulwark and grabbed after any handhold. The deck canted. It spilled men elsewhere into the sea. Sail flapped thunderous, masthead wavered crazily across the stars and then swept downward like a spear dropped by a warrior who has taken an arrow in the belly. Now the deck slipped about and canted forward. Riwal lost his grip and tumbled back into the bows. There the starboard bulwark stood splintered above timbers torn loose from their fastenings. Through it he saw the boat. Her prow was deep in the hull of *Brennilis*. Impact had sheared loose her own mast, it lay in a tangle of rigging and sailcloth alongside, waves made it a ram to batter the ship. One billow cataracted across him. He heard a huge noise of water pouring in. Ballasted and laden, the ship was going down by the head.

From the helm of the boat flitted a whiteness that might have been foam. Riwal lost sight of it. Then suddenly it was over the rail and aboard with him.

Clouds broke from the moon. By its wanness he spied a couple of men amidships. They clung to the lashing of the lifeboat, which they were trying to cut. The nearer man was big—Evirion? The white thing passed up the slanted, sluggishly rolling deck. Wind blew the long hair from the shape of a naked woman.

Riwal screamed. The brawl of sea, the groan and sundering of wood smothered it. He cowered into the angle where he clung, and the mast cut off sight of what happened yonder. Maybe, whirled in his nightmare, maybe she wouldn't notice him. Maybe she would swim off, sated; and at least a part of the ship might float a derelict till it washed ashore, Epona, Christ, give this, make it be!

A wave overran him. He got it in his open mouth and strangled. Somehow he coughed the water out and caught a breath before the next whelming.

The next, the next, the next, each deeper and wrenching harder than the last.

A weight ground its way along the splintered planks. He looked and saw the lifeboat, free of its moorings, somehow turned right side up. It slid forward at every pitch, cut-water aimed at him where he lay tumbled and trapped in the bows.

Blindly, he clawed himself up and went over the side. The sea swallowed him. He could swim, he flailed through the swirls of the dark and broke out into moonlight. In a black-and-white blur he saw waves heave, spindrift fly, *Brennilis* with stern aloft, a last bit of the craft that had gored her, and the boat, the boat. As the ship rolled, the boat slipped through a gap in the bulwark and floated free.

It floated toward him where he threshed.

She leaned forth and laid hold of his tunic. By the gibbous moon he saw her smile. She hauled him aboard, he fell into the bilge, and for a spell nothing was but a blackness that wailed.

When he crept back to himself he found mast stepped and sail full of wind. The boat bounded easily over long rollers where foam sparkled. They rushed and lulled. The moon shone ahead. Wind had swung clear around and now bore for Ys.

The woman sat at the helm. Moonlight quivered on her wet whiteness. She saw him see her and smiled. She was wholly beautiful, but he still burned from the cold of her touch.

He huddled where he was, afraid to stir or cry out.

Clouds blew away. The Milky Way shone across the great wheel of the stars. The moon climbed until it was crooked and tiny on high, then sank toward Ocean aft. Winter's Orion strode gigantic up from the east. Wind boomed softly. Riwal began to feel no more chill, no more fear. Finally, corpse-numb, he felt no more time.

Point Vanis and Cape Rach followed Orion into heaven. The boat glided between their bulks and wove among the remains of Ys. Faint as a gnat's football, Riwal heard its keel plow into the shore. The wind fell, the sail dropped lifeless. The moon was sunken but waters were metallic with the earliest dawnlight above eastern hills.

She left the tiller, stood up, beckoned to him. His cramped legs would barely move. He lurched to the rail, fell over, sprattled for a moment before he could reel to his feet.

She was gone. He blinked in dim puzzlement. Where was she? What did she want of him? He was hers. The sea had washed everything but obedience out of him.

She appeared from behind what had been a gateway and flowed over sand, cobbles, weed, shells, pieces of wreckage, to him. There was now enough light that he could see the gold of her hair; but no color was in lips or nipples or nails, and the blue of the eyes had no depth, it was as blank as Ocean under a dead calm. Though the air lay murmurous, pierced by the mew of an early wakened gull, silence and cold enclosed her.

In her right hand she held something which she reached toward him. He stared. It was a small carving in wood, long since waterlogged and gone to the bottom. Paint was worn off and worms had riddled it, but the thought trickled through him that this was once a prancing horse, playfully shaped, with jointed legs, toy for a child.

She thrust it at him. His fingers closed on its soddenness. Hers brushed them, and the chill jagged to his heart. It shocked him back into terror. She gestured imperiously. He turned and shambled off inland as she commanded. Never did he dare look back to see if those empty eyes gazed after him. But as he, having passed the amphitheater, climbed to what was left of the eastbound road on the heights, his glance fell over the bay, and all he saw move there in the strengthening light were waves and a flight of cormorants.

~ 5 ~

Equinox almost a month behind them, nights drew in fast. The sun was down when Tera reached the shieling at the meadows. Autumn colors in the woods had gone dun, though as yet crowns were limned sharp against a sky where a yellowish glow lingered. A breeze sighed bleak over the grass. Fallen leaves rustled.

Candleglow spilled around Nemeta's slight figure and burned in her tresses as she opened the door to the newcomer's knock. "Welcome, oh, welcome." Her tones shook. "Come in. My house is yours."

"We'll have scant need of it, I think," said the stocky woman. Nonetheless she entered. Smoke off the hearthfire stung her at first; she sneezed and wiped a hand below her pug nose while she leaned her staff against the wall. Otherwise she carried an emptied water bag and a sack with lumpy things in it, tied to her back. Her weather-whitened mane was the brightest sight among the shadows. The years had begun to dull it.

"I have wine, food," Nemeta offered.

Tera shook her head. "We'll eat otherwise this night. Have you brought the foal I wanted?" After Nemeta had sent a runner to her, carrying simply the spoken appeal, "Please let me hear from you," messages more confidential had gone between them on the tongue of her oldest son.

"Aye. He's tethered behind the house. The horses are in winter quarters nearer Confluentes— But how have you fared? We've not met for long and long."

"Since Maeloch's death."

"I should have sought you out," Nemeta said contritely. "You earned my abiding thanks once."

"Well, you've had full days of your own, dear, and—" The round face tightened briefly into a frown. "Some signs made me believe 'twere best to leave you to yourself." A sad smile. "But that's all past. We who remember Ys should stand together."

"How *have* you fared?"

"Well enough. Drusus is a kindly man. My children are not ill content either, save that 'tis plain the son of Maeloch will never make a farmer." Tera looked hard at Nemeta. The fire wavered and sputtered. "But you, lass, you're more gaunt than ever, and you tremble as you stand there. What is it?"

"I want—I need—" Nemeta twisted her head right and left. "You know why I asked you here!"

"Somewhat," Tera answered slowly. "News does reach us, though drop by drop and often muddied. A madman came back to Confluentes

from the sea. You'd have me help you divine what it means because...
he'd sailed with your man."

Nemeta's neck stiffened. She stared before her into the darknesses
that wove over the cob wall and said fast: "Riwal, he is, or was, a
Briton who moved hither several years ago. He was with a mission my
Evirion led to his country a score of days past—less two—oh, I've
counted, I've counted every one. A shepherd found him rambling
aimlessly in the high pastures some leagues east of Ys. He was half
dead and could only mumble and moan. Folk nourished a little strength
into him and brought him to Confluentes, where he was known—family,
friends— When I heard, I dared go there myself, by day. He was under
care at the church, but no physician could mend his wits, nor could
Bishop Corentinus drive any demon out of him. All he can tell is that
'she' gave him something he must bring back. When pressed to say
more, he falls into a weeping, whimpering fit. Otherwise he's quiet,
aye, sits unstirring for hours on end and gapes at the air. He knows
the names of wife and children and likes it when they are nigh; he
has a few words of his own and obeys simple commands as a dog
might; Corentinus thinks he may in time be able to do rough labor
for his keep.

"And he sailed with my man!" she yelled, flung herself on Tera's
broad bosom, clung tight with her good arm, and let the sobs shake her.

"Poor lamb. Easy, easy. Come, let's sit." Tera guided her to the
bed, where they could be close.

In sawtoothed fragments, the story came out. Tera had only heard
rumors of Dahut's doings after the battle at Ys where Maeloch drowned.
"Aye," she said starkly, "She killed him and more, she lamed you and
keeps you afraid, now you fear what she may have done to your Evirion,
aye, aye. The dead bitch that will not lie down, can your Christian
priests do naught against her?"

"I asked the bishop." Nemeta had regained will. She sat straight in
the circle of the other woman's arm and spoke in a hard, low voice.
"I begged of him. He told me these things are forbidden Christian
souls to ransack. His God has sent him no vision. He cannot, may not
conjure, and from the power that is in his prayers she need merely
swim away. He bade me abide, with my trust in Christ. Then I bethought
me of you."

"But you and, and Evirion are Christian yourselves, nay?"

Nemeta nodded. "We are, and for what I seek to do, I must answer
heavily to God. Yet I cannot wait and wait, alone each night in this
bed we shared, not knowing what—she—has done to him. Nor what
she may do to us all. Tera, I carry Evirion's child. Lately I've been
sure of it. Evirion's child, Grallon's grandchild. What shall *his* lot be
in a land where she haunts the shores?"

"I am no Queen of Ys, darling, nor even a witch like what you
were."

Nemeta looked at her. "But you serve the old Gods yet," she whispered. "Not the Gods of Ys but of your own people, Cernunnos, Epona, Teutatis, Those Who once were mighty here and may still keep a little, little strength to help Their last few worshippers. And I forswore my witchcraft, but for this, for Evirion and the damning of Dahut, I will call back what I can of it. Together we may do something. I know not what, but—for your own children, Tera, and for Maeloch's ghost, wherever he wanders this night—will you stand by me?"

—It was the dark of the moon, as it must be, but crystalline, starthronged, the River of Tiamat frozen to bright ice. Light edged the upper blackness of forest and made the rime on turf and stones shimmer. Maybe Tera could have done without the torch that Nemeta held for her while she squatted at a stacked pile of wood and, with a drill whereon signs were carved, kindled the needfire. Flames burned quietly, standing tall now that wind had died away. The faint blood-tinge of them rose high in the smoke until it lost itself among stars.

From the shieling she fetched a cauldron, too big for a one-armed woman to carry, but it was Nemeta who went to and fro bringing water from the pond while Tera sat cross-legged and shut-eyed, lips forming ancient unspoken sounds. When at length the water seethed and steam lent its whiteness to the smoke, they both paced around and around. Tera had brought the dried borage, nettle, mandrake root that they cast in, but the chant, high and ululating, was Nemeta's.

It hurt her when they led the foal to the fire. He was a fine young stallion, roan with a silver blaze, get of Favonius. She felt she betrayed her father's trust. Gratillonius had left her here after Evirion departed, rather than returning the former watchman. She fought back the tears. Beneath her heart she carried his grandchild.

The colt tossed his head, rolled his eyes, whinnied, alarmed by this strangeness. She gripped the bridle tightly, rubbed her head against his neck, crooned comfort, soothed him.

"We call," said Tera, and Nemeta stepped aside. Her companion raised a sledge hammer in both strong hands. Old stains were on haft and head. She smashed it forward. The horse screamed and went down. Tera leaped on him, knife drawn, and struck. The blood spouted. A while he struggled, then shivered and lay still. The blood that pooled around him steamed like the kettle. The women marked themselves with it.

Did a shadow of antlers rise athwart the stars? Did hoofs gallop? A wolf howled. Not for years had men heard wolves this near their city.

Tera butchered the sacrifice quickly and roughly, and cast the meat in the cauldron, while Nemeta cursed the Gods of Ys and summoned the Old Folk from their dolmens. They did not cook the food long before they forced down as much of it as they were able. Afterward they ate the holy toadstools, rolled themselves in blankets by the waning fire, and invoked sleep. It thundered upon them.

—Stars glimmered yet in the west, but had fled the pallor of the east. Hoarfrost crusted every blade of grass. Ice had formed on the stiffened blood around guts, hide, half-stripped bones. It made a skin over the stew in the kettle. Dust drifted on a dawn breeze from the ash underneath.

The women huddled close in their coverings, as if a wraith of heat lingered for them. They shook with weariness. Breath smoked at each hoarse word.

"So we know," Tera said. "Dahut brought my Maeloch onto the rocks, and herself bore him below. She rammed *Brennilis* with a craft she'd robbed from some fishers she drew to Ys for this, and herself bore Evirion below. Everyone aboard was lost save for Riwal. Him she ferried ashore. We know not why that was."

"And we know," Nemeta joined in, "that she bore Rufinus below, but her vengefulness was unquenchable and so she led the Scoti to Audiarna. We know of other wreck and ruin she has wrought among humble folk whom nobody mourned but those that loved them. We know the evil of her can only end with herself; for the Gods of Ys have made her Their revenge on the world."

"But how can we seek her out?"

"*We* cannot. The One God gives her leave to be. We know not why. By His might alone may her sea take her back to it forever."

Tera shuddered. "Are her powers that great?"

"She swims untiring," said Nemeta's toneless chant, "but she cannot long endure sun, nor be on land more than a very little span. Where she goes, she commands the wind, though she breathes no longer. She lures, enchants, dazzles, terrifies. Nonetheless men have wrenched themselves from her call, and to it a saint would be deaf. With a single prayer he could destroy her."

"She will ken him from afar, and flee."

"She is of the moon. Ever its fullness draws her back to Ys, where she died, that she may drink its light upon that bay. By a gibbous moon she sought out Rufinus on the bridge and led the Scoti to Audiarna, but afterward she left them and returned home, that she might swim in its fullness among the ruins of Ys. There and then can someone find her."

"But still she will know him, and escape into Ocean."

Nemeta slumped before the ashes. Exhaustion dragged down her voice. "More I cannot say. Nor did the Horned One have more to give your dreams, did He? Let us go indoors and seek mortal sleep."

Tera rose. "And what next will you do, lonely dear?" she asked. "Me, I'll trudge back to the farm, but you?"

"I will seek Bishop Corentinus," Nemeta answered. "I will tell him what we have learned, and beg his forgiveness, and Christ's, and Christ's help against yonder thing."

XXV

~ 1 ~

The day before solstice hung still and murky. Breath misted, but there was no real sense of cold, nor of wetness, and noises all seemed hushed. The rivers glided iron-dark under earthen walls of Confluentes where summer's grass had gone sere, and, mingled together, on past Aquilo toward the sea. Folk in the streets and shops went about their work unwontedly subdued, though none could have said why. It was as if the world lay waiting.

Suddenly, far down the Venetorum road, against bare brown fields and skeleton trees, color burst forth. Red-bordered gold with black emblem, the wolf banner flew at the head of a mounted troop. Behind it, cloaks billowed rainbow-colored; tunics and breeks proclaimed clans by the interwoven hues; metal winked, helmets, mailcoats, spearheads that rose and fell and rose again to the rocking rhythm of the horses. Hoofs thudded. Even the baggage mules were eager. A horn sang, a shout lifted, for the men of Gradlon saw home before them.

Sentinels of the city cried answer and winded trumpets of their own. News washed like a wave between the turrets. Men, women, children dropped whatever they were at and swarmed forth. Their cheers defied the sullen sky. "He comes! The King is back!"—not the Duke, as he named himself, but the King, as they did.

Ever louder through hoofbeats, creak of leather, jangle of iron, whoops out of throats, the sound of his cities reached Gratillonius. His vision strained forward. How well he knew each battlement, each timber in the portal and stone in the bridge. Behind them reached the ways he had laid out, the buildings he had watched grow, the people for whom he had been riding, hearthfires and hope. O Verania! What was Marcus up to, how much bigger was Maria?

Ahead laired trouble, toil, much anger, some heartbreak. You didn't get away from any of those, this side of Heaven. But he felt ready to meet them. Eastward he left a good job of work, alliances firmly forged. In doing it he had shored up the spirit within himself. Today was the day when he would again embrace Verania.

For an instant Dahilis flitted through his awareness. He thought she smiled and waved. A farewell? She was gone. He signalled his trumpeter to sound gallop. Favonius surged.

His hoofs thundered on the bridge. Gratillonius glanced left. Several boats were moored at the wharf, a couple of them large enough to be called small ships, but mostly the piers were winter-empty.

Brennilis was not there.

The shock made him rein in with needless force. Favonius neighed angrily, reared, went on at a skittish walk. Turbulence erupted as the troopers filed off to cross. Everybody was impatient. Hurrahs gusted from the open gate.

Had the weather proven too fierce around Britannia? It had continued benign on the mainland. Only yesterday, Gratillonius had with a breastful of anxiety inquired of the villagers near whom he camped, and heard that it had also been mild hereabouts. Misfortune? Pirates would scarcely have been out so late in the year; if any were, they'd scarcely attack a craft as redoubtable as *Brennilis*. Evirion would be wary of ambushes ashore. The Britons might reject Gratillonius's offer at once, unlikely though that seemed, but they wouldn't harm the bearer, would they?

He rode through the gate. Guardsmen fenced Principal Way with their pikeshafts, holding back the crowd on either side. The street was clear for him—and there, where it crossed Market Way, on which their house stood, there waited Verania in the middle of the intersection. She carried Maria in her arms. Marcus hopped and shouted on her right. Tall on her left, his cloak a splash of springtime green, was Salomon. Across the yards between, Gratillonius knew them. He must hold Favonius in. He might trample them if he went too fast. Another minute.

Bishop Corentinus stepped out of Apostolic Way and stopped. "Whoa!" Barely, Gratillonius halted.

The man afoot must look up at the man on horseback, yet somehow it was as if their eyes met on a level: for all at once the walls, the tumult, everything receded from Gratillonius and they two were alone in a strange place. Corentinus wore sandals on his bare feet and a coarse black robe over his rawboned height. He had thrown a cloak across his shoulders, and put a wide-brimmed hat on his head. Hair and beard were more white than gray. His right hand gripped a staff, his left was upraised, palm outward, a command to stop. It was eerie how Gratillonius came to think of the Germanic God Wotan the Wanderer, Who leads the dead away.

"Hail," he said. Seeing this confrontation, the people fell piecemeal silent, until they stood staring under the low dark sky.

"Welcome back," replied Corentinus with never a smile. "Did you succeed in your mission?"

"I did, but—"

"That is well; for much here is ill. Listen. You can see for yourself that your family is hale. I'm sorry to bar you from them, but there are tidings I think you'd best have first,—" Sternness fell from voice and

1107

craggy face. "—old friend. It needn't take long, then you can rejoin them. Will you follow me now?"

Gratillonius sat hearing the pulse in his head. It felt like a while and a while before he said, "As you will," and turned about to give the troop into charge of his deputy.

Likewise he gave the reins of Favonius, and dismounted. As he left with the bishop, he looked toward Verania. She waved at him, as his memory of Dahilis had waved.

—Corentinus had moved from Aquilo to a house newly erected beside the cathedral in Confluentes. It was a good-sized building and decently, if austerely, furnished, for he received men of importance, on matters temporal as well as spiritual, and his flock would have him do so in such manner as to reflect credit on their community. At the rear, however, he had had made a room that was his alone, for prayer, meditation, and sleep. It was a mere cell, its window a single uncovered slit. The dirt floor held one stool and a straw pallet with a thin blanket. Walls and ceiling were bare plaster. Above the bed hung a small, roughly whittled wooden cross which holy Martinus had blessed. A clay lamp on a shelf burned the poorest sort of fat. Today it flickered alight because else men would have been like moles. Dankness and chill were gathered as thick as the gloom.

"Here we'll talk," Corentinus said, "for I may hope a faintest breath of sanctity is present, and what we have to speak of is terrible."

Gratillonius sat hunched on the stool and regarded the guttering yellow flame. Corentinus loomed above him. In a few words, the tale came out.

"Oh, no," Gratillonius whispered. "No, no."

"So it is, my son."

Gratillonius twisted his neck around and peered upward. He saw only the hair, the beard, a glint of eyes. "Nemeta, how is she?"

"Sorrowful but in health."

"I must go to her. Is she still out at the pastures? What have you done about, about her sin? Do you think she's lost?"

Corentinus shook his head. "No. She's a valiant lass. I've never seen more bravery than was in her when she came to confess to me. She thought she might well be damned, and was ready take that, if the Church would receive her child." A knobby hand reached down to squeeze the shoulder beneath. "She did what she did largely for you, Gratillonius."

Unshed tears can fill the gullet. "Wha-what did you do?"

"I told her to sin no more. And yet—she acted less in fear or hatred than out of love. That was why she could not wholly repent." A rusty chuckle. "I asked her if she was sorry she could not, and this she agreed to. So then and there I baptized her."

Gratillonius caught hold of the hand that clasped him, and pressed it hard.

"I'll provide for her, of course," he said when he was able. "She can't stay on alone in that wretched shack."

"She dares not come into town at all anymore, now that she carries Evirion's child," said Corentinus harshly. "And Verania wonders whether your children and she are safe, even within the walls. She will no longer let them out, no, not to the manor house where they've had pleasure, certainly not across the bridge and down along the river to see their grandmother. Dwellers on the coast live in fright, worse than any barbarians ever brought them, for barbarians are at least human and—do not stalk the shores in winter."

As he listened, a tide rose in Gratillonius. He heard it roar, he felt himself drowning in it. "Dahut," he called across the wild waters, "Dahut."

"You cannot keep hiding from this," the relentless voice marched on above him. "We must destroy that hell-creature or perish in trying."

Gratillonius sprang up. "We can't!" he yelled. "There is no way!" He struck his fist against the wall. Plaster cracked apart and fell. The cross shivered.

"There is, with God's help," said Corentinus at his back. "Nemeta staked her soul to discover it."

Gratillonius leaned head on arm and shut his eyes.

The bishop's tone gentled a little. "She did not see this herself, and best we keep the secret between us. I did not either, at first, nor is it entirely clear to me yet. We've a fouled line to untangle, you and I, and afterward a hard course to steer. It may well end in wreck for us too."

Somehow the warning put a measure of strength back in Gratillonius. He turned from the wall.

"Good man, oh, good man," murmured Corentinus. "I need your counsel. Can you give it? Afterward I'll let you go home."

Gratillonius forced a nod.

"I haven't told you quite everything about poor mad Riwal," said the other. "He was carrying something when the shepherd found him, and wouldn't let slip of it. As I tried to speak with him later, he mouthed broken words about Dahut, the White One, bringing him ashore. Well, I've told you that. I thought, as I imagine you do, she did this—for Nemeta's vision declared it was true she did—in refined cruelty. She'd leave no doubt that she, and nothing mortal or natural, had sunken the ship and murdered the crew. But then I looked at the thing in his hand, and the peasant who'd brought him in explained about it. When I asked, he gave it to me, no, forced it on me. 'For Gradlon,' he babbled, 'for Gradlon.' I still don't understand. But here it is."

He stooped with an aged man's stiffness and from beneath the blanket fetched a small object which he proffered. Gratillonius took it and held it near the lamp to see. Rotten wood was damp and spongy between his fingers. Decayed, worm-eaten, battered, the thing had scant form left. And yet he knew it. Suddenly he was cold down into his bones, sea-bottom cold.

"It doesn't seem like a cult object or a magical tool, does it?" he heard across immensities. "Almost a toy."

"That's what it is," he heard inside his skull. "A horse figure I made for her when she was a little girl."

"Why on—earth—would she send it to you? A taunt? A challenge?"

"I think not," said Gratillonius from somewhere outside himself. "My daughter was always glad of my gifts. She was so proud that her Papa could make them. This one was her special favorite. I think she's calling me."

~ 2 ~

Snow began to fall as the couple neared the top of Mons Ferruginus. It dropped through windless quiet in flakes tiny but teeming. Beyond a few yards there soon was white blindness. Ground vanished beneath it and the bare boughs of trees and shrubs bore a new flowering. A measure of warmth had stolen into the air.

Gratillonius halted on the trail. "We may as well go back," he said.

"I'm sorry," Verania replied. "You wanted so much a view over your country."

He glanced down at her. She looked up from within her snow-dusted cowl. The cloak happened to be black, and winter always paled her fair skin, so lips and hazel eyes and a stray brown lock bore all the colors he saw in a world of gray and white.

"Did I say that?" he asked.

"No, not really. But I could tell."

"You notice more than you let on."

She shook her head. "I only pay attention—to you, my dearest."

"Ah, well," he sighed, "I've plenty memories from here." With a grave smile: "Besides, what I most wanted was to get off alone with you."

She came to him and laid her cheek against his breast. For a moment they held each other, then started homeward, hand in hand. The trail being narrow, often one of them must go off it into brush which scratched and crackled unnaturally loud; but neither let go.

"Anyhow," Gratillonius said, "now I'll have more time with the children before we tuck them in."

"They're lucky," she answered. "My father was like you in this, if little else. It's a rare kind."

"Aw," he mumbled.

Her grip tightened. Abruptly her voice grew shrill. "Come back to us!"

He stopped again. Her delicate features worked until she could stiffen them. Tears glinted on the lashes. "Of course I will," he promised.

"How do I know?" The words tumbled forth. "You haven't told me anything except that you're leaving already."

It tore away the visor he had lowered against her. "I haven't dared," he rasped. "Nobody. Nor can I speak till afterward."

"You are going—"

"To deal with a certain menace. It won't take long."

"Unless you're the one who dies."

He shrugged.

"It could be worse than death," she said frantically. "Gradlon, that evil is not of this world."

"You notice too much," he snapped.

She looked from him, and back at him, shuddered within the cloak, finally said low, "And I think about it."

He tugged at her hand. "Come," he proposed. They went on downhill through the snowfall.

When he thought she had calmed a bit, he said, "You've always been wise for your age, Verania. Have you the wisdom now to keep silence?"

She nodded.

Her fingers, which had gone icy, seemed pace by pace to thaw in his. At last she gave him a smile.

The snowfall thickened.

"Strange," he said slowly. "All at once I remember. Today is the Birthday of Mithras."

Alarm touched her tone. "You don't follow that God any longer!"

"Certainly not. But it seems to me somehow as though this, everything that matters to me, it began that selfsame day, five-and-twenty years ago. I stood guard on the Wall....And soon, one way or another it will end."

"It won't!" she cried. "Not for you!" Her face lifted toward hidden heaven. Snow struck it, melted, ran down in rain. "Holy Maria, Mother of God," she appealed, "we've only had four years."

In a way he did not understand but that was like a smith quenching a newly forged sword, it hardened his will for that to which he had plighted himself.

~ 3 ~

Midwinter nights fell early and dwelt late in Armorica, day hardly more than a glimmer between them, but this one was ice-clear. Stars thronged the dark, so bright that he could see colors in some, blue like steel, yellow like brass, red like rust. Their brilliance was also in the Milky Way, which to Ys had been the River of Tiamat, primordial Serpent of Chaos, but which elsewhere was the bridge by which the dead leave our world. Snow on the ground caught the light from above, glowed and glittered. It was a crust frozen hard, crunching underhoof; the earth beneath it boomed. Gratillonius rode easily across a vast unreal sweep of hills above the whitened valley. He was aware of the cold around him but did not feel it; he went as if in a dream.

The moon rose full, immense, over the eastern range as Favonius started down Aquilonian Way. Night became yet the more luminous, dazzlingly; but now there were fewer stars and many crooked shadows. The stallion slowed, for scattered or broken paving blocks, holes, and brambles made this part of the road treacherous. Below the thuds and the vaporous breathing, his rider began to hear the sea.

Tide was about two hours into ebb, water still well up the bay. Radiance ran across it where wave crests caught moonbeams. The wet strand shimmered. He could make out the last few rubble-bulks as blacknesses unstirring amidst that mercury fluidity. Right and left, the cliffs also denied the light. Their brutal masses shouldered into a sky that Ocean walled off afar.

He came down onto level ground and turned again west. The amphitheater huddled in its congealed marsh under a ragged blanket of snow. He glimpsed stars through gaps in the sides. Demolition had continued since he fought his battle here. By the time of his death, likely no trace whatsoever of Ys would remain.

That was supposing he reached a fairly ripe age. He might die this hour. No fear of it was in him. He had dropped such human things on the journey from Confluentes. They waited for him at home.

The amphitheater fell behind. Snow dwindled to patches and then to naught, washed away by sea-spray. Frost sparkled on rocks and leafless shrubs. The murmur he heard from the heights had become deep, multitudinously whispery at the shore, rumbling and roaring farther out. Phantoms leaped where combers broke on skerries.

"Whoa," said Gratillonius, and drew rein. He sprang from the saddle and tethered Favonius to a bush at the rim of the beach. His cloak he unfastened and laid across the horse's withers for whatever slight warmth it might give. It could hamper him. He wore simply Gallic tunic, breeks, soft shoes that let his feet grip the soil. Roman sword and Celtic dirk were at his belt, but he did not think he would have use for either.

Favonius whickered. Gratillonius stroked a hand down the head and over the soft nose. "Good luck, old buddy," he said. "God keep you."

He turned and walked over sand and shingle toward the water. They gritted. Kelp coiled snakish. Cold such as this deadened most odors, but his nostrils drank a sharpness of salt.

Two hillocks marked where High Gate formerly stood. Passing between, he saw more. On his left, that one had been the royal palace; on his right, that one had been the Temple of Belisama. A vague track and two or three cracked slabs told him that he betrod Lir Way. Moored to a stump of stone lay a boat—aye, the lifeboat from *Brennilis*.

At the water's edge he halted and looked outward. Receding, Ocean nonetheless cast small waves that licked his ankles. He did not mark their chill. Froth roiled around pieces of wall and a single pillar.

Here I am, Dahut, his spirit called. I have come in answer to your bidding.

For a span that seemed long, nothing stirred but the waves. He was without expectations. How could a mortal man foreknow what would travel through this night? Witchcraft had told that she would be in her Ys, but Satan was the wellspring of untruth. Gratillonius had arrived at moonrise to make doubly sure, and to see as well as might be, little though he wanted to. He was himself burdened with sin, and unbaptized; she ought not to fear him. Though she had knowledge of where those were whom she hated, he did not believe she could hear their thoughts; else she would scarcely have sent her token to him. But what did he know?

His task was to keep her heedful of him; how?

He waited.

A wave, yonder where the gate once opened to the sea? A riptide? Seal-swift it flowed his way. A wake shone brokenly behind. Now he saw an arm uplifted, now he saw the thick, rippling hair. She reached the shallows, a few yards from him, halted, and stood.

The tide swirled around her waist. The light poured over her face, her breasts, the arms she held toward him. White she was as the snow or the waves that shattered on the skerries, save for the mane that he knew was golden and the eyes that he knew were summer-blue. So had he last seen her, demonic at the Bridge of Sena, and the worst horror of it had been the lust that raged aloft in him.

But tonight it was not thus at all. She was merely and wholly beautiful. The whiteness was purity. Her sea had washed her clean; she was renewed, Princess of Ys, and she smiled across the water like that little girl for whom he carved a wooden horse. She was his daughter, born to Dahilis, and she needed him.

Her song went high and sweet over the shout and thunder below the cliffs.

"Out of this moonlight on the sea,
Sundered from you ashore,
Father, I call you, come to me
And give me your love once more.

"Though I have left your world of man,
Flung on the wind like foam,
Do you remember how I ran
To meet you when you came home?

"Lullaby now is wave on reef,
Hollow and comfortless.
Yours was the laugh that healed all grief,
And there was no loneliness.

"Cold were those years when I at sea
Longed, and yet could not weep.
Father, I call you come to me
And rock me again to sleep."

By the mercy of Christ. No, he could not judge that. He must not utter it.

She stood waiting for him. If he stayed on the land that was forbidden her, she would soon swim away, alone forever.

He waded forth. The bottom sloped steeply. A few feet past her, he would be over his depth. Salt drops stung his lips.

Joy pulsed from her. She leaned forward, as if she could go no higher. The hands trembled that reached for him. Her smile outshone the stars that wreathed her hair.

He opened his arms. She fell into them. He held her tightly against him. Her embrace around his neck, her head on his breast, stabbed with chill. "Dahut," he said, "oh, Dahut."

She wrenched herself loose. Her scream clawed. Never had he beheld such terror on any face.

Not looking around, he knew that his follower Corentinus had reached the strand and begun the exorcism.

Dahut dived. She had time to flee.

Gratillonius snatched after her. His fingers closed in the streaming tresses. Her strength hauled him under. Blind, the breath gone from him, he tumbled with her, outward over the deeps. His free hand found solidness, curve of flesh. He locked a leg around those that kicked at him.

Heads came above water. He saw her eyes wide, mouth open, before the struggle whirled him toward the moon and its whiteness dazed sight of her. He gasped air full of froth churned up. Her nails raked him. It smote through his awareness. Once she cried for me to draw her from the sea. Tonight at last I do.

The voice resounded through the surf: "I exorcise you, unclean spirit, in the name of Jesus Christ, Who did cast forth demons, and by the power that He gave unto His holy Church, against which the gates of hell shall not prevail. Begone, creature of Satan, he the enemy of God and of mankind, he whose rebellion brought war in Heaven and whose falseness brought death into the world, he the root of evil, discord, and misery. Begone to him. Begone. Amen. Amen. Amen."

Dahut shrieked. It echoed off the cliffs and flew out over Ocean. She writhed and slumped.

Gratillonius felt hardness underfoot, a fallen shard of Ys. He regained balance and stood there on it, the tide up to his heart, in his arms a dead young woman.

1114

At dawn the sea was withdrawing anew, gray and white between darkling cliffs and among the rocks. It drummed an undertone to a silence otherwise broken by only the earliest of the gulls. A breeze blew sharp down the valley.

Stiffly, Gratillonius rose. Corentinus did too, and gave him an anxious look. The bishop had built and tended a small fire above the strand. He had gone after his own mount and the pack animal, with dry clothes which he forced his companion to don. Afterward no word passed from one of them to the other. Corentinus prayed through the night while Gratillonius sat beside that which he had wrapped in his cloak.

"You really should get some sleep before we start back," the bishop said.

"No need," Gratillonius replied.

"Food?" Corentinus gestured at their rations.

"No."

"Well, then, let's load our stuff."

"Not that either."

Corentinus raised his brows. "What?"

Gratillonius pointed to the object at his feet. "Dahut. I have to bury her."

"I thought we'd bring her with us."

Now the voice clanged: "Slung over a horse's rump? To be jeered and cursed and lie like a beast in unhallowed ground? No. She's going home to the Queens of Ys."

"But without that shown them, will the people believe?" Corentinus protested. "They may think she haunts these waters yet."

"Let them. Some bold sailors will take our word. When no harm comes, the rest will soon take ship likewise."

Corentinus stood meditative a while before he sighed, "Ah, well... So be it. They'll remember her with Ys, a legend, a hearthside story on winter nights."

Gratillonius stared at the bundle. "That's all that will be left."

Corentinus blinked hard. "My son—" He must try afresh. "I can barely guess, old childless I, what wounds you carry. May they heal in you. The scars of them will be a pledge of your reward in Heaven, my son."

"My daughter—" Gratillonius lifted his head and met those eyes. "There at the end, she told me she loved me."

The response was rough. "Another snare of hers."

"I don't know," Gratillonius said. "I never will, unless after I'm dead myself. *Should* I have held her for you?"

Corentinus nodded. "You should. No matter what. It was your duty."

Gratillonius spread his hands. "If she did speak the truth—if she did—is she in hell? Might God have taken her to Him after all?"

"It is not for us to set bounds on His mercy," Corentinus answered low. What else could he say? Louder: "But in His name, Gratillonius, and for everyone's sake, do not brood on this."

The father grinned. "Oh, I'll have enough else to do. There will be war again in spring."

He bent down at the knees, gathered the body, bore it across the strand to the water. The lifeboat still floated at a few inches' depth. He laid his burden within. Searching about, he found a stone of the size he wanted. It was off the capital of a pillar, the eroded image of a flower. He put it in the boat and hauled himself after. Unstepped mast, yardarm, furled sail, oars were neatly lashed in place. He freed the oars, cast off, and bent to the rowing. The ebb tide helped. Corentinus watched from shore till he must go sit down. His years were heavy upon him.

Past the ruins, over the sea gate, and on outward Gratillonius went. Oars creaked and thumped between their tholes, for the wind stiffened, to make the boat roll and pitch. Waves tramped by, gray-green and wrinkled, spindrift blown off their crests. They snarled and crashed on rocks, flinging whiteness high for the wind to catch. It was a chill morning, the sun wan above the snow.

Presently he reached the funeral grounds of Ys, where the bottom plunged to depths unknown. He shipped his oars and let the boat swing adrift. Far off to the west he spied a streak of darkness that was Sena.

He cut a length from the lashings, made stone fast to ankles, wound the line up the shrouding cloak but stopped short. Ys had had her own service for the dead. *Gods of mystery, Gods of life and death, sea that nourishes Ys, take this my beloved—* But he must not say such words. Nor would he if he might.

A prayer to Christ? Somehow that wasn't right either.

He folded back the cloth. The hours had smoothed her face. With eyes closed and jaw bound, she lay in that inhuman peacefulness which dwells for a time before dissolution begins. He kissed her brow. She was no colder than the wind.

He covered her again, made the cord secure, and on his knees— because to stand would have been dangerous, and he had duties—lifted her up and dropped her over the side. She sank at once. A gull mewed.

He settled onto his thwart, took the oars, rowed back.

It was a long haul against the flow of air and water, that brought him a blessed weariness. When at last he grounded, he could roll into a blanket and sleep an hour or two.

Rousing, for a moment he was full of gladness. Then he remembered. But miles lay ahead, to Audiarna where he and his companion would rest before going on to Confluentes. When he was at home with Verania he could weep; and she would make all things good.

Favonius pawed the ground, eager to be off. Corentinus had gotten the baggage ready. The men departed. Sundown at their backs, they rode into night.

Would you know the dog from the wolf? You may look at his paw,
Comparing the claw and the pad; you may measure his stride;
You may handle his coat and his ears; you may study his jaw;
And yet what you seek is not found in his bones or his hide,
For between the Dog and the Wolf there is only the Law.

AFTERWORD

The Breton folk tell many different tales about the sunken city of Ys, its king, and his daughter. Bearing in mind that these often disagree, let us give a synopsis of the basic medieval story.

Grallon (sometimes rendered "Gradlon") was ruler of Cornouaille, along the southwestern shore of Brittany, with his seat at Quimper, which some say he helped found. Once he took a great fleet overseas and made war on Malgven, Queen of the North. In conquering her country he also won her heart, as she did his. They started off together for his home, but terrible weather kept them at sea for a year. During this time Malgven bore a girl child, and died in so doing. When the heartbroken Grallon finally returned, he could deny nothing to his daughter Dahut (in some versions, Ahes). She grew up beautiful and evil.

While hunting, Grallon met a hermit, Corentin, who lived in the forest. This man was miraculously nourished; each day he drew a fish from the water, ate half, and threw the other half back, whereupon it became whole and alive again. However, it was his wisdom that most impressed the king. Grallon persuaded Corentin to join him in Quimper, and there the holy man won the people over to righteous ways. Other legends maintain that he was the actual founder or cofounder of the city, and its first bishop.

Dahut felt oppressed by the piety all around her, and begged her father to give her a place of her own. He built Ys on the shore—Ys of the hundred towers, walled against the waters that forever threatened its splendor. Hung upon his breast, Grallon kept the silver key that alone could unlock the sea gate. Otherwise he gave Dahut free rein and turned a blind eye to her wickedness.

Led by her, Ys became altogether iniquitous. The rich ground down the poor, gave themselves to licentious pleasures, forgot their duty to God, and even blasphemed Him. Dahut herself took a different lover every night, and in the morning had him cast to his death in the sea.

Another holy man, St. Guénolé, was stirred to enter the city and plead with the people to mend their ways. For a while he did succeed in frightening many into reform; but the baneful influence of Dahut was too strong, and they drifted back into sin.

At last God determined to destroy Ys, and gave the Devil leave to carry out the mission. Taking the guise of a handsome young man, he sought Dahut in her palace and was soon welcomed into her bed. Him she did not have killed. Rather, she fell wildly in love. He demanded, as a sign of her affection, that she bring him the key Grallon bore. Dahut stole it while the king was asleep and gave it to her lover. The

1118

night was wild with storm. He slipped out and unlocked the gate. The sea raged in and overwhelmed Ys.

It had no power over St. Guénolé, who awakened innocent Grallon and warned him to flee. Barely did the king's great charger carry him through the waters as they surged in between the city walls. Dahut screamed in terror. Her father saw, and tried to save her. The saint told him he must not, for the weight of her sins would drag him down too; and she was swept away from his grasp. None but Grallon and Guénolé escaped, as Ys went under the waves.

Guénolé laid the doom on the city that it would remain sunken until a Mass was said in it upon a Good Friday. Dahut became a siren, haunting the coast, luring sailors to shipwreck among the many rocks thereabouts. Grallon gave up his crown and ended his days in the abbey of Landevennec which Guénolé had founded.

A later story relates how one mariner was borne benath the water by certain strange swimmers. Somehow he did not drown, and they led him to the sunken city and into a church where a service was going on. He was afraid to give the responses, when no one else did. Afterward his guides brought him ashore and let him go; but first they asked sadly, "Why did you not say what you should have at the Mass? Then we would all have been released."

Ys is still there under the sea.

Thus far the tradition. As for its origin, the prosaic fact is that stories about submerged towns are common along the Welsh and Cornish coasts. Folk from those parts could well have carried the idea with them during their massive emigration to Armorica in the fifth and sixth centuries. In the course of time it came to be associated with Grallon and with several of the host of Breton saints. On the other hand, the tale could conceivably have been a native one which the Bretons found when they arrived, and this we have assumed for our purposes.

Among the disagreements between versions of the legend, conspicuous is that concerning the site. Some accounts put Ys on the Baie de Douarnenez, others on the Baie d'Audierne, still others on the Baie des Trépassés. We have chosen the last of these.

Obviously we have made a good many more choices! First and foremost, we have imagined that there really was an Ys.

If so, when did it perish? Saints Corentin and Guénolé are assigned to the fifth and sixth centuries respectively; therefore they could not both have been involved. We picked the earlier era. (If nothing else, the farther back in time, the more plausible it is that no record would survive of the city and its destruction. At that, we have had to offer some explanation of why the Romans left none.) Therefore Corentin must needs assume the role that folklore gives to Guénolé. Besides, legend associates him with the founding of Quimper and makes St. Martin consecrate him its bishop.

Since no kingdom of Cornouaille existed at this time, our Grallon would have had to begin as the ruler of Ys, which must thus have been flourishing long before his birth. He in turn would have had no reason to start a settlement at what was to become Quimper until after the loss of his realm. The need for a new stronghold, in the chaos that was spreading through Gaul, would be clear to him if he was himself a Roman, as we have supposed.

From the first-century geographer Pomponius Mela we have adopted and adapted the Gallicenae. True, he describes them as vestal virgins, but with his own sources all being indirect, he was not necessarily right about this. The sixth-century historian Procopius gives an account of the Ferriers of the Dead; he says they took their unseen passengers from Gaul to Britain, but we depict men so engaged between Ys and the Île de Sein. The king who must win and defend his crown in mortal combat is best known from Lake Nemi, as described by Sir James Frazer in *The Golden Bough*. However, the practice has occurred elsewhere too, in various guises, around the world, so we could reasonably attribute it to Ys.

Aside from such modifications, logically required, we have stayed as close as possible to the legends. After all, this is a fantasy. Yet we have at the same time tried to keep it within the framework of facts that are well established.

For us it all began one day in 1979, when we were staying on a farm near Médréac in Brittany and Karen, on impulse, wrote the poem with which our story ends. Earlier in the same trip we had visited a number of Roman remains in England and stood on Hadrian's Wall. Now somehow this came together with Ys, of which our surroundings reminded us, and the first dim outlines of the tale appeared. At home we thought and talked about it more and more often, until by 1982 our ideas were clear enough that we returned to Brittany for a look at sites we had not examined before. There followed about a year's worth of book research, and then the actual writing—occasionally interrupted to meet other commitments—lasted into the spring of 1987. The whole business has been a strange and rewarding experience. We hope readers will enjoy what has come out of it.

NOTES

Although our aim has been to make the text of this novel self-explanatory, certain historical details may surprise some readers, who may thereupon think we are in error. Other readers may simply wish to learn a little more about the era. Nobody has to look at these notes, but anybody who wishes to is welcome.

A word about nomenclature. In the story we generally give place names the forms they had at the time, rather than use their English versions. This is for the sake of accuracy as well as color. After all, the boundaries of most cities, territories, etc. were seldom quite identical with those of their modern counterparts, and the societies occupying them were entirely different. There are a few exceptions, such as "Rome" or the names of famous tribes, where insistence on the ancient rendering would have been pedantic.

As for personal names, the story uses original forms throughout. Most are attested, a few represent conjectures by us. Ysan names are imaginary but not arbitrary; they are supposed to show the Celtic and Semitic roots of the language, plus later Graeco-Roman influences. "Ys" itself is pronounced, approximately, "eess," though the vowel is pure, not a diphthong of the English sort. The French "ice," as in "justice," comes close.

ROMA MATER

I

Mithras (or *Mithra*): A deity of ancient Aryan origin whose cult reached Rome by way of Persia. Especially popular among soldiers, it became for a time the most important rival of Christianity, with which it had much in common.

The Birthday of Mithras: 25 December. Formerly it had been celebrated on the winter solstice, but precession of the equinoxes caused the latter to move backward through the calendar. About 274 A.D. the Emperor Aurelian fixed the birthday of Sol Invictus as the 25th, a date which the related Mithraic faith adopted. The Christian Church would not settle on it for the Nativity of Christ until much later; in the fourth century, that event was still considered of secondary importance.

Gaius Valerius Gratillonius: Throughout the lands that the Empire ruled, inhabitants belonging to the upper and middle classes, and often persons more humble, generally imitated Roman nomenclature. Here "Gaius" is the given name—which, however, men did not much use, if only because the selection was small. "Valerius" belongs to a Roman *gens*, and indicates that at some time in the past someone of that tribe patronized, adopted, or freed a British ancestor. "Gratillonius" is the cognomen, the family name, and is a Latinization of a native one (in this case, postulated rather than historically attested, in order to account for the later form "Grallon"). Admittedly, by the time of our story, the system was breaking down and there were many exceptions to it; but provincials would tend to be conservative.

Borcovicium (also recorded as *Vorcovicium, Vorcovicum,*etc.): Housesteads.

Mail: Heavy infantrymen of this period generally wore coats of mail, not the loricated cuirasses of an earlier day. A centurion was outfitted differently from those under him. The crest on his helmet, detachable for combat, arched side-to-side rather than front-to-back; greaves protected his shins; his sword hung from a baldric, and on the left instead of the right; he did not carry the two javelins, light and heavy, but did bear a twisted vinestaff as emblem of authority and instrument of immediate punishment for infractions.

Cliff: Where nature had not provided such a barrier, a deep ditch paralleled Hadrian's Wall on the north. Another, with earthen ramparts, ran at some distance to the south.

Fifteen feet: Post-Roman quarrying has much brought down what is left of the Wall, but this was its original height, more or less, along most of its length. As for that length, from Wallsend on the Tyne to Bowness on the Solway it is 73 English or about 77 Roman miles.

Eboracum (or *Eburacum*): York.

Other legions in Britain: Besides the Sixth, those permanently stationed there were the Twentieth Valeria Victrix, based at Deva (Chester), and the Second Augusta, based at Isca Silurum (Caerleon). Evidence indicates that a vexillation, a detachment, of the latter was called to Housesteads in the emergency of 382 A.D. As elsewhere throughout the Empire in its later days, legionary regulars were outnumbered by auxiliaries from all over, equipped and operating in their native styles.

Duke: At this time the *Dux Britanniarum* commanded the Roman forces in the provinces of Britain, with his seat in York.

Vindolanda: This site is today occupied by the farm Chesterholm.

Tungri: A tribe in the Low Countries.

Basilica: Originally this word meant an administrative center, civil or military.

Base: Contrary to modern popular impressions, Hadrian's Wall was not intended as a line of defense, and hardly ever served as one. It provided a means of controlling peacetime traffic between Roman Britain and the tribes to the north; in the event of hostilities, it was a base out of which soldiers operated, taking war to the enemy rather than waiting for an attack.

Highlanders: The country of the Picts (a name loosely bestowed by the Romans) lay well to the north of Hadrian's Wall. Another common misconception makes them dwarfish; they were actually a rather tall people.

Warriors from across the water: The Scots were at this time living in what is now Ireland, except perhaps for an enclave on the Argyll coast. As the Empire declined, they came more and more to raid it, much in the style of the vikings centuries later.

Praetorium: The commandant's house in a legionary fortress. It doubtless had other uses as well.

Principia: The headquarters block, generally comprising three buildings around a courtyard.

Isca Silurum: Caerleon in southeastern Wales.

Hispania Tarraconensis: A Roman province occupying a large piece of Spain, in the northeast and east.

Clean-shaven: To judge by contemporary portraits, many Roman men of this period were, though closely trimmed beards may have been a little more common.

Cunedag: Better known as Cunedda, but that is a later form of the name. His move to northern Wales with a following of his native Votadini (sometimes rendered "Otadini") is historical; there he drove out the Scots and founded the kingdom of Venedotia, which eventually became Gwynedd. The Roman intention was that this should be a foederate, a closely controlled ally, but when the Empire receded it naturally became independent. Most authorities take for granted that the move was at the instigation of Stilicho, not Maximus. However, this is not certain; and Maximus himself did enter Welsh legend as Maxen Wledig, a prince who did something wonderful though unspecified for that country. Could it have been providing the leadership and organization from which the medieval kingdom developed?

Ordovices: The people occupying northern Wales. Roman practice was to convert native tribes into local units of government, somewhat like Swiss cantons.

Dumnonii: The people occupying, approximately, Cornwall and Devon.

Language: It is not quite certain, but it is not unlikely that there was a single Celtic language, with mutually intelligible dialects, throughout England and southern Scotland.

Stools: Chairs were not in common use. People ordinarily sat on stools, benches, or even floors.

Hivernia (or *Hibernia*): Ireland.

Wine: The Romans favored wines so sweet and thick that they were best watered.

Mediolanum: Milan.

Augusta Treverorum: Trier.

Arians: Christians following the doctrine of Arius, which the Council of Nicea had declared heretical.

Silures: The people occupying southern Wales.

Belgae: These folk held a broad territory in the South, ranging approximately from Somerset through Hampshire. They were the last Celts to reach the island, just a couple of centuries before the Roman conquest, and their Continental kin retained the same name. The Belgae claimed a strong Germanic strain in their ancestry.

British soldiers: For reasons uncertain today, auxiliaries of British birth, unlike most such, seem hardly ever to have been stationed in their home country. However, probably this was not so general a rule for regular legionaries.

Aquae Sulis: Bath.

Dacia: Approximately, modern Romania. In the later fourth century, the Empire had almost entirely abandoned this province.

Nervii: A tribe in the Low Countries.

Abonae: A small town on the river Avon (Latin *Abona*) in Somerset, near the meeting of this stream with the Mouth of the Severn (Latin *Sabrina*), which gives on the Bristol Channel and thus the sea.

Armorica: Brittany.

Gesoriacum: Boulogne.

Condate Redonum: Rennes.

Vorgium: Carhaix. In Roman times, until it was sacked, it was the most important city in western Brittany...except Ys!

Caledonians: A confederacy in the far North. However, the name was often given generally to the peoples beyond Hadrian's Wall.

Temenos: The hallowed ground before or around a temple.

Parnesius: Kipling makes him a centurion of the Thirtieth Legion, which was stationed in the Rhineland; we have found no confirmation of T.S. Eliot's assertion that it, or a vexillation of it, was on Hadrian's Wall at any time. Rather than leave Parnesius entirely out of the story, we suggest that he actually belonged to the Twentieth.

Serfs: Latin *coloni* (singular *colonus*), tenant farmers and their families whom the "reforms" of Diocletian had bound to the soil they cultivated, as their descendants would be bound for the next thousand years and more.

Ahura-Mazda: The supreme god of Mithraism.

Pronaos: An entrance hall above or adjoining the inner sanctum of a temple.

Tauroctony: A representation of Mithras slaying the primordial Bull.

II

The history of Ireland from the earliest times through the heroic age, and even the beginnings of the Christian era, is obscure, often totally confused. Such sagas, poems, and chronicles as we have were written down centuries after the events they purport to describe. Taken as a whole, they are full of contradictions as well as anachronisms and outright impossibilities. Moreover, it is clear that the medieval recorders misunderstood much, deliberately changed much else as being too pagan or otherwise unedifying, and supplied numerous inventions of their own. Foreign historians are of small help, because Ireland never came under Roman rule. Archaeology supplies some clues, as well as data about everyday life. One can also extrapolate backward from the oldest extant documents, notably the Brehon Laws, and from customs and beliefs reported by observers almost until the present day. Anthropology, with parallels to draw from other parts of the world, gives many hints as well.

In general, for this novel we have chosen those interpretations and hypotheses which best fit our story. Various authorities would disagree with us on various points. We will try to discuss briefly the most controversial matters as we go along.

The Irish still have no unanimity on how to spell Gaelic. The basic problem is that this is a language which does not lend itself well to the Roman alphabet. Besides, historical and dialectical variations are great. Our characters speak a forerunner of the language known as Old Irish, which itself is at least as different from modern Gaelic as Old Norse is from modern Danish. For a single example, the medieval and modern "mac," meaning "son of," was earlier "maqq," pronounced approximately "makw." We are indebted to Celtologist Alexi Kondratiev for what knowledge of the ancient forms we have, but he must not be held responsible for our mistakes and deliberate modifications. Notably, we use the name "Niall," although the older version is "Néll," because its bearer looms so large in Irish history and tradition.

Imbolc: In the modern calendar, 1 February. The pagan festival must have taken place approximately then. Our guess is that it, like others, was determined by the moon. The customs mentioned flourished as late as the early twentieth century. They look very ancient, only slightly Christianized.

Manandan(maqq Leri): Later called Manannan mac Lir; a major Irish god, associated with the sea.

Brigit: Originally an Irish goddess. She appears to have been tripartite, as many Celtic deities were. Her name passed to a Christian saint— nowadays Brighid or Bridget—who was especially popular and whose feast day was 1 February. The spring tide nearest this date bore her name and was believed to be the greatest of the year.

Condacht (or *Olnegmacht*): Connaught, west central Ireland, still a recognized division of the country. We will presently discuss the Fifths.

Mumu: Munster, southwestern Ireland. Like "Leinster" and "Ulster," the modern form of the name traces back to the Danes, as does, for that matter, "Ireland" itself.

Tuath: This word is often rendered "tribe," but that is somewhat misleading. A tuath, consisting of families with an intricate social ranking, was a political unit occupying a definite territory, but not otherwise especially distinct from others of its kind. Each tuath had a king (*rí*), who owed allegiance to the King of the Fifth, about which arrangement there is a later note. (The ancient form is *tótha*.)

Temir (later *Teamhair*): Now called Tara, this hill is located about 15 miles northwest of Dublin (which, of course, did not exist in our period; early Ireland had no towns). It had been used, if not continuously occupied, at least since megalithic times, and was regarded as especially charged with *mana*. However, tradition says that it was not until a few generations before Niall that a dynasty from Connaught established itself here.

King: The institution of the High King (*Ard-rí*) of Ireland did not exist even in theory until a much later date, and was never really very effective. In ancient times, at best the principal king of a Fifth commanded the allegiance of various lower-ranking kings, each of whom led a tuath or an alliance of several tuaths. (More grades of royalty eventually developed.) The King of a Fifth might, though, have additional powers or claims outside its borders. Allegiance amounted to little more than the payment of tribute—with the overlord expected to give a smaller amount of goods in return—and military service on strictly limited terms. Basically, any king lived off the proceeds of his own holdings, off certain payments from those beneath him, and off whatever he could plunder in wartime. His function was at last as much sacral as political.

Niall maqq Echach ("Echach" is the genitive of "Eochaid"): Later famous as Niall of the Nine Hostages, ancestor of the Uí Néill dynasties. On the whole, we have followed traditional accounts of his life and exploits. Certain modern scholars maintain that these date him a generation or two too early; a few doubt that he is historical at all. It is true that many contradictions and other puzzles in the medieval chronicles can be resolved by some such theory, and we do not venture to say this is mistaken. Yet perhaps it gives certain annals more weight, at the expense of others, than they deserve. There are authorities who think so. Discounting the fabulous elements that have crept in, the old stories about Niall look plausible enough. The real problems arise with some about his successor Nath Í, which are scarcely to be taken seriously. For that matter, the chronology and the very identity of St. Patrick are in confusion. Given all this, we have felt free to chose, from among the different accounts of Niall, those parts that accord with our story. Of course, we have added inventions of our own, beginning with his son Breccan, but these are not incompatible with our sources.

Ollam (or *olave*): The highest grade of any profession considered learned or skilled.

Free tenants: Land was held in ancient Ireland under a system too complicated to describe here. Briefly and incompletely put, however: land was inalienable from the tuath, which held in common the nonarable parts suitable for rough grazing, peat and wood gathering, etc. Farmland and the richer pastures were usually the property of some "noble"—whether the king, a *flaith*, or a learned man such as a judge, poet, physician, etc.—who, though, basically held the acreage in trust for his family. Otherwise real estate belonged to a sept, who subdivided it from time to time among different members. Land not directly used by the owner(s) was rented out to tenants, who paid in kind and in services, since the early Irish did not coin money. A free tenant (*soer-céli*) supplied all or most of his own stock, paid moderate rent, enjoyed a good social standing, and might often be wealthy. A bond tenant (*doer-céli*), to whom the landlord must furnish "starting capital," paid a much higher rent and ranked much lower. Both classes had other obligations, but those of the free tenant were lighter, and his rights and privileges under the law were far more. Nevertheless, the bond tenant was in no sense a serf; the relationship was contractual, and either party could terminate it. Indeed, there appears to have been social mobility, with poor men occasionally bettering their lot. Slaves, without rights and set to tasks nobody wanted, were generally captives taken in wars or raids, or children of these.

Mide: Occupying approximately modern Counties Meath, Westmeath, Longford, parts of Kildare and Offaly, it is supposed to have been carved out of Connaught, Leinster, and Ulster by the upstart Tara dynasty. Whether or not it actually existed as such an entity in our period is uncertain, but we assume that it did.

The Lagini: The people of Leinster, southeastern Ireland. Their territory was known as "Qóiqet Lagin," i.e. "the fifth of the Lagini." The later form is "Cóiced Laigen."

The Ulati: The people of Ulster, northeastern Ireland. Their territory was Qóiqet nUlat.

Fifths: According to tradition, Ireland was anciently divided into five parts, the Fifths. Though their inhabitants had much in common with each other, four of these regions had quite distinct histories and, in some particulars, ways of life. Those were Ulster, Leinster, Munster, and Connaught, which retain a meaningful existence to this day. The medieval chronicles state that Mide was formed out of parts of them, mostly Leinster, by a dynasty originating in Connaught. This dynasty took possession of holy Tara and eventually produced the High Kings who theoretically were supreme over all lesser kings throughout Ireland. Boundaries were ill-defined and often variable, not identical with those of the four modern provinces. Thus, at times Munster was divided in two, and Ulster shrank under the impact of the Uí Néill. As we have remarked above, at best the Fifths corresponded only roughly to separate kingdoms, as limited as royal powers were; and the High Kingship, which did not appear until well after Niall's time, was more a legal fiction than a working institution. (Some modern scholars argue that the chronicles must be wrong and that Connaught actually developed out of Mide. It may be so; but as far as possible, we have chosen to follow the traditional accounts.)

Emain Macha: The seat of the Ulster kings, near modern Armagh.

Hill fort sacred to Medb: The ruins of this are now known as Rath Maeve (a later form of the name "Medb"). They may or may not be contemporary with the main earthworks on Tara; our guess is that they are older, but were maintained. The attribution to Medb may well be right. She has been identified with the wife of Airt the Lonely, father of Corbmaqq (later called Cormac), but we suspect that originally the dedication was to Medb, tutelary goddess of Mide.

Forest: Unlike the country today, ancient Ireland was thickly wooded.

Boand's River: The Boyne, of which Boand was the goddess.

Great Rath: The remnants of this are now called the Ráth na Ríogh, or Royal Enclosure, but that is pure guesswork. "Rath" means such an enclosure, surrounded by an earthen wall—usually circular— which was originally topped by a palisade and often ringed by a fosse. It might protect anything from a single farmstead to a whole group of houses.

Pigs: The early Irish kept swine not only for food and leather, but occasionally as pets.

Heads: Like their Continental cousins before the Roman conquest, the Celts of Ireland were headhunters until they became Christian.

Flaw: No man could be king who had any serious deformity or disability. Some kings abdicated after suffering mutilation in war or accident, rather than risk expulsion.

Hostages: Alliances, subjugations, etc. were cemented by exchange of hostages, generally from leading families—unless a victor took his without giving any in return. As a rule, provided the terms of agreement were observed, they were well treated.

Bodyguards and champion: Besides his retinue of full-time warriors, an Irish king had several bodyguards—the number four is in the annals—who were with him whenever he went forth, as much for his dignity as his protection. For similar reasons, he kept a champion to deal with challenges to single combat, as opposed to war. Incidentally, aggrieved parties could not bring lawsuits against him, but could do so against his steward. In case of adverse judgement, naturally the king put up the compensation. The British monarchy preserves a version of this custom.

Equipment of the warriors: Contrary to Giraldus Cambrensis, the Irish used battle-axes before the viking invasions; but they did not wear armor, except occasionally helmets or greaves.

Royal Guesthouse; King's quarters: It is merely our suggestion that these may correspond to what are now dubbed, respectively, the Forradh and Teach Cormaic. Some scholars question whether Tara was ever actually occupied, proposing instead that it served just for meetings and ceremonies. But not only are there raths, there are traces of actual buildings. Our idea is that, at least after the establishment of a dynasty centered here, a maintenance staff lived permanently on the hill, while aristocrats and their retainers came for short periods during the year.

Mound of the Kings: Today called the Mound of the Hostages, because of a story that a dormitory for hostages stood upon it. This is impossible; it is far too small. Another story says that hostages who died while in captivity were buried here; but excavation has turned only a few post-Neolithic skeletons. Undeniably, this mound had some kind of sacredness from of old. Archaeology has revealed that it consists of earth heaped over a megalithic passage grave. Our guess is that this led to a reverence for it which grew over the years, until it was the site chosen for consecrating new kings at Tara.

Phallus: The Lia Fáil, Stone of Destiny. It stands on the Teach Cormaic, but was moved there in the eighteenth century; earlier, it seems to have been on or near the Mound of the Hostages. The name "Phallus of Fergus" was local in recent times, and probably well founded. Certainly this upright pillar could not have been a stone on which kings stood at their consecrations, as they did throughout early Ireland. The legend that it roared upon contact with a true king is ancient; we have borrowed a modern idea that in fact somebody swung a bullroarer. The "coronation" stone on top of the mound is our own notion; nothing of the kind is there now.

Rath of the Warriors: Today called Rath of the Synods. More guesswork on our part: if kings stayed on Tara for any length of time at all, their military retinues would have needed some shelter, and this earthwork could have enclosed their barracks.

Dall and Dercha: The names of these two small burial mounds may or may not go back to our period.

Druid (actually the plural, *drui* being the original singular): Unlike their Continental (and probably British) counterparts before the Romans, Irish druids were not priests. Rather, they were repositories of knowledge, tradition, and wisdom, who had undergone a long and arduous education. Some were female; women had a high standing in this society. Druids served as teachers and counselors. In the earliest times they were also poets, judges, physicians, etc., but these gradually became separate specialists. They were believed to have powers of divination and magic. We might note that they did not collect mistletoe—a plant introduced into Ireland much later—nor pay any special regard to the oak; the trees that the Irish considered powerful were the hazel, yew, and rowan.

Ogamm (later *Ogham*): A primitive alphabet, its signs consisting of strokes and dots along a central line. It seems to have been used almost entirely for memorial and magical inscriptions.

The Mórrigu (or *Morrigan*): The goddess of war. She seems to have had three aspects or avatars with different names. It has been suggested more than once that Morgan le Fay of Arthurian legend is a later version of her.

Taking valor: Ancient Irish of the warrior classes often put their sons through a ceremony of "knighthood" as early as the age of seven.

Poets: A top-ranking poet (*fili*) was an awesome figure; in some respects, he was more powerful than any king. Like a druid, he had survived a relentless course of training and commanded incredible linguistic and mnemonic skills. His words could make or break a reputation; if he was angered and composed a satire, its effects were believed to be physically destructive. Probably the worst crime in old Ireland was to offer violence to a poet, druid, or other learned person. There was a lower class of versifiers, whom we may as well call bards, but they, although respected, were essentially just entertainers.

Senchaide (or *shanachie*): Today, simply a storyteller, albeit often a delightful one. Very few remain active. In ancient times he was historian and genealogist to a basically illiterate society; he carried the annals of the country in his head.

The Feasting Hall: More guesswork on our part. What is now called the Banquet Hall (Teach Miodhchuarta) is the remnant of a great oblong earthwork, of approximately the dimensions that old stories ascribe to the hall where the Kings of Tara held their feasts. Some modern scholars think this was merely an open-air meeting site—but then why the ramparts? Others say the banks were formerly higher, which they doubtless were, and roofed over—but then why no traces of wood, when these have been identified elsewhere on Tara? Now it is attested in later history that the Irish could and did raise quite impressive temporary buildings, e.g., on one occasion to receive the King of England. Therefore we suggest that anciently they would erect such a hall within the elongated rath, demolishing and rebuilding it every three years for the triennial fair.

The feast: Unlike many peoples, the Irish generally took their principal meal of the day in the evening.

The cookhouse: Because of the fire hazard, cooking was usually done in a separate structure.

Battle-scarred women: Celtic women not uncommonly fought side by side with their men.

Laidchenn's verse: The syllabic prosody and interknit alliterations attempt to suggest one of the numerous early Irish poetic forms. Laidchenn himself figures in the sagas.

Lúg: A primary god of all the Celts, remembered in place names as far off as the south of France (Lyons, which was known to the Romans as Lugdunum).

Magimedon: A nickname meaning "servant (or slave) of Medon," who was presumably a god. Another interpretation is "master of slaves."

Carenn (or *Cairinn*): Laidchenn is relating the legends about Niall's early life that have come down to us today. It is not implausible that these would have cropped up almost at once; examples of the same thing are everywhere around in our own era, usually less close to the facts than tales of him may have been. We have modified them only slightly, in order to rationalize the chronology. Our assumption is that listeners, including Niall himself, accepted even the most fantastic parts as being metaphorically if not always literally true; moreover, there could well have been a considerable amount of selective recall and actual self-hypnosis, phenomena which are also common enough today. As for his mother, the medieval account calls her a Saxon princess, but this is most unlikely. On the other hand, if we take her name to be an Irish rendition of "Carina," she could have been Romano-British—perhaps the daughter of some tribal chieftain, or even a princess.

Succession of kings: Kingship, whether over a tuath or a larger polity, was inherent in a particular family: that is, a particular line of descent on the male side. Otherwise it was elective, and illegitimacy was no barrier.

Marrying the land: Well into Christian times, Irish kings at their inaugurations went through a ceremony of "marrying the tuath" or "the realm." This was purely symbolic; but the earlier pagans doubtless enacted it literally, choosing some maiden to embody the goddess, with whom the new king spent a night. The patron deity of the Tara line, and so presumably of Mide, was Medb. Thus legend says that Niall coupled with her, despite her disguise; and whether or not he believed this happened in fact, he did with her mortal representative.

Dál Riata (or *Dalriada*): A kingdom of eastern Ulster which founded a colony of the same name in Argyll, the first important settlement of Scots in what was to become Scotland. The date of the founding is quite uncertain. Since the colony enters into the traditional story, we perforce assume that it was already in existence by Niall's time. This is debatable but not impossible.

Gess (later *geas*; plural *Gessa*): A kind of taboo; a prohibition laid upon an individual or a class. It might be traditional or might be imposed by one person on another. Sometimes the gessa look very strange. For example, another of those on the King of Tara was that he must never travel widdershins around North Leinster; and the hero Finn mac Cumail (Old Irish form) was forbidden to sleep more than nine nights running at Allen. To break a gess was thought to bring disaster, and would certainly be disgraceful unless one was forced to it by trickery or circumstance, as various legendary figures were.

III

Burdigala: Bordeaux.

(Gallia) Narbonensis: A Roman province incorporating part of southwestern France.

Wine: This was produced in southern Britain under the Romans, and well into medieval times, after which the climate became too severe. With conditions now again milder, some is once more being made.

Fish and Chi Rho: These ancient Christian symbols were still in common use, whereas the crucifix was not yet so, and the cross not often.

Villa: To the Romans, this word meant a farm, not a house—especially a farm of some size.

Solidus: A gold coin, one of the few that had not been debased, therefore valuable and hard to come by.

Saddles: It is not certain whether the Mediterranean civilizations had yet adopted the Asian invention of stirrups; but improved saddles were already making cavalry more important than it had ever been before.

Cataphracts: Heavy-armored cavalrymen. Such a corps may have been the historical original of Arthur's knights, half a century or so after our story closes.

Ard: A primitive plow, wheelless, and possessing merely a pointed end. The moldboard plow appears to have been a Celtic invention, not much employed by the Romans except in areas where heavy soil gave it the advantage. Since no effective horse collar existed, an ox was the usual draft animal.

Curials: The curials, also called decurions, were those men of a city and its hinterland who had a certain amount of property. That is, they corresponded more or less to the middle class of modern Western civilization. They were expected to be active in local government and to meet various public expenses out of their own coffers. The caste system imposed by Diocletian froze them into this station, while the decay of the economy and the inordinate taxes of the state gradually ruined them.

Londinium: London. Its official Roman name, Augusta, was falling out of use.

Senators: In the late Empire, senatorial rank was conferred as often as it was inherited, carried privileges and exemptions rather than obligations, and was frequently attained by corrupt means.

Theater: Despite the generally moralistic atmosphere of the late Empire, performances—supposedly of classic stories—were apt to be as raw as anything on our contemporary screens.

Navicularius: A shipowner. Such persons were tightly organized into a guild. Theoretically they were born to their status and could not get out of it, but in practice there must have been exceptions.

1132

Dubris: Dover. Rutupiae (Richborough) had supplanted it as a major military base, but being a fort of the Saxon Shore it must have kept a garrison, and it was still an active seaport.

Navigation: The ancient mariners generally avoided sailing in autumn and winter less for fear of storms than because weather was too likely to hide the landmarks and heavens by which they found their way.

(Gallia) Lugdunensis: A Roman province incorporating much of northern and part of central France.

Wives: In contrast to the practice of earlier times, soldiers of the later Empire were allowed to marry during their terms of service. Doubtless this was meant as an inducement to enlist, for conscription was seldom resorted to anymore, and when it was oftenest out of subject peoples. Wives and children lived near the base, husbands joining them when off duty.

Gesocribate: It is not certain whether this town developed into the modern Brest, or was simply near the site of the latter.

Count (Latin *comes*): An official in charge of the defenses of a particular area. Best known to English-speaking moderns is the Count of the Saxon Shore, who governed the fortresses along the southeastern coast of Britain.

Foederate (Latin *civitas foederata*): A nation allied with or satellite to Rome. The word was also used for troops recruited from such peoples.

Gratillonius and his men: The army of the late Empire was organized differently in some respects from that of the Republic or Principate. Eight men of a legion formed a *contubernium*, sharing a tent and pack horse; in barracks they also shared two rooms, one for equipment and one for sleeping. Ten such parties made up the usual century (*centuria*), commanded by a centurion: thus numbering 80 rather than the original 100. Six centuries were grouped in three pairs (*maniples*) to form a cohort, and ten cohorts comprised a legion. The first cohort was larger than the rest, being made up five double centuries, because it included all the technicians and clerks of headquarters. Hence the legion contained about 5300 infantrymen. In addition there were 120 horsemen—orderlies, scouts, and dispatch carriers rather than cavalry—distributed among the various centuries; there were also higher officers and their staffs, specialists, etc. Altogether a legion was from about 5500 to 6000 strong. As political, economic, and military conditions worsened, the actual total often became less.

The backbone of the legion was its centurions, most of whom had risen from the ranks. The senior centurions (primi ordines) were in the first cohort, whose first century was commanded by the chief centurion (primus pilus), a trusted and honored veteran who, after a year, might go on to become camp prefect (praefectus

1133

castrorum), in charge of the legion's internal organization and operations—or might take some equally responsible post, if he did not simply retire on his savings and a large gratuity given him.

Originally the commandant of the legion was the legate (legatus), who was a political appointee of senatorial rank, although he was expected to have served before as a military tribune—staff officer—and so to have learned generalship. Since the reign of Gallienus, the camp prefect had supplanted him. There is no need here to describe other functionaries.

Many legions had existed for hundreds of years, and some had been based at their sites for almost as long. Strangely enough, considering the vital function of the centurions, they were quite commonly assigned and reassigned to different legions, sometimes across the width of the Empire. Probably the government did not want too close bonds of mutual personal loyalty between such career officers and the enlisted men. Gratillonius had not held the rank sufficiently long for this to have happened to him, but likely it would have if Maximus had not entrusted him with a mission that brought him to an unforeseen fate.

Or perhaps it would not have happened. What we have just been describing no longer existed in the eastern part of the Empire. There infantry was largely made up of limitanei, reservists who were called on to fight only in the areas where they lived, while the core of the armed forces was the cavalry, composed mostly of Germanic mercenaries. By the end of the fourth century, the strength of a legion was no more than 1500 men, set to garrison and other minor duty.

However, though these transformations were also taking place in the West, the were much slower, and quite likely had scarcely begun in Britain or northwestern Gaul. For one thing, there the principal menaces to Rome—Saxons, Franks, Alemanni, etc.—were not yet horsemen. Military reforms like those enacted at Constantinople were indeed imperative, but the enfeebled government of the West was incapable of doing anything quickly or efficiently. Thus a soldier such as Gratillonius could have begun his service in a unit in a legion not very different from, say, one of Marcus Aurelius's—aside from the large number of auxiliary troops—and ended it in an army not vastly different from, say, William the Conqueror's.

IV

Sails: Roman transport ships did not use oars, except for steering. Warcraft generally did, making sails the auxiliary power. It is worth remarking that the rowers were free men, and rather well paid. Galley slaves did not appear until the Middle Ages.

Pharos: Lighthouse. The beacon was a fire on its top after dark; by day, the tower was a landmark helpful to navigators. The Dover pharos, of which a part still exists, was about 80 feet high.

Dobunni: A tribe occupying, approximately, Gloucestershire, Herefordshire, and some adjacent areas.

Deputy: Second in command of a century, chosen by the centurion himself, hence the Latin name *optio*.

Regnenses: A tribe in Sussex.

Demetae: A tribe in the western part of southern Wales.

Coritani: A tribe occupying, approximately, Lincolnshire and adjacent territories.

Navy: The *classis Britannica* that guarded the coasts around the Channel and the North Sea approaches disappears from history about the middle of the third century. Its former base at Dover, abandoned even earlier, was converted to a fort of the Saxon Shore. However, Dover remained a seaport, and surely the military still needed some ships of their own.

Prefect of the cohort (praefectus cohortis): Commander of a unit of infantry auxiliaries. The word *"praefectus"* was used in a number of different contexts.

Lanterns: These, with panes of glass or thin-scraped horn, were known to the Romans. Some were quite elaborately made.

Hostel: (Latin *mansio*): Accommodations for person travelling on business of the state were maintained at rather frequent intervals along major routes. It seems reasonable to us that the one closest to a small city such as Gesoriacum would be outside rather than inside the walls, to save valuable building space and for the benefit of persons who arrived belatedly. On the other hand, there would probably have been at least one hostel near the center of any large and important city.

Candles: The Romans had both wax and tallow candles. The latter, at least, were considered much inferior to lamps, if only because of the smell, while the single material available for the former, beeswax, was too expensive for any but the richest people. Nevertheless tallow candles were much used, especially in areas where oil for lamps was scarce and thus costly.

Publican: The publicans of the Bible were not jolly taverners, as many moderns suppose, but tax farmers. Only Jesus, among decent people, could find it in his heart to associate with them. Their circumstances and practices changed as the Empire grew old, but not their spirit.

Tax in kind: This had become especially important as debasement made currency increasingly worthless. Diocletian and Constantine had reformed the coinage, but honest money remained scarce.

Couriers: The Roman postal service must still have been functioning reasonably well in most areas, since we have a considerable volume of correspondence among clergy and other learned men. Graffiti show that literacy was not confined to the upper classes, either. However, in regions as distressed as the northern Gallic littoral now was, the mails had surely deteriorated.

Massiiia: Marseilles.

(Civitas) Baiocassium: Bayeux.

Hoofs: Horseshoes had not yet been invented, but a kind of sandals or slippers were sometimes put on the animals when ground was bad.

Standard bearer: The *signifer* wore an animal skin of a sort traditional for his unit. In a small detachment like this, it would make sense to rotate the duty. The standard was not the legionary eagle but a banner.

Rations: Archaeology has revealed that the legions enjoyed a more varied diet, with more meat in it, than historians had thought.

Beans: Broadbeans (fava), the only kind known in Europe before the discovery of America.

Lent: As yet, the formula for calculating the date of Easter had not been finally settled upon, but varied from area to area and was the subject of much controversy. Nor was there agreement on how long a period of abstention should precede it, or on what austerities should be minimally required. For that matter, there was no standardized weekly practice of self-denial, such as the meatless Friday of later centuries. One may presume that even soldiers who were devout would not trouble themselves about that, at least while on duty. However, Easter, the holiest day in the Church calendar, and observances directly related to it, would be of concern. Strictly speaking, therefore, our use of the word "Lent" is anachronistic—but it conveys, in brief, approximately what Budic had in mind.

Sunday: The week as we know it had not yet been officially taken into the Roman calendar, though of course it was ancient in the East. One may well wonder how many ordinary soldiers were conscious of it, especially when in the field.

Nodens: A Celtic god, especially revered at the Severn mouth, in which flow great tidal bores.

Leagues: The Gallic *leuga* equalled 1.59 English or 1.68 Roman mile.

Rhenus: Rhine.

Caletes: A tribe in northeastern Gallia Lugdunensis, occupying approximately Seine-Maritime, Oise, and Somme.

Osismii: A tribe in the far west of Brittany, occupying approximately Finistère and part of Côtes-du-Nord. Place names and other clues seem to show they were not purely Celtic, nor were neighboring tribes. Rather, Celtic invaders probably imposed an aristocracy which interbred and became identified with the people. Meanwhile the language, too, became largely Celtic. The earlier race was not necessarily descended straight from the megalith builders; there could have been more than one set of newcomers over the centuries. Yet nothing appears to forbid our supposition that the Armoricans *believed* the "Old Folk" were among their ancestors. An analogous traditions exists in Ireland.

Honestiores: Great landholders, virtual feudal overlords.

Alani: An Iranian-Altaic people, originally living in what is now southern Russia. Under pressure from the Huns, the western branch of them mingled with the Germans and joined these in that great migration into Roman territory which was just getting well under way at the time of our story.

Ingena: Avranches. Today it is Norman rather than Breton, but of course neither of those peoples had yet reached France.

Vorgium (later *Osismii*): Carhaix. Folk etymology derives the present name from "Ker-Ahes" ("Strong-hold of Ahes," the latter name being given to Dahut in some versions of the Ys legend), but this is false.

Mauretania: Approximately, northern Morocco.

Condate Redonum: Rennes.

Veneti: A tribe in south Brittany, occupying approximately Morbihan.

Fanum Martis: Corseul. The tower is still there, in remarkably good condition.

Garomagus: There was a Roman town of some small importance—as we describe later—in the area of modern Douarnenez, but its name is not known. "Garomagus" is our conjecture, referring to its production of *garum*, a fish sauce which was a major item of Armorican trade.

Passage grave occupied by refugees: A case of this is known. There were probably more.

Ahriman: The supreme lord of evil in the Zoroastrian religion and its Mithraic offshoot, as Ahura-Mazda (or Ormazd) was the lord of good.

Franks in Condate Redonum: Those tribes lumped together as Franks (Latin *Franci*) originated in western Germany and the Netherlands. As yet they had not overrun Gaul, but some had entered and settled in various areas. The laeti at Rennes and their open paganism, including even human sacrifice, just at the time when Gratillonius passed through, are attested.

V

Sena: Île de Sein. Archeology shows it to have been occupied since prehistoric times, but we suppose that for several centuries it was reserved exclusively for the use of the Gallicenae—as the first-century geographer Pomponius Mela says was the case in his own period.

House: There are traces, now submerged, of what is believed to have been a Roman building at Île de Sein. Was this actually the sanctuary of its priestesses, remodeled under Roman influence?

Stones: These two megaliths are still on the island.

Cernunnos: A major Celtic god, represented as a man with stag's antlers.

Yes, yea, aye: You may have noticed that hitherto no person in the story has used any of these words. This is because Latin and the Celtic languages have no exact equivalent. We suppose that Semitic influence on the evolution of the Ysan tongue, otherwise basically Celtic, produced such words in it, just as the Germanic example would cause the Romance languages to develop them. Latin and Celtic do not employ a simple "No" either when giving a negative response. However, we have supplied it in rendering the former, in order that that may seem colloquial to the modern reader, and have also provided Ysan with it.

VI

Astrology: Belief in this prevailed throughout the late Roman Empire, along with countless other superstitions. Since it appears to have been part of the Mithraic faith, Gratillonius was heterodox in his reservations about it.

Book: The codex may go back as far as the first century. Toward the end of the fourth it had displaced the scroll except for legal and other special purposes. Elaborate illumination of the medieval sort was not yet done, but illustration of a simpler kind was, and it seems quite likely that the binding of some religious manuscripts was ornate and costly.

Twenty miles: Roman miles, of course.

Gobaean Promontory (Promontorium Gobaeum): The Cap Sizun area.

AVC: Anno Urbis Conditae ("V" was habitually used for "U" in inscriptions), year after the founding of Rome, for which the traditional date corresponded to 753 B.C. The Romans themselves rarely counted time from this baseline, but the reference was not unknown.

SPQR: Senatus Populusque Romanus: "The Roman Senate and People," proud motto of the Republic, long borne on standards of the legions.

Fortress and maritime station: The remnant of the fortress can still be seen on Pointe de Castelmeur. There must have been more of it extant in Gratillonius's day. The station is rather conjectural.

Key: By Roman times, locks had developed into bolt-and-pin types not too unlike modern sorts. Their keys had corresponding prongs. When a key was inserted, these prongs pushed up the pins, where upon a sidewise pull drew back the bolt.

VII

Fresh-made laurel wreath: The laurel is an evergreen.

Cape Rach: Pointe du Raz (hypothetical reconstruction of the aboriginal name). The *ch* is supposed to be as in modern Scottish or German.

Refusing the crown: While today our knowledge of Mithraism is scanty, this detail is attested.

VIII

Point Vanis: Pointe du Van (hypothetical reconstruction of the aboriginal name).

Billon: Debased coin metal used by the late Empire. It took more than 14,000 nummi to equal one gold solidus. Archeology shows that Gresham's Law was as operative in Roman times as it is now.

Thule: It is not certain what the Classical geographers meant by this name. Iceland and Norway are among the more common suggestions. We incline toward the latter.

The sea gate of Ys: Today one would solve the problem of protecting a harbor from overwhelming tides by constructing locks. These, however, were not developed until much later.

Saxon (Saxones): This name did not distinguish any single tribe or kingdom. Rather, it was a general term used by the Romans for all those robbers and invaders who came across the North Sea from the northern Netherlands, the German littoral, Jutland, and possibly regions still more distant.

IX

Soap: This appears to have been a Gallic invention, regarded by the Romans more often as a medicinal for the skin than as a cleansing agent.

Basilica: In this period and earlier, the word referred to a building for public business—administration, trials at law, etc.

The layout of the church: Private homes were frequently converted for this purpose, but it is clear that no one in Ys who might be willing to make such a donation possessed a suitable one; so, as happened elsewhere (for example, to the Parthenon), this pagan temple was expropriated by Imperial decree. Normally there would be a baptistry, but in Ys there was no resident bishop, and a chorepiscopus had no authority to administer this sacrament—which was not usually given children anyway. *Vide infra.* Believers who had not received it could enter no farther than the porch or vestibule, and were dismissed before the Communion service began in the sanctuary. Even in the great churches, furniture was basically the same as described here. Such amenities as pews were for a later era.

Redonic: Of the tribe of the Redones, around Rennes.

Audiarna: Audierne, on the River Goyen, some nine English miles east of the Baie des Trépassés. There are traces of Roman occupation. Our Latin name is conjectural, and we assume the name of St. Audierne comes from the town rather than vice versa.

Consecrated bread and wine: At this period, only a bishop could consecrate the bread and wine for the Eucharist, or perform several other important functions. This consecration was generally of large quantities at a time, which were then distributed among churches. Eucherius would seldom have to restock. Not only was his congregation tiny, but the majority of it were unbaptized, having only the status of catechumens and therefore unqualified to partake of the Lord's Supper. Baptism was a rite regarded with great awe. It must be done by a bishop or, at least under the supervision of one; as a rule, this was just once or twice a year, notably at Easter. Most believers received it comparatively late in life, not uncommonly when on their deathbeds—as in the case of Constantine I. After all, it washed away prior sins, but was of no avail against any that might be committed afterward, which indeed would then be the deadlier.

Eucherius's heresy: It anticipated that of Pelagius, in some small degree; such ideas were in the air.

The appointment of Eucherius: At this time the Church organization that we know today, including the Papacy itself, was still nascent. Originally each congregation had had its own bishop, the priests and deacons being merely his councillors and assistants, but eventually the numbers of the faithful were such as to require something more elaborate, which naturally came to be modeled on the Roman state. The process was under way in the decades around 400 A.D., but as yet there was a great deal of local variation, arbitrariness, and outright irregularity. For example, St. Patrick may well have consecrated himself a bishop. The chorepiscopus served most of the functions later assigned the parish priest, but by no means all of them.

Neapolis: Naples.

(Gallia) Aquitania: A Roman province occupying, approximately, the part of France south of the Loire, west of the Allier, and north of the Pyrenees.

Tamesis: The Thames.

The Hooded Three: The *genii cucullati*, a trio of gods (?) in Britain about which we have little more information than some representations and votive inscriptions.

Handclasp: The handshake as we know it seems to be of Germanic origin, but might have appeared independently in Ys, or been observed by travelers and become a custom at home.

Niall and the women: In sleeping with women of various households, the King was not exerting any special prerogative nor giving any offense. Early Irish society gave a great deal of freedom to women other than slaves, including the right to choose which of several different forms of marriage or cohabitation they wanted. Wives often took lovers, with their husbands' knowledge and consent.

Mag Slecht: In present-day County Cavan. Cromb Cróche (later Crom Cruach) and the twelve attendant divinities were probably pillar stones, sheathed in gold and bronze. There will be more about them later.

Ruirthech: The Liffey.

Clón Tarui: Now Clontarf, a district of Dublin on the north shore of the bay. It became the site of a famous battle in the year 1016.

Public hostel: There were several classes of these in early Ireland, endowed by kings or communities with enough land to support the provision of free food and to all travellers. Such hospitality was required to maintain honor; and, to be sure, it encouraged trade. The innkeepers were usually men, but sometimes women.

Border of the Lagini: The River Liffey does *not* mark the border of modern-day Leinster. It did, though, come to form one frontier of lands subject to the southern Uí Néill. Given the enormous uncertainties about conditions at the time of their great ancestor, we think it reasonable to suppose that Mide extended this far. After all, Niall could scarcely have ravaged Britain as repeatedly and thoroughly as the chronicles say, did he not have at least one port of embarkation on the east coast of Ireland.

Bóru tribute: About this, more later. Imposed of old by Connaught on Leinster, it came to be claimed by the Tara kings, but more often than not they had to collect it by force, and oftener still it went unpaid. In large part this was because it was exorbitant (though one need not take literally the traditional list of cattle and other treasure). King Brian, eleventh-century victor at Clontarf, got the nickname Bóruma—now usually rendered as Boru—because he did succeed in exacting it.

Smoke: Modern experiments have shown that primitive Celtic houses could not have had vent holes as more elaborate halls did. Instead, smoke simply filtered out through the conical thatch roofs, killing vermin on the way.

Horseblanket: The ancient Irish seem to have used merely a pad when riding. It is not certain whether they had saddles by the time of our story, but if they did, the use of these could not have been common.

X

Greenish light: Even the best Roman window glass had such a tinge.

Diocese: A division of the Empire. In our period there were fifteen, of which Britain constituted one. Each was governed by a vicarius, who was responsible to a praetorian prefect. The praetorian prefect of Gaul, residing in Trier, also administered Britain and Iberia. A diocese was subdivided into provinces, whose governors, called praesides, had civil but not military authority.

Triclinium: The dining room in a Roman house. However, the basic layout of an Ysan home was different from that of a typical Roman one.

XI

Ishtar: The recorded Carthaginian form of this name is "Ashtoreth" or something similar, but we assume "Ishtar" was the older version; and Babylonian immigrants to Ys would have reinforced its use.

Sea level: This has varied considerably in historical time, presumably because of melting and refreezing of polar ice as climate passes through cycles of warmth and cold. In the late fourth century it was at, or not long past a peak. Western Brittany, where the tidefall is always great, would be especially affected—above all in small bays with steeply shelving bottoms between sheer headlands.

XII

Lutetia Parisiorum: Paris.

Draughts: Board games of various sorts were popular in antiquity, though none seem to have been identical with any played nowadays. However, versions of what we now call draughts or checkers go back to Pharaonic Egypt.

XIII

Noble landowners: A *flaith* was a man who actually owned land, normally by right of inheritance although subject to the claims of his kindred and tuath. He rented out most of it to others, for payment in kind and in services.

Beltene (also spelled *Beltane, Beltine,* etc.): In the modern calendar, 1 May. In pagan times the date may have been set according to the moon, but would have fallen approximately the same. Most lunar calendars count from the new moon, which is the phase most readily identifiable, but we assume that the northern Celts, at least, wanted a full moon at their great festivals, to help light ceremonies held after dark. They could have added fourteen or fifteen days to the time when they observed the new one—or they may simply have taken advantage of the fact that the full one is less often completely lost to sight in the wet climate of their homelands. Second only to Samain in importance, Beltene carried with it many beliefs and customs which survived, somewhat Christianized, almost until the present day. We have extrapolated backward in order to suggest what various features may originally have been like.

Marriage: In ancient Ireland this had several different forms. Among them was not only the usual arrangement negotiated by parents with an eye to advantageous alliance between families, but unions for a limited span, freely entered into by the individuals concerned. While women did not have all the rights of men, on the whole they enjoyed—if freeborn—more liberty than their sex would again, in most of the world, until the twentieth century.

Needfire: Before the invention of matches, kindling a fire was a laborious and oftimes precarious task, therefore a serious matter. If a hearthfire went out, it was generally easiest to borrow coals from a neighbor to restart it. Deliberately extinguishing it, in order to begin quite afresh, was an act fraught with religious and magical significance.

Rath of Gráinne and Sloping Trenches: These are present-day names of ruined works on Tara which were probably burial rather than dwelling sites. People in Niall's day may already have been telling much the same stories about them that we now hear.

Síd (later *sidhe*): "Fairy mounds" or, in general, underground habitations of supernatural beings, to whom the same word is applied as a name. They appear to have been originally megalithic tombs, although later they included natural hills. When Christianity had prevailed in Ireland, the síd folk became largely identified with the Tuatha Dé Danaan, tribes possessing magical powers who had retreated into these fastnesses after suffering defeat in war, but still came forth on occasion for good or ill. It is clear that those were, mainly, the old gods themselves, slightly disguised. To the pagan Irish, the síd folk were presumably ghosts and other such night-wanderers.

Conaire: The story of this king and his death at the destruction of Dá Derga's hostel appears to be so ancient that it was already a myth among the Irish of Niall's time.

Samain (today usually spelled *Samhain*): In the modern calendar, 1 November. It was the most important and awesome of the Celtic festivals. Many beliefs and practices associated with it continued through the Christian era virtually to the present day.

Diarmait (later *Diarmuid*) and *Gráinne*: A legendary pair of lovers, with whom folklore associates the Rath of Gráinne.

Liger: The Loire.

XIV

Bare marble: The classical Greeks generally painted their statues and buildings. The Romans did likewise for sculpture, but as for buildings, at least in the later part of their history, they were more apt to make the stone itself the decoration, frequently as a facing on a concrete structure.

Portus Namnetum: Nantes. Condovincum, uphill, was later incorporated.

Shield grip: Celtic and Nordic shields were not held by loops for the arm but simply grasped by a handle. The Romans added a shoulder strap.

Breccan maqq Nélli: Breccan son of Niall, "Nélli" being the genitive.

Tír innan Oac: The Land of Youth, one of several paradises which Celtic mythology located afar in the western ocean.

1143

Milesians: In Irish legend, the last wave of invaders (prior to the vikings). A number of tuaths, especially in Connaught, claimed descent from them, and looked down on "Firbolg" who could not.

Following the wind: It is not clear whether Germanic galleys and Irish currachs (or "curraghs" or "coracles") could tack at all. Roman square-riggers could get no closer than seven points off the wind, and had the advantage of comparatively deep draught, in that era when the keel was not yet designed to help. Sprit-riggers did better. As for currachs, Tim Severin put leeboards on his *Brendan* but admits this may be an anachronism, since there is no evidence for them until well into the Middle Ages. We therefore suppose that they did not exist in our period. Under sail, doing anything but running straight downwind, crews would have used their oars for lateral resistance to keep on a broad reach, which was probably the best they could achieve; without a wind from astern, they struck their sails and rowed. It must have been likewise for Germanic galleys. Certain archaeologists doubt that those even had sails until just before the viking era, but we think that at least some had primitive rigs in imitation of the Romans.

Christian Scoti: It appears that there was a significant Christian community in Munster, if not in the rest of Ireland, well before St. Patrick.

Wolf: We know that the bad reputation of this animal is undeserved. However, until recent times most people dreaded and hated it, and there is reason to believe that wolves did occasionally attack humans—especially in hard winters when they could get no other food—as well as raid livestock. Firearms have changed that; the wolf is quite able to learn a lesson and teach its young.

XV

Maze: Intricate sets of paths had been laid out in northern as well as southern Europe since neolithic times, probably for religious or magical use.

XVI

Funeral societies: A Roman legionary was expected to belong to a military funeral association, the dues of which were stopped from his pay. When he died it gave him a proper burial.

Sena: Implicit are various topographical differences from today's Île de Sein. It is most unlikely that so low and small an island, constantly battered by waves which storms sometimes dash clear across, would remain for centuries unchanged.

XVII

Mithraism: Little is known today about the doctrines of this religion. We present those which are reasonably well attested. Their parallels to Christianity were remarked upon at the time, in writings which survive, and are presumably due to common origins of the ideas in question. As for the rites, there is virtually no record, aside from some propagandistic Christian references. Out of these we have taken what looks plausible, and added thereto a good deal of conjecture.

XVIII

Planets: In classical astrology and astronomy, the sun and the moon counted as planets, making—with Mercury, Venus, Mars, Jupiter, and Saturn—seven in all.

Carthaginian abhorrence: It is not certain what the actual attitude of the Carthaginians was toward homosexuality. The Mosaic prohibition suggests that they may have tried to ban it like their fellow Semites the Jews, if only as part of a general reaction against the Graeco-Roman world, but this is perhaps a mistaken idea. However, in any case Ysans who did disapprove—conceivably as a legacy from the Celtic side of their descent—would naturally attribute the same feeling to the founders of their city. As for contemporary Romans, although bisexuality among men, especially in the form of pederasty, had been widespread in the late Republic and the Principate, under the Dominate Christian influence and a generally puritanical mind-set eventually drove it underground.

XIX

"Tene, Mithra," etc.: The line is adapted from Kipling's poem "A Song to Mithras"—"Mithras, also a soldier, keep us true to our vows!"

XX

Theater: Where there was a curtain in a Classical theater, it was generally deployed from below rather than above, since the building was roofless. The Ysan theater is unique in several respects, perhaps most notably in allowing women—preferably respectable women—to perform. Among the Greeks and Romans, they only did so in pornographic shows; otherwise female roles were played by boys.

Feast of Lúg: Known to the Irish of recent times as Lugnasad, it is now fixed at 1 August, although we are again assuming that originally the date varied. We also suppose that the Continental Celts pronounced the name differently from their insular cousins.

XXI

C. Valerius Gratillonius: The name "Gaius" was abbreviated "C.," a relic of times before the Roman alphabet possessed a letter "G."

XXII

Guilt and expiation: Some modern Christian apologists have maintained disapprovingly, and some neo-pagans have maintained approvingly, that the ancients had little or no concept of sin, few sexual inhibitions, etc. This is utter nonsense, as even a superficial study of their writings, onward from the oldest Mesopotamian and Egyptian texts, will show. For that matter, anthropologists have found that the concept of any noble savages living anywhere in happy innocence and harmony with nature is equally ludicrous.

Dahilis forbidden to Gratillonius: Present-day medical doctrine allows sexual intercourse, if there are no complications, practically to the end of pregnancy; but this is a very recent idea, as your authors can attest with some ruefulness. In most societies, abstinence has been urged or commanded for expectant mothers during the last several weeks or months. Given the limited capabilities of physicians and rudimentary knowledge of sanitation in the ancient world, this was probably wise then.

Falernian wine: Renowned in Roman times, it came from an area within Campania, which was a region including modern Capua and Naples. Today's Campania, in turn, includes ancient Campania in a larger territory.

XXIII

Black Months: The Breton expression for this time of year may well have ancient origins.

Dál Riata: A kingdom in Ulster, or its colony of the same name, across the North Channel on the shore of what is now Scotland.

Mandrake: Beside its alleged magical properties, mandrake root was anciently used as an emetic, purgative, and narcotic. The *Encyclopaedia Britannica* (11th ed.) observes, "...it has fallen into well-earned disrepute."

Pellitory: Pyrethrum parthenium, Shakespeare's "feverfew," related to the chrysanthemum.

Money in circulation: The economic depression in the Roman Empire, with more and more trade being in kind, inevitably affected other states. Coins, especially those least debased, tended to accumulate in hoards such as later ages have unearthed. However, a society whose institutions were still basically sound would respond to any stimulus given its businesses.

Opium: This was known to the ancients in the forms of extract from either the whole plant or the capsule, but apparently used only as an analgesic. The source being Asia Minor, where the opium poppy was native, supply to Western Europe must have cut off as trade declined.

XXV

Teeth cleansers: The Romans had versions of tooth-brushes and dentrifices.

Toys: If Gratillonius appears unsentimental about Innilis's miscarriage, one should remember that attitudes toward such things, and toward infants, were different then. Prior to modern medicine and sanitation, mortality was so high that parents dared not invest much love in a child until it was old enough to have a reasonable chance of living further.

Snow and ice: These are not especially common in Breton winters, which are oftener rainy, but do occur sometimes.

Caesar: The Caesarian section gets its name not because Julius was thus born—he wasn't—but because he re-established the old Royal Law that when a woman died in late pregnancy, a surgical attempt should be made to save her child. The first recorded operation on a living woman occurred in the sixteenth century, and until recent times the fatality rate was so high that it was a last-choice procedure. Nowadays, of course, it is almost routine.

Bay of Aquitania: Sinus Aquitanicus, the Bay of Biscay.

Wet nurse: For a newborn infant, it would naturally be preferable to have a woman who had herself given birth very recently.

The Birthday of Mithras: As we have stated before, this was fixed at 25 December—but in the Julian calendar, which was already out of step with astronomical time. Hence the date of the full moon following was earlier than a modern ephemeris for the fourth century, using the Gregorian calendar, indicates. Throughout the writing of this book, we have tried to be as accurate as possible about all verifiable details.

GALLICENAE

I

Chairs: In the ancient world these were usually reserved for persons of status. Ordinary folk sat on stools, benches, or the floor.

Augustus: At this time there was more than one Roman Emperor. The senior of two was titled "Augustus," his colleague and heir apparent "Caesar." Usually both the Western and Eastern parts of the Empire had such a double monarchy. (Occasionally a given Augustus had two or more Caesars, each responsible for a part of his domains.) Hence the name "Tetrarchy." Evidently Maximus's designation as Augustus amounted to recognition that the Empire had now split into three coequal realms, *de facto* if not quite *de jure*. St. Ambrose, bishop of Milan, had played a leading role in persuading him to settle for that, rather than trying to take over the entire West. In 387 he would break the agreement and invade Italy.

Augusta Treverorum: Trier (Trêves).

Early this year: Maximus made his terms with Valentinian and Theodosius late in 384 or early in 385; the date is uncertain, like the dates of many events in this era.

Africa: North Africa, exclusive of Egypt and Ethiopia.

Illyricum: A Roman diocese (major administrative division) occupying, approximately, most of the territory now comprising Yugoslavia and Greece.

Lugdunum: Lyons.

Burdigala: Bordeaux.

Sena: Île de Sein.

Sign of the Ram, etc: Precessing, the vernal equinox moved from Aries to Pisces about the time of Christ, and by the fourth century was well within the latter. To populations obsessed with astrology, this had an obscure but apocalyptic significance. It may in some degree have aided the initial spread of the Christian religion and (together with the ICHTHYS acronym) influenced the adoption of the fish as a symbol of Christ.

Gallia: Gaul.

Pagans in high Roman office: Symmachus is best known from this time, but there were numerous others, despite Christianity being now the state religion and attempts made to proscribe all the rest.

Empire: The Roman state still called itself a republic, but had of course long ceased to be any such thing. Nobody took the fiction seriously. So, to avoid confusing modern readers, we have our characters speak the word which was actually in their minds.

Italian Mediolanum: Milan. Several cities bore that name.

Ambrosius: Today known as St. Ambrose.

(Gallia) Lugdunensis: A province of Gaul, comprising most of what is now northern and a fair portion of central France.

(Gallia) Aquitania: A province of Gaul, bounded approximately by the Atlantic Ocean and the Garonne and Loire Rivers.

Osismii: A tribe occupying the western end of Britanny, hence the immediate neighbors of Ys.

Ahriman: The supreme lord of evil in the Mithraic religion.

II

Tuba: In the Roman world, this was a long, straight trumpet, used especially by the military for commanding, signalling, setting cadence, etc.

Pontus: A Roman diocese, comprising Anatolia.

Hispania: A Roman diocese, comprising what are now Spain and Portugal.

Caledonia: A loose term, referring more or less to what is now Scotland. Cf. the notes to *Roma Mater*.

Condate Redonum: Rennes.

Liger: The River Loire.

Juliomagus: Angers.

Namnetes: A tribe occupying the right bank of the Loire from the seashore to its confluence with the Mayenne.

Caesarodunum Turonum: Tours. At this time, those parts of city names that designated local tribes were increasingly displacing those parts the Romans had bestowed. Thus they often became the ancestors of the present-day names.

Laeti: Barbarians allowed to settle within the Empire on condition that they give it allegiance—a proviso observed only loosely, at best.

Jerkin: No such garment is attested until a much later date, but something of the kind must have been in use long before.

Gesoriacum: Boulogne.

Redones: A tribe occupying the area around Rennes.

Maedraeacum: Médréac, a village near which we once spent a pleasant week in a *gîte*. The reconstruction of the ancient name is entirely conjectural, as is the history. However, many such communities did originate as latifundia.

Last Day: Chiliasm was rampant in this era. About 380, St. Martin of Tours told a disciple that the Antichrist had been born. Countless people, high and low, educated and ignorant, were finding their own portents of the imminent end of the world. Like numerous other features of late West Roman society, this one looks rather familiar to an inhabitant of the late twentieth century.

Organization of the Bacaudae (also spelled *Bagaudae*): Little is recorded about this. A couple of chronicles mention an "emperor," though that word (Latin *imperator*) may simply have its original meaning of "commander." Since the Bacaudae persisted for a long time and occasionally won pitched battles, they must have had more structure than, say, the medieval Jacquerie. But we can scarcely compare them to modern guerrillas; they lacked both a formalized ideology and the assistance of powerful foreign states. Our guess is that, as more and more individuals fled from an oppressive civilization and then perforce turned about to prey on it, they necessarily and almost blindly developed primitive institutions and a moralistic rationalization of their actions.

Hand to arm: The Roman equivalent of the later handshake.

III

Martinus: Today know as St. Martin of Tours.

The appearance of St. Martin: At this time there were not yet any particular vestments or other distinguishing marks for the clergy. Indeed, most still earned their livelihoods in ordinary ways and preached in their spare time; many were married; some of the married, when the husband had been ordained, vowed sexual abstention, but not all did by any means. Likewise, tonsures for cenobites were neither standardized nor universal. The kind adopted by St. Martin, which he may have originated, became that of the Celtic Church, eventually superseded by the Roman form with which we today are more familiar. Martin's looks and traits are described by his disciple and biographer Sulpicius Severus.

Martin's elevation to bishop: This story, given us by Sulpicius, is not as incredible as it looks. Ecclesiastical procedures were often *ad hoc*, especially in the provinces, and there are well-attested cases of laymen being called to the episcopate and only then receiving baptism. A full bishop had so much secular importance that ordinary people sometimes demanded a voice in the choosing of him.

Pannonia: A Roman province occupying an area now shared by parts of Hungary, Austria, and Czechoslovakia. Its inhabitants at the time were largely, if not exclusively, Celtic.

Avela (or *Abula*): Ávila.

Ossanuba: Faro, Portugal.

Manicheanism: A religion which was, like Mithraism, of Iranian origin, but if anything more of a threat to Christianity, since it incorporated important elements of the latter. Throughout the centuries, under one name or another, it has been a recurrent heresy. Among other deviations, it attributes creative powers to Satan.

Gates of Trier: In Roman Imperial times there were four of these, of which the Porta Nigra survives as a ruin. Its name is medieval; originally it was not blackened by centuries of smoke.

Mosella: The River Moselle (or Mosel).

Rhenus: The River Rhine.

Bonna: Bonn.

Juthungi: A Germanic tribe living near Raetia.

Raetia (or *Rhaetia*): A Roman province covering, approximately, what is now Bavaria.

Basilica: Originally this word meant an administrative center, civil or military.

The fate of the Priscillianists: Much is uncertain about events surrounding this trial, the historical importance of which includes the fact that it is the first recorded persecution of Christians by other Christians. The dates and the very year are debatable. We have chosen the 385 favored by most scholars and assumed that, because so much had been going on before, the trial took place rather late in that year. Some accounts say the heretics were burned, but it seems likelier that they were beheaded; the stake did not come into vogue until the Middle Ages.

IV

Fortifications: Legionaries on campaign had normally dug a trench and erected an earthwork around every camp, then levelled these upon leaving to keep an enemy from taking them over. By the late fourth century this cannot have been a common practice, for the old-style legion was on the way out. We assume that it lasted later in Britain than elsewhere.

Lugdunum (or *Lugudunum*): Lyons. Several other cities bore this name.

Vienna: Vienne (Wien in Austria, Vienna to speakers of English, was then Vindobona.) Remnants of a Mithraeum, such as are not found in Lyons, suggested that the cult persisted there, though by the time of Gratillonius's visit it had been driven into a private home.

Rhodanus: The River Rhône.

Circus: A space with tiers of seats on three sides, divided lengthwise by a barrier, for races, games, and shows.

Asiatic: By "Asia" the Romans meant what we now call "Asia Minor" or "the Near East."

The Mithraeum in Vienne: As the model for this hypothetical last survivor, we have chosen some that have been excavated in Ostia.

Tauroctony: A depiction of Mithras slaying the primordial Bull.

Burdigala: Bordeaux.

Rhetoric: Occasionally one sees classical schools of rhetoric, such as the great one at Bordeaux, referred to as universities. This is anachronistic, but only mildly so. Rhetoric, the study of persuasive argument, embraced not just oratory, but languages, logic, history, literature, and much else. Thus a mastery of it amounted to a liberal education.

Garumna: The River Garonne.

Paulinus: Ausonius's grandson grew up into the kind of life that the old man envisioned, but it was shattered by the arrival of the Visigoths and other calamities.

Duranius: The River Dordogne.

V

Mumu: Munster. The boundaries were probably less definite than in later times. Its association with women, musicians, and magic was ancient, and persisted into the Middle Ages.

Ériu: Ireland.

Children of Danu: Best known by a later name, the Tuatha Dé Danaan. According to legend, this race, the tuaths (only approximately equivalent to tribes; see the notes to *Roma Mater*) descended from the goddess Danu, held Ireland before the Milesians arrived from Spain. Overcome by the invaders, they retreated to the *sid*, mounds and hills whose interiors they made their dwellings. They themselves became the fairy folk. Most modern commentators think they are a Christian euhemerization of the pagan gods, and doubtless there is much truth in this view. However, the tradition of a war between them and the newcomers is so basic to Irish mythology that it must have some foundation in fact. Successive Celtic peoples did enter, taking land by force of arms. Our guess is that one or more of the earlier peoples, to whom their conquerors attributed magical powers, became conflated with the old gods, but that this had not yet happened at the time of our story.

Children of Ír and Éber: Later called the Milesians; tradition makes them last invaders of Ireland before the Vikings.

The Mountain of Fair Women: Now Slievenamon, southwest of Cashel.

Síd (or sídh): Singular of *sídhe*. Both are pronounced, approximately, "shee."

Condacht: Connaught.

Qóiquet Lagini: Leinster.

Mide: A realm carved out of Connaught and Leinster, centered on Tara.

The Ulati: The people of Ulster (*Qóiqet nUlat*). It should be remembered that the boundaries of all these territories were vague, and generally not identical with those of the modern provinces.

Trade between Munster and Egypt: Potsherds up to the early Islamic period have been found.

Christianity: The histories indicate that there was already an established and growing body of Christians in Munster, if not elsewhere in Ireland. For one thing, Palladius was sent to minister to them; and other bishops are mentioned, together with Irish clergymen serving on the Continent—all before the mission of St. Patrick.

Conual Corcc (today usually rendered as *Conall Corc*): His dates are still more uncertain than Niall's, and the stories about him that have come down to us are even more confused and contradictory. In both cases, we have tried to put together versions that make some logical sense.

Fostering: Children in ancient Ireland, at least among the upper classes, more often that not were raised in other homes than their parents'. The ties thus created between families were as sacred as those of blood kinship.

Alba: The early Irish name for what is now, more or less, Scotland. Sometimes "Alba" also included England and Wales. The name "Scotland" comes from its heavy colonization by Scoti, i.e., people from Ireland—just as Armorica was to become Brittany (Breizh, in its own language) after immigrants from Britain took it over. At the time of our story, the Scotic settlement amounted largely to an extension, into what is now Argyll, of the kingdom of Dál Riata, in what is now northern Antrim. (Some authorities put its founding as late as 500 A.D., but the event would have become possible soon after the Romans abandoned the Antonine Wall toward the end of the second century, and a date in the middle fourth century is consistent with other assumptions we have made for story purposes.) However, a king from Mide, adventuring in Alba, could well have defeated a Pictish leader and imposed an alliance in which the latter was a junior partner.

The ogamm (today *ogham*) *shield*: This is evidently a Celtic form of an ancient and widespread story. Quite possibly the Vikings, in their day, brought it back to Denmark from Ireland. "Hamlet"—"Amleth(us)" in Saxo Grammaticus, Shakespeare's ultimate source—is not a name otherwise found; one scholar has suggested that it may be a Scandinavian reading of the Gaelic spelling of the Nordic "Olaf"! Ogham was a very primitive and limited form of writing, so to alter it would not have been difficult.

Ordovices and Silures: Tribes inhabiting what is now Wales.

VI

Éndae Qennsalach: Perhaps historical, perhaps not. The second half of his name refers to his ancestry.

Founding of Mide: This is the legendary version. See the notes to *Roma Mater*.

Origin of the Bóruma: This is also a legend, of course, but one which people of Niall's time may well have believed. The tribute itself and its evil consequences are historical fact.

Niall's warfare: The sources say nothing specific; but given our story assumptions, campaigns like these are plausible.

Ruirthech: The River Liffey. Then it seems to have marked the northern frontier of Leinster.

Chariots: Roman tactics had long since made the military chariot obsolete, but it persisted in Ireland, where it did not have to face well-drilled infantry and cavalry, until past our time. As for other equipment, see the notes to *Roma Mater*.

Niall's two Queens: Not only concubinage but polygyny was accepted in ancient Ireland, even after the conversion to Christianity. (For a while canon law decreed that a *priest* could have only one wife!) The chronicles say that Niall had fourteen sons by two wives, whom we suppose to have been more or less contemporaneous. Surely he had daughters too, and children by other women.

Nobles and tenants: For a brief description of the classes *flaith, soer-céli,* and *doer-céli*, see the notes to *Roma Mater*.

Combat tactics: Like the equipment, these too were little changed in Ireland from the old Celtic forms.

Lifting a knee: Stools and tables were very low. To rise when a visitor appeared was a token of full respect. Short of this, though still polite, was to raise a knee, as if about to get up.

Verse: Like Nordic skalds of a later date, early Irish poets used intricate forms, yet were expected to be able to compose within those forms on a moment's notice. Our rendition here is a much simplified version of one scheme. Each stanza, expressing a complete thought, consists of four seven-syllabled lines. Besides the alliteration and rhyme, it is required that end-words of the second and fourth lines have one more syllable than those of the first and third. Oral skill such as this is entirely possible and historically attested. The poet naturally had to have an innate gift together with long and arduous training.

Satire: The Celtic peoples were great believers in word magic. Well into Christian times, satirists were dreaded in Ireland. To a modern mind, it is not implausible that they could bring on psychosomatic disorders, even wasting illness. Our story supposes their powers went beyond that.

VII

Odita: The River Odet. (Our Latin name is conjectural.) The distances mentioned have been rounded off, as they would be in the mind of any ordinary traveler. It should be noted that this stream was deeper then than it is now, when impoundments in the watershed have diminished its sources.

Stegir: The River Steir. (This is also conjectural on our part.)

Aquilo: Locmaria, now a district at the south end of Quimper. While the existence of Roman Aquilo is attested, our history and description of it are still more conjecture.

Mons Ferruginus: Mont Frugy. More conjecture, this time based on the fact that there is iron ore in the area.

Durocotorum: Rheims.

Apuleius Vero: The ancient tripartite system of nomenclature had long since broken down. Some people still employed it, but others, in the upper classes, did not. "Vero" is a hypothetical Gallo-Roman name commemorating the family's most important connection of that kind. "Apuleius," the old *gens* name, now went from father to eldest son, much as the same given and middle names may pass through several generations in our own era. Upon succeeding to the paternal estate, this Apuleius dropped whatever other names he had borne, if any. In this as in several more significant respects, he typifies a man of his time, place, and station in life. More provincial and thus more conservative, the Gratillonii of Britain clung to traditional usages.

The Duke of the Armorican Tract: The Roman military official in charge of defense of the entire area. (This is a shortened version of the actual title, such as we suppose people employed in everyday speech.) Armorica was, in fact, considered a military district, not a political entity. Ravages along the coats indicate that at this time the Duke's efforts were concentrated in the east and the interior of the peninsula.

This was doubtless because resources were limited and, terrible though the depredations of pirates often were, they seemed less of a threat than a possible Germanic invasion overland. Gaul had already suffered the latter, again and again, and sometimes the Romans had managed only barely and slowly to drive the barbarians back. Under such circumstances, the Duke might be glad to delegate authority in the west to some competent leader. Our idea that this particular Duke was covertly opposed to Maximus is a guess—nothing is known for certain—but not unreasonable.

Troops: Increasingly, locally recruited soldiers were providing garrisons such as here described. Not being attached to any legion, they were known as *numeri* or *cunei* rather than auxiliaries. Civilian men, *limitanei*, were being made into reservists. These processes had gone much further in the Eastern half of the Empire than they had, as yet, in the West.

The Pulcher villa: Baths, such as would have belonged to a substantial estate, have been excavated at Poulker (near Benodet). The form of this place name is unusual in Brittany. However, we only venture a guess as to its possible origin.

The defenses of Aquilo: Our idea of what these may have amounted to is based on the lack of archeological evidence for anything else. Actually, the Gallic wall was a good, solid structure.

Corentinus: Known in France at the present day as St. Corentin. His historicity is uncertain, but there are many legends about him, including that of the miracle of the fish and his later career as the first bishop of Quimper. For reasons discussed in the Afterword to the last of these volumes, we have conflated him with the equally enigmatic figure of St. Guénolé.

Smoke: As we remarked in the notes to *Roma Mater*, primitive Celtic dwellings neither needed nor had vent holes for smoke. It filtered out through the thatch, killing vermin along the way.

Pictavum: Poitiers.

Pomoerium: The space kept clear just inside and outside a defensive wall.

Consecration of the Mithraeum: Our description of this draws in part on our imaginations, but largely on the ideas of such authorities as Cumont, Stewardson, and Saunders.

Pater and Heliodromos: Father and Runner (or Courier) of the Sun, the first and second degrees of a Mithraic congregation. Although knowledge of this religion is, today, fragmentary, what we do possess shows its many resemblances to Christianity, not only in belief but in liturgy, organization, and requirements laid upon the faithful.

VIII

Lugdunensis Tertia: The Roman province comprising northwestern France.

Church buildings: Most were quite small. The cathedral in Tours may have been the size of a fairly large present-day house.

Samarobriva: Amiens.

St. Martin as a military physician: This is not in the chronicles, but some modern biographers think it is probable.

Exorcists: In this era, such priests were not specifically charged with driving out demons, but simply with the supervision of the energumens and similar duties.

The service: Obviously this was very different from today's ritual. It varied from place to place; what we have sketched was the so-called Gallic Mass. Strictly speaking, though, the Mass was the Communion service, reserved for the baptized.

Biblical texts: Respectively Amos viii, 8; I Corinthians ii, 14 and Matthew viii, 8.

Martin and the bishops: His refusal to attend any synods after the Priscillian affair is attested.

Greater Monastery: Majus Monasterium, which probably is the origin of the place name "Marmoutier," although some scholars derive it from "Martin."

Chorespiscopus: The powers granted priests in the early Church were very limited. A chorepiscopus, "country bishop," ranked above them but below a full bishop. He had most of the powers later given a parish priest, but not all. See the notes to *Roma Mater*.

Paenula: A poncholike outer garment. From everyday garb of this period and later derived the priestly vestments of the Church. The paenula became the chasuble.

Cernunnos: An ancient Gallic god.

IX

Sarmatian: What people the Classical geographers meant by this name is obscure, and evidently varied over the centuries. To Corentinus, we suppose, the word would designate one of those Slavic tribes that were drifting into what is now Poland and Prussia as the Germanic inhabitants moved elsewhere.

Suebian Sea: The Baltic *(Mare Suebicum)*.

Cimbrian Chersonese: Jutland. The Heruls, whom tradition says once inhabited the adjacent islands, had by now migrated south, and the Danes were moving in from what is now Sweden. Jutes and Angles were still at home, although soon many of them would be among the invaders of Britain.

Franks: This word *(Franci)* was a generic Roman term for Germanic tribes originating north of the River Main and along the North Sea. Moving into Gaul, they eventually gave that name to the entire country of France. Our account of their pagan religious practices draws on descriptions from other times and places; but it seems plausible to us. Whatever the details, we have scarcely exaggerated the brutality of the Franks. It was notorious. Even after they had become Christian, the history of the early Merovingians is a catalogue of horrors.

Cataphract: A heavy cavalryman.

Aquileia: Near present-day Trieste.

Death of Maximus and Victor: Authorities disagree on the precise date and manner of this, but it occurred in the summer of 388.

XI

The defeat of Maximus: According to one source, only two Romans died at Aquileia, Maximus and Victor. This implies that both armies were composed entirely of barbarian mercenaries, which seems to us unlikely in the extreme. Surely Maximus, at least, would have needed legionaries to drive Valentinian out of Italy, and then, lacking effective cavalry such as Theodosius possessed, would have brought them to meet the latter.

Maximus's veterans: There is a tradition that they were settled in Armorica, and some modern historians consider it plausible. If this did happen, then doubtless the involuntary colonists included certain of the troops Maximus had left behind in Gaul, though probably only those whose loyalty to the re-established Imperium of the West was very questionable.

The gravestone: Roman epitaphs, especially when military, were generally short and employed abbreviations. Expanded and translated, this one reads TO QUINTUS JUNIUS EPPILUS / OPTIO (deputy) IN THE SECOND LEGION AUGUSTA / HIS FELLOW SOLDIERS MADE THIS.

XII

Thracia: Thrace, occupying approximately what are now the northeastern end of Greece, the northwestern end of Turkey, and southern Bulgaria.

Saxons in Britain: There is good evidence for some colonization, as well as piracy, by these barbarians as early as the later fourth century. Be that as it may, Stilicho had hard fights against them.

Sabrina: The River Severn.

Silures: The British tribe inhabiting what is now, more or less, Glamorganshire and Monmouth.

Sucat (or *Succat*): Birth name of St. Patrick. As nearly as possible, we follow traditional accounts of him, including that interpretation of them which makes the year of his capture, rather than his birth, 389. It must be added that a number of modern scholars have called into question all the dates and other details of his story; some actually challenge his historicity. His appearances before Niall is our own idea. Even tradition does not make clear where he passed his time of servitude. Somewhat arbitrarily, we adopt the suggestion that was in County Mayo.

Temir: Tara.

Cú Culanni: Today better known as Cuchulainn, the greatest hero of the Ulster cycle. His king, Conchobar, was said by medieval writers to have died of fury at hearing that Christ had been crucified, though he himself was a pagan. This at least gives some hint at the time that tradition assigned to these sagas.

Emain Macha: The ancient seat of the supreme Ulster kings, near present-day Armagh. The Red Branch (more accurately, but hardly ever, rendered as Royal Branch) was the lodge where their chief warriors met.

Fifth: For the ancient division of Ireland into five parts, autonomous if not exactly nation-states, see the notes to *Roma Mater*.

Qóiqet nUlat: The Fifth of the Ulati people.

Cruthini and Firi Bolg: There were Picts (whom the Irish called Cruthini) in Ireland as well as in Scotland-to-be—and, for that matter, in northern Gaul. As we have noted earlier, they were not at all the dwarfs of modern folklore, nor backward with respect to the Gaels; however, they were a distinct people. The Firi Bolg were, in legend, the first colonists of Ireland, subjugated by the invading Children of Danu. Perhaps this tale embodies a dim folk memory of an aboriginal population whom the first wave or waves of incoming Celts overran and intermarried with. If so, pride of ancestry persisted well into historical times; and to this day, there do appear to be at least two racial types native to the country.

Conduct of the Ulati: Tradition does not say that the upper classes in Ulster were especially oppressive. However, the Uí Néill seem to have had little difficulty in keeping the Aregésla (or Airgialla), about whom more later, a puppet power. This has given some modern writers the idea that a malcontent population was present in the first place—a suggestion we have followed. Granted, at the worst the yoke would have been far lighter than that upon the peoples of the Roman Empire or, for that matter, virtually everybody today. The Irish aristocrats were not saints or libertarians, but they lacked the apparatus available to organized governments.

Starving: Among the early Irish, a man who had a grievance against one more powerful, and could not otherwise get redress, often sat down at the door of the latter and fasted. If this did not shame the second party into making a settlement, then he too was expected to deny himself food, and it became an endurance contest.

Sinand: The River Shannon. The territory we have described Niall as taking includes present-day County Cavan and part of Monaghan. Of course, our depiction of events is purely conjectural, and some modern scholars deny that it could have happened this way at all.

Mag Slecht: The "Plain of Prostrations," In County Cavan, where stood the idols of Cromb Cróche (or Crom Cruach) and his twelve attendants. The chronicles say these were the most powerful and revered gods in Ireland until St. Patrick overthrew them.

The lunar eclipse: This took place on 13 July 390 (Gregorian calendar).

The comet of 390: It is recorded as having been visible from 22 August to 17 September (Gregorian dates). The magnitude is not known, but it was presumably conspicuous.

Polaris: Prior to the development of elevators, locations in a tall building were less desirable the farther up they were. Structures of this height were forbidden in Rome as being too hazardous, but we suppose the Ysans had more confidence in their architects, and knew how to make self-bracing frameworks.

Corentinus's sermon: Few if any Christians of this period denied the reality of pagan gods. Sometimes they were considered to be mere euhemerizations, but oftener demons or, at best, beings with certain powers and perhaps without evil intentions, to whom it was nevertheless wrong to pay divine honors.

XIII

Lúgnassat (later *Lugnasad*): A harvest festival taking its name from the god Lúg. In Christian times it occurred on 1 August. The English know it as Lammas, though that name has another derivation. Lacking the Roman calendar, the pagan Celts must have set the date some other way; we guess that the moon helped determine it.

Fairs: The ancient Irish held a number of such events, at various localities each year. Religious as well as secular, they were open to all.

Cromb Cróche and the death of Domnuald: Our description of the sanctuary and the ceremonies that took place there is conjectural, though based on the chronicles, on local traditions in the area said to have held it, and on similar things in other milieus. Domnuald and his fate are imaginary, but the story does go that the slaying of a son of his made Niall ready to kill the hostages he had from the folk of the murderers.

Éricc (later *eraic*): Akin to the Teutonic weregild, a payment to an injured party of his heirs, the amount depending on the actual harm done and the possible provocation.

Honor price: Unlike the Germanic peoples, the Irish made some effort to equalize justice between rich and poor. A man of rank, who owed an éricc, must pay in addition an amount of goods which increased with his social standing.

Clón Tarui: Now Clontarf, a district of Dublin.

Tallten: Now Teltown, on the River Blackwater in County Meath. Our description of the size and importance of the fair (*óenach*) there is not exaggerated; like its counterparts, it continued for centuries after Ireland became Christian, so reliable records exist. That an eponymous goddess should have been buried at the site is not unique. For example, though the Nordic god Baldr died in the early days of the world, he seems to have had a cult.

The Dagdae (later *Dagda*): A god especially wise. His well is our invention.

Mag Mell: The Plain of Honey, one of the paradises that Celtic myth located afar in the western ocean. Sometimes the name was applied to all of them together. The Celts do not appear to have had any clear or consistent ideas about an afterlife. There are mentions of favored persons whose souls were borne west to abide a while before returning and being reincarnated. Probably the most usual supposition was that the dead inhabited their graves, coming out to spook around on the eves of Beltene and Samain.

Irish arts and crafts: The glorious works that remain to us prove that, for all its violence and technological backwardness, this society had as keen a sense for beauty as ever the Greeks did.

Expulsion of the Irish from Wales: This is attested.

Eóganachta: The royal family, or rather set of families claiming a common ancestor, in Munster.

Tanist: The heir apparent of an Irish king, chosen well beforehand. It was doubtless done in the hope of an orderly succession. Any man with royal blood and no physical impairment, whether born in or out of wedlock, could become king if he had the power to enforce his claim. This could easily lead to war between rival pretenders. The laws and institutions of Rome had decayed so far that the Empire must needs invent something of the kind for itself, the Caesar associated with the Augustus.

Nath Í: Tradition says that this nephew of Niall succeeded him. The medieval account of his career creates so many chronological problems that several modern scholars have decided he must be purely fictional and that Niall—if he himself ever lived—should be dated a generation later than he is in the chronicles. It may be; or it may not. Given all the uncertainties, we have felt free to stay with the tradition, which better fits our story, and to put in modifications or new material of our own. The contradictions in the sources *could* mainly be due to their authors, drawing on oral history handed down for lifetimes, getting different persons and their acts confused with each other.

The Walls of the Ulati: Known as the Black Pig's Dyke, remnants of ancient fortifications—earthen walls and fosses—occur approximately along the southern boundary of Ulster. They may have been raised in imitation of Roman works, or they may be older than that. They were probably not a continuous line of defense, but rather a set of strongpoints for controlling movement along the main routes of travel. Elsewhere, forest, bog and other natural obstacles would have sufficiently hindered invaders or retreating cattle rustlers.

Commandments and prohibitions laid on royal persons: Those mentioned here are in the annals. A taboo applying to an individual or a class of people was known as a *gess* (later *geas*), plural *gessa*.

The redemption of the hostages: This is in the tradition, though it does not state where they were from. We have put the incident just after Lúgnassat, partly so we could describe a little of the fair, partly because the chronicles say that the Rock of Cashel was revealed "when the leaves were yellow," which must have been in autumn.

Darioritum (Venetorum): Vannes.

Tambilis and Gratillonius: Most peoples, including our own until recent times, have considered a girl of sixteen to be nubile.

Veneti: A tribe in southern Brittany. Under the Empire, tribes had no independence and their identities gradually eroded, but they did constitute units of local government, not totally unlike American states.

XIV

The Síd Drommen (or *Sídhe Druimm*): This is one of several names the great rock originally bore. They all suggest the supernatural.

The finding of Cashel: We have tried to synthesize the legends, omitting Christian elements that the chroniclers inserted. There are enough pagan ones. Swine were anciently associated with the dead, which may be why kings could not own them. The yew, one of the three trees the Irish held sacred (together with the hazel and the rowan), was a patron of the Eóganachta; the name of their ancestor, Eógan, means "yew." At his ceremony of accession, a new king always stood on a flagstone (*lecc*).

The career of Conual: It is not known when or how Cashel and the kingdom that grew from it were actually founded. We have followed tradition as far as possible, including parts that some modern scholars hold to be purely mythical. For example, Byrne considers Conual's second wife, Ámend, a humanized sun goddess, daughter of the lightning (Bolg). That may be. Yet it seems quite plausible that Conual made a political marriage, and that his early successes were in large part due to the awe inspired by the seemingly supernatural circumstances of his advent—circumstances that may have been accidental or may have been engineered, but that he, who had been exposed to Roman civilization, was quick to take advantage of. Some authorities suggest that he was a Christian. We suppose not, if only because the chronicles declare that his grandson was the first king of Cashel to take the Faith, and the tale of that baptism by St. Patrick is too delightful to give up willingly. Hardly any historian disputes that a Roman-style fortress was erected on the outcrop sometime in the late fourth or early fifth century; that the name Cassel, later Caisel, now Cashel, derives from Latin *Castellum*, meaning such a stronghold; and that from this nucleus developed the kingdom of Munster. Eventually deeded to the Church, the rock became an important ecclesiastical site.

Aregésla (later *Airgialla*): Occupying, approximately, what are now Counties Monaghan, Cavan, and Leitrim, this kingdom does appear to have been established as a puppet of Niall or his sons. Our account of the founding is conjectural. Giving local chieftains authority over the rites of Mag Slecht would not have debarred the kings of Tara from that ready access to Crom Cruach which the legend of St. Patrick says they had.

Niall of the Nine Hostages: By this name is the ancestor of the Uí Néill dynasties known to history. Just when or how he got the sobriquet is unknown. At any given time, any king of importance surely held more than nine individual hostages. Hence the reference must be to some who were especially significant. According to one chronicle, Niall had them from each of the Fifths of Ireland, and four from Britain; according to another, besides the five Irish, they were from Scotland (the Picts), the Britons, the Saxons, and the Franks. This makes little or no sense. For once we go along with modern commentators and suppose that the nine were of the Aregésla, whose establishment as subordinate allies marked a turning part in the destiny of the Uí Néill.

The hallowing of the newborn: There is no reason why a healthy woman who has given birth should not get up and walk about, at least for fairly short distances, a few hours later.

Niall Náegéslach (later *Nóigiallach*): Niall of the Nine Hostages. It is our conjecture that he took advantage of Stilicho's departure to ravage Britain and so assert his power in the face of Conual Corcc's spectacular successes. It squares with the tradition. Certainly Scotic raids increased about this time.

The Loígis: Presumably this set of tribes gave their name to present-day County Laoighis; but the sources indicate that they held the western frontiers of Leinster as far down as the sea.

Ossraige: A kingdom occupying the western parts of what are now Counties Laoighis and Kilkenny. Apparently it had a subordinate relation to the Leinster high kings, somewhat like that of the Aregésla to the Uí Néill.

The origin of the Lagini: We repeat the legends.

Dún Alinni: Near present-day Kildare.

Fomóri: A legendary race who harassed the Firi Bolg in ancient times and whom the Children of Danu expelled.

Eochaid's raid: This, and its aftermath, are traditional tales, though of course we have filled in many details as best we could.

XV

Menstrual pad: Today's convenient sanitary napkins and tampons are quite a recent development, but people have always had the problem to cope with as best they could, and we may suppose the upper-class Ysan women had arrangements available to them that were better than most.

Vervain: Now more commonly known as verbena. Both the Romans and the Gauls credited it with numerous wonderful properties.

Irish gold: The country was rich in this metal, though in the course of centuries the sources would be exhausted.

Praetorian prefect: For some discussion of this high office, see the notes to *Roma Mater*.

Salomon: A form of the name closer to the original than "Solomon" and still common on the Continent. The early Church made little use of the Old Testament, except for a few lyrical and prophetic parts, so it is natural that Gratillonius would be ignorant of ancient Jewish history, while a scholarly sort like Apuleius could be well versed in it.

XVI

Carsa: Another conjectural family name. We fancy that it could relate to Carsac, a village in the Dordogne where we have spent pleasant days.

Cadurci: A Gallic tribe inhabiting the Dordogne.

Garumna: The River Garonne.

The Armorican run: Archeological evidence shows that commerce was still going on between southern France and Brittany.

The shipping season: In the ancient world, this was generally from April through October. The virtual cessation of maritime traffic in the winter was less for fear of storms—most ships were quite seaworthy—than because weather made navigation difficult.

Tonnage: Mediterranean grain ships had burdens of up to 1200 tons. Oceangoing vessels were doubtless smaller, but not too much so. A typical merchantman is described in *Roma Mater*.

Speed: Merchantmen could do four or five knots under good conditions. They could point up to the wind to a limited extent and lie hove to, after a fashion, when that was the prudent thing to do.

Periplus: A set of sailing directions for a given route, describing landmarks, hazards, etc. Maps were so crude as to be virtually useless to navigators.

Clerestory: Rome also had adopted this useful Egyptian technique for lighting interiors.

Sucat and Martin: Again we are forced to select from among the often contradictory stories about St. Patrick; but we have invented essentially nothing. He may actually have been an Armorican rather than a Briton, and he may have been born as late as 389. However, this would probably rule out the kinship to St. Martin which tradition gives him, and certainly the story that he became a disciple of the latter. His career after escape from captivity is obscure in the extreme. The reconstruction that we employ has him come to Marmoutier in 396, seeking holy orders, and live there until the bishop's death, after which he went south to pursue his studies and devotions.

Banaventa (or *Bannauenta* or other variants): Mentioned in Patrick's *Confessions* (which some modern scholars consider spurious), this may have been Daventry, but may also have been one of three places in Glamorganshire called Banwent; we assume the latter. It is described as the home of his mother's parents, whom he was visiting when the raiders struck, but this does not seem to square with the claim that she was Martin's niece, so we follow the school of thought that makes Banaventa his father's and his own dwelling place.

Sucat's future: He spent many years on the Continent. Legend declares that Pope Celestine, in consecrating him for his mission, gave him the new name Patricius—now Patrick. There is reason to think he may have assumed it himself and, indeed, even consecrated himself a bishop. The traditional date for his return to Ireland is 432, for his death 461. Thus he, like Martin, had a long life, active until the very end.

XVII

Garomagus: Our conjectural name for a Roman town that, archeology has revealed, existed on the site of present-day Douarnenez. In fact, the entire littoral of the bay there was reasonably populous and prosperous in the heyday of the Empire. Local tradition makes the city Douarnenez the seat of legendary King Mark, and the islet bears the name of his nephew Tristan. This suggests that the area has ancient magical associations.

Roman Bay: Baie de Douarnenez. This is the Ysan name; what the Romans called it is not known.

Goat Foreland: Cap de la Chèvre. We are supposing that a name Gallic or even older has kept the same meaning though languages have changed—unless the identity is coincidental.

DAHUT

I

The Feast of Lug: Known in modern Ireland as Lugnasad, its date fixed at 1 August, it was originally widespread among Celts, honoring one of their greatest gods. Nobody today knows how the pagans set the times of their festivals, but we assume that a full moon was among the parameters. In the present case we spell the name "Lug" without a diacritical mark, as a suggestion that the pronounciation differed between Ireland and the Continent.

Artemon: A bowsprit sail, chiefly an aid to steering.

Ériu: Early Gaelic name of Ireland.

Manandan maqq Léri: A god associated with the sea, later known as Manannan mac Lir.

Maia: Bowness, on Solway Firth.

Dál Riata: The first important Scotic settlement in what is now Scotland, on the Argyll coast, an offshoot of a realm in Ulster with the same name. It may not have been in existence this early, but we follow the tradition that says it was.

Kilts: Until recent times the kilt was no mere skirt, but a great piece of wool that could cover most of the body and was often a poor man's only garment.

Lúguvallium: Carlisle.

Emain Macha: The ancient seat of the supreme Ulster kings, near present-day Armagh.

Hunter's Moon: We assume that, prior to Christianity and the Julian calendar, this set the date of Samain (or Samhain), the Celtic festival of the dead and turn of the year. It was later fixed at 1 November, but remained important in Ireland. Hallowe'en is a degenerate survival of Samain Eve.

The prayer of Corentinus: Not until about 800 A.D. are Christians known to have brought their hands together when praying, and the custom did not become common until about 1300. Early Christians, like pagans, raised their arms while standing, a gesture of supplication seen in many Egyptian tomb paintings.

II

Duke of the Armorican Tract: Roman commander of the defenses of the Peninsula, which was considered a military district rather than a province, politically belonging in Lúgdunensis Tertia.

Corbilo: St. Nazaire. The exact year of the Saxon takeover is not known, but it was about the end of the fourth century.

Liger: The River Loire.

Laeti: Barbarians granted permission to settle in Roman lands on condition of providing defense forces. Increasingly often, such an agreement was mere face-saving on the part of the Romans, who were unable to keep the newcomers out.

The Roman campaign in Britain: Little is known about it except the dates, 396-398. A panegyric by one Claudian implies that Stilicho was personally in charge throughout, which he could not have been, and that he delivered the diocese from Scots, Picts, and Saxons, which at best was a very short-lived accomplishment. We propose that the effort met with even less success than that.

Africa: To the Romans, this meant what we call North Africa, exclusive of Egypt and Ethiopia. The rest of the continent was unknown to them.

African revolt: Led by one Gildo, this rebellion appears to have been instigated by Constantinople in hopes of outflanking the Western Empire; relations were increasingly strained. Stilicho suppressed it.

Diocese: A major administrative subdivision of the Empire.

Corentinus's advice: It was by no means uncommon for Christian married couples to vow perpetual sexual abstinence, especially if they had lost a child or suffered some equal tragedy.

Prophetic dreams: The early Irish believed that one way to have these was to eat almost to the bursting point just before sleeping.

Cromb Cróche: Later known as Crom Cruach. See the notes to *Gallicenae*.

Aregésla: The "Givers of Hostages," Niall's earliest important conquests, who became loyal followers of him and his descendants. See the notes to *Gallicenae*.

The stockpen: Now known as the Dorsey, this is a great earthwork forming an enclosure within which little sign of habitation has been found, but which was obviously important—as not only its size but its name (meaning "the doors") imply. Our suggestion is that besides being a strongpoint, it held livestock in times of crisis, to feed the army. In like manner, we have supposed Niall would bring some supplies with him, though of course this would not have been as well organized as a Roman baggage train.

Niall's campaign: Even the Roman army was hampered by inadequate communications. Among the barbarians of Europe, war was generally a matter of mobs engaging in a series of brawls. However, a leader such as Niall, adding foreign experience to innate military genius, and taking advantage of the somewhat disciplined cadre comprising his household troops, could presumably impose a measure of order and direction on the rest of his followers.

The outer defenses of Emain Macha: What we have in mind is one of the two sets of earthworks now known as the Dane's Cast, this being about four miles south of Armagh. Of course, we have had to guess as just what it was like in its heyday.

The fall of Emain Macha: Perhaps even more mystery and controversy surround this event than any other in early Irish history (or, rather, late Irish prehistory). Now called Navan Fort, the site is a mile and a half west of Armagh. Its impressiveness joins with tradition to leave no reasonable doubt that it was in fact the seat of power in Ulster and had been since before the time of Christ. Nor is there any doubt that it was overthrown, and that in the course of time the Uí Néill parceled most of Ulster out among themselves. Eventually the old northern rulers held only Counties Antrim and Down. The story that the Ulati themselves fired Emain Macha is ancient. But when and how did this first disaster come about? One account makes it the work of three brothers named Colla, before the time of Niall; another says it was due his three eldest sons, whenever they may have flourished, and (what is probable) that the three Collas are mere doublets of them, invented long afterward. Then some modern scholars argue that Emain Macha must still have been extant and important in the time of St. Patrick, and therefore fell victim to the Uí Néill proper, the grandsons or later descendants of Niall. Once again, we have had to make our own choices and suggestions.

Lúgnassat: Early Irish form of "Lúgnasad."

III

Redonian: A person of the tribe of the Redones, inhabiting eastern and central Brittany—though the interior of the peninsula was very thinly populated.

Gess (later *geas*): A taboo, which could be inherited, go with a certain position, or be laid by one person on another. See the notes to *Roma Mater*.

Ruirthech: The River Liffey. It does not set the northern boundary of Leinster today, but we hypothesize that it did in the days when Mide (Meath) was coequal.

Ollam (or *ollave*): Of the highest standing in a profession regarded as learned or skilled.

Brithem (later *brehon*): A man empowered to hear disputes, give judgments, and, in a basically illiterate society, know just what the law was.

The number of the colors: How many colors might be displayed in garments depended on rank. A king could have up to seven. The various customs and rules such as this that we have attempted to show are, in general, attested for early Christian Ireland, so doubtless prevailed in late pagan times.

The Mórrigu (or *Morrigan*): The great goddess of war.

Éricc and honor price: Compensations for wrongdoing paid to injured parties. See the notes to *Gallicenae*.

Trumpets: Roman trumpets were, of course, different from modern ones. The principal types were the cornu, tuba, and buccina.

Events: Eochaid's escape, the murder he committed, and Laidchenn's satire are in the legends that have been written down, though naturally we have supplied nearly all the details. As for the motivation of Eochaid's crime, hideous by the standards of his culture, he had been cruelly imprisoned for a long time; he was a desperate and starveling fugitive; his ambitions had been shattered. Among the ancient Irish, a king must be without visible blemish.

Ordovices, Demetae, Silures, Dumnonii: Tribes in western Britain. See the notes to *Roma Mater*.

Laidchenn's satire: The Irish believed, well into the Christian period, that a satire (*áer*) composed by a poet who had the power not only brought disgrace, but could be physically destructive. In suggesting what this one may have been like, we again employ, as nearly as possible to us, a verse form of that country and era.

IV

Imbolc: A festival set in Christian times at 1 February. Again we suppose the pagan original varied the date somewhat according to the moon.

Siuir: The River Suir. The different spellings indicate different pronunciations. Something is known about the language prior to Old Irish from ogamm (ogham) inscriptions and other clues.

Niall and Sadb: The early Irish appear to have had a great deal of sexual freedom. Women, married or no, could bestow their favors as readily as men, without it being thought in any way scandalous. In previous volumes we have mentioned the variety of marriage arrangements. This does not appear to have prevented intense love relationships. See, for example, the story of Derdriu (Deirdre) and Noisiu (Naoise) or Cú Culanni (Cuchulainn) and Emer.

Clepsydra: A kind of water clock.

V

Basilica: The building in a city devoted to governmental offices, law courts, etc.

Procurator: Like "prefect" (*praefectus*), this title had a rather wide range of meanings. Here it indicates the official in charge of fiscal and related matters, possessing considerable administrative powers.

Lúgdunensis Tertia: A province, within the diocese of Gallia, embracing Brittany and some other parts of northwestern France. For lack of historical records, we have had to invent its governor and procurator.

The decree of Honorius: Paganism had been banned from time to time by previous Emperors, with limited success. However, each such attempt had its lasting effects, and Honorius's of 399 may be regarded as completing the process. To be sure, it would take a long time yet before all the people in the Western Empire were converted.

Lake Nemi: Here the best-known King of the Wood held forth. Accounts of him inspired Sir James Frazer to those studies which produced *The Golden Bough*.

Aurochs: The European wild ox. It became extinct in the seventeenth century, but in the twentieth has been bred back out of domestic cattle with which its bloodlines had intermingled.

Audiarna: Audierne (hypothetical Latin original of the name).

Mag Mell: One of the paradises that Celtic mythology located afar in the western ocean.

VI

Darioritum Venetorum: Vannes. As in many other instances, the tribal name in its genitive case was displacing the Roman one, to become ancestral to the modern name.

Audiarna on the River Goana: Audierne on the Goyen. Our reconstruction of the Latin names is hypothetical, as is our picture of the community, its garrison, its officiating clergyman, etc. However, we model all this on what was usual for minor provincial cities.

Francisca: A battle-ax intended to be thrown at the enemy, characteristic of the Frankish warrior's equipment.

Redonia: The territory of the Redones.

Mediolanum: Milan. At this time it, not Rome, was the capital of the Western Empire—to which, however, "Rome" was still commonly applied.

VIII

Calends: The first day of a month. The Romans generally specified a date with respect to the calends, the nones, or the ides. The sixteenth day of every month was especially sacred in the Mithraic religion. Of course, people were using the Julian calendar.

Mithraic hymns: None survive. Our bit of reconstruction employs the *versus popularis* form, which was used for centuries in a number of legionary songs, sometimes at the triumph of a Caesar, as well as in civilian poetry.

The bull sacrifice: This is entirely conjectural. Nothing is known today about how such a rite was conducted, or even whether it still ever was by the end of the fourth century. We suggest it could have been, on extraordinary occasions, and that it amounted to a re-enactment of the scene so often depicted in religious art.

Epictetus: For this passage we employ the 1890 translation by Thomas Wentworth Higginson.

Venetic: The tribe of the Veneti inhabited the southern coast of Brittany and its hinterland, east of the Osismii.

The Place of the Old Ones: The area around Carnac. It is probable that the entire Gulf of Morbihan has been submerged by rising sea level within historic times.

IX

Gratillonius's actions: Readers may think that a sacral king who defied the religion that had been his *raison d'etre* would undermine or even destroy his own power. This is not necessarily true. For example, in 1819 Kamehameha II of Hawaii publicly broke ancient taboos, and thereafter ordered demolition of the pagan temples and cessation of rites. Nor did he decree any new faith; the country was almost a religious vacuum until Christian missionaries arrived in some numbers. Nevertheless the monarchy remained unquestioned until 1840, when Kamehameha III voluntarily handed down a constitution granting civil right to the people.

Roman authorities: An Imperial diocese was generally under the overall control of its vicarius. Above him was a praetorian prefect, who in this case had charge of Britain, Gaul, and Iberia.

Corentinus's wish: At this time Christianity had not yet developed concepts of the afterlife as elaborate as those we find in Dante. Even on points of doctrine that had supposedly been settled, e.g., by the Council of Nicea, ideas kept springing up that were not instantly identifiable as heretical. Furthermore, comparatively few clergymen had much education in what theology there was, especially not those out on the fringes of civilization.

X

Rivelin's medical practices: They were as good as anything known in the Roman world, except that we assume the Ysans had a more effective pharmacopoeia. Because of their long isolation, together with the conservatism of the medical profession and, now, the internal decay of the Empire, use of these materials had not spread through Europe.

XI

Samain (now usually *Samhain*): We can only conjecture what the beliefs and customs of the pagan Irish were with respect to this most important time of their year—doubtless there was considerable variation from place to place—but our guesses do draw on what is known from later centuries. The word "Samain" (pronounced, approximately, "Saow-*ween*" and signifying "End of Summer") may date from then rather than from earlier. Its vigil was also known as *Oiche Shamhna*, "Hallowe'en," and *Oiche no Sprideanna*, "Spirit Night," but these names are Christian. Samain appears to have been the first day of the Celtic year or, rather, half-year. This timing, like that of Beltene, gives good reason to believe that the calendar was devised by and for a pastoral, not an agricultural people; and in fact, until well beyond the period of our story, the Irish were herders more than they were farmers. Our reconstruction of pagan beliefs and practices is based on what is recorded of the Christian, as well as mention of pre-Christian ones (e.g., the ceremonial sharpening of weapons) and, inevitably, guesses of our own.

Firi Bolg and Fomóri: In the legend, these were early inhabitants of Ireland; the Fomóri had a sinister repute. Such stories probably stemmed from vague tribal recollections of populations in the island before the Celts.

The cemetery at Teltown: Little or no trace survives, which has led some modern scholars to maintain that the tradition is wrong and the royal burials were actually elsewhere. However, if they were relatively modest in size—and the evidence is that they were—then it is reasonable to suppose that the agriculture of later centuries obliterated them, a process common enough throughout Europe.

Brug (now *Brugh*): On the Boyne, this is the site of remarkable neolithic tombs and other monuments, of which Newgrange is the most famous. Legend associates them with the Dedannans, the godlike race who held Ireland before the Milesians arrived and overthrew them.

Mongfind: Modern scholars generally take for granted that she is purely mythical, as witness the fact that she had a cult of some kind which emphasized rites at Samain. They suppose that her identity as a mortal queen and association with Niall are inventions of later storytellers. For our purposes, we have assumed that there is at least a core of truth in the legends. Niall's elevation of her from revenant to demigoddess is, of course, entirely our idea.

The sacrifice: The sacrifice of horses does not seem to have been as central to the Celtic religions as it was to the Germanic, but it did sometimes occur, and a passage in Giraldus Cambrensis suggests that it may have had more importance in Ireland than in Britain or on the continent.

The vision: We have noted earlier that one ancient Irish method of seeking prophetic dreams was to overeat just before going to sleep.

Music: Although ancient writers agreed on the nature and use of the musical "modes," they never described just what those were. We only know that they were not the same as the similarly named "modes" of plainsong, which were constructed on very different principles.

XIII

Slings: The sling, especially the staff sling, was a formidable weapon. Ranges of 200 yards or more are known. Europeans of the nineteenth and early twentieth centuries who encountered slings in such areas as the Near East and Madagascar considered them as dangerous as firearms of that time. Like the longbow in the Middle Ages, this weapon seems to have been limited in its military uses by the fact that training from boyhood on was required for real proficiency. Hence corps of slingers were recruited from regions where it was traditional.

XIV

Opium, etc: We have noted before that opium was used as an analgesic, in the form of an extract. Licorice was also known. Both being from the Mediterranean, they must have become scarce and costly in northern Europe as commerce declined. Willowbark yields a material akin to aspirin.

Birthday of Mithras: 25 December. The Christian Church had not yet settled on a date for the Nativity, but some congregations were observing this one, whether in imitation or because both religions drew on pervasive Near Eastern traditions. It does not accord well with Luke's narrative. We might mention that the practice of counting years from the putative birth of Christ had not yet developed.

The lunar eclipse: For the date and hour of this, as well as for other astronomical information, we are indebted to Bing F. Quock of the Morrison Planetarium, San Francisco. He is not responsible for any mistakes we may have made in using it, such as in converting to the Julian calendar. Given modern knowledge and technology, prediction and postdiction of celestial events is fairly simple. The ancients were handicapped in several ways, including a shortage of data; only about half of all occurrences were ever visible to them, and surely bad weather hid many that might have been seen.

XV

Germanic Sea: Roman name (*Oceanus Germanicus*) for the North Sea.

The foreign ship: Not much is known about Scandinavian shipbuilding prior to the viking era. We base this description primarily on two finds at Kvalsund, Norway, and a picture carved in a stone at Bro on Gotland (Sweden).

The Jews: Although they had long been widespread in the Mediterranean countries, few if any had yet reached northern Europe. Budic's ignorance is also due to the fact that early Christians made only limited use of the Old Testament.

Germans in Britain: As mentioned in a previous note, there is reason to believe that some colonization had already begun.

Scandia (or *Scania*): Now the southernmost part of Sweden, this territory was Danish until 1658 and may well have been the aboriginal home of the Danes, that people who made themselves supreme in the islands and eventually Jutland, thereby giving their name to the entire country. In our time they had not yet done so.

Outlawry: Among the early Scandinavians, well into their Christian era a man whom the folkmoot found guilty of a serious offense was often condemned to outlawry—removal of any legal recourse for whatever somebody might do to him—for a specified time. If he could, he usually went abroad until the term was up.

Finnaithae: This Roman word presumably refers either to Finns or Lapps.

Anglic laeti: The Angli supplied many post-Roman migrants to Britain; the name "England" derives from them. Earlier they lived near the southern end of the Jutland peninsula.

Icenian coast: Along Norfolk and Suffolk.

Treverian: Member of a German tribe occupying the area around Trier.

Suebian Sea (Mare Suebicum): Roman name of the Baltic Sea.

Danuvius: The River Danube.

Cenabum: Orleans. In the fifth century its name was changed to Aurelianum, whence comes the modern version.

Sequana: The River Seine.

Lutetia Parisiorum: Paris. At this time it was of minor importance.

Maedraeacum: Médréac, now a village not far from Rennes. Our reconstruction of the name is hypothetical. Where such communities have originated as latifundia, their names are often traceable to the names of the families who owned them, as recorded on Roman tax rolls. However, this one looks as if it has a more ancient origin, in the name of a Gallic god. Then in the course of generations, though the inhabitants were reduced to servitude under the Sicori, the traditional appellation persisted.

Comet: For details of what is known about the comet of 400 we are indebted to David Levy, discoverer of more than one. He is not responsible for any mistakes in our use of the information. The comet is recorded between 19 March and 10 April (Gregorian dates). Apart from the obvious fact that it was visible to the naked eye, we can only guess at its appearance. However, there is reason to think that large, bright comets were commoner in the past than they are now. Each passage close to the sun diminishes such a body. Occasionally new ones are perturbed into the inner regions of the Solar System, but this does not appear to have happened very often for a historically long time.

Wind and wave: Although hurricane-force winds are much less frequent along the coasts of northern Europe than in certain other parts of the world, they do sometimes occur. One may or may not have struck in the spring of 400; the records are silent. However, some meteorologists find reason to believe that weather was more stormy, on the average, than now. (Reference is to the Petterson theory of climatic cycles.) In any case, such an event is possible. Tide tables for the Audierne area indicate that, unless conditions have changed considerably, there was a spring high tide in the Baie des Trépassés shortly before moonset on the night of 26-27 March (Gregorian dates). With such weather at its back, it could well have been disastrous.

THE DOG AND THE WOLF

I

The plight of the Ysans: While the Osismii were friendly enough, it should be remembered that the concept of foreign aid did not exist. True, the Roman Empire often supplied grain (or money) to client states, but this was a subsidy and depended on their being perceived as useful.

Suffetes: Members of the thirteen aristocratic Ysan families. See the earlier books.

Emain Macha: The central stronghold of the Ulati. See *Dahut*.

Gess (now *geas*): A kind of taboo; a prohibition laid upon an individual or a class. See *Roma Mater*.

Corentinus's warning: As we have remarked before, the early Christian Church did not deny that most pagan gods were real, but tended to consider them demons intent on misleading men. Euhemerism sometimes provided an alternative explanation, as in the *Heimskringla*.

Kilt: This was originally no mere skirt, but a garment—often a poor man's only garment—ample to cover most of the body and to serve as a bedroll at night.

II

Chorepiscopus: In the early Church, a cleric with rank between that of a priest and a bishop. See the notes to *Roma Mater*. Corentinus had been the chorepiscopus at Ys.

Iron ore: This was generally bog iron, collected rather than mined.

Garrison troops: According to an extant record, as of about 425 A.D. there were fourteen units of *limitanei*, totaling less than 10,000 men, in Sequania, Moguntiacum, Belgica, and Armorica. It seems unlikely that there were many more a quarter century earlier. To be sure, they were supplemented by native *numeri* (regulars) and other outfits, but these had nothing like the effectiveness of the old legions.

Comet: The comet of 400 is known to have been visible from 19 March to 10 April (Gregorian dates); the actual span may have been longer.

Robin: The European bird, smaller than the North American and of a different genus, is meant.

Summoning the gods: Gallic beliefs and practices, especially on extra-ordinary occasions, are scarcely known; one must guess. Besides, they probably varied with time and from tribe to tribe.

Crossbow: Versions of this weapon existed from quite ancient times, though it use did not become widespread until the Middle Ages.

Britannic Sea (Oceanus Britannicus): The English Channel.

The Islands of Crows (in Latin, *Corvorum Insulae*, this word order being preferred in such cases): The Channel Islands. Almost nothing is known of their history prior to the medieval period. There are traces of Roman occupation, but slight, indicating that it was nominal and came to an end before the Empire did. It is our own idea that they thereupon became a haunt of pirates and so acquired the nickname we use.

German Sea (Oceanus Germanicus): The North Sea.

Celtic Languages: Through closely related, these had enough differences from each other to make them distinct. We suppose that a speaker of the Irish tongue could acquire a Continental one fairly easily, and vice versa.

Danes (Dani): For a brief discussion of this people, see the notes to *Dahut*. While the viking era would not commence for several centuries, it is reasonable to suppose that some Scandinavians joined the Western Germanic sailors already harrying the Empire.

Tungri and Continental Belgae: Tribes inhabiting what are now the Low Countries and the adjacent part of France. Belgae had also established themselves quite powerfully in Britain before the Roman conquest.

III

Liguria: A region of Italy which at this time included what is now Lombardy. Modern Liguria is only a seaboard strip.

Mediolanum: Milan. Very little is known of it layout or appearance in Roman times.

Alaric: Visigothic king whose armies repeatedly invaded Italy, beginning as early as 401. In between hostilities there was occasional uneasy alliance with the Romans.

(The next few entries repeat, briefly, explanations made in earlier volumes.)

Ruirthech: The River Liffey. Today it does *not* mark the border of Leinster, but we suppose that the Tara dynasty carved most of Mide out of the latter.

Kings: Each tuath in early Ireland had its own king, who was little more than a wartime leader and peacetime arbitrator. Such kings generally owed allegiance to more powerful ones, among whom the strongest might dominate a realm; but he was in no sense a monarch.

Mumu: Approximately, Munster. At this time the chief king was Conual Corcc, whom we suppose to have been friendly toward both Niall and Ys.

Temir: Tara.

Women in early Ireland: They had almost as many rights and as much freedom as men, including sexually, even after marriage.

IV

The turf wall: We base our description on the experimental work of Robin Birley and his team. A turf cut to the regulation Roman army size of 18" x 12" x 6" weighs about 2-1/4 stone, or a little over 30 pounds. Edward Luttwak has pointed out that the real value of the perimeter defense of a legionary camp was its enabling most men to get a good night's sleep.

Darioritum Venetorum: Vannes.

Vorgium: Carhaix.

Gesoscribate: A Roman port on or near the site of present-day Brest.

Jecta: The River Jet (conjectural from aqua iacta, "water thrown in a straight line," thence Jecta, and so on to the modern form).

Postal privileges: The Imperial mails went via frequent relay stations where fresh horses, relief riders, and, at longer intervals, lodging were available. The system was reserved for official communications, but favored persons were occasionally allowed to use it. Ordinary people employed private carriers.

Dumnoniic shore: The Dumnonii inhabited what is now Cornwall and Devon. It seems believable that, under Roman influence, they were sometimes building better boats than their Irish cousins—although the currach is itself very seaworthy.

Egyptians: Egypt was largly Christian by the early fourth century, and remained so under its early Moslem rulers.

V

Indiction: (Latin *indictio*): The decree issued every fifteen years by the Roman Emperors, establishing property and head taxes on the basis of census reports; also, the taxes themselves, collected annually and for the most part in kind. The indiction was by no means the only levy, and often superindictions were added. The year 402 was one of indiction.

Fundus: A landed estate. See *Roma Mater*.

Gong: Bells were probably not yet known. The earliest date suggested by any evidence is the late fourth century, and the actual date may well lie a hundred or more years later. Certainly bells would not be found in Armorica at the time of our story.

Seating: As we have observed before, chairs were not common (except in Ys) until fairly recent times. People ususally sat on benches or stools, though for the well-to-do these might be elaborately made and upholstered. The floor was quite often used, expecially by the poor, and to offer a visitor nothing better would be a blunt subordination of him.

Sucat: St. Patrick to be. See *Gallicenae.*

Stories of St. Martin: These two—that Satan appeared to him in the guise of Christ but was identified and dismissed, and that he raised and exorcised the ghost of a false saint—occur in his legend.

Confluentes Cornuales: The Breton name "Kemper," which French renders "Quimper," means "confluence." We have supposed that there was a Latin original with the same meaning, most likely in the plural form as is permissible in that language. Our historical analogue is Koblenz in Germany. The general area in which Quimper lies is known as Cornuaille. This is not a version of "Cornwall," bestowed by immigrants from Britain, as is often said; its source is obscure. That the region came to be called Dogwood Land, Terra Cornualis, in late Roman times, and thus eventually Cornouaille, is our own idea.

VII

The high Mass: This scene represents our reconstruction of a Gallic Mass, which was quite different from forms elsewhere and those that developed later. Much is uncertain about it, and there appears to have been considerable variation from time to time and place to place.

Corentinus a bishop: There is no record of a bishop of Quimper in the fifth century. Yet Breton tradition holds that St. Corentin held the office, having been consecrated by St. Martin. If this is true, as we assume in the story, perhaps it fell vacant for a long time after his death. Alternatively, it may have happened that no bishop of Quimper attended a synod—as Martin himself did not subsequent to the Priscillianist affair—throughout the same period, and hence none is mentioned in what chronicles and lists have survived. Political and ethnic divisions might account for the absences.

A carcass breeds maggots: This belief was widespread before the life cycle was understood.

Vienna: The River Vienne.

Liger: The River Loire.

Death of St. Martin: Our account follows that of Sulpicius, with a few slight adaptations. The date was probably 8 November. (A modern biography gives it as the 11th, but this was likelier the date of burial.) However, a calendrical inconsistency in the chronicle makes the year uncertain. Depending on how one reads, it was either 397 or 400. We have chosen the latter.

VIII

The Biblical verse: Hebrews xiii.

Exorcism: In the early Church, this was repeatedly done over candidates for baptism, at least if they were adult and if time allowed.

Baptism: As we have observed before, the usual practice even in Christian families had been to defer baptism until the person and his bishop agreed he was ready—often quite late in life. This remained common in the East, but in the West the earliest possible christening came to be more and more favored, until by about 400 it was generally done for infants. Most converts were still first given some instruction, which included the exorcisms mentioned.

Piracy: Throughout history, pirates have raided the land much more frequently than they have attacked ships at sea.

Church organization: We have already explained that this was different from what it later became. Priests were essentially assistants to the bishop, ranking above deacons but without certain of the powers, such as independently administering baptism, that later became theirs.

Baptismal rites: These varied considerably from time to time, place to place, and according to circumstances. What we have depicted is a variant of a form commonly employed; the modifications for women are rather conjectural, but may well have been ordered by some if not all bishops. Holy Saturday was the favored time. From the preceding period of instruction and abstinence developed, quite probably, many Lenten practices that later became general.

Drusus's farm: It is not typically Celtic in its layout nor Roman in its legal standing. However, under peculiar conditions such as prevailed around Aquilo at the time, something like this was a logical development among new settlers.

Paganism: Though pagan rites were now illegal, the law was seldom enforceable, except against conspicuous centers; and baptism was not yet compulsory.

IX

Sprit rig: Formerly this was through to be a Dutch invention of the late Middle Ages, but archeological evidence has come to light that the Romans knew it, as well as a version of the lateen sail.

Artemon: A small square sail hung from the bowsprit to aid in steering.

Roman Bay: Baie de Douarnenez. The name that the Romans themselves gave it is unknown.

Goat Foreland: Cap de la Chêvre. We suppose that the Ysans and their neighbors gave it a name with the same meaning.

Sapa: Pliny describes this substance, its preparation and uses. In terms of modern chemistry, the active ingredients were organic lead salts. Lead is an abortifacient; when it lightens the complexion, it does so by causing anemia.

Johannes: Latin form of "John," in this case John the Baptist. His feast day is not now precisely at the solstice, but Midsummer Night rituals connected with it persisted until quite recent times, and in some areas the bonfires are still lighted.

Marriage: Church doctrine and practice with respect to matrimony in the early fifth century are discussed in a later note.

X

The witch: It is unlikely that medieval witchcraft represented a widespread, underground Old Religion, as is often claimed. Granted, there were pagan survivals in the practice of it, but so there were in Christianity. Doubtless some witches and their male counterparts were outright pagans, like Nemeta, though probably more were henotheistic and still more thought of themselves as Christian (or, in some cases, Jewish). Certain monkish chroniclers seem to have greatly exaggerated the significance of magic and passed on the wildest rumors. Despite this, the fact is that for centuries magic was generally tolerated, provided it was not openly blasphemous— which would scarcely have been so if the Church saw it as a threat. There were actually stories of pious wizards such as Merlin. Full persecution of witches and alleged witches was a phenomenon of the Reformation era, and did not succeed in extirpating them everywhere. Within living memory, some parts of southern Europe had their village witches whose spells were supposed to help people with minor problems. This is not to say that *no* witches and warlocks were ever feared, or that horrid rites and malign intent never happened. Evil occurs in all walks of life.

Egyptian malady: Diphtheria, described under this name by Aretaeus in the second century. There is much uncertainty about the epidemiology of the ancient world. The devastating plague in the reign of Marcus Aurelius does not appear to have been bubonic, which is first unequivocally documented in Europe in the sixth century. Smallpox seems to have entered from Asia about a hundred years later than that.

Imperial tax agent: At this period, tax collection was as a general rule the responsibility of the curials of each locality. They might sometimes engage a man to go about the countryside performing the duty, and he might take a considerable rakeoff, thus in a way reviving the tax farming of the Republic and early Empire. Laws, such as those which supposedly forbade the selling of children above the age of ten into slavery, could be ignored when the poor had no access to higher authroity and might not even know the laws were on the books. Lúgotorix in *Roma Mater* is a publican of this kind. In addition, special tax officers reported directly to provincial or diocesal officialdom. One class of these collected arrears, another oversaw the whole process and kept the curials up to the mark. Or so the theory went; in practice, they often terrorized everybody, screening their peculations and extortions with bureaucratic obfuscation. A common way for them to grow rich was to convert arrears of taxes into private debts at huge rates of interest. Nagon has been appointed to such a provincial office.

Dál Riata: As we have explained earlier, this was the first Irish colony in what is now Scotland, on the Argyll coast, founded by emigrants from an Ulster kingdom of that name and for a long time considered part of it. The date of the settlement is uncertain. Some authorities place it a century or more after the time of our story, but we are here following traditional accounts.

Aryagalatis: The chronicle calls him Gabran, but we follow the suggestion of Alexei Kondratiev as to what the earlier form of the name had been. (Admittedly, we are inconsistent in that we do not do likewise for the name "Niall" and for a few such words as "tuath," but these, like "Rome" and "Constantinople," are familiar enough that we would rather not risk seeming pedantic.) Though he bore that title, he was not a sovereign monarch. Any man of the right descent, leading any group from a tuath upward, was called its king (*rí*). His powers were always strictly limited; see earlier parts of this story for details. Aryagalatis would have been essentially the chief warlord and sacral figure of the colonial tuaths and whatever natives they subdued. The medieval story says he gave Eochaid refuge after the latter must flee Ireland becaue of having murdered the poet's son. That Eochaid first roamed about as a pirate is our idea, but quite possible.

Alba: The early Gaelic name for what is now Scotland; sometimes it was extended to include England and Wales.

Cruthini: The Irish name for that people, or those tribes, the Romans lumped together as Picts. Prior to the great Irish (Scotic) immigration early in the Dark Ages, they formed most of the population of what the Irish called Alba and we today call Scotland. Smaller numbers of them also lived here and there in Gaul and in Ireland itself.

XI

The first Visigothic invasion of Italy: Dates are not quite cetain, but most authorities put in in November, 401.

Illyricum: The political status and official boundaries of this region varied in the course of history, but in general it comprised much of the Balkan area. Around 400 it was a prefecture, divided between the Western and Eastern Empires. (So they were by that time, although theoretically still one.)

Rhenus: The River Rhine.

Danuvius: The River Danube.

Euxinus: The Black Sea.

Deva: Chester.

The legion at Chester: As admirers of the work of Stephen Vincent Benét, we regretted making the discovery that the Twentieth Valeria Victrix was not, after all, the last legion to depart from Britain.

Etruria: Tuscany and northern Latium.

Histria (later Istria): The area around what is now Trieste.

Rhaetia (or Raetia): An area occupying what are now known as the Grisons of eastern Switzerland, much of the Tyrol of Austria, and part of Lombardy.

Iron ore: This was usually bog iron, collected rather than mined.

Durotriges: A British tribe occupying, approximately, Dorset.

British immigration into Armorica: This is generally supposed to have gone on in the fifth and sixth centuries, but there is evidence that it began earlier. Some modern scholars believe that it had actually become overwhelming by about 400, but we stay with the traditional view.

German Sea (Oceanus Germanicus): The North Sea.

Cimbrian peninsula: Jutland.

Thule: It is not known what Classical geographers meant by this, and they themselves may well have been unsure or in disagreement. We accept the idea that it was in Norway.

XII

The Republic: Even this late, the Western Empire, at least, maintained the fiction that it was a republic, the Emperor its chief magistrate although sanctified by the office and surrounded by the trappings of Oriental monarchy.

Churching: The rite readmitting a woman to services after she had given birth.

Deacon: As explained previously, clergy of the early church, below the rank of bishop, had usually had mundane occupations by which they earned their livings. By the time of our story, priests were supposed to receive stipends, but it is doubtful that deacons did, unless perhaps in the wealthiest churches.

Bricius: Now known as St. Brice, this bishop relaxed the strict rules of his predecessor St. Martin. He was later accused of immorality. The Pope absolved him but he never returned to his see, which suggests he had in fact been guilty.

Paenula: A poncholike outer garment.

XIII

The move to Ravenna: Its date is not certain, but was probably in summer or autumn of 402.

The case against Cadoc: Breton legend relates how King Grallon cleared St. Ronan of a similar charge by similar means. We are supposing that the story derives from an actual incident and was later transferred to the canonized churchman.

Duke: The Duke of the Armorican Tract, director of defense in that district of Lúgdunensis Tertia province.

XIV

The obliteration of Ys: Greater cities than this have been lost from the face of the earth. Archeologists in modern times have identified the sites and uncovered traces of a number of them, but not yet all, and this has generally been with historical records to provide clues.

XV

Postal couriers: These frequently doubled as intelligence agents for the civil authorities.

Savus: The River Drava.

Dalmatia: A province occupying, approximately, what is now most of Yugoslavia.

Pannonia: A province occupying, approximately, what is now Hungary with parts of Austria and Yugoslavia (Croatia).

Resettlement of the Visigoths: Stilicho's repeated leniency toward Alaric was most likely prompted by a desire to make an ally of him for a drive that would establish the supremacy of the Western over the Eastern Empire. The policy was to prove disastrously mistaken.

Procedures possible against the Confluentians: If these seem limited to the modern reader, one should bear in mind that, while the Romans developed many instruments of tyranny with the inevitable social consequences, the idea of income tax as we know it never occurred to them. Besides, they would have lacked the technology to enforce it.

The wedding: To the Romans, until very late in their history, marriage was a civil contract. Since Tertullian, Christians believed the public blessing of the Church was necessary to make it valid (a view somewhat modified today), but not until after St. Augustine did they consider it a sacrament in itself. Then marriages with pagans and heretics came to be disallowed. However, this had not yet happened at the time of our story. (Augustine issued his *De Bono Conjugali* in 401; it would hardly have reached Armorica by 403, let alone become a basis of doctrine.) Observances surely varied from place to place and time to time. Our version derives in large part from ancient customs, but we suppose that the new religion and the special circumstances caused these to be a little altered.

The prayer: As we have explained before, early Christians had not ordinarily knelt to pray. Except when they prostrated themselves, they stood upright with arms lifted. Kneeling, though not folding of hands, presently came into use in church, but individuals alone probably, as a rule, continued the older practice.

The Virgin Mary: Adoration of her seems to have begun in earnest during the fourth century. It was not yet anything like what it became in the Middle Ages, not could it yet have had much currency in the North; but Gratillonius's impulse seems to us a very natural one under the circumstances.

XVI

Head of navigation: As we have explained earlier, today this is at Locmaria (Aquilo), and then only at high tide and for rather small craft; but apparently the Odet and, perhaps, the Steir were larger and deeper in the past, and ancient vessels generally drew less water than today's. A change in the harbor site helps explain how Quimper (Confluentes) came to overshadow and eventually absorb the older settlement.

Bridge of Sena: Pont de Sein. We suppose that this is the French form of a name going back to ancient time.

XVII

Brigantes: A tribe occupying a substantial part of Britain just south of Hadrian's Wall.

Laégare (later rendered *Laoghaire,* now sometimes *Leary*). According to the traditional histories, he was King at Tara when St. Patrick returned to Ireland. He became friendly with the missionaries and put no obstacles in their path. Indeed, he got Patrick to help him reform and write down the Brehon Laws, the ancient Irish code, which continued in effect for centuries thereafter. However, he himself never accepted baptism. When he died he was buried according to his wish, upright in full battle gear, facing his hereditary enemies the Leinstermen.

Fox and hare: Within living memory in Ireland, it was believed unlucky if either of these animals crossed one's path. Galway fishermen bound for their boats would often turn home.

Lúg's Chariot, etc: It is not known what constellations the Irish and other Celts actually invented. We do know that, while ancient mariners hugged the coasts as much as possible, the Mediterranean civilizations had developed means of measuring the altitudes of heavenly bodies with some precision, and so estimating latitude. The voyages made by more primitive sailors such as the Irish and Saxons show that they must have possessed a smiliar capability, perhaps learned from the Romans.

Corbilo: Mentioned by Strabo as an important maritime city of Gaul, it seems to have occupied the site of present-day St. Nazaire. About the end of the fourth century, when its circumstances must have been much reduced, it was taken over by Saxons, presumably laeti but evidently with effective autonomy, since they were not converted for another one or two hundred years.

The hour between dog and wolf: This French phrase for twilight, *"l'heure entre chien et loup,"* may have ancient origins.

Torna Éces: According to legend, this greatest of the ancient poets was foster-father to both Niall and Conual, and lamented them both after their deaths. The implied lifespan is great, but not impossible.

XVIII

Sanctuary: This issue was an early one in that conflict between Church and state which was to dominate Western history for centuries and shape much of the new civilization. At the time of our story, a bishop was virtually sovereign with respect to ecclesiastical matters within his (religious) diocese, and had great temporal authority and influence as well. The Pope was only *primus inter pares*, the final arbiter of disputes between bishops but otherwise with little power unique to his office.

Arelate: Arles. The date when it supplanted Trier is not known exactly, but 404 is a reasonable guess.

Exorcism: Corentinus's opinion may not seem canonical to a modern Catholic, but it should be remembered that in the fifth century much doctrine was still unformulated, disagreements and heresies were rife. Moreover, Dahut's case may have been unique in demonology.

Milk: Children were nursed for a long time by modern standards, well after they began to take solid foods—which were not pressed on them in the manner of today. Lactation does in fact often inhibit impregnation.

Danastris: The River Dniester.

Danuvius: The River Danube. It seems likely that the Goths did not slow themselves by much plundering along the way, but pushed on to catch the Romans ill-prepared in Italy.

XIX

Terms of enlistment: These are attested, and help show how desperate the situation was.

Niall's successor: According to the Irish chronicles, he was Nath Í (or Nathi or Dathi), a fierce warrior who perished in 428 when struck by lightning on an expedition into the Alps. This is almost surely a copyist's error for "Alba," Scotland or England. His successor in turn was Niall's son Laégare, in whose reign St. Patrick began his mission.

Gesocribate: Virtually nothing is known of this city. Even its location is uncertain, though at or near the site of Brest. Its oblivion indicates that it was probably rather small, and may well have been repeatedly sacked until at last it was abandoned.

Crossbow: Little is known about the ancient form of this weapon. Apparently it was drawn by hand rather than wound like the medieval arbalest, but by the fifth century it may sometimes have possessed a pawl. Given sufficient pull, arrows can certainly penetrate mail. Although the rate of discharge is low, the crossbow has an advantage in requiring less skill, hence less training, than the straight bow does.

Holy Georgios: St. George, patron of soldiers. While the cult of saints had not yet approached its medieval intensity, unless perhaps in Egypt, the idea of their intercession, implicit in Scripture, was taking hold widely. No doubt the evangelization of the rural Empire strengthened it. Pagan halidoms were rededicated to specific saints, and people continued to seek help there.

XX

Scythia: At this time it was a rather vague designation; but the Alani, an Iranian people with some Altaic admixture, originated north of the Caspian Sea and spread into the steppes of Russia. Some eventually reached Germanic lands and there joined in the Völkerwanderung.

Moguntiacum: Mainz.

XXI

Vorgium: Carhaix.

Brains: Galen, in the second century, taught that the brain is the seat of consciousness, and his medical works became canonical, although doubtless the uneducated in the fifth century clung to older concepts.

Durocortorum: Reims.

Samarobriva: Amiens.

Nemetacum: Arras.

Turnacum: Tournay.

Eboracum (or *Eburacum*): York.

Constantinus: Today called Constantine III or Constantine the Usurper. Virtually nothing is known about the events leading up to his try for the purple, except the names of his predecessors Marcus and Gratian, and that the latter reigned for four months (which implies that the former was no more durable). Constantine's origin is equally obscure. Little has been recorded of his character, and that by hostile writers. He is said to have been a common soldier, but this can scarcely mean that he was when the legions hailed him. We have supplied him with a career that brought him up from the ranks. The fact that he had two sons who took an active part in his campaigns gives a clue to his age at the time. A tradition holds that he was himself a son of Magnus Maximus, who had become a folk hero among the Britons (at least, in the West: see *Roma Mater*). This seems implausible to us, but perhaps there was some more distant kinship, such as Maximus's wife having been Constantine's aunt.

Saxon and Scotian: Unlettered, ferocious, and impulsive though they were, the barbarian leaders cannot often have been stupid. Else the migration of whole tribes could not have happened. Spies, scouts, talkative traders, and other such sources must have given them some idea of what was going on in those parts of the Empire that interested them. The Romans can hardly ever have been able to keep events secret. Even the huge alliance that crossed the Rhine at the end of 406 would have had intelligence of what to expect.

Gesoriacum: Boulogne (not to be confused with Gesocribate).

Pyrenaei Mountains: The Pyrenees.

XXII

Lemovicium: Limoges. Earlier it was Augustoritum but in the fourth century, like so many other cities, it came to be called after the tribe in whose ancient territory it lay.

The Feast of Lug: As we have observed before, the harvest festival known in Ireland as Lugnasad and in England as Lammas has long been fixed at 1 August. (The customs we mention were Irish until recent times and must have been of very old Celtic origin.) We hypothesize that, like other such dates, this one was established with Christianity and the Roman calendar, and that originally it was determined by the moon.

Salaun: Breton form of the name "Salomon," which belonged to the legendary first King of Brittany. We shall have more to say about him later in these notes.

XXIII

The Armorican revolt of 407: Nothing is really known about the circumstances. The chronicles say merely that Roman officials were expelled and independence declared; they attribute this to Bacaudae. That seems absured if taken literally. There could not have been that many outlaws, nor would they have been well enough organized, nor does it appear likely they would have refrained from massacring those they looked on oppressors. "Bacaudae" must be esentially a swear word, though perhaps with more meaning where it comes to things that happened elsewhere or later. We think our reconstruction of events that year in Armorica is plausible. Of course, all the details are fictional.

Pictavum: Poiters. The older name was Limonum. The Pictones of Gaul were not related to the Picts of Alba, "Picta" being a name bestowed by the Romans on the latter, the "painted people." However, apparently some tribes related to them did live in Gaul and Ireland as well as Scotland.

Prince (Latin *princeps*): Orginally an honorific, meaning "first," applied to various persons such as the first senator on the censor's list in the Republic (*princeps senatus*), later under the Empire as a title of various civil and military officials. Thus in our period it did not yet connote superiority or royal blood. Still, Armoricans might very naturally apply it to the associate and prospective successor of the man they regarded as their Duke (*dux,* "leader," especially a military leader, though this inevitably gave him command over certain civil functions as well).

Hawking: Falconry was practiced by the Romans, albeit the slight and vague mentions of it that we have from them, and the lack of artistic representations, indicate that it had nothing like the popularity it gained during the Middle Ages.

Gelding: Given the lack of what we consider basic prophylaxis, the death rate among new castrates—at least, human ones—was extremely high. Moreover, Roman law forbade the operation on citizens. Eunuchs were either prisoners of war or, oftener, imported from abroad, especially Persia. In consequence, they were expensive. The restrictions were later lifted.

XXIV

The Race of Sena: Raz de Sein, between the island and the mainland.

Garrison in Britain: Virtually nothing is known for certain, but there is some reason to suppose Constantine left a few soldiers behind— much too few to be effective, as the course of events shows.

British-Armorican alliance: Obviously this did not come to pass in 407, but there is mention (date not deducible, reliability somewhat questionable) of joint action against the Germans in Gaul, and more than this may have taken place. If so, it was probably after 410, when Homorius's rescript gave the Britons leave to defend themselves.

Caletes: A tribe occupying what is now, approximately, Seine-Maritime.

Sequana: The River Seine. Apparently the revolt in Gaul reached at least this far; and areas farther off had their own uprisings.

Rotomagus: Rouen.

Beltane: We use this variant spelling to indicate a difference between the languages of the insular and the Continental Celts.

Infantry: There was no possibility of re-creating anything like the old Roman legions, and the military future for almost the next thousand years belonged to the heavy cavalryman. The independent Gauls could scarcely raise such a corps either; at best, they may have developed some reasonably good light horse. The bulk of their forces must have been foot. Still, given training and equipment, these could meet the Germans and the seaborne raiders on equal terms.

The Gallic revolt: One should beware of identifying the many different rebellions in the ancient world with any revolution in the modern, such as the American, French, Russian, or Philippine, to name jsut four widely divergent examples. Each case in the period of our story and earlier was probably unique too. Nothing is really known about the Gallic instance. By analogy with events in Britain, we suppose that ancient tribalism awoke and asserted itself among people who had despaired of Rome. In both countries there appears also to have been a certain amount of nascent nationalism, though it never developed into anything as strong as the modern form.

West Island: Ushant (hypothetical; its name in Roman times is unknown).

XXV

Wotan: This god appears to have been originally a conductor of the dead like Hermes or Mercury, with whom the Romans therefore identified him. We suppose that in the fifth century he had not yet gained those other, overshadowing attributes we know of in his late version, Odin of the viking era.

The moon: It was full on 30 December 407 (Gregorian calendar).

The exorcism: This is not the present-day formula, which is of rather recent origin. There does not seem to have been a standard one in the fifth century; ours is conjectural.

The aftermath: In 408 Stilicho married his second daughter Thermantia to Honorius, but soon afterward the machinations of his rivals achieved their purpose. He was accused of treasonous dealings with Alaric the Visigoth, his troops mutinied, and he was assassinated in August of that year. There followed such a wave of anti-German feeling and persecution that the soldiers of that origin and their families went over to Alaric. He marched on Rome, and only an exorbitant payment turned him from it. The next year he came back and set up a puppet emperor whom the Senate perforce acknowledged but quickly thereafter disowned. Alaric returned in 410, captured and sacked Rome, and was on his way through Italy to invade North Africa when he died.

Meanwhile Constantine III established himself in Arles and, defeating forces sent against him by Honorius, wrung from the government the consulship of 409 and recognition as an Imperial colleague; he and his older son proclaimed themselves Augusti. He defended the Rhine frontier rather ably and brought the Germans who had invaded Gaul under a measure of control. Intrigue and attacks led to his overthrow in 411. He surrendered to Honorius, who, repudiating a guarantee of safety, had him executed.

The year 410 was also when Honorius sent his famous rescript to the Britons, granting them the right to organize their own defenses because the help for which they appealed would not be forthcoming. It appears they were temporarily victorious about the middle of the century and this is the seed from which the Arthurian legend sprang. Germans continued to enter Roman territory on the Continent and founded independent kingdoms in it, the Burgundians as early as 413. The Huns, sometimes allies of the Empire, become more and more often its ravishers.

Nevertheless a chronicle declares that in or about 417 the Romans regained Armorica and other secessionist parts of Gaul. No details are given. It seems probable to us that, if this did happen, the submission was nominal, the result of a mutually advantageous compromise, and that the Armoricans retained essential autonomy. Honorius could not very well punish an uprising which had, after all, been against the usurper Constantine; nor could he have spared troops to occupy the region and compel subservience. (He died unlamented in 423.) There is mention of later revolts of "Bacaudae" in various areas, but these may have been incidents of jacquerie.

According to the Breton accounts, Salaun (Salomon) reigned as King from 421 to 435; he abolished the Roman practice of selling children into slavery to pay taxes, but was killed by pagans who resented his efforts to Christianize the country. If this can be trusted, and it looks no more unreliable than the Mediterranean sources, it bears out the idea of a free Armorica. Still more does an extant roll of the nations that sent men to join Aëtius in his historic battle against the Huns, 451. "The Armoricans" are listed like any others, implying that they were sovereign allies.

Equally suggestive is the heavy immigration from Britain in this and the subsequent century. It would scarcely have gone in the direction of more oppression and less security. Of course, it resulted in the flooding of the small native population. Armorica became known as Breizh (Bretagne in French, Brittany in English) and the Celtic language still spoken there is of southwestern British origin. A few traditions survive from ancient times—among them, perhaps, the story of Ys.

GEOGRAPHICAL GLOSSARY

These equivalents are for the most part only approximations. For further details, see the Notes.

Abona: The River Avon in Somerset.

Abonae: Sea Mills.

Africa: North Africa, exclusive of Egypt and Ethiopia.

Alba: Scotic name of what is now Scotland, sometimes including England and Wales.

Aquae Sulis: Bath.

Aquileia: Near present-day Trieste.

Aquilo: Locmaria, now a district at the south end of Quimper.

Aquitania: See *Gallia Aquitania.*

Aregésla: Counties Monaghan, Cavan, and Leitrim in Ireland.

Arelate: Arles.

Armorica: Brittany.

Asia: Asia Minor

Audiarna: Audierne (hypothetical).

Augusta Treverorum: Trier.

Avela: Ávila

Bay of Aquitania (Sinus Aquitanicus): Bay of Biscay.

Boand's River: The River Boyne.

Bonna: Bonn

Borcovicium: Housesteads, at Hadrian's Wall.

Bridge of Sena: Pont de Sein.

Britannia: The Roman part of Britain, essentially England and Wales.

Britannic Sea (Oceanus Britannicus): The English Channel.

Burdigala: Bordeaux.

Caesarodunum Turonum: Tours.

Caledonia: Roman name of Scotland.

Campania: A district of Italy including modern Capua and Naples.

Cape Rach: Pointe du Raz (hypothetical).

Cassel: Cashel.

Castellum: Original form of "Cassel."

Cenabum: Orleans

Cimbrian Chersonese, Cimbrian peninsula: Jutland.

Clón Tarui: Clontarf, now a district of Dublin.

Condacht: Connaught.

Condate Redonum: Rennes.

Condevincum: A small city, now part of Nantes.

Confluentes: Quimper (hypothetical).

Corbilo: St. Nazaire.

Dacia: Romania.

Dalmatia: A province occupying, approximately, what is now much of Yugoslavia.

Dál Riata: A realm in Ulster, or its colony on the Argyll coast.

Danastris: The River Dniester.

Danuvius: The River Danube.

Darioritum Venetorum: Vannes.

Deva: Chester.

Dochaldun: An Osismiic village (imaginary).

Dubris: Dover.

Dún Alinni: Near present-day Kildare.

Duranius: The River Dordogne.

Durocotorum: Reims.

Eboracum: York.

Emain Macha: Seat of the principal Ulster kings, near present-day Armagh.

Ériu: Early Gaelic name of Ireland.

Etruria: Tuscany and northern Latium.

Euxinus: The Black Sea.

Falernia: An area in Campania, noted for wine.

Fanum Martis: Corseul.

Gallia: Gaul, including France and parts of Belgium, Germany, and Switzerland.

Gallia Aquitania: A province of Gaul, bounded approximately by the Atlantic Ocean and the Garonne and Loire Rivers.

Gallia Lugdunensis: A province of Gaul, comprising most of what is now northern and a fair portion of central France.

Gallia Narbonensis: A province in southwestern France.

Garomagus: A town at or near present-day Douarnenez (hypothetical).

Garumna: The River Garonne.

German Sea (Oceanus Germanicus): The North Sea.

Gesocribate: A seaport at or near the site of Brest.

Gesoriacum: Boulogne.

Goana: The River Goyen (hypothetical).

Goat Foreland: Cap de la Chêvre (hypothetical).

Gobaean Promontory (Promontorium Gobaeum): Cap Sizun.

Hispania Tarraconensis: A province in the northeast and east of Spain.

Hispania: Spain and Portugal.

Histria: The area around what is now Trieste.

Hivernia: Roman name of Ireland.

Icenia: Norfolk and Suffolk.

Illyricum: A Roman diocese (major administrative division) occupying, approximately, Greece and much of Yugoslavia.

Ingena: Avranches.

Isca Silurum: Caerleon

Islands of Crows: The Channel Islands (hypothetical nickname).
Jecta: The River Jet (hypothetical).
Juliomagus: Angers.
Lemovicium: Limoges.
Liger: The River Loire.
Liguria: A region of Italy including Lombardy and present day Liguria.
Londinium: London.
Lugdunensis: See *Gallia Lugdunensis.*
Lugdunensis Tertia: A Roman province comprising northwestern France.
Lugdunum: Lyons.
Lugovallium: Carlisle.
Lutetia Parisiorum: Paris (in part).
Maedraecum: Médréac (hypothetical).
Mag Slecht: A pagan sanctuary in County Cavan, Ireland.
Maia: Bowness.
Massilia: Marseilles.
Mauretania: Northern Morocco.
Mediolanum: Milan.
Mide: A kingdom occupying present-day Counties Meath, Westmeath, and Longford, with parts of Kildare and Offaly, Ireland.
Moguntiacum: Mainz.
Mons Ferruginus: Mont Frugy (hypothetical).
Mosella: The River Moselle (or Mosel).
Mumu: Munster.
Namnetum: See *Portus Namnetum.*
Narbonensis: See *Gallia Narbonensis.*
Neapolis: Naples.
Nemetacum: Arras.
Odita: The River Odet (hypothetical).
Osismia: The country of the Osismii, in western Britanny.
Osismiis: Later name of Vorgium (q.v.)
Ossanuba: Faro, Portugal.
Ossraige: A realm occupying the western part of Counties Laoighis and Kilkenny, Ireland.
Pannonia: A Roman province occupying parts of Hungary, Austria, and Yugoslavia.
Pergamum: A former kingdom in western Anatolia, eventually assimilated by Rome.
Pictavum: Poitiers.
Point Vanis: Pointe du Van (hypothetical).
Portus Namnetum: Nantes (in part).
Pyrenaei Mountains: The Pyrenees.
Qóiqet Lagini: Leinster (in part).
Qóiqet nUlat: Ulster.
Race of Sena: Raz de Sein.

Raetia (or Rhaetia): A Roman province occupying the eastern Alps and western Tyrol.

Redonia: The country of the Redones, in eastern Brittany.

Redonum: See *Condate Redonum.*

Rhenus: The River Rhine.

Rhodanus: The River Rhone.

Roman Bay: Baie de Douarnenez (hypothetical).

Rotomagus: Rouen.

Ruirthech: The River Liffey.

Sabrina: The River Severn.

Samarobriva: Amiens.

Savus: The River Drava.

Scandia: The southern part of the Scandinavian peninsula.

Scot's Landing: A fisher hamlet near Ys (imaginary).

Sena: Île de Sein.

Sequana: The River Seine.

Sinand: The River Shannon.

Stag Run: An Osismiic village (imaginary).

Stegir: The River Steir (hypothetical).

Suebian Sea (Mare Suebicum): The Baltic Sea.

Tallten: Teltown, in County Meath, Ireland.

Tamesis: The River Thames.

Tarraconensis: See *Hispania Tarraconensis.*

Temir: Tara.

Teutoburg Forest: Scene of a Roman military disaster at German hands in the reign of Augustus Caesar.

Thracia: Thrace, occupying approximately the northeastern end of Greece, the northwestern end of Turkey, and a part of Bulgaria.

Treverorum: See *Augusta Treverorum.*

Turnacum: Tournay.

Turonum: See *Caesarodunum Turonum.*

Venetorum: See *Darioritum Venetorum.*

Vienna: Vienne.

Vindolanda: Chesterholm, at Hadrian's Wall.

Vindoval: An Osismiic village (imaginary).

Vindovaria: A village in Britain (imaginary).

Vorgium: Carhaix.

Whalestrand: A fisher hamlet in western Britanny (imaginary).

Ys: City-state at the far western end of Brittany (legendary).

DRAMATIS PERSONAE

Where characters are fictional or legendary, their names are in Roman lower case; where historical (in the opinion of most authorities), in Roman capitals; where of doubtful or debatable historicity, in italics. When a full name has not appeared in the text, it is generally not here either, for it was of no great importance even to the bearer.

Adminius: A legionary from Londinium in Britannia, second in comand (deputy) of Gratillonius's detachment in Ys.

Adruval Tyri: Sea Lord of Ys, head of the navy and marines.

Aébell: A daughter of Cellach.

Aed: A tuathal king in Munster.

AETHBE: A wife of Niall (name conjectural).

ALARIC: King of the Visigoths.

Allil: A half-brother of Niall.

Amair: A daughter of Fennalis by Hoel.

AMBROSIUS: Bishop of Milan, today known as St. Ambrose.

Ámend: Second wife of Conual Corcc.

Amreth Taniti: Commander of the surviving Ysan marines.

Anmureg maqq Cerballi: A sea rover from Mide.

Antonia: (1) A sister of Gratillonis; (2) Second daughter of Guilvilis and Gratillonius.

Apuleius Vero: A senator in Aquilo and a tribune of the city.

Arator: A Gallo-Roman prelate.

Arban Cartagi: An Ysan Suffete, husband of Talavair, father of Korai.

ARBOGAST: A Frankish general in the Roman army.

ARCADIUS, FLAVIUS: A son of Theodosius and his successor as Augustus of the East.

Ardens, Septimius Cornelius: Praetorian prefect of Gallia, Hispania, and Britannia.

Arel: Father of Donnerch.

Artorius: The former steward of the Gratillonius estate.

Aryagalatis maqq Irgalato: King of Dál Riata in Alba.

Audrenius: A Gallo-Roman dealer in fuel.

Audris: Dauther of Innilis by Hoel.

Augustina: Daughter of Vindilis and Gratillonius.

AUSONIUS, DECIMUS MAGNUS: Gallo-Roman poet, scholar, teacher, and sometime Imperial officer.

Avonis: Sister of Herun, eventually wife of Adminius.

Bacca, Quintus Domitius: Procurator of Lugdunensis Tertia.

Bannon: Headman of Dochaldun.

Barak Tyri: A young man of Ys.

Belcar: A legendary Ysan hero.

Betha: Wife of Maeloch.

Blodvin: Osismiic maidservant of Fennalis.

Bodilis: A Queen of Ys; daughter of Tambilis by Wulfgar.

Boia: A daughter of Lanarvilis by Hoel.

Bolce Ben-bretnach: Mother of Conual Corcc.

Bomatin Kusuri: A Suffete of Ys, a sea captain and Mariner delegate to the Council.

Borsus: An Ysan.

Bran maqq Anmerech: A hostelkeeper in Mide.

Breccan maqq Nélli: Eldest son of Niall, killed in battle at Ys.

Breifa: A female servant of Bodilis.

Brennilis: Leader of the Gallicenae at the time of Julius and Augustus Caesar, responsible for the building of the sea wall and gate.

Bresslan: A man of Carpre's.

BRICIUS: Successor of Martinus; known today as St. Brice.

Briga: Osismiic maidservant of Forsquilis.

Brión: A half-brother of Niall.

Budic: A legionary in Gratillonius's detachment at Ys, of the Coritanean tribe in Britain; killed by Gratillonius in combat at the Wood of the King.

Cadoc Himilco: A young Ysan of Suffete family.

Cael maqq Eriai: An ollam poet at Niall's court

Calloch: A Gaul, former King of Ys, father of Fennalis and Morvanalis.

CALVINUS: An agent of Maximus's secret police.

CALPURNIUS: Father of Sucat.

Camilla: (1) A sister of Gratillonius; (2) Third daughter of Guilvilis and Gratillonius.

Carenn: Mother of Niall.

Carpre maqq Nélli: A son of Niall.

Carsa, Aulus Metellus: A young Gallo-Roman seaman from Burdigala, stationed in Ys; killed by Gratillonius in combat at the Wood of the King.

Carsa, Tiberius Metellus: A Gallo-Roman sea captain, father of the above.

Cata: A female worker at the Apuleius manor house.

Catellan: A Ysan.

Cathual: Charioteer to Niall.

Catto: A fisherman from Whalestrand.

Catualorig: A former Bacauda.

Cellach maqq Blathmaic: The hostelkeeper at Clón Tarui.

Cernach maqq Durthact: A merchant skipper of Munster.

Childeric: A son of Merowech.

Chramn: A Frankish warrior.

Cian: A name used by Dahut.

Claudia: A woman mentioned by Eucherius.

Clothair: A Frank settled in the Redonic canton; father of Chramn.

Colconor: A Gaul, King of Ys at the time of Gratillonius's arrival; slain by Gratillonius.

Commius: A Romano-Brittanic senator.

CONCHESSA: Niece of Martinus and mother of Sucat.

CONSTANTINUS, CONSTANS: Elder son of Flavius Claudius Constantinus.

CONSTANTINUS, FLAVIUS CLAUDIUS: A Roman army officer in Britannia, later a usurper known as CONSTANTINUS III.

CONSTANTINUS, JULIANUS: Younger son of Flavius Claudius Constantinus.

CONUAL CORCC MAQQ LUGTHACI: Principal king in Mumu, founder of the kingdom at Cashel.

Conual Gulban maqq Nélli: A son of Niall.

Corbmaqq (later *Cormac*): An ancestor of Niall, remembered to this day as having reigned gloriously.

Corentinus: A holy man, chorepiscopus at Ys, later bishop of Confluentes and Aquilo, known today as St. Corentin.

Coriran: A swineherd in Munster.

Cothortin Rosmertai: Lord of Works in Ys, head of civil service.

Cotta: A Mithraist in Vienne.

Craumthan maqq Fidaci: Brother of Mongfind, successor to King Eochaid maqq Muredach.

CUNEDAG: A leader of the Votadini, settled in Western Britannia to be an ally of Rome.

Cynan: (1) A legionary in Gratillonius's detachment at Ys, of the Demetic tribe in Britain, and a convert to Mithraisim; (2) A centurion in Constantinus's army.

Dahilis: A Queen of Ys, daughter of Tambilis by Hoel, mother of Dahut by Gratillonius.

Dahut: Daughter of Dahilis and Gratillonius.

DAMASUS: Pope, 366-384.

Dardriu: A swineherd in Munster.

Dauvinach: An Ysan.

Davona: A minor priestess in Ys.

DELPHINUS: Late friend of Ausonius.

Dion: A youth from Neapolis.

Docca: A Dumnonic woman, once nurse to Gratillonius.

Domnuald maqq Nélli: A son of Niall.

Donalis: A former Queen of Ys, mother of Quistilis by Wulfgar.

Donan: A member of Maeloch's crew.

Donnerch: A carter in Ys.

Doranius: A young man from Gesocribate.

Drach: Father of Vellano.

Drusus, Publius Flavius: A Britannic centurion of the Sixth under Maximus and a friend of Gratillonius, later a settler in Armorica.

Elissa: (1) Birth name of Lanarvilis; (2) Daughter of Lanarvilis by Lugaid.

Einiaunus, Valerius: A Britannic official in Constantinus's service.

Éndae maqq Nélli: A son of Niall.

Éndae Qennsalach: Principal king in Qóiqet Lagini (Leinster).

Eochaid maqq Éndae: A son of Éndae Qennsalach, exiled for murder of a poet and implacable enemy of Niall.

Eochaid maqq Muredach: A former King at Temir (Tara), father of Niall.

Eógan maqq Nélli: A son of Niall.

Eppillus, Quintus Junius: A Dobunnic legionary in Gratillonius's detachment, his deputy at the time, killed in battle at Ys.

Esmunin Sironai: Chief astrologer in Ys.

Estar: (1) Birth name of Dahilis; (2) Second daughter of Gratillonius and Tambilis.

Esun: A son of Catto.

Étain: A female druid at Niall's court.

Ethniu: A former concubine of Niall, mother of Breccan.

Eucherius: Christian minister (chorepiscopus) in Ys at the time of Gratillonius's arrival.

EUGENIUS: Briefly Augustus of the West, as a puppet of Arbogast.

Evana: Daughter of Vallilis and Wulfgar, mother of Joreth.

Evar: A maidservant of Innilis.

Evirion Baltisi: A young Ysan sea captain.

Ewein: A neighbor of the Gratilloni in Britannia.

Favonius: Gratillonius's favorite horse.

Faustina: A sister of Gratillonius.

Féchra: A late half-brother of Niall.

Fedelmm: A witch, foster-mother of Conual Corcc.

FELIX: A clergyman who became bishop of Trier.

Fennalis: A Queen of Ys, daughter of Ochtalis by Calloch.

Fergus Fogae: Supreme King in Ulster; a half-brother of Niall.

Fland Dub maqq Ninnedo: Murderer of Domnuald.

Florus: A Gallo-Roman merchant.

Fogartach: A follower of Eochaid.

Forsquilis: A Queen of Ys, daughter of Karilis by Lugaid, mother of Nemeta.

Fredegond: A son of Merowech.

Gaetulius: A Mauretanian, former King of Ys, father of Maldunilis, Vindilis, and Innilis.

GAINAS: A Roman general of Gothic origin.

Galith: A name used by Dahut.

Glabrio, Titus Scribona: Governor of Lugdunensis Tertia.

Gladwy: Birth name of Quinipilis.

Goban: An Osismiic boatman and deacon to Corentinus.

Gradlon: An Armorican version of "Gratillonius."

Grallon: An Ysan version of "Gratillonius."

GRATIANUS, FLAVIUS: A legionary officer in Britannia, co-Emperor of the West with Valentinianus; defeated by Maximus and murdered.

Gratillonius, Gaius Valerius: A Romano-Briton of the Belgic tribe, centurion in the Second Legion Augusta. Sent by Maximus to be the Roman prefect in Ys and caused by the Gallicenae to become its King.

Gratillonius, Lucius Valerius: Older brother of the above.

Gratillonius, Marcus Valerius: Father of the two above.

Guennellius: A Britannic curial.

Guentius: A Britannic legionary in Gratillonius' detachment.

Guilvilis: A Queen of Ys.

Gunnung Ivarsson: A Danic skipper and sea rover.

Gwynmael: Gamekeeper, later groom on the Gratillonius estate.

Hannon Baltisi: Lir Captain in Ys.

Herun Taniti: An officer in the Ysan navy.

Hilketh Eliuni: Former Transporter delegate to the Council of Suffetes in Ys.

Hoel: A Gaul, King of Ys before Colconor; father of Dahilis.

HONORIUS, FLAVIUS: A son of Theodosius, by him made Augustus of the West.

Hornach: An Osismian who would be King.

Innilis: A Queen of Ys, daughter of Donalis by Gaetulius.

Innloc: Father of Maeloch.

Intil: An Ysan fisherman.

Iram Eliuni: Lord of Gold in Ys, head of the treasury.

Ita: Late sister of Rufinus.

ITHACIUS: Bishop of Faro.

Janatha: An Ysan.

Johannes: Son of Julia and Cadoc.

Jonan: A laborer in Ys.

Joreth: A courtesan in Ys.

Julia: (1) Mother of Gratillonius; (2) Daughter of Lanarvilis and Gratillonius.

JULIANUS, FLAVIUS CLAUDIUS: Today known as Julian the Apostate, this Emperor (361-363) tried to revive paganism under the auspices of the state.

Kadrach: A cooper in Ys.

Karilis: A former Queen of Ys, mother of Forsquilis by Lugaid.

Keban: A former prostitute in Ys, converted to Christianity and married to Budic largely at the instigation of Corentinus.

Kel Cartagi: A young man of Ys.

Kerna: Second daughter of Bodilis by Hoel.

Korai: Granddaughter of Bodilis.
LAÉGARE MAQQ NÉLLI: Youngest (?) son of Niall.
Laidchenn maqq Barchedo: An ollam poet of Munster, attached to Niall's court.
Lanarvilis: A Queen of Ys, daughter of Fennalis by Wulfgar, mother of Julia.
Laurentinus: A Britannic curial.
Lavinia: A lady of Mediolanum.
Lorcann maqq Flandi: A Scotic warrior.
Lugaid: A Scotian, forner King of Ys, father of Forsquilis.
Lugotorix, Sextus Titius: A Gallo-Roman publican.
Lugthach maqq Aillelo: A king in Munster, father of Conual Corcc.
Lydris: Wife of Nagon Demari.
Lyria: Birth name of Karilis.
Maclavius: A Britannic legionary in Gratillonius's detachment and fellow Mithraist.
Maecius: Chorepiscopus at Aquilo, presently retired.
Maeloch: An Ysan fisher captain and formerly a Ferrier of the Dead.
Maldunilis: A Queen of Ys, daughter of Quistilis by Gaetulius.
Malthi: A maidservant of Fennalis.
Marcus: Son of Verania and Gratillonius.
MARCUS: A legionary officer in Britannia, briefly claimant of the purple.
Maria. Daughter of Verania and Gratillonius.
MARIA: First daughter of Stilicho, who became wife of Honorius.
MARTINUS: Bishop of Turonum (Tours) and founder of the monastery at Marmoutier; today known as St. Martin of Tours.
MAXIMUS, MAGNUS CLEMENS: Commander of Roman forces in Britannia, who later forcibly took power as co-Emperor but was overthrown and executed by Theodosius the Great.
Mella: A servant and medical assistant of Innilis.
Merowech: A leader of the Frankish laeti around Redonum; father of Theuderich.
Mílchu: Owner of Sucat when the latter was a slave.
Miraine: A daughter of Lanarvilis by Hoel.
Mochta: An Osismiic prostitute in Ys.
Moethaire of the Corco Óchae: Father of Fedelmm.
Mongfind: Stepmother of Niall, long dead, said to have been a witch.
Morvanalis: A former Queen of Ys, mother of Guilvilis by Hoel.
Muton Rosmertai: A Suffete of Ys and convert to Mithraism.
Murena, Flaminius: Duke of the Armorican Tract.
Nagon Demari: A Suffete and the Labor Councillor in Ys, self-exiled during Graillonius's reign and bitterly hostile to him.
Namma: Cook in the Apuleius household.
Nath Í: Nephew, tanist, and eventual successor of Niall.
Nathach: A painter in Ys.

...nain maqq Aedo: Chief druid at Niall's court.
...meta: Daughter of Forsquilis and Gratillonius.
NIALL MAQQ ECHACH, also known as NIALL OF THE NINE HOSTAGES: King at Temir (Tara) and overlord of Mide in Ireland.
Norom: A crewman of Maeloch's.
Ochtalis: A former Queen of Ys, mother of Morvanalis and Fennalis by Calloch.
Oengus Bolg: A king in Munster, father of Ámend.
Ogotorig: A hunter, formerly a Bacauda.
Olath Cartagi: An Ysan survivor who became an ironmaker.
Osrach Taniti: Fisher Councillor in Ys.
Parnesius: A Romano-Britannic centurion, friend of Gratillonius in his youth.
PATRICIUS: An advocate in the service of Maximus.
PAULINUS: A grandson of Ausonius.
Pertinax: A Romano-Britannic centurion, friend of Parnesius.
Philippus: An exorcist in Turonum.
PRISCILLIANUS: Heretical bishop of Ávila, executed by Maximus.
Prudentius: A Redonian, deacon to Eucherius.
Quanis: A demonic mermaid in Ysan legend.
Quinipilis: A Queen of Ys, daughter of Redorix, mother unspecified.
Quintilius: A courtier in Mediolanum.
Quistilis: A former Queen of Ys, mother of Maldunilis by Wulfgar.
RADAGAISUS: A Gothic warlord.
Radoch: A manservant of Vindilis.
Rael: A prostitute in Ys.
Ramas Tyri: Former Artisan delegate to the Council of Suffetes in Ys.
Redorix: A Gaul, former King of Ys, father of Quinipilis.
Rivelin: Royal surgeon in Ys.
Riwal: A Durotrigian (from Britannia) who moved to Confluentes.
Ronach: An Osismiic Mithraist.
Rovinda: Wife of Apuleius Vero.
Rufinus: A Redonian, formerly a Bacauda, henchman of Gratillonius.
RUFINUS: Praetorian prefect of Arcadius, overthrown by Stilicho.
Rullus, Septimius: A curial in Gesocribate.
Runa: (1) Birth name of Vindilis; (2) Daughter of Vindilis by Hoel.
Sadb: Wife of Cernach.
Salaun: An Armorican version of "Salomon."
Salomon: Son of Rovinda and Apuleius Vero.
Saphon: A former Ysan fisher captain.
Sasai: (1) Birth name of Guilvilis; (2) First daughter of Guilvilis and Gratillonius.
Semuramat: (1) Third daughter of Bodilis by Hoel, later known as Tambilis; (2) First daughter of her and Gratillonius.
SERENA: Wife of Stilicho; niece and adopted daughter of Theo-dosius.
Sicorus: The large landowner at Maedraecum.

Sigo, Quintus Flavius: An Imperial courier.

Silis: A prostitute in Ys.

Soren Cartagi: Speaker for Taranis in Ys, Timberman delegate to the Council.

Sosir: A painter in Ys.

STILICHO, FLAVIUS: A Roman general, half Vandal by birth, who became effectively the dictator of the West Roman Empire.

Subne maqq Dúnchado: A follower of Eochaid.

SUCAT (or SUCCAT): A young holy man, later called Patricius; known today as St. Patrick.

Surach: A son of Catto.

Syrus, Lucas Orgetuorig: Mithraic Father in Vienne.

Taenus Himilco: A Suffete of Ys, Landholder Councillor; father of Cadoc.

Talavair: (1) Birth name of Bodilis; (2) First daughter of Bodilis and Hoel.

Taltha: A courtesan in Ys.

Tambilis: (1) A Queen of Ys, daughter of Bodilis and Hoel; (2) A former Queen, grandmother of this one; mother of Bodilis by Wulfgar and Dahilis by Hoel.

Tardelbach: A man of Carpre's.

Targorix: An early Celtic king.

Tasciovanus: A Britannic curial.

Temesa: A maidservant of Quinipilis.

Tera: An Ysan countrywoman.

THEODOSIUS, FLAVIUS: Today known as the Great; Augustus of the East; eventually, briefly, sole Roman Emperor.

Theuderich: A son of Merowech; a leader of the Frankish laeti around Redonum.

Tigernach maqq Laidchinni: A son and pupil of Laidchenn, murdered by Eochaid.

Timbro: A follower of Ullus.

Tommaltach maqq Donngalii: A young Scotian living in Ys, killed by Gratillonius in combat at the Wood of the King.

Torna Éces: Greatest poet in Ériu, foster-father of Niall and Conual and teacher of Laidchenn.

Tóthual the Desired: Founder of Mide.

Tronan Sironai: Late husband of Runa.

Uail maqq Carbri: Henchman of Niall.

Udach: A servant of Gratillonius.

Ullus: A bully from Audiarna.

Una: (1) Daughter of Bodilis and Gratillonius; (2) A Britannic girl, daughter of Ewein; sweetheart of Gratillonius in his youth.

Usun: An Ysan fisherman, Maeloch's mate on *Osprey.*

Utican the Wanderer: An Ysan poet.

VALENTINIANUS, FLAVIUS: Co-Emperor of the West.

eria: Fourth daughter of Guilvilis and Gratillonius.
ilis: A former Queen of Ys, mother of Tambilis by Wulfgar.
Vellano: A Redonian who moved to Confluentes.
Verania: Daughter of Rovinda and Apuleius Vero.
Verica: A Britannic legionary in Gratillonius's detachment and fellow Mithraist.
VICTOR: A son of Maximus.
Vindilis: A Queen of Ys, daughter of Quinipilis by Gaetulius, mother of Runa.
Vindolenus: A former Bacauda.
Vindomarix: Druid to Targorix.
Vortivir, Flavius: Tribune at Darioritum Venetorum.
Witch-Hanai: An Ysan poet.
Wulfgar: A Saxon, former King of Ys; father of Tambilis, Quistilis, Karilis, Lanarvilis, and Bodilis.
Zeugit: An Ysan, landlord of the Green Whale.
Zisa: First daughter of Maldunilis and Gratillonius.